# Stewart Edward White,
## Collection novels

**In this book:**
**The Forest**
**Arizona Nights**
**The Killer**
**The Forty-Niners A Chronicle**
**of the California Trail and El Dorado**
**African Camp Fires**
**The Blazed Trail**
**The Land of Footprints**
**The Riverman**

Stewart Edward White (1873 – 1946) was an American writer, novelist, and spiritualist. White's books were popular at a time when America was losing its vanishing wilderness. He was a keen observer of the beauties of nature and human nature, yet could render them in a plain-spoken style. Based on his own experience, whether writing camping journals or Westerns, he included pithy and fun details about cabin-building, canoeing, logging, gold-hunting, and guns and fishing and hunting. He also interviewed people who had been involved in the fur trade, the California gold rush and other pioneers which provided him with details that give his novels verisimilitude.

# In this book:

# The Forest

## I.
## THE CALLING.

"The Red Gods make their medicine again."

Some time in February, when the snow and sleet have shut out from the wearied mind even the memory of spring, the man of the woods generally receives his first inspiration. He may catch it from some companion's chance remark, a glance at the map, a vague recollection of a dim past conversation, or it may flash on him from the mere pronouncement of a name. The first faint thrill of discovery leaves him cool, but gradually, with the increasing enthusiasm of cogitation, the idea gains body, until finally it has grown to plan fit for discussion.

Of these many quickening potencies of inspiration, the mere name of a place seems to strike deepest at the heart of romance. Colour, mystery, the vastnesses of unexplored space are there, symbolized compactly for the aliment of imagination. It lures the fancy as a fly lures the trout. Mattágami, Peace River, Kánanaw, the House of the Touchwood Hills, Rupert's House, the Land of Little Sticks, Flying Post, Conjuror's House--how the syllables roll from the tongue, what pictures rise in instant response to their suggestion! The journey of a thousand miles seems not too great a price to pay for the sight of a place called the Hills of Silence, for acquaintance with the people who dwell there, perhaps for a glimpse of the saga-spirit that so named its environment. On the other hand, one would feel but little desire to visit Muggin's Corners, even though at their crossing one were assured of the deepest flavour of the Far North.

The first response to the red god's summons is almost invariably the production of a fly-book and the complete rearrangement of all its contents. The next is a resumption of practice with the little pistol. The third, and last, is pencil and paper, and lists of grub and duffel, and estimates of routes and expenses, and correspondence with men who spell queerly, bear down heavily with blunt pencils, and agree to be at Black Beaver Portage on a certain date. Now, though the February snow and sleet still shut him in, the spring has draw very near. He can feel the warmth of her breath rustling through his reviving memories.

There are said to be sixty-eight roads to heaven, of which but one is the true way, although here and there a by-path offers experimental variety to the restless and bold. The true way for the man in the woods to attain the elusive best of his wilderness experience is to go as light as possible, and the by-paths of departure from that principle lead only to the slightly increased carrying possibilities of open-water canoe trips, and permanent camps.

But these prove to be not very independent side paths, never diverging so far from the main road that one may dare hope to conceal from a vigilant eye that he is *not* going light.

To go light is to play the game fairly. The man in the woods matches himself against the forces of nature. In the towns he is warmed and fed and clothed so spontaneously and easily that after a time he perforce begins to doubt himself, to wonder whether his powers are not atrophied from disuse. And so, with his naked soul, he fronts the wilderness. It is a test, a measuring of strength, a proving of his essential pluck and resourcefulness and manhood, an assurance of man's highest potency, the ability to endure and to take care of himself. In just so far as he substitutes the ready-made of civilization for the wit-made of the forest, the pneumatic bed for the balsam boughs, in just so far is he relying on other men and other men's labour to take care of him. To exactly that extent is the test invalidated. He has not proved a courteous antagonist, for he has not stripped to the contest.

To go light is to play the game sensibly. For even when it is not so earnest, nor the stake so high, a certain common-sense should take the place on a lower plane of the fair-play sense on the higher. A great many people find enjoyment in merely playing with nature. Through vacation they relax their minds, exercise mildly their bodies, and freshen the colours of their outlook on life. Such people like to live comfortably, work little, and enjoy existence lazily. Instead of modifying themselves to fit the life of the wilderness, they modify their city methods to fit open-air conditions. They do not need to strip to the contest, for contest there is none, and Indian packers are cheap at a dollar a day. But even so the problem of the greatest comfort--defining comfort as an accurate balance of effort expended to results obtained--can be solved only by the one formula. And that formula is, again, *go light*, for a superabundance of paraphernalia proves always more of a care than a satisfaction. When the woods offer you a thing ready made, it is the merest foolishness to transport that same thing a hundred miles for the sake of the manufacturer's trademark.

I once met an outfit in the North Woods, plodding diligently across portage, laden like the camels of the desert. Three Indians swarmed back and forth a half-dozen trips apiece. An Indian can carry over two hundred pounds. That evening a half-breed and I visited their camp and examined their outfit, always with growing wonder. They had tent-poles and about fifty pounds of hardwood tent pegs--in a wooded country where such things can be had for a clip of the axe. They had a system of ringed iron bars which could be so fitted together as to form a low open grill on which trout could be broiled--weight twenty pounds, and split wood necessary for its efficiency. They had air mattresses and camp-chairs and oil lanterns. They had corpulent duffel bags apiece that would stand alone, and enough changes of clothes to last out dry-skinned a week's rain. And the leader of the party wore the wrinkled brow of tribulation. For he had to keep track of everything and see that package number twenty-eight was not left, and that package number sixteen did not get wet; that the pneumatic bed did not get punctured, and that the canned goods did. Beside which, the caravan was moving at the majestic rate of about five miles a day.

3

Now tent-pegs can always be cut, and trout broiled beautifully by a dozen other ways, and candle lanterns fold up, and balsam can be laid in such a manner as to be as springy as a pneumatic mattress, and camp-chairs, if desired, can be quickly constructed with an axe, and clothes can always be washed or dried as long as fire burns and water runs, and any one of fifty other items of laborious burden could have been ingeniously and quickly substituted by any one of the Indians. It was not that we concealed a bucolic scorn of effete but solid comfort; only it did seem ridiculous that a man should cumber himself with a fifth wheel on a smoothly macadamized road.

The next morning Billy and I went cheerfully on our way. We were carrying an axe, a gun, blankets, an extra pair of drawers and socks apiece, a little grub, and an eight-pound shelter tent. We had been out a week, and we were having a good time.

## II.

THE SCIENCE OF GOING LIGHT.

"Now the Four-Way lodge is opened--now the smokes of Council rise--
Pleasant smokes ere yet 'twixt trail and trail they choose."

You can no more be told how to go light than you can be told how to hit a ball with a bat. It is something that must be lived through, and all advice on the subject has just about the value of an answer to a bashful young man who begged from one of our woman's periodicals help in overcoming the diffidence felt on entering a crowded room. The reply read: "Cultivate an easy, graceful manner." In like case I might hypothecate, "To go light, discard all but the really necessary articles."

The sticking-point, were you to press me close, would be the definition of the word "necessary," for the terms of such definition would have to be those solely and simply of a man's experience. Comforts, even most desirable comforts, are not necessities. A dozen times a day trifling emergencies will seem precisely to call for some little handy contrivance that would be just the thing, were it in the pack rather than at home. A disgorger does the business better than a pocket-knife; a pair of oilskin trousers turns the wet better than does kersey; a camp-stove will burn merrily in a rain lively enough to drown an open fire. Yet neither disgorger, nor oilskins, nor camp-stove can be considered in the light of necessities, for the simple reason that the conditions of their use occur too infrequently to compensate for the pains of their carriage. Or, to put it the other way, a few moments' work with a knife, wet knees occasionally, or an infrequent soggy meal are not too great a price to pay for unburdened shoulders.

Nor on the other hand must you conclude that because a thing is a mere luxury in town, it is nothing but that in the woods. Most woodsmen own some little ridiculous item of outfit without which they could not be happy. And when a man cannot be happy lacking a thing, that thing becomes a necessity. I knew one who never stirred without borated talcum powder; another who must have his mouth-organ; a third who was miserable without a small bottle of salad dressing; I confess to a pair of light buckskin gloves. Each man must decide for himself--remembering always the endurance limit of human shoulders.

A necessity is that which, *by your own experience*, you have found you cannot do without. As a bit of practical advice, however, the following system of elimination may be recommended. When you return from a trip, turn your duffel bag upside down on the floor. Of the contents make three piles--three piles conscientiously selected in the light of what has happened rather than what ought to have happened, or what might have happened. It is difficult to do this. Preconceived notions, habits of civilization, theory for future, imagination, all stand in the eye of your honesty. Pile number one should comprise those articles you have used every day; pile number two, those you have used occasionally; pile number three, those you have not used at all. If you are resolute and singleminded, you will at once discard the latter two.

Throughout the following winter you will be attacked by misgivings. To be sure, you wore the mosquito hat but once or twice, and the fourth pair of socks not at all; but then the mosquitoes might be thicker next time, and a series of rainy days and cold nights might make it desirable to have a dry pair of socks to put on at night. The past has been $x$, but the future might be $y$. One by one the discarded creep back into the list. And by the opening of next season you have made toward perfection by only the little space of a mackintosh coat and a ten-gauge gun.

But in the years to come you learn better and better the simple woods lesson of substitution or doing without. You find that discomfort is as soon forgotten as pain; that almost anything can be endured if it is but for the time being; that absolute physical comfort is worth but a very small price in avoirdupois. Your pack shrinks.

In fact, it really never ceases shrinking. Only last summer taught me the uselessness of an extra pair of trousers. It rains in the woods; streams are to be waded; the wetness of leaves is greater than the wetness of many rivers. Logically, naturally, inevitably, such conditions point to change of garments when camp is made. We always change our clothes when we get wet in the city. So for years I carried those extra nether garments--and continued in the natural exposure to sun and wind and camp-fire to dry off before change time, or to hang the damp clothes from the ridge-pole for resumption in the morning. And then one day the web of that particular convention broke. We change wet trousers in the town; we do not in the woods. The extras were relegated to pile number three, and my pack, already apparently down to a minimum, lost a few pounds more.

You will want a hat, a *good* hat to turn rain, with a medium brim. If you are wise, you will get it too small for your head, and rip out the lining. The felt will cling tenaciously to your hair, so that you will find the snatches of the brush and the wind generally unavailing.

By way of undergarments wear woollen. Buy winter weights even for midsummer. In travelling with a pack a man is going to sweat in streams, no matter what he puts on or takes off, and the thick garment will be found no more oppressive than the thin. And then in the cool of the woods or of the evening he avoids a chill. And he can plunge into the coldest water with impunity, sure that ten minutes of the air will dry him fairly well. Until you have shivered in clammy cotton, you cannot realize the importance of this point. Ten minutes of cotton underwear in cold water will chill. On the other hand, suitably clothed in wool, I have waded the ice water of north country streams when the thermometer was so low I could see my breath in the air, without other discomfort than a cold ring around my legs to mark the surface of the water, and a slight numbness in my feet when I emerged. Therefore, even in hot weather, wear heavy wool. It is the most comfortable. Undoubtedly you will come to believe this only by experience.

Do not carry a coat. This is another preconception of civilization, exceedingly difficult to get rid of. You will never wear it while packing. In a rain you will find that it wets through so promptly as to be of little use; or, if waterproof, the inside condensation will more than equal the rain-water. In camp you will discard it because it will impede the swing of your arms. The end of that coat will be a brief half-hour after supper, and a makeshift roll to serve as a pillow during the night. And for these a sweater is better in every way.

In fact, if you feel you must possess another outside garment, let it be an extra sweater. You can sleep in it, use it when your day garment is soaked, or even tie things in it as in a bag. It is not necessary, however.

One good shirt is enough. When you wash it, substitute the sweater until it dries. In fact, by keeping the sweater always in your waterproof bag, you possess a dry garment to change into. Two handkerchiefs are enough. One should be of silk, for neck, head, or--in case of cramps or intense cold--the *stomach*; the other of coloured cotton for the pocket. Both can be quickly washed, and dried *en route*. Three pairs of heavy wool socks will be enough--one for wear, one for night, and one for extra. A second pair of drawers supplements the sweater when a temporary day change is desirable. Heavy kersey "driver's" trousers are the best. They are cheap, dry very quickly, and are not easily "picked out" by the brush.

The best blanket is that made by the Hudson's Bay Company for its servants--a "three-point" for summer is heavy enough. The next best is our own gray army blanket. One of rubber should fold about it, and a pair of narrow buckle straps is handy to keep the bundle right and tight and waterproof. As for a tent, buy the smallest shelter you can get along with, have it made of balloon silk well waterproofed, and supplement it with a duplicate tent of light cheesecloth to suspend inside as a fly-proof defence. A seven-by-seven three-man A-tent, which would weigh between twenty and thirty pounds if made of duck, means only about eight pounds constructed of this material. And it is waterproof. I own one which I have used for three seasons. It has been employed as tarpaulin, fly, even blanket on a pinch; it has been packed through the roughest country; I have even pressed it into service as a sort of canoe lining; but it is still as good as ever. Such a tent sometimes condenses a little moisture in a cold rain, but it never "sprays" as does a duck shelter; it never leaks simply because you have accidentally touched its under-surface; and, best of all, it weighs no more after a rain than before it. This latter item is perhaps its best recommendation. The confronting with equanimity of a wet day's journey in the shower-bath brush of our northern forests requires a degree of philosophy which a gratuitous ten pounds of soaked-up water sometimes most effectually breaks down. I know of but one place where such a tent can be bought. The address will be gladly sent to any one practically interested.

As for the actual implements of the trade, they are not many, although of course the sporting goods stores are full of all sorts of "handy contrivances." A small axe--one of the pocket size will do, if you get the right shape and balance, although a light regulation axe is better; a thin-bladed sheath-knife of the best steel; a pocket-knife; a compass; a waterproof match-safe; fishing-tackle; firearms; and cooking utensils comprise the list. All others belong to permanent camps, or open-water cruises--not to "hikes" in the woods.

The items, with the exception of the last two, seem to explain themselves. During the summer months in the North Woods you will not need a rifle. Partridges, spruce hens, ptarmigan, rabbits, ducks, and geese are usually abundant enough to fill the provision list. For them, of course, a shotgun is the thing; but since such a weapon weighs many pounds, and its ammunition many more, I have come gradually to depend entirely on a pistol. The instrument is single shot, carries a six-inch barrel, is fitted with a special butt, and is built on the graceful lines of a 38-calibre Smith and Wesson revolver. Its cartridge is the 22 long-rifle, a target size, that carries as accurately as you can hold for upwards of a hundred yards. With it I have often killed a half-dozen of partridges from the same tree. The ammunition is light. Altogether it is a most satisfactory, convenient, and accurate weapon, and quite adequate to all small game. In fact, an Indian named Tawabinisáy, after seeing it perform, once borrowed it to kill a moose.

"I shootum in eye," said he.

By way of cooking utensils, buy aluminium. It is expensive, but so light and so easily cleaned that it is well worth all you may have to pay. If you are alone you will not want to carry much hardware. I made a twenty-day trip once with nothing but a tin cup and a frying-pan. Dishes, pails, wash-basins, and other receptacles can always be made of birch bark and cedar withes--by one who knows how. The ideal outfit for two or three is a cup, fork, and spoon apiece, one tea-pail, two kettle-pails, and a frying-pan. The latter can be used as a bread-oven.

A few minor items, of practically no weight, suggest themselves--toilet requisites, fly-dope, needle and thread, a cathartic, pain-killer, a roll of surgeon's bandage, pipe and tobacco. But when the pack is made up, and the duffel bag tied, you find that, while fitted for every emergency but that of catastrophe, you are prepared to "go light."

5

## THE JUMPING-OFF PLACE.

Sometime, no matter how long your journey, you will reach a spot whose psychological effect is so exactly like a dozen others that you will recognize at once its kinship with former experience. Mere physical likeness does not count at all. It may possess a water-front of laths and sawdust, or an outlook over broad, shimmering, heat-baked plains. It may front the impassive fringe of a forest, or it may skirt the calm stretch of a river. But whether of log or mud, stone or unpainted board, its identity becomes at first sight indubitably evident. Were you, by the wave of some beneficent wand, to be transported direct to it from the heart of the city, you could not fail to recognize it. "The jumping-off place!" you would cry ecstatically, and turn with unerring instinct to the Aromatic Shop.

For here is where begins the Long Trail. Whether it will lead you through the forests, or up the hills, or over the plains, or by invisible water paths; whether you will accomplish it on horseback, or in canoe, or by the transportation of your own two legs; whether your companions shall be white or red, or merely the voices of the wilds--these things matter not a particle. In the symbol of this little town you loose your hold on the world of made things, and shift for yourself among the unchanging conditions of nature.

Here the faint forest flavour, the subtle, invisible breath of freedom, stirs faintly across men's conventions. The ordinary affairs of life savour of this tang--a trace of wildness in the domesticated berry. In the dress of the inhabitants is a dash of colour, a carelessness of port; in the manner of their greeting is the clear, steady-eyed taciturnity of the silent places; through the web of their gray talk of ways and means and men's simpler beliefs runs a thread of colour. One hears strange, suggestive words and phrases--arapajo, capote, arroyo, the diamond hitch, cache, butte, coulé, muskegs, portage, and a dozen others coined into the tender of daily use. And occasionally, when the expectation is least alert, one encounters suddenly the very symbol of the wilderness itself--a dust-whitened cowboy, an Indian packer with his straight, fillet-confined hair, a voyageur gay in red sash and ornamented moccasins, one of the Company's canoemen, hollow-cheeked from the river--no costumed show exhibit, but fitting naturally into the scene, bringing something of the open space with him--so that in your imagination the little town gradually takes on the colour of mystery which an older community utterly lacks.

But perhaps the strongest of the influences which unite to assure the psychological kinships of the jumping-off places is that of the Aromatic Shop. It is usually a board affair, with a broad high sidewalk shaded by a wooden awning. You enter through a narrow door, and find yourself facing two dusky aisles separated by a narrow division of goods, and flanked by wooden counters. So far it is exactly like the corner store of our rural districts. But in the dimness of these two aisles lurks the spirit of the wilds. There in a row hang fifty pair of smoke-tanned moccasins; in another an equal number of oil-tanned; across the background you can make out snowshoes. The shelves are high with blankets--three-point, four-point--thick and warm for the out-of-doors. Should you care to examine, the storekeeper will hook down from aloft capotes of different degrees of fineness. Fathoms of black tobacco-rope lie coiled in tubs. Tump-lines welter in a tangle of dimness. On a series of little shelves is the ammunition, fascinating in the attraction of mere numbers--44 Winchester, 45 Colt, 40-82, 30-40, 44 S. & W.--they all connote something to the accustomed mind, just as do the numbered street names of New York.

An exploration is always bringing something new to light among the commonplaces of ginghams and working shirts, and canned goods and stationery, and the other thousands of civilized drearinesses to found in every country store. From under the counter you drag out a mink skin or so; from the dark corner an assortment of steel traps. In a loft a birch-bark mokok, fifty pounds heavy with granulated maple sugar, dispenses a faint perfume.

For this is, above all, the Aromatic Shop. A hundred ghosts of odours mingle to produce the spirit of it. The reek of the camp-fires is in its buckskin, of the woods in its birch bark, of the muskegs in its sweet grass, of the open spaces in its peltries, of the evening meal in its coffees and bacons, of the portage trail in the leather of the tump-lines. I am speaking now of the country of which we are to write. The shops of the other jumping-off places are equally aromatic--whether with the leather of saddles, the freshness of ash paddles, or the pungency of marline; and once the smell of them is in your nostrils you cannot but away.

The Aromatic Shop is always kept by the wisest, the most accommodating, the most charming shopkeeper in the world. He has all leisure to give you, and enters into the innermost spirit of your buying. He is of supernal sagacity in regard to supplies and outfits, and if he does not know all about routes, at least he is acquainted with the very man who can tell you everything you want to know. He leans both elbows on the counter, you swing your feet, and together you go over the list, while the Indian stands smoky and silent in the background. "Now, if I was you," says he, "I'd take just a little more pork. You won't be eatin' so much yourself, but these Injuns ain't got no bottom when it comes to sow-belly. And I wouldn't buy all that coffee. You ain't goin' to want much after the first edge is worn off. Tea's the boy." The Indian shoots a few rapid words across the discussion. "He says you'll want some iron shoes to fit on canoe poles for when you come back up-stream," interprets your friend. "I guess that's right. I ain't got none, but th' blacksmith'll fit you out all right. You'll find him just below--never mind, don't you bother, I'll see to all that for you."

The next morning he saunters into view at the river-bank. "Thought I'd see you off," he replies to your expression of surprise at his early rising. "Take care of yourself." And so the last hand-clasp of civilization is extended to you from the little Aromatic Shop.

Occasionally, however, though very rarely, you step to the Long Trail from the streets of a raw modern town. The chance presence of some local industry demanding a large population of workmen, combined with first-class railroad transportation, may plant an electric-lighted, saloon-lined, brick-hoteled city in the middle of the wilderness. Lumber, mines--especially of the baser metals or commercial minerals--fisheries, a terminus of water freightage, may one or all call into existence a community a hundred years in advance of its environment. Then you lose the savour of the jump-off. Nothing can quite take the place of the instant plunge into the wilderness, for you must travel three or four days from such a place before you sense the forest in its vastness, even though deer may eat the cabbages at the edge of town. Occasionally, however, by force of crude contrast to the brick-heated atmosphere, the breath of the woods reaches your cheek, and always you own a very tender feeling for the cause of it.

Dick and myself were caught in such a place. It was an unfinished little town, with brick-fronted stores, arc-lights swaying over fathomless mud, big superintendent's and millowner's houses of bastard architecture in a blatant superiority of hill location, a hotel whose office chairs supported a variety of cheap drummers, and stores screeching in an attempt at metropolitan smartness. We inspected the standpipe and the docks, walked a careless mile of board walk, kicked a dozen pugnacious dogs from our setter, Deuce, and found ourselves at the end of our resources. As a crowd seemed to be gathering about the wooden railway station, we joined it in sheer idleness.

It seemed that an election had taken place the day before, that one Smith had been chosen to the Assembly, and that, though this district had gone anti-Smith, the candidate was expected to stop off an hour on his way to a more westerly point. Consequently the town was on hand to receive him.

The crowd, we soon discovered, was bourgeois in the extreme. Young men from the mill escorted young women from the shops. The young men wore flaring collars three sizes too large; the young women white cotton mitts three sizes too small. The older men spat, and talked through their noses; the women drawled out a monotonous flow of speech concerning the annoyances of domestic life. A gang of uncouth practical jokers, exploding in horse-laughter, skylarked about, jostling rudely. A village band, uniformed solely with cheap carriage-cloth caps, brayed excruciatingly. The reception committee had decorated, with red and white silesia streamers and rosettes, an ordinary side-bar buggy, to which a long rope had been attached, that the great man might be dragged by his fellow-citizens to the public square.

Nobody seemed to be taking the affair too seriously. It was evidently more than half a joke. Anti-Smith was more good-humouredly in evidence than the winning party. Just this touch of buffoonery completed our sense of the farce-comedy character of the situation. The town was tawdry in its preparations--and knew it; but half sincere in its enthusiasm--and knew it. If the crowd had been composed of Americans, we should have anticipated an unhappy time for Smith; but good, loyal Canadians, by the limitations of temperament, could get no further than a spirit of manifest irreverence.

In the shifting of the groups Dick and I became separated, but shortly I made him out worming his way excitedly toward me, his sketch-book open in his hand.

"Come here," he whispered. "There's going to be fun. They're going to open up on old Smith after all."

I followed. The decorated side-bar buggy might be well meant; the village band need not have been interpreted as an ironical compliment; the rest of the celebration might indicate paucity of resource rather than facetious intent; but surely the figure of fun before us could not be otherwise construed than as a deliberate advertising in the face of success of the town's real attitude toward the celebration.

The man was short. He wore a felt hat, so big that it rested on his ears. A gray wool shirt hung below his neck. A cutaway coat miles too large depended below his knees and to the first joints of his fingers. By way of official uniform his legs were incased in an ordinary rough pair of miller's white trousers, on which broad strips of red flannel had been roughly sewn. Everything was wrinkled in the folds of too-bigness. As though to accentuate the note, the man stood very erect, very military, and supported in one hand the staff of an English flag. This figure of fun, this man made from the slop-chest, this caricature of a scarecrow, had been put forth by heavy-handed facetiousness to the post of greatest honour. He was Standard-Bearer to the occasion! Surely subtle irony could go no further.

A sudden movement caused the man to turn. One sleeve of the faded, ridiculous old cutaway was empty. He turned again. From under the ear-flanging hat looked unflinchingly the clear, steady blue eye of the woodsman. And so we knew. This old soldier had come in from the Long Trail to bear again the flag of his country. If his clothes were old and ill-fitting, at least they were his best, and the largeness of the empty sleeve belittled the too-largeness of the other. In all this ribald, laughing, irreverent, commonplace, semi-vicious crowd he was the one note of sincerity. To him this was a real occasion, and the exalted reverence in his eye for the task he was so simply performing was Smith's real triumph--if he could have known it. We understood now, we felt the imminence of the Long Trail. For the first time the little brick, tawdry town gripped our hearts with the well-known thrill of the Jumping-Off Place. Suddenly the great, simple, unashamed wilderness drew near us as with the rush of wings.

*IV.*

ON MAKING CAMP.

"Who hath smelt wood-smoke at twilight? Who hath
heard the birch log burning?
Who is quick to read the noises of the night?

7

Let him follow with the others, for the young men's feet are turning
To the camps of proved desire and known delight."

In the Ojibway language *wigwam* means a good spot for camping, a place cleared for a camp, a camp as an abstract proposition, and a camp in the concrete as represented by a tent, a thatched shelter, or a conical tepee. In like manner, the English word *camp* lends itself to a variety of concepts. I once slept in a four-poster bed over a polished floor in an elaborate servant-haunted structure which, mainly because it was built of logs and overlooked a lake, the owner always spoke of as his camp. Again, I once slept on a bed of prairie grass, before a fire of dried buffalo chips and mesquite, wrapped in a single light blanket, while a good vigorous rain-storm made new cold places on me and under me all night. In the morning the cowboy with whom I was travelling remarked that this was "sure a lonesome proposition as a camp."

Between these two extremes is infinite variety, grading upwards through the divers bivouacs of snow, plains, pines, or hills to the bark shelter; past the dog-tent, the A-tent, the wall-tent, to the elaborate permanent canvas cottage of the luxurious camper, the dug-out winter retreat of the range cowboy, the trapper's cabin, the great log-built lumber-jack communities, and the last refinements of sybaritic summer homes in the Adirondacks. All these are camps. And when you talk of making camp you must know whether that process is to mean only a search for rattlesnakes and enough acrid-smoked fuel to boil tea, or a winter's consultation with an expert architect; whether your camp is to be made on the principle of Omar's one-night Sultan, or whether it is intended to accommodate the full days of an entire summer.

But to those who tread the Long Trail the making of camp resolves itself into an algebraical formula. After a man has travelled all day through the Northern wilderness he wants to rest, and anything that stands between himself and his repose he must get rid of in as few motions as is consistent with reasonable thoroughness. The end in view is a hot meal and a comfortable dry place to sleep. The straighter he can draw the line to those two points the happier he is.

Early in his woods experience, Dick became possessed with the desire to do everything for himself. As this was a laudable striving for self-sufficiency, I called a halt at about three o'clock one afternoon in order to give him plenty of time.

Now Dick is a good, active, able-bodied boy, possessed of average intelligence and rather more than average zeal. He even had theory of a sort, for he had read various "Boy Campers, or the Trapper's Guide," "How to Camp Out," "The Science of Woodcraft," and other able works. He certainly had ideas enough and confidence enough. I sat down on a log.

At the end of three hours' flusteration, heat, worry, and good hard work, he had accomplished the following results: A tent, very saggy, very askew, covered a four-sided area--it was not a rectangle--of very bumpy ground. A hodge-podge bonfire, in the centre of which an inaccessible coffee-pot toppled menacingly, alternately threatened to ignite the entire surrounding forest or to go out altogether through lack of fuel. Personal belongings strewed the ground near the fire, and provisions cumbered the entrance to the tent. Dick was anxiously mixing batter for the cakes, attempting to stir a pot of rice often enough to prevent it from burning, and trying to rustle sufficient dry wood to keep the fire going. This diversity of interests certainly made him sit up and pay attention. At each instant he had to desert his flour-sack to rescue the coffee-pot, or to shift the kettle, or to dab hastily at the rice, or to stamp out the small brush, or to pile on more dry twigs. His movements were not graceful. They raised a scurry of dry bark, ashes, wood dust, twigs, leaves, and pine needles, a certain proportion of which found their way into the coffee, the rice, and the sticky batter, while the smaller articles of personal belonging, hastily dumped from the duffel-bag, gradually disappeared from view in the manner of Pompeii and ancient Vesuvius. Dick burned his fingers and stumbled about and swore, and looked so comically-pathetically red-faced through the smoke that I, seated on the log, at the same time laughed and pitied. And in the end, when he needed a continuous steady fire to fry his cakes, he suddenly discovered that dry twigs do not make coals, and that his previous operations had used up all the fuel within easy circle of the camp.

So he had to drop everything for the purpose of rustling wood, while the coffee chilled, the rice cooled, the bacon congealed, and all the provisions, cooked and uncooked, gathered entomological specimens. At the last, the poor bedeviled theorist made a hasty meal of scorched food, brazenly postponed the washing of dishes until the morrow, and coiled about his hummocky couch to dream the nightmares of complete exhaustion.

Poor Dick! I knew exactly how he felt, how the low afternoon sun scorched, how the fire darted out at unexpected places, how the smoke followed him around, no matter on which side of the fire he placed himself, how the flies all took to biting when both hands were occupied, and how they all miraculously disappeared when he had set down the frying-pan and knife to fight them. I could sympathize, too, with the lonely, forlorn, lost-dog feeling that clutched him after it was all over. I could remember how big and forbidding and unfriendly the forest had once looked to me in like circumstances, so that I had felt suddenly thrust outside into empty spaces. Almost was I tempted to intervene; but I liked Dick, and I wanted to do him good. This experience was harrowing, but it prepared his mind for the seeds of wisdom. By the following morning he had chastened his spirit, forgotten the assurance breathed from the windy pages of the Boy Trapper Library, and was ready to learn.

Have you ever watched a competent portraitist at work? The infinite pains a skilled man spends on the preliminaries before he takes one step towards a likeness nearly always wears down the patience of the sitter. He measures with his eye, he plumbs, he sketches tentatively, he places in here a dab, there a blotch, he puts behind him apparently unproductive hours--and then all at once he is ready to begin something that will not have to be done over again. An amateur, however, is carried away by his desire for results. He dashes in a hit-or-miss early effect, which grows into an approximate likeness almost immediately, but which will require infinite labour, alteration, and anxiety to beat into finished shape.

The case of the artist in making camps is exactly similar, and the philosophical reasons for his failure are exactly the same. To the superficial mind a camp is a shelter, a bright fire, and a smell of cooking. So when a man is very tired he cuts across lots to those three results. He pitches his tent, lights his fire, puts over his food--and finds himself drowned in detail, like my friend Dick.

The following is, in brief, what during the next six weeks I told that youth, by precept, by homily, and by making the solution so obvious that he could work it out for himself.

When five or six o'clock draws near, begin to look about you for a good level dry place, elevated some few feet above the surroundings. Drop your pack or beach your canoe. Examine the location carefully. You will want two trees about ten feet apart, from which to suspend your tent, and a bit of flat ground underneath them. Of course the flat ground need not be particularly unencumbered by brush or saplings, so the combination ought not to be hard to discover. Now return to your canoe. Do not unpack the tent.

With the little axe clear the ground thoroughly. By bending a sapling over strongly with the left hand, clipping sharply at the strained fibres, and then bending it as strongly the other way to repeat the axe stroke on the other side, you will find that treelets of even two or three inches diameter can be felled by two blows. In a very few moments you will have accomplished a hole in the forest, and your two supporting trees will stand sentinel at either end of a most respectable-looking clearing. Do not unpack the tent.

Now, although the ground seems free of all but unimportant growths, go over it thoroughly for little shrubs and leaves. They look soft and yielding, but are often possessed of unexpectedly abrasive roots. Besides, they mask the face of the ground. When you have finished pulling them up by the roots, you will find that your supposedly level plot is knobby with hummocks. Stand directly over each little mound; swing the back of your axe vigorously against it, adze-wise, between your legs. Nine times out of ten it will crumble, and the tenth time means merely a root to cut or a stone to pry out. At length you are possessed of a plot of clean, fresh earth, level and soft, free from projections. But do not unpack your tent.

Lay a young birch or maple an inch or so in diameter across a log. Two clips will produce you a tent-peg. If you are inexperienced, and cherish memories of striped lawn marquees, you will cut them about six inches long. If you are wise and old and gray in woods experience, you will multiply that length by four. Then your loops will not slip off, and you will have a real grip on mother earth, than which nothing can be more desirable in the event of a heavy rain and wind squall about midnight. If your axe is as sharp as it ought to be, you can point them more neatly by holding them suspended in front of you while you snip at their ends with the axe, rather than by resting them against a solid base. Pile them together at the edge of the clearing. Cut a crotched sapling eight or ten feet long. Now unpack your tent.

In a wooded country you will not take the time to fool with tent-poles. A stout line run through the eyelets and along the apex will string it successfully between your two trees. Draw the line as tight as possible, but do not be too unhappy if, after your best efforts, it still sags a little. That is what your long crotched stick is for. Stake out your four corners. If you get them in a good rectangle, and in such relation to the apex as to form two isosceles triangles of the ends, your tent will stand smoothly. Therefore, be an artist and do it right. Once the four corners are well placed, the rest follows naturally. Occasionally in the North Country it will be found that the soil is too thin over the rocks to grip the tent-pegs. In that case drive them at a sharp angle as deep as they will go, and then lay a large flat stone across the slant of them. Thus anchored, you will ride out a gale. Finally, wedge your long sapling crotch under the line--outside the tent, of course--to tighten it. Your shelter is up. If you are a woodsman, ten or fifteen minutes has sufficed to accomplish all this.

There remains the question of a bed, and you'd better attend to it now, while your mind is still occupied with the shelter problem. Fell a good thrifty young balsam and set to work pulling off the fans. Those you cannot strip off easily with your hands are too tough for your purpose. Lay them carelessly crisscross against the blade of your axe and up the handle. They will not drop off, and when you shoulder that axe you will resemble a walking haystack, and will probably experience a genuine emotion of surprise at the amount of balsam that can be thus transported. In the tent lay smoothly one layer of fans, convex side up, butts toward the foot. Now thatch the rest on top of this, thrusting the butt ends underneath the layer already placed in such a manner as to leave the fan ends curving up and down towards the foot of your bed. Your second emotion of surprise will assail you as you realize how much spring inheres in but two or three layers thus arranged. When you have spread your rubber blanket, you will be possessed of a bed as soft and a great deal more aromatic and luxurious than any you would be able to buy in town.

Your next care is to clear a living space in front of the tent. This will take you about twenty seconds, for you need not be particular as to stumps, hummocks, or small brush. All you want is room for cooking, and suitable space for spreading out your provisions. But do not unpack anything yet.

Your fireplace you will build of two green logs laid side by side. The fire is to be made between them. They should converge slightly, in order that the utensils to be rested across them may be of various sizes. If your vicinity yields flat stones, they build up even better than the logs--unless they happen to be of granite. Granite explodes most disconcertingly. Poles sharpened, driven upright into the ground, and then pressed down to slant over the fireplace, will hold your kettles a suitable height above the blaze.

Fuel should be your next thought. A roll of birch bark first of all. Then some of the small, dry, resinous branches that stick out from the trunks of medium-sized pines, living or dead. Finally, the wood itself. If you are merely cooking supper, and have no thought for a warmth-fire or a friendship-fire, I should advise you to stick to the dry pine branches, helped out, in the interest of coals for frying, by a little dry maple or birch. If you need more of a blaze, you will have to search out, fell, and split a standing dead tree. This is not at all necessary. I have travelled many weeks in the woods without using a more formidable implement than a one-pound hatchet. Pile your fuel--a complete supply, all you are

9

going to need--by the side of your already improvised fireplace. But, as you value your peace of mind, do not fool with matches.

It will be a little difficult to turn your mind from the concept of fire, to which all these preparations have compellingly led it--especially as a fire is the one cheerful thing your weariness needs the most at this time of day--but you must do so. Leave everything just as it is, and unpack your provisions.

First of all, rinse your utensils. Hang your tea-pail, with the proper quantity of water, from one slanting pole, and your kettle from the other. Salt the water in the latter receptacle. Peel your potatoes, if you have any; open your little provision sacks; puncture your tin cans, if you have any; slice your bacon; clean your fish; pluck your birds; mix your dough or batter; spread your table tinware on your tarpaulin or a sheet of birch bark; cut a kettle-lifter; see that everything you are going to need is within direct reach of your hand as you squat on your heels before the fireplace. Now light your fire.

The civilized method is to build a fire and then to touch a match to the completed structure. If well done and in a grate or steve, this works beautifully. Only in the woods you have no grate. The only sure way is as follows: Hold a piece of birch bark in your hand. Shelter your match all you know how. When the bark has caught, lay it in your fireplace, assist it with more bark, and gradually build up, twig by twig, stick by stick, from the first pin-point of flame, all the fire you are going to need. It will not be much. The little hot blaze rising between the parallel logs directly against the aluminium of your utensils will do the business in a very short order. In fifteen minutes at most your meal is ready. And you have been able to attain to hot food thus quickly because you were prepared.

In case of very wet weather the affair is altered somewhat. If the rain has just commenced, do not stop to clear out very thoroughly, but get your tent up as quickly as possible, in order to preserve an area of comparatively dry ground. But if the earth is already soaked, you had best build a bonfire to dry out by, while you cook over a smaller fire a little distance removed, leaving the tent until later. Or it may be well not to pitch the tent at all, but to lay it across slanting supports at an angle to reflect the heat against the ground.

It is no joke to light a fire in the rain. An Indian can do it more easily than a white man, but even an Indian has more trouble than the story-books acknowledge. You will need a greater quantity of birch bark, a bigger pile of resinous dead limbs from the pine trees, and perhaps the heart of a dead pine stub or stump. Then, with infinite patience, you may be able to tease the flame. Sometimes a small dead birch contains in the waterproof envelope of its bark a species of powdery, dry touchwood that takes the flame readily. Still, it is easy enough to start a blaze--a very fine-looking, cheerful, healthy blaze; the difficulty is to prevent its petering out the moment your back is turned.

But the depths of woe are sounded and the limit of patience reached when you are forced to get breakfast in the dripping forest. After the chill of early dawn you are always reluctant in the best of circumstances to leave your blankets, to fumble with numbed fingers for matches, to handle cold steel and slippery fish. But when every leaf, twig, sapling, and tree contains a douche of cold water; when the wetness oozes about your moccasins from the soggy earth with every step you take; when you look about you and realize that somehow, before you can get a mouthful to banish that before-breakfast ill-humour, you must brave cold water in an attempt to find enough fuel to cook with, then your philosophy and early religious training avail you little. The first ninety-nine times you are forced to do this you will probably squirm circumspectly through the bush in a vain attempt to avoid shaking water down on yourself; you will resent each failure to do so, and at the end your rage will personify the wilderness for the purpose of one sweeping anathema. The hundredth time will bring you wisdom. You will do the anathema--rueful rather than enraged--from the tent opening. Then you will plunge boldly in and get wet. It is not pleasant, but it has to be done, and you will save much temper, not to speak of time.

Dick and I earned our diplomas at this sort of work. It rained twelve of the first fourteen days we were out. Towards the end of that two weeks I doubt if even an Indian could have discovered a dry stick of wood in the entire country. The land was of Laurentian rock formation, running in parallel ridges of bare stone separated by hollows carpeted with a thin layer of earth. The ridges were naturally ill-adapted to camping, and the cup hollows speedily filled up with water until they became most creditable little marshes. Often we hunted for an hour or so before we could find any sort of a spot to pitch our tent. As for a fire, it was a matter of chopping down dead trees large enough to have remained dry inside, of armfuls of birch bark, and of the patient drying out, by repeated ignition, of enough fuel to cook very simple meals. Of course we could have kept a big fire going easily enough, but we were travelling steadily and had not the time for that. In these trying circumstances, Dick showed that, no matter how much of a tenderfoot he might be, he was game enough under stress.

But to return to our pleasant afternoon. While you are consuming the supper you will hang over some water to heat for the dish-washing, and the dish-washing you will attend to the moment you have finished eating. Do not commit the fallacy of sitting down for a little rest. Better finish the job completely while you are about it. You will appreciate leisure so much more later. In lack of a wash-rag you will find that a bunch of tall grass bent double makes an ideal swab.

Now brush the flies from your tent, drop the mosquito-proof lining, and enjoy yourself. The whole task, from first to last, has consumed but a little over an hour. And you are through for the day.

In the woods, as nowhere else, you will earn your leisure only by forethought. Make no move until you know it follows the line of greatest economy. To putter is to wallow in endless desolation. If you cannot move directly and swiftly and certainly along the line of least resistance in everything you do, take a guide with you; you are not of the woods people. You will never enjoy doing for yourself, for your days will be crammed with unending labour.

It is but a little after seven. The long crimson shadows of the North Country are lifting across the aisles of the forest. You sit on a log, or lie on your back, and blow contented clouds straight up into the air. Nothing can disturb you now. The wilderness is yours, for you have taken from it the essentials of primitive civilization--shelter, warmth, and food. An hour ago a rainstorm would have been a minor catastrophe. Now you do not care. Blow high, blow low, you have made for yourself an abiding-place, so that the signs of the sky are less important to you than to the city dweller who wonders if he should take an umbrella. From your doorstep you can look placidly out on the great unknown. The noises of the forest draw close about you their circle of mystery, but the circle cannot break upon you, for here you have conjured the homely sounds of kettle and crackling flame to keep ward. Thronging down through the twilight steal the jealous woodland shadows, awful in the sublimity of the Silent Places, but at the sentry outposts of your firelit trees they pause like wild animals, hesitating to advance. The wilderness, untamed, dreadful at night, is all about; but this one little spot you have reclaimed. Here is something before unknown to the eerie spirits of the woods. As you sleepily knock the ashes from the pipe, you look about on the familiar scene with accustomed satisfaction. You are at home.

## V.

### ON LYING AWAKE AT NIGHT.

"Who hath lain alone to hear the wild goose cry?"

About once in so often you are due to lie awake at night. Why this is so I have never been able to discover. It apparently comes from no predisposing uneasiness of indigestion, no rashness in the matter of too much tea or tobacco, no excitation of unusual incident or stimulating conversation. In fact, you turn in with the expectation of rather a good night's rest. Almost at once the little noises of the forest grow larger, blend in the hollow bigness of the first drowse; your thoughts drift idly back and forth between reality and dream; when--snap!--you are broad awake!

Perhaps the reservoir of your vital forces is full to the overflow of a little waste; or perhaps, more subtly, the great Mother insists thus that you enter the temple of her larger mysteries.

For, unlike mere insomnia, lying awake at night in the woods is pleasant. The eager, nervous straining for sleep gives way to a delicious indifference. You do not care. Your mind is cradled in an exquisite poppy-suspension of judgment and of thought. Impressions slip vaguely into your consciousness and as vaguely out again. Sometimes they stand stark and naked for your inspection; sometimes they lose themselves in the midst of half-sleep. Always they lay soft velvet fingers on the drowsy imagination, so that in their caressing you feel the vaster spaces from which they have come. Peaceful-brooding your faculties receive. Hearing, sight, smell--all are preternaturally keen to whatever of sound and sight and woods perfume is abroad through the night; and yet at the same time active appreciation dozes, so these things lie on it sweet and cloying like fallen rose leaves.

In such circumstance you will hear what the *voyageurs* call the voices of the rapids. Many people never hear them at all. They speak very soft and low and distinct beneath the steady roar and dashing, beneath even the lesser tinklings and gurglings whose quality superimposes them over the louder sounds. They are like the tear-forms swimming across the field of vision, which disappear so quickly when you concentrate your sight to look at them, and which reappear so magically when again your gaze turns vacant. In the stillness of your hazy half-consciousness they speak; when you bend your attention to listen, they are gone, and only the tumults and the tinklings remain.

But in the moments of their audibility they are very distinct. Just as often an odour will wake all a vanished memory, so these voices, by the force of a large impressionism, suggest whole scenes. Far off are the cling-clang-cling of chimes and the swell-and-fall murmur of a multitude *en fête*, so that subtly you feel the gray old town, with its walls, the crowded marketplace, the decent peasant crowd, the booths, the mellow church building with its bells, the warm, dust-moted sun. Or, in the pauses between the swish-dash-dashings of the waters, sound faint and clear voices singing intermittently, calls, distant notes of laughter, as though many canoes were working against the current; only the flotilla never gets any nearer, nor the voices louder. The *voyageurs* call these mist people the Huntsmen, and look frightened. To each is his vision, according to his experience. The nations of the earth whisper to their exiled sons through the voices of the rapids. Curiously enough, by all reports, they suggest always peaceful scenes--a harvest field, a street fair, a Sunday morning in a cathedral town, careless travellers--never the turmoils and struggles. Perhaps this is the great Mother's compensation in a harsh mode of life.

Nothing is more fantastically unreal to tell about, nothing more concretely real to experience, than this undernote of the quick water. And when you do lie awake at night, it is always making its unobtrusive appeal. Gradually its hypnotic spell works. The distant chimes ring louder and nearer as you cross the borderland of sleep. And then outside the tent some little woods noise snaps the thread. An owl hoots, a whippoorwill cries, a twig cracks beneath the cautious prowl of some night creature--at once the yellow sunlit French meadows puff away--you are staring at the blurred image of the moon spraying through the texture of your tent.

The voices of the rapids have dropped into the background, as have the dashing noises of the stream. Through the forest is a great silence, but no stillness at all. The whippoorwill swings down and up the short curve of his regular song; over and over an owl says his rapid *whoo, whoo, whoo*. These, with the ceaseless dash of the rapids, are the web on which the night traces her more delicate embroideries of the unexpected. Distant crashes, single and impressive; stealthy footsteps near at hand; the subdued scratching of claws; a faint *sniff! sniff! sniff!* of inquiry; the sudden clear tin-horn *ko-ko-ko-óh* of the little owl; the mournful, long-drawn-out cry of the loon, instinct with the spirit of loneliness; the ethereal call-note of the birds of passage high in the air; a *patter, patter, patter* among the dead leaves, immediately stilled; and then at the last, from the thicket close at hand, the beautiful silver purity of the white-throated sparrow--the nightingale of

**11**

the North--trembling with the ecstasy of beauty, as though a shimmering moonbeam had turned to sound; and all the while the blurred figure of the moon mounting to the ridge-line of your tent--these things combine subtly, until at last the great Silence of which they are a part overarches the night and draws you forth to contemplation.

No beverage is more grateful than the cup of spring water you drink at such a time; no moment more refreshing than that in which you look about you at the darkened forest. You have cast from you with the warm blanket the drowsiness of dreams. A coolness, physical and spiritual, bathes you from head to foot. All your senses are keyed to the last vibrations. You hear the littler night prowlers, you glimpse the greater. A faint, searching woods perfume of dampness greets your nostrils. And somehow, mysteriously, in a manner not to be understood, the forces of the world seem in suspense, as though a touch might crystallize infinite possibilities into infinite power and motion. But the touch lacks. The forces hover on the edge of action, unheeding the little noises. In all humbleness and awe, you are a dweller of the Silent Places.

At such a time you will meet with adventures. One night we put fourteen inquisitive porcupines out of camp. Near M'Gregor's Bay I discovered in the large grass park of my camp-site nine deer, cropping the herbage like so many beautiful ghosts. A friend tells me of a fawn that every night used to sleep outside his tent and within a foot of his head, probably by way of protection against wolves. Its mother had in all likelihood been killed. The instant my friend moved toward the tent opening the little creature would disappear, and it was always gone by earliest daylight. Nocturnal bears in search of pork are not uncommon. But even though your interest meets nothing but the bats and the woods shadows and the stars, that few moments of the sleeping world forces is a psychical experience to be gained in no other way. You cannot know the night by sitting up; she will sit up with you. Only by coming into her presence from the borders of sleep can you meet her face to face in her intimate mood.

The night wind from the river, or from the open spaces of the wilds, chills you after a time. You begin to think of your blankets. In a few moments you roll yourself in their soft wool. Instantly it is morning.

And, strange to say, you have not to pay by going through the day unrefreshed. You may feel like turning in at eight instead of nine, and you may fall asleep with unusual promptitude, but your journey will begin clear-headedly, proceed springily, and end with much in reserve. No languor, no dull headache, no exhaustion, follows your experience. For this once your two hours of sleep have been as effective as nine.


## VI.

THE 'LUNGE.


"Do you know the chosen water where the ouananiche is waiting?"


Dick and I travelled in a fifteen-foot wooden canoe, with grub, duffel, tent, and Deuce, the black-and-white setter dog. As a consequence we were pretty well down toward the water-line, for we had not realized that a wooden canoe would carry so little weight for its length in comparison with a birch-bark. A good heavy sea we could ride--with proper management and a little baling; but sloppy waves kept us busy.

Deuce did not like it at all. He was a dog old in the wisdom of experience. It had taken him just twenty minutes to learn all about canoes. After a single tentative trial he jumped lightly to the very centre of his place, with the lithe caution of a cat. Then if the water happened to be smooth, he would sit gravely on his haunches, or would rest his chin on the gunwale to contemplate the passing landscape. But in rough weather he crouched directly over the keel, his nose between his paws, and tried not to dodge when the cold water dashed in on him. Deuce was a true woodsman in that respect. Discomfort he always bore with equanimity, and he must often have been very cold and very cramped.

For just over a week we had been travelling in open water, and the elements had not been kind to us at all. We had crept up under rock-cliff points; had weathered the rips of white water to shelter on the other side; had struggled across open spaces where each wave was singly a problem to fail in whose solution meant instant swamping; had baled, and schemed, and figured, and carried, and sworn, and tried again, and succeeded with about two cupfuls to spare, until we as well as Deuce had grown a little tired of it. For the lust of travel was on us.

The lust of travel is a very real disease. It usually takes you when you have made up your mind that there is no hurry. Its predisposing cause is a chart or map, and its main symptom is the feverish delight with which you check off the landmarks of your journey. A fair wind of some force is absolutely fatal. With that at your back you cannot stop. Good fishing, fine scenery, interesting bays, reputed game, even camps where friends might be visited--all pass swiftly astern. Hardly do you pause for lunch at noon. The mad joy of putting country behind you eats all other interests. You recover only when you have come to your journey's end a week too early, and must then search out new voyages to fill in the time.

All this morning we had been bucking a strong north wind. Fortunately, the shelter of a string of islands had given us smooth water enough, but the heavy gusts sometimes stopped us as effectively as though we had butted solid land. Now about noon we came to the last island, and looked out on a five-mile stretch of tumbling seas. We landed the canoe and mounted a high rock.

"Can't make it like this," said I. "I'll take the outfit over and land it, and come back for you and the dog. Let's see that chart."

We hid behind the rock and spread out the map.

"Four miles," measured Dick. "It's going to be a terror."

We looked at each other vaguely, suddenly tired.

"We can't camp here--at this time of day," objected Dick, to our unspoken thoughts.

And then the map gave him an inspiration. "Here's a little river," ruminated Dick, "that goes to a little lake, and then there's another little river that flows from the lake and comes out about ten miles above here."

"It's a good thirty miles," I objected.

"What of it?" asked Dick calmly.

So the fever-lust of travel broke. We turned to the right behind the last island, searched out the reed-grown opening to the stream, and paddled serenely and philosophically against the current. Deuce sat up and yawned with a mighty satisfaction.

We had been bending our heads to the demon of wind; our ears had been filled with his shoutings, our eyes blinded with tears, our breath caught away from us, our muscles strung to the fiercest endeavour. Suddenly we found ourselves between the ranks of tall forest trees, bathed in a warm sunlight, gliding like a feather from one grassy bend to another of the laziest little stream that ever hesitated as to which way the grasses of its bed should float. As for the wind, it was lost somewhere away up high, where we could hear it muttering to itself about something.

The woods leaned over the fringe of bushes cool and green and silent. Occasionally through tiny openings we caught instant impressions of straight column trunks and transparent shadows. Miniature grass marshes jutted out from the bends of the little river. We idled along as with a homely rustic companion through the aloofness of patrician multitudes.

Every bend offered us charming surprises. Sometimes a muskrat swam hastily in a pointed furrow of ripple; vanishing wings, barely sensed in the flash, left us staring; stealthy withdrawals of creatures, whose presence we realized only in the fact of those withdrawals, snared our eager interest; porcupines rattled and rustled importantly and regally from the water's edge to the woods; herons, ravens, an occasional duck, croaked away at our approach; thrice we surprised eagles, once a tassel-eared Canada lynx. Or, if all else lacked, we still experienced the little thrill of pleased novelty over the disclosure of a group of silvery birches on a knoll; a magnificent white pine towering over the beech and maple forest; the unexpected aisle of a long, straight stretch of the little river.

Deuce approved thoroughly. He stretched himself and yawned and shook off the water, and glanced at me open-mouthed with doggy good-nature, and set himself to acquiring a conscientious olfactory knowledge of both banks of the river. I do not doubt he knew a great deal more about it than we did. Porcupines aroused his special enthusiasm. Incidentally, two days later he returned to camp after an expedition of his own, bristling as to the face with that animal's barbed weapons. Thenceforward his interest waned.

We ascended the charming little river two or three miles. At a sharp bend to the east a huge sheet of rock sloped from a round grass knoll sparsely planted with birches directly down into a pool. Two or three tree trunks jammed directly opposite had formed a sort of half dam under which the water lay dark. A tiny grass meadow forty feet in diameter narrowed the stream to half its width.

We landed. Dick seated himself on the shelving rock. I put my fish-rod together. Deuce disappeared.

Deuce always disappeared whenever we landed. With nose down, hind quarters well tucked under him, ears flying, he quartered the forest at high speed, investigating every nook and cranny of it for the radius of a quarter of a mile. When he has quite satisfied himself that we were safe for the moment, he would return to the fire, where he would lie, six inches of pink tongue vibrating with breathlessness, beautiful in the consciousness of virtue. Dick generally sat on a rock and thought. I generally fished.

After a time Deuce returned. I gave up flies, spoons, phantom minnows, artificial frogs, and crayfish. As Dick continued to sit on the rock and think, we both joined him. The sun was very warm and grateful, and I am sure we both acquired an added respect for Dick's judgment.

Just when it happened neither of us was afterwards able to decide. Perhaps Deuce knew. But suddenly, as often a figure appears in a cinematograph, the diminutive meadow thirty feet away contained two deer. They stood knee-deep in the grass, wagging their little tails in impatience of the flies.

"Look a' there!" stammered Dick aloud.

Deuce sat up on his haunches.

I started for my camera.

The deer did not seem to be in the slightest degree alarmed. They pointed four big ears in our direction, ate a few leisurely mouthfuls of grass, sauntered to the stream for a drink of water, wagged their little tails some more, and quietly faded into the cool shadows of the forest.

An hour later we ran out into reeds, and so to the lake. It was a pretty lake, forest-girt. Across the distance we made out a moving object which shortly resolved itself into a birch canoe. The canoe proved to contain an Indian, an Indian boy of about ten years, a black dog, and a bundle. When within a few rods of each other we ceased paddling, and drifted by with the momentum. The Indian was a fine-looking man of about forty, his hair bound with a red fillet, his feet incased in silk-worked moccasins, but otherwise dressed in white men's garments. He smoked a short pipe, and contemplated us gravely.

"Bo' jou', bo' jou'," we called in the usual double-barrelled North Country salutation.

"Bo' jou', bo' jou'," he replied.

"Kée-gons?" we inquired as to the fishing in the lake.

"Áh-hah," he assented.

13

We drifted by each other without further speech. When the decent distance of etiquette separated us we resumed our paddles.

I produced a young cable terminated by a tremendous spoon and a solid brass snell as thick as a telegraph wire. We had laid in this formidable implement in hopes of a big muscallunge. It had been trailed for days at a time. We had become used to its vibration, which actually seemed to communicate itself to every fibre of the light canoe. Every once in a while we would stop with a jerk that would nearly snap our heads off. Then we would know we had hooked the American continent. We had become used to that also. It generally happened when we attempted a little burst of speed. So when the canoe brought up so violently that all our tinware rolled on Deuce, Dick was merely disgusted.

"There she goes again," he grumbled. "You've hooked Canada."

Canada held quiescent for about three seconds. Then it started due south.

"Suffering serpents!" shrieked Dick.

"Paddle, you sulphurated idiot!" yelled I.

It was most interesting. All I had to do was to hang on and try to stay in the boat. Dick paddled and fumed and splashed water and got more excited. Canada dragged us bodily backward.

Then Canada changed his mind and started in our direction. I was plenty busy taking in slack, so I did not notice Dick. Dick was absolutely demented. His mind automatically reacted in the direction of paddling. He paddled, blindly, frantically. Canada came surging in, his mouth open, his wicked eyes flaming, a tremendous indistinct body lashing foam. Dick glanced once over his shoulder, and let out a frantic howl.

"You've got the sea-serpent!" he shrieked.

I turned to fumble for the pistol. We were headed directly for a log stranded on shore, and about ten feet from it.

"Dick!" I yelled in warning.

He thrust his paddle out forward just in time. The stout maple bent and cracked. The canoe hit with a bump that threw us forward. I returned to the young cable. It came in limp and slack.

We looked at each other sadly.

"No use," sighed Dick at last. "They've never invented the words, and we'd upset if we kicked the dog."

I had the end of the line in my hands.

"Look here!" I cried. That thick brass wire had been as cleanly bitten through as though it had been cut with clippers. "He must have caught sight of you," said I.

Dick lifted up his voice in lamentation. "You had four feet of him out of water," he wailed, "and there was a lot more."

"If you had kept cool," said I severely, "we shouldn't have lost him. You don't want to get rattled in an emergency; there's no sense in it."

"What were you going to do with that?" asked Dick, pointing to where I had laid the pistol.

"I was going to shoot him in the head," I replied with dignity. "It's the best way to land them."

Dick laughed disagreeably. I looked down. At my side lay our largest iron spoon.

We skirted the left-hand side of the lake in silence. Far out from shore the water was ruffled where the wind swept down, but with us it was as still and calm as the forest trees that looked over into it. After a time we turned short to the left through a very narrow passage between two marshy shores, and so, after a sharp bend of but a few hundred feet, came into the other river.

This was a wide stream, smoothly hurrying, without rapids or tumult. The forest had drawn to either side to let us pass. Here were the wilder reaches after the intimacies of the little river. Across stretches of marsh we could see an occasional great blue heron standing mid-leg deep. Long strings of ducks struggled quacking from invisible pools. The faint marsh odour saluted our nostrils from the point where the lily-pads flashed broadly, ruffling in the wind. We dropped out the smaller spoon and masterfully landed a five-pound pickerel. Even Deuce brightened. He cared nothing for raw fish, but he knew their possibilities. Towards evening we entered the hilly country, and so at the last turned to the left into a sand cove where grew maples and birches in beautiful park order under a hill. There we pitched camp, and, as the flies lacked, built a friendship-fire about which to forgather when the day was done.

Dick still vocally regretted the muscallunge told him of my big bear.

One day, late in the summer, I was engaged in packing some supplies along an old fur trail north of Lake Superior. I had accomplished one back-load, and with empty straps was returning to the cache for another. The trail at one point emerged into and crossed an open park some hundreds of feet in diameter, in which the grass grew to the height of the knee. When I was about halfway across, a black bear arose to his hind legs not ten feet from me, and remarked *Woof!* in a loud tone of voice. Now, if a man were to say *woof* to you unexpectedly, even in the formality of an Italian garden or the accustomedness of a city street, you would be somewhat startled. So I went to camp. There I told them about the bear. I tried to be conservative in my description, because I did not wish to be accused of exaggeration. My impression of the animal was that he and a spruce tree that grew near enough for ready comparison were approximately of the same stature. We returned to the grass park. After some difficulty we found a clear footprint. It was a little larger than that made by a good-sized coon.

"So, you see," I admonished didactically, "that lunge probably was not quite so large as you thought."

"It may have been a Chinese bear," said Dick dreamily--"a Chinese lady bear of high degree."

I                    gave                    him                    up.

## VII.

ON OPEN-WATER CANOE TRAVELLING.

"It is there that I am going, with an extra hand to bail her-- Just one single long-shore loafer that I know. He can take his chance of drowning while I sail and sail and sail her, For the Red Gods call me out, and I must go."

The following morning the wind had died, but had been succeeded by a heavy pall of fog. After we had felt our way beyond the mouth of the river we were forced to paddle north-west by north, in blind reliance on our compass. Sounds there were none. Involuntarily we lowered our voices. The inadvertent click of the paddle against the gunwale seemed to desecrate a foreordained stillness.

Occasionally to the right hand or the left we made out faint shadow-pictures of wooded islands that endured but a moment and then deliberately faded into whiteness. They formed on the view exactly as an image develops on a photographic plate. Sometimes a faint *lisp-lisp-lisp* of tiny waves against a shore nearer than it seemed cautioned us anew not to break the silence. Otherwise we were alone, intruders, suffered in the presence of a brooding nature only as long as we refrained from disturbances.

Then at noon the vapours began to eddy, to open momentarily in revelation of vivid green glimpses, to stream down the rising wind. Pale sunlight dashed fitfully across us like a shower. Somewhere in the invisibility a duck quacked. Deuce awoke, looked about him, and *yow-yow-yowed* in doggish relief. Animals understand thoroughly these subtleties of nature.

In half an hour the sun was strong, the air clear and sparkling, and a freshening wind was certifying our prognostications of a lively afternoon.

A light canoe will stand almost anything in the way of a sea, although you may find it impossible sometimes to force it in the direction you wish to go. A loaded canoe will weather a great deal more than you might think. However, only experience in balance and in the nature of waves will bring you safely across a stretch of whitecaps.

With the sea dead ahead you must not go too fast; otherwise you will dip water over the bow. You must trim the craft absolutely on an even keel; otherwise the comb of the wave, too light to lift you, will slop in over one gunwale or the other. You must be perpetually watching your chance to gain a foot or so between the heavier seas.

With the sea over one bow you must paddle on the leeward side. When the canoe mounts a wave, you must allow the crest to throw the bow off a trifle, but the moment it starts down the other slope you must twist your paddle sharply to regain the direction of your course. The careening tendency of this twist you must counteract by a corresponding twist of your body in the other direction. Then the hollow will allow you two or three strokes wherewith to assure a little progress. The double twist at the very crest of the wave must be very delicately performed, or you will ship water the whole length of your craft.

With the sea abeam you must simply paddle straight ahead. The adjustment is to be accomplished entirely by the poise of the body. You must prevent the capsize of your canoe when clinging to the angle of a wave by leaning to one side. The crucial moment, of course, is that during which the peak of the wave slips under you. In case of a breaking comber, thrust the flat of your paddle deep in the water to prevent an upset, and lean well to leeward, thus presenting the side and half the bottom of the canoe to the shock of water. Your recovery must be instant, however. If you lean a second too long, over you go. This sounds more difficult than it is. After a time you do it instinctively, as a skater balances. With the sea over the quarter you have merely to take care that the waves do not slue you around sidewise, and that the canoe does not dip water on one side or the other under the stress of your twists with the paddle. Dead astern is perhaps the most difficult of all, for the reason that you must watch both gunwales at once, and must preserve an absolutely even keel, in spite of the fact that it generally requires your utmost strength to steer. In really heavy weather one man only can do any work. The other must be content to remain passenger, and he must be trained to absolute immobility. No matter how dangerous a careen the canoe may take, no matter how much good cold water may pour in over his legs, he must resist his tendency to shift his weight. The entire issue depends on the delicacy of the steersman's adjustments, so he must be given every chance.

The main difficulty rests in the fact that such canoeing is a good deal like air-ship travel--there is not much opportunity to learn by experience. In a four-hour run across an open bay you will encounter somewhat over a thousand waves, no two of which are exactly alike, and any one of which can fill you up only too easily if it is not correctly met. Your experience is called on to solve instantly and practically a thousand problems. No breathing-space in which to recover is permitted you between them. At the end of the four hours you awaken to the fact that your eyes are strained from intense concentration, and that you taste copper.

Probably nothing, however, can more effectively wake you up to the last fibre of your physical, intellectual, and nervous being. You are filled with an exhilaration. Every muscle, strung tight, answers immediately and accurately to the slightest hint. You quiver all over with restrained energy. Your mind thrusts behind you the problem of the last wave as soon as solved, and leaps with insistent eagerness to the next. You attain that superordinary condition when your faculties react instinctively, like a machine. It is a species of intoxication. After a time you personify each wave; you grapple with it as with a personal adversary; you exult as, beaten and broken, it hisses away to leeward. "Go it, you son of a gun!" you shout. "Ah, you would, would you! think you can, do you?" and in the roar and rush of wind and water you crouch like a boxer on the defence, parrying the blows, but ready at the slightest opening to gain a stroke of the paddle.

In such circumstances you have not the leisure to consider distance. You are too busily engaged in slaughtering waves to consider your rate of progress. The fact that slowly you are pulling up on your objective point does not occur to you until you are within a few hundred yards of it. Then, unless you are careful, you are undone.

Probably the most difficult thing of all to learn is that the waves to be encountered in the last hundred yards of an open sweep are exactly as dangerous as those you dodged so fearfully four miles from shore. You are so nearly in that you unconsciously relax your efforts. Calmly, almost contemptuously, a big roller rips along your gunwale. You are wrecked--fortunately within easy swimming distance. But that doesn't save your duffel. Remember this: be just as careful with the very last wave as you were with the others. Get inside before you draw that deep breath of relief.

Strangely enough, in out-of-door sports, where it would seem that convention would rest practically at the zero point, the bugbear of good form, although mashed and disguised, rises up to confuse the directed practicality. The average man is wedded to his theory. He has seen a thing done in a certain way, and he not only always does it that way himself, but he is positively unhappy at seeing any one else employing a different method. From the swing at golf to the manner of lighting a match in the wind, this truism applies. I remember once hearing a long argument with an Eastern man on the question of the English riding-seat in the Western country.

"Your method is all very well," said the Westerner, "for where it came from. In England they ride to hunt, so they need a light saddle and very short stirrups set well forward. That helps them in jumping. But it is most awkward. Out here you want your stirrups very long and directly under you, so your legs hang loose, and you depend on your balance and the grip of your thighs--not your knees. It is less tiring, and better sense, and infinitely more graceful, for it more nearly approximates the bareback seat. Instead of depending on stirrups, you are part of the horse. You follow his every movement. And as for your rising trot, I'd like to see you accomplish it safely on our mountain trails, where the trot is the only gait practicable, unless you take for ever to get anywhere." To all of which the Easterner found no rebuttal except the, to him, entirely efficient plea that his own method was good form.

Now, of course, it is very pleasant to do things always accurately, according to the rules of the game, and if you are out merely for sport, perhaps it is as well to stick to them. But utility is another matter. Personally, I do not care at all to kill trout unless by the fly; but when we need meat and they do not need flies, I never hesitate to offer them any kind of doodle-bug they may fancy. I have even at a pinch clubbed them to death in a shallow, land-locked pool. Time will come in your open-water canoe experience when you will pull into shelter half full of water, when you will be glad of the fortuity of a chance cross-wave to help you out, when sheer blind luck, or main strength and awkwardness, will be the only reasons you can honestly give for an arrival, and a battered and dishevelled arrival at that. Do not, therefore, repine, or bewail your awkwardness, or indulge in undue self-accusations of "tenderfoot." Method is nothing; the arrival is the important thing. You are travelling, and if you can make time by nearly swamping yourself, or by dragging your craft across a point, or by taking any other base advantage of the game's formality, by all means do so. Deuce used to solve the problem of comfort by drinking the little pool of cold water in which he sometimes was forced to lie. In the woods, when a thing is to be done, do not consider how you have done it, or how you have seen it done, or how you think it ought to be done, but how it *can* be accomplished. Absolute fluidity of expedient, perfect adaptability, is worth a dozen volumes of theoretical knowledge. "If you can't talk," goes the Western expression, "raise a yell; if you can't yell, make signs; if you can't make signs, wave a bush."

And do not be too ready to take advice as to what you can or cannot accomplish, even from the woods people. Of course the woods Indians or the *voyageurs* know all about canoes, and you would do well to listen to them. But the mere fact that your interlocutor lives in the forest, while you normally inhabit the towns, does not necessarily give him authority. A community used to horses looks with horror on the instability of all water craft less solid than canal boats. Canoemen stand in awe of the bronco. The fishermen of the Georgian Bay, accustomed to venture out with their open sailboats in weather that forces the big lake schooners to shelter, know absolutely nothing about canoes. Dick and I made an eight-mile run from the Fox island to Killarney in a trifling sea, to be cheered during our stay at the latter place by doleful predictions of an early drowning. And this from a seafaring community. It knew all about boats; it knew nothing about canoes; and yet the unthinking might have been influenced by the advice of these men simply because they had been brought up on the water. The point is obvious. Do not attempt a thing unless you are sure of yourself; but do not relinquish it merely because some one else is not sure of you.

The best way to learn is with a bathing-suit. Keep near shore, and try everything. Don't attempt the real thing until your handling in a heavy sea has become as instinctive as snap-shooting or the steps of dancing. Remain on the hither side of caution when you start out. Act at first as though every wavelet would surely swamp you. Extend the scope of your operations very gradually, until you know just what you can do. *Never* get careless. Never take any *real* chances. That's all.


## VIII.

## THE STRANDED STRANGERS.


As we progressed, the country grew more and more solemnly aloof. In the Southland is a certain appearance of mobility, lent by the deciduous trees, the warm sun, the intimate nooks in which grow the commoner homely weeds and flowers, the abundance of bees and musical insects, the childhood familiarity of the well-known birds, even the pleasantly fickle aspects of the skies. But the North wraps itself in a mantle of awe. Great hills rest not so much in the stillness of sleep as in the calm of a mighty comprehension. The pines, rank after rank, file after file, are always trooping somewhere, up the slope, to pause at the crest before descending on the other side into the unknown. Bodies of water exactly of the size, shape, and general appearance we are accustomed to see dotted with pleasure craft and bordered with wharves, summer cottages, pavilions, and hotels, accentuate by that very fact a solitude that harbours only a pair of weirdly laughing loons. Like the hills, these lakes are lying in a deep, still repose, but a repose that somehow suggests the comprehending calm of those behind the veil. The whole country seems to rest in a suspense of waiting. A shot breaks the stillness for an instant, but its very memory is shadowy a moment after the echoes die. Inevitably the traveller feels thrust in upon himself by a neutrality more deadly than open hostility would be. Hostility at least supposes recognition of his existence, a rousing of forces to oppose him. This ignores. One can no longer wonder at the taciturnity of the men who dwell here; nor does one fail to grasp the eminent suitability to the country of its Indian name--the Silent Places.

Even the birds, joyful, lively, commonplace little people that they are, draw some of this aloofness to themselves. The North is full of the homelier singers. A dozen species of warblers lisp music-box phrases, two or three sparrows whistle a cheerful repertoire, the nuthatches and chickadees toot away in blissful *bourgeoisie*. And yet, somehow, that very circumstance thrusts the imaginative voyager outside the companionship of their friendliness. In the face of the great gods they move with accustomed familiarity. Somehow they possess in their little experience that which explains the mystery, so that they no longer stand in its awe. Their everyday lives are spent under the shadow of the temple whither you dare not bend your footsteps. The intimacy of occult things isolates also these wise little birds.

The North speaks, however, only in the voices of three--the two thrushes, and the white-throated sparrow. You must hear these each at his proper time.

The hermit thrush you will rarely see. But late some afternoon, when the sun is lifting along the trunks of the hardwood forest, if you are very lucky and very quiet, you will hear him far in the depth of the blackest swamps. Musically expressed, his song is very much like that of the wood thrush--three cadenced liquid notes, a quivering pause, then three more notes of another phrase, and so on. But the fineness of its quality makes of it an entirely different performance. If you symbolize the hermit thrush by the flute, you must call the wood thrush a chime of little tinkling bells. One is a rendition; the other the essence of liquid music. An effect of gold-embroidered richness, of depth going down to the very soul of things, a haunting suggestion of having touched very near to the source of tears, a conviction that the just interpretation of the song would be an equally just interpretation of black woods, deep shadows, cloistered sunlight, brooding hills--these are the subtle and elusive impressions you will receive in the middle of the ancient forest.

The olive-backed thrush you will enjoy after your day's work is quite finished. You will see him through the tobacco haze, perched on a limb against the evening sky. He utters a loud joyful *chirp* pauses for the attention he thus solicits, and then deliberately runs up five mellow double notes, ending with a metallic "*ting* chee chee chee" that sounds as though it had been struck on a triangle. Then a silence of exactly nine seconds and repeat. As regularly as clock-work this performance goes on. Time him as often as you will, you can never convict him of a second's variation. And he is so optimistic and willing, and his notes are so golden with the yellow of sunshine!

The white-throated sparrow sings nine distinct variations of the same song. He may sing more, but that is all I have counted. He inhabits woods, berry-vines, brulés, and clearings. Ordinarily he is cheerful, and occasionally aggravating. One man I knew he drove nearly crazy. To that man he was always saying, "*And he never heard the man say drink and the----.*" Toward the last my friend used wildly to offer him a thousand dollars if he would, if he only *would*, finish that sentence. But occasionally, in just the proper circumstances, he forgets his stump corners, his vines, his jolly sunlight, and his delightful bugs to become the intimate voice of the wilds. It is night, very still, Very dark. The subdued murmur of the forest ebbs and flows with the voices of the furtive folk--an undertone fearful to break the night calm. Suddenly across the dusk of silence flashes a single thread of silver, vibrating, trembling with some unguessed ecstasy of emotion: "*Ah! poor Canada Canada Canada Canada!*" it mourns passionately, and falls silent. That is all.

You will hear at various times other birds peculiarly of the North. Loons alternately calling and uttering their maniac laughter; purple finches or some of the pine sparrows warbling high and clear; the winter wren, whose rapturous ravings never fail to strike the attention of the dullest passer; all these are exclusively Northern voices, and each expresses some phase or mood of the Silent Places. But none symbolizes as do the three. And when first you hear one of them after an absence, you are satisfied that things are right in the world, for the North Country's spirit is as it was.

Now ensued a spell of calm weather, with a film of haze over the sky. The water lay like quicksilver, heavy and inert. Toward afternoon it became opalescent. The very substance of the liquid itself seemed impregnated with dyes ranging in shade from wine colour to the most delicate lilac. Through a smoke veil the sun hung, a ball of red, while beneath every island, every rock, every tree, every wild fowl floating idly in a medium apparently too delicate for its support, lurked the beautiful crimson shadows of the North.

Hour after hour, day after day, we slipped on. Point after point, island after island, presented itself silently to our inspection and dropped quietly astern. The beat of paddles fitted monotonously into the almost portentous stillness. It seemed that we might be able to go on thus for ever, lapped in the dream of some forgotten magic that had stricken breathless the life of the world. And then, suddenly, three weeks on our journey, we came to a town.

It was not the typical fur town of the Far North, but it lay at the threshold. A single street, worn smooth by the feet of men and dogs, but innocent of hoofs, fronted the channel. A board walk, elevated against the snows, bordered a row of whitewashed log and frame houses, each with its garden of brilliant flowers. A dozen wharves of various sizes, over whose edges peeped the double masts of Mackinaw boats, spoke of a fishing community. Between the roofs one caught glimpses of a low sparse woods and some thousand-foot hills beyond. We subsequently added the charm of isolation in learning that the nearest telegraph line was fifteen miles distant, while the railroad passed some fifty miles away.

**17**

Dick immediately went wild. It was his first glimpse of the mixed peoples. A dozen loungers, handsome, careless, graceful with the inimitable elegance of the half-breed's leisure, chatted, rolled cigarettes, and surveyed with heavy-eyed indolence such of the town as could be viewed from the shade in which they lay. Three girls, in whose dark cheeks glowed a rich French comeliness, were comparing purchases near the store. A group of rivermen, spike-booted, short-trousered, reckless of air, with their little round hats over one ear, sat chair-tilted outside the "hotel." Across the dividing fences of two of the blazoned gardens a pair of old crones gossiped under their breaths. Some Indians smoked silently at the edge of one of the docks. In the distance of the street's end a French priest added the quaintness of his cassock to the exotic atmosphere of the scene. At once a pack of the fierce sledge-dogs left their foraging for the offal of the fisheries, to bound challenging in the direction of poor Deuce. That highbred animal fruitlessly attempted to combine dignity with a discretionary lurking between our legs. We made demonstrations with sticks, and sought out the hotel, for it was about time to eat.

We had supper at a table with three Forest Rangers, two lumber-jacks, and a cat-like handsome "breed" whose business did not appear. Then we lit up and strolled about to see what we could see.

On the text of a pair of brass knuckles hanging behind the hotel bar I embroidered many experiences with the lumberjack. I told of a Wisconsin town where an enforced wait of five hours enabled me to establish the proportion of fourteen saloons out of a total of twenty frame buildings. I descanted craftily on the character of the woodsman out of the woods and in the right frame of mind for deviltry. I related how Jack Boyd, irritated beyond endurance at the annoyances of a stranger, finally with the flat of his hand boxed the man's head so mightily that he whirled around twice and sat down.

"Now," said Jack softly, "be more careful, my friend, or next time I'll *hit* you." Or of a little Irishman who shouted to his friends about to pull a big man from pounding the life quite out of him, "Let him alone! let him alone! I may be on top myself in a few minutes!" And of Dave Walker, who fought to a standstill with his bare fists alone five men who had sworn to kill him. And again of that doughty knight of the peavie who, when attacked by an axe, waved aside interference with the truly dauntless cry, "Leave him be, boys; there's an axe between us!"

I tried to sketch, too, the drive, wherein a dozen times in an hour these men face death with a smile or a curse--the raging untamed river, the fierce rush of the logs, the cool little human beings poising with a certain contemptuous preciosity on the edge of destruction as they herd their brutish multitudes.

There was Jimmy, the river boss, who could not swim a stroke, and who was incontinently swept over a dam and into the boiling back-set of the eddy below. Three times, gasping, strangling, drowning, he was carried in the wide swirl of the circle, sometimes under, sometimes on top. Then his knee touched a sand-bar, and he dragged himself painfully ashore. He coughed up a quantity of water, and gave vent to his feelings over a miraculous escape. "Damn it all!" he wailed, "I lost my peavie!"

"On the Paint River drive one spring," said I, "a jam formed that extended up river some three miles. The men were working at the breast of it, some underneath, some on top. After a time the jam apparently broke, pulled downstream a hundred feet or so, and plugged again. Then it was seen that only a small section had moved, leaving the main body still jammed, so that between the two sections lay a narrow stretch of open water. Into this open water one of the men had fallen. Before he could recover, the second or tail section of the jam started to pull. Apparently nothing could prevent him from being crushed. A man called Sam--I don't know his last name--ran down the tail of the first section, across the loose logs bobbing in the open water, seized the victim of the accident by the collar, desperately scaled the face of the moving jam, and reached the top just as the two sections ground together with the brutish noise of wrecking timbers. It was a magnificent rescue. Any but these men of iron would have adjourned for thanks and congratulations.

"Still retaining his hold on the other man's collar, Sam twisted him about and delivered a vigorous kick. '*There*, damn you!' said he. That was all. They fell to work at once to keep the jam moving."

I instanced, too, some of the feats of river-work these men could perform. Of how Jack Boyd has been known to float twenty miles without shifting his feet, on a log so small that he carried it to the water on his shoulder; of how a dozen rivermen, one after the other, would often go through the chute of a dam standing upright on single logs; of O'Donnell, who could turn a somersault on a floating pine log; of the birling matches, wherein two men on a single log try to throw each other into the river by treading, squirrel fashion, in faster and faster rotation; of how a riverman and spiked boots and a saw-log can do more work than an ordinary man with a rowboat.

I do not suppose Dick believed all this--although it was strictly and literally true--but his imagination was impressed. He gazed with respect on the group at the far end of the street, where fifteen or twenty lumber-jacks were interested in some amusement concealed from us.

"What do you suppose they are doing?" murmured Dick, awestricken.

"Wrestling, or boxing, or gambling, or jumping," said I.

We approached. Gravely, silently, intensely interested, the cock-hatted, spikeshod, dangerous men were playing--croquet!

The sight was too much for our nerves. We went away.

The permanent inhabitants of the place we discovered to be friendly to a degree.

The Indian strain was evident in various dilution through all. Dick's enthusiasm grew steadily until his artistic instincts became aggressive, and he flatly announced his intention of staying at least four days for the purpose of making sketches. We talked the matter over. Finally it was agreed. Deuce and I were to make a wide circle to the north and west as far as the Hudson's Bay post of Cloche, while Dick filled his notebook. That night we slept in beds for the first time.

That is to say, we slept until about three o'clock. Then we became vaguely conscious, through a haze of drowse--as one becomes conscious in the pause of a sleeping-car--of voices outside our doors. Some one said something about its being hardly much use to go to bed. Another hoped the sheets were not damp. A succession of lights twinkled across the walls of our room, and were vaguely explained by the coughing of a steamboat. We sank into oblivion until the calling-bell brought us to our feet.

I happened to finish my toilet a little before Dick, and so descended to the sunlight until he might be ready. Roosting on a gray old boulder ten feet outside the door were two figures that made me want to rub my eyes.

The older was a square, ruddy-faced man of sixty, with neatly trimmed, snow-white whiskers. He had on a soft Alpine hat of pearl gray, a modishly cut gray homespun suit, a tie in which glimmered an opal pin, wore tan gloves, and had slung over one shoulder by a narrow black strap a pair of field-glasses.

The younger was a tall and angular young fellow, of an eager and sophomoric youth. His hair was very light and very smoothly brushed, his eyes blue and rather near-sighted, his complexion pink, with an obviously recent and superficial sunburn, and his clothes, from the white Panama to the broad-soled low shoes, of the latest cut and material. Instinctively I sought his fraternity pin. He looked as though he might say "Rah! Rah!" something or other. A camera completed his outfit.

Tourists! How in the world did they get here? And then I remembered the twinkle of the lights and the coughing of the steamboat. But what in time could they be doing here? Picturesque as the place was, it held nothing to appeal to the Baedeker spirit. I surveyed the pair with some interest.

"I suppose there is pretty good fishing around here," ventured the elder.

He evidently took me for an inhabitant. Remembering my faded blue shirt and my floppy old hat and the red handkerchief about my neck and the moccasins on my feet, I did not blame him.

"I suppose there are bass among the islands," I replied.

We fell into conversation. I learned that he and his son were from New York.

He learned, by a final direct question which was most significant of his not belonging to the country, who I was. By chance he knew my name. He opened his heart.

"We came down on the *City of Flint*," said he. "My son and I are on a vacation. We have been as far as the Yellowstone, and thought we would like to see some of this country. I was assured that on this date I could make connection with the *North Star* for the south. I told the purser of the *Flint* not to wake us up unless the *North Star* was here at the docks. He bundled us off here at three in the morning. The *North Star* was not here; it is an outrage!"

He uttered various threats.

"I thought the *North Star* was running away south around the Perry Sound region," I suggested.

"Yes, but she was to begin to-day, June 16, to make this connection." He produced a railroad folder. "It's in this," he continued.

"Did you go by that thing?" I marvelled.

"Why, of course," said he.

"I forgot you were an American," said I. "You're in Canada now."

He looked his bewilderment, so I hunted up Dick. I detailed the situation. "He doesn't know the race," I concluded. "Soon he will be trying to get information out of the agent. Let's be on hand."

We were on hand. The tourist, his face very red, his whiskers very white and bristly, marched importantly to the agent's office. The latter comprised also the post-office, the fish depot, and a general store. The agent was for the moment dickering *in re* two pounds of sugar. This transaction took five minutes to the pound. Mr. Tourist waited. Then he opened up. The agent heard him placidly, as one who listens to a curious tale.

"What I want to know is, where's that boat?" ended the tourist.

"Couldn't say," replied the agent.

"Aren't you the agent of this company?"

"Sure," replied the agent.

"Then why don't you know something about its business and plans and intentions?"

"Couldn't say," replied the agent.

"Do you think it would be any good to wait for the *North Star*? Do you suppose they can be coming? Do you suppose they've altered the schedule?"

"Couldn't say," replied the agent.

"When is the next boat through here?"

I listened for the answer in trepidation, for I saw that another "Couldn't say" would cause the red-faced tourist to blow up. To my relief, the agent merely inquired,--

"North or south?"

"South, of course. I just came from the north. What in the name of everlasting blazes should I want to go north again for?"

"Couldn't say," replied the agent. "The next boat south gets in next week, Tuesday or Wednesday."

"Next week!" shrieked the tourist.

"When's the next boat north?" interposed the son.

"To-morrow morning."

"What time?"

"Couldn't say; you'd have to watch for her."

"That's our boat, dad," said the young man.

"But we've just *come* from there!" snorted his father; "it's three hundred miles back. It'll put us behind two days. I've got to be in New York Friday. I've got an engagement." He turned suddenly to the agent. "Here, I've got to send a telegram."

The agent blinked placidly. "You'll not send it from here. This ain't a telegraph station."

"Where's the nearest station?"

"Fifteen mile."

Without further parley the old man turned and walked, stiff and military, from the place. Near the end of the broad walk he met the usual doddering but amiable oldest inhabitant.

"Fine day," chirped the patriarch in well-meant friendliness. "They jest brought in a bear cub over to Antoine's. If you'd like to take a look at him, I'll show you where it is."

The tourist stopped short and glared fiercely.

"Sir," said he, "damn your bear!" Then he strode on, leaving grandpa staring after him.

In the course of the morning we became quite well acquainted, and he resigned. The son appeared to take somewhat the humorous view all through the affair, which must have irritated the old gentleman. They discussed it rather thoroughly, and finally decided to retrace their steps for a fresh start over a better-known route. This settled, the senior seemed to feel relieved of a weight. He even saw and relished certain funny phases of the incident, though he never ceased to foretell different kinds of trouble for the company, varying in range from mere complaints to the most tremendous of damage suits.

He was much interested, finally, in our methods of travel, and then, in logical sequence, with what he could see about him. He watched curiously my loading of the canoe, for I had a three-mile stretch of open water, and the wind was abroad. Deuce's empirical boat wisdom aroused his admiration. He and his son were both at the shore to see me off.

Deuce settled himself in the bottom. I lifted the stern from the shore and gently set it afloat. In a moment I was ready to start.

"Wait a minute! Wait a minute!" suddenly cried the father.

I swirled my paddle back. The old gentleman was hastily fumbling in his pockets. After an instant he descended to the water's edge.

"Here," said he, "you are a judge of fiction; take this."

It was his steamboat and railway folder.


## IX.

ON FLIES.


All the rest of the day I paddled under the frowning cliffs of the hill ranges. Bold, bare, scarred, seamed with fissures, their precipice rocks gave the impression of ten thousand feet rather that only so many hundreds. Late in the afternoon we landed against a formation of basaltic blocks cut as squarely up and down as a dock, and dropping off into as deep water. The waves *chug-chug-chugged* sullenly against them, and the fringe of a dark pine forest, drawn back from a breadth of natural grass, lowered across the horizon like a thunder-cloud.

Deuce and I made camp with the uneasy feeling of being under inimical inspection. A cold wind ruffled lead-like waters. No comfort was in the prospect, so we retired early. Then it appeared that the coarse grass of the park had bred innumerable black flies, and that we had our work cut out for us.

The question of flies--using that, to a woodsman, eminently connotive word in its wide embracement of mosquitoes, sandflies, deer-flies, black flies, and midges--is one much mooted in the craft. On no subject are more widely divergent ideas expressed. One writer claims that black flies' bites are but the temporary inconvenience of a pin-prick; another tells of boils lasting a week as the invariable result of their attentions; a third sweeps aside the whole question as unimportant to concentrate his anathemas on the musical mosquito; still a fourth descants on the maddening midge, and is prepared to defend his claims against the world. A like dogmatic partisanship obtains in the question of defences. Each and every man possessed of a tongue wherewith to speak or a pen wherewith to write, heralds the particular merits of his own fly-dope, head-net, or mosquito-proof tent-lining. Eager advocates of the advantages of pork fat, kerosene, pine tar, pennyroyal, oil of cloves, castor oil, lollacapop, or a half hundred other concoctions, will assure you, tears in eyes, that his is the only true faith. So many men, so many minds, until the theorist is confused into doing the most uncomfortable thing possible--that is, to learn by experience.

As for the truth, it is at once in all of them and in none of them. The annoyance of after-effects from a sting depends entirely on the individual's physical makeup. Some people are so poisoned by mosquito bites that three or four on the forehead suffice to close entirely the victim's eyes. On others they leave but a small red mark without swelling. Black flies caused festering sores on one man I accompanied to the woods. In my own case they leave only a tiny blood-spot the size of a pin-head, which bothers me not a bit. Midges nearly drove crazy the same companion of mine, so that finally he jumped into the river, clothes and all, to get rid of them. Again, merely my own experience would lead me to regard them as a tremendous nuisance, but one quite bearable. Indians are less susceptible than whites; nevertheless I have seen them badly swelled behind the ears from the bites of the big hardwood mosquito.

**20**

You can make up your mind to one thing: from the first warm weather until August you must expect to cope with insect pests. The black fly will keep you busy until late afternoon; the midges will swarm you about sunset; and the mosquito will preserve the tradition after you have turned in. As for the deer-fly, and others of his piratical breed, he will bite like a dog at any time.

To me the most annoying species is the mosquito. The black fly is sometimes most industrious--I have seen trout fishermen come into camp with the blood literally streaming from their faces--but his great recommendation is that he holds still to be killed. No frantic slaps, no waving of arms, no muffled curses. You just place your finger calmly and firmly on the spot. You get him every time. In this is great, heart-lifting joy. It may be unholy joy, perhaps even vengeful, but it leaves the spirit ecstatic. The satisfaction of *murdering* the beast that has had the nerve to light on you just as you are reeling in almost counterbalances the pain of a sting. The midge, again, or punkie, or "no-see-'um," just as you please, swarms down upon you suddenly and with commendable vigour, so that you feel as though red-hot pepper were being sprinkled on your bare skin; and his invisibility and intangibility are such that you can never tell whether you have killed him or not; but he doesn't last long, and dope routs him totally. Your mosquito, however, is such a deliberate brute. He has in him some of that divine fire which causes a dog to turn around nine times before lying down.

Whether he is selecting or gloating I do not know, but I do maintain that the price of your life's blood is often not too great to pay for the cessation of that hum.

"Eet is not hees bite," said Billy the half-breed to me once--"eet is hees sing."

I agree with Billy. One mosquito in a tent can keep you awake for hours.

As to protection, it is varied enough in all conscience, and always theoretically perfect. A head-net falling well down over your chest, or even tied under your arm-pits, is at once the simplest and most fallacious of these theories. It will keep vast numbers of flies out, to be sure. It will also keep the few adventurous discoverers in, where you can neither kill nor eject. Likewise you are deprived of your pipe; and the common homely comfort of spitting on your bait is totally denied you. The landscape takes on the prismatic colours of refraction, so that, while you can easily make out red, white, and blue Chinese dragons and mythological monsters, you are unable to discover the more welcome succulence, say, of a partridge on a limb. And the end of that head-net is to be picked to holes by the brush, and finally to be snatched from you to sapling height, whence your pains will rescue it only in a useless condition. Probably then you will dance the war-dance of exasperation on its dismembered remains. Still, there are times--in case of straight-away river paddling, or open walking, or lengthened waiting--when the net is a great comfort. And it is easily included in the pack.

Next in order come the various "dopes." And they are various. From the stickiest, blackest pastes to the silkiest, suavest oils they range, through the grades of essence, salve, and cream. Every man has his own recipe--the infallible. As a general rule, it may be stated that the thicker kinds last longer and are generally more thoroughly effective, but the lighter are pleasanter to wear, though requiring more frequent application. At a pinch, ordinary pork fat is good. The Indians often make temporary use of the broad caribou leaf, crushing it between their palms and rubbing the juices on the skin. I know by experience that this is effective, but very transitory. It is, however, a good thing to use when resting on the trail, for, by the grace of Providence, flies are rarely bothersome as long as you are moving at a fair gait.

This does not always hold good, however, any more than the best fly-dope is always effective. I remember most vividly the first day of a return journey from the shores of the Hudson Bay. The weather was rather oppressively close and overcast.

We had paddled a few miles up river from the fur trading-post, and then had landed in order to lighten the canoe for the ascent against the current. At that point the forest has already begun to dwindle towards the Land of Little Sticks, so that often miles and miles of open muskegs will intervene between groups of the stunted trees. Jim and I found ourselves a little over waist deep in luxuriant and tangled grasses that impeded and clogged our every footstep. Never shall I forget that country--its sad and lonely isolation, its dull lead sky, its silence, and the closeness of its stifling atmosphere--and never shall I see it otherwise than as in a dense brown haze, a haze composed of swarming millions of mosquitoes. There is not the slightest exaggeration in the statement. At every step new multitudes rushed into our faces to join the old. At times Jim's back was so covered with them that they almost overlaid the colour of the cloth. And as near as we could see, every square foot of the thousands of acres quartered its hordes.

We doped liberally, but without the slightest apparent effect. Probably two million squeamish mosquitoes were driven away by the disgust of our medicaments, but what good did that do us when eight million others were not so particular? At the last we hung bandanas under our hats, cut fans of leaves, and stumbled on through a most miserable day until we could build a smudge at evening.

For smoke is usually a specific. Not always, however: some midges seem to delight in it. The Indians make a tiny blaze of birch bark and pine twigs deep in a nest of grass and caribou leaves. When the flame is well started, they twist the growing vegetation canopy-wise above it.

In that manner they gain a few minutes of dense, acrid smoke, which is enough for an Indian. A white man, however, needs something more elaborate.

The chief reason for your initial failure in making an effective smudge will be that you will not get your fire well started before piling on the damp smoke-material. It need not be a conflagration, but it should be bright and glowing, so that the punk birch or maple wood you add will not smother it entirely. After it is completed, you will not have to sit coughing in the thick of fumigation, as do many, but only to leeward and underneath. Your hat used as a fan will eddy the smoke temporarily into desirable nooks and crevices. I have slept without annoyance on the Great Plains, where the mosquitoes seem to go in organized and predatory bands, merely by lying beneath a smudge that passed at least five feet above me. You will find the frying-pan a handy brazier for the accommodation of a movable smoke to be transported to the interior of the tent. And it does not in the least hurt the frying-pan. These be hints, briefly spoken, out of which at times you may have to construct elaborate campaigns.

But you come to grapples in the defence of comfort when night approaches. If you can eat and sleep well, you can stand almost any hardship. The night's rest is as carefully to be fore-assured as the food that sustains you. No precaution is too elaborate to certify unbroken repose. By dark you will discover the peak of your tent to be liberally speckled with insects of all sorts. Especially is this true of an evening that threatens rain. Your smudge-pan may drive away the mosquitoes, but merely stupefies the other varieties. You are forced to the manipulation of a balsam fan.

In your use of this simple implement you will betray the extent of your experience. Dick used at first to begin at the rear peak and brush as rapidly as possible toward the opening. The flies, thoroughly aroused, eddied about a few frantic moments, like leaves in an autumn wind, finally to settle close to the sod in the crannies between the tent-wall and the ground. Then Dick would lie flat on his belly in order to brush with equal vigour at these new lurking-places. The flies repeated the autumn-leaf effect, and returned to the rear peak. This was amusing to me, and furnished the flies with healthful, appetizing exercise, but was bad for Dick's soul. After a time he discovered the only successful method is the gentle one. Then he began at the peak and brushed forward slowly, very, very slowly, so that the limited intellect of his visitors did not become confused. Thus when they arrived at the opening they saw it and used it, instead of searching frantically for corners in which to hide from apparently vengeful destruction. Then he would close his tent-flap securely, and turn in at once. So he was able to sleep until earliest daylight. At that time the mosquitoes again found him out.

Nine out of ten--perhaps ninety-nine out of a hundred--sleep in open tents. For absolute and perfect comfort proceed as follows:--Have your tent-maker sew you a tent of cheese-cloth* with the same dimensions as your shelter, except that the walls should be loose and voluminous at the bottom. It should have no openings.

* Do not allow yourself to be talked into substituting mosquito-bar or bobinet. Any mesh coarser than cheese-cloth will prove pregnable to the most enterprising of the smaller species.

Suspend this affair inside your tent by means of cords or tapes. Drop it about you. Spread it out. Lay rod-cases, duffel-bags, or rocks along its lower edges to keep it spread. You will sleep beneath it like a child in winter. No driving out of reluctant flies; no enforced early rising; no danger of a single overlooked insect to make the midnight miserable. The cheese-cloth weighs almost nothing, can be looped up out of the way in the daytime, admits the air readily. Nothing could fill the soul with more ecstatic satisfaction than to lie for a moment before going to sleep listening to a noise outside like an able-bodied sawmill that indicates the *ping-gosh* are abroad.

It would be unfair to leave the subject without a passing reference to its effect on the imagination. We are all familiar with comic paper mosquito stories, and some of them are very good. But until actual experience takes you by the hand and leads you into the realm of pure fancy, you will never know of what improvisation the human mind is capable.

The picture rises before my mind of the cabin of a twenty-eight-foot cutter-sloop just before the dawn of a midsummer day. The sloop was made for business, and the cabin harmonized exactly with the sloop--painted pine, wooden bunks without mattresses, camp-blankets, duffel-bags slung up because all the floor place had been requisitioned for sleeping purposes. We were anchored a hundred feet off land from Pilot Cove, on the uninhabited north shore. The mosquitoes had adventured on the deep. We lay half asleep.

"On the middle rafter," murmured the Football Man, "is one old fellow giving signals."

"A quartette is singing drinking-songs on my nose," muttered the Glee Club Man.

"We won't need to cook," I suggested somnolently. "We can run up and down on deck with our mouths open and get enough for breakfast."

The fourth member opened one eye. "Boys," he breathed, "we won't be able to go on to-morrow unless we give up having any more biscuits."

After a time some one murmured, "Why?"

"We'll have to use all the lard on the mast. They're so mad because they can't get at us that they're biting the mast. It's already swelled up as big as a barrel. We'll never be able to get the mainsail up. Any of you boys got any vaseline? Perhaps a little fly-dope--"

But we snored vigorously in unison. The Indians say that when Kitch' Manitou had created men he was dissatisfied, and so brought women into being. At once love-making began, and then, as now, the couples sought solitude for their exchanges of vows, their sighings to the moon, their claspings of hands. Marriages ensued. The situation remained unchanged. Life was one perpetual honeymoon. I suppose the novelty was fresh and the sexes had not yet realized they would not part as abruptly as they had been brought together. The villages were deserted, while the woods and bushes were populous with wedded and unwedded lovers. Kitch' Manitou looked on the proceedings with disapproval. All this was most romantic and beautiful, no doubt, but in the meantime mi-dáw-min, the corn, mi-nó-men, the rice, grew rank and uncultivated; while bis-íw, the lynx, and swingwáage, the wolverine, and me-én-gan, the wolf, committed unchecked depredations among the weaker forest creatures. The business of life was being sadly neglected. So Kitch' Manitou took counsel with himself, and created sáw-gi-may, the mosquito, to whom he gave as dwelling the woods and bushes. That took the romance out of the situation. As my narrator grimly expressed it, "Him come back, go to work."

Certainly it should be most effective. Even the thick-skinned moose is not exempt from discomfort. At certain seasons the canoe voyager in the Far North will run upon a dozen in the course of a day's travel, standing nose-deep in the river merely to escape the insect pests.

However, this is to be remembered: after the first of August they bother very little; before that time the campaign I have outlined is effective; even in fly season the worst days are infrequent. In the woods you must expect to pay a certain price in discomfort for a very real and very deep pleasure. Wet, heat, cold, hunger, thirst, difficult travel, insects, hard beds, aching muscles--all these at one time or another will be your portion. If you are of the class that cannot have a good time unless everything is right with it, stay out of the woods. One thing at least will always be wrong. When you have gained the faculty of ignoring the one disagreeable thing and concentrating your powers on the compensations, then you will have become a true woodsman, and to your desires the forest will always be calling.

## X.

CLOCHE.

Imagine a many-armed lake, like a starfish, nested among rugged Laurentian hills, whose brows are bare and forbidding, but whose concealed ravines harbour each its cool screen of forest growth. Imagine a brawling stream escaping at one of the arms, to tumble, intermittently visible among the trees, down a series of cascades and rapids, to the broad, island-dotted calm of the big lake. Imagine a meadow at the mouth of this stream, and on the meadow a single white dot. Thus you will see Cloche, a trading-post of the Honourable the Hudson's Bay Company, as Deuce and I saw it from the summit of the hills.

We had accomplished a very hard scramble, which started well enough in a ravine so leafy and green and impenetrable that we might well have imagined ourselves in a boundless forest. Deuce had scented sundry partridges, which he had pointed with entire deference to the good form of a sporting dog's conventions. As usual, to Deuce's never-failing surprise and disgust, the birds had proved themselves most uncultivated and rude persons by hopping promptly into trees instead of lying to point and then flushing as a well-taught partridge should. I had refused to pull pistol on them. Deuce's heart was broken. Then, finally, we came to cliffs up which we had to scale, and boulders which we had to climb, and fissures which we had to jump or cross on fallen trees, and wide, bare sweeps of rock and blueberry bushes which we had to cover, until at last we stood where we could look all ways at once.

The starfish thrust his insinuating arms in among the distant hills to the north. League after league, rising and falling and rising again into ever bluer distance, forest-covered, mysterious, other ranges and systems lifted, until at last, far out, nearly at the horizon-height of my eye, flashed again the gleam of water. And so the starfish arms of the little lake at my feet seemed to have plunged into this wilderness tangle only to reappear at greater distance. Like swamp-fire, it lured the imagination always on and on and on through the secret waterways of the uninhabited North. It was as though I stood on the dividing ridge between the old and the new. Through the southern haze, hull down, I thought to make out the smoke of a Great Lake freighter; from the shelter of a distant cove I was not surprised a moment later to see emerge a tiny speck whose movements betrayed it as a birch canoe. The great North was at this, the most southern of the Hudson's Bay posts, striking a pin-point of contact with the world of men.

Deuce and I angled down the mountain toward the stream. Our arrival coincided with that of the canoe. It was of the Ojibway three-fathom pattern, and contained a half-dozen packs, a sledge-dog, with whom Deuce at once opened guarded negotiations, an old Indian, a squaw, and a child of six or eight. We exchanged brief greetings. Then I sat on a stump and watched the portage.

These were evidently "Woods Indians," an entirely different article from the "Post Indians." They wore their hair long, and bound by a narrow strip or fillet; their faces were hard and deeply lined, with a fine, bold, far-seeing look to the eyes which comes only from long woods dwelling. They walked, even under heavy loads, with a sagging, springy gait, at once sure-footed and swift. Instead of tump-lines the man used his sash, and the woman a blanket knotted loosely together at the ends. The details of their costumes were interesting in combination of jeans and buckskin, broadcloth and blanket, stroud and a material evidently made from the strong white sacking in which flour intended for frontier consumption is always packed. After the first double-barrelled "bo' jou', bo' jou'," they paid no further attention to me. In a few moments the portage was completed. The woman thrust her paddle against the stream's bottom and the canoe, and so embarked. The man stepped smoothly to his place like a cat leaping from a chair. They shot away with the current, leaving behind them a strange and mysterious impression of silence.

I followed down a narrow but well-beaten trail, and so at the end of a half-mile came to the meadow and the post of Cloche.

The building itself was accurately of the Hudson Bay type--a steep, sloping roof greater in front than behind, a deep recessed veranda, squared logs sheathed with whitewashed boards. About it was a little garden, which, besides the usual flowers and vegetables, contained such exotics as a deer confined to a pen and a bear chained to a stake. As I approached, the door opened and the Trader came out.

Now, often along the southern fringe your Hudson's Bay Trader will prove to be a distinct disappointment. In fact, one of the historic old posts is now kept by a pert little cockney Englishman, cringing or impudent as the main chance seems to advise. When you have penetrated further into the wilderness, however, where the hardships of winter and summer travel, the loneliness of winter posts, the necessity of dealing directly with savage men and savage nature, develops the quality of a man or wrecks him early in the game, you will be certain of meeting your type. But here, within fifty miles of the railroad!

The man who now stepped into view, however, preserved in his appearance all the old traditions. He was, briefly, a short black-and-white man built very square. Immense power lurked in the broad, heavy shoulders, the massive chest, the thick arms, the sturdy, column-like legs. As for his face, it was almost entirely concealed behind a curly square black beard that grew above his cheek-bones nearly to his eyes. Only a thick hawk nose, an inscrutable pair of black eyes under phenomenally heavy eyebrows, and a short black pipe showed plainly from the hirsute tangle. He was lock, stock, and barrel of the Far North, one of the old *régime*. I was rejoiced to see him there, but did not betray a glimmer of interest. I knew my type too well for that.

"How are you?" he said grudgingly.

"Good-day," said I.

We leaned against the fence and smoked, each contemplating carefully the end of his pipe. I knew better than to say anything. The Trader was looking me over, making up his mind about me. Speech on my part would argue lightness of disposition, for it would seem to indicate that I was not also making up my mind about him.

In this pause there was not the least unfriendliness. Only, in the woods you prefer to know first the business and character of a chance acquaintance. Afterwards you may ingratiate to his good will. All of which possesses a beautiful simplicity, for it proves that good or bad opinion need not depend on how gracefully you can chatter assurances. At the end of a long period the Trader inquired, "Which way you headed?"

"Out in a canoe for pleasure. Headed almost anywhere."

Again we smoked.

"Dog any good?" asked the Trader, removing his pipe and pointing to the observant Deuce.

"He'll hunt shade on a hot day," said I tentatively. "How's the fur in this district?"

We were off. He invited me in and showed me his bear. In ten minutes we were seated chair-tilted on the veranda, and slowly, very cautiously, in abbreviated syncopation, were feeling our way toward an intimacy.

Now came the Indians I had seen at the lake to barter for some flour and pork. I was glad of the chance to follow them all into the trading-room. A low wooden counter backed by a grill divided the main body of the room from the entrance. It was deliciously dim. All the charm of the Aromatic Shop was in the place, and an additional flavour of the wilds. Everything here was meant for the Indian trade: bolts of bright-patterned ginghams, blankets of red or blue, articles of clothing, boxes of beads for decoration, skeins of brilliant silk, lead bars for bullet-making, stacks of long brass-bound "trade guns" in the corner, small mirrors, red and parti-coloured worsted sashes with tassels on the ends, steel traps of various sizes, and a dozen other articles to be desired by the forest people. And here, unlike the Aromatic Shop, were none of the products of the Far North. All that, I knew, was to be found elsewhere, in another apartment, equally dim, but delightful in the orderly disorder of a storeroom.

Afterwards I made the excuse of a pair of moccasins to see this other room. We climbed a steep, rough flight of stairs to emerge through a sort of trap-door into a space directly under the roof. It was lit only by a single little square at one end. Deep under the eaves I could make out row after row of boxes and chests. From the rafters hung a dozen pair of snow-shoes. In the centre of the floor, half overturned, lay an open box from which tumbled dozens of pairs of moose-hide snow-shoe moccasins.

Shades of childhood, what a place! No one of us can fail to recall with a thrill the delights of a rummage in the attic-- the joy of pulling from some half-forgotten trunk a wholly forgotten shabby garment, which nevertheless has taken to itself from the stillness of undisturbed years the faint aroma of romance; the rapture of discovering in the dusk of a concealed nook some old spur or broken knife or rusty pistol redolent of the open road. Such essentially commonplace affairs they are, after all, in the light of our mature common sense, but such unspeakable ecstasies to the romance-breathing years of fancy. Here would no fancy be required. To rummage in these silent chests and boxes would be to rummage, not in the fictions of imagination, but the facts of the most real picturesque. In yonder square box are the smoke-tanned shoes of silence; that velvet dimness would prove to be the fur of a bear; this birch-bark package contains maple sugar savoured of the wilds. Buckskin, both white and buff, bears' claws in strings, bundles of medicinal herbs, sweet-grass baskets fragrant as an Eastern tale, birch-bark boxes embroidered with stained quills of the porcupines, bows of hickory and arrows of maple, queer half-boots of stiff sealskin from the very shores of the Hudson Bay, belts of beadwork, yellow and green, for the Corn Dance, even a costume or so of buckskin complete for ceremonial--all these the fortunate child would find were he to take the rainy-day privilege in this, the most wonderful attic in all the world. And then, after he had stroked the soft fur, and smelled the buckskin and sweet grasses, and tasted the crumbling maple sugar, and dressed himself in the barbaric splendours of the North, he could flatten his little nose against the dim square of light and look out over the glistening yellow backs of a dozen birchbark canoes to the distant, rain-blurred hills, beyond which lay the country whence all these things had come. Do you wonder that in after years that child hits the Long Trail? Do you still wonder at finding these strange, taciturn, formidable, tender-hearted men dwelling lonely in the Silent Places?

The Trader yanked several of the boxes to the centre and prosaically tumbled about their contents. He brought to light heavy moose-hide moccasins with high linen tops for the snow; lighter buckskin moccasins, again with the high tops, but this time of white tanned doeskin; slipper-like deer-skin moccasins with rolled edges, for the summer; oil-tanned shoepacs, with and without the flexible leather sole; "cruisers" of varying degree of height--each and every sort of footgear in use in the Far North, excepting and saving always the beautiful soft doeskin slippers finished with white fawnskin and ornamented with the Ojibway flower pattern for which I sought. Finally he gave it up.

"I had a few pair. They must have been sent out," said he.

We rummaged a little further for luck's sake, then descended to the outer air. I left him to fetch my canoe, but returned in the afternoon. We became friends. That evening we sat in the little sitting-room and talked far into the night.

He was a true Hudson's Bay man, steadfastly loyal to the Company. I mentioned the legend of *La Longue Traverse*; he stoutly asserted he had never heard of it. I tried to buy a mink-skin or so to hang on the wall as souvenir of my visit; he was genuinely distressed, but had to refuse because the Company had not authorized him to sell, and he had nothing of his own to give. I mentioned the River of the Moose, the Land of Little Sticks; his deep eyes sparkled with excitement, and he asked eagerly a multitude of details concerning late news from the northern posts.

And as the evening dwindled, after the manner of Traders everywhere, he began to tell me the "ghost stories" of this station of Cloche. Every post has gathered a mass of legendary lore in the slow years, but this had been on the route of the *voyageurs* from Montreal and Quebec at the time when the lords of the North journeyed to the scenes of their annual revels at Fort Williams. The Trader had much to say of the magnificence and luxury of these men--their cooks, their silken tents, their strange and costly foods, their rare wines, their hordes of French and Indian canoemen and packers. Then Cloche was a halting-place for the night. Its meadows had blossomed many times with the gay tents and banners of a great company. He told me, as vividly as though he had been an eye-witness, of how the canoes must have loomed up suddenly from between the islands. By-and-by he seized the lamp and conducted me outside, where hung ponderous ornamental steelyards, on which in the old days the peltries were weighed.

"It is not so now," said he. "We buy by count, and modern scales weigh the provisions. And the beaver are all gone."

We re-entered the house in silence. After a while he began briefly to sketch his own career. Then, indeed, the flavour of the Far North breathed its crisp, bracing ozone through the atmosphere of the room.

He had started life at one of the posts of the Far North-West. At the age of twelve he enlisted in the Company. Throughout forty years he had served her. He had travelled to all the strange places of the North, and claimed to have stood on the shores of that half-mythical lake of Yamba Tooh.

"It was snowing at the time," he said prosaically; "and I couldn't see anything, except that I'd have to bear to the east to get away from open water. Maybe she wasn't the lake. The Injins said she was, but I was too almighty shy of grub to bother with lakes."

Other names fell from him in the course of talk, some of which I had heard and some not, but all of which rang sweet and clear with no uncertain note of adventure. Especially haunts my memory an impression of desolate burned trees standing stick-like in death on the shores of Lost River.

He told me he had been four years at Cloche, but expected shortly to be transferred, as the fur was getting scarce, and another post one hundred miles to the west could care for the dwindling trade. He hoped to be sent into the North-West, but shrugged his shoulders as he said so, as though that were in the hands of the gods. At the last he fished out a concertina and played for me. Have you ever heard, after dark, in the North, where the hills grow big at sunset, *à la Claire Fontaine* crooned to such an accompaniment, and by a man of impassive bulk and countenance, but with glowing eyes?

I said good-night, and stumbled, sight-dazed, through the cool dark to my tent near the beach. The weird minor strains breathed after me as I went.

"A la claire fontaine M'en allant promener, J'ai trouvé l'eau si belle Que je m'y suis baigné, Il y a longtemps que je t'aime Jamais je ne t'oublierai."

The next day, with the combers of a howling north-westerly gale clutching at the stern of the canoe, I rode in a glory of spray and copper-tasting excitement back to Dick and his half-breed settlement.

But the incident had its sequel. The following season, as I was sitting writing at my desk, a strange package was brought me. It was wrapped in linen sewn strongly with waxed cord. Its contents lie before me now--a pair of moccasins fashioned of the finest doeskin, tanned so beautifully that the delicious smoke fragrance fills the room, and so effectively that they could be washed with soap and water without destroying their softness. The tongue-shaped piece over the instep is of white fawnskin heavily ornamented in five colours of silk. Where it joins the foot of the slipper it is worked over and over into a narrow cord of red and blue silk. The edge about the ankle is turned over, deeply scalloped, and bound at the top with a broad band of blue silk stitched with pink. Two tiny blue bows at either side the ankle ornament the front. Altogether a most magnificent foot-gear. No word accompanied them, apparently, but after some search I drew a bit of paper from the toe of one of them. It was inscribed simply--"Fort la Cloche."

## XI.

## THE HABITANTS.

During my absence Dick had made many friends. Wherein lies his secret I do not know, but he has a peculiar power of ingratiation with people whose lives are quite outside his experience or sympathies. In the short space of four days he had earned joyous greetings from every one in town. The children grinned at him cheerfully; the old women cackled good-natured little teasing jests to him as he passed; the pretty, dusky half-breed girls dropped their eyelashes fascinatingly across their cheeks, tempering their coyness with a smile; the men painfully demanded information as to artistic achievement which was evidently as well meant as it was foreign to any real thirst for knowledge they might possess; even the lumber-jacks addressed him as "Bub." And withal Dick's methods of approach were radically wrong, for he blundered upon new acquaintance with a beaming smile, which is ordinarily a sure repellent to the cautious, taciturn men of the woods. Perhaps their keenness penetrated to the fact that he was absolutely without guile, and that his kindness was an essential part of himself. I should be curious to know whether Billy Knapp of the Black Hills would surrender his gun to Dick for inspection.

"I want you to go out this afternoon to see some friends of mine," said Dick. "They're on a farm about two miles back in the brush. They're ancestors."

"They're what?" I inquired.

"Ancestors. You can go down to Grosse Point near Detroit, and find people living in beautiful country places next the water, and after dinner they'll show you an old silhouette or a daguerreotype or something like that, and will say to you proudly, 'This is old Jules, my ancestor, who was a pioneer in this country. The Place has been in the family ever since his time.'"

"Well?"

"Well, this is a French family, and they are pioneers, and the family has a place that slopes down to the water through white birch trees, and it is of the kind very tenacious of its own land. In two hundred years this will be a great resort; bound to be--beautiful, salubrious, good sport, fine scenery, accessible--"

"Railroad fifty miles away; boat every once in a while," said I sarcastically.

"Accessible in two hundred years, all right," insisted Dick serenely. "Even Canada can build a quarter of a mile of railway a year. Accessible," he went on; "good shipping-point for country now undeveloped."

"You ought to be a real estate agent," I advised.

"Lived two hundred years too soon," disclaimed Dick. "What more obvious? These are certainly ancestors."

"Family may die out," I suggested.

"It has a good start," said Dick sweetly. "There are eighty-seven in it now."

"What!" I gasped.

"One great-grandfather, twelve grandparents, thirty-seven parents, and thirty-seven children," tabulated Dick.

"I should like to see the great-grandfather," said I; "he must be very old and feeble."

"He is eighty-five years old," said Dick, "and the last time I saw him he was engaged with an axe in clearing trees off his farm."

All of these astonishing statements I found to be absolutely true.

We started out afoot soon after dinner, through a scattering growth of popples that alternately drew the veil of coyness over the blue hills and caught our breath with the delight of a momentary prospect. Deuce, remembering autumn days, concluded partridges, and scurried away on the expert diagonal, his hind legs tucked well under his flanks. The road itself was a mere cutting through the miniature woods, winding to right or left for the purpose of avoiding a log-end or a boulder, surmounting little knolls with an idle disregard for the straight line, knobby with big, round stones, and interestingly diversified by circular mud holes a foot or so in diameter. After a mile and a half we came to the corner of a snake fence. This, Dick informed me, marked the limits of the "farm."

We burst through the screen of popples definitely into the clear. A two-storied house of squared logs crested a knoll in the middle distance. Ten acres of grass marsh, perhaps twenty of ploughed land, and then the ash-white-green of popples. We dodged the grass marsh and gained the house. Dick was at once among friends.

The mother had no English, so smiled expansively, her bony arms folded across her stomach. Her oldest daughter, a frail-looking girl in the twenties, but with a sad and spiritual beauty of the Madonna in her big eyes and straight black hair, gave us a shy good-day. Three boys, just alike in their slender, stolid Indian good looks, except that they differed in size, nodded with the awkwardness of the male. Two babies stared solemnly. A little girl with a beautiful, oval face, large mischievous gray eyes behind long black lashes, a mischievously quirked mouth to match the eyes, and black hair banged straight, both front and behind, in almost mediaeval fashion, twirked a pair of brown bare legs all about us. Another light-haired, curly little girl, surmounted by an old yachting-cap, spread apart sturdy shoes in an attitude at once critical and expectant.

Dick rose to the occasion by sorting out from some concealed recess of his garments a huge paper parcel of candy.

With infinite tact, he presented this bag to Madame rather than the children. Madame instituted judicious distribution and appropriate reservation for the future. We entered the cabin.

Never have I seen a place more exquisitely neat. The floor had not only been washed clean; it had been scrubbed white. The walls of logs were freshly whitewashed. The chairs were polished. The few ornaments were new, and not at all dusty or dingy or tawdry. Several religious pictures, a portrait of royalty, a lithographed advertisement of some buggy, a photograph or so--and then just the fresh, wholesome cleanliness of scrubbed pine. Madame made us welcome with smiles--a faded, lean woman with a remnant of beauty peeping from her soft eyes, but worn down to the first principles of pioneer bone and gristle by toil, care, and the bearing of children. I spoke to her in French, complimenting her on the appearance of the place. She was genuinely pleased, saying in reply that one did one's possible, but that children!--with an expressive pause.

Next we called for volunteers to show us to the great-grandfather. Our elfish little girls at once offered, and went dancing off down the trail like autumn leaves in a wind. Whether it was the Indian in them, or the effects of environment, or merely our own imaginations, we both had the same thought--that in these strange, taciturn, friendly, smiling, pirouetting little creatures was some eerie, wild strain akin to the woods and birds and animals. As they danced on ahead of us, turning to throw us a delicious smile or a half-veiled roguish glance of nascent coquetry, we seemed to swing into an orbit of experience foreign to our own. These bright-eyed woods people were in the last analysis as inscrutable to us as the squirrels.

26

We followed our swirling, airy guides down through a trail to another clearing planted with potatoes. On the farther side of this they stopped, hand in hand, at the woods' fringe, and awaited us in a startlingly sudden repose.

"V'la le gran'père," said they in unison.

At the words a huge gaunt man clad in shirt and jeans arose and confronted us. Our first impression was of a vast framework stiffened and shrunken into the peculiar petrifaction of age; our second, of a Jove-like wealth of iron-gray beard and hair; our third, of eyes, wide, clear, and tired with looking out on a century of the world's time. His movements, as he laid one side his axe and passed a great, gnarled hand across his forehead, were angular and slow. We knew instinctively the quality of his work--a deliberate pause, a mighty blow, another pause, a painful recovery--labour compounded of infinite slow patience, but wonderfully effective in the week's result. It would go on without haste, without pause, inevitable as the years slowly closing about the toiler. His mental processes would be of the same fibre. The apparent hesitation might seem to waste the precious hours remaining, but in the end, when the engine started, it would move surely and unswervingly along the appointed grooves. In his wealth of hair; in his wide eyes, like the mysterious blanks of a marble statue; in his huge frame, gnarled and wasted to the strange, impressive, powerful age-quality of Phidias's old men, he seemed to us to deserve a wreath and a marble seat with strange inscriptions and the graceful half-draperies of another time and a group of old Greeks like himself with whom to exchange slow sentences on the body politic. Indeed, the fact that his seat was of fallen pine, and his draperies of butternut brown, and his audience two half-breed children, an artist, and a writer, and his body politic two hundred acres in the wilderness, did not filch from him the impressiveness of his estate. He was a Patriarch. It did not need the park of birch trees, the grass beneath them sloping down to the water, the wooded knoll fairly insisting on a spacious mansion, to substantiate Dick's fancy that he had discovered an ancestor.

Neat piles of brush, equally neat piles of cord-wood, knee-high stumps as cleanly cut as by a saw, attested the old man's efficiency. We conversed.

Yes, said he, the soil was good. It is laborious to clear away the forest. Still, one arrives. M'sieu has but to look. In the memory of his oldest grandson, even, all this was a forest. Le bon Dieu had blessed him. His family was large. Yes, it was as M'sieu said, eighty-seven--that is, counting himself. The soil was not wonderful. It is indeed a large family and much labour, but somehow there was always food for all. For his part he had a great pity for those whom God had not blessed. It must be very lonesome without children.

We spared a private thought that this old man was certainly in no danger of loneliness.

Yes, he went on, he was old--eighty-five. He was not as quick as he used to be; he left that for the young ones. Still, he could do a day's work. He was most proud to have made these gentlemen's acquaintance. He wished us good-day.

We left him seated on the pine log, his axe between his knees, his great, gnarled brown hands hanging idly. After a time we heard the *whack* of his implement; then after another long time we heard it *whack* again. We knew that those two blows had gone straight and true and forceful to the mark. So old a man had no energy to expend in the indirections of haste.

Our elfish guides led us back along the trail to the farmhouse. A girl of thirteen had just arrived from school. In the summer the little ones divided the educational advantages among themselves, turn and turn about.

The newcomer had been out into the world, and was dressed accordingly. A neat dark-blue cloth dress, plainly made, a dull red and blue checked apron; a broad, round hat, shoes and stockings, all in the best and quietest taste--marked contrast to the usual garish Sunday best of the Anglo-Saxon. She herself exemplified the most striking type of beauty to be found in the mixed bloods. Her hair was thick and glossy and black in the mode that throws deep purple shadows under the rolls and coils. Her face was a regular oval, like the opening in a wishbone. Her skin was dark, but rich and dusky with life and red blood that ebbed and flowed with her shyness. Her lips were full, and of a dark cherry red. Her eyes were deep, rather musing, and furnished with the most gloriously tangling of eyelashes. Dick went into ecstasies, took several photographs which did not turn out well, and made one sketch which did. Perpetually did he bewail the absence of oils. The type is not uncommon, but its beauty rarely remains perfect after the fifteenth year.

We made our ceremonious adieus to the Madame, and started back to town under the guidance of one of the boys, who promised us a short cut.

This youth proved to be filled with the old, wandering spirit that lures so many of his race into the wilderness life. He confided to us as we walked that he liked to tramp extended distances, and that the days were really not made long enough for those who had to return home at night.

"I is been top of dose hills," he said. "Bime by I mak' heem go to dose lak' beyon'."

He told us that some day he hoped to go out with the fur traders. In his vocabulary "I wish" occurred with such wistful frequency that finally I inquired curiously what use he would make of the Fairy Gift.

"If you could have just one wish come true, Pierre," I asked, "what would you desire?"

His answer came without a moment's hesitation.

"I is lak' be one giant," said he.

"Why?" I demanded.

"So I can mak' heem de walk far," he replied simply.

I was tempted to point out to him the fact that big men do not outlast the little men, and that vast strength rarely endures, but then a better feeling persuaded me to leave him his illusions. The power, even in fancy, of striding on seven-league boots across the fascinations spread out below his kindling vision from "dose hills" was too precious a possession lightly to be taken away.

27

Strangely enough, though his woodcraft naturally was not inconsiderable, it did not hold his paramount interest. He knew something about animals and their ways and their methods of capture, but the chase did not appeal strongly to him, nor apparently did he possess much skill along that line. He liked the actual physical labour, the walking, the paddling, the tump-line, the camp-making, the new country, the companionship of the wild life, the wilderness as a whole rather than in any one of its single aspects as Fish Pond, Game Preserve, Picture Gallery. In this he showed the true spirit of the *voyageur*. I should confidently look to meet him in another ten years--if threats of railroads spare the Far North so long--girdled with the red sash, shod in silent moccasins, bending beneath the portage load, trolling *Isabeau* to the silent land somewhere under the Arctic Circle. The French of the North have never been great fighters nor great hunters, in the terms of the Anglo-Saxon frontiersmen, but they have laughed in farther places.

## XII.

## THE RIVER.

At a certain spot on the North Shore--I am not going to tell you where--you board one of the two or three fishing-steamers that collect from the different stations the big ice-boxes of Lake Superior whitefish. After a certain number of hours--I am not going to tell you how many--your craft will turn in toward a semicircle of bold, beautiful hills, that seem at first to be many less miles distant than the reality, and at the last to be many more miles remote than is the fact. From the prow you will make out first a uniform velvet green; then the differentiation of many shades; then the dull neutrals of rocks and crags; finally the narrow white of a pebble beach against which the waves utter continually a rattling undertone. The steamer pushes boldly in. The cool green of the water underneath changes to gray. Suddenly you make out the bottom, as through a thick green glass, and the big suckers and catfish idling over its riffled sands, inconceivably far down through the unbelievably clear liquid. So absorbed are you in this marvellous clarity that a slight, grinding jar alone brings you to yourself. The steamer's nose is actually touching the white strip of pebbles!

Now you can do one of a number of things. The forest slants down to your feet in dwindling scrub, which half conceals an abandoned log structure. This latter is the old Hudson's Bay post. Behind it is the Fur Trail, and the Fur Trail will take you three miles to Burned Rock Pool, where are spring water and mighty trout. But again, half a mile to the left, is the mouth of the River. And the River meanders charmingly through the woods of the flat country over numberless riffles and rapids, beneath various steep gravel banks, until it sweeps boldly under the cliff of the first high hill. There a rugged precipice rises sheer and jagged and damp-dark to overhanging trees clinging to the shoulder of the mountain. And precisely at that spot is a bend where the water hits square, to divide right and left in whiteness, to swirl into convolutions of foam, to lurk darkly for a moment on the edge of tumult before racing away. And there you can stand hip-deep, and just reach the eddy foam with a cast tied craftily of Royal Coachman, Parmachenee Belle, and Montreal.

From that point you are with the hills. They draw back to leave wide forest, but always they return to the River--as you would return season after season were I to tell you how--throwing across your woods-progress a sheer cliff forty or fifty feet high, shouldering you incontinently into the necessity of fording to the other side. More and more jealous they become as you penetrate, until at the Big Falls they close in entirely, warning you that here they take the wilderness to themselves. At the Big Falls anglers make their last camp. About the fire they may discuss idly various academic questions--as to whether the great inaccessible pool below the Falls really contains the legendary Biggest Trout; what direction the River takes above; whether it really becomes nothing but a series of stagnant pools connected by sluggish water-reaches; whether there are any trout above the Falls; and so on.

These questions, as I have said, are merely academic. Your true angler is a philosopher. Enough is to him worth fifteen courses, and if the finite mind of man could imagine anything to be desired as an addition to his present possessions on the River, he at least knows nothing of it. Already he commands ten miles of water--swift, clear water--running over stone, through a freshet bed so many hundreds of feet wide that he has forgotten what it means to guard his back cast. It is to be waded in the riffles, so that he can cross from one shore to the other as the mood suits him. One bank is apt to be precipitous, the other to stretch away in a mile or so of the coolest, greenest, stillest primeval forest to be imagined. Thus he can cut across the wide bends of the River, should he so desire and should haste be necessary to make camp before dark. And, last, but not least by any manner of means, there are trout.

I mean real trout--big fellows, the kind the fishers of little streams dream of but awake to call Morpheus a liar, just as they are too polite to call you a liar when you are so indiscreet as to tell them a few plain facts. I have one solemnly attested and witnessed record of twenty-nine inches, caught in running water. I saw a friend land on one cast three whose aggregate weight was four and one half pounds. I witnessed, and partly shared, an exciting struggle in which three fish on three rods were played in the same pool at the same time. They weighed just fourteen pounds. One pool, a backset, was known as the Idiot's Delight, because any one could catch fish there. I have lain on my stomach at the Burned Rock Pool and seen the great fish lying so close together as nearly to cover the bottom, rank after rank of them, and the smallest not under a half pound. As to the largest--well, every true fisherman knows him!

So it came about for many years that the natural barrier interposed by the Big Falls successfully turned the idle tide of anglers' exploration. Beyond them lay an unknown country, but you had to climb cruelly to see it, and you couldn't gain above what you already had in any case. The nearest settlement was nearly sixty miles away, so even added isolation had not its usual quickening effect on camper's effort. The River is visited by few, anyway. An occasional adventurous steam yacht pauses at the mouth, fishes a few little ones from the shallow pools there, or a few big ones from the reefs, and pushes on. It never dreams of sending an expedition to the interior. Our own people, and two other parties, are all I know of who visit the River regularly. Our camp-sites alone break the forest; our blazes alone continue the initial short cut of the Fur Trail; our names alone distinguish the various pools. We had always been satisfied to compromise with the frowning Hills. In return for the delicious necks and points and forest areas through which our clipped trails ran, we had tacitly respected the mystery of the upper reaches.

This year, however, a number of unusual conditions changed our spirit. I have perhaps neglected to state that our trip up to now had been a rather singularly damp one. Of the first fourteen days twelve had been rainy. This was only a slightly exaggerated sample for the rest of the time. As a consequence we found the River filled even to the limit of its freshet banks. The broad borders of stone beach between the stream's edge and the bushes had quite disappeared; the riffles had become rapids, and the rapids roaring torrents; the bends boiled angrily with a smashing eddy that sucked air into pirouetting cavities inches in depth. Plainly, fly-fishing was out of the question. No self-respecting trout would rise to the surface of such a moil, or abandon for syllabubs of tinsel the magnificent solidities of ground-bait such a freshet would bring down from the hills. Also the River was unfordable.

We made camp at the mouth and consulted together. Billy, the half-breed who had joined us for the labour of a permanent camp, shook his head.

"I t'ink one week, ten day," he vouchsafed. "P'rhaps she go down den. We mus' wait." We did not want to wait; the idleness of a permanent camp is the most deadly in the world.

"Billy," said I, "have you ever been above the Big Falls?"

The half-breed's eyes flashed.

"Non," he replied simply. "Bâ, I lak' mak' heem firs' rate."

"All right, Billy; we'll do it."

The next day it rained, and the River went up two inches. The morning following was fair enough, but so cold you could see your breath. We began to experiment.

Now, this expedition had become a fishing vacation, so we had all the comforts of home with us. When said comforts of home were laden into the canoe, there remained forward and aft just about one square foot of space for Billy and me, and not over two inches of freeboard for the River. We could not stand up and pole; tracking with a tow-line was out of the question, because there existed no banks on which to walk; the current was too swift for paddling. So we knelt and poled. We knew it before, but we had to be convinced by trial, that two inches of freeboard will dip under the most gingerly effort. It did so. We groaned, stepped out into ice-water up to our waists, and so began the day's journey with fleeting reference to Dante's nethermost hell.

Next the shore the water was most of the time a little above our knees, but the swirl of a rushing current brought an apron of foam to our hips. Billy took the bow and pulled; I took the stern and pushed. In places our combined efforts could but just counterbalance the strength of the current. Then Billy had to hang on until I could get my shoulder against the stern for a mighty heave, the few inches gain of which he would guard as jealously as possible, until I could get into position for another shove. At other places we were in nearly to our armpits, but close under the banks where we could help ourselves by seizing bushes.

Sometimes I lost my footing entirely and trailed out behind like a streamer; sometimes Billy would be swept away, the canoe's bow would swing down-stream, and I would have to dig my heels and hang on until he had floundered upright. Fortunately for our provisions, this never happened to both at the same time. The difficulties were still further complicated by the fact that our feet speedily became so numb from the cold that we could not feel the bottom, and so were much inclined to aimless stumblings. By-and-by we got out and kicked trees to start the circulation. In the meantime the sun had retired behind thick, leaden clouds.

At the First Bend we were forced to carry some fifty feet. There the River rushed down in a smooth apron straight against the cliff, where its force actually raised the mass of water a good three feet higher than the level of the surrounding pool. I tied on a bait-hook, and two cartridges for sinkers, and in fifteen minutes had caught three trout, one of which weighed three pounds, and the others two pounds and a pound and a half respectively. At this point Dick and Deuce, who had been paralleling through the woods, joined us. We broiled the trout, and boiled tea, and shivered as near the fire as we could. That afternoon, by dint of labour and labour, and yet more labour, we made Burned Rock, and there we camped for the night, utterly beaten out by about as hard a day's travel as a man would want to undertake.

The following day was even worse, for as the natural bed of the River narrowed, we found less and less footing and swifter and swifter water. The journey to Burned Rock had been a matter of dogged hard work; this was an affair of alertness, of taking advantage of every little eddy, of breathless suspense during long seconds while the question of supremacy between our strength and the stream's was being debated. And the thermometer must have registered well towards freezing. Three times we were forced to cross the River in order to get even precarious footing. Those were the really doubtful moments. We had to get in carefully, to sit craftily, and to paddle gingerly and firmly, without attempting to counteract the downward sweep of the current. All our energies and care were given to preventing those miserable curling little waves from over-topping our precious two inches, and that miserable little canoe from departing even by a hair's-breadth from the exactly level keel. Where we were going did not matter. After an interminable interval the tail of our eyes would catch the sway of bushes near at hand.

"Now," Billy would mutter abstractedly.

With one accord we would arise from six inches of wet and step swiftly into the River. The lightened canoe would strain back; we would brace our legs. The traverse was accomplished.

Being thus under the other bank, I would hold the canoe while Billy, astraddle the other end for the purpose of depressing the water to within reach of his hand, would bail away the consequences of our crossing. Then we would make up the quarter of a mile we had lost.

We quit at the Organ Pool about three o'clock of the afternoon. Not much was said that evening.

The day following we tied into it again. This time we put Dick and Deuce on an old Indian trail that promised a short cut, with instructions to wait at the end of it. In the joyous anticipation of another wet day we forgot they had never before followed an Indian trail. Let us now turn aside to the adventures of Dick and Deuce.

Be it premised here that Dick is a regular Indian of taciturnity when it becomes a question of his own experience, so that for a long time we knew of what follows but the single explanatory monosyllable which you shall read in due time. But Dick has a beloved uncle. In moments of expansion to this relative after his return he held forth as to the happenings of that morning.

Dick and the setter managed the Indian trail for about twenty rods. They thought they managed it for perhaps twice that distance. Then it became borne in on them that the bushes went back, the faint knife-clippings, and the half weather-browned brush-cuttings that alone constitute an Indian trail had taken another direction, and that they had now their own way to make through the forest. Dick knew the direction well enough, so he broke ahead confidently. After a half-hour's walk he crossed a tiny streamlet. After another half-hour's walk he came to another. It was flowing the wrong way.

Dick did not understand this. He had never known of little streams flowing away from rivers and towards eight-hundred-foot hills. This might be a loop, of course. He resolved to follow it up-stream far enough to settle the point. The following brought him in time to a soggy little thicket with three areas of moss-covered mud and two round, pellucid pools of water about a foot in diameter. As the little stream had wound and twisted, Dick had by now lost entirely his sense of direction. He fished out his compass and set it on a rock. The River flows nearly north-east to the Big Falls, and Dick knew himself to be somewhere east of the River. The compass appeared to be wrong. Dick was a youth of sense, so he did not quarrel with the compass; he merely became doubtful as to which was the north end of the needle--the white or the black. After a few moments' puzzling he was quite at sea, and could no more remember how he had been taught as to this than you can clinch the spelling of a doubtful word after you have tried on paper a dozen variations. But being a youth of sense he did not desert the streamlet.

After a short half-mile of stumbling the apparent wrong direction in the brook's bed, he came to the River. The River was also flowing the wrong way, and uphill. Dick sat down and covered his eyes with his hands, as I had told him to do in like instance, and so managed to swing the country around where it belonged.

Now here was the River--and Dick resolved to desert it for no more short cuts--but where was the canoe?

This point remained unsettled in Dick's mind, or rather it was alternately settled in two ways. Sometimes the boy concluded we must be still below him, so he would sit on a rock to wait. Then, after a few moments, inactivity would bring him panic. The canoe must have passed this point long since, and every second he wasted stupidly sitting on that stone separated him farther from his friends and from food. Then he would tear madly through the forest. Deuce enjoyed this game, but Dick did not.

In time Dick found his farther progress along the banks cut off by a hill. The hill ended abruptly at the water's edge in a sheer rock cliff thirty feet high. This was in reality the end of the Indian trail short cut--the point where Dick was to meet us--but he did not know it. He happened for the moment to be obsessed by one of his canoe up-stream panics, so he turned inland to a spot where the hill appeared climbable, and started in to surmount the obstruction.

This was comparatively easy at first. Then the shoulder of the cliff intervened. Dick mounted still a little higher up the hill, then higher, then still higher. Far down to his left, through the trees, broiled the River. The slope of the hill to it had become steeper than a roof, and at the edge of the eaves came a cliff drop of thirty feet. Dick picked his way gingerly over curving moss-beds, assisting his balance by a number of little cedar trees. Then something happened.

Dick says the side of the hill slid out from under him. The fact of the matter is, probably, the skin-moss over loose rounded stones gave way. Dick sat down and began slowly to bump down the slant of the roof. He never really lost his equilibrium, nor until the last ten feet did he abandon the hope of checking his descent. Sometimes he did actually succeed in stopping himself for a moment; but on his attempting to follow up the advantage, the moss always slipped or the sapling let go a tenuous hold and he continued on down. At last the River flashed out below him. He saw the sheer drop. He saw the boiling eddies of the Halfway Pool, capable of sucking down a saw-log. Then, with a final rush of loose round stones, he shot the chutes feet first into space. In the meantime Billy and I repeated our experience of the two previous days, with a few variations caused by the necessity of passing two exceptionally ugly rapids whose banks left little footing. We did this precariously, with a rope. The cold water was beginning to tell on our vitality, so that twice we went ashore and made hot tea. Just below the Halfway Pool we began to do a little figuring ahead, which is a bad thing. The Halfway Pool meant much inevitable labour, with its two swift rapids and its swirling, eddies, as sedulously to be avoided as so many steel bear-traps. Then there were a dozen others, and the three miles of riffles, and all the rest of it. At our present rate it would take us a week to make the Falls. Below the Halfway Pool we looked for Dick. He was not to be seen. This made us cross. At the Halfway Pool we intended to unload for portage, and also to ferry over Dick and the setter in the lightened canoe. The tardiness of Dick delayed the game.

However, we drew ashore to the little clearing of the Halfway Camp, made the year before, and wearily discharged our cargo. Suddenly, upstream, and apparently up in the air, we heard distinctly the excited yap of a dog. Billy and I looked at each other. Then we looked upstream.

Close under the perpendicular wall of rock, and fifty feet from the end of it, waist deep in water that swirled angrily about him, stood Dick.

I knew well enough what he was standing on--a little ledge of shale not over five or six feet in length and two feet wide--for in lower water I had often from its advantage cast a fly down below the big boulder. But I knew it to be surrounded by water fifteen feet deep. It was impossible to wade to the spot, impossible to swim to it. And why in the name of all the woods gods would a man want to wade or swim to it if he could? The affair, to our cold-benumbed intellects, was simply incomprehensible.

Billy and I spoke no word. We silently, perhaps a little fearfully, launched the empty canoe. Then we went into a space of water whose treading proved us no angels. From the slack water under the cliff we took another look. It was indeed Dick. He carried a rod-case in one hand. His fish-creel lay against his hip. His broad hat sat accurately level on his head. His face was imperturbable. Above, Deuce agonized, afraid to leap into the stream, but convinced that his duty required him to do so.

We steadied the canoe while Dick climbed in. You would have thought he was embarking at the regularly appointed rendezvous. In silence we shot the rapids, and collected Deuce from the end of the trail, whither he followed us. In silence we worked our way across to where our duffel lay scattered. In silence we disembarked.

"In Heaven's name, Dick," I demanded at last, "how did you get *there*?"

"Fell," said he, succinctly. And that was all.


## XIII.

## THE HILLS.

We explained carefully to Dick that he had lit on the only spot in the Halfway Pool where the water was at once deep enough to break his fall and not too deep to stand in. We also pointed out that he had escaped being telescoped or drowned by the merest hair's-breadth. From this we drew moral conclusions. It did us good, but undoubtedly Dick knew it already.

Now we gave our attention to the wetness of garments, for we were chilled blue. A big fire and a clothes-rack of forked sticks and a sapling, an open-air change, a lunch of hot tea and trout and cold galette and beans, a pipe--and then the inevitable summing up.

We had in two and a half days made the easier half of the distance to the Falls. At this rate we would consume a week or more in reaching the starting-point of our explorations. It was a question whether we could stand a week of ice-water and the heavy labour combined. Ordinarily we might be able to abandon the canoe and push on afoot, as we were accustomed to do when trout-fishing, but that involved fording the river three times--a feat manifestly impossible in present freshet conditions.

"I t'ink we quit heem," said Billy.

But then I was seized with an inspiration. Judging by the configuration of the hills, the River bent sharply above the Falls. Why would it not be possible to cut loose entirely at this point, to strike across through the forest, and so to come out on the upper reaches? Remained only the probability of our being able, encumbered by a pack, to scale the mountains.

"Billy," said I, "have you ever been over in those hills?".

"No," said he.

"Do you know anything about the country? Are there any trails?"

"Dat countree is belong Tawabinisáy. He know heem. I don' know heem. I t'ink he is have many hills, some lak'."

"Do you think we can climb those hills with packs?"

Billy cast a doubtful glance on Dick. Then his eye lit up.

"Tawabinisáy is tell me 'bout dat Lak' Kawágama. P'rhaps we fine heem."

In so saying Billy decided the attempt. What angler on the River has not discussed--again idly, again academically--that mysterious Lake alive with the burnished copper trout, lying hidden and wonderful in the high hills, clear as crystal, bottomed with gravel like a fountain, shaped like a great crescent whose curves were haunted of forest trees grim and awesome with the solemnity of the primeval? That its exact location was known to Tawabinisáy alone, that the trail to it was purposely blinded and muddled with the crossing of many little ponds, that the route was laborious--all those things, along with the minor details so dear to winter fire-chats, were matters of notoriety. Probably more expeditions to Kawágama have been planned--in February--than would fill a volume with an account of anticipated adventures. Only, none of them ever came off. We were accustomed to gaze at the forbidden cliff ramparts of the hills, to think of the Idiot's Delight, and the Halfway Pool, and the Organ Pool, and the Burned Rock Pool, and the Rolling Stone Pool, and all the rest of them even up to the Big Falls; and so we would quietly allow our February plannings to lapse. One man Tawabinisáy had honoured. But this man, named Clement, a banker from Peoria, had proved unworthy. Tawabinisáy told how he caught trout, many, many trout, and piled them on the shores of Kawágama to defile the air. Subsequently this same "sportsman" buried another big catch on the beach of Superior. These and other exploits finally earned him his exclusion from the delectable land. I give his name because I have personally talked with his guides, and heard their circumstantial accounts of his performances. Unless three or four woodsmen are fearful liars, I do Mr. Clement no injustice.

Since then Tawabinisáy had hidden himself behind his impenetrable grin.

So you can easily see that the discovery of Kawágama would be a feat worthy even high hills.

That afternoon we rested and made our cache. A cache in the forest country is simply a heavily constructed rustic platform on which provisions and clothing are laid and wrapped completely about in sheets of canoe bark tied firmly with strips of cedar bark, or withes made from a bush whose appearance I know well, but whose name I cannot say. In this receptacle we left all our canned goods, our extra clothing, and our Dutch oven. We retained for transportation some pork, flour, rice, baking-powder, oatmeal, sugar, and tea, cooking utensils, blankets, the tent, fishing-tackle, and the little pistol. As we were about to go into the high country where presumably both game and fish might lack, we were forced to take a full supply for four--counting Deuce as one--to last ten days. The packs counted up about one hundred and fifteen pounds of grub, twenty pounds of blankets, ten of tent, say eight or ten of hardware including the axe, about twenty of duffel. This was further increased by the idiosyncrasy of Billy. He, like most woodsmen, was wedded to a single utterly foolish article of personal belonging, which he worshipped as a fetish, and without which he was unhappy. In his case it was a huge winter overcoat that must have weighed fifteen pounds. The total amounted to about one hundred and ninety pounds. We gave Dick twenty, I took seventy-six, and Billy shouldered the rest.

The carrying we did with the universal tump-line. This is usually described as a strap passed about a pack and across the forehead of the bearer. The description is incorrect. It passes across the top of the head. The weight should rest on the small of the back just above the hips--not on the broad of the back as most beginners place it. Then the chin should be dropped, the body slanted sharply forward, and you may be able to stagger forty rods at your first attempt.

Use soon accustoms you to carrying, however. The first time I ever did any packing I had a hard time stumbling a few hundred feet over a hill portage with just fifty pounds on my back. By the end of that same trip I could carry a hundred pounds and a lot of miscellaneous traps, like canoe-poles and guns, without serious inconvenience and over a long portage. This quickly-gained power comes partly from a strengthening of the muscles of the neck, but more from a mastery of balance. A pack can twist you as suddenly and expertly on your back as the best of wrestlers. It has a head lock on you, and you have to go or break your neck. After a time you adjust your movements, just as after a time you can travel on snow-shoes through heavy down timber without taking conscious thought as to the placing of your feet.

But at first packing is as near infernal punishment as merely mundane conditions can compass. Sixteen brand-new muscles ache, at first dully, then sharply, then intolerably, until it seems you cannot bear it another second. You are unable to keep your feet. A stagger means an effort at recovery, and an effort at recovery means that you trip when you place your feet, and that means, if you are lucky enough not to be thrown, an extra tweak for every one of the sixteen new muscles. At first you rest every time you feel tired. Then you begin to feel very tired every fifty feet. Then you have to do the best you can, and prove the pluck that is in you.

Mr. Tom Friant, an old woodsman of wide experience, has often told me with relish of his first try at carrying. He had about sixty pounds, and his companion double that amount. Mr. Friant stood it a few centuries and then sat down. He couldn't have moved another step if a gun had been at his ear.

"What's the matter?" asked his companion.

"Del," said Friant, "I'm all in. I can't navigate. Here's where I quit."

"Can't you carry her any farther?"

"Not an inch."

"Well, pile her on. I'll carry her for you."

Friant looked at him a moment in silent amazement.

"Do you mean to say that you are going to carry your pack and mine too?"

"That's what I mean to say. I'll do it if I have to."

Friant drew a long breath.

"Well," said he at last, "if a little sawed-off cuss like you can wiggle under a hundred and eighty, I guess I can make it under sixty."

"That's right," said Del imperturbably. "*If you think you can, you can.*"

"And I did," ends Friant, with a chuckle.

Therein lies the whole secret. The work is irksome, sometimes even painful, but if you think you can do it, you can, for though great is the protest of the human frame against what it considers abuse, greater is the power of a man's grit.

We carried the canoe above the larger eddies, where we embarked ourselves and our packs for traverse, leaving Deuce under strict command to await a second trip. Deuce disregarded the strict command. From disobedience came great peril, for when he attempted to swim across after us he was carried downstream, involved in a whirlpool, sucked under, and nearly drowned. We could do nothing but watch. When, finally, the River spued out a frightened and bedraggled dog, we drew a breath of very genuine relief, for Deuce was dear to us through much association.

The canoe we turned bottom up and left in the bushes, and so we set off through the forest.

At the end of fifteen minutes we began to mount a gentle ascent. The gentle ascent speedily became a sharp slope, the sharp slope an abrupt hill, and the latter finally an almost sheer face of rock and thin soil. We laid hold doggedly of little cedars; we dug our fingers into little crevices, and felt for the same with our toes; we perspired in streams and breathed in gasps; we held the strained muscles of our necks rigid, for the twisting of a pack meant here a dangerous fall; we flattened ourselves against the face of the mountain with always the heavy, ceaseless pull of the tump-line attempting to tear us backward from our holds. And so at last, when the muscles of our thighs refused to strengthen our legs for the ascent of another foot, we would turn our backs to the slant and sink gratefully into the only real luxury in the world.

For be it known that real luxury cannot be bought; it must be worked for. I refer to luxury as the exquisite savour of a pleasant sensation. The keenest sense-impressions are undoubtedly those of contrast. In looking back over a variety of experience, I have no hesitation at all in selecting as the moment in which I have experienced the liveliest physical pleasure one hot afternoon in July. The thermometer might have stood anywhere. We would have placed childlike trust in any of its statements, even three figures great. Our way had led through unbroken forest oppressed by low brush and an underfooting of brakes. There had been hills. Our clothes were wringing wet, to the last stitch; even the leather of the tump-line was saturated. The hot air we gulped down did not seem to satisfy our craving for oxygen any more than lukewarm water ever seems to cut a real thirst. The woods were literally like an oven in their hot dryness. Finally we skirted a little hill, and at the base of that hill a great tree had fallen, and through the aperture thus made in the forest a tiny current of cool air flowed like a stream. It was not a great current, nor a wide; if we moved three feet in any direction, we were out of it. But we sat us down directly across its flow. And never have dinners or wines or men or women, or talks of books or scenery or adventure or sport, or the softest, daintiest refinements of man's invention given me the half of luxury I drank in from that little breeze. So the commonest things--a dash of cool water on the wrists, a gulp of hot tea, a warm, dry blanket, a whiff of tobacco, a ray of sunshine--are more really the luxuries than all the comforts and sybaritisms we buy. Undoubtedly the latter would also rise to the higher category if we were to work for their essence instead of merely signing club cheques or paying party calls for them.

Which means that when we three would rest our packs against the side of that hill, and drop our head-straps below our chins, we were not at all to be pitied, even though the forest growth denied us the encouragement of knowing how much farther we had to go.

Before us the trees dropped away rapidly, so that twenty feet out in a straight line we were looking directly into their tops. There, quite on an equality with their own airy estate, we could watch the fly-catchers and warblers conducting their small affairs of the chase. It lent us the illusion of imponderability; we felt that we too might be able to rest securely on graceful gossamer twigs. And sometimes, through a chance opening, we could see down over billows of waving leaves to a single little spot of blue, like a turquoise sunk in folds of green velvet, which meant that the River was dropping below us. This, in the mercy of the Red Gods, was meant as encouragement.

The time came, however, when the ramparts we scaled rose sheer and bare in impregnability. Nothing could be done on the straight line, so we turned sharp to the north. The way was difficult, for it lay over great fragments of rock stricken from the cliff by winter, and further rendered treacherous by the moss and wet by a thousand trickles of water. At the end of one hour we found what might be called a ravine, if you happened not to be particular, or a steep cleft in the precipice if you were. Here we deserted the open air for piled-up brushy tangles, many sharp-cornered rock fragments, and a choked streamlet. Finally the whole outfit abruptly ceased. We climbed ten feet of crevices and stood on the ridge.

The forest trees shut us in our own little area, so that we were for the moment unable to look abroad over the country.

The descent, abrupt where we had mounted, stretched away gently toward the north and west. And on that slope, protected as it was from the severer storms that sweep up the open valleys in winter, stood the most magnificent primeval forest it has ever been my fortune to behold. The huge maple, beech, and birch trees lifted column-like straight up to a lucent green canopy, always twinkling and shifting in the wind and the sunlight. Below grew a thin screen of underbrush, through which we had no difficulty at all in pushing, but which threw about us face-high a tender green partition. The effect was that of a pew in an old-fashioned church, so that, though we shared the upper stillnesses, a certain delightful privacy of our own seemed assured us. This privacy we knew to be assured also to many creatures besides ourselves. On the other side of the screen of broad leaves we sensed the presence of life. It did not intrude on us, nor were we permitted to intrude on it. But it was there. We heard it rustling, pattering, scrambling, whispering, scurrying with a rush of wings. More subtly we felt it, as one knows of a presence in a darkened room. By the exercise of imagination and experience we identified it in its manifestations--the squirrel, the partridge, the weasel, the spruce hens, once or twice the deer. We knew it saw us perfectly, although we could not see it, and that gave us an impression of companionship; so the forest was not lonely.

Next to this double sense of isolation and company was the feeling of transparent shadow. The forest was thick and cool. Only rarely did the sun find an orifice in the roof through which to pour a splash of liquid gold. All the rest was in shadow. But the shadow was that of the bottom of the sea--cool, green, and, above all, transparent. We saw into the depth of it, but dimly, as we would see into the green recesses of a tropic ocean. It possessed the same liquid quality. Finally the illusion overcame us completely. We bathed in the shadows as though they were palpable, and from that came great refreshment.

Under foot the soil was springy with the mould of numberless autumns. The axe had never hurried slow old servant decay. Once in a while we came across a prostrate trunk lying in the trough of destruction its fall had occasioned. But the rest of the time we trod a carpet to the making of which centuries of dead forest warriors had wrapped themselves in mould and soft moss and gentle dissolution. Sometimes a faint rounded shell of former fair proportion swelled above the level, to crumble to punkwood at the lightest touch of our feet. Or, again, the simulacrum of a tree trunk would bravely oppose our path, only to melt away into nothing, like the opposing phantoms of Aeneas, when we placed a knee against it for the surmounting.

If the pine woods be characterized by cathedral solemnity, and the cedars and tamaracks by certain horrifical gloom, and the popples by a silvery sunshine, and the berry-clearings by grateful heat and the homely manner of familiar birds, then the great hardwood must be known as the dwelling-place of transparent shadows, of cool green lucency, and the repository of immemorial cheerful forest tradition which the traveller can hear of, but which he is never permitted actually to know.

In this lovable mystery we journeyed all the rest of that morning. The packs were heavy with the first day's weight, and we were tired from our climb; but the deep physical joy of going on and ever on into unknown valleys, down a long, gentle slope that must lead somewhere, through things animate and things of an almost animate life, opening silently before us to give us passage, and closing as silently behind us after we had passed--these made us forget our aches and fatigues for the moment.

At noon we boiled tea near a little spring of clear, cold water. As yet we had no opportunity of seeing farther than the closing in of many trees. We were, as far as external appearances went, no more advanced than our first resting-place after surmounting the ridge. This effect is constant in the great forests. You are in a treadmill--though a pleasant one withal. Your camp of to-day differs only in non-essentials from that of yesterday, and your camp of to-morrow will probably be almost exactly like to-day's. Only when you reach your objective point do you come to a full realization that you have not been the Sisyphus of the Red Gods.

Deuce returning from exploration brought indubitable evidence of porcupines. We picked the barbed little weapons from his face and nose and tongue with much difficulty for ourselves and much pain for Deuce. We offered consolation by voicing for his dumbness his undoubted intention to avoid all future porcupines. Then we took up the afternoon tramp.

Now at last through the trees appeared the gleam of water. Tawabinisáy had said that Kawágama was the only lake in its district. We therefore became quite excited at this sapphire promise. Our packs were thrown aside, and like school-boys we raced down the declivity to the shore.


## XIV.

## ON WALKING THROUGH THE WOODS.


We found ourselves peering through the thicket at a little reed and grass grown body of water a few acres in extent. A short detour to the right led us to an outlet--a brook of width and dash that convinced us the little pond was only a stopping-place in the stream, and not a headwater as we had at first imagined. Then a nearer approach led us past pointed tree-stumps exquisitely chiselled with the marks of teeth; so we knew we looked, not on a natural pond, but on the work of beavers.

I examined the dam more closely. It was a marvel of engineering skill in the accuracy with which the big trees had been felled exactly along the most effective lines, the efficiency of the filling in, and the just estimate of the waste water to be allowed. We named the place obviously Beaver Pond, resumed our packs, and pushed on.

Now I must be permitted to celebrate by a little the pluck of Dick. He was quite unused to the tump-line, comparatively inexperienced in woods-walking, and weighed but one hundred and thirty-five pounds. Yet not once in the course of that trip did he bewail his fate. Towards the close of this first afternoon I dropped behind to see how he was making it. The boy had his head down, his lips shut tight together, his legs well straddled apart. As I watched he stumbled badly over the merest twig.

"Dick," said I, "are you tired?"

"Yes," he confessed frankly.

"Can you make it another half-hour?"

"I guess so; I'll try."

At the end of the half-hour we dropped our packs. Dick had manifested no impatience--not once had he even asked how nearly time was up--but now he breathed a deep sigh of relief.

"I thought you were never going to stop," said he simply.

From Dick those words meant a good deal. For woods-walking differs as widely from ordinary walking as trap-shooting from field-shooting. A good pedestrian may tire very quickly in the forest. No two successive steps are of the same length; no two successive steps fall on the same quality of footing; no two successive steps are on the same level. Those three are the major elements of fatigue. Add further the facts that your way is continually obstructed both by real difficulties--such as trees, trunks, and rocks--and lesser annoyances, such as branches, bushes, and even spider-webs. These things all combine against endurance. The inexperienced does not know how to meet them with a minimum of effort. The tenderfoot is in a constant state of muscular and mental rigidity against a fall or a stumble or a cut across the face from some one of the infinitely numerous woods scourges. This rigidity speedily exhausts the vital force.

So much for the philosophy of it. Its practical side might be infinitely extended. Woodsmen are tough and enduring and in good condition; but no more so than the average college athlete. Time and again I have seen men of the latter class walked to a standstill. I mean exactly that. They knew, and were justly proud, of their physical condition, and they hated to acknowledge, even to themselves, that the rest of us were more enduring. As a consequence they played on their nerve, beyond their physical powers. When the collapse came it was complete. I remember very well a crew of men turning out from a lumber camp on the Sturgeon River to bring in on a litter a young fellow who had given out while attempting to follow Bethel Bristol through a hard day. Bristol said he dropped finally as though he had been struck on the head. The woodsman had thereupon built him a little fire, made him as comfortable as possible with both coats, and hiked for assistance. I once went into the woods with a prominent college athlete. We walked rather hard over a rough country until noon. Then the athlete lay on his back for the rest of the day, while I finished alone the business we had come on.

Now, these instances do not imply that Bristol, and certainly not myself, were any stronger physically, or possessed more nervous force, than the men we had tired out. Either of them on a road could have trailed us, step for step, and as long as we pleased. But we knew the game.

It comes at the last to be entirely a matter of experience. Any man can walk in the woods all day at some gait. But his speed will depend on his skill. It is exactly like making your way through heavy, dry sand. As long as you restrain yourself to a certain leisurely plodding, you get along without extraordinary effort, while even a slight increase of speed drags fiercely at your feet. So it is with the woods. As long as you walk slowly enough, so that you can pick your footing and lift aside easily the branches that menace your face, you will expend little nervous energy. But the slightest pressing, the slightest inclination to go beyond what may be called your physical foresight, lands you immediately in difficulties. You stumble, you break through the brush, you shut your eyes to avoid sharp switchings. The reservoir of your energy is open full cock. In about an hour you feel very, very tired.

This principle holds rigidly true of every one, from the softest tenderfoot to the expertest forest-runner. For each there exists a normal rate of travel, beyond which are penalties. Only, the forest-runner, by long use, has raised the exponent of his powers. Perhaps as a working hypothesis the following might be recommended: *One good step is worth six stumbling steps; go only fast enough to assure that good one.*

You will learn, besides, a number of things practically which memory cannot summon to order for instance here. "Brush slanted across your path is easier lifted over your head and dropped behind you than pushed aside," will do as an example.

A good woods-walker progresses without apparent hurry. I have followed the disappearing back of Tawabinisáy when, as my companion elegantly expressed it, "if you stopped to spit you got lost." Tawabinisáy wandered through the forest, his hands in his pockets, humming a little Indian hymn. And we were breaking madly along behind him with the crashing of many timbers.

Of your discoveries probably one of the most impressive will be that in the bright lexicon of woodscraft the word "mile" has been entirely left out. To count by miles is a useless and ornamental elegance of civilization. Some of us once worked hard all one day only to camp three miles downstream from our resting-place of the night before. And the following day we ran nearly sixty with the current. The space of measured country known as a mile may hold you five minutes or five hours from your destination. The Indian counts by time, and after a little you follow his example. "Four miles to Kettle Portage" means nothing. "Two hours to Kettle Portage" does. Only when an Indian tells you two hours you would do well to count it as four.

Well, our trip practically amounted to seven days to nowhere; or perhaps seven days to everywhere would be more accurate. It was all in the high hills until the last day and a half, and generally in the hardwood forests. Twice we intersected and followed for short distances Indian trails, neither of which apparently had been travelled since the original party that had made them. They led across country for greater or lesser distances in the direction we wished to travel, and then turned aside. Three times we blundered on little meadows of moose-grass. Invariably they were tramped muddy like a cattle-yard where the great animals had stood as lately as the night before. Caribou were not uncommon. There were a few deer, but not many, for the most of the deer country lies to the south of this our district. Partridge, as we had anticipated, lacked in such high country.

In the course of the five days and a half we were in the hills we discovered six lakes of various sizes. The smallest was a mere pond; the largest would measure some three or four miles in diameter. We came upon that very late one afternoon. A brook of some size crossed our way, so, as was our habit, we promptly turned upstream to discover its source. In the high country the head-waters are never more than a few miles distant; and at the same time the magnitude of this indicated a lake rather than a spring as the supply. The lake might be Kawágama.

Our packs had grown to be very heavy, for they had already the weight of nine hours piled on top. And the stream was exceedingly difficult to follow. It flowed in one of those aggravating little ravines whose banks are too high and steep and uneven for good footing, and whose beds are choked with a too abundant growth. In addition, there had fallen many trees over which one had to climb. We kept at it for perhaps an hour. The brook continued of the same size, and the country of the same character. Dick for the first time suggested that it might be well to camp.

"We've got good water here," he argued, quite justly, "and we can push on to-morrow just as well as to-night."

We balanced our packs against a prostrate tree-trunk. Billy contributed his indirect share to the argument.

"I lak' to have the job mak' heem this countree all over," he sighed. "I mak' heem more level."

"All right," I agreed; "you fellows sit here and rest a minute, and I'll take a whirl a little ways ahead."

I slipped my tump-line and started on light. After carrying a heavy pack so long, I seemed to tread on air. The thicket, before so formidable, amounted to nothing at all. Perhaps the consciousness that the day's work was in reality over lent a little factitious energy to my tired legs. At any rate, the projected two hundred feet of my investigations stretched to a good quarter-mile. At the end of that space I debouched on a widening of the ravine. The hardwood ran off into cedars. I pushed through the stiff rods and yielding fans of the latter, and all at once found myself leaning out over the waters of the lake.

It was almost an exact oval, and lay in a cup of hills. Three wooded islands, swimming like ducks in the placid evening waters, added a touch of diversity. A huge white rock balanced the composition to the left, and a single white sea-gull, like a snowflake against pines, brooded on its top.

I looked abroad to where the perfect reflection of the hills confused the shore line. I looked down through five feet of crystal water to where pebbles shimmered in refraction. I noted the low rocks jutting from the wood's shelter whereon one might stand to cast a fly. Then I turned and yelled and yelled and yelled again at the forest.

Billy came through the brush, crashing in his haste. He looked long and comprehendingly. Without further speech, we turned back to where Dick was guarding the packs.

That youth we found profoundly indifferent.

"Kawágama," we cried, "a quarter-mile ahead."

He turned on us a lack-lustre eye.

"You going to camp here?" he inquired dully.

"Course not! We'll go on and camp at the lake."

"All right," he replied.

We resumed our packs, a little stiffly and reluctantly, for we had tasted of woods-travel without them. At the lake we rested.

"Going to camp here?" inquired Dick.

We looked about, but noted that the ground under the cedars was hummocky, and that the hardwood grew on a slope. Besides, we wanted to camp as near the shore as possible. Probably a trifle further along there would be a point of high land and delightful little paper-birches.

"No," we answered cheerfully, "this isn't much good. Suppose we push along a ways and find something better."

"All right," Dick replied.

We walked perhaps a half-mile more to the westward before we discovered what we wanted, stopping from time to time to discuss the merits of this or that place. Billy and I were feeling pretty good. After such a week Kawágama was a tonic. Finally we agreed.

"This'll do," said we.

"Thank God!" said Dick unexpectedly, and dropped his pack to the ground with a thud, and sat on it.

I looked at him closely. Then I undid my own pack. "Billy," said I, "start in on grub. Never mind the tent just now."

"A' right," grinned Billy. He had been making his own observations.

"Dick," said I, "let's go down and sit on the rock over the water. We might fish a little."

"All right," Dick replied.

He stumbled dully after me to the shore.

"Dick," I continued, "you're a kid, and you have high principles, and your mother wouldn't like it, but I'm going to prescribe for you, and I'm going to insist on your following the prescription. This flask does not contain fly-dope--that's in the other flask--it contains whisky. I have had it in my pack since we started, and it has not been opened. I don't believe in whisky in the woods; not because I am temperance, but because a man can't travel on it. But here is where you break your heaven-born principles. Drink."

Dick hesitated, then he drank. By the time grub was ready his vitality had come to normal, and so he was able to digest his food and get some good out of it; otherwise he could not have done so. Thus he furnished an admirable example of the only real use for whisky in woods-travel. Also it was the nearest Dick ever came to being completely played out.

That evening was delightful. We sat on the rock and watched the long North Country twilight steal up like a gray cloud from the east. Two loons called to each other, now in the shrill maniac laughter, now with the long, mournful cry. It needed just that one touch to finish the picture. We were looking, had we but known it, on a lake no white man had ever visited before. Clement alone had seen Kawágama, so in our ignorance we attained much the same mental attitude. For I may as well let you into the secret; this was not the fabled lake after all. We found that out later from Tawabinisáy. But it was beautiful enough, and wild enough, and strange enough in its splendid wilderness isolation to fill the heart of the explorer with a great content.

Having thus, as we thought, attained the primary object of our explorations, we determined on trying now for the second--that is, the investigation of the upper reaches of the River. Trout we had not accomplished at this lake, but the existence of fish of some sort was attested by the presence of the two loons and the gull, so we laid our non-success to fisherman's luck. After two false starts we managed to strike into a good country near enough our direction. The travel was much the same as before. The second day, however, we came to a surveyor's base-line cut through the woods. Then we followed that as a matter of convenience. The base-line, cut the fall before, was the only evidence of man we saw in the high country. It meant nothing in itself, but was intended as a starting-point for the township surveys, whenever the country should become civilized enough to warrant them. That condition of affairs might not occur for years to come. Therefore the line was cut out clear for a width of twenty feet.

We continued along it as along a trail until we discovered our last lake--a body of water possessing many radiating arms. This was the nearest we came to the real Kawágama. If we had skirted the lake, mounted the ridge, followed a creek-bed, mounted another ridge, and descended a slope, we should have made our discovery. Later we did just that, under the guidance of Tawabinisáy himself. Floating in the birch canoe we carried with us we looked back at the very spot on which we stood this morning.

But we turned sharp to the left, and so missed our chance. However, we were in a happy frame of mind, for we imagined we had really made the desired discovery.

Nothing of moment happened until we reached the valley of the River. Then we found we were treed. We had been travelling all the time among hills and valleys, to be sure, but on a high elevation. Even the bottom lands, in which lay the lakes, were several hundred feet above Superior. Now we emerged from the forest to find ourselves on bold mountains at least seven or eight hundred feet above the main valley. And in the main valley we could make out the River.

It was rather dizzy work. Three or four times we ventured over the rounded crest of the hill, only to return after forty or fifty feet because the slope had become too abrupt. This grew to be monotonous and aggravating. It looked as though we might have to parallel the River's course, like scouts watching an army, on the top of the hill. Finally a little ravine gave us hope. We scrambled down it; ended in a very steep slant, and finished at a sheer tangle of cedar-roots. The latter we attempted. Billy went on ahead. I let the packs down to him by means of a tump-line. He balanced them on roof; until I had climbed below him. And so on. It was exactly like letting a bucket down a well. If one of the packs had slipped off the cedar-roots, it would have dropped like a plummet to the valley, and landed on Heaven knows what. The same might be said of ourselves. We did this because we were angry all through.

Then we came to the end of the cedar-roots. Right and left offered nothing; below was a sheer, bare drop. Absolutely nothing remained but to climb back, heavy packs and all, to the top of the mountain. False hopes had wasted a good half day and innumerable foot-pounds. Billy and I saw red. We bowed our heads and snaked those packs to the top of the mountain at a gait that ordinarily would have tired us out in fifty feet. Dick did not attempt to keep up. When we reached the top we sat down to wait for him. After a while he appeared, climbing leisurely. He gazed on us from behind the mask of his Indian imperturbability. Then he grinned. That did us good, for we all three laughed aloud, and buckled down to business in a better frame of mind.

That day we discovered a most beautiful waterfall. A stream about twenty feet in width, and with a good volume of water, dropped some three hundred feet or more into the River. It was across the valley from us, so we had a good view of its beauties. Our estimates of its height were carefully made on the basis of some standing pine that grew near its foot.

And then we entered a steep little ravine, and descended it with misgivings to a cañon, and walked easily down the cañon to a slope that took us by barely sensible gradations to a wooded plain. At six o'clock we stood on the banks of the River, and the hills were behind us.

Of our down-stream travel there is little really to be said. We established a number of facts--that the River dashes most scenically from rapid to rapid, so that the stagnant pool theory is henceforth untenable; that the hills get higher and wilder the farther you penetrate to the interior, and their cliffs and rock-precipices bolder and more naked; that there are trout in the upper reaches, but not so large as in the lower pools; and, above all, that travel is not a joy for ever.

For we could not ford the River above the Falls--it is too deep and swift. As a consequence, we had often to climb, often to break through the narrowest thicket strips, and once to feel our way cautiously along a sunken ledge under a sheer rock cliff. That was Billy's idea. We came to the sheer rock cliff after a pretty hard scramble, and we were most loth to do the necessary climbing. Billy suggested that we might be able to wade. As the pool below the cliff was black water and of indeterminate depth, we scouted the idea. Billy, however, poked around with a stick, and, as I have said, discovered a little ledge about a foot and a half wide and about two feet and a half below the surface. This was spectacular, but we did it. A slip meant a swim and the loss of the pack. We did not happen to slip. Shortly after, we came to the Big Falls, and so after further painful experiment descended joyfully into known country.

The freshet had gone down, the weather had warmed, the sun shone, we caught trout for lunch below the Big Falls; everything was lovely. By three o'clock, after thrice wading the stream, we regained our canoe--now at least forty feet from the water. We paddled across. Deuce followed easily, where a week before he had been sucked down and nearly drowned. We opened the cache and changed our very travel-stained garments. We cooked ourselves a luxurious meal. We built a friendship-fire. And at last we stretched our tired bodies full length on balsam a foot thick, and gazed drowsily at the canvas-blurred moon before sinking to a dreamless sleep.

## XV.

### ON WOODS INDIANS.

Far in the North dwell a people practically unknown to any but the fur-trader and the explorer. Our information as to Mokis, Sioux, Cheyennes Nez Percés, and indirectly many others, through the pages of Cooper, Parkman, and allied writers, is varied enough, so that our ideas of Indians are pretty well established. If we are romantic, we hark back to the past and invent fairy-tales with ourselves anent the Noble Red Man who has Passed Away. If we are severely practical, we take notice of filth, vice, plug-hats, tin cans, and laziness. In fact, we might divide all Indian concepts into two classes, following these mental and imaginative bents. Then we should have quite simply and satisfactorily the Cooper Indian and the Comic Paper Indian. It must be confessed that the latter is often approximated by reality--and everybody knows it. That the former is by no means a myth--at least in many qualities--the average reader might be pardoned for doubting.

Some time ago I desired to increase my knowledge of the Woods Indians by whatever others had accomplished. Accordingly I wrote to the Ethnological Department at Washington asking what had been done in regard to the Ojibways and Wood Crees north of Lake Superior. The answer was "nothing."

And "nothing" is more nearly a comprehensive answer than at first you might believe. Visitors at Mackinac, Traverse, Sault Ste. Marie, and other northern resorts are besought at certain times of the year by silent calico-dressed squaws to purchase basket and bark work. If the tourist happens to follow these women for more wholesale examination of their wares, he will be led to a double-ended Mackinaw-built sailing-craft with red-dyed sails, half pulled out on the beach. In the stern sit two or three bucks wearing shirts, jean trousers, and broad black hats. Some of the oldest men may sport a patched pair of moccasins or so, but most are conventional enough in clumsy shoes. After a longer or shorter stay they hoist their red sails and drift away toward some mysterious destination on the north shore. If the buyer is curious enough and persistent enough, he may elicit the fact that they are Ojibways.

Now, if this same tourist happens to possess a mildly venturesome disposition, a sailing-craft, and a chart of the region, he will sooner or later blunder across the dwelling-place of his silent vendors. At the foot of some rarely-frequented bay he will come on a diminutive village of small whitewashed log houses. It will differ from other villages in that the houses are arranged with no reference whatever to one another, but in the haphazard fashion of an encampment. Its inhabitants are his summer friends. If he is of an insinuating address, he may get a glimpse of their daily life. Then he will go away firmly convinced that he knows quite a lot about the North Woods Indian.

And so he does. But this North Woods Indian is the Reservation Indian. And in the North a Reservation Indian is as different from a Woods Indian as a negro is from a Chinese.

Suppose, on the other hand, your tourist is unfortunate enough to get left at some North Woods railway station where he has descended from the transcontinental to stretch his legs, and suppose him to have happened on a fur-town like Missináibie at the precise time when the trappers are in from the wilds. Near the borders of the village he will come upon a little encampment of conical tepees. At his approach the women and children will disappear into inner darkness. A dozen wolf-like dogs will rush out barking. Grave-faced men will respond silently to his salutation.

These men, he will be interested to observe, wear still the deer or moose skin moccasin--the lightest and easiest foot-gear for the woods; bind their long hair with a narrow fillet, and their waists with a red or striped worsted sash; keep warm under the blanket thickness of a Hudson Bay capote; and deck their clothes with a variety of barbaric ornament. He will see about camp weapons whose acquaintance he has made only in museums, peltries of whose identification he is by no means sure, and as matters of daily use--snow-shoes, bark canoes, bows and arrows--what to him have been articles of ornament or curiosity. To-morrow these people will be gone for another year, carrying with them the results of the week's barter. Neither he nor his kind will see them again, unless they too journey far into the Silent Places. But he has caught a glimpse of the stolid mask of the Woods Indian, concerning whom officially "nothing" is known.

In many respects the Woods Indian is the legitimate descendant of the Cooper Indian. His life is led entirely in the forests; his subsistence is assured by hunting, fishing, and trapping; his dwelling is the wigwam, and his habitation the wide reaches of the wilderness lying between Lake Superior and the Hudson Bay; his relation to humanity confined to intercourse with his own people and acquaintance with the men who barter for his peltries. So his dependence is not on the world the white man has brought, but on himself and his natural environment. Civilization has merely ornamented his ancient manner. It has given him the convenience of cloth, of firearms, of steel traps, of iron kettles, of matches; it has accustomed him to the luxuries of white sugar--though he had always his own maple product--tea, flour, and white man's tobacco. That is about all. He knows nothing of whisky. The towns are never visited by him, and the Hudson's Bay Company will sell him no liquor. His concern with you is not great, for he has little to gain from you.

This people, then, depending on natural resources for subsistence, has retained to a great extent the qualities of the early aborigines.

To begin with, it is distinctly nomadic. The great rolls of birch bark to cover the pointed tepees are easily transported in the bottoms of canoes, and the poles are quickly cut and put in place. As a consequence, the Ojibway family is always on the move. It searches out new trapping-grounds, new fisheries, it pays visits, it seems even to enjoy travel for the sake of exploration. In winter a tepee of double wall is built, whose hollow is stuffed with moss to keep out the cold; but even that approximation of permanence cannot stand against the slightest convenience. When an Indian kills, often he does not transport his game to camp, but moves his camp to the vicinity of the carcass. There are of these woods dwellers no villages, no permanent clearings. The vicinity of a Hudson's Bay post is sometimes occupied for a month or so during the summer, but that is all.

An obvious corollary of this is that tribal life does not consistently obtain. Throughout the summer months, when game and fur are at their poorest, the bands assemble, probably at the times of barter with the traders. Then for the short period of the idling season they drift together up and down the North Country streams, or camp for big pow-wows and conjuring near some pleasant conflux of rivers. But when the first frosts nip the leaves, the families separate to their allotted trapping districts, there to spend the winter in pursuit of the real business of life.

The tribe is thus split into many groups, ranging in numbers from the solitary trapper, eager to win enough fur to buy him a wife, to a compact little group of three or four families closely related in blood. The most striking consequence is that, unlike other Indian bodies politic, there are no regularly constituted and acknowledged chiefs. Certain individuals gain a remarkable reputation and an equally remarkable respect for wisdom, or hunting skill, or power of woodcraft, or travel. These men are the so-called "old men" often mentioned in Indian manifestoes, though age has nothing to do with the deference accorded them. Tawabinisáy is not more than thirty-five years old; Peter, our Hudson Bay Indian, is hardly more than a boy. Yet both are obeyed implicitly by whomever they happen to be with; both lead the way by river or trail; and both, where question arises, are sought in advice by men old enough to be their fathers. Perhaps this is as good a democracy as another.

The life so briefly hinted at in the foregoing lines inevitably develops and fosters an expertness of woodcraft almost beyond belief. The Ojibway knows his environment. The forest is to him so familiar in each and every one of its numerous and subtle aspects that the slightest departure from the normal strikes his attention at once. A patch of brown shadow where green shadow should fall, a shimmering of leaves where should be merely a gentle waving, a cross-light where the usual forest growth should adumbrate, a flash of wings at a time of day when feathered creatures ordinarily rest quiet--these, and hundreds of others which you and I should never even guess at, force themselves as glaringly on an

Indian's notice as a brass band in a city street. A white man *looks* for game; an Indian sees it because it differs from the forest.

That is, of course, a matter of long experience and lifetime habit. Were it a question merely of this, the white man might also in time attain the same skill. But the Indian is a better animal. His senses are appreciably sharper than our own.

In journeying down the Kapúskasíng River, our Indians--who had come from the woods to guide us--always saw game long before we did. They would never point it out to us. The bow of the canoe would swing silently in its direction, there to rest motionless until we indicated we had seen something.

"Where is it, Peter?" I would whisper.

But Peter always remained contemptuously silent.

One evening we paddled directly into the eye of the setting sun across a shallow little lake filled with hardly sunken boulders. There was no current, and no breath of wind to stir the water into betraying riffles. But invariably those Indians twisted the canoe into a new course ten feet before we reached one of the obstructions, whose existence our dazzled vision could not attest until they were actually below us. They *saw* those rocks, through the shimmer of the surface glare.

Another time I discovered a small black animal lying flat on a point of shale. Its head was concealed behind a boulder, and it was so far away that I was inclined to congratulate myself on having differentiated it from the shadow.

"What is it, Peter?" I asked.

Peter hardly glanced at it.

"Ninny-moósh" (dog), he replied.

Now we were a hundred miles south of the Hudson's Bay post, and two weeks north of any other settlement. Saving a horse, a dog would be about the last thing to occur to one in guessing at the identity of any strange animal. This looked like a little black blotch, without form. Yet Peter knew it. It was a dog, lost from some Indian hunting-party, and mightily glad to see us.

The sense of smell, too, is developed to an extent positively uncanny to us who have needed it so little. Your Woods Indian is always sniffing, always testing the impressions of other senses by his olfactories. Instances numerous and varied might be cited, but probably one will do as well as a dozen. It once became desirable to kill a caribou in country where the animals are not at all abundant. Tawabinisáy volunteered to take Jim within shot of one. Jim describes their hunt as the most wonderful bit of stalking he had ever seen. The Indian followed the animal's tracks as easily as you or I could have followed them over snow. He did this rapidly and certainly. Every once in a while he would get down on all fours to sniff inquiringly at the crushed herbage. Always on rising to his feet he would give the result of his investigations. "Ah-téek caribou one hour."

And later, "Ah-téek half hour."

Or again, "Ah-téek quarter hour."

And finally, "Ah-téek over nex' hill."

And it was so.

In like manner, but most remarkable to us because the test of direct comparison with our own sense was permitted us, was their acuteness of hearing. Often while "jumping" a roaring rapids in two canoes, my companion and I have heard our men talking to each other in quite an ordinary tone of voice. That is to say, I could hear my Indian, and Jim could hear his; but personally we were forced to shout loudly to carry across the noise of the stream. The distant approach of animals they announce accurately.

"Wawashkeshí" (deer), says Peter.

And sure enough, after an interval, we too could distinguish the footfalls on the dry leaves.

As both cause and consequence of these physical endowments--which place them nearly on a parity with the game itself--they are most expert hunters. Every sportsman knows the importance--and also the difficulty--of discovering game before it discovers him. The Indian has here an immense advantage. And after game is discovered, he is furthermore most expert in approaching it with all the refined art of the still hunter.

Mr. Caspar Whitney describes in exasperation his experience with the Indians of the Far North-West. He complains that when they blunder on game they drop everything and enter into almost hopeless chase, two legs against four. Occasionally the quarry becomes enough bewildered so that the wild shooting will bring it down. He quite justly argues that the merest pretence at caution in approach would result in much greater success.

The Woods Indian is no such fool. He is a mighty poor shot--and he knows it. Personally I believe he shuts both eyes before pulling trigger. He is armed with a long flint or percussion lock musket, whose gas-pipe barrel is bound to the wood that runs its entire length by means of brass bands, and whose effective range must be about ten yards. This archaic implement is known as a "trade gun" and has the single merit of never getting out of order. Furthermore ammunition is precious. In consequence, the wilderness hunter is not going to be merely pretty sure; he intends to be absolutely certain. If he cannot approach near enough to blow a hole in his prey, he does not fire.

I have seen Peter drop into marsh-grass so thin that apparently we could discern the surface of the ground through it, and disappear so completely that our most earnest attention could not distinguish even a rustling of the herbage. After an interval his gun would go off from some distant point, exactly where some ducks had been feeding serenely oblivious to fate. Neither of us white men would have considered for a moment the possibility of getting any of them. Once I felt rather proud of myself for killing six ruffed grouse out of some trees with the pistol, until Peter drifted in carrying three he had bagged with a stick.

Another interesting phase of this almost perfect correspondence to environment is the readiness with which an Indian will meet an emergency. We are accustomed to rely first of all on the skilled labour of some one we can hire; second, if we undertake the job ourselves, on the tools made for us by skilled labour; and third, on the shops to supply us with the materials we may need. Not once in a lifetime are we thrown entirely on our own resources. Then we improvise bunglingly a makeshift.

The Woods Indian possesses his knife and his light axe. Nails, planes, glue, chisels, vices, cord, rope, and all the rest of it he has to do without. But he never improvises makeshifts. No matter what the exigency or how complicated the demand, his experience answers with accuracy.

Utensils and tools he knows exactly where to find. His job is neat and workmanlike, whether it is a bark receptacle-- water-tight or not--a pair of snow-shoes, the repairing of a badly-smashed canoe, the construction of a shelter, or the fashioning of a paddle. About noon one day Tawabinisáy broke his axe-helve square off. This to us would have been a serious affair. Probably we should, left to ourselves, have stuck in some sort of a rough straight sapling handle which would have answered well enough until we could have bought another. By the time we had cooked dinner that Indian had fashioned another helve. We compared it with the store article. It was as well shaped, as smooth, as nicely balanced. In fact, as we laid the new and the old side by side, we could not have selected, from any evidence of the workmanship, which had been made by machine and which by hand. Tawabinisáy then burned out the wood from the axe, retempered the steel, set the new helve, and wedged it neatly with ironwood wedges. The whole affair, including the cutting of the timber, consumed perhaps half an hour.

To travel with a Woods Indian is a constant source of delight on this account. So many little things that the white man does without, because he will not bother with their transportation, the Indian makes for himself. And so quickly and easily! I have seen a thoroughly waterproof, commodious, and comfortable bark shelter made in about the time it would take one to pitch a tent. I have seen a raft built of cedar logs and cedar bark ropes in an hour. I have seen a badly-stove canoe made as good as new in fifteen minutes. The Indian rarely needs to hunt for the materials he requires. He knows exactly where they grow, and he turns as directly to them as a clerk would turn to his shelves. No problem of the living of physical life is too obscure to have escaped his varied experience. You may travel with Indians for years, and learn something new and delightful as to how to take care of yourself every summer.

The qualities I have mentioned come primarily from the fact that the Woods Indian is a hunter. I have now to instance two whose development can be traced to the other fact--that he is a nomad. I refer to his skill with the bark canoe and his ability to carry.

I was once introduced to a man at a little way station of the Canadian Pacific Railway in the following words:--

"Shake hands with Munson; he's as good a canoeman as an Indian."

A little later one of the bystanders remarked to me:--

"That fellow you was just talking with is as good a canoeman as an Injun."

Still later, at an entirely different place, a member of the bar informed me, in the course of discussion:--

"The only man I know of who can do it is named Munson. He is as good a canoeman as an Indian."

At the time this unanimity of praise puzzled me a little. I thought I had seen some pretty good canoe work, and even cherished a mild conceit that occasionally I could keep right side up myself. I knew Munson to be a great woods-traveller, with many striking qualities, and why this of canoemanship should be so insistently chosen above the others was beyond my comprehension. Subsequently a companion and I journeyed to Hudson Bay with two birch canoes and two Indians. Since that trip I have had a vast respect for Munson.

Undoubtedly among the half-breed and white guides of Lower Canada, Maine, and the Adirondacks are many skilful men. But they know their waters; they follow a beaten track. The Woods Indian--well, let me tell you something of what he does.

We went down the Kapúskasíng River to the Mattágami, and then down that to the Moose. These rivers are at first but a hundred feet or so wide, but rapidly swell with the influx of numberless smaller streams. Two days' journey brings you to a watercourse nearly half a mile in breadth; two weeks finds you on a surface approximately a mile and a half across. All this water descends from the Height of Land to the sea level. It does so through a rock country. The result is a series of roaring, dashing boulder rapids and waterfalls that would make your hair stand on end merely to contemplate from the banks.

The regular route to Moose Factory is by the Missinaíbie. Our way was new and strange. No trails; no knowledge of the country. When we came to a stretch of white water, the Indians would rise to their feet for a single instant's searching examination of the stretch of tumbled water before them. In that moment they picked the passage they were to follow as well as a white man could have done so in half an hour's study. Then without hesitation they shot their little craft at the green water.

From that time we merely tried to sit still, each in his canoe. Each Indian did it all with his single paddle. He seemed to possess absolute control over his craft.

Even in the rush of water which seemed to hurry us on at almost railroad speed, he could stop for an instant, work directly sideways, shoot forward at a slant, swing either his bow or his stern. An error in judgment or in the instantaneous acting upon it meant a hit; and a hit in these savage North Country Rivers meant destruction. How my man kept in his mind the passage he had planned during his momentary inspection was always to me a miracle. How he got so unruly a beast as the birch canoe to follow it in that tearing volume of water was always another. Big boulders he dodged, eddies he took advantage of, slants of current he utilized. A fractional second of hesitation could not be permitted him. But always the clutching of white hands from the rip at the eddy finally conveyed to my spray-drenched faculties that the rapid was safely astern. And this, mind you, in strange waters.

Occasionally we would carry our outfit through the woods, while the Indians would shoot some especially bad water in the light canoe. As a spectacle nothing could be finer. The flash of the yellow bark, the movement of the broken waters, the gleam of the paddle, the tense alertness of the men's figures, their carven, passive faces, with the contrast of the flashing eyes and the distended nostrils, then the leap into space over some half-cataract, the smash of spray, the exultant yells of the canoemen! For your Indian enjoys the game thoroughly. And it requires very bad water indeed to make him take to the brush.

This is, of course, the spectacular. But also in the ordinary gray business of canoe travel the Woods Indian shows his superiority. He is tireless, and composed as to wrist and shoulder of a number of whale-bone springs. From early dawn to dewy eve, and then a few gratuitous hours into the night, he will dig energetic holes in the water with his long, narrow blade. And every stroke counts. The water boils out in a splotch of white air-bubbles, the little suction holes pirouette like dancing-girls, the fabric of the craft itself trembles under the power of the stroke. Jim and I used, in the lake stretches, to amuse ourselves--and probably the Indians--by paddling in furious rivalry one against the other. Then Peter would make up his mind he would like to speak to Jacob. His canoe would shoot up alongside as though the Old Man of the Lake had laid his hand across its stern. Would I could catch that trick of easy, tireless speed! I know it lies somewhat in keeping both elbows always straight and stiff, in a lurch forward of the shoulders at the end of the stroke. But that, and more! Perhaps one needs a copper skin and beady black eyes with surface lights.

Nor need you hope to pole a canoe upstream as do these people. Tawabinisáy uses two short poles, one in either hand, kneels amidships, and snakes that little old canoe of his upstream so fast that you would swear the rapids an easy matter-- until you tried them yourself. We were once trailed up a river by an old Woods Indian and his interesting family. The outfit consisted of canoe Number One--*item*, one old Injin, one boy of eight years, one dog; canoe Number Two--*item*, one old Injin squaw, one girl of eighteen or twenty, one dog; canoe Number Three--*item*, two little girls of ten and twelve, one dog. We tried desperately for three days to get away from this party. It did not seem to work hard at all. We did. Even the two little girls appeared to dip the contemplative paddle from time to time. Water boiled back of our own blades. We started early and quit late, and about as we congratulated ourselves over our evening fire that we had distanced our followers at last, those three canoes would steal silently and calmly about the lower bend to draw ashore below us. In ten minutes the old Indian was delivering an oration to us, squatted in resignation.

The Red Gods alone know what he talked about. He had no English, and our Ojibway was of the strictly utilitarian. But for an hour he would hold forth. We called him Talk-in-the-Face, the Great Indian Chief. Then he would drop a mild hint for sáymon, which means tobacco, and depart. By ten o'clock the next morning he and his people would overtake us in spite of our earlier start. Usually we were in the act of dragging our canoe through an especially vicious rapid by means of a tow-line. Their three canoes, even to the children's, would ascend easily by means of poles. Tow-lines appeared to be unsportsmanlike--like angle-worms. Then the entire nine--including the dogs--would roost on rocks and watch critically our methods.

The incident had one value, however: it showed us just why these people possess the marvellous canoe skill I have attempted to sketch. The little boy in the leading canoe was not over eight or nine years of age, but he had his little paddle and his little canoe-pole, and, what is more, he already used them intelligently and well. As for the little girls-- well, they did easily feats I never hope to emulate, and that without removing the cowl-like coverings from their heads and shoulders.

The same early habitude probably accounts for their ability to carry weights long distances. The Woods Indian is not a mighty man physically. Most of them are straight and well built, but of only medium height, and not wonderfully muscled. Peter was most beautiful, but in the fashion of the flying Mercury, with long smooth panther muscles. He looked like Uncas, especially when his keen hawk-face was fixed in distant attention. But I think I could have wrestled Peter down. Yet time and again I have seen that Indian carry two hundred pounds for some miles through a rough country absolutely without trails. And once I was witness of a feat of Tawabinisáy, when that wily savage portaged a pack of fifty pounds and a two-man canoe through a hill country for four hours and ten minutes without a rest. Tawabinisáy is even smaller than Peter.

So much for the qualities developed by the woods life. Let us now examine what may be described as the inherent characteristics of the people.

## XVI.

ON WOODS INDIANS (*continued*).

It must be understood, of course, that I offer you only the best of my subject. A people counts for what it does well. Also I instance men of standing in the loose Indian body politic. A traveller can easily discover the reverse of the medal. These have their shirks, their do-nothings, their men of small account, just as do other races. I have no thought of glorifying the noble red man, nor of claiming for him a freedom from human imperfection--even where his natural quality and training count the most--greater than enlightenment has been able to reach.

In my experience the honesty of the Woods Indian is of a very high order. The sense of *mine* and *thine* is strongly forced by the exigencies of the North Woods life. A man is always on the move; he is always exploring the unknown countries. Manifestly it is impossible for him to transport the entire sum of his worldly effects. The implements of winter are a burden in summer. Also the return journey from distant shores must be provided for by food-stations, to be relied on. The solution of these needs is the cache.

And the cache is not a literal term at all. It *conceals* nothing. Rather does it hold aloft in long-legged prominence, for the inspection of all who pass, what the owner has seen fit to leave behind. A heavy platform high enough from the ground to frustrate the investigations of animals is all that is required. Visual concealment is unnecessary, because in the North Country a cache is sacred. On it may depend the life of a man. He who leaves provisions must find them on his return, for he may reach them starving, and the length of his out-journey may depend on his certainty of relief at this point on his in-journey. So men passing touch not his hoard, for some day they may be in the same fix, and a precedent is a bad thing.

Thus in parts of the wildest countries of northern Canada I have unexpectedly come upon a birch canoe in capsized suspension between two trees; or a whole bunch of snow-shoes depending fruit-like beneath the fans of a spruce; or a tangle of steel traps thrust into the crevice of a tree-root; or a supply of pork and flour, swathed like an Egyptian mummy, occupying stately a high bier. These things we have passed by reverently, as symbols of a people's trust in its kind.

The same sort of honesty holds in regard to smaller things. I have never hesitated to leave in my camp firearms, fishing-rods, utensils valuable from a woods point of view, even a watch or money. Not only have I never lost anything in that manner, but once an Indian lad followed me some miles after the morning's start to restore to me a half-dozen trout flies I had accidentally left behind.

It might be readily inferred that this quality carries over into the subtleties, as indeed is the case. Mr. MacDonald of Brunswick House once discussed with me the system of credits carried on by the Hudson's Bay Company with the trappers. Each family is advanced goods to the value of two hundred dollars, with the understanding that the debt is to be paid from the season's catch.

"I should think you would lose a good deal," I ventured. "Nothing could be easier than for an Indian to take his two hundred dollars' worth and disappear in the woods. You'd never be able to find him." Mr. MacDonald's reply struck me, for the man had twenty years' trading experience.

"I have never," said he, "in a long woods life known but one Indian liar."

This my own limited woods-wandering has proved to be true to a sometimes almost ridiculous extent. The most trivial statement of fact can be relied on, provided it is given outside of trade or enmity or absolute indifference. The Indian loves to fool the tenderfoot. But a sober, measured statement you can conclude is accurate. And if an Indian promises a thing, he will accomplish it. He expects you to do the same. Watch your lightest words carefully and you would retain the respect of your red associates.

On our way to the Hudson Bay we rashly asked Peter, towards the last, when we should reach Moose Factory. He deliberated.

"T'ursday," said he.

Things went wrong; Thursday supplied a head wind. We had absolutely no interest in reaching Moose Factory next day; the next week would have done as well. But Peter, deaf to expostulation, entreaty, and command, kept us travelling from six in the morning until after twelve at night. We couldn't get him to stop. Finally he drew the canoes ashore.

"Moose-amik quarter hour," said he.

He had kept his word.

The Ojibway possesses a great pride which the unthinking can ruffle quite unconsciously in many ways. Consequently the Woods Indian is variously described as a good guide or a bad one. The difference lies in whether you suggest or command.

"Peter, you've got to make Chicawgun to-night. Get a move on you!" will bring you sullen service, and probably breed kicks on the grub supply, which is the immediate precursor of mutiny.

"Peter, it's a long way to Chicawgun. Do you think we make him to-night?" on the other hand, will earn you at least a serious consideration of the question. And if Peter says you can, you will.

For the proper man the Ojibway takes a great pride in his woodcraft, the neatness of his camps, the savoury quality of his cookery, the expedition of his travel, the size of his packs, the patience of his endurance. On the other hand, he can be as sullen, inefficient, stupid, and vindictive as any man of any race on earth. I suppose the faculty of getting along with men is largely inherent. Certainly it is blended of many subtleties. To be friendly, to retain respect, to praise, to preserve authority, to direct and yet to leave detail, to exact what is due, and yet to deserve it--these be the qualities of a leader, and cannot be taught.

In general the Woods Indian is sober. He cannot get whisky regularly, to be sure, but I have often seen the better class of Ojibways refuse a drink, saying that they did not care for it. He starves well, and keeps going on nothing long after hope is vanished. He is patient--yea, very patient--under toil, and so accomplishes great journeys, overcomes great difficulties, and does great deeds by means of this handmaiden of genius. According to his own standards is he clean. To be sure his baths are not numerous, nor his laundry-days many, but he never cooks until he has washed his hands and arms to the very shoulders. Other details would but corroborate the impression of this instance--that his ideas differ from ours, as is his right, but that he lives up to his ideas. Also is he hospitable, expecting nothing in return. After your canoe is afloat and your paddle in the river, two or three of his youngsters will splash in after you to toss silver fish to your necessities. And so always he will wait until this last moment of departure, in order that you will not feel called on to give him something in return. Which is true tact and kindliness, and worthy of high praise.

Perhaps I have not strongly enough insisted that the Indian nations differ as widely from one another as do unallied races. We found this to be true even in the comparatively brief journey from Chapleau to Moose. After pushing through a trackless wilderness without having laid eyes on a human being, excepting the single instance of three French *voyageurs* going Heaven knows where, we were anticipating pleasurably our encounter with the traders at the Factory, and naturally supposed that Peter and Jacob would be equally pleased at the chance of visiting with their own kind. Not at all. When we reached Moose our Ojibways wrapped themselves in a mantle of dignity, and stalked scornful amidst obsequious clans. For the Ojibway is great among Indians, verily much greater than the Moose River Crees. Had it been a question of Rupert's River Crees with their fierce blood-laws, their conjuring-lodges, and their pagan customs, the affair might have been different.

For, mark you, the Moose River Cree is little among hunters, and he conducts the chase miscellaneously over his district without thought to the preservation of the beaver, and he works in the hay marshes during the summer, and is short, squab, and dirty, and generally *ka-win-ni-shi-shin*. The old sacred tribal laws, which are better than a religion because they are practically adapted to northern life, have among them been allowed to lapse. Travellers they are none, nor do their trappers get far from the Company's pork-barrels. So they inbreed ignobly for lack of outside favour, and are dying from the face of the land through dire diseases, just as their reputations have already died from men's respect.

The great unwritten law of the forest is that, save as provision during legitimate travel, one may not hunt in his neighbour's district. Each trapper has assigned him, or gets by inheritance or purchase, certain territorial power. In his land he alone may trap. He knows the beaver-dams, how many animals each harbours, how large a catch each will stand without diminution of the supply. So the fur is made to last. In the southern district this division is tacitly agreed upon. It is not etiquette to poach. What would happen to a poacher no one knows, simply because the necessity for finding out has not arisen. Tawabinisáy controls from Batchawanúng to Agawa. There old Waboos takes charge. And so on. But in the Far North the control is more often disputed, and there the blood-law still holds. An illegal trapper baits his snares with his life. If discovered, he is summarily shot. So is the game preserved.

The Woods Indian never kills waste-fully. The mere presence of game does not breed in him a lust to slaughter something. Moderation you learn of him first of all. Later, provided you are with him long enough and your mind is open to mystic influence, you will feel the strong impress of his idea--that the animals of the forest are not lower than man, but only different. Man is an animal living the life of the forest; the beasts are also a body politic speaking a different language and with different view-points. Amik, the beaver, has certain ideas as to the conduct of life, certain habits of body, and certain bias of thought. His scheme of things is totally at variance with that held by Me-en-gan, the wolf, but even to us whites the two are on a parity. Man has still another system. One is no better than another. They are merely different. And just as Me-en-gan preys on Amik, so does Man kill for his own uses.

Thence are curious customs. A Rupert River Cree will not kill a bear unless he, the hunter, is in gala attire, and then not until he has made a short speech in which he assures his victim that the affair is not one of personal enmity, but of expedience, and that anyway he, the bear, will be better off in the Hereafter. And then the skull is cleaned and set on a pole near running water, there to remain during twelve moons. Also at the tail-root of a newly-deceased beaver is tied a thong braided of red wool and deerskin. And many other curious habitudes which would be of slight interest here. Likewise do they conjure up by means of racket and fasting the familiar spirits of distant friends or enemies, and on these spirits fasten a blessing or a curse.

From this it may be deduced that missionary work has not been as thorough as might be hoped. That is true. The Woods Indian loves to sing, and possesses quaint melodies, or rather intonations, of his own. But especially does he delight in the long-drawn wail of some of our old-fashioned hymns. The church oftenest reaches him through them. I know nothing stranger than the sight of a little half-lit church filled with Indians swaying unctuously to and fro in the rhythm of a cadence old Watts would have recognized with difficulty. The religious feeling of the performance is not remarkable, but perhaps it does as a starting-point.

Exactly how valuable the average missionary work is I have been puzzled to decide. Perhaps the church needs more intelligence in the men it sends out. The evangelist is usually filled with narrow, preconceived notions as to the proper physical life. He squeezes his savage into log houses, boiled shirts, and boots. When he has succeeded in getting his tuberculosis crop well started, he offers as compensation a doctrinal religion admirably adapted to us, who have within reach of century-trained perceptions a thousand of the subtler associations a savage can know nothing about. If there is enough glitter and tin steeple and high-sounding office and gilt good-behaviour card to it, the red man's pagan heart is tickled in its vanity, and he dies in the odour of sanctity--and of a filth his out-of-door life has never taught him how to avoid. The Indian is like a raccoon: in his proper surroundings he is clean morally and physically because he knows how to be so; but in a cage he is filthy because he does not know how to be otherwise.

I must not be understood as condemning missionary work; only the stupid missionary work one most often sees in the North. Surely Christianity should be adaptable enough in its little things to fit any people with its great. It seems hard for some men to believe that it is not essential for a real Christian to wear a plug-hat. One God, love, kindness, charity, honesty, right living, may thrive as well in the wigwam as in a foursquare house--provided you let them wear moccasins and a *capote* wherewith to keep themselves warm and vital.

Tawabinisáy must have had his religious training at the hands of a good man. He had lost none of his aboriginal virtue and skill, as may be gathered from what I have before said of him, and had gained in addition certain of the gentle qualities. I have never been able to gauge exactly the extent of his religious *understanding*, for Tawabinisáy is a silent individual, and possesses very little English; but I do know that his religious *feeling* was deep and reverent. He never swore in English; he did not drink; he never travelled or hunted or fished on Sunday when he could possibly help it. These virtues he wore modestly and unassumingly as an accustomed garment. Yet he was the most gloriously natural man I have ever met.

The main reliance of his formalism when he was off in the woods seemed to be a little tattered volume, which he perused diligently all Sunday, and wrapped carefully in a strip of oiled paper during the rest of the week. One day I had a chance to look at this book while its owner was away after spring water. Every alternate page was in the phonetic Indian symbols, of which more hereafter. The rest was in French, and evidently a translation. Although the volume was of Roman Catholic origin, creed was conspicuously subordinated to the needs of the class it aimed to reach. A confession of faith, quite simple, in one God, a Saviour, a Mother of Heaven; a number of Biblical extracts rich in imagery and applicability to the experience of a woods-dweller; a dozen simple prayers of the kind the natural man would oftenest find occasion to express--a prayer for sickness, for bounty, for fair weather, for ease of travel, for the smiling face of Providence; and then some hymns. To me the selection seemed most judicious. It answered the needs of Tawabinisáy's habitual experiences, and so the red man was a good and consistent convert. Irresistibly I was led to contemplate the idea of any one trying to get Tawabinisáy to live in a house, to cut cordwood with an axe, to roost on a hard bench under a tin steeple, to wear stiff shoes, and to quit forest roaming.

The written language mentioned above you will see often in the Northland. Whenever an Indian band camps, it blazes a tree and leaves, as record for those who may follow, a message written in the phonetic character. I do not understand exactly the philosophy of it, but I gather that each sound has a symbol of its own, like shorthand, and that therefore even totally different languages--such as Ojibway, the Wood Cree, or the Hudson Bay Eskimos--may all be written in the same character. It was invented nearly a hundred years ago by a priest. So simple is it, and so needed a method of intercommunication, that its use is now practically universal. Even the youngsters understand it, for they are early instructed in its mysteries during the long winter evenings. On the preceding page is a message I copied from a spruce tree two hundred miles from anywhere on the Mattágami River.

Illustration

Besides this are numberless formal symbols in constant use. Forerunners on a trail stick a twig in the ground whose point indicates exactly the position of the sun. Those who follow are able to estimate, by noting how far beyond the spot the twig points to the sun has travelled, how long a period of time has elapsed. A stick pointed in any given direction tells the route, of course. Another planted upright across the first shows by its position how long a journey is contemplated. A little sack suspended at the end of the pointer conveys information as to the state of the larder, lean or fat according as the little sack contains more or less gravel or sand. A shred of rabbit-skin means starvation. And so on in variety useless in any but an ethnological work.

Illustration 1: A short journey.
Illustration 2: A medium journey.
Illustration 3: A long journey.

The Ojibways' tongue is soft, and full of decided lisping and sustained hissing sounds. It is spoken with somewhat of a sing-song drawl. We always had a fancy that somehow it was of forest growth, and that its syllables were intended in the scheme of things to blend with the woods noises, just as the feathers of the mother partridge blend with the woods colours. In general it is polysyllabic. That applies especially to concepts borrowed of the white men. On the other hand, the Ojibways describe in monosyllables many ideas we could express only in phrase. They have a single word for the notion, Place-where-an-animal-slept-last-night. Our "lair," "form," etc., do not mean exactly that. Its genius, moreover, inclines to a flexible verb-form, by which adjectives and substantives are often absorbed into the verb itself, so that one beautiful singing word will convey a whole paragraph of information. My little knowledge of it is so entirely empirical that it can possess small value.

In concluding these desultory remarks, I want to tell you of a very curious survival among the Ojibways and Ottawas of the Georgian Bay. It seems that some hundreds of years ago these ordinarily peaceful folk descended on the Iroquois in what is now New York, and massacred a village or so. Then, like small boys who have thrown only too accurately at the delivery wagon, they scuttled back home again.

Since that time they have lived in deadly fear of retribution. The Iroquois have long since disappeared from the face of the earth, but even to-day the Georgian Bay Indians are subject to periodical spasms of terror. Some wild-eyed and imaginative youth sees at sunset a canoe far down the horizon. Immediately the villages are abandoned in haste, and the entire community moves up to the head-waters of streams, there to lurk until convinced that all danger is past. It does no good to tell these benighted savages that they are safe from vengeance, at least in this world. The dreaded name of Iroquois is potent, even across the centuries.

*XVII.*

THE CATCHING OF A CERTAIN FISH.

We settled down peacefully on the River, and the weather, after so much enmity, was kind to us. Likewise did the flies disappear from the woods utterly.

Each morning we arose as the Red Gods willed; generally early, when the sun was just gilding the peaks to the westward; but not too early, before the white veil had left the River. Billy, with woodsman's contempt for economy, hewed great logs and burned them nobly in the cooking of trout, oatmeal, pancakes, and the like. We had constructed ourselves tables and benches between green trees, and there we ate. And great was the eating beyond the official capacity of the human stomach. There offered little things to do, delicious little things just on the hither side of idleness. A rod wrapping needed more waxed silk; a favourite fly required attention to prevent dissolution; the pistol was to be cleaned; a flag-pole seemed desirable; a trifle more of balsam could do no harm; clothes might stand drying, blankets airing. We accomplished these things leisurely, pausing for the telling of stories, for the puffing of pipes, for the sheer joy of contemplations. Deerskin slipper moccasins and flapping trousers attested our deshabille. And then somehow it was noon, and Billy again at the Dutch oven and the broiler.

Trout we ate, and always more trout. Big fellows broiled with strips of bacon craftily sewn in and out of the pink flesh; medium fellows cut into steaks; little fellows fried crisp in corn-meal; big, medium, and little fellows mingled in component of the famous North Country *bouillon*, whose other ingredients are partridges, and tomatoes, and potatoes, and onions, and salt pork, and flour in combination delicious beyond belief. Nor ever did we tire of them, three times a day, printed statement to the contrary notwithstanding. And besides were many crafty dishes over whose construction the major portion of morning idleness was spent.

Now at two o'clock we groaned temporary little groans; and crawled shrinking into our river clothes, which we dared not hang too near the fire for fear of the disintegrating scorch, and drew on soggy hobnailed shoes with holes cut in the bottom and plunged with howls of disgust into the upper riffles. Then the cautious leg-straddled passage of the swift current, during which we forgot for ever--which eternity alone circles the bliss of an afternoon on the River--the chill of the water, and so came to the trail.

Now, at the Idiot's Delight Dick and I parted company. By three o'clock I came again to the River, far up, halfway to the Big Falls. Deuce watched me gravely. With the first click of the reel he retired to the brush away from the back cast, there to remain until the pool was fished and we could continue our journey.

In the swift leaping water, at the smooth back of the eddy, in the white foam, under the dark cliff shadow, here, there, everywhere the bright flies drop softly like strange snowflakes. The game is as interesting as pistol-shooting. To hit the mark, that is enough. And then a swirl of water and a broad lazy tail wake you to the fact that other matters are yours. Verily the fish of the North Country are mighty beyond all others.

Over the River rests the sheen of light; over the hills rests the sheen of romance. The land is enchanted. Birds dip and sway, advance and retreat; leaves toss their hands in greeting, or bend and whisper one to the other; splashes of sun fall heavy as metal through the yielding screens of branches; little breezes wander hesitatingly here and there to sink like spent kites on the nearest bar of sun-warmed shingle; the stream shouts and gurgles, murmurs, hushes, lies still and secret as though to warn you to discretion, breaks away with a shriek of hilarity when your discretion has been assured. There is in you a great leisure, as though the day would never end. There is in you a great keenness. One part of you is vibrantly alive. Your wrist muscles contract almost automatically at the swirl of a rise, and the hum of life along the gossamer of your line gains its communication with every nerve in your body. The question of gear and method you attack clear-minded. What fly? Montreal, Parmachenee Belle, Royal Coachman, Silver Doctor, Professor, Brown Hackle, Cow-dung--these grand lures for the North Country trout receive each its due test and attention. And on the tail snell what fisherman has not the Gamble--the unusual, obscure, multinamed fly which may, in the occultism of his taste, attract the Big Fellows? Besides, there remains always the handling. Does your trout to-day fancy the skittering of his food, or the withdrawal in three jerks, or the inch-deep sinking of the fly? Does he want it across current or up current; will he rise with a snap, or is he going to come slowly, or is he going to play? These be problems interesting, insistent to be solved, with the ready test within the reach of your skill.

But that alertness is only one side of your mood. No matter how difficult the selection, how strenuous the fight, there is in you a large feeling that might almost be described as Buddhistic. Time has nothing to do with your problems. The world has quietly run down, and has been embalmed with all its sweetness of light and colour and sound in a warm Lethe bath of sun. This afternoon is going to last for ever. You note and enjoy and savour the little pleasures unhurried by the thought that anything else, whether of pleasure or duty, is to follow.

And so for long delicious eons. The River flows on, ever on; the hills watch, watch always; the birds sing, the sun shines grateful across your shoulders; the big trout and the little rise in predestined order, and make their predestined fight, and go their predestined way either to liberty or the creel; the pools and the rapids and the riffles slip by upstream as though they had been withdrawn rather than as though you had advanced.

Then suddenly the day has dropped its wings. The earth moves forward with a jar. Things are to be accomplished; things are being accomplished. The River is hurrying down to the Lake; the birds have business of their own to attend to, an it please you; the hills are waiting for something that has not yet happened, but they are ready. Startled, you look up. The afternoon has finished. Your last step has taken you over the edge of the shadow cast by the setting sun across the range of hills.

For the first time you look about you to see where you are. It has not mattered before. Now you know that shortly it will be dark. Still remain below you four pools. A great haste seizes you.

"If I take my rod apart and strike through the woods," you argue, "I can make the Narrows, and I am sure there is a big trout there."

Why the Narrows should be any more likely to contain a big trout than any of the other three pools you would not be able to explain. In half an hour it will be dark. You hurry. In the forest it is already twilight, but by now you know the forest well. Preoccupied, feverish with your great idea, you hasten on. The birds, silent all in the brooding of night, rise ghostly to right and left. Shadows steal away like hostile spies among the treetrunks. The silver of last daylight gleams ahead of you through the brush. You know it for the Narrows, whither the instinct of your eagerness has led you as accurately as a compass through the forest.

Fervently, as though this were of world's affairs the most important, you congratulate yourself on being in time. Your rod seems to join itself. In a moment the cast drops like a breath on the molten silver. Nothing. Another try a trifle lower down. Nothing. A little wandering breeze spoils your fourth attempt, carrying the leader far to the left. Curses, deep and fervent. The daylight is fading, draining away. A fifth cast falls forty feet out. Slowly you drag the flies across the current, reluctant to recover until the latest possible moment. And so, when your rod is foolishly upright, your line slack, and your flies motionless, there rolls slowly up and over the trout of trouts. You see a broad side, the whirl of a fantail that looks to you to be at least six inches across; and the current slides on, silver-like, smooth, indifferent to the wild leap of your heart.

Like a crazy man you shorten your line. Six seconds later your flies fall skilfully just upstream from where last you saw that wonderful tail.

But six seconds may be a long, long period of time. You have feared and hoped and speculated and realized; feared that the leviathan has pricked himself, and so will not rise again; hoped that his appearance merely indicated curiosity which he will desire further to satisfy; speculated on whether your skill can drop the fly exactly on that spot, as it must be dropped; and realized that, whatever be the truth as to all those fears and hopes and speculations, this is irrevocably your last chance.

For an instant you allow the flies to drift downstream, to be floated here and there by idle little eddies, to be sucked down and spat out of tiny suction-holes. Then cautiously you draw them across the surface of the waters. *Thump--thump--thump*--your heart slows up with disappointment. Then mysteriously, like the stirring of the waters by some invisible hand, the molten silver is broken in its smoothness. The Royal Coachman quietly disappears. With all the brakes shrieking on your desire to shut your eyes and heave a mighty heave, you depress your butt and strike.

Then in the twilight the battle. No leisure is here, only quivering, intense, agonized anxiety. The affair transcends the moment. Purposes and necessities of untold ages have concentrated, so that somehow back of your consciousness rest hosts of disembodied hopes, tendencies, evolutionary progressions, all breathless lest you prove unequal to the struggle for which they have been so long preparing. Responsibility--vast, vague, formless--is yours. Only the fact that you are wholly occupied with the exigence of the moment prevents your understanding of what it is, but it hovers dark and depressing behind your possible failure. You must win. This is no fish; it is opportunity itself, and once gone it will never return. The mysticism of lower dusk in the forest, of upper afterglow on the hills, of the chill of evening waters and winds, of the glint of strange phantoms under the darkness of cliffs, of the whisperings and shoutings of Things you are too busy to identify out in the gray of North Country awe--all these menace you with indeterminate dread. Knee-deep, waist-deep, swift water, slack water, downstream, upstream, with red eyes straining into the dimness, with every muscle taut and every nerve quivering, you follow the ripping of your line. You have consecrated yourself to the uttermost. The minutes stalk by you gigantic. You are a stable pin-point in whirling phantasms. And you are very little, very small, very inadequate among these Titans of circumstance.

Thrice he breaks water, a white and ghostly apparition from the deep. Your heart stops with your reel, and only resumes its office when again the line sings safely. The darkness falls, and with it, like the mysterious strength of Sir Gareth's opponent, falls the power of your adversary. His rushes shorten. The blown world of your uncertainty shrinks to the normal. From the haze of your consciousness, as through a fog, loom the old familiar forest, and the hills, and the River. Slowly you creep from that strange enchanted land. The sullen trout yields. In all gentleness you float him within reach of your net. Quietly, breathlessly you walk ashore, and over the beach, and yet an unnecessary hundred feet from the water lest he retain still a flop. Then you lay him upon the stones and lift up your heart in rejoicing.

How you get to camp you never clearly know. Exultation lifts your feet. Wings, wings, O ye Red Gods, wings to carry the body whither the spirit hath already soared, and stooped, and circled back in impatience to see why still the body lingers! Ordinarily you can cross the riffles above the Halfway Pool only with caution and prayer and a stout staff craftily employed. This night you can--and do--splash across hand-free, as recklessly as you would wade a little brook. There is no stumble in you, for you have done a great deed, and the Red Gods are smiling.

Through the trees glows a light, and in the centre of that light are leaping flames, and in the circle of that light stand, rough-hewn in orange, the tent and the table and the waiting figures of your companions. You stop short, and swallow hard, and saunter into camp as one indifferent.

Carelessly you toss aside your creel--into the darkest corner, as though it were unimportant--nonchalantly you lean your rod against the slant of your tent, wearily you seat yourself and begin to draw off your drenched garments. Billy bends toward the fire. Dick gets you your dry clothes. Nobody says anything, for everybody is hungry. No one asks you any questions, for on the River you get in almost any time of night.

Finally, as you are hanging your wet things near the fire, you inquire casually over your shoulder,--

"Dick, have any luck?"

Dick tells you. You listen with apparent interest. He has caught a three-pounder. He describes the spot and the method and the struggle. He is very much pleased. You pity him.

The three of you eat supper, lots of supper. Billy arises first, filling his pipe. He hangs water over the fire for the dish-washing. You and Dick sit hunched on a log, blissfully happy in the moments of digestion, ruminative, watching the blaze. The tobacco smoke eddies and sucks upward to join the wood smoke. Billy moves here and there in the fulfilment of his simple tasks, casting his shadow wavering and gigantic against the fire-lit trees. By-and-by he has finished. He gathers up the straps of Dick's creel, and turns to the shadow for your own. He is going to clean the fish. It is the moment you have watched for. You shroud yourself in profound indifference.

"*Sacré!*" shrieks Billy.

You do not even turn your head.

"Jumping giraffes! why, it's a whale!" cries Dick.

You roll a *blasé* eye in their direction, as though such puerile enthusiasm wearies you.

"Yes, it's quite a little fish," you concede.

They swarm down upon you, demanding particulars. These you accord laconically, a word at a time, in answer to direct question, between puffs of smoke.

"At the Narrows. Royal Coachman. Just before I came in. Pretty fair fight. Just at the edge of the eddy." And so on. But your soul glories.

The tape-line is brought out. Twenty-nine inches it records. Holy smoke, what a fish! Your air implies that you will probably catch three more just like him on the morrow. Dick and Billy make tracings of him on the birch bark. You retain your lofty calm: but inside you are little quivers of rapture. And when you awake, late in the night, you are conscious, first of all, that you are happy, happy, happy, all through; and only when the drowse drains away do you remember                                                                                                            why.


*XVIII.*

MAN WHO WALKS BY MOONLIGHT.


We had been joined on the River by friends. "Doug," who never fished more than forty rods from camp, and was always inventing water-gauges, patent indicators, and other things, and who wore in his soft slouch hat so many brilliant trout flies that he irresistibly reminded you of flower-decked Ophelia; "Dinnis," who was large and good-natured, and bubbling and popular; Johnny, whose wide eyes looked for the first time on the woods-life, and whose awe-struck soul concealed itself behind assumptions; "Jim," six feet tall and three feet broad, with whom the season before I had penetrated to Hudson Bay; and finally, "Doc," tall, granite, experienced, the best fisherman that ever hit the river. With these were Indians. Buckshot, a little Indian with a good knowledge of English; Johnnie Challán, a half-breed Indian, ugly, furtive, an efficient man about camp; and Tawabinisáy himself. This was an honour due to the presence of Doc. Tawabinisáy approved of Doc. That was all there was to say about it.

After a few days, inevitably the question of Kawágama came up. Billy, Johnnie Challán, and Buckshot squatted in a semi-circle, and drew diagrams in the soft dirt with a stick. Tawabinisáy sat on a log and overlooked the proceedings. Finally he spoke.

"Tawabinisáy" (they always gave him his full title; we called him Tawáb) "tell me lake you find he no Kawágama," translated Buckshot. "He called Black Beaver Lake."

"Ask him if he'll take us to Kawágama," I requested.

Tawabinisáy looked very doubtful.

"Come on, Tawáb," urged Doc, nodding at him vigorously. "Don't be a clam. We won't take anybody else up there."

The Indian probably did not comprehend the words, but he liked Doc.

"A'-right," he pronounced laboriously.

Buckshot explained to us his plans.

"Tawabinisáy tell me," said he, "he don' been to Kawágama seven year. To-morrow he go blaze trail. Nex' day we go."

"How would it be if one or two of us went with him to-morrow to see how he does it?" asked Jim.

Buckshot looked at us strangely.

"*I* don't want to follow him," he replied, with a significant simplicity. "He run like a deer."

"Buckshot," said I, pursuing the inevitable linguistics, "what does Kawágama mean?"

Buckshot thought for quite two minutes. Then he drew a semicircle.

"W'at you call dat?" he asked.

"Crescent, like moon? half-circle? horseshoe? bow?" we proposed.

Buckshot shook his head at each suggestion. He made a wriggling mark, then a wide sweep, then a loop.

"All dose," said he, "w'at you call him?"

"Curve!" we cried.

"Áh hah," assented Buckshot, satisfied.

"Buckshot," we went on, "what does Tawabinisáy mean?"

"Man-who-travels-by-moonlight," he replied promptly.

The following morning Tawabinisáy departed, carrying a lunch and a hand-axe. At four o'clock he was back, sitting on a log and smoking a pipe. In the meantime we had made up our party.

Tawabinisáy himself had decided that the two half-breeds must stay at home. He wished to share his secret only with his own tribesmen. The fiat grieved Billy, for behold he had already put in much time on this very search, and naturally desired to be in at the finish. Dick, too, wanted to go, but him we decided too young and light for a fast march. Dinnis had to leave the River in a day or so; Johnnie was a little doubtful as to the tramp, although he concealed his doubt--at least to his own satisfaction--under a variety of excuses. Jim and Doc would go, of course. There remained Doug.

We found that individual erecting a rack of many projecting arms--like a Greek warrior's trophy--at the precise spot where the first rays of the morning sun would strike it. On the projecting arms he purposed hanging his wet clothes.

"Doug," said we, "do you want to go to Kawágama to-morrow?"

Doug turned on us a sardonic eye. He made no direct answer, but told the following story:--

"Once upon a time Judge Carter was riding through a rural district in Virginia. He stopped at a negro's cabin to get his direction.

"'Uncle,' said he, 'can you direct me to Colonel Thompson's?'

"'Yes, sah,' replied the negro; 'yo' goes down this yah road 'bout two mile till yo' comes to an ol' ailm tree, and then yo' tu'us sha'p to th' right down a lane fo' 'bout a qua'ter of a mile. Thah you sees a big white house. Yo' wants to go through th' ya'd, to a paf that takes you a spell to a gate. Yo' follows that road to th' lef till yo' comes to three roads goin' up a hill; and, jedge, *it don' mattah which one of them thah roads yo' take, yo' gets lost surer 'n hell anyway!*'"

Then Doug turned placidly back to the construction of his trophy.

We interpreted this as an answer, and made up an outfit for five.

The following morning at six o'clock we were under way. Johnnie Challán ferried us across the river in two instalments. We waved our hands and plunged through the brush screen.

Thenceforth it was walk half an hour, rest five minutes, with almost the regularity of clockwork. We timed the Indians secretly, and found they varied by hardly a minute from absolute fidelity to this schedule. We had at first, of course, to gain the higher level of the hills, but Tawabinisáy had the day before picked out a route that mounted as easily as the country would allow, and through a hardwood forest free of underbrush. Briefly indicated, our way led first through the big trees and up the hills, then behind a great cliff knob into a creek valley, through a quarter-mile of bottom-land thicket, then by an open strip to the first little lake. This we ferried by means of the bark canoe carried on the shoulders of Tawabinisáy.

In the course of the morning we thus passed four lakes. Throughout the entire distance to Kawágama were the fresh axe-blazes the Indian had made the day before. These were neither so frequent nor as plainly cut as a white man's trail, but each represented a pause long enough for the clip of an axe. In addition the trail had been made passable for a canoe. That meant the cutting out of overhanging branches wherever they might catch the bow of the craft. In the thicket a little road had been cleared, and the brush had been piled on either side. To an unaccustomed eye it seemed the work of two days at least. Yet Tawabinisáy had picked out his route, cleared and marked it thus, skirted the shores of the lakes we were able to traverse in the canoe, and had returned to the River in less time than we consumed in merely reaching the Lake itself! Truly, as Buckshot said, he must have "run like a deer."

Tawabinisáy has a delightful grin which he displays when pleased or good-humoured or puzzled or interested or comprehending, just as a dog sneezes and wrinkles up his nose in like case. He is essentially kind-hearted. If he likes you and approves of you, he tries to teach you, to help you, to show you things. But he never offers to do any part of your work, and on the march he never looks back to see if you are keeping up. You can shout at him until you are black in the face, but never will he pause until rest-time. Then he squats on his heels, lights his pipe, and grins.

Buckshot adored him. This opportunity of travelling with him was an epoch. He drank in eagerly the brief remarks of his "old man," and detailed them to us with solemnity, prefaced always by his "Tàwabinisáy tell me." Buckshot is of the better class of Indian himself, but occasionally he is puzzled by the woods-noises. Tawabinisáy never. As we cooked lunch, we heard the sound of steady footsteps in the forest--*pat*; then a pause; then *pat*; just like a deer browsing. To make sure I inquired of Buckshot.

"What is it?"

Buckshot listened a moment.

"Deer," said he decisively; then, not because he doubted his own judgment, but from habitual deference, he turned to where Tawabinisáy was frying things.

"Qwaw?" he inquired.

Tawabinisáy never even looked up.

"Adjí-domo" (squirrel), said he.

We looked at each other incredulously. It sounded like a deer. It did not sound in the least like a squirrel. An experienced Indian had pronounced it a deer. Nevertheless it was a squirrel.

We approached Kawágama by way of a gradual slope clothed with a beautiful beech and maple forest whose trees were the tallest of those species I have ever seen. Ten minutes brought us to the shore. There was no abrupt bursting in on Kawágama through screens of leaves; we entered leisurely to her presence by way of an ante-chamber whose spaciousness permitted no vulgar surprises. After a time we launched our canoe from a natural dock afforded by a cedar root, and so stood ready to cross to our permanent camp. But first we drew our knives and erased from a giant birch the half-grown-over name of the banker Clement.

There seems to me little use in telling you that Kawágama is about four miles long by a mile wide, is shaped like a crescent, and lies in a valley surrounded by high hills; nor that its water is so transparent that the bottom is visible until it fades into the sheer blackness of depth; nor that it is alive with trout; nor that its silence is the silence of a vast solitude, so that always, even at daybreak or at high midday, it seems to be late afternoon. That would convey little to you. I will inform you quite simply that Kawágama is a very beautiful specimen of the wilderness lake; that it is as the Lord made it; and that we had a good time.

Did you ever fish with the fly from a birch-bark canoe on absolutely still water? You do not seem to move. But far below you, gliding, silent, ghostlike, the bottom slips beneath. Like a weather-vane in an imperceptible current of air, your bow turns to right or left in apparent obedience to the mere will of your companion. And the flies drop softly like down. Then the silence becomes sacred. You swhisper--although there is no reason for your whispering; you move cautiously, lest your reel scrape the gunwale. An inadvertent click of the paddle is a profanation. The only creatures in all God's world possessing the right to utter aloud a single syllable are the loon, far away, and the winter wren, near at hand. Even the trout fight grimly, without noise, their white bodies flashing far down in the dimness.

Hour after hour we stole here and there like conspirators. Where showed the circles of a fish's rise, thither crept we to drop a fly on their centre as in the bull's-eye of a target. The trout seemed to linger near their latest capture, so often we would catch one exactly where we had seen him break water some little time before. In this was the charm of the still hunt. Shoal water, deep water, it seemed all the same to our fortunes. The lake was full of fish, and beautiful fish they were, with deep, glowing bronze bellies, and all of from a pound to a pound and a half in weight. The lake had not been fished. Probably somewhere in those black depths over one of the bubbling spring-holes that must feed so cold and clear a body of water, are big fellows lying, and probably the crafty minnow or spoon might lure them out. But we were satisfied with our game.

At other times we paddled here and there in exploration of coves, inlets, and a tiny little brook that flowed westward from a reed marsh to join another river running parallel to our own.

The Indians had erected a huge lean-to of birch bark, from the ribs of which hung clothes and the little bags of food. The cooking-fire was made in front of it between two giant birch trees. At evening the light and heat reflected strongly beneath the shelter, leaving the forest in impenetrable darkness. To the very edge of mystery crowded the strange woods noises, the eerie influences of the night, like wolves afraid of the blaze. We felt them hovering, vague, huge, dreadful, just outside the circle of safety our fire had traced about us. The cheerful flames were dancing familiars who cherished for us the home feeling in the middle of a wilderness.

Two days we lingered, then took the back track. A little after noon we arrived at the camp, empty save for Johnnie Challán. Towards dark the fishermen straggled in. Time had been paid them in familiar coinage. They had demanded only accustomed toll of the days, but we had returned laden with strange and glittering memories.

## XIX.

APOLOGIA.

The time at last arrived for departure.

Deep laden were the canoes; heavy laden were we. The Indians shot away down the current. We followed for the last time the dim blazed trail, forded for the last time the shallows of the river. At the Burned Rock Pool we caught our lunch fish from the ranks of leviathans. Then the trodden way of the Fur Trail, worn into a groove so deep and a surface so smooth that vegetation has left it as bare as ever, though the Post has been abandoned these many years. At last the scrub spruce, and the sandy soil, and the blue, restless waters of the Great Lake. With the appearance of the fish-tug early the following day the summer ended.

How often have I ruminated in the long marches the problem of the Forest! Subtle she is, and mysterious, and gifted with a charm that lures. Vast she is, and dreadful, so that man bows before her fiercer moods, a little thing. Gentle she is, and kindly, so that she denies nothing, whether of the material or spiritual, to those of her chosen who will seek. August she is, and yet of a homely, sprightly gentleness. Variable she is in her many moods. Night, day, sun, cloud, rain, snow, wind, lend to her their best of warmth and cold, of comfort and awe, of peace and of many shoutings, and she accepts them, but yet remains greater and more enduring than they. In her is all the sweetness of little things. Murmurs of water and of breeze, faint odours, wandering streams of tepid air, stray bird-songs in fragment as when a door is opened and closed, the softness of moss, the coolness of shade, the glimpse of occult affairs in the woods life, accompany her as Titania her court. How to express these things; how to fix on paper in a record, as one would describe the Capitol at Washington, what the Forest is--that is what I have asked myself often, and that is what I have never yet found out.

This is the wisdom reflection has taught. One cannot imprison the ocean in a vial of sea-water; one cannot imprison the Forest inside the covers of a book.

There remains the second best. I have thought that perhaps if I were to attempt a series of detached impressions, without relation, without sequence; if I were to suggest a little here the beauty of a moon-beam, there the humour of a rainstorm, at the last you might, by dint of imagination and sympathy, get some slight feeling of what the great woods are. It is the method of the painter. Perhaps it may suffice.

For this reason let no old camper look upon this volume as a treatise on woodcraft. Woodcraft there is in it, just as there is woodcraft in the Forest itself, but much of the simplest and most obvious does not appear. The painter would not depict every twig, as would the naturalist.

Equally it cannot be considered a book of travel nor of description. The story is not consecutive; the adventures not exciting; the landscape not denned. Perhaps it may be permitted to call it a book of suggestion. Often on the street we have had opened to us by the merest sketches of incident limitless vistas of memory. A momentary pose of the head of a passer-by, a chance word, the breath of a faint perfume--these bring back to us the entirety of forgotten scenes. Some of these essays may perform a like office for you. I cannot hope to give you the Forest. But perhaps a word or a sentence, an incident, an impression, may quicken your imagination, so that through no conscious direction of my own the wonder of the Forest may fill you, as the mere sight of a conch-shell will sometimes till you with the wonder of the sea.

## SUGGESTIONS FOR OUTFIT.

In reply to inquiries as to necessary outfit for camping and woods-travelling, the author furnishes the following lists:--

1. *Provisions per man, one week.*

7 lbs. flour; 5 lbs. pork; 1-5 lb. tea; 2 lbs. beans; 1 1-2 lbs. sugar; 1 1-2 lbs. rice; 1 1-2 lbs. prunes and raisins; 1-1-2 lb. lard; 1 lb. oatmeal; baking-powder; matches; soap; pepper; salt; 1-3 lb. tobacco--(weight, a little over 20 lbs.). This will last much longer if you get game and fish.

2. *Pack one, or absolute necessities for hard trip.*

*Wear* hat; suit woollen underwear; shirt; trousers; socks; silk handkerchief; cotton handkerchief; moccasins.

*Carry* sweater (3 lbs.); extra drawers (1 1-2 lbs.); 2 extra pairs socks; gloves (buckskin); towel; 2 extra pairs moccasins; surgeon's plaster; laxative; pistol and cartridges; fishing-tackle; blanket (7 1-2 lbs.); rubber blanket (1 lb.); tent (8 lbs.); small axe (2 1-2 lbs.); knife; mosquito-dope; compass; match-box; tooth-brush; comb; small whetstone--(weight, about 25 lbs.); 2 tin or aluminium pails; 1 frying-pan; 1 cup; 1 knife, fork, and spoon--(weight, 4 lbs. if of aluminium).

Whole pack under 50 lbs. In case of two or more people, each pack would be lighter, as tent, tinware, etc., would do for both.

3. *Pack two--for luxuries and easy trips--extra to pack one.*

More fishing-tackle; camera; 1 more pair socks; 1 more suit underclothes; extra sweater; wading-shoes of canvas; large axe; mosquito net; mending materials; kettle; candles; more cooking-utensils; extra shirt; whisky.

## THE END.

# Arizona Nights

## CHAPTER ONE
## THE OLE VIRGINIA

The ring around the sun had thickened all day long, and the turquoise blue of the Arizona sky had filmed. Storms in the dry countries are infrequent, but heavy; and this surely meant storm.

We had ridden since sun-up over broad mesas, down and out of deep canons, along the base of the mountain in the wildest parts of the territory. The cattle were winding leisurely toward the high country; the jack rabbits had disappeared; the quail lacked; we did not see a single antelope in the open.

"It's a case of hole up," the Cattleman ventured his opinion. "I have a ranch over in the Double R. Charley and Windy Bill hold it down. We'll tackle it. What do you think?"

The four cowboys agreed. We dropped into a low, broad watercourse, ascended its bed to big cottonwoods and flowing water, followed it into box canons between rim-rock carved fantastically and painted like a Moorish facade, until at last in a widening below a rounded hill, we came upon an adobe house, a fruit tree, and a round corral. This was the Double R.

Charley and Windy Bill welcomed us with soda biscuits. We turned our horses out, spread our beds on the floor, filled our pipes, and squatted on our heels. Various dogs of various breeds investigated us. It was very pleasant, and we did not mind the ring around the sun.

"Somebody else coming," announced the Cattleman finally.

"Uncle Jim," said Charley, after a glance.

A hawk-faced old man with a long white beard and long white hair rode out from the cottonwoods. He had on a battered broad hat abnormally high of crown, carried across his saddle a heavy "eight square" rifle, and was followed by a half-dozen lolloping hounds.

The largest and fiercest of the latter, catching sight of our group, launched himself with lightning rapidity at the biggest of the ranch dogs, promptly nailed that canine by the back of the neck, shook him violently a score of times, flung him aside, and pounced on the next. During the ensuing few moments that hound was the busiest thing in the West. He satisfactorily whipped four dogs, pursued two cats up a tree, upset the Dutch oven and the rest of the soda biscuits, stampeded the horses, and raised a cloud of dust adequate to represent the smoke of battle. We others were too paralysed to move. Uncle Jim sat placidly on his white horse, his thin knees bent to the ox-bow stirrups, smoking.

In ten seconds the trouble was over, principally because there was no more trouble to make. The hound returned leisurely, licking from his chops the hair of his victims. Uncle Jim shook his head.

"Trailer," said he sadly, "is a little severe."

We agreed heartily, and turned in to welcome Uncle Jim with a fresh batch of soda biscuits.

The old man was one of the typical "long hairs." He had come to the Galiuro Mountains in '69, and since '69 he had remained in the Galiuro Mountains, spite of man or the devil. At present he possessed some hundreds of cattle, which he was reputed to water, in a dry season, from an ordinary dishpan. In times past he had prospected.

That evening, the severe Trailer having dropped to slumber, he held forth on big-game hunting and dogs, quartz claims and Apaches.

"Did you ever have any very close calls?" I asked.

He ruminated a few moments, refilled his pipe with some awful tobacco, and told the following experience:

In the time of Geronimo I was living just about where I do now; and that was just about in line with the raiding. You see, Geronimo, and Ju , and old Loco used to pile out of the reservation at Camp Apache, raid south to the line, slip over into Mexico when the soldiers got too promiscuous, and raid there until they got ready to come back. Then there was always a big medicine talk. Says Geronimo:

"I am tired of the warpath. I will come back from Mexico with all my warriors, if you will escort me with soldiers and protect my people."

"All right," says the General, being only too glad to get him back at all.

So, then, in ten minutes there wouldn't be a buck in camp, but next morning they shows up again, each with about fifty head of hosses.

"Where'd you get those hosses?" asks the General, suspicious.

"Had 'em pastured in the hills," answers Geronimo.

"I can't take all those hosses with me; I believe they're stolen!" says the General.

"My people cannot go without their hosses," says Geronimo.

So, across the line they goes, and back to the reservation. In about a week there's fifty-two frantic Greasers wanting to know where's their hosses. The army is nothing but an importer of stolen stock, and knows it, and can't help it.

Well, as I says, I'm between Camp Apache and the Mexican line, so that every raiding party goes right on past me. The point is that I'm a thousand feet or so above the valley, and the renegades is in such a devil of a hurry about that time that they never stop to climb up and collect me. Often I've watched them trailing down the valley in a cloud of dust. Then, in a day or two, a squad of soldiers would come up, and camp at my spring for a while. They used to send soldiers to guard every water hole in the country so the renegades couldn't get water. After a while, from not being bothered none, I got thinking I wasn't worth while with them.

Me and Johnny Hooper were pecking away at the old Virginia mine then. We'd got down about sixty feet, all timbered, and was thinking of cross-cutting. One day Johnny went to town, and that same day I got in a hurry and left my gun at camp.

I worked all the morning down at the bottom of the shaft, and when I see by the sun it was getting along towards noon, I put in three good shots, tamped 'em down, lit the fusees, and started to climb out.

It ain't noways pleasant to light a fuse in a shaft, and then have to climb out a fifty-foot ladder, with it burning behind you. I never did get used to it. You keep thinking, "Now suppose there's a flaw in that fuse, or something, and she goes off in six seconds instead of two minutes? where'll you be then?" It would give you a good boost towards your home on high, anyway.

So I climbed fast, and stuck my head out the top without looking—and then I froze solid enough. There, about fifty feet away, climbing up the hill on mighty tired hosses, was a dozen of the ugliest Chiricahuas you ever don't want to meet, and in addition a Mexican renegade named Maria, who was worse than any of 'em. I see at once their hosses was tired out, and they had a notion of camping at my water hole, not knowing nothing about the Ole Virginia mine.

For two bits I'd have let go all holts and dropped backwards, trusting to my thick head for easy lighting. Then I heard a little fizz and sputter from below. At that my hair riz right up so I could feel the breeze blow under my hat. For about six seconds I stood there like an imbecile, grinning amiably. Then one of the Chiricahuas made a sort of grunt, and I sabed that they'd seen the original exhibit your Uncle Jim was making of himself.

Then that fuse gave another sputter and one of the Apaches said "Un dah." That means "white man." It was harder to turn my head than if I'd had a stiff neck; but I managed to do it, and I see that my ore dump wasn't more than ten foot away. I mighty near overjumped it; and the next I knew I was on one side of it and those Apaches on the other. Probably I flew; leastways I don't seem to remember jumping.

That didn't seem to do me much good. The renegades were grinning and laughing to think how easy a thing they had; and I couldn't rightly think up any arguments against that notion—at least from their standpoint. They were chattering away to each other in Mexican for the benefit of Maria. Oh, they had me all distributed, down to my suspender buttons! And me squatting behind that ore dump about as formidable as a brush rabbit!

Then, all at once, one of my shots went off down in the shaft.

"Boom!" says she, plenty big; and a slather of rock, and stones come out of the mouth, and began to dump down promiscuous on the scenery. I got one little one in the shoulder-blade, and found time to wish my ore dump had a roof. But those renegades caught it square in the thick of trouble. One got knocked out entirely for a minute, by a nice piece of country rock in the head.

"Otra vez!" yells I, which means "again."

"Boom!" goes the Ole Virginia prompt as an answer.

I put in my time dodging, but when I gets a chance to look, the Apaches has all got to cover, and is looking scared.

"Otra vez!" yells I again.

"Boom!" says the Ole Virginia.

This was the biggest shot of the lot, and she surely cut loose. I ought to have been half-way up the bill watching things from a safe distance, but I wasn't. Lucky for me the shaft was a little on the drift, so she didn't quite shoot my way. But she distributed about a ton over those renegades. They sort of half got to their feet uncertain.

"Otra vez!" yells I once more, as bold as if I could keep her shooting all day.

It was just a cold, raw blazer; and if it didn't go through I could see me as an Apache parlour ornament. But it did. Those Chiricahuas give one yell and skipped. It was surely a funny sight, after they got aboard their war ponies, to see them trying to dig out on horses too tired to trot.

I didn't stop to get all the laughs, though. In fact, I give one jump off that ledge, and I lit a-running. A quarter-hoss couldn't have beat me to that shack. There I grabbed old Meat-in-the-pot and made a climb for the tall country, aiming to wait around until dark, and then to pull out for Benson. Johnny Hooper wasn't expected till next day, which was lucky. From where I lay I could see the Apaches camped out beyond my draw, and I didn't doubt they'd visited the place. Along about sunset they all left their camp, and went into the draw, so there, I thinks, I sees a good chance to make a start before dark. I dropped down from the mesa, skirted the butte, and angled down across the country. After I'd gone a half mile from the cliffs, I ran across Johnny Hooper's fresh trail headed towards camp!

My heart jumped right up into my mouth at that. Here was poor old Johnny, a day too early, with a pack-mule of grub, walking innocent as a yearling, right into the bands of those hostiles. The trail looked pretty fresh, and Benson's a good long day with a pack animal, so I thought perhaps I might catch him before he runs into trouble. So I ran back on the trail as fast as I could make it. The sun was down by now, and it was getting dusk.

I didn't overtake him, and when I got to the top of the canon I crawled along very cautious and took a look. Of course, I expected to see everything up in smoke, but I nearly got up and yelled when I see everything all right, and old Sukey, the pack-mule, and Johnny's hoss hitched up as peaceful as babies to the corral.

"THAT'S all right!" thinks I, "they're back in their camp, and haven't discovered Johnny yet. I'll snail him out of there."

So I ran down the hill and into the shack. Johnny sat in his chair—what there was of him. He must have got in about two hours before sundown, for they'd had lots of time to put in on him. That's the reason they'd stayed so long up the draw. Poor old Johnny! I was glad it was night, and he was dead. Apaches are the worst Injuns there is for tortures. They cut off the bottoms of old man Wilkins's feet, and stood him on an ant-hill—.

In a minute or so, though, my wits gets to work.

"Why ain't the shack burned?" I asks myself, "and why is the hoss and the mule tied all so peaceful to the corral?"

It didn't take long for a man who knows Injins to answer THOSE conundrums. The whole thing was a trap—for me—and I'd walked into it, chuckle-headed as a prairie-dog!

With that I makes a run outside—by now it was dark—and listens. Sure enough, I hears hosses. So I makes a rapid sneak back over the trail.

Everything seemed all right till I got up to the rim-rock. Then I heard more hosses—ahead of me. And when I looked back I could see some Injuns already at the shack, and starting to build a fire outside.

In a tight fix, a man is pretty apt to get scared till all hope is gone. Then he is pretty apt to get cool and calm. That was my case. I couldn't go ahead—there was those hosses coming along the trail. I couldn't go back—there was those Injuns building the fire. So I skirmished around till I got a bright star right over the trail head, and I trained old Meat-in-the-pot to bear on that star, and I made up my mind that when the star was darkened I'd turn loose. So I lay there a while listening. By and by the star was blotted out, and I cut loose, and old Meat-in-the-pot missed fire—she never did it before nor since; I think that cartridge—

Well, I don't know where the Injuns came from, but it seemed as if the hammer had hardly clicked before three or four of them bad piled on me. I put up the best fight I could, for I wasn't figuring to be caught alive, and this miss-fire deal had fooled me all along the line. They surely had a lively time. I expected every minute to feel a knife in my back, but when I didn't get it then I knew they wanted to bring me in alive, and that made me fight harder. First and last, we rolled and plunged all the way from the rim-rock down to the canon-bed. Then one of the Injuns sung out:

"Maria!"

And I thought of that renegade Mexican, and what I'd heard bout him, and that made me fight harder yet.

But after we'd fought down to the canon-bed, and had lost most of our skin, a half-dozen more fell on me, and in less than no time they had me tied. Then they picked me up and carried me over to where they'd built a big fire by the corral.

Uncle Jim stopped with an air of finality, and began lazily to refill his pipe. From the open mud fireplace he picked a coal. Outside, the rain, faithful to the prophecy of the wide-ringed sun, beat fitfully against the roof.

"That was the closest call I ever had," said he at last.

"But, Uncle Jim," we cried in a confused chorus, "how did you get away? What did the Indians do to you? Who rescued you?"

Uncle Jim chuckled.

"The first man I saw sitting at that fire," said he, "was Lieutenant Price of the United States Army, and by him was Tom Horn."

"'What's this?' he asks, and Horn talks to the Injuns in Apache.

"'They say they've caught Maria,' translates Horn back again.

"'Maria-nothing!' says Lieutenant Price. 'This is Jim Fox. I know him.'"

"So they turned me loose. It seems the troops had driven off the renegades an hour before."

"And the Indians who caught you, Uncle Jim? You said they were Indians."

"Were Tonto Basin Apaches," explained the old man—"government scouts under Tom Horn."

Pronounced "Hoo."

CHAPTER TWO
THE EMIGRANTS

After the rain that had held us holed up at the Double R over one day, we discussed what we should do next.

"The flats will be too boggy for riding, and anyway the cattle will be in the high country," the Cattleman summed up the situation. "We'd bog down the chuck-wagon if we tried to get back to the J. H. But now after the rain the weather ought to be beautiful. What shall we do?"

"Was you ever in the Jackson country?" asked Uncle Jim. "It's the wildest part of Arizona. It's a big country and rough, and no one lives there, and there's lots of deer and mountain lions and bear. Here's my dogs. We might have a hunt."

"Good!" said we.

We skirmished around and found a condemned army pack saddle with aparejos, and a sawbuck saddle with kyacks. On these, we managed to condense our grub and utensils. There were plenty of horses, so our bedding we bound flat about their naked barrels by means of the squaw-hitch. Then we started.

That day furnished us with a demonstration of what Arizona horses can do. Our way led first through a canon-bed filled with rounded boulders and rocks, slippery and unstable. Big cottonwoods and oaks grew so thick as partially to conceal the cliffs on either side of us. The rim-rock was mysterious with caves; beautiful with hanging gardens of tree ferns and grasses growing thick in long transverse crevices; wonderful in colour and shape. We passed the little canons fenced off by the rustlers as corrals into which to shunt from the herds their choice of beeves.

The Cattleman shook his head at them. "Many a man has come from Texas and established a herd with no other asset than a couple of horses and a branding-iron," said he.

Then we worked up gradually to a divide, whence we could see a range of wild and rugged mountains on our right. They rose by slopes and ledges, steep and rough, and at last ended in the thousand-foot cliffs of the buttes, running sheer and unbroken for many miles. During all the rest of our trip they were to be our companions, the only constant factors in the tumult of lesser peaks, precipitous canons, and twisted systems in which we were constantly involved.

The sky was sun-and-shadow after the rain. Each and every Arizonan predicted clearing.

"Why, it almost never rains in Arizona," said Jed Parker. "And when it does it quits before it begins."

Nevertheless, about noon a thick cloud gathered about the tops of the Galiuros above us. Almost immediately it was dissipated by the wind, but when the peaks again showed, we stared with astonishment to see that they were white with snow. It was as though a magician had passed a sheet before them the brief instant necessary to work his great transformation. Shortly the sky thickened again, and it began to rain.

Travel had been precarious before; but now its difficulties were infinitely increased. The clay sub-soil to the rubble turned slippery and adhesive. On the sides of the mountains it was almost impossible to keep a footing. We speedily became wet, our hands puffed and purple, our boots sodden with the water that had trickled from our clothing into them.

"Over the next ridge," Uncle Jim promised us, "is an old shack that I fixed up seven years ago. We can all make out to get in it."

Over the next ridge, therefore, we slipped and slid, thanking the god of luck for each ten feet gained. It was growing cold. The cliffs and palisades near at hand showed dimly behind the falling rain; beyond them waved and eddied the storm mists through which the mountains revealed and concealed proportions exaggerated into unearthly grandeur. Deep in the clefts of the box canons the streams were filling. The roar of their rapids echoed from innumerable precipices. A soft swish of water usurped the world of sound.

Nothing more uncomfortable or more magnificent could be imagined. We rode shivering. Each said to himself, "I can stand this—right now—at the present moment. Very well; I will do so, and I will refuse to look forward even five minutes to what I may have to stand," which is the true philosophy of tough times and the only effective way to endure discomfort.

By luck we reached the bottom of that canon without a fall. It was wide, well grown with oak trees, and belly deep in rich horse feed—an ideal place to camp were it not for the fact that a thin sheet of water a quarter of an inch deep was flowing over the entire surface of the ground. We spurred on desperately, thinking of a warm fire and a chance to steam.

The roof of the shack had fallen in, and the floor was six inches deep in adobe mud.

We did not dismount—that would have wet our saddles—but sat on our horses taking in the details. Finally Uncle Jim came to the front with a suggestion.

"I know of a cave," said he, "close under a butte. It's a big cave, but it has such a steep floor that I'm not sure as we could stay in it; and it's back the other side of that ridge."

"I don't know how the ridge is to get back over—it was slippery enough coming this way—and the cave may shoot us out into space, but I'd like to LOOK at a dry place anyway," replied the Cattleman.

We all felt the same about it, so back over the ridge we went. About half way down the other side Uncle Jim turned sharp to the right, and as the "hog back" dropped behind us, we found ourselves out on the steep side of a mountain, the perpendicular cliff over us to the right, the river roaring savagely far down below our left, and sheets of water glazing the footing we could find among the boulders and debris. Hardly could the ponies keep from slipping sideways on the slope, as we proceeded farther and farther from the solidity of the ridge behind us, we experienced the illusion of venturing out on a tight rope over abysses of space. Even the feeling of danger was only an illusion, however, composite of the falling rain, the deepening twilight, and the night that had already enveloped the plunge of the canon below. Finally Uncle Jim stopped just within the drip from the cliffs.

"Here she is," said he.

We descended eagerly. A deer bounded away from the base of the buttes. The cave ran steep, in the manner of an inclined tunnel, far up into the dimness. We had to dig our toes in and scramble to make way up it at all, but we found it dry, and after a little search discovered a foot-ledge of earth sufficiently broad for a seat.

"That's all right," quoth Jed Parker. "Now, for sleeping places."

We scattered. Uncle Jim and Charley promptly annexed the slight overhang of the cliff whence the deer had jumped. It was dry at the moment, but we uttered pessimistic predictions if the wind should change. Tom Rich and Jim Lester had a little tent, and insisted on descending to the canon-bed.

"Got to cook there, anyways," said they, and departed with the two pack mules and their bed horse.

That left the Cattleman, Windy Bill, Jed Parker, and me. In a moment Windy Bill came up to us whispering and mysterious.

"Get your cavallos and follow me," said he.

We did so. He led us two hundred yards to another cave, twenty feet high, fifteen feet in diameter, level as a floor.

"How's that?" he cried in triumph. "Found her just now while I was rustling nigger-heads for a fire."

We unpacked our beds with chuckles of joy, and spread them carefully within the shelter of the cave. Except for the very edges, which did not much matter, our blankets and "so-guns," protected by the canvas "tarp," were reasonably dry. Every once in a while a spasm of conscience would seize one or the other of us.

"It seems sort of mean on the other fellows," ruminated Jed Parker.

"They had their first choice," cried we all.

"Uncle Jim's an old man," the Cattleman pointed out.

But Windy Bill had thought of that. "I told him of this yere cave first. But he allowed he was plumb satisfied."

We finished laying out our blankets. The result looked good to us. We all burst out laughing.

"Well, I'm sorry for those fellows," cried the Cattleman. We hobbled our horses and descended to the gleam of the fire, like guilty conspirators. There we ate hastily of meat, bread and coffee, merely for the sake of sustenance. It certainly amounted to little in the way of pleasure. The water from the direct rain, the shivering trees, and our hat brims accumulated in our plates faster than we could bail it out. The dishes were thrust under a canvas. Rich and Lester decided to remain with their tent, and so we saw them no more until morning.

We broke off back-loads of mesquite and toiled up the hill, tasting thickly the high altitude in the severe labour. At the big cave we dumped down our burdens, transported our fuel piecemeal to the vicinity of the narrow ledge, built a good fire, sat in a row, and lit our pipes. In a few moments, the blaze was burning high, and our bodies had ceased shivering. Fantastically the firelight revealed the knobs and crevices, the ledges and the arching walls. Their shadows leaped, following the flames, receding and advancing like playful beasts. Far above us was a single tiny opening through which the smoke was sucked as through a chimney. The glow ruddied the men's features. Outside was thick darkness, and the swish and rush and roar of rising waters. Listening, Windy Bill was reminded of a story. We leaned back comfortably against the sloping walls of the cave, thrust our feet toward the blaze, smoked, and hearkened to the tale of Windy Bill.

There's a tur'ble lot of water running loose here, but I've seen the time and place where even what is in that drip would be worth a gold mine. That was in the emigrant days. They used to come over south of here, through what they called Emigrant Pass, on their way to Californy. I was a kid then, about eighteen year old, and what I didn't know about Injins and Agency cattle wasn't a patch of alkali. I had a kid outfit of h'ar bridle, lots of silver and such, and I used to ride over and be the handsome boy before such outfits as happened along.

They were queer people, most of 'em from Missoury and such-like southern seaports, and they were tur'ble sick of travel by the time they come in sight of Emigrant Pass. Up to Santa Fe they mostly hiked along any old way, but once there they herded up together in bunches of twenty wagons or so, 'count of our old friends, Geronimo and Loco. A good many of 'em had horned cattle to their wagons, and they crawled along about two miles an hour, hotter'n hell with the blower on, nothin' to look at but a mountain a week way, chuck full of alkali, plenty of sage-brush and rattlesnakes—but mighty little water.

Why, you boys know that country down there. Between the Chiricahua Mountains and Emigrant Pass it's maybe a three or four days' journey for these yere bull-slingers.

Mostly they filled up their bellies and their kegs, hoping to last through, but they sure found it drier than cork legs, and generally long before they hit the Springs their tongues was hangin' out a foot. You see, for all their plumb nerve in comin' so far, the most of them didn't know sic 'em. They were plumb innocent in regard to savin' their water, and Injins, and such; and the long-haired buckskin fakes they picked up at Santa Fe for guides wasn't much better.

That was where Texas Pete made his killing.

Texas Pete was a tough citizen from the Lone Star. He was about as broad as he was long, and wore all sorts of big whiskers and black eyebrows. His heart was very bad. You never COULD tell where Texas Pete was goin' to jump next. He was a side-winder and a diamond-back and a little black rattlesnake all rolled into one. I believe that Texas Pete person cared about as little for killin' a man as for takin' a drink—and he shorely drank without an effort. Peaceable citizens just spoke soft and minded their own business; onpeaceable citizens Texas Pete used to plant out in the sagebrush.

Now this Texas Pete happened to discover a water hole right out in the plumb middle of the desert. He promptly annexed said water hole, digs her out, timbers her up, and lays for emigrants.

He charged two bits a head—man or beast—and nobody got a mouthful till he paid up in hard coin.

Think of the wads he raked in! I used to figure it up, just for the joy of envyin' him, I reckon. An average twenty-wagon outfit, first and last, would bring him in somewheres about fifty dollars—and besides he had forty-rod at four bits a glass. And outfits at that time were thicker'n spatter.

We used all to go down sometimes to watch them come in. When they see that little canvas shack and that well, they begun to cheer up and move fast. And when they see that sign, "Water, two bits a head," their eyes stuck out like two raw oysters.

Then come the kicks. What a howl they did raise, shorely. But it didn't do no manner of good. Texas Pete didn't do nothin' but sit there and smoke, with a kind of sulky gleam in one corner of his eye. He didn't even take the trouble to answer, but his Winchester lay across his lap. There wasn't no humour in the situation for him.

"How much is your water for humans?" asks one emigrant.

"Can't you read that sign?" Texas Pete asks him.

"But you don't mean two bits a head for HUMANS!" yells the man. "Why, you can get whisky for that!"

"You can read the sign, can't you?" insists Texas Pete.

"I can read it all right?" says the man, tryin' a new deal, "but they tell me not to believe more'n half I read."

But that don't go; and Mr. Emigrant shells out with the rest.

I didn't blame them for raisin' their howl. Why, at that time the regular water holes was chargin' five cents a head from the government freighters, and the motto was always "Hold up Uncle Sam," at that. Once in a while some outfit would get mad and go chargin' off dry; but it was a long, long way to the Springs, and mighty hot and dusty. Texas Pete and his one lonesome water hole shorely did a big business.

Late one afternoon me and Gentleman Tim was joggin' along above Texas Pete's place. It was a tur'ble hot day—you had to prime yourself to spit—and we was just gettin' back from drivin' some beef up to the troops at Fort Huachuca. We was due to cross the Emigrant Trail—she's wore in tur'ble deep—you can see the ruts to-day. When we topped the rise we see a little old outfit just makin' out to drag along.

It was one little schooner all by herself, drug along by two poor old cavallos that couldn't have pulled my hat off. Their tongues was out, and every once in a while they'd stick in a chuck-hole. Then a man would get down and put his shoulder to the wheel, and everybody'd take a heave, and up they'd come, all a-trembling and weak.

Tim and I rode down just to take a look at the curiosity.

A thin-lookin' man was drivin', all humped up.

"Hullo, stranger," says I, "ain't you 'fraid of Injins?"

"Yes," says he.

"Then why are you travellin' through an Injin country all alone?"

"Couldn't keep up," says he. "Can I get water here?"

"I reckon," I answers.

He drove up to the water trough there at Texas Pete's, me and Gentleman Tim followin' along because our trail led that way. But he hadn't more'n stopped before Texas Pete was out.

"Cost you four bits to water them hosses," says he.

The man looked up kind of bewildered.

"I'm sorry," says he, "I ain't got no four bits. I got my roll lifted off'n me."

"No water, then," growls Texas Pete back at him.

The man looked about him helpless.

"How far is it to the next water?" he asks me.

"Twenty mile," I tells him.

"My God!" he says, to himself-like.

Then he shrugged his shoulders very tired.

"All right. It's gettin' the cool of the evenin'; we'll make it." He turns into the inside of that old schooner.

"Gi' me the cup, Sue."

A white-faced woman who looked mighty good to us alkalis opened the flaps and gave out a tin cup, which the man pointed out to fill.

"How many of you is they?" asks Texas Pete.

"Three," replies the man, wondering.

"Well, six bits, then," says Texas Pete, "cash down."

At that the man straightens up a little.

"I ain't askin' for no water for my stock," says he, "but my wife and baby has been out in this sun all day without a drop of water. Our cask slipped a hoop and bust just this side of Dos Cabesas. The poor kid is plumb dry."

"Two bits a head," says Texas Pete.

At that the woman comes out, a little bit of a baby in her arms. The kid had fuzzy yellow hair, and its face was flushed red and shiny.

"Shorely you won't refuse a sick child a drink of water, sir," says she.

But Texas Pete had some sort of a special grouch; I guess he was just beginning to get his snowshoes off after a fight with his own forty-rod.

"What the hell are you-all doin' on the trail without no money at all?" he growls, "and how do you expect to get along? Such plumb tenderfeet drive me weary."

"Well," says the man, still reasonable, "I ain't got no money, but I'll give you six bits' worth of flour or trade or an'thin' I got."

"I don't run no truck-store," snaps Texas Pete, and turns square on his heel and goes back to his chair.

"Got six bits about you?" whispers Gentleman Tim to me.

"Not a red," I answers.

Gentleman Tim turns to Texas Pete.

"Let 'em have a drink, Pete. I'll pay you next time I come down."

"Cash down," growls Pete.

"You're the meanest man I ever see," observes Tim. "I wouldn't speak to you if I met you in hell carryin' a lump of ice in your hand."

"You're the softest I ever see," sneers Pete. "Don't they have any genooine Texans down your way?"

"Not enough to make it disagreeable," says Tim.

"That lets you out," growls Pete, gettin' hostile and handlin' of his rifle.

Which the man had been standin' there bewildered, the cup hangin' from his finger. At last, lookin' pretty desperate, he stooped down to dig up a little of the wet from an overflow puddle lyin' at his feet. At the same time the hosses, left sort of to themselves and bein' drier than a covered bridge, drug forward and stuck their noses in the trough.

Gentleman Tim and me was sittin' there on our hosses, a little to one side. We saw Texas Pete jump up from his chair, take a quick aim, and cut loose with his rifle. It was plumb unexpected to us. We hadn't thought of any shootin', and our six-shooters was tied in, 'count of the jumpy country we'd been drivin' the steers over. But Gentleman Tim, who had unslung his rope, aimin' to help the hosses out of the chuckhole, snatched her off the horn, and with one of the prettiest twenty-foot flip throws I ever see done he snaked old Texas Pete right out of his wicky-up, gun and all. The old renegade did his best to twist around for a shot at us; but it was no go; and I never enjoyed hog-tying a critter more in my life than I enjoyed hog-tying Texas Pete. Then we turned to see what damage had been done.

We were some relieved to find the family all right, but Texas Pete had bored one of them poor old crow-bait hosses plumb through the head.

"It's lucky for you you don't get the old man," says Gentleman Tim very quiet and polite.

Which Gentleman Tim was an Irishman, and I'd been on the range long enough with him to know that when he got quiet and polite it was time to dodge behind something.

"I hope, sir" says he to the stranger, "that you will give your wife and baby a satisfying drink. As for your hoss, pray do not be under any apprehension. Our friend, Mr. Texas Pete, here, has kindly consented to make good any deficiencies from his own corral."

Tim could talk high, wide, and handsome when he set out to.

The man started to say something; but I managed to herd him to one side.

"Let him alone," I whispers. "When he talks that way, he's mad; and when he's mad, it's better to leave nature to supply the lightnin' rods."

He seemed to sabe all right, so we built us a little fire and started some grub, while Gentleman Tim walked up and down very grand and fierce.

By and by he seemed to make up his mind. He went over and untied Texas Pete.

"Stand up, you hound," says he. "Now listen to me. If you make a break to get away, or if you refuse to do just as I tell you, I won't shoot you, but I'll march you up country and see that Geronimo gets you."

He sorted out a shovel and pick, made Texas Pete carry them right along the trail a quarter, and started him to diggin' a hole.

Texas Pete started in hard enough, Tim sittin' over him on his hoss, his six-shooter loose, and his rope free. The man and I stood by, not darin' to say a word. After a minute or so Texas Pete began to work slower and slower. By and by he stopped.

"Look here," says he, "is this here thing my grave?"

"I am goin' to see that you give the gentleman's hoss decent interment," says Gentleman Tim very polite.

"Bury a hoss!" growls Texas Pete.

But he didn't say any more. Tim cocked his six-shooter.

"Perhaps you'd better quit panting and sweat a little," says he.

Texas Pete worked hard for a while, for Tim's quietness was beginning to scare him up the worst way. By and by he had got down maybe four or five feet, and Tim got off his hoss.

"I think that will do," says he.

"You may come out. Billy, my son, cover him. Now, Mr. Texas Pete," he says, cold as steel, "there is the grave. We will place the hoss in it. Then I intend to shoot you and put you in with the hoss, and write you an epitaph that will be a comfort to such travellers of the Trail as are honest, and a warnin' to such as are not. I'd as soon kill you now as an hour from now, so you may make a break for it if you feel like it."

He stooped over to look into the hole. I thought he looked an extra long time, but when he raised his head his face had changed complete.

"March!" says he very brisk.

We all went back to the shack. From the corral Tim took Texas Pete's best team and hitched her to the old schooner.

"There," says he to the man. "Now you'd better hit the trail. Take that whisky keg there for water. Good-bye."

We sat there without sayin' a word for some time after the schooner had pulled out. Then Tim says, very abrupt:

"I've changed my mind."

He got up.

"Come on, Billy," says he to me. "We'll just leave our friend tied up. I'll be back to-morrow to turn you loose. In the meantime it won't hurt you a bit to be a little uncomfortable, and hungry—and thirsty."

We rode off just about sundown, leavin' Texas Pete lashed tight.

Now all this knocked me hell-west and crooked, and I said so, but I couldn't get a word out of Gentleman Tim. All the answer I could get was just little laughs.

We drawed into the ranch near midnight, but next mornin' Tim had a long talk with the boss, and the result was that the whole outfit was instructed to arm up with a pick or a shovel apiece, and to get set for Texas Pete's. We got there a little after noon, turned the old boy out—without firearms—and then began to dig at a place Tim told us to, near that grave of Texas Pete's. In three hours we had the finest water-hole developed you ever want to see. Then the boss stuck up a sign that said:

PUBLIC WATER-HOLE. WATER, FREE.

"Now you old skin," says he to Texas Pete, "charge all you want to on your own property. But if I ever hear of your layin' claim to this other hole, I'll shore make you hard to catch."

Then we rode off home. You see, when Gentleman Tim inspected that grave, he noted indications of water; and it struck him that runnin' the old renegade out of business was a neater way of gettin' even than merely killin' him.

Somebody threw a fresh mesquite on the fire. The flames leaped up again, showing a thin trickle of water running down the other side of the cave. The steady downpour again made itself prominent through the re-established silence.

"What did Texas Pete do after that?" asked the Cattleman.

"Texas Pete?" chuckled Windy Bill. "Well, he put in a heap of his spare time lettin' Tim alone."

CHAPTER THREE
THE REMITTANCE MAN

After Windy Bill had finished his story we began to think it time to turn in. Uncle Jim and Charley slid and slipped down the chute-like passage leading from the cave and disappeared in the direction of the overhang beneath which they had spread their bed. After a moment we tore off long bundles of the nigger-head blades, lit the resinous ends at our fire, and with these torches started to make our way along the base of the cliff to the other cave.

Once without the influence of the fire our impromptu links cast an adequate light. The sheets of rain became suddenly visible as they entered the circle of illumination. By careful scrutiny of the footing I gained the entrance to our cave without mishap. I looked back. Here and there irregularly gleamed and spluttered my companions' torches. Across each slanted the rain. All else was of inky blackness except where, between them and me, a faint red reflection shone on the wet rocks. Then I turned inside.

Now, to judge from the crumbling powder of the footing, that cave had been dry since Noah. In fact, its roof was nearly a thousand feet thick. But since we had spread our blankets, the persistent waters had soaked down and through. The thousand-foot roof had a sprung a leak. Three separate and distinct streams of water ran as from spigots. I lowered my torch. The canvas tarpaulin shone with wet, and in its exact centre glimmered a pool of water three inches deep and at least two feet in diameter.

"Well, I'll be," I began. Then I remembered those three wending their way along a wet and disagreeable trail, happy and peaceful in anticipation of warm blankets and a level floor. I chuckled and sat on my heels out of the drip.

First came Jed Parker, his head bent to protect the fire in his pipe. He gained the very centre of the cave before he looked up.

Then he cast one glance at each bed, and one at me. His grave, hawk-like features relaxed. A faint grin appeared under his long moustache. Without a word he squatted down beside me.

Next the Cattleman. He looked about him with a comical expression of dismay, and burst into a hearty laugh.

"I believe I said I was sorry for those other fellows," he remarked.

Windy Bill was the last. He stooped his head to enter, straightened his lank figure, and took in the situation without expression.

"Well, this is handy," said he; "I was gettin' tur'ble dry, and was thinkin' I would have to climb way down to the creek in all this rain."

He stooped to the pool in the centre of the tarpaulin and drank.

But now our torches began to run low. A small dry bush grew near the entrance. We ignited it, and while it blazed we hastily sorted a blanket apiece and tumbled the rest out of the drip.

Our return without torches along the base of that butte was something to remember. The night was so thick you could feel the darkness pressing on you; the mountain dropped abruptly to the left, and was strewn with boulders and blocks of stone. Collisions and stumbles were frequent. Once I stepped off a little ledge five or six feet—nothing worse than a barked shin. And all the while the rain, pelting us unmercifully, searched out what poor little remnants of dryness we had been able to retain.

At last we opened out the gleam of fire in our cave, and a minute later were engaged in struggling desperately up the slant that brought us to our ledge and the slope on which our fire burned.

"My Lord!" panted Windy Bill, "a man had ought to have hooks on his eyebrows to climb up here!"

We renewed the fire—and blessed the back-load of mesquite we had packed up earlier in the evening. Our blankets we wrapped around our shoulders, our feet we hung over the ledge toward the blaze, our backs we leaned against the hollow slant of the cave's wall. We were not uncomfortable. The beat of the rain sprang up in the darkness, growing louder and louder, like horsemen passing on a hard road. Gradually we dozed off.

For a time everything was pleasant. Dreams came fused with realities; the firelight faded from consciousness or returned fantastic to our half-awakening; a delicious numbness overspread our tired bodies. The shadows leaped, became solid, monstrous. We fell asleep.

After a time the fact obtruded itself dimly through our stupor that the constant pressure of the hard rock had impeded our circulation. We stirred uneasily, shifting to a better position.

That was the beginning of awakening. The new position did not suit. A slight shivering seized us, which the drawing closer of the blanket failed to end. Finally I threw aside my hat and looked out. Jed Parker, a vivid patch-work comforter wrapped about his shoulders, stood upright and silent by the fire. I kept still, fearing to awaken the others. In a short time I became aware that the others were doing identically the same thing. We laughed, threw off our blankets, stretched, and fed the fire.

A thick acrid smoke filled the air. The Cattleman, rising, left a trail of incandescent footprints. We investigated hastily, and discovered that the supposed earth on the slant of the cave was nothing more than bat guano, tons of it. The fire, eating its way beneath, had rendered untenable its immediate vicinity. We felt as though we were living over a volcano. How soon our ledge, of the same material, might be attacked, we had no means of knowing. Overcome with drowsiness, we again disposed our blankets, resolved to get as many naps as possible before even these constrained quarters were taken from us.

This happened sooner and in a manner otherwise than we had expected. Windy Bill brought us to consciousness by a wild yell.

Consciousness reported to us a strange, hurried sound like the long roll on a drum. Investigation showed us that this cave, too, had sprung a leak; not with any premonitory drip, but all at once, as though someone had turned on a faucet. In ten seconds a very competent streamlet six inches wide had eroded a course down through the guano, past the fire and to the outer slope. And by the irony of fate that one—and only one—leak in all the roof expanse of a big cave was directly over one end of our tiny ledge. The Cattleman laughed.

"Reminds me of the old farmer and his kind friend," said he. "Kind friend hunts up the old farmer in the village.

"'John,' says he, 'I've bad news for you. Your barn has burned up.'

"'My Lord!' says the farmer.

"'But that ain't the worst. Your cow was burned, too.'

"'My Lord!' says the farmer.

"'But that ain't the worst. Your horses were burned.'

"'My Lord!' says the farmer.

"'But, that ain't the worst. The barn set fire to the house, and it was burned—total loss.'

"'My Lord!' groans the farmer.

"'But that ain't the worst. Your wife and child were killed, too.'

"'At that the farmer began to roar with laughter.

"'Good heavens, man!' cries his friend, astonished, 'what in the world do you find to laugh at in that?'

"'Don't you see?' answers the farmer. 'Why, it's so darn COMPLETE!'

"Well," finished the Cattleman, "that's what strikes me about our case; it's so darn complete!"

"What time is it?" asked Windy Bill.

"Midnight," I announced.

"Lord! Six hours to day!" groaned Windy Bill. "How'd you like to be doin' a nice quiet job at gardenin' in the East where you could belly up to the bar reg'lar every evenin', and drink a pussy cafe and smoke tailor-made cigareets?"

"You wouldn't like it a bit," put in the Cattleman with decision; whereupon in proof he told us the following story:

Windy has mentioned Gentleman Tim, and that reminded me of the first time I ever saw him. He was an Irishman all right, but he had been educated in England, and except for his accent he was more an Englishman than anything else. A freight outfit brought him into Tucson from Santa Fe and dumped him down on the plaza, where at once every idler in town gathered to quiz him.

Certainly he was one of the greenest specimens I ever saw in this country. He had on a pair of balloon pants and a Norfolk jacket, and was surrounded by a half-dozen baby trunks. His face was red-cheeked and aggressively clean, and his eye limpid as a child's. Most of those present thought that indicated childishness; but I could see that it was only utter self-unconsciousness.

It seemed that he was out for big game, and intended to go after silver-tips somewhere in these very mountains. Of course he was offered plenty of advice, and would probably have made engagements much to be regretted had I not taken a strong fancy to him.

"My friend," said I, drawing him aside, "I don't want to be inquisitive, but what might you do when you're home?"

"I'm a younger son," said he. I was green myself in those days, and knew nothing of primogeniture.

"That is a very interesting piece of family history," said I, "but it does not answer my question."

He smiled.

"Well now, I hadn't thought of that," said he, "but in a manner of speaking, it does. I do nothing."

"Well," said I, unabashed, "if you saw me trying to be a younger son and likely to forget myself and do something without meaning to, wouldn't you be apt to warn me?"

"Well, 'pon honour, you're a queer chap. What do you mean?"

"I mean that if you hire any of those men to guide you in the mountains, you'll be outrageously cheated, and will be lucky if you're not gobbled by Apaches."

"Do you do any guiding yourself, now?" he asked, most innocent of manner.

But I flared up.

"You damn ungrateful pup," I said, "go to the devil in your own way," and turned square on my heel.

But the young man was at my elbow, his hand on my shoulder.

"Oh, I say now, I'm sorry. I didn't rightly understand. Do wait one moment until I dispose of these boxes of mine, and then I want the honour of your further acquaintance."

He got some Greasers to take his trunks over to the hotel, then linked his arm in mine most engagingly.

"Now, my dear chap," said he, "let's go somewhere for a B & S, and find out about each other."

We were both young and expansive. We exchanged views, names, and confidences, and before noon we had arranged to hunt together, I to collect the outfit.

The upshot of the matter was that the Honourable Timothy Clare and I had a most excellent month's excursion, shot several good bear, and returned to Tucson the best of friends.

At Tucson was Schiefflein and his stories of a big strike down in the Apache country. Nothing would do but that we should both go to see for ourselves. We joined the second expedition; crept in the gullies, tied bushes about ourselves when monumenting corners, and so helped establish the town of Tombstone. We made nothing, nor attempted to. Neither of us knew anything of mining, but we were both thirsty for adventure, and took a schoolboy delight in playing the game of life or death with the Chiricahuas.

In fact, I never saw anybody take to the wild life as eagerly as the Honourable Timothy Clare. He wanted to attempt everything. With him it was no sooner see than try, and he had such an abundance of enthusiasm that he generally succeeded. The balloon pants soon went. In a month his outfit was irreproachable. He used to study us by the hour, taking in every detail of our equipment, from the smallest to the most important. Then he asked questions. For all his desire to be one of the country, he was never ashamed to acknowledge his ignorance.

"Now, don't you chaps think it silly to wear such high heels to your boots?" he would ask. "It seems to me a very useless sort of vanity."

"No vanity about it, Tim," I explained. "In the first place, it keeps your foot from slipping through the stirrup. In the second place, it is good to grip on the ground when you're roping afoot."

"By Jove, that's true!" he cried.

So he'd get him a pair of boots. For a while it was enough to wear and own all these things. He seemed to delight in his six-shooter and his rope just as ornaments to himself and horse. But he soon got over that. Then he had to learn to use them.

For the time being, pistol practice, for instance, would absorb all his thoughts. He'd bang away at intervals all day, and figure out new theories all night.

"That bally scheme won't work," he would complain. "I believe if I extended my thumb along the cylinder it would help that side jump."

He was always easing the trigger-pull, or filing the sights. In time he got to be a fairly accurate and very quick shot.

The same way with roping and hog-tying and all the rest.

"What's the use?" I used to ask him. "If you were going to be a buckeroo, you couldn't go into harder training."

"I like it," was always his answer.

He had only one real vice, that I could see. He would gamble. Stud poker was his favourite; and I never saw a Britisher yet who could play poker. I used to head him off, when I could, and he was always grateful, but the passion was strong.

After we got back from founding Tombstone I was busted and had to go to work.

"I've got plenty," said Tim, "and it's all yours."

"I know, old fellow," I told him, "but your money wouldn't do for me."

Buck Johnson was just seeing his chance then, and was preparing to take some breeding cattle over into the Soda Springs Valley. Everybody laughed at him—said it was right in the line of the Chiricahua raids, which was true. But Buck had been in there with Agency steers, and thought he knew. So he collected a trail crew, brought some Oregon cattle across, and built his home ranch of three-foot adobe walls with portholes. I joined the trail crew; and somehow or another the Honourable Timothy got permission to go along on his own hook.

The trail was a long one. We had thirst and heat and stampedes and some Indian scares. But in the queer atmospheric conditions that prevailed that summer, I never saw the desert more wonderful. It was like waking to the glory of God to sit up at dawn and see the colours change on the dry ranges.

At the home ranch, again, Tim managed to get permission to stay on. He kept his own mount of horses, took care of them, hunted, and took part in all the cow work. We lost some cattle from Indians, of course, but it was too near the Reservation for them to do more than pick up a few stray head on their way through. The troops were always after them full jump, and so they never had time to round up the beef. But of course we had to look out or we'd lose our hair, and many a cowboy has won out to the home ranch in an almighty exciting race. This was nuts for the Honourable Timothy Clare, much better than hunting silver-tips, and he enjoyed it no limit.

Things went along that way for some time, until one evening as I was turning out the horses a buckboard drew in, and from it descended Tony Briggs and a dapper little fellow dressed all in black and with a plug hat.

"Which I accounts for said hat reachin' the ranch, because it's Friday and the boys not in town," Tony whispered to me.

As I happened to be the only man in sight, the stranger addressed me.

"I am looking," said he in a peculiar, sing-song manner I have since learned to be English, "for the Honourable Timothy Clare. Is he here?"

"Oh, you're looking for him are you?" said I. "And who might you be?"

You see, I liked Tim, and I didn't intend to deliver him over into trouble.

The man picked a pair of eye-glasses off his stomach where they dangled at the end of a chain, perched them on his nose, and stared me over. I must have looked uncompromising, for after a few seconds he abruptly wrinkled his nose so that the glasses fell promptly to his stomach again, felt his waistcoat pocket, and produced a card. I took it, and read:

JEFFRIES CASE, Barrister.

"A lawyer!" said I suspiciously.

"My dear man," he rejoined with a slight impatience, "I am not here to do your young friend a harm. In fact, my firm have been his family solicitors for generations."

"Very well," I agreed, and led the way to the one-room adobe that Tim and I occupied.

If I had expected an enthusiastic greeting for the boyhood friend from the old home, I would have been disappointed. Tim was sitting with his back to the door reading an old magazine. When we entered he glanced over his shoulder.

"Ah, Case," said he, and went on reading. After a moment he said without looking up, "Sit down."

The little man took it calmly, deposited himself in a chair and his bag between his feet, and looked about him daintily at our rough quarters. I made a move to go, whereupon Tim laid down his magazine, yawned, stretched his arms over his head, and sighed.

"Don't go, Harry," he begged. "Well, Case," he addressed the barrister, "what is it this time? Must be something devilish important to bring you—how many thousand miles is it—into such a country as this."

"It is important, Mr. Clare," stated the lawyer in his dry sing-song tones; "but my journey might have been avoided had you paid some attention to my letters."

"Letters!" repeated Tim, opening his eyes. "My dear chap, I've had no letters."

"Addressed as usual to your New York bankers."

Tim laughed softly. "Where they are, with my last two quarters' allowance. I especially instructed them to send me no mail. One spends no money in this country." He paused, pulling his moustache. "I'm truly sorry you had to come so far," he continued, "and if your business is, as I suspect, the old one of inducing me to return to my dear uncle's arms, I assure you the mission will prove quite fruitless. Uncle Hillary and I could never live in the same county, let alone the same house."

"And yet your uncle, the Viscount Mar, was very fond of you," ventured Case. "Your allowances—"

"Oh, I grant you his generosity in MONEY affairs—"

"He has continued that generosity in the terms of his will, and those terms I am here to communicate to you."

"Uncle Hillary is dead!" cried Tim.

"He passed away the sixteenth of last June."

A slight pause ensued.

"I am ready to hear you," said Tim soberly, at last.

The barrister stooped and began to fumble with his bag.

"No, not that!" cried Tim, with some impatience. "Tell me in your own words."

The lawyer sat back and pressed his finger points together over his stomach.

"The late Viscount," said he, "has been graciously pleased to leave you in fee simple his entire estate of Staghurst, together with its buildings, rentals, and privileges. This, besides the residential rights, amounts to some ten thousands pounds sterling per annum."

"A little less than fifty thousand dollars a year, Harry," Tim shot over his shoulder at me.

"There is one condition," put in the lawyer.

61

"Oh, there is!" exclaimed Tim, his crest falling. "Well, knowing my Uncle Hillary—"

"The condition is not extravagant," the lawyer hastily interposed. "It merely entails continued residence in England, and a minimum of nine months on the estate. This provision is absolute, and the estate reverts in its discontinuance, but may I be permitted to observe that the majority of men, myself among the number, are content to spend the most of their lives, not merely in the confines of a kingdom, but between the four walls of a room, for much less than ten thousand pounds a year. Also that England is not without its attractions for an Englishman, and that Staghurst is a country place of many possibilities."

The Honourable Timothy had recovered from his first surprise.

"And if the conditions are not complied with?" he inquired.

"Then the estate reverts to the heirs at law, and you receive an annuity of one hundred pounds, payable quarterly."

"May I ask further the reason for this extraordinary condition?"

"My distinguished client never informed me," replied the lawyer, "but"—and a twinkle appeared in his eye—"as an occasional disburser of funds—Monte Carlo—"

Tim burst out laughing.

"Oh, but I recognise Uncle Hillary there!" he cried. "Well, Mr. Case, I am sure Mr. Johnson, the owner of this ranch, can put you up, and to-morrow we'll start back."

He returned after a few minutes to find me sitting' smoking a moody pipe. I liked Tim, and I was sorry to have him go. Then, too, I was ruffled, in the senseless manner of youth, by the sudden altitude to which his changed fortunes had lifted him. He stood in the middle of the room, surveying me, then came across and laid his arm on my shoulder.

"Well," I growled, without looking up, "you're a very rich man now, Mr. Clare."

At that he jerked me bodily out of my seat and stood me up in the centre of the room, the Irish blazing out of his eyes.

"Here, none of that!" he snapped. "You damn little fool! Don't you 'Mr. Clare' me!"

So in five minutes we were talking it over. Tim was very much excited at the prospect. He knew Staghurst well, and told me all about the big stone house, and the avenue through the trees; and the hedge-row roads, and the lawn with its peacocks, and the round green hills, and the labourers' cottages.

"It's home," said he, "and I didn't realise before how much I wanted to see it. And I'll be a man of weight there, Harry, and it'll be mighty good."

We made all sorts of plans as to how I was going to visit him just as soon as I could get together the money for the passage. He had the delicacy not to offer to let me have it; and that clinched my trust and love of him.

The next day he drove away with Tony and the dapper little lawyer. I am not ashamed to say that I watched the buckboard until it disappeared in the mirage.

I was with Buck Johnson all that summer, and the following winter, as well. We had our first round-up, found the natural increase much in excess of the loss by Indians, and extended our holdings up over the Rock Creek country. We witnessed the start of many Indian campaigns, participated in a few little brushes with the Chiricahuas, saw the beginning of the cattle-rustling. A man had not much opportunity to think of anything but what he had right on hand, but I found time for a few speculations on Tim. I wondered how he looked now, and what he was doing, and how in blazes he managed to get away with fifty thousand a year.

And then one Sunday in June, while I was lying on my bunk, Tim pushed open the door and walked in. I was young, but I'd seen a lot, and I knew the expression of his face. So I laid low and said nothing.

In a minute the door opened again, and Buck Johnson himself came in.

"How do," said he; "I saw you ride up."

"How do you do," replied Tim.

"I know all about you," said Buck, without any preliminaries; "your man, Case, has wrote me. I don't know your reasons, and I don't want to know—it's none of my business—and I ain't goin' to tell you just what kind of a damn fool I think you are—that's none of my business, either. But I want you to understand without question how you stand on the ranch."

"Quite good, sir," said Tim very quietly.

"When you were out here before I was glad to have you here as a sort of guest. Then you were what I've heerd called a gentleman of leisure. Now you're nothin' but a remittance man. Your money's nothin' to me, but the principle of the thing is. The country is plumb pestered with remittance men, doin' nothin', and I don't aim to run no home for incompetents. I had a son of a duke drivin' wagon for me; and he couldn't drive nails in a snowbanks. So don't you herd up with the idea that you can come on this ranch and loaf."

"I don't want to loaf," put in Tim, "I want a job."

"I'm willing to give you a job," replied Buck, "but it's jest an ordinary cow-puncher's job at forty a month. And if you don't fill your saddle, it goes to someone else."

"That's satisfactory," agreed Tim.

"All right," finished Buck, "so that's understood. Your friend Case wanted me to give you a lot of advice. A man generally has about as much use for advice as a cow has for four hind legs."

He went out.

"For God's sake, what's up?" I cried, leaping from my bunk.

"Hullo, Harry," said he, as though he had seen me the day before, "I've come back."

"How come back?" I asked. "I thought you couldn't leave the estate. Have they broken the will?"

"No," said he.

"Is the money lost?"

"No."

"Then what?"

"The long and short of it is, that I couldn't afford that estate and that money."

"What do you mean?"

"I've given it up."

"Given it up! What for?"

"To come back here."

took this all in slowly.

"Tim Clare," said I at last, "do you mean to say that you have given up an English estate and fifty thousand dollars a year to be a remittance man at five hundred, and a cow-puncher on as much more?"

"Exactly," said he.

"Tim," I adjured him solemnly, "you are a damn fool!"

"Maybe," he agreed.

"Why did you do it?" I begged.

He walked to the door and looked out across the desert to where the mountains hovered like soap-bubbles on the horizon. For a long time he looked; then whirled on me.

"Harry," said he in a low voice, "do you remember the camp we made on the shoulder of the mountain that night we were caught out? And do you remember how the dawn came up on the big snow peaks across the way—and all the canon below us filled with whirling mists—and the steel stars leaving us one by one? Where could I find room for that in English paddocks? And do you recall the day we trailed across the Yuma deserts, and the sun beat into our skulls, and the dry, brittle hills looked like papier-mache, and the grey sage-bush ran off into the rise of the hills; and then came sunset and the hard, dry mountains grew filmy, like gauze veils of many colours, and melted and glowed and faded to slate blue, and the stars came out? The English hills are rounded and green and curried, and the sky is near, and the stars only a few miles up. And do you recollect that dark night when old Loco and his warriors were camped at the base of Cochise's Stronghold, and we crept down through the velvet dark wondering when we would be discovered, our mouths sticky with excitement, and the little winds blowing?"

He walked up and down a half-dozen times, his breast heaving.

"It's all very well for the man who is brought up to it, and who has seen nothing else. Case can exist in four walls; he has been brought up to it and knows nothing different. But a man like me—

"They wanted me to canter between hedge-row,—I who have ridden the desert where the sky over me and the plain under me were bigger than the Islander's universe! They wanted me to oversee little farms—I who have watched the sun rising over half a world! Talk of your ten thou' a year and what it'll buy! You know, Harry, how it feels when a steer takes the slack of your rope, and your pony sits back! Where in England can I buy that? You know the rising and the falling of days, and the boundless spaces where your heart grows big, and the thirst of the desert and the hunger of the trail, and a sun that shines and fills the sky, and a wind that blows fresh from the wide places! Where in parcelled, snug, green, tight little England could I buy that with ten thou'—aye, or an hundred times ten thou'? No, no, Harry, that fortune would cost me too dear. I have seen and done and been too much. I've come back to the Big Country, where the pay is poor and the work is hard and the comfort small, but where a man and his soul meet their Maker face to face."

The Cattleman had finished his yarn. For a time no one spoke. Outside, the volume of rain was subsiding. Windy Bill reported a few stars shining through rifts in the showers. The chill that precedes the dawn brought us as close to the fire as the smouldering guano would permit.

"I don't know whether he was right or wrong," mused the Cattleman, after a while. "A man can do a heap with that much money. And yet an old 'alkali' is never happy anywhere else. However," he concluded emphatically, "one thing I do know: rain, cold, hunger, discomfort, curses, kicks, and violent deaths included, there isn't one of you grumblers who would hold that gardening job you spoke of three days!"

CHAPTER FOUR
THE CATTLE RUSTLERS

Dawn broke, so we descended through wet grasses to the canon. There, after some difficulty, we managed to start a fire, and so ate breakfast, the rain still pouring down on us. About nine o'clock, with miraculous suddenness, the torrent stopped. It began to turn cold. The Cattleman and I decided to climb to the top of the butte after meat, which we entirely lacked.

It was rather a stiff ascent, but once above the sheer cliffs we found ourselves on a rolling meadow tableland a half-mile broad by, perhaps, a mile and a half in length. Grass grew high; here and there were small live oaks planted park-like; slight and rounded ravines accommodated brooklets. As we walked back, the edges blended in the edges of the mesa across the canon. The deep gorges, which had heretofore seemed the most prominent elements of the scenery, were lost. We stood, apparently, in the middle of a wide and undulating plain, diversified by little ridges, and running with a free sweep to the very foot of the snowy Galiuros. It seemed as though we should be able to ride horseback in almost any given direction. Yet we knew that ten minutes' walk would take us to the brink of most stupendous chasms—so deep that the water flowing in them hardly seemed to move; so rugged that only with the greatest difficulty could a horseman make his way through the country at all; and yet so ancient that the bottoms supported forests, rich grasses, and rounded, gentle knolls. It was a most astonishing set of double impressions.

We succeeded in killing a nice, fat white-tail buck, and so returned to camp happy. The rain, held off. We dug ditches, organised shelters, cooked a warm meal. For the next day we planned a bear hunt afoot, far up a manzanita canon where Uncle Jim knew of some "holing up" caves.

But when we awoke in the morning we threw aside our coverings with some difficulty to look on a ground covered with snow; trees laden almost to the breaking point with snow, and the air filled with it.

"No bear today" said the Cattleman.

"No," agreed Uncle Jim drily. "No b'ar. And what's more, unless yo're aimin' to stop here somewhat of a spell, we'll have to make out to-day."

We cooked with freezing fingers, ate while dodging avalanches from the trees, and packed reluctantly. The ropes were frozen, the hobbles stiff, everything either crackling or wet. Finally the task was finished. We took a last warming of the fingers and climbed on.

The country was wonderfully beautiful with the white not yet shaken from the trees and rock ledges. Also it was wonderfully slippery. The snow was soft enough to ball under the horses' hoofs, so that most of the time the poor animals skated and stumbled along on stilts. Thus we made our way back over ground which, naked of these difficulties, we had considered bad enough.

Imagine riding along a slant of rock shelving off to a bad tumble, so steep that your pony has to do more or less expert ankle work to keep from slipping off sideways. During the passage of that rock you are apt to sit very light. Now cover it with several inches of snow, stick a snowball on each hoof of your mount, and try again. When you have ridden it—or its duplicate—a few score of times, select a steep mountain side, cover it with round rocks the size of your head, and over that spread a concealing blanket of the same sticky snow. You are privileged to vary these to the limits of your imagination.

Once across the divide, we ran into a new sort of trouble. You may remember that on our journey over we had been forced to travel for some distance in a narrow stream-bed. During our passage we had scrambled up some rather steep and rough slopes, and hopped up some fairly high ledges. Now we found the heretofore dry bed flowing a good eight inches deep. The steep slopes had become cascades; the ledges, waterfalls. When we came to them, we had to "shoot the rapids" as best we could, only to land with a PLUNK in an indeterminately deep pool at the bottom. Some of the pack horses went down, sousing again our unfortunate bedding, but by the grace of fortune not a saddle pony lost his feet.

After a time the gorge widened. We came out into the box canon with its trees. Here the water spread and shoaled to a depth of only two or three inches. We splashed along gaily enough, for, with the exception of an occasional quicksand or boggy spot, our troubles were over.

Jed Parker and I happened to ride side by side, bringing up the rear and seeing to it that the pack animals did not stray or linger. As we passed the first of the rustlers' corrals, he called my attention to them.

"Go take a look," said he. "We only got those fellows out of here two years ago."

I rode over. At this point the rim-rock broke to admit the ingress of a ravine into the main canon. Riding a short distance up the ravine, I could see that it ended abruptly in a perpendicular cliff. As the sides also were precipitous, it became necessary only to build a fence across the entrance into the main canon to become possessed of a corral completely closed in. Remembering the absolute invisibility of these sunken canons until the rider is almost directly over them, and also the extreme roughness and remoteness of the district, I could see that the spot was admirably adapted to concealment.

"There's quite a yarn about the gang that held this hole," said Jed Parker to me, when I had ridden back to him "I'll tell you about it sometime."

We climbed the hill, descended on the Double R, built a fire in the stove, dried out, and were happy. After a square meal—and a dry one—I reminded Jed Parker of his promise, and so, sitting cross-legged on his "so-gun" in the middle of the floor, he told us the following yarn:

There's a good deal of romance been written about the "bad man," and there's about the same amount of nonsense. The bad man is justa plain murderer, neither more nor less. He never does get into a real, good, plain, stand-up gunfight if he can possibly help it. His killin's are done from behind a door, or when he's got his man dead to rights. There's Sam Cook. You've all heard of him. He had nerve, of course, and when he was backed into a corner he made good; he was sure sudden death with a gun. But when he went for a man deliberate, he didn't take no special chances. For a while he was marshal at Willets. Pretty soon it was noted that there was a heap of cases of resisting arrest, where Sam as marshal had to shoot, and that those cases almost always happened to be his personal enemies. Of course, that might be all right, but it looked suspicious. Then one day he killed poor old Max Schmidt out behind his own saloon. Called him out and shot him in the stomach. Said Max resisted arrest on a warrant for keepin' open out of hours! That was a sweet warrant to take out in Willets, anyway! Mrs. Schmidt always claimed that she saw that deal played, and that, while they were talkin' perfectly peacable, Cook let drive from the hip at about two yards' range. Anyway, we decided we needed another marshal. Nothin' else was ever done, for the Vigilantes hadn't been formed, and your individual and decent citizen doesn't care to be marked by a gun of that stripe. Leastwise, unless he wants to go in for bad-man methods and do a little ambusheein' on his own account.

The point is, that these yere bad men are a low-down, miserable proposition, and plain, cold-blood murderers, willin' to wait for a sure thing, and without no compunctions whatsoever. The bad man takes you unawares, when you're sleepin', or talkin', or drinkin', or lookin' to see what for a day it's goin' to be, anyway. He don't give you no show, and sooner or later he's goin' to get you in the safest and easiest way for himself. There ain't no romance about that.

And, until you've seen a few men called out of their shacks for a friendly conversation, and shot when they happen to look away; or asked for a drink of water, and killed when they stoop to the spring; or potted from behind as they go into a room, it's pretty hard to believe that any man can be so plumb lackin' in fair play or pity or just natural humanity.

As you boys know, I come in from Texas to Buck Johnson's about ten year back. I had a pretty good mount of ponies that I knew, and I hated to let them go at prices they were offerin' then, so I made up my mind to ride across and bring them in with me. It wasn't so awful far, and I figured that I'd like to take in what New Mexico looked like anyway.

About down by Albuquerque I tracked up with another outfit headed my way. There was five of them, three men, and a woman, and a yearlin' baby. They had a dozen hosses, and that was about all I could see. There was only two packed, and no wagon. I suppose the whole outfit—pots, pans, and kettles—was worth five dollars. It was just supper when I run across them, and it didn't take more'n one look to discover that flour, coffee, sugar, and salt was all they carried. A yearlin' carcass, half-skinned, lay near, and the fry-pan was, full of meat.

"Howdy, strangers," says I, ridin' up.

They nodded a little, but didn't say nothin'. My hosses fell to grazin', and I eased myself around in my saddle, and made a cigareet. The men was tall, lank fellows, with kind of sullen faces, and sly, shifty eyes; the woman was dirty and generally mussed up. I knowed that sort all right. Texas was gettin' too many fences for them.

"Havin' supper?" says I, cheerful.

One of 'em grunted "Yes" at me; and, after a while, the biggest asked me very grudgin' if I wouldn't light and eat. I told them "No," that I was travellin' in the cool of the evenin'.

"You seem to have more meat than you need, though," says I. "I could use a little of that."

"Help yourself," says they. "It's a maverick we come across."

I took a steak, and noted that the hide had been mighty well cut to ribbons around the flanks and that the head was gone.

"Well," says I to the carcass, "No one's going to be able to swear whether you're a maverick or not, but I bet you knew the feel of a brandin' iron all right."

I gave them a thank-you, and climbed on again. My hosses acted some surprised at bein' gathered up again, but I couldn't help that.

"It looks like a plumb imposition, cavallos," says I to them, "after an all-day, but you sure don't want to join that outfit any more than I do the angels, and if we camp here we're likely to do both."

I didn't see them any more after that until I'd hit the Lazy Y, and had started in runnin' cattle in the Soda Springs Valley. Larry Eagen and I rode together those days, and that's how I got to know him pretty well. One day, over in the Elm Flat, we ran smack on this Texas outfit again, headed north. This time I was on my own range, and I knew where I stood, so I could show a little more curiosity in the case.

"Well, you got this far," says I.

"Yes," says they.

"Where you headed?"

"Over towards the hills."

"What to do?"

"Make a ranch, raise some truck; perhaps buy a few cows."

They went on.

"Truck" says I to Larry, "is fine prospects in this country."

He sat on his horse looking after them.

"I'm sorry for them" says he. "It must he almighty hard scratchin'."

Well, we rode the range for upwards of two year. In that time we saw our Texas friends—name of Hahn—two or three times in Willets, and heard of them off and on. They bought an old brand of Steve McWilliams for seventy-five dollars, carryin' six or eight head of cows. After that, from time to time, we heard of them buying more—two or three head from one man, and two or three from another. They branded them all with that McWilliams iron—T 0—so, pretty soon, we began to see the cattle on the range.

Now, a good cattleman knows cattle just as well as you know people, and he can tell them about as far off. Horned critters look alike to you, but even in a country supportin' a good many thousand head, a man used to the business can recognise most every individual as far as he can see him. Some is better than others at it. I suppose you really have to be brought up to it. So we boys at the Lazy Y noted all the cattle with the new T 0, and could estimate pretty close that the Hahn outfit might own, maybe, thirty-five head all told.

That was all very well, and nobody had any kick comin'. Then one day in the spring, we came across our first "sleeper."

What's a sleeper? A sleeper is a calf that has been ear-marked, but not branded. Every owner has a certain brand, as you know, and then he crops and slits the ears in a certain way, too. In that manner he don't have to look at the brand, except to corroborate the ears; and, as the critter generally sticks his ears up inquirin'-like to anyone ridin' up, it's easy to know the brand without lookin' at it, merely from the ear-marks. Once in a great while, when a man comes across an unbranded calf, and it ain't handy to build a fire, he just ear-marks it and let's the brandin' go till later. But it isn't done often, and our outfit had strict orders never to make sleepers.

Well, one day in the spring, as I say, Larry and me was ridin', when we came across a Lazy Y cow and calf. The little fellow was ear-marked all right, so we rode on, and never would have discovered nothin' if a bush rabbit hadn't jumped and scared the calf right across in front of our hosses. Then we couldn't help but see that there wasn't no brand.

Of course we roped him and put the iron on him. I took the chance to look at his ears, and saw that the marking had been done quite recent, so when we got in that night I reported to Buck Johnson that one of the punchers was gettin' lazy and sleeperin'. Naturally he went after the man who had done it; but every puncher swore up and down, and back and across, that he'd branded every calf he'd had a rope on that spring. We put it down that someone was lyin', and let it go at that.

And then, about a week later, one of the other boys reported a Triangle-H sleeper. The Triangle-H was the Goodrich brand, so we didn't have nothin' to do with that. Some of them might be sleeperin' for all we knew. Three other cases of the same kind we happened across that same spring.

So far, so good. Sleepers runnin' in such numbers was a little astonishin', but nothin' suspicious. Cattle did well that summer, and when we come to round up in the fall, we cut out maybe a dozen of those T 0 cattle that had strayed out of that Hahn country. Of the dozen there was five grown cows, and seven yearlin's.

"My Lord, Jed," says Buck to me, "they's a heap of these youngsters comin' over our way."

But still, as a young critter is more apt to stray than an old one that's got his range established, we didn't lay no great store by that neither. The Hahns took their bunch, and that's all there was to it.

Next spring, though, we found a few more sleepers, and one day we came on a cow that had gone dead lame. That was usual, too, but Buck, who was with me, had somethin' on his mind. Finally he turned back and roped her, and threw her.

"Look here, Jed," says he, "what do you make of this?"

I could see where the hind legs below the hocks had been burned.

"Looks like somebody had roped her by the hind feet," says I.

"Might be," says he, "but her heels lame that way makes it look more like hobbles."

So we didn't say nothin' more about that neither, until just by luck we came on another lame cow. We threw her, too.

"Well, what do you think of this one?" Buck Johnson asks me.

"The feet is pretty well tore up," says I, "and down to the quick, but I've seen them tore up just as bad on the rocks when they come down out of the mountains."

You sabe what that meant, don't you? You see, a rustler will take a cow and hobble her, or lame her so she can't follow, and then he'll take her calf a long ways off and brand it with his iron. Of course, if we was to see a calf of one brand followin' of a cow with another, it would be just too easy to guess what had happened.

We rode on mighty thoughtful. There couldn't be much doubt that cattle rustlers was at work. The sleepers they had ear-marked, hopin' that no one would discover the lack of a brand. Then, after the calf was weaned, and quit followin' of his mother, the rustler would brand it with his own iron, and change its ear-mark to match. It made a nice, easy way of gettin' together a bunch of cattle cheap.

But it was pretty hard to guess off-hand who the rustlers might be. There were a lot of renegades down towards the Mexican line who made a raid once in a while, and a few oilers  livin' near had water holes in the foothills, and any amount of little cattle holders, like this T 0 outfit, and any of them wouldn't shy very hard at a little sleeperin' on the side. Buck Johnson told us all to watch out, and passed the word quiet among the big owners to try and see whose cattle seemed to have too many calves for the number of cows.

The Texas outfit I'm tellin' you about had settled up above in this Double R canon where I showed you those natural corrals this morning. They'd built them a 'dobe, and cleared some land, and planted a few trees, and made an irrigated patch for alfalfa. Nobody never rode over this way very much, 'cause the country was most too rough for cattle, and our ranges lay farther to the southward. Now, however, we began to extend our ridin' a little.

I was down towards Dos Cabesas to look over the cattle there, and they used to send Larry up into the Double R country. One evenin' he took me to one side.

"Look here, Jed," says he, "I know you pretty well, and I'm not ashamed to say that I'm all new at this cattle business— in fact, I haven't been at it more'n a year. What should be the proportion of cows to calves anyhow?"

"There ought to be about twice as many cows as there're calves," I tells him.

"Then, with only about fifty head of grown cows, there ought not to be an equal number of yearlin's?"

"I should say not," says I. "What are you drivin' at?"

"Nothin' yet," says he.

A few days later he tackled me again.

"Jed," says he, "I'm not good, like you fellows are, at knowin' one cow from another, but there's a calf down there branded T 0 that I'd pretty near swear I saw with an X Y cow last month. I wish you could come down with me."

We got that fixed easy enough, and for the next month rammed around through this broken country lookin' for evidence. I saw enough to satisfy me to a moral certainty, but nothin' for a sheriff; and, of course, we couldn't go shoot up a peaceful rancher on mere suspicion. Finally, one day, we run on a four-months' calf all by himself, with the T 0 iron onto him—a mighty healthy lookin' calf, too.

"Wonder where HIS mother is!" says I.

"Maybe it's a 'dogie,'" says Larry Eagen—we calls calves whose mothers have died "dogies."

"No," says I, "I don't hardly think so. A dogie is always under size and poor, and he's layin' around water holes, and he always has a big, sway belly onto him. No, this is no dogie; and, if it's an honest calf, there sure ought to be a T 0 cow around somewhere."

So we separated to have a good look. Larry rode up on the edge of a little rimrock. In a minute I saw his hoss jump back, dodgin' a rattlesnake or somethin', and then fall back out of sight. I jumped my hoss up there tur'ble quick, and looked over, expectin' to see nothin' but mangled remains. It was only about fifteen foot down, but I couldn't see bottom 'count of some brush.

"Are you all right?" I yells.

"Yes, yes!" cries Larry, "but for the love of God, get down here as quick as you can."

I hopped off my hoss and scrambled down somehow.

"Hurt?" says I, as soon as I lit.

"Not a bit—look here."

There was a dead cow with the Lazy Y on her flank.

"And a bullet-hole in her forehead," adds Larry. "And, look here, that T 0 calf was bald-faced, and so was this cow."

"Reckon we found our sleepers," says I.

So, there we was. Larry had to lead his cavallo down the barranca to the main canon. I followed along on the rim, waitin' until a place gave me a chance to get down, too, or Larry a chance to get up. We were talkin' back and forth when, all at once, Larry shouted again.

"Big game this time," he yells. "Here's a cave and a mountain lion squallin' in it."

I slid down to him at once, and we drew our six-shooters and went up to the cave openin', right under the rim-rock. There, sure enough, were fresh lion tracks, and we could hear a little faint cryin' like woman.

"First chance," claims Larry, and dropped to his hands and knees at the entrance.

"Well, damn me!" he cries, and crawls in at once, payin' no attention to me tellin' him to be more cautious. In a minute he backs out, carryin' a three-year-old goat.

"We seem to be in for adventures to-day," says he. "Now, where do you suppose that came from, and how did it get here?"

"Well," says I, "I've followed lion tracks where they've carried yearlin's across their backs like a fox does a goose. They're tur'ble strong."

"But where did she come from?" he wonders.

"As for that," says I, "don't you remember now that T 0 outfit had a yearlin' kid when it came into the country?"

"That's right," says he. "It's only a mile down the canon. I'll take it home. They must be most distracted about it."

So I scratched up to the top where my pony was waitin'. It was a tur'ble hard climb, and I 'most had to have hooks on my eyebrows to get up at all. It's easier to slide down than to climb back. I dropped my gun out of my holster, and she went way to the bottom, but I wouldn't have gone back for six guns. Larry picked it up for me.

So we went along, me on the rim-rock and around the barrancas, and Larry in the bottom carryin' of the kid.

By and by we came to the ranch house, stopped to wait. The minute Larry hove in sight everybody was out to once, and in two winks the woman had that baby. They didn't see me at all, but I could hear, plain enough, what they said. Larry told how he had found her in the cave, and all about the lion tracks, and the woman cried and held the kid close to her, and thanked him about forty times. Then when she'd wore the edge off a little, she took the kid inside to feed it or somethin'.

"Well," says Larry, still laughin', "I must hit the trail."

"You say you found her up the Double R?" asks Hahn. "Was it that cave near the three cottonwoods?"

"Yes," says Larry.

"Where'd you get into the canyon?"

"Oh, my hoss slipped off into the barranca just above."

"The barranca just above," repeats Hahn, lookin' straight at him.

Larry took one step back.

"You ought to be almighty glad I got into the canyon at all," says he.

Hahn stepped up, holdin' out his hand.

"That's right," says he. "You done us a good turn there."

Larry took his hand. At the same time Hahn pulled his gun and shot him through the middle.

It was all so sudden and unexpected that I stood there paralysed.

Larry fell forward the way a man mostly will when he's hit in the stomach, but somehow he jerked loose a gun and got it off twice. He didn't hit nothin', and I reckon he was dead before he hit the ground. And there he had my gun, and I was about as useless as a pocket in a shirt!

No, sir, you can talk as much as you please, but the killer is a low-down ornery scub, and he don't hesitate at no treachery or ingratitude to keep his carcass safe.

**67**

Jed Parker ceased talking. The dusk had fallen in the little room, and dimly could be seen the recumbent figures lying at ease on their blankets. The ranch foreman was sitting bolt upright, cross-legged. A faint glow from his pipe barely distinguished his features.

"What became of the rustlers?" I asked him.

"Well, sir, that is the queer part. Hahn himself, who had done the killin', skipped out. We got out warrants, of course, but they never got served. He was a sort of half outlaw from that time, and was killed finally in the train hold-up of '97. But the others we tried for rustling. We didn't have much of a case, as the law went then, and they'd have gone free if the woman hadn't turned evidence against them. The killin' was too much for her. And, as the precedent held good in a lot of other rustlin' cases, Larry's death was really the beginnin' of law and order in the cattle business."

We smoked. The last light suddenly showed red against the grimy window. Windy Bill arose and looked out the door.

"Boys," said he, returning. "She's cleared off. We can get back to the ranch tomorrow."

"Oilers"—Greasers—Mexicans.

## CHAPTER FIVE
## THE DRIVE

A cry awakened me. It was still deep night. The moon sailed overhead, the stars shone unwavering like candles, and a chill breeze wandered in from the open spaces of the desert. I raised myself on my elbow, throwing aside the blankets and the canvas tarpaulin. Forty other indistinct, formless bundles on the ground all about me were sluggishly astir. Four figures passed and repassed between me and a red fire. I knew them for the two cooks and the horse wranglers. One of the latter was grumbling.

"Didn't git in till moon-up last night," he growled. "Might as well trade my bed for a lantern and be done with it."

Even as I stretched my arms and shivered a little, the two wranglers threw down their tin plates with a clatter, mounted horses and rode away in the direction of the thousand acres or so known as the pasture.

I pulled on my clothes hastily, buckled in my buckskin shirt, and dove for the fire. A dozen others were before me. It was bitterly cold. In the east the sky had paled the least bit in the world, but the moon and stars shone on bravely and undiminished. A band of coyotes was shrieking desperate blasphemies against the new day, and the stray herd, awakening, was beginning to bawl and bellow.

Two crater-like dutch ovens, filled with pieces of fried beef, stood near the fire; two galvanised water buckets, brimming with soda biscuits, flanked them; two tremendous coffee pots stood guard at either end. We picked us each a tin cup and a tin plate from the box at the rear of the chuck wagon; helped ourselves from a dutch oven, a pail, and a coffee pot, and squatted on our heels as close to the fire as possible. Men who came too late borrowed the shovel, scooped up some coals, and so started little fires of their own about which new groups formed.

While we ate, the eastern sky lightened. The mountains under the dawn looked like silhouettes cut from slate-coloured paper; those in the west showed faintly luminous. Objects about us became dimly visible. We could make out the windmill, and the adobe of the ranch houses, and the corrals. The cowboys arose one by one, dropped their plates into the dishpan, and began to hunt out their ropes. Everything was obscure and mysterious in the faint grey light. I watched Windy Bill near his tarpaulin. He stooped to throw over the canvas. When he bent, it was before daylight; when he straightened his back, daylight had come. It was just like that, as though someone had reached out his hand to turn on the illumination of the world.

The eastern mountains were fragile, the plain was ethereal, like a sea of liquid gases. From the pasture we heard the shoutings of the wranglers, and made out a cloud of dust. In a moment the first of the remuda came into view, trotting forward with the free grace of the unburdened horse. Others followed in procession: those near sharp and well defined, those in the background more or less obscured by the dust, now appearing plainly, now fading like ghosts. The leader turned unhesitatingly into the corral. After him poured the stream of the remuda—two hundred and fifty saddle horses— with an unceasing thunder of hoofs.

Immediately the cook-camp was deserted. The cowboys entered the corral. The horses began to circle around the edge of the enclosure as around the circumference of a circus ring. The men, grouped at the centre, watched keenly, looking for the mounts they had already decided on. In no time each had recognised his choice, and, his loop trailing, was walking toward that part of the revolving circumference where his pony dodged. Some few whirled the loop, but most cast it with a quick flip. It was really marvellous to observe the accuracy with which the noose would fly, past a dozen tossing heads, and over a dozen backs, to settle firmly about the neck of an animal perhaps in the very centre of the group. But again, if the first throw failed, it was interesting to see how the selected pony would dodge, double back, twist, turn, and hide to escape second cast. And it was equally interesting to observe how his companions would help him.

They seemed to realise that they were not wanted, and would push themselves between the cowboy and his intended mount with the utmost boldness. In the thick dust that instantly arose, and with the bewildering thunder of galloping, the flashing change of grouping, the rush of the charging animals, recognition alone would seem almost impossible, yet in an incredibly short time each had his mount, and the others, under convoy of the wranglers, were meekly wending their way out over the plain. There, until time for a change of horses, they would graze in a loose and scattered band, requiring scarcely any supervision. Escape? Bless you, no, that thought was the last in their minds.

In the meantime the saddles and bridles were adjusted. Always in a cowboy's "string" of from six to ten animals the boss assigns him two or three broncos to break in to the cow business. Therefore, each morning we could observe a half dozen or so men gingerly leading wicked looking little animals out to the sand "to take the pitch out of them." One small black, belonging to a cowboy called the Judge, used more than to fulfil expectations of a good time.

"Go to him, Judge!" someone would always remark.

"If he ain't goin' to pitch, I ain't goin' to make him", the Judge would grin, as he swung aboard.

The black would trot off quite calmly and in a most matter of fact way, as though to shame all slanderers of his lamb-like character. Then, as the bystanders would turn away, he would utter a squeal, throw down his head, and go at it. He was a very hard bucker, and made some really spectacular jumps, but the trick on which he based his claims to originality consisted in standing on his hind legs at so perilous an approach to the perpendicular that his rider would conclude he was about to fall backwards, and then suddenly springing forward in a series of stiff-legged bucks. The first manoeuvre induced the rider to loosen his seat in order to be ready to jump from under, and the second threw him before he could regain his grip.

"And they say a horse don't think!" exclaimed an admirer.

But as these were broken horses—save the mark!—the show was all over after each had had his little fling. We mounted and rode away, just as the mountain peaks to the west caught the rays of a sun we should not enjoy for a good half hour yet.

I had five horses in my string, and this morning rode "that C S horse, Brown Jug." Brown Jug was a powerful and well-built animal, about fourteen two in height, and possessed of a vast enthusiasm for cow-work. As the morning was frosty, he felt good.

At the gate of the water corral we separated into two groups. The smaller, under the direction of Jed Parker, was to drive the mesquite in the wide flats. The rest of us, under the command of Homer, the round-up captain, were to sweep the country even as far as the base of the foothills near Mount Graham. Accordingly we put our horses to the full gallop.

Mile after mile we thundered along at a brisk rate of speed. Sometimes we dodged in and out among the mesquite bushes, alternately separating and coming together again; sometimes we swept over grassy plains apparently of illimitable extent, sometimes we skipped and hopped and buck-jumped through and over little gullies, barrancas, and other sorts of malpais—but always without drawing rein. The men rode easily, with no thought to the way nor care for the footing. The air came back sharp against our faces. The warm blood stirred by the rush flowed more rapidly. We experienced a delightful glow. Of the morning cold only the very tips of our fingers and the ends of our noses retained a remnant. Already the sun was shining low and level across the plains. The shadows of the canons modelled the hitherto flat surfaces of the mountains.

After a time we came to some low hills helmeted with the outcrop of a rock escarpment. Hitherto they had seemed a termination of Mount Graham, but now, when we rode around them, we discovered them to be separated from the range by a good five miles of sloping plain. Later we looked back and would have sworn them part of the Dos Cabesas system, did we not know them to be at least eight miles' distant from that rocky rampart. It is always that way in Arizona. Spaces develop of whose existence you had not the slightest intimation. Hidden in apparently plane surfaces are valleys and prairies. At one sweep of the eye you embrace the entire area of an eastern State; but nevertheless the reality as you explore it foot by foot proves to be infinitely more than the vision has promised.

Beyond the hill we stopped. Here our party divided again, half to the right and half to the left. We had ridden, up to this time, directly away from camp, now we rode a circumference of which headquarters was the centre. The country was pleasantly rolling and covered with grass. Here and there were clumps of soapweed. Far in a remote distance lay a slender dark line across the plain. This we knew to be mesquite; and once entered, we knew it, too, would seem to spread out vastly. And then this grassy slope, on which we now rode, would show merely as an insignificant streak of yellow. It is also like that in Arizona.

I have ridden in succession through grass land, brush land, flower land, desert. Each in turn seemed entirely to fill the space of the plains between the mountains.

From time to time Homer halted us and detached a man. The business of the latter was then to ride directly back to camp, driving all cattle before him. Each was in sight of his right- and left-hand neighbour. Thus was constructed a drag-net whose meshes contracted as home was neared.

I was detached, when of our party only the Cattleman and Homer remained. They would take the outside. This was the post of honour, and required the hardest riding, for as soon as the cattle should realise the fact of their pursuit, they would attempt to "break" past the end and up the valley. Brown Jug and I congratulated ourselves on an exciting morning in prospect.

Now, wild cattle know perfectly well what a drive means, and they do not intend to get into a round-up if they can help it. Were it not for the two facts, that they are afraid of a mounted man, and cannot run quite so fast as a horse, I do not know how the cattle business would be conducted. As soon as a band of them caught sight of any one of us, they curled their tails and away they went at a long, easy lope that a domestic cow would stare at in wonder. This was all very well; in fact we yelled and shrieked and otherwise uttered cow-calls to keep them going, to "get the cattle started," as they say. But pretty soon a little band of the many scurrying away before our thin line, began to bear farther and farther to the east. When in their judgment they should have gained an opening, they would turn directly back and make a dash for liberty. Accordingly the nearest cowboy clapped spurs to his horse and pursued them.

It was a pretty race. The cattle ran easily enough, with long, springy jumps that carried them over the ground faster than appearances would lead one to believe. The cow-pony, his nose stretched out, his ears slanted, his eyes snapping with joy of the chase, flew fairly "belly to earth." The rider sat slightly forward, with the cowboy's loose seat. A whirl of dust, strangely insignificant against the immensity of a desert morning, rose from the flying group. Now they disappeared in a ravine, only to scramble out again the next instant, pace undiminished. The rider merely rose slightly and threw up his elbows to relieve the jar of the rough gully. At first the cattle seemed to hold their own, but soon the horse began to gain. In a short time he had come abreast of the leading animal.

The latter stopped short with a snort, dodged back, and set out at right angles to his former course. From a dead run the pony came to a stand in two fierce plunges, doubled like a shot, and was off on the other tack. An unaccustomed rider would here have lost his seat. The second dash was short. With a final shake of the head, the steers turned to the proper course in the direction of the ranch. The pony dropped unconcernedly to the shuffling jog of habitual progression.

Far away stretched the arc of our cordon. The most distant rider was a speck, and the cattle ahead of him were like maggots endowed with a smooth, swift onward motion. As yet the herd had not taken form; it was still too widely scattered. Its units, in the shape of small bunches, momently grew in numbers. The distant plains were crawling and alive with minute creatures making toward a common tiny centre.

Immediately in our front the cattle at first behaved very well. Then far down the long gentle slope I saw a break for the upper valley. The manikin that represented Homer at once became even smaller as it departed in pursuit. The Cattleman moved down to cover Homer's territory until he should return—and I in turn edged farther to the right. Then another break from another bunch. The Cattleman rode at top speed to head it. Before long he disappeared in the distant mesquite. I found myself in sole charge of a front three miles long.

The nearest cattle were some distance ahead, and trotting along at a good gait. As they had not yet discovered the chance left open by unforeseen circumstance, I descended and took in on my cinch while yet there was time. Even as I mounted, an impatient movement on the part of experienced Brown Jug told me that the cattle had seen their opportunity.

I gathered the reins and spoke to the horse. He needed no further direction, but set off at a wide angle, nicely calculated, to intercept the truants. Brown Jug was a powerful beast. The spring of his leap was as whalebone. The yellow earth began to stream past like water. Always the pace increased with a growing thunder of hoofs. It seemed that nothing could turn us from the straight line, nothing check the headlong momentum of our rush. My eyes filled with tears from the wind of our going. Saddle strings streamed behind. Brown Jug's mane whipped my bridle band. Dimly I was conscious of soapweed, sacatone, mesquite, as we passed them. They were abreast and gone before I could think of them or how they were to be dodged. Two antelope bounded away to the left; birds rose hastily from the grasses. A sudden chirk, chirk, chirk, rose all about me. We were in the very centre of a prairie-dog town, but before I could formulate in my mind the probabilities of holes and broken legs, the chirk, chirk, chirking had fallen astern. Brown Jug had skipped and dodged successfully.

We were approaching the cattle. They ran stubbornly and well, evidently unwilling to be turned until the latest possible moment. A great rage at their obstinacy took possession of us both. A broad shallow wash crossed our way, but we plunged through its rocks and boulders recklessly, angered at even the slight delay they necessitated. The hardland on the other side we greeted with joy. Brown Jug extended himself with a snort.

Suddenly a jar seemed to shake my very head loose. I found myself staring over the horse's head directly down into a deep and precipitous gully, the edge of which was so cunningly concealed by the grasses as to have remained invisible to my blurred vision. Brown Jug, however, had caught sight of it at the last instant, and had executed one of the wonderful stops possible only to a cow-pony.

But already the cattle had discovered a passage above, and were scrambling down and across. Brown Jug and I, at more sober pace, slid off the almost perpendicular bank, and out the other side.

A moment later we had headed them. They whirled, and without the necessity of any suggestion on my part Brown Jug turned after them, and so quickly that my stirrup actually brushed the ground.

After that we were masters. We chased the cattle far enough to start them well in the proper direction, and then pulled down to a walk in order to get a breath of air.

But now we noticed another band, back on the ground over which we had just come, doubling through in the direction of Mount Graham. A hard run set them to rights. We turned. More had poured out from the hills. Bands were crossing everywhere, ahead and behind. Brown Jug and I went to work.

Being an indivisible unit, we could chase only one bunch at a time; and, while we were after one, a half dozen others would be taking advantage of our preoccupation. We could not hold our own. Each run after an escaping bunch had to be

70

on a longer diagonal. Gradually we were forced back, and back, and back; but still we managed to hold the line unbroken. Never shall I forget the dash and clatter of that morning. Neither Brown Jug nor I thought for a moment of sparing horseflesh, nor of picking a route. We made the shortest line, and paid little attention to anything that stood in the way. A very fever of resistance possessed us. It was like beating against a head wind, or fighting fire, or combating in any other of the great forces of nature. We were quite alone. The Cattleman and Homer had vanished. To our left the men were fully occupied in marshalling the compact brown herds that had gradually massed—for these antagonists of mine were merely outlying remnants.

I suppose Brown Jug must have run nearly twenty miles with only one check. Then we chased a cow some distance and into the dry bed of a stream, where she whirled on us savagely. By luck her horn hit only the leather of my saddle skirts, so we left her; for when a cow has sense enough to "get on the peck," there is no driving her farther. We gained nothing, and had to give ground, but we succeeded in holding a semblance of order, so that the cattle did not break and scatter far and wide. The sun had by now well risen, and was beginning to shine hot. Brown Jug still ran gamely and displayed as much interest as ever, but he was evidently tiring. We were both glad to see Homer's grey showing in the fringe of mesquite.

Together we soon succeeded in throwing the cows into the main herd. And, strangely enough, as soon as they had joined a compact band of their fellows, their wildness left them and, convoyed by outsiders, they set themselves to plodding energetically toward the home ranch.

As my horse was somewhat winded, I joined the "drag" at the rear. Here by course of natural sifting soon accumulated all the lazy, gentle, and sickly cows, and the small calves. The difficulty now was to prevent them from lagging and dropping out. To that end we indulged in a great variety of the picturesque cow-calls peculiar to the cowboy. One found an old tin can which by the aid of a few pebbles he converted into a very effective rattle.

The dust rose in clouds and eddied in the sun. We slouched easily in our saddles. The cowboys compared notes as to the brands they had seen. Our ponies shuffled along, resting, but always ready for a dash in chase of an occasional bull calf or yearling with independent ideas of its own.

Thus we passed over the country, down the long gentle slope to the "sink" of the valley, whence another long gentle slope ran to the base of the other ranges. At greater or lesser distances we caught the dust, and made out dimly the masses of the other herds collected by our companions, and by the party under Jed Parker. They went forward toward the common centre, with a slow ruminative movement, and the dust they raised went with them.

Little by little they grew plainer to us, and the home ranch, hitherto merely a brown shimmer in the distance, began to take on definition as the group of buildings, windmills, and corrals we knew. Miniature horsemen could be seen galloping forward to the open white plain where the herd would be held. Then the mesquite enveloped us; and we knew little more, save the anxiety lest we overlook laggards in the brush, until we came out on the edge of that same white plain.

Here were more cattle, thousands of them, and billows of dust, and a great bellowing, and slim, mounted figures riding and shouting ahead of the herd. Soon they succeeded in turning the leaders back. These threw into confusion those that followed. In a few moments the cattle had stopped. A cordon of horsemen sat at equal distances holding them in.

"Pretty good haul," said the man next to me; "a good five thousand head."

CHAPTER SIX
CUTTING OUT

It was somewhere near noon by the time we had bunched and held the herd of some four or five thousand head in the smooth, wide flat, free from bushes and dog holes. Each sat at ease on his horse facing the cattle, watching lazily the clouds of dust and the shifting beasts, but ready at any instant to turn back the restless or independent individuals that might break for liberty.

Out of the haze came Homer, the round-up captain, on an easy lope. As he passed successively the sentries he delivered to each a low command, but without slacking pace. Some of those spoken to wheeled their horses and rode away. The others settled themselves in their saddles and began to roll cigarettes.

"Change horses; get something to eat," said he to me; so I swung after the file traveling at a canter over the low swells beyond the plain.

The remuda had been driven by its leaders to a corner of the pasture's wire fence, and there held. As each man arrived he dismounted, threw off his saddle, and turned his animal loose. Then he flipped a loop in his rope and disappeared in the eddying herd. The discarded horse, with many grunts, indulged in a satisfying roll, shook himself vigorously, and walked slowly away. His labour was over for the day, and he knew it, and took not the slightest trouble to get out of the way of the men with the swinging ropes.

Not so the fresh horses, however. They had no intention of being caught, if they could help it, but dodged and twisted, hid and doubled behind the moving screen of their friends. The latter, seeming as usual to know they were not wanted, made no effort to avoid the men, which probably accounted in great measure for the fact that the herd as a body remained compact, in spite of the cowboys threading it, and in spite of the lack of an enclosure.

Our horses caught, we saddled as hastily as possible; and then at the top speed of our fresh and eager ponies we swept down on the chuck wagon. There we fell off our saddles and descended on the meat and bread like ravenous locusts on a cornfield. The ponies stood where we left them, "tied to the ground", the cattle-country fashion.

As soon as a man had stoked up for the afternoon he rode away. Some finished before others, so across the plain formed an endless procession of men returning to the herd, and of those whom they replaced coming for their turn at the grub.

We found the herd quiet. Some were even lying down, chewing their cuds as peacefully as any barnyard cows. Most, however, stood ruminative, or walked slowly to and fro in the confines allotted by the horsemen, so that the herd looked from a distance like a brown carpet whose pattern was constantly changing—a dusty brown carpet in the process of being beaten. I relieved one of the watchers, and settled myself for a wait.

At this close inspection the different sorts of cattle showed more distinctly their characteristics. The cows and calves generally rested peacefully enough, the calf often lying down while the mother stood guard over it. Steers, however, were more restless. They walked ceaselessly, threading their way in and out among the standing cattle, pausing in brutish amazement at the edge of the herd, and turning back immediately to endless journeyings. The bulls, excited by so much company forced on their accustomed solitary habit, roared defiance at each other until the air fairly trembled. Occasionally two would clash foreheads. Then the powerful animals would push and wrestle, trying for a chance to gore. The decision of supremacy was a question of but a few minutes, and a bloody topknot the worst damage. The defeated one side-stepped hastily and clumsily out of reach, and then walked away.

Most of the time all we had to do was to sit our horses and watch these things, to enjoy the warm bath of the Arizona sun, and to converse with our next neighbours. Once in a while some enterprising cow, observing the opening between the men, would start to walk out. Others would fall in behind her until the movement would become general. Then one of us would swing his leg off the pommel and jog his pony over to head them off. They would return peacefully enough.

But one black muley cow, with a calf as black and muley as herself, was more persistent. Time after time, with infinite patience, she tried it again the moment my back was turned. I tried driving her far into the herd. No use; she always returned. Quirtings and stones had no effect on her mild and steady persistence.

"She's a San Simon cow," drawled my neighbour. "Everybody knows her. She's at every round-up, just naturally raisin' hell."

When the last man had returned from chuck, Homer made the dispositions for the cut. There were present probably thirty men from the home ranches round about, and twenty representing owners at a distance, here to pick up the strays inevitable to the season's drift. The round-up captain appointed two men to hold the cow-and-calf cut, and two more to hold the steer cut. Several of us rode into the herd, while the remainder retained their positions as sentinels to hold the main body of cattle in shape.

Little G and I rode slowly among the cattle looking everywhere. The animals moved sluggishly aside to give us passage, and closed in as sluggishly behind us, so that we were always closely hemmed in wherever we went. Over the shifting sleek backs, through the eddying clouds of dust, I could make out the figures of my companions moving slowly, apparently aimlessly, here and there.

Our task for the moment was to search out the unbranded J H calves. Since in ranks so closely crowded it would be physically impossible actually to see an animal's branded flank, we depended entirely on the ear-marks.

Did you ever notice how any animal, tame or wild, always points his ears inquiringly in the direction of whatever interests or alarms him? Those ears are for the moment his most prominent feature. So when a brand is quite indistinguishable because, as now, of press of numbers, or, as in winter, from extreme length of hair, the cropped ears tell plainly the tale of ownership. As every animal is so marked when branded, it follows that an uncut pair of ears means that its owner has never felt the iron.

So, now we had to look first of all for calves with uncut ears. After discovering one, we had to ascertain his ownership by examining the ear-marks of his mother, by whose side he was sure, in this alarming multitude, to be clinging faithfully.

Calves were numerous, and J H cows everywhere to be seen, so in somewhat less than ten seconds I had my eye on a mother and son. Immediately I turned Little G in their direction. At the slap of my quirt against the stirrup, all the cows immediately about me shrank suspiciously aside. Little G stepped forward daintily, his nostrils expanding, his ears working back and forth, trying to the best of his ability to understand which animals I had selected. The cow and her calf turned in toward the centre of the herd. A touch of the reins guided the pony. At once he comprehended. From that time on he needed no further directions.

Cautiously, patiently, with great skill, he forced the cow through the press toward the edge of the herd. It had to be done very quietly, at a foot pace, so as to alarm neither the objects of pursuit nor those surrounding them. When the cow turned back, Little G somehow happened always in her way. Before she knew it she was at the outer edge of the herd. There she found herself, with a group of three or four companions, facing the open plain. Instinctively she sought shelter. I felt Little G's muscles tighten beneath me. The moment for action had come. Before the cow had a chance to dodge among her companions the pony was upon her like a thunderbolt. She broke in alarm, trying desperately to avoid the rush. There ensued an exciting contest of dodgings, turnings, and doublings. Wherever she turned Little G was before her. Some of his evolutions were marvellous. All I had to do was to sit my saddle, and apply just that final touch of judgment denied even the wisest of the lower animals. Time and again the turn was so quick that the stirrup swept the ground. At last the cow, convinced of the uselessness of further effort to return, broke away on a long lumbering run to the open plain. She was stopped and held by the men detailed, and so formed the nucleus of the new cut-herd. Immediately Little G, his ears working in conscious virtue, jog-trotted back into the herd, ready for another.

After a dozen cows had been sent across to the cut-herd, the work simplified. Once a cow caught sight of this new band, she generally made directly for it, head and tail up. After the first short struggle to force her from the herd, all I had to do was to start her in the proper direction and keep her at it until her decision was fixed. If she was too soon left to her own devices, however, she was likely to return. An old cowman knows to a second just the proper moment to abandon her.

Sometimes, in spite of our best efforts a cow succeeded in circling us and plunging into the main herd. The temptation was then strong to plunge in also, and to drive her out by main force; but the temptation had to be resisted. A dash into the thick of it might break the whole band. At once, of his own accord, Little G dropped to his fast, shuffling walk, and again we addressed ourselves to the task of pushing her gently to the edge.

This was all comparatively simple—almost any pony is fast enough for the calf cut—but now Homer gave orders for the steer cut to begin, and steers are rapid and resourceful and full of natural cussedness. Little G and I were relieved by Windy Bill, and betook ourselves to the outside of the herd.

Here we had leisure to observe the effects that up to this moment we had ourselves been producing. The herd, restless by reason of the horsemen threading it, shifted, gave ground, expanded, and contracted, so that its shape and size were always changing in the constant area guarded by the sentinel cowboys. Dust arose from these movements, clouds of it, to eddy and swirl, thicken and dissipate in the currents of air. Now it concealed all but the nearest dimly-outlined animals; again it parted in rifts through which mistily we discerned the riders moving in and out of the fog; again it lifted high and thin, so that we saw in clarity the whole herd and the outriders and the mesas far away. As the afternoon waned, long shafts of sun slanted through this dust. It played on men and beasts magically, expanding them to the dimensions of strange genii, appearing and effacing themselves in the billows of vapour from some enchanted bottle.

We on the outside found our sinecure of hot noon-tide filched from us by the cooler hours. The cattle, wearied of standing, and perhaps somewhat hungry and thirsty, grew more and more impatient. We rode continually back and forth, turning the slow movement in on itself. Occasionally some particularly enterprising cow would conclude that one or another of the cut-herds would suit her better than this mill of turmoil. She would start confidently out, head and tail up, find herself chased back, get stubborn on the question, and lead her pursuer a long, hard run before she would return to her companions. Once in a while one would even have to be roped and dragged back. For know, before something happens to you, that you can chase a cow safely only until she gets hot and winded. Then she stands her ground and gets emphatically "on the peck."

I remember very well when I first discovered this. It was after I had had considerable cow work, too. I thought of cows as I had always seen them—afraid of a horseman, easy to turn with the pony, and willing to be chased as far as necessary to the work. Nobody told me anything different. One day we were making a drive in an exceedingly broken country. I was bringing in a small bunch I had discovered in a pocket of the hills, but was excessively annoyed by one old cow that insisted on breaking back. In the wisdom of further experience, I now conclude that she probably had a calf in the brush. Finally she got away entirely. After starting the bunch well ahead, I went after her.

Well, the cow and I ran nearly side by side for as much as half a mile at top speed. She declined to be headed. Finally she fell down and was so entirely winded that she could not get up.

"Now, old girl, I've got you!" said I, and set myself to urging her to her feet.

The pony acted somewhat astonished, and suspicious of the job. Therein he knew a lot more than I did. But I insisted, and, like a good pony, he obeyed. I yelled at the cow, and slapped my bat, and used my quirt. When she had quite recovered her wind, she got slowly to her feet—and charged me in a most determined manner.

Now, a bull, or a steer, is not difficult to dodge. He lowers his head, shuts his eyes, and comes in on one straight rush. But a cow looks to see what she is doing; her eyes are open every minute, and it overjoys her to take a side hook at you even when you succeed in eluding her direct charge.

The pony I was riding did his best, but even then could not avoid a sharp prod that would have ripped him up had not my leather bastos intervened. Then we retired to a distance in order to plan further; but we did not succeed in inducing that cow to revise her ideas, so at last we left her. When, in some chagrin, I mentioned to the round-up captain the fact that I had skipped one animal, he merely laughed.

"Why, kid," said he, "you can't do nothin' with a cow that gets on the prod that away 'thout you ropes her; and what could you do with her out there if you DID rope her?"

So I learned one thing more about cows.

After the steer cut had been finished, the men representing the neighbouring ranges looked through the herd for strays of their brands. These were thrown into the stray-herd, which had been brought up from the bottom lands to receive the new accessions. Work was pushed rapidly, as the afternoon was nearly gone.

In fact, so absorbed were we that until it was almost upon us we did not notice a heavy thunder-shower that arose in the region of the Dragoon Mountains, and swept rapidly across the zenith. Before we knew it the rain had begun. In ten seconds it had increased to a deluge, and in twenty we were all to leeward of the herd striving desperately to stop the drift of the cattle down wind.

We did everything in our power to stop them, but in vain. Slickers waved, quirts slapped against leather, six-shooters flashed, but still the cattle, heads lowered, advanced with slow and sullen persistence that would not be stemmed. If we held our ground, they divided around us. Step by step we were forced to give way—the thin line of nervously plunging horses sprayed before the dense mass of the cattle.

"No, they won't stampede," shouted Charley to my question. "There's cows and calves in them. If they was just steers or grown critters, they might."

The sensations of those few moments were very vivid—the blinding beat of the storm in my face, the unbroken front of horned heads bearing down on me, resistless as fate, the long slant of rain with the sun shining in the distance beyond it.

Abruptly the downpour ceased. We shook our hats free of water, and drove the herd back to the cutting grounds again.

But now the surface of the ground was slippery, and the rapid manoeuvring of horses had become a matter precarious in the extreme. Time and again the ponies fairly sat on their haunches and slid when negotiating a sudden stop, while quick turns meant the rapid scramblings that only a cow-horse could accomplish. Nevertheless the work went forward unchecked. The men of the other outfits cut their cattle into the stray-herd. The latter was by now of considerable size, for this was the third week of the round-up.

Finally everyone expressed himself as satisfied. The largely diminished main herd was now started forward by means of shrill cowboy cries and beating of quirts. The cattle were only too eager to go. From my position on a little rise above the stray-herd I could see the leaders breaking into a run, their heads thrown forward as they snuffed their freedom. On the mesa side the sentinel riders quietly withdrew. From the rear and flanks the horsemen closed in. The cattle poured out in a steady stream through the opening thus left on the mesa side. The fringe of cowboys followed, urging them on. Abruptly the cavalcade turned and came loping back. The cattle continued ahead on a trot, gradually spreading abroad over the landscape, losing their integrity as a herd. Some of the slower or hungrier dropped out and began to graze. Certain of the more wary disappeared to right or left.

Now, after the day's work was practically over, we had our first accident. The horse ridden by a young fellow from Dos Cabesas slipped, fell, and rolled quite over his rider. At once the animal lunged to his feet, only to be immediately seized by the nearest rider. But the Dos Cabesas man lay still, his arms and legs spread abroad, his head doubled sideways in a horribly suggestive manner. We hopped off. Two men straightened him out, while two more looked carefully over the indications on the ground.

"All right," sang out one of them, "the horn didn't catch him."

He pointed to the indentation left by the pommel. Indeed five minutes brought the man to his senses. He complained of a very twisted back. Homer set one of the men in after the bed-wagon, by means of which the sufferer was shortly transported to camp. By the end of the week he was again in the saddle. How men escape from this common accident with injuries so slight has always puzzled me. The horse rolls completely over his rider, and yet it seems to be the rarest thing in the world for the latter to be either killed or permanently injured.

Now each man had the privilege of looking through the J H cuts to see if by chance steers of his own had been included in them. When all had expressed themselves as satisfied, the various bands were started to the corrals.

From a slight eminence where I had paused to enjoy the evening I looked down on the scene. The three herds, separated by generous distance one from the other, crawled leisurely along; the riders, their hats thrust back, lolled in their saddles, shouting conversation to each other, relaxing after the day's work; through the clouds strong shafts of light belittled the living creatures, threw into proportion the vastness of the desert.

CHAPTER SEVEN
A CORNER IN HORSES

It was dark night. The stay-herd bellowed frantically from one of the big corrals; the cow-and-calf-herd from a second. Already the remuda, driven in from the open plains, scattered about the thousand acres of pasture. Away from the conveniences of fence and corral, men would have had to patrol all night. Now, however, everyone was gathered about the camp fire.

Probably forty cowboys were in the group, representing all types, from old John, who had been in the business forty years, and had punched from the Rio Grande to the Pacific, to the Kid, who would have given his chance of salvation if he could have been taken for ten years older than he was. At the moment Jed Parker was holding forth to his friend Johnny Stone in reference to another old crony who had that evening joined the round-up.

"Johnny," inquired Jed with elaborate gravity, and entirely ignoring the presence of the subject of conversation, "what is that thing just beyond the fire, and where did it come from?"

Johnny Stone squinted to make sure.

"That?" he replied. "Oh, this evenin' the dogs see something run down a hole, and they dug it out, and that's what they got."

The newcomer grinned.

"The trouble with you fellows," he proffered "is that you're so plumb alkalied you don't know the real thing when you see it."

"That's right," supplemented Windy Bill drily. "HE come from New York."

"No!" cried Jed. "You don't say so? Did he come in one box or in two?"

Under cover of the laugh, the newcomer made a raid on the dutch ovens and pails. Having filled his plate, he squatted on his heels and fell to his belated meal. He was a tall, slab-sided individual, with a lean, leathery face, a sweeping white moustache, and a grave and sardonic eye. His leather chaps were plain and worn, and his hat had been fashioned by time and wear into much individuality. I was not surprised to hear him nicknamed Sacatone Bill.

"Just ask him how he got that game foot," suggested Johnny Stone to me in an undertone, so, of course, I did not.

Later someone told me that the lameness resulted from his refusal of an urgent invitation to return across a river. Mr. Sacatone Bill happened not to be riding his own horse at the time.

The Cattleman dropped down beside me a moment later.

"I wish," said he in a low voice, "we could get that fellow talking. He is a queer one. Pretty well educated apparently. Claims to be writing a book of memoirs. Sometimes he will open up in good shape, and sometimes he will not. It does no good to ask him direct, and he is as shy as an old crow when you try to lead him up to a subject. We must just lie low and trust to Providence."

A man was playing on the mouth organ. He played excellently well, with all sorts of variations and frills. We smoked in silence. The deep rumble of the cattle filled the air with its diapason. Always the shrill coyotes raved out in the mesquite. Sacatone Bill had finished his meal, and had gone to sit by Jed Parker, his old friend. They talked together low-voiced. The evening grew, and the eastern sky silvered over the mountains in anticipation of the moon.

Sacatone Bill suddenly threw back his head and laughed.

"Reminds me of the time I went to Colorado!" he cried.

"He's off!" whispered the Cattleman.

A dead silence fell on the circle. Everybody shifted position the better to listen to the story of Sacatone Bill.

About ten year ago I got plumb sick of punchin' cows around my part of the country. She hadn't rained since Noah, and I'd forgot what water outside a pail or a trough looked like. So I scouted around inside of me to see what part of the world I'd jump to, and as I seemed to know as little of Colorado and minin' as anything else, I made up the pint of bean soup I call my brains to go there. So I catches me a buyer at Henson and turns over my pore little bunch of cattle and prepared to fly. The last day I hauled up about twenty good buckets of water and threw her up against the cabin. My buyer was settin' his hoss waitin' for me to get ready. He didn't say nothin' until we'd got down about ten mile or so.

"Mr. Hicks," says he, hesitatin' like, "I find it a good rule in this country not to overlook other folks' plays, but I'd take it mighty kind if you'd explain those actions of yours with the pails of water."

"Mr. Jones," says I, "it's very simple. I built that shack five year ago, and it's never rained since. I just wanted to settle in my mind whether or not that damn roof leaked."

So I quit Arizona, and in about a week I see my reflection in the winders of a little place called Cyanide in the Colorado mountains.

Fellows, she was a bird. They wasn't a pony in sight, nor a squar' foot of land that wasn't either street or straight up. It made me plumb lonesome for a country where you could see a long ways even if you didn't see much. And this early in the evenin' they wasn't hardly anybody in the streets at all.

I took a look at them dark, gloomy, old mountains, and a sniff at a breeze that would have frozen the whiskers of hope, and I made a dive for the nearest lit winder. They was a sign over it that just said:

THIS IS A SALOON

I was glad they labelled her. I'd never have known it. They had a fifteen-year old kid tendin' bar, no games goin', and not a soul in the place.

"Sorry to disturb your repose, bub," says I, "but see if you can sort out any rye among them collections of sassapariller of yours."

I took a drink, and then another to keep it company—I was beginnin' to sympathise with anythin' lonesome. Then I kind of sauntered out to the back room where the hurdy-gurdy ought to be.

Sure enough, there was a girl settin' on the pianner stool, another in a chair, and a nice shiny Jew drummer danglin' his feet from a table. They looked up when they see me come in, and went right on talkin'.

"Hello, girls!" says I.

At that they stopped talkin' complete.

"How's tricks?" says I.

"Who's your woolly friend?" the shiny Jew asks of the girls.

I looked at him a minute, but I see he'd been raised a pet, and then, too, I was so hungry for sassiety I was willin' to pass a bet or two.

"Don't you ADMIRE these cow gents?" snickers one of the girls.

"Play somethin', sister," says I to the one at the pianner.

She just grinned at me.

"Interdooce me," says the drummer in a kind of a way that made them all laugh a heap.

"Give us a tune," I begs, tryin' to be jolly, too.

"She don't know any pieces," says the Jew.

"Don't you?" I asks pretty sharp.

"No," says she.

"Well, I do," says I.

I walked up to her, jerked out my guns, and reached around both sides of her to the pianner. I run the muzzles up and down the keyboard two or three times, and then shot out half a dozen keys.

"That's the piece I know," says I.

But the other girl and the Jew drummer had punched the breeze.

The girl at the pianner just grinned, and pointed to the winder where they was some ragged glass hangin'. She was dead game.

"Say, Susie," says I, "you're all right, but your friends is tur'ble. I may be rough, and I ain't never been curried below the knees, but I'm better to tie to than them sons of guns."

"I believe it," says she.

So we had a drink at the bar, and started out to investigate the wonders of Cyanide.

Say, that night was a wonder. Susie faded after about three drinks, but I didn't seem to mind that. I hooked up to another saloon kept by a thin Dutchman. A fat Dutchman is stupid, but a thin one is all right.

In ten minutes I had more friends in Cyanide than they is fiddlers in hell. I begun to conclude Cyanide wasn't so lonesome. About four o'clock in comes a little Irishman about four foot high, with more upper lip than a muley cow, and enough red hair to make an artificial aurorer borealis. He had big red hands with freckles pasted onto them, and stiff red hairs standin' up separate and lonesome like signal stations. Also his legs was bowed.

He gets a drink at the bar, and stands back and yells:

"God bless the Irish and let the Dutch rustle!"

Now, this was none of my town, so I just stepped back of the end of the bar quick where I wouldn't stop no lead. The shootin' didn't begin.

"Probably Dutchy didn't take no note of what the locoed little dogie DID say," thinks I to myself.

The Irishman bellied up to the bar again, and pounded on it with his fist.

"Look here!" he yells. "Listen to what I'm tellin' ye! God bless the Irish and let the Dutch rustle! Do ye hear me?"

"Sure, I hear ye," says Dutchy, and goes on swabbin' his bar with a towel.

At that my soul just grew sick. I asked the man next to me why Dutchy didn't kill the little fellow.

"Kill him!" says this man. "What for?"

"For insultin' of him, of course."

"Oh, he's drunk," says the man, as if that explained anythin'.

That settled it with me. I left that place, and went home, and it wasn't more than four o'clock, neither. No, I don't call four o'clock late. It may be a little late for night before last, but it's just the shank of the evenin' for to-night.

Well, it took me six weeks and two days to go broke. I didn't know sic em, about minin'; and before long I KNEW that I didn't 'know sic 'em. Most all day I poked around them mountains—-not like our'n—too much timber to be comfortable. At night I got to droppin' in at Dutchy's. He had a couple of quiet games goin', and they was one fellow among that lot of grubbin' prairie dogs that had heerd tell that cows had horns. He was the wisest of the bunch on the cattle business. So I stowed away my consolation, and made out to forget comparing Colorado with God's country.

About three times a week this Irishman I told you of—name O'Toole—comes bulgin' in. When he was sober he talked minin' high, wide, and handsome. When he was drunk he pounded both fists on the bar and yelled for action, tryin' to get Dutchy on the peck.

"God bless the Irish and let the Dutch rustle!" he yells about six times. "Say, do you hear?"

"Sure," says Dutchy, calm as a milk cow, "sure, I hears ye!"

I was plumb sorry for O'Toole. I'd like to have given him a run; but, of course, I couldn't take it up without makin' myself out a friend of this Dutchy party, and I couldn't stand for that. But I did tackle Dutchy about it one night when they wasn't nobody else there.

"Dutchy," says I, "what makes you let that bow-legged cross between a bulldog and a flamin' red sunset tromp on you so? It looks to me like you're plumb spiritless."

Dutchy stopped wiping glasses for a minute.

"Just you hold on" says he. "I ain't ready yet. Bimeby I make him sick; also those others who laugh with him."

He had a little grey flicker in his eye, and I thinks to myself that maybe they'd get Dutchy on the peck yet.

As I said, I went broke in just six weeks and two days. And I was broke a plenty. No hold-outs anywhere. It was a heap long ways to cows; and I'd be teetotally chawed up and spit out if I was goin' to join these minin' terrapins defacin' the bosom of nature. It sure looked to me like hard work.

While I was figurin' what next, Dutchy came in. Which I was tur'ble surprised at that, but I said good-mornin' and would he rest his poor feet.

"You like to make some money?" he asks.

"That depends," says I, "on how easy it is."

"It is easy," says he. "I want you to buy hosses for me."

"Hosses! Sure!" I yells, jumpin' up. "You bet you! Why, hosses is where I live! What hosses do you want?"

"All hosses," says he, calm as a faro dealer.

"What?" says I. "Elucidate, my bucko. I don't take no such blanket order. Spread your cards."

"I mean just that," says he. "I want you to buy all the hosses in this camp, and in the mountains. Every one."

"Whew!" I whistles. "That's a large order. But I'm your meat."

"Come with me, then," says he. I hadn't but just got up, but I went with him to his little old poison factory. Of course, I hadn't had no breakfast; but he staked me to a Kentucky breakfast. What's a Kentucky breakfast? Why, a Kentucky breakfast is a three-pound steak, a bottle of whisky, and a setter dog. What's the dog for? Why, to eat the steak, of course.

We come to an agreement. I was to get two-fifty a head commission. So I started out. There wasn't many hosses in that country, and what there was the owners hadn't much use for unless it was to work a whim. I picked up about a hundred head quick enough, and reported to Dutchy.

"How about burros and mules?" I asks Dutchy.

"They goes," says he. "Mules same as hosses; burros four bits a head to you."

At the end of a week I had a remuda of probably two hundred animals. We kept them over the hills in some "parks," as these sots call meadows in that country. I rode into town and told Dutchy.

"Got them all?" he asks.

"All but a cross-eyed buckskin that's mean, and the bay mare that Noah bred to."

"Get them," says he.

"The bandits want too much," I explains.

"Get them anyway," says he.

I went away and got them. It was scand'lous; such prices.

When I hit Cyanide again I ran into scenes of wild excitement. The whole passel of them was on that one street of their'n, talkin' sixteen ounces to the pound. In the middle was Dutchy, drunk as a soldier-just plain foolish drunk.

"Good Lord!" thinks I to myself, "he ain't celebratin' gettin' that bunch of buzzards, is he?"

But I found he wasn't that bad. When he caught sight of me, he fell on me drivellin'.

"Look there!" he weeps, showin' me a letter.

I was the last to come in; so I kept that letter—here she is. I'll read her.

Dear Dutchy:—I suppose you thought I'd flew the coop, but I haven't and this is to prove it. Pack up your outfit and hit the trail. I've made the biggest free gold strike you ever see. I'm sending you specimens. There's tons just like it, tons and tons. I got all the claims I can hold myself; but there's heaps more. I've writ to Johnny and Ed at Denver to come on. Don't give this away. Make tracks. Come in to Buck Canon in the Whetstones and oblige.

Yours                                                                       truly,

Henry Smith

Somebody showed me a handful of white rock with yeller streaks in it. His eyes was bulgin' until you could have hung your hat on them. That O'Toole party was walkin' around, wettin' his lips with his tongue and swearin' soft.

"God bless the Irish and let the Dutch rustle!" says he. "And the fool had to get drunk and give it away!"

The excitement was just started, but it didn't last long. The crowd got the same notion at the same time, and it just melted. Me and Dutchy was left alone.

I went home. Pretty soon a fellow named Jimmy Tack come around a little out of breath.

"Say, you know that buckskin you bought off'n me?" says he, "I want to buy him back."

"Oh, you do," says I.

"Yes," says he. "I've got to leave town for a couple of days, and I got to have somethin' to pack."

"Wait and I'll see," says I.

Outside the door I met another fellow.

"Look here," he stops me with. "How about that bay mare I sold you? Can you call that sale off? I got to leave town for a day or two and—"

"Wait," says I. "I'll see."

By the gate was another hurryin' up.

"Oh, yes," says I when he opens his mouth. "I know all your troubles. You have to leave town for a couple of days, and you want back that lizard you sold me. Well, wait."

After that I had to quit the main street and dodge back of the hog ranch. They was all headed my way. I was as popular as a snake in a prohibition town.

I hit Dutchy's by the back door.

"Do you want to sell hosses?" I asks. "Everyone in town wants to buy."

Dutchy looked hurt.

"I wanted to keep them for the valley market," says he, "but—How much did you give Jimmy Tack for his buckskin?"

"Twenty," says I.

"Well, let him have it for eighty," says Dutchy; "and the others in proportion."

I lay back and breathed hard.

"Sell them all, but the one best hoss," says he—"no, the TWO best."

"Holy smoke!" says I, gettin' my breath. "If you mean that, Dutchy, you lend me another gun and give me a drink."

He done so, and I went back home to where the whole camp of Cyanide was waitin'.

I got up and made them a speech and told them I'd sell them hosses all right, and to come back. Then I got an Injin boy to help, and we rustled over the remuda and held them in a blind canon. Then I called up these miners one at a time, and made bargains with them. Roar! Well, you could hear them at Denver, they tell me, and the weather reports said, "Thunder in the mountains." But it was cash on delivery, and they all paid up. They had seen that white quartz with the gold stickin' into it, and that's the same as a dose of loco to miner gents.

Why didn't I take a hoss and start first? I did think of it—for about one second. I wouldn't stay in that country then for a million dollars a minute. I was plumb sick and loathin' it, and just waitin' to make high jumps back to Arizona. So I wasn't aimin' to join this stampede, and didn't have no vivid emotions.

They got to fightin' on which should get the first hoss; so I bent my gun on them and made them draw lots. They roared some more, but done so; and as fast as each one handed over his dust or dinero he made a rush for his cabin, piled on his saddle and pack, and pulled his freight on a cloud of dust. It was sure a grand stampede, and I enjoyed it no limit.

So by sundown I was alone with the Injin. Those two hundred head brought in about twenty thousand dollars. It was heavy, but I could carry it. I was about alone in the landscape; and there were the two best hosses I had saved out for Dutchy. I was sure some tempted. But I had enough to get home on anyway; and I never yet drank behind the bar, even if I might hold up the saloon from the floor. So I grieved some inside that I was so tur'ble conscientious, shouldered the sacks, and went down to find Dutchy.

I met him headed his way, and carryin' of a sheet of paper.

"Here's your dinero," says I, dumpin' the four big sacks on the ground.

He stooped over and hefted them. Then he passed one over to me.

"What's that for?" I asks.

"For you," says he.

"My commission ain't that much," I objects.

"You've earned it," says he, "and you might have skipped with the whole wad."

"How did you know I wouldn't?" I asks.

"Well," says he, and I noted that jag of his had flew. "You see, I was behind that rock up there, and I had you covered."

I saw; and I began to feel better about bein' so tur'ble conscientious.

We walked a little ways without sayin' nothin'.

"But ain't you goin' to join the game?" I asks.

"Guess not," says he, jinglin' of his gold. "I'm satisfied."

"But if you don't get a wiggle on you, you are sure goin' to get left on those gold claims," says I.

"There ain't no gold claims," says he.

"But Henry Smith—" I cries.

"There ain't no Henry Smith," says he.

I let that soak in about six inches.

"But there's a Buck Canon," I pleads. "Please say there's a Buck Canon."

"Oh, yes, there's a Buck Canon," he allows. "Nice limestone formation—make good hard water."

"Well, you're a marvel," says I.

We walked together down to Dutchy's saloon.

We stopped outside.

"Now," says he, "I'm goin' to take one of those hosses and go somewheres else. Maybe you'd better do likewise on the other."

"You bet I will," says I.

He turned around and taked up the paper he was carryin'. It was a sign. It read:

THE DUTCH HAS RUSTLED

"Nice sentiment," says I. "It will be appreciated when the crowd comes back from that little pasear into Buck Canon. But why not tack her up where the trail hits the camp? Why on this particular door?"

"Well," said Dutchy, squintin' at the sign sideways, "you see I sold this place day before yesterday—to Mike O'Toole."

CHAPTER EIGHT
THE CORRAL BRANDING

All that night we slept like sticks of wood. No dreams visited us, but in accordance with the immemorial habit of those who live out—whether in the woods, on the plains, among the mountains, or at sea—once during the night each of us rose on his elbow, looked about him, and dropped back to sleep. If there had been a fire to replenish, that would have been the moment to do so; if the wind had been changing and the seas rising, that would have been the time to cast an eye aloft for indications, to feel whether the anchor cable was holding; if the pack-horses had straggled from the alpine meadows under the snows, this would have been the occasion for intent listening for the faintly tinkling bell so that next day one would know in which direction to look. But since there existed for us no responsibility, we each reported dutifully at the roll-call of habit, and dropped back into our blankets with a grateful sigh.

I remember the moon sailing a good gait among apparently stationary cloudlets; I recall a deep, black shadow lying before distant silvery mountains; I glanced over the stark, motionless canvases, each of which concealed a man; the air trembled with the bellowing of cattle in the corrals.

Seemingly but a moment later the cook's howl brought me to consciousness again. A clear, licking little fire danced in the blackness. Before it moved silhouettes of men already eating.

I piled out and joined the group. Homer was busy distributing his men for the day. Three were to care for the remuda; five were to move the stray-herd from the corrals to good feed; three branding crews were told to brand the calves we had collected in the cut of the afternoon before. That took up about half the men. The rest were to make a short drive in the salt grass. I joined the Cattleman, and together we made our way afoot to the branding pen.

We were the only ones who did go afoot, however, although the corrals were not more than two hundred yards' distant. When we arrived we found the string of ponies standing around outside. Between the upright bars of greasewood we could see the cattle, and near the opposite side the men building a fire next the fence. We pushed open the wide gate and entered. The three ropers sat their horses, idly swinging the loops of their ropes back and forth. Three others brought wood and arranged it craftily in such manner as to get best draught for heatin,—a good branding fire is most decidedly a work of art. One stood waiting for them to finish, a sheaf of long JH stamping irons in his hand. All the rest squatted on their heels along the fence, smoking cigarettes and chatting together. The first rays of the sun slanted across in one great sweep from the remote mountains.

In ten minutes Charley pronounced the irons ready. Homer, Wooden, and old California John rode in among the cattle. The rest of the men arose and stretched their legs and advanced. The Cattleman and I climbed to the top bar of the gate, where we roosted, he with his tally-book on his knee.

Each rider swung his rope above his head with one hand, keeping the broad loop open by a skilful turn of the wrist at the end of each revolution. In a moment Homer leaned forward and threw. As the loop settled, he jerked sharply upward, exactly as one would strike to hook a big fish. This tightened the loop and prevented it from slipping off. Immediately, and without waiting to ascertain the result of the manoeuvre, the horse turned and began methodically, without undue haste, to walk toward the branding fire. Homer wrapped the rope twice or thrice about the horn, and sat over in one stirrup to avoid the tightened line and to preserve the balance. Nobody paid any attention to the calf. The critter had been caught by the two hind legs. As the rope tightened, he was suddenly upset, and before he could realise that something disagreeable was happening, he was sliding majestically along on his belly. Behind him followed his anxious mother, her head swinging from side to side.

Near the fire the horse stopped. The two "bull-doggers" immediately pounced upon the victim. It was promptly flopped over on its right side. One knelt on its head and twisted back its foreleg in a sort of hammer-lock; the other seized one hind foot, pressed his boot heel against the other hind leg close to the body, and sat down behind the animal. Thus the calf was unable to struggle. When once you have had the wind knocked out of you, or a rib or two broken, you cease to think this unnecessarily rough. Then one or the other threw off the rope. Homer rode away, coiling the rope as he went.

"Hot iron!" yelled one of the bull-doggers.

"Marker!" yelled the other.

Immediately two men ran forward. The brander pressed the iron smoothly against the flank. A smoke and the smell of scorching hair arose. Perhaps the calf blatted a little as the heat scorched. In a brief moment it was over. The brand showed cherry, which is the proper colour to indicate due peeling and a successful mark.

In the meantime the marker was engaged in his work. First, with a sharp knife he cut off slanting the upper quarter of one ear. Then he nicked out a swallow-tail in the other. The pieces he thrust into his pocket in order that at the completion of the work he could thus check the Cattleman's tally-board as to the number of calves branded. The bull-dogger let go. The calf sprang up, was appropriated and smelled over by his worried mother, and the two departed into the herd to talk it over.

It seems to me that a great deal of unnecessary twaddle is abroad as to the extreme cruelty of branding. Undoubtedly it is to some extent painful, and could some other method of ready identification be devised, it might be as well to adopt it in preference. But in the circumstance of a free range, thousands of cattle, and hundreds of owners, any other method is out of the question. I remember a New England movement looking toward small brass tags to be hung from the ear. Inextinguishable laughter followed the spread of this doctrine through Arizona. Imagine a puncher descending to examine politely the ear-tags of wild cattle on the open range or in a round-up.

But, as I have intimated, even the inevitable branding and ear-marking are not so painful as one might suppose. The scorching hardly penetrates below the outer tough skin—only enough to kill the roots of the hair—besides which it must be remembered that cattle are not so sensitive as the higher nervous organisms. A calf usually bellows when the iron bites, but as soon as released he almost invariably goes to feeding or to looking idly about. Indeed, I have never seen one even take the trouble to lick his wounds, which is certainly not true in the case of the injuries they inflict on each other in fighting. Besides which, it happens but once in a lifetime, and is over in ten seconds; a comfort denied to those of us who have our teeth filled.

In the meantime two other calves had been roped by the two other men. One of the little animals was but a few months old, so the rider did not bother with its hind legs, but tossed his loop over its neck. Naturally, when things tightened up,

Mr. Calf entered his objections, which took the form of most vigorous bawlings, and the most comical bucking, pitching, cavorting, and bounding in the air. Mr. Frost's bull-calf alone in pictorial history shows the attitudes. And then, of course, there was the gorgeous contrast between all this frantic and uncomprehending excitement and the absolute matter-of-fact imperturbability of horse and rider. Once at the fire, one of the men seized the tightened rope in one hand, reached well over the animal's back to get a slack of the loose hide next the belly, lifted strongly, and tripped. This is called "bull-dogging." As he knew his business, and as the calf was a small one, the little beast went over promptly, bit the ground with a whack, and was pounced upon and held.

Such good luck did not always follow, however. An occasional and exceedingly husky bull yearling declined to be upset in any such manner. He would catch himself on one foot, scramble vigorously, and end by struggling back to the upright. Then ten to one he made a dash to get away. In such case he was generally snubbed up short enough at the end of the rope; but once or twice he succeeded in running around a group absorbed in branding. You can imagine what happened next. The rope, attached at one end to a conscientious and immovable horse and at the other to a reckless and vigorous little bull, swept its taut and destroying way about mid-knee high across that group. The brander and marker, who were standing, promptly sat down hard; the bull-doggers, who were sitting, immediately turned several most capable somersaults; the other calf arose and inextricably entangled his rope with that of his accomplice. Hot irons, hot language, and dust filled the air.

Another method, and one requiring slightly more knack, is to grasp the animal's tail and throw it by a quick jerk across the pressure of the rope. This is productive of some fun if it fails.

By now the branding was in full swing. The three horses came and went phlegmatically. When the nooses fell, they turned and walked toward the fire as a matter of course. Rarely did the cast fail. Men ran to and fro busy and intent. Sometimes three or four calves were on the ground at once. Cries arose in a confusion: "Marker" "Hot iron!" "Tally one!" Dust eddied and dissipated. Behind all were clear sunlight and the organ roll of the cattle bellowing.

Toward the middle of the morning the bull-doggers began to get a little tired.

"No more necked calves," they announced. "Catch 'em by the hind legs, or bull-dog 'em yourself."

And that went. Once in a while the rider, lazy, or careless, or bothered by the press of numbers, dragged up a victim caught by the neck. The bull-doggers flatly refused to have anything to do with it. An obvious way out would have been to flip off the loop and try again; but of course that would have amounted to a confession of wrong.

"You fellows drive me plumb weary," remarked the rider, slowly dismounting. "A little bit of a calf like that! What you all need is a nigger to cut up your food for you!"

Then he would spit on his hands and go at it alone. If luck attended his first effort, his sarcasm was profound.

"There's yore little calf," said he. "Would you like to have me tote it to you, or do you reckon you could toddle this far with yore little old iron?"

But if the calf gave much trouble, then all work ceased while the unfortunate puncher wrestled it down.

Toward noon the work slacked. Unbranded calves were scarce. Sometimes the men rode here and there for a minute or so before their eyes fell on a pair of uncropped ears. Finally Homer rode over to the Cattleman and reported the branding finished. The latter counted the marks in his tally-book.

"One hundred and seventy-six," he announced.

The markers, squatted on their heels, told over the bits of ears they had saved. The total amounted to but an hundred and seventy-five. Everybody went to searching for the missing bit. It was not forth-coming. Finally Wooden discovered it in his hip pocket.

"Felt her thar all the time," said he, "but thought it must shorely be a chaw of tobacco."

This matter satisfactorily adjusted, the men all ran for their ponies. They had been doing a wrestler's heavy work all the morning, but did not seem to be tired. I saw once in some crank physical culture periodical that a cowboy's life was physically ill-balanced, like an oarsman's, in that it exercised only certain muscles of the body. The writer should be turned loose in a branding corral.

Through the wide gates the cattle were urged out to the open plain. There they were held for over an hour while the cows wandered about looking for their lost progeny. A cow knows her calf by scent and sound, not by sight. Therefore the noise was deafening, and the motion incessant.

Finally the last and most foolish cow found the last and most foolish calf. We turned the herd loose to hunt water and grass at its own pleasure, and went slowly back to chuck.

For the benefit of the squeamish it might be well to note that the fragments of the ears were cartilaginous, and therefore not bloody.

About a week later, in the course of the round-up, we reached the valley of the Box Springs, where we camped for some days at the dilapidated and abandoned adobe structure that had once been a ranch house of some importance.

Just at dusk one afternoon we finished cutting the herd which our morning's drive had collected. The stray-herd, with its new additions from the day's work, we pushed rapidly into one big stock corral. The cows and unbranded calves we urged into another. Fifty head of beef steers found asylum from dust, heat, and racing to and fro, in the mile square wire enclosure called the pasture. All the remainder, for which we had no further use we drove out of the flat into the brush and toward the distant mountains. Then we let them go as best pleased them.

By now the desert bad turned slate-coloured, and the brush was olive green with evening. The hard, uncompromising ranges, twenty miles to eastward, had softened behind a wonderful veil of purple and pink, vivid as the chiffon of a girl's gown. To the south and southwest the Chiricahuas and Dragoons were lost in thunderclouds which flashed and rumbled.

We jogged homewards, our cutting ponies, tired with the quick, sharp work, shuffling knee deep in a dusk that seemed to disengage itself and rise upwards from the surface of the desert. Everybody was hungry and tired. At the chuck wagon we threw off our saddles and turned the mounts into the remuda. Some of the wisest of us, remembering the thunderclouds, stacked our gear under the veranda roof of the old ranch house.

Supper was ready. We seized the tin battery, filled the plates with the meat, bread, and canned corn, and squatted on our heels. The food was good, and we ate hugely in silence. When we could hold no more we lit pipes. Then we had leisure to notice that the storm cloud was mounting in a portentous silence to the zenith, quenching the brilliant desert stars.

"Rolls" were scattered everywhere. A roll includes a cowboy's bed and all of his personal belongings. When the outfit includes a bed-wagon, the roll assumes bulky proportions.

As soon as we had come to a definite conclusion that it was going to rain, we deserted the camp fire and went rustling for our blankets. At the end of ten minutes every bed was safe within the doors of the abandoned adobe ranch house, each owner recumbent on the floor claim he had pre-empted, and every man hoping fervently that he had guessed right as to the location of leaks.

Ordinarily we had depended on the light of camp fires, so now artificial illumination lacked. Each man was indicated by the alternately glowing and waning lozenge of his cigarette fire. Occasionally someone struck a match, revealing for a moment high-lights on bronzed countenances, and the silhouette of a shading hand. Voices spoke disembodied. As the conversation developed, we gradually recognised the membership of our own roomful. I had forgotten to state that the ranch house included four chambers. Outside, the rain roared with Arizona ferocity. Inside, men congratulated themselves, or swore as leaks developed and localised.

Naturally we talked first of stampedes. Cows and bears are the two great cattle-country topics. Then we had a mouth-organ solo or two, which naturally led on to songs. My turn came. I struck up the first verse of a sailor chantey as possessing at least the interest of novelty:

Oh, once we were a-sailing, a-sailing were we,
Blow high, blow low, what care we;
And we were a-sailing to see what we could see,
Down on the coast of the High Barbaree.

I had just gone so far when I was brought up short by a tremendous oath behind me. At the same instant a match flared. I turned to face a stranger holding the little light above his head, and peering with fiery intentness over the group sprawled about the floor.

He was evidently just in from the storm. His dripping hat lay at his feet. A shock of straight, close-clipped vigorous hair stood up grey above his seamed forehead. Bushy iron-grey eyebrows drawn close together thatched a pair of burning, unquenchable eyes. A square, deep jaw, lightly stubbled with grey, was clamped so tight that the cheek muscles above it stood out in knots and welts.

Then the match burned his thick, square fingers, and he dropped it into the darkness that ascended to swallow it.

"Who was singing that song?" he cried harshly. Nobody answered.

"Who was that singing?" he demanded again.

By this time I had recovered from my first astonishment.

"I was singing," said I.

Another match was instantly lit and thrust into my very face. I underwent the fierce scrutiny of an instant, then the taper was thrown away half consumed.

"Where did you learn it?" the stranger asked in an altered voice.

"I don't remember," I replied; "it is a common enough deep-sea chantey."

A heavy pause fell. Finally the stranger sighed.

"Quite like," he said; "I never heard but one man sing it."

"Who in hell are you?" someone demanded out of the darkness.

Before replying, the newcomer lit a third match, searching for a place to sit down. As he bent forward, his strong, harsh face once more came clearly into view.

"He's Colorado Rogers," the Cattleman answered for him; "I know him."

"Well," insisted the first voice, "what in hell does Colorado Rogers mean by bustin' in on our song fiesta that way?"

"Tell them, Rogers," advised the Cattleman, "tell them—just as you told it down on the Gila ten years ago next month."

"What?" inquired Rogers. "Who are you?"

"You don't know me," replied the Cattleman, "but I was with Buck Johnson's outfit then. Give us the yarn."

"Well," agreed Rogers, "pass over the 'makings' and I will."

He rolled and lit a cigarette, while I revelled in the memory of his rich, great voice. It was of the sort made to declaim against the sea or the rush of rivers or, as here, the fall of waters and the thunder—full, from the chest, with the caressing throat vibration that gives colour to the most ordinary statements. After ten words we sank back oblivious of the storm, forgetful of the leaky roof and the dirty floor, lost in the story told us by the Old Timer.

CHAPTER TEN
THE TEXAS RANGERS

I came from Texas, like the bulk of you punchers, but a good while before the most of you were born. That was forty-odd years ago—and I've been on the Colorado River ever since. That's why they call me Colorado Rogers. About a dozen of us came out together. We had all been Texas Rangers, but when the war broke out we were out of a job. We none of us cared much for the Johnny Rebs, and still less for the Yanks, so we struck overland for the West, with the idea of hitting the California diggings.

Well, we got switched off one way and another. When we got down to about where Douglas is now, we found that the Mexican Government was offering a bounty for Apache scalps. That looked pretty good to us, for Injin chasing was our job, so we started in to collect. Did pretty well, too, for about three months, and then the Injins began to get too scarce, or too plenty in streaks. Looked like our job was over with, but some of the boys discovered that Mexicans, having straight black hair, you couldn't tell one of their scalps from an Apache's. After that the bounty business picked up for a while. It was too much for me, though, and I quit the outfit and pushed on alone until I struck the Colorado about where Yuma is now.

At that time the California immigrants by the southern route used to cross just there, and these Yuma Injins had a monopoly on the ferry business. They were a peaceful, fine-looking lot, without a thing on but a gee-string. The women had belts with rawhide strings hanging to the knees. They put them on one over the other until they didn't feel too decollotey. It wasn't until the soldiers came that the officers' wives got them to wear handkerchiefs over their breasts. The system was all right, though. They wallowed around in the hot, clean sand, like chickens, and kept healthy. Since they took to wearing clothes they've been petering out, and dying of dirt and assorted diseases.

They ran this ferry monopoly by means of boats made of tules, charged a scand'lous low price, and everything was happy and lovely. I ran on a little bar and panned out some dust, so I camped a while, washing gold, getting friendly with the Yumas, and talking horse and other things with the immigrants.

About a month of this, and the Texas boys drifted in. Seems they sort of overdid the scalp matter, and got found out. When they saw me, they stopped and went into camp. They'd travelled a heap of desert, and were getting sick of it. For a while they tried gold washing, but I had the only pocket—and that was about skinned. One evening a fellow named Walleye announced that he had been doing some figuring, and wanted to make a speech. We told him to fire ahead.

"Now look here," said he, "what's the use of going to California? Why not stay here?"

"What in hell would we do here?" someone asked. "Collect Gila monsters for their good looks?"

"Don't get gay," said Walleye. "What's the matter with going into business? Here's a heap of people going through, and more coming every day. This ferry business could be made to pay big. Them Injins charges two bits a head. That's a crime for the only way across. And how much do you suppose whisky'd be worth to drink after that desert? And a man's so sick of himself by the time he gets this far that he'd play chuck-a-luck, let alone faro or monte."

That kind of talk hit them where they lived, and Yuma was founded right then and there. They hadn't any whisky yet, but cards were plenty, and the ferry monopoly was too easy. Walleye served notice on the Injins that a dollar a head went; and we all set to building a tule raft like the others. Then the wild bunch got uneasy, so they walked upstream one morning and stole the Injins' boats. The Injins came after them innocent as babies, thinking the raft had gone adrift. When they got into camp our men opened up and killed four of them as a kind of hint. After that the ferry company didn't have any trouble. The Yumas moved up river a ways, where they've lived ever since. They got the corpses and buried them. That is, they dug a trench for each one and laid poles across it, with a funeral pyre on the poles. Then they put the body on top, and the women of the family cut their hair off and threw it on. After that they set fire to the outfit, and, when the poles bad burned through, the whole business fell into the trench of its own accord. It was the neatest, automatic, self-cocking, double-action sort of a funeral I ever saw. There wasn't any ceremony—only crying.

The ferry business flourished at prices which were sometimes hard to collect. But it was a case of pay or go back, and it was a tur'ble long ways back. We got us timbers and made a scow; built a baile and saloon and houses out of adobe; and called her Yuma, after the Injins that had really started her. We got our supplies through the Gulf of California, where sailing boats worked up the river. People began to come in for one reason or another, and first thing we knew we had a store and all sorts of trimmings. In fact we was a real live town.

## CHAPTER ELEVEN
## THE SAILOR WITH ONE HAND

At this moment the heavy beat of the storm on the roof ceased with miraculous suddenness, leaving the outside world empty of sound save for the DRIP, DRIP, DRIP of eaves. Nobody ventured to fill in the pause that followed the stranger's last words, so in a moment he continued his narrative.

We had every sort of people with us off and on, and, as I was lookout at a popular game, I saw them all. One evening I was on my way home about two o'clock of a moonlit night, when on the edge of the shadow I stumbled over a body lying part across the footway. At the same instant I heard the rip of steel through cloth and felt a sharp stab in my left leg. For a minute I thought some drunk had used his knife on me, and I mighty near derringered him as he lay. But somehow I didn't, and looking closer, I saw the man was unconscious. Then I scouted to see what had cut me, and found that the fellow had lost a hand. In place of it he wore a sharp steel hook. This I had tangled up with and gotten well pricked.

I dragged him out into the light. He was a slim-built young fellow, with straight black hair, long and lank and oily, a lean face, and big hooked nose. He had on only a thin shirt, a pair of rough wool pants, and the rawhide home-made zapatos the Mexicans wore then instead of boots. Across his forehead ran a long gash, cutting his left eyebrow square in two.

There was no doubt of his being alive, for he was breathing hard, like a man does when he gets hit over the head. It didn't sound good. When a man breathes that way he's mostly all gone.

Well, it was really none of my business, as you might say. Men got batted over the head often enough in those days. But for some reason I picked him up and carried him to my 'dobe shack, and laid him out, and washed his cut with sour wine. That brought him to. Sour wine is fine to put a wound in shape to heal, but it's no soothing syrup. He sat up as though he'd been touched with a hot poker, stared around wild-eyed, and cut loose with that song you were singing. Only it wasn't that verse. It was another one further along, that went like this:

Their coffin was their ship, and their grave it was the sea,
Blow high, blow low, what care we;
And the quarter that we gave them was to sink them in the sea,
Down on the coast of the High Barbaree.

It fair made my hair rise to hear him, with the big, still, solemn desert outside, and the quiet moonlight, and the shadows, and him sitting up straight and gaunt, his eyes blazing each side his big eagle nose, and his snaky hair hanging over the raw cut across his head. However, I made out to get him bandaged up and in shape; and pretty soon he sort of went to sleep.

Well, he was clean out of his head for nigh two weeks. Most of the time he lay flat on his back staring at the pole roof, his eyes burning and looking like they saw each one something a different distance off, the way crazy eyes do. That was when he was best. Then again he'd sing that Barbaree song until I'd go out and look at the old Colorado flowing by just to be sure I hadn't died and gone below. Or else he'd just talk. That was the worst performance of all. It was like listening to one end of a telephone, though we didn't know what telephones were in those days. He began when he was a kid, and he gave his side of conversations, pausing for replies. I could mighty near furnish the replies sometimes. It was queer lingo—about ships and ships' officers and gales and calms and fights and pearls and whales and islands and birds and skies. But it was all little stuff. I used to listen by the hour, but I never made out anything really important as to who the man was, or where he'd come from, or what he'd done.

At the end of the second week I came in at noon as per usual to fix him up with grub. I didn't pay any attention to him, for he was quiet. As I was bending over the fire he spoke. Usually I didn't bother with his talk, for it didn't mean anything, but something in his voice made me turn. He was lying on his side, those black eyes of his blazing at me, but now both of them saw the same distance.

"Where are my clothes?" he asked, very intense.

"You ain't in any shape to want clothes," said I. "Lie still."

I hadn't any more than got the words out of my mouth before he was atop me. His method was a winner. He had me by the throat with his hand, and I felt the point of the hook pricking the back of my neck. One little squeeze—Talk about your deadly weapons!

But he'd been too sick and too long abed. He turned dizzy and keeled over, and I dumped him back on the bunk. Then I put my six-shooter on.

**83**

In a minute or so he came to.

"Now you're a nice, sweet proposition," said I, as soon as I was sure he could understand me. "Here I pick you up on the street and save your worthless carcass, and the first chance you get you try to crawl my hump. Explain."

"Where's my clothes?" he demanded again, very fierce.

"For heaven's sake," I yelled at him, "what's the matter with you and your old clothes? There ain't enough of them to dust a fiddle with anyway. What do you think I'd want with them? They're safe enough.'"

"Let me have them," he begged.

"Now, look here," said I, "you can't get up to-day. You ain't fit."

"I know," he pleaded, "but let me see them."

Just to satisfy him I passed over his old duds.

"I've been robbed," he cried.

"Well," said I, "what did you expect would happen to you lying around Yuma after midnight with a hole in your head?"

"Where's my coat?" he asked.

"You had no coat when I picked you up," I replied.

He looked at me mighty suspicious, but didn't say anything more—he wouldn't even answer when I spoke to him. After he'd eaten a fair meal he fell asleep. When I came back that evening the bunk was empty and he was gone.

I didn't see him again for two days. Then I caught sight of him quite a ways off. He nodded at me very sour, and dodged around the corner of the store.

"Guess he suspicions I stole that old coat of his," thinks I; and afterwards I found that my surmise had been correct.

However, he didn't stay long in that frame of mind. It was along towards evening, and I was walking on the banks looking down over the muddy old Colorado, as I always liked to do. The sun had just set, and the mountains had turned hard and stiff, as they do after the glow, and the sky above them was a thousand million miles deep of pale green-gold light. A pair of Greasers were ahead of me, but I could see only their outlines, and they didn't seem to interfere any with the scenery. Suddenly a black figure seemed to rise up out of the ground; the Mexican man went down as though he'd been jerked with a string, and the woman screeched.

I ran up, pulling my gun. The Mex was flat on his face, his arms stretched out. On the middle of his back knelt my one-armed friend. And that sharp hook was caught neatly under the point of the Mexican's jaw. You bet he lay still.

I really think I was just in time to save the man's life. According to my belief another minute would have buried the hook in the Mexican's neck. Anyway, I thrust the muzzle of my Colt's into the sailor's face.

"What's this?" I asked.

The sailor looked up at me without changing his position. He was not the least bit afraid.

"This man has my coat," he explained.

"Where'd you get the coat?" I asked the Mex.

"I ween heem at monte off Antonio Curvez," said he.

"Maybe," growled the sailor.

He still held the hook under the man's jaw, but with the other hand he ran rapidly under and over the Mexican's left shoulder. In the half light I could see his face change. The gleam died from his eye; the snarl left his lips. Without further delay he arose to his feet.

"Get up and give it here!" he demanded.

The Mexican was only too glad to get off so easy. I don't know whether he'd really won the coat at monte or not. In any case, he flew poco pronto, leaving me and my friend together.

The man with the hook felt the left shoulder of the coat again, looked up, met my eye, muttered something intended to be pleasant, and walked away.

This was in December.

During the next two months he was a good deal about town, mostly doing odd jobs. I saw him off and on. He always spoke to me as pleasantly as he knew how, and once made some sort of a bluff about paying me back for my trouble in bringing him around. However, I didn't pay much attention to that, being at the time almighty busy holding down my card games.

The last day of February I was sitting in my shack smoking a pipe after supper, when my one-armed friend opened the door a foot, slipped in, and shut it immediately. By the time he looked towards me I knew where my six-shooter was.

"That's all right," said I, "but you better stay right there."

I intended to take no more chances with that hook.

He stood there looking straight at me without winking or offering to move.

"What do you want?" I asked.

"I want to make up to you for your trouble," said he. "I've got a good thing, and I want to let you in on it."

"What kind of a good thing?" I asked.

"Treasure," said he.

"H'm," said I.

I examined him closely. He looked all right enough, neither drunk nor loco.

"Sit down," said I—"over there; the other side the table." He did so. "Now, fire away," said I.

He told me his name was Solomon Anderson, but that he was generally known as Handy Solomon, on account of his hook; that he had always followed the sea; that lately he had coasted the west shores of Mexico; that at Guaymas he had

84

fallen in with Spanish friends, in company with whom he had visited the mines in the Sierra Madre; that on this expedition the party had been attacked by Yaquis and wiped out, he alone surviving; that his blanket-mate before expiring had told him of gold buried in a cove of Lower California by the man's grandfather; that the man had given him a chart showing the location of the treasure; that he had sewn this chart in the shoulder of his coat, whence his suspicion of me and his being so loco about getting it back.

"And it's a big thing," said Handy Solomon to me, "for they's not only gold, but altar jewels and diamonds. It will make us rich, and a dozen like us, and you can kiss the Book on that."

"That may all be true," said I, "but why do you tell me? Why don't you get your treasure without the need of dividing it?"

"Why, mate," he answered, "it's just plain gratitude. Didn't you save my life, and nuss me, and take care of me when I was nigh killed?"

"Look here, Anderson, or Handy Solomon, or whatever you please to call yourself," I rejoined to this, "if you're going to do business with me—and I do not understand yet just what it is you want of me—you'll have to talk straight. It's all very well to say gratitude, but that don't go with me. You've been around here three months, and barring a half-dozen civil words and twice as many of the other kind, I've failed to see any indications of your gratitude before. It's a quality with a hell of a hang-fire to it."

He looked at me sideways, spat, and looked at me sideways again. Then he burst into a laugh.

"The devil's a preacher, if you ain't lost your pinfeathers,'" said he. "Well, it's this then: I got to have a boat to get there; and she must be stocked. And I got to have help with the treasure, if it's like this fellow said it was. And the Yaquis and cannibals from Tiburon is through the country. It's money I got to have, and it's money I haven't got, and can't get unless I let somebody in as pardner."

"Why me?" I asked.

"Why not?" he retorted. "I ain't see anybody I like better."

We talked the matter over at length. I had to force him to each point, for suspicion was strong in him. I stood out for a larger party. He strongly opposed this as depreciating the shares, but I had no intention of going alone into what was then considered a wild and dangerous country. Finally we compromised. A third of the treasure was to go to him, a third to me, and the rest was to be divided among the men whom I should select. This scheme did not appeal to him.

"How do I know you plays fair?" he complained. "They'll be four of you to one of me; and I don't like it, and you can kiss the Book on that."

"If you don't like it, leave it," said I, "and get out, and be damned to you."

Finally he agreed; but he refused me a look at the chart, saying that he had left it in a safe place. I believe in reality he wanted to be surer of me, and for that I can hardly blame him.

## CHAPTER TWELVE
## THE MURDER ON THE BEACH

At this moment the cook stuck his head in at the open door.

"Say, you fellows," he complained, "I got to be up at three o'clock. Ain't you never going to turn in?"

"Shut up, Doctor!" "Somebody kill him!" "Here, sit down and listen to this yarn!" yelled a savage chorus.

There ensued a slight scuffle, a few objections. Then silence, and the stranger took up his story.

I had a chum named Billy Simpson, and I rung him in for friendship. Then there was a solemn, tall Texas young fellow, strong as a bull, straight and tough, brought up fighting Injins. He never said much, but I knew he'd be right there when the gong struck. For fourth man I picked out a German named Schwartz. He and Simpson had just come back from the mines together. I took him because he was a friend of Billy's, and besides was young and strong, and was the only man in town excepting the sailor, Anderson, who knew anything about running a boat. I forgot to say that the Texas fellow was named Denton.

Handy Solomon had his boat all picked out. It belonged to some Basques who had sailed her around from California. I must say when I saw her I felt inclined to renig, for she wasn't more'n about twenty-five feet long, was open except for a little sort of cubbyhole up in the front of her, had one mast, and was pointed at both ends. However, Schwartz said she was all right. He claimed he knew the kind; that she was the sort used by French fishermen, and could stand all sorts of trouble. She didn't look it.

We worked her up to Yuma, partly with oars and partly by sails. Then we loaded her with grub for a month. Each of us had his own weapons, of course. In addition we put in picks and shovels, and a small cask of water. Handy Solomon said that would be enough, as there was water marked down on his chart. We told the gang that we were going trading.

At the end of the week we started, and were out four days. There wasn't much room, what with the supplies and the baggage, for the five of us. We had to curl up 'most anywheres to sleep. And it certainly seemed to me that we were in lots of danger. The waves were much bigger than she was, and splashed on us considerable, but Schwartz and Anderson didn't seem to mind. They laughed at us. Anderson sang that song of his, and Schwartz told us of the placers he had worked. He and Simpson had made a pretty good clean-up, just enough to make them want to get rich. The first day out Simpson showed us a belt with about an hundred ounces of dust. This he got tired of wearing, so he kept it in a compass-box, which was empty.

At the end of the four days we turned in at a deep bay and came to anchor. The country was the usual proposition—very light-brown, brittle-looking mountains, about two thousand feet high; lots of sage and cactus, a pebbly beach, and not a sign of anything fresh and green.

But Denton and I were mighty glad to see any sort of land. Besides, our keg of water was pretty low, and it was getting about time to discover the spring the chart spoke of. So we piled our camp stuff in the small boat and rowed ashore.

Anderson led the way confidently enough up a dry arroyo, whose sides were clay and conglomerate. But, though we followed it to the end, we could find no indications that it was anything more than a wash for rain floods.

"That's main queer," muttered Anderson, and returned to the beach.

There he spread out the chart—the first look at it we'd had—and set to studying it.

It was a careful piece of work done in India ink, pretty old, to judge by the look of it, and with all sorts of pictures of mountains and dolphins and ships and anchors around the edge. There was our bay, all right. Two crosses were marked on the land part—one labelled "oro" and the other "agua."

"Now there's the high cliff," says Anderson, following it out, "and there's the round hill with the boulder—and if them bearings don't point due for that ravine, the devil's a preacher."

We tried it again, with the same result. A second inspection of the map brought us no light on the question. We talked it over, and looked at it from all points, but we couldn't dodge the truth: the chart was wrong.

Then we explored several of the nearest gullies, but without finding anything but loose stones baked hot in the sun.

By now it was getting towards sundown, so we built us a fire of mesquite on the beach, made us supper, and boiled a pot of beans.

We talked it over. The water was about gone.

"That's what we've got to find first," said Simpson, "no question of it. It's God knows how far to the next water, and we don't know how long it will take us to get there in that little boat. If we run our water entirely out before we start, we're going to be in trouble. We'll have a good look to-morrow, and if we don't find her, we'll run down to Mollyhay and get a few extra casks."

"Perhaps that map is wrong about the treasure, too," suggested Denton.

"I thought of that," said Handy Solomon, "but then, thinks I to myself, this old rip probably don't make no long stay here—just dodges in and out like, between tides, to bury his loot. He would need no water at the time; but he might when he came back, so he marked the water on his map. But he wasn't noways particular AND exact, being in a hurry. But you can kiss the Book to it that he didn't make no such mistakes about the swag."

"I believe you're right," said I.

When we came to turn in, Anderson suggested that he should sleep aboard the boat. But Billy Simpson, in mind perhaps of the hundred ounces in the compass-box, insisted that he'd just as soon as not. After a little objection Handy Solomon gave in, but I thought he seemed sour about it. We built a good fire, and in about ten seconds were asleep.

Now, usually I sleep like a log, and did this time until about midnight. Then all at once I came broad awake and sitting up in my blankets. Nothing had happened—I wasn't even dreaming—but there I was as alert and clear as though it were broad noon.

By the light of the fire I saw Handy Solomon sitting, and at his side our five rifles gathered.

I must have made some noise, for he turned quietly toward me, saw I was awake, and nodded. The moonlight was sparkling on the hard stony landscape, and a thin dampness came out from the sea.

After a minute Anderson threw on another stick of wood, yawned, and stood up.

"It's wet," said he; "I've been fixing the guns."

He showed me how he was inserting a little patch of felt between the hammer and the nipple, a scheme of his own for keeping damp from the powder. Then he rolled up in his blanket. At the time it all seemed quite natural—I suppose my mind wasn't fully awake, for all my head felt so clear. Afterwards I realised what a ridiculous bluff he was making: for of course the cap already on the nipple was plenty to keep out the damp. I fully believe he intended to kill us as we lay. Only my sudden awakening spoiled his plan.

I had absolutely no idea of this at the time, however. Not the slightest suspicion entered my head. In view of that fact, I have since believed in guardian angels. For my next move, which at the time seemed to me absolutely aimless, was to change my blankets from one side of the fire to the other. And that brought me alongside the five rifles.

Owing to this fact, I am now convinced, we awoke safe at daylight, cooked breakfast, and laid the plan for the day. Anderson directed us. I was to climb over the ridge before us and search in the ravine on the other side. Schwartz was to explore up the beach to the left, and Denton to the right. Anderson said he would wait for Billy Simpson, who had overslept in the darkness of the cubbyhole, and who was now paddling ashore. The two of them would push inland to the west until a high hill would give them a chance to look around for greenery.

We started at once, before the sun would be hot. The hill I had to climb was steep and covered with chollas, so I didn't get along very fast. When I was about half way to the top I heard a shot from the beach. I looked back. Anderson was in the small boat, rowing rapidly out to the vessel. Denton was running up the beach from one direction and Schwartz from the other. I slid and slipped down the bluff, getting pretty well stuck up with the cholla spines.

At the beach we found Billy Simpson lying on his ace, shot through the back. We turned him over, but he was apparently dead. Anderson had hoisted the sail, had cut loose from the anchor, and was sailing away.

Denton stood up straight and tall, looking. Then he pulled his belt in a hole, grabbed my arm, and started to run up the long curve of the beach. Behind us came Schwartz. We ran near a mile, and then fell among some tules in an inlet at the farther point.

"What is it?" I gasped.

"Our only chance—to get him—" said Denton. "He's got to go around this point—big wind—perhaps his mast will bust—then he'll come ashore—" He opened and shut his big brown hands.

So there we two fools lay, like panthers in the tules, taking our only one-in-a-million chance to lay hands on Anderson. Any sailor could have told us that the mast wouldn't break, but we had winded Schwartz a quarter of a mile back. And so we waited, our eyes fixed on the boat's sail, grudging her every inch, just burning to fix things to suit us a little better. And naturally she made the point in what I now know was only a fresh breeze, squared away, and dropped down before the wind toward Guaymas.

We walked back slowly to our camp, swallowing the copper taste of too hard a run. Schwartz we picked up from a boulder, just recovering. We were all of us crazy mad. Schwartz half wept, and blamed and cussed. Denton glowered away in silence. I ground my feet into the sand in a help less sort of anger, not only at the man himself, but also at the whole way things had turned out. I don't believe the least notion of our predicament had come to any of us. All we knew yet was that we had been done up, and we were hostile about it.

But at camp we found something to occupy us for the moment. Poor Billy was not dead, as we had supposed, but very weak and sick, and a hole square through him. When we returned he was conscious, but that was about all. His eyes were shut, and he was moaning. I tore open his shirt to stanch the blood. He felt my hand and opened his eyes. They were glazed, and I don't think he saw me.

"Water, water!" he cried.

At that we others saw all at once where we stood. I remember I rose to my feet and found myself staring straight into Tom Denton's eyes. We looked at each other that way for I guess it was a full minute. Then Tom shook his head.

"Water, water!" begged poor Billy.

Tom leaned over him.

"My God, Billy, there ain't any water!" said he.

Mulege—I retain the Old Timer's pronunciation.

CHAPTER THIRTEEN
BURIED TREASURE

The Old Timer's voice broke a little. We had leisure to notice that even the drip from the eaves had ceased. A faint, diffused light vouchsafed us dim outlines of sprawling figures and tumbled bedding. Far in the distance outside a wolf yelped.

We could do nothing for him except shelter him from the sun, and wet his forehead with sea-water; nor could we think clearly for ourselves as long as the spark of life lingered in him. His chest rose and fell regularly, but with long pauses between. When the sun was overhead he suddenly opened his eyes.

"Fellows," said he, "it's beautiful over there; the grass is so green, and the water so cool; I am tired of marching, and I reckon I'll cross over and camp."

Then he died. We scooped out a shallow hole above tide-mark, and laid him in it, and piled over him stones from the wash.

Then we went back to the beach, very solemn, to talk it over.

"Now, boys," said I, "there seems to me just one thing to do, and that is to pike out for water as fast as we can."

"Where?" asked Denton.

"Well," I argued, "I don't believe there's any water about this bay. Maybe there was when that chart was made. It was a long time ago. And any way, the old pirate was a sailor, and no plainsman, and maybe he mistook rainwater for a spring. We've looked around this end of the bay. The chances are we'd use up two or three days exploring around the other, and then wouldn't be as well off as we are right now."

"Which way?" asked Denton again, mighty brief.

"Well," said I, "there's one thing I've always noticed in case of folks held up by the desert: they generally go wandering about here and there looking for water until they die not far from where they got lost. And usually they've covered a heap of actual distance."

"That's so," agreed Denton.

"Now, I've always figured that it would be a good deal better to start right out for some particular place, even if it's ten thousand miles away. A man is just as likely to strike water going in a straight line as he is going in a circle; and then, besides, he's getting somewhere."

"Correct," said Denton,

"So," I finished, "I reckon we'd better follow the coast south and try to get to Mollyhay."

"How far is that?" asked Schwartz.

"I don't rightly know. But somewheres between three and five hundred miles, at a guess."

At that he fell to glowering and grooming with himself, brooding over what a hard time it was going to be. That is the way with a German. First off he's plumb scared at the prospect of suffering anything, and would rather die right off than take long chances. After he gets into the swing of it, he behaves as well as any man.

We took stock of what we had to depend on. The total assets proved to be just three pairs of legs. A pot of coffee had been on the fire, but that villain had kicked it over when he left. The kettle of beans was there, but somehow we got the notion they might have been poisoned, so we left them. I don't know now why we were so foolish—if poison was his game, he'd have tried it before—but at that time it seemed reasonable enough. Perhaps the horror of the morning's work, and the sight of the brittle-brown mountains, and the ghastly yellow glare of the sun, and the blue waves racing by outside, and the big strong wind that blew through us so hard that it seemed to blow empty our souls, had turned our judgment. Anyway, we left a full meal there in the beanpot.

So without any further delay we set off up the ridge I had started to cross that morning. Schwartz lagged, sulky as a muley cow, but we managed to keep him with us. At the top of the ridge we took our bearings for the next deep bay. Already we had made up our minds to stick to the sea-coast, both on account of the lower country over which to travel and the off chance of falling in with a fishing vessel. Schwartz muttered something about its being too far even to the next bay, and wanted to sit down on a rock. Denton didn't say anything, but he jerked Schwartz up by the collar so fiercely that the German gave it over and came along.

We dropped down into the gully, stumbled over the boulder wash, and began to toil in the ankle-deep sand of a little sage-brush flat this side of the next ascent. Schwartz followed steadily enough now, but had fallen forty or fifty feet behind. This was a nuisance, as we bad to keep turning to see if he still kept up.

Suddenly he seemed to disappear.

Denton and I hurried back to find him on his hands and knees behind a sagebrush, clawing away at the sand like mad.

"Can't be water on this flat," said Denton; "he must have gone crazy."

"What's the matter, Schwartz?" I asked.

For answer he moved a little to one side, showing beneath his knee one corner of a wooden box sticking above the sand.

At this we dropped beside him, and in five minutes had uncovered the whole of the chest. It was not very large, and was locked. A rock from the wash fixed that, however. We threw back the lid.

It was full to the brim of gold coins, thrown in loose, nigh two bushels of them.

"The treasure!" I cried.

There it was, sure enough, or some of it. We looked the rest through, but found nothing but the gold coins. The altar ornaments and jewels were lacking.

"Probably buried in another box or so," said Denton.

Schwartz wanted to dig around a little.

"No good," said I. "We've got our work cut out for us as it is."

Denton backed me up. We were both old hands at the business, had each in our time suffered the "cotton-mouth" thirst, and the memory of it outweighed any desire for treasure.

But Schwartz was money-mad. Left to himself he would have staid on that sand flat to perish, as certainly as had poor Billy. We had fairly to force him away, and then succeeded only because we let him fill all his pockets to bulging with the coins. As we moved up the next rise, he kept looking back and uttering little moans against the crime of leaving it.

Luckily for us it was winter. We shouldn't have lasted six hours at this time of year. As it was, the sun was hot against the shale and the little stones of those cussed hills. We plodded along until late afternoon, toiling up one hill and down another, only to repeat immediately. Towards sundown we made the second bay, where we plunged into the sea, clothes and all, and were greatly refreshed. I suppose a man absorbs a good deal that way. Anyhow, it always seemed to help.

We were now pretty hungry, and, as we walked along the shore, we began to look for turtles or shellfish, or anything else that might come handy. There was nothing. Schwartz wanted to stop for a night's rest, but Denton and I knew better than that.

"Look here, Schwartz," said Denton, "you don't realise you're entered against time in this race—and that you're a damn fool to carry all that weight in your clothes."

So we dragged along all night.

It was weird enough, I can tell you. The moon shone cold and white over that dead, dry country. Hot whiffs rose from the baked stones and hillsides. Shadows lay under the stones like animals crouching. When we came to the edge of a silvery hill we dropped off into pitchy blackness. There we stumbled over boulders for a minute or so, and began to climb the steep shale on the other side. This was fearful work. The top seemed always miles away. By morning we didn't seem to have made much of anywhere. The same old hollow-looking mountains with the sharp edges stuck up in about the same old places.

We had got over being very hungry, and, though we were pretty dry, we didn't really suffer yet from thirst. About this time Denton ran across some fishhook cactus, which we cut up and chewed. They have a sticky wet sort of inside, which doesn't quench your thirst any, but helps to keep you from drying up and blowing away.

All that day we plugged along as per usual. It was main hard work, and we got to that state where things are disagreeable, but mechanical. Strange to say, Schwartz kept in the lead. It seemed to me at the time that he was using more energy than the occasion called for—just as man runs faster before he comes to the giving-out point. However, the hours went by, and he didn't seem to get any more tired than the rest of us.

We kept a sharp lookout for anything to eat, but there was nothing but lizards and horned toads. Later we'd have been glad of them, but by that time we'd got out of their district. Night came. Just at sundown we took another wallow in the surf, and chewed some more fishhook cactus. When the moon came up we went on.

I'm not going to tell you how dead beat we got. We were pretty tough and strong, for all of us had been used to hard living, but after the third day without anything to eat and no water to drink, it came to be pretty hard going. It got to the point where we had to have some REASON for getting out besides just keeping alive. A man would sometimes rather die than keep alive, anyway, if it came only to that. But I know I made up my mind I was going to get out so I could smash up that Anderson, and I reckon Denton had the same idea. Schwartz didn't say anything, but he pumped on ahead of us, his back bent over, and his clothes sagging and bulging with the gold he carried.

We used to travel all night, because it was cool, and rest an hour or two at noon. That is all the rest we did get. I don't know how fast we went; I'd got beyond that. We must have crawled along mighty slow, though, after our first strength gave out. The way I used to do was to collect myself with an effort, look around for my bearings, pick out a landmark a little distance off, and forget everything but it. Then I'd plod along, knowing nothing but the sand and shale and slope under my feet, until I'd reached that landmark. Then I'd clear my mind and pick out another.

But I couldn't shut out the figure of Schwartz that way. He used to walk along just ahead of my shoulder. His face was all twisted up, but I remember thinking at the time it looked more as if he was worried in his mind than like bodily suffering. The weight of the gold in his clothes bent his shoulders over.

As we went on the country gradually got to be more mountainous, and, as we were steadily growing weaker, it did seem things were piling up on us. The eighth day we ran out of the fishhook cactus, and, being on a high promontory, were out of touch with the sea. For the first time my tongue began to swell a little. The cactus had kept me from that before. Denton must have been in the same fix, for he looked at me and raised one eyebrow kind of humorous.

Schwartz was having a good deal of difficulty to navigate. I will say for him that he had done well, but now I could see that his strength was going on him in spite of himself. He knew it, all right, for when we rested that day he took all the gold coins and spread them in a row, and counted them, and put them back in his pocket, and then all of a sudden snatched out two handfuls and threw them as far as he could.

"Too heavy," he muttered, but that was all he could bring himself to throw away.

All that night we wandered high in the air. I guess we tried to keep a general direction, but I don't know. Anyway, along late, but before moonrise—she was now on the wane—I came to, and found myself looking over the edge of a twenty-foot drop. Right below me I made out a faint glimmer of white earth in the starlight. Somehow it reminded me of a little trail I used to know under a big rock back in Texas.

"Here's a trail," I thought, more than half loco; "I'll follow it!"

At least that's what half of me thought. The other half was sensible, and knew better, but it seemed to be kind of standing to one side, a little scornful, watching the performance. So I slid and slipped down to the strip of white earth, and, sure enough, it was a trail. At that the loco half of me gave the sensible part the laugh. I followed the path twenty feet and came to a dark hollow under the rock, and in it a round pool of water about a foot across. They say a man kills himself drinking too much, after starving for water. That may be, but it didn't kill me, and I sucked up all I could hold. Perhaps the fishhook cactus had helped. Well, sir, it was surprising how that drink brought me around. A minute before I'd been on the edge of going plumb loco, and here I was as clear-headed as a lawyer.

I hunted up Denton and Schwartz. They drank, themselves full, too. Then we rested. It was mighty hard to leave that spring—

Oh, we had to do it. We'd have starved sure, there. The trail was a game trail, but that did us no good, for we had no weapons.

How we did wish for the coffeepot, so we could take some away. We filled our hats, and carried them about three hours, before the water began to soak through. Then we had to drink it in order to save it.

The country fairly stood up on end. We had to climb separate little hills so as to avoid rolling rocks down on each other. It took it out of us. About this time we began to see mountain sheep. They would come right up to the edges of the small cliffs to look at us. We threw stones at them, hoping to hit one in the forehead, but of course without any results.

The good effects of the water lasted us about a day. Then we began to see things again. Off and on I could see water plain as could be in every hollow, and game of all kinds standing around and looking at me. I knew these were all fakes. By making an effort I could swing things around to where they belonged. I used to do that every once in a while, just to be sure we weren't doubling back, and to look out for real water. But most of the time it didn't seem to be worth while. I just let all these visions riot around and have a good time inside me or outside me, whichever it was. I knew I could get rid of them any minute. Most of the time, if I was in any doubt, it was easier to throw a stone to see if the animals were real or not. The real ones ran away.

We began to see bands of wild horses in the uplands. One day both Denton and I plainly saw one with saddle marks on him. If only one of us had seen him, it wouldn't have counted much, but we both made him out. This encouraged us wonderfully, though I don't see why it should have. We had topped the high country, too, and had started down the other side of the mountains that ran out on the promontory. Denton and I were still navigating without any thought of giving up, but Schwartz was getting in bad shape. I'd hate to pack twenty pounds over that country even with rest, food, and water. He was toting it on nothing. We told him so, and he came to see it, but he never could persuade himself to get rid of the gold all at once. Instead he threw away the pieces one by one. Each sacrifice seemed to nerve him up for another heat. I can shut my eyes and see it now—the wide, glaring, yellow country, the pasteboard mountains, we three dragging along, and the fierce sunshine flashing from the doubloons as one by one they went spinning through the air.

## CHAPTER FOURTEEN
## THE CHEWED SUGAR CANE

"I'd like to have trailed you fellows," sighed a voice from the corner.
"Would you!" said Colorado Rogers grimly.

It was five days to the next water. But they were worse than the eight days before. We were lucky, however, for at the spring we discovered in a deep wash near the coast, was the dried-up skull of a horse. It had been there a long time, but a few shreds of dried flesh still clung to it. It was the only thing that could be described as food that had passed our lips since breakfast thirteen days before. In that time we had crossed the mountain chain, and had come again to the sea. The Lord was good to us. He sent us the water, and the horse's skull, and the smooth hard beach, without breaks or the necessity of climbing hills. And we needed it, oh, I promise you, we needed it!

I doubt if any of us could have kept the direction except by such an obvious and continuous landmark as the sea to our left. It hardly seemed worth while to focus my mind, but I did it occasionally just by way of testing myself. Schwartz still threw away his gold coins, and once, in one of my rare intervals of looking about me, I saw Denton picking them up. This surprised me mildly, but I was too tired to be very curious. Only now, when I saw Schwartz's arm sweep out in what had become a mechanical movement, I always took pains to look, and always I saw Denton search for the coin. Sometimes he found it, and sometimes he did not.

The figures of my companions and the yellow-brown tide sand under my feet, and a consciousness of the blue and white sea to my left, are all I remember, except when we had to pull ourselves together for the purpose of cutting fishhook cactus. I kept going, and I knew I had a good reason for doing so, but it seemed too much of an effort to recall what that reason was.

Schwartz threw away a gold piece as another man would take a stimulant. Gradually, without really thinking about it, I came to see this, and then went on to sabe why Denton picked up the coins; and a great admiration for Denton's cleverness seeped through me like water through the sand. He was saving the coins to keep Schwartz going. When the last coin went, Schwartz would give out. It all sounds queer now, but it seemed all right then—and it WAS all right, too.

So we walked on the beach, losing entire track of time. And after a long interval I came to myself to see Schwartz lying on the sand, and Denton standing over him. Of course we'd all been falling down a lot, but always before we'd got up again.

"He's give out," croaked Denton.

His voice sounded as if it was miles away, which surprised me, but, when I answered, mine sounded miles away, too, which surprised me still more.

Denton pulled out a handful of gold coins.

"This will buy him some more walk," said he gravely, "but not much."

I nodded. It seemed all right, this new, strange purchasing power of gold—it WAS all right, by God, and as real as buying bricks—

"I'll go on," said Denton, "and send back help. You come after."

"To Mollyhay!" said I.

This far I reckon we'd hung onto ourselves because it was serious. Now I began to laugh. So did Denton. We laughed and laughed.

> "A damn long way
> To Mollyhay."

said I. Then we laughed some more, until the tears ran down our cheeks, and we had to hold our poor weak sides. Pretty soon we fetched up with a gasp.

> "A damn long way
> To Mollyhay,"

whispered Denton, and then off we went into more shrieks. And when we would sober down a little, one or the other of us would say it again:

> "A damn long way
> To Mollyhay,"

and then we'd laugh some more. It must have been a sweet sight!

At last I realised that we ought to pull ourselves together, so I snubbed up short, and Denton did the same, and we set to laying plans. But every minute or so one of us would catch on some word, and then we'd trail off into rhymes and laughter and repetition.

"Keep him going as long as you can," said Denton.

"Yes."

"And be sure to stick to the beach."

That far it was all right and clear-headed. But the word "beach" let us out.

> "I'm a peach
> Upon the beach,"

sings I, and there we were both off again until one or the other managed to grope his way back to common sense again. And sometimes we crow-hopped solemnly around and around the prostrate Schwartz like a pair of Injins.

But somehow we got our plan laid at last, slipped the coins into Schwartz's pocket, and said good-bye.

"Old socks, good-bye, You bet I'll try,"

yelled Denton, and laughing fit to kill, danced off up the beach, and out into a sort of grey mist that shut off everything beyond a certain distance from me now.

So I kicked Schwartz, he felt in his pocket, threw a gold piece away, and "bought a little more walk."

My entire vision was fifty feet or so across. Beyond that was grey mist. Inside my circle I could see the sand quite plainly and Denton's footprints. If I moved a little to the left, the wash of the waters would lap under the edge of that grey curtain.

If I moved to the right, I came to cliffs. The nearer I drew to them, the farther up I could see, but I could never see to the top. It used to amuse me to move this area of consciousness about to see what I could find. Actual physical suffering was beginning to dull, and my head seemed to be getting clearer.

One day, without any apparent reason, I moved at right angles across the beach. Directly before me lay a piece of sugar cane, and one end of it had been chewed.

Do you know what that meant? Animals don't cut sugar cane and bring it to the beach and chew one end. A new strength ran through me, and actually the grey mist thinned and lifted for a moment, until I could make out dimly the line of cliffs and the tumbling sea.

I was not a bit hungry, but I chewed on the sugar cane, and made Schwartz do the same. When we went on I kept close to the cliff, even though the walking was somewhat heavier.

I remember after that its getting dark and then light again, so the night must have passed, but whether we rested or walked I do not know. Probably we did not get very far, though certainly we staggered ahead after sun-up, for I remember my shadow.

About midday, I suppose, I made out a dim trail leading up a break in the cliffs. Plenty of such trails we had seen before. They were generally made by peccaries in search of cast-up fish—I hope they had better luck than we.

But in the middle of this, as though for a sign, lay another piece of chewed sugar cane.

CHAPTER FIFTEEN
THE CALABASH STEW

I had agreed with Denton to stick to the beach, but Schwartz could not last much longer, and I had not the slightest idea how far it might prove to be to Mollyhay. So I turned up the trail.

We climbed a mountain ten thousand feet high. I mean that; and I know, for I've climbed them that high, and I know just how it feels, and how many times you have to rest, and how long it takes, and how much it knocks out of you. Those are the things that count in measuring height, and so I tell you we climbed that far. Actually I suppose the hill was a couple of hundred feet, if not less. But on account of the grey mist I mentioned, I could not see the top, and the illusion was complete.

We reached the summit late in the afternoon, for the sun was square in our eyes. But instead of blinding me, it seemed to clear my sight, so that I saw below me a little mud hut with smoke rising behind it, and a small patch of cultivated ground.

I'll pass over how I felt about it: they haven't made the words—

Well, we stumbled down the trail and into the hut. At first I thought it was empty, but after a minute I saw a very old man crouched in a corner. As I looked at him he raised his bleared eyes to me, his head swinging slowly from side to side as though with a kind of palsy. He could not see me, that was evident, nor hear me, but some instinct not yet decayed turned him toward a new presence in the room. In my wild desire for water I found room to think that here was a man even worse off than myself.

A vessel of water was in the corner. I drank it. It was more than I could hold, but I drank even after I was filled, and the waste ran from the corners of my mouth. I had forgotten Schwartz. The excess made me a little sick, but I held down what I had swallowed, and I really believe it soaked into my system as it does into the desert earth after a drought.

In a moment or so I took the vessel and filled it and gave it to Schwartz. Then it seemed to me that my responsibility had ended. A sudden great dreamy lassitude came over me. I knew I needed food, but I had no wish for it, and no ambition to search it out. The man in the corner mumbled at me with his toothless gums. I remember wondering if we were all to starve there peacefully together—Schwartz and his remaining gold coins, the man far gone in years, and myself. I did not greatly care.

After a while the light was blotted out. There followed a slight pause. Then I knew that someone had flown to my side, and was kneeling beside me and saying liquid, pitying things in Mexican. I swallowed something hot and strong. In a moment I came back from wherever I was drifting, to look up at a Mexican girl about twenty years old.

She was no great matter in looks, but she seemed like an angel to me then. And she had sense. No questions, no nothing. Just business. The only thing she asked of me was if I understood Spanish.

Then she told me that her brother would be back soon, that they were very poor, that she was sorry she had no meat to offer me, that they were VERY poor, that all they had was calabash—a sort of squash. All this time she was bustling things together. Next thing I know I had a big bowl of calabash stew between my knees.

Now, strangely enough, I had no great interest in that calabash stew. I tasted it, sat and thought a while, and tasted it again. By and by I had emptied the bowl. It was getting dark. I was very sleepy. A man came in, but I was too drowsy to pay any attention to him. I heard the sound of voices. Then I was picked up bodily and carried to an out-building and laid on a pile of skins. I felt the weight of a blanket thrown over me—

I awoke in the night. Mind you, I had practically had no rest at all for a matter of more than two weeks, yet I woke in a few hours. And, remember, even in eating the calabash stew I had felt no hunger in spite of my long fast. But now I found myself ravenous. You boys do not know what hunger is. It HURTS. And all the rest of that night I lay awake chewing on the rawhide of a pack-saddle that hung near me.

Next morning the young Mexican and his sister came to us early, bringing more calabash stew. I fell on it like a wild animal, and just wallowed in it, so eager was I to eat. They stood and watched me—and I suppose Schwartz, too, though I had now lost interest in anyone but myself—glancing at each other in pity from time to time.

When I had finished the man told me that they had decided to kill a beef so we could have meat. They were very poor, but God had brought us to them—

I appreciated this afterward. At the time I merely caught at the word "meat." It seemed to me I could have eaten the animal entire, hide, hoofs, and tallow. As a matter of fact, it was mighty lucky they didn't have any meat. If they had, we'd probably have killed ourselves with it. I suppose the calabash was about the best thing for us under the circumstances.

The Mexican went out to hunt up his horse. I called the girl back.

"How far is it to Mollyhay?" I asked her.

"A league," said she.

So we had been near our journey's end after all, and Denton was probably all right.

The Mexican went away horseback. The girl fed us calabash. We waited.

About one o'clock a group of horsemen rode over the hill. When they came near enough I recognised Denton at their head. That man was of tempered steel—

They had followed back along the beach, caught our trail where we had turned off, and so discovered us. Denton had fortunately found kind and intelligent people.

We said good-bye to the Mexican girl. I made Schwartz give her one of his gold pieces.

But Denton could not wait for us to say "hullo" even, he was so anxious to get back to town, so we mounted the horses he had brought us, and rode off, very wobbly.

We lived three weeks in Mollyhay. It took us that long to get fed up. The lady I stayed with made a dish of kid meat and stuffed olives—

Why, an hour after filling myself up to the muzzle I'd be hungry again, and scouting round to houses looking for more to eat!

We talked things over a good deal, after we had gained a little strength. I wanted to take a little flyer at Guaymas to see if I could run across this Handy Solomon person, but Denton pointed out that Anderson would be expecting just that, and would take mighty good care to be scarce. His idea was that we'd do better to get hold of a boat and some water casks, and lug off the treasure we had stumbled over. Denton told us that the idea of going back and scooping all that dinero up with a shovel had kept him going, just as the idea of getting even with Anderson had kept me going. Schwartz said that after he'd carried that heavy gold over the first day, he made up his mind he'd get the spending of it or bust. That's why he hated so to throw it away.

There were lots of fishing boats in the harbour, and we hired one, and a man to run it for next to nothing a week. We laid a course north, and in six days anchored in our bay.

I tell you it looked queer. There were the charred sticks of the fire, and the coffeepot lying on its side. We took off our hats at poor Billy's grave a minute, and then climbed over the cholla-covered hill carrying our picks and shovels, and the canvas sacks to take the treasure away in.

There was no trouble in reaching the sandy flat. But when we got there we found it torn up from one end to the other. A few scattered timbers and three empty chests with the covers pried off alone remained. Handy Solomon had been there before us.

We went back to our boat sick at heart. Nobody said a word. We went aboard and made our Greaser boatman head for Yuma. It took us a week to get there. We were all of us glum, but Denton was the worst of the lot. Even after we'd got back to town and fallen into our old ways of life, he couldn't seem to get over it. He seemed plumb possessed of gloom, and moped around like a chicken with the pip. This surprised me, for I didn't think the loss of money would hit him so hard. It didn't hit any of us very hard in those days.

One evening I took him aside and fed him a drink, and expostulated with him.

"Oh, HELL, Rogers," he burst out, "I don't care about the loot. But, suffering cats, think how that fellow sized us up for a lot of pattern-made fools; and how right he was about, it. Why all he did was to sail out of sight around the next corner. He knew we'd start across country; and we did. All we had to do was to lay low, and save our legs. He was BOUND to come back. And we might have nailed him when he landed."

"That's about all there was to it," concluded Colorado Rogers, after a pause, "—except that I've been looking for him ever since, and when I heard you singing that song I naturally thought I'd landed."

"And you never saw him again?" asked Windy Bill.

"Well," chuckled Rogers, "I did about ten year later. It was in Tucson. I was in the back of a store, when the door in front opened and this man came in. He stopped at the little cigar-case by the door. In about one jump I was on his neck. I jerked him over backwards before he knew what had struck him, threw him on his face, got my hands in his back-hair, and began to jump his features against the floor. Then all at once I noted that this man had two arms; so of course he was the wrong fellow. "Oh, excuse me," said I, and ran out the back door."

CHAPTER SIXTEEN
THE HONK-HONK BREED

It was Sunday at the ranch. For a wonder the weather had been favourable; the windmills were all working, the bogs had dried up, the beef had lasted over, the remuda had not strayed—in short, there was nothing to do. Sang had given us a baked bread-pudding with raisins in it. We filled it—in a wash basin full of it—on top of a few incidental pounds of chile con, baked beans, soda biscuits, "air tights," and other delicacies. Then we adjourned with our pipes to the shady side of the blacksmith's shop where we could watch the ravens on top the adobe wall of the corral. Somebody told a story about ravens. This led to road-runners. This suggested rattlesnakes. They started Windy Bill.

"Speakin' of snakes," said Windy, "I mind when they catched the great-granddaddy of all the bullsnakes up at Lead in the Black Hills. I was only a kid then. This wasn't no such tur'ble long a snake, but he was more'n a foot thick. Looked just like a sahuaro stalk. Man name of Terwilliger Smith catched it. He named this yere bullsnake Clarence, and got it so plumb gentle it followed him everywhere. One day old P. T. Barnum come along and wanted to buy this Clarence snake—offered Terwilliger a thousand cold—but Smith wouldn't part with the snake nohow. So finally they fixed up a deal so Smith could go along with the show. They shoved Clarence in a box in the baggage car, but after a while Mr. Snake gets so lonesome he gnaws out and starts to crawl back to find his master. Just as he is half-way between the baggage car and the smoker, the couplin' give way—right on that heavy grade between Custer and Rocky Point. Well, sir, Clarence wound his head 'round one brake wheel and his tail around the other, and held that train together to the bottom of the grade. But it stretched him twenty-eight feet and they had to advertise him as a boa-constrictor."

Windy Bill's story of the faithful bullsnake aroused to reminiscence the grizzled stranger, who thereupon held forth as follows:

Wall, I've see things and I've heerd things, some of them ornery, and some you'd love to believe, they was that gorgeous and improbable. Nat'ral history was always my hobby and sportin' events my special pleasure and this yarn of

Windy's reminds me of the only chanst I ever had to ring in business and pleasure and hobby all in one grand merry-go-round of joy. It come about like this:

One day, a few year back, I was sittin' on the beach at Santa Barbara watchin' the sky stay up, and wonderin' what to do with my year's wages, when a little squinch-eye round-face with big bow spectacles came and plumped down beside me.

"Did you ever stop to think," says he, shovin' back his hat, "that if the horsepower delivered by them waves on this beach in one single hour could be concentrated behind washin' machines, it would be enough to wash all the shirts for a city of four hundred and fifty-one thousand one hundred and thirty-six people?"

"Can't say I ever did," says I, squintin' at him sideways.

"Fact," says he, "and did it ever occur to you that if all the food a man eats in the course of a natural life could be gathered together at one time, it would fill a wagon-train twelve miles long?"

"You make me hungry," says I.

"And ain't it interestin' to reflect," he goes on, "that if all the finger-nail parin's of the human race for one year was to be collected and subjected to hydraulic pressure it would equal in size the pyramid of Cheops?"

"Look yere," says I, sittin' up, "did YOU ever pause to excogitate that if all the hot air you is dispensin' was to be collected together it would fill a balloon big enough to waft you and me over that Bullyvard of Palms to yonder gin mill on the corner?"

He didn't say nothin' to that—just yanked me to my feet, faced me towards the gin mill above mentioned, and exerted considerable pressure on my arm in urgin' of me forward.

"You ain't so much of a dreamer, after all," thinks I. "In important matters you are plumb decisive."

We sat down at little tables, and my friend ordered a beer and a chicken sandwich.

"Chickens," says he, gazin' at the sandwich, "is a dollar apiece in this country, and plumb scarce. Did you ever pause to ponder over the returns chickens would give on a small investment? Say you start with ten hens. Each hatches out thirteen aigs, of which allow a loss of say six for childish accidents. At the end of the year you has eighty chickens. At the end of two years that flock has increased to six hundred and twenty. At the end of the third year—" e had the medicine tongue! Ten days later him and me was occupyin' of an old ranch fifty mile from anywhere. When they run stage-coaches this joint used to be a roadhouse. The outlook was on about a thousand little brown foothills. A road two miles four rods two foot eleven inches in sight run by in front of us. It come over one foothill and disappeared over another. I know just how long it was, for later in the game I measured it.

Out back was about a hundred little wire chicken corrals filled with chickens. We had two kinds. That was the doin's of Tuscarora. My pardner called himself Tuscarora Maxillary. I asked him once if that was his real name.

"It's the realest little old name you ever heerd tell of," says he. "I know, for I made it myself—liked the sound of her. Parents ain't got no rights to name their children. Parents don't have to be called them names."

Well, these chickens, as I said, was of two kinds. The first was these low-set, heavyweight propositions with feathers on their laigs, and not much laigs at that, called Cochin Chinys. The other was a tall ridiculous outfit made up entire of bulgin' breast and gangle laigs. They stood about two foot and a half tall, and when they went to peck the ground their tail feathers stuck straight up to the sky. Tusky called 'em Japanese Games.

"Which the chief advantage of them chickens is," says he, "that in weight about ninety per cent of 'em is breast meat. Now my idee is, that if we can cross 'em with these Cochin Chiny fowls we'll have a low-hung, heavyweight chicken runnin' strong on breast meat. These Jap Games is too small, but if we can bring 'em up in size and shorten their laigs, we'll shore have a winner."

That looked good to me, so we started in on that idee. The theery was bully, but she didn't work out. The first broods we hatched growed up with big husky Cochin Chiny bodies and little short necks, perched up on laigs three foot long. Them chickens couldn't reach ground nohow. We had to build a table for 'em to eat off, and when they went out rustlin' for themselves they had to confine themselves to sidehills or flyin' insects. Their breasts was all right, though—"And think of them drumsticks for the boardinghouse trade!" says Tusky.

So far things wasn't so bad. We had a good grubstake. Tusky and me used to feed them chickens twict a day, and then used to set around watchin' the playful critters chase grasshoppers up an' down the wire corrals, while Tusky figgered out what'd happen if somebody was dumfool enough to gather up somethin' and fix it in baskets or wagons or such. That was where we showed our ignorance of chickens.

One day in the spring I hitched up, rustled a dozen of the youngsters into coops, and druv over to the railroad to make our first sale. I couldn't fold them chickens up into them coops at first, but then I stuck the coops up on aidge and they worked all right, though I will admit they was a comical sight. At the railroad one of them towerist trains had just slowed down to a halt as I come up, and the towerist was paradin' up and down allowin' they was particular enjoyin' of the warm Californy sunshine. One old terrapin, with grey chin whiskers, projected over, with his wife, and took a peek through the slats of my coop. He straightened up like someone had touched him off with a red-hot poker.

"Stranger," said he, in a scared kind of whisper, "what's them?"

"Them's chickens," says I.

He took another long look.

"Marthy," says he to the old woman, "this will be about all! We come out from Ioway to see the Wonders of Californy, but I can't go nothin' stronger than this. If these is chickens, I don't want to see no Big Trees."

Well, I sold them chickens all right for a dollar and two bits, which was better than I expected, and got an order for more. About ten days later I got a letter from the commission house.

"We are returnin' a sample of your Arts and Crafts chickens with the lovin' marks of the teeth still onto him," says they. "Don't send any more till they stops pursuin' of the nimble grasshopper. Dentist bill will foller."

With the letter came the remains of one of the chickens. Tusky and I, very indignant, cooked her for supper. She was tough, all right. We thought she might do better biled, so we put her in the pot over night. Nary bit. Well, then we got interested. Tusky kep' the fire goin' and I rustled greasewood. We cooked her three days and three nights. At the end of that time she was sort of pale and frazzled, but still givin' points to three-year-old jerky on cohesion and other uncompromisin' forces of Nature. We buried her then, and went out back to recuperate.

There we could gaze on the smilin' landscape, dotted by about four hundred long-laigged chickens swoopin' here and there after grasshoppers.

"We got to stop that," says I.

"We can't," murmured Tusky, inspired. "We can't. It's born in 'em; it's a primal instinct, like the love of a mother for her young, and it can't be eradicated! Them chickens is constructed by a divine providence for the express purpose of chasin' grasshoppers, jest as the beaver is made for buildin' dams, and the cow-puncher is made for whisky and faro-games. We can't keep 'em from it. If we was to shut 'em in a dark cellar, they'd flop after imaginary grasshoppers in their dreams, and die emaciated in the midst of plenty. Jimmy, we're up agin the Cosmos, the oversoul—" Oh, he had the medicine tongue, Tusky had, and risin' on the wings of eloquence that way, he had me faded in ten minutes. In fifteen I was wedded solid to the notion that the bottom had dropped out of the chicken business. I think now that if we'd shut them hens up, we might have—still, I don't know; they was a good deal in what Tusky said.

"Tuscarora Maxillary," says I, "did you ever stop to entertain that beautiful thought that if all the dumfoolishness possessed now by the human race could be gathered together, and lined up alongside of us, the first feller to come along would say to it 'Why, hello, Solomon!'"

We quit the notion of chickens for profit right then and there, but we couldn't quit the place. We hadn't much money, for one thing, and then we, kind of liked loafin' around and raisin' a little garden truck, and—oh, well, I might as well say so, we had a notion about placers in the dry wash back of the house you know how it is. So we stayed on, and kept a-raisin' these long-laigs for the fun of it. I used to like to watch 'em projectin' around, and I fed 'em twict a day about as usual.

So Tusky and I lived alone there together, happy as ducks in Arizona. About onc't in a month somebody'd pike along the road. She wasn't much of a road, generally more chuckholes than bumps, though sometimes it was the other way around. Unless it happened to be a man horseback or maybe a freighter without the fear of God in his soul, we didn't have no words with them; they was too busy cussin' the highways and generally too mad for social discourses.

One day early in the year, when the 'dobe mud made ruts to add to the bumps, one of these automobeels went past. It was the first Tusky and me had seen in them parts, so we run out to view her. Owin' to the high spots on the road, she looked like one of these movin' picters, as to blur and wobble; sounded like a cyclone mingled with cuss-words, and smelt like hell on housecleanin' day.

"Which them folks don't seem to be enjoyin' of the scenery," says I to Tusky. "Do you reckon that there blue trail is smoke from the machine or remarks from the inhabitants thereof?"

Tusky raised his head and sniffed long and inquirin'.

"It's langwidge," says he. "Did you ever stop to think that all the words in the dictionary stretched end to end would reach—"

But at that minute I catched sight of somethin' brass lyin' in the road. It proved to be a curled-up sort of horn with a rubber bulb on the end. I squoze the bulb and jumped twenty foot over the remark she made.

"Jarred off the machine," says Tusky.

"Oh, did it?" says I, my nerves still wrong. "I thought maybe it had growed up from the soil like a toadstool."

About this time we abolished the wire chicken corrals, because we needed some of the wire. Them long-laigs thereupon scattered all over the flat searchin' out their prey. When feed time come I had to screech my lungs out gettin' of 'em in, and then sometimes they didn't all hear. It was plumb discouragin', and I mighty nigh made up my mind to quit 'em, but they had come to be sort of pets, and I hated to turn 'em down. It used to tickle Tusky almost to death to see me out there hollerin' away like an old bull-frog. He used to come out reg'lar, with his pipe lit, just to enjoy me. Finally I got mad and opened up on him.

"Oh," he explains, "it just plumb amuses me to see the dumfool at his childish work. Why don't you teach 'em to come to that brass horn, and save your voice?"

"Tusky," says I, with feelin', "sometimes you do seem to get a glimmer of real sense."

Well, first off them chickens used to throw back-sommersets over that horn. You have no idee how slow chickens is to learn things. I could tell you things about chickens—say, this yere bluff about roosters bein' gallant is all wrong. I've watched 'em. When one finds a nice feed he gobbles it so fast that the pieces foller down his throat like yearlin's through a hole in the fence. It's only when he scratches up a measly one-grain quick-lunch that he calls up the hens and stands noble and self-sacrificin' to one side. That ain't the point, which is, that after two months I had them long-laigs so they'd drop everythin' and come kitin' at the HONK-HONK of that horn. It was a purty sight to see 'em, sailin' in from all directions twenty foot at a stride. I was proud of 'em, and named 'em the Honk-honk Breed. We didn't have no others, for by now the coyotes and bob-cats had nailed the straight-breds. There wasn't no wild cat or coyote could catch one of my Honk-honks, no, sir!

95

We made a little on our placer—just enough to keep interested. Then the supervisors decided to fix our road, and what's more, THEY DONE IT! That's the only part in this yarn that's hard to believe, but, boys, you'll have to take it on faith. They ploughed her, and crowned her, and scraped her, and rolled her, and when they moved on we had the fanciest highway in the State of Californy.

That noon—the day they called her a job—Tusky and I sat smokin' our pipes as per usual, when way over the foothills we seen a cloud of dust and faint to our ears was bore a whizzin' sound. The chickens was gathered under the cottonwood for the heat of the day, but they didn't pay no attention. Then faint, but clear, we heard another of them brass horns:

"Honk! honk!" says it, and every one of them chickens woke up, and stood at attention.

"Honk! honk!" it hollered clearer and nearer.

Then over the hill come an automobeel, blowin' vigorous at every jump.

"My God!" I yells to Tusky, kickin' over my chair, as I springs to my feet. "Stop 'em! Stop 'em!"

But it was too late. Out the gate sprinted them poor devoted chickens, and up the road they trailed in vain pursuit. The last we seen of 'em was a mingling of dust and dim figgers goin' thirty mile an hour after a disappearin' automobeel.

That was all we seen for the moment. About three o'clock the first straggler came limpin' in, his wings hangin', his mouth open, his eyes glazed with the heat. By sundown fourteen had returned. All the rest had disappeared utter; we never seen 'em again. I reckon they just naturally run themselves into a sunstroke and died on the road.

It takes a long time to learn a chicken a thing, but a heap longer to unlearn him. After that two or three of these yere automobeels went by every day, all a-blowin' of their horns, all kickin' up a hell of a dust. And every time them fourteen Honk-honks of mine took along after 'em, just as I'd taught 'em to do, layin' to get to their corn when they caught up. No more of 'em died, but that fourteen did get into elegant trainin'. After a while they got plumb to enjoyin' it. When you come right down to it, a chicken don't have many amusements and relaxations in this life. Searchin' for worms, chasin' grasshoppers, and wallerin' in the dust is about the limits of joys for chickens.

It was sure a fine sight to see 'em after they got well into the game. About nine o'clock every mornin' they would saunter down to the rise of the road where they would wait patient until a machine came along. Then it would warm your heart to see the enthusiasm of them. With, exultant cackles of joy they'd trail in, reachin' out like quarter-horses, their wings half spread out, their eyes beamin' with delight. At the lower turn they'd quit. Then, after talkin' it over excited-like for a few minutes, they'd calm down and wait for another.

After a few months of this sort of trainin' they got purty good at it. I had one two-year-old rooster that made fifty-four mile an hour behind one of those sixty-horsepower Panhandles. When cars didn't come along often enough, they'd all turn out and chase jack-rabbits. They wasn't much fun at that. After a short, brief sprint the rabbit would crouch down plumb terrified, while the Honk-honks pulled off triumphal dances around his shrinkin' form.

Our ranch got to be purty well known them days among automobeelists. The strength of their cars was horse-power, of course, but the speed of them they got to ratin' by chicken-power. Some of them used to come way up from Los Angeles just to try out a new car along our road with the Honk-honks for pace-makers. We charged them a little somethin', and then, too, we opened up the road-house and the bar, so we did purty well. It wasn't necessary to work any longer at that bogus placer. Evenin's we sat around outside and swapped yarns, and I bragged on my chickens. The chickens would gather round close to listen.

They liked to hear their praises sung, all right. You bet they sabe! The only reason a chicken, or any other critter, isn't intelligent is because he hasn't no chance to expand.

Why, we used to run races with 'em. Some of us would hold two or more chickens back of a chalk line, and the starter'd blow the horn from a hundred yards to a mile away, dependin' on whether it was a sprint or for distance. We had pools on the results, gave odds, made books, and kept records. After the thing got knowed we made money hand over fist.

The stranger broke off abruptly and began to roll a cigarette.

"What did you quit it for, then?" ventured Charley, out of the hushed silence.

"Pride," replied the stranger solemnly. "Haughtiness of spirit."

"How so?" urged Charley, after a pause.

"Them chickens," continued the stranger, after a moment, "stood around listenin' to me a-braggin' of what superior fowls they was until they got all puffed up. They wouldn't have nothin' whatever to do with the ordinary chickens we brought in for eatin' purposes, but stood around lookin' bored when there wasn't no sport doin'. They got to be just like that Four Hundred you read about in the papers. It was one continual round of grasshopper balls, race meets, and afternoon hen-parties. They got idle and haughty, just like folks. Then come race suicide. They got to feelin' so aristocratic the hens wouldn't have no eggs."

Nobody dared say a word.

"Windy Bill's snake—" began the narrator genially.

"Stranger," broke in Windy Bill, with great emphasis, "as to that snake, I want you to understand this: yereafter in my estimation that snake is nothin' but an ornery angleworm!"

## PART II
## THE TWO GUN MAN
### CHAPTER ONE
### THE CATTLE RUSTLERS

Buck Johnson was American born, but with a black beard and a dignity of manner that had earned him the title of Senor. He had drifted into southeastern Arizona in the days of Cochise and Victorio and Geronimo. He had persisted, and so in time had come to control the water—and hence the grazing—of nearly all the Soda Springs Valley. His troubles were many, and his difficulties great. There were the ordinary problems of lean and dry years. There were also the extraordinary problems of devastating Apaches; rivals for early and ill-defined range rights—and cattle rustlers.

Senor Buck Johnson was a man of capacity, courage, directness of method, and perseverance. Especially the latter. Therefore he had survived to see the Apaches subdued, the range rights adjusted, his cattle increased to thousands, grazing the area of a principality. Now, all the energy and fire of his frontiersman's nature he had turned to wiping out the third uncertainty of an uncertain business. He found it a task of some magnitude.

For Senor Buck Johnson lived just north of that terra incognita filled with the mystery of a double chance of death from man or the flaming desert known as the Mexican border. There, by natural gravitation, gathered all the desperate characters of three States and two republics. He who rode into it took good care that no one should ride behind him, lived warily, slept light, and breathed deep when once he had again sighted the familiar peaks of Cochise's Stronghold. No one professed knowledge of those who dwelt therein. They moved, mysterious as the desert illusions that compassed them about. As you rode, the ranges of mountains visibly changed form, the monstrous, snaky, sea-like growths of the cactus clutched at your stirrup, mock lakes sparkled and dissolved in the middle distance, the sun beat hot and merciless, the powdered dry alkali beat hotly and mercilessly back—and strange, grim men, swarthy, bearded, heavily armed, with red-rimmed unshifting eyes, rode silently out of the mists of illusion to look on you steadily, and then to ride silently back into the desert haze. They might be only the herders of the gaunt cattle, or again they might belong to the Lost Legion that peopled the country. All you could know was that of the men who entered in, but few returned.

Directly north of this unknown land you encountered parallel fences running across the country. They enclosed nothing, but offered a check to the cattle drifting toward the clutch of the renegades, and an obstacle to swift, dashing forays.

Of cattle-rustling there are various forms. The boldest consists quite simply of running off a bunch of stock, hustling it over the Mexican line, and there selling it to some of the big Sonora ranch owners. Generally this sort means war. Also are there subtler means, grading in skill from the re-branding through a wet blanket, through the crafty refashioning of a brand to the various methods of separating the cow from her unbranded calf. In the course of his task Senor Buck Johnson would have to do with them all, but at present he existed in a state of warfare, fighting an enemy who stole as the Indians used to steal.

Already he had fought two pitched battles and had won them both. His cattle increased, and he became rich. Nevertheless he knew that constantly his resources were being drained. Time and again he and his new Texas foreman, Jed Parker, had followed the trail of a stampeded bunch of twenty or thirty, followed them on down through the Soda Springs Valley to the cut drift fences, there to abandon them. For, as yet, an armed force would be needed to penetrate the borderland. Once he and his men bad experienced the glory of a night pursuit. Then, at the drift fences, he had fought one of his battles. But it was impossible adequately to patrol all parts of a range bigger than some Eastern States.

Buck Johnson did his best, but it was like stopping with sand the innumerable little leaks of a dam. Did his riders watch toward the Chiricahuas, then a score of beef steers disappeared from Grant's Pass forty miles away. Pursuit here meant leaving cattle unguarded there. It was useless, and the Senor soon perceived that sooner or later he must strike in offence.

For this purpose he began slowly to strengthen the forces of his riders. Men were coming in from Texas. They were good men, addicted to the grass-rope, the double cinch, and the ox-bow stirrup. Senor Johnson wanted men who could shoot, and he got them.

"Jed," said Senor Johnson to his foreman, "the next son of a gun that rustles any of our cows is sure loading himself full of trouble. We'll hit his trail and will stay with it, and we'll reach his cattle-rustling conscience with a rope."

So it came about that a little army crossed the drift fences and entered the border country. Two days later it came out, and mighty pleased to be able to do so. The rope had not been used.

The reason for the defeat was quite simple. The thief had run his cattle through the lava beds where the trail at once became difficult to follow. This delayed the pursuing party; they ran out of water, and, as there was among them not one man well enough acquainted with the country to know where to find more, they had to return.

"No use, Buck," said Jed. "We'd any of us come in on a gun play, but we can't buck the desert. We'll have to get someone who knows the country."

"That's all right—but where?" queried Johnson.

"There's Pereza," suggested Parker. "It's the only town down near that country."

"Might get someone there," agreed the Senor.

Next day he rode away in search of a guide. The third evening he was back again, much discouraged.

"The country's no good," he explained. "The regular inhabitants 're a set of Mexican bums and old soaks. The cowmen's all from north and don't know nothing more than we do. I found lots who claimed to know that country, but when I told 'em what I wanted they shied like a colt. I couldn't hire 'em, for no money, to go down in that country. They ain't got the nerve. I took two days to her, too, and rode out to a ranch where they said a man lived who knew all about it down there. Nary riffle. Man looked all right, but his tail went down like the rest when I told him what we wanted. Seemed plumb scairt to death. Says he lives too close to the gang. Says they'd wipe him out sure if he done it. Seemed plumb SCAIRT." Buck Johnson grinned. "I told him so and he got hosstyle right off. Didn't seem no ways scairt of me. I don't know what's the matter with that outfit down there. They're plumb terrorised."

That night a bunch of steers was stolen from the very corrals of the home ranch. The home ranch was far north, near Fort Sherman itself, and so had always been considered immune from attack. Consequently these steers were very fine ones.

For the first time Buck Johnson lost his head and his dignity. He ordered the horses.

"I'm going to follow that —— into Sonora," he shouted to Jed Parker. "This thing's got to stop!"

"You can't make her, Buck," objected the foreman. "You'll get held up by the desert, and, if that don't finish you, they'll tangle you up in all those little mountains down there, and ambush you, and massacre you. You know it damn well."

"I don't give a —" exploded Senor Johnson, "if they do. No man can slap my face and not get a run for it."

Jed Parker communed with himself.

"Senor," said he, at last, "it's no good; you can't do it. You got to have a guide. You wait three days and I'll get you one."

"You can't do it," insisted the Senor. "I tried every man in the district."

"Will you wait three days?" repeated the foreman.

Johnson pulled loose his latigo. His first anger had cooled.

"All right," he agreed, "and you can say for me that I'll pay five thousand dollars in gold and give all the men and horses he needs to the man who has the nerve to get back that bunch of cattle, and bring in the man who rustled them. I'll sure make this a test case."

So Jed Parker set out to discover his man with nerve.

CHAPTER TWO
THE MAN WITH NERVE

At about ten o'clock of the Fourth of July a rider topped the summit of the last swell of land, and loped his animal down into the single street of Pereza. The buildings on either side were flat-roofed and coated with plaster. Over the sidewalks extended wooden awnings, beneath which opened very wide doors into the coolness of saloons. Each of these places ran a bar, and also games of roulette, faro, craps, and stud poker. Even this early in the morning every game was patronised.

The day was already hot with the dry, breathless, but exhilarating, heat of the desert. A throng of men idling at the edge of the sidewalks, jostling up and down their centre, or eddying into the places of amusement, acknowledged the power of summer by loosening their collars, carrying their coats on their arms. They were as yet busily engaged in recognising acquaintances. Later they would drink freely and gamble, and perhaps fight. Toward all but those whom they recognised they preserved an attitude of potential suspicion, for here were gathered the "bad men" of the border countries. A certain jealousy or touchy egotism lest the other man be considered quicker on the trigger, bolder, more aggressive than himself, kept each strung to tension. An occasional shot attracted little notice. Men in the cow-countries shoot as casually as we strike matches, and some subtle instinct told them that the reports were harmless.

As the rider entered the one street, however, a more definite cause of excitement drew the loose population toward the centre of the road. Immediately their mass blotted out what had interested them. Curiosity attracted the saunterers; then in turn the frequenters of the bars and gambling games. In a very few moments the barkeepers, gamblers, and look-out men, held aloof only by the necessities of their calling, alone of all the population of Pereza were not included in the newly-formed ring.

The stranger pushed his horse resolutely to the outer edge of the crowd where, from his point of vantage, he could easily overlook their heads. He was a quiet-appearing young fellow, rather neatly dressed in the border costume, rode a "centre fire," or single-cinch, saddle, and wore no chaps. He was what is known as a "two-gun man": that is to say, he wore a heavy Colt's revolver on either hip. The fact that the lower ends of his holsters were tied down, in order to facilitate the easy withdrawal of the revolvers, seemed to indicate that he expected to use them. He had furthermore a quiet grey eye, with the glint of steel that bore out the inference of the tied holsters.

The newcomer dropped his reins on his pony's neck, eased himself to an attitude of attention, and looked down gravely on what was taking place. He saw over the heads of the bystanders a tall, muscular, wild-eyed man, hatless, his hair rumpled into staring confusion, his right sleeve rolled to his shoulder, a wicked-looking nine-inch knife in his hand, and a red bandana handkerchief hanging by one corner from his teeth.

"What's biting the locoed stranger?" the young man inquired of his neighbour.

The other frowned at him darkly.

"Dare's anyone to take the other end of that handkerchief in his teeth, and fight it out without letting go."

"Nice joyful proposition," commented the young man.

He settled himself to closer attention. The wild-eyed man was talking rapidly. What he said cannot be printed here. Mainly was it derogatory of the southern countries. Shortly it became boastful of the northern, and then of the man who uttered it.

He swaggered up and down, becoming always the more insolent as his challenge remained untaken.

"Why don't you take him up?" inquired the young man, after a moment.

"Not me!" negatived the other vigorously. "I'll go yore little old gunfight to a finish, but I don't want any cold steel in mine. Ugh! it gives me the shivers. It's a reg'lar Mexican trick! With a gun it's down and out, but this knife work is too slow and searchin'."

The newcomer said nothing, but fixed his eye again on the raging man with the knife.

"Don't you reckon he's bluffing?" he inquired.

"Not any!" denied the other with emphasis. "He's jest drunk enough to be crazy mad."

The newcomer shrugged his shoulders and cast his glance searchingly over the fringe of the crowd. It rested on a Mexican.

"Hi, Tony! come here," he called.

The Mexican approached, flashing his white teeth.

"Here," said the stranger, "lend me your knife a minute."

The Mexican, anticipating sport of his own peculiar kind, obeyed with alacrity.

"You fellows make me tired," observed the stranger, dismounting. "He's got the whole townful of you bluffed to a standstill. Damn if I don't try his little game."

He hung his coat on his saddle, shouldered his way through the press, which parted for him readily, and picked up the other corner of the handkerchief.

"Now, you mangy son of a gun," said he.


CHAPTER THREE
THE AGREEMENT

Jed Parker straightened his back, rolled up the bandana handkerchief, and thrust it into his pocket, hit flat with his hand the touselled mass of his hair, and thrust the long hunting knife into its sheath.

"You're the man I want," said he.

Instantly the two-gun man had jerked loose his weapons and was covering the foreman.

"Am I!" he snarled.

"Not jest that way," explained Parker. "My gun is on my hoss, and you can have this old toad-sticker if you want it. I been looking for you, and took this way of finding you. Now, let's go talk."

The stranger looked him in the eye for nearly a half minute without lowering his revolvers.

"I go you," said he briefly, at last.

But the crowd, missing the purport, and in fact the very occurrence of this colloquy, did not understand. It thought the bluff had been called, and naturally, finding harmless what had intimidated it, gave way to an exasperated impulse to get even.

"You —— bluffer!" shouted a voice, "don't you think you can run any such ranikaboo here!"

Jed Parker turned humorously to his companion.

"Do we get that talk?" he inquired gently.

For answer the two-gun man turned and walked steadily in the direction of the man who had shouted. The latter's hand strayed uncertainly toward his own weapon, but the movement paused when the stranger's clear, steel eye rested on it.

"This gentleman," pointed out the two-gun man softly, "is an old friend of mine. Don't you get to calling of him names."

His eye swept the bystanders calmly.

"Come on, Jack," said he, addressing Parker.

On the outskirts he encountered the Mexican from whom he had borrowed the knife.

"Here, Tony," said he with a slight laugh, "here's a peso. You'll find your knife back there where I had to drop her."

He entered a saloon, nodded to the proprietor, and led the way through it to a boxlike room containing a board table and two chairs.

"Make good," he commanded briefly.

"I'm looking for a man with nerve," explained Parker, with equal succinctness. "You're the man."

"Well?"

"Do you know the country south of here?"

The stranger's eyes narrowed.

"Proceed," said he.

"I'm foreman of the Lazy Y of Soda Springs Valley range," explained Parker. "I'm looking for a man with sand enough and sabe of the country enough to lead a posse after cattle-rustlers into the border country."

"I live in this country," admitted the stranger.

"So do plenty of others, but their eyes stick out like two raw oysters when you mention the border country. Will you tackle it?"

"What's the proposition?"

"Come and see the old man. He'll put it to you."

They mounted their horses and rode the rest of the day. The desert compassed them about, marvellously changing shape and colour, and every character, with all the noiselessness of phantasmagoria. At evening the desert stars shone steady and unwinking, like the flames of candles. By moonrise they came to the home ranch.

The buildings and corrals lay dark and silent against the moonlight that made of the plain a sea of mist. The two men unsaddled their horses and turned them loose in the wire-fenced "pasture," the necessary noises of their movements sounding sharp and clear against the velvet hush of the night. After a moment they walked stiffly past the sheds and cook shanty, past the men's bunk houses, and the tall windmill silhouetted against the sky, to the main building of the home ranch under its great cottonwoods. There a light still burned, for this was the third day, and Buck Johnson awaited his foreman.

Jed Parker pushed in without ceremony.

"Here's your man, Buck," said he.

The stranger had stepped inside and carefully closed the door behind him. The lamplight threw into relief the bold, free lines of his face, the details of his costume powdered thick with alkali, the shiny butts of the two guns in their open holsters tied at the bottom. Equally it defined the resolute countenance of Buck Johnson turned up in inquiry. The two men examined each other—and liked each other at once.

"How are you," greeted the cattleman.

"Good-evening," responded the stranger.

"Sit down," invited Buck Johnson.

The stranger perched gingerly on the edge of a chair, with an appearance less of embarrassment than of habitual alertness.

"You'll take the job?" inquired the Senor.

"I haven't heard what it is," replied the stranger.

"Parker here—?"

"Said you'd explain."

"Very well," said Buck Johnson. He paused a moment, collecting his thoughts. "There's too much cattle-rustling here. I'm going to stop it. I've got good men here ready to take the job, but no one who knows the country south. Three days ago I had a bunch of cattle stolen right here from the home-ranch corrals, and by one man, at that. It wasn't much of a bunch—about twenty head—but I'm going to make a starter right here, and now. I'm going to get that bunch back, and the man who stole them, if I have to go to hell to do it. And I'm going to do the same with every case of rustling that comes up from now on. I don't care if it's only one cow, I'm going to get it back—every trip. Now, I want to know if you'll lead a posse down into the south country and bring out that last bunch, and the man who rustled them?"

"I don't know—" hesitated the stranger.

"I offer you five thousand dollars in gold if you'll bring back those cows and the man who stole 'em," repeated Buck Johnson. "And I'll give you all the horses and men you think you need."

"I'll do it," replied the two-gun man promptly.

"Good!" cried Buck Johnson, "and you better start to-morrow."

"I shall start to-night—right now."

"Better yet. How many men do you want, and grub for how long?"

"I'll play her a lone hand."

"Alone!" exclaimed Johnson, his confidence visibly cooling.

"Alone! Do you think you can make her?"

"I'll be back with those cattle in not more than ten days."

"And the man," supplemented the Senor.

"And the man. What's more, I want that money here when I come in. I don't aim to stay in this country over night."

A grin overspread Buck Johnson's countenance. He understood.

"Climate not healthy for you?" he hazarded. "I guess you'd be safe enough all right with us. But suit yourself. The money will be here."

"That's agreed?" insisted the two-gun man.

"Sure."

"I want a fresh horse—I'll leave mine—he's a good one. I want a little grub."

"All right. Parker'll fit you out."

The stranger rose.

"I'll see you in about ten days."

"Good luck," Senor Buck Johnson wished him.

CHAPTER FOUR
THE ACCOMPLISHMENT

The next morning Buck Johnson took a trip down into the "pasture" of five hundred wire-fenced acres.

"He means business," he confided to Jed Parker, on his return. "That cavallo of his is a heap sight better than the Shorty horse we let him take. Jed, you found your man with nerve, all right. How did you do it?"

The two settled down to wait, if not with confidence, at least with interest. Sometimes, remembering the desperate character of the outlaws, their fierce distrust of any intruder, the wildness of the country, Buck Johnson and his foreman inclined to the belief that the stranger had undertaken a task beyond the powers of any one man. Again, remembering the stranger's cool grey eye, the poise of his demeanour, the quickness of his movements, and the two guns with tied holsters to permit of easy withdrawal, they were almost persuaded that he might win.

"He's one of those long-chance fellows," surmised Jed. "He likes excitement. I see that by the way he takes up with my knife play. He'd rather leave his hide on the fence than stay in the corral."

"Well, he's all right," replied Senor Buck Johnson, "and if he ever gets back, which same I'm some doubtful of, his dinero'll be here for him."

In pursuance of this he rode in to Willets, where shortly the overland train brought him from Tucson the five thousand dollars in double eagles.

In the meantime the regular life of the ranch went on. Each morning Sang, the Chinese cook, rang the great bell, summoning the men. They ate, and then caught up the saddle horses for the day, turning those not wanted from the corral into the pasture. Shortly they jingled away in different directions, two by two, on the slow Spanish trot of the cow-puncher. All day long thus they would ride, without food or water for man or beast, looking the range, identifying the stock, branding the young calves, examining generally into the state of affairs, gazing always with grave eyes on the magnificent, flaming, changing, beautiful, dreadful desert of the Arizona plains. At evening when the coloured atmosphere, catching the last glow, threw across the Chiricahuas its veil of mystery, they jingled in again, two by two, untired, unhasting, the glory of the desert in their deep-set, steady eyes.

And all the day long, while they were absent, the cattle, too, made their pilgrimage, straggling in singly, in pairs, in bunches, in long files, leisurely, ruminantly, without haste. There, at the long troughs filled by the windmill of the blindfolded pump mule, they drank, then filed away again into the mists of the desert. And Senor Buck Johnson, or his foreman, Parker, examined them for their condition, noting the increase, remarking the strays from another range. Later, perhaps, they, too, rode abroad. The same thing happened at nine other ranches from five to ten miles apart, where dwelt other fierce, silent men all under the authority of Buck Johnson.

And when night fell, and the topaz and violet and saffron and amethyst and mauve and lilac had faded suddenly from the Chiricahuas, like a veil that has been rent, and the ramparts had become slate-grey and then black—the soft-breathed night wandered here and there over the desert, and the land fell under an enchantment even stranger than the day's.

So the days went by, wonderful, fashioning the ways and the characters of men. Seven passed. Buck Johnson and his foreman began to look for the stranger. Eight, they began to speculate. Nine, they doubted. On the tenth they gave him up—and he came.

They knew him first by the soft lowing of cattle. Jed Parker, dazzled by the lamp, peered out from the door, and made him out dimly turning the animals into the corral. A moment later his pony's hoofs impacted softly on the baked earth, he dropped from the saddle and entered the room.

"I'm late," said he briefly, glancing at the clock, which indicated ten; "but I'm here."

His manner was quick and sharp, almost breathless, as though he had been running.

"Your cattle are in the corral: all of them. Have you the money?"

"I have the money here," replied Buck Johnson, laying his hand against a drawer, "and it's ready for you when you've earned it. I don't care so much for the cattle. What I wanted is the man who stole them. Did you bring him?"

"Yes, I brought him," said the stranger. "Let's see that money."

Buck Johnson threw open the drawer, and drew from it the heavy canvas sack.

"It's here. Now bring in your prisoner."

The two-gun man seemed suddenly to loom large in the doorway. The muzzles of his revolvers covered the two before him. His speech came short and sharp.

"I told you I'd bring back the cows and the one who rustled them," he snapped. "I've never lied to a man yet. Your stock is in the corral. I'll trouble you for that five thousand. I'm the man who stole your cattle!"

*PART III*

*THE RAWHIDE*

CHAPTER ONE
THE PASSING OF THE COLT'S FORTY-FIVE

The man of whom I am now to tell you came to Arizona in the early days of Chief Cochise. He settled in the Soda Springs Valley, and there persisted in spite of the devastating forays of that Apache. After a time he owned all the wells and springs in the valley, and so, naturally, controlled the grazing on that extensive free range. Once a day the cattle, in twos and threes, in bands, in strings, could be seen winding leisurely down the deep-trodden and converging trails to the water troughs at the home ranch, there leisurely to drink, and then leisurely to drift away into the saffron and violet and amethyst distances of the desert. At ten other outlying ranches this daily scene was repeated. All these cattle belonged to the man, great by reason of his priority in the country, the balance of his even character, and the grim determination of his spirit.

When he had first entered Soda Springs Valley his companions had called him Buck Johnson. Since then his form had squared, his eyes had steadied to the serenity of a great authority, his mouth, shadowed by the moustache and the beard, had closed straight in the line of power and taciturnity. There was about him more than a trace of the Spanish. So now he was known as Senor Johnson, although in reality he was straight American enough.

Senor Johnson lived at the home ranch with a Chinese cook, and Parker, his foreman. The home ranch was of adobe, built with loopholes like a fort. In the obsolescence of this necessity, other buildings had sprung up unfortified. An adobe bunkhouse for the cow-punchers, an adobe blacksmith shop, a long, low stable, a shed, a windmill and pond-like reservoir, a whole system of corrals of different sizes, a walled-in vegetable garden—these gathered to themselves cottonwoods from the moisture of their being, and so added each a little to the green spot in the desert. In the smallest corral, between the stable and the shed, stood a buckboard and a heavy wagon, the only wheeled vehicles about the place. Under the shed were rows of saddles, riatas, spurs mounted with silver, bits ornamented with the same metal, curved short irons for the range branding, long, heavy "stamps" for the corral branding. Behind the stable lay the "pasture," a thousand acres of desert fenced in with wire. There the hardy cow-ponies sought out the sparse, but nutritious, bunch grass, sixty of them, beautiful as antelope, for they were the pick of Senor Johnson's herds.

And all about lay the desert, shimmering, changing, many-tinted, wonderful, hemmed in by the mountains that seemed tenuous and thin, like beautiful mists, and by the sky that seemed hard and polished like a turquoise.

Each morning at six o'clock the ten cow-punchers of the home ranch drove the horses to the corral, neatly roped the dozen to be "kept up" for that day, and rewarded the rest with a feed of grain. Then they rode away at a little fox trot, two by two. All day long they travelled thus, conducting the business of the range, and at night, having completed the circle, they jingled again into the corral.

At the ten other ranches this programme had been duplicated. The half-hundred men of Senor Johnson's outfit had covered the area of a European principality. And all of it, every acre, every spear of grass, every cactus prickle, every creature on it, practically belonged to Senor Johnson, because Senor Johnson owned the water, and without water one cannot exist on the desert.

This result had not been gained without struggle. The fact could be read in the settled lines of Senor Johnson's face, and the great calm of his grey eye. Indian days drove him often to the shelter of the loopholed adobe ranch house, there to await the soldiers from the Fort, in plain sight thirty miles away on the slope that led to the foot of the Chiricahuas. He lost cattle and some men, but the profits were great, and in time Cochise, Geronimo, and the lesser lights had flickered out in the winds of destiny. The sheep terror merely threatened, for it was soon discovered that with the feed of Soda Springs Valley grew a burr that annoyed the flocks beyond reason, so the bleating scourge swept by forty miles away. Cattle rustling so near the Mexican line was an easy matter. For a time Senor Johnson commanded an armed band. He was lord of the high, the low, and the middle justice. He violated international ethics, and for the laws of nations he substituted his own. One by one he annihilated the thieves of cattle, sometimes in open fight, but oftener by surprise and deliberate massacre. The country was delivered. And then, with indefatigable energy, Senor Johnson became a skilled detective. Alone, or with Parker, his foreman, he rode the country through, gathering evidence. When the evidence was unassailable he brought offenders to book. The rebranding through a wet blanket he knew and could prove; the ear-marking of an unbranded calf until it could be weaned he understood; the paring of hoofs to prevent travelling he could tell as far as he could see; the crafty alteration of similar brands—as when a Mexican changed Johnson's Lazy Y to a Dumb-bell Bar—he saw through at a glance. In short, the hundred and one petty tricks of the sneak-thief he ferreted out, in danger of his life. Then he sent to Phoenix for a Ranger—and that was the last of the Dumb-bell Bar brand, or the Three Link Bar brand, or the Hour Glass Brand, or a half dozen others. The Soda Springs Valley acquired a reputation for good order.

Senor Johnson at this stage of his career found himself dropping into a routine. In March began the spring branding, then the corralling and breaking of the wild horses, the summer range-riding, the great fall round-up, the shipping of cattle, and the riding of the winter range. This happened over and over again.

You and I would not have suffered from ennui. The roping and throwing and branding, the wild swing and dash of handling stock, the mad races to head the mustangs, the fierce combats to subdue these raging wild beasts to the saddle, the spectacle of the round-up with its brutish multitudes and its graceful riders, the dust and monotony and excitement and glory of the Trail, and especially the hundreds of incidental and gratuitous adventures of bears and antelope, of thirst and heat, of the joy of taking care of one's self—all these would have filled our days with the glittering, changing throng of the unusual.

But to Senor Johnson it had become an old story. After the days of construction the days of accomplishment seemed to him lean. His men did the work and reaped the excitement. Senor Johnson never thought now of riding the wild horses, of swinging the rope coiled at his saddle horn, or of rounding ahead of the flying herds. His inspections were business inspections. The country was tame. The leather chaps with the silver conchas hung behind the door. The Colt's forty-five depended at the head of the bed. Senor Johnson rode in mufti. Of his cowboy days persisted still the high-heeled boots and spurs, the broad Stetson hat, and the fringed buckskin gauntlets.

The Colt's forty-five had been the last to go. Finally one evening Senor Johnson received an express package. He opened it before the undemonstrative Parker. It proved to contain a pocket "gun"—a nickel-plated, thirty-eight calibre Smith & Wesson "five-shooter." Senor Johnson examined it a little doubtfully. In comparison with the six-shooter it looked like a toy.

"How do you, like her?" he inquired, handing the weapon to Parker.

Parker turned it over and over, as a child a rattle. Then he returned it to its owner.

"Senor," said he, "if ever you shoot me with that little old gun, AND I find it out the same day, I'll just raise hell with you!"

"I don't reckon she'd INJURE a man much," agreed the Senor, "but perhaps she'd call his attention."

However, the "little old gun" took its place, not in Senor Johnson's hip pocket, but inside the front waistband of his trousers, and the old shiny Colt's forty-five, with its worn leather "Texas style" holster, became a bedroom ornament.

Thus, from a frontiersman dropped Senor Johnson to the status of a property owner. In a general way he had to attend to his interests before the cattlemen's association; he had to arrange for the buying and shipping, and the rest was leisure. He could now have gone away somewhere as far as time went. So can a fish live in trees—as far as time goes. And in the daily riding, riding, riding over the range he found the opportunity for abstract thought which the frontier life had crowded aside.

CHAPTER TWO
THE SHAPES OF ILLUSION

Every day, as always, Senor Johnson rode abroad over the land. His surroundings had before been accepted casually as a more or less pertinent setting of action and condition. Now he sensed some of the fascination of the Arizona desert.

He noticed many things before unnoticed. As he jingled loosely along on his cow-horse, he observed how the animal waded fetlock deep in the gorgeous orange California poppies, and then he looked up and about, and saw that the rich colour carpeted the landscape as far as his eye could reach, so that it seemed as though he could ride on and on through them to the distant Chiricahuas. Only, close under the hills, lay, unobtrusive, a narrow streak of grey. And in a few hours he had reached the streak of grey, and ridden out into it to find himself the centre of a limitless alkali plain, so that again it seemed the valley could contain nothing else of importance.

Looking back, Senor Johnson could discern a tenuous ribbon of orange—the poppies. And perhaps ahead a little shadow blotted the face of the alkali, which, being reached and entered, spread like fire until it, too, filled the whole plain, until it, too, arrogated to itself the right of typifying Soda Springs Valley as a shimmering prairie of mesquite. Flowered upland, dead lowland, brush, cactus, volcanic rock, sand, each of these for the time being occupied the whole space, broad as the sea. In the circlet of the mountains was room for many infinities.

Among the foothills Senor Johnson, for the first time, appreciated colour. Hundreds of acres of flowers filled the velvet creases of the little hills and washed over the smooth, rounded slopes so accurately in the placing and manner of tinted shadows that the mind had difficulty in believing the colour not to have been shaded in actually by free sweeps of some gigantic brush. A dozen shades of pinks and purples, a dozen of blues, and then the flame reds, the yellows, and the vivid greens. Beyond were the mountains in their glory of volcanic rocks, rich as the tapestry of a Florentine palace. And, modifying all the others, the tinted atmosphere of the south-west, refracting the sun through the infinitesimal earth motes thrown up constantly by the wind devils of the desert, drew before the scene a delicate and gauzy veil of lilac, of rose, of saffron, of amethyst, or of mauve, according to the time of day. Senor Johnson discovered that looking at the landscape upside down accentuated the colour effects. It amused him vastly suddenly to bend over his saddle horn, the top of his head nearly touching his horse's mane. The distant mountains at once started out into redder prominence; their shadows of purple deepened to the royal colour; the rose veil thickened.

"She's the prettiest country God ever made!" exclaimed Senor Johnson with entire conviction.

And no matter where he went, nor into how familiar country he rode, the shapes of illusion offered always variety. One day the Chiricahuas were a tableland; next day a series of castellated peaks; now an anvil; now a saw tooth; and rarely they threw a magnificent suspension bridge across the heavens to their neighbours, the ranges on the west. Lakes rippling in the wind and breaking on the shore, cattle big as elephants or small as rabbits, distances that did not exist and forests that never were, beds of lava along the hills swearing to a cloud shadow, while the sky was polished like a precious stone—these, and many other beautiful and marvellous but empty shows the great desert displayed lavishly, with the glitter and inconsequence of a dream. Senor Johnson sat on his horse in the hot sun, his chin in his band, his elbow on the pommel, watching it all with grave, unshifting eyes.

Occasionally, belated, he saw the stars, the wonderful desert stars, blazing clear and unflickering, like the flames of candles. Or the moon worked her necromancies, hemming him in by mountains ten thousand feet high through which there was no pass. And then as he rode, the mountains shifted like the scenes in a theatre, and he crossed the little sand dunes out from the dream country to the adobe corrals of the home ranch.

All these things, and many others, Senor Johnson now saw for the first time, although he had lived among them for twenty years. It struck him with the freshness of a surprise. Also it reacted chemically on his mental processes to generate a new power within him. The new power, being as yet unapplied, made him uneasy and restless and a little irritable.

He tried to show some of his wonders to Parker.

"Jed," said he, one day, "this is a great country."

"You KNOW it," replied the foreman.

"Those tourists in their nickel-plated Pullmans call this a desert. Desert, hell! Look at them flowers!"

The foreman cast an eye on a glorious silken mantle of purple, a hundred yards broad.

"Sure," he agreed; "shows what we could do if we only had a little water."

And again: "Jed," began the Senor, "did you ever notice them mountains?"

"Sure," agreed Jed.

"Ain't that a pretty colour?"

"You bet," agreed the foreman; "now you're talking! I always, said they was mineralised enough to make a good prospect."

This was unsatisfactory. Senor Johnson grew more restless. His critical eye began to take account of small details. At the ranch house one evening he, on a sudden, bellowed loudly for Sang, the Chinese servant.

"Look at these!" he roared, when Sang appeared.

Sang's eyes opened in bewilderment.

"There, and there!" shouted the cattleman. "Look at them old newspapers and them gun rags! The place is like a cow-yard. Why in the name of heaven don't you clean up here!"

"Allee light," babbled Sang; "I clean him."

The papers and gun rags had lain there unnoticed for nearly a year. Senor Johnson kicked them savagely.

"It's time we took a brace here," he growled, "we're livin' like a lot of Oilers."

Oilers: Greasers—Mexicans

CHAPTER THREE
THE PAPER A YEAR OLD

Sang hurried out for a broom. Senor Johnson sat where he was, his heavy, square brows knit. Suddenly he stooped, seized one of the newspapers, drew near the lamp, and began to read.

It was a Kansas City paper and, by a strange coincidence, was dated exactly a year before. The sheet Senor Johnson happened to pick up was one usually passed over by the average newspaper reader. It contained only columns of little two- and three-line advertisements classified as Help Wanted, Situations Wanted, Lost and Found, and Personal. The latter items Senor Johnson commenced to read while awaiting Sang and the broom.

The notices were five in number. The first three were of the mysterious newspaper-correspondence type, in which Birdie beseeches Jack to meet her at the fountain; the fourth advertised a clairvoyant. Over the fifth Senor Johnson paused long. It reads

"WANTED.-By an intelligent and refined lady of pleasing appearance, correspondence with a gentleman of means. Object matrimony."

Just then Sang returned with the broom and began noisily to sweep together the debris. The rustling of papers aroused Senor Johnson from his reverie. At once he exploded.

"Get out of here, you debased Mongolian," he shouted; "can't you see I'm reading?"

Sang fled, sorely puzzled, for the Senor was calm and unexcited and aloof in his everyday habit.

Soon Jed Parker, tall, wiry, hawk-nosed, deliberate, came into the room and flung his broad hat and spurs into the corner. Then he proceeded to light his pipe and threw the burned match on the floor.

"Been over to look at the Grant Pass range," he announced cheerfully. "She's no good. Drier than cork legs. Th' country wouldn't support three horned toads."

"Jed," quoth the Senor solemnly, "I wisht you'd hang up your hat like I have. It don't look good there on the floor."

"Why, sure," agreed Jed, with an astonished stare.

Sang brought in supper and slung it on the red and white squares of oilcloth. Then he moved the lamp and retired.

Senor Johnson gazed with distaste into his cup.

"This coffee would float a wedge," he commented sourly.

"She's no puling infant," agreed the cheerful Jed.

"And this!" went on the Senor, picking up what purported to be plum duff: "Bog down a few currants in dough and call her pudding!"

He ate in silence, then pushed back his chair and went to the window, gazing through its grimy panes at the mountains, ethereal in their evening saffron.

"Blamed Chink," he growled; "why don't he wash these windows?"

Jed laid down his busy knife and idle fork to gaze on his chief with amazement. Buck Johnson, the austere, the aloof, the grimly taciturn, the dangerous, to be thus complaining like a querulous woman!

"Senor," said he, "you're off your feed."

Senor Johnson strode savagely to the table and sat down with a bang.

"I'm sick of it," he growled; "this thing will kill me off. I might as well go be a buck nun and be done with it."

With one round-arm sweep he cleared aside the dishes.

"Give me that pen and paper behind you," he requested.

For an hour he wrote and destroyed. The floor became littered with torn papers. Then he enveloped a meagre result. Parker had watched him in silence.

The Senor looked up to catch his speculative eye. His own eye twinkled a little, but the twinkle was determined and sinister, with only an alloy of humour.

"Senor," ventured Parker slowly, "this event sure knocks me hell-west and crooked. If the loco you have culled hasn't paralysed your speaking parts, would you mind telling me what in the name of heaven, hell, and high-water is up?"

"I am going to get married," announced the Senor calmly.

"What!" shouted Parker; "who to?"

"To a lady," replied the Senor, "an intelligent and refined lady—of pleasing appearance."

CHAPTER FOUR
DREAMS

Although the paper was a year old, Senor Johnson in due time received an answer from Kansas. A correspondence ensued. Senor Johnson enshrined above the big fireplace the photograph of a woman. Before this he used to stand for hours at a time slowly constructing in his mind what he had hitherto lacked—an ideal of woman and of home. This ideal he used sometimes to express to himself and to the ironical Jed.

"It must sure be nice to have a little woman waitin' for you when you come in off'n the desert."

Or: "Now, a woman would have them windows just blooming with flowers and white curtains and such truck."

Or: "I bet that Sang would get a wiggle on him with his little old cleaning duds if he had a woman ahold of his jerk line."

Slowly he reconstructed his life, the life of the ranch, in terms of this hypothesised feminine influence. Then matters came to an understanding, Senor Johnson had sent his own portrait. Estrella Sands wrote back that she adored big black beards, but she was afraid of him, he had such a fascinating bad eye: no woman could resist him. Senor Johnson at once took things for granted, sent on to Kansas a preposterous sum of "expense" money and a railroad ticket, and raided

Goodrich's store at Willets, a hundred miles away, for all manner of gaudy carpets, silverware, fancy lamps, works of art, pianos, linen, and gimcracks for the adornment of the ranch house. Furthermore, he offered wages more than equal to a hundred miles of desert to a young Irish girl, named Susie O'Toole, to come out as housekeeper, decorator, boss of Sang and another Chinaman, and companion to Mrs. Johnson when she should arrive.

Furthermore, he laid off from the range work Brent Palmer, the most skilful man with horses, and set him to "gentling" a beautiful little sorrel. A sidesaddle had arrived from El Paso. It was "centre fire," which is to say it had but the single horsehair cinch, broad, tasselled, very genteel in its suggestion of pleasure use only. Brent could be seen at all times of day, cantering here and there on the sorrel, a blanket tied around his waist to simulate the long riding skirt. He carried also a sulky and evil gleam in his eye, warning against undue levity.

Jed Parker watched these various proceedings sardonically.

Once, the baby light of innocence blue in his eye, he inquired if he would be required to dress for dinner.

"If so," he went on, "I'll have my man brush up my low-necked clothes."

But Senor Johnson refused to be baited.

"Go on, Jed," said he; "you know you ain't got clothes enough to dust a fiddle."

The Senor was happy these days. He showed it by an unwonted joviality of spirit, by a slight but evident unbending of his Spanish dignity. No longer did the splendour of the desert fill him with a vague yearning and uneasiness. He looked upon it confidently, noting its various phases with care, rejoicing in each new development of colour and light, of form and illusion, storing them away in his memory so that their recurrence should find him prepared to recognise and explain them. For soon he would have someone by his side with whom to appreciate them. In that sharing he could see the reason for them, the reason for their strange bitter-sweet effects on the human soul.

One evening he leaned on the corral fence, looking toward the Dragoons. The sun had set behind them. Gigantic they loomed against the western light. From their summits, like an aureola, radiated the splendour of the dust-moted air, this evening a deep umber. A faint reflection of it fell across the desert, glorifying the reaches of its nothingness.

"I'll take her out on an evening like this," quoth Senor Johnson to himself, "and I'll make her keep her eyes on the ground till we get right up by Running Bear Knob, and then I'll let her look up all to once. And she'll surely enjoy this life. I bet she never saw a steer roped in her life. She can ride with me every day out over the range and I'll show her the busting and the branding and that band of antelope over by the Tall Windmill. I'll teach her to shoot, too. And we can make little pack trips off in the hills when she gets too hot—up there by Deerskin Meadows 'mongst the high peaks."

He mused, turning over in his mind a new picture of his own life, aims, and pursuits as modified by the sympathetic and understanding companionship of a woman. He pictured himself as he must seem to her in his different pursuits. The picturesqueness pleased him. The simple, direct vanity of the man—the wholesome vanity of a straightforward nature—awakened to preen its feathers before the idea of the mate.

The shadows fell. Over the Chiricahuas flared the evening star. The plain, self-luminous with the weird lucence of the arid lands, showed ghostly. Jed Parker, coming out from the lamp-lit adobe, leaned his elbows on the rail in silent company with his chief. He, too, looked abroad. His mind's eye saw what his body's eye had always told him were the insistent notes—the alkali, the cactus, the sage, the mesquite, the lava, the choking dust, the blinding beat, the burning thirst. He sighed in the dim half recollection of past days.

"I wonder if she'll like the country?" he hazarded.

But Senor Johnson turned on him his steady eyes, filled with the great glory of the desert.

"Like the country!" he marvelled slowly. "Of course! Why shouldn't she?"

CHAPTER FIVE
THE ARRIVAL

The Overland drew into Willets, coated from engine to observation with white dust. A porter, in strange contrast of neatness, flung open the vestibule, dropped his little carpeted step, and turned to assist someone. A few idle passengers gazed out on the uninteresting, flat frontier town.

Senor Johnson caught his breath in amazement. "God! Ain't she just like her picture!" he exclaimed. He seemed to find this astonishing.

For a moment he did not step forward to claim her, so she stood looking about her uncertainly, her leather suit-case at her feet.

She was indeed like the photograph. The same full-curved, compact little figure, the same round face, the same cupid's bow mouth, the same appealing, large eyes, the same haze of doll's hair. In a moment she caught sight of Senor Johnson and took two steps toward him, then stopped. The Senor at once came forward.

"You're Mr. Johnson, ain't you?" she inquired, thrusting her little pointed chin forward, and so elevating her baby-blue eyes to his.

"Yes, ma'am," he acknowledged formally. Then, after a moment's pause: "I hope you're well."

"Yes, thank you."

The station loungers, augmented by all the ranchmen and cowboys in town, were examining her closely. She looked at them in a swift side glance that seemed to gather all their eyes to hers. Then, satisfied that she possessed the universal admiration, she returned the full force of her attention to the man before her.

"Now you give me your trunk checks," he was saying, "and then we'll go right over and get married."

"Oh!" she gasped.

"That's right, ain't it?" he demanded.

"Yes, I suppose so," she agreed faintly.

A little subdued, she followed him to the clergyman's house, where, in the presence of Goodrich, the storekeeper, and the preacher's wife, the two were united. Then they mounted the buckboard and drove from town.

Senor Johnson said nothing, because he knew of nothing to say. He drove skilfully and fast through the gathering dusk. It was a hundred miles to the home ranch, and that hundred miles, by means of five relays of horses already arranged for, they would cover by morning. Thus they would avoid the dust and heat and high winds of the day.

The sweet night fell. The little desert winds laid soft fingers on their checks. Overhead burned the stars, clear, unflickering, like candles. Dimly could be seen the horses, their flanks swinging steadily in the square trot. Ghostly bushes passed them; ghostly rock elevations. Far, in indeterminate distance, lay the outlines of the mountains. Always, they seemed to recede. The plain, all but invisible, the wagon trail quite so, the depths of space—these flung heavy on the soul their weight of mysticism. The woman, until now bolt upright in the buckboard seat, shrank nearer to the man. He felt against his sleeve the delicate contact of her garment and thrilled to the touch. A coyote barked sharply from a neighbouring eminence, then trailed off into the long-drawn, shrill howl of his species.

"What was that?" she asked quickly, in a subdued voice.

"A coyote—one of them little wolves," he explained.

The horses' hoofs rang clear on a hardened bit of the alkali crust, then dully as they encountered again the dust of the plain. Vast, vague, mysterious in the silence of night, filled with strange influences breathing through space like damp winds, the desert took them to the heart of her great spaces.

"Buck," she whispered, a little tremblingly. It was the first time she had spoken his name.

"What is it?" he asked, a new note in his voice.

But for a time she did not reply. Only the contact against his sleeve increased by ever so little.

"Buck," she repeated, then all in a rush and with a sob, "Oh, I'm afraid."

Tenderly the man drew her to him. Her head fell against his shoulder and she hid her eyes.

"There, little girl," he reassured her, his big voice rich and musical. "There's nothing to get scairt of, I'll take care of you. What frightens you, honey?"

She nestled close in his arm with a sigh of half relief.

"I don't know," she laughed, but still with a tremble in her tones. "It's all so big and lonesome and strange—and I'm so little."

"There, little girl," he repeated.

They drove on and on. At the end of two hours they stopped. Men with lanterns dazzled their eyes. The horses were changed, and so out again into the night where the desert seemed to breathe in deep, mysterious exhalations like a sleeping beast.

Senor Johnson drove his horses masterfully with his one free hand. The road did not exist, except to his trained eyes. They seemed to be swimming out, out, into a vapour of night with the wind of their going steady against their faces.

"Buck," she murmured, "I'm so tired."

He tightened his arm around her and she went to sleep, half-waking at the ranches where the relays waited, dozing again as soon as the lanterns dropped behind. And Senor Johnson, alone with his horses and the solemn stars, drove on, ever on, into the desert.

By grey of the early summer dawn they arrived. The girl wakened, descended, smiling uncertainly at Susie O'Toole, blinking somnolently at her surroundings. Susie put her to bed in the little southwest room where hung the shiny Colt's forty-five in its worn leather "Texas-style" holster. She murmured incoherent thanks and sank again to sleep, overcome by the fatigue of unaccustomed travelling, by the potency of the desert air, by the excitement of anticipation to which her nerves had long been strung.

Senor Johnson did not sleep. He was tough, and used to it. He lit a cigar and rambled about, now reading the newspapers he had brought with him, now prowling softly about the building, now visiting the corrals and outbuildings, once even the thousand-acre pasture where his saddle-horse knew him and came to him to have its forehead rubbed. The dawn broke in good earnest, throwing aside its gauzy draperies of mauve. Sang, the Chinese cook, built his fire. Senor Johnson forbade him to clang the rising bell, and himself roused the cow-punchers. The girl slept on. Senor Johnson tiptoed a dozen times to the bedroom door. Once he ventured to push it open. He looked long within, then shut it softly and tiptoed out into the open, his eyes shining.

"Jed," he said to his foreman, "you don't know how it made me feel. To see her lying there so pink and soft and pretty, with her yaller hair all tumbled about and a little smile on her—there in my old bed, with my old gun hanging over her that way—By Heaven, Jed, it made me feel almost HOLY!"

107

About noon she emerged from the room, fully refreshed and wide awake. She and Susie O'Toole had unpacked at least one of the trunks, and now she stood arrayed in shirtwaist and blue skirt.

At once she stepped into the open air and looked about her with considerable curiosity.

"So this is a real cattle ranch," was her comment.

Senor Johnson was at her side pressing on her with boyish eagerness the sights of the place. She patted the stag hounds and inspected the garden. Then, confessing herself hungry, she obeyed with alacrity Sang's call to an early meal. At the table she ate coquettishly, throwing her birdlike side glances at the man opposite.

"I want to see a real cowboy," she announced, as she pushed her chair back.

"Why, sure!" cried Senor Johnson joyously. "Sang! hi, Sang! Tell Brent Palmer to step in here a minute."

After an interval the cowboy appeared, mincing in on his high-heeled boots, his silver spurs jingling, the fringe of his chaps impacting softly on the leather. He stood at ease, his broad hat in both hands, his dark, level brows fixed on his chief.

"Shake hands with Mrs. Johnson, Brent. I called you in because she said she wanted to see a real cow-puncher."

"Oh, BUCK!" cried the woman.

For an instant the cow-puncher's level brows drew together. Then he caught the woman's glance fair. He smiled.

"Well, I ain't much to look at," he proffered.

"That's not for you to say, sir," said Estrella, recovering.

"Brent, here, gentled your pony for you," exclaimed Senor Johnson.

"Oh," cried Estrella, "have I a pony? How nice. And it was so good of you, Mr. Brent. Can't I see him? I want to see him. I want to give him a piece of sugar." She fumbled in the bowl.

"Sure you can see him. I don't know as he'll eat sugar. He ain't that educated. Think you could teach him to eat sugar, Brent?"

"I reckon," replied the cowboy.

They went out toward the corral, the cowboy joining them as a matter of course. Estrella demanded explanations as she went along. Their progress was leisurely. The blindfolded pump mule interested her.

"And he goes round and round that way all day without stopping, thinking he's really getting somewhere!" she marvelled. "I think that's a shame! Poor old fellow, to get fooled that way!"

"It is some foolish," said Brent Palmer, "but he ain't any worse off than a cow-pony that hikes out twenty mile and then twenty back."

"No, I suppose not," admitted Estrella.

"And we got to have water, you know," added Senor Johnson.

Brent rode up the sorrel bareback. The pretty animal, gentle as a kitten, nevertheless planted his forefeet strongly and snorted at Estrella.

"I reckon he ain't used to the sight of a woman," proffered the Senor, disappointed. "He'll get used to you. Go up to him soft-like and rub him between the eyes.'"

Estrella approached, but the pony jerked back his head with every symptom of distrust. She forgot the sugar she had intended to offer him.

"He's a perfect beauty," she said at last, "but, my! I'd never dare ride him. I'm awful scairt of horses."

"Oh, he'll come around all right," assured Brent easily. "I'll fix him."

"Oh, Mr. Brent," she exclaimed, "don't think I don't appreciate what you've done. I'm sure he's really just as gentle as he can be. It's only that I'm foolish."

"I'll fix him," repeated Brent.

The two men conducted her here and there, showing her the various institutions of the place. A man bent near the shed nailing a shoe to a horse's hoof.

"So you even have a blacksmith!" said Estrella. Her guides laughed amusedly.

"Tommy, come here!" called the Senor.

The horseshoer straightened up and approached. He was a lithe, curly-haired young boy, with a reckless, humorous eye and a smooth face, now red from bending over.

"Tommy, shake hands with Mrs. Johnson," said the Senor. "Mrs. Johnson wants to know if you're the blacksmith." He exploded in laughter.

"Oh, BUCK!" cried Estrella again.

"No, ma'am," answered the boy directly; "I'm just tacking a shoe on Danger, here. We all does our own blacksmithing."

His roving eye examined her countenance respectfully, but with admiration. She caught the admiration and returned it, covertly but unmistakably, pleased that her charms were appreciated.

They continued their rounds. The sun was very hot and the dust deep. A woman would have known that these things distressed Estrella. She picked her way through the debris; she dropped her head from the burning; she felt her delicate garments moistening with perspiration, her hair dampening; the dust sifted up through the air. Over in the large corral a bronco buster, assisted by two of the cowboys, was engaged in roping and throwing some wild mustangs. The sight was wonderful, but here the dust billowed in clouds.

"I'm getting a little hot and tired," she confessed at last. "I think I'll go to the house."

But near the shed she stopped again, interested in spite of herself by a bit of repairing Tommy had under way. The tire of a wagon wheel had been destroyed. Tommy was mending it. On the ground lay a fresh cowhide. From this Tommy was cutting a wide strip. As she watched he measured the strip around the circumference of the wheel.

"He isn't going to make a tire of that!" she exclaimed, incredulously.

"Sure," replied Senor Johnson.

"Will it wear?"

"It'll wear for a month or so, till we can get another from town."

Estrella advanced and felt curiously of the rawhide. Tommy was fastening it to the wheel at the ends only.

"But how can it stay on that way?" she objected. "It'll come right off as soon as you use it."

"It'll harden on tight enough."

"Why?" she persisted. "Does it shrink much when it dries?"

Senor Johnson stared to see if she might be joking. "Does it shrink?" he repeated slowly. "There ain't nothing shrinks more, nor harder. It'll mighty nigh break that wood."

Estrella, incredulous, interested, she could not have told why, stooped again to feel the soft, yielding hide. She shook her head.

"You're joking me because I'm a tenderfoot," she accused brightly. "I know it dries hard, and I'll believe it shrinks a lot, but to break wood—that's piling it on a little thick."

"No, that's right, ma'am," broke in Brent Palmer. "It's awful strong. It pulls like a horse when the desert sun gets on it. You wrap anything up in a piece of that hide and see what happens. Some time you take and wrap a piece around a potato and put her out in the sun and see how it'll squeeze the water out of her."

"Is that so?" she appealed to Tommy. "I can't tell when they are making fun of me."

"Yes, ma'am, that's right," he assured her.

Estrella passed a strip of the flexible hide playfully about her wrists.

"And if I let that dry that way I'd be handcuffed hard and fast," she said.

"It would cut you down to the bone," supplemented Brent Palmer.

She untwisted the strip, and stood looking at it, her eyes wide.

"I—I don't know why—" she faltered. "The thought makes me a little sick. Why, isn't it queer? Ugh! it's like a snake!" She flung it from her energetically and turned toward the ranch house.

CHAPTER SEVEN
ESTRELLA

The honeymoon developed and the necessary adjustments took place. The latter Senor Johnson had not foreseen; and yet, when the necessity for them arose, he acknowledged them right and proper.

"Course she don't want to ride over to Circle I with us," he informed his confidant, Jed Parker. "It's a long ride, and she ain't used to riding yet. Trouble is I've been thinking of doing things with her just as if she was a man. Women are different. They likes different things."

This second idea gradually overlaid the first in Senor Johnson's mind. Estrella showed little aptitude or interest in the rougher side of life. Her husband's statement as to her being still unused to riding was distinctly a euphemism. Estrella never arrived at the point of feeling safe on a horse. In time she gave up trying, and the sorrel drifted back to cow-punching. The range work she never understood.

As a spectacle it imposed itself on her interest for a week; but since she could discover no real and vital concern in the welfare of cows, soon the mere outward show became an old story. Estrella's sleek nature avoided instinctively all that interfered with bodily well-being. When she was cool and well-fed and not thirsty, and surrounded by a proper degree of feminine daintiness, then she was ready to amuse herself. But she could not understand the desirability of those pleasures for which a certain price in discomfort must be paid. As for firearms, she confessed herself frankly afraid of them. That was the point at which her intimacy with them stopped.

The natural level to which these waters fell is easily seen. Quite simply, the Senor found that a wife does not enter fully into her husband's workaday life. The dreams he had dreamed did not come true.

This was at first a disappointment to him, of course, but the disappointment did not last. Senor Johnson was a man of sense, and he easily modified his first scheme of married life.

"She'd get sick of it, and I'd get sick of it," he formulated his new philosophy. "Now I got something to come back to, somebody to look forward to. And it's a WOMAN; it ain't one of these darn gangle-leg cowgirls. The great thing is to feel you BELONG to someone; and that someone nice and cool and fresh and purty is waitin' for you when you come in tired. It beats that other little old idee of mine slick as a gun barrel."

So, during this, the busy season of the range riding, immediately before the great fall round-ups, Senor Johnson rode abroad all day, and returned to his own hearth as many evenings of the week as he could. Estrella always saw him coming and stood in the doorway to greet him. He kicked off his spurs, washed and dusted himself, and spent the evening with his wife. He liked the sound of exactly that phrase, and was fond of repeating it to himself in a variety of connections.

"When I get in I'll spend the evening with my wife." "If I don't ride over to Circle I, I'll spend the evening with my wife," and so on. He had a good deal to tell her of the day's discoveries, the state of the range, and the condition of the cattle. To all of this she listened at least with patience. Senor Johnson, like most men who have long delayed marriage, was self-centred without knowing it. His interest in his mate had to do with her personality rather than with her doings.

"What you do with yourself all day to-day?" he occasionally inquired.

"Oh, there's lots to do," she would answer, a trifle listlessly; and this reply always seemed quite to satisfy his interest in the subject.

Senor Johnson, with a curiously instant transformation often to be observed among the adventurous, settled luxuriously into the state of being a married man. Its smallest details gave him distinct and separate sensations of pleasure.

"I plumb likes it all," he said. "I likes havin' interest in some fool geranium plant, and I likes worryin' about the screen doors and all the rest of the plumb foolishness. It does me good. It feels like stretchin' your legs in front of a good warm fire."

The centre, the compelling influence of this new state of affairs, was undoubtedly Estrella, and yet it is equally to be doubted whether she stood for more than the suggestion. Senor Johnson conducted his entire life with reference to his wife. His waking hours were concerned only with the thought of her, his every act revolved in its orbit controlled by her influence. Nevertheless she, as an individual human being, had little to do with it. Senor Johnson referred his life to a state of affairs he had himself invented and which he called the married state, and to a woman whose attitude he had himself determined upon and whom he designated as his wife. The actual state of affairs—whatever it might be—he did not see; and the actual woman supplied merely the material medium necessary to the reality of his idea. Whether Estrella's eyes were interested or bored, bright or dull, alert or abstracted, contented or afraid, Senor Johnson could not have told you. He might have replied promptly enough—that they were happy and loving. That is the way Senor Johnson conceived a wife's eyes.

The routine of life, then, soon settled. After breakfast the Senor insisted that his wife accompany him on a short tour of inspection. "A little pasear," he called it, "just to get set for the day." Then his horse was brought, and he rode away on whatever business called him. Like a true son of the alkali, he took no lunch with him, nor expected his horse to feed until his return. This was an hour before sunset. The evening passed as has been described. It was all very simple.

When the business hung close to the ranch house--as in the bronco busting, the rebranding of bought cattle, and the like—he was able to share his wife's day. Estrella conducted herself dreamily, with a slow smile for him when his actual presence insisted on her attention. She seemed much given to staring out over the desert. Senor Johnson, appreciatively, thought he could understand this. Again, she gave much leisure to rocking back and forth on the low, wide veranda, her hands idle, her eyes vacant, her lips dumb. Susie O'Toole had early proved incompatible and had gone.

"A nice, contented, home sort of a woman," said Senor Johnson.

One thing alone besides the deserts on which she never seemed tired of looking, fascinated her. Whenever a beef was killed for the uses of the ranch, she commanded strips of the green skin. Then, like a child, she bound them and sewed them and nailed them to substances particularly susceptible to their constricting power. She choked the necks of green gourds, she indented the tender bark of cottonwood shoots, she expended an apparently exhaustless ingenuity on the fabrication of mechanical devices whose principle answered to the pulling of the drying rawhide. And always along the adobe fence could be seen a long row of potatoes bound in skin, some of them fresh and smooth and round; some sweating in the agony of squeezing; some wrinkled and dry and little, the last drops of life tortured out of them. Senor Johnson laughed good-humouredly at these toys, puzzled to explain their fascination for his wife.

"They're sure an amusing enough contraption honey," said he, "but what makes you stand out there in the hot sun staring at them that way? It's cooler on the porch."

"I don't know," said Estrella, helplessly, turning her slow, vacant gaze on him. Suddenly she shivered in a strong physical revulsion. "I don't know!" she cried with passion.

After they had been married about a month Senor Johnson found it necessary to drive into Willets.

"How would you like to go, too, and buy some duds?" he asked Estrella.

"Oh!" she cried strangely. "When?"

"Day after tomorrow."

The trip decided, her entire attitude changed. The vacancy of her gaze lifted; her movements quickened; she left off staring at the desert, and her rawhide toys were neglected. Before starting, Senor Johnson gave her a check book. He explained that there were no banks in Willets, but that Goodrich, the storekeeper, would honour her signature.

"Buy what you want to, honey," said he. "Tear her wide open. I'm good for it."

"How much can I draw?" she asked, smiling.

"As much as you want to," he replied with emphasis.

"Take care"—she poised before him with the check book extended—"I may draw—I might draw fifty thousand dollars."

"Not out of Goodrich," he grinned; "you'd bust the game. But hold him up for the limit, anyway."

He chuckled aloud, pleased at the rare, bird-like coquetry of the woman. They drove to Willets. It took them two days to go and two days to return. Estrella went through the town in a cyclone burst of enthusiasm, saw everything, bought everything, exhausted everything in two hours. Willets was not a large place. On her return to the ranch she sat down at once in the rocking-chair on the veranda. Her hands fell into her lap. She stared out over the desert.

Senor Johnson stole up behind her, clumsy as a playful bear. His eyes followed the direction of hers to where a cloud shadow lay across the slope, heavy, palpable, untransparent, like a blotch of ink.

"Pretty, isn't it, honey?" said he. "Glad to get back?"

She smiled at him her vacant, slow smile.

"Here's my check book," she said; "put it away for me. I'm through with it."

"I'll put it in my desk," said he. "It's in the left-hand cubbyhole," he called from inside.

"Very well," she replied.

He stood in the doorway, looking fondly at her unconscious shoulders and the pose of her blonde head thrown back against the high rocking-chair.

"That's the sort of a woman, after all," said Senor Johnson. "No blame fuss about her."

## CHAPTER EIGHT
## THE ROUND-UP

This, as you well may gather, was in the summer routine. Now the time of the great fall round-up drew near. The home ranch began to bustle in preparation.

All through Cochise County were short mountain ranges set down, apparently at random, like a child's blocks. In and out between them flowed the broad, plain-like valleys. On the valleys were the various ranges, great or small, controlled by the different individuals of the Cattlemen's Association. During the year an unimportant, but certain, shifting of stock took place. A few cattle of Senor Johnson's Lazy Y eluded the vigilance of his riders to drift over through the Grant Pass and into the ranges of his neighbour; equally, many of the neighbour's steers watered daily at Senor Johnson's troughs. It was a matter of courtesy to permit this, but one of the reasons for the fall round-up was a redistribution to the proper ranges. Each cattle-owner sent an outfit to the scene of labour. The combined outfits moved slowly from one valley to another, cutting out the strays, branding the late calves, collecting for the owner of that particular range all his stock, that he might select his marketable beef. In turn each cattleman was host to his neighbours and their men.

This year it had been decided to begin the circle of the round-up at the C 0 Bar, near the banks of the San Pedro. Thence it would work eastward, wandering slowly in north and south deviation, to include all the country, until the final break-up would occur at the Lazy Y.

The Lazy Y crew was to consist of four men, thirty riding horses, a "chuck wagon," and cook. These, helping others, and receiving help in turn, would suffice, for in the round-up labour was pooled to a common end. With them would ride Jed Parker, to safeguard his master's interests.

For a week the punchers, in their daily rides, gathered in the range ponies. Senor Johnson owned fifty horses which he maintained at the home ranch for every-day riding, two hundred broken saddle animals, allowed the freedom of the range, except when special occasion demanded their use, and perhaps half a thousand quite unbroken—brood mares, stallions, young horses, broncos, and the like. At this time of year it was his habit to corral all those saddlewise in order to select horses for the round-ups and to replace the ranch animals. The latter he turned loose for their turn at the freedom of the range.

The horses chosen, next the men turned their attention to outfit. Each had, of course, his saddle, spurs, and "rope." Of the latter the chuck wagon carried many extra. That vehicle, furthermore, transported such articles as the blankets, the tarpaulins under which to sleep, the running irons for branding, the cooking layout, and the men's personal effects. All was in readiness to move for the six weeks' circle, when a complication arose. Jed Parker, while nimbly escaping an irritated steer, twisted the high heel of his boot on the corral fence. He insisted the injury amounted to nothing. Senor Johnson however, disagreed.

"It don't amount to nothing, Jed," he pronounced, after manipulation, "but she might make a good able-bodied injury with a little coaxing. Rest her a week and then you'll be all right."

"Rest her, the devil!" growled Jed; "who's going to San Pedro?"

"I will, of course," replied the Senor promptly. "Didje think we'd send the Chink?"

"I was first cousin to a Yaqui jackass for sendin' young Billy Ellis out. He'll be back in a week. He'd do."

"So'd the President," the Senor pointed out; "I hear he's had some experience."

"I hate to have you to go," objected Jed. "There's the missis." He shot a glance sideways at his chief.

"I guess she and I can stand it for a week," scoffed the latter. "Why, we are old married folks by now. Besides, you can take care of her."

"I'll try," said Jed Parker, a little grimly.

## CHAPTER NINE
## THE LONG TRAIL

The round-up crew started early the next morning, just about sun-up. Senor Johnson rode first, merely to keep out of the dust. Then followed Torn Rich, jogging along easily in the cow-puncher's "Spanish trot" whistling soothingly to quiet the horses, giving a lead to the band of saddle animals strung out loosely behind him. These moved on gracefully and lightly in the manner of the unburdened plains horse, half decided to follow Tom's guidance, half inclined to break to right or left. Homer and Jim Lester flanked them, also riding in a slouch of apparent laziness, but every once in a while darting forward like bullets to turn back into the main herd certain individuals whom the early morning of the unwearied day had inspired to make a dash for liberty. The rear was brought up by Jerky Jones, the fourth cow-puncher, and the four-mule chuck wagon, lost in its own dust.

The sun mounted; the desert went silently through its changes. Wind devils raised straight, true columns of dust six, eight hundred, even a thousand feet into the air. The billows of dust from the horses and men crept and crawled with them like a living creature. Glorious colour, magnificent distance, astonishing illusion, filled the world.

Senor Johnson rode ahead, looking at these things. The separation from his wife, brief as it would be, left room in his soul for the heart-hunger which beauty arouses in men. He loved the charm of the desert, yet it hurt him.

Behind him the punchers relieved the tedium of the march, each after his own manner. In an hour the bunch of loose horses lost its early-morning good spirits and settled down to a steady plodding, that needed no supervision. Tom Rich led them, now, in silence, his time fully occupied in rolling Mexican cigarettes with one hand. The other three dropped back together and exchanged desultory remarks. Occasionally Jim Lester sang. It was always the same song of uncounted verses, but Jim had a strange fashion of singing a single verse at a time. After a long interval he would sing another.

> "My Love is a rider
> And broncos he breaks,
> But he's given up riding
> And all for my sake,
> For he found him a horse
> And it suited him so
> That he vowed he'd ne'er ride
> Any other bronco!"

he warbled, and then in the same breath:

"Say, boys, did you get onto the pisano-looking shorthorn at Willets last week?

"Nope."

"He sifted in wearin' one of these hardboiled hats, and carryin' a brogue thick enough to skate on. Says he wants a job drivin' team—that he drives a truck plenty back to St. Louis, where he comes from. Goodrich sets him behind them little pinto cavallos he has. Say! that son of a gun a driver! He couldn't drive nails in a snow bank." An expressive free-hand gesture told all there was to tell of the runaway. "Th' shorthorn landed headfirst in Goldfish Charlie's horse trough. Charlie fishes him out. 'How the devil, stranger,' says Charlie, 'did you come to fall in here?' 'You blamed fool,' says the shorthorn, just cryin' mad, 'I didn't come to fall in here, I come to drive horses.'"

And then, without a transitory pause:

> Oh, my love has a gun
> And that gun he can use,
> ut he's quit his gun fighting
> As well as his booze.
> nd he's sold him his saddle,
> His spurs, and his rope,
> nd there's no more cow-punching
> And that's what I hope."

The alkali dust, swirled back by a little breeze, billowed up and choked him. Behind, the mules coughed, their coats whitening with the powder. Far ahead in the distance lay the westerly mountains. They looked an hour away, and yet every man and beast in the outfit knew that hour after hour they were doomed, by the enchantment of the land, to plod ahead without apparently getting an inch nearer. The only salvation was to forget the mountains and to fill the present moment full of little things.

But Senor Johnson, to-day, found himself unable to do this. In spite of his best efforts he caught himself straining toward the distant goal, becoming impatient, trying to measure progress by landmarks—in short acting like a tenderfoot on the desert, who wears himself down and dies, not from the hardship, but from the nervous strain which he does not know how to avoid. Senor Johnson knew this as well as you and I. He cursed himself vigorously, and began with great resolution to think of something else.

He was aroused from this by Tom Rich, riding alongside. "Somebody coming, Senor," said he.

Senor Johnson raised his eyes to the approaching cloud of dust. Silently the two watched it until it resolved into a rider loping easily along. In fifteen minutes he drew rein, his pony dropped immediately from a gallop to immobility, he swung into a graceful at-ease attitude across his saddle, grinned amiably, and began to roll a cigarette.

"Billy Ellis," cried Rich.

"That's me," replied the newcomer.

"Thought you were down to Tucson?"

"I was."

"Thought you wasn't comin' back for a week yet?"

"Tommy," proffered Billy Ellis dreamily, "when you go to Tucson next you watch out until you sees a little, squint-eyed Britisher. Take a look at him. Then come away. He says he don't know nothin' about poker. Mebbe he don't, but he'll outhold a warehouse."

But here Senor Johnson broke in: "Billy, you're just in time. Jed has hurt his foot and can't get on for a week yet. I want you to take charge. I've got a lot to do at the ranch."

"Ain't got my war-bag," objected Billy.

"Take my stuff. I'll send yours on when Parker goes."

"All right."

"Well, so long."

"So long, Senor." They moved. The erratic Arizona breezes twisted the dust of their going. Senor Johnson watched them dwindle. With them seemed to go the joy in the old life. No longer did the long trail possess for him its ancient fascination. He had become a domestic man.

"And I'm glad of it," commented Senor Johnson.

The dust eddied aside. Plainly could be seen the swaying wagon, the loose-riding cowboys, the gleaming, naked backs of the herd. Then the veil closed over them again. But down the wind, faintly, in snatches, came the words of Jim Lester's song:

"Oh, Sam has a gun
That has gone to the bad,
Which makes poor old Sammy
Feel pretty, damn sad,
For that gun it shoots high,
And that gun it shoots low,
And it wabbles about
Like a bucking bronco!"

Senor Johnson turned and struck spurs to his willing pony.

CHAPTER TEN
THE DISCOVERY

Senor Buck Johnson loped quickly back toward the home ranch, his heart glad at this fortunate solution of his annoyance. The home ranch lay in plain sight not ten miles away. As Senor Johnson idly watched it shimmering in the heat, a tiny figure detached itself from the mass and launched itself in his direction.

"Wonder what's eating HIM!" marvelled Senor Johnson, "—and who is it?"

The figure drew steadily nearer. In half an hour it had approached near enough to be recognised.

"Why, it's Jed!" cried the Senor, and spurred his horse. "What do you mean, riding out with that foot?" he demanded sternly, when within hailing distance.

"Foot, hell!" gasped Parker, whirling his horse alongside. "Your wife's run away with Brent Palmer."

For fully ten seconds not the faintest indication proved that the husband had heard, except that he lifted his bridle-hand, and the well-trained pony stopped.

"What did you say?" he asked finally.

"Your wife's run away with Brent Palmer," repeated Jed, almost with impatience.

Again the long pause.

"How do you know?" asked Senor Johnson, then.

"Know, hell! It's been going on for a month. Sang saw them drive off. They took the buckboard. He heard 'em planning it. He was too scairt to tell till they'd gone. I just found it out. They've been gone two hours. Must be going to make the Limited." Parker fidgeted, impatient to be off. "You're wasting time," he snapped at the motionless figure.

Suddenly Johnson's face flamed. He reached from his saddle to clutch Jed's shoulder, nearly pulling the foreman from his pony.

"You lie!" he cried. "You're lying to me! It ain't SO!"

Parker made no effort to extricate himself from the painful grasp. His cool eyes met the blazing eyes of his chief.

"I wisht I did lie, Buck," he said sadly. "I wisht it wasn't so. But it is."

Johnson's head snapped back to the front with a groan. The pony snorted as the steel bit his flanks, leaped forward, and with head outstretched, nostrils wide, the wicked white of the bronco flickering in the corner of his eye, struck the bee line for the home ranch. Jed followed as fast as he was able.

On his arrival he found his chief raging about the house like a wild beast. Sang trembled from a quick and stormy interrogatory in the kitchen. Chairs had been upset and let lie. Estrella's belongings had been tumbled over. Senor Johnson there found only too sure proof, in the various lacks, of a premeditated and permanent flight. Still he hoped; and as long as he hoped, he doubted, and the demons of doubt tore him to a frenzy. Jed stood near the door, his arms folded, his weight shifted to his sound foot, waiting and wondering what the next move was to be.

Finally, Senor Johnson, struck with a new idea, ran to his desk to rummage in a pigeon-hole. But he found no need to do so, for lying on the desk was what he sought—the check book from which Estrella was to draw on Goodrich for the money she might need. He fairly snatched it open. Two of the checks had been torn out, stub and all. And then his eye caught a crumpled bit of blue paper under the edge of the desk.

He smoothed it out. The check was made out to bearer and signed Estrella Johnson. It called for fifteen thousand dollars. Across the middle was a great ink blot, reason for its rejection.

At once Senor Johnson became singularly and dangerously cool.

"I reckon you're right, Jed," he cried in his natural voice. "She's gone with him. She's got all her traps with her, and she's drawn on Goodrich for fifteen thousand. And SHE never thought of going just this time of month when the miners are in with their dust, and Goodrich would be sure to have that much. That's friend Palmer. Been going on a month, you say?"

"I couldn't say anything, Buck," said Parker anxiously. "A man's never sure enough about them things till afterwards."

"I know," agreed Buck Johnson; "give me a light for my cigarette."

He puffed for a moment, then rose, stretching his legs. In a moment he returned from the other room, the old shiny Colt's forty-five strapped loosely on his hip. Jed looked him in the face with some anxiety. The foreman was not deceived by the man's easy manner; in fact, he knew it to be symptomatic of one of the dangerous phases of Senor Johnson's character.

"What's up, Buck?" he inquired.

"Just going out for a pasear with the little horse, Jed."

"I suppose I better come along?"

"Not with your lame foot, Jed."

The tone of voice was conclusive. Jed cleared his throat.

"She left this for you," said he, proffering an envelope. "Them kind always writes."

"Sure," agreed Senor Johnson, stuffing the letter carelessly into his side pocket. He half drew the Colt's from its holster and slipped it back again. "Makes you feel plumb like a man to have one of these things rubbin' against you again," he observed irrelevantly. Then he went out, leaving the foreman leaning, chair tilted, against the wall.

CHAPTER ELEVEN
THE CAPTURE

Although he had left the room so suddenly, Senor Johnson did not at once open the gate of the adobe wall. His demeanour was gay, for he was a Westerner, but his heart was black. Hardly did he see beyond the convexity of his eyeballs.

The pony, warmed up by its little run, pawed the ground, impatient to be off. It was a fine animal, clean-built, deep-chested, one of the mustang stock descended from the Arabs brought over by Pizarro. Sang watched fearfully from the slant of the kitchen window. Jed Parker, even, listened for the beat of the horse's hoofs.

But Senor Johnson stood stock-still, his brain absolutely numb and empty. His hand brushed against something which fell, to the ground. He brought his dull gaze to bear on it. The object proved to be a black, wrinkled spheroid, baked hard as iron in the sunshine of Estrella's toys, a potato squeezed to dryness by the constricting power of the rawhide. In a row along the fence were others. To Senor Johnson it seemed that thus his heart was being squeezed in the fire of suffering.

But the slight movement of the falling object roused him. He swung open the gate. The pony bowed his head delightedly. He was not tired, but his reins depended straight to the ground, and it was a point of honour with him to stand. At the saddle horn, in its sling, hung the riata, the "rope" without which no cowman ever stirs abroad, but which Senor Johnson had rarely used of late. Senor Johnson threw the reins over, seized the pony's mane in his left hand, held the pommel with his right, and so swung easily aboard, the pony's jump helping him to the saddle. Wheel tracks led down the trail. He followed them.

Truth to tell, Senor Johnson had very little idea of what he was going to do. His action was entirely instinctive. The wheel tracks held to the southwest so he held to the southwest, too.

The pony hit his stride. The miles slipped by. After seven of them the animal slowed to a walk. Senor Johnson allowed him to get his wind, then spurred him on again. He did not even take the ordinary precautions of a pursuer. He did not even glance to the horizon in search.

About supper-time he came to the first ranch house. There he took a bite to eat and exchanged his horse for another, a favourite of his, named Button. The two men asked no questions.

"See Mrs. Johnson go through?" asked the Senor from the saddle.

"Yes, about three o'clock. Brent Palmer driving her. Bound for Willets to visit the preacher's wife, she said. Ought to catch up at the Circle I. That's where they'd all spend the night, of course. So long."

Senor Johnson knew now the couple would follow the straight road. They would fear no pursuit. He himself was supposed not to return for a week, and the story of visiting the minister's wife was not only plausible, it was natural. Jed had upset calculations, because Jed was shrewd, and had eyes in his head. Buck Johnson's first mental numbness was wearing away; he was beginning to think.

The night was very still and very dark, the stars very bright in their candle-like glow. The man, loping steadily on through the darkness, recalled that other night, equally still, equally dark, equally starry, when he had driven out from his accustomed life into the unknown with a woman by his side, the sight of whom asleep had made him feel "almost holy." He uttered a short laugh.

The pony was a good one, well equal to twice the distance he would be called upon to cover this night. Senor Johnson managed him well. By long experience and a natural instinct he knew just how hard to push his mount, just how to keep inside the point where too rapid exhaustion of vitality begins.

Toward the hour of sunrise he drew rein to look about him. The desert, till now wrapped in the thousand little noises that make night silence, drew breath in preparation for the awe of the daily wonder. It lay across the world heavy as a sea of lead, and as lifeless; deeply unconscious, like an exhausted sleeper. The sky bent above, the stars paling. Far away the mountains seemed to wait. And then, imperceptibly, those in the east became blacker and sharper, while those in the west became faintly lucent and lost the distinctness of their outline. The change was nothing, yet everything. And suddenly a desert bird sprang into the air and began to sing.

Senor Johnson caught the wonder of it. The wonder of it seemed to him wasted, useless, cruel in its effect. He sighed impatiently, and drew his hand across his eyes.

The desert became grey with the first light before the glory. In the illusory revealment of it Senor Johnson's sharp frontiersman's eyes made out an object moving away from him in the middle distance. In a moment the object rose for a second against the sky line, then disappeared. He knew it to be the buckboard, and that the vehicle had just plunged into the dry bed of an arroyo.

Immediately life surged through him like an electric shock. He unfastened the riata from its sling, shook loose the noose, and moved forward in the direction in which he had last seen the buckboard.

At the top of the steep little bank he stopped behind the mesquite, straining his eyes; luck had been good to him. The buckboard had pulled up, and Brent Palmer was at the moment beginning a little fire, evidently to make the morning coffee.

Senor Johnson struck spurs to his horse and half slid, half fell, clattering, down the steep clay bank almost on top of the couple below.

Estrella screamed. Brent Palmer jerked out an oath, and reached for his gun. The loop of the riata fell wide over him, immediately to be jerked tight, binding his arms tight to his side.

The bronco-buster, swept from his feet by the pony's rapid turn, nevertheless struggled desperately to wrench himself loose. Button, intelligent at all rope work, walked steadily backward, step by step, taking up the slack, keeping the rope tight as he had done hundreds of times before when a steer had struggled as this man was struggling now. His master leaped from the saddle and ran forward. Button continued to walk slowly back. The riata remained taut. The noose held.

Brent Palmer fought savagely, even then. He kicked, he rolled over and over, he wrenched violently at his pinioned arms, he twisted his powerful young body from Senor Johnson's grasp again and again. But it was no use. In less than a minute he was bound hard and fast. Button promptly slackened the rope. The dust settled. The noise of the combat died. Again could be heard the single desert bird singing against the dawn.

CHAPTER TWELVE
IN THE ARROYO

Senor Johnson quietly approached Estrella. The girl had, during the struggle, gone through an aimless but frantic exhibition of terror. Now she shrank back, her eyes staring wildly, her hands behind her, ready to flop again over the brink of hysteria.

"What are you going to do?" she demanded, her voice unnatural.

She received no reply. The man reached out and took her by the arm.

And then at once, as though the personal contact of the touch had broken through the last crumb of numbness with which shock had overlaid Buck Johnson's passions, the insanity of his rage broke out. He twisted her violently on her face, knelt on her back, and, with the short piece of hard rope the cowboy always carries to "hog-tie" cattle, he lashed her wrists together. Then he arose panting, his square black beard rising and falling with the rise and fall of his great chest.

Estrella had screamed again and again until her face had been fairly ground into the alkali. There she had choked and strangled and gasped and sobbed, her mind nearly unhinged with terror. She kept appealing to him in a hoarse voice, but could get no reply, no indication that he had even heard. This terrified her still more. Brent Palmer cursed steadily and accurately, but the man did not seem to hear him either.

The tempest bad broken in Buck Johnson's soul. When he had touched Estrella he had, for the first time, realised what he had lost. It was not the woman—her he despised. But the dreams! All at once he knew what they had been to him—he understood how completely the very substance of his life had changed in response to their slow soul-action. The new world had been blasted—the old no longer existed to which to return.

Buck Johnson stared at this catastrophe until his sight blurred. Why, it was atrocious! He had done nothing to deserve it! Why had they not left him peaceful in his own life of cattle and the trail? He had been happy. His dull eyes fell on the causes of the ruin.

And then, finally, in the understanding of how he had been tricked of his life, his happiness, his right to well-being, the whole force of the man's anger flared. Brent Palmer lay there cursing him artistically. That man had done it; that man was in his power. He would get even. How?

Estrella, too, lay huddled, helpless and defenseless, at his feet. She had done it. He would get even. How?

He had spoken no word. He spoke none now, either in answer to Estrella's appeals, becoming piteous in their craving for relief from suspense, or in response to Brent Palmer's steady stream of insults and vituperations. Such things were far below. The bitterness and anger and desolation were squeezing his heart. He remembered the silly little row of potatoes sewn in the green hide lying along the top of the adobe fence, some fresh and round, some dripping as the rawhide contracted, some black and withered and very small. A fierce and savage light sprang into his eyes.

CHAPTER THIRTEEN
THE RAWHIDE

First of all he unhitched the horses from the buckboard and turned them loose. Then, since he was early trained in Indian warfare, he dragged Palmer to the wagon wheel, and tied him so closely to it that he could not roll over. For, though the bronco-buster was already so fettered that his only possible movement was of the jack-knife variety, nevertheless he might be able to hitch himself along the ground to a sharp stone, there to saw through the rope about his wrists. Estrella, her husband held in contempt. He merely supplemented her wrist bands by one about the ankles.

Leisurely he mounted Button and turned up the wagon trail, leaving the two. Estrella had exhausted herself. She was capable of nothing more in the way of emotion. Her eyes tight closed, she inhaled in deep, trembling, long-drawn breaths, and exhaled with the name of her Maker.

Brent Palmer, on the contrary, was by no means subdued. He had expected to be shot in cold blood. Now he did not know what to anticipate. His black, level brows drawn straight in defiance, he threw his curses after Johnson's retreating figure.

The latter, however, paid no attention. He had his purposes. Once at the top of the arroyo he took a careful survey of the landscape, now rich with dawn. Each excrescence on the plain his half-squinted eyes noticed, and with instant skill relegated to its proper category of soap-weed, mesquite, cactus. At length he swung Button in an easy lope toward what looked to be a bunch of soap-weed in the middle distance.

But in a moment the cattle could be seen plainly. Button pricked up his ears. He knew cattle. Now he proceeded tentatively, lifting high his little hoofs to avoid the half-seen inequalities of the ground and the ground's growths, wondering whether he were to be called on to rope or to drive. When the rider had approached to within a hundred feet, the cattle started. Immediately Button understood that he was to pursue. No rope swung above his head, so he sheered off and ran as fast as he could to cut ahead of the bunch. But his rider with knee and rein forced him in. After a moment, to his astonishment, he found himself running alongside a big steer. Button had never hunted buffalo—Buck Johnson had.

The Colt's forty-five barked once, and then again. The steer staggered, fell to his knees, recovered, and finally stopped, the blood streaming from his nostrils. In a moment he fell heavily on his side—dead.

Senor Johnson at once dismounted and began methodically to skin the animal. This was not easy for he had no way of suspending the carcass nor of rolling it from side to side. However, he was practised at it and did a neat job. Two or three times he even caught himself taking extra pains that the thin flesh strips should not adhere to the inside of the pelt. Then he smiled grimly, and ripped it loose.

After the hide had been removed he cut from the edge, around and around, a long, narrow strip. With this he bound the whole into a compact bundle, strapped it on behind his saddle, and remounted. He returned to the arroyo.

Estrella still lay with her eyes closed. Brent Palmer looked up keenly. The bronco-buster saw the green hide. A puzzled expression crept across his face.

Roughly Johnson loosed his enemy from the wheel and dragged him to the woman. He passed the free end of the riata about them both, tying them close together. The girl continued to moan, out of her wits with terror.

"What are you going to do now, you devil?" demanded Palmer, but received no reply.

Buck Johnson spread out the rawhide. Putting forth his huge strength, he carried to it the pair, bound together like a bale of goods, and laid them on its cool surface. He threw across them the edges, and then deliberately began to wind around and around the huge and unwieldy rawhide package the strip he had cut from the edge of the pelt.

Nor was this altogether easy. At last Brent Palmer understood. He writhed in the struggle of desperation, foaming blasphemies. The uncouth bundle rolled here and there. But inexorably the other, from the advantage of his position, drew the thongs tighter.

And then, all at once, from vituperation the bronco-buster fell to pleading, not for life, but for death.

"For God's sake, shoot me!" he cried from within the smothering folds of the rawhide. "If you ever had a heart in you, shoot me! Don't leave me here to be crushed in this vise. You wouldn't do that to a yellow dog. An Injin wouldn't do that, Buck. It's a joke, isn't it? Don't go away and leave me, Buck. I've done you dirt. Cut my heart out, if you want to; I won't say a word, but don't leave me here for the sun—"is voice was drowned in a piercing scream, as Estrella came to herself and understood. Always the rawhide had possessed for her an occult fascination and repulsion. She had never been able to touch it without a shudder, and yet she had always been drawn to experiment with it. The terror of her doom had now added to it for her all the vague and premonitory terrors which heretofore she had not understood.

The richness of the dawn had flowed to the west. Day was at hand. Breezes had begun to play across the desert; the wind devils to raise their straight columns. A first long shaft of sunlight shot through a pass in the Chiricahuas, trembled in the dust-moted air, and laid its warmth on the rawhide. Senor Johnson roused himself from his gloom to speak his first words of the episode.

"There, damn you!" said he. "I guess you'll be close enough together now!"

He turned away to look for his horse.

CHAPTER FOURTEEN
THE DESERT

Button was a trusty of Senor Johnson's private animals. He was never known to leave his master in the lurch, and so was habitually allowed certain privileges. Now, instead of remaining exactly on the spot where he was "tied to the ground," he had wandered out of the dry arroyo bed to the upper level of the plains, where he knew certain bunch grasses might be found. Buck Johnson climbed the steep wooded bank in search of him.

The pony stood not ten feet distant. At his master's abrupt appearance he merely raised his head, a wisp of grass in the corner of his mouth, without attempting to move away. Buck Johnson walked confidently to him, fumbling in his side pocket for the piece of sugar with which he habitually soothed Button's sophisticated palate. His hand encountered Estrella's letter. He drew it out and opened it.

"Dear Buck," it read, "I am going away. I tried to be good, but I can't. It's too lonesome for me. I'm afraid of the horses and the cattle and the men and the desert. I hate it all. I tried to make you see how I felt about it, but you couldn't seem to see. I know you'll never forgive me, but I'd go crazy here. I'm almost crazy now. I suppose you think I'm a bad woman, but I am not. You won't believe that. Its' true though. The desert would make anyone bad. I don't see how you stand it. You've been good to me, and I've really tried, but it's no use. The country is awful. I never ought to have come. I'm sorry you are going to think me a bad woman, for I like you and admire you, but nothing, NOTHING could make me stay here any longer." She signed herself simply Estrella Sands, her maiden name.

Buck Johnson stood staring at the paper for a much longer time than was necessary merely to absorb the meaning of the words. His senses, sharpened by the stress of the last sixteen hours, were trying mightily to cut to the mystery of a change going on within himself. The phrases of the letter were bald enough, yet they conveyed something vital to his inner being. He could not understand what it was.

Then abruptly he raised his eyes.

Before him lay the desert, but a desert suddenly and miraculously changed, a desert he had never seen before. Mile after mile it swept away before him, hot, dry, suffocating, lifeless. The sparse vegetation was grey with the alkali dust. The heat hung choking in the air like a curtain. Lizards sprawled in the sun, repulsive. A rattlesnake dragged its loathsome length from under a mesquite. The dried carcass of a steer, whose parchment skin drew tight across its bones, rattled in the breeze. Here and there rock ridges showed with the obscenity of so many skeletons, exposing to the hard, cruel sky the earth's nakedness. Thirst, delirium, death, hovered palpable in the wind; dreadful, unconquerable, ghastly.

The desert showed her teeth and lay in wait like a fierce beast. The little soul of man shrank in terror before it.

Buck Johnson stared, recalling the phrases of the letter, recalling the words of his foreman, Jed Parker. "It's too lonesome for me," "I'm afraid," "I hate it all," "I'd go crazy here," "The desert would make anyone bad," "The country is awful." And the musing voice of the old cattleman, "I wonder if she'll like the country!" They reiterated themselves over and over; and always as refrain his own confident reply, "Like the country? Sure! Why SHOULDN'T she?"

And then he recalled the summer just passing, and the woman who had made no fuss. Chance remarks of hers came back to him, remarks whose meaning he had not at the time grasped, but which now he saw were desperate appeals to his understanding. He had known his desert. He had never known hers.

With an exclamation Buck Johnson turned abruptly back to the arroyo. Button followed him, mildly curious, certain that his master's reappearance meant a summons for himself.

Down the miniature cliff the man slid, confidently, without hesitation, sure of himself. His shoulders held squarely, his step elastic, his eye bright, he walked to the fearful, shapeless bundle now lying motionless on the flat surface of the alkali.

Brent Palmer had fallen into a grim silence, but Estrella still moaned. The cattleman drew his knife and ripped loose the bonds. Immediately the flaps of the wet rawhide fell apart, exposing to the new daylight the two bound together. Buck Johnson leaned over to touch the woman's shoulder.

"Estrella," said he gently.

Her eyes came open with a snap, and stared into his, wild with the surprise of his return.

"Estrella," he repeated, "how old are you?"

She gulped down a sob, unable to comprehend the purport of his question.

"How old are you, Estrella?" he repeated again.

"Twenty-one," she gasped finally.

"Ah!" said he.

He stood for a moment in deep thought, then began methodically, without haste, to cut loose the thongs that bound the two together.

When the man and the woman were quite freed, he stood for a moment, the knife in his hand, looking down on them. Then he swung himself into the saddle and rode away, straight down the narrow arroyo, out beyond its lower widening, into the vast plains the hither side of the Chiricahuas. The alkali dust was snatched by the wind from beneath his horse's feet. Smaller and smaller he dwindled, rising and falling, rising and falling in the monotonous cow-pony's lope. The heat shimmer veiled him for a moment, but he reappeared. A mirage concealed him, but he emerged on the other side of it. Then suddenly he was gone. The desert had swallowed him up.

# The Killer

## CHAPTER I

I want to state right at the start that I am writing this story twenty years after it happened solely because my wife and Señor Buck Johnson insist on it. Myself, I don't think it a good yarn. It hasn't any love story in it; and there isn't any plot. Things just happened, one thing after the other. There ought to be a yarn in it somehow, and I suppose if a fellow wanted to lie a little he could make a tail-twister out of it. Anyway, here goes; and if you don't like it, you know you can quit at any stage of the game.

It happened when I was a kid and didn't know any better than to do such things. They dared me to go up to Hooper's ranch and stay all night; and as I had no information on either the ranch or its owner, I saddled up and went. It was only twelve miles from our Box Springs ranch—a nice easy ride. I should explain that heretofore I had ridden the Gila end of our range, which is so far away that only vague rumours of Hooper had ever reached me at all. He was reputed a tough old devil with horrid habits; but that meant little to me. The tougher and horrider they came, the better they suited me— so I thought. Just to make everything entirely clear I will add that this was in the year of 1897 and the Soda Springs valley in Arizona.

By these two facts you old timers will gather the setting of my tale. Indian days over; "nester" days with frame houses and vegetable patches not yet here. Still a few guns packed for business purposes; Mexican border handy; no railroad in to Tombstone yet; cattle rustlers lingering in the Galiuros; train hold-ups and homicide yet prevalent but frowned upon; favourite tipple whiskey toddy with sugar; but the old fortified ranches all gone; longhorns crowded out by shorthorn blaze-head Herefords or near-Herefords; some indignation against Alfred Henry Lewis's *Wolfville* as a base libel; and, also but, no gasoline wagons or pumps, no white collars, no tourists pervading the desert, and the Injins still wearing blankets and overalls at their reservations instead of bead work on the railway platforms when the Overland goes through. In other words, we were wild and wooly, but sincerely didn't know it.

While I was saddling up to go take my dare, old Jed Parker came and leaned himself up against the snubbing post of the corral. He watched me for a while, and I kept quiet, knowing well enough that he had something to say.

"Know Hooper?" he asked.

"I've seen him driving by," said I.

I had: a little humped, insignificant figure with close-cropped white hair beneath a huge hat. He drove all hunched up. His buckboard was a rattletrap, old, insulting challenge to every little stone in the road; but there was nothing the matter with the horses or their harness. We never held much with grooming in Arizona, but these beasts shone like bronze. Good sizeable horses, clean built—well, I better not get started talking horse! They're the reason I had never really sized up the old man the few times I'd passed him.

"Well, he's a tough bird," said Jed.

"Looks like a harmless old cuss—but mean," says I.

"About this trip," said Jed, after I'd saddled and coiled my rope—"don't, and say you did."

I didn't answer this, but led my horse to the gate.

"Well, don't say as how I didn't tell you all about it," said Jed, going back to the bunk house.

Miserable old coot! I suppose he thought he *had* told me all about it! Jed was always too loquacious!

But I hadn't racked along more than two miles before a man cantered up who was perfectly able to express himself. He was one of our outfit and was known as Windy Bill. Nuff said!

"Hear you're goin' up to stay the night at Hooper's," said he. "Know Hooper?"

"No, I don't," said I, "are you another of these Sunbirds with glad news?"

"Know about Hooper's boomerang?"

"Boomerang!" I replied, "what's that?"

"That's what they call it. You know how of course we all let each other's strays water at our troughs in this country, and send 'em back to their own range at round up."

"Brother, you interest me," said I, "and would you mind informing me further how you tell the dear little cows apart?"

"Well, old Hooper don't, that's all," went on Windy, without paying me any attention. "He built him a chute leading to the water corrals, and half way down the chute he built a gate that would swing across it and open a hole into a dry corral. And he had a high platform with a handle that ran the gate. When any cattle but those of his own brands came along, he had a man swing the gate and they landed up into the dry corral. By and by he let them out on the range again."

"Without water?"

"Sure! And of course back they came into the chute. And so on. Till they died, or we came along and drove them back home."

"Windy," said I, "you're stuffing me full of tacks."

"I've seen little calves lyin' in heaps against the fence like drifts of tumbleweed," said Windy, soberly; and then added, without apparent passion, "The old——!"

Looking at Windy's face, I knew these words for truth.

"He's a bad *hombre*," resumed Windy Bill after a moment. "He never does no actual killing himself, but he's got a bad lot of oilers[A] there, especially an old one named Andreas and another one called Ramon, and all he has to do is to lift one eye at a man he don't like and that man is as good as dead—one time or another."

This was going it pretty strong, and I grinned at Windy Bill.

"All right," said Windy, "I'm just telling you."

"Well, what's the matter with you fellows down here?" I challenged. "How is it he's lasted so long? Why hasn't someone shot him? Are you all afraid of him or his Mexicans?"

"No, it ain't that, exactly. I don't know. He drives by all alone, and he don't pack no gun ever, and he's sort of runty—and—I do'no *why* he ain't been shot, but he ain't. And if I was you, I'd stick home."

Windy amused but did not greatly persuade me. By this time I was fairly conversant with the cowboy's sense of humour. Nothing would have tickled them more than to bluff me out of a harmless excursion by means of scareful tales. Shortly Windy Bill turned off to examine a distant bunch of cattle; and so I rode on alone.

It was coming on toward evening. Against the eastern mountains were floating tinted mists; and the cañons were a deep purple. The cattle were moving slowly so that here and there a nimbus of dust caught and reflected the late sunlight into gamboge yellows and mauves. The magic time was near when the fierce, implacable day-genius of the desert would fall asleep and the soft, gentle, beautiful star-eyed night-genius of the desert would arise and move softly. My pony racked along in the desert. The mass that represented Hooper's ranch drew imperceptibly nearer. I made out the green of trees and the white of walls and building.

---

CHAPTER II

Hooper's ranch proved to be entirely enclosed by a wall of adobe ten feet high and whitewashed. To the outside it presented a blank face. Only corrals and an alfalfa patch were not included. A wide, high gateway, that could be closed by massive doors, let into a stable yard, and seemed to be the only entrance. The buildings within were all immaculate also: evidently Old Man Hooper loved whitewash. Cottonwood trees showed their green heads; and to the right I saw the sloped shingled roof of a larger building. Not a living creature was in sight. I shook myself, saying that the undoubted sinister feeling of utter silence and lifelessness was compounded of my expectations and the time of day. But that did not satisfy me. My aroused mind, casting about, soon struck it: I was missing the swarms of blackbirds, linnets, purple finches, and doves that made our own ranch trees vocal. Here were no birds. Laughing at this simple explanation of my eerie feeling, I passed under the gate and entered the courtyard.

It, too, seemed empty. A stable occupied all one side; the other three were formed by bunk houses and necessary out-buildings. Here, too, dwelt absolute solitude and absolute silence. It was uncanny, as though one walked in a vacuum. Everything was neat and shut up and whitewashed and apparently dead. There were no sounds or signs of occupancy. I was as much alone as though I had been in the middle of an ocean. My mind, by now abnormally sensitive and alert, leaped on this idea. For the same reason, it insisted—lack of life: there were no birds here, not even *flies*! Of course, said I, gone to bed in the cool of evening: why should there be? I laughed aloud and hushed suddenly; and then nearly jumped out of my skin. The thin blue curl of smoke had caught my eye; and I became aware of the figure of a man seated on the ground, in the shadow, leaning against the building. The curl of smoke was from his cigarette. He was wrapped in a *serape* which blended well with the cool colour of shadow. My eyes were dazzled with the whitewash—natural enough—yet the impression of solitude had been so complete. It was uncanny, as though he had materialized out of the shadow itself. Silly idea! I ranged my eye along the row of houses, and I saw three other figures I had missed before, all broodingly immobile, all merged in shadow, all watching me, all with the insubstantial air of having as I looked taken body from thin air.

This was too foolish! I dismounted, dropped my horse's reins over his head, and sauntered to the nearest figure. He was lost in the dusk of the building and of his Mexican hat. I saw only the gleam of eyes.

"Where will I find Mr. Hooper?" I asked.

The figure waved a long, slim hand toward a wicket gate in one side of the enclosure. He said no word, nor made another motion; and the other figures sat as though graved from stone.

After a moment's hesitation I pushed open the wicket gate, and so found myself in a smaller intimate courtyard of most surprising character. Its centre was green grass, and about its border grew tall, bright flowers. A wide verandah ran about three sides. I could see that in the numerous windows hung white lace curtains. Mind you, this was in Arizona of the 'nineties!

I knocked at the nearest door, and after an interval it opened and I stood face to face with Old Man Hooper himself.

He proved to be as small as I had thought, not taller than my own shoulder, with a bent little figure dressed in wrinkled and baggy store clothes of a snuff brown. His bullet head had been cropped so that his hair stood up like a short-bristled white brush. His rather round face was brown and lined. His hands, which grasped the doorposts uncompromisingly to bar the way, were lean and veined and old. But all that I found in my recollections afterward to be utterly unimportant. His eyes were his predominant, his formidable, his compelling characteristic. They were round, the pupils very small, the irises large and of a light flecked blue. From the pupils radiated fine lines. The blank, cold, inscrutable stare of them bored me through to the back of the neck. I suppose the man winked occasionally, but I never got that impression. I've noticed that owls have this same intent, unwinking stare—and wildcats.

"Mr. Hooper," said I, "can you keep me over night?"

It was a usual request in the old cattle country. He continued to stare at me for some moments.

"Where are you from?" he asked at length. His voice was soft and low; rather purring.

I mentioned our headquarters on the Gila: it did not seem worth while to say anything about Box Springs only a dozen miles away. He stared at me for some time more.

"Come in," he said, abruptly; and stood aside.

This was a disconcerting surprise. All I had expected was permission to stop, and a direction as to how to find the bunk house. Then a more or less dull evening, and a return the following day to collect on my "dare." I stepped into the dimness of the hallway; and immediately after into a room beyond.

Again I must remind you that this was the Arizona of the 'nineties. All the ranch houses with which I was acquainted, and I knew about all of them, were very crudely done. They comprised generally a half dozen rooms with adobe walls and rough board floors, with only such furnishings as deal tables, benches, homemade chairs, perhaps a battered old washstand or so, and bunks filled with straw. We had no such things as tablecloths and sheets, of course. Everything was on a like scale of simple utility.

All right, get that in your mind. The interior into which I now stepped, with my clanking spurs, my rattling *chaps*, the dust of my sweat-stained garments, was a low-ceilinged, dim abode with faint, musty aromas. Carpets covered the floors; an old-fashioned hat rack flanked the door on one side, a tall clock on the other. I saw in passing framed steel engravings. The room beyond contained easy chairs, a sofa upholstered with hair cloth, an upright piano, a marble fireplace with a mantel, in a corner a triangular what-not filled with objects. It, too, was dim and curtained and faintly aromatic as had been the house of an old maiden aunt of my childhood, who used to give me cookies on the Sabbath. I felt now too large, and too noisy, and altogether mis-dressed and blundering and dirty. The little old man moved without a sound, and the grandfather's clock outside ticked deliberately in a hollow silence.

I sat down, rather gingerly, in the chair he indicated for me.

"I shall be very glad to offer you hospitality for the night," he said, as though there had been no interim. "I feel honoured at the opportunity."

I murmured my thanks, and a suggestion that I should look after my horse.

"Your horse, sir, has been attended to, and your *cantinas*[B] are undoubtedly by now in your room, where, I am sure, you are anxious to repair."

He gave no signal, nor uttered any command, but at his last words a grave, elderly Mexican appeared noiselessly at my elbow. As a matter of fact, he came through an unnoticed door at the back, but he might as well have materialized from the thin air for the start that he gave me. Hooper instantly arose.

"I trust, sir, you will find all to your liking. If anything is lacking, I trust you will at once indicate the fact. We shall dine in a half hour——"

He seized a small implement consisting of a bit of wire screen attached to the end of a short stick, darted across the room with the most extraordinary agility, thwacked a lone house fly, and returned.

"—and you will undoubtedly be ready for it," he finished his speech, calmly, as though he had not moved from his tracks.

I murmured my acknowledgments. My last impression as I left the room was of the baleful, dead, challenging stare of the man's wildcat eyes.

The Mexican glided before me. We emerged into the court, walked along the verandah, and entered a bedroom. My guide slipped by me and disappeared before I had the chance of a word with him. He may have been dumb for all I know. I sat down and tried to take stock.

---

CHAPTER III

The room was small, but it was papered, it was rugged, its floor was painted and waxed, its window—opening into the court, by the way—was hung with chintz and net curtains, its bed was garnished with sheets and counterpane, its chairs were upholstered and in perfect repair and polish. It was not Arizona, emphatically not, but rather the sweet and garnished and lavendered respectability of a Connecticut village. My dirty old *cantinas* lay stacked against the washstand. At sight of them I had to grin. Of course I travelled cowboy fashion. They contained a toothbrush, a comb, and a change of underwear. The latter item was sheer, rank pride of caste.

It was all most incongruous and strange. But the strangest part, of course, was the fact that I found myself where I was at that moment. Why was I thus received? Why was I, an ordinary and rather dirty cowpuncher, not sent as usual to the men's bunk house? It could not be possible that Old Man Hooper extended this sort of hospitality to every chance wayfarer. Arizona is a democratic country, Lord knows: none more so! But owners are not likely to invite in strange cowboys unless they themselves mess with their own men. I gave it up, and tried unsuccessfully to shrug it off my mind, and sought distraction in looking about me. There was not much to see. The one door and one window opened into the court. The other side was blank except that near the ceiling ran a curious, long, narrow opening closed by a transom-like sash. I had never seen anything quite like it, but concluded that it must be a sort of loop hole for musketry in the old days. Probably they had some kind of scaffold to stand on.

I pulled off my shirt and took a good wash: shook the dust out of my clothes as well as I could; removed my spurs and *chaps*; knotted my silk handkerchief necktie fashion; slicked down my wet hair, and tried to imagine myself decently turned out for company. I took off my gun belt also; but after some hesitation thrust the revolver inside the waistband of my drawers. Had no reason; simply the border instinct to stick to one's weapon.

Then I sat down to wait. The friendly little noises of my own movements left me. I give you my word, never before nor since have I experienced such stillness. In vain I told myself that with adobe walls two feet thick, a windless evening, and an hour after sunset, stillness was to be expected. That did not satisfy. Silence is made up of a thousand little noises so accustomed that they pass over the consciousness. Somehow these little noises seemed to lack. I sat in an aural vacuum. This analysis has come to me since. At that time I only knew that most uneasily I missed something, and that my ears ached from vain listening.

At the end of the half hour I returned to the parlour. Old Man Hooper was there waiting. A hanging lamp had been lighted. Out of the shadows cast from it a slender figure rose and came forward.

"My daughter, Mr.——" he paused.

"Sanborn," I supplied.

"My dear, Mr. Sanborn has most kindly dropped in to relieve the tedium of our evening with his company—his distinguished company." He pronounced the words suavely, without a trace of sarcastic emphasis, yet somehow I felt my face flush. And all the time he was staring at me blankly with his wide, unblinking, wildcat eyes.

The girl was very pale, with black hair and wide eyes under a fair, wide brow. She was simply dressed in some sort of white stuff. I thought she drooped a little. She did not look at me, nor speak to me; only bowed slightly.

We went at once into a dining room at the end of the little dark hall. It was lighted by a suspended lamp that threw the illumination straight down on a table perfect in its appointments of napery, silver, and glass. I felt very awkward and dusty in my cowboy rig; and rather too large. The same Mexican served us, deftly. We had delightful food, well cooked. I do not remember what it was. My attention was divided between the old man and his daughter. He talked, urbanely, of a wide range of topics, displaying a cosmopolitan taste, employing a choice of words and phrases that was astonishing. The girl, who turned out to be very pretty in a dark, pale, sad way, never raised her eyes from her plate.

It was the cool of the evening, and a light breeze from the open window swung the curtains. From the blackness outside a single frog began to chirp. My host's flow of words eddied, ceased. He raised his head uneasily; then, without apology, slipped from his chair and glided from the room. The Mexican remained, standing bolt upright in the dimness.

For the first time the girl spoke. Her voice was low and sweet, but either I or my aroused imagination detected a strained under quality.

"Ramon," she said in Spanish, "I am chilly. Close the window."

The servant turned his back to obey. With a movement rapid as a snake's dart the girl's hand came from beneath the table, reached across, and thrust into mine a small, folded paper. The next instant she was back in her place, staring down as before in apparent apathy. So amazed was I that I recovered barely soon enough to conceal the paper before Ramon turned back from his errand.

The next five minutes were to me hours of strained and bewildered waiting. I addressed one or two remarks to my companion, but received always monosyllabic answers. Twice I caught the flash of lanterns beyond the darkened window; and a subdued, confused murmur as though several people were walking about stealthily. Except for this the night had again fallen deathly still. Even the cheerful frog had hushed.

At the end of a period my host returned, and without apology or explanation resumed his seat and took up his remarks where he had left them.

The girl disappeared somewhere between the table and the sitting room. Old Man Hooper offered me a cigar, and sat down deliberately to entertain me. I had an uncomfortable feeling that he was also amusing himself, as though I were being played with and covertly sneered at. Hooper's politeness and suavity concealed, and well concealed, a bitter irony. His manner was detached and a little precise. Every few moments he burst into a flurry of activity with the fly whacker, darting here and there as his eyes fell upon one of the insects; but returning always calmly to his discourse with an air of never having moved from his chair. He talked to me of Praxiteles, among other things. What should an Arizona cowboy know of Praxiteles? and why should any one talk to him of that worthy Greek save as a subtle and hidden expression of contempt? That was my feeling. My senses and mental apperceptions were by now a little on the raw.

That, possibly, is why I noticed the very first chirp of another frog outside. It continued, and I found myself watching my host covertly. Sure enough, after a few repetitions I saw subtle signs of uneasiness, of divided attention; and soon, again without apology or explanation, he glided from the room. And at the same instant the old Mexican servitor came and pretended to fuss with the lamps.

My curiosity was now thoroughly aroused, but I could guess no means of satisfying it. Like the bedroom, this parlour gave out only on the interior court. The flash of lanterns against the ceiling above reached me. All I could do was to wander about looking at the objects in the cabinet and the pictures on the walls. There was, I remember, a set of carved ivory chessmen and an engraving of the legal trial of some English worthy of the seventeenth century. But my hearing was alert, and I thought to hear footsteps outside. At any rate, the chirp of the frog came to an abrupt end.

Shortly my host returned and took up his monologue. It amounted to that. He seemed to delight in choosing unusual subjects and then backing me into a corner with an array of well-considered phrases that allowed me no opening for reply nor even comment. In one of my desperate attempts to gain even a momentary initiative I asked him, apropos of the piano, whether his daughter played.

"Do you like music?" he added, and without waiting for a reply seated himself at the instrument.

He played to me for half an hour. I do not know much about music; but I know he played well and that he played good things. Also that, for the first time, he came out of himself, abandoned himself to feeling. His close-cropped head swayed from side to side; his staring, wildcat eyes half closed——

He slammed shut the piano and arose, more drily precise than ever.

"I imagine all that is rather beyond your apperceptions," he remarked, "and that you are ready for your bed. Here is a short document I would have you take to your room for perusal. Good-night."

He tendered me a small, folded paper which I thrust into the breast pocket of my shirt along with the note handed me earlier in the evening by the girl. Thus dismissed I was only too delighted to repair to my bedroom.

There I first carefully drew together the curtains; then examined the first of the papers I drew from my pocket. It proved to be the one from the girl, and read as follows:

I am here against my will. I am not this man's daughter. For God's sake if you can help me, do so. But be careful for he is a dangerous man. My room is the last one on the left wing of the court. I am constantly guarded. I do not know what you can do. The case is hopeless. I cannot write more. I am watched.

I unfolded the paper Hooper himself had given me. It was similar in appearance to the other, and read:

I am held a prisoner. This man Hooper is not my father but he is vindictive and cruel and dangerous. Beware for yourself. I live in the last room in the left wing. I am watched, so cannot write more.

The handwriting of the two documents was the same. I stared at one paper and then at the other, and for a half hour I thought all the thoughts appropriate to the occasion. They led me nowhere, and would not interest you.

---

CHAPTER IV

After a time I went to bed, but not to sleep. I placed my gun under my pillow, locked and bolted the door, and arranged a string cunningly across the open window so that an intruder—unless he had extraordinary luck—could not have failed to kick up a devil of a clatter. I was young, bold, without nerves; so that I think I can truthfully say I was not in the least frightened. But I cannot deny I was nervous—or rather the whole situation was on my nerves. I lay on my back staring straight at the ceiling. I caught myself gripping the sheets and listening. Only there was nothing to listen to. The night was absolutely still. There were no frogs, no owls, no crickets even. The firm old adobe walls gave off no creak nor snap of timbers. The world was muffled—I almost said smothered. The psychological effect was that of blank darkness, the black darkness of far underground, although the moon was sailing the heavens.

How long that lasted I could not tell you. But at last the silence was broken by the cheerful chirp of a frog. Never was sound more grateful to the ear! I lay drinking it in as thirstily as water after a day on the desert. It seemed that the world breathed again, was coming alive after syncope. And then beneath that loud and cheerful singing I became aware of duller half-heard movements; and a moment or so later yellow lights began to flicker through the transom high at the blank wall of the room, and to reflect in wavering patches on the ceiling. Evidently somebody was afoot outside with a lantern.

I crept from the bed, moved the table beneath the transom, and climbed atop. The opening was still a foot or so above my head. Being young, strong, and active, I drew myself up by the strength of my arms so I could look—until my muscles gave out!

I saw four men with lanterns moving here and there among some willows that bordered what seemed to be an irrigating ditch with water. They were armed with long clubs. Old Man Hooper, in an overcoat, stood in a commanding position. They seemed to be searching. Suddenly from a clump of bushes one of the men uttered an exclamation of triumph. I saw his long club rise and fall. At that instant my tired fingers slipped from the ledge and I had to let myself drop to the table. When a moment later I regained my vantage point, I found that the whole crew had disappeared.

Nothing more happened that night. At times I dozed in a broken sort of fashion, but never actually fell into sound sleep. The nearest I came to slumber was just at dawn. I really lost all consciousness of my surroundings and circumstances, and was only slowly brought to myself by the sweet singing of innumerable birds in the willows outside the blank wall. I lay in a half stupor enjoying them. Abruptly their music ceased. I heard the soft, flat *spat* of a miniature rifle. The sound was repeated. I climbed back on my table and drew myself again to a position of observation.

Old Man Hooper, armed with a .22 calibre rifle, was prowling along the willows in which fluttered a small band of migratory birds. He was just drawing bead on a robin. At the report the bird fell. The old man darted forward with the impetuosity of a boy, although the bird was dead. An impulse of contempt curled my lips. The old man was childish! Why should he find pleasure in hunting such harmless creatures? and why should he take on triumph over retrieving such petty game? But when he reached the fallen bird he did not pick it up for a possible pot-pie as I thought he would do. He ground it into the soft earth with the heel of his boot, stamping on the poor thing again and again. And never have I seen on human countenance such an expression of satisfied malignity!

I went to my door and looked out. You may be sure that the message I had received from the unfortunate young lady had not been forgotten; but Old Man Hooper's cynical delivery of the second paper had rendered me too cautious to undertake anything without proper reconnaissance. The left wing about the courtyard seemed to contain two apartments—at least there were two doors, each with its accompanying window. The window farthest out was heavily barred. My thrill at this discovery was, however, slightly dashed by the further observation that also all the other windows into the courtyard were barred. Still, that was peculiar in itself, and not attributable—as were the walls and remarkable transoms—to former necessities of defence. My first thought was to stroll idly around the courtyard, thus obtaining a closer inspection. But the moment I stepped into the open a Mexican sauntered into view and began to water the flowers. I can say no more than that in his hands that watering pot looked fairly silly. So I turned to the right and passed through the wicket gate and into the stable yard. It was natural enough that I should go to look after my own horse.

The stable yard was for the moment empty; but as I walked across it one of its doors opened and a very little, wizened old man emerged leading a horse. He tied the animal to a ring in the wall and proceeded at once to currying.

I had been in Arizona for ten years. During that time I had seen a great many very fine native horses, for the stock of that country is directly descended from the barbs of the *conquistadores*. But, though often well formed and as tough and useful as horseflesh is made, they were small. And no man thought of refinements in caring for any one of his numerous mounts. They went shaggy or smooth according to the season; and not one of them could have called a curry comb or brush out of its name.

The beast from which the wizened old man stripped a *bona fide* horse blanket was none of these. He stood a good sixteen hands; his head was small and clean cut with large, intelligent eyes and little, well-set ears; his long, muscular shoulders sloped forward as shoulders should; his barrel was long and deep and well ribbed up; his back was flat and straight; his legs were clean and—what was rarely seen in the cow country—well proportioned—the cannon bone shorter than the leg bone, the ankle sloping and long and elastic—in short, a magnificent creature whose points of excellence appeared one by one under close scrutiny. And the high lights of his glossy coat flashed in the sun like water.

I walked from one side to the other of him marvelling. Not a defect, not even a blemish could I discover. The animal was fairly a perfect specimen of horseflesh. And I could not help speculating as to its use. Old Man Hooper had certainly never appeared with it in public; the fame of such a beast would have spread the breadth of the country.

During my inspection the wizened little man continued his work without even a glance in my direction. He had on riding breeches and leather gaiters, a plaid waistcoat and a peaked cap; which, when you think of it, was to Arizona about as incongruous as the horse. I made several conventional remarks of admiration, to which he paid not the slightest attention. But I know a bait.

"I suppose you claim him as a Morgan," said I.

"Claim, is it!" grunted the little man, contemptuously.

"Well, the Morgan is not a real breed, anyway," I persisted. "A sixty-fourth blood will get one registered. What does that amount to?"

The little man grunted again.

"Besides, though your animal is a good one, he is too short and straight in the pasterns," said I, uttering sheer, rank, wild heresy.

After that we talked; at first heatedly, then argumentatively, then with entire, enthusiastic agreement. I saw to that. Allowing yourself to be converted from an absurd opinion is always a sure way to favour. We ended with antiphonies of praise for this descendant of Justin Morgan.

"You're the only man in all this God-forsaken country that has the sense of a Shanghai rooster!" cried the little man in a glow. "They ride horses and they know naught of them; and they laugh at a horseman! Your hand, sir!" He shook it. "And is that your horse in number four? I wondered! He's the first animal I've seen here properly shod. They use the rasp, sir, on the outside the hoof, and on the clinches, sir; and they burn a seat for the shoe; and they pare out the sole and trim the frog—bah! You shoe your own horse, I take it. That's right and proper! Your hand again, sir. Your horse has been fed this hour agone."

"I'll water him, then," said I.

But when I led him forth I could find no trough or other facilities until the little man led me to a corner of the corral and showed me a contraption with a close-fitting lid to be lifted.

"It's along of the flies," he explained to me. "They must drink, and we starve them for water here, and they go greedy for their poison yonder." He indicated flat dishes full of liquid set on shelves here and about. "We keep them pretty clear."

I walked over, curiously, to examine. About and in the dishes were literally quarts of dead insects, not only flies, but bees, hornets, and other sorts as well. I now understood the deadly silence that had so impressed me the evening before. This was certainly most ingenious; and I said so.

But at my first remark the old man became obstinately silent, and fell again to grooming the Morgan horse. Then I became aware that he was addressing me in low tones out of the corner of his mouth.

"Go on; look at the horse; say something," he muttered, busily polishing down the animal's hind legs. "You're a man who *saveys* a horse—the only man I've seen here who does. *Get out*! Don't ask why. You're safe now. You're not safe here another day. Water your horse; eat your breakfast; then *get out*!"

And not another word did I extract. I watered my horse at the covered trough, and rather thoughtfully returned to the courtyard.

I found there Old Man Hooper waiting. He looked as bland and innocent and harmless as the sunlight on his own flagstones—until he gazed up at me, and then I was as usual disconcerted by the blank, veiled, unwinking stare of his eyes.

"Remarkably fine Morgan stallion you have, sir," I greeted him. "I didn't know such a creature existed in this part of the world."

But the little man displayed no gratification.

"He's well enough. I have him more to keep Tim happy than anything else. We'll go in to breakfast."

I cast a cautious eye at the barred window in the left wing. The curtains were still down. At the table I ventured to ask after Miss Hooper. The old man stared at me up to the point of embarrassment, then replied drily that she always breakfasted in her room. The rest of our conversation was on general topics. I am bound to say it was unexpectedly easy. The old man was a good talker, and possessed social ease and a certain charm, which he seemed to be trying to exert. Among other things, I remember, he told me of the Indian councils he used to hold in the old days.

"They were held on the willow flat, outside the east wall," he said. "I never allowed any of them inside the walls." The suavity of his manner broke fiercely and suddenly. "Everything inside the walls is mine!" he declared with heat. "Mine! mine! mine! Understand? I will not tolerate in here anything that is not mine; that does not obey my will; that does not come when I say come; go when I say go; and fall silent when I say be still!"

A wild and fantastic idea suddenly illuminated my understanding.

"Even the crickets, the flies, the frogs, the birds," I said, audaciously.

He fixed his wildcat eyes upon me without answering.

"And," I went on, deliberately, "who could deny your perfect right to do what you will with your own? And if they did deny that right what more natural than that they should be made to perish—or take their breakfasts in their rooms?"

I was never more aware of the absolute stillness of the house than when I uttered these foolish words. My hand was on the gun in my trouser-band; but even as I spoke a sickening realization came over me that if the old man opposite so willed, I would have no slightest chance to use it. The air behind me seemed full of menace, and the hair crawled on the back of my neck. Hooper stared at me without sign for ten seconds; his right hand hovered above the polished table. Then he let it fall without giving what I am convinced would have been a signal.

"Will you have more coffee—my guest?" he inquired. And he stressed subtly the last word in a manner that somehow made me just a trifle ashamed.

At the close of the meal the Mexican familiar glided into the room. Hooper seemed to understand the man's presence, for he arose at once.

"Your horse is saddled and ready," he told me, briskly. "You will be wishing to start before the heat of the day. Your *cantinas* are ready on the saddle."

He clapped on his hat and we walked together to the corral. There awaited us not only my own horse, but another. The equipment of the latter was magnificently reminiscent of the old California days—gaily-coloured braided hair bridle and reins; silver *conchas*; stock saddle of carved leather with silver horn and cantle; silvered bit bars; gay Navajo blanket as corona; silver corners to skirts, silver *conchas* on the long *tapaderos*. Old Man Hooper, strangely incongruous in his wrinkled "store clothes," swung aboard.

"I will ride with you for a distance," he said.

We jogged forth side by side at the slow Spanish trot. Hooper called my attention to the buildings of Fort Shafter glimmering part way up the slopes of the distant mountains, and talked entertainingly of the Indian days, and how the young officers used to ride down to his ranch for music.

After a half hour thus we came to the long string of wire and the huge, awkward gate that marked the limit of Hooper's "pasture." Of course the open range was his real pasture; but every ranch enclosed a thousand acres or so somewhere near the home station to be used for horses in active service. Before I could anticipate him, he had sidled his horse skillfully alongside the gate and was holding it open for me to pass. I rode through the opening murmuring thanks and an apology. The old man followed me through, and halted me by placing his horse square across the path of mine.

"You are now, sir, outside my land and therefore no longer my guest," he said, and the snap in his voice was like the crackling of electricity. "Don't let me ever see you here again. You are keen and intelligent. You spoke the truth a short time since. You were right. I tolerate nothing in my place that is not my own—no man, no animal, no bird, no insect nor reptile even—that will not obey my lightest order. And these creatures, great or small, who will not—*or even cannot*—obey my orders must go—or die. Understand me clearly?

"You have come here, actuated, I believe, by idle curiosity, but without knowledge. You made yourself—ignorantly—my guest; and a guest is sacred. But now you know my customs and ideas. I am telling you. Never again can you come here in ignorance; therefore never again can you come here as a guest; and never again will you pass freely."

He delivered this drily, precisely, with frost in his tones, staring balefully into my eyes. So taken aback was I by this unleashed hostility that for a moment I had nothing to say.

"Now, if you please, I will take both notes from that poor idiot: the one I handed you and the one she handed you."

I realized suddenly that the two lay together in the breast pocket of my shirt; that though alike in tenor, they differed in phrasing; and that I had no means of telling one from the other.

"The paper you gave me I read and threw away," I stated, boldly. "It meant nothing to me. As to any other, I do not know what you are talking about."

"You are lying," he said, calmly, as merely stating a fact. "It does not matter. It is my fancy to collect them. I should have liked to add yours. Now get out of this, and don't let me see your face again!"

"Mr. Hooper," said I, "I thank you for your hospitality, which has been complete and generous. You have pointed out the fact that I am no longer your guest. I can, therefore, with propriety, tell you that your ideas and prejudices are noted with interest; your wishes are placed on file for future reference; I don't give a damn for your orders; and you can go to hell!"

"Fine flow of language. Educated cowpuncher," said the old man, drily. "You are warned. Keep off. Don't meddle with what does not concern you. And if the rumour gets back to me that you've been speculating or talking or criticizing——"

"Well?" I challenged.

"I'll have you killed," he said, simply; so simply that I knew he meant it.

"You are foolish to make threats," I rejoined. "Two can play at that game. You drive much alone."

"I do not work alone," he hinted, darkly. "The day my body is found dead of violence, that day marks the doom of a long list of men whom I consider inimical to me—like, perhaps, yourself." He stared me down with his unwinking gaze.

---

## CHAPTER V

I returned to Box Springs at a slow jog trot, thinking things over. Old Man Hooper's warning sobered, but did not act as a deterrent of my intention to continue with the adventure. But how? I could hardly storm the fort single handed and carry off the damsel in distress. On the evidence I possessed I could not even get together a storming party. The cowboy is chivalrous enough, but human. He would not uprise spontaneously to the point of war on the mere statement of incarcerated beauty—especially as ill-treatment was not apparent. I would hardly last long enough to carry out the necessary proselyting campaign. It never occurred to me to doubt that Hooper would fulfill his threat of having me killed, or his ability to do so.

So when the men drifted in two by two at dusk, I said nothing of my real adventures, and answered their chaff in kind.

"He played the piano for me," I told them the literal truth, "and had me in to the parlour and dining room. He gave me a room to myself with a bed and sheets; and he rode out to his pasture gate with me to say good-bye," and thereby I was branded a delicious liar.

"They took me into the bunk house and fed me, all right," said Windy Bill, "and fed my horse. And nextmorning that old Mexican Joe of his just nat'rally up and kicked me off the premises."

"Wonder you didn't shoot him," I exclaimed.

"Oh, he didn't use his foot. But he sort of let me know that the place was unhealthy to visit more'n once. And somehow I seen he meant it; and I ain't never had no call to go back."

I mulled over the situation all day, and then could stand it no longer. On the dark of the evening I rode to within a couple of miles of Hooper's ranch, tied my horse, and scouted carefully forward afoot. For one thing I wanted to find out whether the system of high transoms extended to all the rooms, including that in the left wing: for another I wanted to determine the "lay of the land" on that blank side of the house. I found my surmise correct as to the transoms. As to the blank side of the house, that looked down on a wide, green, moist patch and the irrigating ditch with its stunted willows. Then painstakingly I went over every inch of the terrain about the ranch; and might just as well have investigated the external economy of a mud turtle. Realizing that nothing was to be gained in this manner, I withdrew to my strategic base where I rolled down and slept until daylight. Then I saddled and returned toward the ranch.

I had not ridden two miles, however, before in the boulder-strewn wash of Arroyo Seco I met Jim Starr, one of our men.

"Look here," he said to me. "Jed sent me up to look at the Elder Springs, but my hoss has done cast a shoe. Cain't you ride up there?"

"I cannot," said I, promptly. "I've been out all night and had no breakfast. But you can have my horse."

So we traded horses and separated, each our own way. They sent me out by Coyote Wells with two other men, and we did not get back until the following evening.

The ranch was buzzing with excitement. Jim Starr had not returned, although the ride to Elder Springs was only a two-hour affair. After a night had elapsed, and still he did not return, two men had been sent. They found him half way to Elder Springs with a bullet hole in his back. The bullet was that of a rifle. Being plainsmen they had done good detective work of its kind, and had determined—by the direction of the bullet's flight as evidenced by the wound—that it had been fired from a point above. The only point above was the low "rim" that ran for miles down the Soda Springs Valley. It was of black lava and showed no tracks. The men, with a true sense of values, had contented themselves with covering Jim Starr with a blanket, and then had ridden the rim for some miles in both directions looking for a trail. None could be discovered. By this they deduced that the murder was not the result of chance encounter, but had been so carefully planned that no trace would be left of the murderer or murderers.

No theory could be imagined save the rather vague one of personal enmity. Jim Starr was comparatively a newcomer with us. Nobody knew anything much about him or his relations. Nobody questioned the only man who could have told anything; and that man did not volunteer to tell what he knew.

I refer to myself. The thing was sickeningly clear to me. Jim Starr had nothing to do with it. I was the man for whom that bullet from the rim had been intended. I was the unthinking, shortsighted fool who had done Jim Starr to his death. It had never occurred to me that my midnight reconnoitring would leave tracks, that Old Man Hooper's suspicious vigilance would even look for tracks. But given that vigilance, the rest followed plainly enough. A skillful trailer would have found his way to where I had mounted; he would have followed my horse to Arroyo Seco where I had met with Jim Starr. There he would have visualized a rider on a horse without one shoe coming as far as the Arroyo, meeting me, and returning whence he had come; and me at once turning off at right angles. His natural conclusion would be that a messenger had brought me orders and had returned. The fact that we had shifted mounts he could not have read, for the reason—as I only too distinctly remembered—that we had made the change in the boulder and rock stream bed which would show no clear traces.

The thought that poor Jim Starr, whom I had well liked, had been sacrificed for me, rendered my ride home with the convoy more deeply thoughtful than even the tragic circumstances warranted. We laid his body in the small office, pending Buck Johnson's return from town, and ate our belated meal in silence. Then we gathered around the corner fireplace in the bunk house, lit our smokes, and talked it over. Jed Parker joined us. Usually he sat with our owner in the office.

Hardly had we settled ourselves to discussion when the door opened and Buck Johnson came in. We had been so absorbed that no one had heard him ride up. He leaned his forearm against the doorway at the height of his head and surveyed the silenced group rather ironically.

"Lucky I'm not nervous and jumpy by nature," he observed. "I've seen dead men before. Still, next time you want to leave one in my office after dark, I wish you'd put a light with him, or tack up a sign, or even leave somebody to tell me about it. I'm sorry it's Starr and not that thoughtful old horned toad in the corner."

Jed looked foolish, but said nothing. Buck came in, closed the door, and took a chair square in front of the fireplace. The glow of the leaping flames was full upon him. His strong face and bulky figure were revealed, while the other men sat in half shadow. He at once took charge of the discussion.

"How was he killed?" he inquired, "bucked off?"

"Shot," replied Jed Parker.

Buck's eyebrows came together.

"Who?" he asked.

He was told the circumstances as far as they were known, but declined to listen to any of the various deductions and surmises.

"Deliberate murder and not a chance quarrel," he concluded. "He wasn't even within hollering distance of that rim-rock. Anybody know anything about Starr?"

"He's been with us about five weeks," proffered Jed, as foreman. "Said he came from Texas."

"He was a Texican," corroborated one of the other men. "I rode with him considerable."

"What enemies did he have?" asked Buck.

3But it developed that, as far as these men knew, Jim Starr had had no enemies. He was a quiet sort of a fellow. He had been to town once or twice. Of course he might have made an enemy, but it was not likely; he had always behaved himself. Somebody would have known of any trouble——

"Maybe somebody followed him from Texas."

"More likely the usual local work," Buck interrupted. "This man Starr ever met up with Old Man Hooper or Hooper's men?"

But here was another impasse. Starr had been over on the Slick Rock ever since his arrival. I could have thrown some light on the matter, perhaps, but new thoughts were coming to me and I kept silence.

Shortly Buck Johnson went out. His departure loosened tongues, among them mine.

"I don't see why you stand for this old *hombre* if he's as bad as you say," I broke in. "Why don't some of you brave young warriors just naturally pot him?"

And that started a new line of discussion that left me even more thoughtful than before. I knew these men intimately. There was not a coward among them. They had been tried and hardened and tempered in the fierceness of the desert. Any one of them would have twisted the tail of the devil himself; but they were off Old Man Hooper. They did not make that admission in so many words; far from it. And I valued my hide enough to refrain from pointing the fact. But that fact remained: they were off Old Man Hooper. Furthermore, by the time they had finished recounting in intimate detail some scores of anecdotes dealing with what happened when Old Man Hooper winked his wildcat eye, I 3began in spite of myself to share some of their sentiments. For no matter how flagrant the killing, nor how certain morally the origin, never had the most brilliant nor the most painstaking effort been able to connect with the slayers nor their instigator. He worked in the dark by hidden hands; but the death from the hands was as certain as the rattlesnake's. Certain of his victims, by luck or cleverness, seemed to have escaped sometimes as many as three or four attempts but in the end the old man's Killers got them.

A Jew drummer who had grossly insulted Hooper in the Lone Star Emporium had, on learning the enormity of his crime, fled to San Francisco. Three months later Soda Springs awoke to find pasted by an unknown hand on the window of the Emporium a newspaper account of that Jew drummer's taking off. The newspaper could offer no theory and merely recited the fact that the man suffered from a heavy-calibred bullet. But always the talk turned back at last to that crowning atrocity, the Boomerang, with its windrows of little calves, starved for water, lying against the fence.

"Yes," someone unexpectedly answered my first question at last, "someone could just naturally pot him easy enough. But I got a hunch that he couldn't get fur enough away to feel safe afterward. The fellow with a hankering for a good *useful* kind of suicide could get it right there. Any candidates? You-all been looking kinda mournful lately, Windy; s'pose you be the human benefactor and rid the world of this yere reptile."

"Me?" said Windy with vast surprise, "me mournful? Why, I sing at my work like a little dicky bird. I'm so3plumb cheerful bull frogs ain't in it. You ain't talking to me!"

But I wanted one more point of information before the conversation veered.

"Does his daughter ever ride out?" I asked.

"Daughter?" they echoed in surprise.

"Or niece, or whoever she is," I supplemented impatiently.

"There's no woman there; not even a Mex," said one, and "Did you see any sign of any woman?" keenly from Windy Bill.

But I was not minded to be drawn.

"Somebody told me about a daughter, or niece, or something," I said, vaguely.

---

## CHAPTER VI

I lay in my bunk and cast things up in my mind. The patch of moonlight from the window moved slowly across the floor. One of the men was snoring, but with regularity, so he did not annoy me. The outside silence was softly musical with all the little voices that at Hooper's had so disconcertingly lacked. There were crickets—I had forgotten about them—and frogs, and a hoot owl, and various such matters, beneath whose influence customarily my consciousness merged into sleep so sweetly that I never knew when I had lost them. But I was never wider awake than now, and never had I done more concentrated thinking.

For the moment, and for the moment, only, I was safe. Old Man Hooper thought he had put me out of the way. How long would he continue to think so? How long before his men would bring true word of the mistake that had been made? Perhaps the following day would inform him that Jim Starr and not myself had been reached by his killer's bullet. Then, I had no doubt, a second attempt would be made on my life. Therefore, whatever I was going to do must be done quickly.

I had the choice of war or retreat. Would it do me any good to retreat? There was the Jew drummer who was killed in San Francisco; and others whose fates I have not detailed. But why should he particularly desire my extinction? What had I done or what knowledge did I possess that had not been equally done and known by any chance visitor to the ranch? I remembered the notes in my shirt pocket; and, at the risk of awakening some of my comrades, I lit a candle and studied them. They were undoubtedly written by the same hand. To whom had the other been smuggled? and by what means had it come into Old Man Hooper's possession? The answer hit me so suddenly, and seemed intrinsically so absurd, that I blew out the candle and lay again on my back to study it.

And the more I studied it, the less absurd it seemed, not by the light of reason, but by the feeling of pure intuition. I knew it as sanely as I knew that the moon made that patch of light through the window. The man to whom that other note had been surreptitiously conveyed by the sad-eyed, beautiful girl of the iron-barred chamber was dead; and he was dead because Old Man Hooper had so willed. And the former owners of the other notes of the "Collection" concerning which the old man had spoken were dead, too—dead for the same reason and by the same hidden hands.

Why? Because they knew about the girl? Unlikely. Without doubt Hooper had, as in my case, himself made possible that knowledge. But I remembered many things; and I knew that my flash of intuition, absurd as it might seem at first sight, was true. I recalled the swift, darting onslaughts with the fly whackers, the fierce, vindictive slaughter of the frogs, his early-morning pursuit of the flock of migrating birds. Especially came clear to my recollection the words spoken at breakfast:

"Everything inside the walls is mine! Mine! Mine! Understand? I will not tolerate anything that is not mine; that does not obey my will; that does not come when I say come; go when I say go; and fall silent when I say be still!"

My crime, the crime of these men from whose dead hands the girl's appeals had been taken for the "Collection," was that of curiosity! The old man would within his own domain reign supreme, in the mental as in the physical world. The chance cowboy, genuinely desirous only of a resting place for the night, rode away unscathed; but he whom the old man convicted of a prying spirit committed a lese-majesty that could not be forgiven. And I had made many tracks during my night reconnaissance.

And the same flash of insight showed me that I would be followed wherever I went; and the thing that convinced my intuitions—not my reason—of this was the recollection of the old man stamping the remains of the poor little bird into the mud by the willows. I saw again the insane rage of his face; and I felt cold fingers touching my spine.

On this I went abruptly and unexpectedly to sleep, after the fashion of youth, and did not stir until Sing, the cook, routed us out before dawn. We were not to ride the range that day because of Jim Starr, but Sing was a person of fixed habits. I plunged my head into the face of the dawn with a new and light-hearted confidence. It was one of those clear, nile-green sunrises whose lucent depths go back a million miles or so; and my spirit followed on wings. Gone were at once my fine-spun theories and my forebodings of the night. Life was clean and clear and simple. Jim Starr had probably some personal enemy. Old Man Hooper was undoubtedly a mean old lunatic, and dangerous; very likely he would attempt to do me harm, as he said, if I bothered him again, but as for following me to the ends of the earth——

The girl was a different matter. She required thought. So, as I was hungry and the day sparkling, I postponed her and went in to breakfast.

---

By the time the coroner's inquest and the funeral in town were over it was three o'clock of the afternoon. As I only occasionally managed Soda Springs I felt no inclination to hurry on the return journey. My intention was to watch the Overland through, to make some small purchases at the Lone Star Emporium, to hoist one or two at McGrue's, and to dine sumptuously at the best—and only—hotel. A programme simple in theme but susceptible to variations.

The latter began early. After posing kiddishly as a rough, woolly, romantic cowboy before the passengers of the Overland, I found myself chaperoning a visitor to our midst. By sheer accident the visitor had singled me out for an inquiry.

"Can you tell me how to get to Hooper's ranch?" he asked.

So I annexed him promptly in hope of developments.

He was certainly no prize package, for he was small, pale, nervous, shifty, and rat-like; and neither his hands nor his eyes were still for an instant. Further to set him apart he wore a hard-boiled hat, a flaming tie, a checked vest, a coat cut too tight for even his emaciated little figure, and long toothpick shoes of patent leather. A fairer mark for cowboy humour would be difficult to find; but I had a personal interest and a determined character so the gang took a look at me and bided their time.

But immediately I discovered I was going to have my hands full. It seemed that the little, shifty, rat-faced man had been possessed of a small handbag which the negro porter had failed to put off the train; and which was of tremendous importance. At the discovery it was lacking my new friend went into hysterics. He ran a few feet after the disappearing train; he called upon high heaven to destroy utterly the race of negro porters; he threatened terrible reprisals against a delinquent railroad company; he seized upon a bewildered station agent over whom he poured his troubles in one gush; and he lifted up his voice and wept—literally wept! This to the vast enjoyment of my friends.

"What ails the small party?" asked Windy Bill coming up.

"He's lost the family jewels!" "The papers are missing." "Sandy here (meaning me) won't give him his bottle and it's past feeding time." "Sandy's took away his stick of candy and won't give it back." "The little son-of-a-gun's just remembered that he give the nigger porter two bits," were some of the replies he got.

On the general principle of "never start anything you can't finish," I managed to quell the disturbance; I got a description of the bag, and arranged to have it wired for at the next station. On receiving the news that it could not possibly be returned before the following morning, my protégé showed signs of another outburst. To prevent it I took him firmly by the arm and led him across to McGrue's. He was shivering as though from a violent chill.

The multitude trailed interestedly after; but I took my man into one of McGrue's private rooms and firmly closed the door.

"Put that under your belt," I invited, pouring him a half tumbler of McGrue's best, "and pull yourself together."

He smelled it.

"It's only whiskey," he observed, mournfully. "That won't help much."

"You don't know this stuff," I encouraged.

He took off the half tumbler without a blink, shook his head, and poured himself another. In spite of his scepticism I thought his nervousness became less marked.

"Now," said I, "if you don't mind, why do you descend on a peaceful community and stir it all up because of the derelictions of an absent coon? And why do you set such store by your travelling bag? And why do you weep in the face of high heaven and outraged manhood? And why do you want to find Hooper's ranch? And why are you and your vaudeville make up?"

But he proved singularly embarrassed and nervous and uncommunicative, darting his glance here and there about him, twisting his hands, never by any chance meeting my eye. I leaned back and surveyed him in considerable disgust.

"Look here, brother," I pointed out to him. "You don't seem to realize. A man like you can't get away with himself in this country except behind footlights—and there ain't any footlights. All I got to do is to throw open yonder door and withdraw my beneficent protection and you will be set upon by a pack of ravening wolves with their own ideas of humour, among whom I especially mention one Windy Bill. I'm about the only thing that looks like a friend you've got."

He caught at the last sentence only.

"You my friend?" he said, breathlessly, "then tell me: is there a doctor around here?"

"No," said I, looking at him closely, "not this side of Tucson. Are you sick?"

"Is there a drug store in town, then?"

"Nary drug store."

He jumped to his feet, knocking over his chair as he did so.

"My God!" he cried in uncontrollable excitement, "I've got to get my bag! How far is it to the next station where they're going to put it off? Ain't there some way of getting there? I got to get to my bag."

"It's near to forty miles," I replied, leaning back.

"And there's no drug store here? What kind of a bum tank town is this, anyhow?"

"They keep a few patent medicines and such over at the Lone Star Emporium——" I started to tell him. I never had a chance to finish my sentence. He darted around the table, grabbed me by the arm, and urged me to my feet.

"Show me!" he panted.

We sailed through the bar room under full head of steam, leaving the gang staring after us open-mouthed. I could feel we were exciting considerable public interest. At the Lone Star Emporium the little freak looked wildly about him until his eyes fell on the bottle shelves. Then he rushed right in behind the counter and began to paw them over. I headed off Sol Levi, who was coming front making war medicine.

"*Loco*," says I to him. "If there's any damage, I'll settle."

It looked like there was going to be damage all right, the way he snatched up one bottle after the other, read the labels, and thrust them one side. At last he uttered a crow of delight, just like a kid.

"How many you got of these?" he demanded, holding up a bottle of soothing syrup.

"You only take a tablespoon of that stuff——" began Sol.

"How many you got—how much are they?" interrupted the stranger.

"Six—three dollars a bottle," says Sol, boosting the price.

The little man peeled a twenty off a roll of bills and threw it down.

"Keep the other five bottles for me!" he cried in a shaky voice, and ran out, with me after him, forgetting his change and to shut the door behind us.

Back through McGrue's bar we trailed like one of these moving-picture chases and into the back room.

"Well, here we are home again," said I.

The stranger grabbed a glass and filled it half full of soothing syrup.

"Here, you aren't going to drink that!" I yelled at him. "Didn't you hear Sol tell you the dose is a spoonful?"

But he didn't pay me any attention. His hand was shaking so he could hardly connect with his own mouth, and he was panting as though he'd run a race.

"Well, no accounting for tastes," I said. "Where do you want me to ship your remains?"

He drank her down, shut his eyes a few minutes, and held still. He had quit his shaking, and he looked me square in the face.

"What's it *to* you?" he demanded. "Huh? Ain't you never seen a guy hit the hop before?"

He stared at me so truculently that I was moved to righteous wrath; and I answered him back. I told him what I thought of him and his clothes and his conduct at quite some length. When I had finished he seemed to have gained a new attitude of aggravating wise superiority.

"That's all right, kid; that's all right," he assured me; "keep your hair on. I ain't such a bad scout; but you gotta get used to me. Give me my hop and I'm all right. Now about this Hooper; you say you know him?"

"None better," I rejoined. "But what's that to you? That's a fair question."

He bored me with his beady rat eyes for several seconds.

"Friend of yours?" he asked, briefly.

Something in the intonations of his voice induced me to frankness.

"I have good cause to think he's trying to kill me," I replied.

He produced a pocketbook, fumbled in it for a moment, and laid before me a clipping. It was from the Want column of a newspaper, and read as follows:

A.A.B.—Will deal with you on your terms. H.H.

"A.A.B. that's me—Artie Brower. And H.H.—that's him—Henry Hooper," he explained. "And that lil' piece of paper means that's he's caved, come off, war's over. Means I'm rich, that I can have my own ponies if I want to, 'stead of touting somebody else's old dogs. It means that I got old H.H.—Henry Hooper—where the hair is short, and he's got to come my way!"

His eyes were glittering restlessly, and the pupils seemed to be unduly dilated. The whiskey and opium together— probably an unaccustomed combination—were too much for his ill-balanced control. Every indication of his face and his narrow eyes was for secrecy and craft; yet for the moment he was opening up to me, a stranger, like an oyster. Even my inexperience could see that much, and I eagerly took advantage of my chance.

"You are a horseman, then?" I suggested.

"Me a horseman? Say, kid, you didn't get my name. Brower—Artie Brower. Why, I've ridden more winning races than any other man on the Pacific Coast. That's how I got onto old H.H. I rode for him. He knows a good horse all right—the old skunk. Used to have a pretty string."

"He's got at least one good Morgan stallion now," said I. "I've seen him at Hooper's ranch."

"I know the old crock—trotter," scorned the true riding jockey. "Probably old Tim Westmore is hanging around, too. He's in love with that horse."

"Is he in love with Hooper, too?" I asked.

"Just like I am," said the jockey with a leer.

"So you're going to be rich," said I. "How's that?"

He leered at me again, going foxy.

"Don't you wish you knew! But I'll tell you this: old H.H. is going to give me all I want—just because I ask him to."

I took another tack, affecting incredulity.

"The hell he is! He'll hand you over to Ramon and that will be the last of a certain jockey."

"No, he won't do no such trick. I've fixed that; and he knows it. If he kills me, he'll lose *all* he's got 'stead of only part."

"You're drunk or dreaming," said I. "If you bother him, he'll just plain have you killed. That's a little way of his."

"And if he does a friend of mine will just go to a certain place and get certain papers and give 'em to a certain lawyer— and then where's old H.H.? And he knows it, damn well. And he's going to be good to Artie and give him what he wants. We'll get along fine. Took him a long time to come to it; but I didn't take no chances while he was making up his mind; you can bet on that."

"Blackmail, eh?" I said, with just enough of a sneer to fire him.

"Blackmail nothing!" he shouted. "It ain't blackmail to take away what don't belong to a man at all!"

"What don't belong to him?"

"Nothing. Not a damn thing except his money. This ranch. The oil wells in California. The cattle. Not a damn thing. That was the agreement with his pardner when they split. And I've got the agreement! Now what you got to say?"

"Say? Why its *loco*! Why doesn't the pardner raise a row?"

"He's dead."

"His heirs then?"

"He hasn't got but one heir—his daughter." My heart skipped a beat in the amazement of a half idea. "And she knew nothing about the agreement. Nobody knows but old H.H.—and me." He sat back, visibly gloating over me. But his mood was passing. His earlier exhilaration had died, and with it was dying the expansiveness of his confidence. The triumph of his last speech savoured he slipped again into his normal self. He looked at me suspiciously, and raised his whiskey to cover his confusion.

"What's it to yuh, anyway?" he muttered into his glass darkly. His eyes were again shifting here and there; and his lips were snarled back malevolently to show his teeth.

At this precise moment the lords of chance willed Windy Bill and others to intrude on our privacy by opening the door and hurling several whiskey-flavoured sarcasms at the pair of us. The jockey seemed to explode after the fashion of an over-inflated ball. He squeaked like a rat, leaped to his feet, hurled the chair on which he had been sitting crash against the door from which Windy Bill *et al* had withdrawn hastily, and ended by producing a small wicked-looking automatic—then a new and strange weapon—and rushing out into the main saloon. There he announced that he was known to the cognoscenti as Art the Blood and was a city gunman in comparison with which these plain, so-called bad men were as sucking doves to the untamed eagle. Thence he glanced briefly at their ancestry as far as known; and ended by rushing forth in the general direction of McCloud's hotel.

"Suffering giraffes!" gasped Windy Bill after the whirlwind had passed. "Was that the scared little rabbit that wept all them salt tears over at the depot? What brand of licker did you feed him, Sandy?"

I silently handed him the bottle.

"Soothing syrup—my God!" said Windy in hushed tones.

---

CHAPTER VIII

At that epoch I prided myself on being a man of resource; and I proceeded to prove it in a fashion that even now fills me with satisfaction. I annexed the remainder of that bottle of soothing syrup; I went to Sol Levi and easily procured delivery of the other five. Then I strolled peacefully to supper over at McCloud's hotel. Pathological knowledge of dope fiends was outside my ken—I could not guess how soon my man would need another dose of his "hop," but I was positively sure that another would be needed. Inquiry of McCloud elicited the fact that the ex-jockey had swallowed a hasty meal and had immediately retired to Room 4. I found Room 4 unlocked, and Brower lying fully clothed sound asleep across the bed. I did not disturb him, except that I robbed him of his pistol. All looked safe for awhile; but just to be certain I took Room 6, across the narrow hall, and left both doors open. McCloud's hotel never did much of a room business. By midnight the cowboys would be on their way for the ranches. Brower and myself were the only occupants of the second floor.

For two hours I smoked and read. The ex-jockey did not move a muscle. Then I went to bed and to a sound sleep; but I set my mind like an alarm clock, so that the slightest move from the other room would have fetched me broad awake. City-bred people may not know that this can be done by most outdoor men. I have listened subconsciously to horsebells for so many nights, for example, that even on stormy nights the cessation of that faint twinkle will awaken me, while the crash of the elements or even the fall of a tree would not in the slightest disturb my tired slumbers. So now, although the songs and stamping and racket of the revellers below stairs in McCloud's bar did not for one second prevent my falling into deep and dreamless sleep, Brower's softest tread would have reached my consciousness.

However, he slept right through the night, and was still dead to the world when I slipped out at six o'clock to meet the east-bound train. The bag—a small black Gladstone—was aboard in charge of the baggageman. I had no great difficulty in getting it from my friend, the station agent. Had he not seen me herding the locoed stranger? I secreted the black bag with the five full bottles of soothing syrup, slipped the half-emptied bottle in my pocket, and returned to the hotel. There I ate breakfast, and sat down for a comfortable chat with McCloud while awaiting results.

Got them very promptly. About eight o'clock Brower came downstairs. He passed through the office, nodding curtly to McCloud and me, and into the dining room where he drank several cups of coffee. Thence he passed down the street toward Sol Levi's. He emerged rather hurriedly and slanted across to the station.

"In about two minutes," I observed to McCloud, "you're going to observe yon butterfly turn into a stinging lizard. He's going to head in this direction; and he'll probably aim to climb my hump. Such being the case, and the affair being private, you'll do me a favour by supervising something in some remote corner of the premises."

"Sure," said McCloud, "I'll go twist that Chink washee-man. Been intending to for a week." And he stumped out on his wooden foot.

The comet hit at precisely 7:42 by McCloud's big clock. Its head was Brower at high speed and tension; and its tail was the light alkali dust of Arizona mingled with the station agent. No irresistible force and immovable body proposition in mine; I gave to the impact.

"Why, sure, I got 'em for you," I answered. "You left your dope lying around loose so I took care of it for you. As for your bag; you seemed to set such store by it that I got that for you, too."

Which deflated that particular enterprise for the moment, anyway. The station agent, too mad to spit, departed before he should be tempted beyond his strength to resist homicide.

"I suppose you're taking care of my gun for me, too," said Brower; but his irony was weak. He was evidently off the boil.

"Your gun?" I echoed. "Have you lost your gun?"

He passed his hand across his eyes. His super-excitement had passed, leaving him weak and nervous. Now was the time for my counter-attack.

"Here's your gun," said I, "didn't want to collect any lead while you were excited, and I've got your dope," I repeated, "in a safe place." I added, "and you'll not see any of it again until you answer me a few questions, and answer them straight."

"If you think you can roll me for blackmail," he came back with some decision, "you're left a mile."

"I don't want a cent; but I do want a talk."

"Shoot," said he.

"How often do you have to have this dope—for the best results; and how much of it at a shot?"

He stared at me for a moment, then laughed.

"What's it to yuh?" he repeated his formula.

"I want to know."

"I get to needing it about once a day. Three grains will carry me by."

"All right; that's what I want to know. Now listen to me. I'm custodian of this dope, and you'll get your regular ration as long as you stick with me."

"I can always hop a train. This ain't the only hamlet on the map," he reminded me.

"That's always what you can do if you find we can't work together. That's where you've got me if my proposition doesn't sound good."

"What is your proposition?" he asked after a moment.

"Before I tell you, I'm going to give you a few pointers on what you're up against. I don't know how much you know about Old Man Hooper, but I'll bet there's plenty you *don't* know about."

I proceeded to tell him something of the old man's methods, from the "boomerang" to vicarious murder.

"And he gets away with it?" asked Brower when I had finished.

"He certainly does," said I. "Now," I continued, "you may be solid as a brick church, and your plans may be water-tight, and old Hooper may kill the fatted four-year-old, for all I know. But if I were you, I wouldn't go sasshaying all alone out to Hooper's ranch. It's altogether *too* blame confiding and innocent."

"If anything happens to me, I've left directions for those contracts to be recorded," he pointed out. "Old Hooper knows that."

"Oh, sure!" I replied, "just like that! But one day your trustworthy friend back yonder will get a letter in your well-known hand-write that will say that all is well and the goose hangs high, that the old man is a prince and has come through, and that in accordance with the nice, friendly agreement you have reached he—your friend—will hand over the contract to a very respectable lawyer herein named, and so forth and so on, ending with your equally well-known John Hancock."

"Well, that's all right."

"I hadn't finished the picture. In the meantime, you will be getting out of it just one good swift kick, and that is all."

"I shouldn't write any such letter. Not 'till I felt the feel of the dough."

"Not at first you wouldn't," I said, softly. "Certainly not at first. But after a while you would. These renegade Mexicans—like Hooper's Ramon, for example—know a lot of rotten little tricks. They drive pitch-pine splinters into your legs and set fire to them, for one thing. Or make small cuts in you with a knife, and load them up with powder squibs in oiled paper—so the blood won't wet them—and touch them off. And so on. When you've been shown about ten per cent, of what old Ramon knows about such things, you'll write most any kind of a letter."

"My God!" he muttered, thrusting the ridiculous derby to the back of his head.

"So you see you'd look sweet walking trustfully into Hooper's claws. That's what that newspaper ad was meant for. And when the respectable lawyer wrote that the contract had been delivered, do you know what would happen to you?"

The ex-jockey shuddered.

"But you've only told me part of what I want to know," I pursued. "You got me side-tracked. This daughter of the dead pardner—this girl, what about her? Where is she now?"

"Europe, I believe."

"When did she go?"

"About three months ago."

"Any other relatives?"

"Not that I know of."

"H'm," I pondered. "What does she look like?"

"She's about medium height, dark, good figure, good-looking all right. She's got eyes wide apart and a wide forehead. That's the best I can do. Why?"

"Anybody heard from her since she went to Europe?"

"How should I know?" rejoined Brower, impatiently. "What you driving at?"

"I think I've seen her. I believe she's not in Europe at all. I believe she's a prisoner at the ranch."

"My aunt!" ejaculated Brower. His nervousness was increasing—the symptoms I was to recognize so well. "Why the hell don't you just shoot him from behind a bush? I'll do it, if you won't."

"He's too smooth for that." And I told him what Hooper had told me. "His hold on these Mexicans is remarkable. I don't doubt that fifty of the best killers in the southwest have lists of the men Old Man Hooper thinks might lay him out. And every man on that list would get his within a year—without any doubt. I don't doubt that partner's daughter would go first of all. You, too, of course."

"My aunt!" groaned the jockey again.

"He's a killer," I went on, "by nature, and by interest—a bad combination. He ought to be tramped out like a rattlesnake. But this is a new country, and it's near the border. I expect he's got me marked. If I have to I'll kill him just like I would a rattlesnake; but that wouldn't do me a whole lot of good and would probably get a bunch assassinated. I'd like to figure something different. So you see you'd better come on in while the coming is good."

"I see," said the ex-jockey, very much subdued. "What's your idea? What do you want me to do?"

That stumped me. To tell the truth I had no idea at all what to do.

"I don't want you to go out to Hooper's ranch alone," said I.

"Trust me!" he rejoined, fervently.

"I reckon the first best thing is to get along out of town," I suggested. "That black bag all the plunder you got?"

"That's it."

"Then we'll go out a-horseback."

We had lunch and a smoke and settled up with McCloud. About mid-afternoon we went on down to the livery corral. I knew the keeper pretty well, of course, so I borrowed a horse and saddle for Brower. The latter looked with extreme disfavour on both.

"This is no race meet," I reminded him. "This is a means of transportation."

"Sorry I ain't got nothing better," apologized Meigs, to whom I had confided my companion's profession—I had to account for such a figure somehow. "All my saddle hosses went off with a mine outfit yesterday."

"What's the matter with that chestnut in the shed?"

"He's all right; fine beast. Only it ain't mine. It belongs to Ramon."

"Ramon from Hooper's?"

"Yeah."

"I'd let you ride my horse and take Meigs's old skate myself," I said to Brower, "but when you first get on him this bronc of mine is a rip-humming tail twister. Ain't he, Meigs?"

"He's a bad *caballo*," corroborated Meigs.

"Does he buck?" queried Brower, indifferently.

"Every known fashion. Bites, scratches, gouges, and paws. Want to try him?"

"I got a headache," replied Brower, grouchily. "Bring out your old dog."

When I came back from roping and blindfolding the twisted dynamite I was engaged in "gentling," I found that Brower was saddling the mournful creature with my saddle. My expostulation found him very snappy and very arbitrary. His opium-irritated nerves were beginning to react. I realized that he was not far short of explosive obstinacy. So I conceded the point; although, as every rider knows, a cowboy's saddle and a cowboy's gun are like unto a toothbrush when it comes to lending. Also it involved changing the stirrup length on the livery saddle. I needed things just right to ride Tiger through the first five minutes.

When I had completed this latter operation, Brower had just finished drawing tight the cinch. His horse stood dejectedly. When Brower had made fast the latigo, the horse—as such dispirited animals often do—heaved a deep sigh. Something snapped beneath the slight strain of the indrawn breath.

"Dogged if your cinch ain't busted!" cried Meigs with a loud laugh. "Lucky for you your friend did borrow your saddle! If you'd clumb Tiger with that outfit you could just naturally have begun pickin' out the likely-looking she-angels."

I dropped the stirrup and went over to examine the damage. Both of the quarter straps on the off side had given way. I found that they had been cut nearly through with a sharp knife. My eye strayed to Ramon's chestnut horse standing under the shed.

---

CHAPTER IX

We jogged out to Box Springs by way of the lower alkali flats. It is about three miles farther that way; but one can see for miles in every direction. I did not one bit fancy the cañons, the mesquite patches, and the open ground of the usual route.

I beguiled the distance watching Brower. The animal he rode was a hammer-headed, ewe-necked beast with a disconsolate eye and a half-shed winter coat. The ex-jockey was not accustomed to a stock saddle. He had shortened his stirrups beyond all reason so that his knees and his pointed shoes and his elbows stuck out at all angles. He had thrust his derby hat far down over his ears, and buttoned his inadequate coat tightly. In addition, he was nourishing a very considerable grouch, attributable, I suppose, to the fact that his customary dose was just about due. Tiger could not be blamed for dancing wide. Evening was falling, the evening of the desert when mysterious things seem to swell and draw imminent out of unguessed distances. I could not help wondering what these gods of the desert could be thinking of us.

However, as we drew imperceptibly nearer the tiny patch of cottonwoods that marked Box Springs, I began to realize that it would be more to the point to wonder what that gang of hoodlums in the bunk house was going to think of us. The matter had been fairly well carried off up to that moment, but I could not hope for a successful repetition. No man could continue to lug around with him so delicious a vaudeville sketch without some concession to curiosity. Nor could any mortal for long wear such clothes in the face of Arizona without being required to show cause. He had got away with it last night, by surprise; but that would be about all.

At my fiftieth attempt to enter into conversation with him, I unexpectedly succeeded. I believe I was indicating the points of interest. You can see farther in Arizona than any place I know, so there was no difficulty about that. I'd pointed out the range of the Chiracahuas, and Cochise's Stronghold, and the peaks of the Galiuros and other natural sceneries; I had showed him mesquite and yucca, and mescal and soapweed, and sage, and sacatone and niggerheads and all the other known vegetables of the region. Also I'd indicated prairie dogs and squinch owls and Gambel's quail and road runners and a couple of coyotes and lizards and other miscellaneous fauna. Not to speak of naming painstakingly the ranches indicated by the clumps of trees that you could just make out as little spots in the distance—Box Springs, the O.T., the Double H, Fort Shafter, and Hooper's. He waked up and paid a little attention at this; and I thought I might get a little friendly talk out of him. A cowboy rides around alone so much he sort of likes to josh when he has anybody with him. This "strong silent" stuff doesn't go until you've used around with a man quite some time.

I got the talk, all right, but it didn't have a thing to do with topography or natural history. Unless you call the skate he was riding natural history. That was the burden of his song. He didn't like that horse, and he didn't care who knew it. It was an uncomfortable horse to ride on, it required exertion to keep in motion, and it hurt his feelings. Especially the last. He was a horseman, a jockey, he'd ridden the best blood in the equine world; and here he was condemned through no fault of his own to straddle a cross between a llama and a woolly toy sheep. It hurt his pride. He felt bitterly about it. Indeed, he fairly harped on the subject.

"Is that horse of yours through bucking for the day?" he asked at last.

"Certain thing. Tiger never pitches but the once."

"Let me ride him a ways. I'd like to feel a real horse to get the taste of this kangaroo out of my system."

I could see he was jumpy, so I thought I'd humour him.

"Swing on all at once and you're all right," I advised him. "Tiger don't like fumbling in getting aboard."

He grunted scornfully.

"Those stirrups are longer than the ones you've been using. Want to shorten them?"

He did not bother to answer, but mounted in a decisive manner that proved he was indeed a horseman, and a good one. I climbed old crow bait and let my legs hang.

The jockey gathered the reins and touched Tiger with his heels. I kicked my animal with my stock spurs and managed to extract a lumbering sort of gallop.

"Hey, slow up!" I called after a few moments. "I can't keep up with you."

Brower did not turn his head, nor did Tiger slow up. After twenty seconds I realized that he intended to do neither. I ceased urging on my animal, there was no use tiring us both; evidently the jockey was enjoying to the full the exhilaration of a good horse, and we would catch up at Box Springs. I only hoped the boys wouldn't do anything drastic to him before my arrival.

So I jogged along at the little running walk possessed by even the most humble cattle horse, and enjoyed the evening. It was going on toward dusk and pools of twilight were in the bottomlands. For the moment the world had grown smaller, more intimate, as the skies expanded. The dust from Brower's going did not so much recede as grow littler, more toy-like. I watched idly his progress.

At a point perhaps a mile this side the Box Springs ranch the road divides: the right-hand fork leading to the ranch house, the left on up the valley. After a moment I noticed that the dust was on the left-hand fork. I swore aloud.

"The damn fool has taken the wrong road!" and then after a moment, with dismay: "He's headed straight for Hooper's ranch!"

I envisaged the full joy and rapture of this thought for perhaps half a minute. It sure complicated matters, what with old Hooper gunning on my trail, and this partner's daughter shut up behind bars. Me, I expected to last about two days unless I did something mighty sudden. Brower I expected might last approximately half that time, depending on how soon Ramon *et al* got busy. The girl I didn't know anything about, nor did I want to at that moment. I was plenty worried about my own precious hide just then. And if you think you are going to get a love story out of this, I warn you again to quit right now; you are not.

Brower was going to walk into that gray old spider's web like a nice fat fly. And he was going to land without even the aid and comfort of his own particular brand of Dutch courage. For safety's sake, and because of Tiger's playful tendencies when first mounted, we had tied the famous black bag—which now for convenience contained also the soothing syrup—behind the cantle of Meigs's old nag. Which said nag I now possessed together with all appurtenances and attachments thereunto appertaining I tried to speculate on the reactions of Old Man Hooper, Ramon, Brower and no dope, but it was too much for me. My head was getting tired thinking about all these complicated things, anyhow. I was accustomed to nice, simple jobs with my head, like figuring on the shrinkage of beef cattle, or the inner running of a two-card draw. All this annoyed me. I began to get mad. When I got mad enough I cussed and came to a decision: which was to go after Old Man Hooper and all his works that very night. Next day wouldn't do; I wanted action right off quick. Naturally I had no plans, nor even a glimmering of what I was going to do about it; but you bet you I was going to do something! As soon as it was dark I was going right on up there. Frontal attack, you understand. As to details, those would take care of themselves as the affair developed. Having come to which sapient decision I shoved the whole irritating mess over the edge of my mind and rode on quite happy. I told you at the start of this yarn that I was a kid.

My mind being now quite easy as to my future actions, I gave thought to the first step. That was supper. There seemed to me no adequate reason, with a fine, long night before me, why I shouldn't use a little of the shank end of it to stoke up for the rest. So I turned at the right-hand fork and jogged slowly toward our own ranch.

Of course I had the rotten luck to find most of the boys still at the water corral. When they saw who was the lone horseman approaching through the dusk of the spring twilight, and got a good fair look at the ensemble, they dropped everything and came over to see about it, headed naturally by those mournful blights, Windy Bill and Wooden. In solemn silence they examined my outfit, paying not the slightest attention to me. At the end of a full minute they looked at each other.

"What do you think, Sam?" asked Windy.

"My opinion is not quite formed, suh," replied Wooden, who was a Texican. "But my first examination inclines me to the belief that it is a hoss."

"Yo're wrong, Sam," denied Windy, sadly; "yo're judgment is confused by the fact that the critter carries a saddle. Look at the animile itself."

"I have done it," continued Sam Wooden; "at first glance I should agree with you. Look carefully, Windy. Examine the details; never mind the *toot enscramble*. It's got hoofs."

"So's a cow, a goat, a burro, a camel, a hippypottamus, and the devil," pointed out Windy.

"Of course I may be wrong," acknowledged Wooden. "On second examination I probably am wrong. But if it ain't a hoss, then what is it? Do you know?"

"It's a genuine royal gyasticutus," esserted Windy Bill, positively. "I seen one once. It has one peculiarity that you can't never fail to identify it by."

"What's that?"

"It invariably travels around with a congenital idiot."

Wooden promptly conceded that, but claimed the identification not complete as he doubted whether, strictly speaking, I could be classified as a congenital idiot. Windy pointed out that evidently I had traded Tiger for the gyasticutus. Wooden admitted that this proved me an idiot, but not necessarily a congenital idiot.

This colloquy—and more like it—went on with entire gravity. The other men were hanging about relishing the situation, but without a symptom of mirth. I was unsaddling methodically, paying no attention to anybody, and apparently deaf to all that was being said. If the two old fools had succeeded in eliciting a word from me they would have been entirely happy; but I knew that fact, and shut my lips.

I hung my saddle on the rack and was just about to lead the old skate to water when we all heard the sound of a horse galloping on the road.

"It's a light boss," said somebody after a moment, meaning a horse without a burden.

We nodded and resumed our occupation. A stray horse coming in to water was nothing strange or unusual. But an instant later, stirrups swinging, reins flapping, up dashed my own horse, Tiger.

---

CHAPTER X

All this being beyond me, and then some, I proceeded methodically to carry out my complicated plan; which was, it will be remembered, to eat supper and then to go and see about it in person. I performed the first part of this to my entire satisfaction but not to that of the rest. They accused me of unbecoming secrecy; only they expressed it differently. That did not worry me, and in due time I made my escape. At the corral I picked out a good horse, one that I had brought from the Gila, that would stay tied indefinitely without impatience. Then I lighted a cigarette and jogged up the road. I carried with me a little grub, my six-gun, the famous black bag, and an entirely empty head.

The night was only moderately dark, for while there was no moon there were plenty of those candle-like desert stars. The little twinkling lights of the Box Springs dropped astern like lamps on a shore. By and by I turned off the road and made a wide détour down the sacatone bottoms, for I had still some sense; and roads were a little too obvious. The reception committee that had taken charge of my little friend might be expecting another visitor—me. This brought my approach to the blank side of the ranch where were the willow trees and the irrigating ditch. I rode up as close as I thought I ought to. Then I tied my horse to a prominent lone Joshua-tree that would be easy to find, unstrapped the black bag, and started off. The black bag, however, bothered me; so after some thought I broke the lock with a stone and investigated the contents, mainly by feel. There were a lot of clothes and toilet articles and such junk, and a number of undetermined hard things like round wooden boxes. Finally I withdrew to the shelter of a *barranca* where I could light matches. Then I had no difficulty in identifying a nice compact little hypodermic outfit, which I slipped into a pocket. I then deposited the bag in a safe place where I could find it easily.

Leaving my horse I approached the ranch under cover of the willows. Yes, I remembered this time that I left tracks, but I did not care. My idea was to get some sort of decisive action before morning. Once through the willows I crept up close to the walls. They were twelve or fifteen feet high, absolutely smooth; and with one exception broken only by the long, narrow loopholes or transoms I have mentioned before. The one exception was a small wicket gate or door. I remembered the various sorties with torches after the chirping frogs, and knew that by this opening the hunting party had emerged. This and the big main gate were the only entrances to the enclosure.

I retired to the vicinity of the willows and uttered the cry of the barred owl. After ten seconds I repeated it, and so continued. My only regret was that I could not chirp convincingly like a frog. I saw a shadow shift suddenly through one of the transoms, and at once glided to the wall near the little door. After a moment or so it opened to emit Old Man Hooper and another bulkier figure which I imagined to be that of Ramon. Both were armed with shotguns. Suddenly it came to me that I was lucky not to have been able to chirp convincingly like a frog. They hunted frogs with torches and in a crowd. Those two carried no light and they were so intent on making a sneak on the willows and the supposititious owl that I, flattened in the shadow of the wall, easily escaped their notice. I slipped inside the doorway.

This brought me into a narrow passage between two buildings. The other end looked into the interior court. A careful reconnaissance showed no one in sight, so I walked boldly along the verandah in the direction of the girl's room. Her note had said she was constantly guarded; but I could see no one in sight, and I had to take a chance somewhere. Two seconds' talk would do me: I wanted to know in which of the numerous rooms the old man slept. I had a hunch it would be a good idea to share that room with him. What to do then I left to the hunch.

But when I was half way down the verandah I heard the wicket door slammed shut. The owl hunters had returned more quickly than I had anticipated. Running as lightly as possible I darted down the verandah and around the corner of the left wing. This brought me into a narrow little garden strip between the main house and the wall dividing the court from the corrals and stable yards. Footsteps followed me but stopped. A hand tried the door knob to the corner room.

"Nothing," I heard Hooper's voice replying to a question. "Nothing at all. Go to sleep."

The fragrant smell of Mexican tobacco reached my nostrils. After a moment Ramon—it was he—resumed a conversation in Spanish:

"I do not know, señor, who the man was. I could but listen; it was not well to inquire nor to show too much interest. His name, yes; Jim Starr, but who he is——" I could imagine the shrug. "It is of no importance."

"It is of importance that the other man still lives," broke in Hooper's harsher voice. "I will not have it, I say! Are you sure of it?"

"I saw him. And I saw his horse at the Señor Meigs. It was the brown that bucks badly, so I cut the quarter straps of his saddle. It might be that we have luck; I do not count on it. But rest your mind easy, señor, it shall be arranged."

"It better be."

"But there is more, señor. The señor will remember a man who rode in races for him many years ago, one named Artie——"

"Brower!" broke in Hooper. "What about him?"

"He is in town. He arrived yesterday afternoon."

Hooper ejaculated something.

"And more, he is all day and all night with this Sanborn."

Hooper swore fluently in English.

"Look, Ramon!" he ordered, vehemently. "It is necessary to finish this Sanborn at once, without delay."

"*Bueno*, señor."

"It must not go over a single day."

"Haste makes risk, señor."

"The risk must be run."

"*Bueno*, señor. And also this Artie?"

"No! no! no!" hastened Hooper. "Guard him as your life! But send a trusty man for him to-morrow with the buckboard. He comes to see me, in answer to my invitation."

"And if he will not come, señor?" inquired Ramon's quiet voice.

"Why should he not come?"

"He has been much with Sanborn."

"It's necessary that he come," replied Hooper, emphasizing each word.

"*Bueno*, señor."

"Who is to be on guard?"

"Cortinez, señor."

"I will send him at once. Do me the kindness to watch for a moment until I send him. Here is the key; give it to him. It shall be but a moment."

"*Bueno*, señor," replied Ramon.

He leaned against the corner of the house. I could see the half of his figure against the sky and the dim white of the walls.

The night was very still, as always at this ranch. There was not even a breeze to create a rustle in the leaves. I was obliged to hold rigidly motionless, almost to hush my breathing, while the figure bulked large against the whitewashed wall. But my eyes, wide to the dimness, took in every detail of my surroundings. Near me stood a water barrel. If I could get a spring from that water barrel I could catch one of the heavy projecting beams of the roof.

After an apparently interminable interval the sound of footsteps became audible, and a moment later Ramon moved to meet his relief. I seized the opportunity of their conversation and ascended to the roof. It proved to be easy, although the dried-out old beam to which for a moment I swung creaked outrageously. Probably it sounded louder to me than the actual fact. I took off my boots and moved cautiously to where I could look down into the court. Ramon and his companion were still talking under the verandah, so I could not see them; but I waited until I heard one of them move away. Then I went to seat myself on the low parapet and think things over.

The man below me had the key to the girl's room. If I could get the key I could accomplish the first step of my plan—indeed the only step I had determined upon. The exact method of getting the key would have to develop. In the meantime, I gave passing wonder to the fact, as developed by the conversation between Hooper and Ramon, that Brower was not at the ranch and had not been heard of at the ranch. Where had Tiger dumped him, and where now was he lying? I keenly regretted the loss of a possible ally; and, much to my astonishment, I found within myself a little regret for the man himself.

The thought of the transom occurred to me. I tiptoed over to that side and looked down. The opening was about five feet below the parapet. After a moment's thought I tied a bit of stone from the coping in the end of my silk bandana and lowered it at arm's length. By swinging it gently back and forth I determined that the transom was open. With the stub of the pencil every cowboy carried to tally with I scribbled a few words on an envelope which I wrapped about the bit of coping. Something to the effect that I was there, and expected to gain entrance to her room later, and to be prepared. Then I lowered my contraption, caused it to tap gently a dozen times on the edge of the transom, and finally swung it with a rather nice accuracy to fly, bandana and all, through the opening. After a short interval of suspense I saw the reflection of a light and so knew my message had been received.

There was nothing to do now but return to a point of observation. On my way I stubbed my stockinged foot against a stone *metate* or mortar in which Indians and Mexicans make their flour. The heavy pestle was there. I annexed it. Dropped accurately from the height of the roof it would make a very pretty weapon. The trouble, of course, lay in that word "accurately."

But I soon found the fates playing into my hands. At the end of a quarter hour the sentry emerged from under the verandah, looked up at the sky, yawned, stretched, and finally sat down with his back against the wall of the building opposite. Inside of ten minutes he was sound asleep and snoring gently.

I wanted nothing better than that. The descent was a little difficult to accomplish noiselessly, as I had to drop some feet, but I managed it. After crouching for a moment to see if the slight sounds had aroused him, I crept along the wall to where he sat. The stone pestle of the *metate* I had been forced to leave behind me, but I had the heavy barrel of my gun, and I was going to take no chances. I had no compunctions as to what I did to any one of this pack of mad dogs. Cautiously I drew it from its holster and poised it to strike. At that instant I was seized and pinioned from behind.

---

CHAPTER XI

I did not struggle. I would have done so if I had been able, but I was caught in a grip so skillful that the smallest move gave me the most exquisite pain. At that time I had not even heard the words *jiu jitsu*, but I have looked them up since. Cortinez, the sleepy sentry, without changing his position, had opened his eyes and was grinning at me.

I was forced to my feet and marched to the open door of the corner room. There I was released, and turned around to face Hooper himself. The old man's face was twisted in a sardonic half-snarl that might pass for a grin; but there was no smile in his unblinking wildcat eyes. There seemed to be trace neither of the girl nor the girl's occupation.

"Thank you for your warning of your intended visit," said Hooper in silky tones, indicating my bandana which lay on the table. "And now may I inquire to what I owe the honour of this call? Or it may be that the visit was not intended for me at all. Mistake in the rooms, perhaps. I often shift and change my quarters, and those of my household; especially if I suspect I have some reason for doing so. It adds interest to an otherwise uneventful life."

He was eying me sardonically, evidently gloating over the situation as he found it.

"How did you get on that roof? Who let you inside the walls?" he demanded, abruptly.

I merely smiled at him.

"That we can determine later," he observed, resuming command of himself.

I measured my chances, and found them at present a minus quantity. The old man was separated from me by a table, and he held my own revolver ready for instant use. So I stood tight and waited.

The room was an almost exact replica of the one in which I had spent the night so short a time before; the same long narrow transom near the ceiling, the same barred windows opening on the court, the same closet against the blank wall. Hooper had evidently inhabited it for some days, for it was filled with his personal belongings. Indeed he must have moved in *en bloc* when his ward had been moved out, for none of the furnishings showed the feminine touch, and several articles could have belonged only to the old man personally. Of such was a small iron safe in one corner and a tall old-fashioned desk crammed with papers.

But if I decided overt action unwise at this moment, I decidedly went into action the next. Hooper whistled and four Mexicans appeared with ropes. Somehow I knew if they once hog-tied me I would never get another chance. Better dead now than helpless in the morning, for what that old buzzard might want of me.

One of them tossed a loop at me. I struck it aside and sailed in.

It had always been my profound and contemptuous belief that I could lick any four Mexicans. Now I had to take that back. I could not. But I gave the man argument, and by the time they had my elbows lashed behind me and my legs tied to the legs of one of those big solid chairs they like to name as "Mission style," I had marked them up and torn their pretty clothes and smashed a lot of junk around the place and generally got them so mad they would have knifed me in a holy second if it had not been for Old Man Hooper. The latter held up the lamp where it wouldn't get smashed and admonished them in no uncertain terms that he wanted me alive and comparatively undamaged. Oh, sure! they mussed me up, too. I wasn't very pretty, either.

The bravos withdrew muttering curses, as the story books say; and after Hooper had righted the table and stuck the lamp on it, and taken a good look at my bonds, he withdrew also.

Most of my time until the next thing occurred was occupied in figuring on all the things that might happen to me. One thing I acknowledged to myself right off the reel: the Mexicans had sure trussed me up for further orders! I could move my hands, but I knew enough of ropes and ties to realize that my chances of getting free were exactly nothing. My plans had gone perfectly up to this moment. I had schemed to get inside the ranch and into Old Man Hooper's room; and here I was! What more could a man ask?

The next thing occurred so soon, however, that I hadn't had time to think of more than ten per cent. of the things that might happen to me. The outside door opened to admit Hooper, followed by the girl. He stood aside in the most courtly fashion.

"My dear," he said, "here is Mr. Sanborn, who has come to call on you. You remember Mr. Sanborn, I am sure. You met him at dinner; and besides, I believe you had some correspondence with him, did you not? He has taken so much trouble, so very much trouble to see you that I think it a great pity his wish should not be fulfilled. Won't you sit down here, my dear?"

She was staring at me, her eyes gone wide with wonder and horror. Half thinking she took her seat as indicated. Instantly the old man had bound her elbows at the back and had lashed her to the chair. After the first start of surprise she made no resistance.

"There," said Hooper, straightening up after the accomplishment of this task; "now I'm going to leave you to your visit. You can talk it all over. Tell him all you please, my dear. And you, sir, tell her all you know. I think I can arrange so your confidences will go no further."

For the first time I heard him laugh, a high, uncertain cackle. The girl said nothing, but she stared at him with level, blazing eyes. Also for the first time I began to take an interest in her.

"Do you object to smoking?" I asked her, suddenly.

She blinked and recovered.

"Not at all," she answered.

"Well then, old man, be a sport. Give me the makings. I can get my hands to my mouth."

The old man transferred his baleful eyes on me. Then without saying a word he placed in my hands a box of tailor-made cigarettes and a dozen matches.

"Until morning," he observed, his hand on the door knob. He inclined in a most courteous fashion, first to the one of us, then to the other, and went out. He did not lock the door after him, and I could hear him addressing Cortinez outside. The girl started to speak, but I waved my shackled hand at her for silence. By straining my ears I could just make out what was said.

"I am going to bed," Hooper said. "It is not necessary to stand guard. You may get your blankets and sleep on the verandah."

After the old man's footsteps had died, I turned back to the girl opposite me and looked her over carefully. My first impression of meekness I revised. She did not look to be one bit meek. Her lips were compressed, her nostrils wide, her level eyes unsubdued. A person of sense, I said to myself, well balanced, who has learned when it is useless to kick against the pricks, but who has not necessarily on that account forever renounced all kicking. It occurred to me that she must have had to be pretty thoroughly convinced before she had come to this frame of mind. When she saw that I had heard all I wanted of the movements outside, she spoke hurriedly in her low, sweet voice:

"Oh, I am so distressed! This is all my doing! I should have known better——"

"Now," I interrupted her, decisively, "let's get down to cases. You had nothing to do with this; nothing whatever. I visited this ranch the first time out of curiosity, and to-night because I knew that I'd have to hit first to save my own life. You had no influence on me in either case."

"You thought this was my room—I wrote you it was," she countered, swiftly.

"I wanted to see you solely and simply that I might find out how to get at Hooper. This is all my fault; and we're going to cut out the self-accusations and get down to cases."

I afterward realized that all this was somewhat inconsiderate and ungallant and slightly humiliating; I should have taken the part of the knight-errant rescuing the damsel in distress, but at that moment only the direct essentials entered my mind.

"Very well," she assented in her repressed tones.

"Do you think he is listening to what we say; or has somebody listening?"

"I am positive not."

"Why?"

"I lived in this room for two months, and I know every inch of it."

"He might have some sort of a concealed listening hole somewhere, just the same."

"I am certain he has not. The walls are two feet thick."

"All right; let it go at that. Now let's see where we stand. In the first place, how do you dope this out?"

"What do you mean?"

"What does he intend to do with us?"

She looked at me straight, eye to eye.

"In the morning he will kill you—unless you can contrive something."

"Cheering thought."

"There is no sense in not facing situations squarely. If there is a way out, that is the only method by which it may be found."

"True," I agreed, my admiration growing. "And yourself; will he kill you, too?"

"He will not. He does not dare!" she cried, proudly, with a flash of the eyes.

I was not so sure of that, but there was no object in saying so.

"Why has he tied you in that chair, then, along with the condemned?" I asked.

"You will understand better if I tell you who I am."

"You are his deceased partner's daughter; and everybody thinks you are in Europe," I stated.

"How in the world did you know that? But no matter; it is true. I embarked three months ago on the Limited for New York intending, as you say, to go on a long trip to Europe. My father and I had been alone in the world. We were very fond of each other. I took no companion, nor did I intend to. I felt quite independent and able to take care of myself. At the last moment Mr. Hooper boarded the train. That was quite unexpected. He was on his way to the ranch. He persuaded me to stop over for a few days to decide some matters. You know, since my father's death I am half owner."

"Whole owner," I murmured.

"What did you say?"

"Nothing. Go ahead. Sure you don't mind my smoking?" I lit one of the tailor-mades and settled back. Even my inexperienced youth recognized the necessity of relief this long-continued stubborn repression must feel. My companion had as yet told me nothing I did not already know or guess; but I knew it would do her good to talk, and I might learn something valuable.

"We came out to the ranch, and talked matters over quite normally; but when it came time for my departure, I was not permitted to leave. For some unexplained reason I was a prisoner, confined absolutely to the four walls of this enclosure. I was guarded night and day; and I soon found I was to be permitted conversation with two men only, Mexicans named Ramon and Andreas."

"They are his right and left hand," I commented.

"So I found. You may imagine I did not submit to this until I found I had to. Then I made up my mind that the only possible thing to do was to acquiesce, to observe, and to wait my chance."

"You were right enough there. Why do you figure he did this?"

"I don't know!" she cried with a flash of thwarted despair. "I have racked my brains, but I can find no motive. He has not asked me for a thing; he has not even asked me a question. Unless he's stark crazy, I cannot make it out!"

"He may be that," I suggested.

"He may be; and yet I doubt it somehow. I don't know why; but I *feel* that he is sane enough. He is inconceivably cruel and domineering. He will not tolerate a living thing about the place that will not or cannot take orders from him. He kills the flies, the bees, the birds, the frogs, because they are not his. I believe he would kill a man as quickly who stood out even for a second against him here. To that extent I believe he is crazy: a sort of monomania. But not otherwise. That is why I say he will kill you; I really believe he would do it."

"So do I," I agreed, grimly. "However, let's drop that for right now. Do you know a man named Brower, Artie Brower?"

"I don't think I ever heard of him. Why?"

"Never mind for a minute. I've just had a great thought strike me. Just let me alone a few moments while I work it out."

I lighted a second cigarette from the butt of the first and fell into a study. Cortinez breathed heavily outside. Otherwise the silence was as dead as the blackness of the night. The smoke from my cigarettes floated lazily until it reached the influence of the hot air from the lamp; then it shot upward toward the ceiling. The girl watched me from under her level brows, always with that air of controlled restraint I found so admirable.

"I've got it," I said at last, "—or at least I think I have. Now listen to me, and believe what I've got to say. Here are the facts: first, your father and Hooper split partnership a while back. Hooper took his share entirely in cash; your father took his probably part in cash, but certainly all of the ranch and cattle. Get that clear? Hooper owns no part of the ranch and cattle. All right. Your father dies before the papers relating to this agreement are recorded. Nobody knew of those papers except your father and Hooper. So if Hooper were to destroy those papers, he'd still have the cash that had been paid him, and an equal share in the property. That plain?"

"Perfectly," she replied, composedly. "Why didn't he destroy them?"

"Because they had been stolen by this man Brower I asked you about—an ex-jockey of Hooper's. Brower held them for blackmail. Unless Hooper came through Brower would record the papers."

"Where do I come in?"

"Easy. I'm coming to that. But answer me this: who would be your heir in case you died?"

"Why—I don't know!"

"Have you any kin?"

"Not a soul!"

"Did you ever make a will?"

"I never thought of such a thing!"

"Well, I'll tell you. If you were to die your interest in this property would go to Hooper."

"What makes you think so? I thought it would go to the state."

"I'm guessing," I acknowledged, "but I believe I'm guessing straight. A lot of these old Arizona partnerships were made just that way. Life was uncertain out here. I'll bet the old original partnership between your father and Hooper provides that in case of the extinction of one line, the other will inherit. It's a very common form of partnership in a new country like this. You can see for yourself it's a sensible thing to provide."

"You may be right," she commented. "Go on."

"You told me a while ago it was best to face any situation squarely. Now brace up and face this. You said a while ago that Hooper would not dare kill you. That is true for the moment. But there is no doubt in my mind that he has intended from the first to kill you, because by that he would get possession of the whole property."

"I cannot believe it!" she cried.

"Isn't the incentive enough? Think carefully, and answer honestly: don't you think him capable of it?"

"Yes—I suppose so," she admitted, reluctantly, after a moment. She gathered herself as after a shock. "Why hasn't he done so? Why has he waited?"

I told her of the situation as it concerned Brower. While the dissolution of partnership papers still existed and might still be recorded, such a murder would be useless. For naturally the dissolution abrogated the old partnership agreement. The girl's share of the property would, at her demise intestate, go to the state. That is, provided the new papers were ever recorded.

"Then I am safe until——?" she began.

"Until he negotiates or otherwise settles with Brower. Until he has destroyed all evidence."

"Then everything seems to depend on this Brower," she said, knitting her brows anxiously. "Where is he?"

I did not answer this last question. My eyes were riveted on the door knob which was slowly, almost imperceptibly, turning. Cortinez continued to breathe heavily in sleep outside. The intruder was evidently at great pains not to awaken the guard. A fraction of an inch at a time the door opened. A wild-haired, wild-eyed head inserted itself cautiously through the crack. The girl's eyes widened in surprise and, I imagine, a little in fear. I began to laugh, silently, so as not to disturb Cortinez. Mirth overcame me; the tears ran down my cheeks.

"It's so darn complete!" I gasped, answering the girl's horrified look of inquiry. "Miss Emory, allow me to present Mr. Artie Brower!"

---

CHAPTER XII

Brower entered the room quickly but very quietly, and at once came to me. His eyes were staring, his eyelids twitched, his hands shook. I recognized the symptoms.

"Have you got it? Have you got it with you?" he whispered, feverishly.

"It's all right. I can fix you up. Untie me first," I replied.

He began to fumble with the knots of my bonds too hastily and impatiently for effectiveness. I was trying to stoop over far enough to see what he was doing when my eye caught the shadow of a moving figure outside. An instant later Tim Westmore, the English groom attached to the Morgan stallion, came cautiously through the door, which he closed behind him. I attempted unobtrusively to warn Brower, but he only looked up, nodded vaguely, and continued his fumbling efforts to free me. Westmore glanced at us all curiously, but went at once to the big windows, which he proceeded to swing shut. Then he came over to us, pushed Brower one side, and most expeditiously untied the knots. I stood up stretching in the luxury of freedom, then turned to perform a like office for Miss Emory. But Brower was by now frantic. He seized my arm and fairly shook me, big as I was, in the urgence of his desire. He was rapidly losing all control and caution.

"Let him have it, sir," urged Westmore in a whisper. "I'll free the young lady."

I gave Brower the hypodermic case. He ran to the wash bowl for water. During the process of preparation he uttered little animal sounds under his breath. When the needle had sunk home he lay back in a chair and closed his eyes.

In the meantime, I had been holding a whispered colloquy with Westmore.

"He sneaked in on me at dark, sir," he told me, "on foot. I don't know how he got in without being seen. They'd have found his tracks anyway in the morning. I don't think he knew quite what he wanted to do. Him and me were old pals, and he wanted to ask me about things. He didn't expect to stay, I fancy. He told me he had left his horse tied a mile or so down the road. Then a while back orders came to close down, air tight. We're used to such orders. Nobody can go out or come in, you understand. And there are guards placed. That made him uneasy. He told me then he was a hop fiend. I've seen them before, and I got uneasy, too. If he came to the worst I might have to tie and gag him. I know how they are."

"Go ahead," I urged. He had stopped to listen.

"I don't like that Cortinez being so handy like out there," he confessed.

"Hooper told him he could sleep. He's not likely to pay attention to us. Miss Emory and I have been talking aloud."

"I hope not. Well, then, Ramon came by and stopped to talk to me for a minute. I had to hide Artie in a box-stall and hope to God he kept quiet. He wasn't as bad as he is now. Ramon told me about you being caught, and went on. After that nothing must do but find you. He thought you might have his dope. He'd have gone into the jaws of hell after it. So I came along to keep him out of mischief."

"What are you going to do now?" asked the girl, who had kicked off her slippers and had been walking a few paces to and fro.

"I don't know, ma'am. We've got to get away."

"We?"

"You mean me, too? Yes, ma'am! I have stood with the doings of this place as long as I can stand them. Artie has told me some other things. Are you here of your free will, ma'am?" he asked, abruptly.

"No," she replied.

"I suspected as much. I'm through with the whole lot of them."

Brower opened his eyes. He was now quite calm.

"Hooper sold the Morgan stallion," he whispered, smiled sardonically, and closed his eyes again.

"Without telling me a word of it!" added Tim with heat. "He ain't delivered him yet."

"Well, I don't blame you. Now you'd better quietly sneak back to your quarters. There is likely to be trouble before we get through. You, too, Brower. Nobody knows you are here."

Brower opened his eyes again.

"I can get out of this place now I've had me hop," said he, decidedly. "Come on, let's go."

"We'll all go," I agreed; "but let's see what we can find here first. There may be some paper—or something——"

"What do you mean? What sort of papers? Hadn't we better go at once?"

"It is supposed to be well known that the reason Hooper isn't assassinated from behind a bush is because in that case his killers are in turn to assassinate a long list of his enemies. Only nobody is sure: just as nobody is really sure that he has killers at all. You can't get action on an uncertainty."

She nodded. "I can understand that."

"If we could get proof positive it would be no trick at all to raise the country."

"What sort of proof?"

"Well, I mentioned a list. I don't doubt his head man—Ramon, I suppose, the one he'd trust with carrying out such a job—must have a list of some sort. He wouldn't trust to memory."

"And he wouldn't trust it to Ramon until after he was dead!" said the girl with sudden intuition. "If it exists we'll find it here."

She started toward the paper-stuffed desk, but I stopped her.

"More likely the safe," said I.

Tim, who was standing near it, tried the handle.

"It's locked," he whispered.

I fell on my knees and began to fiddle with the dial, of course in vain. Miss Emory, with more practical decision of character, began to run through the innumerable bundles and loose papers in the desk, tossing them aside as they proved unimportant or not germane to the issue. I had not the slightest knowledge of the constructions of safes but whirled the knob hopelessly in one direction or another trying to listen for clicks, as somewhere I had read was the thing to do. As may be imagined, I arrived nowhere. Nor did the girl. We looked at each other in chagrin at last.

"There is nothing here but ranch bills and accounts and business letters," she confessed.

I merely shook my head.

At this moment Brower, whom I had supposed to be sound asleep, opened his eyes.

"Want that safe open?" he asked, drowsily.

He arose, stretched, and took his place beside me on the floor. His head cocked one side, he slowly turned the dials with the tips of fingers I for the first time noticed were long and slim and sensitive. Twice after extended, delicate manipulations he whirled the knob impatiently and took a fresh start. On the proverbial third trial he turned the handle and the door swung open. He arose rather stiffly from his knees, resumed his place in the armchair, and again closed his eyes.

It was a small safe, with few pigeon holes. A number of blue-covered contracts took small time for examination. There were the usual number of mine certificates not valuable enough for a safe deposit, some confidential memoranda and accounts having to do with the ranch.

"Ah, here is something!" I breathed to the eager audience over my shoulder. I held in my hands a heavy manila envelope, sealed, inscribed "Ramon. (To be destroyed unopened.)"

"Evidently we were right: Ramon has the combination and is to be executor," I commented.

I tore open the envelope and extracted from it another of the blue-covered documents.

"It's a copy, unsigned, of that last agreement with your father," I said, after a disappointed glance. "It's worth keeping," and I thrust it inside my shirt.

But this particular pigeon hole proved to be a mine. In it were several more of the same sort of envelope, all sealed, all addressed to Ramon. One was labelled as the Last Will, one as Inventory, and one simply as Directions. This last had a further warning that it was to be opened only by the one addressed. I determined by hasty examination that the first two were only what they purported to be, and turned hopefully to a perusal of the last. It was in Spanish, and dealt at great length with the disposition and management of Hooper's extensive interests. I append a translation of the portion of this remarkable document, having to do with our case.

"These are my directions," it began, "as to the matter of which we have many times spoken together. I have many enemies, and many who think they have cause to wish my death. They are cowards and soft and I do not think they will ever be sure enough to do me harm. I do not fear them. But it may be that one or some of them will find it in their souls to do a deed against me. In that case I shall be content, for neither do I fear the devil. But I shall be content only if you follow my orders. I add here a list of my enemies and of those who have cause to wish me ill. If I am killed, it is probable that some one of these will have done the deed. Therefore they must all die. You must see to it, following them if necessary to the ends of the earth. You will know how; and what means to employ. When all these are gone, then go you to the highest rock on the southerly pinnacle of Cochise's Stronghold. Ten paces northwest is a gray, flat slab. If you lift this slab there will be found a copper box. In the box is the name of a man. You will go to this man and give him the copper box and in return he will give to you one hundred thousand dollars. I know well, my Ramon, that your honesty would not permit you to seek the copper box before the last of my enemies is dead. Nevertheless, that you may admire my recourse, I have made an arrangement. If the gray slab on Cochise's Stronghold is ever disturbed before the whole toll is paid, you will die very suddenly and unpleasantly. I know well that you, my Ramon, would not disturb it; and I hope for your sake that nobody else will do so. It is not likely. No one is fool enough to climb Cochise's Stronghold for pleasure; and this gray slab is one among many."

At this time I did not read carefully the above cheerful document. My Spanish was good enough, but took time in the translating. I dipped into it enough to determine that it was what we wanted, and flipped the pages to come to the list of prospective victims. It covered two sheets, and a glance down the columns showed me that about every permanent inhabitant of the Soda Springs Valley was included. I found my own name in quite fresh ink toward the last.

"This is what we want," I said in satisfaction, rising to my feet. I sketched in a few words the purport of the document.

"Let me see it," said the girl.

I handed it to her. She began to examine carefully the list of names, her face turning paler as she read. Tim Westmore looked anxiously over her shoulder. Suddenly I saw his face congest and his eyes bulge.

"Why! why!" he gasped, "I'm there! What've I ever done, I ask you that? The old——" he choked, at a loss and groping. Then his anger flared up. "I've always served him faithful and done what I was told," he muttered, fiercely. "I'll do him in for this!"

"I am here," observed Miss Emory.

"Yes, and that sot in the chair!" whispered Tim, fiercely.

Again Brower proved he was not asleep by opening one eye.

"Thanks for them kind words," said he.

"We've got to get out of here," stated Tim with conviction.

"That idea just got through your thick British skull?" queried Artie, rousing again.

"I wish we had some way to carry the young lady—she can't walk," said Westmore, paying no attention.

"I have my horse tied out by the lone Joshua-tree," I answered him.

"I'm going to take a look at that Cortinez," said the little Englishman, nodding his satisfaction at my news as to the horse. "I'm not easy about him."

"He'll sleep like a log until morning," Miss Emory reassured me. "I've often stepped right over him where he has been on guard and walked all around the garden."

"Just the same I'm going to take a look," persisted Westmore.

He tiptoed to the door, softly turned the knob and opened it. He found himself face to face with Cortinez.

---

CHAPTER XIII

I had not thought of the English groom as a man of resource, but his action in this emergency proved him. He cast a fleeting glance over his shoulder. Artie Brower was huddled down in his armchair practically out of sight; Miss Emory and I had reseated ourselves in the only other two chairs in the room, so that we were in the same relative positions as when we had been bound and left. Only the confusion of the papers on the floor and the open safe would have struck an observant eye.

"It is well that you come," said Tim to Cortinez in Spanish. "The señor sent me to conduct these two to the East Room and I like not the job alone. Enter."

He held the door with one hand and fairly dragged Cortinez through with the other. Instantly he closed the door and cast himself on Cortinez's back. I had already launched myself at the Mexican's throat.

The struggle was violent but brief. Fortunately I had not missed my spring at our enemy's windpipe, so he had been unable to shout. The noise of our scuffle sounded loud enough within the walls of the room; but those walls were two feet thick, and the door and windows closed.

"Get something to gag him with, and the cords," panted Tim to the girl.

Brower opened his eyes again.

"I can beat that," he announced.

He produced his hypodermic and proceeded to mix a gunful of the dope.

"This'll fix him," he observed, turning back the Mexican's sleeve. "You can lay him outside and if anybody comes along they'll think he's asleep—as usual."

This we did when the dope had worked.

It was now high time to think of our next move. For weapons we had the gun and knife taken from Cortinez and the miserable little automatic belonging to Brower. That was all. It was perfectly evident that we could not get out through the regular doorways, as, by Tim's statement, they were all closed and guarded. On my representation it was decided to try the roof.

We therefore knotted together the cord that had bound me and two sheets from the bed, and sneaked cautiously out on the verandah, around the corner to the water barrel, and so to the vantage point of the roof.

The chill of the night was come, and the stars hung cold in the sky. It seemed that the air would snap and crackle were some little resolving element to be dropped into its suspended hush. Not a sound was to be heard except a slow drip of water from somewhere in the courtyard.

It was agreed that I, as the heaviest, should descend first. I landed easily enough and steadied the rope for Miss Emory who came next. While I was waiting I distinctly heard, from the direction of the willows, the hooting of an owl. Furthermore, it was a great horned owl, and he seemed to have a lot to say. You remember what I told you about setting your mind so that only one sort of noise will arouse it, but that one instantly? I knew perfectly well that Old Man Hooper's mind was set to all these smaller harmless noises that most people never notice at all, waking or sleeping—frogs, crickets, owls. And therefore I was convinced that sooner or later that old man and his foolish ideas and his shotgun would come projecting right across our well-planned getaway. Which was just what happened, and almost at once. Probably that great horned owl had been hooting for some time, but we had been too busy to notice. I heard the wicket door turning on its hinges, and ventured a warning hiss to Brower and Tim Westmore, who had not yet descended. An instant later I could make out shadowy forms stealing toward the willows. Evidently those who served Old Man Hooper were accustomed to broken rest.

We kept very quiet, straining our eyes at the willows. After an interval a long stab of light pierced the dusk and the round detonation of old-fashioned black powder shook the silence. There came to us the babbling of voices released. At the same instant the newly risen moon plastered us against that whitewashed wall like insects pinned in a cork-lined case. The moonlight must have been visibly creeping down to us for some few minutes, but so absorbed had I been in the doings of the party in the willows, and so chuckleheaded were the two on the roof, that actually none of us had noticed!

I dropped flat and dragged the girl down with me. But there remained that ridiculous, plainly visible rope; and anyway a shout relieved me of any doubt as to whether we had been seen. Brower came tumbling down on us, and with one accord we three doubled to the right around the walls of the ranch. A revolver shot sang by us, but we were not immediately pursued. Our antagonists were too few and too uncertain of our numbers and arms.

It was up to us to utilize the few minutes before the ranch should be aroused. We doubled back through the willows and across the mesquite flat toward the lone Joshua-tree where I had left my horse. I held the girl's hand to help her when she stumbled, while Brower scuttled along with surprising endurance for a dope wreck. Nobody said anything, but saved their wind.

"Where's Tim?" I asked at a check when we had to scramble across a *barranca*.

"He went back into the ranch the way we came," replied Artie with some bitterness.

It was, nevertheless, the wisest thing he could have done. He had not been identified with this outfit except by Cortinez, and Cortinez was safe for twelve hours.

We found the Joshua-tree without difficulty.

"Now," said I, "here is the plan. You are to take these papers to Señor Buck Johnson, at the Box Springs ranch. That's the next ranch on the fork of the road. Do you remember it?"

"Yes," said Brower, who had waked up and seemed quite sober and responsible. "I can get to it."

"Wake him up. Show him these papers. Make him read them. Tell him that Miss Emory and I are in the Bat-eye Tunnel. Remember that?"

"The Bat-eye Tunnel," repeated Artie.

"Why don't *you* go?" inquired the girl, anxiously.

"I ride too heavy; and I know where the tunnel is," I replied. "If anybody else was to go, it would be you. But Artie rides light and sure, and he'll have to ride like hell. Here, put these papers inside your shirt. Be off!"

Lights were flickering at the ranch as men ran to and fro with lanterns. It would not take these skilled *vaqueros* long to catch their horses and saddle up. At any moment I expected to see the massive doors swing open to let loose the wolf pack.

Brower ran to my horse—a fool proceeding, especially for an experienced horseman—and jerked loose the tie rope. Badger is a good reliable cow horse, but he's not a million years old, and he's got some natural equine suspicions. I kind of lay a good deal of it to that fool hard-boiled hat. At any rate, he snorted and sagged back on the rope, hit a yucca point, whirled and made off. Artie was game. He hung on until he was drug into a bunch of *chollas*, and then he had to let go. Badger departed into the distance, tail up and snorting.

"Well, you've done it now!" I observed to Brower, who, crying with nervous rage and chagrin, and undoubtedly considerably stuck up with *cholla* spines, was crawling to his feet.

"Can't we catch him? Won't he stop?" asked Miss Emory. "If he gets to the ranch, won't they look for you?"

"He's one of my range ponies: he won't stop short of the Gila."

I cast over the chances in my mind, weighing my knowledge of the country against the probabilities of search. The proportion was small. Most of my riding experience had been farther north and to the west. Such obvious hole-ups as the one I had suggested—the Bat-eye Tunnel—were of course familiar to our pursuers. My indecision must have seemed long, for the girl broke in anxiously on my meditations.

"Oughtn't we to be moving?"

"As well here as anywhere," I replied. "We are under good cover; and afoot we could not much better ourselves as against mounted men. We must hide."

"But they may find the trampled ground where your horse has been tied."

"I hope they do."

"You hope they do!"

"Sure. They'll figure that we must sure have moved away. They'll never guess we'd hide near at hand. At least that's what I hope."

"How about tracks?"

"Not at night. By daylight maybe."

"But then to-morrow morning they can——"

"To-morrow morning is a long way off."

"Look!" cried Brower.

The big gates of the ranch had been thrown open. The glare of a light—probably a locomotive headlight—poured out. Mounted figures galloped forth and swerved to right or left, spreading in a circle about the enclosure. The horsemen reined to a trot and began methodically to quarter the ground, weaving back and forth. Four detached themselves and rode off at a swift gallop to the points of the compass. The mounted men were working fast for fear, I suppose, that we may have possessed horses. Another contingent, afoot and with lanterns, followed more slowly, going over the ground for indications. I could not but admire the skill and thoroughness of the plan.

"Our only chance is in the shadow from the moon," I told my companions. "If we can slip through the riders, and get in their rear, we may be able to follow the *barranca* down. Any of those big rocks will do. Lay low, and after a rider has gone over a spot, try to get to that spot without being seen."

We were not to be kept long in suspense. Out of all the three hundred and sixty degrees of the circle one of the swift outriders selected precisely our direction! Straight as an arrow he came for us, at full gallop. I could see the toss of his horse's mane against the light from the opened door. There was no time to move. All we could do was to cower beneath our rock, muscles tense, and hope to be able to glide around the shadow as he passed.

But he did not pass. Down into the shallow *barranca* he slid with a tinkle of shale, and drew rein within ten feet of our lurking place.

We could hear the soft snorting of his mount above the thumping of our hearts. I managed to get into a position to steal a glimpse. It was difficult, but at length I made out the statuesque lines of the horse, and the rider himself, standing in his stirrups and leaning slightly forward, peering intently about him. The figures were in silhouette against the sky, but nobody ever fooled me as to a horse. It was the Morgan stallion, and the rider was Tim Westmore. Just as the realization came to me, Tim uttered a low, impatient whistle.

It's always a good idea to take a chance. I arose into view—but I kept my gun handy.

"Thank God!" cried Tim, fervently, under his breath. "I remembered you'd left your horse by this Joshua: it's the only landmark in the dark. Saints!" he ejaculated in dismay as he saw us all. "Where's your horse?"

"Gone."

"We can't all ride this stallion——"

"Listen," I cut in, and I gave him the same directions I had previously given Brower. He heard me attentively.

"I can beat that," he cut me off. He dismounted. "Get on here, Artie. Ride down the *barranca* two hundred yards and you'll come to an alkali flat. Get out on that flat and ride like hell for Box Springs."

"Why don't you do it?"

"I'm going back and tell 'em how I was slugged and robbed of my horse."

"They'll kill you if they suspect; dare you go back?"

"I've been back once," he pointed out. He was helping Brower aboard.

"Where did you get that bag?" he asked.

"Found it by the rock where we were hiding: it's mine," replied Brower.

Westmore tried to get him to leave it, but the little jockey was obstinate. He kicked his horse and, bending low, rode away.

"You're right: I beg your pardon," I answered Westmore's remark to me. "You don't look slugged."

"That's easy fixed," said Tim, calmly. He removed his hat and hit his forehead a very solid blow against a projection of the conglomerate boulder. The girl screamed slightly.

"Hush!" warned Tim in a fierce whisper. He raised his hand toward the approaching horsemen, who were now very near. Without attention to the blood streaming from his brow he bent his head to listen to the faint clinking of steel against rock that marked the stallion's progress toward the alkali flat. The searchers were by now dangerously close, and Tim uttered a smothered oath of impatience. But at last we distinctly heard the faint, soft thud of galloping hoofs.

The searchers heard it, too, and reined up to listen. Tim thrust into my hand the 30-30 Winchester he was carrying together with a box of cartridges. Then with a leap like a tiger he gained the rim of the *barranca*. Once there, however, his forces seemed to desert him. He staggered forward calling in a weak voice. I could hear the volley of rapid questions shot at him by the men who immediately surrounded him; and his replies. Then somebody fired a revolver thrice in rapid succession and the whole cavalcade swept away with a mighty crackling of brush. Immediately after Tim rejoined us. I had not expected this.

Relieved for the moment we hurried Miss Emory rapidly up the bed of the shallow wash. The tunnel mentioned was part of an old mine operation, undertaken at some remote period before the cattle days. It entered the base of one of those isolated conical hills, lying like islands in the plain, so common in Arizona. From where we had hidden it lay about three miles to the northeast. It was a natural and obvious hide out, and I had no expectation of remaining unmolested. My hope lay in rescue.

We picked our way under cover of the ravine as long as we could, then struck boldly across the plain. Nobody seemed to be following us. A wild hope entered my heart that perhaps they might believe we had all made our escape to Box Springs.

As we proceeded the conviction was borne in on me that the stratagem had at least saved us from immediate capture. Like most men who ride I had very sketchy ideas of what three miles afoot is like—at night—in high heels. The latter affliction was common to both Miss Emory and myself. She had on a sort of bedroom slipper, and I wore the usual cowboy boots. We began to go footsore about the same time, and the little rolling volcanic rocks among the bunches of *sacatone* did not help us a bit. Tim made good time, curse him. Or rather, bless him; for as I just said, if he had not tolled away our mounted pursuit we would have been caught as sure as God made little green apples. He seemed as lively as a cricket, in spite of the dried blood across his face.

The moon was now sailing well above the horizon, throwing the world into silver and black velvet. When we moved in the open we showed up like a train of cars; but, on the other hand, the shadow was a cloak. It was by now nearly one o'clock in the morning.

Miss Emory's nerve did not belie the clear, steadfast look of her eye; but she was about all in when we reached the foot of Bat-eye Butte. Tim and I had discussed the procedure as we walked. I was for lying in wait outside; but Tim pointed out that the tunnel entrance was well down in the boulders, that even the sharpest outlook could not be sure of detecting an approach through the shadows, and that from the shelter of the roof props and against the light we should be able to hold off a large force almost indefinitely. In any case, we would have to gamble on Brewer's winning through, and having sense enough in his opium-saturated mind to make a convincing yarn of it. So after a drink at the *tenaja* below the mine we entered the black square of the tunnel.

The work was old, but it had been well done. They must have dragged the timbers down from the White Mountains. Indeed a number of unused beams, both trunks of trees and squared, still lay around outside. From time to time, since the original operations, some locoed prospector comes projecting along and does a little work in hopes he may find something the other fellow had missed. So the passage was crazy with props and supports, new and old, placed to brace the ageing overhead timbers. Going in they were a confounded nuisance against the bumped head; but looking back toward the square of light they made fine protections behind which to crouch. In this part of the country any tunnel would be dry. It ran straight for about a hundred and fifty feet.

We groped our way about seventy-five feet, which was as far as we could make out the opening distinctly, and sat down to wait. I still had the rest of the tailor-made cigarettes, which I shared with Tim. We did not talk, for we wished to listen for sounds outside. To judge by her breathing, I think Miss Emory dozed, or even went to sleep.

About an hour later I thought to hear a single tinkle of shale. Tim heard it, too, for he nudged me. Our straining ears caught nothing further, however; and I, for one, had relaxed from my tension when the square of light was darkened by a figure. I was nearest, so I raised Cortinez's gun and fired. The girl uttered a scream, and the figure disappeared. I don't know yet whether I hit him or not; we never found any blood.

We made Miss Emory lie down behind a little slide of rock, and disposed ourselves under shelter.

"We can take them as fast as they come," exulted Tim.

"I don't believe there are more than two or three of them," I observed. "It would be only a scouting party. They will go for help."

As there was no longer reason for concealment, we talked aloud and freely.

Now ensued a long waiting interim. We could hear various sounds outside as of moving to and fro. The enemy had likewise no reason for further concealment.

"Look!" suddenly cried Tim. "Something crawling."

He raised the 30-30 and fired. Before the flash and the fumes had blinded me I, too, had seen indistinctly something low and prone gliding around the corner of the entrance. That was all we could make out of it, for as you can imagine the light was almost non-existent. The thing glided steadily, untouched or unmindful of the shots we threw at it. When it came to the first of the crazy uprights supporting the roof timbers it seemed to hesitate gropingly. Then it drew slowly back a foot or so, and darted forward. The ensuing thud enlightened us. The thing was one of the long, squared timbers we had noted outside; and it was being used as a battering ram.

"They'll bring the whole mountain down on us!" cried Tim, springing forward.

But even as he spoke, and before he had moved two feet, that catastrophe seemed at least to have begun. The prop gave way: the light at the entrance was at once blotted out; the air was filled with terrifying roaring echoes. There followed a succession of crashes, the rolling of rocks over each other, the grinding slide of avalanches great and small. We could scarcely breathe for the dust. Our danger was that now the thing was started it would not stop: that the antique and inadequate supports would all give way, one bringing down the other in succession until we were buried. Would the forces of equilibrium establish themselves through the successive slight resistances of these rotted, worm-eaten old timbers before the constricted space in which we crouched should be entirely eaten away?

After the first great crash there ensued a moment's hesitation. Then a second span succumbed. There followed a series of minor chutes with short intervening silences. At last so long an interval of calm ensued that we plucked up courage to believe it all over. A single stone rolled a few feet and hit the rock floor with a bang. Then, immediately after, the first-deafening thunder was repeated as evidently another span gave way. It sounded as though the whole mountain had moved. I was almost afraid to stretch out my hand for fear it would encounter the wall of débris. The roar ceased as abruptly as it had begun. Followed then a long silence. Then a little cascading tinkle of shale. And another dead silence.

"I believe it's over," ventured Miss Emory, after a long time.

"I'm going to find out how bad it is," I asserted.

I moved forward cautiously, my arms extended before me, feeling my way with my feet. Foot after foot I went, encountering nothing but the props. Expecting as I did to meet an obstruction within a few paces at most, I soon lost my sense of distance; after a few moments it seemed to me that I must have gone much farther than the original length of the tunnel. At last I stumbled over a fragment, and so found my fingers against a rough mass of débris.

"Why, this is fine!" I cried to the others, "I don't believe more than a span or so has gone!"

I struck one of my few remaining matches to make sure. While of course I had no very accurate mental image of the original state of things, still it seemed to me there was an awful lot of tunnel left. As the whole significance of our situation came to me, I laughed aloud.

"Well," said I, cheerfully, "they couldn't have done us a better favour! It's a half hour's job to dig us out, and in the meantime we are safe as a covered bridge. We don't even have to keep watch."

"Provided Brower gets through," the girl reminded us.

"He'll get through," assented Tim, positively. "There's nothing on four legs can catch that Morgan stallion."

I opened my watch crystal and felt of the hands. Half-past two.

"Four or five hours before they can get here," I announced.

"We'd better go to sleep, I think," said Miss Emory.

"Good idea," I approved. "Just pick your rocks and go to it."

I sat down and leaned against one of the uprights, expecting fully to wait with what patience I might the march of events. Sleep was the farthest thing from my thoughts. When I came to I found myself doubled on my side with a short piece of ore sticking in my ribs and eighteen or twenty assorted cramp-pains in various parts of me. This was all my consciousness had room to attend to for a few moments. Then I became dully aware of faint tinkling sounds and muffled shoutings from the outer end of the tunnel. I shouted in return and made my way as rapidly as possible toward the late entrance.

A half hour later we crawled cautiously through a precarious opening and stood blinking at the sunlight.

---

CHAPTER XIV

A group of about twenty men greeted our appearance with a wild cowboy yell. Some of the men of our outfit were there, but not all; and I recognized others from as far south as the Chiracahuas. Windy Bill was there with Jed Parker; but Señor Johnson's bulky figure was nowhere to be seen. The other men were all riders—nobody of any particular standing or authority. The sun made it about three o'clock of the afternoon. Our adventures had certainly brought us a good sleep!

After we had satisfied our thirst from a canteen we began to ask and answer questions. Artie Brower had made the ranch without mishap, had told his story, and had promptly fallen asleep. Buck Johnson, in his usual deliberate manner, read all the papers through twice; pondered for some time while the more excited Jed and Windy fidgeted impatiently; and then, his mind made up, acted with his customary decision. Three men he sent to reconnoitre in the direction of the Bat-eye Tunnel with instructions to keep out of trouble and to report promptly. His other riders he dispatched with an insistent summons to all the leading cattlemen as far south as the Chiracahua Range, as far east as Grant's Pass, as far west as Madrona. Such was Buck Johnson's reputation for level-headedness that without hesitation these men saddled and rode at their best speed. By noon the weightiest of the Soda Spring Valley had gathered in conclave.

"That's where we faded out," said Jed Parker. "They sent us up to see about you-all. The scouts from up here come back with their little Wild West story about knocking down this yere mountain on top of you. We had to believe them because they brought back a little proof with them. Mex guns and spurs and such plunder looted off'n the deceased on the field of battle. Bill here can tell you."

"They was only two of them," said Windy Bill, diffident for the first time in his life, "and we managed to catch one of 'em foul. We been digging here for too long. We ain't no prairie dogs to go delving into the bosom of the earth. We thought you must be plumb deceased anyhow: we couldn't get a peep out of you. I was in favour of leavin' you lay myself. This yere butte seemed like a first-rate imposing tomb; and I was willing myself to carve a few choice sentiments on some selected rock. Sure I can carve! But Jed here allowed that you owed him ten dollars and maybe had some money in your pocket——"

"Shut up, Windy," I broke in. "Can't you see the young lady——"

Windy whirled all contrition and apologies.

"Don't you mind me, ma'am," he begged. "They call me Windy Bill, and I reckon that's about right. I don't mean nothing. And we'd have dug all through this butte before——"

"I know that. It isn't your talk," interrupted Miss Emory, "but the sun is hot—and—haven't you anything at all to eat?"

"Suffering giraffes!" cried Windy above the chorus of dismay. "Lunkheads! chumps! Of all the idiot plays ever made in this territory!" He turned to the dismayed group. "Ain't any one of you boys had sense enough to bring any grub?"

But nobody had. The old-fashioned Arizona cowboy ate only twice a day. It would never occur to him to carry a lunch for noon. Still, they might have considered a rescue party's probable needs.

We mounted and started for the Box Springs ranch. They had at least known enough to bring extra horses.

"Old Hooper knows the cat is out of the bag now," I suggested as we rode along.

"He sure does."

"Do you think he'll stick: or will he get out?"

"He'll stick."

"I don't know——" I argued, doubtfully.

"I do," with great positiveness.

"Why are you so sure?"

"There are men in the brush all around his ranch to see that he does."

"For heaven's sake how many have you got together?" I cried, astonished.

"About three hundred," said Jed.

"What's the plan?"

"I don't know. They were chewing over it when I left. But I'll bet something's going to pop. There's a bunch of 'em on that sweet little list you-all dug up."

We rode slowly. It was near five o'clock when we pulled down the lane toward the big corrals. The latter were full of riding horses, and the fences were topped with neatly arranged saddles. Men were everywhere, seated in rows on top rails, gathered in groups, leaning idly against the ranch buildings. There was a feeling of waiting.

We were discovered and acclaimed with a wild yell that brought everybody running. Immediately we were surrounded. Escorted by a clamouring multitude we moved slowly down the lane and into the enclosure.

There awaited us a dozen men headed by Buck Johnson. They emerged from the office as we drew up. At sight of them the cowboys stopped, and we moved forward alone. For here were the substantial men of this part of the territory, the old timers, who had come in the early days and who had persisted through the Indian wars, the border forays, the cattle rustlings, through drought and enmity and bad years. A grim, elderly, four-square, unsmiling little band of granite-faced pioneers, their very appearance carried a conviction of direct and, if necessary, ruthless action. At sight of them my heart leaped. Twenty-four hours previous my case had seemed none too joyful. Now, mainly by my own efforts, after all, I was no longer alone.

They did not waste time in vain congratulations or query. The occasion was too grave for such side issues. Buck Johnson said something very brief to the effect that he was glad to see us safe.

"If this young lady will come in first," he suggested.

But I was emboldened to speak up.

"This young lady has not had a bite to eat since last night," I interposed.

The señor bent on me his grave look.

"Thank you," said he. "Sing!" he roared, and then to the Chinaman who showed up in a nervous hover: "Give this lady grub, savvy? If you'll go with him, ma'am, he'll get you up something. Then we'd like to see you."

"I can perfectly well wait——" she began.

"I'd rather not, ma'am," said Buck with such grave finality that she merely bowed and followed the cook.

---

CHAPTER XV

They had no tender feelings about me, however. Nobody cared whether I ever ate or not. I was led into the little ranch office and catechized to a fare-ye-well. They sat and roosted and squatted about, emitting solemn puffs of smoke and speaking never a word; and the sun went down in shafts of light through the murk, and the old shadows of former days crept from the corners. When I had finished my story it was dusk.

And on the heels of my recital came the sound of hoofs in a hurry; and presently loomed in the doorway the gigantic figure of Tom Thorne, the sheriff. He peered, seeing nothing through the smoke and the twilight; and the old timers sat tight and smoked.

"Buck Johnson here?" asked Thorne in his big voice.

"Here," replied the señor.

"I am told," said Thorne, directly, "that there is here an assembly for unlawful purposes. If so, I call on you in the name of the law to keep the peace."

"Tom," rejoined Buck Johnson, "I want you to make me your deputy."

"For what purpose?"

"There is a dispossession notice to be served hereabouts; a trespasser who must be put off from property that is not his."

"You men are after Hooper, and I know it. Now you can't run your neighbours' quarrels with a gun, not anymore. This is a country of law now."

"Tom," repeated Buck in a reasoning tone, "come in. Strike a light if you want to: and take a look around. There's a lot of your friends here. There's Jim Carson over in the corner, and Donald Macomber, and Marcus Malley, and Dan Watkins."

At this slow telling of the most prominent names in the southwest cattle industry Tom Thorne took a step into the room and lighted a match. The little flame, held high above his head, burned down to his fingers while he stared at the impassive faces surrounding him. Probably he had thought to interfere dutifully in a local affair of considerable seriousness; and there is no doubt that Tom Thorne was never afraid of his duty. But here was Arizona itself gathered for purposes of its own. He hardly noticed when the flame scorched his fingers.

"Tom," said Buck Johnson after a moment, "I heerd tell of a desperate criminal headed for Grant's Pass, and I figure you can just about catch up with him if you start right now and keep on riding. Only you'd better make me your deputy first. It'll sort of leave things in good legal responsible hands, as you can always easy point out if asked."

Tom gulped.

"Raise your right hand," he commanded, curtly, and administered the oath. "Now I leave it in your hands to preserve the peace," he concluded. "I call you all to witness."

"That's all right, Tom," said Buck, still in his crooning tones, taking the big sheriff by the elbow and gently propelling him toward the door, "now as to this yere criminal over toward Grant's Pass, he was a little bit of a runt about six foot three tall; heavy set, weight about a hundred and ten; light complected with black hair and eyes. You can't help but find him. Tom's a good sort," he observed, coming back, "but he's young. He don't realize yet that when things get real serious this sheriff foolishness just nat'rally bogs down. Now I reckon we'd better talk to the girl."

I made a beeline for the cook house while they did that and filled up for three. By the time I had finished, the conference was raised, and men were catching and saddling their mounts. I did not intend to get left out, you may be sure, so I rustled around and borrowed me a saddle and a horse, and was ready to start with the rest.

We jogged up the road in a rough sort of column, the old timers riding ahead in a group of their own. No injunction had been laid as to keeping quiet; nevertheless, conversation was sparse and low voiced. The men mostly rode in silence smoking their cigarettes. About half way the leaders summoned me, and I trotted up to join them.

They wanted to know about the situation of the ranch as I had observed it. I could not encourage them much. My recollection made of the place a thoroughly protected walled fortress, capable of resisting a considerable assault.

"Of course with this gang we could sail right over them," observed Buck, thoughtfully, "but we'd lose a considerable of men doing it."

"Ain't no chance of sneaking somebody inside?" suggested Watkins.

"Got to give Old Man Hooper credit for some sense," replied the señor, shortly.

"We can starve 'em out," suggested somebody.

"Unless I miss the old man a mile he's already got a messenger headed for the troops at Fort Huachuca," interposed Macomber. "He ain't fool enough to take chances on a local sheriff."

"You're tooting he ain't," approved Buck Johnson. "It's got to be quick work."

"Burn him out," said Watkins.

"It's the young lady's property," hesitated my boss. "I kind of hate to destroy it unless we have to."

At this moment the Morgan stallion, which I had not noticed before, was reined back to join our little group. Atop him rode the diminutive form of Artie Brower whom I had thought down and out. He had evidently had his evening's dose of hop and under the excitement of the first effect had joined the party. His derby hat was flattened down to his ears. Somehow it exasperated me.

"For heaven's sake why don't you get you a decent hat!" I muttered, but to myself. He was carrying that precious black bag.

"Blow a hole in his old walls!" he suggested, cheerfully. "That old fort was built against Injins. A man could sneak up in the shadow and set her off. It wouldn't take but a dash of soup to stick a hole you could ride through a-horseback."

"Soup?" echoed Buck.

"Nitroglycerine," explained Watkins, who had once been a miner.

"Oh, sure!" agreed Buck, sarcastically. "And where'd we get it?"

"I always carry a little with me just for emergencies," asserted Brower, calmly, and patted his black bag.

There was a sudden and unanimous edging away.

"For the love of Pete!" I cried. "Was there some of that stuff in there all the time I've been carrying it around?"

"It's packed good: it can't go off," Artie reassured us. "I know my biz."

"What in God's name do you want such stuff for!" cried Judson.

"Oh, just emergencies," answered Brower, vaguely, but I remembered his uncanny skill in opening the combination of the safe. Possibly that contract between Emory and Hooper had come into his hands through professional activities. However, that did not matter.

"I can make a drop of soup go farther than other men a pint," boasted Artie. "I'll show you: and I'll show that old——"

"You'll probably get shot," observed Buck, watching him closely.

"W'at t'hell," observed Artie with an airy gesture.

"It's the dope he takes," I told Johnson aside. "It only lasts about so long. Get him going before it dies on him."

"I see. Trot right along," Buck commanded.

Taking this as permission Brower clapped heels to the stallion and shot away like an arrow.

"Hold on! Stop! Oh, damn!" ejaculated the señor. "He'll gum the whole game!" He spurred forward in pursuit, realized the hopelessness of trying to catch the Morgan, and reined down again to a brisk travelling canter. We surmounted the long, slow rise this side of Hooper's in time to see a man stand out in the brush, evidently for the purpose of challenging the horseman. Artie paid him not the slightest attention, but swept by magnificently, the great stallion leaping high in his restrained vitality. The outpost promptly levelled his rifle. We saw the vivid flash in the half light. Brower reeled in his saddle, half fell, caught himself by the stallion's mane and clung, swinging to and fro. The horse, freed of control, tossed his head, laid back his ears, and ran straight as an arrow for the great doors of the ranch.

We uttered a simultaneous groan of dismay. Then with one accord we struck spurs and charged at full speed, grimly and silently. Against the gathering hush of evening rose only the drum-roll of our horses' hoofs and the dust cloud of their going. Except that Buck Johnson, rising in his stirrups, let off three shots in the air; and at the signal from all points around the beleagured ranch men arose from the brush and mounted concealed horses, and rode out into the open with rifles poised.

The stallion thundered on; and the little jockey managed to cling to the saddle, though how he did it none of us could tell. In the bottomland near the ranch he ran out of the deeper dusk into a band of the strange, luminous after-glow that follows erratically sunset in wide spaces. Then we could see that he was not only holding his seat, but was trying to do something, just what we could not make out. The reins were flying free, so there was no question of regaining control.

A shot flashed at him from the ranch; then a second; after which, as though at command, the firing ceased. Probably the condition of affairs had been recognized.

All this we saw from a distance. The immensity of the Arizona country, especially at dusk when the mountains withdraw behind their veils and mystery flows into the bottomlands, has always a panoramic quality that throws small any human-sized activities. The ranch houses and their attendant trees look like toys; the bands of cattle and the men working them are as though viewed through the reverse lenses of a glass; and the very details of mesquite or *sacatone* flats, of alkali shallow or of oak grove are blended into broad washes of tone. But now the distant, galloping horse with its swaying mannikin charging on the ranch seemed to fill our world. The great forces of portent that hover aloof in the dusk of the desert stooped as with a rush of wings. The peaceful, wide spaces and the veiled hills and the brooding skies were swept clear. Crisis filled our souls: crisis laid her hand on every living moving thing in the world, stopping it in its tracks so that the very infinities for a brief, weird period seemed poised over the running horse and the swaying, fumbling man.

At least that is the way it affected me; and subsequent talk leads me to believe that that it is how it affected every man jack of us. We all had different ways of expressing it. Windy Bill subsequently remarked: "I felt like some old Injun He-God had just told me to crawl in my hole and give them that knew how a chanct."

But I know we all stopped short, frozen in our tracks, and stared, and I don't believe man, *or* horse, drew a deep breath.

Nearer and nearer the stallion drew to the ranch. Now he was within a few yards. In another moment he would crash head on, at tremendous speed, into the closed massive doors. The rider seemed to have regained somewhat of his strength. He was sitting straight in the saddle, was no longer clinging. But apparently he was making no effort to regain control. His head was bent and he was still fumbling at something. The distance was too great for us to make out what, but that much we could see.

On flew the stallion at undiminished speed. He was running blind; and seemingly nothing could save him from a crash. But at almost the last moment the great doors swung back. Those within had indeed realized the situation and were meeting it. At the same instant Brower rose in his stirrups and brought his arm forward in a wide, free swing. A blinding glare flashed across the world. We felt the thud and heave of a tremendous explosion. Dust obliterated everything.

"Charge, you coyotes! Charge!" shrieked Buck Johnson.

And at full speed, shrieking like fiends, we swept across flats.

---

CHAPTER XVI

There was no general resistance. We tumbled pell mell through the breach into the courtyard, encountering only terror-stricken wretches who cowered still dazed by the unexpectedness and force of the explosion. In the excitement order and command were temporarily lost. The men swarmed through the ranch buildings like locusts. Señor Buck Johnson and the other old timers let them go; but I noticed they themselves scattered here and there keeping a restraining eye on activities. There was to be no looting: and that was early made plain.

But before matters had a chance to go very far we were brought up all standing by the sound of shots outside. A rush started in that direction: but immediately Buck Johnson asserted his authority and took command. He did not intend to have his men shot unnecessarily.

By now it was pitch dark. A reconnaissance disclosed a little battle going on down toward the water corrals. Two of our men, straying in that direction, had been fired upon. They had promptly gone down on their bellies and were shooting back.

"I think they've got down behind the water troughs," one of these men told me as I crawled up alongside. "Cain't say how many there is. They shore do spit fire considerable. I'm just cuttin' loose where I see the flash. When I shoot, you prepare to move and move lively. One of those horned toads can sure shoot some; and it ain't healthy to linger none behind your own flash."

The boys, when I crawled back with my report, were eager to pile in and rush the enemy.

"Just put us a hoss-back, señor," pleaded Windy Bill, "and we'll run right over them like a Shanghai rooster over a little green snake. They can't hit nothing moving fast in the dark."

"You'll do just what I say," rejoined Buck Johnson, fiercely. "Cow hands are scarce, and I don't aim to lose one except in the line of business. If any man gets shot to-night, he's out of luck. He'd better get shot good and dead; or he'll wish he had been. That goes! There can't be but a few of those renegades out there, and we'll tend to them in due order. Watkins," he addressed that old timer, "you tend to this. Feel around cautious. Fill up the place full of lead. Work your men around through the brush until you get them surrounded, and then just squat and shoot and wait for morning."

Watkins sent out a dozen of the nearest men to circle the water troughs in order to cut off further retreat, if that were projected. Then he went about methodically selecting others to whom he assigned various stations.

"Now you get a-plenty of catteridges," he told them, "and you lay low and shoot 'em off. And if any of you gets shot I'll sure skin him alive!"

In the meantime, the locomotive lantern had been lit so that the interior of the courtyard was thrown into brilliant light. Needless to say the opening blown in the walls did *not* face toward the water corrals. Of Artie Brower and the Morgan stallion we found hardly a trace. They had been literally blown to pieces. Not one of us who had known him but felt in his heart a kindly sorrow for the strange little man. The sentry who had fired at him and who had thus, indirectly, precipitated the catastrophe, was especially downcast.

"I told him to stop, and he kep' right on a-going, so I shot at him," he explained. "What else was I to do? How was I to know he didn't belong to that gang? He acted like it."

But when you think of it how could it have come out better? Poor, weak, vice-ridden, likeable little beggar, what could the future have held for him? And it is probable that his death saved many lives.

The prisoners were brought in—some forty of them, for Old Man Hooper maintained only the home ranch and all his cow hands as well as his personal bravos were gathered here. Buck Johnson separated apart seven of them, and ordered the others into the stables under guard.

"Bad *hombres*, all of them," he observed to Jed Parker. "We'll just nat'rally ship them across the line very*pronto*. But these seven are worse than bad *hombres*. We'll have to see about them."

But neither Andreas, Ramon, nor Old Man Hooper himself were among those present.

"Maybe they slipped out through our guards; but I doubt it," said Buck. "I believe we've identified that peevish lot by the water troughs."

The firing went on quite briskly for a while; then slackened, and finally died to an occasioned burst, mainly from our own side. Under our leader's direction the men fed their horses and made themselves comfortable. I was summoned to the living quarters to explain on the spot the events that had gone before. Here we examined more carefully and in detail the various documents—the extraordinary directions to Ramon; the list of prospective victims to be offered at the tomb, so to speak, of Old Man Hooper; and the copy of the agreement between Emory and Hooper. The latter, as I had surmised, stated in so many words that it superceded and nullified an old partnership agreement. This started us on a further search which was at last rewarded by the discovery of that original partnership. It contained, again as I had surmised, the not-uncommon clause that in case of the death of one or the other of the partners without direct heirs the common property should revert to the other. I felt very stuck on myself for a good guesser. The only trouble was that the original of the second agreement was lacking: we had only a copy, and of course without signatures. It will be remembered that Brower said he had deposited it with a third party, and that third party was to us unknown. We could not even guess in what city he lived. Of course we could advertise. But Windy Bill who—leaning his long figure against the wall—had been listening in silence—a pretty fair young miracle in itself—had a good idea, which was the real miracle, in my estimation.

"Look here," he broke in, "if I've been following the plot of this yere dime novel correctly, it's plumb easy. Just catch Jud—Jud—you know, the editor of the *Cochise Branding Iron*, and get him to telegraph a piece to the other papers that Artie Brower, celebrated jockey et ceterer, has met a violent death at Hooper's ranch, details as yet unknown. That's the catch-word, as I *savey* it. When this yere third party sees that, he goes and records the paper, and there you are!"

Windy leaned back dramatically and looked exceedingly pleased with himself.

"Yes, that's it," approved Buck, briefly, which disappointed Windy, who was looking for high encomium.

At this moment a messenger came in from the firing party to report that apparently all opposition had ceased. At least there had been for some time no shooting from the direction of the water troughs; a fact concealed from us by the thickness of the ranch walls. Buck Johnson immediately went out to confer with Watkins.

"I kind of think we've got 'em all," was the latter's opinion. "We haven't had a sound out of 'em for a half hour. It may be a trick, of course."

"Sure they haven't slipped by you?" suggested the señor.

"Pretty certain. We've got a close circle."

"Well, I wouldn't take chances in the dark. Just lay low 'till morning."

We returned to the ranch house where, after a little further discussion, I bedded down and immediately fell into a deep sleep. This was more and longer continued excitement than I was used to.

I was afoot with the first stirrings of dawn, you may be sure, and out to join the party that moved with infiniteprecaution on the water troughs as soon as it was light enough to see clearly. We found them riddled with bullets and the water all run out. Gleaming brass cartridges scattered, catching the first rays of the sun, attested the vigour of the defence. Four bodies lay huddled on the ground under the partial shelter of the troughs. I saw Ramon, his face frowning and sinister even in death, his right hand still grasping tenaciously the stock of his Winchester; and Andreas flat on his face; and two others whom I did not recognize. Ramon had been hit at least four times. But of Hooper himself was no hide nor hair! So certain had we been that he had escaped to this spot with his familiars that we were completely taken aback at his absence.

"We got just about as much sense as a bunch of sheepmen!" cried Buck Johnson, exasperated. "He's probably been hiding out somewhere about the place. God knows where he is by now!"

But just as we were about to return to the ranch house we were arrested by a shout from one of the cowboys who had been projecting around the neighbourhood. He came running to us. In his hand he held a blade of *sacatone* on which he pointed out a single dark spot about the size of the head of a pin. Buck seized it and examined it closely.

"Blood, all right," he said at last. "Where did you get this, son?"

The man, a Chiracahua hand named Curley something-or-other, indicated a *sacatone* bottom a hundred yards to the west.

"You got good eyes, son," Buck complimented him. "Think you can make out the trail?"

"Do'no," said Curley. "Used to do a considerable of tracking."

"Horses!" commanded Buck.

We followed Curley afoot while several men went to saddle up. On the edge of the two-foot jump-off we grouped ourselves waiting while Curley, his brows knit tensely, quartered here and there like a setter dog. He was a good trailer, you could see that in a minute. He went at it right. After quite a spell he picked up a rock and came back to show it. I should never have noticed anything—merely another tiny black spot among other spots—but Buck nodded instantly he saw it.

"It's about ten rods west of whar I found the grass," said Curley. "Looks like he's headed for that water in Cockeye Basin. From thar he could easy make Cochise when he got rested."

"Looks likely," agreed Buck. "Can't you find no footprints?"

"Too much tramped up by cowboys and other jackasses," said Curley. "It'll come easier when we get outside this yere battlefield."

He stood erect, sizing up the situation through half-squinted eyes.

"You-all wait here," he decided. "Chances are he kept right on up the broad wash."

He mounted one of the horses that had now arrived and rode at a lope to a point nearly half a mile west. There he dismounted and tied his horse to the ground. After rather a prolonged search he raised his hand over his head and described several small horizontal circles in the air.

"Been in the army, have you?" muttered Buck; "well, I will say you're a handy sort of leather-leg to have around. He gave the soldier signal for 'assemble'," he answered Jed Parker's question.

We rode over to join Curley.

"It's all right; he came this way," said the latter; but he did not trouble to show us indications. I am a pretty fair game trailer myself, but I could make out nothing.

We proceeded slowly, Curley afoot leading his horse. The direction continued to be toward Cockeye. Sometimes we could all see plain footprints; again the trail was, at least as far as I was concerned, a total loss. Three times we found blood, once in quite a splash. Occasionally even Curley was at fault for a few moments; but in general he moved forward at a rapid walk.

"This Curley person is all right," observed Windy Bill after a while, "I was brung up to find my way about, and I can puzzle out most anywhere a critter has gone and left a sign; but this yere Curley can track a humming bird acrost a granite boulder!"

After a little while Curley stopped for us to catch up.

"Seems to me no manner of doubt but what he's headed for Cockeye," he said. "There ain't no other place for him to go out this way. I reckon I can pick up enough of this trail just riding along. If we don't find no sign at Cockeye, we can just naturally back track and pick up where he turned off. We'll save time that-away, and he's had plenty of time to get thar and back again."

So Curley mounted and we rode on at a walk on the horse trail that led up the broad, shallow wash that came out of Cockeye.

Curley led, of course. Then rode Buck Johnson and Watkins and myself. I had horned in on general principles, and nobody kicked. I suppose they thought my general entanglement with this extraordinary series of events entitled me to more than was coming to me as ordinary cow hand. For a long time we proceeded in silence. Then, as we neared the hills, Buck began to lay out his plan.

"When we come up on Cockeye," he was explaining, "I want you to take a half dozen men or so and throw around the other side on the Cochise trail——"

His speech was cut short by the sound of a rifle shot. The country was still flat, unsuited for concealment or defence. We were riding carelessly. A shivering shock ran through my frame and my horse plunged wildly. For an instant I thought I must be hit, then I saw that the bullet had cut off cleanly the horn of my saddle—within two inches of my stomach!

Surprise paralyzed us for the fraction of a second. Then we charged the rock pile from which the shot had come.

We found there Old Man Hooper seated in a pool of his own blood. He had been shot through the body and was dead. His rifle lay across a rock, trained carefully on the trail. How long he had sat there nursing the vindictive spark of his vitality nobody will ever know—certainly for some hours. And the shot delivered had taken from him the last flicker of life.

"By God, he was sure game!" Buck Johnson pronounced his epitaph.

---

## CHAPTER XVII

We cleaned up at the ranch and herded our prisoners together and rode back to Box Springs. The seven men who had been segregated from the rest by Buck Johnson were not among them. I never found out what had become of them nor who had executed whatever decrees had been pronounced against them. There at the home ranch we found Miss Emory very anxious, excited, and interested. Buck and the others in authority left me to inform her of what had taken place.

I told you some time back that this is no love story; but I may as well let you in on the whole sequel to it, and get it off my chest. Windy's scheme brought immediate results. The partnership agreement was recorded, and after the usual legal red-tape Miss Emory came into the property. She had to have a foreman for the ranch, and hanged if she didn't pick on me! Think of that; me an ordinary, forty-dollar cow puncher! I tried to tell her that it was all plumb foolishness, that running a big cattle ranch was a man-sized job and took experience, but she wouldn't listen. Women are like that. She'd seen me blunder in and out of a series of adventures and she thought that settled it, that I was a great man. After arguing with her quite some time about it, I had to give in; so I spit on my hands and sailed in to do my little darndest. I expected the men who realized fully how little I knew about it all would call me a brash damn fool or anyway give me the horse laugh; but I fooled myself. They were mightily decent. Jed Parker or Sam Wooden or Windy Bill were always just happening by and roosting on the corral rails. Then if I listened to them—and I always did—I learned a heap about what I ought to do. Why, even Buck Johnson himself came and stayed at the ranch with me for more than a week at the time of the fall round-up: and he never went near the riding, but just projected around here and there looking over my works and ways. And in the evenings he would smoke and utter grave words of executive wisdom which I treasured and profited by.

If a man gives his whole mind to it, he learns practical things fast. Even a dumb-head Wop gets his English rapidly when he's where he has to talk that or nothing. Inside of three years I had that ranch paying, and paying big. It was due to my friends whom I had been afraid of, and I'm not ashamed to say so. There's Herefords on our range now instead of that lot of heady long-horns Old Man Hooper used to run; and we're growing alfalfa and hay in quantity for fattening when they come in off the ranges. Got considerable hogs, too, and hogs are high—nothing but pure blood Poland. I figure I've added fully fifty per cent., if not more, to the value of the ranch as it came to me. No, I'm not bragging; I'm explaining how came it I married my wife and figured to keep my self-respect. I'd have married her anyhow. We've been together now fifteen years, and I'm here to say that she's a humdinger of a girl, game as a badger, better looking every day, knows cattle and alfalfa and sunsets and sonatas and Poland hogs—but I said this was no love story, and it isn't!

The day following the taking of the ranch and the death of Old Man Hooper we put our prisoners on horses and started along with them toward the Mexican border. Just outside of Soda Springs whom should we meet up with but big Tom Thorne, the sheriff.

"Evenin', Buck," said he.

"Evenin'," replied the señor.

"What you got here?"

"This is a little band of religious devotees fleein' persecution," said Buck.

"And what are you up to with them?" asked Thorne.

"We're protecting them out of Christian charity from the dangers of the road until they reach the Promised Land."

"I see," said Thorne, reflectively. "Whereabouts lays this Promised Land?"

"About sixty mile due south."

"You sure to get them all there safe and sound—I suppose you'd be willing to guarantee that nothing's going to happen to them, Buck?"

"I give my word on that, Tom."

"All right," said Thorne, evidently relieved. He threw his leg over the horn of his saddle. "How about that little dispossession matter, deputy? You ain't reported on that."

"It's all done and finished."

"Have any trouble?"

"Nary trouble," said Señor Buck Johnson, blandly, "all went off quiet and serene."

---

## THE ROAD AGENT

---

### CHAPTER I

The Sierra Nevadas of California are very wide and very high. Kingdoms could be lost among the defiles of their ranges. Kingdoms have been found there. One of them was Bright's Cove.

It happened back in the seventies. Old Man Bright was prospecting. He had come up from the foothills accompanied by a new but stolid Indian wife. After he had grubbed around a while on old Italian bar and had succeeded in washing out a little colour, she woke up and took a slight interest in the proceedings.

"You like catch dat?" she grunted, contemptuously. "Heap much over dere!"

She waved an arm. Old Man Bright girded his loins and packed his jackass. After incredible scramblings the two succeeded in surmounting the ranges and in dropping sheer to the mile-wide round valley through which flowed the river—the broad, swift mountain river, with the snow-white rapids and the swirling translucent green of very thick grass. They were very glad to reach the grass at the bottom, but a little doubtful on how to get out. The big mountains took root at the very edge of the tiny round valley; the river flowed out of a gorge at one end and into a gorge at the other.

"Guess the sun don't rise here 'til next morning," commented Old Man Bright. The squaw was too busy even to grunt.

In six years Old Man Bright was worth six million dollars, all taken from the ledges of Bright's Cove. Of this amount he had been forced to let go of a small proportion for mill machinery and labour. He had also invested twenty-five thousand dollars in a road. It was a steep road, and a picturesque. It wound in and out and around, by loops, lacets, and hairpins, dropping down the face of the mountain in unheard-of grades and turns. Nothing was ever hauled up it, save yellow bars of bullion—so that did not matter. Down it, with a shriek of brakes, a cloud of dust, a clank of harness and a rumble of oaths, came divers matters, such as machinery, glassware, whiskey, mirrors, ammunition, and pianos. From any one of a dozen bold points on this road one could see far down and far up its entire white, thread-like length. The tiny crawling teams each with its puff of dust crawling with it; the great tumbled peaks of the Sierras; the river so far below as to resemble a little stream, the round Cove with its toy houses and its distant ant-like industry—all these were plainly to be seized by a glance of whatever eye cared to look.

As time went on a great many teams and pack trains and saddle animals climbed up and down that road. Bright's Cove became quite a town. Old Man Bright made six millions; other men aggregated nearly four millions more; still others acquired deep holes and a deficit. It might be remarked in passing that the squaw acquired experience, a calico dress or so, and a final honourable discharge. Being an Indian she quite cheerfully went back to pounding acorns in a *metate*.

In the fifth year of prosperity there drifted into camp two men, possessed of innocence, three mules, and a thousand dollars. They retained the mules; and, it is to be presumed, at least a portion of the innocence.

The thousand dollars went to the purchase of the Lost Dog from Barney Fallan. The Lost Dog consisted quite simply of a hole in the ground guarded by an excellent five stamp-mill. The latter's existence could only be explained by the incurable optimism of Barney Fallan—certainly not by the contents of the hole in the ground. To the older men of the camp it seemed a shame, for the newcomers were nice, fresh-cheeked, clear-eyed lads to whom everything was new and strange and wonderful, their enthusiasm was contagious, and their cheerful command of vernacular exceedingly heart-warming. California John, then a man in his forties, tried to head off the deal.

"Look here, son," said he to Gaynes. "Don't do it. There's nothin' in it. Take my word."

"But Fallan's got a good stamp-mill all ready for business, and the ledge——"

"Son," said California John, "every once in a while the Lord gets to experimentin' makin' brains for a new species of jackass, and when he runs out of donkeys to put 'em in——"

"Meaning me?" demanded Gaynes, his fair skin turning a deep red.

"Not at all. Meanin' Barney Fallan."

Nevertheless the Babes, as the Gaynes brothers were speedily nicknamed, paid over their good thousand for Barney's worthless prospect with the imposing but ridiculous stamp-mill. There they set cheerfully to work. After a week's desperate and clanking experiment they got the machinery under way and began to run rock through the crushers.

"It ain't even ore!" expostulated California John. "Why, son, it's only country rock. Go down on your shaft until you strike a pan test, anyway! You're wasting time and fuel and—Oh, hell!" he broke off hopelessly at the sight of the two cherubic faces upturned respectful but unconvinced.

"But you never can tell where you will find gold," broke in Jimmy, eagerly. "That's been proved over and over again. I heard one fellow say once that they thought they'd never find gold in hornblende. But they did."

California John stumped home in indignant disgust.

"Damn little ijits!" he exploded. "Pigheaded! Stubborn as a pair of mules!" The recollection of the scrubbed red cheeks, the clear, puppy-dog, frank brown eyes, the close-curling brown hair, forced his lips to a wry grin. "Just like I was at that age," he admitted. He sighed. "Well, they'll drop their little pile, of course. The only ray of hope's the experience that old Bible fellow had with them turkey buzzards—or was it ravens?"

The Babes pecked away for about a month, full of tribulation and questions. They seemed to depend almost equally on optimism and chance, in both of which they had supreme faith. A huge horseshoe was tacked over the door of the stamp-mill. Jimmy Gaynes always spat over his right shoulder before doing a day's work. They never walked under the short ladders leading to the hoppers. Neither would they permit visitors to their shafts. To California John and his friend Tibbetts they interposed scandalized objections.

"It's bad luck to let another man in your shaft!" cried George. "I'm no high-brow on this mining proposition, but I know enough for that."

"Bad as playing opposite a cross-eyed man," said Jimmy.

"Or holding Jacks full on Eights," supplemented George, conclusively.

"You're about as wise as a treeful of owls," said California John, sarcastically. "But, Lord love you, I ain't cherishin' any very burnin' ambition to crawl down your snake hole."

The Babes used up their provisions; they went about as far as they could on credit; they harrowed the feelings of the community—and then, in a very mild way, they struck it. Together they drifted down the single street of the camp, arm in arm, an elaborate nonchalance steadying their steps. Near the horse trough they paused.

"Gold," said Jimmy, oracularly, to George, "is where you find it."

"Likewise horse sense," quoth George.

Whereupon they whooped wildly and descended on the astonished group. To it they exhibited yellow dust to the value of an hundred dollars. "And more where that came from," said they.

"What kind of rock did you find it in?" demanded Tibbetts, after he had recovered his breath from the youngsters' enthusiastic man-handling.

"Oh, a kind of red, pasty-looking rock," said they.

"Show us," demanded the miners.

"What?" cried Jimmy, astounded, "and give Old Man Luck the backhand slap just when he's decided to buy a corner lot in the Gaynes Addition? Not on your saccharine existence!"

"But we'll show you some more of this to-morrow Q.M.," said George.

They bought drinks all round, and paid their various bills, and departed again feverishly to the Lost Dog whence rose smoke and clankings. And next day, sure enough, they left their work just long enough to exhibit another respectable little clean-up of fifty dollars or so.

"And we're just getting into it!" said George, triumphantly.

California John and all the rest of his good friends rejoiced exceedingly and genuinely. They liked the Babes. The little strike of the Lost Dog quite overshadowed in importance the fact that old man Bright's "Clarice" had run into a fabulously rich pocket.

The end of the month drew near. The Lost Dog had produced nearly eight hundred dollars. The Babes waxed important and talked largely of their moneyed interests.

"I think," said Jimmy, importantly, "that we will decide to keep three hundred dollars to boost the game; and nail down the rest where moths won't corrupt. Where do you fellows salt your surplus, anyway?"

"There's an express goes out pretty soon," someone explained, "with the clean-up of the Clarice. We send our dust out with that; and I reckon you can fix it with Bright."

They saw Bright, but ran up against an unexpected difficulty. Old Man Bright received them with considerable surliness. He considered himself as the originator, discoverer, inventor, and almost the proprietor of Bright's Cove and all it contained. Therefore, when he first heard of the new strike, he walked up to the Lost Dog to see what it looked like. The Babes, panic stricken at the intended affront to "Old Man Luck," headed him off. Bright had not the least belief in the reason given. He surveyed them with disfavour.

"I can't take your package," he told them. "Send it out yourself."

"And that old skunk has cleaned up a hundred thousand this month!" complained Jimmy, pathetically, to the group around the horse trough. "And he won't even take a pore little five hundred package of dust out to some suffering bank! I suppose I'll have to cache it in a tomato can for Johnson's old billy goat to chew up."

"Bring it over and I'll shove it in with mine," suggested California John.

So it was done. The express, carrying nearly four hundred pounds of gold dust, set forth over the steep road. In two hours the driver and messenger sailed in, bung-eyed with excitement. They had been held up by a single road agent.

"He come out right on that point of rocks where you can see the whole valley," said the driver in answer to many questions, "right where the heavy grade is and the thick chaparral. We was busy climbing; and he had us before we could wink. Made us drop off the dust and 'bout face. He was a big, tall feller; and had a sawed-off Winchester. Once, when we stopped, he dropped a bullet right behind us. He must have watched us all the way to camp."

The camp turned out. As the men passed the Lost Dog someone yelled to the Babes. George, covered with mud, came to the door of the mill.

"Gee!" said he. "Lucky we saved out that three hundred. I'm powerful sorry for that suffering bank. I'll join you as soon as I can get Jimmy up out of the shaft." Before the party had gone a mile they were joined by the brothers boyishly eager over this new excitement.

The men toiled up the road to where the robbery had taken place. Plainly to be seen were the marks of the man's boots. The tracks of a single horse, walking, followed the man.

"He packed off the dust, and he had an almighty big horse to carry it," pronounced someone.

They followed the trail. It led a half mile to a broad sheet of rock. There it disappeared. On one side the bank rose twenty or thirty feet. On the other it fell away nearly a hundred. On the other side of the sheet of rock stretched the dusty road unbroken by anything more recent than the wheel-tracks of the day before. It was as though man and horse had taken unto themselves wings.

Immediately Bright took active charge of the posse.

"Stand here, on this rock," he commanded. "This road's been tracked up too much already. You, John, and Tibbetts and Simmins, there, come 'long with me to see what you can make out."

The old mountaineers retraced their steps, examining carefully every inch of the ground. They returned vastly puzzled.

"No sabe," California John summed up their investigations. "There's the man's track leadin' his hoss. The hoss had on new shoes, and the robber did his own shoeing. So we ain't got any blacksmiths to help us."

"How do you know he shod the horse himself?" asked Jimmy Gaynes.

"Shoes just alike on front and back feet. Shows he must just have tacked on ready-made shoes. A blacksmith shapes 'em different. Those tracks leads right up to this rock: and here they quit. If you can figger how a horse, a man, and nigh four hundredweight of gold dust got off this rock, I'll be obleeged."

The men looked up at the perpendicular cliff to their right; over the sheer precipice at their left; and upon the untracked deep, white dust ahead.

"Furthermore," California John went on, impressively, after a moment, "where did that man and that hoss come from in the beginning? Not from up this way. They's no fresh tracks comin' down the road no more than they's fresh tracks goin' up. Not from camp. They's no tracks whatsomever on the road below, except our'n and the stage outfit's."

"Are you sure of that?" asked Jimmy, his eyes shining with interest.

"Sartin sure," replied California John, positively. "We didn't take no chances on that."

"Then he must have come into the road from up the mountain or down the mountain."

"Where?" demanded California John. "A man afoot might scramble down in one or two places; but not a hoss. They ain't no tracks either side the muss-up where the express was stopped. And at that p'int the mountain is straight up and down, like it is here."

They talked it over, and argued it, and reexamined the evidence, but without avail. The stubborn facts remained: Between the hold-up and the sheet of rock was one set of tracks going one way; elsewhere, nothing.

---

CHAPTER II

Nearly a year passed. If it had not been for the very tangible loss of a hundred and fifty thousand dollars, the little community at Bright's Cove might almost have come to doubt the evidence of their senses and the accuracy of their memories, so fantastic on sober reflection did all the circumstances become. Even the indisputable four hundred pounds of gold could not quite avert an unconfessed suspicion of the uncanny. Miners are superstitious folk. Old Man Bright remembered the parting and involved curses of his squaw before she went back to her acorns and pine nuts. To Tibbetts alone he imparted a vague hint of the imaginings into which he had fallen. But he brooded much, seeking a plausible theory that would not force him back on the powers of darkness. This he did not find.

Nor did any other man. It remained a mystery, a single bizarre anomaly in the life of the camp. For some time thereafter the express went heavily guarded. The road was patrolled. Jimmy or George Gaynes in person accompanied each shipment of dust. Their pay streak held out, increased steadily in value. They would hire no assistance for the actual mining in the shaft, although they had several hands to work at the mill. One month they cleaned up twelve thousand dollars.

"You bet I'm going," said Jimmy, "I don't care if it is only a little compared to what Bright and you fellows are sending. It's a heap sight to us, and I'm going to see it safe to the city. No more spooks in mine. I got my fingers crossed. Allah skazallalum! I don't know what a ghost would want with cash assets, but they seemed to use George's and my little old five hundred, all right."

Twelve months went by. Two expresses a month toiled up the road. Nothing happened. Finally Jimmy decided that four good working days a month were a good deal to pay for apparently useless supervision. Three men comprised the shot-gun guard. They, with the driver, were considered ample.

"You'll have to get on without me," said Jimmy to them in farewell. "Be good boys. We've got the biggest clean-up yet aboard you."

They started on the twenty-fifth trip since the hold-up. After a time, far up the mountain was heard a single shot. Inside of two hours the express drew sorrowfully into camp. The driver appeared to be alone. In the bottom of the wagon were the three guards weak and sick. The gold sacks were very much absent.

"Done it again," said the driver. "Ain't more than got started afore the whole outfit's down with the belly-ache. Too much of that cursed salmon. Told 'em so. I didn't eat none. That road agent hit her lucky this trip sure. He was all organized for business. Never showed himself at all. Just opened fire. Sent a bullet through the top of my hat. He's either a damn good shot or a damn poor one. I hung up both hands and yelled we was down and out. What could I do? This outfit couldn't a fit a bumble bee. And I couldn't git away, or git hold of no gun, or see anything to shoot, if I did. He was behind that big rock."

The men nodded. They were many of them hard hit, but they had lived too long in the West not to recognize the justice of the driver's implied contention that he had done his best.

"He told me to throw out them sacks, and to be damn quick about it," went on the driver. "Then I drove home."

"What sort of a lookin' fellow was he?" asked someone. "Same one as last year?"

"I never seen him," said the driver. "He hung behind his rock. He was organized for shoot, and if the messengers hadn't happened to' a' been out of it, I believe he could have killed us all."

"What did his hoss look like?" inquired California John.

"He didn't have no horse," stated the driver. "Leastways, not near him. There was no cover. He might have been around a p'int. And I can sw'ar to this: there weren't no tracks of no kind from there to camp."

They caught up horses and started out. When they came to the Lost Dog, they stopped and looked at each other.

"Poor old Babes," said Simmins. "Biggest clean-up yet; and first time one of 'em didn't go 'long."

"I'm glad they didn't," said Tibbetts. "That agent would have killed 'em shore!"

They called out the Gaynes brothers and broke the news. For once the jovial youngsters had no joke to make.

"This is getting serious," said Jimmy, seriously. "We can't afford to lose that much."

George whistled dolefully, and went into the corral for the mules.

The party toiled up the mountain. Plainly in the dust could be made out the trail of the express ascending and descending. Plain also were the signs where the driver had dumped out the gold bags and turned around. From that point the tracks of a man and a horse led to the sheet of rock. Beyond that, nothing.

The men stared at each other a little frightened. Somebody swore softly.

"Boys," said Bright in a strained voice, "do you know how much was in that express? A half million! There's nary earthly hoss can carry over half a ton! And this one treads as light as a saddler."

They looked at each other blankly. Several even glanced in apprehension at the sky.

In a perfunctory manner, for the sake of doing something, those skilled in trail-reading went back over the ground. Nothing was added to the first experience. At the point of robbery magically had appeared a man and—if the stage driver's solemn assertion that at the time of the hold-up no animal was in sight could be believed—subsequently, when needed, a large horse. Whence had they come? Not along the road in either direction: the unbroken, deep dust assured that. Not down the mountain from above, for the cliff rose sheer for at least three hundred feet. Jimmy Gaynes, following unconsciously the general train of conjecture, craned his neck over the edge of the road. The broken jagged rock and shale dropped off an hundred feet to a tangle of manzanita and snowbrush.

California John looked over, too.

"Couldn't even get sheep up that," said he, "let alone a sixteen-hand horse."

Old Man Bright was sunk in a superstitious torpor. He had lost hundreds of thousands where he would have hated to spend pennies; yet the financial part of the loss hardly touched him. He mumbled fearfully to himself, and took not the slightest interest in the half-hearted attempts to read the mystery. When the others moved, he moved with them, because he was afraid to be left alone.

After the men had assured themselves again and again that the horse and the man had apparently materialized from thin air exactly at the point of robbery, they again followed the tracks to the broad sheet of rock. Whither had the robber gone? Back into the thin air whence he had come. There was no other solution. No tracks ahead; an absolute and physical impossibility of anything without wings getting up or down the flanking precipices—these were the incontestable facts.

After this second robbery a gloom descended on Bright's Cove which lasted through many months. Old Man Bright hunted out the squaw with whom he had first discovered the diggings, and set her up in an establishment with gay curtains, glass danglers and red doileys. Each month he paid for her provisions and sent to her a sum of money. In this manner, at least, the phantom road agent had furthered the ends of justice. The sop to the powers of darkness appeared to be effective in this respect: no more hold-ups occurred; no more mysterious tracks appeared in the dust; gradually men's minds swung back to the balanced and normal, and the life of the camp went forward on its appointed way.

Nevertheless, certain effects remained. Each express went out heavily guarded, and preceded and followed by men on horseback. Strangely enough the gamblers left camp. In a little more than a year Old Man Bright fell into a settled melancholia from which his millions never helped him to the very day of his death a little more than a year later.

In the meantime, however varied the fortunes of the other mines and prospects, the Lost Dog continued to work toward a steadily increasing paying basis. It never reached the proportions of the Clarice, but turned out an increasing value of dust at each clean-up. The Gaynes boys two years before had been in debt for their groceries. Now they were said to have shipped out something like three or four hundred thousand dollars' worth of gold. Their friends used to wander down for the regular clean-up, just to rejoice over the youngsters' deserved good luck. The little five stamp-mill crunched away steadily; the water flowed; and in the riffles the heavy gold dust accumulated.

"Why don't you-all put up a big mill, throw in a crew of men, and get busy?" they were asked.

"I'll tell you," replied George, "it's because we know a heap sight more about mining than we did when we came here. We have just one claim, and from all indications it's only a pocket. The Clarice is on a genuine lode; but we're likely to run into a 'horse' or pinch out most any minute. When we do, it's all over but a few faint cries of fraud. And we can empty that pocket just as well with a little jerkwater outfit like this as we could with a big crew and a real mill. It'll take a little longer; but we're pulling it and quick enough."

"Those Babes have more sense than we gave 'em credit for," commented California John. "Their heads are level. They're dead right about it's bein' a pocket. The stuff they run through there is the darndest mixture *I* ever see gold in."

Two months after this conversation the Babes drifted into camp to announce that the expected pinch had come.

"We're going," said Jimmy. "We have a heap plenty dust salted away; and there's not a colour left in the Lost Dog. The mill machinery is for sale cheap. Any one can have the Lost Dog who wants it. We're going out to see what makes the wheels go 'round. You boys have a first claim on us wherever you find us. You've sure been good to us. If you catch that spook, send us one of his tail feathers. It would be worth just twelve thousand five hundred to us."

They sold the stamp-mill for almost nothing; packed eight animals with heavy things they had accumulated; and departed up the steep white road, over the rim to the outer world whence came no word of them more. The camp went on prospering. Old Man Bright died. The heavily guarded express continued to drag out yellow gold by the hundredweight.

About six weeks after the departure of the Babes, California John saddled up his best horse, put on his best overalls, strapped about him his shiny worn Colt's .45 and departed for his semi-annual visit to the valleys and the towns. A week later he returned. It was about dusk. At the water trough he dismounted.

"Boys," said he, quietly, "I've been held up." He eyed them quizzically. "Up by the slide rock," he continued, "and by the spook."

"Who was he?" "What was it?" they cried, starting to their feet.

"It was Jimmy Gaynes," replied California John.

"The Babe?" someone broke the stunned silence at last.

"Precisely."

"Well, I'll be damned!" cried Tibbetts.

"Did he get much off you?" asked a miner after another pause.

"He never took a thing."

And on that, being much besieged, California John sat him down and told of his experience.

---

## CHAPTER III

California John was discursive and interested and disinclined to be hurried. He crossed one leg over the other and lit his pipe.

"I was driftin' down the road busy with my own idees—which ain't many," he began, "when I was woke up all to once by someone givin' me advice. I took the advice. Wasn't nothin' else to do. All I could see was a rock and a gun barrel. That was enough. So I histed my hands as per commands and waited for the next move." He chuckled. "I wasn't worryin'. Had to squeeze my dust bag to pay my hotel bill when I left the city."

"'Drop yore gun in the road,' says the agent.

"I done so.

"'Now dismount.'

"I climbed down. And then Jimmy Gaynes rose up from behind that rock and laughed at me.

"'The joke's on me!' said I, and reached down for my gun.

"'Better leave that!' said Jimmy pretty sharp. I know that tone of voice, so I straightened up again.

"'Well, Jimmy,' said I, 'she lays if you say so. But where'd you come from: and what for do you turn road agent and hold up your old friends?'

"'I'm holdin' you up,' Jimmy answered, 'because I want to talk to you for ten minutes. As for where I come from, that's neither here nor there.'

"'Of course,' said I, 'I'm one of these exclusive guys that needs a gun throwed on him before he'll talk with the plain people like you.'

"'Now don't get mad,' says Jimmy. 'But light yore pipe, and set down on that rock, and you'll see in a minute why I *pre*ferred to corner the gatling market.'

"Well, I set down and lit up, and Jimmy done likewise, about ten feet away.

"'I've come back a long ways to talk to one of you boys, and I've shore hung around this road some few hours waitin' for some of you terrapins to come along. Ever found out who done those two hold-ups?'

"'Nope,' said I, 'and don't expect to.'

"'Well, I done it,' says he.

"I looked him in the eye mighty severe.

"'You're one of the funniest little jokers ever hit this trail,' I told him. 'If that's your general line of talkee-talkee I don't wonder you don't want me to have no gun.'

"'Never*the*less,' he insists, 'I done it. And I'll tell you just how it was done. Here's yore old express crawlin' up the road. Here I am behind this little old rock. You know what happened next I reckon—from experience.'

"'I reckon I know that,' says I, 'but how did you get behind that rock without leavin' no tracks?'

157

"I climbed up the cliff out of the cañon, and I just walked up the cañon from the Lost Dog through the brush.'

"'Yes,' says I, 'that might be: a man could make out to shinny up. But how——'

"'One thing to a time. Then I ordered them dust sacks throwed out, and the driver to 'bout-face and retreat.'

"'Sure,' says I, 'simple as a wart on a kid's nose. There was you with a half ton of gold to fly off with! Come again.'

"'I then dropped them sacks off the edge of the cliff where they rolled into the brush. After a while I climbed down after them, and was on hand when your posse started out. Then I carried them home at leisure.'

"'What did you do with your hoss?' I asked him, mighty sarcastic. 'Seems to me you overlook a few bets.'

"'I didn't have no hoss,' says he.

"'But the real hold-up——

"'You mean them tracks. Well, just to amuse you fellows, I walked in the dust up to that flat rock. Then I clamped a big pair of horseshoes on hind-side before and walked back again.'"

California John's audience had been listening intently. Now it could no longer contain itself, but broke forth into exclamations indicative of various emotions.

"That's why them front and back tracks was the same size!" someone cried.

"Gee, you're bright!" said California John. "That's what I told him. I also told him he was a wonder, but how did he manage to slip out near a ton of dust up that road without our knowing it?

"'You did know it,' says he. 'Did you fellows really think there was any gold-bearing ore in the Lost Dog? We just run that dust through the mill along with a lot of worthless rock, and shipped it out open and above board as our own mill run. There never was an ounce of dust come out of the Lost Dog, and there never will.' Then he give me back my gun—emptied—we shook hands, and here I be."

After the next burst of astonishment had ebbed, and had been succeeded by a rather general feeling of admiration, somebody asked California John if Jimmy had come back solely for the purpose of clearing up the mystery. California John had evidently been waiting for this question. He arose and knocked the ashes from his pipe.

"Bring a candle," he requested the storekeeper, and led the way to the abandoned Lost Dog. Into the tunnel he led them, to the very end. There he paused, holding aloft his light. At his feet was a canvas which, being removed, was found to cover neatly a number of heavy sacks.

"Here's our dust," said California John, "every ounce of it, he said. He kept about six hundred thousand or so that belonged to Bright: but he didn't take none of ours. He come back to tell me so."

The men crowded around for closer inspection.

"I wonder why he done that?" Tibbetts marvelled.

"I asked him that," replied California John, grimly, "He said his conscience never would rest easy if he robbed us babes."

Tibbetts broke the ensuing silence.

"Was 'babes' the word he used?" he asked, softly.

"'Babes' was the word," said California John.

----

## THE TIDE

A short story, say the writers of text books and the teachers of sophomores, should deal with but a single episode. That dictum is probably true; but it admits of wider interpretation than is generally given it. The teller of tales, anxious to escape from restriction but not avid of being cast into the outer darkness of the taboo, can in self-justification become as technical as any lawyer. The phrase "a single episode" is loosely worded. The rule does not specify an episode in one man's life; it might be in the life of a family, or a state, or even of a whole people. In that case the action might cover many lives. It is a way out for those who have a story to tell, a limit to tell it within, but who do not wish to embroil themselves too seriously with the august Makers of the Rules.

----

### CHAPTER I

The time was 1850, the place that long, soft, hot dry stretch of blasted desolation known as the Humboldt Sink. The sun stared, the heat rose in waves, the mirage shimmered, the dust devils of choking alkali whirled aloft or sank in suffocation on the hot earth. Thus it had been since in remote ages the last drop of the inland sea had risen into a brazen sky. But this year had brought something new. A track now led across the desert. It had sunk deep into the alkali, and the soft edges had closed over it like snow, so that the wheel marks and the hoof marks and the prints of men's feet looked old. Almost in a straight line it led to the west. Its perspective, dwindling to nothingness, corrected the deceit of the clear air. Without it the cool, tall mountains looked very near. But when the eye followed the trail to its vanishing, then, as though by magic, the Ranges drew back, and before them denied dreadful forces of toil, thirst, exhaustion, and despair. For the trail was marked. If the wheel ruts had been obliterated, it could still have been easily followed. Abandoned goods, furniture, stores, broken-down wagons, bloated carcasses of oxen or horses, bones bleached white, rattling mummies of dried skin, and an almost unbroken line of marked and unmarked graves—like the rout of an army, like the spent wash of a wave that had rolled westward—these in double rank defined the road.

The buzzards sailing aloft looked down on the Humboldt Sink as we would look upon a relief map. Near the centre of the map a tiny cloud of white dust crawled slowly forward. The buzzards stooped to poise above it.

Two ox wagons plodded along. A squirrel—were such a creature possible—would have stirred disproportionately the light alkali dust; the two heavy wagons and the shuffling feet of the beasts raised a cloud. The fitful furnace draught carried this along at the slow pace of the caravan, which could be seen only dimly, as through a dense fog.

The oxen were in distress. Evidently weakened by starvation, they were proceeding only with the greatestdifficulty. Their tongues were out, their legs spread, spasmodically their eyes rolled back to show the whites, from time to time one or another of them uttered a strangled, moaning bellow. They were white with the powdery dust, as were their yokes, the wagons, and the men who plodded doggedly alongside. Finally, they stopped. The dust eddied by; and the blasting sun fell upon them.

The driver of the leading team motioned to the other. They huddled in the scanty shade alongside the first wagon. Both men were so powdered and caked with alkali that their features were indistinguishable. Their red-rimmed, inflamed eyes looked out as though from masks.

The one who had been bringing up the rear looked despairingly toward the mountains.

"We'll never get there!" he cried.

"Not the way we are now," replied the other. "But I intend to get there."

"How?"

"Leave your wagon, Jim; it's the heaviest. Put your team on here."

"But my wagon is all I've got in the world!" cried the other, "and we've got near a keg of water yet! We can make it! The oxen are pulling all right!"

His companion turned away with a shrug, then thought better of it and turned back.

"We've thrown out all we owned except bare necessities," he explained, patiently. "Your wagon is too heavy. The time to change is while the beasts can still pull."

"But I refuse!" cried the other. "I won't do it. Go ahead with your wagon. I'll get mine in, John Gates, you can't bulldoze me."

Gates stared him in the eye.

"Get the pail," he requested, mildly.

He drew water from one of the kegs slung underneath the wagon's body. The oxen, smelling it, strained weakly, bellowing. Gates slowly and carefully swabbed out their mouths, permitted them each a few swallows, rubbed them pityingly between the horns. Then he proceeded to unyoke the four beasts from the other man's wagon and yoked them to his own. Jim started to say something. Gates faced him. Nothing was said.

"Get your kit," Gates commanded, briefly, after a few moments. He parted the hanging canvas and looked into the wagon. Built to transport much freight it was nearly empty. A young woman lay on a bed spread along the wagon bottom. She seemed very weak.

"All right, honey?" asked Gates, gently.

She stirred, and achieved a faint smile.

"It's terribly hot. The sun strikes through," she replied. "Can't we let some air in?"

"The dust would smother you."

"Are we nearly there?"

"Getting on farther every minute," he replied, cheerfully.

Again the smothering alkali rose and the dust cloud crawled.

Four hours later the traveller called Jim collapsed face downward. The oxen stopped. Gates lifted the man by the shoulders. So exhausted was he that he had not the strength nor energy to spit forth the alkali with which his fall had caked his open mouth. Gates had recourse to the water keg. After a little he hoisted his companion to the front seat.

At intervals thereafter the lone human figure spoke the single word that brought his team to an instantaneous dead stop. His first care was then the woman, next the man clinging to the front seat, then the oxen. Before starting he clambered to the top of the wagon and cast a long, calculating look across the desolation ahead. Twice he even further reduced the meagre contents of the wagon, appraising each article long and doubtfully before discarding it. About mid-afternoon he said abruptly:

"Jim, you've got to walk."

The man demurred weakly, with a touch of panic.

"Every ounce counts. It's going to be a close shave. You can hang on to the tail of the wagon."

Yet an hour later Jim, for the fourth time, fell face downward, but now did not rise. Gates, going to him, laid his hand on his head, pushed back one of his eyelids, then knelt for a full half minute, staring straight ahead. Once he made a tentative motion toward the nearly empty water keg, once he started to raise the man's shoulders. The movements were inhibited. A brief agony cracked the mask of alkali on his countenance. Then stolidly, wearily, he arose. The wagon lurched forward. After it had gone a hundred yards and was well under way in its painful forward crawl, Gates, his red-rimmed, bloodshot eyes fixed and glazed, drew the revolver from its holster and went back.

At sundown he began to use the gad. The oxen were trying to lie down. If one of them succeeded, it would never again arise. Gates knew this. He plied the long, heavy whip in both hands. Where the lash fell it bit out strips of hide. It was characteristic of the man that though heretofore he had not in all this day inflicted a single blow on the suffering animals, though his nostrils widened and his terrible red eyes looked for pity toward the skies, yet now he swung mercilessly with all his strength.

Dusk fell, but the hot earth still radiated, the powder dust rose and choked. The desert dragged at their feet; and in the twilight John Gates thought to hear mutterings and the soft sound of wings overhead as the dread spirits of the wastes stooped low. He had not stopped for nearly two hours. This was the last push; he must go straight through or fail.

And when the gleam of the river answered the gleam of the starlight he had again to rouse his drained energies. By the brake, by directing the wagon into an obstruction, by voice and whip he fought the frantic beasts back to a moaning standstill. Then pail by pail he fed them the water until the danger of overdrinking was past. He parted the curtains. In spite of the noise outside the woman, soothed by the breath of cooler air, had fallen asleep.

Some time later he again parted the curtains.

"We're here, honey," he said, "good water, good grass, shade. The desert is past. Wake up and take a little coffee."

She smiled at him.

"I'm so tired."

"We're going to rest here a spell."

She drank the coffee, ate some of the food he brought her, thrust back her hair, breathed deep of the cooling night.

"Where's Jim?" she asked at last.

"Jim got very tired," he said, "Jim's asleep."

---

Three months later. The western slant of the Sierras just where the cañon clefts begin to spread into foothills. On a flat near—too near—the stream-bed was a typical placer-mining camp of the day. That is, three or four large, rough buildings in a row, twenty or thirty log cabins scattered without order, and as many tents.

The whole population was gathered interestedly in the largest structure, which was primarily a dance hall. Ninety-five per cent. were men, of whom the majority were young men. A year ago the percentage would have been nearer one hundred, but now a certain small coterie of women had drifted in, most of them with a keen eye for prosperity. The red or blue shirt, the nondescript hat, and the high, mud-caked boots of the miner preponderated. Here and there in the crowd, however, stood a man dressed in the height of fashion. There seemed no middle ground. These latter were either the professional gamblers, the lawyers, or the promoters.

A trial was in progress, to which all paid deep attention. Two men disputed the ownership of a certain claim. Their causes were represented by ornate individuals whose evident zest in the legal battle was not measured by prospective fees. Nowhere in the domain and at no time in the history of the law has technicality been so valued, has the game of the courts possessed such intellectual interest, has substantial justice been so uncertain as in the California of the early 'fifties. The lawyer could spread himself unhampered; and these were so doing.

In the height of the proceedings a man entered from outside and took his position leaning against the rail of the jury box. That he was a stranger was evident from the glances of curiosity, cast in his direction. He was tall, strong, young, bearded, with a roving, humorous bold eye.

The last word was spoken. A rather bewildered-looking jury filed out. Ensued a wait. The jury came back. It could not agree; it wanted information. Both lawyers supplied it in abundance. The foreman, who happened to be next the rail against which the newcomer was leaning, cast on him a quizzical eye.

"Stranger," said he, "mout you be able to make head er tail of all that air?"

The other shook his head.

"I'm plumb distracted to know what to do; and dear knows we all want to git shet of this job. Thar's a badger fight——"

"Where is this claim, anyway?"

"Right adown the road. Location notice is on the first white oak you come to. Cain't miss her."

"If I were you," said the stranger after a pause, "I'd just declare the claim vacant. Then neither side would win."

At this moment the jury rose to retire again. The stranger unobtrusively gained the attention of the clerk and from him begged a sheet of paper. On this he wrote rapidly, then folded it, and moved to the outer door, against the jamb of which he took his position. After another and shorter wait, the jury returned.

"Have you agreed on your verdict, gentlemen?" inquired the judge.

"We have," replied the lank foreman. "We award that the claim belongs to neither and be declared vacant."

At the words the stranger in the doorway disappeared. Two minutes later the advance guard of the rush that had comprehended the true meaning of the verdict found the white oak tree in possession of a competent individual with a Colt's revolving pistol and a humorous eye.

"My location notice, gentlemen," he said, calling attention to a paper freshly attached by wooden pegs.

"Honey-bug claim'," they read, "'John Gates'," and the usual phraseology.

"But this is a swindle, an outrage!" cried one of the erstwhile owners.

"If so it was perpetrated by your own courts," said Gates, crisply. "I am within my rights, and I propose to defend them."

Thus John Gates and his wife, now strong and hearty, became members of this community. His intention had been to proceed to Sacramento. An incident stopped him here.

The Honey-bug claim might or might not be a good placer mine—time would show—but it was certainly a wonderful location. Below the sloping bench on which it stood the country fell away into the brown heat haze of the lowlands, a curtain that could lift before a north wind to reveal a landscape magnificent as a kingdom.Spreading white oaks gave shade, a spring sang from the side hill on which grew lofty pines, and back to the east rose the dark or glittering Sierras. The meadow at the back was gay with mariposa lilies, melodious with bees and birds, aromatic with the mingled essences of tarweed, lads-love, and the pines. At this happy elevation the sun lay warm and caressing, but the air tasted cool.

"I could love this," said the woman.

"You'll have a chance," said John Gates, "for when we've made our pile, we'll always keep this to come back to."

At first they lived in the wagon, which they drew up under one of the trees, while the oxen recuperated and grew fat on the abundant grasses. Then in spare moments John Gates began the construction of a house. He was a man of tremendous energy, but also of many activities. The days were not long enough for him. In him was the true ferment of constructive civilization. Instinctively he reached out to modify his surroundings. A house, then a picket fence, split from the living trees; an irrigation ditch; a garden spot; fruit trees; vines over the porch; better stables; more fences; the gradual shaping from the wilderness of a home—these absorbed his surplus. As a matter of business he worked with pick and shovel until he had proved the Honey-bug hopeless, then he started a store on credit. Therein he sold everything from hats to 42 calibre whiskey. To it he brought the same overflowing play-spirit that had fashioned his home.

"I'm making a very good living," he answered a question; "that is, if I'm not particular on how well I live," and he laughed his huge laugh.

He was very popular. Shortly they elected him sheriff. He gained this high office fundamentally, of course, by reason of his courage and decision of character; but the immediate and visible causes were the Episode of the Frazzled Mule, and the Episode of the Frying Pan. The one inspired respect; the other amusement.

The freight company used many pack and draught animals. One day one of its mules died. The *mozo* in charge of the corrals dragged the carcass to the superintendent's office. That individual cursed twice; once at the mule for dying, and once at the *mozo* for being a fool. At nightfall another mule died. This time the *mozo*, mindful of his berating, did not deliver the body, but conducted the superintendent to see the sad remains.

"Bury it," ordered the superintendent, disgustedly. Two mules at $350—quite a loss.

But next morning another had died; fairly an epidemic among mules. This carcass also was ordered buried. And at noon a fourth. The superintendent, on his way to view the defunct, ran across John Gates.

"Look here, John," queried he, "do you know anything about mules?"

"Considerable," admitted Gates.

"Well, come see if you can tell me what's killing ours off."

They contemplated the latest victim of the epidemic.

"Seems to be something that swells them up," ventured the superintendent after a while.

John Gates said nothing for some time. Then suddenly he snatched his pistol and levelled it at the shrinking*mozo*.

"Produce those three mules!" he roared, "*mucho pronto*, too!" To the bewildered superintendent he explained. "Don't you see? this is the same old original mule. He ain't never been buried at all. They've been stealing your animals pretending they died, and using this one over and over as proof!"

This proved to be the case; but John Gates was clever enough never to tell how he surmised the truth.

"That mule looked to me pretty frazzled," was all he would say.

The frying-pan episode was the sequence of a quarrel. Gates was bringing home a new frying pan. At the proper point in the discussion he used his great strength to smash the implement over his opponent's head so vigorously that it came down around his neck like a jagged collar! Gates clung to the handle, however, and by it led his man all around camp, to the huge delight of the populace.

As sheriff he was effective, but at times peculiar in his administration. No man could have been more zealous in performing his duty; yet he never would mix in the affairs of foreigners. Invariably in such cases he made out the warrants in blank, swore in the complaining parties themselves as deputies, and told them blandly to do their own arresting! Nor at times did he fail to temper his duty with a little substantial justice of his own. Thus he was once called upon to execute a judgment for $30 against a poor family. Gates went down to the premises, looked over the situation, talked to the man—a poverty-stricken, discouraged, ague-shaken creature—and marched back to the offices of the plaintiffs in the case.

"Here," said he, calmly, laying a paper and a small bag of gold dust on their table, "is $30 and a receipt in full."

The complainant reached for the sack. Gates placed his hand over it.

"Sign the receipt," he commanded. "Now," he went on after the ink had been sanded, "there's your $30. It's yours legally; and you can take it if you want to. But I want to warn you that a thousand-dollar licking goes with it!"

The money—from Gates's own pocket—eventually found its way to the poor family!

They had three children, two boys and a girl of which one boy died.

In five years the placers began to play out. One by one the more energetic of the miners dropped away. The nature of the community changed. Small hill ranches or fruit farms took the place of the mines. The camp became a country village. Old time excitement calmed, the pace of life slowed, the horizon narrowed.

John Gates, clear-eyed, energetic, keen brained, saw this tendency before it became a fact.

"This camp is busted," he told himself.

161

It was the hour to fulfill the purpose of the long, terrible journey across the plains, to carry out the original intention to descend from the Sierras to the golden valleys, to follow the struggle.

"Reckon it's time to be moving," he told his wife.

But now his own great labours asserted their claim. He had put four years of his life into making this farm out of nothing, four years of incredible toil, energy, and young enthusiasm. He had a good dwelling and spacious corrals, an orchard started, a truck garden, a barley field, a pasture, cattle, sheep, chickens, his horses—all his creation from nothing. One evening at sundown he found his wife in the garden weeping softly.

"What is it, honey?" he asked.

"I was just thinking how we'd miss the garden," she replied.

He looked about at the bright, cheerful flowers, the vine-hung picket fence, the cool verandah, the shady fig tree already of some size. Everything was neat and trim, just as he liked it. And the tinkle of pleasant waters, the song of a meadow lark, the distant mellow lowing of cows came to his ears; the smell of tarweed and of pines mingled in his nostrils.

"It's a good place for children," he said, vaguely.

Neither knew it, but that little speech marked the ebb of the wave that had lifted him from his eastern home, had urged him across the plains, had flung him in the almost insolent triumph of his youth high toward the sun. Now the wash receded.

---

CHAPTER II

It was indeed a good place for children. Charley and Alice Gates grew tall and strong, big boned, magnificent, typical California products. They went to the district school, rode in the mountains, helped handle the wild cattle. At the age of twelve Charley began to accompany the summer incursions into the High Sierras in search of feed. At the age of sixteen he was entrusted with a bunch of cattle. In these summers he learned the wonder of the high, glittering peaks, the blueness of the skies in high altitudes, the multitude of the stars, the flower-gemmed secret meadows, the dark, murmuring forests. He fished in the streams, and hunted on the ridges. His camp was pitched within a corral of heavy logs. It was very simple. Utensils depending from trees, beds beneath canvas tarpaulins on pine needles, saddlery, riatas, branding irons scattered about. No shelter but the sky. A wonderful roving life.

It developed taciturnity and individualism. Charley Gates felt no necessity for expression as yet; and as his work required little coöperation from his fellow creatures he acknowledged as little responsibility toward them. Thus far he was the typical mountaineer.

But other influences came to him; as, indeed, they come to all. But young Charley was more susceptible than most, and this—on the impulse of the next tide resurgent—saved him from his type. He liked to read; he did not scorn utterly and boisterously the unfortunate young man who taught the school; and, better than all, he possessed just the questioning mind that refuses to accept on their own asseveration only the conventions of life or the opinions of neighbours. If he were to drink, it would be because he wanted to; not because his companions considered it manly. If he were to enter the sheep war, it would be because he really considered sheep harmful to the range; not because of the overwhelming—and contagious—prejudice.

In one thing only did he follow blindly his sense of loyalty: He hated the Hydraulic Company.

Years after the placers failed someone discovered that the wholesale use of hydraulic "giants" produced gold in paying quantities. Huge streams of water under high pressure were directed against the hills, which melted like snow under the spring sun. The earth in suspension was run over artificial riffles against which the heavier gold collected. One such stream could accomplish in a few hours what would have cost hand miners the better part of a season.

But the débris must go somewhere. A rushing mud and boulder-filled torrent tore down stream beds adapted to a tenth of their volume. It wrecked much of the country below, ripping out the good soil, covering the bottomlands many feet deep with coarse rubble, clay, mud, and even big rocks and boulders. The farmers situated below such operations suffered cruelly. Even to this day the devastating results may be seen above Colfax or Sacramento.

John Gates suffered with the rest. His was not the nature to submit tamely, nor to compromise. He had made his farm with his own hands, and he did not propose to see it destroyed. Much money he expended through the courts; indeed the profits of his business were eaten by a never-ending, inconclusive suit. The Hydraulic Company, securely entrenched behind the barriers of especial privilege, could laugh at his frontal attacks. It was useless to think of force. The feud degenerated into a bitter legal battle and much petty guerrilla warfare on both sides.

To this quarrel Charley had been bred up in a consuming hate of the Hydraulic Company, all its works, officers, bosses, and employees. Every human being in any way connected with it wore horns, hoofs, and a tail. In company with the wild youths of the neighbourhood he perpetrated many a raid on the Company's property. Beginning with boyish openings of corrals to permit stock to stray, these raids progressed with the years until they had nearly arrived at the dignity of armed deputies and bench warrants.

The next day of significance to our story was October 15, 1872. On that date fire started near Flour Gold and swept upward. October is always a bad time of year for fires in foothill California—between the rains, the heat of the year, everything crisp and brown and brittle. This threatened the whole valley and water shed. The Gateses turned out, and all their neighbours, with hoe, mattock, axe, and sacking, trying to beat, cut, or scrape a "break" wide enough to check the flames. It was cruel work. The sun blazed overhead and the earth underfoot. The air quivered as from a furnace. Men gasped at it with straining lungs. The sweat pouring from their bodies combined with the parching of the superheated air induced a raging thirst. No water was to be had save what was brought to them. Young boys and women rode along the line carrying canteens, water bottles, and food. The fire fighters snatched hastily at these, for the attack of the fire permitted no respite. Twice they cut the wide swath across country; but twice before it was completed the fire crept through and roared into triumph behind them. The third time the line held, and this was well into the second day.

Charley Gates had fought doggedly. He had summoned the splendid resources of youth and heritage, and they had responded. Next in line to his right had been a stranger. This latter was a slender, clean-cut youth, at first glance seemingly of delicate physique. Charley had looked upon him with the pitying contempt of strong youth for weak youth. He considered that the stranger's hands were soft and effeminate, he disliked his little trimmed moustache, and especially the cool, mocking, appraising glance of his eyes. But as the day, and the night, and the day following wore away, Charley raised his opinion. The slender body possessed unexpected reserve, the long, lean hands plied the tools unweariedly, the sensitive face had become drawn and tired, but the spirit behind the mocking eyes had not lost the flash of its defiance. In the heat of the struggle was opportunity for only the briefest exchanges. Once, when Charley despairingly shook his empty canteen, the stranger offered him a swallow from his own. Next time exigency crowded them together, Charley croaked:

"Reckon we'll hold her."

Toward evening of the second day the westerly breeze died, and shortly there breathed a gentle air from the mountains. The danger was past.

Charley and the stranger took long pulls from their recently replenished canteens. Then they sank down where they were, and fell instantly asleep. The projecting root of a buckthorn stuck squarely into Charley's ribs, but he did not know it; a column of marching ants, led by a non-adaptable commander, climbed up and over the recumbent form of the stranger, but he did not care.

They came to life in the shiver of gray dawn, wearied, stiffened, their eyes swelled, their mouths dry.

"You're a sweet sight, stranger," observed Charley.

"Same to you and more of 'em," rejoined the other.

Charley arose painfully.

"There's a little water in my canteen yet," he proffered. "What might you call yourself? I don't seem to know you in these parts."

"Thanks," replied the other. "My name's Cathcart; I'm from just above."

He drank, and lowered the canteen to look into the flaming, bloodshot eyes of his companion.

"Are you the low-lived skunk that's running the Hydraulic Company?" demanded Charley Gates.

The stranger laid down the canteen and scrambled painfully to his feet.

"I am employed by the Company," he replied, curtly, "but please to understand I don't permit you to call me names."

"Permit!" sneered Charley.

"Permit," repeated Cathcart.

So, not having had enough exercise in the past two days, these young game cocks went at each other. Charley was much the stronger rough-and-tumble fighter; but Cathcart possessed some boxing skill. Result was that, in their weakened condition, they speedily fought themselves to a standstill without serious damage to either side.

"Now perhaps you'll tell me who the hell you think you are!" panted Cathcart, fiercely.

At just beyond arm's length they discussed the situation, at first belligerently with much recrimination, then more calmly, at last with a modicum of mutual understanding. Neither seceded from his basic opinion. Charley Gates maintained that the Company had no earthly business ruining his property, but admitted that with all that good gold lying there it was a pity not to get it out. Cathcart stoutly defended a man's perfect right to do as he pleased with his own belongings, but conceded that something really ought to be done about overflow waters.

"What are you doing down here fighting fire, anyway?" demanded Charley, suddenly. "It couldn't hurt your property. You could turn the 'giants' on it, if it ever came up your way."

"I don't know. I just thought I ought to help out a little," said Cathcart, simply.

For three years more Charley ran his father's cattle in the hills. Then he announced his intention of going away. John Gates was thunderstruck. By now he was stranded high and dry above the tide, fitting perfectly his surroundings. Vaguely he had felt that his son would stay with him always. But the wave was again surging upward. Charley had talked with Cathcart.

"This is no country to draw a salary in," the latter had told him, "nor to play with farming or cows. It's too big, too new, there are too many opportunities. I'll resign, and you leave; and we'll make our fortunes."

"How?" asked Charley.

"Timber," said Cathcart.

They conferred on this point. Cathcart had the experience of business ways; Charley Gates the intimate knowledge of the country; there only needed a third member to furnish some money. Charley broke the news to his family, packed his few belongings, and the two of them went to San Francisco.

Charley had never seen a big city. He was very funny about it, but not overwhelmed. While willing, even avid, to go the rounds and meet the sporting element, he declined to drink. When pressed and badgered by his new acquaintances, he grinned amiably.

163

"I never play the other fellows' game," he said. "When it gets to be my game, I'll join you."

The new partners had difficulty in getting even a hearing.

"It's a small business," said capitalists, "and will be. The demand for lumber here is limited, and it is well taken care of by small concerns near at hand."

"The state will grow and I am counting on the outside market," argued Cathcart.

But this was too absurd! The forests of Michigan, Wisconsin, and Minnesota were inexhaustible! As for the state growing to that extent; of course we all believe it, but when it comes to investing good money in the belief——

At length they came upon one of the new millionaires created by the bonanzas of Virginia City.

"I don't know a damn thing about your timber, byes," said he, "but I like your looks. I'll go in wid ye. Have a seegar; they cost me a dollar apiece."

The sum invested was absurdly, inadequately small.

"It'll have to spread as thin as it can," said Cathcart.

They spent the entire season camping in the mountains. By the end of the summer they knew what they wanted; and immediately took steps to acquire it. Under the homestead laws each was entitled to but a small tract of Government land. However, they hired men to exercise their privileges in this respect, to take up each his allotted portion, and then to convey his rights to Cathcart and Gates. It was slow business, for the show of compliance with Government regulations had to be made. But in this manner the sum of money at their disposal was indeed spread out very thin.

For many years the small, nibbling lumbering operations their limited capital permitted supplied only a little more than a bare living and the taxes. But every available cent went back into the business. It grew. Band saws replaced the old circulars; the new mills delivered their product into flumes that carried it forty miles to the railroad. The construction of this flume was a tremendous undertaking, but by now the firm could borrow on its timber. To get the water necessary to keep the flume in operation the partners—again by means of "dummies"—filed on the water rights of certain streams. To take up the water directly was without the law; but a show of mineral stain was held to justify a "mineral claim," so patents were obtained under that ruling. Then Charley had a bright idea.

"Look here, Cliff," he said to Cathcart. "I know something about farming; I was brought up on a farm. This country will grow anything anywhere if it has water. That lower country they call a desert, but that's only because it hasn't any rainfall. We're going to have a lot of water at the end of that flume——"

They bought the desert land at fifty cents an acre; scraped ditches and checks; planted a model orchard, and went into the real estate business. In time a community grew up. When hydro-electric power came into its own Cathcart & Gates from their various water rights furnished light for themselves, and gradually for the towns and villages round-about. Thus their affairs spread and became complicated. Before they knew it they were wealthy, very wealthy. Their wives—for in due course each had his romance—began to talk of San Francisco.

All this had not come about easily. At first they had to fight tooth and nail. The conditions of the times were crude, the code merciless. As soon as the firm showed its head above the financial horizon, it was swooped upon. Business was predatory. They had to fight for what they got; had to fight harder to hold it. Cathcart was involved continually in a maze of intricate banking transactions; Gates resisted aggression within and without, often with his own two fists. They learned to trust no man, but they learned also to hate no man. It was all part of the game. More sensitive temperaments would have failed; these succeeded. Cathcart became shrewd, incisive, direct, cold, a little hard; Charley Gates was burly, hearty, a trifle bullying. Both were in all circumstances quite unruffled; and in some circumstances ruthless.

About 1900 the entire holdings of the Company were capitalized, and a stock company was formed. The actual management of the lumbering, the conduct of the farms and ranches, the running of the hydro-electric systems of light and transportation, were placed in the hands of active young men. Charley Gates and his partner exercised over these activities only the slightest supervision; auditing accounts, making an occasional trip of inspection. Affairs would quite well have gone on without them; though they would have disbelieved and resented that statement.

The great central offices in San Francisco were very busy—all but the inner rooms where stood the partners' desks. One day Cathcart lit a fresh cigar, and slowly wheeled his chair.

"Look here, Charley," he proposed, "we've got a big surplus. There's no reason why we shouldn't make a killing on the side."

"As how?" asked Gates.

Cathcart outlined his plan. It was simply stock manipulation on a big scale; although the naked import was somewhat obscured by the complications of the scheme. After he had finished Gates smoked for some time in silence.

"All right, Cliff," said he, "let's do it."

And so by a sentence, as his father before him, he marked the farthest throw of the wave that had borne him blindly toward the shore. In the next ten years Cathcart and Gates made forty million dollars. Charley seemed to himself to be doing a tremendous business, but his real work, his contribution to the episode in the life of the commonwealth, ceased there. Again the wave receded.

---

The third generation of the Gates family consisted of two girls and a boy. They were brought up as to their early childhood in what may be called moderate circumstances. A small home near the little mill town, a single Chinese servant, a setter dog, and plenty of horses formed their entourage. When Charles, Jr., was eleven, and his sisters six and eight, however, the family moved to a pretentious "mansion" on Nob Hill in San Francisco. The environment of childhood became a memory: the reality of life was comprised in the super-luxurious existence on Nob Hill.

It was not a particularly wise existence. Whims were too easily realized, consequences too lightly avoided, discipline too capricious. The children were sent to private schools where they met only their own kind; they were specifically forbidden to mingle with the "hoodlums" in the next street; they became accustomed to being sent here and there in carriages with two servants, or later, in motor cars; they had always spending money for the asking.

"I know what it is like to scrimp and save, and my children are going to be spared that!" was Mrs. Gates's creed in the matter.

The little girls were always dressed alike in elaborately simple clothes, with frilly, starched underpinnies, silk stockings, high boots buttoned up slim legs; and across their shoulders, from beneath wonderful lingerie hats, hung shining curls. The latter were not natural, but had each day to be elaborately constructed. They made a dainty and charming picture.

"Did you ever see anything so sweet in all your life!" was the invariable feminine exclamation.

Clara and Ethel-May always heard these remarks. They conducted themselves with the poise and *savoir faire* of grown women. Before they were twelve they could "handle" servants, conduct polite conversations in a correctly artificial accent, and adapt their manners to another's station in life.

Charley Junior's development was sharply divided into two periods, with the second of which alone we have to do. The first, briefly, was repressive. He was not allowed to play with certain boys, he was not permitted to stray beyond certain bounds, he was kept clean and dressed-up, he was taught his manners. In short, Mrs. Gates tried—without knowing what she was doing—to use the same formula on him as she had on Ethel-May and Clara.

In the second period, he was a grief to his family. Roughly speaking, this period commenced about the time he began to be known as "Chuck" instead of Charley.

There was no real harm in the boy. He was high spirited, full of life, strong as a horse, and curious. Possessed of the patrician haughty good looks we breed so easily from shirtsleeves, free with his money, known as the son of his powerful father, a good boxer, knowing no fear, he speedily became a familiar popular figure around town. It delighted him to play the prince, either incognito or in person; to "blow off the crowd," to battle joyously with longshoremen; to "rough house" the semi-respectable restaurants. The Barbary Coast knew him, Taits, Zinkands, the Poodle Dog, the Cliff House, Franks, and many other resorts not to be spoken of so openly. He even got into the police courts once or twice; and nonchalantly paid a fine, with a joke at the judge and a tip to the policeman who had arrested him. There was too much drinking, too much gambling, too loose a companionship, altogether too much spending; but in this case the life was redeemed from its usual significance by a fantastic spirit of play, a generosity of soul, a regard for the unfortunate, a courtliness toward all the world, a refusal to believe in meanness or sordidness or cruelty. Chuck Gates was inbred with the spirit of *noblesse oblige*.

As soon as motor cars came in Chuck had the raciest possible. With it he managed to frighten a good many people half out of their wits. He had no accidents, partly because he was a very good heady driver, and partly because those whom he encountered were quick witted. One day while touring in the south he came down grade around a bend squarely upon a car ascending. Chuck's car was going too fast to be stopped. He tried desperately to wrench it from the road, but perceived at once that this was impossible without a fatal skid. Fortunately the only turnout for a half mile happened to be just at that spot. The other man managed to jump his car out on this little side ledge and to jam on his brakes at the very brink, just as Chuck flashed by. His mud guards slipped under those at the rear of the other car.

"Close," observed Chuck to Joe Merrill his companion, "I was going a little too fast," and thought no more of it.

But the other man, being angry, turned around and followed him into town. At the garage he sought Chuck out.

"Didn't you pass me on the grade five miles back?" he inquired.

"I may have done so," replied Chuck, courteously.

"Don't you realize that you were going altogether too fast for a mountain grade? that you were completely out of control?"

"I'm afraid I'll have to admit that that is so."

"Well," said the other man, with difficulty suppressing his anger. "What do you suppose would have happened if I hadn't just been able to pull out?"

"Why," replied Chuck, blandly, "I suppose I'd have had to pay heavily; that's all."

"Pay!" cried the man, then checked himself with an effort, "so you imagine you are privileged to the road, do whatever damage you please—and *pay!* I'll just take your number."

"That is unnecessary. My name is Charles Gates," replied Chuck, "of San Francisco."

The man appeared never to have heard of this potent cognomen. A month later the trial came off. It was most inconvenient. Chuck was in Oregon, hunting. He had to travel many hundreds of miles, to pay an expensive lawyer. In the end he was fined. The whole affair disgusted him, but he went through with it well, testified without attempt at evasion. It was a pity; but evidently the other man was no gentleman.

"I acknowledged I was wrong," he told Joe Merrill. He honestly felt that this would have been sufficient had the cases been reversed. In answer to a question as to whether he considered it fair to place the burden of safety on the other man, he replied:

"Among motorists it is customary to exchange the courtesies of the road—and sometimes the discourtesies," he added with a faint scorn.

The earthquake and fire of 1906 caught him in town. During three days and nights he ran his car for the benefit of the sufferers; going practically without food or sleep, exercising the utmost audacity and ingenuity in getting supplies, running fearlessly many dangers.

For the rest he played polo well, shot excellently at the traps, was good at tennis, golf, bridge. Naturally he belonged to the best clubs both city and country. He sailed a yacht expertly, was a keen fisherman, hunted. Also he played poker a good deal and was noted for his accurate taste in dress.

His mother firmly believed that he caused her much sorrow; his sisters looked up to him with a little awe; his father down on him with a fiercely tolerant contempt.

For Chuck had had his turn in the offices. His mind was a good one; his education both formal and informal, had trained it fairly well; yet he could not quite make good. Energetic, ambitious, keen young men, clambering upward from the ruck, gave him points at the game and then beat him. It was humiliating to the old man. He could not see the perfectly normal reason. These young men were striving keenly for what they had never had. Chuck was asked merely to add to what he already had more than enough of by means of a game that itself did not interest him.

Late one evening Chuck and some friends were dining at the Cliff House. They had been cruising up toward Tomales Bay, and had had themselves put ashore here. No one knew of their whereabouts. Thus it was that Chuck first learned of his father's death from apoplexy in the scareheads of an evening paper handed him by the majordomo. He read the article through carefully, then went alone to the beach below. It had been the usual sensational article; and but two sentences clung to Chuck's memory: "This fortunate young man's income will actually amount to about ten dollars a minute. What a significance have now his days—and nights!"

He looked out to sea whence the waves, in ordered rank, cast themselves on the shore, seethed upward along the sands, poised, and receded. His thoughts were many, but they always returned to the same point. Ten dollars a minute—roughly speaking, seven thousand a day! What would he do with it? "What a significance have now his days—and nights!"

His best friend, Joe Merrill, came down the path to him, and stood silently by his side.

"I'm sorry about your governor, old man," he ventured; and then, after a long time:

"You're the richest man in the West."

Chuck Gates arose. A wave larger than the rest thundered and ran hissing up to their feet.

"I wonder if the tide is coming in or going out," said Chuck, vaguely.

---

## CLIMBING FOR GOATS

---

### CHAPTER I

Near the point at which the great Continental Divide of the Rocky Mountains crosses the Canadian border another range edges in toward it from the south. Between these ranges lies a space of from twenty to forty miles; and midway between them flows a clear, wonderful river through dense forests. Into the river empty other, tributary, rivers rising in the bleak and lofty fastnesses of the mountains to right and left. Between them, in turn, run spur systems of mountains only a little less lofty than the parent ranges. Thus the ground plan of the whole country is a good deal like that of a leaf: the main stem representing the big river, the lateral veins its affluents; the tiny veins its torrents pouring from the sides of its mountains and glaciers; and the edges of the leaf and all spaces standing for mountains rising very sheer and abrupt from the floor of the densely forested stream valleys. In this country of forty miles by five hundred, then, are hundreds of distinct ranges, thousands of peaks, and innumerable valleys, pockets, and "parks." A wilder, lonelier, grander country would be hard to find. Save for the Forest Service and a handful of fur trappers, it is uninhabited. Its streams abound in trout; its dense forests with elk and white-tailed deer; its balder hills with blacktail deer; its upper basins with grizzly bears; its higher country with sheep and that dizzy climber the Rocky Mountain goat.

He who would enter this region descends at a little station on the Great Northern, and thence proceeds by pack train at least four days, preferably more, out into the wilderness. The going is through forests, the tree trunks straight and very close together, so that he will see very little of the open sky and less of the landscape. By way of compensation the forest itself is remarkably beautiful. Its undergrowth, though dense, is very low and even, not more than a foot or so off the ground; and in the Hunting Moon the leaves of this undergrowth have turned to purest yellow, without touch or trace of red, so that the sombre forest is carpeted with gold. Here and there shows a birch or aspen, also bright, pure light yellow, as though a brilliant sun were striking down through painted windows. Groups of yellow-leafed larches add to the splendour. And close to the ground grow little flat plants decked out with red or blue or white wax berries, Christmas fashion.

In this green-and-gold room one journeys for days. Occasionally a chance opening affords a momentary glimpse of hills or of the river sweeping below; but not for long. It is a chilly room. The frost has hardened the mud in the trail. One's feet and hands ache cruelly. At night camp is made near the banks of the river, whence always one may in a few moments catch as many trout as are needed, fine, big, fighting trout.

By the end of three or four days the prospect opens out. Tremendous cliffs rise sheer from the bottom of the valley; up tributary cañons one can see a dozen miles to distant snow ranges glittering and wonderful. Nearer at hand the mountains rise above timber line to great buttes and precipices.

---

## CHAPTER II

### THE FIRST CLIMB

Fisher, Frank, and I had been hunting for elk in the dense forests along the foot of one of these mountains; and for a half day, drenched with sweat, had toiled continuously up and down steep slopes, trying to go quietly, trying to keep our wind, trying to pierce the secrets of the leafy screen always about us. We were tired of it.

"Let's go to the top and look for goats," suggested Frank. "There are some goat cliffs on the other side of her. It isn't very far."

It was not very far, as measured by the main ranges, but it was a two hours' steady climb nearly straight up. We would toil doggedly for a hundred feet, or until our wind gave out and our hearts began to pound distressingly; then we would rest a moment. After doing this a few hundred times we would venture a look upward, confidently expecting the summit to be close at hand. It seemed as far as ever. We suffered a dozen or so of these disappointments, and then learned not to look up. This was only after we had risen above timber line to the smooth, rounded rock-and-grass shoulder of the mountain. Then three times we made what we thought was a last spurt, only to find ourselves on a "false summit." After a while we grew resigned, we realized that we were never going to get anywhere, but were to go on forever, without ultimate purpose and without hope, pushing with tired legs, gasping with inadequate lungs. When we had fully made up our minds to that, we arrived. This is typical of all high-mountain climbing—the dogged, hard, hopeless work that can never reach an accomplishment; and then at last the sudden, unexpected culmination.

We topped a gently rounding summit; took several deep breaths into the uttermost cells of our distressed lungs; walked forward a dozen steps—and found ourselves looking over the sheer brink of a precipice. So startlingly unforeseen was the swoop into blue space that I recoiled hastily, feeling a little dizzy. Then I recovered and stepped forward cautiously for another look. As with all sheer precipices, the lip on which we stood seemed slightly to overhang, so that in order to see one had apparently to crane away over, quite off balance. Only by the strongest effort of the will is one able to rid oneself of the notion that the centre of gravity is about to plunge one off head first into blue space. For it was fairly blue space below our precipice. We could see birds wheeling below us; and then below them again, very tiny, the fall away of talus, and the tops of trees in the basin below. And opposite, and all around, even down over the horizon, were other majestic peaks, peers of our own, naked and rugged. From camp the great forests had seemed to us the most important, most dominant, most pervading feature of the wilderness. Now in the high sisterhood of the peaks we saw they were as mantles that had been dropped about the feet.

Across the face of the cliff below us ran irregular tiny ledges; buttresses ended in narrow peaks; "chimneys" ran down irregularly to the talus. Here were supposed to dwell the goats.

We proceeded along the crest, spying eagerly. We saw tracks; but no animals. By now it was four o'clock, and past time to turn campward. We struck down the mountain on a diagonal that should take us home. For some distance all went well enough. To be sure, it was very steep, and we had to pay due attention to balance and sliding. Then a rock wall barred our way. It was not a very large rock wall. We went below it. After a hundred yards we struck another. By now the first had risen until it towered far above us, a sheer, gray cliff behind which the sky was very blue. We skirted the base of the second and lower cliff. It led us to another; and to still another. Each of these we passed on the talus beneath it; but with increasing difficulty, owing to the fact that the wide ledges were pinching out. At last we found ourselves cut off from farther progress. To our right rose tier after tier of great cliffs, serenely and loftily unconscious of any little insects like ourselves that might be puttering around their feet. Straight ahead the ledge ceased to exist. To our left was a hundred-foot drop to the talus that sloped down to the cañon. The cañon did not look so very far away, and we desired mightily to reach it. The only alternative to getting straight down was to climb back the weary way we had come; and that meant all night without food, warm clothing, or shelter on a snow-and-ice mountain.

Therefore, we scouted that hundred-foot drop to our left very carefully. It seemed hopeless; but at last I found a place where a point of the talus ran up to a level not much below our own. The only difficulty was that between ourselves and that point of talus extended a piece of sheer wall. I slung my rifle over my back, and gave myself to a serious consideration of that wall. Then I began to work out across its face.

The principle of safe climbing is to maintain always three points of suspension: that it to say, one should keep either both footholds and one handhold, or both handholds and one foothold. Failing that, one is taking long chances. With this firmly in mind, I spidered out across the wall, testing every projection and cranny before I trusted any weight to it. One apparently solid projection as big as my head came away at the first touch, and went bouncing off into space. Finally I stood, or rather sprawled, almost within arm's length of a tiny scrub pine growing solidly in a crevice just over the talus. Once there, our troubles were over; but there seemed no way of crossing. For the moment it actually looked as though four feet only would be sufficient to turn us back.

At last, however, I found a toehold half way across. It was a very slight crevice, and not more than two inches deep. The toe of a boot would just hold there without slipping. Unfortunately, there were no handholds above it. After thinking the matter over, however, I made up my mind to violate, for this occasion only, the rules for climbing. I inserted the toe, gathered myself, and with one smooth swoop swung myself across and grabbed that tiny pine!

Fisher now worked his way out and crossed in the same manner. But Frank was too heavy for such gymnastics. Fisher therefore took a firm grip on the pine, inserted his toe in the crevice, and hung on with all his strength while Frank crossed on his shoulders!

---

## CHAPTER III

### THE SECOND AND THIRD CLIMBS

Once more, lured by the promise of the tracks we had seen, we climbed this same mountain, but again without results. By now, you may be sure, we had found an easier way home! This was a very hard day's work, but uneventful.

Now, four days later, I crossed the river and set off above to explore in the direction of the Continental Divide. Of course I had no intention of climbing for goats, or, indeed, of hunting very hard for anything. My object was an idle go-look-see. Equally, of course, after I had rammed around most happily for a while up the wooded stream-bed of that cañon, I turned sharp to the right and began to climb the slope of the spur, running out at right angles to the main ranges that constituted one wall of my cañon. It was fifteen hundred nearly perpendicular feet of hard scrambling through windfalls. Then when I had gained the ridge, I thought I might as well keep along it a little distance. And then, naturally, I saw the main peaks not so *very* far away; and was in for it!

On either side of me the mountain dropped away abruptly. I walked on a knife edge, steeply rising. Great cañons yawned close at either hand, and over across were leagues of snow mountains.

In the cañon from which I had emerged a fine rain had been falling. Here it had turned to wet sleet. As I mounted, the slush underfoot grew firmer, froze, then changed to dry, powdery snow. This change was interesting and beautiful, but rather uncomfortable, for my boots, soaked through by the slush, now froze solid and scraped various patches of skin from my feet. It was interesting, too, to trace the change in bird life as the altitude increased. At snow line the species had narrowed down to a few ravens, a Canada jay, a blue grouse or so, nuthatches, and brown creepers. I saw one fresh elk track, innumerable marten, and the pad of a very large grizzly.

The ridge mounted steadily. After I had gained to 2,300 feet above the cañon I found that the ridge dipped to a saddle 600 feet lower. It really grieved me to give up that hard-earned six hundred, and then to buy it back again by another hard, slow, toilsome climb. Again I found my way barred by some unsuspected cliffs about sixty feet in height. Fortunately, they were well broken; and I worked my way to the top by means of ledges.

Atop this the snow suddenly grew deeper and the ascent more precipitous. I fairly wallowed along. The timber line fell below me. All animal life disappeared. My only companions were now at spaced-out and mighty intervals the big bare peaks that had lifted themselves mysteriously from among their lesser neighbours, with which heretofore they had been confused. In spite of very heavy exertions, I began to feel the cold; so I unslung my rucksack and put on my buckskin shirt. The snow had become very light and feathery. The high, still buttes and crags of the main divide were right before me. Light fog wreaths drifted and eddied slowly, now concealing, now revealing the solemn crags and buttresses. Over everything—the rocks, the few stunted and twisted small trees, the very surface of the snow itself—lay a heavy rime of frost. This rime stood out in long, slender needles an inch to an inch and a half in length, sparkling and fragile and beautiful. It seemed that a breath of wind or even a loud sound would precipitate the glittering panoply to ruin; but in all the really awesome silence and hushed breathlessness of that strange upper world there was nothing to disturb them. The only motion was that of the idly-drifting fog wreaths; the only sound was that made by the singing of the blood in my ears! I felt as though I were in a world holding its breath.

It was piercing cold. I ate a biscuit and a few prunes, tramping energetically back and forth to keep warm. I could see in all directions now: an infinity of bare peaks, with hardly a glimpse of forests or streams or places where things might live. Goats are certainly either fools or great poets.

After a half hour of fruitless examination of the cliffs I perforce had to descend. The trip back was long. It had the added interest in that it was bringing me nearer water. No thirst is quite so torturing as that which afflicts one who climbs hard in cold, high altitudes. The throat and mouth seem to shrivel and parch. Psychologically, it is even worse than the desert thirst because in cold air it is unreasonable. Finally it became so unendurable that I turned down from the spur-ridge long before I should otherwise have done so, and did a good deal of extra work merely to reach a little sooner the stream at the bottom of the cañon. When I reached it, I found that here it flowed underground.

## CHAPTER IV

## OTHER CLIMBS

For ten days we hunted and fished. When the opportunity offered, we made a goat-survey of a new place. Finally, as time grew short, we realized that we must concentrate our energies in one effort if we were to get specimens of this most desirable of all American big game. Therefore Fisher, Frank, Harry, and I, leaving our other two companions and the majority of the horses at the base camp, packed a few days' provisions and started in for the highest peaks of all.

We journeyed up an unknown cañon eighteen miles long, heavily wooded in the bottoms, with great mountains overhanging, and with a beautiful clear trout stream singing down its bed. The first day we travelled ten hours. One man was always in front cutting out windfalls or other obstructions. I should be afraid to guess how many trees we chopped through that day. Another man scouted ahead for the best route amid difficulties. The other two performed the soul-destroying task of getting the horses to follow the appointed way. After three o'clock we began to hope for horse feed. At dark we reluctantly gave it up. The forest remained unbroken. We had to tie the poor, unfed horses to trees, while we ourselves searched diligently and with only partial success for tiny spots level enough and clear enough for our beds. It was very cold that night; and nobody was comfortable; the horses least of all.

Next morning we were out and away by daylight. If we could not find horse feed inside of four hours, we would be forced to retreat. Three hours of the four went by. Then Harry and I held the horses while our companions scouted ahead rapidly. We nearly froze, for in that deep valley the sun did not rise until nearly noon. Through an opening we could see back to a tremendous sheer butte rising more than three thousand feet[C] by a series of very narrow terraced ledges. We named it the Citadel, so like was it to an ancient proud fortress.

Fisher reported first. He had climbed a tree, but had seen no feed. Ten minutes later Frank returned. He had found the track of an ancient avalanche close under the mountain, and in that track grew coarse grasses. We pushed on, and there made camp.

It was a queer enough camp. Our beds we spread in the various little spots among the roots and hummocks we imagined to look the most even. The fire we had to build in quite another place. All around us the lodge-pole pines, firs, and larches grew close and dark and damp. Only to the west the snow ranges showed among the treetops like great, looming white clouds.

For two days we lived high among the glaciers and snow crags, taking tremendous tramps, seeing wonderful peaks, frozen lakes, sheer cliffs, the tracks of grizzlies in numbers, the tiny sources of great streams, and the infinity of upper spaces. But no goats; and no tracks of goats. Little by little we eliminated the possibilities of the country accessible to us. Leagues in all directions, as far as the eye could reach, was plenty of other country, all equally good for goats; but it was not within reach of us from this cañon; and our time was up. Finally, we dropped back and made camp at the last feed; a mile or so below the Citadel. Two ranges at right angles here converged, and the Citadel rose like a tower at the corner. Here was our last chance.

## CHAPTER V

## GOATS

As we were finishing breakfast my eye was attracted to a snow speck on the mountainside some two thousand feet above us and slightly westward that somehow looked to me different from other snow specks. For nearly a minute I stared at it through my glasses. At last the speck moved. The game was in sight!

We drew straws for the shot, and Fisher won. Then we began our climb. It was the same old story of pumping lungs and pounding hearts; but with the incentive before us we made excellent time. A shallow ravine and a fringe of woods afforded us the cover we needed. At the end of an hour and a half we crawled out of our ravine and to the edge of the trees. There across a steep cañon and perhaps four hundred yards away were the goats, two of them, lying on the edge of small cliffs. We could see them very plainly, but they were too far for a sure shot. After examining them to our satisfaction we wormed our way back.

"The only sure way," I insisted, "is to climb clear to the top of the ridge, go along it on the other side until we are above and beyond the goats, and then to stalk them down hill."

That meant a lot more hard work; but in the end the plan was adopted. We resumed our interminable and toilsome climbing.

The ridge proved to be of the knife-edge variety, and covered with snow. From a deep, wide, walled-in basin on the other side rose the howling of two brush wolves. We descended a few feet to gain safe concealment; walked as rapidly as possible to the point above the goats; and then with the utmost caution began our descent.

In the last two hundred yards is the essence of big-game stalking. The hunter must move noiselessly, he must keep concealed; he must determine *at each step* just what the effect of that step has been in the matters of noise and of altering the point of view. It is necessary to spy sharply, not only from the normal elevation of a man's shoulders, but also stooping to the waist line, and even down to the knees. An animal is just as suspicious of legs as of heads; and much more likely to see them.

The shoulder of the mountain here consisted of a series of steep grass curves ending in short cliff jump-offs. Scattered and stunted trees and tree groups grew here and there. In thirty minutes we had made our distance and recognized the fact that our goats must be lying at the base of the next ledge. Motioning Harry to the left and Fisher to the front, I myself moved to the right to cut off the game should it run in that direction. Ten seconds later I heard Fisher shoot; then Harry opened up; and in a moment a goat ran across the ledge fifty yards below me. With a thrill of the greatest satisfaction I dropped the gold bead of my front sight on his shoulder!

The bullet knocked him off the edge of the cliff. He fell, struck the steep grass slope, and began to roll. Over and over and over he went, gathering speed like a snowball, getting smaller and smaller until he disappeared in the brush far below, a tiny spot of white.

No one can appreciate the feeling of relaxed relief that filled me. Hard and dangerous climbs, killing work, considerable hardship and discomfort had at length their reward. I could now take a rest. The day was young, and I contemplated with something like rapture a return to camp, and a good puttery day skinning out that goat. In addition I was suffering now from a splitting headache, the effects of incipient snow-blindness, and was generally pretty wobbly.

And then my eye wandered to the left, whence that goat had come. I saw a large splash of blood; at a spot *before* I had fired! It was too evident that the goat had already been wounded by Fisher; and therefore, by hunter's law, belonged to him!

I set my teeth and turned up the mountain to regain the descent we had just made. At the knife-edge top I stopped for a moment to get my breath and to survey the country. Diagonally across the basin where the wolves were howling, half way down the ridge running at right angles to my own, I made out two goats. They were two miles away from me on an air line. My course was obvious. I must proceed along my ridge to the Citadel, keeping always out of sight; surmount that fortress; descend to the second ridge; walk along the other side of it until I was above those goats, and then sneak down on them.

I accomplished the first two stages of my journey all right, though with considerably more difficulty in spots than I should have anticipated. The knife edge was so sharp and the sides so treacherous that at times it was almost impossible to travel anywhere but right on top. This would not do. By a little planning, however, I managed to reach the central "keep" of the Citadel: a high, bleak, broken pile, flat on top, with snow in all the crevices, and small cliffs on all sides. From this advantage I could cautiously spy out the lay of the land.

Below me fifty feet dipped the second ridge, running nearly at right angles. It sloped abruptly to the wolf basin, but fell sheer on the other side to depths I could not at that time guess.[D] A very few scattered, stunted, and twisted trees huddled close down to the rock and snow. This saddle was about fifty feet in width and perhaps five hundred yards in length. It ended in another craggy butte very much like the Citadel.

My first glance determined that my original plan would not do. The goats had climbed from where I had first seen them, and were now leisurely topping the saddle. To attempt to descend would be to reveal myself. I was forced to huddle just where I was. My hope was that the goats would wander along the saddle toward me, and not climb the other butte opposite. Also I wanted them to hurry, please, as the snow in which I sat was cold, and the wind piercing.

This apparently they were not inclined to do. They paused, they nibbled at some scanty moss, they gazed at the scenery, they scratched their ears. I shifted my position cautiously—and saw below me,[E] lying on the snow at the very edge of the cliff, a tremendous billy! He had been there all the time; and I had been looking over him!

At the crack of the Springfield he lurched forward and toppled slowly out of sight over the edge of the cliff. The two I had been stalking instantly disappeared. But on the very top of the butte opposite appeared another. It was a very long shot,[F] but I had to take chances, for I could not tell whether or not the one I had just shot was accessible or not. On a guess I held six inches over his back. The goat gave one leap forward into space. For twenty feet he fell spread-eagled and right side up as though flying. Then he began to turn and whirl. As far as my personal testimony could go, he is falling yet through that dizzy blue abyss.

"Good-bye, billy," said I, sadly. It looked then as though I had lost both.

I worked my way down the face of the Citadel until I was just above the steep snow fields. Here was a drop of six feet. If the snow was soft, all right. If it was frozen underneath, I would be very likely to toboggan off into space. I pried loose a small rock and dropped it, watching with great interest how it lit. It sunk with a dull plunk. Therefore I made my leap, and found myself waist deep in feathery snow.

With what anxiety I peered over the edge of that precipice the reader can guess. Thirty feet below was a four-foot ledge. On the edge of that ledge grew two stunted pines about three feet in height—and only two. Against those pines my goat had lodged! In my exultation I straightened up and uttered a whoop. To my surprise it was answered from behind me. Frank had followed my trail. He had killed a nanny and was carrying the head. Everybody had goats!

After a great deal of manœuvring we worked our way down to the ledge by means of a crevice and a ten-foot pole. Then we tied the goat to the little trees, and set to work. I held Frank while he skinned; and then he held me while I skinned. It was very awkward. The tiny landscape almost directly beneath us was blue with the atmosphere of distance. A solitary raven discovered us, and began to circle and croak and flop.

"You'll get your meal later," we told him.

Far below us, like suspended leaves swirling in a wind, a dense flock of snowbirds fluttered.

We got on well enough until it became necessary to sever the backbone. Then, try as we would, we could not in the general awkwardness reach a joint with a knife. At last we had a bright idea. I held the head back while Frank shot the vertebrae in two with his rifle!

Then we loosed the cords that held the body. It fell six hundred feet, hit a ledge, bounded out, and so disappeared toward the hazy blue map below. The raven folded his wings and dropped like a plummet, with a strange rushing sound. We watched him until the increasing speed of his swoop turned us a little dizzy, and we drew back. When we looked a moment later he had disappeared into the distance—straight down!

Now we had to win our way out. The trophy we tied with a rope. I climbed up the pole, and along the crevice as far as the rope would let me, hauled up the trophy, jammed my feet and back against both sides of the "chimney." Frank then clambered past me; and so repeat.

But once in the saddle we found we could not return the way we had come. The drop-off into the feather snow settled that. A short reconnaissance made it very evident that we would have to go completely around the outside of the Citadel, at the level of the saddle, until we had gained the other ridge. This meant about three quarters of a mile against the tremendous cliff.

We found a ledge and started. Our packs weighed about sixty pounds apiece, and we were forced to carry them rather high. The ledge proved to be from six to ten feet wide, with a gentle slope outward. We could not afford the false steps, nor the little slips, nor the overbalancings so unimportant on level ground. Progress was slow and cautious. We could not but remember the heart-stopping drop of that goat after we had cut the rope; and the swoop of the raven. Especially at the corners did we hug close to the wall, for the wind there snatched at us eagerly.

The ledge held out bravely. It had to; for there was no possible way to get up or down from it. We rounded the shoulder of the pile. Below us now was another landscape into which to fall—the valley of the stream, with its forests and its high cliffs over the way. But already we could see our ridge. Another quarter mile would land us in safety.

Without warning the ledge pinched out. A narrow tongue of shale, on so steep a slope that it barely clung to the mountain, ran twenty feet to a precipice. A touch sent its surface rattling merrily down and into space. It was only about eight feet across; and then the ledge began again.

We eyed it. Three steps would take us across. Alternative: return along the ledge to attack the problem *ab initio*.

"That shale is going to start," said Frank. "If you stop, she'll sure carry you over the ledge. But if you keep right on going, *fast*, I believe your weight will carry you through."

We readjusted our packs so they could not slip and overbalance us; we measured and re-measured with our eyes just where those steps would fall; we took a deep breath—and we *hustled*. Behind us the fine shale slid sullenly in a miniature avalanche that cascaded over the edge. Our "weight had carried us through!"

In camp, we found that Harry's shooting had landed a kid, so that we had a goat apiece.

We rejoined the main camp next day just ahead of a big snowstorm that must have made travel all but impossible. Then for five days we rode out, in snow, sleet, and hail. But we were entirely happy, and indifferent to what the weather could do to us now.

---

## MOISTURE, A TRACE

---

Last fall I revisited Arizona for the first time in many years. My ultimate destination lay one hundred and twenty-eight miles south of the railroad. As I stepped off the Pullman I drew deep the crisp, thin air; I looked across immeasurable distance to tiny, brittle, gilded buttes; I glanced up and down a ramshackle row of wooden buildings with crazy wooden awnings, and I sighed contentedly. Same good old Arizona.

The Overland pulled out, flirting its tail at me contemptuously. A small, battered-looking car, grayed and caked with white alkali dust, glided alongside, and from under its swaying and disreputable top emerged someone I knew. Not individually. But by many campfires of the past I had foregathered with him and his kind. Same old Arizona, I repeated to myself.

This person bore down upon me and gently extracted my bag from my grasp. He stood about six feet three; his face was long and brown and grave; his figure was spare and strong. Atop his head he wore the sacred Arizona high-crowned hat, around his neck a bright bandana; no coat, but an unbuttoned vest; skinny trousers, and boots. Save for lack of spurs and *chaps* and revolver he might have been a moving-picture cowboy. The spurs alone were lacking from the picture of a real one.

He deposited my bag in the tonneau, urged me into a front seat, and crowded himself behind the wheel. The effect was that of a grown-up in a go-cart. This particular brand of tin car had not been built for this particular size of man. His knees were hunched up either side the steering column; his huge, strong brown hands grasped most competently that toy-like wheel. The peak of his sombrero missed the wrinkled top only because he sat on his spine. I reflected that he must have been drafted into this job, and I admired his courage in undertaking to double up like that even for a short journey.

"Roads good?" I asked the usual question as I slammed shut the door.

"Fair, suh," he replied, soberly.

"What time should we get in?" I inquired.

"Long 'bout six o'clock, suh," he informed me.

It was then eight in the morning—one hundred and twenty-eight miles—ten hours—roads good, eh?—hum.

He touched the starter. The motor exploded with a bang. We moved.

I looked her over. On the running board were strapped two big galvanized tanks of water. It was almost distressingly evident that the muffler had either been lost or thrown away. But she was hitting on all four. I glanced at the speedometer dial. It registered the astonishing total of 29,250 miles.

We swung out the end of the main street and sailed down a road that vanished in the endless gentle slope of a"sink." Beyond the sink the bank rose again, gently, to gain the height of the eyes at some *mesas*. Well I know that sort of country. One journeyed for the whole day, and the *mesas* stayed where they were; and in between were successively vast stretches of mesquite, or alkali, or lava outcrops, or *sacatone* bottoms, each seeming, while one was in it, to fill all the world forever, without end; and the day's changes were of mirage and the shifting colours of distant hills.

It was soon evident that my friend's ideas of driving probably coincided with his ideas of going up a mountain. When a mounted cowboy climbs a hill he does not believe in fussing with such nonsense as grades; he goes straight up. Similarly, this man evidently considered that, as roads were made for travel and distance for annihilation, one should turn on full speed and get there. Not one hair's breadth did he deign to swerve for chuck-hole or stone; not one fractional mile per hour did he check for gully or ditch. We struck them head-on, bang! did they happen in our way. Then my head hit the disreputable top. In the mysterious fashion of those who drive freight wagons my companion remained imperturbably glued to his seat. I had neither breath nor leisure for the country or conversation.

Thus one half hour. The speedometer dial showed the figures 29,260. I allowed myself to think of a possible late lunch at my friend's ranch.

We slowed down. The driver advanced the hand throttle the full sweep of the quadrant, steered with his knees, and produced the "makings." The faithful little motor continued to hit on all four, but in slow and painful succession, each explosion sounding like a pistol shot. We had passed already the lowest point of the "sink," and were climbing the slope on the other side. The country, as usual, looked perfectly level, but the motor knew different.

"I like to hear her shoot," said the driver, after his first cigarette. "That's why I chucked the muffler. Its plumb lonesome out yere all by yourself. A hoss is different."

"Who you riding for?"

"Me? I'm riding for me. This outfit is mine."

It didn't sound reasonable; but that's what I heard.

"You mean you drive this car—as a living——"

"Correct."

"I should think you'd get cramped!" I burst out.

"Me? I'm used to it. I bet I ain't missed three days since I got her—and that's about a year ago."

He answered my questions briefly, volunteering nothing. He had never had any trouble with the car; he had never broken a spring; he'd overhauled her once or twice; he averaged sixteen actual miles to the gallon. If I were to name the car I should have to write advt. after this article to keep within the law. I resolved to get one. We chugged persistently along on high gear; though I believe second would have been better.

Presently we stopped and gave her a drink. She was boiling like a little tea kettle, and she was pretty thirsty.

"They all do it," said Bill. Of course his name was Bill. "Especially the big he-ones. High altitude. Going slow with your throttle wide open. You're all right if you got plenty water. If not, why then ketch a cow and use the milk. Only go slow or you'll git all clogged up with butter."

We clambered aboard and proceeded. That distant dreamful *mesa* had drawn very near. It was scandalous. The aloof desert whose terror, whose beauty, whose wonder, whose allure was the awe of infinite space that could be traversed only in toil and humbleness, had been contracted by a thing that now said 29,265.

"At this rate we'll get there before six o'clock," I remarked, hopefully.

"Oh, this is County Highway!" said Bill.

As we crawled along, still on high gear—that tin car certainly pulled strongly—a horseman emerged from a fold in the hills. He was riding a sweat-covered, mettlesome black with a rolling eye. His own eye was bitter, and likewise the other features of his face. After trying in vain to get the frantic animal within twenty feet of our *mitrailleuse*, he gave it up.

"Got anything for me?" he shrieked at Bill.

Bill leisurely turned off the switch, draped his long legs over the side of the car, and produced his makings.

"Nothing, Jim. Expaicting of anything?"

"Sent for a new grass rope. How's feed down Mogallon way?"

"Fair. That a bronco you're riding?"

"Just backed him three days ago."

"Amount to anything?"

"That," said Jim, with an extraordinary bitterness, "is already a gaited hoss. He has fo' gaits now."

"Four gaits," repeated Bill, incredulously. "I'm in the stink wagon business. I ain't aiming to buy no hosses. What four gaits you claim he's got?"

"Start, stumble, fall down *and* git up," said Jim.

172

Shortly after this joyous *rencontre* we topped the rise, and, looking back, could realize the grade we had been ascending.

The road led white and straight as an arrow to dwindle in perspective to a mere thread. The little car leaped forward on the invisible down grade. Again I anchored myself to one of the top supports. A long, rangy fowl happened into the road just ahead of us, but immediately flopped clumsily, half afoot, half a-wing, to one side in the brush, like a stampeded hen.

"Road runner," said Bill, with a short laugh. "Remember how they used to rack along in front of a hoss for miles, keeping just ahead, lettin' out a link when you spurred up? Aggravatin' fowl! They got over tryin' to keep ahead of gasoline."

In the white alkaline road lay one lone, pyramidal rock. It was about the size of one's two fists and all its edges and corners were sharp. Probably twenty miles of clear space lay on either flank of that rock. Nevertheless, our right front wheel hit it square in the middle. The car leaped straight up, the rock popped sidewise, and the tire went off with a mighty bang. Bill put on the brakes, deliberately uncoiled himself, and descended.

"Seems like tires don't last no time at all in this country," he remarked, sadly. He walked around the car and began to examine the four wrecks he carried as spares. After some inspection of their respective merits, he selected one. "I just somehow kain't git over the notion she ought to sidestep them little rocks and holes of her own accord," he exclaimed. "A hoss is a plumb, narrow-minded critter, but he knows enough for that."

While he changed the tire—which incidentally involved patching one of half a dozen over-worn tubes—I looked her over more in detail. The customary frame, strut rods, and torsion rods had been supplemented by the most extraordinary criss-cross of angle-iron braces it has ever been my fortune to behold. They ran from anywhere to everywhere beneath that car. I began to comprehend her cohesiveness.

"Jim Coles, blacksmith at the O T, puts them braces in all our cars," explained Bill. "He's got her down to a system."

The repair finished and the radiator refilled we resumed the journey. It was now just eleven o'clock. The odometer reading was 29,276. The temperature was well up toward 100 degrees. But beneath the disreputable top, and while in motion, the heat was not noticeable. Nevertheless, the brief stop had brought back poignantly certain old days—choking dust, thirst, the heat of a heavy sun, the long day that led one nowhere——

The noon mirages were taking shape, throwing stately and slow their vast illusions across the horizon. Lakes glimmered; distant ranges took on the forms of phantasm, rising higher, flattening, reaching across space the arches of their spans, rendering unreal a world of beauty and dread. That in the old days was the deliberate fashion the desert had of searing men's souls with her majesty. Slowly, slowly, the changes melted one into the other; massively, deliberately the face of the world was altered; so that at last the poor plodding human being, hot, dry, blinded, thirsty, felt himself a nothing in the presence of eternities. Well I knew that old spell of the desert. But now! Honestly, after a few minutes I began to feel sorry for the poor old desert! Its spells didn't work for the simple reason that *we didn't give it time!* We charged down on its phantom lakes and disproved them and forgot them. We broke right in on the dignified and deliberate scene shifting of mountains and *mesas*, showed them up for the brittle, dry hills they were, and left them behind. It was pitiful! It was as though a revered tragedian should overnight find that his vogue had departed; that he was no longer getting over; that an irreverent upstart, breaking in on his most sonorous periods, was getting laughs with slang. We had lots of water; the dust we left behind; it wasn't even hot in the wind of our going!

In the shallow crease of hills a shimmer of white soon changed to evident houses. We drew into a straggling desert town.

It was typical—thirty miles from the railroad, a distributing point for the cattle country. Four broad buildings with peeled, sunburned faces, a wooden house or so, and a dozen flat-roofed adobe huts hung pleasingly with long strips of red peppers. Of course one of the wooden buildings was labelled General Store; and another, smaller, contained a barber shop and postoffice combined. The third was barred and unoccupied. The fourth had been a livery stable but was now a garage. Six saddle horses and six Fords stood outside the General Store, which was a fair division.

Bill slowed down.

"Have a drink," I observed, hospitably.

"Arizona's a dry state," Bill reminded me; but nevertheless stopped and uncoiled. That unbelievable phenomenon had escaped my memory. In the old days I used to shut my eyes and project my soul into what I imagined was the future. I saw Arizona, embottled, dying in the last-wet ditch, while all the rest of the world, even including Milwaukee, bore down on her carrying the banners of Prohibition. So much for prophecy. I voiced a thought.

"There must be an awful lot of old timers died this spring. You can't cut them off short and hope to save them."

Bill grunted.

We entered the store. It smelled good, as such stores always do—soap, leather, ground coffee, bacon, cheese—all sorts of things. On the right ran a counter and shelves of dry goods and clothing; on the left groceries, cigars, and provisions generally. Down the middle saddles, ropes, spurs, pack outfits, harness, hardware. In the rear a glass cubby-hole with a desk inside. All that was customary, right and proper. But I noticed also a glass case with spark plugs and accessories; a rack full of tires; and a barrel of lubricating oil. I did not notice any body polish. By the front door stood a paper-basket whose purport I understood not at all.

Bill led me at once past two or three lounging cow persons to the cubbyhole, where arose a typical old timer.

"Mr. White, meet Mr. Billings," he said.

The old timer grasped me firmly by the right hand and held tight while he demanded, as usual, "What name?" We informed him together. He allowed he was pleased. I allowed the same.

173

"I want to buy a yard of calico," said Bill.

The old timer reached beneath the counter and produced a strip of cloth. It was already cut, and looked to be about a yard long. Also it showed the marks of loving but brutal and soiled hands.

"Wrap it up?" inquired Mr. Billings.

"Nope," said Bill, and handed out three silver dollars. Evidently calico was high in these parts. We turned away.

"By the way, Bill," Mr. Billings called after us, "I got a little present here for you. Some friends sent her in to me the other day. Let me know what you think of it."

We turned. Mr. Billings held in his hand a sealed quart bottle with a familiar and famous label.

"Why, that's kind of you," said Bill, gravely. He took the proffered bottle, turned it upside down, glanced at the bottom, and handed it back. "But I don't believe I'd wish for none of that particular breed. It never did agree with my stummick."

Without a flicker of the eye the storekeeper produced a second sealed bottle, identical in appearance and label with the first.

"Try it," he urged. "Here's one from a different case. Some of these yere vintages is better than others."

"So I've noticed," replied Bill, dryly. He glanced at the bottom and slipped it into his pocket.

We went out. As we passed the door Bill, unobserved, dropped into the heretofore unexplained waste-basket the yard of calico he had just purchased.

"Don't believe I like the pattern for my boudoir," he told me, gravely.

We clambered aboard and shot our derisive exhaust at the diminishing town.

"Thought Arizona was a dry state," I suggested.

"She is. You cain't sell a drop. But you can keep stuff for personal use. There ain't nothing more personal than givin' it away to your friends."

"The price of calico is high down here."

"And goin' up," agreed Bill, gloomily. He drove ten miles in silence while I, knowing my type, waited.

"That old Billings ought to be drug out and buried," he remarked at last. "We rode together on the Chiracahua range. He ought to know better than to try to put it onto me."

"???" said I.

"You saw that first bottle? Just plain forty-rod dog poison—and me payin' three good round dollars!"

"For calico," I reminded.

"Shore. That's why he done it. He had me—if I hadn't called him."

"But that first bottle was identically the same as the one you have in your pocket," I stated.

"Shore?"

"Why, yes—at least—that is, the bottle and label were the same, and I particularly noticed the cork seal looked intact."

"It was," agreed Bill. "That cap hasn't never been disturbed. You're right."

"Then what objection——"

"It's one of them wonders of modern science that spoils the simple life next to Nature's heart," said Bill, unexpectedly. "You hitch a big hollow needle onto an electric light current. When she gets hot enough you punch a hole with her in the bottom of the bottle. Then you throw the switch and let the needle cool off. When she's cool you pour out the real thing for your own use—mebbe. Then you stick in your forty-cent-a-gallon squirrel poison. Heat up your needle again. Draw her out very slow so the glass will close up behind her. Simple, neat, effective, honest enough for down here. Cork still there, seal still there, label still there. Bottle still there, except for a little bit of a wart-lookin' bubble in the bottom."

It was now in the noon hour. Knowing cowboys of old I expected no lunch. We racketed along, and our dust tried to catch us, and sleepy, accustomed jack rabbits made two perfunctory hops as we turned on them the battery of our exhaust.

We dipped down into a carved bottomland, several miles wide, filled with minarets, peaks, vermilion towers, and strange striped labyrinths of many colours above which the sky showed an unbelievable blue. The trunks of colossal trees lay about in numbers. Apparently they had all been cross-cut in sections like those sawed for shake bolts, for each was many times clearly divided. The sections, however, lay all in place; so the trunks of the trees were as they had fallen. About the ground were scattered fragments of rock of all sizes, like lava, but of all the colours of the giddiest parrots. The tiniest piece had at least all the tints of the spectrum; and the biggest seemed to go the littlest several better. They looked to me like beautiful jewels. Bill cast at them a contemptuous glance.

"Every towerist I take in yere makes me stop while he sags down the car with this junk," he said. Whenever I say "Bill said" or "I said," I imply that we shrieked, for always through that great, still country we hustled enveloped in a profanity of explosions, creaks, rattles, and hums. Just now though, on a level, we travelled at a low gear. "Petrified wood," Bill added.

I swallowed guiltily the request I was about to proffer.

The malpais defined itself. We came to a wide, dry wash filled with white sand. Bill brought the little car to a stop.

Well I know that sort of sand! You plunge rashly into it on low gear; you buzz bravely for possibly fifty feet; you slow down, slow down; your driving wheels begin to spin—that finishes you. Every revolution digs a deeper hole. It is useless to apply power. If you are wise you throw out your clutch the instant she stalls, and thus save digging yourself in unnecessarily. But if you are really wise you don't get in that fix at all. The next stage is that wherein you thrust beneath the hind wheels certain expedients such as robes, coats, and so forth. The wheels, when set in motion, hurl these trivialities yards to the rear. The car then settles down with a shrug. About the time the axle is actually resting on the sand you proceed to serious digging, cutting brush, and laying causeways. Some sand you can get out of by these methods,

174

but not dry, stream-bed sand in the Southwest. Finally you reach; the state of true wisdom. Either you sit peacefully in the tonneau and smoke until someone comes along; or, if you are doubtful of that miracle, you walk to the nearest team and rope. And never, never, never are you caught again! A détour of fifty miles is nothing after that!

While Bill manipulated the makings, I examined the prospects. This was that kind of a wash; no doubt of it!

"How far is the nearest crossing?" I asked, returning.

"About eight feet," said he.

My mind, panic-stricken, flew to several things—that bottle (I regret that I failed to record that by test its contents had proved genuine), the cornered rock we had so blithely charged, other evidences of Bill's casual nature. My heart sank.

"You ain't going to tackle that wash!" I cried.

"I shore am," said Bill.

I examined Bill. He meant it.

"How far to the nearest ranch?"

"'Bout ten mile."

I went and sat on a rock. It was one of those rainbow remnants of a bygone past; but my interest in curios had waned.

Bill dove into the grimy mysteries of under the back seat and produced two blocks of wood six or eight inches square and two strong straps with buckles. He inserted a block between the frame of the car and the rear axle; then he ran a strap around the rear spring and cinched on it until the car body, the block, and the axle made one solid mass. In other words, the spring action was entirely eliminated. He did the same thing on the other side.

"Climb in," said he.

We went into low and slid down the steep clay bank into the waiting sand. To me it was like a plunge into ice water. Bill stepped on her. We ploughed out into trouble. The steering wheel bucked and jerked vainly against Bill's huge hands; we swayed like a moving-picture comic; but we forged steadily ahead. Not once did we falter. Our wheels gripped continuously. When we pulled out on the other bank I exhaled as though I, too, had lost my muffler. I believe I had held my breath the whole way across. Bill removed the blocks and gave her more water. Still in low we climbed out of the malpais.

It was now after two o'clock. We registered 29,328. I was getting humble minded. Six o'clock looked good enough to me now.

One thing was greatly encouraging. As we rose again to the main level of the country I recognized over the horizon a certain humped mountain. Often in the "good old days" I had approached this mountain from the south. Beneath its flanks lay my friend's ranch, our destination. Five hours earlier in my experience its distance would have appalled me; but my standards had changed. Nevertheless, it seemed far enough away. I was getting physically tired. There is a heap of exercise in many occupations, such as digging sewers and chopping wood and shopping with a woman; but driving in small Arizona motor cars need give none of these occupations any odds. And of late years I have been accustoming myself to three meals a day.

For this reason there seems no excuse for detailing the next three hours. From three o'clock until sunset the mirages slowly fade away into the many-tinted veils of evening. I know that because I've seen it; but never would I know it whilst an inmate of a gasoline madhouse. We carried our own egg-shaped aura constantly with us, on the invisible walls of which the subtle and austere influences of the desert beat in vain. That aura was composed of speed, bumps, dust, profane noise, and an extreme and exotic busyness. It might be that in a docile, tame, expensive automobile, garnished with a sane and biddable driver, one might see the desert as it is. I don't know whether such a combination exists. But me—I couldn't get into the Officers' Training Camp because of my advanced years: I may be an old fogy, but I cherish a sneaking idea that perhaps you have to buy some of these things at the cost of the aforementioned thirst, heat, weariness, and the slow passing of long days. Still, an Assyrian brick in the British Museum is inscribed by a father to his son away at school with a lament over the passing of the "good old days!"

At any rate, we drew into Spring Creek at five o'clock, shooting at every jump. My friend's ranch was only six miles farther. This was home for Bill, and we were soon surrounded by many acquaintances. He had letters and packages for many of them; and detailed many items of local news. To us shortly came a cowboy who had evidently bought all the calico he could carry. This person was also long and lean and brown; hard bitten; bedecked with worn brown leather *chaps*, and wearing a gun. The latter he unbuckled and cast from him with great scorn.

"And I don't need no gun to do it, neither!" he stated, as though concluding a long conversation.

"Shore not, Slim," agreed one of the group, promptly annexing the artillery. "What is it?"

"Kill that ——— ——— ——— Beck," said Slim, owlishly. "I can do it; and I can do it with my bare hands, b' God!"

He walked sturdily enough in the direction of the General Store across the dusty square. No one paid any further attention to his movements. The man who had picked up the gun belt buckled it around his own waist. Bill refilled the ever-thirsty radiator, peered at his gasoline gauge, leisurely turned down a few grease cups. Ten minutes passed. We were about ready to start.

Back across the square drifted a strange figure. With difficulty we recognized it as the erstwhile Slim. He had no hat. His hair stuck out in all directions. One eye was puffing shut, blood oozed from a cut in his forehead and dripped from his damaged nose. One shirt sleeve had been half torn from its parent at the shoulder. But, most curious of all, Slim's face was evenly marked by a perpendicular series of long, red scratches as though he had been dragged from stem to stern along a particularly abrasive gravel walk. Slim seemed quite calm.

His approach was made in a somewhat strained silence. At length there spoke a dry, sardonic voice.

"Well," said it, "did you kill Beck?"

175

"Naw!" replied Slim's remains disgustedly, "the son of a gun wouldn't fight!"

We reached my friend's ranch just about dusk. He met me at the yard gate.

"Well!" he said, heartily. "I'm glad you're here! Not much like the old days, is it?"

I agreed with him.

"Journey out is dull and uninteresting now. But compared to the way we used to do it, it is a cinch. Just sit still and roll along."

I disagreed with him—mentally.

"The old order has changed," said he.

"Yes," I agreed, "now it's one yard of calico."

---

*THE RANCH*

---

## CHAPTER I

### THE NEW AND THE OLD

The old ranching days of California are to all intents and purposes past and gone. To be sure there remain many large tracts supporting a single group of ranch buildings, and over which the cattle wander "on a thousand hills." There are even a few, a very few—like the ranch of which I am going to write—that are still undivided, still game haunted, still hospitable, still delightful. But in spite of these apparent exceptions, my first statement must stand. About the large tracts swarm real estate men, eager for the chance to subdivide into small farms—and the small farmers pour in from the East at the rate of a thousand a month. No matter how sternly the old land-lords set their faces against the new order of things, the new order of things will prevail; for sooner or late old land-lords must die, and the heirs have not in them the spirit of the ancient tradition. This is, of course, best for the country and for progress; but something passes, and is no more. So the Chino ranch and more recently Lucky Baldwin's broad acres have yielded.

And even in the case of those that still remain intact, whose wide hills and plains graze thousands of head of cattle; whose pastures breed their own cowhorses; whose cowmen, wearing still with a twist of pride the all-but-vanished regalia of their all-but-vanished calling, refuse to drop back to the humdrum status of "farm hands on a cow ranch"; even here has entered a single element powerful enough to change the old to something new. The new may be better—it is certainly more convenient—and perhaps when all is said and done we would not want to go back to the old. But the old is gone. One single modern institution has been sufficient to render it completely of the past. That institution is the automobile.

In the old days—and they are but yesterdays, after all—the ranch was perforce an isolated community. The journey to town was not to be lightly undertaken; indeed, as far as might be, it was obviated altogether. Blacksmithing, carpentry, shoe cobbling, repairing, barbering, and even mild doctoring were all to be done on the premises. Nearly every item of food was raised at home, including vegetables, fruit, meat, eggs, fowl, butter, and honey. Above all, the inhabitants of that ranch settled down comfortably into the realization that their only available community was that immediately about them; and so they both made and were influenced by the individual atmosphere of the place.

In the latter years they have all purchased touring cars, and now they run to town casually, on almost any excuse. They make shopping lists as does the city dweller; they go back for things forgotten; and they return to the ranch as one returns to his home on the side streets of a great city. In place of the old wonderful and impressive expeditions to visit in state the nearest neighbour (twelve miles distant), they drop over of an afternoon for a ten-minutes' chat. The ranch is no longer an environment in which one finds the whole activity of his existence, but a dwelling place from which one goes forth.

I will admit that this is probably a distinct gain; but the fact is indubitable that, even in these cases where the ranch life has not been materially changed otherwise, the automobile has brought about a condition entirely new. And as the automobile has fortunately come to stay, the old will never return. It is of the old, and its charm and leisure, that I wish to write.

---

## CHAPTER II

### THE OLD WEST

I went to the ranch many years ago, stepping from the train somewhere near midnight into a cold, crisp air full of stars. My knowledge of California was at that time confined to several seasons spent on the coast, where the straw hat retires only in deference to a tradition which none of the flowers seem bound to respect. As my dress accorded with this experience, I was very glad to be conducted across the street to a little hotel. My guide was an elderly, very brown man, with a white moustache, and the bearing of an army regular. This latter surmise later proved correct. Manning was one of the numerous old soldiers who had fought through the General's Apache campaigns, and who now in his age had drifted back to be near his old commander. He left me, after many solicitations as to my comfort, and a promise to be back with the team at seven o'clock sharp.

Promptly at that hour he drew up by the curb. My kit bag was piled aboard, and I clambered in beside the driver. Manning touched his team. We were off.

The rig was of the sort usual to the better California ranches of the day, and so, perhaps, worth description. It might best be defined as a rather wide, stiff buckboard set on springs, and supported by stout running gear. The single seat was set well forward, while the body of the rig extended back to receive the light freight an errand to town was sure to accumulate. An ample hood top of gray canvas could be raised for protection against either sun, wind, or rain. Most powerful brakes could be manipulated by a thrust of the driver's foot. You may be sure they were outside brakes. Inside brakes were then considered the weak expedients of a tourist driving mercenary. Generally the tongue and moving gear were painted cream; and the body of the vehicle dark green.

This substantial, practical, and business-like vehicle was drawn by a pair of mighty good bright bay horses, straight backed, square rumped, deep shouldered, with fine heads, small ears, and alert yet gentle eyes of high-bred stock. When the word was given, they fell into a steady, swinging trot. One felt instinctively the power of it, and knew that they were capable of keeping up this same gait all day. And that would mean many miles. Their harness was of plain russet leather, neat and well oiled.

Concerning them I made some remark, trivial yet enough to start Manning. He told me of them, and of their peculiarities and virtues. He descanted at length on their breeding, and whence came they and their fathers and their fathers' fathers even unto the sixth generation. He left me at last with the impression that this was probably the best team in the valley, bar none. It was a good team, strong, spirited, gentle, and enduring.

We swung out from the little town into a straight road. If it has seemed that I have occupied you too exclusively with objects near at hand, the matter could not be helped. There was nothing more to occupy you. A fog held all the land.

It was a dense fog, and a very cold. Twenty feet ahead of the horses showed only a wall of white. To right and left dim, ghostly bushes or fence posts trooped by us at the ordered pace of our trot. An occasional lone poplar tree developed in the mist as an object on a dry plate develops. We splashed into puddles, crossed culverts, went through all the business of proceeding along a road—and apparently got nowhere. The mists opened grudgingly before us, and closed in behind. As far as knowing what the country was like I might as well have been blindfolded.

From Manning I elicited piecemeal some few and vague ideas. This meagreness was not due to a disinclination on Manning's part, but only to the fact that he never quite grasped my interest in mere surroundings. Yes, said he, it was a pretty flat country, and some brush. Yes, there were mountains, some ways off, though. Not many trees, but some—what you might call a few. And so on, until I gave it up. Mountains, trees, brush, and flat land! One could construct any and all landscapes with such building blocks as those.

Now, as has been hinted, I was dressed for southern California; and the fog was very damp and chill. The light overcoat I wore failed utterly to exclude it. At first I had been comfortable enough, but as mile succeeded mile the cold of that winter land fog penetrated to the bone. In answer to my comment Manning replied cheerfully in the words of an old saw:

"*A                                                          winter's                                                          fog
Will freeze a dog,*"

said he.

I agreed with him. We continued to jog on. Manning detailed what I then thought were hunting lies as to the abundance of game; but which I afterward discovered were only sober truths. When too far gone in the miseries of abject cold I remembered his former calling, and glancing sideways at his bronzed, soldierly face, wished I had gumption enough left to start him going on some of his Indian campaigns. It was too late; I had not the gumption; I was too cold.

Now I believe I am fairly well qualified to know when I really feel cold. I have slept out with the thermometer out of sight somewhere down near the bulb; I once snowshoed nine miles; and then overheated from that exertion, drove thirty-five without additional clothing. On various other occasions I have had experiences that might be called frigid. But never have I been quite so deadly cold as on that winter morning's drive through the land fog of semi-tropical California. It struck through to the very heart.

I subsequently discovered that it takes two hours and three quarters to drive to the ranch. That is a long time when one has nothing to look at, and when one is cold. In fact, it is so long that one loses track of time at all, and gradually relapses into that queer condition of passive endurance whereto is no end and no beginning. Therefore the end always comes suddenly, and as a surprise.

So it was in this case. Out of the mists sprang suddenly two tall fan palms, and then two others, and still others. I realized dimly that we were in an avenue of palms. The wheels grated strangely on gravel. We swung sharply to the left between hedges. The mass of a building loomed indistinctly. Manning applied the brakes. We stopped, the steam from the horses' shining backs rising straight up to mingle with the fog.

"Well, here we are!" said Manning.

So we were! I hadn't thought of that. We must be here. After an appreciable moment it occurred to me that perhaps I'd better climb down. I did so, very slowly and stiffly, making the sad mistake of jumping down from the height of the step.

How that did injure my feelings! The only catastrophe I can remember comparable to it was when a teacher rapped my knuckles with a ruler after I had been making snowballs bare handed. My benumbed faculties next swung around to the proposition of proceeding up an interminable gravel walk—(it is twenty-five feet long!) to a forbidding flight of stairs—(porch steps—five of them!) I put this idea into execution. I reached the steps. And then——

The door was flung open from within, I could see the sparkle and leap of a fine big grate fire. The Captain stood in the doorway, a broad smile on his face; my hostess smiled another welcome behind him; the General roared still another from somewhere behind her.

Now I had never met the Captain. He held out both hands in greeting. One of those hands was for me to shake. The other held a huge glass of hot scotch. The hot scotch was in the right hand!

---

## CHAPTER III

### THE PEOPLE AND THE PLACE

They warmed me through, and then another old soldier named Redmond took me up to show me where I lived. We clambered up narrow boxed stairs that turned three ways; we walked down a narrow passage; turned to the right; walked down another narrow passage, climbed three steps to open a door; promptly climbed three steps down again; crossed a screened-in bridge to another wing; ducked through a passageway, and so arrived. The ranch house was like that. Parts of it were built out on stilts. Five or six big cottonwood trees grew right up through the verandahs, and spread out over the roof of the house. There are all sorts of places where you hang coats, or stack guns, or store shells, or find unexpected books; passageways leading to outdoor upstairs screened porches, cubby holes and the like. And whenever you imagine the house must be quite full of guests, they can always discover to you yet another bedroom. It may, at the last, be a very tiny bedroom, with space enough only for a single bed and not much else; and you may get to it only by way of out of doors; and it may be already fairly well occupied by wooden decoys and shotgun shells, but there it is, guests and guests after you thought the house must be full.

Belonging and appertaining unto the house were several fixtures. One of these was old Charley, the Chinese cook. He had been there twenty-five years. In that time he had learned perfect English, acquired our kind of a sense of humour, come to a complete theoretical understanding of how to run a ranch and all the people on it, and taught Pollymckittrick what she knew.

Pollymckittrick was the bereaved widow of the noble pair of yellow and green parrots Noah selected for his ark. At least I think she was that old. She was certainly very wise in both Oriental and Occidental wisdom. Her chief accomplishments, other than those customary to parrots, were the ability to spell, and to sing English songs. "After the Ball" and "Daisy Bell" were her favourites, rendered with occasional jungle variations. She considered Charley her only real friend, though she tolerated some others. Pollymckittrick was a product of artificial civilization. No call of the wild in hers! She preferred her cage, gilded or otherwise. Each afternoon the cage was placed out on the lawn so Pollymckittrick could have her sun bath. One day a big redtail hawk sailed by. Pollymckittrick fell backward off her perch, flat on her back. The sorrowing family gathered to observe this extraordinary case of heart failure. After an interval Pollymckittrick unfilmed one yellow eye.

"Po—o—or Pollymckittrick!" she remarked.

At the sight of that hawk Pollymckittrick had fainted!

The third institution having to do with the house was undoubtedly Redmond. Redmond was another of the old soldiers who had in their age sought out their beloved General. Redmond was a sort of all-round man. He builtthe fires very early in the morning; and he did your boots and hunting clothes, got out the decoys, plucked the ducks, saw to the shells, fed the dogs, and was always on hand at arrival and departure to lend a helping hand. He dwelt in a square room in the windmill tower together with a black cat and all the newspapers in the world. The cat he alternately allowed the most extraordinary liberties or disciplined rigorously. On the latter occasions he invariably seized the animal and hurled it bodily through the open window. The cat took the long fall quite calmly, and immediately clambered back up the outside stairway that led to the room. The newspapers he read, and clipped therefrom items of the most diverse nature to which he deprecatingly invited attention. Once in so often a strange martial fervour would obsess him. Then the family, awakened in the early dawn, would groan and turn over, realizing that its rest was for that morning permanently shattered. The old man had hoisted his colours over the windmill tower, and now in a frenzy of fervour was marching around and around the tower beating the long roll on his drum. After one such outbreak he would be his ordinary, humble, quiet, obliging, almost deprecating self for another month or so. The ranch people took it philosophically.

The fourth institution was Nobo. Nobo was a Japanese woman who bossed the General. She was a square-built person of forty or so who had also been with the family unknown years. Her capabilities were undoubted; as also her faith in them. The hostess depended on her a good deal; and at the same time chafed mildly under her calm assumption that she knew perfectly what the situation demanded. The General took her domination amusedly. To be sure nobody was likely to fool much with the General. His vast good nature had way down beneath it something that on occasion could be stern. Nobo could and would tell the General what clothes to wear, and when to change them, and such matters; but she never ventured to inhibit the General's ideas as to going forth in rains, or driving where he everlastingly dod-blistered pleased, or words to that effect, across country in his magnificently rattletrap surrey, although she often looked very anxious. For she adored the General. But we all did that.

As though the heavy curtain of fog had been laid upon the land expressly that I might get my first impressions of the ranch in due order, about noon the weather cleared. Even while we ate lunch, the sun came out. After the meal we went forth to see what we could see.

The ranch was situated in the middle of a vast plain around three sides of which rose a grand amphitheatre of mountains. The nearest of them was some thirty miles away, yet ordinarily, in this clear, dry, Western atmosphere they were always imminent. Over their eastern ramparts the sun rose to look upon a chill and frosty world; behind their western barriers the sun withdrew, leaving soft air, purple shadows, and the flight of dim, far wildfowl across a saffron sky. To the north was only distance and the fading of the blue of the heavens to the pearl gray of the horizon.

So much if one stepped immediately beyond the ranch itself. The plains were broad. Here and there the flatness broke in a long, low line of cottonwoods marking the winding course of a slough or trace of subsoil water. Mesquite lay in dark patches; sagebrush; the green of pasture-land periodically overflowed by the irrigation water. Nearer at home were occasional great white oaks, or haystacks bigger than a house, and shaped like one.

To the distant eye the ranch was a grove of trees. Cottonwoods and eucalyptus had been planted and had thriven mightily on the abundant artesian water. We have already noticed the six or eight great trees growing fairly up through the house. On the outskirts lay also a fruit orchard of several hundred acres. Opposite the house, and separated from it by a cedar hedge, was a commodious and attractive bungalow for the foreman. Beyond him were the bunk house, cook houses, blacksmith shops, and the like.

We started our tour of inspection by examining and commenting gravely upon the dormant rose garden and equally dormant grape arbour. Through this we came to the big wire corrals in which were kept the dogs. Here I met old Ben.

Old Ben was not very old; but he was different from young Ben. He was a pointer of the old-fashioned, stocky-built, enduring type common—and serviceable—before our bench-show experts began to breed for speed, fineness, small size—and lack of stamina. Ben proved in the event to be a good all-round dog. He combined the attributes of pointer, cocker spaniel, and retriever. In other words, he would hunt quail in the orthodox fashion; or he would rustle into the mesquite thorns for the purpose of flushing them out to us; or he would swim anywhere any number of times to bring out ducks. To be sure he occasionally got a little mixed. At times he might try to flush quail in the open, instead of standing them; or would attempt to retrieve some perfectly lively specimens. Then Ben needed a licking; and generally got it. He lacked in his work some of the finish and style of the dogs we used after grouse in Michigan, but he was a good all-round dog for the work. Furthermore, he was most pleasant personally.

Next door to him lived the dachshunds.

The dachshunds were a marvel, a nuisance, a bone of contention, an anomaly, an accident, and a farce. They happened because somebody had once given the hostess a pair of them. I do not believe she cared particularly for them; but she is good natured, and the ranch is large, and they are rather amusing. At the time of my first visit the original pair had multiplied. Gazing on that yardful of imbecile-looking canines, my admiration for Noah's wisdom increased; he certainly needed no more than a pair to restock the earth. Redmond claimed there were twenty-two of them, though nobody else pretended to have been able to disentangle them enough for a census. They were all light brown in colour; and the aggregation reminded me of a rather disentangled bunch of angle-worms. They lived in a large enclosure; and emerged therefrom only under supervision, for they considered chickens and young pigs their especial prey. The Captain looked upon them with exasperated tolerance; Redmond with affection; the hostess, I think, with a good deal of the partisanship inspired not so much by liking as by the necessity of defending them against ridicule; and the rest of the world with amused expectation as to what they would do next. The Captain was continually uttering half-serious threats as to the different kinds of sudden death he was going to inflict on the whole useless, bandylegged, snipe-nosed, waggle-eared——

The best comment was offered last year by the chauffeur of the automobile. After gazing on the phenomenon of their extraordinary build for some moments he remarked thoughtfully:

"Those dogs have a mighty long wheel base!"

For some reason unknown two of the dachshunds have been elevated from the ranks, and have house privileges. Their names are respectively Pete and Pup. They hate each other, and have sensitive dispositions. It took me just four years to learn to tell them apart. I believe Pete has a slightly projecting short rib on his left side—or is it Pup? It was fatal to mistake.

"Hullo, Pup!" I would cry to one jovially.

"G—r—r—r—!" would remark the dog, retiring under the sofa. Thus I would know it was Pete. The worst of it was that said Pete's feelings were thereby lacerated so deeply that I was not forgiven all the rest of that day.

Beyond the dogs lay a noble enclosure so large that it would have been subdivided into building lots had it been anywhere else. It was inhabited by all sorts of fowl, hundreds of them, of all varieties. There were chickens, turkeys, geese, and a flock of ducks. The Captain pointed out the Rouen ducks, almost exactly like the wild mallards.

"Those are my live decoys," said he.

For the accommodation of this multitude were cities of nest houses, roost houses, and the like. Huge structures elevated on poles swarmed with doves. A duck pond even had been provided for its proper denizens.

Thus we reached the southernmost outpost of our quadrangle, and turned to the west, where an ancient Chinaman and an assistant cultivated minutely and painstakingly a beautiful vegetable garden. Tiny irrigation streams ran here and there, fitted with miniature water locks. Strange and foreign bamboo mattings, withes, and poles performed strange and foreign functions. The gardener, brown and old and wrinkled, his cue wound neatly beneath his tremendous, woven-straw umbrella of a hat, possessing no English, no emotion, no single ray of the sort of intelligence required to penetrate into our Occidental world, bent over his work. When we passed, he did not look up. He dwelt in a shed. At least, such it proved to be, when examined with the cold eye of analysis. In impression it was ancient, exotic, Mongolian, the abode of one of a mysterious and venerable race, a bit of foreign country. By what precise means this was accomplished it would be difficult to say. It is a fact well known to all Californians that a Chinaman can with no more extensive properties than a few pieces of red paper, a partition, a dingy curtain, and a varnished duck transform utterly an American tenement into a Chinese pagoda.

Thence we passed through a wicket and came to the abode of hogs. They dotted the landscape into the far distance, rooting about to find what they could; they lay in wallows; they heaped themselves along fences; they snorted and splashed in sundry shallow pools; a good half mile of maternal hogs occupied a row of kennels from which the various progeny issued forth between the bars. I cannot say I am much interested in hogs, but even I could dimly comprehend the Captain's attitude of swollen pride. They were clean, and black, and more nearly approximated the absurd hog advertisements than I had believed possible. You know the kind I mean; an almost exact rectangle on four short legs.

In the middle distance stood a long, narrow, thatched roof supported on poles. Beneath this, the Captain told me, were the beehives. They proved later to be in charge of a mild-eyed religious fanatic who believed the world to be flat.

We took a cursory glance at a barn filled to the brim with prunes; and the gushing, beautiful artesian well; at the men's quarters; the blacksmith shop, and all the rest. So we rounded the circle and came to the most important single feature of the ranch—the quarters for the horses.

A very long, deep shed, open on all sides, contained a double row of mangers facing each other, and divided into stalls. Here stood and were fed the working horses. By that I mean not only the mule and horse teams, but also the utility driving teams and the saddle horses used by the cowboys. Between each two stalls was a heavy pillar supporting the roof, and well supplied with facilities for hanging up the harness and equipments. As is usual in California, the sides and ends were open to the air; and the floor was simply the earth well bedded.

But over against this shed stood a big barn of the Eastern type. Here were the private equipments.

The Captain is a horseman. He breeds polo ponies after a formula of his own; and so successfully that many of them cross the Atlantic. On the ranch are always several hundred head of beautiful animals; and of these the best are kept up for the use of the Captain and his friends. We looked at them in their clean, commodious stalls; we inspected the harness and saddle room, glistening and satiny with polished metal and well-oiled leather; we examined the half dozen or so of vehicles of all descriptions. The hostess told with relish of her one attempt to be stylish.

"We had such beautiful horses," said she, "that I thought we ought to have something to go with them, so I sent up to the city for my brougham. It made a very neat turnout; and Tom was as proud of it as I was, but when it came to a question of proper garb for Tom I ran up against a deadlock. Tom refused point blank to wear a livery or anything approaching a livery. He was perfectly respectful about it; but he refused. Well, I drove around all that winter, when the weather was bad, in a well-appointed brougham drawn by a good team in a proper harness; and on the box sat a lean-faced cow puncher in sombrero, red handkerchief, and blue jeans!"

Tom led forth the horses one after the other—Kingmaker, the Fiddler, Pittapat, and the others. We spent a delightful two hours. The sun dropped; the shadows lengthened. From the fields the men began to come in. They drove the wagons and hay ricks into the spacious enclosure, and set leisurely about the task of caring for their animals. Chinese and Japanese drifted from the orchards, and began to manipulate the grindstone on their pruning knives. Presently a cowboy jogged in, his spurs and bit jingling. From the cook house a bell began to clang.

We turned back to the house. Before going in I faced the west. The sky had turned a light green full of lucence. The minor sounds of the ranch near by seemed to be surrounded by a sea of silence outside. Single sounds came very clearly across it. And behind everything, after a few moments, I made out a queer, monotonous background of half-croaking calling. For some time this puzzled me. Then at last my groping recollection came to my assistance. I was hearing the calling of myriads of snow geese.

---

CHAPTER IV

**THE EARLY BIRD**

I was awakened rather early by Redmond, who silently entered the room, lit a kerosene stove, closed the windows, and departed. As I was now beneath two blankets and an eiderdown quilt, and my nose was cold, I was duly grateful. Mistaking the rite for a signal to arise, I did so; and shortly descended. The three fireplaces were crackling away merrily, but they had done little to mitigate the atmosphere as yet. Maids were dusting and sweeping. The table was not yet set. Inquiry telling that breakfast was more than an hour later, I took a gun from the rack, pocketed the only five shells in sight, and departed to see what I could see.

The outer world was crisp with frost. I clambered over the corral fence, made my way through a hundred acres or so of slumbering pigs, and so emerged into the open country.

In the middle distance and perhaps a mile away was a low fringe of brush; to the left an equal distance a group of willows; and almost behind me a clump of cottonwoods. I resolved to walk over to the brush, swing around to the willows, turn to the cottonwoods, and so back to the ranch. It looked like about four miles or so. Perhaps with my five shells I might get something. At any rate, I would have a good walk.

The mountains were turning from the rose pink of early morning. I could hear again the bickering cries of the snow geese and sandhill cranes away in an unknown distance, the homelier calls of barnyard fowl nearer at hand. Cattle trotted before me and to right and left, their heads high, their gait swinging with the freedom of the half-wild animals of the ranges. After a few steps they turned to stare at me, eyes and nostrils wide, before making up their minds whether or not it would be wise to put a greater distance between me and them. The close sod was green and strong. It covered the slightly rounding irrigation "checks" that followed in many a curve and double the lines of contours on the flat plain.

The fringe of brush did not amount to anything; it was merely a convenient turning mark for my little walk. Arrived there, I executed a sharp "column left——"

Seven ducks leaped into the air apparently from the bare, open, and dry ground!

Every sportsman knows the scattering effect on the wits of the absolutely unexpected appearance of game. Every sportsman knows also the instinctive reactions that long habit will bring about. Thus, figuratively, I stood with open mouth, heart beating slightly faster, and mind making to itself such imbecile remarks as: "Well, *what* do you think of that! Who in blazes would have expected ducks here?" and other futile remarks. In the meantime, the trained part of me had jerked the gun off my shoulder, pushed forward the safety catch, and prepared for one hasty long shot at the last and slowest of the ducks. Now the instinctive part of one can do the preparations, but the actual shooting requires a more ordered frame of mind. By this time my wits had snapped back into place. I had the satisfaction of seeing the duck's outstretched neck wilt; of hearing him hit the ground with a thud somewhere beyond.

Marking the line of his fall, I stepped confidently forward, and without any warning whatever found myself standing on the bank of an irrigation ditch. It was filled to the brim with placid water on which floated a few downy feathers. On this side was dry sod; and on the other was dry sod. Nothing indicated the presence of that straight band of silvery water until one stood fairly at its brink. To the right I could see its sides narrow to the point of a remote perspective. To the left it ran for a few hundred yards, then apparently came to an abrupt stop where it turned at an angle.

In the meantime, my duck was on the other side; I was in my citizen's clothes.

No solution offered in sight, so I made my way to the left where I could look around the bend. Nearing the bend I was seized with a bright idea. I dropped back below the line of sight, sneaked quietly to the bank, and, my eye almost level with the water, peered down the new vista. Sure enough, not a hundred and fifty yards away floated another band of ducks.

I watched them for a moment until I was sure, by various small landmarks, of their exact location. Then I dropped back far enough so that, even standing erect, I would be below the line of vision of those ducks; strolled along until opposite my landmarks; then, bolt upright, walked directly forward, the gun at ready. When within twenty yards the ducks arose. It was, of course, easy shooting. Both fell across the ditch. That did not worry me; if worst came to worst I could strip and wade.

This seemed to be an exceedingly unique and interesting way to shoot ducks. To be sure, I had only two shells left; but then, it must be almost breakfast time. I repeated the feat a half mile farther on, discovered a flood gate over which I could get to the other side, collected my five ducks, and cut across country to the ranch. The sun was just getting in its work on the frost. Long files of wagons and men could be seen disappearing in the distance. I entered proudly, only ten minutes late.

---

## CHAPTER V

### QUAIL

The family assembled took my statement with extraordinary calm, contenting themselves with a general inquiry as to the species. I was just a trifle crestfallen at this indifference. You see at this time I was not accustomed to the casual duck. My shooting heretofore had been a very strenuous matter. It had involved arising many hours before sun-up, and venturing forth miles into wild marshes; and much endurance of cold and discomfort. To make a bag of any sort we were in the field before the folk knew the night had passed. Upland shooting meant driving long distances, and walking through the heavy hardwood swamps and slashes from dusk to dusk. Therefore I had considered myself in great luck to have blundered upon my ducks so casually; and, furthermore, from the family's general air of leisure and unpreparedness, jumped to the conclusion that no field sport was projected for that day.

Mrs. Kitty presided beside a copper coffee pot with a bell-shaped glass top. As this was also an institution, it merits attention. A small alcohol lamp beneath was lighted. For a long time nothing happened. Then all at once the glass dome clouded, was filled with frantic brown and racing bubbling. Thereupon the hostess turned over a sand glass. When the last grains had run through, the alcohol lamp was turned off. Immediately the glass dome was empty again. From a spigot one drew off coffee.

But if perchance the Captain and I wished to get up before anybody else could be hired to get up, the Dingbat could be so loaded as to give down an automatic breakfast. The evening before the maid charged the affair as usual, and at the last popped four eggs into the glass dome. After the mysterious alchemical perturbations had ceased, we fished out those eggs soft boiled to the second! One day the maid mistook the gasoline bottle for the alcohol bottle. That is a sad tale having to do with running flames, and burned table pieces, not to speak of a melted-down connection or so on the Dingbat. We did not know what was the matter; and our attitude was not so much that of alarm, as of grief and indignation that our good old tried and trained Dingbat should in his old age cut up any such didoes. Especially as there were new guests present.

After breakfast we wandered out on the verandah. Nobody seemed to be in any hurry to start anything. The hostess made remarks to Pollymckittrick; the General read a newspaper; the Captain sauntered about enjoying the sun. After fifteen minutes, as though the notion had just occurred, somebody suggested that we go shooting.

"How about it?" the Captain asked me.

"Surely," I agreed, and added with some surprise out of my other experience, "Isn't it a little late?"

But the Captain misunderstood me.

"I don't mean blind shooting," said he, "just ram around."

He seized a megaphone and bellowed through it at the stables.

"Better get on your war paint," he suggested to me.

I changed hastily into my shooting clothes, and returned to the verandah. After some few moments the Captain joined me. After some few moments more a tremendous rattling came from the stable. A fine bay team swung into the driveway, rounded the circle, and halted. It drew the source of the tremendous rattling.

Thus I became acquainted with the Liver Invigorator. The Invigorator was a buckboard high, wide, and long. It had one wide seat. Aft of that seat was a cage with bars, in which old Ben rode. Astern was a deep box wherein one carried rubber boots, shells, decoys, lunch, game, and the like. The Invigorator was very old, very noisy, and very able. With it we drove cheerfully anywhere we pleased—over plowed land, irrigation checks, through brush thick enough to lift our wheels right off the ground, and down into and out of water ditches so steep that we alternately stood the affair on its head and its tail, and so deep that we had to hold all our belongings in our arms, while old Ben stuck his nose out the top bars of his cage for a breath of air. It could not be tipped over; at least we never upset it. To offset these virtues it rattled like a runaway milk wagon; and it certainly hit the high spots and hit them *hard*. Nevertheless, in a long and strenuous sporting career the Invigorator became endeared through association to many friends. When the Captain proposed a new vehicle with easier springs and less noise, a wail of protest arose from many and distant places. The Invigorator still fulfills its function.

Now there are three major topics on the Ranch: namely, ducks, quail, and ponies. In addition to these are five of minor interest: the mail, cattle, jackrabbits, coons, and wildcats.

I was already familiar with the valley quail, for I had hunted him since I was a small boy with the first sixteen-gauge gun ever brought to the coast. I knew him for a very speedy bird, much faster than our bob white, dwelling in the rounded sagebrush hills, travelling in flocks of from twenty to several thousand, exceedingly given to rapid leg work. We had to climb hard after him, and shoot like lightning from insecure footing. His idiosyncrasies were as strongly impressed on me as the fact that human beings walk upright. Here, however, I had to revise my ideas.

We drove down the avenue of palms, pursued by four or five yapping dachshunds, and so out into a long, narrow lane between pasture fences. Herds of ponies, fuzzy in their long winter coats, came gently to look at us. The sun was high now, so the fur of their backs lay flat. Later, in the chill of evening, the hair would stand out like the nap of velvet, thus providing for additional warmth by the extra air space between the outside of the coat and the skin. It must be very handy to carry this invisible overcoat, ready for the moment's need. Here, too, were cattle standing about. On many of them I recognized the familiar J-I brand of many of my Arizona experiences. Arizona bred and raised them; California fattened them for market. We met a cowboy jingling by at his fox trot; then came to the country road.

Along this we drove for some miles. The country was perfectly flat, but variegated by patches of greasewood, of sagebrush, of Egyptian-corn fields, and occasionally by a long, narrow fringe of trees. Here, too, were many examples of that phenomenon so vigorously doubted by most Easterners: the long rows of trees grown from original cotton wood or poplar fence posts. In the distance always were the mountains. Overhead the sky was very blue. A number of buzzards circled.

After a time we turned off the road and into a country covered over with tumbleweed, a fine umber red growth six or eight inches high, and scattered sagebrush. Inlets, bays, and estuaries of bare ground ran everywhere. The Captain stood up to drive, watching for the game to cross these bare places.

I stood up, too. It is no idle feat to ride the Invigorator thus over hummocky ground. It lurched and bumped and dropped into and out of trouble; and in correspondence I alternately rose up and sat down again, hard. The Captain rode the storm without difficulty. He was accustomed to the Invigorator; and, too, he had the reins to hang on by.

"There they go!" said he, suddenly, bringing the team to a halt.

I looked ahead. Across a ten-foot barren ran the quail, their crests cocked forward, their trim figures held close as a sprinter goes, rank after rank, their heads high in the alert manner of quail.

The Captain sat down, jerked off the brake, and spoke to his horses. I sat down, too; mainly because I had to. The Invigorator leaped from hump to hump. Before those quail knew it we were among them. Right, left, all around us they roared into the air. Some doubled back; some buzzed low to right or left; others rose straight ahead to fly a quarter mile, and then, wings set, to sail another quarter until finally they pitched down into some bit of inviting cover.

The Captain brought his horses to a stand with great satisfaction. We congratulated each other gleefully; and even old Ben, somewhat shaken up in his cage astern, wagged his tail in appreciation of the situation.

For, you see, we had scattered the covey, and now they would lie. If the band had flushed, flown, and lighted as one body, immediately on hitting the ground they would have put their exceedingly competent little legs into action, and would have run so well and so far that, by the time we had arrived on the spot, they would have been a good half mile away. But now that the covey was broken, the individuals and small bands would stay put. If they ran at all, it would be for but a short distance. On this preliminary scattering depends the success of a chase after California quail. I have seen six or eight men empty both barrels of their guns at a range of more than a hundred yards. They were not insane enough to think they would get anything. Merely they hoped that the racket and the dropping of the spent shot would break the distant covey.

We hitched the horses to a tree, released old Ben, and started forth.

For a half hour we had the most glorious sport, beating back and forth over the ground again and again. The birds lay well in the low cover, and the shooting was clean and open. I soon found that the edges of the bare ground were the most likely places. Apparently the birds worked slowly through the cover ahead of us, but hesitated to cross the open spots, and so bunched at the edge. By walking in a zigzag along some of these borders, we gathered in many scattered birds and small bunches. Why the zigzag? Naturally it covers a trifle more ground than a straight course, but principally it seems to confuse the game. If you walk in a straight line, so the quail can foretell your course, it is very apt either to flush wild or to hide so close that you pass it by. The zigzag fools it.

Thus, with varying luck, we made a slow circle back to the wagon. Here we found Mrs. Kitty and Carrie and the lunch awaiting us with the ponies.

These robust little animals were not miniature horses, but genuine ponies, with all the deviltry, endurance, and speed of their kind. They were jet-black, about waist high, and of great intelligence. They drew a neat little rig, capable of accommodating two, at a persistent rapid patter that somehow got over the road at a great gait. And they could keep it up all day. Although perfectly gentle, they were as alert as gamins for mischief, and delighted hugely in adding to the general row and confusion if anything happened to go wrong. Mrs. Kitty drove them everywhere. One day she attempted to cross an irrigation ditch that proved to be deeper than she had thought it. The ponies disappeared utterly, leaving Mrs. Kitty very much astonished. Horses would have drowned in like circumstances, but the ponies, nothing daunted, dug in their hoofs and scrambled out like a pair of dogs, incidentally dipping their mistress on the way.

In the shade of a high greasewood we unpacked the pony carriage. This was before the days of thermos bottles, so we had a most elaborate wicker basket whose sides let down to form a wind shield protecting an alcohol burner and a kettle. When the water boiled, we made hot tea, and so came to lunch.

Strangely enough this was my first experience at having lunch brought out to the field. Ordinarily we had been accustomed to carry a sandwich or so in the side pockets of our shooting coats, which same we ate at any odd moment that offered. Now was disclosed an astonishing variety. There were sandwiches, of course, and a salad, and the tea, but wonderful to contemplate was a deep dish of potted quail, row after row of them, with delicious white sauce. In place of the frugal bite or so that would have left us alert and fit for an afternoon's work, we ate until nothing remained. Then we lit pipes and lay on our backs, and contemplated a cloudless sky. It was the warm time of day. The horses snoozed, a hind leg tucked up; old Ben lay outstretched in doggy content; Mrs. Kitty knit or crocheted or something of that sort; and Carrie and the Captain and I took cat naps. At length, the sun's rays no longer striking warm from overhead, the Captain aroused us sternly.

"You're a nice, energetic, able lot of sportsmen!" he cried with indignation. "Have I got to wait until sunset for you lazy chumps to get a full night's rest?"

"Don't mind him," Mrs. Kitty told me, placidly; "he was sound asleep himself; and the only reason he waked is because he snored and I *punched* him."

She folded up her fancy work, shook out her skirts, and turned to the ponies.

It was now late in the afternoon. We had disgracefully wasted our time, and enjoyed doing it. The Captain decided it to be too late to hunt up a new covey, so we reversed to pick up some of those that had originally doubled back. We flushed forty or fifty of them at the edge of the road. They scattered ahead of us in a forty-acre plowed field.

Until twilight, then, we walked leisurely back and forth, which is the only way to walk in a plowed field, after all. The birds had pitched down into the old furrows, and whenever a tuft of grass, a piece of tumbleweed, or a shallow grassy ditch offered a handful of cover, there the game was to be found. Mrs. Kitty followed at the Captain's elbow, and Carrie at mine. Carrie made a first-rate dog, marking down the birds unerringly. The quail flew low and hard, offering in the gathering twilight and against the neutral-coloured earth marks worthy of good shooting. At last we turned back to our waiting team. The dusk was coming over the land, and the "shadow of the earth" was marking its strange blue arc in the east. As usual the covey was now securely scattered. Of a thousand or so birds we had bagged forty-odd; and yet of the remainder we would have had difficulty in flushing another dozen. It is the mystery of the quail, and one that the sportsman can never completely comprehend. As we clambered into the Invigorator we could hear from all directions the birds signalling each other. Near, far, to right, to left, the call sounded, repeating over and over again a parting, defiant denial that the victory was ours.

"You *can't* shoot! You *can't* shoot! You *can't* shoot!"

And nearer at hand the contented chirping twitter as the covey found itself.

---

# CHAPTER VI

## PONIES

Next morning the Captain decided that he had various affairs to attend to, so we put on our riding clothes and went down to the stables.

The Captain had always forty or fifty polo ponies in the course of education, and he was delighted to have them ridden, once he was convinced of your seat and hands. They were beautiful ponies, generally iron gray in colour, very friendly, very eager, and very lively. Riding them was like flying through the air, for they sailed over rough ground, irrigation checks, and the like without a break in their stride, and without a jar. By the same token it was necessary to ride them. At odd moments they were quite likely to give a wide sidewise bound or a stiff-legged buck from sheer joy of life. One got genuine "horse exercise" out of them.

The Captain, as perhaps I have said, invented these ponies himself. From Chihuahua he brought in some of the best mustang mares he could find; and, in case you have Frederick Remington's pictures of starved winter-range animals in mind, let me tell you a good mustang is a very handsome animal indeed. These he bred to a thoroughbred. The resulting half-breeds grew to the proper age. Then he started to have them broken to the saddle. A start was as far as he ever got, for nobody could ride them. They combined the intelligence and vice of the mustang with the endurance and nervous instability of the thoroughbred. The Captain tried all sorts of men, even sending at last to Arizona for a good bronco buster on the J-I. Only one or two of the many could back the animals at all, though many aspirants made a try at it. After a long series of experiments, the Captain came to the reluctant conclusion that the cross was no good. It seemed a pity, for they were beautiful animals, up to full polo size, deep chested, strong shouldered, close coupled, and speedy.

Then, by way of idleness, he bred some of the half-bred mares. The three-quarter cross proved to be ideal. They were gentle, easily broken, and to the eye differed in no particular from their pure-blooded brothers. So, ever since, the Captain has been raising these most excellent polo ponies to his great honour and profit and the incidental pleasure of his friends who like riding.

One of these ponies was known as the Merry Jest. He had a terrifying but harmless trick. The moment the saddle was cinched, down went his head and he began to buck in the most vicious style. This he would keep up until further orders. In order to put an end to the performance all one had to do was to haul in on the rope, thrust one's foot in the stirrup, and clamber aboard. For, mark you this, Merry Jest in the course of a long and useful life never failed to buck under the empty saddle—and *never* bucked under a rider!

This, of course, constituted the Merry Jest. Its beauty was that it was so safe.

"Want to ride?" asked the Captain.

"Surely," replied the unsuspecting stranger.

The Merry Jest was saddled, brought forth, and exhibited in action.

"There's your horse," remarked the Captain in a matter-of-course tone.

We rode out the corral gate and directly into the open country. The animals chafed to be away; and when we loosened the reins, leaped forward in long bounds. Over the rough country they skimmed like swallows, their hoofs hardly seeming to touch the ground, the powerful muscles playing smoothly beneath us like engines. After a mile of this we pulled up, and set about the serious business of the day.

One after another we oversaw all the major activities of such a ranch; outside, I mean, of the ranch enclosure proper where were the fowls, the vegetable gardens, and the like. Here an immense hay rick was being driven slowly along while two men pitched off the hay to right and left. After it followed a long line of cattle. This manner of feeding obviated the crowding that would have taken place had the hay not been thus scattered. The more aggressive followed close after the rick, snatching mouthfuls of the hay as it fell. The more peaceful, or subdued, or philosophical strung out in a long, thin line, eating steadily at one spot. They got more hay with less trouble, but the other fellows had to maintain reputations for letting nobody get ahead of *them*!

At another point an exceedingly rackety engine ran a hay press, where the constituents of one of the enormous house-like haystacks were fed into a hopper and came out neatly baled. A dozen or so men oversaw the activities of this noisy and dusty machine.

Down by the northerly cottonwoods two miles away we found other men with scrapers throwing up the irrigation checks along the predetermined contour lines. By means of these irregular meandering earthworks the water, admitted from the ditch to the upper end of the field, would work its way slowly from level to level instead of running off or making channels for itself. This job, too, was a dusty one. We could see the smoke of it rising from a long distance; and the horses and men were brown with it.

And again we rode softly for miles over greensward through the cattle, at a gentle fox trot, so as not to disturb them. At several points stood great blue herons, like sentinels, decorative as a Japanese screen, absolutely motionless. The Captain explained that they were "fishing" for gophers; and blessed them deeply. Sometimes our mounts splashed for a long distance through water five or six inches shallow. Underneath the surface we could see the short green grass of the turf that thus received its refreshment. Then somewhere near, silhouetted against the sky or distant mountains, on the slight elevation of the irrigation ditch bank, we were sure to see some of the irrigation Chinamen. They were strange, exotic figures, their skins sunburned and dark, their queues wound around their heads; wearing always the same uniform of blue jeans cut China-fashion, rubber boots, and the wide, inverted bowl Chinese sun hat of straw. By means of shovels wherewith to dig, and iron bars wherewith to raise and lower flood gates, they controlled the artificial rainfall of the region. So accustomed did the ducks become to these amphibious people that they hardly troubled themselves to get out of the way, and were utterly careless of how near they flew. Uncle Jim once disguised himself as an irrigation Chinaman and got all kinds of shooting—until the ducks found him out. Now they seem able to distinguish accurately between a Chinaman with a long shovel and a white man with a shotgun, no matter how the latter is dressed. Ducks, tame and wild, have a lot of sense. It must bore the former to be forced to associate with chickens.

Over in the orchard, of a thousand acres or so, were many more Orientals, and hundreds of wild doves. These Chinese were all of the lower coolie orders, and primitive, not to say drastic in their medical ideas. One evening the Captain heard a fine caterwauling and drum beating over in the quarters, and sallied forth to investigate. In one of the huts he found four men sitting on the outspread legs and arms of a fifth. The latter had been stripped stark naked. A sixth was engaged in placing live coals on the patient's belly, while assorted assistants furnished appropriate music and lamentation. The Captain put a stop to the proceedings and bundled the victim to a hospital where he promptly died. It was considered among Chinese circles that the Captain had killed him by ill-timed interference!

Everywhere we went, and wherever a small clump of trees or even large brush offered space, hung the carcasses of coyotes, wildcats, and lynx. Some were quite new, while others had completely mummified in the dry air of these interior plains. These were the trophies of the professional "varmint killer," a man hired by the month. Of course it would be only too easy for such an official to loaf on his job, so this one had adopted the unique method of proving his activity. Everywhere the Captain rode he could see that his man had been busy.

All this time we had been working steadily away from the ranch. Long zigzags and side trips carried us little forward, and a constant leftward tendency swung us always around, until we had completed a half circle of which the ranch itself was the centre. The irrigated fields had given place to open country of a semi-desert character grown high with patches of greasewood, sagebrush, thorn-bush; with wide patches of scattered bunch grass; and stretches of alkali waste. Here, unexpectedly to me, we stumbled on a strange but necessary industry incidental to so large an estate. Our nostrils were assailed by a mighty stink. We came around the corner of some high brush directly on a small two-story affair with a factory smokestack. It was fenced in, and the fence was covered with drying hides. I will spare you details, but the function of the place was to make glue, soap, and the like of those cattle whose term of life was marked by misfortune rather than by the butcher's knife. The sole workman at this economical and useful occupation did not seem to mind it. The Captain claimed he was as good as a buzzard at locating the newly demised.

Our ponies did not like the place either. They snorted violently, and pricked their ears back and forth, and were especially relieved and eager to obey when we turned their heads away.

We rode on out into the desert, our ponies skipping expertly through the low brush and gingerly over the alkali crust of the open spaces beneath which might be holes. Jackrabbits by the thousand, literally, hopped away in front of us, spreading in all directions as along the sticks of a fan. They were not particularly afraid, so they loped easily in high-bounding leaps, their ears erect. Many of them sat bolt upright, looking at least two feet high. Occasionally we managed really to scare one, and then it was a grand sight to see him open the throttle and scud away, his ears flat back, in the classical and correct attitude of the constantly recurring phrase of the ancients: "belly to earth he flew!"

Jackrabbits are a great nuisance. The Captain had to enclose his precious alfalfa fields with rabbit-proof wire to prevent utter destruction. There was a good deal of fence, naturally, and occasionally the inquiring rabbit would find a hole and crawl through. Then he was in alfalfa, which is, as every Californian knows, much better than being in clover. He ate at first greedily, then more daintily, wandering always farther afield in search of dessert. Never, however, did he forget the precise location of the opening by which he had entered, as was wise of him. For now, behold, enter the dogs. Ordinarily these dogs, who were also wise beasts, passed by the jackrabbit in his abundance with only inhibited longing. Their experience had taught them that to chase jackrabbits in the open with any motive ulterior to that of healthful exercise and the joy of seeing the blame things run was as vain and as puppish as chasing one's tail. But in the alfalfa fields was a chance, for it must be remembered that such fields were surrounded by the rabbit-proof wire in which but a single opening was known to the jack in question. Therefore, with huge delight, the dogs gave chase. Mr. Rabbit bolted back for his opening, his enemies fairly at his heels. Now comes the curious part of the episode. The dogs knew perfectly well that if the rabbit hit the hole in the fence he was safe for all of them; and they had learned, further, that if the rabbit missed his plunge for safety he would collide strongly with that tight-strung wire. When within twenty feet or so of the fence they stopped short in expectation. Probably three times out of five the game made his plunge in safety and scudded away over the open plain outside. Then the dogs turned and trotted philosophically back to the ranch. But the other two times the rabbit would miss. At full speed he would hit the tight-strung mesh, only to be hurled back by its resiliency fairly into the jaws of his waiting pursuers. Though thousands may consider this another nature-fake, I shall always have the comfort of thinking that the Captain and the dogs know it for the truth.

At times jackrabbits get some sort of a plague and die in great numbers. Indeed some years at the ranch they seemed almost to have disappeared. Their carcasses are destroyed almost immediately by the carrion creatures, and their delicate bones, scattered by the ravens, buzzards, and coyotes, soon disintegrate and pass into the soil. One does not find many evidences of the destruction that has been at work; yet he will see tens instead of myriads. I have been at the ranch when one was never out of sight of jackrabbits, in droves, and again I have been there when one would not see a half dozen in a morning's ride. They recover their numbers fast enough, and the chances are that this "narrow-gauge mule" will be always with us. The ranchman would like nothing better than to bid him a last fond but genuine farewell; but I should certainly miss him.

The greasewood and thorn-bush grew in long, narrow patches. The ragweed grew everywhere it pleased, affording grand cover for the quail. The sagebrush occurred singly at spaced intervals, with tiny bare spaces between across which the plumed little rascals scurried hurriedly. The tumbleweed banked high wherever, in the mysterious dispensations of Providence, a call for tumbleweed had made itself heard.

The tumbleweed is a curious vegetable. It grows and flourishes amain, and becomes great even as a sagebrush, and puts forth its blossoms and seeds, and finally turns brown and brittle. Just about as you would conclude it has reached a respectable old age and should settle down by its chimney corner, it decides to go travelling. The first breath of wind that comes along snaps it off close to the ground. The next turns it over. And then, inasmuch as the tumbleweed is roughly globular in shape, some three or four feet in diameter, and exceedingly light in structure, over and over it rolls across the plain! If the wind happens to increase, the whole flock migrates, bounding merrily along at a good rate of speed. Nothing more terrifying to the unaccustomed equine can be imagined than thirty or forty of these formidable-looking monsters charging down upon him, bouncing several feet from the surface of the earth. The experienced horse treats them with the contempt such light-minded senility deserves, and wades through their phantom attack indifferent. After the breeze has died the debauched old tumbleweeds are everywhere to be seen, piled up against brush, choking the ditches, filling the roads. Their beautiful spherical shapes have been frayed out so that they look sodden and weary and done up. But their seeds have been scattered abroad over the land.

Wherever we found water, there we found ducks. The irrigating ditches contained many bands of a dozen or fifteen; the overflow ponds had each its little flock. The sky, too, was rarely empty of them; and the cries of the snow geese and the calls of sandhill cranes were rarely still. I remarked on this abundance.

"Ducks!" replied the Captain, wonderingly. "Why, you haven't *begun* to see ducks! Come with me."

Thereupon we turned sharp to the left. After ten minutes I made out from a slight rise above the plain a black patch lying across the distance. It seemed to cover a hundred acres or so, and to represent a sort of growth we had not before encountered.

"That," said the Captain, indicating, "is a pond covered with ducks."

I did not believe it. We dropped below the line of sight and rode steadily forward.

All at once a mighty roar burst on our ears, like the rush of a heavy train over a high trestle; and immediately the air ahead of us was filled with ducks towering. They mounted, and wheeled, and circled back or darted away. The sky became fairly obscured with them in the sense that it seemed inconceivable that hither space could contain another bird. Before the retina of the eye they swarmed exactly as a nearer cloud of mosquitoes would appear.

Hardly had the shock of this first stupendous rise of wildfowl spent itself before another and larger flight roared up. It seemed that all the ducks in the world must be a-wing; and yet, even after that, a third body arose, its rush sounding like the abrupt, overwhelming noise of a cataract in a sudden shift of wind. I should be afraid to guess how many ducks had been on that lake. Its surface was literally covered, so that nowhere did a glint of water show. I suppose it would be a simple matter to compute within a few thousand how many ducks would occupy so much space; but of what avail? Mere numbers would convey no impression of the effect. Rather fill the cup of heaven with myriads thick as a swarm of gnats against the sun. They swung and circled back and forth before making up their minds to be off, crossing and recrossing the various lines of flight. The first thrice-repeated roar of rising had given place to the clear, sustained whistling of wings, low, penetrating, inspiring. In the last flight had been a band of several hundred snow geese; and against the whiteness of their plumage the sun shone.

"That," observed the Captain with conviction, "is what you might call ducks."

By now it was the middle of the afternoon. We had not thought of lunch. At the ranch lunch was either a major or a minor consideration; there was no middle ground. If possible, we ate largely of many most delicious things. If, on the other hand, we happened to be out somewhere at noon, we cheerfully omitted lunch. So, when we returned to the ranch, the Captain, after glancing at his watch and remarking that it was rather late to eat, proposed that we try out two other ponies with the polo mallets.

This we proceeded to do. After an hour's pleasant exercise on the flat in the "Enclosure," we jogged contentedly back into the corral.

Around the corner of the barn sailed a distracted and utterly stampeded hen. After her, yapping eagerly, came five dachshunds.

Pause and consider the various elements of outrage the situation presented. (A) Dachshunds are, as before quoted, a bunch of useless, bandylegged, snip-nosed, waggle-eared——, anyway, and represent an amiable good-natured weakness on the part of Mrs. Kitty. (B) Dachshunds in general are *not* supposed to run wild all over the place, but to remain in their perfectly good, sufficiently large, entirely comfortable corral, Pete and Pup excepted. (C) Chickens are valuable. (D) Confound 'em! This sort of a performance will be a bad example for Young Ben. First thing we'll know, he'll be chasing chickens, too!

The Captain dropped from his pony and joined the procession. The hen could run just a trifle faster than the dachshunds; and the dachshunds just a trifle faster than the Captain. I always claimed they circled the barn three times, in the order named. The Captain insists with dignity that I exaggerate three hundred per cent. At any rate, the hen finally blundered, the dachshunds fell upon her—and the Captain swung his polo mallet.

Five typical "sickening thuds" were heard; five dachshunds literally sailed through the air to fall in quivering heaps. The Captain, his anger cooled, came back, shaking his head.

"I wouldn't have killed those dogs for anything in the world!" he muttered half to me, half to himself as we took the path to the house. "I don't know what Mrs. Kitty will say to this! I certainly am sorry about it!" and so on, at length.

We turned the corner of the hedge. There in a row on the top step of the verandah sat five dachshunds, their mouths open in a happy smile, six inches of pink tongue hanging, their eyes half closed in good-humoured appreciation.

The Captain approached softly and looked them over with great care. He felt of their ribs. He stared up at me incredulously.

"Is this the same outfit?" he whispered.

"It is," said I, "I know the blaze-face brute."

"But—but——"

"They played 'possum on you, Captain."

The Captain arose and his wrath exploded.

"You miserable hounds!" he roared.

With a wise premonition they decamped.

"I'm going to clean out the whole bandylegged tribe!" threatened the Captain for the fiftieth time in the month. "I won't have them on the ranch!"

That was seven years ago. They are still there—they and numerous descendants.[G]

---

## CHAPTER VII

### DINNER

We washed up and came down stairs. All at once it proved to be drowsy time. The dark had fallen and the lamps were lit. A new fire crackled in the fireplace, anticipating the chill that was already descending. Carrie played the piano in the other room. The General snorted over something in his city paper. Mrs. Kitty had disappeared on household business. Pete and Pup, having been mistaken one for the other by some innocent bystander, gloomed and glowered under chairs.

Both the Captain and myself made some sort of a pretence of reading the papers. It was only a pretence. The grateful warmth, the soothing crackling of the fire, the distant music—and, possibly, our state of starvation—lulled us to a half doze. From this we were aroused by an announcement of dinner.

We had soup and various affairs of that sort; and there was brought on a huge and baronial roast, from which the Captain promptly proceeded to slice generous allowances. With it came vegetables. They were all cooked in cream; not milk, but rich top cream thick enough to cut with a knife. I began to see why all the house servants were plump. Also there were jellies, and little fat hot rolls, and strange pickled products of the soil. I was good and hungry; and I ate thereof.

The plates were removed. I settled back with a sigh of repletion——

The door opened to admit the waitress bearing a huge platter on which reposed, side by side, five ducks. That meant a whole one apiece! To my feeble protest the family turned indignantly.

"Of course you must eat your duck!" Mrs. Kitty settled the whole question at last.

So I ate my duck. It was a very good duck; as indeed it should have been, for it was fattened on Egyptian corn, hung the exact number of days, and cooked by Charley. It had a little spout of celery down which I could pour the abundant juice from its inside; and it was flanked right and left respectively by a piece of lemon liberally sprinkled with red pepper and sundry crisp slabs of fried hominy. Every night of the shooting season each member of the household had "his duck." Later I was shown the screened room wherein hung the game, each dated by a little tag.

After I had made way with most of my duck, and other things, and had had my coffee, and had lighted a cigar, I was entirely willing to sink back to disgraceful ease. But the Captain suddenly developed an inexcusable and fiendish energy.

"No, you don't," said he. "You come with me and Redmond and get out the decoys."

"What for?" I temporized, feebly.

"To keep the moths out of them, of course," replied the Captain with fine sarcasm. "Do you mean to tell me that you can sit still and do nothing after seeing all those ducks this afternoon? You're a fine sportsman! Brace up!"

"Let me finish this excellent cigar," I pleaded. "You gave it to me."

To this he assented. Carrie went back to the piano. The lights were dim. Mrs. Kitty went on finishing her crochet work or whatever it was. Nobody said anything for a long time. The Captain was busy in the gun room with one of the ranch foremen.

But this could not last, and at length I was haled forth to work.

The crisp, sharp air beneath the frosty stars, after the tepid air within, awakened me like the shock of cold water. Redmond was awaiting us with a lantern. By the horse block lay the mass of something indeterminate which I presently saw to be sacks full of something knobby.

"I have six sacks of wooden decoys," said Redmond, "with weights all on them."

The Captain nodded and passed on. We made our way down past the grape arbour, opened the high door leading into chickenville, and stopped at the border of the little pond. On its surface floated a hundred or so tame ducks of all descriptions. By means of clods of earth we woke them up. They came ashore and waddled without objection to a little inclosure. We followed them and shut the gate.

One after another the Captain indicated those he wished to take with him on the morrow. Redmond caught them, inserted them in gunny sacks, two to the sack. They made no great objection to being caught. One or two youngsters flopped and flapped about, and had to be chased into a corner. In general, however, they accepted the situation philosophically, and snuggled down contentedly in their sacks.

"They are used to it," the Captain explained. "Most of these Rouen ducks are old hands at the business; they know what to expect."

He was very particular as to the colouring of the individuals he selected. A single white feather was sufficient to cause the rejection of a female; and even when the colour scheme was otherwise perfect, too light a shade proved undesired.

"I don't know just why it is," said he, "but the wild ducks are a lot more particular about the live decoys than about the wooden. A wooden decoy can be all knocked to pieces, faded and generally disreputable, but it does well enough; but a live decoy must look the part absolutely. That gives us six apiece; I think it will be enough."

Redmond took charge of our capture. We left him with the lantern, stowing away the decoys, live and inanimate, in the Invigorator. Within fifteen minutes thereafter I was sleeping the sleep of the moderately tired and the fully fed.

---

CHAPTER VIII

DUCKS

The Captain rapped on my door. It was pitch dark, and the wind, which had arisen during the night, was sweeping through the open windows, blowing the light curtains about. Also it was very cold.

"All right," I answered, took my resolution in my hands, and stepped forth.

Ten minutes later, by the light of a single candle, we were manipulating the coffee-and-egg machine, and devouring the tall pile of bread-and-butter sandwiches that had been left for us over night. Then, stepping as softly as we could in our clumping rubber boots, our arms burdened with guns and wraps, we stole into the outer darkness.

It was almost black, but we could dimly make out the treetops whipped about by the wind. Over by the stable we caught the intermittent flashes of many lanterns where the teamsters were feeding their stock. Presently a merry and vigorous *rattle—rattle—rattle* arose and came nearer. The Invigorator was ready and under way.

We put on all the coats and sweaters, and climbed aboard. The Captain spoke to his horses, and we were off.

That morning I had my first experience of a phenomenon I have never ceased admiring—and wondering at. I refer to the Captain's driving in the dark.

The night was absolutely black, so that I could hardly make out the horses. In all the world were only two elements, the sky full of stars and the mass of the earth. The value of this latter, as a means of showing us where we were, was nullified by the fact that the skyline consisted, not of recognizable and serviceable landmarks, but of the distant mountains. We went a certain length of time, and bumped over a certain number of things. Then the Captain pulled his team sharp around to the left. Why he did so I could not tell you. We drove an hour over a meandering course.

"Hang tight," remarked the Captain.

I did so. The front end of the Invigorator immediately fell away from under me, so that if I had not been obeying orders by hanging tight I should most certainly have plunged forward against the horses. We seemed to slide and slither down a steep declivity, then hit water with a splash, and began to flounder forward. The water rose high enough to cover the floor of the Invigorator, causing the Captain to speculate on whether Redmond had packed in the shells properly. Then the bow rose with a mighty jerk and we scrambled out the other side.

"That's the upper ford on the Slough," observed the Captain, calmly.

Everywhere else along the Slough, as I subsequently discovered, the banks fell off perpendicular, the water was deep, and the bottom soft. The approach was down no fenced lane, but across the open, with no other landmarks even in daylight than the break of low willows and cottonwoods exactly like a hundred others. Ten minutes later the Captain drew rein.

"Here you are," said he, cautiously. "You can dump your stuff off right here. I can't get through the fence with the team; but it's only a short distance to carry."

Accordingly, in entire faith, I descended and unloaded my three sacks of wooden decoys and my three sacks of live ducks and my gun and shells.

"I'll drive on to another hole," said the Captain. "Good luck!"

"Would you mind," I suggested, meekly, "telling me in which direction this mythical fence is situated; what kind of a fence it is; and where I carry to when I get through it?"

The Captain chuckled.

"Why," he explained, "the fence is straight ahead of you; and it's barbed wire; and as for where you're headed, you'll find the pond where we saw all those ducks last night about a hundred yards or so west."

Where we saw all those ducks! My blood increased its pace through my veins. Now that I was afoot, I could begin to make out things in the starlight—the silhouettes of bushes or brush, and even three or four posts of the fence.

The Invigorator rattled into the distance. I got my stuff the other side of the wires, and, shouldering a sack, plodded away due west.

But now I made out the pond gleaming; and by this and by the dim grayness of the earth immediately about me knew that dawn was at last under way. The night had not yet begun to withdraw, but its first strength was going. Objects in the world about became, not visible, but existent. By the time I had carried my last load the rather liberal hundred yards to the shores of the pond the eastern sky had banished its stars.

My movements had, of course, alarmed the ducks. There were not many of them, as I could judge by the whistling of their departing wings and by the silvery furrows where they had left the water. It is curious how strong the daylight must become before the eye can distinguish a duck in flight. The comparative paucity of numbers, I reflected, was probably due to the fact that the ducks used this pond merely as a loafing place during the day. Therefore I should anticipate a good flight as soon as feeding time should be over; especially as one end of the pond proved to be fairly well sheltered from the high wind.

At once I set to work to build me a blind. This I constructed of tumbleweed and willow shoots, with a lucky sagebrush as a good basis. I made it thick below and thin on top, so I could crouch hidden, and rise easily to shoot. Also I made it hastily, working away with a concentration that would prove very valuable could it be brought to a useful line of work. There can nothing equal the busyness of a man hastening to perfect his arrangements before a flight of ducks is due to start. Every few moments I would look anxiously up to see how things were going with the morning. The light was indubitably increasing. That is to say, I could make out the whole width of the pond, for example, although the farther banks were still in silhouette, and the sky was almost free of stars. Also the perpendicular plane of the mountains to the west, in some subtle manner, was beginning to break. It was not yet daylight; but the dawn was here.

I reached cautiously into one of the sacks and brought forth one of the decoy ducks. Around his neck I buckled a little leather collar to a ring in which had been attached a cord and weight. Then I cautiously waded out and anchored him.

He was delighted, and proceeded immediately to take a bath, ducking his head under and out again, ruffling his wings, and wagging his absurd little tail. Apparently the whole experience was a matter of course to him; but he was willing to show pleasure that this phase of it was over. I anchored out his five companions, and then proceeded to arrange the wooden decoys artistically around the outskirts. By now it was quite genuinely early daylight. Three times the overhead whistle of wings had warned me to hurry; and twice small flocks of ducks had actually swung down within range only to discover me at the last moment and tower away again. When younger, I used, at such junctures, to rush for my gun. That is a puppy stage, for by the time you get your gun those ducks are gone; and by the time you have regained your abandoned task more ducks are in. Therefore one early learns that when he goes out from his blind to pick up ducks, or catch cripples, or arrange decoys, he would better do so, paying no attention whatever to the game that will immediately appear. So now the whistle of wings merely caused me to work the faster. At length I was able to wade ashore and sink into my blind.

Immediately, as usual, the flights ceased for the time being. I had nothing to do but sit tight and wait.

This was no unpleasant task. The mountains to the west had become lucent, and glowed pink in the dawn; those to the east looked like silhouettes of very thin slate-coloured cardboard stuck up on edge, across which a pearl wash had been laid. The flatter world of the plains all about me lay half revealed in an unearthly gray light. The wind swooped and tore away at the brush, sending its fan-shaped cat's-paws across the surface of the pond. My ducks, having finished their ablutions, now gave a leisurely attention to smoothing out their plumes ruffled by the night in the gunnysack. They ran each feather separately through their bills, preening and smoothing. All the time they conversed together in low tones of voice. Whenever one made a rather clever remark, or smoothed to glossiness a particularly rumpled feather, he wagged his short tail vigorously from side to side in satisfaction.

Suddenly the one farthest out in the pond stilled to attention and craned forward his neck.

"*Mark*!" quoth he, loudly, and then again: "*Mark! quok—quok—quok*!"

The other five looked in the same direction, and then they, too, lifted up their voices. Cautiously I turned my head. Low against the growing splendour of the sunrise, wings rigidly set, came a flock of mallards. My ducks fairly stood up on their tails the better to hurl invitations and inducements at their wild brethren. The chorus praising this particular spot was vociferous and unanimous, I wonder what the mallards thought of the other fifty or sixty in my flock, the wooden ones, that sat placidly aloof. Did they consider these remarkably exclusive; or did they perhaps look upon the live ones as the "boosters" committee for this particular piece of duck real estate? At any rate, they dropped in without the slightest hesitation, which shows the value of live decoys. The mallard is ordinarily a wily bird and circles your pond a number of times before deciding to come in to wooden decoys. At the proper moment I got to my feet, and, by good fortune, knocked down two fat green-heads.

They fell with a splash right among my ducks. Did the latter exhibit alarm over either the double concussion of the gun or this fall of defunct game from above? Not at all! they were tickled to death. Each swam vigorously around and around at the limit of his tether, ruffling his plumage and waggling his tail with the utmost vigour.

"Well, I rather think we fooled that bunch!" said they, one to another. "Did you ever see an easier lot? Came right down without a look! If the Captain had been here he'd have killed a half dozen of the chumps before they got out of range!" and so on. For your experienced decoy always seems to enjoy the game hugely, and to enter into it with much enthusiasm and intelligence. And all the while the flock of wooden decoys headed unanimously up wind, and bobbed in the wavelets; and the sun went on gilding the mountains to the west.

Next a flock of teal whirled down wind, stooped, and were gone like a flash. I got in both barrels; and missed both. The dissatisfaction of this was almost immediately mitigated by a fine smash at a flock of sprig that went by overhead at extreme long range, but from which I managed to bring down a fine drake. When the shot hit him he faltered, then, still flying, left the ranks at an acute angle, sloping ever the quicker downward, until he fell on a long slant, his wings set, his neck still outstretched. I marked the direction as well as I could, and immediately went in search of him. Fortunately he lay in the open, quite dead. Looking back, I could see another good flock fairly hovering over the decoys.

The sun came up, and grew warm. The wind died. I took off my sweater. Between flights I basked deliciously. The affair was outside of all precedent and reason. A duck shooter ought to be out in a storm, a good cold storm. He ought to break the scum ice when he puts out his decoys. He ought to sit half frozen in a wintry blast, his fingers numb, his nose blue, his body shivering. That sort of discomfort goes with duck shooting. Yet here I was sitting out in a warm, summerlike day in my shirt sleeves, waiting comfortably—and the ducks were coming in, too!

After a time I heard the mighty rattle of the Invigorator, and the Captain's voice shouting. Reluctantly I disentangled myself from my blind and went over to see what all the row was about.

"Had enough?" he demanded, cheerily.

I saw that I was supposed to say yes; so I said it. The ducks were still coming in fast. You see, I was not yet free from the traditions to which I had been brought up. Back in Michigan, when a man went for a day's shoot, he stayed with it all day. It was serious business. I was not yet accustomed to being so close to the game that the casual expedition was after all the most fun.

So I pulled up my rubber boots, and waded out, gathering in the game. To my immense surprise I found that I had thirty-seven ducks down. It had not occurred to me that I had shot half that number, which is perhaps commentary on how fast ducks had been coming in. It was then only about eight o'clock. After gathering them in, next we performed the slow and very moist task of lifting the wooden decoys and winding their anchor cords around their placid necks. Lastly we gathered in the live ducks. They came, towed at the end of their tethers, with manifest reluctance; hanging back at their strings, flapping their wings, and hissing at us indignantly. I do not think they were frightened, for once we had our hands on them, they resumed their dignified calm. Only they enjoyed the fun outside; and they did not fancy the bags inside; a choice eminently creditable to their sense.

So back we drove to the ranch. The Captain, too, had had good shooting. Redmond appeared with an immense open hamper into which he dumped the birds two by two, keeping tally in a loud voice. Redmond thoroughly enjoyed all the small details.

---

CHAPTER IX

**UNCLE JIM**

Each morning, while we still sat at breakfast, Uncle Jim drove up from the General's in his two-wheeled cart to see if there might be anything doing. Uncle Jim was a solidly built elderly man, with the brown complexion and the quizzical, good-humoured eye of the habitual sportsman. He wore invariably an old shooting coat and a cap that had seen younger, but perhaps not better, days. His vehicle was a battered but serviceable two-wheeled cart drawn by a placid though adequate horse. His weapon for all purposes was a rather ponderous twelve-gauge.

If we projected some sporting expedition Uncle Jim was our man; but if there proved to be nothing in the wind, he disappeared promptly. He conducted various trapping ventures for "varmints," at which he seemed to have moderate success, for he often brought in a wildcat or coyote. In fact, he maintained one of the former in a cage, to what end nobody knew, for it was a harsh and unsociable character. Uncle Jim began to show signs of life about July fifteenth when the dove season opened; he came into his own from the middle of October until the first of February, during which period one can shoot both ducks and quail; he died down to the bare earth when the game season was over, and only sent up a few green shoots of interest in the matter of supplying his wildcat with that innumerable agricultural pest, the blackbird.

Sometimes I accompanied Uncle Jim, occupying the other side of the two-wheeled cart. We never had any definite object in view; we just went forth for adventure. The old horse jogged along very steadily, considering the fact that he was as likely to be put at cross country as a road. We humped up side by side in sociable silence, spying keenly for what we could see. A covey of quail disappearing in the brush caused us to pull up. We hunted them leisurely for a half hour and gathered in a dozen birds. Always we tried to sneak ducks, no matter how hopeless the situation might seem. Once I went on one hand and my knees through three inches of water for three hundred yards, stalking a flock of sprig loafing in an irrigation puddle. There was absolutely no cover; I was in plain sight; from a serious hunting standpoint the affair was quixotic, not to say imbecile. If I had been out with the Captain we should probably not have looked twice at those sprig. Nevertheless, as the general atmosphere of Uncle Jim's expeditions was always one of adventure and forlorn hopes and try-it-anyway, I tried it on. Uncle Jim sat in the cart and chuckled. Every moment I expected the flock to take wing, but they lingered. Finally, when still sixty yards distant, the leaders rose. I cut loose with both barrels for general results. To my vast surprise three came down, one dead, the other two wing-tipped. The two latter led me a merry chase, wherein I managed to splatter the rest of myself. Then I returned in triumph to the cart. The forlorn hope had planted its banner on the walls of achievement. Uncle Jim laughed at me for my idiocy in crawling through water after such a fool chance. I laughed at Uncle Jim because I had three ducks. We drove on, and the warm sun dried me off.

In this manner we made some astonishing bags; astonishing not by their size, but by the manner of their accomplishment.

We were entirely open minded. Anything that came along interested us. We investigated all the holes in all the trees, in hopes of 'coons or honey or something or other. We drove gloriously through every patch of brush. Sometimes an unseen hummock would all but upset us; so we had to scramble hastily to windward to restore our equilibrium.

The country was gridironed with irrigation ditches. They were eight to ten feet deep, twenty or thirty feet wide, and with elevated, precipitous banks. One could cross them almost anywhere—except when they were brimful, of course. The banks were so steep that, once started, the vehicle had to go, but so short that it must soon reach bottom. On the other side the horse could attain the top by a rush; after which, having gained at least a front footing over the bank, he could draw the light vehicle by dead weight the rest of the distance. Naturally, the driver had to take the course at exactly right angles, or he capsized ingloriously.

One day Uncle Jim and I started to cross one of these ditches that had long been permitted to remain dry. Its bottom was covered by weeds six inches high, and looked to be about six feet down. We committed ourselves to the slope. Then, when too late to reconsider, we discovered that the apparent six-inch growth of weeds was in reality one of four or five feet. The horse discovered it at the same time. With true presence of mind, he immediately determined that it was up to him to leap that ditch. Only the fact that he was hitched to the cart prevented him from doing so; but he made a praiseworthy effort.

The jerk threw me backward, and had I not grabbed Uncle Jim I would most certainly have fallen out behind. As for Uncle Jim, he would most certainly have fallen out behind, too, if he had not clung like grim death to the reins. And as for the horse, alarmed by the check and consequent scramble, he just plain bolted, fortunately straight ahead. We hit the opposite bank with a crash, sailed over it, and headed across country.

Consider us as we went. Feet in air, I was poised on the end of my backbone in a state of exact equilibrium. A touch would tumble me out behind; an extra ounce would tip me safely into the cart; my only salvation was my hold on Uncle Jim. I could not apply that extra ounce for the simple reason that Uncle Jim also, feet in air, was poised exactly on the end of his backbone. If the reins slackened an inch, over he went; if he could manage to pull up the least bit in the world, in he came! So we tore across country for several hundred yards, unable to recover and most decidedly unwilling to fall off on the back of our heads. It must have been a grand sight; and it seemed to endure an hour. Finally, imperceptibly we overcame the opposing forces. We were saved!

Uncle Jim cursed out "Henry" with great vigour. Henry was the mare we drove. Uncle Jim, in his naming of animals, always showed a stern disregard for the female sex. Then, as usual, we looked about to see what we could see.

Over to the left grew a small white oak. About ten or twelve feet from the ground was a hole. That was enough; we drove over to investigate that hole. It was not an easy matter, for we were too lazy to climb the tree unless we had to. Finally we drove close enough so that, by standing on extreme tip-toe atop the seat of the cart, I could get a sort of sidewise, one-eyed squint at that hole.

"If," I warned Uncle Jim, "Henry leaves me suspended in mid-air I'll bash her fool head in!"

"No, you won't," chuckled Uncle Jim, "it's too far home."

It was a very dark hole, and for a moment I could see nothing. Then, all at once, I made out two dull balls of fire glowing steadily out of the blackness. That was as long as I could stand stretching out my entire anatomy to look down any hole.

On hearing my report, Uncle Jim phlegmatically thrust the flexible whip down the hole.

"'Coon," he pronounced, after listening to the resultant remarks from within.

And then the same bright idea struck us both.

"Mrs. Kitty here makes good with those angleworms," Uncle Jim voiced the inspiration.

We blocked up the hole securely; and made rapid time back to the ranch.

---

CHAPTER X

**THE MEDIUM-SIZE GAME**

Against many attacks and accusations of uselessness cast at her dachshunds, Mrs. Kitty had always stoutly opposed the legend of "medium-size game." The dachshunds may look like bologna sausages on legs, ran the gist of her argument; and they may progress like rather lively measuring worms; and the usefulness of their structure may seem to limit itself to a facility for getting under furniture without stooping, *but*—Mrs. Kitty's eloquence always ended by convincing herself, and she became very serious—but that is not the dogs' fault. Rather it is the fault of their environment to which they have been transplanted. Back in their own native vaterland they were always used for medium-sized game. And what is more they are *good* at it! Come here, Pete, they shan't abuse you!

Coyotes and bobcats are medium-size game, someone ventured to point out.

Not at all, medium-size game should live in holes, like badgers. Dachshunds are evidently built for holes. They are long and low, and they have spatulate feet for digging, and their bandy legs enable them to throw the dirt out behind them. Their long, sharp noses are like tweezers to seize upon the medium-size game. In short, by much repetition, a legend had grown up around the dachshunds, a legend of fierceness inhibited only by circumstances, of pathetic deprivation of the sports of their native land. If only we could have a badger, we could almost hear them say to each other in dog language, a strong, morose, savage badger! Alas! we are wasting our days in idleness, our talents rust from disuse! Finally, Uncle Jim remained the only frankly skeptical member.

At this time there visited the ranch two keen sportsmen whom we shall call Charley and Tommy; as also several girls. We burst on the assembled multitude with our news. Immediately a council of war was called. After the praetors and tribunes of the people had uttered their opinions, Uncle Jim arose and spoke as follows:

"Here is your chance to make good," said he, addressing Mrs. Kitty. "Those badger hounds of yours, according to you, have just been fretting for medium-size game. Well, here's some. Bring out the whole flock, and let's see them get busy."

The proposition was received with a shout of rapture Uncle Jim smiled grimly.

"Well, they'll do it!" cried Mrs. Kitty, with spirit.

Preparations were immediately under way. In half an hour the army debouched from the ranch and strung out single file across the plain.

First came Uncle Jim and myself in the two-wheeled cart as scouts and guides.

Followed the General in his surrey. The surrey had originally been intended for idle dalliance along country lanes. In the days of its glory it had been upholstered right merrily, and around its flat top had dangled a blithesome fringe. Both the upholstery and fringe were still somewhat there. Of the glory that was past no other reminder had persisted. The General sat squarely in the middle of the front seat, very large, erect, and imposing, driving with a fine military disregard of hummocks or the laws of equilibrium. In or near the back seat hovered a tiny Japanese boy to whom the General occasionally issued short, sharp, military comments or commands.

Then came Mrs. Kitty and the ponies with Carrie beside her. Immediately astern of the pony cart followed a three-seated carry-all with assorted guests. This was flanked by the Captain and Charley as outriders. The rear was closed by the Invigorator rilled with dachshunds. Their pointed noses poked busily through the slats of the cage, and sniffed up over the edge of the wagon box.

The rear, did I say? I had forgotten Mithradates Antikamia Briggs. The latter polysyllabic person was a despised, apologetic, rangy, black-and-white mongrel hound said to have belonged somewhere to a man named Briggs. I think the rest of his name was intended as an insult. Ordinarily Mithradates hung around the men's quarters where he was liked. Never had he dared seek either solace or sympathy at the doors of the great house; and never, never had he remotely dreamed of following any of the numerous hunting expeditions. That would have been lese-majesty, high treason, sublime impudence, and intolerable nuisance to be punished by banishment or death. Mithradates realized this perfectly; and never did he presume to raise his eyes to such high and shining affairs.

But to-day he followed. Nobody was subsequently able to explain why Mithradates Antikamia should on this one occasion so have plucked up heart. My private opinion is that he saw the dachshunds being taken, and, in his uncultivated manner, communed with himself as follows:

"Well, will you gaze on that! I don't pretend to be in the same class with Old Ben or Young Ben, or even of the fox terriers; but if I'm not more of a dog than that lot of splay-footed freaks, I'll go bite myself! If they're *that* hard up for dogs, I'll be cornswizzled if I don't go myself!"

Which he did. We did not want him; this was distinctly the dachshunds' party, and we did not care to have any one messing in. The Captain tried to drive him back. Mithradates Antikamia would not go. The Captain dismounted and tried force. Mithradates shut both eyes, crouched to the ground, and immediately weighed a half ton. When punished he rolled over and held all four paws in the air. The minute the Captain turned his back, after stern admonitions to "go home!" and "down, charge!" and the like, Mithradates crawled slowly forward to the waiting line, ducking his head, wrinkling his upper lips ingratiatingly, and sneezing in the most apologetic tones. Finally we gave it up.

"But," we "saved our face," "you'll have to behave when we get there!"

So, as has been said, Mithradates Antikamia Briggs brought up the rear.

Arrived at the tree the whole procession drew into a half circle. We unblocked the opening, and the Invigorator was driven to a spot beneath it so each person could take his turn at standing on the seat and peering down the hole. The eyes still glowed like balls of fire.

Next the dachshunds were lifted up one by one and given a chance to smell at the game. This was to make them keen. Held up by means of a hand held either side their chests, they curled up their hind legs and tails and seemed to endure. Mrs. Kitty explained that they had never been so far off the ground in their lives, and so were naturally preoccupied by the new sensation. This sounded reasonable, so we placed them on the ground. There they sat in a circle looking up at our performances, a solemn and mild interest expressing itself in their lugubrious countenances. A dachshund has absolutely no sense of humour or lightness of spirits. He never cavorts.

By sounding carefully with a carriage whip we determined the depth of the hole, and proceeded to cut through to the bottom. This was quite a job, for the oak was tough, and the position difficult. Tommy had ascended the tree, and proclaimed loudly the first signs of daylight as the axe bit through. Mine happened to be the axe work; so when I had finished a neat little orifice, I swung up beside Tommy, and the Invigorator drove out of the way.

My elevated position was a good one; and as Tommy was peering eagerly down the hole, I had nothing to do but survey the scene.

The rigs were drawn up in a semi-circle twenty yards away. Next the horses' heads stood the drivers of the various vehicles, anxious to miss none of the fun. The dachshunds sat on their haunches, looking up, and probably wondering why their friend, Tommy, insisted on roosting up a tree. The Captain and Charley were immediately below, engaged in an earnest effort to poke the 'coon into ascending the hole. Tommy was reporting the result of these efforts from above.

The General, his feet firmly planted, had unlimbered a huge ten-bore shotgun, so as to be ready for anything. Uncle Jim stood by, smoking his pipe. Mithradates Antikamia Briggs sat sadly apart.

The poking efforts accomplished little. Occasionally the 'coon made a little dash or scramble, but never went far. There was a great deal of talking, shouting, and advice.

At last Uncle Jim, knocking the ashes from his pipe, moved into action. He plucked a double handful of the tall, dry grass, touched a match to it, and thrust it in the nick.

Without the slightest hesitation the 'coon shot out at the top!

Now just at that moment Tommy happened to be leaning over for a right *good* look down the hole. He received thirty pounds or so of agitated 'coon square in the chest. Thereupon he fell out of the tree incontinently, with the 'coon on top of him.

We caught our breath in horror. Although we could plainly see that Tommy was in no degree injured by his short fall, yet we all realized that it was going to be serious to be mixed up with a raging, snarling beast fight of twenty-two members. When the dachshunds should pounce on their natural prey, the medium-size game, poor Tommy would be at the bottom of the heap. Several even started forward to restrain the dogs, but stopped as they realized the impossibilities.

Tommy and the 'coon hit with a thump. The dachshunds took one horrified look; then with the precision of a drilled manœuvre they unanimously turned tail and plunged into the tall grass. From my elevated perch I could see it waving agitatedly as they made their way through it in the direction of the distant ranch.

For a moment there was astounded silence. Then there arose a shriek of delight. The Captain rolled over and over and clutched handfuls of turf in his joy. The General roared great salvos of laughter. Tommy, still seated where he had fallen, leaned weakly against the tree, the tears coursing down his cheeks. The rest of the populace lifted up their voices and howled. Even Uncle Jim, who rarely laughed aloud, although his eyes always smiled, emitted great Ho! ho!'s. Only Mrs. Kitty, dumb with indignation, stared speechless after that wriggling mess of fugitives.

The occasion was too marvellous. We enjoyed it to the full. Whenever the rapture sank somewhat, someone would gasp out a half-remembered bit of Mrs. Kitty's former defences.

"Their long, sharp noses are like tweezers to seize the game!" declaimed Charley, weakly. Spasm by the audience.

"Their spatulate feet are meant for digging," the Captain took up the tale. Another spasm.

"Their bandy legs enabled them to throw the dirt out behind them—as they ran," suggested Tommy.

"If *only* they could have had a badger they'd have beaten all records!" we chorused.

And then finally we wiped our eyes and remembered that there used to be a 'coon. At the same time we became conscious of a most unholy row in the offing: the voice of Mithradates Antikamia.

"If you people want your 'coon," he was remarking in a staccato and exasperated voice, "you'd better come and lend a hand. *I* can't manage him alone! The blame thing has bitten me in three places already. Of course, I like to see people have a good time, and I hope you won't curtail your enjoyment on my account; but if you've had *quite* enough of those made-in-Germany imitations, perhaps you'll just stroll over and see what one good American-built DOG can do!"

---

CHAPTER XI

## IN SEARCH OF ADVENTURE

Uncle Jim had friends everywhere. Continually we were pulling up by one of the tiny two-roomed shacks wherein dwelt the small settlers. The houses were always of new boards, unpainted, perched on four-by-fours, in the middle of bare ground, perhaps surrounded by young poplars or cottonwoods, but more likely fully exposed to the sun. A trifling open shed protected a battered buggy on the thills and wheels of which perched numerous chickens. A rough corral and windmill completed the arrangements. Near the house was usually a small patch of alfalfa. Farther out the owner was engaged in the strenuous occupation of brushing and breaking a virgin country.

To greet us rushed forth a half-dozen mongrel dogs, and appeared a swarm of children, followed by the woman of the place. Uncle Jim knew them all by name, including even the dogs. He carefully wound the reins around the whip, leaned forward comfortably, and talked. Henry dozed; and I listened with interest. Uncle Jim had the natural gift of popularity. By either instinct or a wide experience he knew just what problems and triumphs, disappointments and perplexities these people were encountering; and he plunged promptly into the discussion of them. Also, I was never able to make out whether Uncle Jim was a conscious or unconscious diplomat; but certainly he knew how judiciously to make use of the subtle principle, so well illustrated by Molière, that it pleases people to confer small favours. Thus occasionally he gravely "borrowed" a trifle of axle grease, which we immediately applied, or a cup of milk, or a piece of string to mend something. When finally our leisurely roadside call was at an end, we rolled away from unanimously hearty signals of farewell.

In accordance with our settled feeling of taking things as they came, and trying for everything, we blundered into varied experiences, none of which arrange themselves in recollection with any pretence of logical order. Perhaps it might not be a bad idea to copy our method, to set forth and see where we land.

One of the most amusing happened when we were out with my younger, but not smaller, brother. This youth was at that time about eighteen years old, and six feet two in height. His age *plus* his stature *equalled* a certain lankiness. As we drove peacefully along the highway we observed in the adjacent field a coyote. The animal was some three or four hundred yards away, lying down, his head between his paws, for all the world like a collie dog. Immediately the lad was all excitement. We pointed out the well-known facts that the coyote is no fool and is difficult to stalk at best; that while he is apparently tame as long as the wagon keeps moving, he decamps when convinced that his existence is receiving undue attention; that in the present instance the short grass would not conceal a snake; and that, finally, a 16-gauge gun loaded with number-six shot was not an encouraging coyote weapon. He brushed them aside as mere details. So we let him out.

He dropped into the grass and commenced his stalk. This he accomplished on his elbows and knees. A short review of the possibilities will convince you that the sight was unique. Although the boy's head and shoulders were thus admirably close to the ground, there followed an extremely abrupt apex. Add the fact that the canvas shooting coat soon fell forward over his shoulders.

The coyote at first paid no attention. As this strange object worked nearer, he raised his head to take a look. Then he sat up on his haunches to take a better look. At this point we expected him to lope away instead of which he trotted forward a few feet and stopped, his ears pricked forward. There he sat, his shrewd brain alive with conjecture until, at thirty-five yards, the kid emptied both barrels. Thereupon he died, his curiosity as to what a movable brown pyramid might be still unsatisfied.

Uncle Jim, the kid, and I had great fun cruising for jackrabbits. Uncle Jim sat in the middle and drove while the kid and I hung our feet over the sides and constituted ourselves the port and starboard batteries. Bumping and banging along at full speed over the uneven country, we jumped the rabbits, and opened fire as they made off. Each had to stick to his own side of the ship, of course. Uncle Jim's bird dog, his head between our feet, his body under the seat, watched the proceedings, whining. It looked like good fun to him, but it was forbidden. A jackrabbit arrested in full flight by a charge of shot turns a very spectacular somersault. The dog would standabout five rabbits. As the sixth turned over, he executed a mad struggle, accomplished a flying leap over the front wheel, was rolled over and over by the forward momentum of the moving vehicle, scrambled to his feet, pounced on that rabbit, and most everlastingly and savagely shook it up! Then Uncle Jim descended and methodically and dispassionately licked the dog.

Jackrabbits were good small-rifle game. They started away on a slow lope, but generally stopped and sat up if not too seriously alarmed. A whistle sometimes helped bring them to a stand. After a moment's inspection they went away, rapidly. With a .22 automatic one could turn loose at all sorts of ranges at all speeds. It was a good deal of fun, too, sneaking about afoot through the low brush, making believe that the sage was a jungle, the tiny pellets express bullets, the rabbits magnified—I am sorry for the fellow who cannot have fun sometimes "pretending!" In the brush, too, dwelt little cottontails, very good to eat. The jackrabbit was a pest, but the cottontail was worth getting. We caught sight of him first in the bare open spaces between the bushes, whereupon he proceeded rapidly to cover. It was necessary to shoot rather quickly. The inexperienced would be apt to run forward eagerly, hoping to catch a glimpse of the cottontail on the other side; but always it would be in vain. That would be owing to the fact that the little rabbit has a trick of apparently running through a brush at full speed, but in reality of stopping abruptly and squatting at the roots. Often it is possible to get a shot by scrutinizing carefully the last place he was seen. He can stop as suddenly as a cow pony.

Often and often, like good strategic generals, we were induced by circumstances to change our plans or our method of attack at the last moment. On several occasions, while shooting in the fields of Egyptian corn, I have killed a quail with my right barrel and a duck with my left! Continually one was crouching in hopes, when some unexpected flock stooped toward him as he walked across country. These hasty concealments were in general quite futile, for it is a fairly accurate generalization that, in the open, game will see you before you see it. This is not always true. I have on several occasions stood stock still in the open plain until a low-flying mallard came within easy range. Invariably the bird was flying toward the setting sun, so I do not doubt his vision was more or less blinded.

The most ridiculous effort of this sort was put into execution by the Captain and myself.

Be it premised that while, in the season, the wildfowl myriads were always present, it by no means followed that the sportsman was always sure of a bag. The ducks followed the irrigation water. One week they might be here in countless hordes; the next week might see only a few coots and hell divers left, while the game was reported twenty miles away. Furthermore, although fair shooting—of the pleasantest sort, in my opinion—was always to be had by jumping small bands and singles from the "holes" and ditches, the big flocks were quite apt to feed and loaf in the wide spaces discouragingly free of cover. Irrigation was done on a large scale. A section of land might be submerged from three inches to a foot in depth. In the middle of this temporary pond and a half dozen others like it fed the huge bands of ducks. What could you do? There was no cover by which to sneak them. You might build a blind, but before the ducks could get used to its strange presence in a flat and featureless landscape the water would be withdrawn from that piece of land. Only occasionally, when a high wind drove them from the open, or when the irrigation water happened to be turned in to a brushy country, did the sportsman get a chance at the great swarms. Since a man could get all the ducks he could reasonably require, there was no real reason why he should look with longing on these inaccessible packs, but we all did. It was not that we wanted more ducks; for we held strictly within limits, but we wanted to get in the thick of it.

On the occasion of which I started to tell, the Captain and I were returning from somewhere. Near the Lakeside ranch we came across a big tract of land overflowed by not deeper than two or three inches of water. The ducks were everywhere on it. They sat around fat and solemn in flocks; they swirled and stooped and lit and rose again; they fed busily; they streamed in from all points of the compass, cleaving the air with a whistling of wings.

Cover there was none. It was exactly like a big, flat cow pasture without any fences. We pulled up the Invigorator and eyed the scene with speculative eyes. Finally, we did as follows:

Into the middle of that field waded we. The ducks, of course, arose with a roar, circled once out of range, and departed. We knew that in less than a minute the boldest would return to see if, perchance, we might have been mere passers-by. Finding us still there, they would, in the natural course of events, circle once or twice and then depart for good.

Now we had noticed this: ducks will approach to within two or three hundred yards of a man standing upright, but they will come within one hundred—or almost in range—if he squats and holds quite still. This, we figured, is because he is that much more difficult to recognize as a man, even though he is in plain sight. We had to remain in plain sight; but could we not make ourselves more difficult to recognize?

After pulling up our rubber boots carefully, we knelt in the two inches of water, placed our chests across two wooden shell boxes we had brought for the purpose, ducked our heads, and waited. After a few moments overhead came the peculiar swift whistle of wings. We waited, rigid. When that whistle sounded very loud indeed, we jerked ourselves upright and looked up. Immediately above us, already towering frantically, was a flock of sprig. They were out of range, but we were convinced that this was only because we had mistakenly looked up too soon.

It was fascinating work, for we had to depend entirely on the sense of hearing. The moment we stirred in the slightest degree away went the ducks. As it took an appreciable time to rise to our feet, locate the flock, and get into action, we had to guess very accurately. We fired a great many times, and killed a very few; but each duck was an achievement.

Though the bag could not be guaranteed, the sight of ducks could. When my brother went with me to the ranch, the duck shooting was very poor. This was owing to the fact that sudden melting of the snows in the Sierras had overflowed an immense tract of country to form a lake eight or nine miles across. On this lake the ducks were safe, and thither they resorted in vast numbers. As a consequence, the customary resorts were deserted. We could see the ducks, and that was about all. Realizing the hopelessness of the situation we had been confining ourselves so strictly to quail that my brother had begun to be a little sceptical of our wildfowl tales. Therefore, one day, I took him out and showed him ducks.

They were loafing in an angle of the lake formed by the banks of two submerged irrigating ditches, so we were enabled to measure them accurately. After they had flown we paced off their bulk. They had occupied a space on the bank and in the water three hundred yards long by fifty yards wide; and they were packed in there just about as thick as ducks could crowd together. An able statistician might figure out how many there were. At any rate, my brother agreed that he had seen some ducks.

There was one thing about Uncle Jim's expeditions: they were cast in no rigid lines. Their direction, scope, or purpose could be changed at the last moment should circumstances warrant.

One day Uncle Jim came after me afoot, with the quiet assurance that he knew where there were "some ducks."

"Tommy is down there now," said he, "in a blind. We'll make a couple more blinds across the pond, and in that way one or the other of us is sure to get a shot at everything that comes in. And the way they're coming in is scand'lous!"

Therefore I filled my pockets with duck shells, seized my close-choked 12-bore, and followed Uncle Jim. We walked across three fields.

"Those ducks are acting mighty queer," proffered Uncle Jim in puzzled tones.

We stopped a moment to watch. Flock after flock stooped toward the little pond, setting their wings and dropping with the extraordinary confidence wildfowl sometimes exhibit. At a certain point, however, and while still at a good elevation, they towered swiftly and excitedly.

"Doesn't seem like they'd act so scared even if Tommy wasn't well hid," puzzled Uncle Jim.

We proceeded cautiously, keeping out of sight behind some greasewood, until we could see the surface of the pond. There were Tommy's decoys, and there was Tommy's blind. We could not see but that it was a well-made blind. Even as we looked another flock of sprig sailed down wind, stopped short at a good two hundred yards, towered with every appearance of lively dismay, and departed. Tommy's head came above the blind, gazing after them.

"They couldn't act worse if Tommy was out waving his hat at 'em," said Uncle Jim.

We climbed a fence. This brought us to a slight elevation, but sufficient to enable us to see abroad over the flat landscape.

Immediately beyond Tommy was a long, low irrigation check grown with soft green sod. On the farther slope thereof were the girls. They had brought magazines and fancy work, and evidently intended to spend the afternoon in the open, enjoying the fresh air and the glad sunshine and the cheerful voices of God's creatures. They were, of course, quite unconscious of Tommy's sporting venture not a hundred feet away. Their parasols were green, red, blue, and other explosive tints.

Uncle Jim and I sat for a few moments on the top of that fence enjoying the view. Then we climbed softly down and went away. We decided tacitly not to shoot ducks. The nature of the expedition immediately changed. We spent the rest of the afternoon on quail. To be sure number-five shot in a close-choked twelve is not an ideal load for the purpose; but by care in letting our birds get far enough away we managed to have a very good afternoon's sport. And whenever we would make a bad miss we had ready consolation: the thought of Tommy waiting and wondering and puzzling in his blind.

## THE GRAND TOUR

Almost always our sporting expeditions were of this casual character, sandwiched in among other occupations. Guns were handy, as was the game. To seize the one and pursue the other on the whim of the moment was the normal and usual thing. Thus one day Mrs. Kitty drove me over to look at a horse I was thinking of buying. On the way home, in a corner of brush, I hopped out and bagged twelve quail; and a little farther on, by a lucky sneak, I managed to gather in five ducks from an irrigation pond. On another occasion, having a spare hour before lunch, I started out afoot from the ranch house at five minutes past eleven, found my quail within a quarter mile, had luck in scattering them, secured my limit of twenty-five, and was back at the house at twelve twenty-five! Before this I had been to drive with Mrs. Kitty; and after lunch we drove twelve miles to call on a neighbour. Although I had enjoyed a full day's quail shoot, it had been, as it were, merely an interpolation.

Occasionally, however, it was elected to make a grand and formal raid on the game. This could be either a get-up-early-in-the-morning session in the blinds, a formal quail hunt, or the Grand Tour.

To take the Grand Tour we got out the Liver Invigorator and as many saddle horses as might be needed to accommodate the shooters. On reaching the hog field it was proper to disembark, and to line up for an advance on the corner of the irrigation ditch where I had so unexpectedly jumped the ducks my first morning on the ranch. In extended order we approached. If ducks were there, they got a great hammering. Everybody shot joyously—whether in sure range or not, it must be confessed. The birds went into a common bag, for it would be impossible to say who had killed what. After congratulations and reproaches, both of which might be looked upon as sacrifices to the great god Josh, we swung to the left and tramped a half mile to the artesian well. The Invigorator and saddle horses followed at a respectful distance. When we had investigated the chances at the well, we climbed aboard again and rattlety-banged across country to the Slough.

The Slough comprised a wide and varied country. In proper application it was a little winding ravine sunk eight or ten feet below the flat plain, and filled with water. This water had been grown thick with trees, but occasionally, for some reason to me unknown, the growth gave space for tiny open ponds or channels. These were further screened by occasional willows or greasewood growing on the banks. They were famous loafing places for mallards.

It was great fun to slip from bend to bend of the Slough, peering keenly, moving softly, trying to spy through the thick growth to a glimpse of the clear water. The ducks were very wary. It was necessary to know the exact location of each piece of open water, its surroundings, and how best it was to be approached. Only too often, peer as cautiously as we might, the wily old mallards would catch a glimpse of some slight motion. At once they would begin to swim back and forth uneasily. Always then we would withdraw cautiously, hoping against hope that suspicion would die. It never did. Our stalk would disclose to us only a troubled surface of water on which floated lightly a half dozen feathers.

But when things went right we had a beautiful shot. The ducks towered straight up, trying to get above the level of the brush, affording a shot at twenty-five or thirty yards' range. We always tried to avoid shooting at the same bird, but did not always succeed. Old Ben delighted in this work, for now he had a chance to plunge in after the fallen. As a matter of fact, it would have been quite useless to shoot ducks in these circumstances had we not possessed a good retriever like Old Ben.

The Slough proper was about two miles long, and had probably eight or ten "holes" in which ducks might be expected. The region of the Slough was, however, a different matter.

It was a fascinating stretch of country, partly marshy, partly dry, but all of it overgrown with tall and rustling tules. These reeds were sometimes so dense that one could not force his way through them; at others so low and thin that they barely made good quail cover. Almost everywhere a team could be driven; and yet there were soft places and water channels and pond holes in which a horse would bog down hopelessly. From a point on the main north-and-south ditch a man afoot left the bank to plunge directly into a jungle of reeds ten feet tall. Through them narrow passages led him winding and twisting and doubting in a labyrinth. He waded in knee-deep water, but confidently, for he knew the bottom to be solid beneath his feet. On either side, fairly touching his elbows, the reeds stood tall and dense, so that it seemed to him that he walked down a narrow and winding hallway. And every once in a while the hallway debouched into a secret shallow pond lying in the middle of the tule jungle in which might or might not be ducks. If there were ducks, it behooved him to shoot very, very quickly, for those that fell in the tules were probably not to be recovered. Then more narrow passages led to other ponds.

Always the footing was good, so that a man could strike forward confidently. But again there are other places in the Slough region where one has to walk for half a mile to pass a miserable little trickle only just too wide to step across. The watercress grows thick against either oozy bank, leaving a clear of only a foot. Yet it is bottomless.

The Captain knew this region thoroughly, and drove in it by landmarks of his own. After many visits I myself got to know the leading "points of interest" and how to get to them by a set route; but their relations one to another have always remained a little vague.

For instance, there was an earthen reservoir comprising two circular connecting ponds, elevated slightly above the surrounding flats, so that a man ascended an incline to stand on its banks. One half of this reservoir is bordered thickly by tules; but the other half is without growth. We left the Invigorator at some hundreds of yards distance; and, single file, followed the Captain. We stopped when he did, crawled when he did, watched to see what dry and rustling footing he avoided, every sense alert to play accurately this unique game of "follow my leader." He alone kept watch of the cover, the game, and the plan of attack. We were like the tail of a snake, merely following where the head directed. This was not because the Captain was so much more expert than ourselves, but so as to concentrate the chances of remaining undiscovered. If each of us had worked out his own stalk we should have multiplied the chances of alarming the game; we should have created the necessity for signals; and we should have had the greatest difficulty in synchronizing our arrival at the shooting point. We moved a step at a time, feeling circumspectly before resting our weight. At the last moment the Captain motioned with his hand. Wriggling forward, we came into line. Then, very cautiously, we crawled up the bank of the reservoir and peered over! That was the supreme moment! The wildfowl might arise in countless numbers; in which case we shot as carefully and as quickly as possible, reloading and squatting motionless in the almost certain hope of a long-range shot or so at a straggler as the main body swung back over us. Or, again, our eager eyes were quite likely to rest upon nothing but a family party of mud-hens gossiping sociably.

Just beyond the reservoir on the other side was an overflowed small flat. It was simply hummocky solid ground with a little green grass and some water. Behind the hummocks, even after a cannonade at the reservoir, we were almost certain to jump two or three single spoonbills or teal. Why they stayed there, I could not tell you; but stay they did. We walked them up one at a time, as we would quail. The range was long. Sometimes we got them; and sometimes we did not.

From the reservoir we drove out into the illimitable tules. The horses went forward steadily, breasting the rustling growth. Behind them the Invigorator rocked and swayed like a small boat in a tide rip. We stayed in as best we could, our guns bristling up in all directions. The Captain drove from a knowledge of his own. After some time, across the yellow, waving expanse of the rushes, we made out a small dead willow stub slanted rakishly. At sight of this we came to a halt. Just beyond that stub lay a denser thicket of tules, and in the middle of them was known to be a patch of open water about twenty feet across. There was not much to it; but invariably a small bunch of fat old greenheads were loafing in the sun.

It now became, not a question of game, for it was always there, but a question of getting near enough to shoot. To be sure, the tiny pond was so well covered that a stranger to the country would actually be unaware of its existence until he broke through the last barrier of tules; but, by the same token, that cover was the noisiest cover invented for the protection of ducks. Often and often, when still sixty or seventy yards distant, we heard the derisive *quack, quack, quack,* with which a mallard always takes wing, and, a moment later, would see those wily birds rising above the horizon. A false step meant a crackle; a stumble meant a crash. We fairly wormed our way in by inches. Each yard gained was a triumph. When, finally, after a half hour of Indian work, we had managed to line up ready for the shot, we felt that we had really a few congratulations coming. We knew that within fifteen or twenty feet floated the wariest of feathered game; and *absolutely unconscious of our presence.*

"Now!" the Captain remarked, aloud, in conversational tones.

We stood up, guns at present. The Captain's command was answered by the instant beat of wings and the confused quicker calling of alarm. In the briefest fraction of a second the ducks appeared above the tules. They had to tower straight up, for the pond was too small and the reeds too high to permit of any sneaking away. So close were they that we could see the markings of every feather—the iridescence of the heads, the delicate, wave-marked cinnamons and grays and browns, even the absurd little curled plumes over the tails. The guns cracked merrily, the shooters aiming at the up-stretched necks. Down came the quarry with mighty splashes that threw the water high. The remnant of the flock swung away. We stood upright and laughed and joked and exulted after the long strain of our stalk. Ben plunged in again and again, bringing out the game.

Of these tule holes there were three. When we had visited them each in turn we swung back toward the west. There, after much driving, we came to the land of irrigation ditches again. At each new angle one of us would descend, sneak cautiously to the bank and, bending low, peer down the length of the ditch. If ducks were in sight, he located them carefully and then we made our sneak. If not, we drove on to the next bend. Once we all lay behind an embankment like a lot of soldiers behind a breastwork while one of us made a long détour around a big flock resting in an overflow across the ditch. The ruse was successful. The ducks, rising at sight of the scout, flew high directly over the ambuscade. A battery of six or eight guns thereupon opened up. I believe we killed three or four ducks among us; but if we had not brought down a feather we should have been satisfied with the fact that our stratagem succeeded.

So at the last, just as the sun was setting, we completed the circle and landed at the ranch. We had been out all day in the warm California sun and the breezes that blow from the great mountains across the plains; we had worked hard enough to deserve an appetite; we had in a dozen instances exercised our wit or our skill against the keen senses of wild game; we had used our ingenuity in meeting unexpected conditions; we had had a heap of companionship and good-natured fun one with another; we had seen a lot of country. This was much better than sitting solitary anchored in a blind. To be sure a man could kill more ducks from a blind; but what of that?

---

CHAPTER XIII

**RANCH ACTIVITIES**

Big as it was, the ranch was only a feeder for the open range. Way down in southeastern Arizona its cattle had their birth and grew to their half-wild maturity. They won their living where they could, fiercely from the fierce desert. On the broad plains they grazed during the fat season; and as the feed shortened and withered, they retired slowly to the barren mountains. In long lines they plodded to the watering places; and in long, patient lines they plodded their way back again, until deep and indelible troughs had been worn in the face of the earth. Other living creatures they saw few, save the coyotes that hung on their flanks, the jackrabbits, the prairie dogs, the birds strangely cheerful in the face of the mysterious and solemn desert. Once in a while a pair of mounted men jog-trotted slowly here and there among them. They gave way to right and left, swinging in the free trot of untamed creatures, their heads high, their eyes wild. Probably they remembered the terror and ignominy and temporary pain of the branding. The men examined them with critical eye, and commented technically and passed on.

This was when the animals were alive with the fat grasses. But as the drought lengthened, they pushed farther into the hills until the boldest or hardiest of them stood on the summits, and the weakest merely stared dully as the mounted men jingled by. The desert, kind in her bounty, was terrible in her wrath. She took her toll freely and the dried bones of her victims rattled in the wind. The fittest survived. Durham died, Hereford lived through, and turned up after the first rains wiry, lean, and active.

Then came the round-up. From the hidden defiles, the buttes and ranges, the hills and plains, the cowboys drew their net to the centre. Each "drive" brought together on some alkali flat thousands of the restless, milling, bawling cattle. The white dust rose in a cloud against the very blue sky. Then, while some of the cowboys sat their horses as sentinels, turning the herd back on itself, others threaded a way through the multitude, edging always toward the border of the herd some animal uneasy in the consciousness that it was being followed. Surrounding the main herd, and at some distance from it, other smaller herds rapidly formed from the "cut." Thus there was one composed entirely of cows and unbranded calves; another of strays from neighbouring ranges; and a third of the steers considered worthy of being made into beef cattle.

In due time the main herd was turned back on the range; the strays had been cut out and driven home by the cowboys of their several owners; the calves had been duly branded and sent out on the desert to grow up. But there remained still compact the beef herd. When all the excitement of the round-up had died, it showed as the tangible profit of the year.

Its troubles began. Driven to the railroad and into the corrals, it next had to be urged to its first experience of sidedoor Pullmans. There the powerful beasts went frantic. Pike poles urged them up the chute into the cars. They rushed, and hesitated, and stopped and turned back in a panic. At times it seemed impossible to get them started into the narrow chute. On the occasion of one after-dark loading old J.B., the foreman, discovered that the excited steers would charge a lantern light. Therefore he posted himself, with a lantern, in the middle of the chute. Promply the maddened animals rushed at him. He skipped nimbly one side, scaled the fence of the chute. "Now keep 'em coming, boys!" he urged.

The boys did their best, and half filled the car. Then some other impulse seized the bewildered rudimentary brains; the cattle balked. J.B. did it again, and yet again, until the cars were filled.

You have seen the cattle trains, rumbling slowly along, the crowded animals staring stupidly through the bars. They are not having a particularly hard time, considering the fact that they are undergoing their first experience in travelling. Nowadays they are not allowed to become thirsty; and they are too car sick to care about eating. Car sick? Certainly; just as you or I are car sick, no worse; only we do not need to travel unless we want to. At the end of the journey, often, they are too wobbly to stand up. This is not weakness, but dizziness from the unwonted motion. Once a fool S.P.C.A. officer ordered a number of the Captain's steers shot on the ground that they were too weak to live. That greenhorn got into fifty-seven varieties of trouble.

Arrived at their journey's end the steers were permitted six to twelve individuals. The man in charge had to know mules—which is no slight degree of special wisdom; had to know loads; had to understand conditioning. His lantern was the first to twinkle in the morning as he doled out corn to his charges.

Then came the ruck of field hands of all types. The average field hand in California is a cross between a hobo and a labourer. He works probably about half the year. The other half he spends on the road, tramping it from place to place. Like the common hobo, he begs his way when he can; catches freight train rides; consorts in thickets with his kind. Unlike the common hobo, however, he generally has money in his pocket and always carries a bed-roll. The latter consists of a blanket or so, or quilt, and a canvas strapped around the whole. You can see him at any time plodding along the highways and railroads, the roll slung across his back. He much appreciates a lift in your rig; and sometimes proves worth the trouble. His labour raises him above the level degradation of the ordinary tramp; the independence of his spirit gives his point of view an originality; the nomadic stirring of his blood keeps him going. In the course of years he has crossed the length and breadth of the state a half dozen times. He has harvested apples in Siskiyou and oranges in Riverside; he has chopped sugar pine in the snows of the Sierras and manzanita on the blazing hillsides of San Bernardino; he has garnered the wheat of the great Santa Clara Valley and the alfalfa of San Fernando. And whenever the need for change or the desire for a drink has struck him, he has drawn his pay, strapped his bed roll, and cheerfully hiked away down the long and dusty trail.

That is his chief defect as a field hand—his unreliability. He seems to have no great pride in finishing out a job, although he is a good worker while he is at it. The Captain used to send in the wagon to bring men out, but refused absolutely to let any man ride in anything going the other way. Nevertheless the hand, when the wanderlust hit him, trudged cheerfully the long distance to town. I am not sure that a new type is not thus developing, a type as distinct in its way as the riverman or the cowboy. It is not as high a type, of course, for it has not the strength either of sustained and earnest purpose nor of class loyalty; but still it makes for new species. The California field hand has mother-wit, independence, a certain reckless, you-be-damned courage, a wandering instinct. He quits work not because he wants to loaf, but because he wants to go somewhere else. He is always on the road travelling, travelling, travelling. It is not hope of gain that takes him, for in the scarcity of labour wages are as high here as there. It is not desire for dissipation that lures him from labour; he drinks hard enough, but the liquor is as potent here as two hundred miles away. He looks you steadily enough in the eye; and he begs his bread and commits his depredations half humorously, as though all this were fooling that both you and he understood. What his impelling motive is, I cannot say; nor whether he himself understands it, this restlessness that turns his feet ever to the pleasant California highways, an Ishmael of the road.

But this very unreliability forces the ranchman to the next element in our consideration of the ranch's people—the Orientals. They are good workers, these little brown and yellow men, and unobtrusive and skilled. They do not quit until the job is done; they live frugally; they are efficient. The only thing we have against them is that we are afraid of them. They crowd our people out. Into a community they edge themselves little by little. At the end of two years they have saved enough capital to begin to buy land. At the end of ten years they have taken up all the small farms from the whites who cannot or will not live in competition with Oriental frugality. The valley, or cove, or flat has become Japanese. They do not amalgamate. Their progeny are Japanese unchanged; and their progeny born here are American citizens. In the face of public sentiment, restriction, savage resentment they have made head. They are continuing to make head. The effects are as yet small in relation to the whole of the body politic; but more and more of the fertile, beautiful little farm centres of California are becoming the breeding grounds of Japanese colonies. As the pressure of population on the other side increases, it is not difficult to foresee a result. We are afraid of them.

The ranchmen know this. "We would use white labour," say they, "if we could get it, and rely on it. But we cannot; and we *must* have labour!" The debt of California to the Orientals can hardly be computed. The citrus crop is almost entirely moved by them; and all other produce depends so largely on them that it would hardly be an exaggeration to say that without them a large part of the state's produce would rot in fields. We do not want the Oriental; and yet we must have him, must have more of him if we are to reach our fullest development. It is a dilemma; a paradox.

And yet, it seems to me, the paradox only exists because we will not face facts in a commonsense manner. As I remember it, the original anti-Oriental howl out here made much of the fact that the Chinaman and Japanese saved his money and took it home with him. In the peculiar circumstances we should not object to that. We cannot get our work done by our own people; we are forced to hire in outsiders to do it; we should expect, as a country, to pay a fair price for what we get. It is undoubtedly more desirable to get our work done at home; but if we cannot find the help, what more reasonable than that we should get it outside, and pay for it? If we insist that the Oriental is a detriment as a permanent resident, and if at the same time we need his labour, what else is there to do but pay him and let him go when he has done his job?

And he will go *if pay is all he gets*. Only when he is permitted to settle down to his favourite agriculture in a fertile country does he stay permanently. To be sure a certain number of him engages in various other commercial callings, but that number bears always a very definite proportion to the Oriental population in general. And it is harmless. It is not absolute restriction of immigration we want—although I believe immigration should be numerically restricted, but absolute prohibition of the right to hold real estate. To many minds this may seem a denial of the "equal rights of man." I doubt whether in some respects men have equal rights. Certainly Brown has not an equal right with Jones to spank Jones's small boy; nor do I believe the rights of any foreign nation paramount to our own right to safeguard ourselves by proper legislation.

These economics have taken us a long distance from the ranch and its Orientals. The Japanese contingent were mainly occupied with the fruit, possessing a peculiar deftness in pruning and caring for the prunes and apricots. The Chinese had to do with irrigation and with the vegetables. Their broad, woven-straw hats and light denim clothes lent the particular landscape they happened for the moment to adorn a peculiarly foreign and picturesque air.

And outside of these were various special callings represented by one or two men: such as the stable men, the bee keeper, the blacksmith and wagon-wright, the various cooks and cookees, the gardeners, the "varmint catcher," and the like.

Nor must be forgotten the animals, both wild and tame. Old Ben and Young Ben and Linn, the bird dogs; the dachshunds; the mongrels of the men's quarters; all the domestic fowls; the innumerable and blue-blooded hogs; the polo ponies and brood mares, the stud horses and driving horses and cow horses, colts, yearlings, the young and those enjoying a peaceful and honourable old age; Pollymckittrick; Redmond's cat and fifty others, half-wild creatures; vireos and orioles in the trees around the house; thousands and thousands of blackbirds rising in huge swarms like gnats; full-voiced meadowlarks on the fence posts; herons stalking solemnly, or waiting like so many Japanese bronzes for a chance at a gopher; red-tailed hawks circling slowly; pigeon hawks passing with their falcon dart; little gaudy sparrow hawks on top the telephone poles; buzzards, stately and wonderful in flight, repulsive when at rest; barn-owls dwelling in the haystacks, and horned owls in the hollow trees; the game in countless numbers; all the smaller animals and tiny birds in species too numerous to catalogue, all these drew their full sustenance of life from the ranch's smiling abundance.

And the mules; I must not forget them. I have the greatest respect for a mule. He knows more than the horse; just as the goose or the duck knows more than the chicken. Six days the mules on the ranch laboured; but on the seventh they were turned out into the pastures to rest and roll and stand around gossiping sociably, rubbing their long, ridiculous Roman noses together, or switching the flies off one another with their tasselled tails. Each evening at sunset all the various teams came in from different directions, converging at the lane, and plodding dustily up its length to the sheds and their night's rest. Five evenings thus they come in silence. But on the sixth each and every mule lifted up his voice in rejoicing over the morrow. The distant wayfarer—familiar with ranch ways—hearing this strident, discordant, thankful chorus far across the evening peace of the wide country, would thus have known this was Saturday night, and that to-morrow was the Sabbath, the day of rest!

## THE HEATHEN

This must be mainly discursive and anecdotal, for no one really knows much more than externals concerning the Chinese. Some men there are, generally reporters on the big dailies, who have been admitted to the tongs; who can take you into the exclusive Chinese clubs; who are everywhere in Chinatown greeted cordially, treated gratis to strange food and drink, and patted on the back with every appearance of affection. They can tell you of all sorts of queer, unknown customs and facts, and can show you all sorts of strange and unusual things. Yet at the last analysis these are also discursions and anecdotes. We gather empirical knowledge: only rarely do we think we get a glimpse of how the delicate machinery moves behind those twinkling eyes.

I am led to these remarks by the contemplation of Chinese Charley at the ranch. He has been with Mrs. Kitty twenty-five years; he wears American clothes; he speaks English with hardly a trace of either accent or idiom; he has long since dropped the deceiving Oriental stolidity and weeps out his violent Chinese rages unashamed. Yet even now Mrs. Kitty's summing up is that Charley is a "queer old thing."

If you start out with a good Chinaman, you will always have good Chinamen; if you draw a poor one, you will probably be cursed with a succession of mediocrities. They pass you along from one to another of the same "family"; and, short of the adoption of false whiskers and a change of name, you can find no expedient to break the charm. When one leaves of his own accord, he sends you another boy to take his place. When he is discharged, he does identically that, although you may not know it. Down through the list of Gins or Sings or Ungs you slide comfortably or bump disagreeably according to your good fortune or deserts.

Another feature to which you must become accustomed is that of the Unexpected Departure. Everything is going smoothly, and you are engaged in congratulating yourself. To you appears Ah Sing.

"I go San Flancisco two o'clock tlain," he remarks. And he does.

In vain do you point to the inconvenience of guests, the injustice thus of leaving you in the lurch; in vain do you threaten detention of wages due unless he gives you what your servant experience has taught you is a customary "week's warning." He repeats his remark: and goes. At two-fifteen another bland and smiling heathen appears at your door. He may or may not tell you that Ah Sing sent him. Dinner is ready on time. The household work goes on without a hitch or a tiniest jar.

"Ah Sing say you pay me his money," announces this new heathen.

If you are wise, you abandon your thoughts of fighting the outrage. You pay over Ah Sing's arrears.

"By the way," you inquire of your new retainer, "what's your name?"

"My name Lum Sing," the newcomer replies.

That is about the way such changes happen. If by chance you are in the good graces of heathendom, you will be given an involved and fancy reason for the departure. These generally have to do with the mysterious movements of relatives.

"My second-uncle, he come on ship to San Flancisco. I got to show him what to do," explains Ah Sing.

If they like you very much, they tell you they will come back at the end of a month. They never do, and by the end of the month the new man has so endeared himself to you that Ah Sing is only a pleasant memory.

The reasons for these sudden departures are two-fold as near as I can make out. Ah Sing may not entirely like the place; or he may have received orders from his tong to move on—probably the latter. If both Ah Sing and his tong approve of you and the situation, he will stay with you for many years. Our present man once remained but two days at a place. The situation is an easy one; Toy did his work well; the relations were absolutely friendly. After we had become intimate with Toy, he confided to us his reasons:

"I don' like stay at place where nobody laugh," said he.

As servants the Chinese are inconceivably quick, deft, and clean. One good man will do the work of two white servants, and do it better. Toy takes care of us absolutely. He cooks, serves, does the housework, and with it all manages to get off the latter part of the afternoon and nearly every evening. At first, with recollections of the rigidly defined "days off" of the East, I was a little inclined to look into this. I did look into it; but when I found all the work done, without skimping, I concluded that if the man were clever enough to save his time, he had certainly earned it for himself. Systematizing and no false moves proved to be his method.

Since this is so, it follows, quite logically and justly, that the Chinese servant resents the minute and detailed supervision some housewives delight in. Show him what you want done; let him do it; criticize the result—but do not stand around and make suggestions and offer amendments. Some housekeepers, trained to make of housekeeping an end rather than a means, can never keep Chinese. This does not mean that you must let them go at their own sweet will: only that you must try as far as possible to do your criticizing and suggesting before or after the actual performance.

I remember once Billy came home from some afternoon tea where she had been talking to a number of "conscientious" housekeepers of the old school until she had been stricken with a guilty feeling that she had been loafing on the job. To be sure the meals were good, and on time; the house was clean; the beds were made; and the comforts of life seemed to be always neatly on hand; but what of that? The fact remained that Billy had time to go horseback riding, to go swimming, to see her friends, and to shoot at a mark. Every other housekeeper was busy from morning until night; and then complained that somehow or other she never could get finished up! It was evident that somehow Billy was not doing her full duty by the sphere to which woman was called, etc.

So home she came, resolved to do better. Toy was placidly finishing up for the afternoon. Billy followed him around for a while, being a housekeeper. Toy watched her with round, astonished eyes. Finally he turned on her with vast indignation.

"Look here, Mis' White," said he. "What a matter with you? You talk just like one old woman!"

Billy paused in her mad career and considered. That was just what she was talking like. She laughed. Toy laughed. Billy went shooting.

After your Chinaman becomes well acquainted with you, he develops human traits that are astonishing only in contrast to his former mask of absolute stolidity. To the stranger the Oriental is as impassive and inscrutable as a stone Buddha, so that at last we come to read his attitude into his inner life, and to conclude him without emotion. This is also largely true of the Indian. As a matter of fact, your heathen is rather vividly alive inside. His enjoyment is keen, his curiosity lively, his emotions near the surface. If you have or expect to have visitors, you must tell Ah Sing all about them—their station in life, their importance, and the like. He will listen, keenly interested, gravely nodding his pig-tailed, shaven head. Then, if your visitors are from the East, you inform them of what every Californian knows—that each and every member of a household must say "good morning" ceremoniously to Ah Sing. And Ah Sing will smile blandly and duck his pig-tailed, shaven head, and wish each member "good morning" back again. It is sometimes very funny to hear the matin chorus of a dozen people crying out their volley of salute to ceremony; and to hear again the Chinaman's conscientious reply to each in turn down the long table—"*Good* mo'ning, Mr. White; *good* mo'ning, Mis' White; *good* mo'ning, Mr. Lewis——" and so on, until each has been remembered. There are some families that, either from ignorance or pride, omit this and kindred little human ceremonials. The omission is accepted; but that family is never "my family" to the servant within its gates.

For your Chinaman is absolutely faithful and loyal and trustworthy. He can be allowed to handle any amount of money for you. We ourselves are away from home a great deal. When we get ready to go, we simply pack our trunks and depart. Toy then puts away the silver and valuables and places them in the bank vaults, closes the house, and puts all in order. A week or so before our return we write him. Thereupon he cleans things up, reclaims the valuables, rearranges everything. His wonderful Chinese memory enables him to replace every smallest item exactly as it was. If I happen to have left seven cents and an empty .38 cartridge on the southwestern corner of the bureau, there they will be. It is difficult to believe that affairs have been at all disturbed. Yet probably, if our stay away has been of any length, everything in the house has been moved or laid away.

Furthermore, Toy reads and writes English, and enjoys greatly sending us wonderful and involved reports. One of them ended as follows: "The weather is doing nicely, the place is safely well, and the dogs are happy all the while." It brings to mind a peculiarly cheerful picture.

One of the familiar and persistent beliefs as to Chinese traits is that they are a race of automatons. "Tell your Chinaman exactly what you want done, and how you want it done," say your advisors, "for you will never be able to change them once they get started." And then they will adduce a great many amusing and true incidents to illustrate the point.

The facts of the case are undoubted, but the conclusions as to the invariability of the Chinese mind are, in my opinion, somewhat exaggerated.

It must be remembered that almost all Chinese customs and manners of thought are the direct inverse of our own. When announcing or receiving a piece of bad news, for example, it is with them considered polite to laugh; while intense enjoyment is apt to be expressed by tears. The antithesis can be extended almost indefinitely by the student of Oriental manners. Contemplate, now, the condition of the young Chinese but recently arrived. He is engaged by some family to do its housework; and, as he is well paid and conscientious, he desires to do his best. But in this he is not permitted to follow his education. Each, move he makes in initiative is stopped and corrected. To his mind there seems no earthly sense or logic in nine tenths of what we want; but he is willing to do his best.

"Oh, well," says he to himself, "these people do things crazily; and no well-regulated Chinese mind could possibly either anticipate how they desire things done, or figure out why they want them that way. I give it up! I'll just follow things out exactly as I am told"—and he does so!

This condition of affairs used to be more common than it is now. Under the present exclusion law no fresh immigration is supposed to be possible. Most of the Chinese servants are old timers, who have learned white people's ways, and—what is more important—understand them. They are quite capable of initiative; and much more intelligent than the average white servant.

But a green Chinaman is certainly funny. He does things forever-after just as you show him the first time; and a cataclysm of nature is required to shake his purpose. Back in the middle 'eighties my father, moving into a new house, dumped the ashes beside the kitchen steps pending the completion of a suitable ash bin. When the latter had been built, he had Gin Gwee move the ashes from the kitchen steps to the bin. This happened to be of a Friday. Ever after Gin Gwee deposited the ashes by the kitchen steps every day; and on Friday solemnly transferred them to the ash bin! Nor could anything persuade him to desist.

Again he was given pail, soap, and brush, shown the front steps and walk leading to the gate, and set to work. Gin Gwee disappeared. When we went to hunt him up, we found him half way down the block, still scrubbing away. I was in favour of letting him alone to see how far he would go, but mother had other ideas as to his activities.

These stories could be multiplied indefinitely; and are detailed by the dozen as proof of the "stupidity" of the Chinese. The Chinese are anything but stupid; and, as I have said before, when once they have grasped the logic of the situation, can figure out a case with the best of them.

They are, however, great sticklers for formalism; and disapprove of any short cuts in ceremony. As soon leave with the silver as without waiting for the finger bowls. A friend of mine, training a new man by example, as new men of this nationality are always trained, was showing him how to receive a caller. Therefore she rang her own doorbell, presented a card; in short, went through the whole performance. Tom understood perfectly. That same afternoon Mrs. G——, a next-door neighbour and intimate friend, ran over for a chat. She rang the bell. Tom appeared.

"Is Mrs. B—— at home?" inquired the friend.

Tom planted himself square in the doorway. He surveyed her with a cold and glittering eye.

"You got ticket?" he demanded. "You no got ticket, you no come in!"

On another occasion two ladies came to call on Mrs. B—— but by mistake blundered to the kitchen door. Mrs. B——'s house is a bungalow and on a corner. Tom appeared.

"Is Mrs. B—— at home?" they asked.

"This kitchen door; you go front door," requested Tom, politely.

The callers walked around the house to the proper door, rang, and waited. After a suitable interval Tom appeared again.

"Is Mrs. B—— at home?" repeated the visitors.

"No, Mrs. B—— she gone out," Tom informed them. The proper ceremonials had been fulfilled.

To one who appreciates what he can do, and how well he does it; who can value absolute faithfulness and honesty; who confesses a sneaking fondness for the picturesque as nobly exemplified in a clean and starched or brocaded heathen; who understands how to balance the difficult poise, supervision, and interference, the Chinese servant is the best on the continent. But to one who enjoys supervising every step or who likes well-trained ceremony, "good form" in minutiæ, and the deference of our kind of good training the heathen is likely to prove disappointing. When you ring your friend's door-bell, you are quite apt to be greeted by a cheerful and smiling "hullo!" I think most Californians rather like the entirely respectful but freshly unconventional relationship that exists between the master and his Chinese servant. I do.[H]

---

CHAPTER XV

**THE LAST HUNT**

Of all ranch visits the last day neared. Always we forgot it until the latest possible moment; for we did not like to think of it. Then, when the realization could be no longer denied, we planned a grand day just to finish up on. The telephone's tiny, thin voice returned acceptances from distant neighbours; so bright and early we waited at the cross-roads rendezvous.

And from the four directions they came, jogging along in carts or spring-wagons, swaying swiftly in automobiles whose brass flashed back the early sun. As each vehicle drew up, the greetings flew, charged electrically with the dry, chaffing humour of the out of doors. When we finally climbed the fence into the old cornfield we were almost a dozen. There were the Captain, Uncle Jim, and myself from the ranch; and T and his three sons and two guests from Stockdale ranch; the sporting parson of the entire neighbourhood, and Dodge and his three beautiful dogs.

Spread out in a rough line we tramped away through the dried and straggling ranks of the Egyptian corn. Quail buzzed all around us like angry hornets. We did not fire a shot. Each had his limit of twenty-five still before him, and each wanted to have all the fun he could out of getting them. Shooting quail in Egyptian corn is, comparatively speaking, not much fun. We joked each other, and whistled and sang, and trudged manfully along, gun over shoulder. The pale sun was strengthening; the mountains were turning darker as they threw aside the filmy rose of early day; in treetops a row of buzzards sat, their wings outspread like the heraldic devices of a foreign nation. Thousands of doves whistled away; thousands of smaller birds rustled and darted before our advancing lines; tens of thousands of blackbirds sprinkled the bare branches of single trees, uttering the many-throated multitude call; underneath all this light and joyous life the business-like little quail darted away in their bullet flight.

Always they bore across our front to the left; for on that side, paralleling our course, ran a long ravine or "dry slough." It was about ten feet deep on the average, probably thirty feet wide, and was densely grown with a tangle of willows, berry vines, creepers, wild grape, and the like. Into this the quail pitched.

By the time we had covered the mile length of that cornfield we had dumped an unguessable number of quail into that slough.

Then we walked back the entire distance—still with our guns over our shoulders—but this time along the edge of the ravine. We shouted and threw clods, and kicked on the trees, and rattled things, urging the hidden quail once more to flight. The thicket seemed alive with them. We caught glimpses as they ran before us, pacing away at a great rate, their feathers sleek and trim; they buzzed away at bewildering pitches and angles; they sprang into the tops of bushes, cocking their head plumes forward. Their various clicking undercalls, chatterings, and chirrings filled the thicket as full of sound as of motion. And in the middle distance before and behind us they mocked us with their calls.

"You *can't* shoot! You *can't* shoot!"

Some of them flew ever ahead, some of them doubled-back and dropped into the slough behind us; but a proportion broke through the thicket and settled in the wide fields on the other side. After them we went, and for the first time opened our guns and slipped the yellow shells into the barrels.

For this field on the other side was the wide, open plain; and it was grown over by tiny, half-knee high thickets of tumbleweed with here and there a trifle of sagebrush. Between these miniature thickets wound narrow strips of sandy soil, like streams and bays and estuaries in shape. We knew that the quail would lie well here, for they hate to cross bare openings.

Therefore, we threw out our skirmish line, and the real advance in force began.

Every man retrieved his own birds, a matter of some difficulty in the tumbleweed. While one was searching, the rest would get ahead of him. The line became disorganized, broke into groups, finally disintegrated entirely. Each man hunted for himself, circling the tumbleweed patches, combing carefully their edges for the quail that sometimes burst into the air fairly at his feet. When he had killed one, he walked directly to the spot. On the way he would flush two or three more. They were tempting; but we were old hands at the sport, and we knew only too well that if we yielded so far as to shoot a second before we had picked up the first, the probabilities were strong that the first would never be found. In this respect such shooting requires good judgment. It is generally useless to try to shoot a double, even though a dozen easy shots are in the air at once; and yet, occasionally, on a day when Koos-ey-oonek is busy elsewhere, it may happen that the birds flush across a wide, bare space. It is well to keep a weather eye open for such chances.

With a green crowd and in different cover such shooting might have been dangerous; but with an abundance of birds, in this wide, open prairie, cool heads knew enough to keep wide apart and to look before they shot. The fun grew fast and furious; and the guns popped away like firecrackers. In fact, the fun grew a little too fast and furious to suit Dodge.

Dodge had beautiful and well-trained dogs. Ordinarily any one of us would have esteemed it a high privilege to shoot over them. In fact, I have often declared myself to the effect that of the three elements of pleasure comprehended in field shooting that of working the dogs was the chief. Just as it is better to catch one yellowtail on a nine-ounce rod than twenty on a hand line, so it is better to kill one quail over a well-trained dog than a half dozen "Walking 'em up." But this particular case was different. We were out for a high old time; and part of a high old time was a wild and reckless disregard of inhibitive sporting conventions. The birds were here literally in thousands. Not a third had left the slough for this open country; we could not shoot at a tenth of those flushed, yet the guns were popping continuously. Everybody was shooting and laughing and running about. The game was to pelt away, retrieve your bird as quickly as you could, and pelt away again. The dogs, working up to their points carefully and stylishly, as good dogs should, were being constantly left in the rear. They drew down to their points—and behold nobody but their devoted master would pay any attention to their bird! Everybody else was engaged busily in popping away at any one of the dozen-odd other birds to be had for the selection!

Poor Dodge, being somewhat biased by the accident of ownership, looked on us as a lot of barbarians—as, for the time being, we were; nice, happy barbarians having a good time. He worked his dogs conscientiously, and muttered in his beard. The climax came when, in the joyous excitement of the occasion, someone threw out a chance remark on "those —— dogs" being in the way. Then Dodge withdrew with dignity. Having a fellow-feeling as a dog-handler I went over to console him. He was inconsolable; and so remained until after lunch.

In this manner we made our way slowly down the length of the slough, and then slowly back again. Of the birds originally flushed from the Egyptian corn into the thicket but a small proportion had left that thicket for the open country of the tumbleweed and sage; and of the latter we had been able to shoot at a very, very small percentage. Nevertheless, when we emptied our pockets, we found that each had made his bag. We counted them out, throwing them into one pile.

"Twenty-four," counted the Captain.

"Twenty-four," Tom enumerated.

"Twenty-four," Uncle Jim followed him.

We each had twenty-four. And then it developed that every man had saved just one bird of his limit until after lunch. No one wanted to be left out of *all* the shooting while the rest filled their bags; and no one had believed that anybody but himself had come so close to the limit.

So we laughed, and shouldered our guns, and trudged across country to the clump of cottonwood where already the girls had spread lunch.

That was a good lunch. We sat under shady trees, and the sunlit plains stretched away and away to distant calm mountains. Near at hand the sparse gray sagebrush reared its bonneted heads; far away it blurred into a monochrome where the plains lifted and flowed molten into the cañons and crevices of the foothills. Numberless crows, blackbirds, and wildfowl crossed and recrossed the very blue sky. A gray jackrabbit, thinking himself concealed by a very creditable imitation of a *sacatone* hummock, sat motionless not seventy yards away.

After lunch we moved out leisurely to get our one bird apiece. Some of the girls followed us. We were now epicures of shooting, and each let many birds pass before deciding to fire. Some waited for cross shots, some for very easy shots, some for the most difficult shots possible. Each suited his fancy.

"I'm all in," remarked each, as he pocketed his bird; and followed to see the others finish.

---

Next day, our baggage piled in most anywhere, our farewells all said, we bowled away toward town in the brand-new machine. Redmond sat in the front seat with the chauffeur. It was his first experience in an automobile, and he sat very rigidly upright, eyes front, his moustaches bristling.

Now at a certain point on the road lived a large black dog—just plain ranch dog—who was accustomed to come bounding out to the road to run alongside and bark for an appropriate interval. This was an unvarying ceremony. He was a large and prancing dog; and, I suppose from his appearance, must have been named Carlo. In the course of our many visits to the ranch we grew quite fond of the dog, and always looked as hard for him to come out as he did for us to come along.

This day also the dog came forth; but now he had no steady-trotting ranch team to greet. The road was smooth and straight, and the car was hitting thirty-five miles an hour. The dog bounded confidently down the front walk, leaping playfully in the air, opened his mouth to bark—and, behold! the vehicle was not within range any more, but thirty yards away and rapidly departing. So Carlo shut his mouth and got down to business. For three hundred yards he managed to keep pace alongside; but the effort required all his forces; not once did he manage to gather wind for even a single bark.

Redmond in the front seat sat straighter than ever. From his lordly elevation he waved a lordly hand at the poor dog.

"Useless! Useless!" said he, loftily.

And looking back at the dog seated panting in a rapidly disappearing distance, we saw that he also knew that the Old Order had changed.

THE END

# The Forty-Niners A Chronicle
# of the California Trail and El Dorado

## CHAPTER I

### SPANISH DAYS

The dominant people of California have been successively aborigines, *conquistadores*, monks, the dreamy, romantic, unenergetic peoples of Spain, the roaring melange of Forty-nine, and finally the modern citizens, who are so distinctive that they bid fair to become a subspecies of their own. This modern society has, in its evolution, something unique. To be sure, other countries also have passed through these same phases. But while the processes have consumed a leisurely five hundred years or so elsewhere, here they have been subjected to forced growth.

The tourist traveler is inclined to look upon the crumbling yet beautiful remains of the old missions, those venerable relics in a bustling modern land, as he looks upon the enduring remains of old Rome. Yet there are today many unconsidered New England farmhouses older than the oldest western mission, and there are men now living who witnessed the passing of Spanish California.

Though the existence of California had been known for centuries, and the dates of her first visitors are many hundreds of years old, nevertheless Spain attempted no actual occupation until she was forced to it by political necessity. Until that time she had little use for the country. After early investigations had exploded her dream of more treasure cities similar to those looted by Cortés and Pizarro, her interest promptly died.

But in the latter part of the eighteenth century Spain began to awake to the importance of action. Fortunately ready to her hand was a tried and tempered weapon. Just as the modern statesmen turn to commercial penetration, so Spain turned, as always, to religious occupation. She made use of the missionary spirit and she sent forth her expeditions ostensibly for the purpose of converting the heathen. The result was the so-called Sacred Expedition under the leadership of Junípero Serra and Portolá. In the face of incredible hardships and discouragements, these devoted, if narrow and simple, men succeeded in establishing a string of missions from San Diego to Sonoma. The energy, self-sacrifice, and persistence of the members of this expedition furnish inspiring reading today and show clearly of what the Spanish character at its best is capable.

For the next thirty years after the founding of the first mission in 1769, the grasp of Spain on California was assured. Men who could do, suffer, and endure occupied the land. They made their mistakes in judgment and in methods, but the strong fiber of the pioneer was there. The original *padres* were almost without exception zealous, devoted to poverty, uplifted by a fanatic desire to further their cause. The original Spanish temporal leaders were in general able, energetic, courageous, and not afraid of work or fearful of disaster.

At the end of that period, however, things began to suffer a change. The time of pioneering came to an end, and the new age of material prosperity began. Evils of various sorts crept in. The pioneer priests were in some instances replaced by men who thought more of the flesh-pot than of the altar, and whose treatment of the Indians left very much to be desired. Squabbles arose between the civil and the religious powers. Envy of the missions' immense holdings undoubtedly had its influence. The final result of the struggle could not be avoided, and in the end the complete secularization of the missions took place, and with this inevitable change the real influence of these religious outposts came to an end.

Thus before the advent in California of the American as an American, and not as a traveler or a naturalized citizen, the mission had disappeared from the land, and the land was inhabited by a race calling itself the *gente de razón*, in presumed contradistinction to human beasts with no reasoning powers. Of this period the lay reader finds such conflicting accounts that he either is bewildered or else boldly indulges his prejudices. According to one school of writers—mainly those of modern fiction—California before the advent of the *gringo*was a sort of Arcadian paradise, populated by a people who were polite, generous, pleasure-loving, high-minded, chivalrous, aristocratic, and above all things romantic. Only with the coming of the loosely sordid, commercial, and despicable American did this Arcadia fade to the strains of dying and pathetic music. According to another school of writers—mainly authors of personal reminiscences at a time when growing antagonism was accentuating the difference in ideals—the "greaser" was a dirty, idle, shiftless, treacherous, tawdry vagabond, dwelling in a disgracefully primitive house, and backward in every aspect of civilization.

The truth, of course, lies somewhere between the two extremes, but its exact location is difficult though not impossible to determine. The influence of environment is sometimes strong, but human nature does not differ much from age to age. Racial characteristics remain approximately the same. The Californians were of several distinct classes. The upper class, which consisted of a very few families, generally included those who had held office, and whose pride led them to intermarry. Pure blood was exceedingly rare. Of even the best the majority had Indian blood; but the slightest mixture of Spanish was a sufficient claim to gentility. Outside of these "first families," the bulk of the population came from three sources: the original military adjuncts to the missions, those brought in as settlers, and convicts imported to support one side or another in the innumerable political squabbles. These diverse elements shared one sentiment only—an aversion to work. The feeling had grown up that in order to maintain the prestige of the soldier in the eyes of the natives it was highly improper that he should ever do any labor. The settlers, of whom there were few, had themselves been induced to immigrate by rather extravagant promises of an easy life. The convicts were only what was to be expected.

If limitations of space and subject permitted, it would be pleasant to portray the romantic life of those pastoral days. Arcadian conditions were then more nearly attained than perhaps at any other time in the world's history. The picturesque, easy, idle, pleasant, fiery, aristocratic life has been elsewhere so well depicted that it has taken on the quality of rosy legend. Nobody did any more work than it pleased him to do; everybody was well-fed and happy; the women were beautiful and chaste; the men were bold, fiery, spirited, gracefully idle; life was a succession of picturesque merrymakings, lovemakings, intrigues, visits, lavish hospitalities, harmless politics, and revolutions. To be sure, there were but few signs of progressive spirit. People traveled on horseback because roads did not exist. They wore silks and diamonds, lace and satin, but their houses were crude, and conveniences were simple or entirely lacking. Their very vehicles, with wooden axles and wheels made of the cross-section of a tree, were such as an East African savage would be ashamed of. But who cared? And since no one wished improvements, why worry about them?

Certainly, judged by the standards of a truly progressive race, the Spanish occupation had many shortcomings. Agriculture was so little known that at times the country nearly starved. Contemporary travelers mention this fact with wonder. "There is," says Ryan, "very little land under cultivation in the vicinity of Monterey. That which strikes the foreigner most is the utter neglect in which the soil is left and the indifference with which the most charming sites are regarded. In the hands of the English and Americans, Monterey would be a beautiful town adorned with gardens and orchards and surrounded with picturesque walks and drives. The natives are, unfortunately, too ignorant to appreciate and too indolent even to attempt such improvement." And Captain Charles Wilkes asserts that "notwithstanding the immense number of domestic animals in the country, the Californians were too lazy to make butter or cheese, and even milk was rare. If there was a little good soap and leather occasionally found, the people were too indolent to make them in any quantity. The earth was simply scratched a few inches by a mean and ill-contrived plow. When the ground had been turned up by repeated scratching, it was hoed down and the clods broken by dragging over it huge branches of trees. Threshing was performed by spreading the cut grain on a spot of hard ground, treading it with cattle, and after taking off the straw throwing the remainder up in the breeze, much was lost and what was saved was foul."

General shiftlessness and inertia extended also to those branches wherein the Californian was supposed to excel. Even in the matter of cattle and sheep, the stock was very inferior to that brought into the country by the Americans, and such a thing as crossing stock or improving the breed of either cattle or horses was never thought of. The cattle were long-horned, rough-skinned animals, and the beef was tough and coarse. The sheep, while of Spanish stock, were very far from being Spanish merino. Their wool was of the poorest quality, entirely unfit for exportation, and their meat was not a favorite food.

There were practically no manufactures on the whole coast. The inhabitants depended for all luxuries and necessities on foreign trade, and in exchange gave hide and tallow from the semi-wild cattle that roamed the hills. Even this trade was discouraged by heavy import duties which amounted at times to one hundred per cent of the value. Such conditions naturally led to extensive smuggling which was connived at by most officials, high and low, and even by the monks of the missions themselves.

Although the chief reason for Spanish occupancy was to hold the country, the provisions for defense were not only inadequate but careless. Thomes says, in *Land and Sea*, that the fort at Monterey was "armed with four long brass nine-pounders, the handsomest guns that I ever saw all covered with scroll work and figures. They were mounted on ruined and decayed carriages. Two of them were pointed toward the planet Venus, and the other two were depressed so that had they been loaded or fired the balls would have startled the people on the other side of the hemisphere." This condition was typical of those throughout the so-called armed forts of California.

The picture thus presented is unjustly shaded, of course, for Spanish California had its ideal, noble, and romantic side. In a final estimate no one could say where the balance would be struck; but our purpose is not to strike a final balance. We are here endeavoring to analyze the reasons why the task of the American conquerors was so easy, and to explain the facility with which the original population was thrust aside.

It is a sometimes rather annoying anomaly of human nature that the races and individuals about whom are woven the most indestructible mantles of romance are generally those who, from the standpoint of economic stability or solid moral quality, are the most variable. We staid and sober citizens are inclined to throw an aura of picturesqueness about such creatures as the Stuarts, the dissipated Virginian cavaliers, the happy-go-lucky barren artists of the Latin Quarter, the fiery touchiness of that so-called chivalry which was one of the least important features of Southern life, and so on. We staid and sober citizens generally object strenuously to living in actual contact with the unpunctuality, unreliability, unreasonableness, shiftlessness, and general irresponsibility that are the invariable concomitants of this picturesqueness. At a safe distance we prove less critical. We even go so far as to regard this unfamiliar life as a mental anodyne or antidote to the rigid responsibility of our own everyday existence. We use these historical accounts for moral relaxation, much as some financiers or statisticians are said to read cheap detective stories for complete mental relaxation.

But, the Californian's undoubtedly admirable qualities of generosity, kindheartedness (whenever narrow prejudice or very lofty pride was not touched), hospitality, and all the rest, proved, in the eyes of a practical people confronted with a large and practical job, of little value in view of his predominantly negative qualities. A man with all the time in the world rarely gets on with a man who has no time at all. The newcomer had his house to put in order; and it was a very big house. The American wanted to get things done at once; the Californian could see no especial reason for doing them at all. Even when his short-lived enthusiasm happened to be aroused, it was for action tomorrow rather than today.

For all his amiable qualities, the mainspring of the Californian's conduct was at bottom the impression he could make upon others. The magnificence of his apparel and his accoutrement indicated no feeling for luxury but rather a fondness for display. His pride and quick-tempered honor were rooted in a desire to stand well in the eyes of his equals, not in a desire to stand well with himself. In consequence he had not the builder's fundamental instinct. He made no effort to supply himself with anything that did not satisfy this amiable desire. The contradictions of his conduct, therefore, become comprehensible. We begin to see why he wore silks and satins and why he neglected what to us are necessities. We see why he could display such admirable carriage in rough-riding and lassoing grizzlies, and yet seemed to possess such feeble military efficiency. We comprehend his generous hospitality coupled with his often narrow and suspicious cruelty. In fact, all the contrasts of his character and action begin to be clear. His displacement was natural when confronted by a people who, whatever their serious faults, had wants and desires that came from within, who possessed the instinct to create and to hold the things that would gratify those desires, and who, in the final analysis, began to care for other men's opinions only after they had satisfied their own needs and desires.

CHAPTER II

## THE AMERICAN OCCUPATION

From the earliest period Spain had discouraged foreign immigration into California. Her object was neither to attract settlers nor to develop the country, but to retain political control of it, and to make of it a possible asylum for her own people. Fifty years after the founding of the first mission at San Diego, California had only thirteen inhabitants of foreign birth. Most of these had become naturalized citizens, and so were in name Spanish. Of these but three were American!

Subsequent to 1822, however, the number of foreign residents rapidly increased. These people were mainly of substantial character, possessing a real interest in the country and an intention of permanent settlement. Most of them became naturalized, married Spanish women, acquired property, and became trusted citizens. In marked contrast to their neighbors, they invariably displayed the greatest energy and enterprise. They were generally liked by the natives, and such men as Hartnell, Richardson, David Spence, Nicholas Den, and many others, lived lives and left reputations to be envied.

Between 1830 and 1840, however, Americans of a different type began to present themselves. Southwest of the Missouri River the ancient town of Santa Fé attracted trappers and traders of all nations and from all parts of the great West. There they met to exchange their wares and to organize new expeditions into the remote territories. Some of them naturally found their way across the western mountains into California. One of the most notable was James Pattie, whose personal narrative is well worth reading. These men were bold, hardy, rough, energetic, with little patience for the refinements of life—in fact, diametrically opposed in character to the easy-going inhabitants of California. Contempt on the one side and distrust on the other were inevitable. The trappers and traders, together with the deserters from whalers and other ships, banded together in small communities of the rough type familiar to any observer of our frontier communities. They looked down upon and despised the "greasers," who in turn did everything in their power to harass them by political and other means.

At first isolated parties, such as those of Jedediah Smith, the Patties, and some others, had been imprisoned or banished eastward over the Rockies. The pressure of increasing numbers, combined with the rather idle carelessness into which all California-Spanish regulations seemed at length to fall, later nullified this drastic policy. Notorious among these men was one Isaac Graham, an American trapper, who had become weary of wandering and had settled near Natividad. There he established a small distillery, and in consequence drew about him all the rough and idle characters of the country. Some were trappers, some sailors; a few were Mexicans and renegade Indians. Over all of these Graham obtained an absolute control. They were most of them of a belligerent nature and expert shots, accustomed to taking care of themselves in the wilds. This little band, though it consisted of only thirty-nine members, was therefore considered formidable.

A rumor that these people were plotting an uprising for the purpose of overturning the government aroused Governor Alvarado to action. It is probable that the rumors in question were merely the reports of boastful drunken vaporings and would better have been ignored. However, at this time Alvarado, recently arisen to power through the usual revolutionary tactics, felt himself not entirely secure in his new position. He needed some distraction, and he therefore seized upon the rumor of Graham's uprising as a means of solidifying his influence—an expedient not unknown to modern rulers. He therefore ordered the prefect Castro to arrest the party. This was done by surprise. Graham and his companions were taken from their beds, placed upon a ship at Monterey, and exiled to San Blas, to be eventually delivered to the Mexican authorities. There they were held in prison for some months, but being at last released through the efforts of an American lawyer, most of them returned to California rather better off than before their arrest. It is typical of the vacillating Californian policy of the day that, on their return, Graham and his riflemen were at once made use of by one of the revolutionary parties as a reinforcement to their military power!

By 1840 the foreign population had by these rather desultory methods been increased to a few over four hundred souls. The majority could not be described as welcome guests. They had rarely come into the country with the deliberate intention of settling but rather as a traveler's chance. In November, 1841, however, two parties of quite a different character arrived. They were the first true immigrants into California, and their advent is significant as marking the beginning of the end of the old order. One of these parties entered by the Salt Lake Trail, and was the forerunner of the many pioneers over that great central route. The other came by Santa Fé, over the trail that had by now become so well marked that they hardly suffered even inconvenience on their journey. The first party arrived at Monte Diablo in the north, the other at San Gabriel Mission in the south. Many brought their families with them, and they came with the evident intention of settling in California.

The arrival of these two parties presented to the Mexican Government a problem that required immediate solution. Already in anticipation of such an event it had been provided that nobody who had not obtained a legal passport should be permitted to remain in the country; and that even old settlers, unless naturalized, should be required to depart unless they procured official permission to remain. Naturally none of the new arrivals had received notice of this law, and they were in consequence unprovided with the proper passports. Legally they should have been forced at once to turn about and return by the way they came. Actually it would have been inhuman, if not impossible, to have forced them at that season of the year to attempt the mountains. General Vallejo, always broad-minded in his policies, used discretion in the matter and provided those in his district with temporary permits to remain. He required only a bond signed by other Americans who had been longer in the country.

Alvarado and Vallejo at once notified the Mexican Government of the arrival of these strangers, and both expressed fear that other and larger parties would follow. These fears were very soon realized. Succeeding expeditions settled in the State with the evident intention of remaining. No serious effort was made by the California authorities to keep them out. From time to time, to be sure, formal objection was raised and regulations were passed. However, as a matter of plain practicability, it was manifestly impossible to prevent parties from starting across the plains, or to inform the people living in the Eastern States of the regulations adopted by California. It must be remembered that communication at that time was extraordinarily slow and broken. It would have been cruel and unwarranted to drive away those who had already arrived. And even were such a course to be contemplated, a garrison would have been necessary at every mountain pass on the East and North, and at every crossing of the Colorado River, as well as at every port along the coast. The government in California had not men sufficient to handle its own few antique guns in its few coastwise forts, let alone a surplus for the purpose just described. And to cap all, provided the garrisons had been available and could have been placed, it would have been physically impossible to have supplied them with provisions for even a single month.

Truth to tell, the newcomers of this last class were not personally objectionable to the Californians. The Spanish considered them no different from those of their own blood. Had it not been for an uneasiness lest the enterprise of the American settlers should in time overcome Californian interests, had it not been for repeated orders from Mexico itself, and had it not been for reports that ten thousand Mormons had recently left Illinois for California, it is doubtful if much attention would have been paid to the first immigrants.

Westward migration at this time was given an added impetus by the Oregon question. The status of Oregon had long been in doubt. Both England and the United States were inclined to claim priority of occupation. The boundary between Canada and the United States had not yet been decided upon between the two countries. Though they had agreed upon the compromise of joint occupation of the disputed land, this arrangement did not meet with public approval. The land-hungry took a particular interest in the question and joined their voices with those of men actuated by more patriotic motives. In public meetings which were held throughout the country this joint occupation convention was explained and discussed, and its abrogation was demanded. These meetings helped to form the patriotic desire. Senator Tappan once said that thirty thousand settlers with their thirty thousand rifles in the valley of the Columbia would quickly settle all questions of title to the country. This saying was adopted as the slogan for a campaign in the West. It had the same inspiring effect as the later famous "54-40 or fight." People were aroused as in the olden times they had been aroused to the crusades. It became a form of mental contagion to talk of, and finally to accomplish, the journey to the Northwest. Though no accurate records were kept, it is estimated that in 1843 over 800 people crossed to Willamette Valley. By 1845 this immigration had increased to fully 3000 within the year.

Because of these conditions the Oregon Trail had become a national highway. Starting at Independence, which is a suburb of the present Kansas City, it set out over the rolling prairie. At that time the wide plains were bright with wild flowers and teeming with game. Elk, antelope, wild turkeys, buffalo, deer, and a great variety of smaller creatures supplied sport and food in plenty. Wood and water were in every ravine; the abundant grass was sufficient to maintain the swarming hordes of wild animals and to give rich pasture to horses and oxen. The journey across these prairies, while long and hard, could rarely have been tedious. Tremendous thunderstorms succeeded the sultry heat of the West, an occasional cyclone added excitement; the cattle were apt to stampede senselessly; and, while the Indian had not yet developed the hostility that later made a journey across the plains so dangerous, nevertheless the possibilities of theft were always near enough at hand to keep the traveler alert and interested. Then there was the sandy country of the Platte River with its buffalo—buffalo by the hundreds of thousands, as far as the eye could reach—a marvelous sight: and beyond that again the Rockies, by way of Fort Laramie and South Pass.

Beyond Fort Hall the Oregon Trail and the trail for California divided. And at this point there began the terrible part of the journey—the arid, alkaline, thirsty desert, short of game, horrible in its monotony, deadly with its thirst. It is no wonder that, weakened by their sufferings in this inferno, so many of the immigrants looked upon the towering walls of the Sierras with a sinking of the heart.

While at first most of the influx of settlers was by way of Oregon, later the stories of the new country that made their way eastward induced travelers to go direct to California itself. The immigration, both from Oregon in the North and by the route over the Sierras, increased so rapidly that in 1845 there were probably about 700 Americans in the district. Those coming over the Sierras by the Carson Sink and Salt Lake trails arrived first of all at the fort built by Captain Sutter at the junction of the American and Sacramento rivers.

Captain Sutter was a man of Swiss parentage who had arrived in San Francisco in 1839 without much capital and with only the assets of considerable ability and great driving force. From the Governor he obtained grant of a large tract of land "somewhere in the interior" for the purposes of colonization. His colonists consisted of one German, four other white men, and eight Kanakas. The then Governor, Alvarado, thought this rather a small beginning, but advised him to take out naturalization papers and to select a location. Sutter set out on his somewhat vague quest with a four-oared boat and two small schooners, loaded with provisions, implements, ammunition, and three small cannon. Besides his original party he took an Indian boy and a dog, the latter proving by no means the least useful member of the company. He found at the junction of the American and Sacramento rivers the location that appealed to him, and there he established himself. His knack with the Indians soon enlisted their services. He seems to have been able to keep his agreements with them and at the same time to maintain rigid discipline and control.

Within an incredibly short time he had established a feudal barony at his fort. He owned eleven square leagues of land, four thousand two hundred cattle, two thousand horses, and about as many sheep. His trade in beaver skins was most profitable. He maintained a force of trappers who were always welcome at his fort, and whom he generously kept without cost to themselves. He taught the Indians blanket-weaving, hat-making, and other trades, and he even organized them into military companies. The fort which he built was enclosed on four sides and of imposing dimensions and convenience. It mounted twelve pieces of artillery, supported a regular garrison of forty in uniform, and contained within its walls a blacksmith shop, a distillery, a flour mill, a cannery, and space for other necessary industries. Outside the walls of the fort Captain Sutter raised wheat, oats, and barley in quantity, and even established an excellent fruit and vegetable garden.

Indeed, in every way Captain Sutter's environment and the results of his enterprises were in significant contrast to the inactivity and backwardness of his neighbors. He showed what an energetic man could accomplish with exactly the same human powers and material tools as had always been available to the Californians. Sutter himself was a rather short, thick-set man, exquisitely neat, of military bearing, carrying himself with what is called the true old-fashioned courtesy. He was a man of great generosity and of high spirit. His defect was an excess of ambition which in the end o'erleaped itself. There is no doubt that his first expectation was to found an independent state within the borders of California. His loyalty to the Americans was, however, never questioned, and the fact that his lands were gradually taken from him, and that he died finally in comparative poverty, is a striking comment on human injustice.

The important point for us at present is that Sutter's Fort happened to be exactly on the line of the overland immigration. For the trail-weary traveler it was the first stopping-place after crossing the high Sierras to the promised land. Sutter's natural generosity of character induced him always to treat these men with the greatest kindness. He made his profits from such as wished to get rid of their oxen and wagons in exchange for the commodities which he had to offer. But there is no doubt that the worthy captain displayed the utmost liberality in dealing with those whom poverty had overtaken. On several occasions he sent out expeditions at his personal cost to rescue parties caught in the mountains by early snows or other misfortunes along the road, Especially did he go to great expense in the matter of the ill-fated Donner party, who, it will be remembered, spent the winter near Truckee, and were reduced to cannibalism to avoid starvation.

1: See *The Passing of the Frontier*, in "The Chronicles of America."

Now Sutter had, of course, been naturalized in order to obtain his grant of land. He had also been appointed an official of the California-Mexican Government. Taking advantage of this fact, he was accustomed to issue permits or passports to the immigrants, permitting them to remain in the country. This gave the immigrants a certain limited standing, but, as they were not Mexican citizens, they were disqualified from holding land. Nevertheless Sutter used his good offices in showing desirable locations to the would-be settlers.

2: It is to be remarked that, prior to the gold rush, American settlements did not take place in the Spanish South but in the unoccupied North. In 1845 Castro and Castillero made a tour through the Sacramento Valley and the northern regions to inquire about the new arrivals. Castro displayed no personal uneasiness at their presence and made no attempt or threat to deport them.

As far as the Californians were concerned, there was little rivalry or interference between the immigrants and the natives. Their interests did not as yet conflict. Nevertheless the central Mexican Government continued its commands to prevent any and all immigration. It was rather well justified by its experience in Texas, where settlement had ended by final absorption. The local Californian authorities were thus thrust between the devil and the deep blue sea. They were constrained by the very positive and repeated orders from their home government to keep out all immigration and to eject those already on the ground. On the other hand, the means for doing so were entirely lacking, and the present situation did not seem to them alarming.

209

Thus matters drifted along until the Mexican War. For a considerable time before actual hostilities broke out, it was well known throughout the country that they were imminent. Every naval and military commander was perfectly aware that, sooner or later, war was inevitable. Many had received their instructions in case of that eventuality, and most of the others had individual plans to be put into execution at the earliest possible moment. Indeed, as early as 1842 Commodore Jones, being misinformed of a state of war, raced with what he supposed to be English war-vessels from South America, entered the port of Monterey hastily, captured the fort, and raised the American flag. The next day he discovered that not only was there no state of war, but that he had not even raced British ships! The flag was thereupon hauled down, the Mexican emblem substituted, appropriate apologies and salutes were rendered, and the incident was considered closed. The easy-going Californians accepted the apology promptly and cherished no rancor for the mistake.

In the meantime Thomas O. Larkin, a very substantial citizen of long standing in the country, had been appointed consul, and in addition received a sum of six dollars a day to act as secret agent. It was hoped that his great influence would avail to inspire the Californians with a desire for peaceful annexation to the United States. In case that policy failed, he was to use all means to separate them from Mexico, and so isolate them from their natural alliances. He was furthermore to persuade them that England, France, and Russia had sinister designs on their liberty. It was hoped that his good offices would slowly influence public opinion, and that, on the declaration of open war with Mexico, the United States flag could be hoisted in California not only without opposition but with the consent and approval of the inhabitants. This type of peaceful conquest had a very good chance of success. Larkin possessed the confidence of the better class of Californians and he did his duty faithfully.

Just at this moment a picturesque, gallant, ambitious, dashing, and rather unscrupulous character appeared inopportunely on the horizon. His name was John C. Frémont. He was the son of a French father and a Virginia mother. He was thirty-two years old, and was married to the daughter of Thomas H. Benton, United States Senator from Missouri and a man of great influence in the country. Possessed of an adventurous spirit, considerable initiative, and great persistence Frémont had already performed the feat of crossing the Sierra Nevadas by way of Carson River and Johnson Pass, and had also explored the Columbia River and various parts of the Northwest. Frémont now entered California by way of Walker Lake and the Truckee, and reached Sutter's Fort in 1845. He then turned southward to meet a division of his party under Joseph Walker.

His expedition was friendly in character, with the object of surveying a route westward to the Pacific, and then northward to Oregon. It supposedly possessed no military importance whatever. But his turning south to meet Walker instead of north, where ostensibly his duty called him, immediately aroused the suspicions of the Californians. Though ordered to leave the district, he refused compliance, and retired to a place called Gavilán Peak, where he erected fortifications and raised the United States flag. Probably Frémont's intentions were perfectly friendly and peaceful. He made, however, a serious blunder in withdrawing within fortifications. After various threats by the Californians but no performance in the way of attack, he withdrew and proceeded by slow marches to Sutter's Fort and thence towards the north. Near Klamath Lake he was overtaken by Lieutenant Gillespie, who delivered to him certain letters and papers. Frémont thereupon calmly turned south with the pick of his men.

In the meantime the Spanish sub-prefect, Guerrero, had sent word to Larkin that "a multitude of foreigners, having come into California and bought property, a right of naturalized foreigners only, he was under necessity of notifying the authorities in each town to inform such purchasers that the transactions were invalid, and that they themselves were subject to be expelled." This action at once caused widespread consternation among the settlers. They remembered the deportation of Graham and his party some years before, and were both alarmed and thoroughly convinced that defensive measures were necessary. Frémont's return at precisely this moment seemed to them very significant. He was a United States army officer at the head of a government expedition. When on his way to the North he had been overtaken by Gillespie, an officer of the United States Navy. Gillespie had delivered to him certain papers, whereupon he had immediately returned. There seemed no other interpretation of these facts than that the Government at Washington was prepared to uphold by force the American settlers in California.

This reasoning, logical as it seems, proves mistaken in the perspective of the years. Gillespie, it is true, delivered some letters to Frémont, but it is extremely unlikely they contained instructions having to do with interference in Californian affairs. Gillespie, at the same time that he brought these dispatches to Frémont, brought also instructions to Larkin creating the confidential agency above described, and these instructions specifically forbade interference with Californian affairs. It is unreasonable to suppose that contradictory dispatches were sent to one or another of these two men. Many years later Frémont admitted that the dispatch to Larkin was what had been communicated to him by Gillespie. His words are: "This officer Gillespie informed me also that he was directed by the Secretary of State to acquaint me with his instructions to the consular agent, Mr. Larkin." Reading Frémont's character, understanding his ambitions, interpreting his later lawless actions that resulted in his court-martial, realizing the recklessness of his spirit, and his instinct to take chances, one comes to the conclusion that it is more than likely that his move was a gamble on probabilities rather than a result of direct orders.

Be this as it may, the mere fact of Frémont's turning south decided the alarmed settlers, and led to the so-called "Bear Flag Revolution." A number of settlers decided that it would be expedient to capture Sonoma, where under Vallejo were nine cannon and some two hundred muskets. It was, in fact, a sort of military station. The capture proved to be a very simple matter. Thirty-two or thirty-three men appeared at dawn, before Vallejo's house, under Merritt and Semple. They entered the house suddenly, called upon Jacob Leese, Vallejo's son-in-law, to interpret, and demanded immediate surrender. Richman says "Leese was surprised at the 'rough looks' of the Americans. Semple he describes as 'six feet six inches tall, and about fifteen inches in diameter, dressed in greasy buckskin from neck to foot, and with a fox-skin cap.'"

The prisoners were at once sent by these raiders to Frémont, who was at that time on the American River. He immediately disclaimed any part in the affair. However, instead of remaining entirely aloof, he gave further orders that Leese, who was still in attendance as interpreter, should be arrested, and also that the prisoners should be confined in Sutter's Fort. He thus definitely and officially entered the movement. Soon thereafter Frémont started south through Sonoma, collecting men as he went.

The following quotation from a contemporary writer is interesting and illuminating. "A vast cloud of dust appeared at first, and thence in long files emerged this wildest of wild parties. Frémont rode ahead, a spare active looking man, with such an eye! He was dressed in a blouse and leggings, and wore a felt hat. After him came five Delaware Indians who were his bodyguard. They had charge of two baggage-horses. The rest, many of them blacker than Indians, rode two and two, the rifle held by one hand across the pummel of the saddle. The dress of these men was principally a long loose coat of deerskin tied with thongs in front, trousers of the same. The saddles were of various fashions, though these and a large drove of horses and a brass field gun were things they had picked up in California."

Meantime, the Americans who had collected in Sonoma, under the lead of William B. Ide, raised the flag of revolution—"a standard of somewhat uncertain origin as regards the cotton cloth whereof it was made," writes Royce. On this, they painted with berry juice "something that they called a Bear." By this capture of Sonoma, and its subsequent endorsement by Frémont, Larkin's instructions—that is, to secure California by quiet diplomatic means—were absolutely nullified. A second result was that Englishmen in California were much encouraged to hope for English intervention and protection. The Vallejo circle had always been strongly favorable to the United States. The effect of this raid and capture by United States citizens, with a United States officer endorsing the action, may well be guessed.

Inquiries and protests were lodged by the California authorities with Sloat and Lieutenant Montgomery of the United States naval forces. Just what effect these protests would have had, and just the temperature of the hot water in which the dashing Frémont would have found himself, is a matter of surmise. He had gambled strongly—on his own responsibility or at least at the unofficial suggestion of Benton—on an early declaration of war with Mexico. Failing such a declaration, he would be in a precarious diplomatic position, and must by mere force of automatic discipline have been heavily punished. However the dice fell for him. War with Mexico was almost immediately an actual fact. Frémont's injection into the revolution had been timed at the happiest possible moment for him.

The Bear Flag Revolution took place on June 14,1846. On July 7 the American flag was hoisted over the post at Monterey by Commodore Sloat. Though he had knowledge from June 5 of a state of war, this knowledge, apparently, he had shared neither with his officers nor with the public, and he exhibited a want of initiative and vigor which is in striking contrast to Frémont's ambition and overzeal.

Shortly after this incident Commodore Sloat was allowed to return "by reason of ill health," as has been heretofore published in most histories. His undoubted recall gave room to Commodore Robert Stockton, to whom Sloat not only turned over the command of the naval forces, but whom he also directed to "assume command of the forces and operations on shore."

Stockton at once invited Frémont to enlist under his command, and the invitation was accepted. The entire forces moved south by sea and land for the purpose of subduing southern California. This end was temporarily accomplished with almost ridiculous ease. At this distance of time, allowing all obvious explanations of lack of training, meager equipment, and internal dissension, we find it a little difficult to understand why the Californians did not make a better stand. Most of the so-called battles were a sort of *opera bouffe*. Californians entrenched with cannon were driven contemptuously forth, without casualties, by a very few men. For example, a lieutenant and nine men were sufficient to hold Santa Barbara in subjection. Indeed, the conquest was too easy, for, lulled into false security, Stockton departed, leaving as he supposed sufficient men to hold the country. The Californians managed to get some coherence into their councils, attacked the Americans, and drove them forth from their garrisons.

Stockton and Frémont immediately started south. In the meantime an overland party under General Kearny had been dispatched from the East. His instructions were rather broad. He was to take in such small sections of the country as New Mexico and Arizona, leaving sufficient garrisons on his way to California. As a result, though his command at first numbered 1657 men, he arrived in the latter state with only about 100. From Warner's Ranch in the mountains he sent word to Stockton that he had arrived. Gillespie, whom the Commodore at once dispatched with thirty-nine men to meet and conduct him to San Diego, joined Kearny near San Luis Rey Mission.

A force of Californians, however, under command of one Andrés Pico had been hovering about the hills watching the Americans. It was decided to attack this force. Twenty men were detailed under Captain Johnston for the purpose. At dawn on the morning of the 6th of December the Americans charged upon the Californian camp. The Californians promptly decamped after having delivered a volley which resulted in killing Johnston. The Americans at once pursued them hotly, became much scattered, and were turned upon by the fleeing enemy. The Americans were poorly mounted after their journey, their weapons were now empty, and they were unable to give mutual aid. The Spanish were armed with lances, pistols, and the deadly riata. Before the rearguard could come up, sixteen of the total American force were killed and nineteen badly wounded. This battle of San Pascual, as it was called, is interesting as being the only engagement in which the Californians got the upper hand. Whether their Parthian tactics were the result of a preconceived policy or were merely an expedient of the moment, it is impossible to say. The battle is also notable because the well-known scout, Kit Carson, took part in it.

The forces of Stockton and Kearny joined a few days later, and very soon a conflict of authority arose between the leaders. It was a childish affair throughout, and probably at bottom arose from Frémont's usual over-ambitious designs. To Kearny had undoubtedly been given, by the properly constituted authorities, the command of all the land operations.

Stockton, however, claimed to hold supreme land command by instructions from Commodore Sloat already quoted. Through the internal evidence of Stockton's letters and proclamations, it seems he was a trifle inclined to be bombastic and high-flown, to usurp authority, and perhaps to consider himself and his operations of more importance than they actually were. However, he was an officer disciplined and trained to obedience, and his absurd contention is not in character. It may be significant that he had promised to appoint Frémont Governor of California, a promise that naturally could not be fulfilled if Kearny's authority were fully recognized.

Furthermore, at this moment Frémont was at the zenith of his career, and his influence in such matters was considerable. As Hittell says, "At this time and for some time afterwards, Frémont was represented as a sort of young lion. The several trips he had made across the continent, and the several able and interesting reports he had published over his name attracted great public attention. He was hardly ever mentioned except in a high-flown hyperbolical phrase. Benton was one of the most influential men of his day, and it soon became well understood that the surest way of reaching the father-in-law's favor was by furthering the son-in-law's prospects; everybody that wished to court Benton praised Frémont. Besides this political influence Benton exerted in Frémont's behalf, there was an almost equally strong social influence." It might be added that the nature of his public service had been such as to throw him on his own responsibility, and that he had always gambled with fortune, as in the Bear Flag Revolution already mentioned. His star had ever been in the ascendant. He was a spoiled child of fortune at this time, and bitterly and haughtily resented any check to his ambition. The mixture of his blood gave him that fine sense of the dramatic which so easily descends to posing. His actual accomplishment was without doubt great; but his own appreciation of that accomplishment was also undoubtedly great. He was one of those interesting characters whose activities are so near the line between great deeds and charlatanism that it is sometimes difficult to segregate the pose from the performance.

The end of this row for precedence did not come until after the so-called battles at the San Gabriel River and on the Mesa on January 8 and 9, 1847. The first of these conflicts is so typical that it is worth a paragraph of description.

The Californians were posted on the opposite bank of the river. They had about five hundred men, and two pieces of artillery well placed. The bank was elevated some forty feet above the stream and possibly four or six hundred back from the water. The American forces, all told, consisted of about five hundred men, but most of them were dismounted. The tactics were exceedingly simple. The Americans merely forded the river, dragged their guns across, put them in position, and calmly commenced a vigorous bombardment. After about an hour and a half of circling about and futile half-attacks, the Californians withdrew. The total American loss in this and the succeeding "battle," called that of the Mesa, was three killed and twelve wounded.

After this latter battle, the Californians broke completely and hurtled toward the North. Beyond Los Angeles, near San Fernando, they ran head-on into Frémont and his California battalion marching overland from the North. Frémont had just learned of Stockton's defeat of the Californians and, as usual, he seized the happy chance the gods had offered him. He made haste to assure the Californians through a messenger that they would do well to negotiate with him rather than with Stockton. To these suggestions the Californians yielded. Commissioners appointed by both sides then met at Cahuenga on January 13, and elaborated a treaty by which the Californians agreed to surrender their arms and not to serve again during the war, whereupon the victors allowed them to leave the country. Frémont at once proceeded to Los Angeles, where he reported to Kearny and Stockton what had happened.

In accordance with his foolish determination, Stockton still refused to acknowledge Kearny's direct authority. He appointed Frémont Governor of California, which was one mistake; and Frémont accepted, which was another. Undoubtedly the latter thought that his pretensions would be supported by personal influence in Washington. From former experience he had every reason to believe so. In this case, however, he reckoned beyond the resources of even his powerful father-in-law. Kearny, who seems to have been a direct old war-dog, resolved at once to test his authority. He ordered Frémont to muster the California battalion into the regular service, under his (Kearny's) command; or, if the men did not wish to do this, to discharge them. This order did not in the least please Frémont. He attempted to open negotiations, but Kearny was in no manner disposed to talk. He said curtly that he had given his orders, and merely wished to know whether or not they would be obeyed. To this, and from one army officer to another, there could be but one answer, and that was in the affirmative.

Colonel Mason opportunely arrived from Washington with instructions to Frémont either to join his regiment or to resume the explorations on which he had originally been sent to this country. Frémont was still pretending to be Governor, but with nothing to govern. His game was losing at Washington. He could not know this, however, and for some time continued to persist in his absurd claims to governorship. Finally he begged permission of Kearny to form an expedition against Mexico. But it was rather late in the day for the spoiled child to ask for favors, and the permission was refused. Upon his return to Washington under further orders, Frémont was court-martialed, and was found guilty of mutiny, disobedience, and misconduct. He was ordered dismissed from the service, but was pardoned by President Polk in view of his past services. He refused this pardon and resigned.

Frémont was a picturesque figure with a great deal of personal magnetism and dash. The halo of romance has been fitted to his head. There is no doubt that he was a good wilderness traveler, a keen lover of adventure, and a likable personality. He was, however, over-ambitious; he advertised himself altogether too well; and he presumed on the undoubtedly great personal influence he possessed. He has been nicknamed the Pathfinder, but a better title would be the Pathfollower. He found no paths that had not already been traversed by men before him. Unless the silly sentiment that persistently glorifies such despicable characters as the English Stuarts continues to surround this interesting character with fallacious romance, Frémont will undoubtedly take his place in history below men now more obscure but more solid than he was. His services and his ability were both great. If he, his friends, and historians had been content to rest his fame on actualities, his position would be high and honorable. The presumption of so much more than the man actually did or was has the unfortunate effect of minimizing his real accomplishment.

CHAPTER III

*LAW—MILITARY AND CIVIL*

The military conquest of California was now an accomplished fact. As long as hostilities should continue in Mexico, California must remain under a military government, and such control was at once inaugurated. The questions to be dealt with, as may well be imagined, were delicate in the extreme. In general the military Governors handled such questions with tact and efficiency. This ability was especially true in the case of Colonel Mason, who succeeded General Kearny. The understanding displayed by this man in holding back the over-eager Americans on one side, and in mollifying the sensitive Californians on the other, is worthy of all admiration.

The Mexican laws were, in lack of any others, supposed to be enforced. Under this system all trials, except of course those having to do with military affairs, took place before officials called *alcades*, who acknowledged no higher authority than the Governor himself, and enforced the laws as autocrats. The new military Governors took over the old system bodily and appointed new *alcaldes* where it seemed necessary. The new *alcaldes* neither knew nor cared anything about the old Mexican law and its provisions. This disregard cannot be wondered at, for even a cursory examination of the legal forms convinces one that they were meant more for the enormous leisure of the old times than for the necessities of the new. In the place of Mexican law each *alcalde* attempted to substitute his own sense of justice and what recollection of common-law principles he might be able to summon. These common-law principles were not technical in the modern sense of the word, nor were there any printed or written statutes containing them. In this case they were simply what could be recalled by non-technical men of the way in which business had been conducted and disputes had been arranged back in their old homes. But their main reliance was on their individual sense of justice. As Hittell points out, even well-read lawyers who happened to be made*alcaldes* soon came to pay little attention to technicalities and to seek the merit of cases without regard to rules or forms. All the administration of the law was in the hands of these *alcaldes*. Mason, who once made the experiment of appointing a special court at Sutter's Fort to try a man known as Growling Smith for the murder of Indians, afterwards declared that he would not do it again except in the most extraordinary emergency, as the precedent was bad.

As may well be imagined, this uniquely individualistic view of the law made interesting legal history. Many of the incumbents were of the rough diamond type. Stories innumerable are related of them. They had little regard for the external dignity of the court, but they strongly insisted on its discipline. Many of them sat with their feet on the desk, chewing tobacco, and whittling a stick. During a trial one of the counsel referred to his opponent as an "oscillating Tarquín." The judge roared out "A what?"

"An oscillating Tarquín, your honor."

The judge's chair came down with a thump.

"If this honorable court knows herself, and she thinks she do, that remark is an insult to this honorable court, and you are fined two ounces."

Expostulation was cut short.

"Silence, sir! This honorable court won't tolerate cussings and she never goes back on her decisions!"

And she didn't!

Nevertheless a sort of rough justice was generally accomplished. These men felt a responsibility. In addition they possessed a grim commonsense earned by actual experience.

There is an instance of a priest from Santa Clara, sued before the *alcalde* of San José for a breach of contract. His plea was that as a churchman he was not amenable to civil law. The American decided that, while he could not tell what peculiar privileges a clergyman enjoyed as a priest, it was quite evident that when he departed from his religious calling and entered into a secular bargain with a citizen he placed himself on the same footing as the citizen, and should be required like anybody else to comply with his agreement. This principle, which was good sense, has since become good law.

The *alcalde* refused to be bound by trivial concerns. A Mexican was accused of stealing a pair of leggings. He was convicted and fined three ounces for stealing, while the prosecuting witness was also fined one ounce for bothering the court with such a complaint. On another occasion the defendant, on being fined, was found to be totally insolvent. The *alcalde* thereupon ordered the plaintiff to pay the fine and costs for the reason that the court could not be expected to sit without remuneration. Though this naive system worked out well enough in the new and primitive community, nevertheless thinking men realized that it could be for a short time only.

As long as the war with Mexico continued, naturally California was under military Governors, but on the declaration of peace military government automatically ceased. Unfortunately, owing to strong controversies as to slavery or non-slavery, Congress passed no law organizing California as a territory; and the status of the newly-acquired possession was far from clear. The people held that, in the absence of congressional action, they had the right to provide for their own government. On the other hand, General Riley contended that the laws of California obtained until supplanted by act of Congress. He was under instructions as Governor to enforce this view, which was, indeed, sustained by judicial precedents. But for precedents the inhabitants cared little. They resolved to call a constitutional convention. After considerable negotiation and thought, Governor Riley resolved to accede to the wishes of the people. An election of delegates was called and the constitutional convention met at Monterey, September 1, 1849.

Parenthetically it is to be noticed that this event took place a considerable time after the first discovery of gold. It can in no sense be considered as a sequel to that fact. The numbers from the gold rush came in later. The constitutional convention was composed mainly of men who had previous interests in the country. They were representative of the time and place. The oldest delegate was fifty-three years and the youngest twenty-five years old. Fourteen were lawyers, fourteen were farmers, nine were merchants, five were soldiers, two were printers, one was a doctor, and one described himself as "a gentleman of elegant leisure."

The deliberations of this body are very interesting reading. Such a subject is usually dry in the extreme; but here we have men assembled from all over the world trying to piece together a form of government from the experiences of the different communities from which they originally came. Many Spanish Californians were represented on the floor. The different points brought up and discussed, in addition to those finally incorporated in the constitution, are both a valuable measure of the degree of intelligence at that time, and an indication of what men considered important in the problems of the day. The constitution itself was one of the best of the thirty-one state constitutions that then existed. Though almost every provision in it was copied from some other instrument, the choice was good. A provision prohibiting slavery was carried by a unanimous vote. When the convention adjourned, the new commonwealth was equipped with all the necessary machinery for regular government.

3: The constitution was ratified by popular vote, November 13, 1849; and the machinery of state government was at once set in motion, though the State was not admitted into the Union until September 9. 1850.

It is customary to say that the discovery of gold made the State of California. As a matter of fact, it introduced into the history of California a new solvent, but it was in no sense a determining factor in either the acquisition or the assuring of the American hold. It must not be forgotten that a rising tide of American immigration had already set in. By 1845 the white population had increased to about eight thousand. At the close of hostilities it was estimated that the white population had increased to somewhere between twelve and fifteen thousand. Moreover this immigration, though established and constantly growing, was by no means topheavy. There was plenty of room in the north for the Americans, and they were settling there peaceably. Those who went south generally bought their land in due form. They and the Californians were getting on much better than is usual with conquering and conquered peoples.

But the discovery of gold upset all this orderly development. It wiped out the usual evolution. It not only swept aside at once the antiquated Mexican laws, but it submerged for the time being the first stirrings of the commonwealth toward due convention and legislation after the American pattern. It produced an interim wherein the only law was that evolved from men's consciences and the Anglo-Saxon instinct for order. It brought to shores remote from their native lands a cosmopolitan crew whose only thought was a fixed determination to undertake no new responsibilities. Each man was living for himself. He intended to get his own and to protect his own, and he cared very little for the difficulties of his neighbors. In other words, the discovery of gold offered California as the blank of a mint to receive the impress of a brand new civilization. And furthermore it gave to these men and, through them, to the world an impressive lesson that social responsibility can be evaded for a time, to be sure, but only for a time; and that at the last it must be taken up and the arrears must be paid.

CHAPTER IV

*GOLD*

The discovery of gold—made, as everyone knows, by James Marshall, a foreman of Sutter's, engaged in building a sawmill for the Captain—came at a psychological time. The Mexican War was just over and the adventurous spirits, unwilling to settle down, were looking for new excitement. Furthermore, the hard times of the Forties had blanketed the East with mortgages. Many sober communities were ready, deliberately and without excitement, to send their young men westward in the hope of finding a way out of their financial difficulties. The Oregon question, as has been already indicated, had aroused patriotism to such an extent that westward migration had become a sort of mental contagion.

: January 24, 1848, is the date usually given.

It took some time for the first discoveries to leak out, and to be believed after they had gained currency. Even in California itself interest was rather tepid at first. Gold had been found in small quantities many years before, and only the actual sight of the metal in considerable weight could rouse men's imaginations to the blazing point.

Among the most enthusiastic protagonists was one Sam Brannan, who often appeared afterwards in the pages of Californian history. Brannan was a Mormon who had set out from New York with two hundred and fifty Mormons to try out the land of California as a possible refuge for the persecuted sect. That the westward migration of Mormons stopped at Salt Lake may well be due to the fact that on entering San Francisco Bay, Brannan found himself just too late. The American flag was already floating over the Presidio. Eye-witnesses say that Brannan dashed his hat to the deck, exclaiming, "There is that damned rag again." However, he proved an adaptable creature, for he and his Mormons landed nevertheless, and took up the industries of the country.

Brannan collected the usual tithes from these men, with the ostensible purpose of sending them on to the Church at Salt Lake. This, however, he consistently failed to do. One of the Mormons, on asking Sutter how long they should be expected to pay these tithes, received the answer, "As long as you are fools enough to do so." But they did not remain fools very much longer, and Brannan found himself deprived of this source of revenue. On being dunned by Brigham Young for the tithes already collected, Brannan blandly resigned from the Church, still retaining the assets. With this auspicious beginning, aided by a burly, engaging personality, a coarse, direct manner that appealed to men, and an instinct for the limelight, he went far. Though there were a great many admirable traits in his character, people were forced to like him in spite of rather than because of them. His enthusiasm for any public agitation was always on tap.

In the present instance he rode down from Sutter's Fort, where he then had a store, bringing with him gold-dust and nuggets from the new placers. "Gold! Gold! Gold from the American River!" shouted Brannan, as he strode down the street, swinging his hat in one hand and holding aloft the bottle of gold-dust in the other. This he displayed to the crowd that immediately gathered. With such a start, this new interest brought about a stampede that nearly depopulated the city.

The fever spread. People scrambled to the mines from all parts of the State. Practically every able-bodied man in the community, except the Spanish Californians, who as usual did not join this new enterprise with any unanimity, took at least a try at the diggings. Not only did they desert almost every sort of industry, but soldiers left the ranks and sailors the ships, so that often a ship was left in sole charge of its captain. All of American and foreign California moved to the foothills.

Then ensued the brief period so affectionately described in all literalness as the Arcadian Age. Men drank and gambled and enjoyed themselves in the rough manner of mining camps; but they were hardly ever drunken and in no instance dishonest. In all literalness the miners kept their gold-dust in tin cans and similar receptacles, on shelves, unguarded in tents or open cabins. Even quarrels and disorder were practically unknown. The communities were individualistic in the extreme, and yet, with the Anglo-Saxon love of order, they adopted rules and regulations and simple forms of government that proved entirely adequate to their needs. When the "good old days" are mentioned with the lingering regret associated with that phrase, the reference is to this brief period that came between the actual discovery and appreciation of gold and the influx from abroad that came in the following years.

This condition was principally due to the class of men concerned. The earliest miners were a very different lot from the majority of those who arrived in the next few years. They were mostly the original population, who had come out either as pioneers or in the government service. They included the discharged soldiers of Stevenson's regiment of New York Volunteers, who had been detailed for the war but who had arrived a little late, the so-called Mormon Battalion, Sam Brannan's immigrants, and those who had come as settlers since 1842. They were a rough lot with both the virtues and the defects of the pioneer. Nevertheless among their most marked characteristics were their honesty and their kindness. Hittell gives an incident that illustrates the latter trait very well. "It was a little camp, the name of which is not given and perhaps is not important. The day was a hot one when a youth of sixteen came limping along, footsore, weary, hungry, and penniless. There were at least thirty robust miners at work in the ravine and it may well be believed they were cheerful, probably now and then joining in a chorus or laughing at a joke. The lad as he saw and heard them sat down upon the bank, his face telling the sad story of his misfortunes. Though he said nothing he was not unobserved. At length one of the miners, a stalwart fellow, pointing up to the poor fellow on the bank, exclaimed to his companions, 'Boys, I'll work an hour for that chap if you will.' All answered in the affirmative and picks and shovels were plied with even more activity than before. At the end of an hour a hundred dollars' worth of gold-dust was poured into his handkerchief. As this was done the miners who had crowded around the grateful boy made out a list of tools and said to him: 'You go now and buy these tools and come back. We'll have a good claim staked out for you; then you've got to paddle for yourself.'"

Another reason for this distinguished honesty was the extent and incredible richness of the diggings, combined with the firm belief that this richness would last forever and possibly increase. The first gold was often found actually at the roots of bushes, or could be picked out from the veins in the rocks by the aid of an ordinary hunting-knife. Such pockets were, to be sure, by no means numerous; but the miners did not know that. To them it seemed extremely possible that gold in such quantities was to be found almost anywhere for the mere seeking. Authenticated instances are known of men getting ten, fifteen, twenty, and thirty thousand dollars within a week or ten days, without particularly hard work. Gold was so abundant it was much easier to dig it than to steal it, considering the risks attendant on the latter course. A story is told of a miner, while paying for something, dropping a small lump of gold worth perhaps two or three dollars. A bystander picked it up and offered it to him. The miner, without taking it, looked at the man with amazement, exclaiming: "Well, stranger, you are a curiosity. I guess you haven't been in the diggings long. You had better keep that lump for a sample."

These were the days of the red-shirted miner, of romance, of Arcadian simplicity, of clean, honest working under blue skies and beneath the warm California sun, of immense fortunes made quickly, of faithful "pardners," and all the rest. This life was so complete in all its elements that, as we look back upon it, we unconsciously give it a longer period than it actually occupied. It seems to be an epoch, as indeed it was; but it was an epoch of less than a single year, and it ended when the immigration from the world at large began.

The first news of the gold discovery filtered to the east in a roundabout fashion through vessels from the Sandwich Islands. A Baltimore paper published a short item. Everybody laughed at the rumor, for people were already beginning to discount California stories. But they remembered it. Romance, as ever, increases with the square of the distance; and this was a remote land. But soon there came an official letter written by Governor Mason to the War Department wherein he said that in his opinion, "There is more gold in the country drained by the Sacramento and San Joaquín rivers than would pay the cost of the late war with Mexico a hundred times over." The public immediately was alert. And then, strangely enough, to give direction to the restless spirit seething beneath the surface of society, came a silly popular song. As has happened many times before and since, a great movement was set to the lilt of a commonplace melody. Minstrels started it; the public caught it up. Soon in every quarter of the world were heard the strains of *Oh, Susannah!* or rather the modification of it made to fit this case:

"I'll scrape the mountains clean, old girl,
I'll drain the rivers dry.
I'm off for California, Susannah, don't you cry.
Oh, Susannah, don't you cry for me,
I'm off to California with my wash bowl on my
   knee!"

The public mind already prepared for excitement by the stirring events of the past few years, but now falling into the doldrums of both monotonous and hard times, responded eagerly. Every man with a drop of red blood in his veins wanted to go to California. But the journey was a long one, and it cost a great deal of money, and there were such things as ties of family or business impossible to shake off. However, those who saw no immediate prospect of going often joined the curious clubs formed for the purpose of getting at least one or more of their members to the El Dorado. These clubs met once in so often, talked over details, worked upon each other's excitement even occasionally and officially sent some one of their members to the point of running amuck. Then he usually broke off all responsibilities and rushed headlong to the gold coast.

The most absurd ideas obtained currency. Stories did not lose in travel. A work entitled *Three Weeks in the Gold Mines*, written by a mendacious individual who signed himself H.I. Simpson, had a wide vogue. It is doubtful if the author had ever been ten miles from New York; but he wrote a marvelous and at the time convincing tale. According to his account, Simpson had only three weeks for a tour of the gold-fields, and considered ten days of the period was all he could spare the unimportant job of picking up gold. In the ten days, however, with no other implements than a pocket-knife, he accumulated fifty thousand dollars. The rest of the time he really preferred to travel about viewing the country! He condescended, however, to pick up incidental nuggets that happened to lie under his very footstep. Said one man to his friend: "I believe I'll go. I know most of this talk is wildly exaggerated, but I am sensible enough to discount all that sort of thing and to disbelieve absurd stories. I shan't go with the slightest notion of finding the thing true, but will be satisfied if I do reasonably well. In fact, if I don't pick up more than a hatful of gold a day I shall be perfectly satisfied."

Men's minds were full of strange positive knowledge, not only as to the extent of the goldmines, but also as to theory and practice of the actual mining. Contemporary writers tell us of the hundreds and hundreds of different strange machines invented for washing out the gold and actually carried around the Horn or over the Isthmus of Panama to San Francisco. They were of all types, from little pocket-sized affairs up to huge arrangements with windmill arms and wings. Their destination was inevitably the beach below the San Francisco settlement, where, half buried in the sand, torn by the trade winds, and looted for whatever of value might inhere in the metal parts, they rusted and disintegrated, a pathetic and grisly reminder of the futile greed of men.

Nor was this excitement confined to the eastern United States. In France itself lotteries were held, called, I believe, the Lotteries of the Golden Ingot. The holders of the winning tickets were given a trip to the gold-fields. A considerable number of French came over in that manner, so that life in California was then, as now, considerably leavened by Gallicism. Their ignorance of English together with their national clannishness caused them to stick together in communities. They soon became known as Keskydees. Very few people knew why. It was merely the frontiersmen's understanding of the invariable French phrase *"Qu'est-ce qu'il dit?"* In Great Britain, Norway, to a certain extent in Germany, South America, and even distant Australia, the adventurous and impecunious were pricking up their ears and laying their plans.

There were offered three distinct channels for this immigration. The first of these was by sailing around Cape Horn. This was a slow but fairly comfortable and reasonably safe route. It was never subject to the extreme overcrowding of the Isthmus route, and it may be dismissed in this paragraph. The second was by the overland route, of which there were several trails. The third was by the Isthmus of Panama. Each of these two is worth a chapter, and we shall take up the overland migration first.

CHAPTER V

*ACROSS THE PLAINS*

The overland migration attracted the more hardy and experienced pioneers, and also those whose assets lay in cattle and farm equipment rather than in money. The majority came from the more western parts of the then United States, and therefore comprised men who had already some experience in pioneering. As far as the Mississippi or even Kansas these parties generally traveled separately or in small groups from a single locality. Before starting over the great plains, however, it became necessary to combine into larger bands for mutual aid and protection. Such recognized meeting-points were therefore generally in a state of congestion. Thousands of people with their equipment and animals were crowded together in some river-bottom awaiting the propitious moment for setting forth.

The journey ordinarily required about five months, provided nothing untoward happened in the way of delay. A start in the spring therefore allowed the traveler to surmount the Sierra Nevada mountains before the first heavy snowfalls. One of the inevitable anxieties was whether or not this crossing could be safely accomplished. At first the migration was thoroughly orderly and successful. As the stories from California became more glowing, and as the fever for gold mounted higher, the pace accelerated.

A book by a man named Harlan, written in the County Farm to which his old age had brought him, gives a most interesting picture of the times. His party consisted of fourteen persons, one of whom, Harlan's grandmother, was then ninety years old and blind! There were also two very small children. At Indian Creek in Kansas they caught up with the main body of immigrants and soon made up their train. He says: "We proceeded very happily until we reached the South Platte. Every night we young folks had a dance on the green prairie." Game abounded, the party was in good spirits and underwent no especial hardships, and the Indian troubles furnished only sufficient excitement to keep the men interested and alert. After leaving Salt Lake, however, the passage across the desert suddenly loomed up as a terrifying thing. "We started on our passage over this desert in the early morning, trailed all next day and all night, and on the morning of the third day our guide told us that water was still twenty-five miles away. William Harlan here lost his seven yoke of oxen. The man who was in charge of them went to sleep, and the cattle turned back and recrossed the desert or perhaps died there…. Next day I started early and drove till dusk, as I wished to tire the cattle so that they would lie down and give me a chance to sleep. They would rest for two or three hours and then try to go back home to their former range." The party won through, however, and descended into the smiling valleys of California, ninety-year-old lady and all.

These parties which were hastily got together for the mere purpose of progress soon found that they must have some sort of government to make the trip successful. A leader was generally elected to whom implicit obedience was supposed to be accorded. Among independent and hot-headed men quarrels were not infrequent. A rough sort of justice was, however, invoked by vote of the majority. Though a "split of blankets" was not unknown, usually the party went through under one leadership. Fortunate were those who possessed experienced men as leaders, or who in hiring the services of one of the numerous plains guides obtained one of genuine experience. Inexperience and graft were as fatal then as now. It can well be imagined what disaster could descend upon a camping party in a wilderness such as the Old West, amidst the enemies which that wilderness supported. It is bad enough today when inexperienced people go to camp by a lake near a farm-house. Moreover, at that time everybody was in a hurry, and many suspected that the other man was trying to obtain an advantage.

Hittell tells of one ingenious citizen who, in trying to keep ahead of his fellow immigrants as he hurried along, had the bright idea of setting on fire and destroying the dry grass in order to retard the progress of the parties behind. Grass was scarce enough in the best circumstances, and the burning struck those following with starvation. He did not get very far, however, before he was caught by a posse who mounted their best horses for pursuit. They shot him from his saddle and turned back. This attempt at monopoly was thus nipped in the bud.

Probably there would have been more of this sort of thing had it not been for the constant menace of the Indians. The Indian attack on the immigrant train has become so familiar through Wild West shows and so-called literature that it is useless to redescribe it here. Generally the object was merely the theft of horses, but occasionally a genuine attack, followed in case of success by massacre, took place. An experience of this sort did a great deal of good in holding together not only the parties attacked, but also those who afterwards heard of the attempt.

There was, however, another side to the shield, a very encouraging and cheerful side. For example, some good-hearted philanthropist established a kind of reading-room and post-office in the desert near the headwaters of the Humboldt River. He placed it in a natural circular wall of rock by the road, shaded by a lone tree. The original founder left a lot of newspapers on a stone seat inside the wall with a written notice to "Read and leave them for others."

Many trains, well equipped, well formed, well led, went through without trouble—indeed, with real pleasure. Nevertheless the overwhelming testimony is on the other side. Probably this was due in large part to the irritability that always seizes the mind of the tenderfoot when he is confronted by wilderness conditions. A man who is a perfectly normal and agreeable citizen in his own environment becomes a suspicious half-lunatic when placed in circumstances uncomfortable and unaccustomed. It often happened that people were obliged to throw things away in order to lighten their loads. When this necessity occurred, they generally seemed to take an extraordinary delight in destroying their property rather than in leaving it for anybody else who might come along. Hittell tells us that sugar was often ruined by having turpentine poured over it, and flour was mixed with salt and dirt; wagons were burned; clothes were torn into shreds and tatters. All of this destruction was senseless and useless, and was probably only a blind and instinctive reaction against hardships.

Those hardships were considerable. It is estimated that during the height of the overland migration in the spring of 1849 no less than fifty thousand people started out. The wagon trains followed almost on one another's heels, so hot was the pace. Not only did the travelers wish to get to the Sierras before the snows blocked the passes, not only were they eager to enter the gold mines, but they were pursued by the specter of cholera in the concentration camps along the

Mississippi Valley. This scourge devastated these gatherings. It followed the men across the plains like some deadly wild beast, and was shaken off only when the high clear climate of desert altitude was eventually reached.

But the terrible part of the journey began with the entrance into the great deserts, like that of the Humboldt Sink. There the conditions were almost beyond belief. Thousands were left behind, fighting starvation, disease, and the loss of cattle. Women who had lost their husbands from the deadly cholera went staggering on without food or water, leading their children. The trail was literally lined with dead animals. Often in the middle of the desert could be seen the camps of death, the wagons drawn in a circle, the dead animals tainting the air, every living human being crippled from scurvy and other diseases. There was no fodder for the cattle, and very little water The loads had to be lightened almost every mile by the discarding of valuable goods. Many of the immigrants who survived the struggle reached the goal in an impoverished condition. The road was bordered with an almost unbroken barrier of abandoned wagons, old mining implements, clothes, provisions, and the like. As the cattle died, the problem of merely continuing the march became worse. Often the rate of progress was not more than a mile every two or three hours. Each mile had to be relayed back and forth several times. And when this desert had sapped their strength, they came at last to the Sink itself, with its long white fields of alkali with drifts of ashes across them, so soft that the cattle sank half-way to their bellies. The dust was fine and light and rose chokingly; the sun was strong and fierce. All but the strongest groups of pioneers seemed to break here. The retreats became routs. Each one put out for himself with what strength he had left. The wagons were emptied of everything but the barest necessities. At every stop some animal fell in the traces and had to be cut out of the yoke. If a wagon came to a full stop, it was abandoned. The animals were detached and driven forward. And when at last they reached the Humboldt River itself, they found it almost impossible to ford. The best feed lay on the other side. In the distance the high and forbidding ramparts of the Sierra Nevadas reared themselves.

One of these Forty-niners, Delano, a man of some distinction in the later history of the mining communities, says that five men drowned themselves in the Humboldt River in one day out of sheer discouragement. He says that he had to save the lives of his oxen by giving Indians fifteen dollars to swim the river and float some grass across to him. And with weakened cattle, discouraged hearts, no provisions, the travelers had to tackle the high rough road that led across the mountains.

Of course, the picture just drawn is of the darkest aspect. Some trains there were under competent pioneers who knew their job; who were experienced in wilderness travel; who understood better than to chase madly away after every cut-off reported by irresponsible trappers; who comprehended the handling and management of cattle; who, in short, knew wilderness travel. These came through with only the ordinary hardships. But take it all in all, the overland trail was a trial by fire. One gets a notion of its deadliness from the fact that over five thousand people died of cholera alone. The trail was marked throughout its length by the shallow graves of those who had succumbed. He who arrived in California was a different person from the one who had started from the East. Experience had even in so short a time fused his elements into something new. This alteration must not be forgotten when we turn once more to the internal affairs of the new commonwealth.

CHAPTER VI

## *THE MORMONS*

In the westward overland migration the Salt Lake Valley Mormons played an important part. These strange people had but recently taken up their abode in the desert. That was a fortunate circumstance, as their necessities forced them to render an aid to the migration that in better days would probably have been refused.

The founder of the Mormon Church, Joseph Smith, Jr., came from a commonplace family.

Apparently its members were ignorant and superstitious. They talked much of hidden treasure and of supernatural means for its discovery. They believed in omens, signs, and other superstitions. As a boy Joseph had been shrewd enough and superstitious enough to play this trait up for all it was worth. He had a magic peep-stone and a witch-hazel divining-rod that he manipulated so skillfully as to cause other boys and even older men to dig for him as he wished. He seemed to delight in tricking his companions in various ways, by telling fortunes, reeling off tall yarns, and posing as one possessed of occult knowledge.

According to Joseph's autobiography, the discovery of the Mormon Bible happened in this wise: on the night of September 21, 1823, a vision fell upon him; the angel Moroni appeared and directed him to a cave on the hillside; in this cave he found some gold plates, on which were inscribed strange characters, written in what Smith described as "reformed Egyptian"; they were undecipherable except by the aid of a pair of magic peep-stones named Urim and Thummim, delivered him for the purpose by the angel at Palmyra; looking through the hole in these peep-stones, he was able to interpret the gold plates. This was the skeleton of the story embellished by later ornamentation in the way of golden breastplates, two stones bright and shining, golden plates united at the back by rings, the sword of Laban, square stone boxes, cemented clasps, invisible blows, suggestions of Satan, and similar mummery born from the quickened imagination of a zealot.

Smith succeeded in interesting one Harris to act as his amanuensis in his interpretation of these books of Mormon. The future prophet sat behind a screen with the supposed gold plates in his hat. He dictated through the stones Urim and Thummim. With a keen imagination and natural aptitude for the strikingly dramatic, he was able to present formally his ritual, tabernacle, holy of holies, priesthood and tithings, constitution and councils, blood atonement, anointment, twelve apostles, miracles, his spiritual manifestations and revelations, all in reminiscence of the religious tenets of many lands.

Such religious movements rise and fall at periodic intervals. Sometimes they are never heard of outside the small communities of their birth; at other times they arise to temporary nation-wide importance, but they are unlucky either in leadership or environment and so perish. The Mormon Church, however, was fortunate in all respects. Smith was in no manner a successful leader, but he made a good prophet. He was strong physically, was a great wrestler, and had an abundance of good nature; he was personally popular with the type of citizen with whom he was thrown. He could impress the ignorant mind with the reality of his revelations and the potency of his claims. He could impress the more intelligent, but half unscrupulous, half fanatical minds of the leaders with the power of his idea and the opportunities offered for leadership.

Two men of the latter type were Parley P. Pratt and Sidney Rigdon. The former was of the narrow, strong, fanatic type; the latter had the cool constructive brain that gave point, direction, and consistency to the Mormon system of theology. Had it not been for such leaders and others like them, it is quite probable that the Smith movement would have been lost like hundreds of others. That Smith himself lasted so long as the head of the Church, with the powers and perquisites of that position, can be explained by the fact that, either by accident or shrewd design, his position before the unintelligent masses had been made impregnable. If it was not true that Joseph Smith had received the golden plates from an angel and had translated them—again with the assistance of an angel—and had received from heaven the revelations vouchsafed from time to time for the explicit guidance of the Church in moral, temporal, and spiritual matters, then there was no Book of Mormon, no new revelation, no Mormon Church. The dethronement of Smith meant that there could be no successor to Smith, for there would be nothing to which to succeed. The whole church structure must crumble with him.

The time was psychologically right. Occasionally a contagion of religious need seems to sweep the country. People demand manifestations and signs, and will flock to any who can promise them. To this class the Book of Mormon, with its definite sort of mysticism, appealed strongly. The promises of a new Zion were concrete; the power was centralized, so that people who had heretofore been floundering in doubt felt they could lean on authority, and shake off the personal responsibility that had weighed them down. The Mormon communities grew fast, and soon began to send out proselyting missionaries. England was especially a fruitful field for these missionaries. The great manufacturing towns were then at their worst, containing people desperately ignorant, superstitious, and so deeply poverty-stricken that the mere idea of owning land of their own seemed to them the height of affluence. Three years after the arrival of the missionaries the general conference reported 4019 converts in England alone. These were good material in the hands of strong, fanatical, or unscrupulous leaders. They were religious enthusiasts, of course, who believed they were coming to a real city of Zion. Most of them were in debt to the Church for the price of their passage, and their expenses. They were dutiful in their acceptance of miracles, signs, and revelations. The more intelligent among them realized that, having come so far and invested in the enterprise their all, it was essential that they accept wholly the discipline and authority of the Church.

Before their final migration to Utah, the Mormons made three ill-fated attempts to found the city of Zion, first in Ohio, then in western Missouri, and finally, upon their expulsion from Missouri, at Nauvoo in Illinois. In every case they both inspired and encountered opposition and sometimes persecution. As the Mormons increased in power, they became more self-sufficient and arrogant. They at first presumed to dictate politically, and then actually began to consider themselves a separate political entity. One of their earliest pieces of legislation, under the act incorporating the city of Nauvoo, was an ordinance to protect the inhabitants of the Mormon communities from all outside legal processes. No writ for the arrest of any Mormon inhabitants of any Mormon city could be executed until it had received the mayor's approval. By way of a mild and adequate penalty, anyone violating this ordinance was to be imprisoned for life with no power of pardon in the governor without the mayor's consent.

Of course this was a welcome opportunity for the lawless and desperate characters of the surrounding country. They became Mormon to a man. Under the shield of Mormon protection they could steal and raid to their heart's content. Land speculators also came into the Church, and bought land in the expectation that New Zion property would largely rise. Banking grew somewhat frantic. Complaints became so bitter that even the higher church authorities were forced to take cognizance of the practices. In 1840 Smith himself said: "We are no longer at war, and you must stop stealing. When the right time comes, we will go in force and take the whole State of Missouri. It belongs to us as our inheritance, but I want no more petty stealing. A man that will steal petty articles from his enemies will, when occasion offers, steal from his brethren too. Now I command you that have stolen must steal no more."

At Nauvoo, on the eastern bank of the Mississippi, they built a really pretentious and beautiful city, and all but completed a temple that was, from every account, creditable. However, their arrogant relations with their neighbors and the extreme isolation in which they held themselves soon earned them the dislike and distrust of those about them. The practice of polygamy had begun, although even to the rank and file of the Mormons themselves the revelation commanding it was as yet unknown. Still, rumors had leaked forth. The community, already severely shocked in its economic sense, was only too ready to be shocked in its moral sense, as is the usual course of human nature. The rather wild vagaries of the converts, too, aroused distrust and disgust in the sober minds of the western pioneers. At religious meetings converts would often arise to talk in gibberish—utterly nonsensical gibberish. This was called a "speaking with tongues," and could be translated by the speaker or a bystander in any way he saw fit, without responsibility for the saying. This was an easy way of calling a man names without standing behind it, so to speak. The congregation saw visions, read messages on stones picked up in the field—messages which disappeared as soon as interpreted. They had fits in meetings, they chased balls of fire through the fields, they saw wonderful lights in the air, in short they went through all the hysterical vagaries formerly seen also in the Methodist revivals under John Wesley.

Turbulence outside was accompanied by turbulence within. Schisms occurred. Branches were broken off from the Church. The great temporal power and wealth to which, owing to the obedience and docility of the rank and file, the leaders had fallen practically sole heirs, had gone to their heads. The Mormon Church gave every indication of breaking up into disorganized smaller units, when fortunately for it the prophet Joseph Smith and his brother Hyrum were killed by a mob. This martyrdom consolidated the church body once more; and before disintegrating influences could again exert themselves, the reins of power were seized by the strong hand of a remarkable man, Brigham Young, who thrust aside the logical successor, Joseph Smith's son.

Young was an uneducated man, but with a deep insight into human nature. A shrewd practical ability and a rugged intelligence, combined with absolute cold-blooded unscrupulousness in attaining his ends, were qualities amply sufficient to put Young in the front rank of the class of people who composed the Mormon Church. He early established a hierarchy of sufficient powers so that always he was able to keep the strong men of the Church loyal to the idea he represented. He paid them well, both in actual property and in power that was dearer to them than property. Furthermore, whether or not he originated polygamy, he not only saw at once its uses in increasing the population of the new state and in taking care of the extra women such fanatical religions always attract, but also, more astutely, he realized that the doctrine of polygamy would set his people apart from all other people, and probably call down upon them the direct opposition of the Federal Government. A feeling of persecution, opposition, and possible punishment were all potent to segregate the Mormon Church from the rest of humanity and to assure its coherence. Further, he understood thoroughly the results that can be obtained by coöperation of even mediocre people under able leadership. He placed his people apart by thoroughly impressing upon their minds the idea of their superiority to the rest of the world. They were the chosen people, hitherto scattered, but now at last gathered together. His followers had just the degree of intelligence necessary to accept leadership gracefully and to rejoice in a supposed superiority because of a sense of previous inferiority.

This ductile material Brigham welded to his own forms. He was able to assume consistently an appearance of uncouth ignorance in order to retain his hold over his uncultivated flock. He delivered vituperative, even obscene sermons, which may still be read in his collected works. But he was able also on occasions, as when addressing agents of the Federal Government or other outsiders whom he wished to impress, to write direct and dignified English. He was resourceful in obtaining control over the other strong men of his Church; but by his very success he was blinded to due proportions. There can be little doubt that at one time he thought he could defy the United States by force of arms. He even maintained an organization called the Danites, sometimes called the Destroying Angels, who carried out his decrees.

: The Mormon Church has always denied the existence of any such organization; but the weight of evidence is against the Church. In one of his discourses, Young seems inadvertently to have admitted the existence of the Danites. The organization dates from the sojourn of the Mormons in Missouri. See Linn, *The Story of the Mormons*, pp. 189-192.

Brigham could welcome graciously and leave a good impression upon important visitors. He was not a good business man, however, and almost every enterprise he directly undertook proved to be a complete or partial failure. He did the most extraordinarily stupid things, as, for instance, when he planned the so-called Cottonwood Canal, the mouth of which was ten feet higher than its source! Nevertheless he had sense to utilize the business ability of other men, and was a good accumulator of properties. His estate at his death was valued at between two and three million dollars. This was a pretty good saving for a pioneer who had come into the wilderness without a cent of his own, who had always spent lavishly, and who had supported a family of over twenty wives and fifty children—all this without a salary as an officer. Tithes were brought to him personally, and he rendered no accounting. He gave the strong men of his hierarchy power and opportunity, played them against each other to keep his own lead, and made holy any of their misdeeds which were not directed against himself.

The early months of 1846 witnessed a third Mormon exodus. Driven out of Illinois, these Latter-day Saints crossed the Mississippi in organized bands, with Council Bluffs as their first objective. Through the winter and spring some fifteen thousand Mormons with three thousand wagons found their way from camp to camp, through snow, ice, and mud, over the weary stretch of four hundred miles to the banks of the Missouri. The epic of this westward migration is almost biblical. Hardship brought out the heroic in many characters. Like true American pioneers, they adapted themselves to circumstances with fortitude and skill. Linn says: "When a halt occurred, a shoemaker might be seen looking for a stone to serve as a lap-stone in his repair work, or a gunsmith mending a rifle, or a weaver at a wheel or loom. The women learned that the jolting wagons would churn their milk, and when a halt occurred it took them but a short time to heat an oven hollowed out of the hillside, in which to bake the bread already raised." Colonel Kane says that he saw a piece of cloth, the wool for which was sheared, dyed, spun, and woven, during the march.

After a winter of sickness and deprivation in camps along "Misery Bottom," as they called the river flats, during which malaria carried off hundreds, Brigham Young set out with a pioneer band of a hundred and fifty to find a new Zion. Toward the end of July, this expedition by design or chance entered Salt Lake Valley. At sight of the lake glistening in the sun, "Each of us," wrote one of the party, "without saying a word to the other, instinctively, as if by inspiration, raised our hats from our heads, and then, swinging our hats, shouted, 'Hosannah to God and the Lamb!'"

Meantime the first emigration from winter quarters was under way, and in the following spring Young conducted a train of eight hundred wagons across the plains to the great valley where a city of adobe and log houses was already building. The new city was laid off into numbered lots. The Presidency had charge of the distribution of these lots. You may be sure they did not reserve the worst for their use, nor did they place about themselves undesirable neighbors. Immediately after the assignments had been made, various people began at once to speculate in buying and selling according to the location. The spiritual power immediately anathematized this. No one was permitted to trade over property. Any sales were made on a basis of the first cost plus the value of the improvement. A community admirable in almost every way was improvised as though by magic. Among themselves the Mormons were sober, industrious, God-fearing, peaceful. Their difficulties with the nation were yet to come.

Throughout the year, 1848, the weather was propitious for ploughing and sowing. Before the crops could be gathered, however, provisions ran so low that the large community was in actual danger of starvation. Men were reduced to eating skins of slaughtered animals, the raw hides from the roofs of houses, and even a wild root dug by the miserable Ute Indians. To cap the climax, when finally the crops ripened, they were attacked by an army of crickets that threatened to destroy them utterly. Prayers of desperation were miraculously answered by a flight of white sea-gulls that destroyed the invader and saved the crop. Since then this miracle has been many times repeated.

It was in August, 1849, that the first gold rush began. Some of Brannan's company from California had already arrived with samples of gold-dust. Brigham Young was too shrewd not to discourage all mining desires on the part of his people, and he managed to hold them. The Mormons never did indulge in gold-mining. But the samples served to inflame the ardor of the immigrants from the east. Their one desire at once became to lighten their loads so that they could get to the diggings in the shortest possible time. Then the Mormons began to reap their harvest. Animals worth only twenty-five or thirty dollars would bring two hundred dollars in exchange for goods brought in by the travelers. For a light wagon the immigrants did not hesitate to offer three or four heavy ones, and sometimes a yoke of oxen to boot. Such very desirable things to a new community as sheeting, or spades and shovels, since the miners were overstocked, could be had for almost nothing. Indeed, everything, except coffee and sugar, was about half the wholesale rate in the East. The profit to the Mormons from this migration was even greater in 1850. The gold-seeker sometimes paid as high as a dollar a pound for flour; and, conversely, as many of the wayfarers started out with heavy loads of mining machinery and miscellaneous goods, as is the habit of the tenderfoot camper even unto this day, they had to sell at the buyers' prices. Some of the enterprising miners had even brought large amounts of goods for sale at a hoped-for profit in California. At Salt Lake City, however, the information was industriously circulated that shiploads of similar, merchandise were on their way round the Horn, and consequently the would-be traders often sacrificed their own stock.

: Linn, *The Story of the Mormons*, 406.

This friendly condition could not, of course, long obtain. Brigham Young's policy of segregation was absolutely opposed to permanent friendly relations. The immigrants on the other hand were violently prejudiced against the Mormon faith. The valley of the Salt Lake seemed to be just the psychological point for the breaking up into fragments of the larger companies that had crossed the plains. The division of property on these separations sometimes involved a considerable amount of difficulty. The disputants often applied to the Mormon courts for decision. Somebody was sure to become dissatisfied and to accuse the courts of undue influence. Rebellion against the decision brought upon them the full force of civil power. For contempt of court they were most severely fined. The fields of the Mormons were imperfectly fenced; the cattle of the immigrants were very numerous. Trespass cases brought heavy remuneration, the value being so much greater for damages than in the States that it often looked to the stranger like an injustice. A protest would be taken before a bishop who charged costs for his decision. An unreasonable prejudice against the Mormons often arose from these causes. On the other hand there is no doubt that the immigrants often had right on their side. Not only were the Mormons human beings, with the usual qualities of love of gain and desire to take advantage of their situation; but, further, they belonged to a sect that fostered the belief that they were superior to the rest of mankind, and that it was actually meritorious to "spoil the Philistines."

Many gold-diggers who started out with a complete outfit finished their journey almost on foot. Some five hundred of these people got together later in California and compared notes. Finally they drew up a series of affidavits to be sent back home. A petition was presented to Congress charging that many immigrants had been murdered by the Mormons; that, when members of the Mormon community became dissatisfied and tried to leave, they were subdued and killed; that a two per cent tax on the property was levied on those immigrants compelled to stay through the winter; that justice was impossible to obtain in the Mormon courts; that immigrants' mail was opened and destroyed; and that all Mormons were at best treasonable in sentiment. Later the breach between the Mormons and the Americans became more marked, until it culminated in the atrocious Mountain Meadows massacre, which was probably only one of several similar but lesser occurrences. These things, however, are outside of our scope, as they occurred later in history. For the moment, it is only necessary to note that it was extremely fortunate for the gold immigrants, not only that the half-way station had been established by the Mormons, but also that the necessities of the latter forced them to adopt a friendly policy. By the time open enmity had come, the first of the rush had passed and other routes had been well established.

# CHAPTER VII

## *THE WAY BY PANAMA*

Of the three roads to California that by Panama was the most obvious, the shortest, and therefore the most crowded. It was likewise the most expensive. To the casual eye this route was also the easiest. You got on a ship in New York, you disembarked for a very short land journey, you re-embarked on another ship, and landed at San Francisco. This route therefore attracted the more unstable elements of society. The journey by the plains took a certain grim determination and courage; that by Cape Horn, a slow and persistent patience.

The route by the Isthmus, on the other hand, allured the impatient, the reckless, and those who were unaccustomed to and undesirous of hardships. Most of the gamblers and speculators, for example, as well as the cheaper politicians, went by Panama.

In October, 1848, the first steamship of the Pacific Steamship Company began her voyage from New York to Panama and San Francisco, and reached her destination toward the end of February. On the Atlantic every old tub that could be made to float so far was pressed into service. Naturally there were many more vessels on the Atlantic side than on the Pacific side, and the greatest congestion took place at Panama. Every man was promised by the shipping agent a through passage, but the shipping agent was careful to remain in New York.

The overcrowded ships were picturesque though uncomfortable. They were crowded to the guards with as miscellaneous a lot of passengers as were ever got together. It must be remembered that they were mostly young men in the full vigor of youth and thoroughly imbued with the adventurous spirit. It must be remembered again, if the reader can think back so far in his own experience, that youth of that age loves to deck itself out both physically and mentally in the trappings of romance. Almost every man wore a red shirt, a slouch hat, a repeating pistol, and a bowie-knife; and most of them began at once to grow beards. They came from all parts of the country. The lank Maine Yankee elbowed the tall, sallow, black-haired Southerner. Social distinctions soon fell away and were forgotten. No one could tell by speech, manners, or dress whether a man's former status was lawyer, physician, or roustabout. The days were spent in excited discussions of matters pertaining to the new country and the theory and practice of gold-mining. Only two things were said to be capable of breaking in on this interminable palaver. One was dolphins and the other the meal-gong. When dolphins appeared, each passenger promptly rushed to the side of the ship and discharged his revolver in a fusillade that was usually harmless. Meal time always caught the majority unawares. They tumbled and jostled down the companionway only to find that the wise and forethoughtful had preëmpted every chair. There was very little quarreling. A holiday spirit seemed to pervade the crowd. Everybody was more or less elevated in mood and everybody was imbued with the same spirit of comradeship in adventure.

But with the sight of shore, the low beach, and the round high bluffs with the castle atop that meant Chagres, this comradeship rather fell apart. Soon a landing was to be made and transportation across the Isthmus had to be obtained. Men at once became rivals for prompt service. Here, for the first time, the owners of the weird mining-machines already described found themselves at a disadvantage, while those who carried merely the pick, shovel, and small personal equipment were enabled to make a flying start. On the beach there was invariably an immense wrangle over the hiring of boats to go up the river. These were a sort of dug-out with small decks in the bow and in the stern, and with low roofs of palmetto leaves amidships. The fare to Cruces was about fifteen dollars a man. Nobody was in a hurry but the Americans.

Chagres was a collection of cane huts on level ground, with a swamp at the back. Men and women clad in a single cotton garment lay about smoking cigars. Naked and pot-bellied children played in the mud. On the threshold of the doors, in the huts, fish, bullock heads, hides, and carrion were strewn, all in a state of decomposition, while in the rear was the jungle and a lake of stagnant water with a delicate bordering of greasy blue mud. There was but one hotel, called the Crescent City, which boasted of no floor and no food. The newcomers who were unsupplied with provisions had to eat what they could pick up. Unlearned as yet in tropical ways, they wasted a tremendous lot of nervous energy in trying to get the natives started. The natives, calm in the consciousness that there was plenty of demand, refused to be hurried. Many of the travelers, thinking that they had closed a bargain, returned from sightseeing only to find their boat had disappeared. The only safe way was to sit in the canoe until it actually started.

With luck they got off late in the afternoon, and made ten or twelve miles to Gatun. The journey up the lazy tropical river was exciting and interesting. The boatmen sang, the tropic forests came down to the banks with their lilies, shrubs, mangoes, cocos, sycamores, palms; their crimson, purple, and yellow blossoms; their bananas with torn leaves; their butterflies and paroquets; their streamers and vines and scarlet flowers. It was like a vision of fairyland.

Gatun was a collection of bamboo huts, inhabited mainly by fleas. One traveler tells of attempting to write in his journal, and finding the page covered with fleas before he had inscribed a dozen words. The gold seekers slept in hammocks, suspended at such a height that the native dogs found them most convenient back-scratchers. The fleas were not inactive. On all sides the natives drank, sang, and played monte. It generally rained at night, and the flimsy huts did little to keep out the wet. Such things went far to take away the first enthusiasm and to leave the travelers in rather a sad and weary-eyed state.

By the third day the river narrowed and became swifter. With luck the voyagers reached Gorgona on a high bluff. This was usually the end of the river journey. Most people bargained for Cruces six miles beyond, but on arrival decided that the Gorgona trail would be less crowded, and with unanimity went ashore there. Here the bargaining had to be started all over again, this time for mules. Here also the demand far exceeded the supply, with the usual result of arrogance, indifference, and high prices. The difficult ride led at first through a dark deep wood in clay soil that held water in every depression, seamed with steep eroded ravines and diversified by low passes over projecting spurs of a chain of mountains. There the monkeys and parrots furnished the tropical atmosphere, assisted somewhat by innumerable dead mules along the trail. Vultures sat in every tree waiting for more things to happen. The trail was of the consistency of very thick mud. In this mud the first mule had naturally left his tracks; the next mules trod carefully in the first mule's footprints, and all subsequent mules did likewise. The consequence was a succession of narrow deep holes in the clay into which an animal sank half-way to the shoulder. No power was sufficient to make these mules step anywhere else. Each hole was full of muddy water. When the mule inserted his hoof, water spurted out violently as though from a squirt-gun. Walking was simply impossible.

All this was merely adventure for the young, strong, and healthy; but the terrible part of the Panama Trail was the number of victims claimed by cholera and fever. The climate and the unwonted labor brought to the point of exhaustion men unaccustomed to such exertions. They lay flat by the trail as though dead. Many actually did die either from the jungle fever or the yellow-jack. The universal testimony of the times is that this horseback journey seemed interminable; and many speak of being immensely cheered when their Indian stopped, washed his feet in a wayside mudhole, and put on his pantaloons. That indicated the proximity, at last, of the city of Panama.

It was a quaint old place. The two-story wooden houses with corridor and verandah across the face of the second story, painted in bright colors, leaned crazily out across the streets. Narrow and mysterious alleys led between them. Ancient cathedrals and churches stood gray with age before the grass-grown plazas. In the outskirts were massive masonry ruins of great buildings, convents, and colleges, some of which had never been finished. The immense blocks lay about the ground in confusion, covered by thousands of little plants, or soared against the sky in broken arches and corridors. But in the body of the town, the old picturesque houses had taken on a new and temporary smartness which consisted mostly of canvas signs. The main street was composed of hotels, eating-houses, and assorted hells. At times over a thousand men were there awaiting transportation. Some of them had been waiting a long time, and had used up all their money. They were broke and desperate. A number of American gambling-houses were doing business, and of course the saloons were much in evidence. Foreigners kept two of the three hotels; Americans ran the gambling joints; French and Germans kept the restaurants. The natives were content to be interested but not entirely idle spectators. There was a terrible amount of sickness aggravated by American quack remedies. Men rejoiced or despaired according to their dispositions. Every once in a while a train of gold bullion would start back across the Isthmus with mule-loads of huge gold bars, so heavy that they were safe, for no one could carry them off to the jungle. On the other hand there were some returning Californians, drunken and wretched. They delighted in telling with grim joy of the disappointments of the diggings. But probably the only people thoroughly unhappy were the steamship officials. These men had to bear the brunt of disappointment, broken promises, and savage recrimination, if means for going north were not very soon forthcoming. Every once in a while some ship, probably an old tub, would come wallowing to anchor at the nearest point, some eleven miles from the city. Then the raid for transportation took place all over again. There was a limited number of small boats for carrying purposes, and these were pounced on at once by ten times the number they could accommodate. Ships went north scandalously overcrowded and underprovisioned. Mutinies were not infrequent. It took a good captain to satisfy everybody, and there were many bad ones. Some men got so desperate that, with a touching ignorance of geography, they actually started out in small boats to row to the north. Others attempted the overland route. It may well be believed that the reaction from all this disappointment and delay lifted the hearts of these argonauts when they eventually sailed between the Golden Gates.

This confusion, of course, was worse at the beginning. Later the journey was to some extent systematized. The Panama route subsequently became the usual and fashionable way to travel. The ship companies learned how to handle and treat their patrons. In fact, it was said that every jewelry shop in San Francisco carried a large stock of fancy silver speaking-trumpets because of the almost invariable habit of presenting one of these to the captain of the ship by his grateful passengers. One captain swore that he possessed eighteen of them!

CHAPTER VIII

*THE DIGGINGS*

The two streams of immigrants, by sea and overland, thus differed, on the average, in kind. They also landed in the country at different points. The overlanders were generally absorbed before they reached San Francisco. They arrived first at Fort Sutter, whence they distributed themselves; or perhaps they even stopped at one or another of the diggings on their way in.

Of those coming by sea all landed at San Francisco. A certain proportion of the younger and more enthusiastic set out for the mines, but only after a few days had given them experience of the new city and had impressed them with at least a subconscious idea of opportunity. Another certain proportion, however, remained in San Francisco without attempting the mines. These were either men who were discouraged by pessimistic tales, men who had sickened of the fever, or more often men who were attracted by the big opportunities for wealth which the city then afforded. Thus at once we have two different types to consider, the miner and the San Franciscan.

The mines were worked mostly by young men. They journeyed up to the present Sacramento either by river-boats or afoot. Thence they took their outfits into the diggings. It must have seemed a good deal like a picnic. The goal was near; rosy hope had expanded to fill the horizon; breathless anticipation pervaded them—a good deal like a hunting-party starting off in the freshness of the dawn.

The diggings were generally found at the bottoms of the deep river-beds and ravines. Since trails, in order to avoid freshets and too many crossings of the water-courses, took the higher shoulder of the hill, the newcomer ordinarily looked down upon his first glimpse of the mines. The sight must have been busy and animated. The miners dressed in bright-colored garments, and dug themselves in only to the waist or at most to the shoulders before striking bed rock, so that they were visible as spots of gaudy color. The camps were placed on the hillsides or little open flats, and occasionally were set in the bed of a river. They were composed of tents, and of rough log or bark structures.

The newcomers did not spend much time in establishing themselves comfortably or luxuriously. They were altogether too eager to get at the actual digging. There was an immense excitement of the gamble in it all. A man might dig for days without adequate results and then of a sudden run into a rich pocket. Or he might pan out an immense sum within the first ten minutes of striking his pick to earth. No one could tell. The fact that the average of all the days and all the men amounted to very little more than living wages was quite lost to sight. At first the methods were very crude. One man held a coarse screen of willow branches which he shook continuously above an ordinary cooking pot, while his partner slowly shovelled earth over this impromptu sieve. When the pots were filled with siftings, they were carried to the river, where they were carefully submerged, and the contents were stirred about with sticks. The light earth was thus flowed over the rims of the pots. The residue was then dried, and the lighter sand was blown away. The result was gold, though of course with a strong mixture of foreign substance. The pan miners soon followed; and the cradle or rocker with its riffle-board was not long delayed. The digging was free. At first it was supposed that a new holding should not be started within fifteen feet of one already in operation. Later, claims of a definite size were established. A camp, however, made its own laws in regard to this and other matters.

Most of the would-be miners at first rather expected to find gold lying on the surface of the earth, and were very much disappointed to learn that they actually had to dig for it. Moreover, digging in the boulders and gravel, under the terrific heat of the California sun in midsummer, was none too easy; and no matter how rich the diggings averaged—short of an actual bonanza—the miner was disappointed in his expectations. One man is reported saying: "They tell me I can easily make there eleven hundred dollars a day. You know I am not easily moved by such reports. I shall be satisfied if I make three hundred dollars per day." Travelers of the time comment on the contrast between the returning stream of discouraged and disgruntled men and the cheerfulness of the lot actually digging. Nobody had any scientific system to go on. Often a divining-rod was employed to determine where to dig. Many stories were current of accidental finds; as when one man, tiring of waiting for his dog to get through digging out a ground squirrel, pulled the animal out by the tail, and with it a large nugget. Another story is told of a sailor who asked some miners resting at noon where he could dig and as a joke was directed to a most improbable side hill. He obeyed the advice, and uncovered a rich pocket. With such things actually happening, naturally it followed that every report of a real or rumored strike set the miners crazy. Even those who had good claims always suspected that they might do better elsewhere. It is significant that the miners of that day, like hunters, always had the notion that they had come out to California just one trip too late for the best pickings.

The physical life was very hard, and it is no wonder that the stragglers back from the mines increased in numbers as time went on. It was a true case of survival of the fittest. Those who remained and became professional miners were the hardiest, most optimistic, and most persistent of the population. The mere physical labor was very severe. Any one not raised as a day laborer who has tried to do a hard day's work in a new garden can understand what pick and shovel digging in the bottoms of gravel and boulder streams can mean. Add to this the fact that every man overworked himself under the pressure of excitement; that he was up to his waist in the cold water from the Sierra snows, with his head exposed at the same time to the tremendous heat of the California sun; throw in for good measure that he generally cooked for himself, and that his food was coarse and badly prepared; and that in his own mind he had no time to attend to the ordinary comforts and decencies of life. It can well be imagined that a man physically unfit must soon succumb. But those who survived seemed to thrive on these hardships.

California camps by their very quaint and whimsical names bear testimony to the overflowing good humor and high spirits of the early miners. No one took anything too seriously, not even his own success or failure. The very hardness of the life cultivated an ability to snatch joy from the smallest incident. Some of the joking was a little rough, as when some merry jester poured alcohol over a bully's head, touched a match to it, and chased him out of camp yelling, "Man on fire—put him out!" It is evident that the time was not one for men of very refined or sensitive nature, unless they possessed at bottom the strong iron of character. The ill-balanced were swept away by the current of excitement, and fell readily into dissipation. The pleasures were rude; the life was hearty; vices unknown to their possessors came to the surface. The most significant tendency, and one that had much to do with later social and political life in California, was the leveling effect of just this hard physical labor. The man with a strong back and the most persistent spirit was the superior of the man with education but with weaker muscles. Each man, finding every other man compelled to labor, was on a social equality with the best. The usual superiority of head-workers over hand-workers disappeared. The low-grade man thus felt himself the equal, if not the superior, of any one else on earth, especially as he was generally able to

224

put his hand on what were to him comparative riches. The pride of employment disappeared completely. It was just as honorable to be a cook or a waiter in a restaurant as to dispense the law,—where there was any. The period was brief, but while it lasted, it produced a true social democracy. Nor was there any pretense about it. The rudest miner was on a plane of perfect equality with lawyers, merchants, or professional men. Some men dressed in the very height of style, decking themselves out with all the minute care of a dandy; others were not ashamed of, nor did they object to being seen in, ragged garments. No man could be told by his dress.

The great day of days in a mining-camp was Sunday. Some over-enthusiastic fortune-seekers worked the diggings also on that day; but by general consent—uninfluenced, it may be remarked, by religious considerations—the miners repaired to their little town for amusement and relaxation. These little towns were almost all alike. There were usually two or three combined hotels, saloons, and gambling-houses, built of logs, of slabs, of canvas, or of a combination of the three. There was one store that dispensed whiskey as well as dryer goods, and one or two large places of amusement. On Sunday everything went full blast. The streets were crowded with men; the saloons were well patronized; the gambling games ran all day and late into the night. Wrestling-matches, jumping-matches, other athletic tests, horse-races, lotteries, fortune-telling, singing, anything to get a pinch or two of the dust out of the good-natured miners—all these were going strong. The American, English, and other continentals mingled freely, with the exception of the French, who kept to themselves. Successful Germans or Hollanders of the more stupid class ran so true to type and were so numerous that they earned the generic name of "Dutch Charley." They have been described as moon-faced, bland, bullet-headed men, with walrus moustaches, and fatuous, placid smiles. Value meant nothing to them. They only knew the difference between having money and having no money. They carried two or three gold watches at the end of long home-made chains of gold nuggets fastened together with links of copper wire. The chains were sometimes looped about their necks, their shoulders, and waists, and even hung down in long festoons. When two or three such Dutch Charleys inhabited one camp, they became deadly rivals in this childlike display, parading slowly up and down the street, casting malevolent glances at each other as they passed. Shoals of phrenologists, fortune-tellers, and the like, generally drunken old reprobates on their last legs, plied their trades. One artist, giving out under the physical labor of mining, built up a remarkably profitable trade in sketching portraits. Incidentally he had to pay two dollars and a half for every piece of paper! John Kelly, a wandering minstrel with a violin, became celebrated among the camps, and was greeted with enthusiasm wherever he appeared. He probably made more with his fiddle than he could have made with his shovel. The influence of the "forty-two caliber whiskey" was dire, and towards the end of Sunday the sports became pretty rough.

This day was also considered the time for the trial of any cases that had arisen during the week. The miners elected one of their number to act as presiding judge in a "miners' meeting." Justice was dealt out by this man, either on his own authority with the approval of the crowd, or by popular vote. Disputes about property were adjudicated as well as offenses against the criminal code. Thus a body of precedent was slowly built up. A new case before the *alcalde* of Hangtown was often decided on the basis of the procedure at Grub Gulch. The decisions were characterized by direct common sense. It would be most interesting to give adequate examples here, but space forbids. Suffice it to say that a Mexican horse-thief was convicted and severely flogged; and then a collection was taken up for him on the ground that he was on the whole unfortunate. A thief apprehended on a steamboat was punished by a heavy fine for the benefit of a sick man on board.

Sunday evening usually ended by a dance. As women were entirely lacking at first, a proportion of the men was told off to represent the fair sex. At one camp the invariable rule was to consider as ladies those who possessed patches on the seats of their trousers. This was the distinguishing mark. Take it all around, the day was one of noisy, good-humored fun. There was very little sodden drunkenness, and the miners went back to their work on Monday morning with freshened spirits. Probably just this sort of irresponsible ebullition was necessary to balance the hardness of the life.

In each mining-town was at least one Yankee storekeeper. He made the real profits of the mines. His buying ability was considerable; his buying power was often limited by what he could get hold of at the coast and what he could transport to the camps. Often his consignments were quite arbitrary and not at all what he ordered. The story is told of one man who received what, to judge by the smell, he thought was three barrels of spoiled beef. Throwing them out in the back way, he was interested a few days later to find he had acquired a rapidly increasing flock of German scavengers. They seemed to be investigating the barrels and carrying away the spoiled meat. When the barrels were about empty, the storekeeper learned that the supposed meat was in reality sauerkraut!

The outstanding fact about these camps was that they possessed no solidarity. Each man expected to exploit the diggings and then to depart for more congenial climes. He wished to undertake just as little responsibility as he possibly could. With so-called private affairs other than his own he would have nothing to do. The term private affairs was very elastic, stretching often to cover even cool-blooded murder. When matters arose affecting the whole public welfare in which he himself might possibly become interested, he was roused to the point of administering justice. The punishments meted out were fines, flogging, banishment, and, as a last resort, lynching. Theft was considered a worse offense than killing. As the mines began to fill up with the more desperate characters who arrived in 1850 and 1851, the necessity for government increased. At this time, but after the leveling effect of universal labor had had its full effect, the men of personality, of force and influence, began to come to the front. A fresh aristocracy of ability, of influence, of character was created.

225

## CHAPTER IX

## *THE URBAN FORTY-NINER*

In popular estimation the interest and romance of the Forty-niners center in gold and mines. To the close student, however, the true significance of their lives is to be found even more in the city of San Francisco.

At first practically everybody came to California under the excitement of the gold rush and with the intention of having at least one try at the mines. But though gold was to be found in unprecedented abundance, the getting of it was at best extremely hard work. Men fell sick both in body and spirit. They became discouraged. Extravagance of hope often resulted, by reaction, in an equal exaggeration of despair. The prices of everything were very high. The cost of medical attendance was almost prohibitory. Men sometimes made large daily sums in the placers; but necessary expenses reduced their net income to small wages. Ryan gives this account of an interview with a returning miner: "He readily entered into conversation and informed us that he had passed the summer at the mines where the excessive heat during the day, and the dampness of the ground where the gold washing is performed, together with privation and fatigue, had brought on fever and ague which nearly proved fatal to him. He had frequently given an ounce of gold for the visit of a medical man, and on several occasions had paid two and even three ounces for a single dose of medicine. He showed us a pair of shoes, nearly worn out, for which he had paid twenty-four dollars." Later Ryan says: "Only such men as can endure the hardship and privation incidental to life in the mines are likely to make fortunes by digging for the ore. I am unequal to the task … I think I could within an hour assemble in this very place from twenty to thirty individuals of my own acquaintance who had all told the same story. They were thoroughly dissatisfied and disgusted with their experiment in the gold country. The truth of the matter is that only traders, speculators, and gamblers make large fortunes." Only rarely did men of cool enough heads and far enough sight eschew from the very beginning all notion of getting rich quickly in the placers, and deliberately settle down to make their fortunes in other ways.

This conclusion of Ryan's throws, of course, rather too dark a tone over the picture. The "hardy miner" was a reality, and the life in the placers was, to such as he, profitable and pleasant. However, this point of view had its influence in turning back from the mines a very large proportion of those who first went in. Many of them drifted into mercantile pursuits. Harlan tells us: "During my sojourn in Stockton I mixed freely with the returning and disgusted miners from whom I learned that they were selling their mining implements at ruinously low prices. An idea struck me one day which I immediately acted upon for fear that another might strike in the same place and cause an explosion. The heaven-born idea that had penetrated my cranium was this: start in the mercantile line, purchase the kits and implements of the returning miners at low figures and sell to the greenhorns en route to the mines at California prices." In this manner innumerable occupations supplying the obvious needs were taken up by many returned miners. A certain proportion drifted to crime or shady devices, but the large majority returned to San Francisco, whence they either went home completely discouraged, or with renewed energy and better-applied ability took hold of the destinies of the new city. Thus another sort of Forty-niner became in his way as significant and strong, as effective and as romantic as his brother, the red-shirted Forty-niner of the diggings.

But in addition to the miners who had made their stakes, who had given up the idea of mining, or who were merely waiting for the winter's rains to be over to go back again to the diggings, an ever increasing immigration was coming to San Francisco with the sole idea of settling in that place. All classes of men were represented. Many of the big mercantile establishments of the East were sending out their agents. Independent merchants sought the rewards of speculation. Gamblers also perceived opportunities for big killings. Professional politicians and cheap lawyers, largely from the Southern States, unfortunately also saw their chance to obtain standing in a new community, having lost all standing in their own. The result of the mixing of these various chemical elements of society was an extraordinary boiling and bubbling.

When Commander Montgomery hoisted the American flag in 1846, the town of Yerba Buena, as San Francisco was called, had a population of about two hundred. Before the discovery of gold it developed under the influence of American enterprise normally and rationally into a prosperous little town with two hotels, a few private dwellings, and two wharves in the process of construction. Merchants had established themselves with connections in the Eastern States, in Great Britain, and South America. Just before the discovery of gold the population had increased to eight hundred and twelve.

The news of the placers practically emptied the town. It would be curious to know exactly how many human souls and chickens remained after Brannan's *California Star* published the authentic news. The commonest necessary activities were utterly neglected, shops were closed and barricaded, merchandise was left rotting on the wharves and the beaches, and the prices of necessities rose to tremendous altitudes. The place looked as a deserted mining-camp does now. The few men left who would work wanted ten or even twenty dollars a day for the commonest labor.

However, the early pioneers were hard-headed citizens. Many of the shopkeepers and merchants, after a short experience of the mines, hurried back to make the inevitable fortune that must come to the middleman in these extraordinary times. Within the first eight weeks of the gold excitement two hundred and fifty thousand dollars in gold dust reached San Francisco, and within: the following eight weeks six hundred thousand dollars more came in. All of this was to purchase supplies at any price for the miners.

This was in the latter days of 1848. In the first part of 1849 the immigrants began to arrive. They had to have places to sleep, things to eat, transportation to the diggings, outfits of various sorts. In the first six months of 1849 ten thousand

**226**

people piled down upon the little city built to accommodate eight hundred. And the last six months of the year were still more extraordinary, as some thirty thousand more dumped themselves on the chaos of the first immigration. The result can be imagined. The city was mainly of canvas either in the form of tents or of crude canvas and wooden houses. The few substantial buildings stood like rocks in a tossing sea. No attempt, of course, had been made as yet toward public improvements. The streets were ankle-deep in dust or neck-deep in mud. A great smoke of dust hung perpetually over the city, raised by the trade winds of the afternoon. Hundreds of ships lay at anchor in the harbor. They had been deserted by their crews, and, before they could be re-manned, the faster clipper ships, built to control the fluctuating western trade, had displaced them, so that the majority were fated never again to put to sea.

Newcomers landed at first on a flat beach of deep black sand, where they generally left their personal effects for lack of means of transportation. They climbed to a ragged thoroughfare of open sheds and ramshackle buildings, most of them in the course of construction. Beneath crude shelters of all sorts and in great quantities were goods brought in hastily by eager speculators on the high prices. The four hundred deserted ships lying at anchor in the harbor had dumped down on the new community the most ridiculous assortment of necessities and luxuries, such as calico, silk, rich furniture, mirrors, knock-down houses, cases and cases of tobacco, clothing, statuary, mining-implements, provisions, and the like.

The hotels and lodging houses immediately became very numerous. Though they were in reality only overcrowded bunk-houses, the most enormous prices were charged for beds in them. People lay ten or twenty in a single room—in row after row of cots, in bunks, or on the floor. Between the discomfort of hard beds, fleas, and overcrowding, the entire populace spent most of its time on the street or in the saloons and gambling, houses. As some one has pointed out, this custom added greatly to the apparent population of the place. Gambling was the gaudiest, the best-paying, and the most patronized industry. It occupied the largest structures, and it probably imported and installed the first luxuries. Of these resorts the El Dorado became the most famous. It occupied at first a large tent but soon found itself forced to move to better quarters. The rents paid for buildings were enormous. Three thousand dollars a month in advance was charged for a single small store made of rough boards. A two-story frame building on Kearny Street near the Plaza paid its owners a hundred and twenty thousand dollars a year rent. The tent containing the El Dorado gambling saloon was rented for forty thousand dollars a year. The prices sky-rocketed still higher. Miners paid as high as two hundred dollars for an ordinary gold rocker, fifteen or twenty dollars for a pick, the same for a shovel, and so forth. A copper coin was considered a curiosity, a half-dollar was the minimum tip for any small service, twenty-five cents was the smallest coin in circulation, and the least price for which anything could be sold. Bread came to fifty cents a loaf. Good boots were a hundred dollars.

Affairs moved very swiftly. A month was the unit of time. Nobody made bargains for more than a month in advance. Interest was charged on money by the month. Indeed, conditions changed so fast that no man pretended to estimate them beyond thirty days ahead, and to do even that was considered rather a gamble. Real estate joined the parade of advance. Little holes in sand-hills sold for fabulous prices. The sick, destitute, and discouraged were submerged beneath the mounting tide of vigorous optimism that bore on its crest the strong and able members of the community. Every one either was rich or expected soon to be so. Opportunity awaited every man at every corner. Men who knew how to take advantage of fortune's gifts were assured of immediate high returns. Those with capital were, of course, enabled to take advantage of the opportunities more quickly; but the ingenious mind saw its chances even with nothing to start on.

One man, who landed broke but who possessed two or three dozen old newspapers used as packing, sold them at a dollar and two dollars apiece and so made his start. Another immigrant with a few packages of ordinary tin tacks exchanged them with a man engaged in putting up a canvas house for their exact weight in gold dust. Harlan tells of walking along the shore of Happy Valley and finding it lined with discarded pickle jars and bottles. Remembering the high price of pickles in San Francisco, he gathered up several hundred of them, bought a barrel of cider vinegar from a newly-arrived vessel, collected a lot of cucumbers, and started a bottling works. Before night, he said, he had cleared over three hundred dollars. With this he made a corner in tobacco pipes by which he realized one hundred and fifty dollars in twenty-four hours.

Mail was distributed soon after the arrival of the mail-steamer. The indigent would often sit up a day or so before the expected arrival of the mail-steamer holding places in line at the post-office. They expected no letters but could sell the advantageous positions for high prices when the mail actually arrived. He was a poor-spirited man indeed who by these and many other equally picturesque means could not raise his gold slug in a reasonable time; and, possessed of fifty dollars, he was an independent citizen. He could increase his capital by interest compounded every day, provided he used his wits; or for a brief span of glory he could live with the best of them. A story is told of a new-come traveler offering a small boy fifty cents to carry his valise to the hotel. The urchin looked with contempt at the coin, fished out two fifty-cent pieces, handed them to the owner of the valise, saying "Here's a dollar; carry it yourself."

One John A. McGlynn arrived without assets. He appreciated the opportunity for ordinary teaming, and hitching California mules to the only and exceedingly decrepit wagon to be found he started in business. Possessing a monopoly, he charged what he pleased, so that within a short time he had driving for him a New York lawyer, whom he paid a hundred and seventy-five dollars a month. His outfit was magnificent. When somebody joked with him about his legal talent, he replied, "The whole business of a lawyer is to know how to manage mules and asses so as to make them pay." When within a month plenty of wagons were imported, McGlynn had so well established himself and possessed so much character that he became *ex officio* the head of the industry. He was evidently a man of great and solid sense and was looked up to as one of the leading citizens.

Every human necessity was crying out for its ordinary conveniences. There were no streets, there were no hotels, there were no lodging-houses, there were no warehouses, there were no stores, there was no water, there was no fuel. Any one who could improvise anything, even a bare substitute, to satisfy any of these needs, was sure of immense returns. In addition, the populace was so busy—so overwhelmingly busy—with its own affairs that it literally could not spare a moment to govern itself. The professional and daring politicians never had a clearer field. They went to extraordinary lengths in all sorts of grafting, in the sale of public real estate, in every "shenanigan" known to skillful low-grade politicians. Only occasionally did they go too far, as when, in addition to voting themselves salaries of six thousand dollars apiece as aldermen, they coolly voted themselves also gold medals to the value of one hundred and fifty dollars apiece "for public and extra services." Then the determined citizens took an hour off for the council chambers. The medals were cast into the melting-pot.

All writers agree, in their memoirs, that the great impression left on the mind by San Francisco was its extreme busyness. The streets were always crammed full of people running and darting in all directions. It was, indeed, a heterogeneous mixture. Not only did the Caucasian show himself in every extreme of costume, from the most exquisite top-hatted dandy to the red-shirted miner, but there were also to be found all the picturesque and unknown races of the earth, the Chinese, the Chileño, the Moor, the Turk, the Mexican, the Spanish, the Islander, not to speak of ordinary foreigners from Russia, England, France, Belgium, Germany, Italy, and the out-of-the-way corners of Europe. All these people had tremendous affairs to finish in the least possible time. And every once in a while some individual on horseback would sail down the street at full speed, scattering the crowd left and right. If any one remarked that the marauding individual should be shot, the excuse was always offered, "Oh, well, don't mind him. He's only drunk," as if that excused everything. Many of the activities of the day also were picturesque. As there were no warehouses in which to store goods, and as the few structures of the sort charged enormous rentals, it was cheaper to auction off immediately all consignments. These auctions were then, and remained for some years, one of the features of the place. The more pretentious dealers kept brass bands to attract the crowd. The returning miners were numerous enough to patronize both these men and the cheap clothing stores, and having bought themselves new outfits, generally cast the old ones into the middle of the street. Water was exceedingly scarce and in general demand, so that laundry work was high. It was the fashion of these gentry to wear their hair and beards long. They sported red shirts, flashy Chinese scarves around their waists, black belts with silver buckles, six-shooters and bowie-knives, and wide floppy hats.

The business of the day over, the evening was open for relaxation. As the hotels and lodging-houses were nothing but kennels, and very crowded kennels, it followed that the entire population gravitated to the saloons and gambling places. Some of these were established on a very extensive scale. They had not yet attained the magnificence of the Fifties, but it is extraordinary to realize that within so few months and at such a great distance from civilization, the early and enterprising managed to take on the trappings of luxury. Even thus early, plate-glass mirrors, expensive furniture, the gaudy, tremendous oil paintings peculiar to such dives, prism chandeliers, and the like, had made their appearance. Later, as will be seen, these gambling dens presented an aspect of barbaric magnificence, unique and peculiar to the time and place. In 1849, however gorgeous the trappings might have appeared to men long deprived of such things, they were of small importance compared with the games themselves. At times the bets were enormous. Soulé tells us that as high as twenty thousand dollars were risked on the turn of one card. The ordinary stake, however, was not so large, from fifty cents to five dollars being about the usual amount. Even at this the gamblers were well able to pay the high rents. Quick action was the word. The tables were always crowded and bystanders many deep waited to lay their stakes. Within a year or so the gambling resorts assumed rather the nature of club-rooms, frequented by every class, many of whom had no intention of gambling. Men met to talk, read the newspapers, write letters, or perhaps take a turn at the tables. But in 1849 the fever of speculation held every man in its grip.

Again it must be noted how wide an epoch can be spanned by a month or two. The year 1849 was but three hundred and sixty-five days long, and yet in that space the community of San Francisco passed through several distinct phases. It grew visibly like the stalk of a century plant.

Of public improvements there were almost none. The few that were undertaken sprang from absolute necessity. The town got through the summer season fairly well, but, as the winter that year proved to be an unusually rainy time, it soon became evident that something must be done. The streets became bottomless pits of mud. It is stated, as plain and sober fact, that in some of the main thoroughfares teams of mules and horses sank actually out of sight and were suffocated. Foot travel was almost impossible unless across some sort of causeway. Lumber was so expensive that it was impossible to use it for the purpose. Fabulous quantities of goods sent in by speculators loaded the market and would sell so low that it was actually cheaper to use bales of them than to use planks. Thus one muddy stretch was paved with bags of Chilean flour, another with tierces of tobacco, while over still another the wayfarers proceeded on the tops of cook stoves. These sank gradually in the soft soil until the tops were almost level with the mud. Of course one of the first acts of the merry jester was to shy the stove lids off into space. The footing especially after dark can be imagined. Crossing a street on these things was a perilous traverse watched with great interest by spectators on either side. Often the hardy adventurer, after teetering for some time, would with a descriptive oath sink to his waist in the slimy mud. If the wayfarer was drunk enough, he then proceeded to pelt his tormentors with missiles of the sticky slime. The good humor of the community saved it from absolute despair. Looked at with cold appraising eye, the conditions were decidedly uncomfortable. In addition there was a grimmer side to the picture. Cholera and intermittent fever came, brought in by ships as well as by overland immigrants, and the death-rate rose by leaps and bounds.

The greater the hardships and obstacles, the higher the spirit of the community rose to meet them. In that winter was born the spirit that has animated San Francisco ever since, and that so nobly and cheerfully met the final great trial of the earthquake and fire of 1906.

About this time an undesirable lot of immigrants began to arrive, especially from the penal colonies of New South Wales. The criminals of the latter class soon became known to the populace as "Sydney Ducks." They formed a nucleus for an adventurous, idle, pleasure-loving, dissipated set of young sports, who organized themselves into a loose band very much on the order of the East Side gangs in New York or the "hoodlums" in later San Francisco, with the exception, however, that these young men affected the most meticulous nicety in dress. They perfected in the spring of 1849 an organization called the Regulators, announcing that, as there was no regular police force, they would take it upon themselves to protect the weak against the strong and the newcomer against the bunco man. Every Sunday they paraded the streets with bands and banners. Having no business in the world to occupy them, and holding a position unique in the community, the Regulators soon developed into practically a band of cut-throats and robbers, with the object of relieving those too weak to bear alone the weight of wealth. The Regulators, or Hounds, as they soon came to be called, had the great wisdom to avoid the belligerent and resourceful pioneer. They issued from their headquarters, a large tent near the Plaza, every night. Armed with clubs and pistols, they descended upon the settlements of harmless foreigners living near the outskirts, relieved them of what gold dust they possessed, beat them up by way of warning, and returned to headquarters with the consciousness of a duty well done. The victims found it of little use to appeal to the *alcalde*, for with the best disposition in the world the latter could do nothing without an adequate police force. The ordinary citizen, much too interested in his own affairs, merely took precautions to preserve his own skin, avoided dark and unfrequented alleyways, barricaded his doors and windows, and took the rest out in contemptuous cursing.

Encouraged by this indifference, the Hounds naturally grew bolder and bolder. They considered they had terrorized the rest of the community, and they began to put on airs and swagger in the usual manner of bullies everywhere. On Sunday afternoon of July 15, they made a raid on some California ranchos across the bay, ostensibly as a picnic expedition, returning triumphant and very drunk. For the rest of the afternoon with streaming banners they paraded the streets, discharging firearms and generally shooting up the town. At dark they descended upon the Chilean quarters, tore down the tents, robbed the Chileans, beat many of the men to insensibility, ousted the women, killed a number who had not already fled, and returned to town only the following morning.

This proved to be the last straw. The busy citizens dropped their own affairs for a day and got together in a mass meeting at the Plaza. All work was suspended and all business houses were closed. Probably all the inhabitants in the city with the exception of the Hounds had gathered together. Our old friend, Sam Brannan, possessing the gift of a fiery spirit and an arousing tongue, addressed the meeting. A sum of money was raised for the despoiled foreigners. An organization was effected, and armed *posses* were sent out to arrest the ringleaders. They had little difficulty. Many left town for foreign parts or for the mines, where they met an end easily predicted. Others were condemned to various punishments. The Hounds were thoroughly broken up in an astonishingly brief time. The real significance of their great career is that they called to the attention of the better class of citizens the necessity for at least a sketchy form of government and a framework of law. Such matters as city revenue were brought up for practically the first time. Gambling-houses were made to pay a license. Real estate, auction sales, and other licenses were also taxed. One of the ships in the harbor was drawn up on shore and was converted into a jail. A district-attorney was elected, with an associate. The whole municipal structure was still about as rudimentary as the streets into which had been thrown armfuls of brush in a rather hopeless attempt to furnish an artificial bottom. It was a beginning, however, and men had at last turned their eyes even momentarily from their private affairs to consider the welfare of this unique society which was in the making.

CHAPTER X

***ORDEAL BY FIRE***

San Francisco in the early years must be considered, aside from the interest of its picturesqueness and aside from its astonishing growth, as a crucible of character. Men had thrown off all moral responsibility. Gambling, for example, was a respectable amusement. People in every class of life frequented the gambling saloons openly and without thought of apology. Men were leading a hard and vigorous life; the reactions were quick; and diversions were eagerly seized. Decent women were absolutely lacking, and the women of the streets had as usual followed the army of invasion. It was not considered at all out of the ordinary to frequent their company in public, and men walked with them by day to the scandal of nobody. There was neither law nor restraint. Most men were drunk with sudden wealth. The battle was, as ever, to the strong.

There was every inducement to indulge the personal side of life. As a consequence, many formed habits they could not break, spent all of their money on women and drink and gambling, ruined themselves in pocket-book and in health, returned home broken, remained sodden and hopeless tramps, or joined the criminal class. Thousands died of cholera or pneumonia; hundreds committed suicide; but those who came through formed the basis of a race remarkable today for its strength, resourcefulness, and optimism. Characters solid at bottom soon come to the inevitable reaction. They were the forefathers of a race of people which is certainly different from the inhabitants of any other portion of the country.

The first public test came with the earliest of the big fires that, within the short space of eighteen months, six times burned San Francisco to the ground. This fire occurred on December 4, 1849. It was customary in the saloons to give negroes a free drink and tell them not to come again. One did come again to Dennison's; he was flogged, and knocked over a lamp. Thus there started a conflagration that consumed over a million dollars' worth of property. The valuable part of the property, it must be confessed, was in the form of goods, is the light canvas and wooden shacks were of little worth. Possibly the fire consumed enough germs and germ-breeding dirt to pay partially for itself. Before the ashes had cooled, the enterprising real estate owners were back reërecting the destroyed structures.

This first fire was soon followed by others, each intrinsically severe. The people were splendid in enterprise and spirit of recovery; but they soon realized that not only must the buildings be made of more substantial material, but also that fire-fighting apparatus must be bought. In June, 1850, four hundred houses were destroyed; in May, 1851, a thousand were burned at a loss of two million and a half; in June, 1851, the town was razed to the water's edge. In many places the wharves were even disconnected from the shore. Everywhere deep holes were burned in them, and some people fell through at night and were drowned. In this fire a certain firm, Dewitt and Harrison, saved their warehouse by knocking in barrels of vinegar and covering their building with blankets soaked in that liquid. Water was unobtainable. It was reported that they thus used eighty thousand gallons of vinegar, but saved their warehouse.

The loss now had amounted to something like twelve million dollars for the large fires. It became more evident that something must be done. From the exigencies of the situation were developed the volunteer companies, which later became powerful political, as well as fire-fighting, organizations. There were many of these. In the old Volunteer Department there were fourteen engines, three hook-and-ladder companies, and a number of hose companies. Each possessed its own house, which was in the nature of a club-house, well supplied with reading and drinking matter. The members of each company were strongly partisan. They were ordinarily drawn from men of similar tastes and position in life. Gradually they came to stand also for similar political interests, and thus grew to be, like New York's Tammany Hall, instruments of the politically ambitious.

On an alarm of fire the members at any time of the day and night ceased their occupation or leaped from their beds to run to the engine-house. Thence the hand-engines were dragged through the streets at a terrific rate of speed by hundreds of yelling men at the end of the ropes. The first engine at a fire obtained the place of honor; therefore every alarm was the signal for a breakneck race. Arrived at the scene of fire, the water-box of one engine was connected by hose with the reservoir of the next, and so water was relayed from engine to engine until it was thrown on the flames. The motive power of the pump was supplied by the crew of each engine. The men on either side manipulated the pump by jerking the hand-rails up and down. Putting out the fire soon became a secondary matter. The main object of each company was to "wash" its rival; that is, to pump water into the water box of the engine ahead faster than the latter could pump it out, thus overflowing and eternally disgracing its crew. The foremen walked back and forth between the rails, as if on quarter-decks, exhorting their men. Relays in uniform stood ready on either side to take the place of those who were exhausted. As the race became closer, the foremen would get more excited, begging their crews to increase the speed of the stroke, beating their speaking trumpets into shapeless and battered relics.

In the meantime the hook-and-ladder companies were plying their glorious and destructive trade. A couple of firemen would mount a ladder to the eaves of the house to be attacked, taking with them a heavy hook at the end of a long pole or rope. With their axes they cut a small hole in the eaves, hooked on this apparatus, and descended. At once as many firemen and volunteers as could get hold of the pole and the rope began to pull. The timbers would crack, break; the whole side of the house would come out with a grand satisfying smash. In this way the fire within was laid open to the attack of the hose-men. This sort of work naturally did little toward saving the building immediately affected, but it was intended to confine or check the fire within the area already burning. The occasion was a grand jubilation for every boy in the town—which means every male of any age. The roar of the flames, the hissing of the steam, the crash of the timber, the shrieks of the foremen, the yells of applause or of sarcastic comment from the crowd, and the thud of the numerous pumps made a glorious row. Everybody, except the owners of the buildings, was hugely delighted, and when the fire was all over it was customary for the unfortunate owner further to increase the amount of his loss by dealing out liquid refreshments to everybody concerned. On parade days each company turned out with its machine brought to a high state of polish by varnish, and with the members resplendent in uniform, carrying pole-axes and banners. If the rivalries at the fire could only be ended in a general free fight, everybody was the better satisfied.

Thus by the end of the first period of its growth three necessities had compelled the careless new city to take thought of itself and of public convenience. The mud had forced the cleaning and afterwards the planking of the principal roads; the Hounds had compelled the adoption of at least a semblance of government; and the repeated fires had made necessary the semiofficial organization of the fire department.

By the end of 1850 we find that a considerable amount of actual progress has been made. This came not in the least from any sense of civic pride but from the pressure of stern necessity. The new city now had eleven wharves, for example, up to seventeen hundred feet in length. It had done no little grading of its sand-hills. The quagmire of its streets had been filled and in some places planked. Sewers had been installed. Flimsy buildings were being replaced by substantial structures, for which the stones in some instances were imported from China.

Yet it must be repeated that at this time little or no progress sprang from civic pride. Each man was for himself. But, unlike the native Californian, he possessed wants and desires which had to be satisfied, and to that end he was forced, at least in essentials, to accept responsibility and to combine with his neighbors.

The machinery of this early civic life was very crude. Even the fire department, which was by far the most efficient, was, as has been indicated, more occupied with politics, rivalry, and fun, than with its proper function. The plank roads were good as long as they remained unworn, but they soon showed many holes, large and small, jagged, splintered, ugly holes going down into the depths of the mud. Many of these had been mended by private philanthropists; many more had been labeled with facetious signboards. There were rough sketches of accidents taken from life, and various legends such as "Head of Navigation," "No bottom," "Horse and dray lost here," "Take sounding," "Storage room, inquire below," "Good fishing for teal," and the like. As for the government, the less said about that the better. Responsibility was still in embryo; but politics and the law, as an irritant, were highly esteemed. The elections of the times were a farce and a holiday; nobody knew whom he was voting for nor what he was shouting for, but he voted as often and shouted as loud as he could. Every American citizen was entitled to a vote, and every one, no matter from what part of the world he came, claimed to be an American citizen and defied any one to prove the contrary. Proof consisted of club, sling-shot, bowie, and pistol. A grand free fight was a refreshment to the soul. After "a pleasant time by all was had," the populace settled down and forgot all about the officers whom it had elected. The latter went their own sweet way, unless admonished by spasmodic mass-meetings that some particularly unscrupulous raid on the treasury was noted and resented. Most of the revenue was made by the sale of city lots. Scrip was issued in payment of debt. This bore interest sometimes at the rate of six or eight per cent a month.

In the meantime, the rest of the crowd went about its own affairs. Then, as now, the American citizen is willing to pay a very high price in dishonesty to be left free for his own pressing affairs. That does not mean that he is himself either dishonest or indifferent. When the price suddenly becomes too high, either because of the increase in dishonesty or the decrease in value of his own time, he suddenly refuses to pay. This happened not infrequently in the early days of California.

CHAPTER XI

*THE VIGILANTES OF '51*

In 1851 the price for one commodity became too high. That commodity was lawlessness.

In two years the population of the city had vastly increased, until it now numbered over thirty thousand inhabitants. At an equal or greater pace the criminal and lawless elements had also increased. The confessedly criminal immigrants were paroled convicts from Sydney and other criminal colonies. These practiced men were augmented by the weak and desperate from other countries. Mexico, especially, was strongly represented. At first few in numbers and poverty-stricken in resources, these men acted merely as footpads, highwaymen, and cheap crooks. As time went on, however, they gradually became more wealthy and powerful, until they had established a sort of caste. They had not the social importance of many of the "higher-ups" of 1856, but they were crude, powerful, and in many cases wealthy. They were ably seconded by a class of lawyers which then, and for some years later, infested the courts of California. These men had made little success at law, or perhaps had been driven forth from their native haunts because of evil practices. They played the game of law exactly as the cheap criminal lawyer does today, but with the added advantage that their activities were controlled neither by a proper public sentiment nor by the usual discipline of better colleagues. Unhappily we are not yet far enough removed from just this perversion to need further explanation of the method. Indictments were fought for the reason that the murderer's name was spelled wrong in one letter; because, while the accusation stated that the murderer killed his victim with a pistol, it did not say that it was by the discharge of said pistol; and so on. But patience could not endure forever. The decent element of the community was forced at last to beat the rascals. Its apparent indifference had been only preoccupation.

The immediate cause was the cynical and open criminal activity of an Englishman named James Stuart. This man was a degenerate criminal of the worst type, who came into a temporary glory through what he considered the happy circumstances of the time. Arrested for one of his crimes, he seemed to anticipate the usual very good prospects of escaping all penalties. There had been dozens of exactly similar incidents, but this one proved to be the spark to ignite a long gathering pile of kindling. One hundred and eighty-four of the wealthiest and most prominent men of the city formed themselves into a secret Committee of Vigilance. As is usual when anything of importance is to be done, the busiest men of the community were summoned and put to work. Strangely enough, the first trial under this Committee of Vigilance resulted also in a divided jury. The mob of eight thousand or more people who had gathered to see justice done by others than the appointed court finally though grumblingly acquiesced. The prisoners were turned over to the regular authorities, and were eventually convicted and sentenced.

So far from being warned by this popular demonstration, the criminal offenders grew bolder than ever. The second great fire, in May, 1851, was commonly believed to be the work of incendiaries. Patience ceased to be a virtue. The time for resolute repression of crime had arrived. In June the Vigilance Committee was formally organized. Our old and picturesque friend Sam Brannan was deeply concerned. In matters of initiative for the public good, especially where a limelight was concealed in the wing, Brannan was an able and efficient citizen. Headquarters were chosen and a formal organization was perfected. The Monumental Fire Engine Company bell was to be tolled as a summons for the Committee to meet.

231

Even before the first meeting had adjourned, this signal was given. A certain John Jenkins had robbed a safe and was caught after a long and spectacular pursuit. Jenkins was an Australian convict and was known to numerous people as an old offender in many ways. He was therefore typical of the exact thing the Vigilance Committee had been formed to prevent. By eleven o'clock the trial, which was conducted with due decorum and formality, was over. Jenkins was adjudged guilty. There was no disorder either before or after Jenkins's trial. Throughout the trial and subsequent proceedings Jenkins's manner was unafraid and arrogant. He fully expected not only that the nerve of the Committee would give out, but that at any moment he would be rescued. It must be remembered that the sixty or seventy men in charge were known as peaceful unwarlike merchants, and that against them were arrayed all the belligerent swashbucklers of the town. While the trial was going on, the Committee was informed by its officers outside that already the roughest characters throughout the city had been told of the organization, and were gathering for rescue. The prisoner insulted his captors, still unconvinced that they meant business; then he demanded a clergyman, who prayed for three-quarters of an hour straight, until Mr. Ryckman, hearing of the gathering for rescue, no longer contained himself. Said he: "Mr. Minister, you have now prayed three-quarters of an hour. I want you to bring this prayer business to a halt. I am going to hang this man in fifteen minutes."

The Committee itself was by no means sure at all times. Bancroft tells us that "one time during the proceedings there appeared some faltering on the part of the judges, or rather a hesitancy to take the lead in assuming responsibility and braving what might be subsequent odium. It was one thing for a half-drunken rabble to take the life of a fellow man, but quite another thing for staid church-going men of business to do it. Then it was that William A. Howard, after watching the proceedings for a few moments, rose, and laying his revolver on the table looked over the assembly. Then with a slow enunciation he said, 'Gentlemen, as I understand it, we are going to hang somebody.' There was no more halting."

While these things were going on, Sam Brannan was sent out to communicate to the immense crowd the Committee's decision. He was instructed by Ryckman, "Sam, you go out and harangue the crowd while we make ready to move." Brannan was an ideal man for just such a purpose. He was of an engaging personality, of coarse fiber, possessed of a keen sense of humor, a complete knowledge of crowd psychology, and a command of ribald invective that carried far. He spoke for some time, and at the conclusion boldly asked the crowd whether or not the Committee's action met with its approval. The response was naturally very much mixed, but like a true politician Sam took the result he wanted. They found the lovers of order had already procured for them two ropes, and had gathered into some sort of coherence. The procession marched to the Plaza where Jenkins was duly hanged. The lawless element gathered at the street corners, and at least one abortive attempt at rescue was started. But promptness of action combined with the uncertainty of the situation carried the Committee successfully through. The coroner's jury next day brought in a verdict that the deceased "came to his death on the part of an association styling themselves a Committee on Vigilance, of whom the following members are implicated." And then followed nine names. The Committee immediately countered by publishing its roster of one hundred and eighty names in full.

The organization that was immediately perfected was complete and interesting. This was an association that was banded together and close-knit, and not merely a loose body of citizens. It had headquarters, company organizations, police, equipment, laws of its own, and a regular routine for handling the cases brought before it. Its police force was large and active. Had the Vigilance movement in California begun and ended with the Committee of 1851, it would be not only necessary but most interesting to follow its activities in detail. But, as it was only the forerunner and trail-blazer for the greater activities of 1856, we must save our space and attention for the latter. Suffice it to say that, with only nominal interference from the law, the first Committee hanged four people and banished a great many more for the good of their country. Fifty executions in the ordinary way would have had little effect on the excited populace of the time; but in the peculiar circumstances these four deaths accomplished a moral regeneration. This revival of public conscience could not last long, to be sure, but the worst criminals were, at least for the time being, cowed.

Spasmodic efforts toward coherence were made by the criminals, but these attempts all proved abortive. Inflammatory circulars and newspaper articles, small gatherings, hidden threats, were all freely indulged in. At one time a rescue of two prisoners was accomplished, but the Monumental bell called together a determined band of men who had no great difficulty in reclaiming their own. The Governor of the State, secretly in sympathy with the purposes of the Committee, was satisfied to issue a formal proclamation.

It must be repeated that, were it not for the later larger movement of 1856, this Vigilance Committee would merit more extended notice. It gave a lead, however, and a framework on which the Vigilance Committee of 1856 was built. It proved that the better citizens, if aroused, could take matters into their own hands. But the opposing forces of 1851 were very different from those of five years later. And the transition from the criminal of 1851 to the criminal of 1856 is the history of San Francisco between those two dates.

CHAPTER XII

*SAN FRANCISCO IN TRANSITION*

By the mid-fifties San Francisco had attained the dimensions of a city. Among other changes of public interest within the brief space of two or three years were a hospital, a library, a cemetery, several churches, public markets, bathing establishments, public schools, two race-courses, twelve wharves, five hundred and thirty-seven saloons, and about eight thousand women of several classes. The population was now about fifty thousand. The city was now of a fairly substantial character, at least in the down-town districts. There were many structures of brick and stone. In many directions the sand-hills had been conveniently graded down by means of a power shovel called the Steam Paddy in contradistinction to the hand Paddy, or Irishman with a shovel. The streets were driven straight ahead regardless of contours. It is related that often the inhabitants of houses perched on the sides of the sand-hills would have to scramble to safety as their dwellings rolled down the bank, undermined by some grading operation below. A water system had been established, the nucleus of the present Spring Valley Company. The streets had nearly all been planked, and private enterprise had carried the plank toll-road even to the Mission district. The fire department had been brought to a high state of perfection. The shallow waters of the bay were being filled up by the rubbish from the town and by the débris from the operations of the Steam Paddies. New streets were formed on piles extended out into the bay. Houses were erected, also on piles and on either side of these marine thoroughfares. Gradually the rubbish filled the skeleton framework. Occasionally old ships, caught by this seaward invasion, were built around, and so became integral parts of the city itself.

The same insistent demand that led to increasing the speed of the vessels, together with the fact that it cost any ship from one hundred to two hundred dollars a day to lie at any of the wharves, developed an extreme efficiency in loading and unloading cargoes. Hittell says that probably in no port of the world could a ship be emptied as quickly as at San Francisco. For the first and last time in the history of the world the profession of stevedore became a distinguished one. In addition to the overseas trade, there were now many ships, driven by sail or steam, plying the local routes. Some of the river steamboats had actually been brought around the Horn. Their free-board had been raised by planking-in the lower deck, and thus these frail vessels had sailed their long and stormy voyage—truly a notable feat.

It did not pay to hold goods very long. Eastern shippers seemed, by a curious unanimity, to send out many consignments of the same scarcity. The result was that the high prices of today would be utterly destroyed by an oversupply of tomorrow. It was thus to the great advantage of every merchant to meet his ship promptly, and to gain knowledge as soon as possible of the cargo of the incoming vessels. For this purpose signal stations were established, rowboat patrols were organized, and many other ingenious schemes was applied to the secret service of the mercantile business. Both in order to save storage and to avoid the possibility of loss from new shipments coming in, the goods were auctioned off as soon as they were landed.

These auctions were most elaborate institutions involving brass bands, comfortable chairs, eloquent "spielers," and all the rest. They were a feature of the street life, which in turn had an interest all its own. The planking threw back a hollow reverberating sound from the various vehicles. There seemed to be no rules of the road. Omnibuses careered along, every window rattling loudly; drays creaked and strained; non-descript delivery wagons tried to outrattle the omnibuses; horsemen picked their way amid the mêlée. The din was described as something extraordinary—hoofs drumming, wheels rumbling, oaths and shouts, and from the sidewalk the blare and bray of brass bands before the various auction shops. Newsboys and bootblacks darted in all directions. Cigar boys, a peculiar product of the time, added to the hubbub. Bootblacking stands of the most elaborate description were kept by French and Italians. The town was full of characters who delighted in their own eccentricities, and who were always on public view. One individual possessed a remarkably intelligent pony who every morning, without guidance from his master, patronized one of the shoe-blacking stands to get his front hoofs polished. He presented each one in turn to the foot-rest, and stood like a statue until the job was done.

Some of the numberless saloons already showed signs of real magnificence. Mahogany bars with brass rails, huge mirrors in gilt frames, pyramids of delicate crystal, rich hangings, oil paintings of doubtful merit but indisputable interest, heavy chandeliers of glass prisms, the most elaborate of free lunches, skillful barkeepers who mixed drinks at arm's length, were common to all the better places. These things would not be so remarkable in large cities at the present time, but in the early Fifties, only three years after the tent stage, and thousands of miles from the nearest civilization, the enterprise that was displayed seemed remarkable. The question of expense did not stop these early worthies. Of one saloonkeeper it is related that, desiring a punch bowl and finding that the only vessel of the sort was a soup-tureen belonging to a large and expensive dinner set, he bought the whole set for the sake of the soup-tureen. Some of the more pretentious places boasted of special attractions: thus one supported its ceiling on crystal pillars; another had dashing young women to serve the drinks, though the mixing was done by men as usual; a third possessed a large musical-box capable of playing several very noisy tunes; a fourth had imported a marvelous piece of mechanism run by clockwork which exhibited the sea in motion, a ship tossing on the waves, on shore a windmill in action, a train of cars passing over a bridge, a deer chased by hounds, and the like.

But these bar-rooms were a totally different institution from the gambling resorts. Although gambling was not now considered the entirely worthy occupation of a few years previous, and although some of the better citizens, while frequenting the gambling halls, still preferred to do their own playing in semi-private, the picturesqueness and glory of these places had not yet been dimmed by any general popular disapproval. The gambling halls were not only places to risk one's fortune, but they were also a sort of evening club. They usually supported a raised stage with footlights, a negro minstrel troop, or a singer or so. On one side elaborate bars of rosewood or mahogany ran the entire length, backed by big mirrors of French plate. The whole of the very large main floor was heavily carpeted. Down the center generally ran two rows of gambling tables offering various games such as faro, keeno, roulette, poker, and the dice games. Beyond these tables, on the opposite side of the room from the bar, were the lounging quarters, with small tables, large easy-chairs, settees, and fireplaces. Decoration was of the most ornate. The ceilings and walls were generally white with a great deal of gilt. All classes of people frequented these places and were welcomed there. Some were dressed in the height of fashion, and some wore the roughest sort of miners' clothes—floppy old slouch hats, flannel shirts, boots to which the dried mud was clinging or from which it fell to the rich carpet. All were considered on an equal plane. The professional gamblers came to represent a type of their own,—weary, indifferent, pale, cool men, who had not only to keep track of the game and the bets, but also to assure control over the crowd about them. Often in these places immense sums were lost or won; often in these places occurred crimes of shooting and stabbing; but also into these places came many men who rarely drank or gambled at all. They assembled to enjoy each other's company, the brightness, the music, and the sociable warmth.

On Sunday the populace generally did one of two things: either it sallied out in small groups into the surrounding country on picnics or celebrations at some of the numerous road-houses; or it swarmed out the plank toll-road to the Mission. To the newcomer the latter must have been much the more interesting. There he saw a congress of all the nations of the earth: French, Germans, Italians, Russians, Dutchmen, British, Turks, Arabs, Negroes, Chinese, Kanakas, Indians, the gorgeous members of the Spanish races, and all sorts of queer people to whom no habitat could be assigned. Most extraordinary perhaps were the men from the gold mines of the Sierras. The miners had by now distinctly segregated themselves from the rest of the population. They led a hardier, more laborious life and were proud of the fact. They attempted generally to differentiate themselves in appearance from all the rest of the human race, and it must be confessed that they succeeded. The miners were mostly young and wore their hair long, their beards rough; they walked with a wide swagger; their clothes were exaggeratedly coarse, but they ornamented themselves with bright silk handkerchiefs, feathers, flowers, with squirrel or buck tails in their hats, with long heavy chains of nuggets, with glittering and prominently displayed pistols, revolvers, stilettos, knives, and dirks. Some even plaited their beards in three tails, or tied their long hair under their chins; but no matter how bizarre they made themselves, nobody on the streets of *blasé* San Francisco paid the slightest attention to them. The Mission, which they, together with the crowd, frequented, was a primitive Coney Island. Bear pits, cockfights, theatrical attractions, side-shows, innumerable hotels and small restaurants, saloons, races, hammer-striking, throwing balls at negroes' heads, and a hundred other attractions kept the crowds busy and generally good-natured. If a fight arose, "it was," as the Irishman says, "considered a private fight," and nobody else could get in it. Such things were considered matters for the individuals themselves to settle.

The great feature of the time was its extravagance. It did not matter whether a man was a public servant, a private and respected citizen, or from one of the semi-public professions that cater to men's greed and dissipation, he acted as though the ground beneath his feet were solid gold. The most extravagant public works were undertaken without thought and without plan. The respectable women vied in the magnificence and ostentation of their costumes with the women of the lower world. Theatrical attractions at high prices were patronized abundantly. Balls of great magnificence were given almost every night. Private carriages of really excellent appointment were numerous along the disreputable planked roads or the sandy streets strewn with cans and garbage.

The feverish life of the times reflected itself domestically. No live red-blooded man could be expected to spend his evenings reading a book quietly at home while all the magnificent, splendid, seething life of down-town was roaring in his ears. All his friends would be out; all the news of the day passed around; all the excitements of the evening offered themselves. It was too much to expect of human nature. The consequence was that a great many young wives were left alone, with the ultimate result of numerous separations and divorces. The moral nucleus of really respectable society— and there was a noticeable one even at that time—was overshadowed and swamped for the moment. Such a social life as this sounds decidedly immoral but it was really unmoral, with the bright, eager, attractive unmorality of the vigorous child. In fact, in that society, as some one has expressed it, everything was condoned except meanness.

It was the era of the grandiose. Even conversation reflected this characteristic. The myriad bootblacks had grand outfits and stands. The captain of a ship offered ten dollars to a negro to act as his cook. The negro replied, "If you will walk up to my restaurant, I'll set you to work at twenty-five dollars immediately." From men in such humble stations up to the very highest and most respected citizens the spirit of gambling, of taking chances, was also in the air.

As has been pointed out, a large proportion of the city's wealth was raised not from taxation but from the sale of its property. Under the heedless extravagance of the first government the municipal debt rose to over one million dollars. Since interest charged on this was thirty-six per cent annually, it can be seen that the financial situation was rather hopeless. As the city was even then often very short of funds, it paid for its work and its improvements in certificates of indebtedness, usually called "scrip." Naturally this scrip was held below par—a condition that caused all contractors and supply merchants to charge two or three hundred per cent over the normal prices for their work and commodities in order to keep even. And this practice, completing the vicious circle, increased the debt. An attempt was made to fund the city debt by handing in the scrip in exchange for a ten per cent obligation. This method gave promise of success; but a number of holders of scrip refused to surrender it, and brought suit to enforce payment. One of these, a physician named Peter Smith, was owed a considerable sum for the care of indigent sick. He obtained a judgment against the city, levied on some of its property, and proceeded to sell. The city commissioners warned the public that titles under the Smith claim were not legal, and proceeded to sell the property on their own account. The speculators bought claims under Peter Smith amounting to over two millions of dollars at merely nominal rates. For example, one parcel of city lots sold at less than ten cents per lot. The prices were so absurd that these sales were treated as a joke. The joke came in on the other side, however, when the officials proceeded to ratify these sales. The public then woke up to the fact that it had been fleeced. Enormous prices were paid for unsuitable property, ostensibly for the uses of the city. After the money had passed, these properties were often declared unsuitable and resold at reduced prices to people already determined upon by the ring.

Nevertheless commercially things went well for a time. The needs of hundreds of thousands of newcomers, in a country where the manufactures were practically nothing, were enormous. It is related that at first laundry was sent as far as the Hawaiian Islands. Every single commodity of civilized life, such as we understand it, had to be imported. As there was then no remote semblance of combination, either in restraint of or in encouragement of trade, it followed that the market must fluctuate wildly. The local agents of eastern firms were often embarrassed and overwhelmed by the ill-timed consignments of goods. One Boston firm was alleged to have sent out a whole shipload of women's bonnets—to a community where a woman was one of the rarest sights to be found! Not many shipments were as silly as this, but the fact remains that a rumor of a shortage in any commodity would often be followed by rush orders on clipper ships laden to the guards with that same article. As a consequence the bottom fell out of the market completely, and the unfortunate consignee found himself forced to auction off the goods much below cost.

During the year 1854, the tide of prosperity began to ebb. A dry season caused a cessation of mining in many parts of the mountains. Of course it can be well understood that the immense prosperity of the city, the prosperity that allowed it to recover from severe financial disease, had its spring in the placer mines. A constant stream of fresh gold was needed to shore up the tottering commercial structure. With the miners out of the diggings, matters changed. The red-shirted digger of gold had little idea of the value of money. Many of them knew only the difference between having money and having none. They had to have credit, which they promptly wasted. Extending credit to the miners made it necessary that credit should also be extended to the sellers, and so on back. Meanwhile the eastern shippers continued to pour goods into the flooded market. An auction brought such cheap prices that they proved a temptation even to an overstocked public. The gold to pay for purchases went east, draining the country of bullion. One or two of the supposedly respectable and polished citizens such as Talbot Green and "honest Harry Meiggs" fell by the wayside. The confidence of the new community began to be shaken. In 1854 came the crisis. Three hundred out of about a thousand business houses shut down. Seventy-seven filed petitions in insolvency with liabilities for many millions of dollars. In 1855 one hundred and ninety-seven additional firms and several banking houses went under.

There were two immediate results of this state of affairs. In the first place, every citizen became more intensely interested and occupied with his own personal business than ever before; he had less time to devote to the real causes of trouble, that is the public instability; and he grew rather more selfish and suspicious of his neighbor than ever before. The second result was to attract the dregs of society. The pickings incident to demoralized conditions looked rich to these men. Professional politicians, shyster lawyers, political gangsters, flocked to the spoil. In 1851 the lawlessness of mere physical violence had come to a head. By 1855 and 1856 there was added to a recrudescence of this disorder a lawlessness of graft, of corruption, both political and financial, and the overbearing arrogance of a self-made aristocracy. These conditions combined to bring about a second crisis in the precarious life of this new society.

CHAPTER XIII

*THE STORM GATHERS*

The foundation of trouble in California at this time was formal legalism. Legality was made a fetish. The law was a game played by lawyers and not an attempt to get justice done. The whole of public prosecution was in the hands of one man, generally poorly paid, with equally underpaid assistants, while the defense was conducted by the ablest and most enthusiastic men procurable. It followed that convictions were very few. To lose a criminal case was considered even mildly disgraceful. It was a point of professional pride for the lawyer to get his client free, without reference to the circumstances of the time or the guilt of the accused. To fail was a mark of extreme stupidity, for the game was considered an easy and fascinating one. The whole battery of technical delays was at the command of the defendant. If a man had neither the time nor the energy for the finesse that made the interest of the game, he could always procure interminable delays during which witnesses could be scattered or else wearied to the point of non-appearance. Changes of venue to courts either prejudiced or known to be favorable to the technical interpretation of the law were very easily procured. Even of shadier expedients, such as packing juries, there was no end.

With these shadier expedients, however, your high-minded lawyer, moving in the best society, well dressed, proud, looked up to, and today possessing descendants who gaze back upon their pioneer ancestors with pride, had little directly to do. He called in as counsel other lawyers, not so high-minded, so honorable, so highly placed. These little lawyers, shoulder-strikers, bribe-givers and takers, were held in good-humored contempt by the legal lights who employed them. The actual dishonesty was diluted through so many agents that it seemed an almost pure stream of lofty integrity. Ordinary jury-packing was an easy art. Of course the sheriff's office must connive at naming the talesmen; therefore it was necessary to elect the sheriff; consequently all the lawyers were in politics. Of course neither the lawyer nor the sheriff himself ever knew of any individual transaction! A sum of money was handed by the leading counsel to his next in command and charged off as "expense." This fund emerged considerably diminished in the sheriff's office as "perquisites."

Such were the conditions in the realm of criminal law, the realm where the processes became so standardized that between 1849 and 1856 over one thousand murders had been committed and only one legal conviction had been secured! Dueling was a recognized institution, and a skillful shot could always "get" his enemy in this formal manner; but if time or skill lacked, it was still perfectly safe to shoot him down in a street brawl—provided one had money enough to employ talent for defense.

But, once in politics, the law could not stop at the sheriff's office. It rubbed shoulders with big contracts and big financial operations of all sorts. The city was being built within a few years out of nothing by a busy, careless, and shifting population. Money was still easy, people could and did pay high taxes without a thought, for they would rather pay well to be let alone than be bothered with public affairs. Like hyenas to a kill, the public contractors gathered. Immense public works were undertaken at enormous prices. To get their deals through legally it was, of course, necessary that officials, councilmen, engineers, and others should be sympathetic. So, naturally, the big operators as well as the big lawyers had to go into politics. Legal efficiency coupled with the inefficiency of the bench, legal corruption, and the arrogance of personal favor, dissolved naturally into political corruption.

The elections of those days would have been a joke had they been not so tragically significant. They came to be a sheer farce. The polls were guarded by bullies who did not hesitate at command to manhandle any decent citizen indicated by the local leaders. Such men were openly hired for the purposes of intimidation. Votes could be bought in the open market. "Floaters" were shamelessly imported into districts that might prove doubtful; and, if things looked close, the election inspectors and the judges could be relied on to make things come out all right in the final count. One of the exhibits later shown in the Vigilante days of 1856 was an ingenious ballot box by which the goats could be segregated from the sheep as the ballots were cast. You may be sure that the sheep were the only ones counted. Election day was one of continuous whiskey drinking and brawling so that decent citizens were forced to remain within doors. The returns from the different wards were announced as fast as the votes were counted. It was therefore the custom to hold open certain wards until the votes of all the others were known. Then whatever tickets were lacking to secure the proper election were counted from the packed ballot box in the sure ward. In this manner five hundred votes were once returned from Crystal Springs precinct where there dwelt not over thirty voters. If some busybody made enough of a row to get the merry tyrants into court, there were always plenty of lawyers who could play the ultra-technical so well that the accused were not only released but were returned as legally elected as well.

With the proper officials in charge of the executive end of the government and with a trained crew of lawyers making their own rules as they went along, almost any crime of violence, corruption, theft, or the higher grades of finance could be committed with absolute impunity. The state of the public mind became for a while apathetic. After numberless attempts to obtain justice, the public fell back with a shrug of the shoulders. The men of better feeling found themselves helpless. As each man's safety and ability to resent insult depended on his trigger finger, the newspapers of that time made interesting but scurrilous and scandalous reading. An appetite for personalities developed, and these derogatory remarks ordinarily led to personal encounters. The streets became battle-grounds of bowie-knives and revolvers, as rivals hunted each other out. This picture may seem lurid and exaggerated, but the cold statistics of the time supply all the details.

The politicians of the day were essentially fighting men. The large majority were low-grade Southerners who had left their section, urged by unmistakable hints from their fellow-citizens. The political life of early California was colored very largely by the pseudo-chivalry which these people used as a cloak. They used the Southern code for their purposes very thoroughly, and bullied their way through society in a swashbuckling manner that could not but arouse admiration. There were many excellent Southerners in California in those days, but from the very start their influence was overshadowed by the more unworthy. Unfortunately, later many of the better class of Southerners, yielding to prejudice and sectional feeling, joined the so-called "Law and Order" party.

It must be remembered, however, that whereas the active merchants and industrious citizens were too busy to attend to local politics, the professional low-class Southern politician had come out to California for no other purpose. To be successful, he had to be a fighting man. His revolver and his bowie-knife were part of his essential equipment. He used the word "honor" as a weapon of defense, and battered down opposition in the most high-mannered fashion by the simple expedient of claiming that he had been insulted. The fire-eater was numerous in those days. He dressed well, had good manners and appearance, possessed abundant leisure, and looked down scornfully on those citizens who were busy building the city, "low Yankee shopkeepers" being his favorite epithet.

Examined at close range, in contemporary documents, this individual has about him little of romance and nothing whatever admirable. It would be a great pity, were mistaken sentimentality allowed to clothe him in the same bright-hued garments as the cavaliers of England in the time of the Stuarts. It would be an equal pity, were the casual reader to condemn all who eventually aligned themselves against the Vigilance movement as of the same stripe as the criminals who menaced society. There were many worthy people whose education thoroughly inclined them towards formal law, and who, therefore, when the actual break came, found themselves supporting law instead of justice.

As long as the country continued to enjoy the full flood of prosperity, these things did not greatly matter. The time was individualistic, and every man was supposed to take care of himself. But in the year 1855 financial stringency overtook the new community. For lack of water many of the miners had stopped work and had to ask for credit in buying their daily necessities. The country stores had to have credit from the city because the miners could not pay, and the wholesalers of the city again had to ask extension from the East until their bills were met by the retailers. The gold of the country went East to pay its bills. Further to complicate the matter, all banking was at this time done by private firms. These could take deposits and make loans and could issue exchange, but they could not issue bank-notes. Therefore the currency was absolutely inelastic.

Even these conditions failed to shake the public optimism, until out of a clear sky came announcement that Adams and Company had failed. Adams and Company occupied in men's minds much the same position as the Bank of England. If Adams and Company were vulnerable, then nobody was secure. The assets of the bankrupt firm were turned over to one Alfred Cohen as receiver, with whom Jones, a member of the firm of Palmer, Cook, and Company, and a third individual were associated as assignees. On petition of other creditors the judge of the district court removed Cohen and appointed one Naglee in his place. This new man, Naglee, on asking for the assets was told that they had been deposited with Palmer, Cook, and Company. The latter firm refused to give them up, denying Naglee's jurisdiction in the matter. Naglee then commenced suit against the assignees and obtained a judgment against them for $269,000. On their refusal to pay over this sum, Jones and Cohen were taken into custody. But Palmer, Cook, and Company influenced the courts, as did about every large mercantile or political firm. They soon secured the release of the prisoners, and in the general scramble for the assets of Adams and Company they secured the lion's share.

It was the same old story. An immense amount of money had disappeared. Nobody had been punished, and it was all strictly legal. Failures resulted right and left. Even Wells, Fargo, and Company closed their doors but reopened them within a few days. There was much excitement which would probably have died as other excitement had died before, had not the times produced a voice of compelling power. This voice spoke through an individual known as James King of William.

King was a man of keen mind and dauntless courage, who had tried his luck briefly at the mines, realized that the physical work was too much for him, and had therefore returned to mercantile and banking pursuits in San Francisco. His peculiar name was said to be due to the fact that at the age of sixteen, finding another James King in his immediate circle, he had added his father's name as a distinguishing mark. He was rarely mentioned except with the full designation—James King of William. On his return he opened a private banking-house, brought out his family, and entered the life of the town. For a time his banking career prospered and he acquired a moderate fortune, but in 1854 unwise investments forced him to close his office. In a high-minded fashion, very unusual in those times and even now somewhat rare, he surrendered to his creditors everything on earth he possessed. He then accepted a salaried position with Adams and Company, which he held until that house also failed. Since to the outside world his connection with the firm looked dubious, he exonerated himself through a series of pamphlets and short newspaper articles. The vigor and force of their style arrested attention, so that when his dauntless crusading spirit, revolting against the carnival of crime both subtle and obvious, desired to edit a newspaper, he had no difficulty in raising the small sum of money necessary. He had always expressed his opinions clearly and fearlessly, and the public watched with the greatest interest the appearance of the new sheet.

The first number of the *Daily Evening Bulletin* appeared on October 8, 1855. Like all papers of that day and like many of the English papers now, its first page was completely covered with small advertisements. A thin driblet of local items occupied a column on the third and fourth pages, and a single column of editorials ran down the second. As a newspaper it seemed beneath contempt, but the editorials made men sit up and take notice. King started with an attack on Palmer, Cook, and Company's methods. He said nothing whatever about the robberies. He dealt exclusively with the excessive rentals for postal boxes charged the public by Palmer, Cook, and Company. That seemed a comparatively small and harmless matter, but King made it interesting by mentioning exact names, recording specific instances, avoiding any generalities, and stating plainly that this was merely a beginning in the exposure of methods. Jones of Palmer, Cook, and Company—that same Jones who had been arrested with Cohen—immediately visited King in his office with the object of either intimidating or bribing him as the circumstances seemed to advise. He bragged of horsewhips and duels, but returned rather noncommittal. The next evening the *Bulletin* reported Jones's visit simply as an item of news, faithfully, sarcastically, and in a pompous vein. There followed no comment whatever. The next number, now eagerly purchased by every one, was more interesting because of its hints of future disclosures rather than because of its actual information. One of the alleged scoundrels was mentioned by name, and then the subject was dropped. The attention of the City Marshal was curtly called to disorderly houses and the statutes concerning them, and it was added "for his information" that at a certain address, which was given, a structure was then actually being built for improper purposes. Then, without transition, followed a list of official bonds and sureties for which Palmer, Cook, and Company were giving vouchers, amounting to over two millions. There were no comments on this list, but the inference was obvious that the firm had the whip-hand over many public officials.

The position of the new paper was soon formally established. It possessed a large subscription list; it was eagerly bought on its appearance in the street; and its advertising was increasing. King again turned his attention to Palmer, Cook, and Company. Each day he explored succinctly, clearly, without rhetoric, some single branch of their business. By the time he had finished with them, he had not only exposed all their iniquities, but he had, which was more important, educated the public to the financial methods of the time. It followed naturally in this type of exposure that King should criticize some of the legal subterfuges, which in turn brought him to analysis of the firm's legal advisers, who had previously enjoyed a good reputation. From such subjects he drifted to dueling, venal newspapers, and soon down to the ordinary criminals such as Billy Mulligan, Wooley Kearny, Casey, Cora, Yankee Sullivan, Ned McGowan, Charles Duane, and many others. Never did he hesitate to specify names and instances. He never dealt in innuendoes. This was bringing him very close to personal danger, for worthies of the class last mentioned were the sort who carried their pistols and bowie-knives prominently displayed and handy for use. As yet no actual violence had been attempted against him. Other methods of reprisal that came to his notice King published without comment as items of news.

Mere threats had little effect in intimidating the editor. More serious means were tried. A dozen men publicly announced that they intended to kill him—and the records of the dozen were pretty good testimonials to their sincerity. In the gambling resorts and on the streets bets were made and pools formed on the probable duration of King's life. As was his custom, he commented even upon this. Said the *Bulletin's* editorial columns: "Bets are now being offered, we have been told, that the editor of the *Bulletin* will not be in existence twenty days longer. And the case of Dr. Hogan of the Vicksburg paper who was murdered by gamblers of that place is cited as a warning. Pah!… War then is the cry, is it? War between the prostitutes and gamblers on one side and the virtuous and respectable on the other! Be it so, then! Gamblers of San Francisco, you have made your election and we are ready on our side for the issue!" A man named Selover sent a challenge to King. King took this occasion to announce that he would consider no challenges and would fight no duels. Selover then announced his intention of killing King on sight. Says the *Bulletin*: "Mr. Selover, it is said, carries a knife. We carry a pistol. We hope neither will be required, but if this rencontre cannot be avoided, why will Mr. Selover persist in imperiling the lives of others? We pass every afternoon about half-past four to five o'clock along Market Street from Fourth to Fifth Streets. The road is wide and not so much frequented as those streets farther in town. If we are to be shot or cut to pieces, for heaven's sake let it be done there. Others will not be injured, and in case we fall our house is but a few hundred yards beyond and the cemetery not much farther." Boldness such as this did not act exactly as a soporific.

About this time was perpetrated a crime of violence no worse than many hundreds which had preceded it, but occurring at a psychological time. A gambler named Charles Cora shot and killed William Richardson, a United States marshal. The shooting was cold-blooded and without danger to the murderer, for at the time Richardson was unarmed. Cora was at once hustled to jail, not so much for confinement as for safety against a possible momentary public anger. Men had been shot on the street before—many men, some of them as well known and as well liked as Richardson—but not since public sentiment had been aroused and educated as the *Bulletin* had aroused and educated it. Crowds commenced at once to gather. Some talk of lynching went about. Men made violent street-corner speeches. The mobs finally surged to the jail, but were firmly met by a strong armed guard and fell back. There was much destructive and angry talk.

But to swing a mob into action there must be determined men at its head, and this mob had no leader. Sam Brannan started to say something, but was promptly arrested for inciting riot. Though the situation was ticklish, the police seem to have handled it well, making only a passive opposition and leaving the crowd to fritter its energies in purposeless cursing, surging to and fro, and harmless threatenings. Nevertheless this crowd persisted longer than most of them.

The next day the *Bulletin* vigorously counseled dependence upon the law, expressed confidence in the judges who were to try the case—Hager and Norton—and voiced a personal belief that the day had passed when it would ever be necessary to resort to arbitrary measures. It may hence be seen how far from a contemplation of extra legal measures was King in his public attitude. Nevertheless he added a paragraph of warning: "Hang Billy Mulligan—that's the word. If Mr. Sheriff Scannell does not remove Billy Mulligan from his present post as keeper of the County Jail and Mulligan lets Cora escape, hang Billy Mulligan, and if necessary to get rid of the sheriff, hang him—hang the sheriff!"

Public excitement died. Conviction seemed absolutely certain. Richardson had been a public official and a popular one. Cora's action had been cold-blooded and apparently without provocation. Nevertheless he had remained undisturbed. He had retained one of the most brilliant lawyers of the time, James McDougall. McDougall added to his staff the most able of the younger lawyers of the city. Immense sums of money were available. The source is not exactly known, but a certain Belle Cora, a prostitute afterwards married by Cora, was advancing large amounts. A man named James Casey, bound by some mysterious obligation, was active in taking up general collections. Cora lived in great luxury at the jail. He had long been a close personal friend of the sheriff and his deputy, Mulligan. When the case came to trial, Cora escaped conviction through the disagreement of the jury.

This fiasco, following King's editorials, had a profound effect on the public mind. King took the outrage against justice as a fresh starting-point for new attacks. He assailed bitterly and fearlessly the countless abuses of the time, until at last he was recognized as a dangerous opponent by the heretofore cynically amused higher criminals. Many rumors of plots against King's life are to be found in the detailed history of the day. Whether his final assassination was the result of one of these plots, or simply the outcome of a burst of passion, matters little. Ultimately it had its source in the ungoverned spirit of the times.

Four months after the farce of the Cora trial, on May 14, King published an attack on the appointment of a certain man to a position in the federal custom house. The candidate had happened to be involved with James P. Casey in a disgraceful election. Casey was at that time one of the supervisors. Incidental to his attack on the candidate, King wrote as follows: "It does not matter how bad a man Casey had been, or how much benefit it might be to the public to have him out of the way, we cannot accord to any one citizen the right to kill him or even beat him, without justifiable provocation. The fact that Casey has been an inmate of Sing Sing prison in New York is no offense against the laws of this State; nor is the fact of his having stuffed himself through the ballot box, as elected to the Board of Supervisors from a district where it is said he was not even a candidate, any justification for Mr. Bagley to shoot Casey, however richly the latter may deserve to have his neck stretched for such fraud on the people."

Casey read this editorial in full knowledge that thousands of his fellow-citizens would also read it. He was at that time, in addition to his numerous political cares, editor of a small newspaper called *The Sunday Times*. This had been floated for the express purpose of supporting the extremists of the legalists' party, which, as we have explained, now included the gambling and lawless element. How valuable he was considered is shown by the fact that at a previous election Casey had been returned as elected supervisor, although he had not been a candidate, his name had not been on the ticket, and subsequent private investigations could unearth no man who would acknowledge having voted for him. Indeed, he was not even a resident of that district. However, a slick politician named Yankee Sullivan, who ran the election, said officially that the most votes had been counted for him; and so his election was announced. Casey was a handy tool in many ways, rarely appearing in person but adept in selecting suitable agents. He was personally popular. In appearance he is described as a short, slight man with a keen face, a good forehead, a thin but florid countenance, dark curly hair, and blue eyes; a type of unscrupulous Irish adventurer, with perhaps the dash of romantic idealism sometimes found in the worst scoundrels. Like most of his confreres, he was particularly touchy on the subject of his "honor."

On reading the *Bulletin* editorials, he proceeded at once to King's office, announcing his intention of shooting the editor on sight. Probably he would have done so except for the accidental circumstance that King happened to be busy at a table with his back turned squarely to the door. Even Casey could not shoot a man in the back, without a word of warning. He was stuttering and excited. The interview was overheard by two men in an adjoining office.

"What do you mean by that article?" cried Casey.

"What article?" asked King.

"That which says I was formerly an inmate of Sing Sing."

"Is it not true?" asked King quietly.

"That is not the question. I don't wish my past acts raked up. On that point I am sensitive."

A slight pause ensued.

"Are you done?" asked King quietly. Then leaping from the chair he burst suddenly into excitement.

"There's the door, go! And never show your face here again."

Casey had lost his advantage. At the door he gathered himself together again.

"I'll say in my paper what I please," he asserted with a show of bravado.

King was again in control of himself.

"You have a perfect right to do so," he rejoined. "I shall never notice your paper."

Casey struck himself on the breast.

"And if necessary I shall defend myself," he cried.

King bounded again from his seat, livid with anger.

"Go," he commanded sharply, and Casey went.

Outside in the street Casey found a crowd waiting. The news of his visit to the *Bulletin* office had spread. His personal friends crowded around asking eager questions. Casey answered with vague generalities: he wasn't a man to be trifled with, and some people had to find out! Blackmailing was not a healthy occupation when it aimed at a gentleman! He left the general impression that King had apologized. Bragging in this manner, Casey led the way to the Bank Exchange, the fashionable bar not far distant. Here he remained drinking and boasting for some time.

In the group that surrounded him was a certain Judge Edward McGowan, a jolly, hard-drinking, noisy individual. He had been formerly a fugitive from justice. However, through the attractions of a gay life, a combination of bullying and intrigue, he had made himself a place in the new city and had at last risen to the bench. He was apparently easy to fathom, but the stream really ran deep. Some historians claim that he had furnished King the document which proved Casey an ex-convict. It is certain that now he had great influence with Casey, and that he drew him aside from the bar and talked with him some time in a low voice. Some people insist that he furnished the navy revolver with which a few moments later Casey shot King. This may be so, but every man went armed in those days, especially men of Casey's stamp.

It is certain, however, that after his interview with McGowan, Casey took his place across the street from the Bank Exchange. There, wrapped in his cloak, he awaited King's usual promenade home.

That for some time his intention was well known is proved by the group that little by little gathered on the opposite side of the street. It is a matter of record that a small boy passing by was commandeered and sent with a message for Peter Wrightman, a deputy sheriff. Pete, out of breath, soon joined the group. There he idled, also watching,—an official charged with the maintenance of the law of the land!

At just five o'clock King turned the corner, his head bent. He started to cross the street diagonally and had almost reached the opposite sidewalk when he was confronted by Casey who stepped forward from his place of concealment behind a wagon.

"Come on," he said, throwing back his cloak, and immediately fired. King, who could not have known what Casey was saying, was shot through the left breast, staggered, and fell. Casey then took several steps toward his victim, looked at him closely as though to be sure he had done a good job, let down the hammer of his pistol, picked up his cloak, and started for the police-station. All he wanted now was a trial under the law.

The distance to the station-house was less than a block. Instantly at the sound of the shot his friends rose about him and guarded him to the shelter of the lock-up. But at last the public was aroused. Casey had unwittingly cut down a symbol of the better element, as well as a fearless and noble man. Someone rang the old Monumental Engine House bell—the bell that had been used to call together the Vigilantes of 1851. The news spread about the city like wildfire. An immense mob appeared to spring from nowhere.

The police officials were no fools; they recognized the quality of the approaching hurricane. The city jail was too weak a structure. It was desirable to move the prisoner at once to the county jail for safe-keeping. A carriage was brought to the entrance of an alley next the city jail; the prisoner, closely surrounded by armed men, was rushed to it; and the vehicle charged out through the crowd. The mob, as yet unorganized, recoiled instinctively before the plunging horses and the presented pistols. Before anybody could gather his wits, the equipage had disappeared.

The mob surged after the disappearing vehicle, and so ended up finally in the wide open space before the county jail. The latter was a solidly built one-story building situated on top of a low cliff. North, the marshal, had drawn up his armed men. The mob, very excited, vociferated, surging back and forth, though they did not rush, because as yet they had no leaders. Attempts were made to harangue the gathering, but everywhere the speeches were cut short. At a crucial moment the militia appeared. The crowd thought at first that the volunteer troops were coming to uphold their own side, but were soon undeceived. The troops deployed in front of the jail and stood at guard. Just then the mayor attempted to address the crowd.

"You are here creating an excitement," he said, "which may lead to occurrences this night which will require years to wipe out. You are now laboring under great excitement and I advise you to quietly disperse. I assure you the prisoner is safe. Let the law have its course and justice will be done."

He was listened to with respect, up to this point, but here arose such a chorus of jeers that he retired hastily.

"How about Richardson?" they demanded of him. "Where is the law in Cora's case? To hell with such justice!"

More and more soldiers came into the square, which was soon filled with bayonets. The favorable moment had passed and this particular crisis was, like all the other similar crises, quickly over. But the city was aroused. Mass meetings were held in the Plaza and in other convenient localities. Many meetings took place in rooms in different parts of the city. Men armed by the thousands. Vehement orators held forth from every balcony. Some of these people were, as a chronicler of the times quaintly expressed it, "considerably tight." There was great diversity of opinion. All night the city seethed with ill-directed activity. But men felt helpless and hopeless for want of efficient organization.

The so-called Southern chivalry called this affair a "fight." Indeed the *Herald* in its issue of the next morning, mistaking utterly the times, held boldly along the way of its sympathies. It also spoke of the assassination as an "affray," and stated emphatically its opinion that, "now that justice is regularly administered," there was no excuse for even the threat of public violence. This utter blindness to the meaning of the new movement and the far-reaching effect of King's previous campaign proved fatal to the paper. It declined immediately. In the meantime, attended by his wife and a whole score of volunteer physicians, King, lying in a room in the Montgomery block, was making a fight for his life.

Then people began to notice a small advertisement on the first page of the morning papers, headed *The Vigilance Committee*.

"The members of the Vigilance Committee in good standing will please meet at number 105-1/2 Sacramento Street, this day, Thursday, fifteenth instant, at nine o'clock A.M. By order of the COMMITTEE OF THIRTEEN."

People stood still in the streets, when this notice met the eye. If this was actually the old Committee of 1851, it meant business. There was but one way to find out and that was to go and see. Number 105-1/2 Sacramento Street was a three-story barn-like structure that had been built by a short-lived political party called the "Know-Nothings." The crowd poured into the hall to its full capacity, jammed the entrance ways, and gathered for blocks in the street. There all waited patiently to see what would happen.

Meantime, in the small room back of the stage, about a score of men gathered. Chief among all stood William T. Coleman. He had taken a prominent part in the old Committee of '51. With him were Clancey Dempster, small and mild of manner, blue-eyed, the last man in the room one would have picked for great stamina and courage, yet playing one of the leading roles in this crisis; the merchant Truett, towering above all the rest; Farwell, direct, uncompromising, inspired with tremendous single-minded earnestness; James Dows, of the rough and ready, humorous, blasphemous, horse-sense type; Hossefross, of the Committee of '51; Dr. Beverly Cole, high-spirited, distinguished-looking, and courtly; Isaac Bluxome, whose signature of "33 Secretary" was to become terrible, and who also had served well in 1851. These and many more of their type were considering the question dispassionately and earnestly.

"It is a serious business," said Coleman, summing up. "It is no child's play. It may prove very serious. We may get through quickly and safely, or we may so involve ourselves as never to get through."

"The issue is not one of choice but of expediency," replied Dempster. "Shall we have vigilance with order or a mob with anarchy?"

In this spirit Coleman addressed the crowd waiting in the large hall.

"In view of the miscarriage of justice in the courts," he announced briefly, "it has been thought expedient to revive the Vigilance Committee. An Executive Council should be chosen, representative of the whole body. I have been asked to take charge. I will do so, but must stipulate that I am to be free to choose the first council myself. Is that agreed?"

He received a roar of assent.

"Very well, gentlemen, I shall request you to vacate the hall. In a short time the books will be open for enrollment."

With almost disciplined docility the crowd arose and filed out, joining the other crowd waiting patiently in the street.

After a remarkably short period the doors were again thrown open. Inside the passage stood twelve men later to be known as the Executive Committee. These held back the rush, admitting but one man at a time. The crowd immediately caught the idea and helped. There was absolutely no excitement. Every man seemed grimly in earnest. Cries of "Order, order, line up!" came all down the street. A rough queue was formed. There were no jokes or laughing; there was even no talk. Each waited his turn. At the entrance every applicant was closely scrutinized and interrogated. Several men were turned back peremptorily in the first few minutes, with the warning not to dare make another attempt. Passed by this Committee, the candidate climbed the stairs. In the second story behind a table sat Coleman, Dempster, and one other. These administered to him an oath of secrecy and then passed him into another room where sat Bluxome behind a ledger. Here his name was written and he was assigned a number by which henceforth in the activities of the Committee he was to be known. Members were instructed always to use numbers and never names in referring to other members.

Those who had been enrolled waited for some time, but finding that with evening the applicants were still coming in a long procession, they gradually dispersed. No man, however, departed far from the vicinity. Short absences and hastily snatched meals were followed by hurried returns, lest something be missed. From time to time rumors were put in circulation as to the activities of the Executive Committee, which had been in continuous session since its appointment. An Examining Committee had been appointed to scrutinize the applicants. The number of the Executive Committee had been raised to twenty-six; a Chief of Police had been chosen, and he in turn appointed messengers and policemen, who set out in search of individuals wanted as door-keepers, guards, and so forth. Only registered members were allowed on the floor of the hall. Even the newspaper reporters were gently but firmly ejected. There was no excitement or impatience.

At length, at eight o'clock, Coleman came out of one of the side-rooms and, mounting a table, called for order. He explained that a military organization had been decided upon, advised that numbers 1 to 100 inclusive should assemble in one corner of the room, the second hundred at the first window, and so on. An interesting order was his last. "Let the French assemble in the middle of the hall," he said in their language—an order significant of the great numbers of French who had first answered the call of gold in '49, and who now with equal enthusiasm answered the call for essential justice. Each company was advised to elect its own officers, subject to ratification by the Executive Committee. It was further stated that arrangements had been made to hire muskets to the number of several thousands from one George Law. These were only flintlocks, but efficient enough in their way, and supplied with bayonets. They were discarded government weapons, brought out some time ago by Law to arm some mysterious filibustering expedition that had fallen through. In this manner, without confusion, an organization of two thousand men was formed—sixteen military companies.

By Saturday morning, May 17, the Committee rooms were overwhelmed by crowds of citizens who desired to be enrolled. Larger quarters had already been secured in a building on the south side of Sacramento Street. Thither the Committee now removed *en masse*, without interrupting their labors. These new headquarters soon became famous in the history of this eventful year.

In the meantime the representatives of the law had not been less alert. The regular police force was largely increased. The sheriff issued thousands of summonses calling upon citizens for service as deputies. These summonses were made out in due form of law. To refuse them meant to put oneself outside the law. The ordinary citizen was somewhat puzzled by the situation. A great many responded to the appeal from force of habit. Once they accepted the oath these new deputies were confronted by the choice between perjury, and its consequences, or doing service. On the other hand, the issue of the summonses forced many otherwise neutral men into the ranks of the Vigilantes. If they refused to act when directly summoned by law, that very fact placed them on the wrong side of the law. Therefore they felt that joining a party pledged to what practically amounted to civil war was only a short step further. Against these the various military companies were mustered, reminded of their oath, called upon to fulfill their sworn duty, and sent to various strategic points about the jail and elsewhere. The Governor was informally notified of a state of insurrection and was requested to send in the state militia. By evening all the forces of organized society were under arms, and the result was a formidable, apparently impregnable force.

Nor was the widespread indignation against the shooting of James King of William entirely unalloyed by bitterness. King had been a hard hitter, an honest man, a true crusader; but in the heat of battle he had not always had time to make distinctions. Thus he had quite justly attacked the *Times* and other venal newspapers, but in so doing had, by too general statements, drawn the fire of every other journal in town. He had attacked with entire reason a certain Catholic priest, a man the Church itself would probably soon have disciplined, but in so doing had managed to enrage all Roman Catholics. In like manner his scorn of the so-called "chivalry" was certainly well justified, but his manner of expression offended even the best Southerners. Most of us see no farther than the immediate logic of the situation. Those perfectly worthy citizens were inclined to view the Vigilantes, not as a protest against intolerable conditions, but rather as personal champions of King.

In thus relying on the strength of their position the upholders of law realized that there might be fighting, and even severe fighting, but it must be remembered that the Law and Order party loved fighting. It was part of their education and of their pleasure and code. No wonder that they viewed with equanimity and perhaps with joy the beginning of the Vigilance movement of 1856.

The leaders of the Law and Order party chose as their military commander William Tecumseh Sherman, whose professional ability and integrity in later life are unquestioned, but whose military genius was equaled only by his extreme inability to remember facts. When writing his *Memoirs*, the General evidently forgot that original documents existed or that statements concerning historical events can often be checked up. A mere mob is irresponsible and anonymous. But it was not a mob with whom Sherman was faced, for, as a final satisfaction to the legal-minded, the men of the Vigilance Committee had put down their names on record as responsible for this movement, and it is upon contemporary record that the story of these eventful days must rely for its details.

## CHAPTER XIV

## *THE STORM BREAKS*

The Governor of the State at this time was J. Neely Johnson, a politician whose merits and demerits were both so slight that he would long since have been forgotten were it not for the fact that he occupied office during this excitement. His whole life heretofore had been one of trimming. He had made his way by this method, and he gained the Governor's chair by yielding to the opinion of others. He took his color and his temporary belief from those with whom he happened to be. His judgment often stuck at trifles, and his opinions were quickly heated but as quickly cooled. The added fact that his private morals were not above criticism gave men an added hold over him.

On receipt of the request for the state militia by the law party, but not by the proper authorities. Governor Johnson hurried down from Sacramento to San Francisco. Immediately on arriving in the city he sent word to Coleman requesting an interview. Coleman at once visited him at his hotel. Johnson apparently made every effort to appear amiable and conciliatory. In answer to all questions Coleman replied:

"We want peace, and if possible without a struggle."

"It is all very well," said Johnson, "to talk about peace with an army of insurrection newly raised. But what is it you actually wish to accomplish?"

"The law is crippled," replied Coleman. "We want merely to accomplish what the crippled law should do but cannot. This done, we will gladly retire. Now you have been asked by the mayor and certain others to bring out the militia and crush this movement. I assure you it cannot be done, and, if you attempt it, it will cause you and us great trouble. Do as Governor McDougal did in '51. See in this movement what he saw in that—a local movement for a local reform in which the State is not concerned. We are not a mob. We demand no overthrow of institutions. We ask not a single court to adjourn. We ask not a single officer to vacate his position. We demand only the enforcement of the law which we have made."

This expression of intention, with a little elaboration and argument, fired Johnson to enthusiasm. He gave his full support, unofficially of course, to the movement.

"But," he concluded, "hasten the undertaking as much as you can. The opposition is stronger than you suppose. The pressure on me is going to be terrible. What about the prisoners in the jail?"

Coleman evaded this last question by saying that the matter was in the hands of the Committee, and he then left the Governor.

Coleman at once returned to headquarters where the Executive Committee was in session, getting rid of its routine business. After a dozen matters were settled, it was moved "that the Committee as a body shall visit the county jail at such time as the Executive Committee might direct, and take thence James P. Casey and Charles Cora, give them a fair trial, and administer such punishment as justice shall demand."

This, of course, was the real business for which all this organization had been planned. A moment's pause succeeded the proposal, but an instantaneous and unanimous assent followed the demand for a vote. At this precise instant a messenger opened the door and informed them that Governor Johnson was in the building requesting speech with Coleman.

Coleman found Johnson, accompanied by Sherman and a few others, lounging in the anteroom. The Governor sprawled in a chair, his hat pulled over his eyes, a cigar in the corner of his mouth. His companions arose and bowed gravely as Coleman entered the room, but the Governor remained seated and nodded curtly with an air of bravado. Without waiting for even the ordinary courtesies he burst out.

"We have come to ask what you intend to do," he demanded.

Coleman, thoroughly surprised, with the full belief that the subject had all been settled in the previous interview, replied curtly.

"I agree with you as to the grievances," rejoined the Governor, "but the courts are the proper remedy. The judges are good men, and there is no necessity for the people to turn themselves into a mob."

"Sir!" cried Coleman. "This is no mob!—You know this is no mob!"

The Governor went on to explain that it might become necessary to bring out all the force at his command. Coleman, though considerably taken aback, recovered himself and listened without comment. He realized that Sherman and the other men were present as witnesses.

"I will report your remark to my associates," he contented himself with saying. The question of witnesses, however, bothered Coleman. He darted in to the committee room and shortly returned with witnesses of his own.

"Let us now understand each other clearly," he resumed. "As I understand your proposal, it is that, if we make no move, you guarantee no escape, an immediate trial, and instant execution?"

Johnson agreed to this.

"We doubt your ability to do this," went on Coleman, "but we are ready to meet you half-way. This is what we will promise: we will take no steps without first giving you notice. But in return we insist that ten men of our own selection shall be added to the sheriff's force within the jail."

Johnson, who was greatly relieved and delighted, at once agreed to this proposal, and soon withdrew. But the blunder he had made was evident enough. With Coleman, who was completely outside the law, he, as an executive of the law, had no business treating or making agreements at all. Furthermore, as executive of the State, he had no legal right to interfere with city affairs unless he were formally summoned by the authorities. Up to now he had merely been notified by private citizens. And to cap the whole sheaf of blunders, he had now in this private interview treated with rebels, and to their advantage. For, as Coleman probably knew, the last agreement was all for the benefit of the Committee. They gained the right to place a personal guard over the prisoners. They gave in return practically only a promise to withdraw that guard before attacking the jail—a procedure which was eminently practical if they cared anything for the safety of the guard.

Johnson was thoroughly pleased with himself until he reached the hotel where the leaders of the opposition were awaiting him. Their keen legal minds saw at once the position in which he had placed himself. After a hasty discussion, it was decided to claim that the Committee had waived all right of action, and that they had promised definitely to leave the case to the courts. When this statement had been industriously circulated and Coleman had heard of it, he is said to have exclaimed:

"The time has come. After that, it is either ourselves or a mob."

He proceeded at once to the Vigilance headquarters and summoned Olney, the appointed guardian of the jail. Him he commanded to get together sixty of the best men possible. A call was sent out for the companies to assemble. They soon began to gather, coming some in rank as they had gathered in their headquarters outside, others singly and in groups. Doorkeepers prevented all exit: once a man was in, he was not permitted to go out. Each leader received explicit directions as to what was to be done. He was instructed as to precisely when he and his command were to start; from what given point; along exactly what route to proceed; and at just what time to arrive at a given point—not a moment sooner or later. The plan for concerted action was very carefully and skillfully worked out. Olney's sixty men were instructed to lay aside their muskets and, armed only with pistols, to make their way by different routes to the jail.

Sunday morning dawned fair and calm. But as the day wore on, an air of unrest pervaded the city. Rumors of impending action were already abroad. The jail itself hummed like a hive. Men came and went, busily running errands, and darting about through the open door. Armed men were taking their places on the flat roof. Meantime the populace gathered slowly. At first there were only a score or so idling around the square; but little by little they increased in numbers. Black forms began to appear on the rooftops all about; white faces showed at the windows; soon the center of the square had filled; the converging streets became black with closely packed people. The windows and doors and balconies, the copings and railings, the slopes of the hills round about were all occupied. In less than an hour twenty thousand people had gathered. They took their positions quietly and waited patiently. It was evident that they had assembled in the rôle of spectators only, and that action had been left to more competent and better organized men. There was no shouting, no demonstration, and so little talking that it amounted only to a low murmur. Already the doors of the jail had been closed. The armed forces on the roof had been increased.

After a time the congested crowd down one of the side-streets was agitated by the approach of a body of armed men. At the same instant a similar group began to appear at the end of another and converging street. The columns came steadily forward, as the people gave way. The men wore no uniforms, and the glittering steel of their bayonets furnished the only military touch. The two columns reached the convergence of the street at the same time and as they entered the square before the jail a third and a fourth column debouched from other directions, while still others deployed into view on the hills behind. They all took their places in rank around the square.

Among the well-known characters of the times was a certain Colonel Gift. Mr. Hubert H. Bancroft, the chronicler of these events, describes him as "a tall, lank, empty-boweled, tobacco-spurting Southerner, with eyes like burning black balls, who could talk a company of listeners into an insane asylum quicker than any man in California, and whose blasphemy could not be equaled, either in quantity or quality, by the most profane of any age or nation." He remarked to a friend nearby, as he watched the spectacle below: "When you see these damned psalm-singing Yankees turn out of their churches, shoulder their guns, and march away of a Sunday, you may know that hell is going to crack shortly."

For some time the armed men stood rigid, four deep all around the square. Behind them the masses of the people watched. Then at a command the ranks fell apart and from the side-streets marched the sixty men chosen by Olney, dragging a field gun at the end of a rope. This they wheeled into position in the square and pointed it at the door of the jail. Quite deliberately, the cannon was loaded with powder and balls. A man lit a slow match, blew it to a glow, and took his position at the breech. Nothing then happened for a full ten minutes. The six men stood rigid by the gun in the middle of the square. The sunlight gleamed from the ranks of bayonets. The vast multitude held its breath. The wall of the jail remained blank and inscrutable.

Then a man on horseback was seen to make his way through the crowd. This was Charles Doane, Grand Marshal of the Vigilantes. He rode directly to the jail door, on which he rapped with the handle of his riding-whip. After a moment the wicket in the door opened. Without dismounting, the rider handed a note within, and then, backing his horse the length of the square, came to rest.

Again the ranks parted and closed, this time to admit of three carriages. As they came to a stop, the muskets all around the square leaped to "present arms!" From the carriages descended Coleman, Truett, and several others. In dead silence they walked to the jail door, Olney's men close at their heels. For some moments they spoke through the wicket; then the door swung open and the Committee entered.

Up to this moment Casey had been fully content with the situation. He was, of course, treated to the best the jail or the city could afford. It was a bother to have been forced to shoot James King of William; but the nuisance of incarceration for a time was a small price to pay. His friends had rallied well to his defense. He had no doubt whatever, that, according to the usual custom, he would soon work his way through the courts and stand again a free man. His first intimation of trouble was the hearing of the resonant tramp of feet outside. His second was when Sheriff Scannell stood before him with the Vigilantes' note in his hand. Casey took one glance at Scannell's face.

"You aren't going to betray me?" he cried. "You aren't going to give me up?"

"James," replied Scannell solemnly, "there are three thousand armed men coming for you and I have not thirty supporters around the jail."

"Not thirty!" cried Casey astonished. For a moment he appeared crushed; then he leaped to his feet flourishing a long knife. "I'll not be taken from this place alive!" he cried. "Where are all you brave fellows who were going to see me through this?"

At this moment Coleman knocked at the door of the jail. The sheriff hurried away to answer the summons.

Casey took the opportunity to write a note for the Vigilantes which he gave to the marshal. It read:

"*To the Vigilante Committee.* GENTLEMEN:—I am willing to go before you if you will let me speak but ten minutes. I do not wish to have the blood of any man upon my head."

On entering the jail door Coleman and his companions bowed formally to the sheriff.

"We have come for the prisoner Casey," said Coleman. "We ask that he be peaceably delivered us handcuffed at the door immediately."

"Under existing circumstances," replied Scannell, "I shall make no resistance. The prison and its contents are yours."

But Truett would have none of this. "We want only the man Casey at present," he said. "For the safety of all the rest we hold you strictly accountable."

They proceeded at once to Casey's cell. The murderer heard them coming and sprang back from the door holding his long knife poised. Coleman walked directly to the door, where he stopped, looking Casey in the eye. At the end of a full minute he exclaimed sharply:

"Lay down that knife!"

As though the unexpected tones had broken a spell, Casey flung the knife from him and buried his face in his hands. Then, and not until then, Coleman informed him curtly that his request would be granted.

They took Casey out through the door of the jail. The crowd gathered its breath for a frantic cheer. The relief from tension must have been great, but Coleman, bareheaded, raised his hand and, in instant obedience to the gesture, the cheer was stifled. The leaders then entered the carriage, which immediately turned and drove away.

Thus Casey was safely in custody. Charles Cora, who, it will be remembered, had killed Marshal Richardson and who had gained from the jury a disagreement, was taken on a second trip.

The street outside headquarters soon filled with an orderly crowd awaiting events. There was noticeable the same absence of excitement, impatience, or tumult so characteristic of the popular gatherings of that time, except perhaps when the meetings were conducted by the partisans of Law and Order. After a long interval one of the Committee members appeared at an upper window.

"It is not the intention of the Committee to be hasty," he announced. "Nothing will be done today."

This statement was received in silence. At last someone asked:

"Where are Casey and Cora?"

"The Committee hold possession of the jail. All are safe," said the Committee man.

With this simple statement the crowd was completely satisfied, and dispersed quietly and at once.

Of the three thousand enrolled men, three hundred were retained under arms at headquarters, a hundred surrounded the jail, and all the rest were dismissed. Next day, Monday, headquarters still remained inscrutable; but large patrols walked about the city, collecting arms. The gunshops were picketed and their owners were warned under no circumstances to sell weapons. Towards evening the weather grew colder and rain came on. Even this did not discourage the crowd, which stood about in its sodden clothes waiting. At midnight it reluctantly dispersed, but by daylight the following morning the streets around headquarters were blocked. Still it rained, and still apparently nothing happened. All over the city business was at a standstill. Men had dropped their affairs, even the most pressing, either to take part in this movement or to lend the moral support of their presence and their interest. The partisans of Law and Order, so called, were also abroad. No man dared express himself in mixed company openly. The courts were empty. Some actually closed down, with one excuse or another; but most of them pretended to go through the forms of business. Many judges took the occasion to leave town—on vacation, they announced. These incidents occasioned lively comment. As our chronicler before quoted tells us: "A good many who had things on their minds left for the country." Still it rained steadily, and still the crowds waited.

The prisoners, Casey and Cora, had expected, when taken from the jail, to be lynched at once. But, since the execution had been thus long postponed, they began to take heart. They understood that they were to have a clear trial "according to law"—a phrase which was in those days immensely cheering to malefactors. They were not entirely cut off from outside communication. Casey was allowed to see several men on pressing business, and permitted to talk to them freely, although before a witness from the Committee. Cora received visits from Belle Cora, who in the past had spent thousands on his legal defense. Now she came to see him faithfully and reported every effort that was being made.

On Tuesday, the 20th, Cora was brought before the Committee. He asked for counsel, and Truett was appointed to act for him. A list of witnesses demanded by Cora was at once summoned, and a sub-committee was sent to bring them before the board of trial. All the ordinary forms of law were closely followed, and all the essential facts were separately brought out. It was the same old Cora trial over again with one modification; namely, that all technicalities and technical delays were eliminated. Not an attempt was made to confine the investigation to the technical trial. By dusk the case for the prosecution was finished, and that for the defense was supposed to begin.

During all this long interim the Executive Committee had sat in continuous session. They had agreed that no recess of more than thirty minutes should be taken until a decision had been reached. But of all the long list of witnesses submitted by Cora for the defense not one could be found. They were in hiding and afraid. The former perjurers would not appear.

It was now falling dusk. The corners of the great room were in darkness. Beneath the elevated desk, behind which sat Coleman, Bluxome, the secretary, lighted a single oil lamp, the better to see his notes. In the interest of the proceedings a general illumination had not been ordered. Within the shadow, the door opened and Charles Doane, the Grand Marshal of the Vigilantes, advanced three steps into the room.

"Mr. President," he said clearly, "I am instructed to announce that
James King of William is dead."

The conviction of both men took place that night, and the execution was ordered, but in secret.

Thursday noon had been set for the funeral of James King of William. This ceremony was to take place in the Unitarian church. A great multitude had gathered to attend. The church was filled to overflowing early in the day. But thousands of people thronged the streets round about, and stood patiently and seriously to do the man honor. Historians of the time detail the names of many marching bodies from every guild and society in the new city. Hundreds of horsemen, carriages, and foot marchers got themselves quietly into the line. They also were excluded from the funeral ceremonies by lack of room, but wished to do honor to the cortège. This procession is said to have been over two miles in length. Each man wore a band of crêpe around his left arm. All the city seemed to be gathered there. And yet the time for the actual funeral ceremony was still some hours distant.

Nevertheless the few who, hurrying to the scene, had occasion to pass near the Vigilante headquarters, found the silent square guarded on all sides by a triple line of armed men. The side-streets also were filled with them. They stood in the exact alignment their constant drill had made possible, with bayonets fixed, staring straight ahead. Three thousand were under arms. Like the vast crowd a few squares away, they, too, stood silent and patiently waiting.

At a quarter before one the upper windows of the headquarters building were thrown open and small planked platforms were thrust from two of them. Heavy beams were shoved out from the flat roof directly over the platforms. From the ends of the beams dangled nooses of rope. After this another wait ensued. Across the silence of the intervening buildings could be heard faintly from the open windows of the church the sound of an organ, and then the measured cadences of an oration. The funeral services had begun. As though this were a signal, the blinds that had closed the window openings were thrown back and Cora was conducted to the end of one of the little platforms. His face was covered with a white handkerchief and he was bound. A moment later Casey appeared. He had asked not to be blindfolded. Cora stood bolt upright, motionless as a stone, but Casey's courage broke. If he had any hope that the boastful promises of his friends would be fulfilled by a rescue, that hope died as he looked down on the set, grim faces, on the sinister ring of steel. His nerve then deserted him completely and he began to babble.

"Gentlemen," he cried at them, "I am not a murderer! I do not feel afraid to meet my God on a charge of murder! I have done nothing but what I thought was right! Whenever I was injured I have resented it! It has been part of my education during twenty-nine years! Gentlemen, I forgive you this persecution! O God! My poor Mother! O God!"

It is to be noted that he said not one word of contrition nor of regret for the man whose funeral services were then going on, nor for the heartbroken wife who knelt at that coffin. His words found no echo against that grim wall of steel. Again ensued a wait, apparently inexplicable. Across the intervening housetops the sound of the oration ceased. At the door of the church a slight commotion was visible. The coffin was being carried out. It was placed in the hearse. Every head was bared. There followed a slight pause; then from overhead the church-bell boomed out once. Another bell in the next block answered; a third, more distant, chimed in. From all parts of the city tolled the requiem.

At the first stroke of the bell the funeral cortège moved forward toward Lone Mountain cemetery. At the first stroke the Vigilantes as one man presented arms. The platforms dropped, and Casey and Cora fell into eternity.

CHAPTER XV

*THE VIGILANTES OF '56*

This execution naturally occasioned a great storm of indignation among the erstwhile powerful adherents of the law. The ruling, aristocratic class, the so-called chivalry, the best element of the city, had been slapped deliberately in the face, and this by a lot of Yankee shopkeepers. The Committee were stigmatized as stranglers. They ought to be punished as murderers! They should be shot down as revolutionists! It was realized, however, that the former customary street-shooting had temporarily become unsafe. Otherwise there is no doubt that brawls would have been more frequent than they were.

An undercurrent of confidence was apparent, however. The Law and Order men had been surprised and overpowered. They had yielded only to overwhelming odds. With the execution of Cora and Casey accomplished, the Committee might be expected to disband. And when the Committee disbanded, the law would have its innings. Its forces would then be better organized and consolidated, its power assured. It could then safely apprehend and bring to justice the ringleaders of this undertaking. Many of the hotheads were in favor of using armed force to take Coleman and his fellow-conspirators into custody. But calmer spirits advised moderation for the present, until the time was more ripe.

But to the surprise and indignation of these people, the Vigilantes showed no intention of disbanding. Their activities extended and their organization strengthened. The various military companies drilled daily until they went through the manual with all the precision of regular troops. The Committee's book remained opened, and by the end of the week over seven thousand men had signed the roll. Loads of furniture and various supplies stopped at the doors of headquarters and were carried in by members of the organization. No non-member ever saw the inside of the building while it was occupied by the Committee of Vigilance. So cooking utensils, cot-beds, provisions, blankets, bulletin-boards, arms, chairs and tables, field-guns, ammunition, and many other supplies seemed to indicate a permanent occupation. Doorkeepers were always in attendance, and sentinels patrolled in the streets and on the roof. Every day the Executive Committee was in session for all of the daylight hours. A blacklist was in preparation. Orders were issued for the Vigilante police to arrest certain men and to warn certain others to leave town immediately. A choice haul was made of the lesser lights of the ward-heelers and chief politicians. A very good sample was the notorious Yankee Sullivan, an ex-prize-fighter, ward-heeler, ballot-box stuffer, and shoulder-striker. He, it will be remembered, was the man who returned Casey as supervisor in a district where, as far as is known, Casey was not a candidate and no one could be found who had voted for him. This individual went to pieces completely shortly after his arrest. He not only confessed the details of many of his own crimes but, what was more important, disclosed valuable information as to others. His testimony was important, not necessarily as final proof against those whom he accused, but as indication of the need of thorough investigation. Then without warning he committed suicide in his cell. On investigation it turned out that he had been accustomed to from sixty to eighty drinks of whiskey each day, and the sudden and complete deprivation had unhinged his mind. Warned by this unforeseen circumstance, the Committee henceforth issued regular rations of whiskey to all its prisoners, a fact which is a striking commentary on the character of the latter. It is to be noted, furthermore, that liquor of all sorts was debarred from the deliberations of the Vigilantes themselves.

Trials went briskly forward in due order, with counsel for defense and ample opportunity to call witnesses. There were no more capital punishments. It was made known that the Committee had set for itself a rule that capital punishment would be inflicted by it only for crimes so punishable by the regular law. But each outgoing ship took a crowd of the banished. The majority of the first sweepings were low thugs—"Sydney Ducks," hangers-on, and the worst class of criminals; but a certain number were taken from what had been known as the city's best. In the law courts these men would have been declared as white as the driven snow; in fact, that had actually happened to some of them. But they were plainly undesirable citizens. The Committee so decided and bade them depart. Among the names of men who were prominent and influential in the early history of the city, but who now were told to leave, were Charles Duane, Woolley Kearny, William McLean, J.D. Musgrave, Peter Wightman, James White, and Edward McGowan. Hundreds of others left the city of their own accord. Terror spread among the inhabitants of the underworld. Some of the minor offenders brought in by the Vigilante police were turned over by the Executive Committee to the regular law courts. It is significant that, whereas convictions had been almost unknown up to this time, every one of these offenders was promptly sentenced by those courts.

But though the underworld was more or less terrified, the upper grades were only the further aroused. Many sincerely believed that this movement was successful only because it was organized, that the people of the city were scattered and powerless, that they needed only to be organized to combat the forces of disorder. In pursuance of the belief that the public at large needed merely to be called together loyally to defend its institutions, a meeting was set for June 2, in Portsmouth Square. Elaborate secret preparations, including the distribution of armed men, were made to prevent interference. Such preparations were useless. Immediately after the appearance of the notice the Committee of Vigilance issued orders that the meeting was to be in no manner discouraged or molested.

It was well attended. Enormous crowds gathered, not only in and around the Square itself, but in balconies and windows and on housetops. It was a very disrespectful crowd, evidently out for a good time. On the platform within the Square stood or sat the owners of many of the city's proud names. Among them were well-known speakers, men who had never failed to hold and influence a crowd. But only a short distance away little could be heard. It early became evident that, though there would be no interference, the sentiment of the crowd was adverse. And what must have been particularly maddening was that the sentiment was good-humored. Colonel Edward Baker came forward to speak. The Colonel was a man of great eloquence, so that in spite of his considerable lack of scruples he had won his way to a picturesque popularity and fame. But the crowd would have little of him this day, and an almost continuous uproar drowned out his efforts. The usual catch phrases, such as "liberty." "Constitution," "habeas corpus," "trial by jury," and "freedom," occasionally became audible, but the people were not interested. "See Cora's defender!" cried someone, voicing the general suspicion that Baker had been one of the little gambler's hidden counsel. "Cora!" "Ed. Baker!" "$10,000!" "Out of that, you old reprobate!" He spoke ten minutes against the storm and then yielded, red-faced and angry. Others tried but in vain. A Southerner, Benham, inveighing passionately against the conditions of the city, in throwing back his coat happened inadvertently to reveal the butt of a Colt revolver. The bystanders immediately caught the point. "There's a pretty Law and Order man!" they shouted. "Say, Benham, don't you know it's against the law to go armed?"

"I carry this weapon," he cried, shaking his fist, "not as an instrument to overthrow the law, but to uphold it."

Someone from a balcony nearby interrupted: "In other words, sir, you break the law in order to uphold the law. What more are the Vigilantes doing?"

The crowd went wild over this response. The confusion became worse. Upholders of Law and Order thrust forward Judge Campbell in the hope that his age and authority on the bench would command respect. He was unable, however, to utter even two consecutive sentences.

"I once thought," he interrupted himself piteously, "that I was the free citizen of a free country. But recent occurrences have convinced me that I am a slave, more a slave than any on a Southern plantation, for they know their masters, but I know not mine!"

But his auditors refused to be affected by pathos.

"Oh, yes you do," they informed him. "You know your masters as well as anybody. Two of them were hanged the other day!"

Though this attempt at home to gain coherence failed, the partisans at Sacramento had better luck. They collected, it was said, five hundred men hailing from all quarters of the globe, but chiefly from the Southeast and Texas. All of them were fire-eaters, reckless, and sure to make trouble. Two pieces of artillery were reported coming down the Sacramento to aid all prisoners, but especially Billy Mulligan. The numbers were not in themselves formidable as opposed to the enrollment of the Vigilance Committee, but it must be remembered that the city was full of scattered warriors and of cowed members of the underworld waiting only leaders and a rallying point. Even were the Vigilantes to win in the long run, the material for a very pretty civil war was ready to hand. Two hundred men were hastily put to filling gunnybags with sand and to fortifying not only headquarters but the streets round about. Cannon were mounted, breastworks were piled, and embrasures were cut. By morning Fort Gunnybags, as headquarters was henceforth called, had come into existence.

The fire-eaters arrived that night, but they were not five hundred strong, as excited rumor had it. They disembarked, greeting the horde of friends who had come to meet them, marched in a body to Fort Gunnybags, looked it over, stuck their hands into their pockets, and walked peacefully away to the nearest bar-rooms. This was the wisest move on their part, for by now the disposition of the Vigilante men was so complete that nothing short of regularly organized troops could successfully have dislodged them.

Behind headquarters was a long shed and stable In which were to be found at all hours saddle horses and artillery horses, saddled and bridled, ready for instant use. Twenty-six pieces of artillery, most of them sent in by captains of vessels in the harbor, were here parked. Other cannon were mounted for the defense of the fort itself. Muskets, rifles, and sabers had been accumulated. A portable barricade had been constructed in the event of possible street fighting—a sort of wheeled framework that could be transformed into litters or scaling-ladders at will. Mess offices and kitchens were there that could feed a small army. Flags and painted signs carrying the open eye that had been adopted as emblematic of vigilance decorated the main room. A huge alarm bell had been mounted upon the roof. Mattresses, beds, cots, and other furniture necessary to accommodate whole companies on the premises themselves, had been provided. A completely equipped armorers' shop and a hospital with all supplies occupied the third story. The forces were divided into four companies of artillery, one squadron and two troops of cavalry, four regiments and thirty-two companies of infantry, besides the small but very efficient police organization. A tap on the bell gathered these men in an incredibly short space of time. Bancroft says that, as a rule, within fifteen minutes of the first stroke seven-tenths of the entire forces would be on hand ready for combat.

The Law and Order people recognized the strength of this organization and realized that they must go at the matter in a more thorough manner. They turned their attention to the politics of the structure, and here they had every reason to hope for success. No matter how well organized the Vigilantes might be or how thoroughly they might carry the sympathies of the general public, there was no doubt that they were acting in defiance of constituted law, and therefore were nothing less than rebels. It was not only within the power, but it was also a duty, of the Governor to declare the city in a condition of insurrection. When he had done this, the state troops must put down the insurrection; and, if they failed, then the Federal Government itself should be called on. Looked at in this way, the small handful of disturbers, no matter how well armed and disciplined, amounted to very little.

Naturally the Governor had first to be won over. Accordingly all the important men of San Francisco took the steamer *Senator* for Sacramento where they met Judge Terry, of the Supreme Court of California, Volney Howard, and others of the same ilk. No governor of Johnson's nature could long withstand such pressure. He promised to issue the required proclamation of insurrection as soon as it could be "legally proved" that the Vigilance Committee had acted outside the law. The small fact that it had already hanged two and deported a great many others, to say nothing of taking physical possession of the city, meant little to these legal minds.

In order that all things should be technically correct, then, Judge Terry issued a writ of habeas corpus for William Mulligan and gave it into the hands of Deputy Sheriff Harrison for service on the Committee. It was expected that the Committee would deny the writ, which would constitute legal defiance of the State. The Governor would then be justified in issuing the proclamation. If the state troops proved unwilling or inadequate, as might very well be, the plan was then to call on the United States. The local representatives of the central government were at that time General Wool commanding the military department of California, and Captain David Farragut in command of the navy-yard. Within their command was a force sufficient to subdue three times the strength of the Vigilance Committee. William Tecumseh Sherman, then in private life, had been appointed major-general of a division of the state militia. As all this was strictly legal, the plan could not possibly fail.

Harrison took the writ of habeas corpus and proceeded to San Francisco. He presented himself at headquarters and offered his writ. Instead of denying it, the Committee welcomed him cordially and invited him to make a thorough search of the premises. Of course Harrison found nothing—the Committee had seen to that—and departed. The scheme had failed. The Committee had in no way denied his authority or his writ. But Harrison saw clearly what had been expected of him. To Judge Terry he unblushingly returned the writ endorsed "prevented from service by armed men." For the sake of his cause, Harrison had lied. However, the whole affair was now regarded as legal.

Johnson promptly issued his proclamation. The leaders, in high feather, as promptly turned to the federal authorities for the assistance they needed. As yet they did not ask for troops but only for weapons with which to arm their own men. To their blank dismay General Wool refused to furnish arms. He took the position that he had no right to do so without orders from Washington. There is no doubt, however, that this technical position cloaked the doughty warrior's real sympathies. Colonel Baker and Volney Howard were instructed to wait on him. After a somewhat lengthy conversation, they made the mistake of threatening him with a report to Washington for refusing to uphold the law.

"I think, gentlemen," flashed back the veteran indignantly, "I know my duty and in its performance dread no responsibility!" He promptly bowed them out.

In the meantime the Executive Committee had been patiently working down through its blacklist. It finally announced that after June 24 it would consider no fresh cases, and a few days later it proclaimed an adjournment parade on July 4. It considered its work completed and the city safe.

It may be readily imagined that this peaceful outcome did not in the least suit the more aristocratic members of the Law and Order party. They were a haughty, individualistic, bold, forceful, sometimes charming band of fire-eaters. In their opinion they had been deeply insulted. They wanted reprisal and punishment.

When therefore the Committee set a definite day for disbanding, the local authorities and upholders of law were distinctly disappointed. They saw slipping away the last chance for a clash of arms that would put these rebels in their places. There was some thought of arresting the ringleaders, but the courts were by now so well terrorized that it was by no means certain that justice as defined by the Law and Order party could be accomplished. And even if conviction could be secured, the representatives of the law found little satisfaction in ordinary punishment. What they wanted was a fight.

General Sherman had resigned his command of the military forces in disgust. In his stead was chosen General Volney Howard, a man typical of his class, blinded by his prejudices and his passions, filled with a sense of the importance of his caste, and without grasp of the broader aspects of the situation. In the Committee's present attitude he saw not the signs of a job well done, but indications of weakening, and he considered this a propitious moment to show his power. In this attitude he received enthusiastic backing from Judge Terry and his narrow coterie. Terry was then judge of the Supreme Court; and a man more unfitted for the position it would be difficult to find. A tall, attractive, fire-eating Texan with a charming wife, he stood high in the social life of the city. His temper was undisciplined and completely governed his judgment. Intensely partisan and, as usual with his class, touchy on the point of honor, he did precisely the wrong thing on every occasion where cool decision was demanded.

It was so now. The Law and Order party persuaded Governor Johnson to order a parade of state troops in the streets of San Francisco. The argument used was that such a parade of legally organized forces would overawe the citizens. The secret hope, however, which was well founded, was that such a display would promote the desired conflict. This hope they shared with Howard, after the Governor's orders had been obtained. Howard's vanity jumped with his inclination. He consented to the plot. A more ill-timed, idiotic maneuver, with the existing state of the public mind, it would be impossible to imagine. Either we must consider Terry and Howard weak-minded to the point of an inability to reason from cause to effect, or we must ascribe to them more sinister motives.

By now the Law and Order forces had become numerically more formidable. The lower element flocked to the colors through sheer fright. A certain proportion of the organized remained in the ranks, though a majority had resigned. There was, as is usual in a new community, a very large contingent of wild, reckless young men without a care in the world, with no possible interest in the rights and wrongs of the case, or, indeed, in themselves. They were eager only for adventure and offered themselves just as soon as the prospects for a real fight seemed good. Then, too, they could always count on the five hundred Texans who had been imported.

There were plenty of weapons with which to arm these partisans. Contrary to all expectations, the Vigilance Committee had scrupulously refrained from interfering with the state armories. All the muskets belonging to the militia were in the armories and were available in different parts of the city. In addition, the State, as a commonwealth, had a right to a certain number of federal weapons stored in arsenals at Benicia. These could be requisitioned in due form.

But at this point, it has been said, the legal minds of the party conceived a bright plan. The muskets at Benicia on being requisitioned would have to cross the bay in a vessel of some sort Until the muskets were actually delivered they were federal property. Now if the Vigilance Committee were to confiscate the arms while on the transporting vessel, and while still federal property, the act would be piracy; the interceptors, pirates. The Law and Order people could legally call on the federal forces, which would be compelled to respond. If the Committee of Vigilance did not fall into this trap, then the Law and Order people would have the muskets anyway.

: Mr. H.H. Bancroft, in his *Popular Tribunals*, holds that no proof of this plot exists.

To carry out this plot they called in a saturnine, lank, drunken individual whose name was Hube Maloney. Maloney picked out two men of his own type as assistants. He stipulated only that plenty of "refreshments" should be supplied. According to instructions Maloney was to operate boldly and flagrantly in full daylight. But the refreshment idea had been rather liberally interpreted. By six o'clock Rube had just sense enough left to anchor off Pueblo Point. There all gave serious attention to the rest of the refreshments, and finally rolled over to sleep off the effects.

In the meantime news of the intended shipment had reached the headquarters of the Vigilantes.

The Executive Committee went into immediate session. It was evident that the proposed disbanding would have to be postponed. A discussion followed as to methods of procedure to meet this new crisis. The Committee fell into the trap prepared for it. Probably no one realized the legal status of the muskets, but supposed them to belong already to the State. Marshal Doane was instructed to capture them. He called to him the chief of the harbor police. "Have you a small vessel ready for immediate service?" he asked this man. "Yes, a sloop, at the foot of this street." "Be ready to sail in half an hour."

Doane then called to his assistance a quick-witted man named John Durkee. This man had been a member of the regular city police until the shooting of James King of William. At that time he had resigned his position and joined the Vigilance police. He was loyal by nature, steady in execution, and essentially quick-witted, qualities that stood everybody in very good stead as will be shortly seen. He picked out twelve reliable men to assist him, and set sail in the sloop.

For some hours he beat against the wind and the tide; but finally these became so strong that he was forced to anchor in San Pablo Bay until conditions had modified. Late in the afternoon he was again able to get under way. Several of the tramps sailing about the bay were overhauled and examined, but none proved to be the prize. About dark the breeze died, leaving the little sloop barely under steerageway. A less persistent man than Durkee would have anchored for the night, but Durkee had received his instructions and intended to find the other sloop, and it was he himself who first caught the loom of a shadow under Pueblo Point.

He bore down and perceived it to be the sloop whose discovery he desired. The twelve men boarded with a rush, but found themselves in possession of an empty deck. The fumes of alcohol and the sound of snoring guided the boarding-party to the object of their search and the scene of their easy victory. Durkee transferred the muskets and prisoners to his own craft; and returned to the California Street wharf shortly after daylight. A messenger was dispatched to headquarters. He returned with instructions to deliver the muskets but to turn loose the prisoners. Durkee was somewhat astonished at the latter order but complied.

"All right," he is reported to have said. "Now, you measly hounds, you've got just about twenty-eight seconds to make yourselves as scarce as your virtues."

Maloney and his crew wasted few of the twenty-eight seconds in starting, but once out of sight they regained much of their bravado. A few drinks restored them to normal, and enabled them to put a good face on the report they now made to their employers. Maloney and his friends then visited in turn all the saloons. The drunker they grew, the louder they talked, reviling the Committee collectively and singly, bragging that they would shoot at sight Coleman, Truett, Durkee, and several others whom they named. They flourished weapons publicly, and otherwise became obstreperous. The Committee decided that their influence was bad and instructed Sterling Hopkins, with four others, to arrest the lot and bring them in.

The news of this determination reached the offending parties. They immediately fled to their masters like cur dogs. Their masters, who included Terry, Bowie, and a few others, happened to be discussing the situation in the office of Richard Ashe, a Texan. The crew burst into this gathering very much scared, with a statement that a "thousand stranglers" were at their heels. Hopkins, having left his small posse at the foot of the stairs, knocked and entered the room. He was faced by the muzzles of half a dozen pistols and told to get out of there. Hopkins promptly obeyed.

If Terry had possessed the slightest degree of leadership he would have seen that this was the worst of all moments to precipitate a crisis. The forces of his own party were neither armed nor ready. But here, as in all other important crises of his career, he was governed by the haughty and headstrong passion of the moment.

Hopkins left his men on guard at the foot of the stairs, borrowed a horse from a passer-by, and galloped to headquarters. There he was instructed to return and stay on watch, and was told that reinforcements would soon follow. He arrived before the building in which Ashe's office was located in time to see Maloney, Terry, Ashe, McNabb, Bowie, and Howe, all armed with shot-guns, just turning a far corner. He dismounted and called on his men, who followed. The little posse dogged the judge's party for some distance. For a little time no attention was paid to them. But as they pressed closer, Terry, Ashe, and Maloney turned and presented their shot-guns. This was probably intended only as a threat, but Hopkins, who was always overbold, lunged at Maloney. Terry thrust his gun at a Vigilante who seized it by the barrel. At the same instant Ashe pressed the muzzle of his weapon against the breast of a man named Bovee, but hesitated to pull the trigger. It was not at that time as safe to shoot men in the open street as it had been formerly. Barry covered Rowe with a pistol. Rowe dropped his gun and ran towards the armory. The accidental discharge of a pistol seemed to unnerve Terry. He whipped out a long knife and plunged it into Hopkins's neck. Hopkins relaxed his hold on Terry's shot-gun and staggered back.

"I am stabbed! Take them, Vigilantes!" he said.

He dropped to the sidewalk. Terry and his friends ran towards the armory. Of the Vigilante posse only Bovee and Barry remained, but these two pursued the fleeing Law and Order men to the very doors of the armory itself. When the portals were slammed in their faces they took up their stand outside; and alone these two men held imprisoned several hundred men! During the next few minutes several men attempted entrance to the armory, among them our old friend Volney Howard. All were turned back and were given the impression that the armory was already in charge, of the Vigilantes. After a little, however, doubtless to the great relief of the "outside garrison" of the armory, the great Vigilante bell began to boom out its signals: *one, two, three*—rest; *one, two, three*—rest; and so on.

Instantly the streets were alive with men. Merchants left their customers, clerks their books, mechanics their tools. Draymen stripped their horses of harness, abandoned their wagons, and rode away to join their cavalry. Within an incredibly brief space of time everybody was off for the armory, the military companies marching like veterans, the artillery rumbling over the pavement. The cavalry, jogging along at a slow trot, covered the rear. A huge and roaring mob accompanied them, followed them, raced up the side-streets to arrive at the armory at the same time as the first files of the military force. They found the square before the building entirely deserted except for the dauntless Barry and Bovee, who still marched up and down singlehanded, holding the garrison within. They were able to report that no one had either entered or left the armory.

Inside the building the spirit had become one of stubborn sullenness. Terry was very sorry—as, indeed, he well might be—a Judge of the Supreme Court, who had no business being in San Francisco at all. Sworn to uphold the law, and ostensibly on the side of the Law and Order party, he had stepped out from his jurisdiction to commit as lawless and as idiotic a deed of passion and prejudice as could well have been imagined. Whatever chances the Law and Order party might have had heretofore were thereby dissipated. Their troops were scattered in small units; their rank and file had disappeared no one knew where; their enemies were fully organized and had been mustered by the alarm bell to their usual alertness and capability; and Terry's was the hand that had struck the bell!

He was reported as much chagrined.

"This is very unfortunate, very unfortunate," he said; "but you shall not imperil your lives for me. It is I they want. I will surrender to them."

Instead of the prompt expostulations which he probably expected, a dead silence greeted these words.

"There is nothing else to do," agreed Ashe at last.

An exchange of notes in military fashion followed. Ashe, as commander of the armory and leader of the besieged party, offered to surrender to the Executive Committee of the Vigilantes if protected from violence. The Executive Committee demanded the surrender of Terry, Maloney, and Philips, as well as of all arms and ammunition, promising that Terry and Maloney should be protected against persons outside the organization. On receiving this assurance, Ashe threw open the doors of the armory and the Vigilantes marched in.

"All present were disarmed," writes Bancroft. "Terry and Maloney were taken charge of and the armory was quickly swept of its contents. Three hundred muskets and other munitions of war were carried out and placed on drays. Two carriages then drove up, in one of which was placed Maloney and in the other Terry. Both were attended by a strong escort, Olney forming round them with his Citizens' Guard, increased to a battalion. Then in triumph the Committee men, with their prisoners and plunder enclosed in a solid body of infantry and these again surrounded by cavalry, marched back to their rooms."

Nor was this all. Coleman, like a wise general, realizing that compromise was no longer possible, sent out his men to take possession of all the encampments of the Law and Order forces. The four big armories were cleaned out while smaller squads of men combed the city house by house for concealed arms. By midnight the job was done. The Vigilantes were in control of the situation.

CHAPTER XVI

### *THE TRIUMPH OF THE VIGILANTES*

Judge Terry was still a thorny problem to handle. After all, he was a Judge of the Supreme Court. At first his attitude was one of apparent humility, but as time went on he regained his arrogant attitude and from his cell issued defiances to his captors. He was aided and abetted by his high-spirited wife, and in many ways caused the members of the Committee a great deal of trouble. If Hopkins were to die, they could do no less than hang Terry in common consistency and justice. But they realized fully that in executing a Justice of the Supreme Court they would be wading into pretty deep water. The state and federal authorities were inclined to leave them alone and let them work out the manifestly desirable reform, but it might be that such an act would force official interference. As one member of the Committee expressed it, "They had gone gunning for ferrets and had coralled a grizzly." Nevertheless Terry was indicted before the Committee on the following counts, a statement of which gives probably as good a bird's eye view of Terry as numerous pages of personal description:

Resisting with violence the officers of the Vigilance Committee
while in the discharge of their duties.

Committing an assault with a deadly weapon with intent to kill
Sterling A. Hopkins on June 21, 1856.

Various breaches of the peace and attacks upon citizens while in
the discharge of their duties, specified as follows:

1. Resistance in 1853 to a writ of habeas corpus on account of which one Roach escaped from the custody of the law, and the infant heirs of the Sanchez family were defrauded of their rights.

2. An attack in 1853 on a citizen of Stockton named Evans.

3. An attack in 1853 on a citizen in San Francisco named Purdy.

4. An attack at a charter election on a citizen of Stockton named King.

5. An attack in the court house of Stockton on a citizen named Broadhouse.

Before Terry's case came to trial it was known that Hopkins was not fatally wounded. Terry's confidence immediately rose. Heretofore he had been somewhat, but not much, humbled. Now his haughty spirit blazed forth as strongly as ever. He was tried in due course, and was found guilty on the first charge and on one of the minor charges. On the accusation of assault with intent to kill, the Committee deliberated a few days, and ended by declaring him guilty of simple assault. He was discharged and told to leave the State. But, for some reason or other, the order was not enforced.

Undoubtedly he owed his discharge in this form to the evident fact that the Committee did not know what to do with him. Terry at once took the boat for Sacramento, where for some time he remained in comparative retirement. Later he emerged in his old rôle, and ended his life by being killed at the hands of an armed guard of Justice Stephen Field whom Terry assaulted without giving Field a chance to defend himself.

While these events were going forward, the Committee had convicted and hanged two other men, Hetherington and Brace. In both instances the charge was murder of the most dastardly kind. The trials were conducted with due regard to the forms of law and justice, and the men were executed in an orderly fashion. These executions would not be remarkable in any way, were it not for the fact that they rounded out the complete tale of executions by the Vigilance Committee. Four men only were hanged in all the time the Committee held its sway. Nevertheless the manner of the executions and the spirit that actuated all the officers of the organization sufficed to bring about a complete reformation in the administration of justice.

About this time also the danger began to manifest itself that some of the less conscientious and, indeed, less important members of the Committee might attempt through political means to make capital of their connections. A rule was passed that no member of the Committee of Vigilance should be allowed to hold political office. Shortly after this decision, William Rabe was suspended for "having attempted to introduce politics into this body and for attempting to overawe the Executive Committee."

After the execution of the two men mentioned, the interesting trial of Durkee for piracy, the settlement by purchase of certain private claims against city land, and the deportation of a number of undesirable citizens, the active work of the Committee was practically over. It held complete power and had also gained the confidence of probably nine-tenths of the population. Even some of the erstwhile members of the Law and Order party, who had adhered to the forms of legality through principle, had now either ceased opposition, or had come over openly to the side of the Committee. Another date of adjournment was decided upon. The gunnybag barricades were taken down on the fourteenth of August. On the sixteenth, the rooms of the building were ordered thrown open to all members of the Committee, their friends, their families, for a grand reception on the following week. It was determined then not to disorganize but to adjourn *sine die*. The organization was still to be held, and the members were to keep themselves ready whenever the need should arise. But preparatory to adjournment it was decided to hold a grand military review on the eighteenth of August. This was to leave a final impression upon the public mind of the numbers and powder of the Committee.

The parade fulfilled its function admirably. The Grand Marshal and his staff led, followed by the President and the Military Commanding General with his staff. Then marched four companies of artillery with fifteen mounted cannon. In their rear was a float representing Fort Gunnybags with imitation cannon. Next came the Executive Committee mounted, riding three abreast; then cavalry companies and the medical staff, which consisted of some fifty physicians of the town. Representatives of the Vigilance Committee of 1851 followed in wagons with a banner; then four regiments of infantry, more cavalry, citizen guards, pistol men, Vigilante police. Over six thousand men were that day in line, all disciplined, all devoted, all actuated by the highest motives, and conscious of a job well done.

The public reception at Fort Gunnybags was also well attended. Every one was curious to see the interior arrangement. The principal entrance was from Sacramento Street and there was also a private passage from another street. The doorkeeper's box was prominently to the front where each one entering had to give the pass-word. He then proceeded up the stairs to the floor above. The first floor was the armory and drill-room. Around the sides were displayed the artillery harness, the flags, bulletin-boards, and all the smaller arms. On one side was a lunch stand where coffee and other refreshments were dispensed to those on guard. On the opposite side were offices for every conceivable activity. An immense emblematic eye painted on the southeast corner of the room glared down on each as he entered. The front of the second floor was also a guard-room, armory, and drilling floor. Here also was painted the eye of Vigilance, and here was exhibited the famous ballot-box whose sides could separate the good ballots from the bad ballots. Here also were the meeting-rooms for the Executive Committee and a number of cells for the prisoners. The police-office displayed many handcuffs, tools of captured criminals, relics, clothing with bullet holes, ropes used for hanging, bowie-knives, burglar's tools, brass knuckles, and all the other curiosities peculiar to criminal activities. The third story of the building had become the armorer's shop, and the hospital. Eight or ten workmen were employed in the former and six to twenty cots were maintained in the latter. Above all, on the roof, supported by a strong scaffolding, hung the Monumental bell whose tolling summoned the Vigilantes when need arose.

Altogether the visitors must have been greatly impressed, not only with the strength of the organization, but also with the care used in preparing it for every emergency, the perfection of its discipline, and the completeness of its equipment.

When the Committee of Vigilance of 1856 adjourned subject to further call, there must have been in most men's minds the feeling that such a call could not again arise for years to come.

Yet it was not so much the punishment meted out to evil-doers that measures the success of the Vigilante movement. Only four villains were hanged; not more than thirty were banished. But the effect was the same as though four hundred had been executed. It is significant that not less than eight hundred went into voluntary exile.

"What has become of your Vigilance Committee?" asked a stranger naïvely, some years later.

# African Camp Fires

## PART I

TO THE ISLAND OF WAR.

---

*I.*

THE OPEN DOOR.

There are many interesting hotels scattered about the world, with a few of which I am acquainted and with a great many of which I am not. Of course all hotels are interesting, from one point of view or another. In fact, the surest way to fix an audience's attention is to introduce your hero, or to display your opening chorus in the lobby or along the façade of a hotel. The life, the movement and colour, the drifting individualities, the pretence, the bluff, the self-consciousness, the independence, the *ennui*, the darting or lounging servants, the very fact that of those before your eyes seven out of ten are drawn from distant and scattered places, are sufficient in themselves to invest the smallest hostelry with glamour. It is not of this general interest that I would now speak. Nor is it my intention at present to glance at the hotels wherein "quaintness" is specialized, whether intentionally or no. There are thousands of them; and all of them well worth the discriminating traveller's attention. Concerning some of them—as the old inns at Dives-sur-Mer and at Mont St. Michel—whole books have been written. These depend for their charm on a mingled gift of the unusual and the picturesque. There are, as I have said, thousands of them; and of their cataloguing, should one embark on so wide a sea, there could be no end. And, again, I must for convenience exclude the altogether charming places, like the Tour d'Argent of Paris, Simpson's of the Strand, and a dozen others that will spring to every traveller's memory, where the personality of the host, or of a chef, or even a waiter, is at once a magnet for the attraction of visitors and a reward for their coming. These, too, are many. In the interest to which I would draw attention, the hotel as a building or as an institution has little part. It is indeed a façade, a *mise en scène* before which play the actors that attract our attention and applause. The set may be as modernly elaborate as Peacock Alley of the Waldorf or the templed lobby of the St. Francis; or it may present the severe and Elizabethan simplicity of the stone-paved veranda of the Norfolk at Nairobi—the matter is quite inessential to the spectator. His appreciation is only slightly and indirectly influenced by these things. Sunk in his armchair—of velvet or of canvas—he puffs hard and silently at his cigar, watching and listening as the pageant and the conversation eddy by.

Of such hotels I number that gaudy and polysyllabic hostelry the Grand Hôtel du Louvre et de la Paix at Marseilles. I am indifferent to the facts that it is situated on that fine thoroughfare, the Rue de Cannebière, which the proud and untravelled native devoutly believes to be the finest street in the world; that it possesses a dining-room of gilded and painted *repoussé* work so elaborate and wonderful that it surely must be intended to represent a tinsmith's dream of heaven; that its concierge is the most impressive human being on earth except Ludwig von Kampf (whom I have never seen); that its head waiter is sadder and more elderly and forgiving than any other head waiter; and that its hushed and cathedral atmosphere has been undisturbed through immemorial years. That is to be expected; and elsewhere to be duplicated in greater or lesser degree. Nor in the lofty courtyard, or the equally lofty halls and reading-rooms, is there ever much bustle and movement. People sit quietly, or move with circumspection. Servants glide. The fall of a book or teaspoon, the sudden closing of a door, are events to be remarked. Once a day, however, a huge gong sounds, the glass doors of the inner courtyard are thrown open with a flourish, and enters the huge bus fairly among those peacefully sitting at the tables, horses' hoofs striking fire, long lash-cracking volleys, wheels roaring amid hollow reverberations. From the interior of this bus emerge people; and from the top, by means of a strangely-constructed hooked ladder, are decanted boxes, trunks, and appurtenances of various sorts. In these people, and in these boxes, trunks, and appurtenances, are the real interest of the Grand Hôtel du Louvre et de la Paix of the marvellous Rue Cannebière of Marseilles.

For at Marseilles land ships, many ships, from all the scattered ends of the earth; and from Marseilles depart trains for the North, where is home, or the way home for many peoples. And since the arrival of ships is uncertain, and the departure of trains fixed, it follows that everybody descends for a little or greater period at the Grand Hôtel du Louvre et de la Paix.

They come lean and quiet and a little yellow from hard climates, with the names of strange places on their lips, and they speak familiarly of far-off things. Their clothes are generally of ancient cut, and the wrinkles and camphor aroma of a long packing away are yet discernible. Often they are still wearing sun helmets or double terai hats, pending a descent on a Piccadilly hatter two days hence. They move slowly and languidly; the ordinary piercing and dominant English enunciation has fallen to modulation; their eyes, while observant and alert, look tired. It is as though the far countries have sucked something from the pith of them in exchange for great experiences that nevertheless seem of little value; as though these men, having met at last face to face the ultimate of what the earth has to offer in the way of danger, hardship, difficulty, and the things that try men's souls, having unexpectedly found them all to fall short of both the importance and the final significance with which human-kind has always invested them, were now just a little at a loss. Therefore they stretch their long, lean frames in the wicker chairs, they sip the long drinks at their elbows, puff slowly at their long, lean cheroots, and talk spasmodically in short sentences.

Of quite a different type are those going out—young fellows full of northern health and energy, full of the eagerness of anticipation, full of romance skilfully concealed, self-certain, authoritative, clear voiced. Their exit from the bus is followed by a rain of hold-alls, bags, new tin boxes, new gun cases, all lettered freshly—an enormous kit doomed to diminution. They overflow the place, ebb towards their respective rooms; return scrubbed and ruddy, correctly clad, correctly unconscious of everybody else; sink into more wicker chairs. The quiet brown and yellow men continue to puff at their cheroots, quite eclipsed. After a time one of them picks up his battered old sun helmet and goes out into the street. The eyes of the newcomers follow him. They fall silent; and their eyes, under cover of pulled moustache, furtively glance towards the lean man's companions. Then on that office falls a great silence, broken only by the occasional rare remarks of the quiet men with the cheroots. The youngsters are listening with all their ears, though from their appearance no one would suspect that fact. Not a syllable escapes them. These quiet men have been there; they have seen with their own eyes; their lightest word is saturated with the mystery and romance of the unknown. Their easy, matter-of-fact, everyday knowledge is richly wonderful. It would seem natural for these young-young men to question these old-young men of that which they desire so ardently to know; but that isn't done, you know. So they sit tight, and pretend they are not listening, and feast their ears on the wonderful syllables—Ankobar, Kabul, Peshawur, Annam, Nyassaland, Kerman, Serengetti, Tanganika, and many others. On these beautiful syllables must their imaginations feed, for that which is told is as nothing at all. Adventure there is none, romance there is none, mention of high emprise there is none. Adventure, romance, high emprise have to these men somehow lost their importance. Perhaps such things have been to them too common—as well mention the morning egg. Perhaps they have found that there is no genuine adventure, no real romance except over the edge of the world where the rainbow stoops.

The bus rattles in and rattles out again. It takes the fresh-faced young men down past the inner harbour to where lie the tall ships waiting. They and their cargo of exuberance, of hope, of energy, of thirst for the bubble adventure, the rainbow romance, sail away to where these wares have a market. And the quiet men glide away to the North. Their wares have been marketed. The sleepy, fierce, passionate, sunny lands have taken all they had to bring. And have given in exchange? Indifference, ill-health, a profound realization that the length of days are as nothing at all; a supreme agnosticism as to the ultimate value of anything that a single man can do, a sublime faith that it must be done, the power to concentrate, patience illimitable; contempt for danger, disregard of death, the intention to live; a final, weary estimate of the fact that mere things are as unimportant here as there, no matter how quaintly or fantastically they are dressed or named, and a corresponding emptiness of anticipation for the future—these items are only a random few of the price given by the ancient lands for that which the northern races bring to them. What other alchemical changes have been wrought only these lean and weary men could know—if they dared look so far within themselves. And even if they dared, they would not tell.

FOOTNOTES:

In old days before the "improvements."

---

## II.

THE FAREWELL.

We boarded ship, filled with a great, and what seemed to us, an unappeasable curiosity as to what we were going to see. It was not a very big ship, in spite of the grandiloquent descriptions in the advertisements, or the lithograph wherein she cut grandly and evenly through huge waves to the manifest discomfiture of infinitesimal sailing craft bobbing alongside. She was manned entirely by Germans. The room stewards waited at table, cleaned the public saloons, kept the library, rustled the baggage, and played in the band. That is why we took our music between meals. Our staterooms were very tiny indeed. Each was provided with an electric fan; a totally inadequate and rather aggravating electric fan once we had entered the Red Sea. Just at this moment we paid it little attention, for we were still in full enjoyment of sunny France, where, in our own experience, it had rained two months steadily. Indeed, at this moment it was raining, raining a steady, cold, sodden drizzle that had not even the grace to pick out the surface of the harbour in the jolly dancing staccato that goes far to lend attraction to a genuinely earnest rainstorm.

Down the long quay splashed cabs and omnibuses, their drivers glistening in wet capes, to discharge under the open shed at the end various hasty individuals who marshalled long lines of porters with astonishing impedimenta and drove them up the gang-plank. A half-dozen roughs lounged aimlessly. A little bent old woman with a shawl over her head searched here and there. Occasionally she would find a twisted splinter of wood torn from the piles by a hawser or gouged from the planking by heavy freight, or kicked from the floor by the hoofs of horses. This she deposited carefully in a small covered market basket. She was entirely intent on this minute and rather pathetic task, quite unattending the greatness of the ship, or the many people the great hulk swallowed or spat forth.

Near us against the rail leaned a dark-haired young Englishman whom later every man on that many-nationed ship came to recognize and to avoid as an insufferable bore. Now, however, the angel of good inspiration stooped to him. He tossed a copper two-sou piece down to the bent old woman. She heard the clink of the fall, and looked up bewildered. One of the waterside roughs slouched forward. The Englishman shouted a warning and a threat, indicating in pantomime for whom the coin was intended. To our surprise that evil-looking wharf rat smiled and waved his hand reassuringly, then took the old woman by the arm to show her where the coin had fallen. She hobbled to it with a haste eloquent of the horrible Marseillaise poverty-stricken alleys, picked it up joyously, turned—and with a delightful grace kissed her finger-tips towards the ship.

Apparently we all of us had a few remaining French coins; and certainly we were all grateful to the young Englishman for his happy thought. The sous descended as fast as the woman could get to where they fell. So numerous were they that she had no time to express her gratitude except in broken snatches or gesture, in interrupted attitudes of the most complete thanksgiving. The day of miracles for her had come; and from the humble poverty that valued tiny and infrequent splinters of wood she had suddenly come into great wealth. Everybody was laughing, but in a very kindly sort of way it seemed to me; and the very wharf rats and gamins, wolfish and fierce in their everyday life of the water-front, seemed to take a genuine pleasure in pointing out to her the resting-place of those her dim old eyes had not seen. Silver pieces followed. These were too wonderful. She grew more and more excited, until several of the passengers leaning over the rail began to murmur warningly, fearing harm. After picking up each of these silver pieces, she bowed and gestured very gracefully, waving both hands outward, lifting eyes and hands to heaven, kissing her fingers, trying by every means in her power to express the dazzling wonder and joy that this unexpected marvel was bringing her. When she had done all these things many times, she hugged herself ecstatically. A very well-dressed and prosperous-looking Frenchman standing near seemed to be a little afraid she might hug him. His fear had, perhaps, some grounds, for she shook hands with everybody all around, and showed them her wealth in her kerchief, explaining eagerly, the tears running down her face.

Now the gang-plank was drawn aboard, and the band struck up the usual lively air. At the first notes the old woman executed a few feeble little jig steps in sheer exuberance. Then the solemnity of the situation sobered her. Her great, wealthy, powerful, kind friends were departing on their long voyage over mysterious seas. Again and again, very earnestly, she repeated the graceful, slow pantomime—the wave of the arms outward, the eyes raised to heaven, the hands clasped finally over her head. As the brown strip of water silently widened between us it was strangely like a stage scene—the roofed sheds of the quay, the motionless groups, the central figure of the old woman depicting emotion.

Suddenly she dropped her hands and hobbled away at a great rate, disappearing finally into the maze of the street beyond. Concluding that she had decided to get quickly home with her great treasure, we commended her discretion and gave our attention to other things.

The drizzle fell uninterruptedly. We had edged sidewise the requisite distance, and were now gathering headway in our long voyage. The quail was beginning to recede and to diminish. Back from the street hastened the figure of the little old woman. She carried a large white cloth, of which she had evidently been in quest. This she unfolded and waved vigorously with both hands. Until we had passed quite from sight she stood there signalling her farewell. Long after we were beyond distinguishing her figure we could catch the flutter of white. Thus that ship's company, embarking each on his Great Adventure, far from home and friends, received their farewell, a very genuine farewell, from one poor old woman. B. ventured the opinion that it was the best thing we had bought with our French money.

---

### III.

PORT SAID.

The time of times to approach Port Said is just at the fall of dusk. Then the sea lies in opalescent patches, and the low shores fade away into the gathering night. The slanting masts and yards of the dhows silhouette against a sky of the deepest translucent green; and the heroic statue of De Lesseps, standing for ever at the Gateway he opened, points always to the mysterious East.

The rhythmical, accustomed chug of the engines had fallen to quarter speed, leaving an uncanny stillness throughout the ship. Silently we slipped between the long piers, drew up on the waterside town, seized the buoy, and came to rest. All around us lay other ships of all sizes, motionless on the inky water. The reflections from their lights seemed to be thrust into the depths, like stilts; and the few lights from the town reflected shiveringly across. Along the water-front all was dark and silent. We caught the loom of buildings; and behind them a dull glow as from a fire, and guessed tall minarets, and heard the rising and falling of chanting. Numerous small boats hovered near, floating in and out of the patches of light we ourselves cast, waiting for permission to swarm at the gang-plank for our patronage.

We went ashore, passed through a wicket gate, and across the dark buildings to the heart of the town, whence came the dull glow and the sounds of people.

Here were two streets running across one another, both brilliantly lighted, both thronged, both lined with little shops. In the latter one could buy anything, in any language, with any money. In them we saw cheap straw hats made in Germany hung side by side with gorgeous and beautiful stuffs from the Orient; shoddy European garments and Eastern jewels; cheap celluloid combs and curious embroideries. The crowd of passers-by in the streets were compounded in the same curiously mixed fashion; a few Europeans, generally in white, and then a variety of Arabs, Egyptians, Somalis, Berbers, East Indians and the like, each in his own gaudy or graceful costume. It speaks well for the accuracy of feeling, anyway, of our various "Midways," "Pikes," and the like of our world's expositions that the streets of Port Said looked like Midways raised to the nth power. Along them we sauntered with a pleasing feeling of self-importance. On all sides we were gently and humbly besought—by the shopkeepers, by the sidewalk vendors, by would-be guides, by fortune-tellers, by jugglers, by magicians; all soft-voiced and respectful; all yielding as water to rebuff, but as quick as water to glide back again. The vendors were of the colours of the rainbow, and were heavily hung with long necklaces of coral or amber, with scarves, with strings of silver coins, with sequinned veils and silks, girt with many dirks and knives, furnished out in concealed pockets with scarabs, bracelets, sandalwood boxes or anything else under the broad canopy of heaven one might or might not desire. Their voices were soft and pleasing, their eyes had the beseeching quality of a good dog's, their anxious and deprecating faces were ready at the slightest encouragement to break out into the friendliest and most intimate of smiles. Wherever we went we were accompanied by a retinue straight out of the Arabian Nights, patiently awaiting the moment when we should tire; should seek out the table of a sidewalk café; and should, in our relaxed mood, be ready to unbend to our royal purchases.

At that moment we were too much interested in the town itself. The tiny shops, with their smiling and insinuating Oriental keepers, were fascinating in their displays of carved woods, jewellery, perfumes, silks, tapestries, silversmiths' work, ostrich feathers, and the like. To either side the main street lay long narrow dark alleys, in which flared single lights, across which flitted mysterious long-robed figures, from which floated stray snatches of music either palpitatingly barbaric or ridiculously modern. There the authority of the straight, soldierly-looking Soudanese policemen ceased, and it was not safe to wander unarmed or alone.

Besides these motley variegations of the East and West, the main feature of the town was the street car. It was an open-air structure of spacious dimensions, as though benches and a canopy had been erected rather haphazard on a small dancing platform. The track is absurdly narrow in gauge; and as a consequence the edifice swayed and swung from side to side. A single mule was attached to it loosely by about ten feet of rope. It was driven by a gaudy ragamuffin in a turban. Various other gaudy ragamuffins lounged largely and picturesquely on the widely spaced benches. Whence it came or whither it went I do not know. Its orbit swung into the main street, turned a corner, and disappeared. Apparently Europeans did not patronize this picturesque wreck, but drove elegantly but mysteriously in small open cabs conducted by totally incongruous turbaned drivers.

We ended finally at an imposing corner hotel, where we dined by an open window just above the level of the street. A dozen upturned faces besought us silently during the meal. At a glance of even the mildest interest a dozen long brown arms thrust the spoils of the East upon our consideration. With us sat a large benign Swedish professor whose erudition was encyclopaedic, but whose kindly humanity was greater. Uttering deep, cavernous chuckles, the professor bargained. A red coral necklace for the moment was the matter of interest. The professor inspected it carefully, and handed it back.

"I doubt if id iss coral," said he simply.

The present owner of the beads went frantic with rapid-fire proof and vociferation. With the swiftness and precision of much repetition he fished out a match, struck it, applied the flame to the alleged coral, and blew out the match; cast the necklace on the pavement, produced mysteriously a small hammer, and with it proceeded frantically to pound the beads. Evidently he was accustomed to being doubted, and carried his materials for proof around with him. Then, in one motion, the hammer disappeared, the beads were snatched up, and again offered, unharmed, for inspection.

"Are those good tests for genuineness?" we asked the professor, aside.

"As to that," he replied regretfully, "I do not know. I know of coral only that is the hard calcareous skeleton of the marine coelenterate polyps; and that this red coral iss called of a sclerobasic group; and other facts of the kind; but I do not know if it iss supposed to resist impact and heat. Possibly," he ended shrewdly, "it is the common imitation which does *not* resist impact and heat. At any rate they are pretty. How much?" he demanded of the vendor, a bright-eyed Egyptian waiting patiently until our conference should cease.

"Twenty shillings," he replied promptly.

The professor shook with one of his cavernous chuckles.

"Too much," he observed, and handed the necklace back through the window.

The Egyptian would by no means receive it.

"Keep! keep!" he implored, thrusting the mass of red upon the professor with both hands. "How much you give?"

"One shilling," announced the professor firmly.

The coral necklace lay on the edge of the table throughout most of our leisurely meal. The vendor argued, pleaded, gave it up, disappeared in the crowd, returned dramatically after an interval. The professor ate calmly, chuckled much, and from time to time repeated firmly the words, "One shilling." Finally, at the cheese, he reached out, swept the coral into his pocket, and laid down two shillings. The Egyptian deftly gathered the coin, smiled cheerfully, and produced a glittering veil, in which he tried in vain to enlist Billy's interest.

For coffee and cigars we moved to the terrace outside. Here an orchestra played, the peoples of many nations sat at little tables, the peddlers, fakirs, jugglers, and fortune-tellers swarmed. A half-dozen postal cards seemed sufficient to set a small boy up in trade, and to imbue him with all the importance and insistence of a merchant with jewels. Other ten-year-old ragamuffins tried to call our attention to some sort of sleight-of-hand with poor downy little chickens. Grave, turbaned, and polite Indians squatted cross-legged at our feet, begging to give us a look into the future by means of the only genuine hall-marked Yogi-ism; a troupe of acrobats went energetically and hopefully through quite a meritorious performance a few feet away; a deftly triumphant juggler did very easily, and directly beneath our watchful eyes, some really wonderful tricks. A butterfly-gorgeous swarm of insinuating smiling peddlers of small things dangled and spread their wares where they thought themselves most sure of attention. Beyond our own little group we saw slowly passing in the lighted street outside the portico the variegated and picturesque loungers. Across the way a phonograph bawled; our stringed orchestra played "The Dollar Princess;" from somewhere over in the dark and mysterious alleyways came the regular beating of a tom-tom. The magnificent and picturesque town car with its gaudy ragamuffins swayed by in train of its diminutive mule.

Suddenly our persistent and amusing *entourage* vanished in all directions. Standing idly at the portico was a very straight, black Soudanese. On his head was the usual red fez; his clothing was of trim khaki; his knees and feet were bare, with blue puttees between; and around his middle was drawn close and smooth a blood-red sash at least a foot and a half in breadth. He made a fine upstanding Egyptian figure, and was armed with pride, a short sheathed club, and a great scorn. No word spoke he, nor command; but merely jerked a thumb towards the darkness, and into the darkness our many-hued horde melted away. We were left feeling rather lonesome!

Near midnight we sauntered down the street to the quay, whence we were rowed to the ship by another turbaned, long-robed figure, who sweetly begged just a copper or so "for poor boatman."

We found the ship in the process of coaling, every porthole and doorway closed, and heavy canvas hung to protect as far as possible the clean decks. Two barges were moored alongside. Two blazing braziers lighted them with weird red and flickering flames. In their depths, cast in black and red shadows, toiled half-guessed figures; from their depths, mounting a single steep plank, came an unbroken procession of natives, naked save for a wisp of cloth around the loins. They trod closely on each other's heels, carrying each his basket atop his head or on one shoulder, mounted a gang-plank, discharged their loads into the side of the ship, and descended again to the depths by way of another plank. The lights flickered across their dark faces, their gleaming teeth and eyes. Somehow the work demanded a heap of screeching, shouting, and gesticulation; but somehow also it went forward rapidly. Dozens of unattached natives lounged about the gunwales with apparently nothing to do but to look picturesque. Shore boats moved into the narrow circle of light, drifted to our gangway, and discharged huge crates of vegetables, sacks of unknown stuffs, and returning passengers. A vigilant police boat hovered near to settle disputes, generally with the blade of an oar. For a long time we leaned over the rail watching them, and the various reflected lights in the water, and the very clear, unwavering stars. Then, the coaling finished, and the portholes once more opened, we turned in.

---

## IV.

SUEZ.

Some time during the night we must have started, but so gently had we slid along it fractional speed that until I raised my head and looked out I had not realized the fact. I saw a high sandbank. This glided monotonously by until I grew tired of looking at it and got up.

After breakfast, however, I found that the sandbank had various attractions all of its own. Three camels laden with stone and in convoy of white-clad figures shuffled down the slope at a picturesque angle. Two cowled women in black, veiled to the eyes in gauze heavily sewn with sequins, barefooted, with massive silver anklets, watched us pass. Hindu workmen in turban and loin-cloth furnished a picturesque note, but did not seem to be injuring themselves by over-exertion. Naked small boys raced us for a short distance. The banks glided by very slowly and very evenly, the wash sucked after us like water in a slough after a duck boat, and the sky above the yellow sand looked extremely blue.

At short and regular intervals, half-way up the miniature sandhills, heavy piles or snubbing-posts had been planted. For these we at first could guess no reason. Soon, however, we had to pass another ship; and then we saw that one of us must tie up to avoid being drawn irresistibly by suction into collision with the other. The craft sidled by, separated by only a few feet, so that we could look across to each other's decks and exchange greetings. As the day grew this interest grew likewise. Dredgers in the canal; rusty tramps flying unfamiliar flags of strange tiny countries; big freighters, often with Greek or Turkish characters on their sterns; small dirty steamers of suspicious business; passenger ships like our own, returning from the tropics, with white-clad, languid figures reclining in canvas chairs; gunboats of this or that nation bound on mysterious affairs; once a P. & O. converted into a troopship, from whose every available porthole, hatch, deck, and shroud laughing, brown, English faces shouted chaff at our German decks—all these either tied up for us, or were tied up for by us. The only craft that received no consideration on our part were the various picturesque Arab dhows, with their single masts and the long yards slanting across them. Since these were very small, our suction dragged at them cruelly. As a usual thing four vociferous figures clung desperately to a rope passed around one of the snubbing-posts ashore, while an old man shrieked syllables at them from the dhow itself. As they never by any chance thought of mooring her both stem and stern, the dhow generally changed ends rapidly, shipping considerable water in the process. It must be very trying to get so excited in a hot climate.

The high sandbanks of the early part of the day soon dropped lower to afford us a wider view. In its broad, general features the country was, quite simply, the desert of Arizona over again. There were the same high, distant, and brittle-looking mountains, fragile and pearly; the same low, broken half-distances; the same wide sweeps; the same wonderful changing effects of light, colour, shadow, and mirage; the same occasional strips of green marking the watercourses and oases. As to smaller detail, we saw many interesting divergences. In the foreground constantly recurred the Bedouin brush shelters, each with its picturesque figure or so in flowing robes, and its grumpy camels. Twice we saw travelling caravans, exactly like the Bible pictures. At one place a single burnoused Arab, leaning on his elbows, reclined full length on the sky-line of a clean-cut sandhill. Glittering in the mirage, half-guessed, half-seen, we made out distant little white towns with slender palm trees. At places the water from the canal had overflowed wide tracts of country. Here, along the shore, we saw thousands of the water-fowl already familiar to us, as well as such strangers as gaudy kingfishers, ibises, and rosy flamingoes.

The canal itself seemed to be in a continual state of repair. Dredgers were everywhere; some of the ordinary shovel type, others working by suction, and discharging far inland by means of weird huge pipes that apparently meandered at will over the face of nature. The control stations were beautifully French and neat, painted yellow, each with its gorgeous bougainvilleas in flower, its square-rigged signal masts, its brightly painted extra buoys standing in a row, its wharf—and its impassive Arab fishermen thereon. We reclined in our canvas chairs, had lemon squashes brought to us, and watched the entertainment steadily and slowly unrolled before us.

We reached the end of the canal about three o'clock of the afternoon, and dropped anchor off the low-lying shores. Our binoculars showed us white houses in apparently single rank along a far-reaching narrow sand spit, with sparse trees and a railroad line. That was the town of Suez, and seemed so little interesting that we were not particularly sorry that we could not go ashore. Far in the distance were mountains; and the water all about us was the light, clear green of the sky at sunset.

Innumerable dhows and row-boats swarmed down, filled with eager salesmen of curios and ostrich plumes. They had not much time in which to bargain, so they made it up in rapid-fire vociferation. One very tall and dignified Arab had as sailor of his craft the most extraordinary creature, just above the lower limit of the human race. He was of a dull coal black, without a single high light on him anywhere, as though he had been sand-papered, had prominent teeth, like those of a baboon, in a wrinkled, wizened monkey face, across which were three tattooed bands, and possessed a little, long-armed, spare figure, bent and wiry. He clambered up and down his mast, fetching things at his master's behest; leapt nonchalantly for our rail or his own spar, as the case might be, across the staggering abyss; clung so well with his toes that he might almost have been classified with the quadrumana; and between times squatted humped over on the rail, watching us with bright, elfish, alien eyes.

At last the big German sailors bundled the whole variegated horde overside. It was time to go, and our anchor chain was already rumbling in the hawse pipes. They tumbled hastily into their boats; and at once swarmed up their masts, whence they feverishly continued their interrupted bargaining. In fact, so fully embarked on the tides of commerce were they, that they failed to notice the tides of nature widening between us. One old man, in especial, at the very top of his mast, jerked hither and thither by the sea, continued imploringly to offer an utterly ridiculous carved wooden camel long after it was impossible to have completed the transaction should anybody have been moonstruck enough to have desired it. Our ship's prow swung; and just at sunset, as the lights of Suez were twinkling out one by one, we headed down the Red Sea.

---

*V.*

THE RED SEA.

Suez is indeed the gateway to the East. In the Mediterranean often the sea is rough, the winds cold, passengers are not yet acquainted, and hug the saloons or the leeward side of the deck. Once through the canal and all is changed by magic. The air is hot and languid; the ship's company down to the very scullions appear in immaculate white; the saloon chairs and transoms even are put in white coverings; electric fans hum everywhere; the run on lemon squashes begins; and many quaint and curious customs of the tropics obtain.

For example: it is etiquette that before eight o'clock one may wander the decks at will in one's pyjamas, converse affably with fair ladies in pigtail and kimono, and be not abashed. But on the stroke of eight bells it is also etiquette to disappear very promptly and to array one's self for the day; and it is very improper indeed to see or be seen after that hour in the rather extreme *negligée* of the early morning. Also it becomes the universal custom, or perhaps I should say the necessity, to slumber for an hour after the noon meal. Certainly sleep descending on the tropical traveller is armed with a bludgeon. Passengers, crew, steerage, "deck," animal, and bird fall down then in an enchantment. I have often wondered who navigates the ship during that sacred hour, or, indeed, if anybody navigates it at all. Perhaps that time is sacred to the genii of the old East, who close all prying mortal eyes, but in return lend a guiding hand to the most pressing of mortal affairs. The deck of the ship is a curious sight between the hours of half-past one and three. The tropical siesta requires no couching of the form. You sit down in your chair, with a book—you fade slowly into a deep, restful slumber. And yet it is a slumber wherein certain small pleasant things persist from the world outside. You remain dimly conscious of the rhythmic throbbing of the engines, of the beat of soft, warm air on your cheek.

At three o'clock or thereabout you rise as gently back to life, and sit erect in your chair without a stretch or a yawn in your whole anatomy. Then is the one time of day for a display of energy—if you have any to display. Ship games, walks—fairly brisk—explorations to the forecastle, a watch for flying fish or Arab dhows, anything until tea-time. Then the glowing sunset; the opalescent sea, and the soft afterglow of the sky—and the bugle summoning you to dress. That is a mean job. Nothing could possibly swelter worse than the tiny cabin. The electric fan is an aggravation. You reappear in your fresh "whites" somewhat warm and flustered in both mind and body. A turn around the deck cools you off; and dinner restores your equanimity—dinner with the soft, warm tropic air breathing through all the wide-open ports; the electric fans drumming busily; the men all in clean white; the ladies, the very few precious ladies, in soft, low gowns. After dinner the deck, as near cool as it will be, and heads bare to the breeze of our progress, and glowing cigars. At ten or eleven o'clock the groups begin to break up, the canvas chairs to empty. Soon reappears a pyjamaed figure followed by a steward carrying a mattress. This is spread, under its owner's direction, in a dark corner forward. With a sigh you in your turn plunge down into the sweltering inferno of your cabin, only to reappear likewise with a steward and a mattress. The latter, if you are wise, you spread where the wind of the ship's going will be full upon you. It is a strong wind and blows upon you heavily, so that the sleeves and legs of your pyjamas flop, but it is a soft, warm wind, and beats you as with muffled fingers. In no temperate clime can you ever enjoy this peculiar effect of a strong breeze on your naked skin without even the faintest surface chilly sensation. So habituated has one become to feeling cooler in a draught that the absence of chill lends the night an unaccustomedness, the more weird in that it is unanalyzed, so that one feels definitely that one is in a strange, far country. This is intensified by the fact that in these latitudes the moon, the great, glorious, calm tropical moon, is directly overhead—follows the centre line of the zenith—instead of being, as with us in our temperate zone, always more or less declined to the horizon. This, too, lends the night an exotic quality, the more effective in that at first the reason for it is not apprehended.

A night in the tropics is always more or less broken. One awakens, and sleeps again. Motionless white-clad figures, cigarettes glowing, are lounging against the rail looking out over a molten sea. The moonlight lies in patterns across the deck, shivering slightly under the throb of the engines, or occasionally swaying slowly forward or slowly back as the ship's course changes, but otherwise motionless, for here the sea is always calm. You raise your head, look about, sprawl in a new position on your mattress, fall asleep. On one of these occasions you find unexpectedly that the velvet-gray night has become steel-gray dawn, and that the kindly old quartermaster is bending over you. Sleepily, very sleepily, you stagger to your feet and collapse into the nearest chair. Then to the swish of water, as the sailors sluice the decks all around and under you, you fall into a really deep sleep.

At six o'clock this is broken by chota-hazri, another tropical institution, consisting merely of clear tea and biscuits. I never could get to care for it, but nowhere in the tropics could I head it off. No matter how tired I was or how dead sleepy, I had to receive that confounded chota-hazri. Throwing things at the native who brought it did no good at all. He merely dodged. Admonition did no good, nor prohibition in strong terms. I was but one white man of the whole white race; and I had no right to possess idiosyncrasies running counter to dastur, the custom. However, as the early hours are profitable hours in the tropics, it did not drive me to homicide.

The ship's company now developed. Our two prize members, fortunately for us, sat at our table. The first was the Swedish professor aforementioned. He was large, benign, paternal, broad in mind, thoroughly human and beloved, and yet profoundly erudite. He was our iconoclast in the way of food; for he performed small but illuminating dissections on his plate, and announced triumphantly results that were not a bit in accordance with the menu. A single bone was sufficient to take the pretension out of any fish. Our other particular friend was C., with whom later we travelled in the interior of Africa. C. is a very celebrated hunter and explorer, an old Africander, his face seamed and tanned by many years in a hard climate. For several days we did not recognize him, although he sat fairly alongside, but put him down as a shy man, and let it go at that. He never stayed for the long *table d'hôte* dinners, but fell upon the first solid course and made a complete meal from that. When he had quite finished eating all he could, he drank all he could; then he departed from the table, and took up a remote and inaccessible position in the corner of the smoking-room. He was engaged in growing the beard he customarily wore in the jungle—a most fierce outstanding Mohammedan-looking beard that terrified the intrusive into submission. And yet Bwana C. possesses the kindest blue eyes in the world, full of quiet patience, great understanding, and infinite gentleness. His manner was abrupt and uncompromising, but he would do anything in the world for one who stood in need of him. From women he fled; yet Billy won him with infinite patience, and in the event they became the closest of friends. Withal he possessed a pair of the most powerful shoulders I have ever seen on a man of his frame; and in the depths of his mild blue eyes flickered a flame of resolution that I could well imagine flaring up to something formidable. Slow to make friends, but staunch and loyal; gentle and forbearing, but fierce and implacable in action; at once loved and most terribly feared; shy as a wild animal, but straightforward and undeviating in his human relations; most remarkably quiet and unassuming, but with tremendous vital force in his deep eyes and forward-thrust jaw; informed with the widest and most understanding humanity, but unforgiving of evildoers;

259

and with the most direct and absolute courage, Bwana C. was to me the most interesting man I met in Africa, and became the best of my friends.

The only other man at our table happened to be, for our sins, the young Englishman mentioned as throwing the first coin to the old woman on the pier at Marseilles. We will call him Brown, and, because he represents a type, he is worth looking upon for a moment.

He was of the super-enthusiastic sort; bubbling over with vitality, in and out of everything; bounding up at odd and languid moments. To an extraordinary extent he was afflicted with the spiritual blindness of his class. Quite genuinely, quite seriously, he was unconscious of the human significance of beings and institutions belonging to a foreign country or even to a class other than his own. His own kind he treated as complete and understandable human creatures. All others were merely objective. As we, to a certain extent, happened to fall in the former category, he was as pleasant to us as possible—that is, he was pleasant to us in his way, but had not insight enough to guess at how to be pleasant to us in our way. But as soon as he got out of his own class, or what he conceived to be such, he considered all people as "outsiders." He did not credit them with prejudices to rub, with feelings to hurt, indeed hardly with ears to overhear. Provided his subject was an "outsider," he had not the slightest hesitancy in saying exactly what he thought about any one, anywhere, always in his high clear English voice, no matter what the time or occasion. As a natural corollary he always rebuffed beggars and the like brutally, and was always quite sublimely doing little things that thoroughly shocked our sense of the other fellow's rights as a human being. In all this he did not mean to be cruel or inconsiderate. It was just the way he was built; and it never entered his head that "such people" had ears and brains.

In the rest of the ship's company were a dozen or so other Englishmen of the upper classes, either army men on shooting trips, or youths going out with some idea of settling in the country. They were a clean-built, pleasant lot; good people to know anywhere, but of no unusual interest. It was only when one went abroad into the other nations that inscribable human interest could be found.

There was the Greek, Scutari, and his bride, a languorous rather opulent beauty, with large dark eyes for all men, and a luxurious manner of lying back and fanning herself. She talked, soft-voiced, in half a dozen languages, changing from one to the other without a break in either her fluency or her thought. Her little lithe, active husband sat around and adored her. He was apparently a very able citizen indeed, for he was going out to take charge of the construction work on a German railway. To have filched so important a job from the Germans themselves shows that he must have had ability. With them were a middle-aged Holland couple, engaged conscientiously in travelling over the globe. They had been everywhere—the two American hemispheres, from one Arctic Sea to another, Siberia, China, the Malay Archipelago, this, that, and the other odd corner of the world. Always they sat placidly side by side, either in the saloon or on deck, smiling benignly, and conversing in spaced, comfortable syllables with everybody who happened along. Mrs. Breemen worked industriously on some kind of feminine gear, and explained to all and sundry that she travelled "to see de sceenery wid my hoos-band."

Also in this group was a small wiry German doctor, who had lived for many years in the far interior of Africa, and was now returning after his vacation. He was a little man, bright-eyed and keen, with a clear complexion and hard flesh, in striking and agreeable contrast to most of his compatriots. The latter were trying to drink all the beer on the ship; but as she had been stocked for an eighty-day voyage, of which this was but the second week, they were not making noticeable headway. However, they did not seem to be easily discouraged. The Herr Doktor was most polite and attentive, but as we did not talk German nor much Swahili, and he had neither English nor much French, we had our difficulties. I have heard Billy in talking to him scatter fragments of these four languages through a single sentence!

For several days we drifted down a warm flat sea. Then one morning we came on deck to find ourselves close aboard a number of volcanic islands. They were composed entirely of red and dark purple lava blocks, rugged, quite without vegetation save for occasional patches of stringy green in a gully; and uninhabited except for a lighthouse on one, and a fishing shanty near the shores of another. The high mournful mountains, with their dark shadows, seemed to brood over hot desolation. The rusted and battered stern of a wrecked steamer stuck up at an acute angle from the surges. Shortly after we picked up the shores of Arabia.

Note the advantages of a half ignorance. From early childhood we had thought of Arabia as the "burning desert"—flat, of course—and of the Red Sea as bordered by "shifting sands" alone. If we had known the truth—if we had not been half ignorant—we would have missed the profound surprise of discovering that in reality the Red Sea is bordered by high and rugged mountains, leaving just space enough between themselves and the shore for a sloping plain on which our glasses could make out occasional palms. Perhaps the "shifting sands of the burning desert" lie somewhere beyond; but somebody might have mentioned these great mountains! After examining them attentively we had to confess that if this sort of thing continued farther north the children of Israel must have had a very hard time of it. Mocha shone white, glittering, and low, with the red and white spire of a mosque rising brilliantly above it.

---

## VI.

ADEN.

It was cooler; and for a change we had turned into our bunks, when B. pounded on our stateroom door.

"In the name of the Eternal East," said he, "come on deck!"

We slipped on kimonos, and joined the row of scantily draped and interested figures along the rail.

The ship lay quite still on a perfect sea of moonlight, bordered by a low flat distant shore on one side, and nearer mountains on the other. A strong flare, centred from two ship reflectors overside, made a focus of illumination that subdued, but could not quench, the soft moonlight with which all outside was silvered. A dozen boats, striving against a current or clinging as best they could to the ship's side, glided into the light and became real and solid; or dropped back into the ghostly white unsubstantiality of the moon. They were long, narrow boats, with small flush decks fore and aft. We looked down on them from almost directly above, so that we saw the thwarts and the ribs and the things they contained.

Astern in each stood men, bending gracefully against the thrust of long sweeps. About their waists were squares of cloth, wrapped twice and tucked in. Otherwise they were naked, and the long smooth muscles of their slender bodies rippled under the skin. The latter was of a beautiful fine texture, and chocolate brown. These men had keen, intelligent, clear-cut faces, of the Greek order, as though the statues of a garden had been stained brown and had come to life. They leaned on their sweeps, thrusting slowly but strongly against the little wind and current that would drift them back.

In the body of the boats crouched, sat, or lay a picturesque mob. Some pulled spasmodically on the very long limber oars; others squatted doing nothing; some, huddled shapelessly underneath white cloths that completely covered them, slept soundly in the bottom. We took these for merchandise until one of them suddenly threw aside his covering and sat up. Others, again, poised in proud and graceful attitudes on the extreme prows of their bobbing craft. Especially decorative were two, clad only in immense white turbans and white cloths about the waist. An old Arab with a white beard stood midships in one boat, quite motionless, except for the slight swaying necessary to preserve his equilibrium, his voluminous white draperies fluttering in the wind, his dark face just distinguishable under his burnouse. Most of the men were Somalis, however. Their keen small faces, slender but graceful necks, slim, well-formed torsos bending to every movement of the boat, and the white or gaudy draped nether garments were as decorative as the figures on an Egyptian tomb. One or two of the more barbaric had made neat headdresses of white clay plastered in the form of a skull-cap.

After an interval a small and fussy tugboat steamed around our stern and drew alongside the gangway. Three passengers disembarked from her and made their way aboard. The main deck of the craft under an awning was heavily encumbered with trunks, tin boxes, hand baggage, tin bath-tubs, gun cases, and all sorts of impedimenta. The tugboat moored itself to us fore and aft, and proceeded to think about discharging. Perhaps twenty men in accurate replica of those in the small boats had charge of the job. They had their own methods. After a long interval devoted strictly to nothing, some unfathomable impulse would incite one or two or three of the natives to tackle a trunk. At it they tugged and heaved and pushed in the manner of ants making off with a particularly large fly or other treasure trove, tossing it up the steep gangway to the level of our decks. The trunks once safely bestowed, all interest, all industry, died. We thought that finished it, and wondered why the tug did not pull out of the way. But always, after an interval, another bright idea would strike another native or natives. He—or they—would disappear beneath the canvas awning over the tug's deck, to emerge shortly, carrying almost anything, from a parasol to a heavy chest.

On close inspection they proved to be a very small people. The impression of graceful height had come from the slenderness and justness of their proportions, the smallness of their bones, and the upright grace of their carriage. After standing alongside one, we acquired a fine respect for their ability to handle those trunks at all.

Moored to the other side of the ship we found two huge lighters, from which bales of goods were being hoisted aboard. Two camels and a dozen diminutive mules stood in the waist of one of these craft. The camels were as sniffy and supercilious and scornful as camels always are; and everybody promptly hated them with the hatred of the abysmally inferior spirit for something that scorns it, as is the usual attitude of the human mind towards camels. We waited for upwards of an hour, in the hope of seeing those camels hoisted aboard; but in vain. While we were so waiting one of the deck passengers below us, a Somali in white clothes and a gorgeous cerise turban, decided to turn in. He spread a square of thin matting atop one of the hatches, and began to unwind yards and yards of the fine silk turban. He came to the end of it—whisk! he sank to the deck; the turban, spread open by the resistance of the air, fluttered down to cover him from head to foot. Apparently he fell asleep at once, for he did not again move nor alter his position. He, as well as an astonishingly large proportion of the other Somalis and Abyssinians we saw, carried a queer, well-defined, triangular wound in his head. It had long since healed, was an inch or so across, and looked as though a piece of the skull had been removed. If a conscientious enemy had leisure and an icepick he would do just about that sort of a job. How its recipient had escaped instant death is a mystery.

At length, about three o'clock, despairing of the camels, we turned in.

After three hours' sleep we were again on deck. Aden by daylight seemed to be several sections of a town tucked into pockets in bold, raw, lava mountains that came down fairly to the water's edge. Between these pockets ran a narrow shore road; and along the road paced haughty camels hitched to diminutive carts. On contracted round bluffs towards the sea were various low bungalow buildings which, we were informed, comprised the military and civil officers' quarters. The real Aden has been built inland a short distance at the bottom of a cup in the mountains. Elaborate stone reservoirs have been constructed to catch rain water, as there is no other natural water supply whatever. The only difficulty is that it practically never rains; so the reservoirs stand empty, the water is distilled from the sea, and the haughty camels and the little carts do the distributing.

The lava mountains occupy one side of the spacious bay or gulf. The foot of the bay and the other side are flat, with one or two very distant white villages, and many heaps of glittering salt as big as houses.

We waited patiently at the rail for an hour more to see the camels slung aboard by the crane. It was worth the wait. They lost their impassive and immemorial dignity completely, sprawling, groaning, positively shrieking in dismay. When the solid deck rose to them, and the sling had been loosened, however, they regained their poise instantaneously. Their noses went up in the air, and they looked about them with a challenging, unsmiling superiority, as though to dare any one of us to laugh. Their native attendants immediately squatted down in front of them, and began to feed them with convenient lengths of what looked like our common marsh cat-tails. The camels did not even then manifest the slightest interest in the proceedings. Indeed, they would not condescend to reach out three inches for the most luscious tit-bit held that far from their aristocratic noses. The attendants had actually to thrust the fodder between their jaws. I am glad to say they condescended to chew.

---

## VII.

THE INDIAN OCEAN.

Leaving Aden, and rounding the great promontory of Cape Guardafui, we turned south along the coast of Africa. Off the cape were strange, oily cross rips and currents on the surface of the sea; the flying-fish rose in flocks before our bows; high mountains of peaks and flat table tops thrust their summits into clouds; and along the coast the breakers spouted like whales. For the first time, too, we began to experience what our preconceptions had imagined as tropical heat. Heretofore we had been hot enough, in all conscience, but the air had felt as though wafted from an opened furnace door—dry and scorching. Now, although the temperature was lower, the humidity was greater. A swooning languor was abroad over the spellbound ocean, a relaxing mist of enchantment.

My glasses were constantly clouding over with a fine coating of water drops; exposed metal rusted overnight; the folds in garments accumulated mildew in an astonishingly brief period of time. There was never even the suggestion of chill in this dampness. It clung and enveloped like a grateful garment; and seemed only to lack sweet perfume.

At this time, by good fortune, it happened that the moon came full. We had enjoyed its waxing during our voyage down the Red Sea; but now it had reached its greatest phase, and hung over the slumbering tropic ocean like a lantern. The lazy sea stirred beneath it, and the ship glided on, its lights fairly subdued by the splendour of the waters. Under the awnings the ship's company lounged in lazy attitudes or promenaded slowly, talking low voiced, cigars glowing in the splendid dusk. Overside, in the furrow of the disturbed waters, the phosphorescence flashed perpetually beneath the shadow of the ship.

The days passed by languidly and all alike. On the chart outside the smoking-room door the procession of tiny German flags on pins marched steadily, an inch at a time, towards the south. Otherwise we might as well have imagined ourselves midgets afloat in a pond and getting nowhere.

Somewhere north of the equator—before Father Neptune in ancient style had come aboard and ducked the lot of us— we were treated to the spectacle of how the German "sheep" reacts under a joke. Each nation has its type of fool; and all, for the joyousness of mankind, differ. On the bulletin board one evening appeared a notice to the effect that the following morning a limited number of sportsmen would be permitted ashore for the day. Each was advised to bring his own lunch, rifle, and drinks. The reason alleged was that the ship must round a certain cape across which the sportsmen could march afoot in sufficient time to permit them a little shooting.

Now aboard ship were a dozen English, four Americans, and thirty or forty Germans. The Americans and English looked upon that bulletin, smiled gently, and went to order another round of lemon squashes. It was a meek, mild, little joke enough; but surely the bulletin board was as far as it could possibly go. Next morning, however, we observed a half-dozen of our German friends in khaki and sun helmet, very busy with lunch boxes, bottles of beer, rifles, and the like. They said they were going ashore as per bulletin. We looked at each other and hied us to the upper deck. There we found one of the boats slung overside, with our old friend the quartermaster ostentatiously stowing kegs of water, boxes, and the like.

"When," we inquired gently, "does the expedition start?"

"At ten o'clock," said he.

It was now within fifteen minutes of that hour.

We were at the time fully ten miles off shore, and forging ahead full speed parallel with the coast.

We pointed out this fact to the quartermaster, but found, to our sorrow, that the poor old man had suddenly gone deaf! We therefore refrained from asking several other questions that had occurred to us—such as, why the cape was not shown on the map.

"Somebody," said one of the Americans, a cowboy going out second class on the look for new cattle country, "is a goat. It sure looks to me like it was these yere steamboat people. They can't expect to rope nothing on such a raw deal as this!"

To which the English assented, though in different idiom.

But now up the companion ladder struggled eight serious-minded individuals herded by the second mate. They were armed to the teeth, and thoroughly equipped with things I had seen in German catalogues, but in whose existence I had never believed. A half-dozen sailors eagerly helped them with their multitudinous effects. Not a thought gave they to the fact that we were ten miles off the coast, that we gave no indication of slackening speed, that it would take the rest of the day to row ashore, that there was no cape for us to round, that if there were—oh! all the other hundred improbabilities peculiar to the situation. Under direction of the mate they deposited their impedimenta beneath a tarpaulin, and took their places in solemn rows amidships across the thwarts of the boat slung overside. The importance of the occasion sat upon them heavily; they were going ashore—in Africa—to Slay Wild Beasts. They looked upon themselves as of bolder, sterner stuff than the rest of us.

When the procession first appeared, our cowboy's face for a single instant had flamed with amazed incredulity. Then a mask of expressionless stolidity fell across his features, which in no line thereafter varied one iota.

"What are they going to do with them?" murmured one of the Englishmen, at a loss.

"I reckon," said the cowboy, "that they look on this as the easiest way to drown them all to onct."

Then from behind one of the other boats suddenly appeared a huge German sailor with a hose. The devoted imbeciles in the shore boat were drenched as by a cloud-burst. Back and forth and up and down the heavy stream played, while every other human being about the ship shrieked with joy. Did the victims rise up in a body and capture that hose nozzle and turn the stream to sweep the decks? Did they duck for shelter? Did they at least know enough to scatter and run? They did none of these things; but sat there in meek little rows like mannikins until the boat was half full of water and everything awash. Then, when the sailor shut off the stream, they continued to sit there until the mate came to order them out. Why? I cannot tell you. Perhaps that is the German idea of how to take a joke. Perhaps they were afraid worse things might be consequent on resistance. Perhaps they still hoped to go ashore. One of the Englishmen asked just that question.

"What," he demanded disgustedly, "what is the matter with the beggars?"

Our cowboy may have had the correct solution. He stretched his long legs and jumped down from the rail.

"Nothing stirring above the ears," said he.

It is customary in books of travel to describe this part of the journey somewhat as follows: "Skirting the low and uninteresting shores of Africa we at length reached," etc. Low and uninteresting shores! Through the glasses we made out distant mountains far beyond nearer hills. The latter were green-covered with dense forests whence rose mysterious smokes. Along the shore we saw an occasional cocoanut plantation to the water's edge and native huts and villages of thatch. Canoes of strange models lay drawn up on shelving beaches; queer fish-pounds of brush reached out considerable distances from the coast. The white surf pounded on a yellow beach.

All about these things was the jungle, hemming in the plantations and villages, bordering the lagoons, creeping down until it fairly overhung the yellow beaches; as though, conqueror through all the country beyond, it were half-inclined to dispute dominion with old Ocean himself. It looked from the distance like a thick, soft coverlet thrown down over the country; following—or, rather, suggesting—the inequalities. Through the glasses we were occasionally able to peep under the edge of this coverlet, and see where the fringe of the jungle drew back in a little pocket, or to catch the sheen of mysterious dark rivers slipping to the sea. Up these dark rivers, by way of the entrances of these tiny pockets, the imagination then could lead on into the dimness beneath the sunlit upper surfaces.

Towards the close of one afternoon we changed our course slightly, and swung in on a long slant towards the coast. We did it casually; too casually for so very important an action, for now at last we were about to touch the mysterious continent. Then we saw clearer the fine, big groves of palm and the luxuriance of the tropical vegetation. Against the greenery, bold and white, shone the buildings of Mombasa; and after a little while we saw an inland glitter that represented her narrow, deep bay, the stern of a wreck against the low, green cliffs, and strange, fat-trunked squat trees without leaves. Straight past all this we glided at half speed, then turned sharp to the right to enter a long wide expanse like a river, with green banks, twenty feet or so in height, grown thickly with the tall cocoanut palms. These gave way at times into broad, low lagoons, at the end of which were small beaches and boats, and native huts among more cocoanut groves. Through our glasses we could see the black men watching us, quite motionless, squatted on their heels.

It was like suddenly entering another world, this gliding from the open sea straight into the heart of a green land. The ceaseless wash of waves we had left outside with the ocean; our engines had fallen silent. Across the hushed waters came to us strange chantings and the beating of a tom-tom, an occasional shrill shout from the unknown jungle. The sun was just set, and the tops of the palms caught the last rays; all below was dense green shadow. Across the surface of the water glided dug-out canoes of shapes strange to us. We passed ancient ruins almost completely dismantled, their stones half smothered in green rank growth. The wide river-like bay stretched on before us as far as the waning light permitted us to see; finally losing itself in the heart of mystery.

Steadily and confidently our ship steamed forward, until at last, when we seemed to be afloat in a land-locked lake, we dropped anchor and came to rest.

Darkness fell utterly before the usual quarantine regulations had been carried through. Active and efficient agents had already taken charge of our affairs, so we had only to wait idly by the rail until summoned. Then we jostled our way down the long gangway, passed and repassed by natives carrying baggage or returning for more baggage, stepped briskly aboard a very bobby little craft, clambered over a huge pile of baggage, and stowed ourselves as best we could. A figure in a long white robe sat astern, tiller ropes in hand; two half-naked blacks far up towards the prow manipulated a pair of tremendous sweeps. With a vast heaving, jabbering, and shouting, our boat disengaged itself from the swarm of other craft. We floated around the stern of our ship, and were immediately suspended in blackness dotted with the stars and their reflections, and with various twinkling scattered lights. To one of these we steered, and presently touched at a stone quay with steps. At last we set foot on the land to which so long we had journeyed and towards which our expectations had grown so great. We experienced "the pleasure that touches the souls of men landing on strange shores."

FOOTNOTES:

82-88° degrees in daytime, and 75-83° degrees at night.

---

## VIII.

## MOMBASA.

A single light shone at the end of the stone quay, and another inside a big indeterminate building at some distance. We stumbled towards this, and found it to be the biggest shed ever constructed out of corrugated iron. A bearded Sikh stood on guard at its open entrance. He let any one and every one enter, with never a flicker of his expressionless black eyes; but allowed no one to go out again without the closest scrutiny for dutiable articles that lacked the blue customs plaster. We entered. The place was vast and barnlike and dim, and very, very hot. A half-dozen East Indians stood behind the counters; another, a babu, sat at a little desk ready to give his clerical attention to what might be required. We saw no European; but next morning found that one passed his daylight hours in this inferno of heat. For the moment we let our main baggage go, and occupied ourselves only with getting through our smaller effects. This accomplished, we stepped out past the Sikh into the grateful night.

We had as guide a slender and wiry individual clad in tarboush and long white robe. In a vague, general way we knew that the town of Mombasa was across the island and about four miles distant. In what direction or how we got there we had not the remotest idea.

The guide set off at a brisk pace with which we tried in vain to keep step. He knew the ground, and we did not; and the night was black dark. Commands to stop were of no avail whatever; nor could we get hold of him to restrain him by force. When we put on speed he put on speed too. His white robe glimmered ahead of us just in sight; and in the darkness other white robes, passing and crossing, glimmered also. At first the ground was rough, so that we stumbled outrageously. Billy and B. soon fell behind, and I heard their voices calling plaintively for us to slow down a bit.

"If I ever lose this nigger, I'll never find him again," I shouted back, "but I can find you. Do the best you can!"

We struck a smoother road that led up a hill on a long slant. Apparently for miles we followed thus, the white-robed individual ahead still deaf to all commands and the blood-curdling threats I had now come to uttering. All our personal baggage had long since mysteriously disappeared, ravished away from us at the customs house by a ragged horde of blacks. It began to look as though we were stranded in Africa without baggage or effects. Billy and B. were all the time growing fainter in the distance, though evidently they too had struck the long, slanting road.

Then we came to a dim, solitary lantern glowing feebly beside a bench at what appeared to be the top of the hill. Here our guide at last came to a halt and turned to me a grinning face.

"Samama hapa," he observed.

There! That was the word I had been frantically searching my memory for! Samama—stop!

The others struggled in. We were very warm. Up to the bench led a tiny car track, the rails not over two feet apart, like the toy railroads children use. This did not look much like grownup transportation, but it and the bench and the dim lantern represented all the visible world.

We sat philosophically on the bench and enjoyed the soft tropical night. The air was tepid, heavy with unknown perfume, black as a band of velvet across the eyes, musical with the subdued undertones of a thousand thousand night insects. At points overhead the soft blind darkness melted imperceptibly into stars.

After a long interval we distinguished a distant faint rattling, that each moment increased in loudness. Shortly came into view along the narrow tracks a most extraordinary vehicle. It was a small square platform on wheels, across which ran a bench seat, and over which spread a canopy. It carried also a dim lantern. This rumbled up to us and stopped. From its stern hopped two black boys. Obeying a smiling invitation, we took our places on the bench. The two boys immediately set to pushing us along the narrow track.

We were off at an astonishing speed through the darkness. The night was deliciously tepid; and, as I have said, absolutely dark. We made out the tops of palms and the dim loom of great spreading trees, and could smell sweet, soft odours. The bare-headed, lightly-clad boys pattered alongside whenever the grade was easy, one hand resting against the rail; or pushed mightily up little hills; or clung alongside like monkeys while we rattled and swooped and plunged down hill into the darkness. Subsequently we learned that a huge flat beam projecting amidships from beneath the seat operated a brake which we above were supposed to manipulate; but being quite ignorant as to the ethics and mechanics of this strange street-car system, we swung and swayed at times quite breathlessly.

After about fifteen minutes we began to pick up lights ahead, then to pass dimly-seen garden walls with trees whose brilliant flowers the lantern revealed fitfully. At last we made out white stucco houses, and shortly drew up with a flourish before the hotel itself.

This was a two-story stucco affair, with deep verandas sunken in at each story. It fronted a wide white street facing a public garden; and this, we subsequently discovered, was about the only clear and open space in all the narrow town. Antelope horns were everywhere hung on the walls; and teakwood easy-chairs, with rests on which comfortably to elevate your feet above your head, stood all about. We entered a bare, brick-floored dining-room, and partook of tropical fruits quite new to us—papayes, mangoes, custard apples, pawpaws, and the small red eating bananas too delicate for export. Overhead the punkahs swung back and forth in lazy hypnotic rhythm. We could see the two blacks at the ends of the punkah cords outside on the veranda, their bodies swaying lithely in alternation as they threw their weight against the light ropes. Other blacks, in the long white robes and exquisitely worked white skull caps of the Swahili, glided noiselessly on bare feet, serving.

After dinner we sat out until midnight in the teakwood chairs of the upper gallery, staring through the arches into the black, mysterious night, for it was very hot, and we rather dreaded the necessary mosquito veils as likely to prove stuffy. The mosquitoes are few in Mombasa, but they are very deadly—very. At midnight the thermometer stood 87° F.

Our premonitions as to stuffiness were well justified. After a restless night we came awake at daylight to the sound of a fine row of some sort going on outside in the streets. Immediately we arose, threw aside the lattices, and hung out over the sill.

The chalk-white road stretched before us. Opposite was a public square, grown with brilliant flowers, and flowering trees. We could not doubt the cause of the trouble. An Indian on a bicycle, hurrying to his office, had knocked down a native child. Said child, quite naked, sat in the middle of the white dust and howled to rend the heavens—whenever he felt himself observed. If, however, the attention of the crowd happened for the moment to be engrossed with the babu, the injured one sat up straight and watched the row with interested, rolling, pickaninny eyes. A native policeman made the centre of a whirling, vociferating group. He was a fine-looking chap, straight and soldierly, dressed in red tarboosh, khaki coat bound close around the waist by yards and yards of broad red webbing, loose, short drawers of khaki, bare knees and feet, and blue puttees between. His manner was inflexible. The babu jabbered excitedly; telling, in all probability, how he was innocent of fault, was late for his work, etc. In vain. He had to go; also the kid, who now, seeing himself again an object of interest, recommended his howling. Then the babu began frantically to indicate members of the crowd whom he desired to retain as witnesses. Evidently not pleased with the prospect of appearing in court, those indicated promptly ducked and ran. The policeman as promptly pursued and collared them one by one. He was a long-legged policeman, and he ran well. The moment he laid hands on a fugitive, the latter collapsed; whereupon the policeman dropped him and took after another. The joke of it was that the one so abandoned did not try again to make off, but stayed as though he had been tagged at some game. Finally the whole lot, still vociferating, moved off down the white road.

For over an hour we hung from our window sill, thoroughly interested and amused by the varied life that deployed before our eyes. The morning seemed deliciously cool after the hot night, although the thermometer stood high. The sky was very blue, with big piled white clouds down near the horizon. Dazzling sun shone on the white road, the white buildings visible up and down the street, the white walls enclosing their gardens, and the greenery and colours of the trees within them. For from what we could see from our window we immediately voted tropical vegetation quite up to advertisement: whole trees of gaudy red or yellow or bright orange blossoms, flowering vines, flowering shrubs, peered over the walls or through the fences; and behind them rose great mangoes or the slenderer shafts of bananas and cocoanut palms.

Up and down wandered groups of various sorts of natives. A month later we would have been able to identify their different tribes and to know more about them; but now we wondered at them, as strange and picturesque peoples. They impressed us in general as being a fine lot of men, for they were of good physique, carried themselves well, and looked about them with a certain dignity and independence, a fine free pride of carriage and of step. This fact alone differentiated them from our own negroes; but, further, their features were in general much finer, and their skins of a clear mahogany beautiful in its satiny texture. Most—and these were the blackest—wore long white robes and fine openwork skull caps. They were the local race, the Swahili, had we but known it; the original "Zanzibari" who furnished Livingstone, Stanley, Speke, and the other early explorers with their men. Others, however, were much less "civilized." We saw one "Cook's tour from the jungle" consisting of six savages, their hair twisted into innumerable points, their ear lobes stretched to hang fairly to their shoulders, wearing only a rather neglectful blanket, adorned with polished wire, carrying war clubs and bright spears. They followed, with eyes and mouths open, a very sophisticated-looking city cousin in the usual white garments, swinging a jaunty, light bamboo cane. The cane seems to be a distinguishing mark of the leisured class. It not only means that you are not working, but also that you have no earthly desire to work.

About this time one of the hotel boys brought the inevitable chota-hazri—the tea and biscuits of early morning. For this once it was very welcome.

Our hotel proved to be on the direct line of freighting. There are no horses or draught animals in Mombasa; the fly is too deadly. Therefore all hauling is done by hand. The tiny tracks of the unique street car system run everywhere any one would wish to go; branching off even into private grounds and to the very front doors of bungalows situated far out of town. Each resident owns his own street car, just as elsewhere a man has his own carriage. There are, of course, public cars also, each with its pair of boys to push it; and also a number of rather decrepit rickshaws. As a natural corollary to the passenger traffic, the freighting also is handled by the blacks on large flat trucks with short guiding poles. These men

265

are quite naked save for a small loin cloth; are beautifully shaped; and glisten all over with perspiration shining in the sun. So fine is the texture of their skins, the softness of their colour—so rippling the play of muscles—that this shining perspiration is like a beautiful polish. They rush from behind, slowly and steadily, and patiently and unwaveringly, the most tremendous loads of the heaviest stuffs. When the hill becomes too steep for them, they turn their backs against the truck; and by placing one foot behind the other, a few inches at a time, they edge their burden up the slope.

The steering is done by one man at the pole or tongue in front. This individual also sets the key to the song by which in Africa all heavy labour is carried forward. He cries his wavering shrill-voiced chant; the toilers utter antiphony in low gruff tones. At a distance one hears only the wild high syncopated chanting; but as the affair draws slowly nearer, he catches the undertone of the responses. These latter are cast in the regular swing and rhythm of effort; but the steersman throws in his bit at odd and irregular intervals. Thus:

Headman (shrill): "Hay, ah mon!"

Pushers (gruff in rhythm): "Tunk!—tunk!—tunk!—" or:

Headman (and wavering minor chant): "Ah—nah—nee—e-e-e!"

Pushers (undertone): "Umbwa—jo-e! Um-bwa—jo—e!"

These wild and barbaric chantings—in the distance; near at hand; dying into distance again—slow, dogged, toilsome, came to be to us one of the typical features of the place.

After breakfast we put on our sun helmets and went forth curiously to view the town. We found it roughly divided into four quarters—the old Portuguese, the Arabic, the European, and the native. The Portuguese comprises the outer fringe next the water-front of the inner bay. It is very narrow of street, with whitewashed walls, balconies, and wonderful carven and studded doors. The business of the town is done here. The Arabic quarter lies back of it—a maze of narrow alleys winding aimlessly here and there between high white buildings, with occasionally the minarets and towers of a mosque. This district harboured, besides the upper-class Swahilis and Arabs, a large number of East Indians. Still back of this are thousands of the low grass, or mud and wattle huts of the natives, their roofs thatched with straw or palm. These are apparently arranged on little system. The small European population lives atop the sea bluffs beyond the old fort in the most attractive bungalows. This, the most desirable location of all, has remained open to them because heretofore the fierce wars with which Mombasa, "the Island of Blood," has been swept have made the exposed seaward lands impossible.

No idle occupation can be more fascinating than to wander about the mazes of this ancient town. The variety of race and occupation is something astounding. Probably the one human note that, everywhere persisting, draws the whole together is furnished by the water-carriers. Mombasa has no water system whatever. The entire supply is drawn from numberless picturesque wells scattered everywhere in the crowded centre, and distributed mainly in Standard Oil cans suspended at either end of a short pole. By dint of constant daily exercise, hauling water up from a depth and carrying it various distances, these men have developed the most beautifully powerful figures. They proceed at a half trot, the slender poles, with forty pounds at either end, seeming fairly to cut into their naked shoulders, muttering a word of warning to the loiterers at every other breath—semeelay! semeelay! No matter in what part of Mombasa you may happen to be, or at what hour of the day or night, you will meet these industrious little men trotting along under their burdens.

Everywhere also are the women, carrying themselves proudly erect, with a free swing of the hips. They wear invariably a single sheet of cotton cloth printed in blue or black with the most astonishing borders and spotty designs. This is drawn tight just above the breasts, leaving the shoulders and arms bare. Their hair is divided into perhaps a dozen parts running lengthwise of the head from the forehead to the nape of the neck, after the manner of the stripes on a watermelon. Each part then ends in a tiny twisted pigtail not over an inch long. The lobes of their ears have been stretched until they hold thick round disks about three inches in diameter, ornamented by concentric circles of different colours, with a red bull's eye for a centre. The outer edges of the ears are then further decorated with gold clasps set closely together. Many bracelets, necklaces, and armlets complete the get-up. They are big women, with soft velvety skins and a proud and haughty carriage—the counterparts of the men in the white robes and caps.

By the way, it may be a good place here to remark that these garments, and the patterned squares of cloth worn by the women, are invariably most spotlessly clean.

These, we learned, were the Swahilis, the ruling class, the descendants of the slave traders. Beside them are all sorts and conditions. Your true savage pleased his own fancy as to dress and personal adornment. The bushmen generally shaved the edges of their wool to leave a nice close-fitting natural skull cap, wore a single blanket draped from one shoulder, and carried a war club. The ear lobe seemed always to be stretched; sometimes sufficiently to have carried a pint bottle. Indeed, white marmalade jars seemed to be very popular wear. One ingenious person had acquired a dozen of the sort of safety pins used to fasten curtains to their rings. These he had snapped into the lobes, six on a side.

We explored for some time. One of the Swahilis attached himself to us so unobtrusively that before we knew it we had accepted him as guide. In that capacity he realized an ideal, for he never addressed a word to us, nor did he even stay in sight. We wandered along at our sweet will, dawdling as slowly as we pleased. The guide had apparently quite disappeared. Look where we would we could in no manner discover him. At the next corner we would pause, undecided as to what to do; there, in the middle distance, would stand our friend, smiling. When he was sure we had seen him, and were about to take the turn properly, he would disappear again. Convoyed in this pleasant fashion we wound and twisted up and down and round and about through the most appalling maze. We saw the native markets with their vociferating sellers seated cross-legged on tables behind piles of fruit or vegetables, while an equally vociferating crowd surged up and down the aisles. Gray parrots and little monkeys perched everywhere about. Billy gave one of the monkeys a banana. He peeled it exactly as a man would have done, smelt it critically, and threw it back at her in the most insulting fashion. We saw also the rows of Hindu shops open to the street, with their gaudily dressed children of blackened eyelids, their stolid dirty proprietors, and their women marvellous in bright silks and massive bangles. In the thatched native quarter were more of the fine Swahili women sitting cross-legged on the earth under low verandas, engaged in different handicrafts; and chickens; and many amusing naked children. We made friends with many of them, communicating by laughter and by signs, while our guide stood unobtrusively in the middle distance waiting for us to come on. Just at sunset he led us out to a great open space, with a tall palm in the centre of it and the gathering of a multitude of people. A mollah was clambering into a high scaffold built of poles, whence shortly he began to intone a long-drawn-out "Allah! Allah! il Allah!" The cocoanut palms cut the sunset, and the boabab trees—the fat, lazy boababs—looked more monstrous than ever. We called our guide and conferred on him the munificent sum of sixteen and a half cents; with which, apparently much pleased, he departed. Then slowly we wandered back to the hotel.

---

## PART II.

THE SHIMBA HILLS.

---

### IX.

A TROPICAL JUNGLE.

Many months later, and after adventures elsewhere described, besides others not relevant for the moment, F., an Englishman, and I returned to Mombasa. We came from some hundred odd miles in the interior where we had been exploring the sources and the course of the Tsavo River. Now our purpose was to penetrate into the low, hot, wooded country along the coast known as the Shimba Hills in quest of a rare beast called the sable antelope.

These hills could be approached in one of two ways—by crossing the harbour, and then marching two days afoot; or by voyaging up to the very end of one of the long arms of the sea that extend many miles inland. The latter involved dhows, dependence on uncertain winds, favourable tides, and a heap of good luck. It was less laborious but most uncertain. At this stage of the plan the hotel manager came forward with the offer of a gasoline launch, which we gladly accepted.

We embarked about noon, storing our native carriers and effects aboard a dhow hired for the occasion. This we purposed towing. A very neatly uniformed Swahili bearing on his stomach a highly-polished brass label as big as a door plate—"Harbour Police"—threw duck fists over what he called overloading the boat. He knew very little about boats, but threw very competent duck fists. As we did know something about boats, we braved unknown consequences by disregarding him utterly. No consequences ensued—unless perhaps to his own health. When everything was aboard, that dhow was pretty well down, but still well afloat. Then we white men took our places in the launch.

This was a long narrow affair with a four-cylinder thirty-horsepower engine. As she possessed no speed gears, she had either to plunge ahead full speed or come to a stop; there were no compromises. Her steering was managed by a tiller instead of a wheel, so that a mere touch sufficed to swerve her ten feet from her course. As the dhow was in no respects built on such nervous lines, she did occasionally some fancy and splashing curves.

The pilot of the launch turned out to be a sandy-haired Yankee who had been catching wild animals for Barnum and Bailey's circus. While waiting for his ship, he, being a proverbial handy Yankee, had taken on this job. He became quite interested in telling us this, and at times forgot his duties at the tiller. Then that racing-launch would take a wild swoop; the clumsy old dhow astern would try vainly, with much spray and dangerous careening, to follow; the compromise course would all but upset her; the spray would fly; the safari boys would take their ducking; the boat boys would yell and dance and lean frantically against the two long sweeps with which they tried to steer. In this wild and untrammelled fashion we careered up the bay, too interested in our own performances to pay much attention to the scenery. The low shores, with their cocoanut groves gracefully rising above the mangrove tangle, slipped by, and the distant blue Shimba Hills came nearer.

After a while we turned into a narrower channel with a good many curves and a quite unknown depth of water. Down this we whooped at the full speed of our thirty-horsepower engine. Occasional natives, waist deep and fishing, stared after us open-eyed. The Yankee ventured a guess as to how hard she would hit on a mudbank. She promptly proved his guess a rank underestimate by doing so. We fell in a heap on the bottom. The dhow bore down on us with majestic momentum. The boat boys leaned frantically on their sweeps, and managed just to avoid us. The dhow also rammed the mudbank. A dozen reluctant boys hopped overboard and pushed us off. We pursued our merry way again. On either hand now appeared fish weirs of plaited coco fibre; which, being planted in the shallows, helped us materially to guess at the channel. Naked men, up to their shoulders in the water, attended to some mysterious need of the nets, or emerged dripping and sparkling from the water with baskets of fish atop their heads. The channel grew even narrower, and the mudbanks more frequent. We dodged a dozen in our headlong course. Our local guide, a Swahili in tarboosh and a beautiful saffron robe, showed signs of strong excitement. We were to stop, he said, around the next bend; and at this rate we never could stop. The Yankee remarked, superfluously, that it would be handy if this dod-blistered engine had a clutch; adding, as an afterthought, that no matter how long he stayed in the tropics his nose peeled. We asked what we should do if we over-carried our prospective landing-place. He replied that the dod-blistered thing did have a reverse. While thus conversing we shot around a corner into a complete cul-de-sac! Everything was shut off hastily, and an instant later we and the dhow smashed up high and dry on a cozy mud beach! We drew a deep breath and looked around us.

Mangrove thicket to the edge of the slimy ooze; trees behind—that was all we could see. We gave our attention to the business of getting our men, our effects, and ourselves ashore. The ooze proved to be just above knee deep. The porters had a fearful and floundering time, and received much obvious comment from us perched in the bow of the launch. Finally everything was debarked. F. and I took off our boots; but our gunbearers expressed such horror at the mere thought of our plunging into the mud, that we dutifully climbed them pick-a-back and were carried. The hard shell beach was a hundred feet away, occupying a little recess where the persistent tough mangroves drew back. From it led a narrow path through the thicket. We waved and shouted a farewell to the crews of the launch and the dhow.

The path for a hundred feet was walled in by the mangroves through which scuttled and rattled the big land crabs. Then suddenly we found ourselves in a story-book tropical paradise. The tall coco palms rose tufted above everything; the fans of the younger palms waved below; bananas thrust the banners of their broad leaves wherever they could find space; creepers and vines flung the lush luxuriance of their greenery over all the earth and into the depths of all the half-guessed shadows. In no direction could one see unobstructed farther than twenty feet, except straight up; and there one could see just as far as the tops of the palms. It was like being in a room—a green, hot, steamy, lovely room. Very bright-coloured birds that ought really to have been at home in their cages fluttered about.

We had much vigorous clearing to do to make room for our tents. By the time the job was finished we were all pretty hot. Several of the boys made vain attempts to climb for nuts, but without success. We had brought them with us from the interior, where cocoanuts do not grow; and they did not understand the method. They could swarm up the tall slim stems all right, but could not manage to get through the downward-pointing spikes of the dead leaves. F. tried and failed, to the great amusement of the men, but to the greater amusement of myself. I was a wise person, and lay on my back on a canvas cot, so it was not much bother to look up and enjoy life. Not to earn absolutely the stigma of laziness, I tried to shoot some nuts down. This did not work either, for the soft, spongy stems closed around the bullet holes. Then a little wizened monkey of a Swahili porter, having watched our futile performances with interest, nonchalantly swarmed up; in some mysterious manner he wriggled through the defences, and perched in the top, whence he dropped to us a dozen big green nuts. Our men may not have been much of a success at climbing for nuts; but they were passed masters at the art of opening them. Three or four clips from their awkward swordlike pangas, and we were each presented with a clean, beautiful, natural goblet brimming full of a refreshing drink.

About this time a fine figure of a man drifted into camp. He was very smooth-skinned, very dignified, very venerable. He was pure Swahili, though of the savage branch of that race, and had none of the negro type of countenance. In fact, so like was he in face, hair, short square beard and genial dignity to a certain great-uncle of mine that it was very hard to remember that he had on only a small strip of cloth, that he was cherishing as a great treasure a piece of soap box he had salvaged from the shore, and that his skin was red chocolate. I felt inclined to talk to him as to an intellectual equal, especially as he had a fine resonant bass voice that in itself lent his remarks some importance. However, I gave him two ordinary wood screws, showed him how they screwed in and out, and left him happy.

After supper the moon rose, casting shadows of new and unknown shapes through this strangely new and unknown forest. A thin white mist ascending everywhere from the soil tempered but could not obscure the white brilliance. The thermometer stood now only at 82°, but the dripping tropical sweat-bath in which our camp was pitched considerably raised the sensible heat. A bird with a most diabolical shrieking note cursed in the shadows. Another, a pigeon-like creature, began softly, and continued to repeat in diminishing energy until it seemed to have run down, like a piece of clockwork.

Our way next morning led for some time through this lovely but damp jungle. Then we angled up the side of a hill to emerge into the comparatively open country atop what we Westerners would call a "hog's back"—a long narrow spurlike ridge mounting slowly to the general elevation of the main hills. Here were high green bushes, with little free open passages between them, and occasionally meadow-like openings running down the slopes on one side or the other. Before us, some miles distant, were the rounded blue hills.

We climbed steadily. It was still very early morning, but already the day was hot. Pretty soon we saw over the jungle to the gleaming waters of the inlet, and then to the sea. Our "hog's back" led us past a ridge of the hills, and before we knew it we had been deposited in a shallow valley three or four miles wide between parallel ridges; the said valley being at a considerable elevation, and itself diversified with rolling hills, ravines, meadow land, and wide flats. On many of the ridges were scattered cocoanut palms, and occasional mango groves, while many smokes attested the presence of natives.

These we found in shambas or groups of little farms, huddled all together, with wilderness and brush and trees, or the wide open green grass lawn between. The houses were very large and neat-looking. They were constructed quite ingeniously from coco branches. Each branch made one mat. The leaves were all brought over to the same side of the stem, and then plaited. The resulting mat was then six or seven feet long by from twelve to sixteen inches broad, and could be used for a variety of purposes. Indeed, we found Melville's chapter in "Typhee" as to the various uses of the cocoanut palm by no means exaggerated. The nuts, leaves, and fibre supplied every conceivable human want.

The natives were a pleasant, friendly, good-looking lot. In fact, so like was their cast of countenance to that of the white-skinned people we were accustomed to see that we had great difficulty in realizing that they were mere savages, costume—or lack of it—to the contrary notwithstanding. Under a huge mango tree two were engaged in dividing a sheep. Sixty or seventy others stood solemnly around watching. It may have been a religious ceremony, for all I know; but the affair looked to be about two parts business to sixty of idle and cheerful curiosity. We stopped and talked to them a little, chaffed the pretty girls—they were really pretty—and marched on.

About noon our elegant guide stopped, struck an attitude, and pointed with his silver-headed rattan cane.

"This," said he, "is where we must camp."

We marched through a little village. A family party sat beneath the veranda of a fine building—a very old wrinkled couple; two stalwart beautiful youths; a young mother suckling her baby; two young girls; and eight or ten miscellaneous and naked youngsters. As the rest of the village appeared to be empty, I imagined this to be the caretaker's family, and the youngsters to belong to others. We stopped and spoke, were answered cheerfully, suggested that we might like to buy chickens, and offered a price. Instantly with a whoop of joy the lot of them were afoot. The fowl waited for no further intimations of troublous times, but fled squawking. They had been there before. So had our hosts; for inside a minute they had returned, each with a chicken—and a broad grin.

After due payment we proceeded on a few hundred yards, and pitched camp beneath two huge mango trees.

Besides furnishing one of the most delicious of the tropical fruits, the mango is also one of the most beautiful of trees. It is tall, spreads very wide, and its branches sweep to within ten feet of the ground. Its perfect symmetry combined with the size and deep green of its leaves causes it to resemble, from a short distance, a beautiful green hill. Beneath its umbrella one finds dense shade, unmottled by a single ray of sunlight, so that one can lie under it in full confidence. For, parenthetically, even a single ray of this tropical sunlight is to the unprotected a very dangerous thing. But the leaves of the mango have this peculiarity, which distinguishes it from all other trees—namely, that they grow only at the very ends of the small twigs and branches. As these, of course, grow only at the ends of the big limbs, it follows that from beneath the mango looks like a lofty green dome, a veritable pantheon of the forest.

We made our camp under one of these trees; gave ourselves all the space we could use; and had plenty left over—five tents and a cook camp, with no crowding. It was one of the pleasantest camps I ever saw. Our green dome overhead protected us absolutely from the sun; high sweet grass grew all about us; the breeze wandered lazily up from the distant Indian Ocean. Directly before our tent door the slope fell gently away through a sparse cocoanut grove whose straight stems panelled our view, then rose again to the clear-cut outline of a straight ridge opposite. The crest of this was sentinelled by tall scattered cocoanut trees, the "bursting star" pyrotechnic effect of their tops being particularly fine against the sky.

After a five hours' tropical march uphill we were glad to sit under our green dome, to look at our view, to enjoy the little breeze, and to drink some of the cocoanuts our friends the villagers brought in.

---

## X.

### THE SABLE.

About three o'clock I began to feel rested and ambitious. Therefore I called up our elegant guide and Memba Sasa, and set out on my first hunt for sable. F. was rather more done up by the hard morning, and so did not go along. The guide wore still his red tarboosh, his dark short jacket, his saffron yellow nether garment—it was not exactly a skirt—and his silver-headed rattan cane. The only change he made was to tuck up the skirt, leaving his long legs bare. It hardly seemed altogether a suitable costume for hunting; but he seemed to know what he was about.

We marched along ridges, and down into ravines, and across gulleys choked with brush. Horrible thickets alternated with and occasionally surrounded open green meadows hanging against the side hills. As we proceeded, the country became rougher, the ravines more precipitous. We struggled up steep hills, fairly bucking our way through low growth that proved all but impenetrable. The idea was to find a sable feeding in one of the little open glades; but whenever I allowed myself to think of the many adverse elements of the game, the chances seemed very slim. It took a half-hour to get from one glade to the next; there were thousands of glades. The sable is a rare shy animal that likes dense cover fully as well if not better than the open. Sheer rank bull luck alone seemed the only hope. And as I felt my strength going in that vicious struggle against heavy brush and steep hills, I began to have very strong doubts indeed as to that sable.

For it was cruel, hard work. In this climate one hailed a car or a rickshaw to do an errand two streets away, and considered oneself quite a hero if one took a leisurely two-mile stroll along the cliff heads at sunset. Here I was, after a five-hour uphill march, bucking into brush and through country that would be considered difficult going even in Canada. At the end of twenty minutes my every garment was not wringing but dripping wet, so that when I carried my rifle over my arm water ran down the barrel and off the muzzle in a steady stream. After a bit of this my knees began to weaken;

and it became a question of saving energy, of getting along somehow, and of leaving the actual hunting to Memba Sasa and the guide. If they had shown me a sable, I very much doubt if I could have hit it.

However, we did not see one, and I staggered into camp at dusk pretty well exhausted. From the most grateful hot bath and clean clothes I derived much refreshment. Shortly I was sitting in my canvas chair, sipping a cocoanut, and describing the condition of affairs to F., who was naturally very curious as to how the trick was done.

"Now," I concluded, "I know just about what I can and what I cannot do. Three days more of this sort of work will feed me up. If we do not run across a sable in that time, I'm afraid we don't get any."

"Two days will do for me," said he.

We called up the guide and questioned him closely. He seemed quite confident; and asserted that in this country sable were found, when they were found at all, which was not often. They must be discovered in the small grassy openings. We began to understand why so very few people get sable.

We dismissed the guide, and sat quietly smoking in the warm soft evening. The air was absolutely still save for various night insects and birds, and the weird calling of natives across the valleys. Far out towards the sea a thunderstorm flashed; and after a long interval the rumblings came to us. So very distant was it that we paid it little attention, save as an interesting background to our own still evening. Almost between sentences of our slow conversation, however, it rushed up to the zenith, blotting out the stars. The tall palms began to sway and rustle in the forerunning breeze. Then with a swoop it was upon us, a tempest of fury. We turned in; and all night long the heavy deluges of rain fell, roaring like surf on an unfriendly coast.

By morning this had fallen to a light, steady drizzle in which we started off quite happily. In this climate one likes to get wet. The ground was sodden and deep with muck. Within a mile of camp we saw many fresh buffalo tracks.

This time we went downhill and still downhill through openings among batches of great forest trees. The new leaves were just coming out in pinks and russets, so that the effect at a little distance was almost precisely that of our autumn foliage in its duller phases. So familiar were made some of the low rounded knolls that for an instant we were respectively back in the hills of Surrey or Michigan, and told each other so.

Thus we moved slowly out from the dense cover to the grass openings. Far over on another ridge F. called my attention to something jet-black and indeterminate. In another country I should have named it as a charred log on an old pine burning, for that was precisely what it looked like. We glanced at it casually through our glasses. It was a sable buck lying down right out in the open. He was black and sleek, and we could make out his sweeping scimitar horns.

Memba Sasa and the Swahili dropped flat on their faces while F. and I crawled slowly and cautiously through the mud until we had gained the cover of a shallow ravine that ran in the beast's general direction. Noting carefully a certain small thicket as landmark, we stooped and moved as fast as we could down to that point of vantage. There we cautiously parted the grasses and looked. The sable had disappeared. The place where he had been lying was plainly to be identified, and there was no cover save a tiny bush between two and three feet high. We were quite certain he had neither seen nor winded us. Either he had risen and fled forward into the ravine up which we had made our stalk, or else he had entered the small thicket. F. agreed to stay on watch where he was, while I slipped back and examined the earth to leeward of the thicket.

I had hardly crawled ten yards, however, before the gentle snapping of F.'s fingers recalled me to his side.

"He's behind that bush," he whispered in my ear.

I looked. The bush was hardly large enough to conceal a setter dog, and the sable is somewhat larger than our elk. Nevertheless F. insisted that the animal was standing behind it, and that he had caught the toss of its head. We lay still for some time, while the soft, warm rain drizzled down on us, our eyes riveted on the bush. And then we caught the momentary flash of curved horns as the sable tossed his head. It seemed incredible even then that the tiny bush should conceal so large a beast. As a matter of fact we later found that the bush grew on a slight elevation, behind which was a depression. In this the sable stood, patiently enduring the drizzle.

We waited some time in hopes he would move forward a foot or so; but apparently he had selected his loafing place with care, and liked it. The danger of a shift of wind was always present. Finally I slipped back over the brink of the ravine, moved three yards to the left, and crawled up through the tall dripping grass to a new position behind a little bush. Cautiously raising my head, I found I could see plainly the sable's head and part of his shoulders. My position was cramped and out of balance for offhand shooting; but I did my best, and heard the loud plunk of the hit. The sable made off at a fast though rather awkward gallop, wheeled for an instant a hundred yards farther on, received another bullet in the shoulder, and disappeared over the brow of the hill. We raced over the top to get in another shot, and found him stone dead.

He was a fine beast, jet-black in coat, with white markings on the face, red-brown ears, and horns sweeping up and back scimitar fashion. He stood four feet and six inches at the shoulder, and his horns were the second best ever shot in British East Africa. This beast has been described by Heller as a new subspecies, and named Rooseveltii. His description was based upon an immature buck and a doe shot by Kermit Roosevelt. The determination of subspecies on so slight evidence seems to me unscientific in the extreme. While the immature males do exhibit the general brown tone relied on by Mr. Heller, the mature buck differs in no essential from the tropical sable. I find the alledged subspecies is not accepted by European scientists.

A MARCH ALONG THE COAST.

With a most comfortable feeling that my task was done, that suddenly the threatening clouds of killing work had been cleared up, I was now privileged to loaf and invite my soul on this tropical green hilltop while poor F. put in the days trying to find another sable. Every morning he started out before daylight. I could see the light of his lantern outside the tent; and I stretched myself in the luxurious consciousness that I should hear no deprecating but insistent "hodie" from my boy until I pleased to invite it. In the afternoon or evening F. would return, quite exhausted and dripping, with only the report of new country traversed. No sable; no tracks of sable; no old signs, even, of sable. Gradually it was borne in on me how lucky I was to have come upon my magnificent specimen so promptly and in such favourable circumstances.

A leisurely breakfast alone, with the sun climbing; then the writing of notes, a little reading, and perhaps a stroll to the village or along the top of the ridge. At the heat of noon a siesta with a cool cocoanut at my elbow. The view was beautiful on all sides; our great tree full of birds; the rising and dying winds in the palms like the gathering oncoming rush of the rains. From mountain to mountain sounded the wild, far-carrying ululations of the natives, conveying news or messages across the wide jungle. Towards sunset I wandered out in the groves, enjoying the many bright flowers, the tall, sweet grasses, and the cocoa-palms against the sky. Piles of cocoanuts lay on the ground, covered each with a leaf plaited in a peculiarly individual manner to indicate ownership. Small boys, like little black imps, clung naked half-way up the slim trunks of the palms, watching me bright-eyed above the undergrowth. In all directions, crossing and recrossing, ran a maze of beaten paths. Each led somewhere, but it would require the memory of—well, of a native, to keep all their destinations in mind.

I used to follow some of them to their ending in little cocoa-leaf houses on the tops of knolls or beneath mangoes; and would talk with the people. They were very grave and very polite, and seemed to be living out their lives quite correctly according to their conceptions. Again, it was borne in on me that these people are not stumbling along the course of evolution in our footsteps, but have gone as far in their path as we have in ours; that they have reached at least as complete a correspondence with their environment as we with our own.

If F. had not returned by the time I reached camp, I would seat myself in my canvas chair, and thence dispense justice, advice, or medical treatment. If none of these things seemed demanded, I smoked my pipe. To me one afternoon came a big-framed, old, dignified man, with the heavy beard, the noble features, the high forehead, and the blank statue eyes of the blind Homer. He was led by a very small, very bright-eyed naked boy. At some twenty feet distance he squatted down cross-legged before me. For quite five minutes he sat there silent, while I sat in my camp chair, smoked and waited. At last he spoke in a rolling deep bass voice rich and vibrating—a delight to hear.

"Jambo (greeting)!" said he.

"Jambo!" I replied mildly.

Again a five-minute silence. I had begun reading, and had all but forgotten his presence.

"Jambo bwana (greeting, master)!" he rolled out.

"Jambo!" I repeated.

The same dignified, unhasting pause.

"Jambo bwana m'kubwa (greeting, great master)!"

"Jambo!" quoth I, and went on reading. The sun was dropping, but the old man seemed in no hurry.

"Jambo bwana m'kubwa sana (greeting, most mighty master)!" he boomed at last.

"Jambo!" said I.

This would seem to strike the superlative, and I expected now that he would state his business, but the old man had one more shot in his locker.

"Jambo bwana m'kubwa kabeesa sana (greeting, mightiest possible master)!" it came.

Then in due course he delicately hinted that a gift of tobacco would not come amiss.

F. returned a trifle earlier than usual, to admit that his quest was hopeless, that his physical forces were for the time being at an end, and that he was willing to go home.

Accordingly very early next morning we set out by the glimmer of a lantern, hoping to get a good start on our journey before the heat of the day became too severe. We did gain something, but performed several unnecessary loops and semicircles in the maze of beaten paths before we finally struck into one that led down the slope towards the sea. Shortly after the dawn came up "like thunder" in its swiftness, followed almost immediately by the sun.

Our way now led along the wide flat between the seashore and the Shimba Hills, in which we had been hunting. A road ten feet wide and innocent of wheels ran with obstinate directness up and down the slight contours and through the bushes and cocoanut groves that lay in its path. So mathematically straight was it that only when perspective closed it in, or when it dropped over the summit of a little rise, did the eye lose the effect of its interminability. The country through which this road led was various—open bushy veld with sparse trees, dense jungle, cocoanut groves, tall and cool. In the shadows of the latter were the thatched native villages. To the left always ran the blue Shimba Hills; and far away to the right somewhere we heard the grumbling of the sea.

Every hundred yards or so we met somebody. Even thus early the road was thronged. By far the majority were the almost naked natives of the district, pleasant, brown-skinned people with good features. They carried things. These things varied from great loads balanced atop to dainty impromptu baskets woven of cocoa-leaves and containing each a single cocoanut. They smiled on us, returned our greeting, and stood completely aside to let us pass. Other wayfarers were of more importance. Small groups of bearded dignitaries, either upper-class Swahili or pure Arabs, strolled slowly along, apparently with limitless leisure, but evidently bound somewhere, nevertheless. They replied to our greetings with great dignity. Once, also, we overtook a small detachment of Sudanese troops moving. They were scattered over several miles of road. A soldier, most impressive and neat in khaki and red tarboosh and sash; then two or three of his laughing, sleek women, clad in the thin, patterned "'Mericani," glittering with gold ornaments; then a half dozen ragged porters carrying official but battered painted wooden kit boxes, or bags, or miscellaneous curious plunder; then more troopers; and so on for miles. They all drew aside for us most respectfully; and the soldiers saluted, very smart and military.

Under the broad-spreading mangoes near the villages we came upon many open markets in full swing. Each vendor squatted on his heels behind his wares, while the purchasers or traders wandered here and there making offers. The actual commerce compared with the amount of laughing, joking, shrieking joy of the occasion as one to a thousand.

Generally three or four degenerate looking dirty East Indians slunk about, very crafty, very insinuating, very ready and skilful to take what advantages they could. I felt a strong desire to kick every one of them out from these joyful concourses of happy people. Generally we sat down for a while in these markets, and talked to the people a little, and perhaps purchased some of the delicious fruit. They had a small delicate variety of banana, most wonderful, the like of which I have seen nowhere else. We bought forty of these for a coin worth about eight cents. Besides fruit they offered cocoanuts in all forms, grain, woven baskets, small articles of handicraft—and fish. The latter were farther from the sea than they should have been! These occasional halts greatly refreshed us for more of that endless road.

For all this time we were very hot. As the sun mounted, the country fairly steamed. From the end of my rifle barrel, which I carried across my forearm, a steady trickle of water dripped into the road. We neither of us had a dry stitch on us, and our light garments clung to us thoroughly wet through. At first we tried the military method, and marched fifty minutes to rest ten, but soon discovered that twenty-five minutes' work to five minutes off was more practical. The sheer weight of the sun was terrific; after we had been exposed to it for any great length of time—as across several wide open spaces—we entered the steaming shade of the jungle with gratitude. At the end of seven hours, however, we most unexpectedly came through a dense cocoanut grove plump on the banks of the harbour at Kilindini.

Here, after making arrangements for the transport of our safari, when it should arrive, we entrusted ourselves to a small boy and a cranky boat. An hour later, clad in tropical white, with cool drinks at our elbows, we sat in easy-chairs on the veranda of the Mombasa Club.

The clubhouse is built on a low cliff at the water's edge. It looks across the blue waters of the bay to a headland crowned with cocoa-palms, and beyond the headland to the Indian Ocean. The cool trades sweep across that veranda. We idly watched a lone white oarsman pulling strongly against the wind through the tide rips, evidently bent on exercise. We speculated on the incredible folly of wanting exercise; and forgot him. An hour later a huge saffron yellow squall rose from China 'cross the way, filled the world with an unholy light, lashed the reluctant sea to white-caps, and swooped screaming on the cocoa-palms. Police boats to rescue the idiot oarsman! Much minor excitement! Great rushing to and fro! We continued to sit in our lounging chairs, one hand on our cool long drinks.

---

## XII.

THE FIRE.

We were very tired, so we turned in early. W Unfortunately, our rooms were immediately over the billiard room, where a bibulous and cosmopolitan lot were earnestly endeavouring to bolster up by further proof the fiction that a white man cannot retain his health in the tropics. The process was pretty rackety, and while it could not keep us awake, it prevented us from falling thoroughly asleep. At length, and suddenly, the props of noise fell away from me, and I sank into a grateful, profound abyss.

Almost at once, however, I was dragged back to consciousness. Mohammed stood at my bedside.

"Bwana," he proffered to my rather angry inquiry, "all the people have gone to the fire. It is a very large fire. I thought you would like to see it."

I glanced out of the window at the reddening sky, thrust my feet into a pair of slippers, and went forth in my pyjamas to see what I could see.

We threaded our way through many narrow dark and deserted streets, beneath balconies that overhung, past walls over which nodded tufted palms, until a loud and increasing murmuring told us we were nearing the centre of disturbance. Shortly, we came to the outskirts of the excited crowd, and beyond them saw the red furnace glow.

"Semeelay! Semeelay!" warned Mohammed authoritatively; and the bystanders, seeing a white face, gave me passage.

All of picturesque Mombasa was afoot—Arabs, Swahilis, Somalis, savages, Indians—the whole lot. They moved restlessly in the narrow streets; they hung over the edges of balconies; they peered from barred windows; interested dark faces turned up everywhere in the flickering light. One woman, a fine, erect, biblical figure, stood silhouetted on a flat housetop and screamed steadily. I thought she must have at least one baby in the fire, but it seems she was only excited.

The fire was at present confined to two buildings, in which it was raging fiercely. Its spread, however, seemed certain; and, as it was surrounded by warehouses of valuable goods, moving was in full swing. A frantic white man stood at the low doorway of one of these dungeon-like stores hastening the movements of an unending string of porters. As each emerged bearing a case on his shoulder, the white man urged him to a trot. I followed up the street to see where these valuables were being taken, and what were the precautions against theft. Around the next corner, it seemed. As each excited perspiring porter trotted up, he heaved his burden from his head or his shoulders, and promptly scampered back for another load. They were loyal and zealous men; but their headpieces were deficient inside. For the burdens that they saved from the fire happened to be cases of gin in bottles. At least, it was in bottles until the process of saving had been completed. Then it trickled merrily down the gutter. I went back and told the frantic white man about it. He threw up both hands to heaven and departed.

By dodging from street to street Mohammed and I succeeded in circling the whole disturbance, and so came at length to a public square. Here was a vast throng, and a very good place, so I climbed atop a rescued bale of cotton the better to see.

Mombasa has no water system, but a wonderful corps of water-carriers. These were in requisition to a man. They disappeared down through the wide gates of the customs enclosure, their naked, muscular, light-brown bodies gleaming with sweat, their Standard Oil cans dangling merrily at the ends of slender poles. A moment later they emerged, the cans full of salt water from the bay, the poles seeming fairly to butt into their bare shoulders as they teetered along at their rapid, swaying, burdened gait.

The moment they entered the square they were seized upon from a dozen different sides. There was no system at all. Every owner of property was out for himself, and intended to get as much of the precious water as he could. The poor carriers were pulled about, jerked violently here and there, besought, commanded, to bring their loads to one or the other of the threatened premises. Vociferations, accusations, commands arose to screams. One old graybeard occupied himself by standing on tiptoe and screeching, "Maji! maji! maji!" at the top of his voice, as though that added anything to the visible supply. The water-carrier of the moment disappeared in a swirl of excited contestants. He was attending strictly to business, looking neither to right nor to left, pushing forward as steadily as he could, gasping mechanically his customary warning, "Semeelay! Semeelay!" Somehow, eventually, he and his comrades must have got somewhere; for after an interval he returned with empty buckets. Then every blessed fool of a property owner took a whack at his bare shoulders as he passed, shrieking hysterically, "Haya! haya! pesi! pesi!" and the like to men already doing their best. It was a grand sight!

In the meantime the fire itself was roaring away. The old graybeard suddenly ceased crying "maji," and darted forward to where I stood on the bale of cotton. With great but somewhat flurried respect he begged me to descend. I did so, somewhat curious as to what he might be up to, for the cotton was at least two hundred feet from the fire. Immediately he began to tug and heave; the bale was almost beyond his strength; but after incredible exertions he lifted one side of it, poised it for a moment, got his shoulder under it, and rolled it over once. Then he darted away and resumed his raucous cry for water. I climbed back again. Thrice more, at intervals, he repeated this performance. The only result was to daub with mud every possible side of that bale. I hope it was his property.

You must remember that I was observing the heavy artillery of the attack on the conflagration. Individual campaigns were everywhere in progress. I saw one man standing on the roof of a threatened building. He lowered slowly, hand over hand, a small tea-kettle at the end of a string. This was filled by a friend in the street, whereupon the man hauled it up again, slowly, hand over hand, and solemnly dashed its contents into the mouth of the furnace. Thousands of other men on roofs, in balconies, on the street, were doing the same thing. Some had ordinary cups which they filled a block away! The limit of efficiency was a pail. Nobody did anything in concert with anybody else. The sight of these thousands of little midgets each with his teacup, or his teapot, or his tin pail, throwing each his mite of water—for which he had to walk a street or so—into the ravening roaring furnace of flame was as pathetic or as comical as you please. They did not seem to have a show in the world.

Nevertheless, to my vast surprise, the old system of the East triumphed at last. The system of the East is that if you get *enough* labour you can accomplish anything. Little by little those thousands of tea kettles of water had their aggregate effect. The flames fed themselves out and died down leaving the contiguous buildings unharmed save for a little scorching. In two hours all was safe, and I returned to the hotel, having enjoyed myself hugely. I had, however, in the interest and excitement, forgotten how deadly is the fever of Mombasa. Midnight in pyjamas did the business; and shortly I paid well for the fun.

---

*PART III.*

NAIROBI.

---

273

UP FROM THE COAST.

Nairobi is situated at the far edge of the great Athi Plains and just below a range of hills. It might about as well have been anywhere else, and perhaps better a few miles back in the higher country. Whether the funny little narrow-gauge railroad exists for Nairobi, or Nairobi for the railroad, it would be difficult to say. Between Mombasa and this interior placed-to-order town, certainly, there is nothing, absolutely nothing, either in passengers or freight, to justify building the line. That distance is, if I remember it correctly, about three hundred and twenty miles. A dozen or so names of stations appear on the map. These are water tanks, telegraph stations, or small groups of tents in which dwell black labourers— on the railroad.

The way climbs out from the tropical steaming coast belt to and across the high scrub desert, and then through lower rounded hills to the plains. On the desert is only dense thorn brush—and a possibility that the newcomer, if he looks very closely, may to his excitement see his first game in Africa. This is a stray duiker or so, tiny grass antelopes a foot high. Also in this land is thirst; so that alongside the locomotives, as they struggle up grade, in bad seasons, run natives to catch precious drops. An impalpable red dust sifts through and into everything. When a man descends at Voi for dinner he finds his fellow-travellers have changed complexion. The pale clerk from indoor Mombasa has put on a fine healthy sunburn; and the company in general present a rich out-of-doors bloom. A chance dab with a white napkin comes away like fresh paint, however.

You clamber back into the compartment, with its latticed sun shades and its smoked glass windows; you let down the narrow canvas bunk; you unfold your rug, and settle yourself for repose. It is a difficult matter. Everything you touch is gritty. The air is close and stifling, like the smoke-charged air of a tunnel. If you try to open a window you are suffocated with more of the red dust. At last you fall into a doze; to awaken nearly frozen! The train has climbed into what is, after weeks of the tropics, comparative cold; and if you have not been warned to carry wraps, you are in danger of pneumonia.

The gray dawn comes, and shortly, in the sudden tropical fashion, the full light. You look out on a wide smiling grass country, with dips and swales, and brushy river bottoms, and long slopes and hills thrusting up in masses from down below the horizon, and singly here and there in the immensities nearer at hand. The train winds and doubles on itself up the gentle slopes and across the imperceptibly rising plains. But the interest is not in these wide prospects, beautiful and smiling as they may be, but in the game. It is everywhere. Far in the distance the herds twinkle, half guessed in the shimmer of the bottom lands or dotting the sides of the hills. Nearer at hand it stares as the train rumbles and sways laboriously past. Occasionally it even becomes necessary to whistle aside some impertinent kongoni that has placed himself between the metals! The newcomer has but a theoretical knowledge at best of all these animals; and he is intensely interested in identifying the various species. The hartebeeste and the wildebeeste he learns quickly enough, and of course the zebra and the giraffe are unmistakable; but the smaller gazelles are legitimate subjects for discussion. The wonder of the extraordinary abundance of these wild animals mounts as the hours slip by. At the stops for water or for orders the passengers gather from their different compartments to detail excitedly to each other what they have seen. There is always an honest superenthusiast who believes he has seen rhinoceroses, lions, or leopards. He is looked upon with envy by the credulous, and with exasperation by all others.

So the little train puffs and tugs along. Suddenly it happens on a barbed wire fence, and immediately after enters the town of Nairobi. The game has persisted right up to that barbed wire fence.

The station platform is thronged with a heterogeneous multitude of people. The hands of a dozen raggetty black boys are stretched out for luggage. The newcomer sees with delight a savage with a tin can in his stretched ear lobe; another with a set of wooden skewers set fanwise around the edge of the ear; he catches a glimpse of a beautiful naked creature very proud, very decorated with beads and heavy polished wire. Then he is ravished away by the friend, or agent, or hotel representative who has met him, and hurried out through the gates between the impassive and dignified Sikh sentries to the cab. I believe nobody but the newcomer ever rides in the cab; and then but once, from the station to the hotel. After that he uses rickshaws. In fact it is probable that the cab is maintained for the sole purpose of giving the newcomer a grand and impressive entrance. This brief fleeting quarter hour of glory is unique and passes. It is like crossing the Line, or the first kiss, something that in its nature cannot be repeated.

The cab was once a noble vehicle, compounded of opulent curves, with a very high driver's box in front, a little let-down bench, and a deep, luxurious, shell-shaped back seat, reclining in which one received the adulation of the populace. That was in its youth. Now in its age the varnish is gone; the upholstery of the back seat frayed; the upholstery of the small seat lacking utterly, so that one sits on bare boards. In place of two dignifiedly spirited fat white horses, it is drawn by two very small mules in a semi-detached position far ahead. And how it rattles!

Between the station and the hotel at Nairobi is a long straight wide well-made street, nearly a mile long, and bordered by a double row of young eucalyptus. These latter have changed the main street of Nairobi from the sunbaked array of galvanized houses described by travellers of a half dozen years back to a thoroughfare of great charm. The iron houses and stores are now in a shaded background; and the attention is freed to concentrate on the vivid colouring, the incessant movement, the great interest of the people moving to and fro. When I left Nairobi the authorities were considering the removal of these trees, because one row of them had been planted slightly within the legal limits of the street. What they could interfere with in a practically horseless town I cannot imagine, but I trust this stupidity gave way to second thought.

The cab rattles and careers up the length of the street, scattering rickshaws and pedestrians from before its triumphant path. To the left opens a wide street of little booths under iron awnings, hung with gay colour and glittering things. The street is thronged from side to side with natives of all sorts. It whirls past, and shortly after the cab dashes inside a fence and draws up before the low stone-built, wide-verandahed hotel.

FOOTNOTES:

The Government does much nowadays by means of tank cars.

---

## XIV.

## A TOWN OF CONTRASTS.

It has been, as I have said, the fashion to speak of Nairobi as an ugly little town. This was probably true when the first corrugated iron houses huddled unrelieved near the railway station. It is not true now. The lower part of town is well planted, and is always picturesque as long as its people are astir. The white population have built in the wooded hills some charming bungalows surrounded by bright flowers or lost amid the trunks of great trees. From the heights on which is Government House one can, with a glass, watch the game herds feeding on the plains. Two clubs, with the usual games of golf, polo, tennis—especially tennis—football and cricket; a weekly hunt, with jackals instead of foxes; a bungalow town club on the slope of a hill; an electric light system; a race track; a rifle range; frilly parasols and the latest fluffiest summer toilettes from London and Paris—I mention a few of the refinements of civilization that offer to the traveller some of the most piquant of contrasts.

For it must not be forgotten that Nairobi, in spite of these things—due to the direct but slender thread of communication by railroad and ships—is actually in the middle of an African wilderness—is a black man's town, as far as numbers go.

The game feeds to its very outskirts, even wanders into the streets at night. Lions may be heard roaring within a mile or so of town; and leopards occasionally at night come on the verandas of the outlying dwellings. Naked savages from the jungle untouched by civilization in even the minutest particular wander the streets unabashed.

It is this constantly recurring, sharply drawn contrast that gives Nairobi its piquant charm. As one sits on the broad hotel veranda a constantly varied pageant passes before him. A daintily dressed, fresh-faced Englishwoman bobs by in a smart rickshaw drawn by two uniformed runners; a Kikuyu, anointed, curled, naked, brass adorned, teeters along, an expression of satisfaction on his face; a horseman, well appointed, trots briskly by followed by his loping syce; a string of skin-clad women, their heads fantastically shaved, heavily ornamented, lean forward under the burden of firewood for the market; a beautiful baby in a frilled perambulator is propelled by a tall, solemn, fine-looking black man in white robe and cap; the driver of a high cart tools his animal past a creaking, clumsy, two-wheeled wagon drawn by a pair of small humpbacked native oxen. And so it goes, all day long, without end. The public rickshaw boys just across the way chatter and game and quarrel and keep a watchful eye out for a possible patron on whom to charge vociferously and full tilt. Two or three old-timers with white whiskers and red faces continue to slaughter thousands and thousands and thousands of lions from the depths of their easy chairs.

The stone veranda of that hotel is a very interesting place. Here gather men from all parts of East Africa, from Uganda, and the jungles of the Upper Congo. At one time or another all the famous hunters drop into its canvas chairs— Cunninghame, Allan Black, Judd, Outram, Hoey, and the others; white traders with the natives of distant lands; owners of farms experimenting bravely on a greater or lesser scale in a land whose difficulties are just beginning to be understood; great naturalists and scientists from the governments of the earth, eager to observe and collect this interesting and teeming fauna; and sportsmen just out and full of interest, or just returned and modestly important. More absorbing conversation can be listened to on this veranda than in any other one place in the world. The gathering is cosmopolitan; it is representative of the most active of every social, political, and racial element; it has done things; it contemplates vital problems from the vantage ground of experience. The talk veers from pole to pole—and returns always to lions.

Every little while a native—a raw savage—comes along and takes up a stand just outside the railing. He stands there mute and patient for five minutes—a half hour—until some one, any one, happens to notice him.

"N'jo!—come here!" commands this person.

The savage silently proffers a bit of paper on which is written the name of the one with whom he has business.

"Nenda officie!" indicates the charitable person waving his hand towards the hotel office.

Then, and not until this permission has been given by some one, dares the savage cross the threshold to do his errand.

If the messenger happens to be a trained houseboy, however, dressed in his uniform of khaki or his more picturesque white robe and cap, he is privileged to work out his own salvation. And behind the hotel are rows and rows of other

275

boys, each waiting patiently the pleasure of his especial bwana lounging at ease after strenuous days. At the drawling shout of "boy!" one of them instantly departs to find out which particular boy is wanted.

The moment any white man walks to the edge of the veranda a half-dozen of the rickshaws across the street career madly around the corners of the fence, bumping, colliding, careening dangerously, to drop beseechingly in serried confusion close around the step. The rickshaw habit is very strong in Nairobi. If a man wants to go a hundred yards down the street he takes a rickshaw for that stupendous journey. There is in justification the legend that the white man should not exert himself in the tropics. I fell into the custom of the country until I reflected that it would hardly be more fatal to me to walk a half-hour in the streets of Nairobi than to march six or seven hours—as I often did—when on safari or in the hunting field. After that I got a little exercise, to the vast scandal of the rickshaw boys. In fact, so unusual was my performance that at first I had fairly to clear myself a way with my kiboko. After a few experiences they concluded me a particularly crazy person and let me alone.

Rickshaws, however, are very efficient and very cheap. The runners, two in number, are lithe little round-headed Kavirondos, generally, their heads shaved to leave a skull cap, clad in scant ragged garments, and wearing each an anklet of little bells. Their passion for ornament they confine to small bright things in their hair and ears. They run easily, with a very long stride. Even steep hills they struggle up somehow, zigzagging from one side of the road to the other, edging along an inch or so at a time. In such places I should infinitely have preferred to have walked, but that would have lost me caste everywhere. There are limits even to a crazy man's idiosyncrasies. For that reason I never thoroughly enjoyed rickshaws, save along the level ways with bells jingling and feet patpatting a rapid time. Certainly I did not enjoy them going down the steep hills. The boy between the shafts in front hits the landscape about every forty feet. I do not really object to sudden death, but this form of it seemed unfair to some poor hungry lion.

However, the winding smooth roads among the forested, shaded bungalows of the upper part of town were very attractive, especially towards evening. At that time the universal sun-helmet or double terai could be laid aside for straw hats, cloth caps, or bare heads. People played the more violent games, or strolled idly. At the hotel there was now a good deal of foolish drinking; foolish, because in this climate it is very bad for the human system, and in these surroundings of much interest and excitement the relief of its exaltation from monotony or ennui or routine could hardly be required.

FOOTNOTES:

Fifteen hundred whites to twelve thousand natives, approximately.

This happened twice while I was in the country.

---

## XV.

PEOPLE.

Considered as a class rather than as individuals, the dark-skinned population is easily the more interesting. Considered as individuals, the converse is true. Men like Sir Percy Girouard, Hobley, Jackson, Lord Delamere, McMillan, Cunninghame, Allan Black, Leslie Tarleton, Vanderweyer, the Hill cousins, Horne, and a dozen others are nowhere else to be met in so small a community. But the whites have developed nothing in their relations one to another essentially different. The artisan and shopkeeping class dwell on the flats; the Government people and those of military connections live on the heights on one side of the little stream; the civil service and bigger business men among the hills on the other. Between them all is a little jealousy, and contempt, and condescension; just as there is jealousy, and contempt, and condescension elsewhere. They are pleasant people, and hospitable, and some of them very distinguished in position or achievement; and I am glad to say I have good friends among them.

But the native is the joy, and the never-ceasing delight. For his benefit is the wide, glittering, colourful, insanitary bazaar, with its dozens of little open-air veranda shops, its "hotels" where he can sit in a real chair and drink real tea, its cafes, and the dark mysteries of its more doubtful amusements. The bazaar is right in the middle of town, just where it ought not to be, and it is constantly being quarantined, and threatened with removal. It houses a large population mysteriously, for it is of slight extent. Then on the borders of town are the two great native villages—one belonging to the Somalis, and the other hospitably accommodating the swarms of caravan porters and their families. For, just as in old days Mombasa and Zanzibar used to be the points from which caravans into the interior would set forth, now Nairobi outfits the majority of expeditions. Probably ten thousand picked natives of various tribes are engaged in the profession. Of course but a small proportion of this number is ever at home at any one time; but the village is a large one. Both these villages are built in the native style, of plaster and thatch; have their own headman government—under supervision— and are kept pretty well swept out and tidy. Besides these three main gathering places are many camps and

276

"shambas" scattered everywhere; and the back country counts millions of raw jungle savages, only too glad to drift in occasionally for a look at the metropolis.

At first the newcomer is absolutely bewildered by the variety of these peoples; but after a little he learns to differentiate. The Somalis are perhaps the first recognizable, with their finely chiselled, intelligent, delicate brown features, their slender forms, and their strikingly picturesque costumes of turbans, flowing robes, and embroidered sleeveless jackets. Then he learns to distinguish the savage from the sophisticated dweller of the town. Later comes the identification of the numerous tribes.

The savage comes in just as he has been for, ethnologists alone can guess, how many thousands of years. He is too old an institution to have been affected as yet by this tiny spot of modernity in the middle of the wilderness. As a consequence he startles the newcomer even more than the sight of giraffes on the sky-line.

When the shenzi—wild man—comes to town he gathers in two or three of his companions, and presents himself as follows: His hair has been grown quite long, then gathered in three tight pigtails wound with leather, one of which hangs over his forehead, and the other two over his ears. The entire head he has then anointed with a mixture of castor oil and a bright red colouring earth. This is wiped away evenly all around the face, about two inches below the hair, to leave a broad, bandlike glistening effect around the entire head. The ears are most marvellous. From early youth the lobes have been stretched, until at last they have become like two long elastic loops, hanging down upon the shoulder, and capable of accommodating anything up to and including a tomato can. When in fatigue uniform these loops are caught up over the tops of the ears, but on dress parade they accommodate almost anything considered ornamental. I have seen a row of safety pins clasped in them or a number of curtain rings; or a marmalade jar, or the glittering cover of a tobacco tin. The edges of the ears, all around to the top, are then pierced. Then the insertion of a row of long white wooden skewers gives one a peculiarly porcupinish look; or a row of little brass danglers hints of wealth. Having thus finished off his head, your savage clasps around his neck various strings of beads; or collars of iron or copper wire, polished to the point of glitter; puts on a half-dozen armlets and leglets of the same; ties on a narrow bead belt, in which is thrust a short sword; anoints himself all over with reddened castor oil until he glistens and shines in the sun; rubs his legs with white clay and traces patterns therein; seizes his long-bladed spear, and is ready for the city. Oh, no! I forgot—and he probably came near doing so—his strip of 'Mericani. This was originally white, but constant wear over castor oil has turned it a uniform and beautiful brown.

The purpose of this is ornament, and it is so worn. There has been an attempt, I understand, to force these innocent children to some sort of conventional decency while actually in the streets of Nairobi. It was too large an order. Some bring in clothes, to be sure, because the white man asks it; but why no sensible man could say. They are hung from one shoulder, flap merrily in the breeze, and are always quite frankly tucked up about the neck or under the arms when the wearer happens to be in haste. As a matter of fact these savages are so beautifully and smoothly formed; their red-brown or chocolate-brown skin is so fine in texture, and their complete unconsciousness so genuine that in an hour the newcomer is quite accustomed to their nakedness.

These proud youths wander mincingly down the street with an expression of the most fatuous and good-natured satisfaction with themselves. To their minds they have evidently done every last thing that human ingenuity or convention could encompass.

These young men are the dandies, the proud young aristocracy of wealth and importance; and of course they may differ individually or tribally from the sample I have offered. Also there are many other social grades. Those who care less for dress or have less to get it with can rub along very cheaply. The only real essentials are (*a*) something for the ear—a tomato can will do; (*b*) a trifle for clothing—and for that a scrap of gunny sacking will be quite enough.

The women to be seen in the streets of Nairobi are mostly of the Kikuyu tribe. They are pretty much of a pattern. Their heads are shaven, either completely or to leave only ornamental tufts; and are generally bound with a fine wire fillet so tightly that the strands seem to sink into the flesh. A piece of cotton cloth, dyed dark umber red, is belted around the waist, and sometimes, but not always, another is thrown about the shoulder. They go in for more hardware than do the men. The entire arms and the calves of the legs are encased in a sort of armour made of quarter-inch wire wound closely, and a collar of the same material stands out like a ruff eight or ten inches around the neck. This is wound on for good; and must be worn day and night and all the time, a cumbersome and tremendously heavy burden. A dozen large loops of coloured beads strung through the ears, and various strings and necklaces of beads, cowrie shells, and the like finish them out in all their gorgeousness. They would sink like plummets. Their job in life, besides lugging all this stuff about, is to carry in firewood and forage. At any time of the day long files of them can be seen bending forward under their burdens. These they carry on their backs by means of a strap across the tops of their heads; after the fashion of the Canadian tump line.

The next cut above the shenzi, or wild man, is the individual who has been on safari as carrier, or has otherwise been much employed around white men. From this experience he has acquired articles of apparel and points of view. He is given to ragged khaki, or cast-off garments of all sorts, but never to shoes. This hint of the conventional only serves to accent the little self-satisfied excursions he makes into barbarism. The shirt is always worn outside, the ear ornaments are as varied as ever, the head is shaved in strange patterns, a tiny tight tuft on the crown is useful as fastening for feathers or little streamers or anything else that will wave or glitter. One of these individuals wore a red label he had, with patience and difficulty, removed from one of our trunks. He had pasted it on his forehead; and it read "Baggage Room. Not Wanted." These people are, after all, but modified shenzis. The modification is nearly always in the direction of the comic.

277

Now we step up to a class that would resent being called shenzis as it would resent an insult. This is the personal servant class. The members are of all tribes, with possibly a slight preponderance of Swahilis and Somalis. They are a very clean, well-groomed, self-respecting class, with a great deal of dignity, and a great deal of pride in their bwanas. Also they are exceedingly likely to degenerate unless ruled with a firm hand and a wise head. Very rarely are they dishonest as respects the possessions of their own masters. They understand their work perfectly, and the best of them get the equivalent of from eight to ten dollars a month. Every white individual has one or more of them; even the tiny children with their ridiculous little sun helmets are followed everywhere by a tall, solemn, white-robed black. Their powers of divination approach the uncanny. About the time you begin to think of wanting something, and are making a first helpless survey of a boyless landscape, your own servant suddenly, mysteriously, and unobtrusively appears from nowhere. Where he keeps himself, where he feeds himself, where he sleeps you do not know. These beautifully clean, trim, dignified people are always a pleasant feature in the varied picture.

The Somalis are a clan by themselves. A few of them condescend to domestic service, but the most prefer the free life of traders, horse dealers, gunbearers, camel drivers, labour go-betweens, and similar guerrilla occupations. They are handsome, dashing, proud, treacherous, courageous, likeable, untrustworthy. They career around on their high, short-stirruped saddles; they saunter indolently in small groups; they hang about the hotel hoping for a dicker of some kind. There is nothing of the savage about them, but much of the true barbarism, with the barbarian's pride, treachery, and love of colour.

FOOTNOTES:

Native farmlets, generally temporary.

White cotton cloth.

---

## XVI.

### RECRUITING.

To the traveller Nairobi is most interesting as the point from which expeditions start and to which they return. Doubtless an extended stay in the country would show him that problems of administration and possibilities of development could be even more absorbing; but such things are very sketchy to him at first.

As a usual thing, when he wants porters he picks them out from the throng hanging around the big outfitters' establishments. Each man is then given a blanket—cotton, but of a most satisfying red—a tin water bottle, a short stout cord, and a navy blue jersey. After that ceremony he is yours.

But on the occasion of one three months' journey into comparatively unknown country we ran up against difficulties. Some two weeks before our contemplated start two or three cases of bubonic plague had been discovered in the bazaar, and as a consequence Nairobi was quarantined. This meant that a rope had been stretched around the infected area, that the shops had been closed, and that no native could—officially—leave Nairobi. The latter provision affected us; for under it we should be unable to get our bearers out.

As a matter of fact, the whole performance—unofficially—was a farce. Natives conversed affably at arm's length across the ropes; hundreds sneaked in and out of town at will; and from the rear of the infected area I personally saw beds, chests, household goods, blankets, and clothes passed to friends outside the ropes. When this latter condition was reported, in my presence, to the medical officers, they replied that this was a matter for police cognizance! But the brave outward show of ropes, disinfectants, gorgeous sentries—in front—and official inspection went solemnly on. Great, even in Africa, is the god of red tape.

Our only possible plan, in the circumstances, was to recruit the men outside the town, to camp them somewhere, march them across country to a way station, and there embark them. Our goods and safari stores we could then ship out to them by train.

Accordingly we rode on bicycles out to the Swahili village.

This is, as I have said, composed of large "beehive" houses thatched conically with straw. The roofs extend to form verandas beneath which sit indolent damsels, their hair divided in innumerable tiny parts running fore and aft like the stripes on a water melon; their figured 'Mericani garments draped gracefully. As befitted the women of plutocrats, they wore much jewellery, some of it set in their noses. Most of them did all of nothing, but some sat half buried in narrow strips of bright-coloured tissue paper. These they were pasting together like rolls of tape, the coloured edges of the paper forming concentric patterns on the resultant discs—an infinite labour. The discs, when completed, were for insertion in the lobes of the ears.

When we arrived the irregular "streets" of the village were nearly empty, save for a few elegant youths, in long kanzuas, or robes of cinnamon colour and spotless white, on their heads fezzes or turbans, in their hands slender rattan canes. They were very busy talking to each other, and of course did not notice the idle beauties beneath the verandas.

Hardly had we appeared, however, when mysteriously came forth the headman—a bearded, solemn, Arab-like person with a phenomenally ugly face but a most pleasing smile. We told him we wanted porters. He clapped his hands. To the four young men who answered this summons he gave a command. From sleepy indolence they sprang into life. To the four cardinal points of the compass they darted away, running up and down the side streets, beating on the doors, screaming at the tops of their lungs the word "Cazi" over and over again.

The village hummed like a wasps' nest. Men poured from the huts in swarms. The streets were filled; the idle sauntering youths were swamped, and sunk from view. Clamour and shouting arose where before had been a droning silence. The mob beat up to where we stood, surrounding us, shouting at us. From somewhere some one brought an old table and two decrepit chairs, battered and rickety in themselves, but symbols of great authority in a community where nobody habitually used either. Two naked boys proudly took charge of our bicycles.

We seated ourselves.

"Fall in!" we yelled.

About half the crowd fell into rough lines. The rest drew slightly to one side. Nobody stopped talking for a single instant.

We arose and tackled our job. The first part of it was to segregate the applicants into their different tribes.

"Monumwezi hapa!" we yelled; and the command was repeated and repeated again by the headman, by his four personal assistants, by a half-dozen lesser headmen. Slowly the Monumwezi drew aside. We impressed on them emphatically they must stay thus, and went after, in turn, the Baganda, the Wakamba, the Swahilis, the Kavirondo, the Kikuyu. When we had them grouped, we went over them individually. We punched their chests, we ran over all their joints, we examined their feet, we felt their muscles. Our victims stood rigidly at inspection, but their numerous friends surrounded us closely, urging the claims of the man to our notice. It was rather confusing, but we tried to go at it as though we were alone in a wilderness. If the man passed muster we motioned him to a rapidly growing group.

When we had finished we had about sixty men segregated. Then we went over this picked lot again. This time we tried not only to get good specimens, but to mix our tribes. At last our count of twenty-nine was made up, and we took a deep breath. But to us came one of them complaining that he was a Monumwezi, and that we had picked only three Monumwezi, and—We cut him short. His contention was quite correct. A porter tent holds five, and it does not do to mix tribes. Reorganization! Cut out two extra Kavirondos, and include two more Monumwezi. "Bass! finished! Now go get your effects. We start immediately."

As quickly as it had filled, the street cleared. The rejected dived back into their huts, the newly enlisted carriers went to collect their baggage. Only remained the headman and his fierce-faced assistants, and the splendid youths idling up and down—none of them had volunteered, you may be sure—and the damsels of leisure beneath the porticos. Also one engaging and peculiar figure hovering near.

This individual had been particularly busy during our recruiting. He had hustled the men into line, he had advised us for or against different candidates, he had loudly sung my praises as a man to work for, although, of course, he knew nothing about me. Now he approached, saluted, smiled. He was a tall, slenderly-built person, with phenomenally long, thin legs, slightly rounded shoulders, a forward thrust, keen face, and remarkably long, slim hands. With these he gesticulated much, in a right-angled fashion, after the manner of Egyptian hieroglyphical figures. He was in no manner shenzi. He wore a fez, a neat khaki coat and shorts, blue puttees and boots. Also a belt with leather pockets, a bunch of keys, a wrist watch, and a seal ring. His air was of great elegance and social ease. We took him with us as C.'s gunbearer. He proved staunch, a good tracker, an excellent hunter, and a most engaging individual. His name was Kongoni, and he was a Wakamba.

But now we were confronted with a new problem: that of getting our twenty-nine chosen ones together again. They had totally disappeared. In all directions we had emissaries beating up the laggards. As each man reappeared carrying his little bundle, we lined him up with his companions. Then when we turned our backs we lost him again; he had thought of another friend with whom to exchange farewells. At the long last, however, we got them all collected. The procession started, the naked boys proudly wheeling our bikes alongside. We saw them fairly clear of everything, then turned them over to Kongoni, while we returned to Nairobi to see after our effects.

FOOTNOTES:

Work.

## PART IV. A LION HUNT ON KAPITI.

## AN OSTRICH FARM AT MACHAKOS.

This has to do with a lion hunt on the Kapiti Plains. On the veranda at Nairobi I had some time previous met Clifford Hill, who had invited me to visit him at the ostrich farm he and his cousin were running in the mountains near Machakos. Some time later, a visit to Juja Farm gave me the opportunity. Juja is only a day's ride from the Hills'. So an Africander, originally from the south, Captain D., and I sent across a few carriers with our personal effects, and ourselves rode over on horseback.

Juja is on the Athi Plains. Between the Athi and Kapiti Plains runs a range of low mountains around the end of which one can make his way as around a promontory. The Hills' ostrich farm was on the highlands in the bay on the other side of the promontory.

It was towards the close of the rainy season, and the rivers were up. We had to swim our horses within a half-mile of Juja, and got pretty wet. Shortly after crossing the Athi, however, five miles on, we emerged on the dry, drained slopes from the hills. Here the grass was long, and the ticks plentiful. Our horses' legs and chests were black with them; and when we dismounted for lunch we ourselves were almost immediately alive with the pests. In this very high grass the game was rather scarce, but after we had climbed by insensible grades to the shorter growth we began to see many hartebeeste, zebra, and gazelles, and a few of the wildebeeste, or brindled gnus. Travel over these great plains and through these leisurely low hills is a good deal like coastwise sailing—the same apparently unattainable landmarks which, nevertheless, are at last passed and left astern by the same sure but insensible progress. Thus we drew up on apparently continuous hills, found wide gaps between them, crossed them, and turned to the left along the other side of the promontory. About five o'clock we came to the Hills'.

The ostrich farm is situated on the very top of a conical rise that sticks up like an island close inshore to the semicircle of mountains in which end the vast plains of Kapiti. Thus the Hills have at their backs and sides these solid ramparts and face westward the immensities of space. For Kapiti goes on over the edge of the world to unknown, unguessed regions, rolling and troubled like a sea. And from that unknown, on very still days, the snowy peak of Kilimanjaro peers out, sketched as faintly against the sky as a soap bubble wafted upward and about to disappear. Here and there on the plains kopjes stand like islands, their stone tops looking as though thrust through the smooth prairie surface from beneath. To them meandered long, narrow ravines full of low brush, like thin, wavering streaks of gray. On these kopjes—each of which had its name—and in these ravines we were to hunt lions.

We began the ascent of the cone on which dwelt our hosts. It was one of those hills that seem in no part steep, and yet which finally succeed in raising one to a considerable height. We passed two ostrich herds in charge of savages, rode through a scattered native village, and so came to the farm itself, situated on the very summit.

The house consisted of three large circular huts, thatched neatly with papyrus stalks, and with conical roofs. These were arranged as a triangle, just touching each other; and the space between had been roofed over to form a veranda. We were ushered into one of these circular rooms. It was spacious and contained two beds, two chairs, a dresser, and a table. Its earth floor was completely covered by the skins of animals. In the corresponding room, opposite, slept our hosts; while the third was the living and dining room. A long table, raw-hide bottomed chairs, a large sideboard, bookcases, a long easy settee with pillows, gun racks, photographs in and out of frames, a table with writing materials, and books and magazines everywhere—not to speak of again the skins of many animals completely covering the floor. Out behind, in small, separate buildings, laboured the cook, and dwelt the stores, the bath-tub, and other such necessary affairs.

As soon as we had consumed the usual grateful lime juice and sparklets, we followed our hosts into the open air to look around.

On this high, airy hill top the Hills some day are going to build them a real house. In anticipation they have laid out grounds and have planted many things. In examining these my California training stood by me. Out there, as here, one so often examines his own and his neighbours' gardens, not for what they are but for what they shall become. His imagination can exalt this tiny seedling to the impressiveness of spreading noontime shade; can magnify yonder apparent duplicate to the full symmetry of a shrub; can ruthlessly diminish the present importance of certain grand and lofty growths to its true status of flower or animal. So from a dead uniformity of size he casts forward in the years to a pleasing variation of shade, of jungle, of open glade, of flowered vista; and he goes away full of expert admiration for "X.'s bully garden." With this solid training beneath me I was able on this occasion to please immensely.

From the house site we descended the slope to where the ostriches and the cattle and the people were in the late sunlight swarming upward from the plains pastures below. These people were, to the chief extent, Wakamba, quite savage, but attracted here by the justness and fair dealing of the Hills. Some of them farmed on shares with the Hills, the white men furnishing the land and seed, and the black men the labour; some of them laboured on wage; some few herded cattle or ostriches; some were hunters and took the field only when, as now, serious business was afoot. They had their complete villages, with priests, witch doctors, and all; and they seemed both contented and fond of the two white men.

As we walked about we learned much of the ostrich business; and in the course of our ten days' visit we came to a better realization of how much there is to think of in what appears basically so simple a proposition.

In the nesting time, then, the Hills went out over the open country, sometimes for days at a time, armed with long high-power telescopes. With these fearsome and unwieldy instruments they surveyed the country inch by inch from the advantage of a kopje. When thus they discovered a nest, they descended and appropriated the eggs. The latter, hatched at home in an incubator, formed the nucleus of a flock.

Pass the raising of ostrich chicks to full size through the difficulties of disease, wild beasts, and sheer cussedness. Of the resultant thirty birds or so of the season's catch, but two or three will even promise good production. These must be bred in captivity with other likely specimens. Thus after several years the industrious ostrich farmer may become possessed of a few really prime birds. To accumulate a proper flock of such in a new country is a matter of a decade or so. Extra prime birds are as well known and as much in demand for breeding as any blood horse in a racing country. Your true ostrich enthusiast, like the Hills, possesses trunks full of feathers not good commercially, but intensely interesting for comparison and for the purposes of prophecy. While I stayed with them came a rumour of a very fine plucking a distant neighbour had just finished from a likely two-year-old. The Hills were manifestly uneasy until one of them had ridden the long distance to compare this newcomer's product with that of their own two-year-olds. And I shall never forget the reluctantly admiring shake of the head with which he acknowledged that it was indeed a "very fine feather!"

But getting the birds is by no means all of ostrich farming, as many eager experimenters have discovered to their cost. The birds must have a certain sort of pasture land; and their paddocks must be built on an earth that will not soil or break the edges of the new plumes.

And then there is the constant danger of wild beasts. When a man has spent years in gathering suitable flocks, he cannot be blamed for wild anger when, as happened while I was in the country, lions kill sixty or seventy birds in a night. The ostrich seems to tempt lions greatly. The beasts will make their way through and over the most complicated defences. Any ostrich farmer's life is a constant warfare against them. Thus the Hills had slain sixty-eight lions in and near their farm—a tremendous record. Still the beasts continued to come in. My hosts showed me, with considerable pride, their arrangements finally evolved for night protection.

The ostriches were confined in a series of heavy corrals, segregating the birds of different ages. Around the outside of this group of enclosures ran a wide ring corral in which were confined the numerous cattle; and as an outer wall to this were built the huts of the Wakamba village. Thus to penetrate to the ostriches the enterprising lion would have to pass both the people, the cattle, and the strong thorn and log structures that contained them.

This subject brings me to another set of acquaintances we had already made—the dogs.

These consisted of an Airedale named Ruby; two setters called Wayward and Girlie; a heavy black mongrel, Nero; ditto brindle, Ben; and a smaller black and white ditto, Ranger. They were very nice friendly doggy dogs, but they did not look like lion hunters. Nevertheless, Hill assured us that they were of great use in the sport, and promised us that on the following day we should see just how.

---

## XVIII

THE FIRST LIONESS.

At an early hour we loaded our bedding, food, tents, and camp outfit on a two-wheeled wagon drawn by four of the humpbacked native oxen, and sent it away across the plains, with instructions to make camp on a certain kopje. Clifford Hill and myself, accompanied by our gunbearers and syces, then rode leisurely down the length of a shallow brushy cañon for a mile or so. There we dismounted and sat down to await the arrival of the others. These—including Harold Hill, Captain D., five or six Wakamba spearmen, our own carriers, and the dogs—came along more slowly, beating the bottoms on the off chance of game.

The sun was just warming, and the bees and insects were filling the air with their sleepy droning sounds. The hillside opposite showed many little outcrops of rocks so like the hills of our own Western States that it was somewhat difficult to realize that we were in Africa. For some reason the delay was long. Then suddenly all four of us simultaneously saw the same thing. A quarter-mile away and on the hillside opposite a magnificent lioness came loping easily along through the grass. She looked very small at that distance, like a toy, and quite unhurried. Indeed, every few moments she paused to look back in an annoyed fashion over her shoulder in the direction of the row behind her.

There was nothing to do but sit tight and wait. The lioness was headed exactly to cross our front; nor, except at one point, was she at all likely to deviate. A shallow tributary ravine ran into our own about two hundred yards away. She might possibly sneak down the bed of this. It seemed unlikely. The going was bad, and in addition she had no idea as yet that she had been sighted. Indeed, the chances were that she would come to a definite stop before making the crossing, in which case we would get a shot.

"And if she does go down the donga," whispered Hill, "the dogs will locate her."

Sitting still while things approach is always exciting. This is true of ducks; but when you multiply ducks by lions it is still more true. We all crouched very low in the grass. She leapt without hesitation into the ravine—and did not emerge.

This was a disappointment. We concluded she must have entered the stream bottom, and were just about to move when Memba Sasa snapped his fingers. His sharp eyes had discovered her sneaking along, belly to the ground, like the

281

cat she was. The explanation of this change in her gait was simple. Our companions had rounded the corner of the hill and were galloping in plain view a half-mile away. The lioness had caught sight of them.

She was gliding by, dimly visible, through thick brush seventy yards distant. Now I could make out a tawny patch that faded while I looked; now I could merely guess at a melting shadow.

"Stir her up," whispered Hill. "Never mind whether you hit. She'll sneak away."

At the shot she leaped fully out into the open with a snarl. Promptly I planted a Springfield bullet in her ribs. She answered slightly to the hit, but did not shift position. Her head up, her tail thrashing from side to side, her ears laid back, she stood there looking the landscape over carefully point by point. She was searching for us, but as yet could not locate us. It was really magnificent.

I attempted to throw in another cartridge, but because of my desire to work the bolt quietly, in order not to attract the lioness's attention, I did not pull it back far enough, and the cartridge jammed in the magazine. As evidence of Memba Sasa's coolness and efficiency, it is to be written that he became aware of this as soon as I did. He thrust the.405 across my right side, at the same time withdrawing the Springfield on the left. The motion was slight, but the lioness caught it. Immediately she dropped her head and charged.

For the next few moments, naturally, I was pretty intent on lions. Nevertheless a corner of my mind was aware of Memba Sasa methodically picking away at the jammed rifle, and paying no attention whatever to the beast. Also I heard Hill making picturesque remarks about his gunbearer, who had bolted with his second gun.

The lioness charged very fast, but very straight, about in the tearing, scrambling manner of a terrier after a thrown ball. I got in the first shot as she came, the bullet ranging back from the shoulder, and Hill followed it immediately with another from his.404 Jeffrey. She growled at the bullets, and checked very slightly as they hit, but gave no other sign. Then our second shots hit her both together. The mere shock stopped her short, but recovering instantly, she sprang forward again. Hill's third shot came next, and perceptibly slowed and staggered, but did not stop her. By this time she was quite close, and my own third shot reached her brain. She rolled over dead.

Decidedly she was a game beast, and stood more hammering than any other lion I killed or saw killed. Before the final shot in the brain she had taken one light bullet and five heavy ones with hardly a wince. Memba Sasa uttered a loud grunt of satisfaction when she went down for good. He had the Springfield reloaded and cocked, right at my elbow.

Hill's gunboy hovered uncertainly some distance in the rear. The sight of the charging lioness had been too much for him and he had bolted. He was not actually up a tree; but he stood very near one. He lost the gun and acquired a swift kick.

Our friends and the men now came up. The dogs made a great row over the dead lioness. She was measured and skinned to accompaniment of the usual low-hummed chantings. We had with us a small boy of ten or twelve years whose job it was to take care of the dogs and to remove ticks. In fact he was known as the Tick Toto. As this was his first expedition afield, his father took especial pains to smear him with fat from the lioness. This was to make him brave. I am bound to confess the effect was not immediate.

---

## XIX.

THE DOGS.

I soon discovered that we were hunting lions with the assistance of the dogs; not that the dogs were hunting lions. They had not lost any lions, not they! My mental pictures of the snarling, magnificent king of beasts surrounded by an equally snarling, magnificent pack vanished into thin air.

Our system was to cover as much likely country as we could, and to let the dogs have a good time. As I have before indicated, they were thoroughly doggy dogs, and interested in everything—except able-bodied lions. None of the stick-at-your-heels in their composition. They ranged far and wide through all sorts of cover, seeking what they could find in the way of porcupines, mongoose, hares, birds, cats, and whatever else should interest any healthy-minded dog. If there happened to be any lions in the path of these rangings, the dogs retired rapidly, discreetly, and with every symptom of horrified disgust. If a dog came sailing out of a thicket, ki-yi-ing agitatedly, and took up his position, tail between his legs, behind his master, we knew there was probably a lion about. Thus we hunted lions with dogs.

But in order to be fair to these most excellent canines, it should be recorded that they recovered a certain proportion of their nerve after a rifle had been fired. They then returned warily to the—not attack—reconnaissance. This trait showed touching faith, and was a real compliment to the marksmanship of their masters. Some day it will be misplaced. A little cautious scouting on their part located the wounded beast; whereupon, at a respectful distance, they lifted their voices. As a large element of danger in case of a wounded lion is the uncertainty as to his whereabouts, it will be seen that the dogs were very valuable indeed. They seemed to know exactly how badly hit any animal might happen to be, and to gauge their distance accordingly, until at last, when the quarry was hammered to harmlessness, they closed in and began to worry the nearly lifeless carcass. By this policy the dogs had a lot of fun hunting on their own hook, preserved their lives from otherwise inevitable extinction, and were of great assistance in saving their masters' skins.

One member of the pack, perhaps two, were, however, rather pathetic figures. I refer to the setters, Wayward and Girlie. Ranger, Ruby, Ben, and Nero scampered merrily over the landscape after anything that stirred, from field mice to serval cats. All was game to their catholic tastes; and you may be sure, in a country like Africa, they had few dull moments. But Wayward and Girlie had been brought up in a more exclusive manner. Their early instincts had been supplemented by a rigorous early training. Game to them meant birds, and birds only. Furthermore, they had been solemnly assured by human persons in whom they had the utmost confidence, that but one sequence of events was permissible or even thinkable in the presence of game. The Dog at first intimation by scent must convey the fact to the Man, must proceed cautiously to locate exactly, must then stiffen to a point which he must hold staunchly, no matter how distracting events might turn out, or how long an interval might elapse. The Man must next walk up the birds; shoot at them, perhaps kill one, then command the Dog to retrieve. The Dog must on no account move from his tracks until such command is given. All the affair is perfectly simple; but quite inflexible. Any variation in this procedure fills the honest bird dog's mind with the same horror and dismay experienced by a well-brought-up young man who discovers that he has on shoes of the wrong colour. It isn't done, you know.

Consider, then, Wayward and Girlie in a country full of game birds. They quarter wide to right, then cross to left, their heads high, their feather tails waving in the most approved good form. When they find birds they draw to their points in the best possible style; stiffen out—and wait. It is now, according to all good ethics, up to the Man. And the Man and his companions go right on by, paying absolutely no attention either to the situation or one's own magnificent piece of work! What is one to conclude? That our early training is all wrong? that we are at one experience to turn apostate to the settled and only correct order of things? Or that our masters are no gentlemen? That is a pretty difficult thing, an impossible thing, to conclude of one's own master. But it leaves one in a fearful state mentally; and one has no idea of what to do!

Wayward was a perfect gentleman, and he played the game according to the very best traditions. He conscientiously pointed every bird he could get his nose on. Furthermore he was absolutely staunch, and held his point even when the four non-bird dogs rushed in ahead of him. The expression of puzzlement, grief, shock, and sadness in his eyes deepened as bird after bird soared away without a shot. Girlie was more liberal-minded. She pointed her birds, and backed Wayward at need, but when the other dogs rushed her point, she rushed too. And when we swept on by her, leaving her on point, instead of holding it quixotically, as did Wayward, until the bird sneaked away, she merely waited until we were out of sight, and then tried to catch it. Finally Captain D. remarked that, lions or no lions, he was not going to stand it any longer. He got out a shotgun, and all one afternoon killed grouse over Wayward, to the latter's intense relief. His ideals had been rehabilitated.

---

## XX.

BONDONI.

We followed many depressions, in which might be lions, until about three o'clock in the afternoon. Then we climbed the gently-rising long slope that culminated, far above the plains, in the peak of a hill called Bondoni. From a distance it was steep and well defined; but, like most of these larger kopjes, its actual ascent, up to the last few hundred feet, was so gradual that we hardly knew we were climbing. At the summit we found our men and the bullock cart. There also stood an oblong blockhouse of stone, the walls two feet thick and ten feet high. It was entered only by a blind angle passage, and was strong enough, apparently, to resist small artillery. This structure was simply an ostrich corral, and bitter experience had shown the massive construction absolutely necessary as adequate protection, in this exposed and solitary spot, against the lions.

We had some tea and bread and butter, and then Clifford Hill and I set out afoot after meat. Only occasionally do these hard-working settlers get a chance for hunting on the plains so near them; and now they had promised their native retainers that they would send back a treat of game. To carry this promised luxury, a number of the villagers had accompanied the bullock wagon. As we were to move on next day, it became very desirable to get the meat promptly while still near home.

We slipped over to the other side, and by good fortune caught sight of a dozen zebras feeding in scrub half-way down the hill. They were out of their proper environment up there, but we were glad of it. Down on our tummies, then, we dropped, and crawled slowly forward through the high, sweet grasses. We were in the late afternoon shadow of the hill, and we enjoyed the mild skill of the stalk. Taking advantage of every cover, slipping over into little ravines, lying very flat when one of the beasts raised his head, we edged nearer and nearer. We were already well within range, but it amused us to play the game. Finally, at one hundred yards, we came to a halt. The zebra showed very handsome at that range, for even their smaller leg stripes were all plainly visible. Of course at that distance there could be small chance of missing, and we owned one each. The Wakamba, who had been watching eagerly, swarmed down, shouting.

We dined just at sunset under a small tree at the very top of the peak. Long bars of light shot through the western clouds; the plain turned from solid earth to a mysterious sea of shifting twilights; the buttes stood up, wrapped in veils of soft desert colours; Kilimanjaro hung suspended like a rose-coloured bubble above the abyss beyond the world.

## XXI.

RIDING THE PLAINS.

From the mere point of view of lions, lion A hunting was very slow work indeed. It meant riding the whole of long days, from dawn until dark, investigating miles of country that looked all alike and in which we seemed to get nowhere. One by one the long billows of plain fell behind, until our camp hill had turned blue behind us, and we seemed to be out in illimitable space, with no possibility, in an ordinary lifetime, of ever getting in touch with anything again. What from above had looked as level as a floor now turned into a tremendously wide and placid ground swell. As a consequence we were always going imperceptibly up and up and up to a long-delayed sky-line, or tipping as gently down the other side of the wave. From crest to crest of these long billows measured two or three miles. The vertical distance in elevation from trough to top was perhaps not over fifty to one hundred feet.

Slowly we rode along the shallow grass and brush ravines in the troughs of the low billows, while the dogs worked eagerly in and out of cover, and our handful of savages cast stones and shouted. Occasionally we divided forces, and beat the length of a hill, two of us lying in wait at one end for the possible lion, the rest sweeping the sides and summits. Many animals came bounding along, but no lions. Then Harold Hill, unlimbering a huge, many-jointed telescope, would lie flat on his back, and sight the fearsome instrument over his crossed feet, in a general bird's-eye view of the plains for miles around. While he was at it we were privileged to look about us, less under the burden of responsibility. We could make out the game as little, light-coloured dots and speckles, thousands upon thousands of them, thicker than cattle ever grazed on the open range, and as far as the eye could make them out, and then a glance through our glasses picked them up again for mile after mile. Even the six-power could go no farther. The imagination was left the vision of more leagues of wild animals even to the half-guessed azure mountains—and beyond. I had seen abundant game elsewhere in Africa, but nothing like the multitudes inhabiting the Kapiti Plains at that time of year. In other seasons this locality is comparatively deserted.

The glass revealing nothing in our line, we rode again to the lower levels, and again took up our slow, painstaking search.

But although three days went by in this manner without our getting a glimpse of lions, they were far from being days lost. Minor adventure filled our hours. What elsewhere would be of major interest and strange and interesting experience met us at every turn. The game, while abundant, was very shy. This had nothing to do with distrust of hunters, but merely with the fact that it was the season of green grass. We liked to come upon animals unexpectedly, to see them buck-jump and cavort.

Otherwise we rode in a moving space cleared of animals, the beasts unobtrusively giving way before us, and as unobtrusively closing in behind. The sun flashed on the spears of savages travelling single file across the distance. Often we stopped short to gaze upon a wild and tumbled horizon of storm that Gustave Doré might have drawn.

The dogs were always joyously routing out some beast, desirable from their point of view, and chasing it hopelessly about, to our great amusement. Once they ran into a giant porcupine-about the size a setter would be, with shorter legs-which did not understand running away. They came upon it in a dense thicket, and the ensuing row was unholy. They managed to kill the porcupine among them, after which we plucked barbed quills from some very grieved dogs. The quills were large enough to make excellent penholders. The dogs also swore by all canine gods that they wouldn't do a thing to a hyena, if only they could get hold of one. They never got hold of one, for the hyena is a coward. His skull and teeth, however, are as big and powerful as those of a lioness; so I do not know which was luckier in his avoidance of trouble—he or the dogs.

Nor from the shooting standpoint did we lack for sport. We had to shoot for our men, and we occasionally needed meat ourselves. It was always interesting, when such necessities arose, to stalk the shy buck and do long-range rifle practice. This shooting, however, was done only after the day's hunt was over. We had no desire to spoil our lion chances.

The long circle towards our evening camp always proved very long indeed. We arrived at dusk to find supper ready for us. As we were old campaigners we ate this off chop boxes as tables, and sat on the ground. It was served by a Wakamba youth we had nicknamed Herbert Spencer, on account of his gigantic intellect. Herbert meant well, but about all he succeeded in accomplishing was a pathetically wrinkled brow of care and scared eyes. He had never been harshly treated by any of us, but he acted as though always ready to bolt. If there were twenty easy right methods of doing a thing and one difficult wrong method, Herbert would get the latter every time. No amount of experience could teach him the logic of our simplest ways. One evening he brought a tumbler of mixed water and condensed milk. Harold Hill glanced into the receptacle.

"Stir it," he commanded briefly.

Herbert Spencer obeyed. We talked about something else. Some five or ten minutes later one of us noticed that Herbert was still stirring, and called attention to the fact. When the latter saw our eyes were on him he speeded up until the spoon fairly rattled in the tumbler. Then, when he thought our attention had relaxed again, he relaxed also his efforts—the spoon travelled slower and slower in its dreamy circle. We amused ourselves for some time thus. Then we became so weak from laughter that we fell backward off our seats, and some one gasped a command that Herbert cease.

I am afraid, after a little, that we rather enjoyed mildly tormenting poor Herbert Spencer. He tried so hard, and looked so scared, and was so unbelievably stupid! Almost always he had to pick his orders word by word from a vast amount of high-flown, unnecessary English.

"O Herbert Spencer," the command would run, "if you would condescend to bend your mighty intellect to the lowly subject of maji, and will snatch time from your profound cerebrations to assure its being moto sans, I would esteem it infinite condescension on your part to let pesi pesi."

And Herbert, listening to all this with a painful, strained intensity, would catch the six-key words, and would falter forth a trembling "N'dio bwana."

Somewhere down deep within Herbert Spencer's make up, however, was a sense of moral duty. When we finally broke camp for good, on the great hill of Lucania, Herbert Spencer, relieved from his job, bolted like a shot. As far as we could see him he was running at top speed. If he had not possessed a sense of duty, he would have done this long ago.

We camped always well up on some of the numerous hills; for, although anxious enough to find lions in the daytime, we had no use for them at all by night. This usually meant that the boys had to carry water some distance. We kept a canvas bath-tub full for the benefit of the dogs, from which they could drink at any time. This necessary privilege after a hard day nearly drove Captain D. crazy. It happened like this:

We were riding along the slope of a hillside, when in the ravine, a half mile away and below us, we saw something dark pop up in sight and then down again. We shouted to some of the savage Wakamba to go and investigate. They closed in from all sides, their long spears poised to strike. At the last moment out darted, not an animal, but a badly frightened old man armed with bow and arrow. He dashed out under the upraised spears, clasped one of the men around the knees, and implored protection. Our savages, their spears ready, glanced over their shoulders for instruction. They would have liked nothing better than to have spitted the poor old fellow.

We galloped down as fast as possible to the rescue. With reluctance our spearmen drew back, releasing their prize. We picked up his scattered bows and arrows, restored them to him, and uttered many reassurances. He was so badly frightened that he could not stand for the trembling of his knees. Undoubtedly he thought that war had broken out, and that he was the first of its unconscious victims. After calming him down, we told him what we were doing, and offered to shoot him meat if he cared to accompany us. He accepted the offer with joy. So pleased and relieved was he, that he skipped about like a young and nimble goat. His hunting companion, who all this time had stood atop of a hill at a safe distance, viewed these performances with concern. Our captive shouted loudly for him to come join us and share in the good fortune. Not he! He knew a trap when he saw one! Not a bit disturbed by the tales this man would probably carry back home, our old fellow attached himself to us for three days!

Near sundown, to make our promise good, and also to give our own men a feast, I shot two hartebeeste near camp.

The evening was beautiful. The Machakos Range, miles distant across the valley, was mantled with thick, soft clouds. From our elevation we could see over them, and catch the glow of moonlight on their upper surfaces. We were very tired, so we turned in early and settled ourselves for a good rest.

Outside our tent the little "Injun fire" we had built for our own comfort died down to coals. A short distance away, however, was a huge bonfire around which all the savages were gathered. They squatted comfortably on their heels, roasting meat. Behind each man was planted his glittering long-bladed spear. The old man held the place of honour, as befitted his flirtation with death that morning. Everybody was absolutely happy—a good fire, plenty of meat, and strangers with whom to have a grand "shauri." The clatter of tongues was a babel, for almost every one talked at once and excitedly. Those who did not talk crooned weird, improvised chants, in which they detailed the doings of the camp.

We fell very quickly into the half doze of too great exhaustion. It never became more than a half doze. I suppose every one who reads this has had at some time the experience of dropping asleep to the accompaniment of some noise that ought soon to cease—a conversation in the next room, singing, the barking of a dog, the playing of music, or the like. The fact that it ought soon to cease, permits the falling asleep. When, after an interval, the subconsciousness finds the row still going on, inexcusable and unabated, it arouses the victim to staring exasperation. That was our case here. Those natives should have turned in for sleep after a reasonable amount of pow-wow. They did nothing of the kind. On the contrary, I dragged reluctantly back to consciousness and the realization that they had quite happily settled down to make a night of it. I glanced across the little tent to where Captain D. lay on his cot. He was staring straight upward, his eyes wide open.

After a few seconds he slipped out softly and silently. Our little fire had sunk to embers. A dozen sticks radiated from the centre of coals. Each made a firebrand with one end cool to the grasp. Captain D. hurled one of these at the devoted and unconscious group.

It whirled through the air and fell plunk in the other fire, scattering sparks and coals in all directions. The second was under way before the first had landed. It hit a native with similar results, plus astonished and grieved language. The rest followed in rapid-magazine-fire. Every one hit its mark fair and square. The air was full of sparks exploding in all directions. The brush was full of Wakamba, their blankets flapping in the breeze of their going. The convention was adjourned. There fell the sucking vacuum of a great silence. Captain D., breathing righteous wrath, flopped heavily and determinedly down on his cot. I caught a faint snicker from the tent next door.

Captain D. sighed deeply, turned over, and prepared to sleep. Then one of the dogs uprose—I think it was Ben—stretched himself, yawned, approached deliberately, and began to drink from the canvas bath-tub just outside. He drank—lap, lap, lap, lap—for a very long time. It seemed incredible that any mere dog—or canvas bath-tub—could hold so much water. The steady repetition of this sound long after it should logically have ceased was worse than the shenzi gathering around the fire. Each lap should have been the last, but it was not. The shenzi convention had been abated with firebrands, but the dog was strictly within his rights. The poor pups had had a long day with little water, and they could hardly be blamed for feeling a bit feverish now. At last Ben ceased. Next morning Captain D. claimed vehemently that he had drunk two hours forty-nine minutes and ten seconds. With a contented sigh Ben lay down. Then Ruby got up, shook herself, and yawned. A bright idea struck her. She too went over and had a drink. After that I, personally, went to sleep. But in the morning I found Captain D. staring-eyed and strung nearly to madness, trying feverishly to calculate how seven dogs drinking on an average of three hours apiece could have finished by morning. When Harold Hill innocently asked if he had slept well, the captain threw the remaining but now extinct firebrand at him.

One of the safari boys, a big Baganda, had twisted his foot a little, and it had swelled up considerably. In the morning he came to have it attended to. The obvious treatment was very hot water and rest; but it would never do to tell him so. The recommendation of so simple a remedy would lose me his faith. So I gave him a little dab of tick ointment wrapped in a leaf.

"This," said I, "is most wonderful medicine; but it is also most dangerous. If you were to rub it on your foot or your hand or any part of you, that part would drop off. But if you wash the part in very hot water continuously for a half hour, and then put on the medicine, it is good, and will cure you very soon." I am sure I do not know what they put in tick ointment; nor, for the purpose, did it greatly matter. That night, also, Herbert Spencer reached the climax of his absurdities. The chops he had cooked did not quite suffice for our hunger, so we instructed him to give us some of the leg. By this we meant steak, of course. Herbert Spencer was gone so long a time that finally we went to see what possibly could be the matter. We found him trying desperately to cook the whole leg in a frying-pan!

---

## XXII.

### THE SECOND LIONESS.

Now our luck changed most abruptly. We had been riding since early morning over the wide plains. By and by we came to a wide, shallow, flood-water course carpeted with lava boulders and scant, scattered brush. Two of us took one side of it, and two the other. At this we were just within hailing distance. The boys wandered down the middle.

Game was here very abundant, and in this broken country proved quite approachable. I saw one Grant's gazelle head, in especial, that greatly tempted me; but we were hunting lions, and other shooting was out of place. Also the prospects for lions had brightened, for we were continually seeing hyenas in packs of from three to six. They lay among the stones, but galloped away at our approach. The game paid not the slightest attention to these huge, skulking brutes. One passed within twenty feet of a hartebeeste; the latter hardly glanced at him. As the hyena is lazy as well as cowardly, and almost never does his killing, we inferred a good meat supply to gather so many of them in one place. From a tributary ravine we flushed nineteen!

Harold Hill was riding with me on the right bank. His quick eye caught a glimpse of something beyond our companions on the left side. A glance through the glasses showed me that it was a lion, just disappearing over the hill. At once we turned our horses to cross. It was a heavy job. We were naturally in a tremendous hurry; and the footing among those boulders and rounded rocks was so vile that a very slow trot was the best we could accomplish. And that was only by standing in our stirrups, and holding up our horses' heads by main strength. We reached the sky-line in time to see a herd of game stampeding away from a depression a half-mile away. We fixed our eyes on that point, and a moment later saw the lion or lioness, as it turned out, leap a gully and come out the other side.

The footing down this slope, too, was appalling, consisting mainly of chunks of lava interspersed with smooth, rounded stones and sparse tufts of grass. In spite of the stones we managed a sort of stumbling gallop. Why we did not all go down in a heap I do not know. At any rate we had no chance to watch our quarry, for we were forced to keep our eyes strictly to our way. When finally we emerged from that tumble of rocks, she had disappeared.

Either she had galloped out over the plains, or she had doubled back to take cover in the ravine. In the latter case she would stand. Our first job, therefore, was to determine whether she had escaped over the open country. To this end we galloped our horses madly in four different directions, pushing them to the utmost, swooping here and there in wide circles. That was an exhilarating ten minutes until we had surmounted every billow of the plain, spied in all directions, and assured ourselves beyond doubt that she had not run off. The horses fairly flew, spurning the hard sod, leaping the rock dikes, skipping nimbly around the pig holes, turning like cow-ponies under pressure of knee and rein. Finally we drew up, converged, and together jogged our sweating horses back to the ravine. There we learned from the boys that nothing more had been seen of our quarry.

We dismounted, handed our mounts to their syces, and prepared to make afoot a clean sweep of the wide, shallow ravine. Here was where the dogs came in handy. We left a rearguard of two men, and slowly began our beat.

The ravine could hardly be called a ravine; rather a shallow depression with banks not over a foot high, and with a varying width of from two to two hundred feet. The grass grew very patchy, and not very high; in fact, it seemed hardly tall enough to conceal anything as large as a lioness. We men walked along the edge of this depression, while the dogs ranged back and forth in its bottom.

We had gone thus a quarter-mile when one of the rearguard came running up.

"Bwana," said he, "we have seen the lioness. She is lying in a patch of grass. After you had passed, we saw her raise her head."

It seemed impossible that she should have escaped both our eyes and the dogs' noses, but we returned. The man pointed out a thin growth of dried, yellow grass ten feet in diameter. Then it seemed even more incredible. Apparently we could look right through every foot of it. The man persisted, so we advanced in battle array. At thirty yards Captain D. saw the black tips of her ears. We all looked hard, and at last made her out, lying very flat, her head between her paws. Even then she was shadowy and unreal, and, as I have said, the cover did not look thick enough to conceal a good-sized dog.

As though she realized she had been sighted, she at this moment leapt to her feet. Instantly I put a.405 bullet into her shoulder. Any other lion I ever saw or heard of would in such circumstances and at such a distance immediately have charged home. She turned tail and ran away. I missed her as she ran, then knocked her down with a third shot. She got up again, but was immediately hit by Captain D.'s.350 Magnum and brought to a halt. The dogs, seeing her turn tail and hearing our shots, had scrambled madly after her. We dared not shoot again for fear of hitting one of them, so we dashed rapidly into the grass and out the other side. Before we could get to her, she had sent Ruby flying through the air, and had then fallen over dead. Ruby got off lucky with only a deep gash the length of her leg.

This was the only instance I experienced of a wounded lion showing the white feather. She was, however, only about three-quarters grown, and was suffering from diarrhoea.

---

## XXIII.

THE BIG LION.

The boys skinned her while we ate lunch. Then we started several of them back towards camp with the trophy, and ourselves cut across country to a small river known as the Stony Athi. There we dismounted from our horses, and sent them and the boys atop the ridge above the stream, while we ourselves explored afoot the hillside along the river.

This was a totally different sort of country from that to which we had been accustomed. Imagine a very bouldery hillside planted thickly with knee-high brambles and more sparsely with higher bushes. They were not really brambles, of course, but their tripping, tangling, spiky qualities were the same. We had to force our way through these, or step from boulder to boulder. Only very rarely did we get a little rubbly clear space to walk in, and then for only ten or twenty feet. We tried in spaced intervals to cover the whole hillside. It was very hard work. The boys, with the horses, kept pace with us on the sky-line atop, and two or three hundred yards away.

We had proceeded in this fashion for about a mile, when suddenly, and most unexpectedly, the biggest lion I ever saw leapt straight up from a bush twenty-five yards in front of me, and with a tremendous roar vanished behind another bush. I had just time to throw up the.405 shotgun-fashion and let drive a snapshot. Clifford Hill, who was ten yards to my right, saw the fur fly, and we all heard the snarl as the bullet hit. Naturally we expected an instant charge, but, as things turned out, it was evident the lion had not seen us at all. He had leapt at the sight of our men and horses on the sky-line, and when the bullet hit he must have ascribed it to them. At any rate, he began to circle through the tangled vines in their direction.

From their elevation they could follow his movements. At once they set up howls of terror and appeals for help. Some began frantically to run back and forth. None of them tried to run away; there was nowhere to go! The only thing that saved them was the thick and spiky character of the cover. The lion, instead of charging straight and fast, was picking an easy way.

We tore directly up hill as fast as we were able, leaping from rock to rock, and thrusting recklessly through the tangle. About half-way up I jumped to the top of a high, conical rock, and thence by good luck caught sight of the lion's great yellow head advancing steadily about eighty yards away. I took as good a sight as I could and pulled trigger. The recoil knocked me clear off the boulder, but as I fell I saw his tail go up and knew that I had hit. At once Clifford Hill and I jumped up on the rock again, but the lion had moved out of sight. By this time, however, the sound of the shots and the smell of blood had caused the dogs to close in. They did not, of course, attempt to attack the lion, nor even to get very near him, but their snarling and barking showed us the beast's whereabouts. Even this much is bad judgment on their part, as a number of them have been killed at it. The thicket burst into an unholy row.

We all manoeuvred rapidly for position. Again luck was with me, for again I saw his great head, the mane standing out all around it; and for the second time I planted a heavy bullet square in his chest. This stopped his advance; he lay down. His head was up and his eyes glared, as he uttered the most reverberating and magnificent roars and growls. The dogs leapt and barked around him. We came quite close, and I planted my fourth bullet in his shoulder. Even this was not enough. It took a fifth in the same place to finish him, and he died at last biting great chunks of earth.

The howls from the hill top ceased. All gathered to marvel at the lion's immense size. He measured three feet nine inches at the shoulder, and nine feet eleven inches between stakes, or ten feet eleven inches along contour. This is only five inches under record. We weighed him piecemeal, after a fashion, and put him between 550 and 600 pounds.

But these are only statistics, and mean little unless a real attempt is made to visualize them. As a matter of fact, his mere height—that of a medium-size zebra-was little unless accented by the impression of his tremendous power and quickness.

We skinned him, and then rode four long hours to camp. We arrived at dark, and at once set to work preparing the trophy. A dozen of us squatted around the skin, working by lantern light. Memba Sasa had had nothing to eat since before dawn, but in his pride and delight he refused to touch a mouthful until the job was finished. Several times we urged him to stop long enough for even a bite. He steadily declined, and whetted his knife, his eyes gleaming with delight, his lips crooning one of his weird Monumwezi songs. At eleven o'clock the task was done. Then I presented Memba Sasa with a tall mug of coffee and lots of sugar. He considered this a great honour.

---

## XXIV.

### THE FIFTEEN LIONS.

Two days before Captain D. and I were to return to Juja we approached, about eleven o'clock in the morning, a long, low, rugged range of hills called Lucania. They were not very high, but bold with cliffs, buttes, and broken rocky stretches. Here we were to make our final hunt.

We led our safari up to the level of a boulder flat between two deep cañons that ran down from the hills. Here should be water, so we gathered under a lone little tree, and set about directing the simple disposition of our camp. Herbert Spencer brought us a cold lunch, and we sat down to rest and refreshment before tackling the range.

Hardly had we taken the first mouthfuls, however, when Memba Sasa, gasping for breath, came tearing up the slope from the cañon where he had descended for a drink. "Lions!" he cried, guardedly. "I went to drink, and I saw four lions. Two were lying under the shade, but two others were playing like puppies, one on its back."

While he was speaking a lioness wandered out from the cañon and up the opposite slope. She was somewhere between six and nine hundred yards away, and looked very tiny; but the binoculars brought us up to her with a jump. Through them she proved to be a good one. She was not at all hurried, but paused from time to time to yawn and look about her. After a short interval, another, also a lioness, followed in her footsteps. She too had climbed clear when a third, probably a full-grown but still immature lion, came out, and after him the fourth.

"You were right," we told Memba Sasa, "there are your four."

But while we watched, a fifth, again at the spaced interval, this time a maned lion, clambered leisurely up in the wake of his family; and after him another, and another, and yet another! We gasped, and sat down, the better to steady our glasses with our knees. There seemed no end to lions. They came out of that apparently inexhaustible cañon bed one at a time and at the same regular intervals; perhaps twenty yards or so apart. It was almost as though they were being released singly. Finally we had *fifteen* in sight.

It was a most magnificent spectacle, and we could enjoy it unhurried by the feeling that we were losing opportunities. At that range it would be silly to open fire. If we had descended to the cañon in order to follow them out the other side, they would merely have trotted away. Our only chance was to wait until they had disappeared from sight, and then to attempt a wide circle in order to catch them from the flank. In the meantime we had merely to sit still.

Therefore we stared through our glasses, and enjoyed to the full this most unusual sight. There were four cubs about as big as setter dogs, four full-grown but immature youngsters, four lionesses, and three male lions. They kept their spaced, single file formation for two-thirds the ascent of the hill—probably the nature of the ground forced them to it—and then gradually drew together. Near the top, but still below the summit, they entered a jumble of boulders and stopped. We could make out several of them lying down. One fine old yellow fellow stretched himself comfortably atop a flat rock, in the position of a bronze lion on a pedestal. We waited twenty minutes to make sure they were not going to move. Then, leaving all our men except the gunbearers under the tree, we slipped back until out of sight, and began to execute our flank movement. The chances seemed good. The jumble of boulders was surrounded by open country, and it was improbable the lions could leave it without being seen. We had arranged with our men a system of signals.

For two hours we walked very hard in order to circle out of sight, down wind, and to gain the other side of the ridge back of the lions. We purposed slipping over the ridge and attacking from above. Even this was but a slight advantage. The job was a stiff one, for we might expect certainly the majority to charge.

Therefore, when we finally deployed in skirmish order and bore down on that patch of brush and boulders, we were braced for the shock of battle. We found nothing. Our men, however, signalled that the lions had not left cover. After a little search, however, we discovered a very shallow depression running slantwise up the hill and back of the cover. So slight it was that even the glasses had failed to show it from below. The lions had in all probability known about us from the start, and were all the time engaged in withdrawing after their leisurely fashion.

288

Of course we hunted for them; in fact, we spent two days at it; but we never found trace of them again. The country was too hard for tracking. They had left Lucania. Probably by the time we had completed our two hours of flanking movement they were five miles away. The presence of cubs would account for this. In ordinary circumstances we should have had a wonderful and exciting fight. But the sight of those fifteen great beasts was one I shall never forget.

After we had hunted Lucania thoroughly we parted company with the Hills, and returned to Juja Farm.

---

## PART V.

## THE TSAVO RIVER.

---

## XXV.

## VOI.

Part way up the narrow-gauge railroad from the coast is a station called Voi. On his way to the interior the traveller stops there for an evening meal. It is served in a high, wide stone room by white-robed Swahilis under command of a very efficient and quiet East Indian. The voyager steps out into the darkness to look across the way upon the outlines of two great rounded hills against an amethyst sky. That is all he ever sees of Voi, for on the down trip he passes through it about two o'clock in the morning.

At that particularly trying hour F. and I descended, and attempted, by the light of lanterns, to sort out twenty safari boys strange to us, and miscellaneous camp stores. We did not entirely succeed. Three men were carried on down the line, and the fly to our tent was never seen again.

The train disappeared. Our boys, shivering, crept into corners. We took possession of the dak-bungalow maintained by the railroad for just such travellers as ourselves. It was simply a high stone room, with three iron beds, and a corner so cemented that one could pour pails of water over one's self without wetting the whole place. The beds were supplied with mosquito canopies and strong wire springs. Over these we spread our own bedding, and thankfully resumed our slumbers.

The morning discovered to us Voi as the station, the district commissioner's house on a distant side hill, and a fairly extensive East Indian bazaar. The keepers of the latter traded with the natives. Immediately about the station grew some flat shady trees. All else was dense thorn scrub pressing close about the town. Opposite were the tall, rounded mountains.

Nevertheless, in spite of its appearance, Voi has its importance in the scheme of things. From it, crossing the great Serengetti desert, runs the track to Kilimanjaro and that part of German East Africa. The Germans have as yet no railroad; so they must perforce patronize the British line thus far, and then trek across. As the Kilimanjaro district is one rich in natives and trade, the track is well used. Most of the transport is done by donkeys—either in carts or under the pack saddle. As the distance from water to water is very great, the journey is a hard one. This fact, and the incidental consideration that from fly and hardship the mortality in donkeys is very heavy, pushes the freight rates high. And that fact accounts for the motor car, which has been my point of aim from the beginning of this paragraph.

The motor car plies between Voi and the German line at exorbitant rates. Our plan was to have it take us and some galvanized water tanks out into the middle of the desert and dump us down there. So after breakfast we hunted up the owner.

He proved to be a very short, thick-set, blond German youth who justified Weber and Fields. In fact, he talked so exactly like those comedians that my task in visualizing him to you is somewhat lightened. If all, instead of merely a majority of my readers, had seen Weber and Fields that task would vanish.

We explained our plan, and asked him his price.

"Sefen hundert and feefty rupees," said he uncompromisingly.

He was abrupt, blunt, and insulting. As we wanted transportation very much—though not seven hundred and fifty rupees' worth—we persisted. He offered an imperturbable take-it-or-leave-it stolidity. The motor truck stood near. I said something technical about the engine; then something more. He answered these remarks, though grudgingly. I suggested that it took a mighty good driver to motor through this rough country. He mentioned a particular hill. I proposed that we should try the station restaurant for beer while he told me about it. He grunted, but headed for the station.

For two hours we listened to the most blatant boasting. He was a great driver; he had driven for M., the American millionaire; for the Chinese Ambassador to France; for Grand-Duke Alexis; for the Kaiser himself! We learned how he had been the trusted familiar of these celebrities, how on various occasions—all detailed at length—he had been treated by them as an equal; and he told us sundry sly, slanderous, and disgusting anecdotes of these worthies, his forefinger laid one side his nose. When we finally got him worked up to the point of going to get some excessively bad photographs, "I haf daken myself!" we began to have hopes. So we tentatively approached once more the subject of transportation.

Then the basis of the trouble came out. One Davis, M.P. from England, had also dealt with our friend. Davis, as we reconstructed him, was of the blunt type, with probably very little feeling of democracy for those in subordinate positions, and with, most certainly, a good deal of insular and racial prejudice. Evidently a rather vague bargain had been struck, and the motor had set forth. Then ensued financial wranglings and disputes as to terms. It ended by useless hauteur on Davis's part, and inexcusable but effective action by the German. For Davis found himself dumped down on the Serengetti desert and left there.

We heard all this in excruciatingly funny Weberandfieldese, many times repeated. The German literally beat his breast and cried aloud against Davis. We unblushingly sacrificed a probably perfectly worthy Davis to present need, and cried out against him too.

"Am I like one dog?" demanded the German fervently.

"Certainly not," we cried with equal fervour. We both like dogs.

Then followed wearisomely reiterated assurances that we, at least, knew how a gentleman should be treated, and more boasting of proud connections in the past. But the end of it was a bargain of reasonable dimensions for ourselves, our personal boys, and our loads. Under plea of starting our safari boys off we left him, and crept, with shattered nerves, around the corner of the dak-bungalow. There we lurked, busy at pretended affairs, until our friend swaggered away to the Hindu quarters, where, it seems, he had his residence.

About ten o'clock a small safari marched in afoot. It had travelled all of two nights across the Thirst, and was glad to get there. The single white man in charge had been three years alone among the natives near Kilimanjaro, and he was now out for a six months' vacation at home. Two natives in the uniform of Sudanese troops hovered near him very sorrowful. He splashed into the water of the dak-bungalow, and then introduced himself. We sat in teakwood easy-chairs and talked all day. He was a most interesting, likeable, and cordial man, at any stage of the game. The game, by means of French vermouth—of all drinks!—progressed steadily. We could hardly blame him for celebrating. By the afternoon he wanted to give things away. So insistent was he that F. finally accepted an ebony walking-stick, and I an ebony knife inset with ivory. If we had been the least bit unscrupulous, I am afraid the relatives at home would have missed their African souvenirs. He went out *viâ* freight car, all by himself, seated regally in a steamer chair between two wide-open side doors, one native squatted on either side to see that he did not lurch out into the landscape.

FOOTNOTES:

Fifty pounds.

---

## XXVI.

### THE FRINGE-EARED ORYX.

At ten o'clock the following morning we started. On the high front seat, under an awning, sat the German, F., and I. The body of the truck was filled with safari loads, Memba Sasa, Simba Mohammed, and F.'s boy, whose name I have forgotten. The arrangement on the front seat was due to a strike on the part of F.

"Look here," said he to me, "you've got to sit next that rotter. We want him to bring us back some water from the other side, and I'd break his neck in ten minutes. You sit next him and give him your motor car patter."

Therefore I took the middle seat and played chorus. The road was not a bad one, as natural mountain roads go; I have myself driven worse in California. Our man, however, liked to exaggerate all the difficulties, and while doing it to point to himself with pride as a perfect wonder. Between times he talked elementary mechanics.

"The inflammation of the sparkling plugs?" was one of his expressions that did much to compensate.

The country mounted steadily through the densest thorn scrub I have ever seen. It was about fifteen feet high, and so thick that its penetration, save by made tracks, would have been an absolute impossibility. Our road ran like a lane between two spiky jungles. Bold bright mountains cropped up, singly and in short ranges, as far as the eye could see them.

This sort of thing for twenty miles—more than a hard day's journey on safari. We made it in a little less than two hours; and the breeze of our going kept us reasonably cool under our awning. We began to appreciate the real value of our diplomacy.

At noon we came upon a series of unexpectedly green and clear small hills just under the frown of a sheer rock cliff. This oasis in the thorn was occupied by a few scattered native huts and the usual squalid Indian dukka, or trading store. At this last our German friend stopped. From under the seat he drew out a collapsible table and a basket of provisions. These we were invited to share. Diplomacy's highest triumph!

After lunch we surmounted our first steep grade to the top of a ridge. This we found to be the beginning of a long elevated plateau sweeping gently downward to a distant heat mist, which later experience proved a concealment to snowcapped Kilimanjaro. This plateau also looked to be covered with scrub. As we penetrated it, however, we found the bushes were more or less scattered, while in the wide, shallow dips between the undulations were open grassy meadows. There was no water. Isolated mountains or peaked hills showed here and there in the illimitable spaces, some of them fairly hull down, all of them toilsomely distant. This was the Serengetti itself.

In this great extent of country somewhere were game herds. They were exceedingly migratory, and nobody knew very much about them. One of the species would be the rare and localized fringe-eared oryx. This beast was the principal zoological end of our expedition; though, of course, as always, we hoped for a chance lion. Geographically we wished to find the source of the Swanee River, and to follow that stream down to its joining with the Tsavo. About half-past one we passed our safari boys. We had intended to stop and replenish their canteens from our water-drums; but they told us they had encountered a stray and astonishing shower, and did not need more. We left them trudging cheerfully across the desert. They had travelled most of the night before, would do the same in the night to come, and should reach our camping-place about noon of the next day.

We ourselves stopped about four o'clock. In a few hours we had come a hard three days' march. Over the side went our goods. We bade the German a very affectionate farewell; for he was still to fill our drums from one of the streams out of Kilimanjaro and deliver them to us on his return trip next day. We then all turned to and made camp. The scrub desert here was exactly like the scrub desert for the last sixty miles.

The next morning we were up and off before sunrise. In this job time was a very large element of the contract. We must find our fringe-eared oryx before our water supply gave out. Therefore we had resolved not to lose a moment.

The sunrise was most remarkable—lace work, flat clouds, with burnished copper-coloured clouds behind glowing through the lace. We admired it for some few moments. Then one of us happened to look higher. There, above the sky of the horizon, apparently suspended in mid-air half-way to the zenith, hung like delicate bubbles the double snow-cloud peaks of Kilimanjaro. Between them and the earth we could apparently see clear sky. It was in reality, of course, the blue-heat haze that rarely leaves these torrid plains. I have seen many mountains in all parts of the world, but none as fantastically insubstantial; as wonderfully lofty; as gracefully able to yield, before clouds and storms and sunrise glows, all the space in infinity they could possibly use, and yet to tower above them serene in an upper space of its own. Nearly every morning of our journey to come we enjoyed this wonderful vision for an hour or so. Then the mists closed in. The rest of the day showed us a grayish sky along the western horizon, with apparently nothing behind it.

In the meantime we were tramping steadily ahead over the desert; threading the thorn scrub, crossing the wide shallow grass-grown swales; spying about us for signs of game. At the end of three or four miles we came across some ostrich and four hartebeeste. This encouraged us to think we might find other game soon, for the hartebeeste is a gregarious animal. Suddenly we saw a medium-sized squat beast that none of us recognized, trundling along like a badger sixty yards ahead. Any creature not easily identified is a scientific possibility in Africa. Therefore we fired at once. One of the bullets hit his foreleg paw. Immediately this astonishing small creature turned and charged us! If his size had equalled his ferocity, he would have been a formidable opponent. We had a lively few minutes. He rushed us again and again, uttering ferocious growls. We had to step high and lively to keep out of his way. Between charges he sat down and tore savagely at his wounded paw. We wanted him as nearly perfect a specimen as possible, so tried to rap him over the head with a club. Owing to remarkably long teeth and claws, this was soon proved impracticable; so we shot him. He weighed about fifty pounds, and we subsequently learned that he was a honey badger, an animal very rarely captured.

We left the boys to take the whole skin and skull of this beast, and strolled forward slowly. The brush ended abruptly in a wide valley. It had been burnt over, and the new grass was coming up green. We gave one look, and sank back into cover.

The sparse game of the immediate vicinity had gathered to this fresh feed. A herd of hartebeeste and gazelle were grazing, and five giraffe adorned the sky-line. But what interested us especially was a group of about fifty cob-built animals with the unmistakable rapier horns of the oryx. We recognized them as the rarity we desired.

The conditions were most unfavourable. The cover nearest them gave a range of three hundred yards, and even this would bring them directly between us and the rising sun. There was no help for it, however. We made our way to the bushes nearest the herd, and I tried to align the blurs that represented my sights. At the shot, ineffective, they raced to the right across our front. We lay low. As they had seen nothing they wheeled and stopped after two hundred yards of flight. This shift had brought the light into better position. Once more I could define my sights. From the sitting position I took careful aim at the largest buck. He staggered twenty feet and fell dead. The distance was just 381 paces. This shot was indeed fortunate, for we saw no more fringe-eared oryx.

---

## XXVII.

## ACROSS THE SERENGETTI.

We arrived in camp about noon, almost exhausted with the fierce heat and a six hours' tramp, to find our German friend awaiting us. By an irony of fate the drums of water he had brought back with him were now unnecessary; we had our oryx. However, we wearily gave him lunch and listened to his prattle, and finally sped him on his way, hoping never to see him again.

About three o'clock our men came in. We doled out water rations, and told them to rest in preparation for the morrow.

Late that night we were awakened by a creaking and snorting and the flash of torches passing. We looked out, to see a donkey transport toiling slowly along, travelling thus at night to avoid the terrific day heats. The two-wheeled carts with their wild and savage drivers looked very picturesque in the flickering lights. We envied them vaguely their defined route that permitted night travel, and sank to sleep.

In the morning, however, we found they had left with us new responsibilities in the shape of an elderly Somali, very sick, and down with the fever. This was indeed a responsibility. It was manifestly impossible for us to remain there with him; we should all die of thirst. It was equally impossible to take him with us, for he was quite unfit to travel under the sun. Finally, as the best solution of a bad business, we left him five gallons of water, some food, and some quinine, together with the advice to rest until night, and then to follow his companions along the beaten track. What between illness and wild beasts his chances did not look very good, but it was the best we could do for him. This incident exemplifies well the cruelty of this singular people. They probably abandoned the old man because his groans annoyed them, or because one of them wanted to ride in his place on the donkey cart.

We struck off as early as possible through the thorn scrub on a compass bearing that we hoped would bring us to a reported swamp at the head of the Swanee River. The Swanee River was one of the sources of the Tsavo. Of course this was guesswork. We did not know certainly the location of the swamp, its distance from us, nor what lay between us and it. However, we loaded all our transportable vessels with water, and set forth.

The scrub was all alike; sometimes thinner, sometimes thicker. We marched by compass until we had raised a conical hill above the horizon, and then we bore just to the left of that. The surface of the ground was cut by thousands of game tracks. They were all very old, however, made after a rain; and it was evident the game herds venture into this country only when it contains rainwater. After two hours, however, we did see one solitary hartebeeste, whom we greeted as an old friend in desolation. Shortly afterwards we ran across one oribi, which I shot for our own table.

At the end of two hours we sat down. The safari of twenty men was a very miscellaneous lot, consisting of the rag-tag-and-bobtail of the bazaars picked up in a hurry. They were soft and weak, and they straggled badly. The last weakling—prodded along by one of our two askaris—limped in only at the end of half an hour. Then we took a new start.

The sun was by now up and hot. The work was difficult enough at best, but the weight of the tropics was now cast in the scale. Twice more within the next two hours we stopped to let every one catch up. Each time this required a longer interval. In the thorn it was absolutely essential to keep in touch with every member of the party. A man once lost would likely remain so, for we could not afford to endanger all for the sake of one.

Time wore on until noon. Had it not been for a thin film of haze that now overspread the sky, I think the sun would have proved too much for some of the men. Four or five straggled so very badly that we finally left them in charge of one of our two askaris, with instructions to follow on as fast as they could. In order to make this possible, we were at pains to leave a well-marked trail.

After this fashion, slowly, and with growing anxiety for some of the men, we drew up on our landmark hill. There our difficulties increased; the thorn brush thickened. Only by a series of short zigzags, and by taking advantage of every rhino trail going in our direction, could we make our way through it at all; while to men carrying burdens on their heads the tangle aloft must have been fairly maddening. So slow did our progress necessarily become, and so difficult was it to keep in touch with everybody, that F. and I finally halted for consultation. It was decided that I should push on ahead with Memba Sasa to make certain that we were not on the wrong line, while F. and the askaris struggled with the safari.

Therefore I took my compass bearing afresh, and plunged into the scrub. The sensation was of hitting solid ground after a long walk through sand. We seemed fairly to shoot ahead and out of sight. Whenever we came upon earth we marked it deeply with our heels; we broke twigs downwards, and laid hastily-snatched bunches of grass to help the trail we were leaving for the others to follow. This, in spite of our compass, was a very devious track. Besides, the thorn bushes were patches of spiky aloe coming into red flower, and the spears of sisal.

After an hour's steady, swift walking the general trend of the country began to slope downwards. This argued a watercourse between us and the hills around Kilimanjaro. There could be no doubt that we would cut it; the only question was whether it, like so many desert watercourses, might not prove empty. We pushed on the more rapidly. Then we caught a glimpse through a chance opening, of the tops of trees below us. After another hour we suddenly burst from the scrub to a strip of green grass beyond which were the great trees, the palms, and the festooned vines of a watercourse. Two bush bucks plunged into the thicket as we approached, and fifteen or twenty mongooses sat up as straight and stiff as so many picket pins the better to see us.

For a moment my heart sank. The low undergrowth beneath the trees apparently swept unbroken from where we stood to the low bank opposite. It was exactly like the shallow, damp but waterless ravines at home, filled with black berry vines. We pushed forward, however, and found ourselves looking down on a smooth, swift flowing stream.

It was not over six feet wide, grown close with vines and grasses, but so very deep and swift and quiet that an extraordinary volume of water passed, as through an artificial aqueduct. Furthermore, unlike most African streams, it was crystal clear. We plunged our faces and wrists in it, and took long, thankful draughts. It was all most grateful after the scorching desert. The fresh trees meeting in canopy overhead were full of monkeys and bright birds; festooned vines swung their great ropes here and there; long heavy grass carpeted underfoot.

After we had rested a few minutes we filled our empty canteens, and prepared to start back for our companions. But while I stood there, Memba Sasa—good, faithful Memba Sasa—seized both canteens and darted away.

"Lie down!" he shouted back at me, "I will go back."

Without protest—which would have been futile anyway—I sank down on the grass. I was very tired. A little breeze followed the watercourse; the grass was soft; I would have given anything for a nap. But in wild Africa a nap is not healthy; so I drowsily watched the mongooses that had again come out of seclusion, and the monkeys, and the birds. At the end of a long time, and close to sundown, I heard voices. A moment later F., Memba Sasa, and about three-quarters of the men came in. We all, white and black, set to work to make camp. Then we built smudges and fired guns in the faint hope of guiding in the stragglers. As a matter of fact we had not the slightest faith in these expedients. Unless the men were hopelessly lost they should be able to follow our trail. They might be almost anywhere out in that awful scrub. The only course open to them would be to climb thorn trees for the night. Next day we would organize a formal search for them.

In the meantime, almost dead from exhaustion, we sprawled about everywhere. The men, too dispirited even to start their own camp-fires, sat around resting as do boxers between rounds. Then to us came Memba Sasa, who had already that day made a double journey, and who should have been the most tired of all.

"Bwana," said he, "if you will lend me Winchi, and a lantern, I will bring in the men."

We lent him his requirements, and he departed. Hours later he returned, carefully leaned "Winchi" in the corner of the tent, deposited the lantern, and stood erect at attention.

"Well, Memba Sasa," I inquired.

"The men are here."

"They were far?"

"Very far."

"Verna, Memba Sasa, assanti sana."

That was his sole—and sufficient—reward.

FOOTNOTES:

I have just heard that this old man survived, and has been singing our praises in Nairobi as the saviour of his life.

His name for the.405 Winchester.

"Very good, Memba Sasa, thanks very much."

---

## XXVIII.

DOWN THE RIVER.

Relieved now of all anxiety as to water, we had merely to make our way downstream. First, however, there remained the interesting task of determining its source.

Accordingly next day we and our gunbearers left the boys to a well-earned rest, and set out upstream. At first we followed the edge of the river jungle, tramping over hard hot earth, winding in and out of growths of thorn scrub and brilliant aloes. We saw a herd of impallas gliding like phantoms; and as we stood in need of meat, I shot at one of them but missed. The air was very hot and moist. At five o'clock in the morning the thermometer had stood at 78 degrees; and by noon it had mounted to 106 degrees. In addition the atmosphere was filled with the humidity that later in the day was to break in extraordinary deluges. We moved slowly, but even then our garments were literally dripping wet.

At the end of three miles the stream bed widened. We came upon beautiful, spacious, open lawns of from eighty to one hundred acres apiece, separated from each other by narrow strips of tall forest trees. The grass was high, and waved in the breeze like planted grain; the boundary trees resembled artificial wind-breaks of eucalyptus or Normandy poplar. One might expect a white ranch house beyond some low clump of trees, and chicken runs, and corrals.

Along these apparent boundaries of forest trees our stream divided, and divided again, so that we were actually looking upon what we had come to seek—the source of the Swanee branch of the Tsavo River. In these peaceful, protected meadows was it cradled. From them it sprang full size out into the African wilderness.

A fine impalla buck grazed in one of these fields. I crept as near him as I could behind one of the wind-break rows of trees. It was not very near, and for the second time I missed. Thereupon we decided two things: that we were not really meat hungry, and that yesterday's hard work was not conducive to to-day's good shooting.

Having thus accomplished the second object of our expedition, we returned to camp. From that time begins a regular sequence of events on which I look back with the keenest of pleasure. The two constant factors were the river and the great dry country on either side. Day after day we followed down the one, and we made brief excursions out into the other. Each night we camped near the sound of the swift running water, where the winds rustled in the palms, the acacias made lacework across the skies, and the jungle crouched in velvet blackness close to earth like a beast.

Our life in its routine was regular; in its details bizarre and full of the unexpected. Every morning we arose an hour before day, and ate by lantern light and the gleam of fires. At the first gray we were afoot and on the march. F. and I, with our gunbearers, then pushed ahead down the river, leaving the men to come along as fast or as slowly as they pleased. After about six hours or so of marching, we picked out a good camp site, and lay down to await the safari. By two o'clock in the afternoon camp was made. Also it was very hot. After a light lunch we stripped to the skin, lay on our cots underneath the mosquito canopies, and tried to doze or read. The heat at this time of day was blighting. About four o'clock, if we happened to be inspired by energy, one or the other of us strolled out at right angles to the stream to see what we could see. The evening was tepid and beautiful. Bathed and pyjama-clad we lolled in our canvas chairs, smoking, chatting or listening to the innumerable voices of the night.

Such was the simple and almost invariable routine of our days. But enriching it, varying it, disguising it even—as rain-squalls, sunshine cloud shadow, and unexpected winds modify the landscape so well known from a study window— were the incredible incidents and petty adventures of African travel.

The topography of the river itself might be divided very roughly into three: the headwater country down to its junction with the Tsavo the palm-elephant-grass stretch, and the gorge and hill district just before it crosses the rail road.

The headwater country is most beautiful The stream is not over ten feet wide, but very deep, swift, and clear. It flows between defined banks and is set in a narrow strip of jungle. In places the bed widens out to a carpet of the greenest green grass sown with flowers; at other places it offers either mysterious thickets, spacious cathedrals, or snug bowers. Immediately beyond the edge of this river jungle begins the thorn scrub, more or less dense. Distant single mountains or buttes serve as landmarks in a brush-grown, gently rising, strongly rolling country. Occasional alluvial flats draw back to low cliffs not over twenty feet high.

After the junction of the Tsavo, palms of various sorts replace to a large extent the forest trees. Naturally also the stream widens and flows more slowly. Outside the palms grow tall elephant-grass and bush. Our marching had generally to be done in the narrow, neutral space between these two growths. It was pleasant enough, with the river snatching at the trailing branches, and the birds and animals rustling away. Beyond the elephant-grass flats low ridges ran down to the river, varying in width, but carrying always with them the dense thorn. Between them ran recesses, sometimes three or four hundred acres in extent, high with elephant-grass or little trees like alders. So much for the immediate prospect on our right as we marched. Across the river to our left were huge riven mountains, with great cliffs and cañons. As we followed necessarily every twist and turn of the river, sometimes these mountains were directly ahead of us, then magically behind, so that we thought we had passed them by. But the next hour threw them again across our trail. The ideal path would, of course, have cut across all the bends and ridges; but the thorn of the ridges and the elephant-grass of the flats forbade it. So we marched ten miles to gain four.

After days of struggle and deception we passed those mountains. Then we entered a new type of country where the Tsavo ran in cañons between hills. The high cliffs often towered far above us; we had to pick our way along narrow river ledges; again the river ran like a trout stream over riffles and rapids, while we sauntered along cleared banks beneath the trees. Had we not been making a forced march under terrific heat at just that time, this last phase of the river might have been the pleasantest of all.

Throughout the whole course of our journey the rhinoceros was the most abundant of the larger animals. The indications of old tracks proved that at some time of the year, or under some different conditions, great herds of the more gregarious plains antelope and zebra visited the river, but at the time of our visit they were absent. The rhinoceroses, however, in incredible numbers came regularly to water. Paradoxically, we saw very few of them, and enjoyed comparative immunity from their charges. This was due to the fact that their habits and ours swung in different orbits. The rhinoceros, after drinking, took to the hot, dry thorn scrub in the low hills; and as he drank at night, we rarely encountered him in the river bottoms where we were marching. This was very lucky, for the cover was so dense that a meeting must necessarily be at close quarters. Indeed these large and truculent beasts were rather a help than a hindrance, for we often made use of their wide, clear paths to penetrate some particularly distressing jungle. However, we had several small adventures with them: just enough to keep us alert in rounding corners or approaching bushes—and nine-tenths of our travel was bushes and corners. The big, flat footsteps, absolutely fresh in the dust, padded methodically ahead of us down the only way until it seemed that we could not fail to plump upon their maker around the next bend. We crept forward foot by foot, every sense alert, finger on trigger. Then after a time the spoor turned off to the right, towards the hills. We straightened our backs and breathed a sigh of relief. This happened over and over again. At certain times of year also elephants frequent the banks of the Tsavo in considerable numbers We saw many old signs, and once came upon the fresh path of a small herd. The great beasts had passed by that very morning. We gazed with considerable awe on limbs snatched bodily from trees; on flat-topped acacias a foot in diameter pulled up by the roots and stood up side down; on tree trunks twisted like ropes.

Of the game by far the most abundant were the beautiful red impalla. We caught glimpses of their graceful bodies gliding in and out of sight through the bushes; or came upon them standing in small openings, their delicate ears pointed to us. They and the tiny dikdik furnished our table; and an occasional water-buck satisfied the men. One day we came on one of the latter beasts sound asleep in a tiny open space. He was lying down, and his nose rested against the earth just like a very old family horse in a paddock.

Besides these common species were bush-buck wart-hog, lesser kudu, giraffe, and leopard. The bush-buck we jumped occasionally quite near at hand. They ducked their heads low and rushed tearingly to the next cover. The leopard was heard sighing every night, and saw their pad marks next day; but only twice did we catch glimpses of them. One morning we came upon the fresh-killed carcass of a female lesser kudu from which, evidently, we had driven the slayer.

These few species practically completed the game list. They were sufficient for our needs; and the lesser kudu was a prize much desired for our collection. But by far the most interesting to me were the smaller animals, the birds, and the strange, innumerable insects.

We saw no natives in the whole course of our journey.

The valley of the river harboured many monkeys. They seemed to be of two species, blue and brown, but were equally noisy and amusing. They retired ahead of our advance with many remarks, or slipped past us to the rear without any comments whatever. When we made camp they retired with indignant protests, and when we had quite settled down they returned as near as they dared.

One very hot afternoon I lay on my canvas cot in the open, staring straight upward into the overarching greenery of the trees. This is a very pleasant thing to do. The beautiful up-spreading, outstretching of the tree branches and twigs intrigue the eye; the leaves make fascinating, hypnotically waving patterns against a very blue sky; and in the chambers and galleries of the upper world the birds and insects carry on varied businesses of their own. After a time the corner of my eye caught a quick movement far to the left and in a shadow. At once I turned my attention that way. After minute scrutiny I at length made out a monkey. Evidently considering himself quite unobserved, he was slowly and with great care stalking our camp. Inch by inch he moved, taking skilful advantage of every bit of cover, flattening himself along the limbs, hunching himself up behind bunches of leaves, until he had gained a big limb directly overhead. There he stretched flat, staring down at the scene that had so strongly aroused his curiosity. I lay there for over two hours reading and dozing. My friend aloft never stirred. When dusk fell he was still there. Some time after dark he must have regained his band, for in the morning the limb was vacant.

Now comes the part of this story that really needs a witness, not to veracity perhaps, but to accuracy of observations. Fortunately I have F. About noon next day the monkey returned to his point of observation. He used the same precautions as to concealment; he followed his route of the day before; he proceeded directly to his old conning tower on the big limb. It did not take him quite so long to get there, for he had already scouted out the trail. *And close at his heels followed two other monkeys*! They crawled where he crawled; they crouched where he crouched; they hid where he hid; they flattened themselves out by him on the big limb, and all three of them passed the afternoon gazing down on the strange and fascinating things below. Whether these newcomers were part of the first one's family out for a treat, or whether they were Cook's Tourists of the Jungle in charge of my friend's competence as a guide, I do not know.

Farther down the river F. and I stopped for some time to watch the crossing of forty-odd of the little blue monkeys. The whole band clambered to near the top of a tall tree growing by the water's edge. There, one by one, they ran out on a straight overhanging limb and cast themselves into space. On the opposite bank of the river, and leaning well out, grew a small springy bush. Each monkey landed smash in the middle of this, clasped it with all four hands, swayed alarmingly, recovered, and scampered ashore. It was rather a nice problem in ballistics this, for a mistake in calculation of a foot in distance or a pound in push would land Mr. Monkey in the water. And the joke of it was that directly beneath that bush lay two hungry-looking crocodiles! As each tiny body hurtled through the air I'll swear a look of hope came into the eyes of those crocs. We watched until the last had made his leap. There were no mistakes. The joke was against the crocodiles.

We encountered quite a number of dog-faced baboons. These big apes always retreated very slowly and noisily. Scouts in the rearguard were continually ascending small trees or bushes for a better look at us, then leaping down to make disparaging remarks. One lot seemed to show such variation in colour from the usual that we shot one. The distance was about two hundred and fifty yards. Immediately the whole band—a hundred or so strong—dropped on all fours and started in our direction. This was rather terrifying. However, as we stood firm, they slowly came to a halt at about seventy yards, barked and chattered for a moment, then hopped away to right and left.

---

## XXIX.

THE LESSER KUDU.

About eight o'clock, the evening of our first day on the Swanee, the heat broke in a tropical downpour. We heard it coming from a long distance, like the roar of a great wind. The velvet blackness, star hung, was troubled by an invisible blurring mist, evidenced only through a subtle effect on the subconsciousness. Every leaf above us, in the circle of our firelight, depended absolutely motionless from its stem. The insects had ceased their shrilling; the night birds their chirping; the animals, great and small, their callings or their stealthy rustling to and fro. Of the world of sound there remained only the crackling of our fires, the tiny singing of the blood in our ears, and that far-off portentous roar. Our simple dispositions were made. Trenches had been dug around the tents; the pegs had been driven well home; our stores had been put in shelter. We waited silently, puffing away our pipes.

The roaring increased in volume. Beneath it we began to hear the long, rolling crash of thunder. Overhead the stars, already dimmed, were suddenly blotted from existence. Then came the rain, in a literal deluge, as though the god of floods had turned over an entire reservoir with one twist of his mighty hand. Our fire went out instantly; the whole world went out with it. We lay on our canvas cots unable to see a foot beyond our tent opening; unable to hear anything but the insistent, terrible drumming over our heads; unable to think of anything through the tumult of waters. As a man's body might struggle from behind a waterfall through the torrents, so our imaginations, half drowned, managed dimly to picture forth little bits—the men huddled close in their tiny tents, their cowled blankets over their heads. All the rest of the universe had gone.

After a time the insistent beat and rush of waters began to wear through our patience. We willed that this wracking tumult should cease; we willed it with all the force that was in us. Then, as this proved vain, we too humped our spiritual backs, cowled our souls with patience, and waited dumbly for the force of the storm to spend itself. Our faculties were quite as effectually drowned out by the unceasing roar and crash of the waters as our bodily comfort would have been had we lacked the protection of our tent.

Abruptly the storm passed. It did not die away slowly in the diminuendo of ordinary storms. It ceased as though the reservoir had been tipped back again. The rapid *drip, drip, drip* of waters now made the whole of sound; all the rest of the world lay breathless. Then, inside our tent, a cricket struck up bravely.

This homely, cheerful little sound roused us. We went forth to count damages and to put our house in order. The men hunted out dry wood and made another fire; the creatures of the jungle and the stars above them ventured forth.

Next morning we marched into a world swept clean. The ground was as smooth as though a new broom had gone over it. Every track now was fresh, and meant an animal near at hand. The bushes and grasses were hung with jewels. Merry little showers shook down from trees sharing a joke with some tiny wind. White steam rose from a moist, fertile-looking soil. The smell of greenhouses was in the air. Looking back, we were stricken motionless by the sight of Kilimanjaro, its twin peaks suspended a clean blue sky, fresh snow mantling its shoulders.

This day, so cheeringly opened, was destined to fulfil its promise. In the dense scrub dwell a shy and rare animal called the lesser kudu specimens of which we greatly desired. The beast keeps to the thickest and driest cove where it is impossible to see fifty yards ahead but where the slightest movement breaks the numberless dry interlacements of which the place seems made. To move really quietly one could not cover over a half-mile in an hour. As the countryside extends a thousand square miles or more, and the lesser kudu is rare, it can be seen that hunting them might have to be a slow and painful process. We had twice seen the peculiar tracks.

On this morning, however, we caught a glimpse of the beast itself. A flash of gray, with an impression of the characteristic harness-like stripes—that was all. The trail, in the ground, was of course very plain. I left the others and followed it into the brush. As usual the thorn scrub was so thick that I had to stoop and twist to get through it at all, and so brittle that the least false move made a crackling like a fire. The rain of the night before had, however, softened the *débris* lying on the ground. I moved forward as quickly as I could, half suffocated in the steaming heat of the dense thicket. After three or four hundred yards the beast fell into a walk, so I immediately halted. I reasoned that after a few steps at this gait he would look back to see whether or not he was followed. If his scouting showed him nothing he might throw off suspicion. After ten minutes I crept forward again. The spoor showed my surmises to be correct, for I came to where the animal had turned, behind a small bush, and had stood for a few minutes. Taking up the tracks from this point, I was delighted to find that the kudu had forgotten its fear, and was browsing. At the end of five minutes more of very careful work, I was fortunate enough to see it, feeding from the top of a small bush thirty-five yards away. The raking shot from the Springfield dropped it in its tracks.

It proved to be a doe, a great prize of course, but not to be compared with the male. We skinned her carefully, and moved on, delighted to have the species.

Our luck was not over, however. At the end of six hours we picked our camp in a pretty grove by the swift-running stream. There we sat down to await the safari. The tree-tops were full of both the brown and blue monkeys, baboons barked at us from a distance, the air was musical with many sweet birds. Big thunder-clouds were gathering around the horizon.

The safari came in. Mohammed immediately sought us out to report, in great excitement, that he had seen five kudu across the stream. He claimed to have watched them even after the safari had passed, and that they had not been alarmed. The chance was slight that the kudu could be found, but still it was a chance. Accordingly we rather reluctantly gave up our plans for a loaf and a nap. Mohammed said the place was an hour back; we had had six hours march already. However, about two o'clock we set out. Before we had arrived quite at the spot we caught a glimpse of the five kudu as they dashed across a tiny opening ahead of us. They had moved downstream and crossed the river.

It seemed rather hopeless to follow them into that thick country once they had been alarmed, but the prize was great. Therefore Memba Sasa and I took up the trail. We crept forward a mile, very quiet, very tense—very sweaty. Then simultaneously, through a chance opening and a long distance away, we caught a patch of gray with a single transverse white stripe. There was no chance to ascertain the sex of the beast, nor what part of its anatomy was thus exposed. I took a bull's eye chance on that patch of gray; had the luck to hit it in the middle. The animal went down. Memba Sasa leapt forward like a madman; I could not begin to keep pace with him. When I had struggled through the thorn, I found him dancing with delight.

"Monuome, bwana! buck, master!" he cried as soon as he saw me, and made a spiral gesture in imitation of the male's beautiful corkscrew horns.

While the men prepared the trophy, F. and I followed on after the other four to see what they would do, and speedily came to the conclusion that we were lucky to land two of the wily beasts. The four ran compactly together and in a wide curve for several hundred yards. Then two faced directly back, while the other two, one on either side, made a short detour out and back to guard the flanks.

We did not get back to camp until after dark. A tremendous pair of electric storms were volleying and roaring at each other across the space of night; leopards were crying; a pack of wild dogs were barking vociferously. The camp, as we approached it, was a globe of light in a bower of darkness. The fire, shining and flickering on the under sides of the leaves, lent them a strangely unreal stage-like appearance; the porters, their half-naked bodies and red blankets catching the blaze, roasted huge chunks of meat over little fires.

We ate a belated supper in comfort, peace, and satisfaction. Then the storms joined forces and fell upon us.

---

## XXX.

ADVENTURES BY THE WAY.

We journeyed slowly on down the stream. Interesting things happened to us. The impressions of that journey are of two sorts: the little isolated details and the general background of our day's routine, with the gray dawn, the great heats of the day, the blessed evening and its fireflies; the thundering of heaven's artillery, and the downpour of torrents; the hot, high, crackling thorn scrub into which we made excursions; the swift-flowing river with its palms and jungles; outleaning palms trailing their fronds just within the snatch of the flood waters; wide flats in the embrace of the river bends, or extending into the low hills, grown thick with lush green and threaded with rhinoceros paths; the huge sheer cliff mountains over the way; distant single hills far down. The mild discomfort of the start before daylight clearly revealed the thorns and stumbling blocks; the buoyant cheerfulness of the first part of the day, with the grouse rocketing straight up out of the elephant grass, the birds singing everywhere, and the beasts of the jungle still a-graze at the edges; the growing weight of the sun, as though a great pressing hand were laid upon the shoulders; the suffocating, gasping heat of afternoon, and the; gathering piling black and white clouds; the cool evening in pyjamas with the fireflies flickering; among the bushes, the river singing, and little; breezes wandering like pattering raindrops in the dry palm leaves—all these, by repetition of main elements, blend in my memory to form a single image. To be sure each day the rock pinnacles over the way changed slightly their compass bearings, and little variations of contour lent variety to the procession of days. But in essentials they were of one kin.

But here and there certain individual scenes and incidents stand out clearly and alone. Without reference to my notebook I could not tell you their chronological order, nor the days of their happening. They occurred, without correlation.

Thus one afternoon at the loafing hour, when F. was sound asleep under his mosquito bar, and I in my canvas chair was trying to catch the breeze from an approaching deluge, to me came a total stranger in a large turban. He was without arms or baggage of any sort, an alien in a strange and savage country.

"Jambo, bwana m'kubwa (greeting, great master)!" said he.

"Jambo," said I, as though his existence were not in the least surprising, and went on reading. This showed him that I was indeed a great master.

After a suitable interval I looked up.

"Wataka neenee (what do you want)?" I demanded.

"Nataka sema qua heri (I want to say good-bye)," said this astonishing individual.

I had, until that moment, been quite unaware of his existence. As he had therefore not yet said "How do you do," I failed to fathom his reasons for wanting to say "good-bye." However, far be it from me to deny any one innocent pleasure, so I gravely bade him good-bye, and he disappeared into the howling wilderness whence he had come.

---

One afternoon we came upon two lemurs seated gravely side by side on a horizontal limb ten feet up a thorn tree. They contemplated us with the preternatural gravity of very young children, and without the slightest sign of fear. We coveted them as pets for Billy, but soon discovered that their apparent tameness was grounded on good, solid common sense. The thorns of that thorn tree! We left them sitting upright, side by side.

A little farther on, and up a dry earthy hillside, a medium-sized beast leapt from an eroded place fairly under my feet and made off with a singularly familiar kiyi. It was a strange-looking animal, apparently brick red in colour. When I had collected myself I saw it was a wild dog. It had been asleep in a warm hollow of red clay, and had not awakened until I was fairly upon it. We had heard these beasts nearly every night, but this was the first we had seen. Some days later we came upon the entire pack drinking at the river. They leapt suddenly across our front eighty yards away, their heads all turned towards us truculently, barking at us like so many watch dogs. They made off, but not as though particularly alarmed.

---

One afternoon I had wounded a good wart-hog across the river, and had gone downstream to find a dry way over. F., more enthusiastic, had plunged in and promptly attacked the wart-hog. He was armed with the English service revolver shooting the.455 Ely cartridge. It is a very short, stubby bit of ammunition. I had often cast doubt on its driving power as compared to the.45 Colt, for example. F., as a loyal Englishman, had, of course, defended his army's weapon. When I reached the centre of disturbance I found that F. had emptied his revolver three times—eighteen shots—into the head and forequarters of that wart-hog without much effect. Incidentally the wart-hog had given him a good lively time, charging again and again. The weapon has not nearly the shock power of even our.38 service—a cartridge classified as too light for serious business.

---

One afternoon I gave my shotgun to one of the porters to carry afield, remarking facetiously to all and sundry that he looked like a gunbearer. After twenty minutes we ran across a rhinoceros. I spent some time trying to manoeuvre into position for a photograph of the beast. However, the attempt failed. We managed to dodge his rush. Then, after the excitement had died, we discovered the porter and the shotgun up a tree. He descended rather shamefaced. Nobody said anything about it. A half-hour later we came upon another rhinoceros. The beast was visible at some distance, and downhill. Nevertheless the porter moved a little nearer a tree. This was too much for Memba Sasa. All the rest of the afternoon he "ragged" that porter in much the same terms we would have employed in the same circumstances.

"That place ahead," said he, "looks like a good place for rhinoceros. Perhaps you'd better climb a tree."

"There is a dikdik; a bush is big enough to climb for him."

"Are you afraid of jackals, too?"

---

The fireflies were our regular evening companions. We caught one or two of them for the pleasure of watching them alternately igniting and extinguishing their little lamps. Even when we put them in a bottle they still kept up their performance bravely.

But besides them we had an immense variety of evening visitors. Beetles of the most inconceivable shapes and colours, all sorts of moths, and numberless strange things—leaf insects, walking-stick insects (exactly like dry twigs), and the fierce, tall, praying mantis with their mock air of meekness and devotion. Let one of the other insects stray within reach and their piety was quickly enough abandoned! One beetle about three-eighths of an inch across was oblong in shape and of pure glittering gold. His wing covers, on the other hand, were round and transparent. The effect was of a jewel under a tiny glass case. Other beetles were of red dotted with black, or of black dotted with red; they sported stripes, or circles of plain colours; they wore long, slender antennae, or short knobby horns; they carried rapiers or pinchers, long legs or short. In fact they ran the gamut of grace and horror, so that an inebriate would find here a great rest for the imagination.

After we had gone to bed we noticed more pleasantly our cricket. He piped up, you may remember, the night of the first great storm. That evening he took up his abode in some fold or seam of our tent, and there stayed throughout all the rest of the journey. Every evening he tuned up cheerfully, and we dropped to sleep to the sound of his homelike piping. We grew very fond of him, as one does of everything in this wild and changing country that can represent a stable point of habitude.

Nor must I forget one evening when all of a sudden out of the darkness came a tremendous hollow booming, like the beating of war drums or the bellowing of some strange great beast. At length we identified the performer as an unfamiliar kind of frog!

---

## XXXI.

THE LOST SAFARI.

We were possessed of a map of sorts, consisting mostly of wide blank spaces, with an occasional tentative mountain, or the probable course of streams marked thereon. The only landmark that interested us was a single round peak situated south of our river and at a point just before we should cross the railroad at Tsavo Station. There came a day when, from the top of a hill where we had climbed for the sake of the outlook, we thought we recognized that peak. It was about five miles away as the crow flies.

Then we returned to camp and made the fatal mistake of starting to figure. We ought to cover the distance, even with the inevitable twists and turns, in a day; the tri-weekly train passed through Tsavo the following night; if we could catch that we would save a two days' wait for the next train. You follow the thought. We arose very early the next morning to get a good start on our forced march.

There is no use in spinning out a sad tale. We passed what we thought must be our landmark hill just eleven times. The map showed only one butte; as a matter of fact there were dozens. At each disappointment we had to reconstruct our theories. It is the nature of man to do this hopefully—Tsavo Station must be just around the next bend. We marched six hours without pause; then began to save ourselves a little. By all the gods of logical reasoning we *proved* Tsavo just beyond a certain fringe of woods. When we arrived we found that there the river broke through a range of hills by way of a deep gorge. It was a change from the everlasting scrub, with its tumbling waters, its awful cliffs, its luxuriant tropical growths; but it was so much the more difficult to make our way through. Beyond the gorge we found any amount of hills, kopjes, buttes, sugar loaves, etc., each isolated from its fellows, each perfectly competent to serve as the map's single landmark.

We should have camped, but we were very anxious to catch that train; and we were convinced that now, after all that work, Tsavo could not be far away. It would be ridiculous and mortifying to find we had camped almost within sight of our destination!

The heat was very bad and the force of the sun terrific. It seemed to possess actual physical weight, and to press us down from above. We filled our canteens many times at the swift-running stream, and emptied them as often. By two o'clock F. was getting a little wobbly from the sun. We talked of stopping, when an unexpected thunder shower rolled out from behind the mountains, and speedily overcast the entire heavens. This shadow relieved the stress. F., much revived, insisted that we proceed. So we marched and passed many more hills.

In the meantime it began to rain, after the whole-hearted tropical fashion. In two minutes we were drenched to the skin. I kept my matches and notebook dry by placing them in the crown of my cork helmet. After the intense heat this tepid downpour seemed to us delicious.

And then, quite unexpectedly, of course, we came around a bend to make out through the sheets of rain the steel girders of the famous Tsavo bridge.

We clambered up a steep, slippery bank to the right-of-way, along which we proceeded half a mile to the station. This consisted of two or three native huts, a house for the East Indian in charge, and the station building itself. The latter was a small frame structure with a narrow floorless veranda. There was no platform. Drawing close on all sides was the interminable thorn scrub. Later, when the veil of rain had been drawn aside, we found that Tsavo, perched on a hillside, looked abroad over a wide prospect. For the moment all we saw was a dark, dismal, dripping station, wherein was no sign of life.

We were beginning to get chilly, and we wanted very much some tea, fire, a chance to dry, pending the arrival of our safari. We jerked open the door and peered into the inky interior.

"Babu!" yelled F., "Babu!"

From an inner back room came the faint answer in most precise English,—

"I can-not come; I am pray-ing."

There followed the sharp, quick tinkle of a little bell—the Indian manner of calling upon the Lord's attention.

We both knew better than to hustle the institutions of the East; so we waited with what patience we had, listening to the intermittent tinkling of the little bell. At the end of fully fifteen minutes the devotee appeared. He proved to be a mild, deprecating little man, very eager to help, but without resources. He was a Hindu, and lived mainly on tea and rice. The rice was all out, but he expected more on the night train. There was no trading store here. He was the only inhabitant. After a few more answers he disappeared, to return carrying two pieces of letter paper on which were tea and a little coarse native sugar. These, with a half-dozen very small potatoes, were all he had to offer.

It did not look very encouraging. We had absolutely nothing in which to boil water. Of course we could not borrow of our host; caste stood in the way there. If we were even to touch one of his utensils, that utensil was for him defiled for ever. Nevertheless, as we had eaten nothing since four o'clock that morning, and had put a hard day's work behind us, we made an effort. After a short search we captured a savage possessed of a surfuria, or native cooking pot. Memba Sasa scrubbed this with sand. First we made tea in it, and drank turn about, from its wide edge. This warmed us up somewhat. Then we dumped in our few potatoes and a single guinea fowl that F. had decapitated earlier in the day. We ate; and passed the pot over to Memba Sasa.

So far, so good; but we were still very wet, and the uncomfortable thought would obtrude itself that the safari might not get in that day. It behoved us at least to dry what we had on. I hunted up Memba Sasa, whom I found in a native hut. A fire blazed in the middle of the floor. I stooped low to enter, and squatted on my heels with the natives. Slowly I steamed off the surface moisture. We had rather a good time chatting and laughing. After a while I looked out. It had stopped raining. Therefore I emerged and set some of the men collecting firewood. Shortly I had a fine little blaze going under the veranda roof of the station. F. and I hung out our breeches to dry, and spread the tails of our shirts over the heat. F. was actually the human chimney, for the smoke was pouring in clouds from the breast and collar of his shirt. We were fine figures for the public platform of a railway station!

We had just about dried off and had reassumed our thin and scanty garments, when the babu emerged. We stared in drop-jawed astonishment. He had muffled his head and mouth in a most brilliant scarf, as if for zero weather; although dressed otherwise in the usual pongee. Under one arm he carried a folded clumsy cotton umbrella; around his waist he had belted a huge knife; in his other hand he carried his battle-axe. I mean just that—his battle-axe. We had seen such things on tapestries or in museums, but did not dream that they still existed out of captivity. This was an Oriental looking battle-axe with a handle three feet long, a spike on top, a spike out behind, and a half-moon blade in front. The babu had with a little of his signal paint done the whole thing, blade and all, to a brilliant window-shutter green.

As soon as we had recovered our breath, we asked him very politely the reason for these stupendous preparations. It seemed that it was his habit to take a daily stroll just before sunset, "for the sake of the health," as he told us in his accurate English.

"The bush is full of bad men," he explained, "who would like to kill me; but when they see this axe and this knife they say to each other, 'There walks a very bad man. We dare not kill him.'"

He marched very solemnly a quarter-mile up the track and back, always in plain view. Promptly on his return he dived into his little back room where the periodic tinkling of his praying bell for some time marked his gratitude for having escaped the "bad men."

The bell ceased. Several times he came to the door, eyed us timidly, and bolted back into the darkness. Finally he approached to within ten feet, twisted his hands and giggled in a most deprecating fashion.

"What is the use of this killing game?" he gabbled as rapidly as he could. "Man should not destroy what man cannot first create." After which he giggled again and fled.

His conscience, evidently, had driven him to this defiance of our high mightinesses against his sense of politeness and his fears.

About this time my boy Mohammed and the cook drifted in. They reported that they had left the safari not far back. Our hopes of supper and blankets rose. They declined, however, with the gathering darkness, and were replaced by wrath against the faithless ones. Memba Sasa, in spite of his long day, took a gun and disappeared in the darkness. He did not get back until nine o'clock, when he suddenly appeared in the doorway to lean the gun in the corner, and to announce, "Hapana safari."

We stretched ourselves on a bench and a table—the floor was impossible—and took what sleep we could. In the small hours the train thundered through, the train we had hoped to catch!

FOOTNOTES:

This is the point at which construction was stopped by man-eating lions. See Patterson's "The Man-eaters of Tsavo."

---

## XXXII.

THE BABU.

We stretched ourselves stiffly in the first gray of dawn, wondering where we could get a mouthful of breakfast. On emerging from the station a strange and gladsome sight met our eyes—namely, chop boxes and gun cases belonging to some sportsman not yet arrived. Necessity knows no law; so we promptly helped ourselves to food and gun-cleaning implements. Much refreshed, we lit our pipes and settled ourselves to wait for our delinquents.

Shortly after sunrise an Indian track inspector trundled in on a handcar propelled by two natives. He was a suave and corpulent person with a very large umbrella and beautiful silken garments. The natives upset the handcar off the track, and the newcomer settled himself for an enjoyable morning. He and the babu discussed ethics and metaphysical philosophy for three solid hours. Evidently they came from different parts of India, and their only common language was English. Through the thin partition in the station building we could hear plainly every word. It was very interesting. Especially did we chortle with delight when the inspector began one of his arguments somewhat as follows:—

"Now the two English who are here. They possess great sums of wealth"—F. nudged me delightedly—"and they have weapons to kill, and much with which to do things, yet their savage minds—"

It was plain, rank, eavesdropping, but most illuminating, thus to get at first hand the Eastern point of view as to ourselves; to hear the bloodless, gentle shell of Indian philosophy described by believers. They discussed the most minute and impractical points, and involved themselves in the most uncompromising dilemmas.

Thus the gist of one argument was as follows: "All sexual intercourse is sin, but the race must go forward by means of sexual intercourse; therefore the race is conceived in sin and is sinful; but it is a great sin for me, as an individual, not to carry forward the race, since the Divine Will decrees that in some way the race is necessary to it. *Therefore* it would seem that man is in sin whichever way you look at it—"

"But," interposes the inspector firmly but politely, "is it not possible that sexual sin and the sin of opposing Divine Will may be of balance in the spirit, so that in resisting one sort a man acquires virtue to commit the other without harm—" And so on for hours.

At twelve-thirty the safari drifted in. Consider that fact and what it meant. The plain duty of the headman was, of course, to have seen that the men followed us in the day before. But allowing, for the sake of argument, that this was impossible, and that the men had been forced by the exhaustion of some of their number to stop and camp, if they had arisen betimes they should have completed the journey in two hours at most. That should have brought them in by half-past seven or eight o'clock. But a noon arrival condemned them without the necessity of argument. They had camped early, had risen very, very late, and had dawdled on the road.

We ourselves gave the two responsible headmen twenty lashes apiece; then turned over to them the job of thrashing the rest. Ten per man was the allotment. They expected the punishment; took it gracefully. Some even thanked us when it was over! The babu disappeared in his station.

About an hour later he approached us, very deprecating, and handed us a telegram. It was from the district commissioner at Voi ordering us to report for flogging "porters on the Tsavo Station platform."

"I am truly sorry, I am truly sorry," the babu was murmuring at our elbows.

"What does this mean?" we demanded of him.

He produced a thick book.

"It is in here—the law," he explained. "You must not flog men on the station platform. It was my duty to report."

"How did we know that? Why didn't you tell us?"

"If you had gone there"—he pointed ten feet away to a spot exactly like all other spots—"it would have been off the platform. Then I had nothing to say."

We tried to become angry.

"But why in blazes couldn't you have told us of that quietly and decently? We'd have moved."

"It is the law" He tapped his thick book.

"But we cannot be supposed to know by heart every law in that book. Why didn't you warn us before reporting?" we insisted.

"I am truly sorry," he repeated. "I hope and trust it will not prove serious. But it is in the book."

We continued in the same purposeless fashion for a moment or so longer. Then the babu ended the discussion thus,—

"It was my duty. I am truly sorry. Suppose I had not reported and should die to-day, and should go to heaven, and God should ask me, 'Have you done your duty to-day?' what should I say to Him?"

We gave it up; we were up against Revealed Religion.

So that night we took a freight train southward to Voi, leaving the babu and his prayer-bell, and his green battle-axe and his conscience alone in the wilderness. We had quite a respect for that babu.

The district commissioner listened appreciatively to our tale.

"Of course I shall not carry the matter further," he told us, "but having known the babu, you must see that once he had reported to me I was compelled to order you down here. I am sorry for the inconvenience."

And when we reflected on the cataclysmic upheaval that babu would have undergone had we not been summoned after breaking one of The Laws in the Book, we had to admit the district commissioner was right.

---

## PART VI.

IN MASAILAND.

---

## XXXIII.

OVER THE LIKIPIA ESCARPMENT.

Owing to an outbreak of bubonic plague, and consequent quarantine, we had recruited our men outside Nairobi, and had sent them, in charge of C., to a little station up the line.

Billy and I saw to the loading of our equipment on the train, and at two o'clock, in solitary state, set forth. Our only attendants were Mohammed and Memba Sasa, who had been fumigated and inoculated and generally Red-Crossed for the purpose.

The little narrow-gauge train doubled and twisted in its climb up the range overlooking Nairobi and the Athi Plains. Fields of corn grew so tall as partially to conceal villages of round, grass-thatched huts with conical roofs; we looked down into deep ravines where grew the broad-leaved bananas; the steep hillsides had all been carefully cultivated. Savages leaning on spears watched us puff heavily by. Women, richly ornamented with copper wire or beads, toiled along bent under loads carried by means of a band across the top of the head. Naked children rushed out to wave at us. We were steaming quite comfortably through Africa as it had been for thousands of years before the white man came.

At Kikuyu Station we came to a halt. Kikuyu Station ordinarily embarks about two passengers a month, I suppose. Now it was utterly swamped with business, for on it had descended all our safari of thirty-nine men and three mules.

Thirty of the thirty-nine yelled and shrieked and got in the wrong place, as usual. C. and the train men and the stationmaster and our responsible boys heaved and tugged and directed, ordered, commanded. At length the human element was loaded to its places and locked in. Then the mules had to be urged up a very narrow gang-lank into a dangerous-looking car. Quite sensibly they declined to take chances. We persuaded them. The process was quite simple. Two of the men holding the ends at a safe distance stretched a light strong cord across the beasts' hind legs, and sawed it back and forth.

We clanged the doors shut, climbed aboard, and the train at last steamed on. Now bits of forest came across our way, deep, shaded, with trailing curtain vines, and wide leaves as big as table tops, and high, lush, impenetrable undergrowth full of flashing birds, fathomless shadows, and inquisitive monkeys. Occasionally we emerged to the edge of a long oval meadow, set in depressions among hills, like our Sierra meadows. Indeed so like were these openings to those in our own wooded mountains that we always experienced a distinct shock of surprise as the familiar woods parted to disclose a dark solemn savage with flashing spear.

We stopped at various stations, and descended and walked about in the gathering shadows of the forest. It was getting cool. Many little things attracted our attention, to remain in our memories as isolated pictures. Thus I remember one grave savage squatted by the track playing on a sort of mandoline-shaped instrument. It had two strings, and he twanged these alternately, without the slightest effort to change their pitch by stopping with his fingers. He bent his head sidewise, and listened with the meticulous attention of a connoisseur. We stopped at that place for fully ten minutes, but not for a second did he leave off twanging his two strings, nor did he even momentarily relax his attention.

It was now near sundown. We had been climbing steadily. The train shrieked twice, and unexpectedly slid out to the edge of the Likipia Escarpment. We looked down once more into the great Rift Valley.

The Rift Valley is as though a strip of Africa—extending half the length of the continent—had in time past sunk bodily some thousands of feet, leaving a more or less sheer escarpment on either side, and preserving intact its own variegated landscape in the bottom. We were on the Likipia Escarpment. We looked across to the Mau Escarpment, where the country over which our train had been travelling continued after its interruption by the valley. And below us were mountains, streams, plains. The westering sun threw strong slants of light down and across.

The engine shut off its power, and we slid silently down the rather complicated grades and curves of the descent. A noble forest threw its shadows over us. Through the chance openings we caught glimpses of the pale country far below. Across high trestle bridges we rattled, and craned over to see the rushing white water of the mountain torrents a hundred feet down. The shriek of our engine echoed and re-echoed weirdly from the serried trunks of trees and from the great cliffs that seemed to lift themselves as we descended.

We debarked at Kijabe well after dark. It is situated on a ledge in the escarpment, is perhaps a quarter-mile wide, and includes nothing more elaborate than the station, a row of Indian dukkas, and two houses of South Africans set back towards the rise in the cliffs. A mile or so away, and on a little higher level, stand the extensive buildings of an American mission. It is, I believe, educational as well as sectarian, is situated in one of the most healthful climates of East Africa, and is prosperous.

At the moment we saw none of these things. We were too busy getting men, mules, and equipment out of the train. Our lanterns flared in the great wind that swept down the defile; and across the track little fires flared too. Shortly we made the acquaintance of the South Africander who furnished us our ox teams and wagon; and of a lank, drawling youth who was to be our "rider." The latter was very anxious to get started, so we piled all our stores and equipment but those immediately necessary for the night aboard the great wagon. Then we returned to the dak-bungalow for a very belated supper. While eating this we discussed our plans.

These were in essence very simple. Somewhere south of the Great Thirst of the Sotik a river called the Narossara. Back of the river were high mountains, and down the river were benches dropping off by thousands of feet to the barren country of Lake Magadhi. Over some of this country ranged the Greater Kudu, easily the prize buck of East Africa. We intended to try for a Greater Kudu.

People laughed at us. The beast is extremely rare; it ranges over a wide area; it inhabits the thickest sort of cover in a sheer mountainous country; its senses are wonderfully acute; and it is very wary. A man *might*, once in a blue moon, get one by happening upon it accidentally, but deliberately to go after it was sheer lunacy. So we were told. As a matter of fact, we thought so ourselves, but Greater Kudu was as good an excuse as another.

The most immediate of our physical difficulties was the Thirst. Six miles from Kijabe we would leave the Kedong River. After that was no more water for two days and nights. During that time we should be forced to travel and rest in alternation day and night, with a great deal of travel and very little rest. We should be able to carry for the men a limited amount of water on the ox wagon, but the cattle could not drink. It was a hard, anxious grind. A day's journey beyond the first water after the Thirst we should cross the Southern Guaso Nyero River. Then two days should land us at the Narossara. There we must leave our ox wagon and push on with our tiny safari. We planned to relay back for porters from our different camps.

That was our whole plan. Our transport rider's object in starting this night was to reach the Kedong River, and there to outspan until our arrival next day. The cattle would thus get a good feed and rest. Then at four in the afternoon we would set out to conquer the Thirst. After that it would be a question of travelling to suit the oxen.

Next morning, when we arose, we found one of the wagon Kikuyus awaiting us. His tale ran that after going four miles, the oxen had been stampeded by lions. In the mix-up the dusselboom had been broken. He demanded a new dusselboom. I looked as wise as though I knew just what that meant; and told him largely, to help himself. Shortly he departed carrying what looked to be the greater part of a forest tree.

We were in no hurry, so we did not try to get our safari under way before eight o'clock. It consisted of twenty-nine porters, the gunbearers, three personal boys, three syces, and the cook. Of this lot some few stand out from the rest, and deserve particular attention.

Of course I had my veterans, Memba Sasa and Mohammed. There was also Kongoni, gunbearer, elsewhere described. The third gunbearer was Marrouki, a Wakamba. He was the personal gunbearer of a Mr. Twigg, who very courteously loaned him for this trip as possessing some knowledge of the country. He was a small person, with stripes about his eyes; dressed in a Scotch highland cap, khaki breeches, and a shooting coat miles too big for him. His soul was earnest, his courage great, his training good, his intelligence none too brilliant. Timothy, our cook, was pure Swahili. He was a thin, elderly individual, with a wrinkled brow of care. This represented a conscientious soul. He tried hard to please, but he never could quite forget that he had cooked for the Governor's safari. His air was always one of silent disapproval of our modest outfit. So well did he do, however, often under trying circumstances, that at the close of the expedition Billy presented him with a very fancy knife. To her vast astonishment he burst into violent sobs.

"Why, what is it?" she asked.

"Oh, memsahib," he wailed, "I wanted a watch!"

As personal boy Billy had a Masai named Geyeye. The members of this proud and aristocratic tribe rarely condescend to work for the white man; but when they do, they are very fine servants, for they are highly intelligent. Geyeye was short and very, very ugly. Perhaps this may partly explain his leaving tribal life, for the Masai generally are over six feet.

C.'s man was an educated Coast Swahili named Abba Ali. This individual was very smart. He wore a neatly-trimmed Vandyke beard, a flannel boating hat, smart tailored khakis, and carried a rattan cane. He was alert, quick, and intelligent. His position was midway between that of personal boy and headman.

Of the rank and file we began with twenty-nine. Two changed their minds before we were fairly started, and departed in the night. There was no time to get regular porters; but fortunately a Kikuyu chief detailed two wild savages from his tribe to act as carriers. These two children of nature drifted in with pleasant smiles and little else save knick-knacks. From our supplies we gave them two thin jerseys, reaching nearly to the knees. Next day they appeared with broad tucks sewed around the middle! They looked like "My Mama didn't use wool soap." We then gave it up, and left them free and untrammelled.

They differed radically. One was past the first enthusiasms and vanities of youth. He was small, unobtrusive, unornamented. He had no possessions save the jersey, the water-bottle, and the blanket we ourselves supplied. The blanket he crossed bandolier fashion on one shoulder. It hung down behind like a tasselled sash. His face was little and wizened and old. He was quiet and uncomplaining, and the "easy mark" for all the rest. We had constantly to be interfering to save him from imposition as to too heavy loads, too many jobs, and the like. Nearing the close of the long expedition, when our loads were lighter and fewer, one day C. spoke up.

"I'm going to give the old man a good time," said he. "I doubt if he's ever had one before, or if he ever will again. He's that sort of a meek damnfool."

So it was decreed that Kimau should carry nothing for the rest of the trip, was to do no more work, was to have all he wanted to eat. It was a treat to see him. He accepted these things without surprise, without spoken thanks; just as he would have accepted an increased supply of work and kicks. Before his little fire he squatted all day, gazing vacantly off into space, or gnawing on a piece of the meat he always kept roasting on sticks. He spoke to no one; he never smiled or displayed any obvious signs of enjoyment; but from him radiated a feeling of deep content.

His companion savage was a young blood, and still affected by the vanities of life. His hair he wore in short tight curls, resembling the rope hair of a French poodle, liberally anointed with castor-oil and coloured with red-paint clay. His body, too, was turned to bronze by the same method, so that he looked like a beautiful smooth metal statue come to life. To set this quality off he wore glittering collars, bracelets, and ear ornaments of polished copper and brass. When he joined us his sole costume was a negligent two-foot strip of cotton cloth. After he had received his official jersey, he carefully tied the cloth over his wonderful head; nor as far as we knew did he again remove it until the end of the expedition. All his movements were inexpressibly graceful. They reminded one somehow of Flaxman's drawings of the Greek gods. His face, too, was good-natured and likeable. A certain half feminine, wild grace, combined with the queer effect of his headgear, caused us to name him Daphne. At home he was called Kingangui. At first he carried his burden after the fashion of savages—on the back; and kept to the rear of the procession; and at evening consorted only with old Lightfoot. As soon as opportunity offered, he built himself a marvellous iridescent ball of marabout feathers. Each of these he split along the quill, so that they curled and writhed in the wind. This picturesque charm he suspended from a short pole in front of his tent. Also, he belonged to the Kikuyu tribe; he ate no game meat, but confined his diet to cornmeal porridge. We were much interested in watching Daphne's gradual conversion from savage ways to those of the regular porter. Within two weeks he was carrying his load on his head or shoulder, and trying to keep up near the head of the safari. The charm of feathers disappeared shortly after, I am sorry to say. He took his share of the meat. Within two months Daphne was imitating as closely as possible the manners and customs of his safari mates. But he never really succeeded in looking anything but the wild and graceful savage he was.

FOOTNOTES:

After the fashion of the Canadian tump line.

Pronounce all the syllables.


An entirely different stream from that flowing north of Mt. Kenia.


Pronounce *every* syllable.


His official name was Lightfoot, Queen of the Fairies, because of his ballet-like costume.

---

## XXXIV.

TO THE KEDONG.


For four hours we descended the valley through high thorn scrub or the occasional grassy openings. We were now in the floor of the Rift Valley, and both along the escarpments and in the floor of the great blue valley itself mountains were all about us. Most of the large ones were evidently craters; and everywhere were smaller kopjes or buttes, that in their day had also served as blow holes for subterranean fires.

At the end of this time we arrived at the place where we were supposed to find the wagon. No wagon was there.

The spot was in the middle of a level plain on which grew very scattered bushes, a great deal like the sparser mesquite growths of Arizona. Towards the Likipia Escarpment, and about half-way to its base, a line of trees marked the course of the Kedong River. Beyond that, fairly against the mountain, we made out a settler's house.

Leaving Billy and the safari, C. and I set out for this house. The distance was long, and we had not made half of it before thunder clouds began to gather. They came up thick and black behind the escarpment, and rapidly spread over the entire heavens. We found the wagon shortly, still mending its dusselboom, or whatever the thing was. Leaving instructions for it to proceed to a certain point on the Kedong River, we started back for our safari.

It rained. In ten minutes the dusty plains, as far as the eye could reach, were covered with water two or three inches deep, from which the sparse bunches of grasses grew like reeds in a great marshy lake. We splashed along with the water over our ankles. The channels made by the game trails offered natural conduits, and wherever there was the least grade they had become rushing brooks. We found the safari very bedraggled. Billy had made a mound of valuables, atop which she perched, her waterproof cape spread as wide as possible, a good deal like a brooding hen. We set out for the meeting-point on the Kedong. In half an hour we had there found a bit of higher ground and had made camp.

As suddenly as they had gathered the storm clouds broke away. The expiring sun sent across the valley a flood of golden light, that gilded the rugged old mountain of Suswa over the way.

"Directly on the other side of Suswa," C. told me, "there is a 'pan' of hard clay. This rain will fill it, and we shall find water there. We can take a night's rest, and set off comfortably in the morning."

So the rain that had soaked us so thoroughly was a blessing after all. While we were cooking supper the wagon passed us, its wheels and frame creaking, its great whip cracking like a rifle, its men shrieking at the imperturbable team of eighteen oxen. It would travel until the oxen wanted to graze, or sleep, or scratch an ear, or meditate on why is a Kikuyu. Thereupon they would be outspanned and allowed to do it, whatever it was, until they were ready to go on again. Then they would go on. These sequences might take place at any time of the day or night, and for greater or lesser intervals of time. That was distinctly up to the oxen; the human beings had mighty little to say in the matter. But transport riding, from the point of view of the rank outsider, really deserves a chapter of its own.

---

## XXXV.

THE TRANSPORT RIDER.


The wagon is one evolved in South Africa—a long, heavily-constructed affair, with ingenious braces and timbers so arranged as to furnish the maximum clearance with the greatest facility for substitution in case the necessity for repairs might arise. The whole vehicle can be dismounted and reassembled in a few hours; so that unfordable streams or impossible bits of country can be crossed piecemeal. Its enormous wheels are set wide apart. The brake is worked by a crank at the rear, like a reversal of the starting mechanism of a motor car. Bolted to the frame on either side between the front and rear wheels are capacious cupboards, and two stout water kegs swing to and fro when the craft is under way. The net carrying capacity of such a wagon is from three to four thousand pounds.

This formidable vehicle, in our own case, was drawn by a team of eighteen oxen. The biggest brutes, the wheelers, were attached to a tongue, all the others pulled on a long chain. The only harness was the pronged yoke that fitted just forward of the hump. Over rough country the wheelers were banged and jerked about savagely by the tongue; they did not seem to mind it but exhibited a certain amount of intelligence in manipulation.

To drive these oxen we had one white man named Brown, and two small Kikuyu savages. One of these worked the brake crank in the rear while the other preceded the lead cattle. Brown exercised general supervision, a long-lashed whip and Boer-Dutch expletives and admonitions.

In transport riding, as this game is called, there is required a great amount of especial skill though not necessarily a high degree of intelligence. Along the flats all goes well enough, but once in the unbelievable rough country of a hill trek the situation alters. A man must know cattle and their symptoms. It is no light feat to wake up eighteen sluggish bovine minds to the necessity for effort, and then to throw so much dynamic energy into the situation that the whole eighteen will begin to pull at once. That is the secret, unanimity; an ox is the most easily discouraged working animal on earth. If the first three couples begin to haul before the others have aroused to their effort, they will not succeed in budging the wagon an inch, but after a moment's struggle will give up completely. By that time the leaders respond to the command and throw themselves forward in the yoke. In vain. They cannot pull the wagon and their wheel comrades too. Therefore they give up. By this time, perhaps, the lash has aroused the first lot to another effort. And so they go, pulling and hauling against each other, getting nowhere, until the end is an exhausted team, a driver half insane, and a great necessity for unloading.

A good driver, on the other hand, shrieks a few premonitory Dutch words—and then! I suppose inside those bovine heads the effect is somewhat that of a violent electric explosion. At any rate it hits them all at once, and all together, in response, they surge against their yokes. The heavily laden wagon creaks, groans, moves forward. The hurricane of Dutch and the volleys of whip crackings rise to a crescendo. We are off!

To perform just this little simple trick of getting the thing started requires not only a peculiar skill or gift, but also lungs of brass and a throat of iron. A transport rider without a voice is as a tenor in the same fix. He may—and does—get so hoarse that it is a pain to hear him; but as long as he can croak in good volume he is all right. Mere shouting will not do. He must shriek, until to the sympathetic bystander it seems that his throat must split wide open. Furthermore, he must shriek the proper things. It all sounds alike to every one but transport riders and oxen; but as a matter of fact it is Boer-Dutch, nicely assorted to suit different occasions. It is incredible that oxen should distinguish; but, then, it is also incredible that trout should distinguish the nice differences in artificial flies.

After the start has been made successfully, the craft must be kept under way. To an unbiassed bystander the whole affair looks insane. The wagon creaks and sways and groans and cries aloud as it bumps over great boulders in the way; the leading Kikuyu dances nimbly and shrills remarks at the nearest cattle; the tail Kikuyu winds energetically back and forth on his little handle, and tries to keep his feet. And Brown! he is magnificent! His long lash sends out a volley of rifle reports, down, up, ahead, back; his cracked voice roars out an unending stream of apparent gibberish. Back and forth along the line of the team he skips nimbly, the sweat streaming from his face. And the oxen plod along, unhasting, unexcited, their eyes dreamy, chewing the cud of yesterday's philosophic reflections. The situation conveys the general impression of a peevish little stream breaking against great calm cliffs. All this frantic excitement and expenditure of energy is so apparently purposeless and futile, the calm cattle seem so aloof and superior to it all, so absolutely unaffected by it. They are going slowly, to be sure; their gait may be maddeningly deliberate, but evidently they do not intend to be hurried. Why not let them take their own speed?

But all this hullabaloo means something after all. It does its business, and the top of the boulder-strewn hill is gained. Without it the whole concern would have stopped, and then the wagon would have to be unloaded before a fresh start could have been made. Results with cattle are not shown by facial expression nor by increased speed, but simply by continuance. They will plod up steep hills or along the level at the same placid gait. Only in the former case they require especial treatment.

In case the wagon gets stuck on a hill, as will occasionally happen, so that all the oxen are discouraged at once, we would see one of the Kikuyus leading the team back and forth, back and forth, on the side hill just ahead of the wagon. This is to confuse their minds, cause them to forget their failure, and thus to make another attempt.

At one stretch we had three days of real mountains. N'gombe Brown shrieked like a steam calliope all the way through. He lasted the distance, but had little camp-fire conversation even with his beloved Kikuyus.

When the team is outspanned, which in the waterless country of forced marches is likely to be almost any time of the day or night, N'gombe Brown sought a little rest. For this purpose he had a sort of bunk that let down underneath the wagon. If it were daytime, the cattle were allowed to graze under supervision of one of the Kikuyus. If it was night time they were tethered to the long chain, where they lay in a somnolent double row. A lantern at the head of the file and one at the wagon's tail were supposed to discourage lions. In a bad lion country fires were added to these defences.

N'gombe Brown thus worked hard through varied and long hours in strict intimacy with stupid and exasperating beasts. After working hours he liked to wander out to watch those same beasts grazing! His mind was as full of cattle as that! Although we offered him reading matter, he never seemed to care for it, nor for long-continued conversation with white people not of his trade. In fact the only gleam of interest I could get out of him was by commenting on the qualities or peculiarities of the oxen. He had a small mouth-organ on which he occasionally performed, and would hold forth for hours with his childlike Kikuyus. In the intelligence to follow ordinary directions he was an infant. We had to iterate and reiterate in words of one syllable our directions as to routes and meeting-points, and then he was quite as apt to go wrong as right. Yet, I must repeat, he knew thoroughly all the ins and outs of a very difficult trade, and understood, as well, how to keep his cattle always fit and in good condition. In fact he was a little hipped on what the "dear n'gombes" should or should not be called upon to do.

One incident will illustrate all this better than I could explain it. When we reached the Narossara River we left the wagon and pushed on afoot. We were to be gone an indefinite time, and we left N'gombe Brown and his outfit very well fixed. Along the Narossara ran a pleasant shady strip of high jungle; the country about was clear and open; but most important of all, a white man of education and personal charm occupied a trading boma, or enclosure, near at hand. An accident changed our plans and brought us back unexpectedly at the end of a few weeks. We found that N'gombe Brown had trekked back a long day's journey, and was encamped alone at the end of a spur of mountains. We sent native runners after him. He explained his change of base by saying that the cattle feed was a little better at his new camp! Mind you this: at the Narossara the feed was quite good enough, the oxen were doing no work, there was companionship, books, papers, and even a phonograph to while away the long weeks until our return. N'gombe Brown quite cheerfully deserted all this to live in solitude where he imagined the feed to be microscopically better!

FOOTNOTES:

N'gombe = oxen.

---

## XXXVI.

ACROSS THE THIRST.

We were off, a bright, clear day after the rains. Suswa hung grayish pink against the bluest of skies. Our way slanted across the Rift Valley to her base, turned the corner, and continued on the other side of the great peak until we had reached the rainwater "pan" on her farther side. It was a long march.

The plains were very wide and roomy. Here and there on them rose many small cones and craters, lava flows and other varied evidences of recent volcanic activity. Geologically recent, I mean. The grasses of the flowing plains were very brown, and the molehill craters very dark; the larger craters blasted and austere; the higher escarpment in the background blue with a solemn distance. The sizes of things were not originally fitted out for little tiny people like human beings. We walked hours to reach landmarks apparently only a few miles away.

In this manner we crept along industriously until noon, by which time we had nearly reached the shoulder of Suswa, around which we had to double. The sun was strong, and the men not yet hardened to the work. We had many stragglers. After lunch Memba Sasa and I strolled along on a route flanking that of the safari, looking for the first of our meat supply. Within a short time I had killed a Thompson's gazelle. Some solemn giraffes looked on at the performance, and then moved off like mechanical toys.

The day lengthened. We were in the midst of wonderful scenery. Our objection grew to be that it took so long to put any of it behind us. Insensibly, however, we made progress. Suddenly, as it seemed, we found ourselves looking at the other side of Suswa, and various brand-new little craters had moved up to take the places of our old friends. At last, about half-past four, we topped the swell of one of the numerous and interminable land billows that undulate across all plains countries here, and saw a few miles away the wagon outspanned. We reached it about sunset, to be greeted by the welcome news that there was indeed water in the pan.

We unsaddled just before dark, and I immediately started towards the game herds, many of which were grazing a half-mile away. The gazelle would supply our own larder, but meat for hard-worked man was very desirable. I shot a hartebeeste, made the prearranged signal for men to carry meat, and returned to camp.

Even yet the men were not all in. We took lanterns and returned along the road, for the long marches under a desert sun are no joke. At last we had accounted for all but two. These we had to abandon. Next day we found their loads, but never laid eyes on them again. Thus early our twenty-nine became twenty-seven.

About nine o'clock, just as we were turning, a number of lions began to roar. Usually a lion roars once or twice by way of satisfaction after leaving a kill. These, however, were engaged in driving game, and hence trying to make as much noise as possible. We distinguished plainly seven individuals, perhaps more. The air trembled with the sound as to the deepest tones of a big organ, only the organ is near and enclosed, while these vibrations were in the open air and remote. For a few moments the great salvos would boom across the veld, roll after roll of thunder; then would ensue a momentary dead silence; then a single voice would open, to be joined immediately by the others.

We awoke next day to an unexpected cold drizzle. This was a bit uncomfortable, from one point of view, and most unusual, but it robbed the thirst of its terrors. We were enabled to proceed leisurely, and to get a good sleep near water every night. The wagon had, as usual, pulled out some time during the night.

Our way led over a succession of low rolling ridges each higher than its predecessor. Game herds fed in the shallow valleys between. At about ten o'clock we came to the foot of the Mau Escarpment, and also to the unexpected sight of the wagon outspanned. N'gombe Brown explained to us that the oxen had refused to proceed farther in face of a number of lions that came around to sniff at them. Then the rain had come on, and he had been unwilling to attempt the Mau while the footing was slippery. This sounded reasonable; in fact, it was still reasonable. The grass was here fairly neck high, and we found a rain-filled water-hole. Therefore we decided to make camp. C. and I wandered out in search of game. We tramped a great deal of bold, rugged country, both in cañon bottoms and along the open ridges, but found only a rhinoceros, one bush-buck and a dozen hartebeeste. African game, as a general rule, avoids a country where the grass grows very high. We enjoyed, however, some bold and wonderful mountain scenery, and obtained glimpses through the flying murk of the vast plains and the base of Suswa. On a precipitous cañon cliff we found a hanging garden of cactus and of looped cactus-like vines that was a marvel to behold. We ran across the hartebeeste on our way home. Our men were already out of meat; the hartebeeste of yesterday had disappeared. These porters are a good deal like the old-fashioned Michigan lumberjacks—they take a good deal of feeding for the first few days. When we came upon the little herd in the neck-high grass, I took a shot. At the report the animal went down flat. We wandered over slowly. Memba Sasa whetted his knife and walked up. Thereupon Mr. Hartebeeste jumped to his feet, flirted his tail gaily, and departed. We followed him a mile or so, but he got stronger and gayer every moment, until at last he frisked out of the landscape quite strong and hearty. In all my African experience I lost only six animals hit by bullets, as I took infinite pains and any amount of time to hunt down wounded beasts. This animal was, I think, "creased" by too high a shot. Certainly he was not much injured; but certainly he got a big shock to start with.

The little herd had gone on. I got down and crawled on hands and knees in the thick grass. It was slow work, and I had to travel by landmarks. When I finally reckoned I had about reached the proper place, I stood up suddenly, my rifle at ready. So dense was the cover and so still the air that I had actually crawled right into the middle of the band! While we were cutting up the meat the sun broke through strongly.

Therefore the wagon started on up the Mau at six o'clock. Twelve hours later we followed. The fine drizzle had set in again. We were very glad the wagon had taken advantage of the brief dry time.

From the top of the sheer rise we looked back for the last time over the wonderful panorama of the Rift Valley. Before us were wide rounded hills covered with a scattered small growth that in general appearance resembled scrub oak. It sloped away gently until it was lost in mists. Later, when these cleared, we saw distant blue mountains across a tremendous shallow basin. We were nearly on a level with the summit of Suswa itself, nor did we again drop much below that altitude. After five or six miles we overtook the wagon outspanned. The projected all-night journey had again been frustrated by the lions. These beasts had proved so bold and menacing that finally the team had been forced to stop in sheer self-defence. However, the day was cool and overcast, so nothing was lost.

After topping the Mau we saw a few gazelle, zebra, and hartebeeste, but soon plunged into a bush country quite destitute of game. We were paralleling the highest ridge of the escarpment, and so alternated between the crossing of cañons and the travelling along broad ridges between them. In lack of other amusement for a long time I rode with the wagon. The country was very rough and rocky. Everybody was excited to the point of frenzy, except the wagon. It had a certain Dutch stolidity in its manner of calmly and bumpily surmounting such portions of the landscape as happened in its way.

After a very long, tiresome march we camped above a little stream. Barring our lucky rain this would have been the first water since leaving the Kedong River. Here were hundreds of big blue pigeons swooping in to their evening drink.

For two days more we repeated this sort of travel, but always with good camps at fair-sized streams. Gradually we slanted away from the main ridge, though we still continued cross-cutting the swells and ravines thrown off its flanks. Only the ravines hour by hour became shallower, and the swells lower and broader. On their tops the scrub sometimes gave way to openings of short grass. On these fed a few gazelle of both sorts, and an occasional zebra or so. We saw also four topi, a beast about the size of our wapiti, built on the general specifications of a hartebeeste, but with the most beautiful iridescent plum-coloured coat. This quartette was very wild. I made three separate stalks on them, but the best I could do was 360 paces, at which range I missed.

Finally we surmounted the last low swell to look down a wide and sloping plain to the depression in which flowed the principal river of these parts, the Southern Guaso Nyero. Beyond it stretched the immense oceanlike plains of the Loieta, from which here and there rose isolated hills, very distant, like lonesome ships at sea. A little to the left, also very distant, we could make out an unbroken blue range of mountains. These were our ultimate destination.

---

## XXXVII.

### THE SOUTHERN GUASO NYERO.

The Southern Guaso Nyero, unlike its northern namesake, is a sluggish, muddy stream, rather small, flowing between abrupt clay banks. Farther down it drops into great cañons and eroded abysses, and acquires a certain grandeur. But here, at the ford of Agate's Drift, it is decidedly unimpressive. Scant greenery ornaments its banks. In fact, at most places they run hard and baked to a sheer drop-off of ten or fifteen feet. Scattered mimosa trees and aloes mark its course. The earth for a mile or so is trampled by thousands of Masai cattle that at certain seasons pass through the funnel of this, the only ford for miles. Apparently insignificant, it is given to sudden, tremendous rises. These originate in the rainfalls of the upper Mau Escarpment, many miles away. It behooves the safari to cross promptly if it can, and to camp always on the farther bank.

This we did, pitching our tents in a little opening, between clumps of pretty flowering aloes and the mimosas. Here, as everywhere in this country, until we had passed the barrier of the Narossara mountains, the common horseflies were a plague. They follow the Masai cattle. I can give you no better idea of their numbers than to tell you two isolated facts: I killed twenty-one at one blow; and in the morning, before sunrise, the apex of our tent held a solid black mass of the creatures running the length of the ridge pole, and from half an inch to two inches deep! Every pack was black with them on the march, and the wagon carried its millions. When the shadow of a branch would cross that slowly lumbering vehicle, the swarm would rise and bumble around distractedly for a moment before settling down again. They fairly made a nimbus of darkness.

After we had made camp we saw a number of Masai warriors hovering about the opposite bank, but they did not venture across. Some of their women did, however, and came cheerily into camp. These most interesting people are worth more than a casual word, so I shall reserve my observations on them until a later chapter. One of our porters, a big Baganda named Sabakaki, was suffering severely from pains in the chest that subsequently developed into pleurisy. From the Masai women we tried to buy some of the milk they carried in gourds; at first they seemed not averse, but as soon as they realized the milk was not for our own consumption, they turned their backs on poor Sabakaki and refused to have anything more to do with us.

These Masai are very difficult to trade with. Their only willing barter is done in sheep. These they seem to consider legitimate objects of commerce. A short distance from our camp stood three whitewashed round houses with thatched, conical roofs, the property of a trader named Agate. He was away at the time of our visit.

After an early morning, but vain, attempt to get Billy a shot at a lion we set out for our distant blue mountains. The day was a journey over plains of great variegation. At times they were covered with thin scrub; at others with small groves; or again, they were open and grassy. Always they undulated gently, so from their tops one never saw as far as he thought he was going to see. As landmark we steered by a good-sized butte named Donga Rasha.

Memba Sasa and I marched ahead on foot. In this thin scrub we got glimpses of many beasts. At one time we were within fifty yards of a band of magnificent eland. By fleeting glimpses we saw also many wildebeeste and zebra, with occasionally one of the smaller grass antelope. Finally, in an open glade we caught sight of something tawny showing in the middle of a bush. It was too high off the ground to be a buck. We sneaked nearer. At fifty yards we came to a halt, still puzzled. Judging by its height and colour, it should be a lion, but try as we would we could not make out what part of his anatomy was thus visible. At last I made up my mind to give him a shot from the Springfield, with the ·405 handy. At the shot the tawny patch heaved and lay still. We manoeuvred cautiously, and found we had killed stone dead not a lion, but a Bohur reed-buck lying atop an ant hill concealed in the middle of the bush. This accounted for its height above the ground. As it happened, I very much wanted one of these animals as a specimen, so everybody was satisfied.

Shortly after, attracted by a great concourse of carrion birds, both on trees and in the air, we penetrated a thicket to come upon a full-grown giraffe killed by lions. The claw marks and other indications were indubitable. The carcass had been partly eaten, but was rapidly vanishing under the attacks of the birds.

Just before noon we passed Donga Rasha and emerged on the open plains. Here I caught sight of some Roberts' gazelle, a new species to me, and started alone in pursuit. They, as usual, trotted over the nearest rise, so with due precautions I followed after. At the top of that rise I lay still in astonishment. Before me marched solemnly an unbroken single file of game, reaching literally to my limit of vision in both directions. They came over the land swell a mile to my left, and they were disappearing over another land swell a mile and a half to my right. It was rigidly single file, except for the young; the nose of one beast fairly touching the tail of the one ahead, and it plodded along at a businesslike walk. There were but three species represented—the gnu, the zebra, and the hartebeeste. I did not see the head of the procession, for it had gone from sight before I arrived; nor did I ever see the tail of it either, for the safari appearing inopportunely broke its continuance. But I saw two miles and a half, solid, of big game. It was a great and formal trek, probably to new pastures.

Then I turned my attention to the Roberts' gazelle, and my good luck downed a specimen at 273 yards. This, with the Bohur reed-buck, made the second new species for the day. Our luck was not yet over, however. We had proceeded but a few miles when Kongoni discovered a herd of topi. The safari immediately lay down, while I went ahead. There was little cover, and I had a very hard time to get within range, especially as a dozen zebras kept grazing across the line of my stalks. The topi themselves were very uneasy, crossing and recrossing and looking doubtfully in my direction. I had a number of chances at small bucks, but refused them in my desire to get a shot at the big leader of the herd. Finally he separated from the rest and faced in my direction at just 268 yards. At the shot he fell dead.

For the first time we had an opportunity to admire the wonderful pelt. It is beautiful in quality, plum colour, with iridescent lights and wavy "water marks" changing to pearl colour on the four quarters, with black legs. We were both struck with the gorgeousness of a topi motor-rug made of three skins, with these pearl spots as accents in the corners. To our ambitions and hopes we added more topi.

Our journey to the Narossara River lasted three days in all. We gained an outlying spur of the blue mountains, and skirted their base. The usual varied foothill country led us through defiles, over ridges, and by charming groves. We began to see Masai cattle in great herds. The gentle humpbacked beasts were held in close formation by herders afoot, tall, lithe young savages with spears. In the distance and through the heat haze the beasts shimmered strangely, their glossy reds and whites and blacks blending together. In this country of wide expanses and clear air we could thus often make out a very far-off herd simply as a speck of rich colour against the boundless rolling plains.

Here we saw a good variety of game. Zebras, of course, and hartebeeste; the Roberts' gazelle, a few topi, a good many of the gnu or wildebeeste discovered and named by Roosevelt; a few giraffes, klipspringer on the rocky buttes, cheetah, and the usual jackals, hyenas, etc. I killed one very old zebra. So ancient was he that his teeth had worn down to the level of the gums, which seemed fairly on the point of closing over. Nevertheless he was still fat and sleek. He could not much longer have continued to crop the grass. Such extreme age in wild animals is, in Africa at least, most remarkable, for generally they meet violent deaths while still in their prime.

About three o'clock of the third afternoon we came in sight of a long line of forest trees running down parallel with the nearest mountain ranges. These marked the course of the Narossara, and by four o'clock we were descending the last slope.

---

## XXXVIII.

### THE LOWER BENCHES.

The Narossara is really only about creek size, but as it flows the whole year round it merits the title of river. It rises in the junction of a long spur with the main ranges, cuts straight across a wide inward bend of the mountains, joins them again, plunges down a deep and tremendous cañon to the level of a second bench below great cliffs, meanders peacefully in flowery meadows and delightful glades for some miles, and then once more, and most unexpectedly, drops eighteen hundred feet by waterfall and precipitous cascade to join the Southern Guaso Nyero. The country around this junction is some of the roughest I saw in Africa.

We camped at the spot where the river ran at about its maximum distance from the mountains. Our tents were pitched beneath the shade of tall and refreshing trees.

A number of Masai women visited us, laughing and joking with Billy in their quizzically humorous fashion. Just as we were sitting down at table an Englishman wandered out of the greenery and approached. He was a small man with a tremendous red beard, wore loose garments and tennis shoes, and strolled up, his hands in his pockets and smoking a cigarette. This was V., a man of whom we had heard. A member of a historical family, officer in a crack English regiment, he had resigned everything to come into this wild country. Here he had built a boma, or enclosed compound, and engaged himself in acquiring Masai sheep in exchange for beads, wire, and cloth. Obviously the profits of such transactions could not be the temptation. He liked the life, and he liked his position of influence with these proud and savage people. Strangely enough, he cared little for the sporting possibilities of the country, though of course he did a little occasional shooting; but was quite content with his trading, his growing knowledge of and intimacy with the Masai, and his occasional tremendous journeys. To the casual and infrequent stranger his attitude was reported most uncertain.

We invited him to tea, which he accepted, and we fell into conversation. He and C. were already old acquaintances. The man, I found, was shy about talking of the things that interested him; but as they most decidedly interested us also we managed to convey an impression of our sincerity. Thereafter he was most friendly. His helpfulness, kindness, and courtesy could not have been bettered. He lent us his own boy as guide down through the cañons of the Narossara to the Lower Benches, where we hoped to find kudu; he offered store-room to such of our supplies as we intended holding in reserve; he sent us sheep and eggs as a welcome variety to our game diet; and in addition he gave us Masai implements and ornaments we could not possibly have acquired in any other way. It is impossible to buy the personal belongings of this proud and independent people at any price. The price of a spear ordinarily runs about two rupees' worth, when one trades with any other tribe. I know of a case where a Masai was offered fifty rupees for his weapon, but refused scornfully. V. acquired these things through friendship; and after we had gained his, he was most generous with them. Thus he presented us with a thing almost impossible to get and seen rarely outside of museums—the Masai war bonnet, made of the mane of a lion. It is in shape and appearance, though not in colour, almost exactly like the grenadier's shako of the last century. In addition to this priceless trophy, V. also gave us samples of the cattle bells, both wooden and metal, ivory ear ornaments, bead bracelets, steel collars, circumcision knives, sword belts, and other affairs of like value. But I think that the *apogée* of his kindliness was reached when much later he heard from the native tribes that we were engaged in penetrating the defiles of the higher mountains. Then he sent after us a swift Masai runner bearing to us a bottle of whisky and a message to the effect that V. was afraid we would find it very cold up there! Think of what that meant; turn it well over in your mind, with all the circumstances of distance from supplies, difficulty of transportation and all! We none of us used whisky in the tropics, so we later returned it with a suitable explanation and thanks as being too good to waste.

Next morning, under guidance of our friend's boy, we set out for the Lower Benches, leaving N'gombe Brown and his outfit to camp indefinitely until we needed him for the return journey.

The whole lie of the land hereabout is, roughly speaking, in a series of shelves. Behind us were the high mountains—the Fourth Bench; we had been travelling on the plateau of the Loieta—the Third Bench; now we were to penetrate some apparently low hills down an unexpected thousand feet to the Second Bench. This was smaller, perhaps only five miles at its widest. Its outer rim consisted also of low hills concealing a drop of precipitous cliffs. There were no passes nor cañons here—the streams dropped over in waterfalls—and precarious game trails offered the only chance for descent. The First Bench was a mere ledge, a mile or so wide. From it one looked down into the deep gorge of the Southern Guaso Nyero, and across to a tangle of eroded mountains and malpais that filled the eye. Only far off in an incredible distance were other blue mountains that marked the other side of the great Rift Valley.

Our present task was to drop from the Third Bench to the Second. For some distance we followed the Narossara; then, when it began to drop into its tremendous gorge, we continued along the hillsides above it until, by means of various "hogs' backs" and tributary cañons, we were able to regain its level far below. The going was rough and stony, and hard on the porters, but the scenery was very wild and fine. We met the river bottom again in the pleasantest oval meadow with fine big trees. The mountains quite surrounded us, towering imminent above our heads. Ahead of us the stream broke through between portals that rose the full height of the ranges. We followed it, and found ourselves on the Second Bench.

Here was grass, high grass in which the boys were almost lost to sight. Behind us the ramparts rose sheer and high, and over across the way were some low fifty-foot cliffs that marked a plateau land. Between the plateau and the ranges from which we had descended was a sort of slight flat valley through which meandered the forest trees that marked the stream.

We turned to the right and marched an hour. The river gradually approached the plateau, thus leaving between it and the ramparts a considerable plain, and some low foothills. These latter were reported to be one of the feeding grounds of the greater kudu.

We made a most delightful camp at the edge of great trees by the stream. The water flowed at the bottom of a little ravine, precipitous in most places, but with gently sloping banks at the spot we had chosen. It flowed rapidly over clean gravel, with a hurrying, tinkling sound. A broad gravel beach was spread on the hither side of it, like a spacious secret room in the jungle. Here too was a clear little slope on which to sit, with the thicket all about, the clean, swift little stream below, the high forest arches above, and the inquisitive smaller creatures hovering near. Others had been here before us, the wild things, taking advantage of the easy descent to drinking water—eland, buffalo, leopard, and small bucks. The air was almost cloyingly sweet with a perfume like sage-brush honey.

Our first task was to set our boys to work clearing a space; the grass was so high and rank that mere trampling had little effect on it. The Baganda, Sabakaki, we had been compelled to leave with the ox team. So our twenty-seven had become twenty-six.

Next morning C. and I started out very early with one gunbearer. The direction of the wind compelled us to a two hours' walk before we could begin to hunt. The high grass was soaked with a very heavy dew, and shortly we were as wet as though we had fallen into the river. A number of hornbills and parrots followed us for some distance, but soon left us in peace. We saw the Roberts' gazelle and some hartebeeste.

When we had gained a point of vantage, we turned back and began to work slowly along the base of the mountains. We kept on a general level a hundred feet or so up their slope, just high enough to give us a point of overlook for anything that might stir either in the flat plateau foothills or the plains. We also kept a sharp lookout for signs.

We had proceeded in this manner for an hour when in an opening between two bushes below us, and perhaps five hundred yards away, we saw a leopard standing like a statue, head up, a most beautiful spectacle. While we watched her through the glasses, she suddenly dropped flat out of sight. The cause we discovered to be three hartebeeste strolling sociably along, stopping occasionally to snatch a mouthful, but headed always in the direction of the bushes behind which lay the great cat. Much interested, we watched them. They disappeared behind the screen. A sudden flash marked the leopard's spring. Two badly demoralized hartebeeste stamped out into the open and away; two only. The kill had been made.

We had only the one rifle with us, for we were supposed to be out after kudu only, and were travelling as light as possible. No doubt the Springfield would kill a leopard, if the bullet landed in the right place. We discussed the matter. It ended, of course, in our sneaking down there; I with the Springfield, and C. with his knife unsheathed. Our precautions and trepidations were wasted. The leopard had carried the hartebeeste bodily some distance, had thrust it under a bush, and had departed. C. surmised it would return towards evening.

Therefore we continued after kudu. We found old signs, proving that the beasts visited this country, but nothing fresh. We saw, however, the first sing-sing, some impalla, some klipspringer, and Chanler's reed-buck.

At evening we made a crafty stalk atop the mesa-like foothills to a point overlooking the leopard's kill. We lay here looking the place over inch by inch through our glasses, when an ejaculation of disgust from Kongoni called our attention. There at another spot that confounded beast sat like a house cat watching us cynically. Either we had come too soon, or she had heard us and retired to what she considered a safe distance. There was of course no chance of getting nearer; so I sat down, for a steadier hold, and tried her anyway. At the shot she leaped high in the air, rolled over once, then recovered her feet and streaked off at full speed. Just before disappearing over a slight rise, she stopped to look back. I tried her again. We concluded this shot a miss, as the distance and light were such that only sheer luck could have landed the bullet. However, that luck was with us. Later developments showed that both shots had hit. One cut a foreleg, but without breaking a bone, and the other had hit the paunch. One was at 380 paces and the other at 490.

We found blood on the trail, and followed it a hundred yards and over a small ridge to a wide patch of high grass. It was now dark, the grass was very high, and the animal probably desperate. The situation did not look good to us, badly armed as we were. So we returned to camp, resolved to take up the trail again in the morning.

Every man in camp turned out next day to help beat the grass. C., with the ·405, stayed to direct and protect the men; while I, with the Springfield, sat down at the head of the ravine. Soon I could hear the shrieks, rattles, shouts, and whistles of the line of men as they beat through the grass. Small grass bucks and hares bounded past me; birds came whirring by. I sat on a little ant hill spying as hard as I could in all directions. Suddenly the beaters fell to dead silence. Guessing this as a signal to me that the beast had been seen, I ran to climb a higher ant hill to the left. From there I discerned the animal plainly, sneaking along belly to earth, exactly in the manner of a cat after a sparrow. It was not a woods-leopard, but the plains-leopard, or cheetah, supposed to be a comparatively harmless beast.

At my shot she gave one spring forward and rolled over into the grass. The nearest porters yelled, and rushed in. I ran, too, as fast as I could, but was not able to make myself heard above the row. An instant later the beast came to its feet with a savage growl and charged the nearest of the men. She was crippled, and could not move as quickly as usual, but could hobble along faster than her intended victim could run. This was a tall and very conceited Kavirondo. He fled, but ran around in circles in and out of his excited companions. The cheetah followed him, and him only, with most single-minded purpose.

I dared not shoot while men were in the line of fire even on the other side of the cheetah, for I knew the high-power bullet would at that range go right on through, and I fairly split my throat trying to clear the way. It seemed five minutes, though it was probably only as many seconds, before I got my chance. It was high time. The cheetah had reared to strike the man down. My shot bowled her over. She jumped to her feet again, made another dash at the thoroughly scared Kavirondo, and I killed her just at his coat-tails.

The cheetahs ordinarily are supposed to be cowards, although their size and power are equal to that of other leopards. Nobody is afraid of them. Yet this particular animal charged with all the ferocity and determination of the lion, and would certainly have killed or badly mauled my man. To be sure it had been wounded, and had had all night to think about it.

In the relief from the tension we all burst into shrieks of laughter; all except the near-victim of the scrimmage, who managed only a sickly smile. Our mirth was short. Out from a thicket over a hundred yards away walked one of the men, who had been in no way involved in the fight, calmly announcing that he had been shot. We were sceptical, but he turned his back and showed us the bullet hole at the lower edge of the ribs. One of my bullets, after passing through the cheetah, had ricocheted and picked this poor fellow out from the whole of an empty landscape. And this after I had delayed my rescue fairly to the point of danger in order to avoid all chance of hurting some one!

We had no means of telling how deeply the bullet had penetrated; so we reassured the man, and detailed two men to assist him back to camp by easy stages. He did not seem to be suffering much pain, and he had lost little strength.

At camp, however, we found that the wound was deep. C. generously offered to make a forced march in order to get the boy out to a hospital. By hitting directly across the rough country below the benches it was possible to shorten the journey somewhat, provided V. could persuade the Masai to furnish a guide. The country was a desert, and the water scarce. We lined up our remaining twenty-six men and selected the twelve best and strongest. These we offered a month and a half's extra wages for the trip. We then made a hammock out of one of the ground cloths, and the same afternoon C. started. I sent with him four of my own men as far as the ox-wagon for the purpose of bringing back more supplies. They returned the next afternoon bringing also a report from C. that all was well so far, and that he had seen a lion. He made the desert trip without other casualty than the lost of his riding mule, and landed the wounded man in the hospital all right. In spite of C.'s expert care on the journey out, and the best of treatment later, the boy, to my great distress, died eleven days after reaching the hospital. C. was gone just two weeks.

In the meantime I sent out my best trackers in all directions to look for kudu signs, conceiving this the best method of covering the country rapidly. In this manner I shortly determined that chances were small here, and made up my mind to move down to the edge of the bench where the Narossara makes its plunge. Before doing so, however, I hunted for and killed a very large eland bull reported by Mavrouki. This beast was not only one of the largest I ever saw, but was in especially fine coat. He stood five feet six inches high at the shoulder; was nine feet eight inches long, without the tail; and would weigh twenty-five hundred pounds. The men were delighted with this acquisition. I now had fourteen porters, the three gunbearers, the cook, and the two boys. They surrounded each tiny fire with switches full of roasting meat; they cut off great hunks for a stew; they made quantities of biltong, or jerky.

Next day I left Kongoni and one porter at the old camp, loaded my men with what they could carry, and started out. We marched a little over two hours; then found ourselves beneath a lone mimosa tree about a quarter-mile from the edge of the bench. At this point the stream drops into a little cañon preparatory to its plunge; and the plateau rises ever so gently in tremendous cliffs. I immediately dispatched the porters back for another load. A fine sing-sing lured me across the river. I did not get the sing-sing, but had a good fight with two lions, as narrated elsewhere.A

In this spot we camped a number of days; did a heap of hard climbing and spying; killed another lion out of a band of eight; thoroughly determined that we had come at the wrong time for kudu, and decided on another move.

This time our journey lasted five hours, so that our relaying consumed three days. We broke back through the ramparts, by means of another pass we had discovered when looking for kudu, to the Third Bench again. Here we camped in the valley of Lengeetoto.

This valley is one of the most beautiful and secluded in this part of Africa. It is shaped like an ellipse, five or six miles long by about three miles wide, and is completely surrounded by mountains. The ramparts of the western side—those forming the walls of the Fourth Bench—rise in sheer rock cliffs, forest crowned. To the east, from which direction we had just come, were high, rounded mountains. At sunrise they cut clear in an outline of milky slate against the sky.

The floor of this ellipse was surfaced in gentle undulations, like the low swells of a summer sea. Between each swell a singing, clear-watered brook leapt and dashed or loitered through its jungle. Into the mountains ran broad upward-flung valleys of green grass; and groves of great forest trees marched down cañons and out a short distance into the plains. Everything was fresh and green and cool. We needed blankets at night, and each morning the dew was cool and sparkling, and the sky very blue. Underneath the forest trees of the stream beds and the cañon were leafy rooms as small as a closet, or great as cathedral aisles. And in the short brush dwelt rhinoceros and impalla; in the jungles were buffalo and elephant; on the plains we saw giraffe, hartebeeste, zebra, duiker; and in the bases of the hills we heard at evening and early morning the roaring of lions.

In this charming spot we lingered eight days. Memba Sasa and I spent most of our time trying to get one of the jungle-dwelling buffalo without his getting us. In this we were finally successful. Then, as it was about time for C. to return, we moved back to V.'s boma on the Narossara; relaying, as usual, the carrying of our effects. At this time I had had to lay off three more men on account of various sorts of illness, so was still more cramped for transportation facilities. As we were breaking camp a lioness leaped to her feet from where she had been lying under a bush. So near was it to camp that I had not my rifle ready. She must have been lying there within two hundred yards of our tents, watching all our activities.

We drew into V.'s boma a little after two o'clock. The man in charge of our tent did not put in an appearance until next day. Fortunately V. had an extra tent, which he lent us. We camped near the river, just outside the edge of the river forest. The big trees sent their branches out over us very far above, while a winding path led us to the banks of the river where was a dingle like an inner room. After dark we sat with V. at our little camp fire. It was all very beautiful—the skyful of tropical stars, the silhouette of the forest shutting them out, the velvet blackness of the jungle flickering with fireflies, the purer outlines of the hilltops and distant mountains to the left, the porters' tiny fires before the little white tents; and in the distance, from the direction of V.'s boma, the irregular throb of the dance drum and the occasional snatch of barbaric singing borne down on the night wind from where his Wakambas were holding an n'goma. A pair of ibis that had been ejected when we made camp contributed intermittent outraged and raucous squawks from the tiptop of some neighbouring tree.

FOOTNOTES:

This is an interesting fact—that she reared to strike instead of springing.

It must be remembered that this beast had the evening before killed a 350-pound hartebeeste with ease.

---

## XXXIX.

NOTES ON THE MASAI.

It is in no way my intention to attempt a comprehensive description of this unique people. My personal observation is, of course, inadequate to that task, and the numerous careful works on the subject are available to the interested reader.

The southern branch of the race, among whom we were now travelling, are very fine physically. Men close to seven feet in height are not at all uncommon, and the average is well above six. They are strongly and lithely made. Their skins are a red-brown or bronze, generally brought to a high state of polish by liberal anointing. In feature they resemble more the Egyptian or Abyssinian than the negro cast of countenance. The women are tall and well formed, with proud, quaintly quizzical faces. Their expressions and demeanour seem to indicate more independence and initiative than is usual with most savage women, but whether this is actually so or not I cannot say.

On this imposing and pleasing physical foundation your true Masai is content to build a very slight superstructure of ornament. His ear-lobes are always stretched to hang down in long loops, in which small medals, ornaments, decorated blocks of wood, or the like, are inserted. Long, heavy ovals of ivory, grooved to accommodate the flesh loop, very finely etched in decorative designs, are occasionally worn as "stretchers." Around the neck is a slender iron collar, and on the arms are one or two glittering bracelets. The sword belt is of leather heavily beaded, with a short dangling fringe of steel beads. Through this the short blade is thrust. When in full dress the warrior further sports a hollow iron knee bell, connected with the belt by a string of cowrie shells or beads. Often is added a curious triangular strip of skin fitting over the chest, and reaching about to the waist. A robe or short cloak of short-haired sheepskin is sometimes carried for warmth, but not at all for modesty. The weapons are a long, narrow-bladed heavy spear, the buffalo hide shield, the short sword, and the war club or rungs. The women are always shaven-headed, wear voluminous robes of soft leather, and carry a great weight of heavy wire wound into anklets and stockings, and brought to a high state of polish. So extensive are these decorations that they really form a sort of armour, with breaks only for the elbow and the knee joints. The married women wear also a great outstanding collar.

The Masai are pastoral, and keep immense herds and flocks. Therefore they inhabit the grazing countries, and are nomadic. Their villages are invariably arranged in a wide circle, the low huts of mud and wattles facing inwards. The spaces between the huts are filled in with thick dense thorn brush, thus enclosing a strong corral, or boma. These villages are called manyattas. They are built by the women in an incredibly brief space of time. Indeed, an overchief stopping two days at one place has been known to cause the construction of a complete village, to serve only for that period. He then moved on, and the manyatta was never used again! Nevertheless these low rounded huts, in shape like a loaf of bread, give a fictitious impression of great strength and permanency. The smooth and hardened mud resembles masonry or concrete work. As a matter of fact it is the thinnest sort of a shell over plaited withies. The single entrance to this compound may be closed by thorn bush, so that at night, when the lions are abroad, the Masai and all his herds dwell quite peaceably and safely inside the boma. Twelve to twenty huts constitute a village.

When the grass is fed down, the village moves to a new location. There is some regulation about this, determined by the overchiefs, so that one village does not interfere with another. Beside the few articles of value or of domestic use, the only things carried away from an old village are the strongly-woven shield-shaped doors. These are strapped along the flanks of the donkeys, while the other goods rest between. A donkey pack, Masai fashion, is a marvellous affair that would not stay on ten minutes for a white man.

The Masai perform no agriculture whatever, nor will they eat game meat. They have no desire whatever for any of the white man's provisions except sugar. In fact; their sole habitual diet is mixed cow's blood and milk—no fruits, no vegetables, no grains, rarely flesh; a striking commentary on extreme vegetarian claims. The blood they obtain by shooting a very sharp-pointed arrow into the neck vein of the cow. After the requisite amount has been drained, the wound is closed and the animal turned into the herd to recuperate. The blood and milk are then shaken together in long gourds. Certainly the race seems to thrive on this strange diet. Only rarely, on ceremonial occasions or when transportation is difficult, do they eat mutton or goat flesh, but never beef.

Of labour, then, about a Masai village, it follows that there is practically none. The women build the manyattas; there is no cooking, no tilling of the soil, no searching for wild fruits. The herd have to be watched by day, and driven in at the fall of night; that is the task of the boys and the youths who have not gone through with the quadriennial circumcision ceremonies and become El-morani, or warriors. Therefore the grown men are absolutely and completely gentlemen of leisure. In civilization, the less men do the more important they are inclined to think themselves. It is so here. Socially the Masai consider themselves several cuts above anybody else in the country. As social superiority lies mostly in thinking so hard enough—so that the inner belief expresses itself in the outward attitude and manner—the Masai carry it off. Their haughtiness is magnificent. Also they can look as unsmiling and bored as anybody anywhere. Consequently they are either greatly admired, or greatly hated and feared, as the case happens to be, by all the other tribes. The Kikuyu young men frankly ape the customs and ornaments of their powerful neighbours. Even the British Government treats them very gingerly indeed, and allows these economically useless savages a latitude the more agricultural tribes do not enjoy. Yet I submit that any people whose property is in immense herds can more easily be brought to terms than those who have nothing so valuable to lose.

As a matter of fact the white man and the Masai have never had it out. When the English, a few years since, were engaged in opening the country they carried on quite a stoutly contested little war with the Wakamba. These people put up so good a fight that the English anticipated a most bitter struggle with the Masai, whose territory lay next beyond. To their surprise the Masai made peace.

"We have watched the war with the Wakamba," they said, in effect, "and we have seen the Wakamba kill a great many of your men. But more of your men came in always, and there were no more Wakamba to come in and take the places of those who were killed. We are not afraid. If we should war with you, we would undoubtedly kill a great many of you, and you would undoubtedly kill a great many of us. But there can be no use in that. We want the ranges for our cattle; you want a road. Let us then agree."

The result is that to-day the Masai look upon themselves as an unconquered people, and bear themselves—*towards the other tribes*—accordingly. The shrewd common sense and observation evidenced above must have convinced them that war now would be hopeless.

This acute intelligence is not at all incompatible with the rather bigoted and narrow outlook on life inevitable to a people whose ideals are made up of fancied superiorities over the rest of mankind. Witness, the feudal aristocracies of the Middle Ages.

With this type the underlying theory of masculine activity is the military. Some outlet for energy was needed, and in war it was found. Even the ordinary necessities of primitive agriculture and of the chase were lacking. The Masai ate neither vegetable, grain, nor wild game. His whole young manhood, then, could be spent in no better occupation than the pursuit of warlike glory—and cows.

On this rested the peculiar social structure of the people. In perusing the following fragmentary account the reader must first of all divest his mind of what he would, according to white man's standards, consider moral or immoral. Such things must be viewed from the standpoint of the people believing in them. The Masai are moral in the sense that they very rigorously live up to their own customs and creeds. Their women are strictly chaste in the sense that they conduct no affairs outside those permitted within the tribe. No doubt, from the Masai point of view, we are ourselves immoral.

The small boy, as soon as he is big enough to be responsible—and that is very early in life—is given, in company with others, charge of a flock of sheep. Thence he graduates to the precious herds of cows. He wears little or nothing; is armed with a throwing club (a long stick), or perhaps later a broad-bladed, short-headed spear of a pattern peculiar to boys and young men. His life is thus over the free open hills and veld until, somewhere between the ages of eighteen and twenty-one, the year of the circumcision comes. Then he enters on the long ceremonies that initiate him into the warrior class. My knowledge of the details of this subject is limited; for while I had the luck to be in Masailand on the fourth year, such things are not exhibited freely. The curious reader can find more on the subject in other books; but as this is confined to personal experiences I will tell only what I have myself elicited.

The youth's shaved head is allowed to grow its hair. He hangs around his brow a dangling string of bright-coloured bird skins stuffed out in the shape of little cylinders, so that at a short distance they look like curls. For something like a month of probation he wears these, then undergoes the rite. For ten days thereafter he and his companions, their heads daubed with clay and ashes, clad in long black robes, live out in the brush. They have no provision, but are privileged to steal what they need. At the end of the ten days they return to the manyattas. A three-day n'goma, or dance, now completes their transformation to the El-morani class. It finishes by an obscene night dance, in the course of which the new warriors select their partners.

For ten or twelve years these young men are El-morani. They dwell in a separate manyatta. With them dwell promiscuously all the young unmarried women of the tribe. There is no permanent pairing off, no individual property, no marriage. Nor does this constitute flagrant immorality, difficult as it may be for us to see that fact. The institution, like all national institutions, must have had its origin in a very real need and a very practical expediency. The fighting strength of the tribe must be kept up, and by the young and vigorous stock. On the other hand, every man of military age must be foot free to serve in the constant wars and forays. This institution is the means. And, mind you, unchastity in the form of illicit intercourse outside the manyatta of the El-morani, whether with her own or another tribe, subjects the women to instant death.

The El-morani in full fighting rig are imposing. They are, as I have explained, tall and of fine physique. The cherished and prized weapon is the long, narrow-bladed spear. This is five and six feet long, with a blade over three feet by as many inches, and with a long iron shoe. In fact, only a bare hand-hold of wood is provided. It is of formidable weight, but so well balanced that a flip cast with the wrist will drive it clear through an enemy. A short sword and a heavy-headed war club complete the offensive weapons. The shield is of buffalo hide, oval in shape, and decorated with a genuine heraldry, based on genealogy. A circlet of black ostrich feathers in some branches surrounds the face and stands high above the head. In the southern districts the warriors wear two single black ostrich plumes tied one either side the head, and slanting a little backwards. They walk with a mincing step, so that the two feathers bob gently up and down like the waving of the circus equestrienne's filmy skirts.

Naturally the Masai with the Zulu were the most dreaded of all the tribes of Africa. They were constantly raiding in all directions as far as their sphere of operations could reach, capturing cattle and women as the prizes of war. Now that the white man has put a stop to the ferocious intertribal wars, the El-morani are out of a job. The military organization is still carried on as before. What will happen to the morals of the people it would be difficult to say. The twelve years of imposed peace have not been long enough seriously to deteriorate the people; but, inevitably, complete idleness will tell. Either the people must change their ideals and become industrious—which is extremely unlikely—or they will degenerate.

As a passing thought, it is a curious and formidable fact that the prohibition of intertribal wars and forays all through East Central Africa had already permitted the population to increase to a point of discomfort. Many of the districts are becoming so crowded as to overflow. What will happen in the long run only time can tell—famines are weakening things, while war at least hardens a nation's fibre. This is not necessarily an argument for war. Only everywhere in the world the white man seems, with the best of intentions, to be upsetting natural balances without substituting anything for them. We are better at preventing things than causing them.

At the age of thirty, or thereabout, the El-morani becomes an Elder. He may now drink and smoke, vices that in the Spartan days of his military service were rigorously denied him. He may also take a wife or wives, according to his means, and keep herds of cattle. His wives he purchases from their parents, the usual medium of payment being cows or sheep. The young women who have been living in the El-morani village are considered quite as desirable as the young virgins. If there are children, these are taken over by the husband. They are considered rather a recommendation than a detriment, for they prove the girl is fruitful.

Relieved of all responsibility, the ex-warrior now has full leisure to be a gentleman. He drinks a fermented liquor made from milk; he takes snuff or smokes the rank native tobacco; he conducts interminable diplomatic negotiations; he oversees minutely the forms of ceremonials; he helps to shape the policies of his manyatta, and he gives his attention to the accumulation of cows.

The cow is the one thing that arouses the Masai's full energies. He will undertake any journey, any task, any danger, provided the reward therefor is horned cattle. And a cow is the one thing he will on no account trade, sell, destroy. A very few of them he milks, and a very few of them he periodically bleeds; but the majority, to the numbers of thousands upon thousands, live uselessly until they die of old age. They are branded, generally on the flanks or ribs, with strange large brands, and are so constantly handled that they are tamer and more gentle than sheep. I have seen upwards of a thousand head in sole charge of two old women on foot. These ancient dames drove the beasts in a long file to water, then turned them quite easily and drove them back again. Opposite our camp they halted their charges and came to make us a long visit. The cattle stood in their tracks until the call was over; not one offered even to stray off the baked earth in search of grasses.

314

The Masai cattle king knows his property individually. Each beast has its name. Some of the wealthier are worth in cattle, at settler's prices, close to a hundred thousand dollars. They are men of importance in their own council huts, but they lack many things dear to the savage heart simply because they are unwilling to part with a single head of stock in order to procure them.

In the old days forays and raids tended more or less to keep the stock down. Since the White Man's Peace the herds are increasing. In the country between the Mau Escarpment and the Narossara Mountains we found the feed eaten down to the earth two months before the next rainy season. In the meantime the few settlers are hard put to it to buy cattle at any price wherewith to stock their new farms. The situation is an anomaly which probably cannot continue. Some check will have eventually to be devised, either limiting the cattle, or compelling an equitable sale of the surplus. Certainly the present situation represents a sad economic waste—of the energies of a fine race destined to rust away, and of the lives of tens of thousands of valuable beasts brought into existence only to die of old age. If these matchless herders and cattle breeders could be brought into relation with the world's markets everybody would be the better.

Besides his sacred cattle the Masai raises also lesser herds of the hairy sheep of the country. These he used for himself only on the rare occasions of solitary forced marches away from his herds, or at the times of ceremony. Their real use is as a trading medium—for more cattle! Certain white men and Somalis conduct regular trading expeditions into Masailand, bringing in small herds of cows bought with trade goods from the other tribes. These they barter with the Masai for sheep. In Masai estimation a cow is the most valuable thing on earth, while a sheep is only a medium of exchange. With such notions it is easy to see that the white man can make an advantageous exchange, in spite of the Masai's well-known shrewdness at a bargain. Each side is satisfied. There remains only to find a market for the sheep— an easy matter. A small herd of cows will, in the long run, bring quite a decent profit.

The Masai has very little use for white man's products. He will trade for squares of cloth, beads of certain kinds and in a limited quantity, brass and iron wire of heavy gauge, blankets and sugar. That, barring occasional personal idiosyncrasy, is about all. For these things he will pay also in sheep. Masai curios are particularly difficult to get hold of. I rather like them for their independence in that respect. I certainly should refuse to sell my tennis shoes from my feet merely because some casual Chinaman happened to admire them!

The women seem to occupy a position quite satisfactory to themselves. To be sure they do the work; but there is not much work! They appear to be well treated; at least they are always in good spirits, laughing and joking with each other, and always ready with quick repartee to remarks flung at them by the safari boys. They visited camp freely, and would sit down for a good lively afternoon of joking. Their expressions were quizzical, with a shy intelligent humour. In spite of the apparent unabashed freedom of their deportment they always behaved with the utmost circumspection; nor did our boys ever attempt any familiarity. The unobtrusive lounging presence in the background of two warriors with long spears may have had something to do with this.

The Masai government is centred in an overlord or king. His orders seemed to be implicitly obeyed. The present king I do not know, as the old king, Lenani, had just died at an advanced age. In former days the traveller on entering Masailand was met by a sub-chief. This man planted his long spear upright in the ground, and the intending traveller flung over it coils of the heavy wire. A very generous traveller who completely covered the spear then had no more trouble. One less lavish was likely to be held up for further impositions as he penetrated the country. This tax was called the honga.

The Masai language is one of the most difficult of all the native tongues. In fact, the white man is almost completely unable even to pronounce many of the words. V., who is a "Masai-man," who knows them intimately, and who possesses their confidence, does not pretend to talk with them in their own tongue, but employs the universal Swahili.

---

## XL.

### THROUGH THE ENCHANTED FOREST.

We delayed at V.'s boma three days, waiting for C. to turn up. He maintained a little force of Wakamba, as the Masai would not take service. The Wakamba are a hunting tribe, using both the spear and the poisoned arrow to kill their game. Their bows are short and powerful, and the arrows exceedingly well fashioned. The poison is made from the wood of a certain fat tree, with fruit like gigantic bologna sausages. It is cut fine, boiled, and the product evaporated away until only a black sticky substance remains. Into this the point of the arrow is dipped; and the head is then protected until required by a narrow strip of buckskin wound around and around it. I have never witnessed the effects of this poison; but V. told me he had seen an eland die in twenty-two minutes from so slight a wound in the shoulder that it ran barely a hundred yards before stopping. The poison more or less loses its efficiency, however, after the sticky, tarlike substance has dried out.

I offered a half-rupee as a prize for an archery competition, for I was curious to get a view of their marksmanship. The bull's-eye was a piece of typewriter paper at thirty paces. This they managed to puncture only once out of fifteen tries, though they never missed it very widely. V. seemed quite put out at this poor showing, so I suppose they can ordinarily do better; but I imagine they are a good deal like our hunting Indians—poor shots, but very skilful at stalking close to a beast.

Our missing porter, with the tent, was brought in next afternoon by Kongoni, who had gone in search of him. The man was a big, strong Kavirondo. He was sullen, and merely explained that he was "tired." This excuse for a five hours' march after eight days' rest! I fined him eight rupees, which I gave Kongoni, and ordered him twenty-five lashes. Six weeks later he did the same trick. C. allotted him fifty lashes, and had him led thereafter by a short rope around the neck. He was probably addicted to opium. This was the only man to be formally kibokoed on the whole trip—a good testimony at once to C.'s management, the discrimination we had used in picking them out, and the settled reputations we had by now acquired.

After C.'s return we prepared to penetrate straight back through the great rampart of mountains to the south and west.

We crossed the bush-grown plains, and entered a gently rising long cañon flanked on either side by towering ranges that grew higher and higher the farther we proceeded. In the very centre of the mountains, apparently, this cañon ended in a small round valley. There appeared to be no possible exit, save by the way we had come, or over the almost perpendicular ridges a thousand feet or more above. Nevertheless, we discovered a narrow ravine that slanted up into the hills to the left. Following it we found ourselves very shortly in a great forest on the side of a mountain. Hanging creepers brushed our faces, tangled vines hung across our view, strange and unexpected openings offered themselves as a means through which we could see a little closer into the heart of mystery. The air was cool and damp and dark. The occasional shafts of sunlight or glimpses of blue sky served merely to accentuate the soft gloom. Save that we climbed always, we could not tell where we were going.

The ascent occupied a little over an hour. Then through the tree trunks and undergrowth we caught the sky-line of the crest. When we topped this we took a breath, and prepared ourselves for a corresponding descent. But in a hundred yards we popped out of the forest to find ourselves on a new level. The Fourth Bench had been attained.

It was a grass country of many low, rounded hills and dipping valleys, with fine isolated oaklike trees here and there in the depressions, and compact, beautiful oaklike groves thrown over the hills like blankets. Well-kept, green, trim, intimate, it should have had church spires and gray roofs in appropriate spots. It was a refreshment to the eye after the great and austere spaces among which we had been dwelling, repose to the spirit after the alert and dangerous lands. The dark-curtained forest seemed, fancifully, an enchantment through which we had gained to this remote smiling land, nearest of all to the blue sky.

We continued south for two days; and then, as the narrative will show, were forced to return. We found it always the same type; pleasant sleepy little valleys winding around and between low hills crowned with soft groves and forests. It was for all the world like northern Surrey, or like some of the live oak country of California. Only this we soon discovered: in spite of the enchantment of the magic-protecting forest, the upper benches too were subject to the spell that lies over all Africa. These apparently little valleys were in reality the matter of an hour's journey to cross; these rounded hills, to all seeming only two good golf strokes from bottom to top, were matters of serious climbing; these compact, squared groves of oaklike trees were actually great forests of giants in which one could lose one's self for days, in which roamed herds of elephant and buffalo. It looked compact because we could see all its constituent elements. As a matter of fact, it was neat and tidy; only we were, as usual, too small for it.

At the end of two hours' fast marching we had made the distance, say, from the clubhouse to the second hole. Then we camped in a genuinely little grove of really small trees overlooking a green valley bordered with wooded hills. The prospect was indescribably delightful; a sort of Sunday-morning landscape of groves and green grass and a feeling of church bells.

Only down the valley, diminished by distance, all afternoon Masai warriors, in twos and threes, trooped by, mincing along so that their own ostrich feathers would bob up and down, their spears held aslant.

We began to realize that we were indeed in a new country when our noon thermometer registered only 66 degrees, and when at sunrise the following morning it stood at 44 degrees. To us, after eight months under the equator, this was bitter weather!

FOOTNOTES:

Eight by ten and a half inches.

---

## XLI.

NAIOKOTUKU.

Next morning we marched on up the beautiful valley through shoulder-high grasses wet with dew. At the end of two hours we came to the limit of Leyeye's knowledge of the country. It would now be necessary to find savage guides.

Accordingly, while we made camp, C., with Leyeye as interpreter, departed in search of a Masai village. So tall and rank grew the grass, that we had to clear it out as one would clear brushwood in order to make room for our tents.

Several hours later C. returned. He had found a very large village; but unfortunately the savages were engaged in a big n'goma which could not be interrupted by mere business. However, the chief was coming to make a friendly call. When the n'goma should be finished, he would be delighted to furnish us with anything we might desire.

Almost on the heels of this the chief arrived. He was a fine old savage, over six feet tall, of well proportioned figure, and with a shrewd, intelligent face. The n'goma had him to a limited extent, for he stumbled over tent ropes, smiled a bit uncertainly, and slumped down rather suddenly when he had meant to sit. However, he stumbled, smiled, and slumped with unassailable dignity.

From beneath his goatskin robe he produced a long ornamented gourd, from which he offered us a drink of fermented milk. He took our refusal good-naturedly. The gourd must have held a gallon, but he got away with all of its contents in the course of the interview; also several pints of super-sweetened coffee which we doled out to him a little at a time, and which he seemed to appreciate extravagantly.

Through Leyeye we exchanged the compliments of the day, and, after the African custom, told each other how important we were. Our visitor turned out to be none other than the brother of Lenani, the paramount chief of all the Masai. I forget what I was, either the brother of King George or the nephew of Theodore Roosevelt—the only two white men *every* native has heard of. It may be that both of us were mistaken, but from his evident authority over a very wide district we were inclined to believe our visitor.

We told him we wanted guides through the hills to the southward. He promised them in a most friendly fashion.

"I do not know the white man," said he. "I live always in these mountains. But my brother Lenani told me ten years ago that some day the white man would come into my country. My brother told me that when the white man came travelling in my country I must treat him well, for the white man is a good friend but a bad enemy. I have remembered my brother Lenani's words, though they were spoken a long time ago. The white man has been very long in coming; but now he is here. Therefore I have brought you milk to-day, and to-morrow I will send you sheep; and later I will send young men who know the hills to take you where you wish to go."

We expressed gratification, and I presented him with a Marble fish knife. The very thin blade and the ingenious manner in which the two halves of the handle folded forward over it pleased him immensely.

"No one but myself shall ever use this knife," said he.

He had no pockets, but he tucked it away in his armpit, clamped the muscles down over it, and apparently forgot it. At least he gave it no further attention, used his hands as usual, but retained it as securely as in a pocket.

"To-morrow," he promised at parting, "very early in the morning, I will send my own son and another man to guide you; and I will send a sheep for your meat."

We arose "very early," packed our few affairs, picked out four porters—and sat down to wait. Our plan was to cruise for five days with as light and mobile an outfit as possible, and then to return for fresh supplies. Billy would take charge of the main camp during our absence. As advisers, we left her Abba Ali, Memba Sasa, and Mohammed.

At noon we were still waiting. The possibility of doing a full day's journey was gone, but we thought we might at least make a start. At one o'clock, just as we had about given up hope, the Masai strolled in. They were beautiful, tall, straight youths, finely formed, with proud features and a most graceful carriage. In colour they were as though made of copper bronze, with the same glitter of high lights from their fine-textured skins. Even in this chilly climate they were nearly naked. One carried a spear, the other a bow and arrow.

Joyously we uprose—and sat down again. We had provided an excellent supply of provisions for our guides; but on looking over the lot they discovered nothing—absolutely nothing—that met their ideas.

"What *do* they want?" we asked Leyeye in despair.

"They say they will eat nothing but sheep," he reported.

We remembered old Naiokotuku's promise of sending us sheep, sneered cynically at the faith of savages, and grimly set forth to see what we could buy in the surrounding country. But we wronged the old man. Less than a mile from camp we met men driving in as presents not one, but *two* sheep. So we abandoned our shopping tour and returned to camp. By the time one of the sheep had been made into mutton it was too late to start. The Masai showed symptoms of desiring to go back to the village for the night. This did not please us. We called them up, and began extravagantly to admire their weapons, begging to examine them. Once we had them in our hands we craftily discoursed as follows:—

"These are beautiful weapons, the most beautiful we have ever seen. Since you are going so spend the night in our camp, and since we greatly fear that some of our men might steal these beautiful weapons, we will ourselves guard them for you carefully from theft until morning."

So saying, we deposited them inside the tent. Then we knew we had our Masai safe. They would never dream of leaving while the most cherished of their possessions were in hostage.

---

## XLII.

SCOUTING IN THE ELEPHANT FOREST.

Here we were finally off at dawn. It was a very chilly, wet dawn, with the fog so thick that we could see not over ten feet ahead. We had four porters, carrying about twenty-five pounds apiece of the bare necessities, Kongoni, and Leyeye. The Masai struck confidently enough through the mist. We crossed neck-deep grass flats—where we were thoroughly soaked—climbed hills through a forest, skirted apparently for miles an immense reed swamp. As usual when travelling strange country in a fog, we experienced that queer feeling of remaining in the same spot while fragments of near-by things are slowly paraded by. When at length the sun's power cleared the mists, we found ourselves in the middle of a forest country of high hills.

Into this forest we now plunged, threading our way here and there where the animal trails would take us, looking always for fresh elephant spoor. It would have been quite impossible to have moved about in any other fashion. The timber grew on hillsides, and was very lofty and impressive; and the tropical undergrowth grew tall, rank, and impenetrable. We could proceed only by means of the kind assistance of the elephant, the buffalo, and the rhinoceros.

Elephant spoor we found, but none made later than three weeks before. The trails were broad, solid paths through the forest, as ancient and beaten as though they had been in continuous use for years. Unlike the rhino and buffalo trails, they gave us head room and to spare. The great creatures had by sheer might cut their way through the dense, tough growth, leaving twisted, splintered, wrecked jungle behind them, but no impediment.

By means of these beautiful trails we went quietly, penetrating farther and farther into the jungle. Our little procession of ten made no noise. If we should strike fresh elephant tracks, thus would we hunt them, with all our worldly goods at our backs, so that at night we could camp right on the trail.

The day passed almost without incident.

Once a wild crash and a snort told of a rhinoceros, invisible, but very close. We huddled together, our rifles ready, uncertain whether or not the animal would burst from the leafy screen at our very faces. The Masai stood side by side, the long spear poised, the bow bent, fine, tense figures in bronze.

Near sundown we found ourselves by a swift little stream in the bottom of a deep ravine. Here we left the men to make camp, and ourselves climbed a big mountain on the other side. It gave us a look abroad over a wilderness of hills, forested heavily, and a glimpse of the landfall far away where no white man had ever been. This was as far south as we were destined to get, though at the time we did not know it. Our plan was to push on two days more. Near the top of the ridge we found the unmistakable tracks of the bongo. This is interesting to zoologists in that it extends the southward range of this rare and shy beast.

Just at dark we regained our camp. It was built California fashion—for the first and last time in Africa: blankets spread on canvas under the open sky and a gipsy fire at our feet, over which I myself cooked our very simple meal. As we were smoking our pipes in sleepy content, Leyeye and the two Masai appeared for a shauri. Said the Masai,—

"We have taken you over the country we know. There are elephants there sometimes, but there are no elephants there now. We can take you farther, and if you wish us to do so, we will do so; but we know no more of the country than you do. But now if we return to the manyatta to-morrow, we can march two hours to where are some Wanderobo; and the Wanderobo know this country and will take you through it. If it pleases you, one of us will go get the Wanderobo, and the other will stay with you to show good faith."

We rolled our eyes at each other in humorous despair. Here at the very beginning of the reconnaissance we had run against the stone wall of African indirectness and procrastination. And just as we thought we had at last settled everything!

"Why," we inquired, "were not the Wanderobo sent at first, instead of yourselves?"

"Because," they replied, with truly engaging frankness, "our chief, Naiokotuku, thought that perhaps we might find elephant here in the country we know; and then we should get for ourselves all the presents you would give for finding elephant. But the elephant are not here now, so the Wanderobo will get part of the present."

That was certainly candid. After some further talk we decided there was no help for it; we must return to camp for a new start.

At this decision the Masai brightened. They volunteered to set off early with Leyeye, to push ahead of us rapidly, and to have the Wanderobo in camp by the time we reached there. We concealed somewhat cynical smiles, and agreed.

The early start was made, but when we reached camp we found, not the Wanderobo, but Leyeye and the Masai huddled over a fire. This was exasperating, but we could not say much. After all, the whole matter was no right of ours, but a manifestation of friendship on the part of Naiokotuku. In the early afternoon the sky cleared, and the ambassadors departed, promising faithfully to be back before we slept. We spent the day writing and in gazing at the vivid view of the hillside, the forest, and the distant miniature prospect before us. Finally we discovered what made it in essence so strangely familiar. In vividness and clarity—even in the crudity of its tones—it was exactly like a coloured photograph!

Of course the savages did not return that evening, nor did we really expect them. Just as a matter of form we packed up the next morning, and sat down to wait. Shortly before noon Leyeye and the Masai returned, bringing with them two of the strange, shy, forest hunters.

But by this time we had talked things over thoroughly. The lure of the greater kudu was regaining the strength it had lost by a long series of disappointments. We had not time left for both a thorough investigation of the forests and a raid in the dry hills of the west after kudu. Mavrouki said he knew of a place where that animal ranged. So we had come to a decision.

We called the Masai and Wanderobo before us. They squatted in a row, their spears planted before them. We sat in canvas chairs. Leyeye standing, translated. The affair was naturally of the greatest deliberation. In the indirect African manner we began our shauri.

We asked one simple question at a time, dealing with one simple phase of the subject. This phase we treated from several different points of view, in order to be absolutely certain that it was understood. To these questions we received replies in this manner:—

"Yes, the Wanderobo told us," they knew the forest; they knew how to go about in the forest; they understood how to find their way in the forest. They knew the elephant; they had seen the elephant many times in the forest; they knew where the elephant ranged in the forest—and so on through every piece of information we desired. It is the usual and only sure way of questioning natives.

Thus we learned that the elephant range extended south through the forests for about seven days' travel; that at this time of year the beasts might be anywhere on that range. This confirmed our decision. Then said we to Leyeye:—

"Tell the Masai that the bwana m'kubwa is most pleased with them, and that he is pleased with the way they have worked for him, and that he is pleased with the presents they have brought him. Tell them that he has no goods here with him, but that he has sent men back to the boma of bwana Kingozi for blankets and wire and cloth, and when those men return he will make a good present to these Masai and to Naiokotuku, their chief.

"Tell the Wanderobo that the bwana m'kubwa is pleased with them, and that he thanks them for coming so far to tell him of the elephant, and that he believes they have told him the truth. Tell them the bwana m'kubwa will not fight the elephant now, because he has not the time, but must go to attend to his affairs. But later, when two years have gone, he will make another safari, and will come back to this country, and will again ask these men to lead him out where he can fight the elephant. And in the meantime he will give them rupees with which to pay their hut tax to the Government."

After various compliments the sitting rose. Then we packed up for a few hours' march. In a short time we passed the chief's village. He came out to say good-bye. A copper bronze youth accompanied him, lithe as a leopard.

"My men have told me your words," said he. "I live always in these mountains, and my young men will bring me word when you return. I am glad the white men have come to see me. I shall have the Wanderobo ready to take you to fight the elephant when you return."

He then instructed the young man to accompany us for the purpose of bringing back the presents we had promised. We shook hands in farewell, and so parted from this friendly and powerful chief.

FOOTNOTES:

V.'s native name—the Master with the Red Beard.

---

## XLIII.

## THE TOPI CAMP.

At the next camp we stayed for nearly a week.

The country was charming. Mountains surrounded the long ellipse, near one edge of which we had pitched our tents. The ellipse was some ten miles long by four or five wide, and its surface rolled in easy billows to a narrow neck at the lower end. There we could just make out in the far distance a conical hill partly closing the neck. Atop the hill was a Masai manyatta, very tiny, with indistinct crawling red and brown blotches that meant cattle and sheep. Beyond the hill, and through the opening in the ellipse, we could see to another new country of hills and meadows and forest groves. In this clear air they were microscopically distinct. No blue of atmosphere nor shimmer of heat blurred their outlines. They were merely made small.

Our camp was made in the open above a tiny stream. We saw wonderful sunrises and sunsets, and always spread out before us was the sweep of our plains and the unbroken ramparts that hemmed us in. From these mountains meandered small stream-ways marked by narrow strips of trees and brush, but the most of the valley was of high green grass. Occasional ant hills ten feet tall rose conical from the earth; and the country was pleasingly broken and modelled, so that one continually surmounted knolls, low, round ridges, and the like. Of such conditions are surprises made.

The elevation here was some 7,000 feet, so that the nights were cold and the days not too warm. Our men did not fancy this change of weather. A good many of them came down with the fever always latent in their systems, and others suffered from bronchial colds.

At one time we had down sick eleven men out of our slender total. However, I believe, in spite of these surface symptoms, that the cold air did them good. It certainly improved our own appetites and staying power.

In the thirty or forty square miles of our valley were many herds of varied game. We here for the first time found Neuman's hartebeeste. The type at Narossara, and even in Lengetto, was the common Coke's hartebeeste, so that between these closely allied species there interposes at this point only the barriers of a climb and a forest. These animals and the zebra were the most plentiful of the game. The zebra were brilliantly white and black, with magnificent coats. Thompson's and Roberts' gazelles were here in considerable numbers, eland, Roosevelt's wildebeeste, giraffe, the smaller grass antelopes, and a fair number of topi. In the hills we saw buffalo sign, several cheetah, and heard many lions.

It had been our first plan that C. should return immediately to V.'s boma after supplies, but in view of the abundance of game we decided to wait over a day. We much desired to get four topi, and this seemed a good chance to carry some of them out. Also we wished to decide for certain whether or not the hartebeeste here was really of the Neuman variety.

We had great luck. Over the very first hill from camp we came upon a herd of about a dozen topi, feeding on a hill across the way. I knocked down the first one standing at just 250 paces. The herd then split and broke to right and left. By shooting very carefully and steadily I managed to kill three more before they were out of range. The last shot was at 325 paces. In all I fired seven shots, and hit six times. This was the best shooting I did in Africa—or anywhere else—and is a first-rate argument for the Springfield and the high velocity, sharp-pointed bullet.

Overjoyed at our luck in collecting these animals so promptly, so near camp, and at a time so very propitious for handling the trophies, we set to the job of skinning and cutting up. The able-bodied men all came out from camp to carry in the meat. They appeared, grinning broadly, for they had had no meat since leaving the Narossara. C. and I saw matters well under way, and then went on to where I had seen a cheetah the day before. Hardly were we out of sight when two lions sauntered over the hill and proceeded to appropriate the meat! The two men in charge promptly withdrew. A moment later a dozen porters on their way out from camp topped the hill and began to yell at the lions. The latter then slowly and reluctantly retreated.

We were very sorry we had not stayed. The valley seemed populated with lions, but in general they were, for some reason, strictly nocturnal. By day they inhabited the fastnesses of the mountain ranges. We never succeeded in tracing them in that large and labyrinthine country; nor at any time could we induce them to come to kills. Either their natural prey was so abundant that they did not fancy ready-killed food; or, what is more likely, the cold nights prevented the odour of the carcasses from carrying far. We heard lions every night; and every morning we conscientiously turned out before daybreak to crawl up to our bait through the wet, cold grass, but with no results. That very night we were jerked from a sound sleep by a tremendous roar almost in camp. So close was it that it seemed to each of us but just outside the tent. We came up all standing. The lion, apparently, was content with that practical joke, for he moved off quietly. Next morning we found where the tracks had led down to water, not ten yards away.

We spent the rest of that day spying on the game herds. It is fascinating work, to lie belly down on a tall ant hill, glasses steadied by elbows, picking out the individual animals and discussing them low-voiced with a good companion. C. and I looked over several hundred hartebeeste, trying to decide their identity. We were neither of us familiar with the animal, and had only recollections of the book distinctions. Finally I picked out one that seemed to present the most marked characteristics—and missed him clean at 280 yards. Then I took three shots at 180 yards to down a second choice. The poor shooting was forgotten, however, in our determination that this was indeed Neumanii.

A vain hunt for lions occupied all the next day. The third morning C. started for the boma, leaving Billy and me to look about us as we willed. Shortly after he had departed a delegation of Masai came in, dressed in their best, and bearing presents of milk. Leyeye was summoned as interpreter.

The Masai informed us that last night a lion had leapt the thorn walls of their boma, had pressed on through the fires, had seized a two-year-old steer, and had dragged the beast outside. Then the pursuit with spears and firebrands had become too hot for him, so that he had dropped his victim and retired. They desired (a) medicine for the steer, (b) magic to keep that lion away, (c) that I should assist them in hunting the lion down.

I questioned them closely, and soon discovered both that the lion must have been very bold, and also that he had received a pretty lively reception. Magic to keep him away seemed like a safe enough proposition, for the chances were he would keep himself away.

Therefore I filled a quart measure with clear water, passed my hand across its untroubled surface—and lo! it turned a clear bright pink!

Long-drawn exclamations of "Eigh! Eigh!" greeted this magic, performed by means of permanganate crystals held between the fingers.

"With this bathe the wounds of your steer. Then sprinkle the remainder over your cattle. The lion will not return," said I. Then reflecting that I was to be some time in the country, and that the lion might get over his scare, I added, "The power of this magic is three days."

They departed very much impressed. A little later Memba Sasa and I followed them. The manyatta was most picturesquely placed atop the conical hill at the foot of the valley. From its elevation we could see here and there in the distance the variegated blotches of red and white and black that represented the cattle herds. Innumerable flocks of sheep and goats, under charge of the small boys and youths, fed nearer at hand. The low smooth-plastered huts, with their abattis of thorn bush between, crowned the peak like a chaplet. Outside it sat a number of elders sunning themselves, and several smiling, good-natured young women, probably the spoiled darlings of these plutocrats. One of these damsels spake Swahili, so we managed to exchange compliments. They told us exactly when and how the lion had gone. Three nimble old gentlemen accompanied us when we left. They were armed with spears; and they displayed the most extraordinary activity, skipping here and there across the ravines and through the brush, casting huge stones into likely cover, and generally making themselves ubiquitous. However, we did not come up with the lion.

In our clinic that evening appeared one of the men claiming to suffer from rheumatism. I suspected him, and still suspect him, of malingering in advance in order to get out of the hard work we must soon undertake, but had no means of proving my suspicion. However, I decided to administer asperin. We possessed only the powdered form of the drug. I dumped about five grains on his tongue, and was about to proffer him the water with which to wash it down—when he inhaled sharply! I do not know the precise effect of asperin in the windpipe, but it is not pleasant. The boy thought himself bewitched. His eyes stuck out of his head; he gasped painfully; he sank to the ground; he made desperate efforts to bolt out into the brush. By main strength we restrained him, and forced him to swallow the water. Little by little he recovered. Next night I missed him from the clinic, and sent Abba Ali in search. The man assured Abba Ali most vehemently that the medicine was wonderful, that every trace of rheumatism had departed, that he never felt better in his life, and that (important point) he was perfectly able to carry a load on the morrow.

---

## XLIV.

THE UNKNOWN LAND.

C. returned the next day from V.'s boma, bringing more potio and some trade goods. We sent a good present back to Naiokotuku, and prepared for an early start into the new country.

We marched out of the lower end of our elliptical valley towards the miniature landscape we had seen through the opening. But before we reached it we climbed sharp to the right around the end of the mountains, made our way through a low pass, and so found ourselves in a new country entirely. The smooth, undulating green-grass plains were now superseded by lava expanses grown with low bushes. It was almost exactly like the sage-brush deserts of Arizona and New Mexico—the same coarse sand and lava footing, the same deeply eroded barrancas, the same scattered round bushes dotted evenly over the scene. We saw here very little game. Across the way lay another range of low mountains clothed darkly with dull green, like the chaparral-covered coast ranges of California. In one place was a gunsight pass through which we could see other distant blue mountains. We crossed the arid plain and toiled up through the notch pass.

The latter made very difficult footing indeed, for the entire surface of the ground was covered with smooth, slippery boulders and rocks of iron and quartz. What had so smoothed them I do not know, for they seemed to be ill-placed for water erosion. The boys with their packs atop found this hard going, and we ourselves slipped and slid and bumped in spite of our caution.

Once through the pass we found ourselves overlooking a wide prospect of undulating thorn scrub from which rose occasional bushy hills, solitary buttes, and bold cliffs. It was a thick-looking country to make a way through.

Nevertheless somewhere here dwelt the Kudu, so in we plunged. The rest of the day—and of days to follow—we spent in picking a way through the thorn scrub and over loose rocks and shifting stones. A stream bed contained an occasional water hole. Tall aloes were ablaze with red flowers. The country looked arid, the air felt dry, the atmosphere was so clear that a day's journey seemed—usually—but the matter of a few hours. Only rarely did we enjoy a few moments of open travel. Most of the time the thorns caught at us. In the mountain passes were sometimes broad trails of game or of the Masai cattle. The country was harsh and dry and beautiful with the grays and dull greens of arid-land brush, or with the soft atmospheric tints of arid-land distances. Game was fairly common, but rather difficult to find. There were many buffalo, a very few zebra, leopards, hyenas, plenty of impalla, some sing-sing, a few eland, abundant wart-hog, Thompson's gazelle, and duiker. We never lacked for meat when we dared shoot it, but we were after nobler game. The sheep given us by Naiokotuku followed along under charge of the syces.

When we should run quite out of meat, we intended to eat them. We delayed too long, however. One evening the fool boy tied them to a thorn bush; one of them pulled back, the thorns bit, and both broke loose and departed into the darkness. Of course everybody pursued, but we could not recapture them. Ten minutes later the hyenas broke into the most unholy laughter. We could not blame them; the joke was certainly on us.

In passing, the cachinnations of the laughing hyena are rather a series of high-voiced self-conscious titters than laughter. They sound like the stage idea of a lot of silly and rather embarrassed old maids who have been accused by some rude man of "taking notice." This call is rarely used; indeed, I never heard it but the once. The usual note is a sort of moaning howl, impossible to describe, but easy to recognize.

Thus we penetrated gradually deeper and deeper into this wild country; through low mountains, over bush-clad plains, into thorn jungles, down wide valleys, over hill-divided plateaus. Late in the afternoon we would make camp. Sometimes we had good water; more often not. In the evening the throb of distant drums and snatches of intermittent wailing song rose and fell with the little night breezes.

---

## XLV.

THE ROAN.

Our last camp, before turning back, we pitched about two o'clock one afternoon. Up to this time we had marched steadily down wide valleys, around the end of mountain ranges, moving from one room to the other of this hill-divided plateau. At last we ended on a slope that descended gently to water. It was grown sparingly with thorn trees, among which we raised our tents. Over against us, and across several low swells of grass and scrub-grown hills, was a range of mountains. Here, Mavrouki claimed, dwelt roan antelope.

We settled down quite happily. The country round about was full of game; the weather was cool, the wide sweeps of country, the upward fling of mountains and buttes were much like some parts of our great West. Almost every evening the thunderstorms made gorgeous piled effects in the distance. At night the lions and hyenas roared or howled, and some of the tiny fever owls impudently answered them back.

Various adventures came our way, some of which have been elsewhere narrated. Here we killed the very big buffalo that nearly got Billy. In addition, we collected two more specimens of the Neuman's hartebeeste, and two Chanler's reed buck.

But Mavrouki's glowing predictions as to roan were hardly borne out by facts. According to him the mountains simply swarmed with them—he had seen thirty-five in one day, etc. Of course we had discounted this, but some old tracks had to a certain extent borne out his statement.

Lunch time one day, however, found us on top of the highest ridge. Here we hunted up a bit of shade, and spent two hours out of the noon sun. While we lay there the sky slowly overcast, so that when we aroused ourselves to go on, the dazzling light had softened. As time was getting short, we decided to separate. Memba Sasa and Mavrouki were to go in one direction, while C., Kongoni and I took the other.

Before we started I remarked that I was offering two rupees for the capture of a roan.

We had not gone ten minutes when Kongoni turned his head cautiously and grinned back at us.

"My rupees," said he.

A fine buck roan stood motionless beneath a tree in the valley below us. He was on the other side of the stream jungle, and nearly a mile away. While we watched him, he lay down.

Our task now was to gain the shelter of the stream jungle below without being seen, to slip along it until opposite the roan, and then to penetrate the jungle near enough to get a shot. The first part of this contract seemed to us the most difficult, for we were forced to descend the face of the hill, like flies crawling down a blackboard, plain for him to see.

We slid cautiously from bush to bush; we moved by imperceptible inches across the numerous open spaces. About half-way down we were arrested by a violent snort ahead. Fifteen or twenty zebras nooning in the brush where no zebras were supposed to be, clattered down the hill like an avalanche. We froze where we were. The beasts ran fifty yards, then wheeled, and started back up the hill, trying to make us out. For twenty minutes all parties to the transaction remained stock still, the zebras staring, we hoping fervently they would decide to go down the valley and not up it, the roan dozing under his distant tree.

By luck our hopes were fulfilled. The zebra turned downstream, walking sedately away in single file. When we were certain they had all quite gone, we resumed our painful descent.

At length we dropped below the screen of trees, and could stand upright and straighten the kinks out of our backs. But now a new complication arose. The wind, which had been the very basis of our calculations, commenced to chop and veer. Here it blew from one quarter, up there on the side hill from another, and through the bushes in quite another direction still. Then without warning they would all shift about. We watched the tops of the grasses through our binoculars, hoping to read some logic into the condition. It was now four o'clock—our stalk had thus far consumed two hours—and the roan must soon begin to feed. If we were going to do anything, we must do it soon.

Therefore we crept through a very spiky, noisy jungle to its other edge, sneaked along the edge until we could make out the tree, and raised ourselves for a look. Through the glass I could just make out the roan's face stripe. He was still there!

Quite encouraged, I instantly dropped down and crawled to within range. When again I raised my head the roan had disappeared. One of these aggravating little side puffs of breeze had destroyed our two hours' work.

The outlook was not particularly encouraging. We had no means of telling how far the animal would go, nor into what sort of country; and the hour was well advanced toward sunset. However, we took up the track, and proceeded to follow it as well as we could. That was not easy, for the ground was hard and stony. Suddenly C. threw himself flat. Of course we followed his example. To us he whispered that he thought he had caught a glimpse of the animal through an opening and across the stream bed. We stalked carefully, and found ourselves in the middle of a small herd of topis, one of which, half concealed in the brush, had deceived C. This consumed valuable time. When again we had picked up the spoor, it was agreed that I was to still-hunt ahead as rapidly as I could, while C. and Kongoni would puzzle out the tracks as far as possible before dark.

Therefore I climbed the little rocky ridge on our left, and walked along near its crest, keeping a sharp lookout over the valley below—much as one would hunt August bucks in California. After two or three hundred yards I chanced on a short strip of soft earth in which the fresh tracks of the roan going uphill were clearly imprinted. I could not without making too much noise inform the others that I had cut in ahead of them; so I followed the tracks as cautiously and quietly as I could. On the very top of the hill the roan leapt from cover fifty yards away, and with a clatter of rocks dashed off down the ridge. The grass was very high, and I could see only his head and horns, but I dropped the front sight six inches and let drive at a guess. The guess happened to be a good one, for he turned a somersault seventy-two yards away.

C. and Kongoni came up. The sun had just set. In fifteen minutes it would be pitch dark. We dispatched Kongoni for help and lanterns, and turned to on the job of building a signal fire and skinning the trophy.

The reason for our strangely chopping wind now became apparent. From our elevation we could see piled thunder-clouds looming up from the west. They were spreading upward and outward in the swift, rushing manner of tropic storms; and I saw I must hustle if I was to get my fire going at all. The first little blaze was easy, and after that I had to pile on quantities of any wood I could lay my hands to. The deluge blotted out every vestige of daylight and nearly drowned out my fire. I had started to help C. with the roan, but soon found that I had my own job cut out for me, and so went back to nursing my blaze. The water descended in sheets. We were immediately soaked through, and very cold. The surface of the ground was steep and covered with loose round rocks, and in my continuous trips for firewood I stumbled and slipped and ran into thorns miserably.

After a long interval of this the lanterns came bobbing through the darkness, and a few moments later the dim light revealed the shining rain-soaked faces of our men.

We wasted no time in the distribution of burdens. C. with one of the lanterns brought up the rear, while I with the other went on ahead.

Now as Kongoni had but this minute completed the round trip to camp, we concluded that he would be the best one to give us a lead. This was a mistake. He took us out of the hills well enough, and a good job that was, for we could not see the length of our arms into the thick, rainy blackness, and we had to go entirely by the slants of the country. But once in the more open, sloping country, with its innumerable bushy or wooded ravines, he began to stray. I felt this from the first; but Kongoni insisted strongly he was right, and in the rain and darkness we had no way of proving him wrong. In fact I had no reason for thinking him wrong; I only felt it. This sense of direction is apparently a fifth wheel or extra adjustment some people happen to possess. It has nothing to do with acquired knowledge, as is very well proved by the fact that in my own case it acts only as long as I do not think about it. As soon as I begin consciously to consider the matter I am likely to go wrong. Thus many, many times I have back-tracked in the dark over ground I had traversed but once before, and have caught myself turning out for bushes or trees I could not see, but which my subconscious memory recalled. This would happen only when I would think of something besides the way home. As soon as I took charge, I groped as badly as the next man. It is a curious and sometimes valuable extra, but by no means to be depended upon.

Now, however, as I was following Kongoni, this faculty had full play, and it assured me vehemently that we were wrong. I called C. up from the rear for consultation. Kongoni was very positive he was right; but as we had now been walking over an hour, and camp should not have been more than three miles from where we had killed the roan, we were inclined towards my instinct. So we took the compass direction, in order to assure consistency at least, and struck off at full right angles to the left.

So we tramped for a long time. Every few moments Kongoni would want another look at that compass. It happened that we were now going due north, and his notion was that the needle pointed the way to camp. We profoundly hoped that his faith in white man's magic would not be shattered. At the end of an hour the rain let up, and it cleared sufficiently to disclose some of the mountain outlines. They convinced us that we were in the main right; though just where, to the north, camp now lay was beyond our power to determine. Kongoni's detour had been rather indeterminate in direction and distance.

The country now became very rough, in a small way. The feeble light of our leading lantern revealed only ghosts and phantoms and looming, warning suggestions of things which the shadows confused and shifted. Heavily laden men would have found it difficult travelling by prosaic daylight; but now, with the added impossibility of picking a route ahead, we found ourselves in all sorts of trouble. Many times we had to back out and try again. The ghostly flickering tree shapes against the fathomless black offered us apparently endless aisles that nevertheless closed before us like the doors of a trap when we attempted to enter them.

We kept doggedly to the same general northerly direction. When you are lost, nothing is more foolish than to make up your mind hastily and without due reflection; and nothing is more foolish than to change your mind once you have made it up. That way vacillation, confusion, and disaster lie. Should you decide, after due consideration of all the elements of the problem, that you should go east, then east you go, and nothing must turn you. You may get to the Atlantic Ocean if nothing else. And if you begin to modify your original plan, then you begin to circle. Believe me; I know.

Kongoni was plainly sceptical, and said so until I shut him up with some rather peremptory sarcasm. The bearers, who had to stumble in the dark under heavy burdens, were good-natured and joking. This we appreciated. One can never tell whether or not he is popular with a native until he and the native are caught in a dangerous or disagreeable fix.

We walked two hours as in a treadmill. Then that invaluable though erratic sixth sense of mine awoke. I stopped short.

"I believe we've come far enough," I shouted back to C., and fired my rifle.

We received an almost immediate answer from a short distance to the left. Not over two hundred yards in that direction we met our camp men bearing torches, and so were escorted in triumph after a sixteen-hour day.

Six months after I had reached home, one of these thorns worked its way out of the calf of my leg.

---

## XLVI.

THE GREATER KUDU.

Next morning, in a joking manner, I tried to impress Kongoni with a sense of delinquency in not knowing better his directions, especially as he had twice traversed the route. He declined to be impressed.

"It is not the business of man to walk at night," he replied with dignity.

And when you stop to think of it, it certainly is not—in Africa.

At this camp we lingered several days. The great prize of our journeying was still lacking, and, to tell the truth, we had about given up hope, if not our efforts. Almost we had begun to believe our friends in Nairobi who had scoffed at the uselessness of our quest. Always we conscientiously looked over good kudu country, hundreds of miles of it, and always with the same lack of result, or even of encouragement. Other game we saw in plenty, of a dozen different varieties, large and small; but our five weeks' search had thus far yielded us only the sight of the same old, old sign, made many months before. If you had stood with us atop one of the mountains, and with us had looked abroad on the countless leagues of rolling brush-clothed land, undulating away in all directions over a far horizon, you must with us have estimated as very slight the chances of happening on the exact pin point where the kudu at that moment happened to be feeding. For the beast is shy, it inhabits the densest, closest mountain cover, it possesses the keen eyesight and sense of smell of the bush-dwelling deer and antelope, and more than the average sense of hearing. There are very few of him. But the chief discouragement is that arising from his roaming tendencies. Other rare animals are apt to "use" about one locality, so that once the hunter finds tracks, new or old, his game is one of patient, skilful search. The greater kudu, however, seems in this country at least to be a wanderer. He is here to-day and gone to-morrow. Systematic search seems as foolish as in the case of the proverbial needle in the haystack. The only method is to sift constantly, and trust to luck. One cannot catch fish with the fly in the book, but one has at least a chance if one keeps it on the water.

Mavrouki was the only one among us who had the living faith that comes from having seen the animal in the flesh. That is a curious bit of hunter psychology. When a man is out after a species new to him, it is only by the utmost stretch of the imagination that he is able to realize that such an animal can exist at all. He cannot prefigure it, somehow. He generally exaggerates to himself the difficulty of making it out, of approaching it, of getting his shot; until at last, if he happens to have hunted some time in vain, the beast becomes almost mythical and unbelievable. Once he has seen the animal, whether he gets a shot or not, all this vanishes. The strain on faith relaxes. He knows what to look for, and what to expect; and even if he sees no other specimen for a month, he nevertheless goes about the business with a certain confidence.

One afternoon we had been hunting carefully certain low mountains, and were headed for camp, walking rather carelessly along the bed of a narrow, open valley below the bush-covered side hills. The sun had disappeared behind the ranges, and the dusk of evening was just beginning to rise like a mist from the deeps of the cañons. We had ceased hunting—it was time to hurry home—and happened not to be talking only because we were tired. By sheerest idle luck I chanced to look up to the densely covered face of the mountain. Across a single tiny opening in the tall brush five or six hundred yards away, I caught a movement. Still idly I lifted my glasses for a look at what I thought would prove the usual impala or sing-sing, and was just in time to catch the spirals of a magnificent set of horns. It was the greater kudu at last!

I gave a little cluck of caution; and instantly, without question, after the African fashion, the three men ahead of me sank to the ground. C. looked at me inquiringly. I motioned with my eyes. He raised his glasses for one look.

"That's the fellow," he said quietly.

The kudu, as though he had merely stepped into the opening to give us a sight of him, melted into the brush.

It was magnificent and exciting to have seen this wonderful beast after so long a quest, but by the same token it was not very encouraging for all that. If we had had all the daylight we needed, and unlimited time, it would have been quite a feat to stalk the wary beast in that thick, noisy cover. Now it was almost dark, and would be quite dark within the half-hour. The kudu had moved out of sight. Whether he had gone on some distance, or whether he still lingered near the edge of the tiny opening was another matter to be determined, and to be determined quickly.

Leaving Kongoni and Mavrouki, C. and I wriggled pantingly up the hill, as fast and at the same time as cautiously as we could. At the edge of the opening we came to a halt, belly down, and began eagerly to scrutinize the brush across the way. If the kudu still lingered we had to find it out before we ventured out of cover to take up his trail. Inch by inch we scrutinized every possible concealment. Finally C. breathed sharp with satisfaction. He had caught sight of the tip of one horn. With some difficulty he indicated to me where. After staring long enough, we could dimly make out the kudu himself browsing, from the tender branch-ends.

All we could do was to lie low. If the kudu fed on out of sight into the cover, we could not possibly get a shot; if he should happen again to cross the opening, we would get a good shot. No one but a hunter can understand the panting, dry-mouthed excitement of those minutes; five weeks' hard work hung in the balance. The kudu did neither of these things; he ceased browsing, took three steps forward, and stood.

The game seemed blocked. The kudu had evidently settled down for a snooze; it was impossible, in the situation, to shorten the distance without being discovered; the daylight was almost gone; we could make out no trace of him except through our glasses. Look as hard as we could, we could see nothing with the naked eye. Unless something happened within the next two minutes, we would bring nothing into camp but the memory of a magnificent beast. And next day he would probably be inextricably lost in the wilderness of mountains.

It was a time for desperate measures, and, to C.'s evident doubtful anxiety, I took them. Through the glasses the mane of the kudu showed as a dim gray streak. Carefully I picked out two twigs on a bush fifteen feet from me, and a tuft of grass ten yards on, all of which were in line with where the shoulder of the kudu ought to be. Then I lowered my glasses. The gray streak of the kudu's mane had disappeared in the blending twilight, but I could still see the tips of the twigs and the tuft of grass. Very carefully I aligned the sights with these; and, with a silent prayer to the Red Gods, loosed the bullet into the darkness.

At the crack of the rifle the kudu leapt into plain sight.

"Hit!" rasped C. in great excitement.

I did not wait to verify this, but fired four times more as fast as I could work the bolt. Three of the bullets told. At the last shot he crumpled and came rolling down the slope. We both raised a wild whoop of triumph, which was answered at once by the expectant gunbearers below.

The finest trophy in Africa was ours!

FOOTNOTES:

Trailing for any distance was impossible on account of the stony soil.

---

## XLVII.

### THE MAGIC PORTALS CLOSE.

It seemed hopeless to try for a picture. Nevertheless I opened wide my lens, steadied the camera, and gave it a half-second. The result was fairly good. So much for a high grade lens. We sent Kongoni into camp for help, and ourselves proceeded to build up the usual fire for signal and for protection against wild beasts. Then we sat down to enjoy the evening, while Mavrouki skinned the kudu.

We looked abroad over a wide stretch of country. Successive low ridges crossed our front, each of a different shade of slate gray from its neighbours, and a gray half-luminous mist filled the valley between them. The edge of the world was thrown sharp against burnished copper. After a time the moon rose.

Memba Sasa arrived before the lanterns, out of breath, his face streaming with perspiration. Poor Memba Sasa! this was almost the only day he had not followed close at my heels, and on this day we had captured the Great Prize. No thought of that seemed to affect the heartiness of his joy. He rushed up to shake both my hands; he examined the kudu with an attention that was held only by great restraint; he let go that restrain to shake me again enthusiastically by the hands. After him, up the hill, bobbed slowly the lanterns. The smiling bearers shouldered the trophy and the meat, and we stumbled home through the half shadows and the opalescences of the moonlight.

Our task in this part of the country was now finished. We set out on the return journey. The weather changed. A beautiful, bright-copper sunset was followed by a drizzle. By morning this had turned into a heavy rain. We left the topi camp, to which we had by now returned, cold and miserable. C. and I had contributed our waterproofs to protect the precious trophies, and we were speedily wet through. The grass was long. This was no warm and grateful tropical rain, but a driving, chilling storm straight out from the high mountains.

We marched up the long plain, we turned to the left around the base of the ranges, we mounted the narrow grass valley, we entered the forest—the dark, dripping, and unfriendly forest. Over the edge we dropped and clambered down through the hanging vines and the sombre trees. By-and-by, we emerged on the open plains below, the plains on the hither side of the Narossara, the Africa we had known so long. The rain ceased. It was almost as though a magic portal had clicked after us. Behind it lay the wonderful secret upper country of the unknown.

---

## XLVIII.

### THE LAST TREK.

Some weeks later we camped high on the slopes of Suswa, the great mountain of the Rift Valley, only one day's march from the railroad. After the capture of the kudu Africa still held for us various adventures—a buffalo, a go of fever, and the like—but the culmination had been reached. We had lingered until the latest moment, reluctant to go. Now in the gray dawn we were filing down the slopes of the mountains for the last trek. A low, flowing mist marked the distant

Kedong; the flames of an African sunrise were revelling in the eastern skies. All our old friends seemed to be bidding us good-bye. Around the shoulder of the mountains a lion roared, rumble upon rumble. Two hyenas leapt from the grass, ran fifty yards, and turned to look at us.

"Good-bye, simba! good-bye, fice!" we cried to them sadly.

A little farther we saw zebra, and the hartebeeste, and the gazelles. One by one appeared and disappeared again the beasts with which we had grown so familiar during our long months in the jungle. So remarkable was the number of species that we both began to comment upon the fact, to greet the animals, to bid them farewell, as though they were reporting in order from the jungle to bid us God-speed. Half in earnest we waved our hands to them and shouted our greetings to them in the native—punda milia, kongoni, pa-a, fice, m'pofu, twiga, simba, n'grooui, and the rest. Before our eyes the misty ranges hardened and stiffened under the fierce sun. Our men marched steadily, cheerfully, beating their loads in rhythm with their safari sticks, crooning under their breaths, and occasionally breaking into full-voiced chant. They were glad to be back from the long safari, back from across the Thirst, from the high, cold country, from the dangers and discomforts of the unknown. We rode a little wistfully, for these great plains and mysterious jungles, these populous, dangerous, many-voiced nights, these flaming, splendid dawnings and day-falls, these fierce, shimmering noons we were to know no more.

Two days we had in Nairobi before going to the coast. There we paid off and dismissed our men, giving them presents according to the length and faithfulness of their service. They took them and departed, eagerly, as was natural, to the families and the pleasures from which they had been so long separated. Mohammed said good-bye, and went, and was sorry; Kongoni departed, after many and sincere protestations; quiet little Mavrouki came back three times to shake hands again, and disappeared reluctantly—but disappeared; Leyeye went; Abba Ali followed the service of his master, C.; "Timothy" received his present—in which he was disappointed—and departed with salaams. Only Memba Sasa remained. I paid him for his long service, and I gave him many and rich presents, and bade farewell to him with genuine regret and affection.

Memba Sasa had wives and a farm near town, neither of which possessions he had seen for a very long while. Nevertheless he made no move to see them. When our final interview had terminated with the usual "Bass" (It is finished), he shook hands once more and withdrew, but only to take his position across the street. There he squatted on his heels, fixed his eyes upon me, and remained. I went down town on business. Happening to glance through the office window I caught sight of Memba Sasa again across the street, squatted on his heels, his gaze fixed unwaveringly on my face. So it was for two days. When I tried to approach him, he glided away, so that I got no further speech with him; but always, quietly and unobtrusively, he returned to where he could see me plainly. He considered that our interview had terminated our official relations, but he wanted to see the last of the bwana with whom he had journeyed so far.

One makes many acquaintances as one knocks about the world; and once in a great many moons one finds a friend—a man the mere fact of whose existence one is glad to realize, whether one ever sees him again or not. These are not many, and they are of various degree. Among them I am glad to number this fierce savage. He was efficient, self-respecting, brave, staunch, and loyal with a great loyalty. I do not think I can better end this book than by this feeble tribute to a man whose opportunities were not many, but whose soul was great.


THE END

# The Blazed Trail

## Chapter I

When history has granted him the justice of perspective, we shall know the American Pioneer as one of the most picturesque of her many figures. Resourceful, self-reliant, bold; adapting himself with fluidity to diverse circumstances and conditions; meeting with equal cheerfulness of confidence and completeness of capability both unknown dangers and the perils by which he has been educated; seizing the useful in the lives of the beasts and men nearest him, and assimilating it with marvellous rapidity; he presents to the world a picture of complete adequacy which it would be difficult to match in any other walk of life. He is a strong man, with a strong man's virtues and a strong man's vices. In him the passions are elemental, the dramas epic, for he lives in the age when men are close to nature, and draw from her their forces. He satisfies his needs direct from the earth. Stripped of all the towns can give him, he merely resorts to a facile substitution. It becomes an affair of rawhide for leather, buckskin for cloth, venison for canned tomatoes. We feel that his steps are planted on solid earth, for civilizations may crumble without disturbing his magnificent self-poise. In him we perceive dimly his environment. He has something about him which other men do not possess—a frank clearness of the eye, a swing of the shoulder, a carriage of the hips, a tilt of the hat, an air of muscular well-being which marks him as belonging to the advance guard, whether he wears buckskin, mackinaw, sombrero, or broadcloth. The woods are there, the plains, the rivers. Snow is there, and the line of the prairie. Mountain peaks and still pine forests have impressed themselves subtly; so that when we turn to admire his unconsciously graceful swing, we seem to hear the ax biting the pine, or the prospector's pick tapping the rock. And in his eye is the capability of quiet humor, which is just the quality that the surmounting of many difficulties will give a man.

Like the nature he has fought until he understands, his disposition is at once kindly and terrible. Outside the subtleties of his calling, he sees only red. Relieved of the strenuousness of his occupation, he turns all the force of the wonderful energies that have carried him far where other men would have halted, to channels in which a gentle current makes flood enough. It is the mountain torrent and the canal. Instead of pleasure, he seeks orgies. He runs to wild excesses of drinking, fighting, and carousing—which would frighten most men to sobriety—with a happy, reckless spirit that carries him beyond the limits of even his extraordinary forces.

This is not the moment to judge him. And yet one cannot help admiring the magnificently picturesque spectacle of such energies running riot. The power is still in evidence, though beyond its proper application.

## Chapter II

In the network of streams draining the eastern portion of Michigan and known as the Saginaw waters, the great firm of Morrison & Daly had for many years carried on extensive logging operations in the wilderness. The number of their camps was legion, of their employees a multitude. Each spring they had gathered in their capacious booms from thirty to fifty million feet of pine logs.

Now at last, in the early eighties, they reached the end of their holdings. Another winter would finish the cut. Two summers would see the great mills at Beeson Lake dismantled or sold, while Mr. Daly, the "woods partner" of the combination, would flit away to the scenes of new and perhaps more extensive operations. At this juncture Mr. Daly called to him John Radway, a man whom he knew to possess extensive experience, a little capital, and a desire for more of both.

"Radway," said he, when the two found themselves alone in the mill office, "we expect to cut this year some fifty millions, which will finish our pine holdings in the Saginaw waters. Most of this timber lies over in the Crooked Lake district, and that we expect to put in ourselves. We own, however, five million on the Cass Branch which we would like to log on contract. Would you care to take the job?"

"How much a thousand do you give?" asked Radway.

"Four dollars," replied the lumberman.

"I'll look at it," replied the jobber.

So Radway got the "descriptions" and a little map divided into townships, sections, and quarter sections; and went out to look at it. He searched until he found a "blaze" on a tree, the marking on which indicated it as the corner of a section. From this corner the boundary lines were blazed at right angles in either direction. Radway followed the blazed lines. Thus he was able accurately to locate isolated "forties" (forty acres), "eighties," quarter sections, and sections in a primeval wilderness. The feat, however, required considerable woodcraft, an exact sense of direction, and a pocket compass.

These resources were still further drawn upon for the next task. Radway tramped the woods, hills, and valleys to determine the most practical route over which to build a logging road from the standing timber to the shores of Cass Branch. He found it to be an affair of some puzzlement. The pines stood on a country rolling with hills, deep with pot-holes. It became necessary to dodge in and out, here and there, between the knolls, around or through the swamps, still keeping, however, the same general direction, and preserving always the requisite level or down grade. Radway had no vantage point from which to survey the country. A city man would promptly have lost himself in the tangle; but the woodsman emerged at last on the banks of the stream, leaving behind him a meandering trail of clipped trees that wound, twisted, doubled, and turned, but kept ever to a country without steep hills. From the main road he purposed arteries to tap the most distant parts.

"I'll take it," said he to Daly.

Now Radway happened to be in his way a peculiar character. He was acutely sensitive to the human side of those with whom he had dealings. In fact, he was more inclined to take their point of view than to hold his own. For that reason, the subtler disputes were likely to go against him. His desire to avoid coming into direct collision of opinion with the other man, veiled whatever of justice might reside in his own contention. Consequently it was difficult for him to combat sophistry or a plausible appearance of right. Daly was perfectly aware of Radway's peculiarities, and so proceeded to drive a sharp bargain with him.

Customarily a jobber is paid a certain proportion of the agreed price as each stage of the work is completed—so much when the timber is cut; so much when it is skidded, or piled; so much when it is stacked at the river, or banked; so much when the "drive" down the waters of the river is finished. Daly objected to this method of procedure.

"You see, Radway," he explained, "it is our last season in the country. When this lot is in, we want to pull up stakes, so we can't take any chances on not getting that timber in. If you don't finish your Job, it keeps us here another season. There can be no doubt, therefore, that you finish your job. In other words, we can't take any chances. If you start the thing, you've got to carry it 'way through."

"I think I can, Mr. Daly," the jobber assured him.

"For that reason," went on Daly, "we object to paying you as the work progresses. We've got to have a guarantee that you don't quit on us, and that those logs will be driven down the branch as far as the river in time to catch our drive. Therefore I'm going to make you a good price per thousand, but payable only when the logs are delivered to our rivermen."

Radway, with his usual mental attitude of one anxious to justify the other man, ended by seeing only his employer's argument. He did not perceive that the latter's proposition introduced into the transaction a gambling element. It became possible for Morrison & Daly to get a certain amount of work, short of absolute completion, done for nothing.

"How much does the timber estimate?" he inquired finally.

"About five millions."

"I'd need a camp of forty or fifty men then. I don't see how I can run such a camp without borrowing."

"You have some money, haven't you?"

"Yes; a little. But I have a family, too."

"That's all right. Now look here." Daly drew towards him a sheet of paper and began to set down figures showing how the financing could be done. Finally it was agreed. Radway was permitted to draw on the Company's warehouse for what provisions he would need. Daly let him feel it as a concession.

All this was in August. Radway, who was a good practical woodsman, set about the job immediately. He gathered a crew, established his camp, and began at once to cut roads through the country he had already blazed on his former trip.

Those of us who have ever paused to watch a group of farmers working out their road taxes, must have gathered a formidable impression of road-clearing. And the few of us who, besides, have experienced the adventure of a drive over the same highway after the tax has been pronounced liquidated, must have indulged in varied reflections as to the inadequacy of the result.

Radway's task was not merely to level out and ballast the six feet of a road-bed already constructed, but to cut a way for five miles through the unbroken wilderness. The way had moreover to be not less than twenty-five feet wide, needed to be absolutely level and free from any kind of obstructions, and required in the swamps liberal ballasting with poles, called corduroys. To one who will take the trouble to recall the variety of woods, thickets, and jungles that go to make up a wooded country—especially in the creek bottoms where a logging road finds often its levelest way—and the piles of windfalls, vines, bushes, and scrubs that choke the thickets with a discouraging and inextricable tangle, the clearing of five miles to street width will look like an almost hopeless undertaking. Not only must the growth be removed, but the roots must be cut out, and the inequalities of the ground levelled or filled up. Reflect further that Radway had but a brief time at his disposal,—but a few months at most,—and you will then be in a position to gauge the first difficulties of those the American pioneer expects to encounter as a matter of course. The cutting of the road was a mere incident in the battle with the wilderness.

The jobber, of course, pushed his roads as rapidly as possible, but was greatly handicapped by lack of men. Winter set in early and surprised him with several of the smaller branches yet to finish. The main line, however, was done.

At intervals squares were cut out alongside. In them two long timbers, or skids, were laid andiron-wise for the reception of the piles of logs which would be dragged from the fallen trees. They were called skidways. Then finally the season's cut began.

The men who were to fell the trees, Radway distributed along one boundary of a "forty." They were instructed to move forward across the forty in a straight line, felling every pine tree over eight inches in diameter. While the "saw-gangs," three in number, prepared to fell the first trees, other men, called "swampers," were busy cutting and clearing of roots narrow little trails down through the forest from the pine to the skidway at the edge of the logging road. The trails were perhaps three feet wide, and marvels of smoothness, although no attempt was made to level mere inequalities of the ground. They were called travoy roads (French "travois"). Down them the logs would be dragged and hauled, either by means of heavy steel tongs or a short sledge on which one end of the timber would be chained.

Meantime the sawyers were busy. Each pair of men selected a tree, the first they encountered over the blazed line of their "forty." After determining in which direction it was to fall, they set to work to chop a deep gash in that side of the trunk.

Tom Broadhead and Henry Paul picked out a tremendous pine which they determined to throw across a little open space in proximity to the travoy road. One stood to right, the other to left, and alternately their axes bit deep. It was a beautiful sight this, of experts wielding their tools. The craft of the woodsman means incidentally such a free swing of the shoulders and hips, such a directness of stroke as the blade of one sinks accurately in the gash made by the other, that one never tires of watching the grace of it. Tom glanced up as a sailor looks aloft.

"She'll do, Hank," he said.

The two then with a dozen half clips of the ax, removed the inequalities of the bark from the saw's path. The long, flexible ribbon of steel began to sing, bending so adaptably to the hands and motions of the men manipulating, that it did not seem possible so mobile an instrument could cut the rough pine. In a moment the song changed timbre. Without a word the men straightened their backs. Tom flirted along the blade a thin stream of kerosene oil from a bottle in his hip pocket, and the sawyers again bent to their work, swaying back and forth rhythmically, their muscles rippling under the texture of their woolens like those of a panther under its skin. The outer edge of the saw-blade disappeared.

"Better wedge her, Tom," advised Hank.

They paused while, with a heavy sledge, Tom drove a triangle of steel into the crack made by the sawing. This prevented the weight of the tree from pinching the saw, which is a ruin at once to the instrument and the temper of the filer. Then the rhythmical z-z-z! z-z-z! again took up its song.

When the trunk was nearly severed, Tom drove another and thicker wedge.

"Timber!" hallooed Hank in a long-drawn melodious call that melted through the woods into the distance. The swampers ceased work and withdrew to safety.

But the tree stood obstinately upright. So the saw leaped back and forth a few strokes more.

"Crack!" called the tree.

Hank coolly unhooked his saw handle, and Tom drew the blade through and out the other side.

The tree shivered, then leaded ever so slightly from the perpendicular, then fell, at first gently, afterwards with a crescendo rush, tearing through the branches of other trees, bending the small timber, breaking the smallest, and at last hitting with a tremendous crash and bang which filled the air with a fog of small twigs, needles, and the powder of snow, that settled but slowly. There is nothing more impressive than this rush of a pine top, excepting it be a charge of cavalry or the fall of Niagara. Old woodsmen sometimes shout aloud with the mere excitement into which it lifts them.

Then the swampers, who had by now finished the travoy road, trimmed the prostrate trunk clear of all protuberances. It required fairly skillful ax work. The branches had to be shaved close and clear, and at the same time the trunk must not be gashed. And often a man was forced to wield his instrument from a constrained position.

The chopped branches and limbs had now to be dragged clear and piled. While this was being finished, Tom and Hank marked off and sawed the log lengths, paying due attention to the necessity of avoiding knots, forks, and rotten places. Thus some of the logs were eighteen, some sixteen, or fourteen, and some only twelve feet in length.

Next appeared the teamsters with their little wooden sledges, their steel chains, and their tongs. They had been helping the skidders to place the parallel and level beams, or skids, on which the logs were to be piled by the side of the road. The tree which Tom and Hank had just felled lay up a gentle slope from the new travoy road, so little Fabian Laveque, the teamster, clamped the bite of his tongs to the end of the largest, or butt, log.

"Allez, Molly!" he cried.

The horse, huge, elephantine, her head down, nose close to her chest, intelligently spying her steps, moved. The log half rolled over, slid three feet, and menaced a stump.

"Gee!" cried Laveque.

Molly stepped twice directly sideways, planted her fore foot on a root she had seen, and pulled sharply. The end of the log slid around the stump.

"Allez!" commanded Laveque.

And Molly started gingerly down the hill. She pulled the timber, heavy as an iron safe, here and there through the brush, missing no steps, making no false moves, backing, and finally getting out of the way of an unexpected roll with the ease and intelligence of Laveque himself. In five minutes the burden lay by the travoy road. In two minutes more one end of it had been rolled on the little flat wooden sledge and, the other end dragging, it was winding majestically down through the ancient forest. The little Frenchman stood high on the forward end. Molly stepped ahead carefully, with the strange intelligence of the logger's horse. Through the tall, straight, decorative trunks of trees the little convoy moved with the massive pomp of a dead warrior's cortege. And little Fabian Laveque, singing, a midget in the vastness, typified the indomitable spirit of these conquerors of a wilderness.

When Molly and Fabian had travoyed the log to the skidway, they drew it with a bump across the two parallel skids, and left it there to be rolled to the top of the pile.

Then Mike McGovern and Bob Stratton and Jim Gladys took charge of it. Mike and Bob were running the cant-hooks, while Jim stood on top of the great pile of logs already decked. A slender, pliable steel chain, like a gray snake, ran over the top of the pile and disappeared through a pulley to an invisible horse,—Jenny, the mate of Molly. Jim threw the end of this chain down. Bob passed it over and under the log and returned it to Jim, who reached down after it with the hook of his implement. Thus the stick of timber rested in a long loop, one end of which led to the invisible horse, and the other Jim made fast to the top of the pile. He did so by jamming into another log the steel swamp-hook with which the chain was armed. When all was made fast, the horse started.

"She's a bumper!" said Bob. "Look out, Mike!"

The log slid to the foot of the two parallel poles laid slanting up the face of the pile. Then it trembled on the ascent. But one end stuck for an instant, and at once the log took on a dangerous slant. Quick as light Bob and Mike sprang forward, gripped the hooks of the cant-hooks, like great thumbs and forefingers, and, while one held with all his power, the other gave a sharp twist upward. The log straightened. It was a master feat of power, and the knack of applying strength justly.

At the top of the little incline, the timber hovered for a second.

"One more!" sang out Jim to the driver. He poised, stepped lightly up and over, and avoided by the safe hair's breadth being crushed when the log rolled. But it did not lie quite straight and even. So Mike cut a short thick block, and all three stirred the heavy timber sufficiently to admit of the billet's insertion.

Then the chain was thrown down for another.

Jenny, harnessed only to a straight short bar with a hook in it, leaned to her collar and dug in her hoofs at the word of command. The driver, close to her tail, held fast the slender steel chain by an ingenious hitch about the ever-useful swamp-hook. When Jim shouted "whoa!" from the top of the skidway, the driver did not trouble to stop the horse,—he merely let go the hook. So the power was shut off suddenly, as is meet and proper in such ticklish business. He turned and walked back, and Jenny, like a dog, without the necessity of command, followed him in slow patience.

Now came Dyer, the scaler, rapidly down the logging road, a small slender man with a little, turned-up mustache. The men disliked him because of his affectation of a city smartness, and because he never ate with them, even when there was plenty of room. Radway had confidence in him because he lived in the same shanty with him. This one fact a good deal explains Radway's character. The scaler's duty at present was to measure the diameter of the logs in each skidway, and so compute the number of board feet. At the office he tended van, kept the books, and looked after supplies.

He approached the skidway swiftly, laid his flexible rule across the face of each log, made a mark on his pine tablets in the column to which the log belonged, thrust the tablet in the pocket of his coat, seized a blue crayon, in a long holder, with which he made an 8 as indication that the log had been scaled, and finally tapped several times strongly with a sledge hammer. On the face of the hammer in relief was an M inside of a delta. This was the Company's brand, and so the log was branded as belonging to them. He swarmed all over the skidway, rapid and absorbed, in strange contrast of activity to the slower power of the actual skidding. In a moment he moved on to the next scene of operations without having said a word to any of the men.

"A fine t'ing!" said Mike, spitting.

So day after day the work went on. Radway spent his time tramping through the woods, figuring on new work, showing the men how to do things better or differently, discussing minute expedients with the blacksmith, the carpenter, the cook.

He was not without his troubles. First he had not enough men; the snow lacked, and then came too abundantly; horses fell sick of colic or caulked themselves; supplies ran low unexpectedly; trees turned out "punk"; a certain bit of ground proved soft for travoying, and so on. At election-time, of course, a number of the men went out.

And one evening, two days after election-time, another and important character entered the North woods and our story.

### Chapter III

On the evening in question, some thirty or forty miles southeast of Radway's camp, a train was crawling over a badly laid track which led towards the Saginaw Valley. The whole affair was very crude. To the edge of the right-of-way pushed the dense swamp, like a black curtain shutting the virgin country from the view of civilization. Even by daylight the sight could have penetrated but a few feet. The right-of-way itself was rough with upturned stumps, blackened by fire, and gouged by many and varied furrows. Across the snow were tracks of animals.

The train consisted of a string of freight cars, one coach divided half and half between baggage and smoker, and a day car occupied by two silent, awkward women and a child. In the smoker lounged a dozen men. They were of various sizes and descriptions, but they all wore heavy blanket mackinaw coats, rubber shoes, and thick German socks tied at the knee. This constituted, as it were, a sort of uniform. The air was so thick with smoke that the men had difficulty in distinguishing objects across the length of the car.

The passengers sprawled in various attitudes. Some hung their legs over the arms of the seats; others perched their feet on the backs of the seats in front; still others slouched in corners, half reclining. Their occupations were as diverse. Three nearest the baggage-room door attempted to sing, but without much success. A man in the corner breathed softly through a mouth organ, to the music of which his seat mate, leaning his head sideways, gave close attention. One big fellow with a square beard swaggered back and forth down the aisle offering to everyone refreshment from a quart bottle. It was rarely refused. Of the dozen, probably three quarters were more or less drunk.

After a time the smoke became too dense. A short, thick-set fellow with an evil dark face coolly thrust his heel through a window. The conductor, who, with the brakeman and baggage master, was seated in the baggage van, heard the jingle of glass. He arose.

"Guess I'll take up tickets," he remarked. "Perhaps it will quiet the boys down a little."

The conductor was a big man, raw-boned and broad, with a hawk face. His every motion showed lean, quick, panther-like power.

"Let her went," replied the brakeman, rising as a matter of course to follow his chief.

The brakeman was stocky, short, and long armed. In the old fighting days Michigan railroads chose their train officials with an eye to their superior deltoids. A conductor who could not throw an undesirable fare through a car window lived a short official life. The two men loomed on the noisy smoking compartment.

"Tickets, please!" clicked the conductor sharply.

Most of the men began to fumble about in their pockets, but the three singers and the one who had been offering the quart bottle did not stir.

"Ticket, Jack!" repeated the conductor, "come on, now."

The big bearded man leaned uncertainly against the seat.

"Now look here, Bud," he urged in wheedling tones, "I ain't got no ticket. You know how it is, Bud. I blows my stake." He fished uncertainly in his pocket and produced the quart bottle, nearly empty, "Have a drink?"

"No," said the conductor sharply.

"A' right," replied Jack, amiably, "take one myself." He tipped the bottle, emptied it, and hurled it through a window. The conductor paid no apparent attention to the breaking of the glass.

"If you haven't any ticket, you'll have to get off," said he.

The big man straightened up.

"You go to hell!" he snorted, and with the sole of his spiked boot delivered a mighty kick at the conductor's thigh.

The official, agile as a wild cat, leaped back, then forward, and knocked the man half the length of the car. You see, he was used to it. Before Jack could regain his feet the official stood over him.

The three men in the corner had also risen, and were staggering down the aisle intent on battle. The conductor took in the chances with professional rapidity.

"Get at 'em, Jimmy," said he.

And as the big man finally swayed to his feet, he was seized by the collar and trousers in the grip known to "bouncers" everywhere, hustled to the door, which someone obligingly opened, and hurled from the moving train into the snow. The conductor did not care a straw whether the obstreperous Jack lit on his head or his feet, hit a snowbank or a pile of ties. Those were rough days, and the preservation of authority demanded harsh measures.

Jimmy had got at 'em in a method of his own. He gathered himself into a ball of potential trouble, and hurled himself bodily at the legs of his opponents which he gathered in a mighty bear hug. It would have been poor fighting had Jimmy to carry the affair to a finish by himself, but considered as an expedient to gain time for the ejectment proceedings, it was admirable. The conductor returned to find a kicking, rolling, gouging mass of kinetic energy knocking the varnish off all one end of the car. A head appearing, he coolly batted it three times against a corner of the seat arm, after which he pulled the contestant out by the hair and threw him into a seat where he lay limp. Then it could be seen that Jimmy had clasped tight in his embrace a leg each of the other two. He hugged them close to his breast, and jammed his face down against them to protect his features. They could pound the top of his head and welcome. The only thing he really feared was a kick in the side, and for that there was hardly room.

The conductor stood over the heap, at a manifest advantage.

"You lumber-jacks had enough, or do you want to catch it plenty?"

The men, drunk though they were, realized their helplessness. They signified they had had enough. Jimmy thereupon released them and stood up, brushing down his tousled hair with his stubby fingers.

"Now is it ticket or bounce?" inquired the conductor.

After some difficulty and grumbling, the two paid their fare and that of the third, who was still dazed. In return the conductor gave them slips. Then he picked his lantern from the overhead rack whither he had tossed it, slung it on his left arm, and sauntered on down the aisle punching tickets. Behind him followed Jimmy. When he came to the door he swung across the platform with the easy lurch of the trainman, and entered the other car, where he took the tickets of the two women and the boy. One sitting in the second car would have been unable to guess from the bearing or manner of the two officials that anything had gone wrong.

The interested spectators of the little drama included two men near the water-cooler who were perfectly sober. One of them was perhaps a little past the best of life, but still straight and vigorous. His lean face was leather-brown in contrast to a long mustache and heavy eyebrows bleached nearly white, his eyes were a clear steady blue, and his frame was slender but wiry. He wore the regulation mackinaw blanket coat, a peaked cap with an extraordinarily high crown, and buckskin moccasins over long stockings.

The other was younger, not more than twenty-six perhaps, with the clean-cut, regular features we have come to consider typically American. Eyebrows that curved far down along the temples, and eyelashes of a darkness in contrast to the prevailing note of his complexion combined to lend him a rather brooding, soft, and melancholy air which a very cursory second examination showed to be fictitious. His eyes, like the woodsman's, were steady, but inquiring. His jaw was square and settled, his mouth straight. One would be likely to sum him up as a man whose actions would be little influenced by glamour or even by the sentiments. And yet, equally, it was difficult to rid the mind of the impression produced by his eyes. Unlike the other inmates of the car, he wore an ordinary business suit, somewhat worn, but of good cut, and a style that showed even over the soft flannel shirt. The trousers were, however, bound inside the usual socks and rubbers.

The two seat mates had occupied their time each in his own fashion. To the elder the journey was an evil to be endured with the patience learned in watching deer runways, so he stared straight before him, and spat with a certain periodicity into the centre of the aisle. The younger stretched back lazily in an attitude of ease which spoke of the habit of travelling. Sometimes he smoked a pipe. Thrice he read over a letter. It was from his sister, and announced her arrival at the little rural village in which he had made arrangements for her to stay. "It is interesting,—now," she wrote, "though the resources do not look as though they would wear well. I am learning under Mrs. Renwick to sweep and dust and bake and stew and do a multitude of other things which I always vaguely supposed came ready-made. I like it; but after I have learned it all, I do not believe the practise will appeal to me much. However, I can stand it well enough for a year or two or three, for I am young; and then you will have made your everlasting fortune, of course."

Harry Thorpe experienced a glow of pride each time he read this part of the letter. He liked the frankness of the lack of pretence; he admired the penetration and self-analysis which had taught her the truth that, although learning a new thing is always interesting, the practising of an old one is monotonous. And her pluck appealed to him. It is not easy for a girl to step from the position of mistress of servants to that of helping about the housework of a small family in a small town for the sake of the home to be found in it.

"She's a trump!" said Thorpe to himself, "and she shall have her everlasting fortune, if there's such a thing in the country."

He jingled the three dollars and sixty cents in his pocket, and smiled. That was the extent of his everlasting fortune at present.

The letter had been answered from Detroit.

"I am glad you are settled," he wrote. "At least I know you have enough to eat and a roof over you. I hope sincerely that you will do your best to fit yourself to your new conditions. I know it is hard, but with my lack of experience and my ignorance as to where to take hold, it may be a good many years before we can do any better."

When Helen Thorpe read this, she cried. Things had gone wrong that morning, and an encouraging word would have helped her. The somber tone of her brother's communication threw her into a fit of the blues from which, for the first time, she saw her surroundings in a depressing and distasteful light. And yet he had written as he did with the kindest possible motives.

Thorpe had the misfortune to be one of those individuals who, though careless of what people in general may think of them, are in a corresponding degree sensitive to the opinion of the few they love. This feeling was further exaggerated by a constitutional shrinking from any outward manifestation of the emotions. As a natural result, he was often thought indifferent or discouraging when in reality his natural affections were at their liveliest. A failure to procure for a friend certain favors or pleasures dejected him, not only because of that friend's disappointment, but because, also, he imagined the failure earned him a certain blame. Blame from his heart's intimates he shrank from. His life outside the inner circles of his affections was apt to be so militant and so divorced from considerations of amity, that as a matter of natural reaction he became inclined to exaggerate the importance of small objections, little reproaches, slight criticisms from his real friends. Such criticisms seemed to bring into a sphere he would have liked to keep solely for the mutual reliance of loving kindness, something of the hard utilitarianism of the world at large. In consequence he gradually came to choose the line of least resistance, to avoid instinctively even the slightly disagreeable. Perhaps for this reason he was never entirely sincere with those he loved. He showed enthusiasm over any plan suggested by them, for the reason that he never dared offer a merely problematical anticipation. The affair had to be absolutely certain in his own mind before he ventured to admit anyone to the pleasure of looking forward to it,—and simply because he so feared the disappointment in case anything should go wrong. He did not realize that not only is the pleasure of anticipation often the best, but that even disappointment, provided it happen through excusable causes, strengthens the bonds of affection through sympathy. We do not want merely results from a friend—merely finished products. We like to be in at the making, even though the product spoil.

This unfortunate tendency, together with his reserve, lent him the false attitude of a rather cold, self-centered man, discouraging suggestions at first only to adopt them later in the most inexplicable fashion, and conferring favors in a ready-made impersonal manner which destroyed utterly their quality as favors. In reality his heart hungered for the affection which this false attitude generally repelled. He threw the wet blanket of doubt over warm young enthusiasms because his mind worked with a certain deliberateness which did not at once permit him to see the practicability of the scheme. Later he would approve. But by that time, probably, the wet blanket had effectually extinguished the glow. You cannot always savor your pleasures cold.

So after the disgrace of his father, Harry Thorpe did a great deal of thinking and planning which he kept carefully to himself. He considered in turn the different occupations to which he could turn his hand, and negatived them one by one. Few business firms would care to employ the son of as shrewd an embezzler as Henry Thorpe. Finally he came to a decision. He communicated this decision to his sister. It would have commended itself more logically to her had she been able to follow step by step the considerations that had led her brother to it. As the event turned, she was forced to accept it blindly. She knew that her brother intended going West, but as to his hopes and plans she was in ignorance. A little sympathy, a little mutual understanding would have meant a great deal to her, for a girl whose mother she but dimly remembers, turns naturally to her next of kin. Helen Thorpe had always admired her brother, but had never before needed him. She had looked upon him as strong, self-contained, a little moody. Now the tone of his letter caused her to wonder whether he were not also a trifle hard and cold. So she wept on receiving it, and the tears watered the ground for discontent.

At the beginning of the row in the smoking car, Thorpe laid aside his letter and watched with keen appreciation the direct practicality of the trainmen's method. When the bearded man fell before the conductor's blow, he turned to the individual at his side.

"He knows how to hit, doesn't he!" he observed. "That fellow was knocked well off his feet."

"He does," agreed the other dryly.

They fell into a desultory conversation of fits and starts. Woodsmen of the genuine sort are never talkative; and Thorpe, as has been explained, was constitutionally reticent. In the course of their disjointed remarks Thorpe explained that he was looking for work in the woods, and intended, first of all, to try the Morrison & Daly camps at Beeson Lake.

"Know anything about logging?" inquired the stranger.

"Nothing," Thorpe confessed.

"Ain't much show for anything but lumber-jacks. What did you think of doing?"

"I don't know," said Thorpe, doubtfully. "I have driven horses a good deal; I thought I might drive team."

The woodsman turned slowly and looked Thorpe over with a quizzical eye. Then he faced to the front again and spat.

"Quite like," he replied still more dryly.

The boy's remark had amused him, and he had showed it, as much as he ever showed anything. Excepting always the riverman, the driver of a team commands the highest wages among out-of-door workers. He has to be able to guide his horses by little steps over, through, and around slippery and bristling difficulties. He must acquire the knack of facing them square about in their tracks. He must hold them under a control that will throw into their collars, at command, from five pounds to their full power of pull, lasting from five seconds to five minutes. And above all, he must be able to keep them out of the way of tremendous loads of logs on a road which constant sprinkling has rendered smooth and glassy, at the same time preventing the long tongue from sweeping them bodily against leg-breaking debris when a curve in the road is reached. It is easier to drive a fire engine than a logging team.

But in spite of the naivete of the remark, the woodsman had seen something in Thorpe he liked. Such men become rather expert in the reading of character, and often in a log shanty you will hear opinions of a shrewdness to surprise you. He revised his first intention to let the conversation drop.

"I think M. & D. is rather full up just now," he remarked. "I'm walkin'-boss there. The roads is about all made, and road-making is what a greenhorn tackles first. They's more chance earlier in the year. But if the OLD Fellow" (he strongly accented the first word) "h'aint nothin' for you, just ask for Tim Shearer, an' I'll try to put you on the trail for some jobber's camp."

The whistle of the locomotive blew, and the conductor appeared in the doorway.

"Where's that fellow's turkey?" he inquired.

Several men looked toward Thorpe, who, not understanding this argot of the camps, was a little bewildered. Shearer reached over his head and took from the rack a heavy canvas bag, which he handed to the conductor.

"That's the 'turkey'—" he explained, "his war bag. Bud'll throw it off at Scott's, and Jack'll get it there."

"How far back is he?" asked Thorpe.

"About ten mile. He'll hoof it in all right."

A number of men descended at Scott's. The three who had come into collision with Jimmy and Bud were getting noisier. They had produced a stone jug, and had collected the remainder of the passengers,—with the exception of Shearer and Thorpe,—and now were passing the jug rapidly from hand to hand. Soon they became musical, striking up one of the weird long-drawn-out chants so popular with the shanty boy. Thorpe shrewdly guessed his companion to be a man of weight, and did not hesitate to ascribe his immunity from annoyance to the other's presence.

"It's a bad thing," said the walking-boss, "I used to be at it myself, and I know. When I wanted whisky, I needed it worse than a scalded pup does a snow bank. The first year I had a hundred and fifty dollars, and I blew her all in six days. Next year I had a little more, but she lasted me three weeks. That was better. Next year, I says to myself, I'll just save fifty of that stake, and blow the rest. So I did. After that I got to be scaler, and sort've quit. I just made a deal with the Old Fellow to leave my stake with headquarters no matter whether I call for it or not. I got quite a lot coming, now."

"Bees'n Lake!" cried Jimmy fiercely through an aperture of the door.

"You'll find th' boardin'-house just across over the track," said the woodsman, holding out his hand, "so long. See you again if you don't find a job with the Old Fellow. My name's Shearer."

"Mine is Thorpe," replied the other. "Thank you."

The woodsman stepped forward past the carousers to the baggage compartment, where he disappeared. The revellers stumbled out the other door.

Thorpe followed and found himself on the frozen platform of a little dark railway station. As he walked, the boards shrieked under his feet and the sharp air nipped at his face and caught his lungs. Beyond the fence-rail protection to the side of the platform he thought he saw the suggestion of a broad reach of snow, a distant lurking forest, a few shadowy buildings looming mysterious in the night. The air was twinkling with frost and the brilliant stars of the north country.

Directly across the track from the railway station, a single building was picked from the dark by a solitary lamp in a lower-story room. The four who had descended before Thorpe made over toward this light, stumbling and laughing uncertainly, so he knew it was probably in the boarding-house, and prepared to follow them. Shearer and the station agent,—an individual much muffled,—turned to the disposition of some light freight that had been dropped from the baggage car.

The five were met at the steps by the proprietor of the boarding-house. This man was short and stout, with a harelip and cleft palate, which at once gave him the well-known slurring speech of persons so afflicted, and imparted also to the timbre of his voice a peculiarly hollow, resonant, trumpet-like note. He stumped about energetically on a wooden leg of home manufacture. It was a cumbersome instrument, heavy, with deep pine socket for the stump, and a projecting brace which passed under a leather belt around the man's waist. This instrument he used with the dexterity of a third hand. As Thorpe watched him, he drove in a projecting nail, kicked two "turkeys" dexterously inside the open door, and stuck the armed end of his peg-leg through the top and bottom of the whisky jug that one of the new arrivals had set down near the door. The whisky promptly ran out. At this the cripple flirted the impaled jug from the wooden leg far out over the rail of the verandah into the snow.

A growl went up.

"What'n hell's that for I!" snarled one of the owners of the whisky threateningly.

"Don't allow no whisky here," snuffed the harelip.

The men were very angry. They advanced toward the cripple, who retreated with astonishing agility to the lighted room. There he bent the wooden leg behind him, slipped the end of the brace from beneath the leather belt, seized the other, peg end in his right hand, and so became possessed of a murderous bludgeon. This he brandished, hopping at the same time back and forth in such perfect poise and yet with so ludicrous an effect of popping corn, that the men were surprised into laughing.

"Bully for you, peg-leg!" they cried.

"Rules 'n regerlations, boys," replied the latter, without, however, a shade of compromising in his tones. "Had supper?"

On receiving a reply in the affirmative, he caught up the lamp, and, having resumed his artificial leg in one deft motion, led the way to narrow little rooms.

### Chapter IV

Thorpe was awakened a long time before daylight by the ringing of a noisy bell. He dressed, shivering, and stumbled down stairs to a round stove, big as a boiler, into which the cripple dumped huge logs of wood from time to time. After breakfast Thorpe returned to this stove and sat half dozing for what seemed to him untold ages. The cold of the north country was initiating him.

Men came in, smoked a brief pipe, and went out. Shearer was one of them. The woodsman nodded curtly to the young man, his cordiality quite gone. Thorpe vaguely wondered why. After a time he himself put on his overcoat and ventured out into the town. It seemed to Thorpe a meager affair, built of lumber, mostly unpainted, with always the dark, menacing fringe of the forest behind. The great saw mill, with its tall stacks and its row of water-barrels—protection against fire—on top, was the dominant note. Near the mill crouched a little red-painted structure from whose stovepipe a column of white smoke rose, attesting the cold, a clear hundred feet straight upward, and to whose door a number of men were directing their steps through the snow. Over the door Thorpe could distinguish the word "Office." He followed and entered.

In a narrow aisle railed off from the main part of the room waited Thorpe's companions of the night before. The remainder of the office gave accommodation to three clerks. One of these glanced up inquiringly as Thorpe came in.

"I am looking for work," said Thorpe.

"Wait there," briefly commanded the clerk.

In a few moments the door of the inner room opened, and Shearer came out. A man's head peered from within.

"Come on, boys," said he.

The five applicants shuffled through. Thorpe found himself in the presence of a man whom he felt to be the natural leader of these wild, independent spirits. He was already a little past middle life, and his form had lost the elastic vigor of youth. But his eye was keen, clear, and wrinkled to a certain dry facetiousness; and his figure was of that bulk which gives an impression of a subtler weight and power than the merely physical. This peculiarity impresses us in the portraits of such men as Daniel Webster and others of the old jurists. The manner of the man was easy, good-natured, perhaps a little facetious, but these qualities were worn rather as garments than exhibited as characteristics. He could afford them, not because he had fewer difficulties to overcome or battles to fight than another, but because his strength was so sufficient to them that mere battles or difficulties could not affect the deliberateness of his humor. You felt his superiority even when he was most comradely with you. This man Thorpe was to meet under other conditions, wherein the steel hand would more plainly clink the metal.

He was now seated in a worn office chair before a littered desk. In the close air hung the smell of stale cigars and the clear fragrance of pine.

"What is it, Dennis?" he asked the first of the men.

"I've been out," replied the lumberman. "Have you got anything for me, Mr. Daly?"

The mill-owner laughed.

"I guess so. Report to Shearer. Did you vote for the right man, Denny?"

The lumberman grinned sheepishly. "I don't know, sir. I didn't get that far."

"Better let it alone. I suppose you and Bill want to come back, too?" he added, turning to the next two in the line. "All right, report to Tim. Do you want work?" he inquired of the last of the quartette, a big bashful man with the shoulders of a Hercules.

"Yes, sir," answered the latter uncomfortably.

"What do you do?"

"I'm a cant-hook man, sir."

"Where have you worked?"

"I had a job with Morgan & Stebbins on the Clear River last winter."

"All right, we need cant-hook men. Report at 'seven,' and if they don't want you there, go to 'thirteen.'"

Daly looked directly at the man with an air of finality. The lumberman still lingered uneasily, twisting his cap in his hands.

"Anything you want?" asked Daly at last.

"Yes, sir," blurted the big man. "If I come down here and tell you I want three days off and fifty dollars to bury my mother, I wish you'd tell me to go to hell! I buried her three times last winter!"

Daly chuckled a little.

"All right, Bub," said he, "to hell it is."

The man went out. Daly turned to Thorpe with the last flickers of amusement in his eyes.

"What can I do for you?" he inquired in a little crisper tones. Thorpe felt that he was not treated with the same careless familiarity, because, potentially, he might be more of a force to deal with. He underwent, too, the man's keen scrutiny, and knew that every detail of his appearance had found its comment in the other's experienced brain.

"I am looking for work," Thorpe replied.

"What kind of work?"

"Any kind, so I can learn something about the lumber business."

The older man studied him keenly for a few moments.

"Have you had any other business experience?"

"None."

"What have you been doing?"

"Nothing."

The lumberman's eyes hardened.

"We are a very busy firm here," he said with a certain deliberation; "we do not carry a big force of men in any one department, and each of those men has to fill his place and slop some over the sides. We do not pretend or attempt to teach here. If you want to be a lumberman, you must learn the lumber business more directly than through the windows of a bookkeeper's office. Go into the woods. Learn a few first principles. Find out the difference between Norway and white pine, anyway."

Daly, being what is termed a self-made man, entertained a prejudice against youths of the leisure class. He did not believe in their earnestness of purpose, their capacity for knowledge, nor their perseverance in anything. That a man of twenty-six should be looking for his first situation was incomprehensible to him. He made no effort to conceal his prejudice, because the class to which the young man had belonged enjoyed his hearty contempt.

The truth is, he had taken Thorpe's ignorance a little too much for granted. Before leaving his home, and while the project of emigration was still in the air, the young fellow had, with the quiet enthusiasm of men of his habit of mind, applied himself to the mastering of whatever the books could teach. That is not much. The literature on lumbering seems to be singularly limited. Still he knew the trees, and had sketched an outline into which to paint experience. He said nothing of this to the man before him, because of that strange streak in his nature which prompted him to conceal what he felt most strongly; to leave to others the task of guessing out his attitude; to stand on appearances without attempting to justify them, no matter how simple the justification might be. A moment's frank, straightforward talk might have caught Daly's attention, for the lumberman was, after all, a shrewd reader of character where his prejudices were not concerned. Then events would have turned out very differently.

After his speech the business man had whirled back to his desk.

"Have you anything for me to do in the woods, then?" the other asked quietly.

"No," said Daly over his shoulder.

Thorpe went out.

Before leaving Detroit he had, on the advice of friends, visited the city office of Morrison & Daly. There he had been told positively that the firm were hiring men. Now, without five dollars in his pocket, he made the elementary discovery that even in chopping wood skilled labor counts. He did not know where to turn next, and he would not have had the money to go far in any case. So, although Shearer's brusque greeting that morning had argued a lack of cordiality, he resolved to remind the riverman of his promised assistance.

That noon he carried out his resolve. To his surprise Shearer was cordial—in his way. He came afterward to appreciate the subtle nuances of manner and treatment by which a boss retains his moral supremacy in a lumber country,—repels that too great familiarity which breeds contempt, without imperiling the trust and comradeship which breeds willingness. In the morning Thorpe had been a prospective employee of the firm, and so a possible subordinate of Shearer himself. Now he was Shearer's equal.

"Go up and tackle Radway. He's jobbing for us on the Cass Branch. He needs men for roadin', I know, because he's behind. You'll get a job there."

"Where is it?" asked Thorpe.

"Ten miles from here. She's blazed, but you better wait for th' supply team, Friday. If you try to make her yourself, you'll get lost on some of th' old loggin' roads."

Thorpe considered.

"I'm busted," he said at last frankly.

"Oh, that's all right," replied the walking-boss. "Marshall, come here!"

The peg-legged boarding-house keeper stumped in.

"What is it?" he trumpeted snufflingly.

"This boy wants a job till Friday. Then he's going up to Radway's with the supply team. Now quit your hollerin' for a chore-boy for a few days."

"All right," snorted Marshall, "take that ax and split some dry wood that you'll find behind the house."

"I'm very much obliged to you," began Thorpe to the walking-boss, "and—"

"That's all right," interrupted the latter, "some day you can give me a job."


*Chapter V*

For five days Thorpe cut wood, made fires, drew water, swept floors, and ran errands. Sometimes he would look across the broad stump-dotted plain to the distant forest. He had imagination. No business man succeeds without it. With him the great struggle to wrest from an impassive and aloof nature what she has so long held securely as her own, took on the proportions of a battle. The distant forest was the front. To it went the new bands of fighters. From it came the caissons for food, that ammunition of the frontier; messengers bringing tidings of defeat or victory; sometimes men groaning on their litters from the twisting and crushing and breaking inflicted on them by the calm, ruthless enemy; once a dead man bearing still on his chest the mark of the tree that had killed him. Here at headquarters sat the general, map in hand, issuing his orders, directing his forces.

And out of the forest came mystery. Hunters brought deer on sledges. Indians, observant and grave, swung silently across the reaches on their snowshoes, and silently back again carrying their meager purchases. In the daytime ravens wheeled and croaked about the outskirts of the town, bearing the shadow of the woods on their plumes and of the north-wind in the somber quality of their voices; rare eagles wheeled gracefully to and fro; snow squalls coquetted with the landscape. At night the many creatures of the forest ventured out across the plains in search of food,—weasels; big white hares; deer, planting daintily their little sharp hoofs where the frozen turnips were most plentiful; porcupines in quest of anything they could get their keen teeth into;—and often the big timber wolves would send shivering across the waste a long whining howl. And in the morning their tracks would embroider the snow with many stories.

The talk about the great stove in the boarding-house office also possessed the charm of balsam fragrance. One told the other occult facts about the "Southeast of the southwest of eight." The second in turn vouchsafed information about another point of the compass. Thorpe heard of many curious practical expedients. He learned that one can prevent awkward air-holes in lakes by "tapping" the ice with an ax,—for the air must get out, naturally or artificially; that the top log on a load should not be large because of the probability, when one side has dumped with a rush, of its falling straight down from its original height, so breaking the sleigh; that a thin slice of salt pork well peppered is good when tied about a sore throat; that choking a horse will cause him to swell up and float on the top of the water, thus rendering it easy to slide him out on the ice from a hole he may have broken into; that a tree lodged against another may be brought to the ground by felling a third against it; that snowshoes made of caribou hide do not become baggy, because caribou shrinks when wet, whereas other rawhide stretches. These, and many other things too complicated to elaborate here, he heard discussed by expert opinion. Gradually he acquired an enthusiasm for the woods, just as a boy conceives a longing for the out-of-door life of which he hears in the conversation of his elders about the winter fire. He became eager to get away to the front, to stand among the pines, to grapple with the difficulties of thicket, hill, snow, and cold that nature silently interposes between the man and his task.

At the end of the week he received four dollars from his employer; dumped his valise into a low bobsleigh driven by a man muffled in a fur coat; assisted in loading the sleigh with a variety of things, from Spearhead plug to raisins; and turned his face at last toward the land of his hopes and desires.

The long drive to camp was at once a delight and a misery to him. Its miles stretched longer and longer as time went on; and the miles of a route new to a man are always one and a half at least. The forest, so mysterious and inviting from afar, drew within itself coldly when Thorpe entered it. He was as yet a stranger. The snow became the prevailing note. The white was everywhere, concealing jealously beneath rounded uniformity the secrets of the woods. And it was cold. First Thorpe's feet became numb, then his hands, then his nose was nipped, and finally his warm clothes were lifted from him by invisible hands, and he was left naked to shivers and tremblings. He found it torture to sit still on the top of the bale of hay; and yet he could not bear to contemplate the cold shock of jumping from the sleigh to the ground,—of touching foot to the chilling snow. The driver pulled up to breathe his horses at the top of a hill, and to fasten under one runner a heavy chain, which, grinding into the snow, would act as a brake on the descent.

"You're dressed pretty light," he advised; "better hoof it a ways and get warm."

The words tipped the balance of Thorpe's decision. He descended stiffly, conscious of a disagreeable shock from a six-inch jump.

In ten minutes, the wallowing, slipping, and leaping after the tail of the sled had sent his blood tingling to the last of his protesting members. Cold withdrew. He saw now that the pines were beautiful and solemn and still; and that in the temple of their columns dwelt winter enthroned. Across the carpet of the snow wandered the trails of her creatures,—the stately regular prints of the partridge; the series of pairs made by the squirrel; those of the weasel and mink, just like the squirrels' except that the prints were not quite side by side, and that between every other pair stretched the mark of the animal's long, slender body; the delicate tracery of the deer mouse; the fan of the rabbit; the print of a baby's hand that the raccoon left; the broad pad of a lynx; the dog-like trail of wolves;—these, and a dozen others, all equally unknown, gave Thorpe the impression of a great mysterious multitude of living things which moved about him invisible. In a thicket of cedar and scrub willow near the bed of a stream, he encountered one of those strangely assorted bands of woods-creatures which are always cruising it through the country. He heard the cheerful little chickadee; he saw the grave nuthatch with its appearance of a total lack of humor; he glimpsed a black-and-white woodpecker or so, and was reviled by a ribald blue jay. Already the wilderness was taking its character to him.

After a little while, they arrived by way of a hill, over which they plunged into the middle of the camp. Thorpe saw three large buildings, backed end to end, and two smaller ones, all built of heavy logs, roofed with plank, and lighted sparsely through one or two windows apiece. The driver pulled up opposite the space between two of the larger buildings, and began to unload his provisions. Thorpe set about aiding him, and so found himself for the first time in a "cook camp."

It was a commodious building,—Thorpe had no idea a log structure ever contained so much room. One end furnished space for two cooking ranges and two bunks placed one over the other. Along one side ran a broad table-shelf, with other shelves over it and numerous barrels underneath, all filled with cans, loaves of bread, cookies, and pies. The center was occupied by four long bench-flanked tables, down whose middle straggled utensils containing sugar, apple-butter, condiments, and sauces, and whose edges were set with tin dishes for about forty men. The cook, a rather thin-faced man with a mustache, directed where the provisions were to be stowed; and the "cookee," a hulking youth, assisted Thorpe and the driver to carry them in. During the course of the work Thorpe made a mistake.

"That stuff doesn't come here," objected the cookee, indicating a box of tobacco the newcomer was carrying. "She goes to the 'van.'"

Thorpe did not know what the "van" might be, but he replaced the tobacco on the sleigh. In a few moments the task was finished, with the exception of a half dozen other cases, which the driver designated as also for the "van." The horses were unhitched, and stabled in the third of the big log buildings. The driver indicated the second.

"Better go into the men's camp and sit down 'till th' boss gets in," he advised.

Thorpe entered a dim, over-heated structure, lined on two sides by a double tier of large bunks partitioned from one another like cabins of boats, and centered by a huge stove over which hung slender poles. The latter were to dry clothes on. Just outside the bunks ran a straight hard bench. Thorpe stood at the entrance trying to accustom his eyes to the dimness.

"Set down," said a voice, "on th' floor if you want to; but I'd prefer th' deacon seat."

Thorpe obediently took position on the bench, or "deacon seat." His eyes, more used to the light, could make out a thin, tall, bent old man, with bare cranium, two visible teeth, and a three days' stubble of white beard over his meager, twisted face.

He caught, perhaps, Thorpe's surprised expression.

"You think th' old man's no good, do you?" he cackled, without the slightest malice, "looks is deceivin'!" He sprang up swiftly, seized the toe of his right foot in his left hand, and jumped his left foot through the loop thus formed. Then he sat down again, and laughed at Thorpe's astonishment.

"Old Jackson's still purty smart," said he. "I'm barn-boss. They ain't a man in th' country knows as much about hosses as I do. We ain't had but two sick this fall, an' between you an' me, they's a skate lot. You're a greenhorn, ain't you?"

"Yes," confessed Thorpe.

"Well," said Jackson, reflectively but rapidly, "Le Fabian, he's quiet but bad; and O'Grady, he talks loud but you can bluff him; and Perry, he's only bad when he gets full of red likker; and Norton he's bad when he gets mad like, and will use axes."

Thorpe did not know he was getting valuable points on the camp bullies. The old man hitched nearer and peered in his face.

"They don't bluff you a bit," he said, "unless you likes them, and then they can back you way off the skidway."

Thorpe smiled at the old fellow's volubility. He did not know how near to the truth the woodsman's shrewdness had hit; for to himself, as to most strong characters, his peculiarities were the normal, and therefore the unnoticed. His habit of thought in respect to other people was rather objective than subjective. He inquired so impersonally the significance of whatever was before him, that it lost the human quality both as to itself and himself. To him men were things. This attitude relieved him of self-consciousness. He never bothered his head as to what the other man thought of him, his ignorance, or his awkwardness, simply because to him the other man was nothing but an element in his problem. So in such circumstances he learned fast. Once introduce the human element, however, and his absurdly sensitive self-consciousness asserted itself. He was, as Jackson expressed it, backed off the skidway.

At dark the old man lit two lamps, which served dimly to gloze the shadows, and thrust logs of wood into the cast-iron stove. Soon after, the men came in. They were a queer, mixed lot. Some carried the indisputable stamp of the frontiersman in their bearing and glance; others looked to be mere day-laborers, capable of performing whatever task they were set to, and of finding the trail home again. There were active, clean-built, precise Frenchmen, with small hands and feet, and a peculiarly trim way of wearing their rough garments; typical native-born American lumber-jacks powerful in frame, rakish in air, reckless in manner; big blonde Scandinavians and Swedes, strong men at the sawing; an Indian or so, strangely in contrast to the rest; and a variety of Irishmen, Englishmen, and Canadians. These men tramped in without a word, and set busily to work at various tasks. Some sat on the "deacon seat" and began to take off their socks and rubbers; others washed at a little wooden sink; still others selected and lit lanterns from a pendant row near the window, and followed old Jackson out of doors. They were the teamsters.

"You'll find the old man in the office," said Jackson.

Thorpe made his way across to the small log cabin indicated as the office, and pushed open the door. He found himself in a little room containing two bunks, a stove, a counter and desk, and a number of shelves full of supplies. About the walls hung firearms, snowshoes, and a variety of clothes.

A man sat at the desk placing figures on a sheet of paper. He obtained the figures from statistics pencilled on three thin leaves of beech-wood riveted together. In a chair by the stove lounged a bulkier figure, which Thorpe concluded to be that of the "old man."

"I was sent here by Shearer," said Thorpe directly; "he said you might give me some work."

So long a silence fell that the applicant began to wonder if his question had been heard.

"I might," replied the man drily at last.

"Well, will you?" Thorpe inquired, the humor of the situation overcoming him.

"Have you ever worked in the woods?"

"No."

The man smoked silently.

"I'll put you on the road in the morning," he concluded, as though this were the deciding qualification.

One of the men entered abruptly and approached the counter. The writer at the desk laid aside his tablets.

"What is it, Albert?" he added.

"Jot of chewin'," was the reply.

The scaler took from the shelf a long plug of tobacco and cut off two inches.

"Ain't hitting the van much, are you, Albert?" he commented, putting the man's name and the amount in a little book. Thorpe went out, after leaving his name for the time book, enlightened as to the method of obtaining supplies. He promised himself some warm clothing from the van, when he should have worked out the necessary credit.

At supper he learned something else,—that he must not talk at table. A moment's reflection taught him the common-sense of the rule. For one thing, supper was a much briefer affair than it would have been had every man felt privileged to take his will in conversation; not to speak of the absence of noise and the presence of peace. Each man asked for what he wanted.

"Please pass the beans," he said with the deliberate intonation of a man who does not expect that his request will be granted.

Besides the beans were fried salt pork, boiled potatoes, canned corn, mince pie, a variety of cookies and doughnuts, and strong green tea. Thorpe found himself eating ravenously of the crude fare.

That evening he underwent a catechism, a few practical jokes, which he took good-naturedly, and a vast deal of chaffing. At nine the lights were all out. By daylight he and a dozen other men were at work, hewing a road that had to be as smooth and level as a New York boulevard.

### Chapter VI

Thorpe and four others were set to work on this road, which was to be cut through a creek bottom leading, he was told, to "seventeen." The figures meant nothing to him. Later, each number came to possess an individuality of its own. He learned to use a double-bitted ax.

Thorpe's intelligence was of the practical sort that wonderfully helps experience. He watched closely one of the older men, and analyzed the relation borne by each one of his movements to the object in view. In a short time he perceived that one hand and arm are mere continuations of the helve, attaching the blade of the ax to the shoulder of the wielder; and that the other hand directs the stroke. He acquired the knack thus of throwing the bit of steel into the gash as though it were a baseball on the end of a string; and so accomplished power. By experiment he learned just when to slide the guiding hand down the helve; and so gained accuracy. He suffered none of those accidents so common to new choppers. His ax did not twist itself from his hands, nor glance to cut his foot. He attained the method of the double bit, and how to knock roots by alternate employment of the edge and flat. In a few days his hands became hard and used to the cold.

From shortly after daylight he worked. Four other men bore him company, and twice Radway himself came by, watched their operations for a moment, and moved on without comment. After Thorpe had caught his second wind, he enjoyed his task, proving a certain pleasure in the ease with which he handled his tool.

At the end of an interminable period, a faint, musical halloo swelled, echoed, and died through the forest, beautiful as a spirit. It was taken up by another voice and repeated. Then by another. Now near at hand, now far away it rang as hollow as a bell. The sawyers, the swampers, the skidders, and the team men turned and put on their heavy blanket coats.

Down on the road Thorpe heard it too, and wondered what it might be.

"Come on, Bub! she means chew!" explained old man Heath kindly. Old man Heath was a veteran woodsman who had come to swamping in his old age. He knew the game thoroughly, but could never save his "stake" when Pat McGinnis, the saloon man, enticed him in. Throughout the morning he had kept an eye on the newcomer, and was secretly pleased in his heart of the professional at the readiness with which the young fellow learned.

Thorpe resumed his coat, and fell in behind the little procession. After a short time he came upon a horse and sledge. Beyond it the cookee had built a little camp fire, around and over which he had grouped big fifty-pound lard-tins, half full of hot things to eat. Each man, as he approached, picked up a tin plate and cup from a pile near at hand.

338

The cookee was plainly master of the situation. He issued peremptory orders. When Erickson, the blonde Swede, attempted surreptitiously to appropriate a doughnut, the youth turned on him savagely.

"Get out of that, you big tow-head!" he cried with an oath.

A dozen Canada jays, fluffy, impatient, perched near by or made little short circles over and back. They awaited the remains of the dinner. Bob Stratton and a devil-may-care giant by the name of Nolan constructed a joke wherewith to amuse the interim. They cut a long pole, and placed it across a log and through a bush, so that one extremity projected beyond the bush. Then diplomacy won a piece of meat from the cookee. This they nailed to the end of the pole by means of a pine sliver. The Canada jays gazed on the morsel with covetous eyes. When the men had retired, they swooped. One big fellow arrived first, and lit in defiance of the rest.

"Give it to 'im!" whispered Nolan, who had been watching.

Bob hit the other end of the pole a mighty whack with his ax. The astonished jay, projected straight upward by the shock, gave a startled squawk and cut a hole through the air for the tall timber. Stratton and Nolan went into convulsions of laughter.

"Get at it!" cried the cookee, as though setting a pack of dogs on their prey.

The men ate, perched in various attitudes and places. Thorpe found it difficult to keep warm. The violent exercise had heated him through, and now the north country cold penetrated to his bones. He huddled close to the fire, and drank hot tea, but it did not do him very much good. In his secret mind he resolved to buy one of the blanket mackinaws that very evening. He began to see that the costumes of each country have their origin in practicality.

That evening he picked out one of the best. As he was about to inquire the price, Radway drew the van book toward him, inquiring,

"Let's see; what's the name?"

In an instant Thorpe was charged on the book with three dollars and a half, although his work that day had earned him less than a dollar. On his way back to the men's shanty he could not help thinking how easy it would be for him to leave the next morning two dollars and a half ahead. He wondered if this method of procedure obtained in all the camps.

The newcomer's first day of hard work had tired him completely. He was ready for nothing so much as his bunk. But he had forgotten that it was Saturday night. His status was still to assure.

They began with a few mild tricks. Shuffle the Brogan followed Hot Back. Thorpe took all of it good-naturedly. Finally a tall individual with a thin white face, a reptilian forehead, reddish hair, and long baboon arms, suggested tossing in a blanket. Thorpe looked at the low ceiling, and declined.

"I'm with the game as long as you say, boys," said he, "and I'll have as much fun as anybody, but that's going too far for a tired man."

The reptilian gentleman let out a string of oaths whose meaning might be translated, "We'll see about that!"

Thorpe was a good boxer, but he knew by now the lumber-jack's method of fighting,—anything to hurt the other fellow. And in a genuine old-fashioned knock-down-and-drag-out rough-and-tumble your woodsman is about the toughest customer to handle you will be likely to meet. He is brought up on fighting. Nothing pleases him better than to get drunk and, with a few companions, to embark on an earnest effort to "clean out" a rival town. And he will accept cheerfully punishment enough to kill three ordinary men. It takes one of his kind really to hurt him.

Thorpe, at the first hostile movement, sprang back to the door, seized one of the three-foot billets of hardwood intended for the stove, and faced his opponents.

"I don't know which of you boys is coming first," said he quietly, "but he's going to get it good and plenty."

If the affair had been serious, these men would never have recoiled before the mere danger of a stick of hardwood. The American woodsman is afraid of nothing human. But this was a good-natured bit of foolery, a test of nerve, and there was no object in getting a broken head for that. The reptilian gentleman alone grumbled at the abandonment of the attack, mumbling something profane.

"If you hanker for trouble so much," drawled the unexpected voice of old Jackson from the corner, "mebbe you could put on th' gloves."

The idea was acclaimed. Somebody tossed out a dirty torn old set of buckskin boxing gloves.

The rest was farce. Thorpe was built on the true athletic lines, broad, straight shoulders, narrow flanks, long, clean, smooth muscles. He possessed, besides, that hereditary toughness and bulk which no gymnasium training will ever quite supply. The other man, while powerful and ugly in his rushes, was clumsy and did not use his head. Thorpe planted his hard straight blows at will. In this game he was as manifestly superior as his opponent would probably have been had the rules permitted kicking, gouging, and wrestling. Finally he saw his opening and let out with a swinging pivot blow. The other picked himself out of a corner, and drew off the gloves. Thorpe's status was assured.

A Frenchman took down his fiddle and began to squeak. In the course of the dance old Jackson and old Heath found themselves together, smoking their pipes of Peerless.

"The young feller's all right," observed Heath; "he cuffed Ben up to a peak all right."

"Went down like a peck of wet fish-nets," replied Jackson tranquilly.

339

In the office shanty one evening about a week later, Radway and his scaler happened to be talking over the situation. The scaler, whose name was Dyer, slouched back in the shadow, watching his great honest superior as a crafty, dainty cat might watch the blunderings of a St. Bernard. When he spoke, it was with a mockery so subtle as quite to escape the perceptions of the lumberman. Dyer had a precise little black mustache whose ends he was constantly twisting into points, black eyebrows, and long effeminate black lashes. You would have expected his dress in the city to be just a trifle flashy, not enough so to be loud, but sinning as to the trifles of good taste. The two men conversed in short elliptical sentences, using many technical terms.

"That 'seventeen' white pine is going to underrun," said Dyer. "It won't skid over three hundred thousand."

"It's small stuff," agreed Radway, "and so much the worse for us; but the Company'll stand in on it because small stuff like that always over-runs on the mill-cut."

The scaler nodded comprehension.

"When you going to dray-haul that Norway across Pike Lake?"

"To-morrow. She's springy, but the books say five inches of ice will hold a team, and there's more than that. How much are we putting in a day, now?"

"About forty thousand."

Radway fell silent.

"That's mighty little for such a crew," he observed at last, doubtfully.

"I always said you were too easy with them. You got to drive them more."

"Well, it's a rough country," apologized Radway, trying, as was his custom, to find excuses for the other party as soon as he was agreed with in his blame, "there's any amount of potholes; and, then, we've had so much snow the ground ain't really froze underneath. It gets pretty soft in some of them swamps. Can't figure on putting up as much in this country as we used to down on the Muskegon."

The scaler smiled a thin smile all to himself behind the stove. Big John Radway depended so much on the moral effect of approval or disapproval by those with whom he lived. It amused Dyer to withhold the timely word, so leaving the jobber to flounder between his easy nature and his sense of what should be done.

Dyer knew perfectly well that the work was behind, and he knew the reason. For some time the men had been relaxing their efforts. They had worked honestly enough, but a certain snap and vim had lacked. This was because Radway had been too easy on them.

Your true lumber-jack adores of all things in creation a man whom he feels to be stronger than himself. If his employer is big enough to drive him, then he is willing to be driven to the last ounce of his strength. But once he gets the notion that his "boss" is afraid of, or for, him or his feelings or his health, he loses interest in working for that man. So a little effort to lighten or expedite his work, a little leniency in excusing the dilatory finishing of a job, a little easing-up under stress of weather, are taken as so many indications of a desire to conciliate. And conciliation means weakness every time. Your lumber-jack likes to be met front to front, one strong man to another. As you value your authority, the love of your men, and the completion of your work, keep a bluff brow and an unbending singleness of purpose.

Radway's peculiar temperament rendered him liable to just this mistake. It was so much easier for him to do the thing himself than to be harsh to the point of forcing another to it, that he was inclined to take the line of least resistance when it came to a question of even ordinary diligence. He sought often in his own mind excuses for dereliction in favor of a man who would not have dreamed of seeking them for himself. A good many people would call this kindness of heart. Perhaps it was; the question is a little puzzling. But the facts were as stated.

Thorpe had already commented on the feeling among the men, though, owing to his inexperience, he was not able to estimate its full value. The men were inclined to a semi-apologetic air when they spoke of their connection with the camp. Instead of being honored as one of a series of jobs, this seemed to be considered as merely a temporary halting-place in which they took no pride, and from which they looked forward in anticipation or back in memory to better things.

"Old Shearer, he's the bully boy," said Bob Stratton. "I remember when he was foremap for M. & D. at Camp 0. Say, we did hustle them saw-logs in! I should rise to remark! Out in th' woods by first streak o' day. I recall one mornin' she was pretty cold, an' the boys grumbled some about turnin' out. 'Cold,' says Tim, 'you sons of guns! You got your ch'ice. It may be too cold for you in the woods, but it's a damm sight too hot fer you in hell, an' you're going to one or the other!' And he meant it too. Them was great days! Forty million a year, and not a hitch."

One man said nothing in the general discussion. It was his first winter in the woods, and plainly in the eyes of the veterans this experience did not count. It was a "faute de mieux," in which one would give an honest day's work, and no more.

As has been hinted, even the inexperienced newcomer noticed the lack of enthusiasm, of unity. Had he known the loyalty, devotion, and adoration that a thoroughly competent man wins from his "hands," the state of affairs would have seemed even more surprising. The lumber-jack will work sixteen, eighteen hours a day, sometimes up to the waist in water full of floating ice; sleep wet on the ground by a little fire; and then next morning will spring to work at daylight with an "Oh, no, not tired; just a little stiff, sir!" in cheerful reply to his master's inquiry,—for the right man! Only it must be a strong man,—with the strength of the wilderness in his eye.

The next morning Radway transferred Molly and Jenny, with little Fabian Laveque and two of the younger men, to Pike Lake. There, earlier in the season, a number of pines had been felled out on the ice, cut in logs, and left in expectation of ice thick enough to bear the travoy "dray." Owing to the fact that the shores of Pike Lake were extremely precipitous, it had been impossible to travoy the logs up over the hill.

Radway had sounded carefully the thickness of the ice with an ax. Although the weather had of late been sufficiently cold for the time of year, the snow, as often happens, had fallen before the temperature. Under the warm white blanket, the actual freezing had been slight. However, there seemed to be at least eight inches of clear ice, which would suffice.

Some of the logs in question were found to be half imbedded in the ice. It became necessary first of all to free them. Young Henrys cut a strong bar six or eight feet long, while Pat McGuire chopped a hole alongside the log. Then one end of the bar was thrust into the hole, the logging chain fastened to the other; and, behold, a monster lever, whose fulcrum was the ice and whose power was applied by Molly, hitched to the end of the chain. In this simple manner a task was accomplished in five minutes which would have taken a dozen men an hour. When the log had been cat-a-cornered from its bed, the chain was fastened around one end by means of the ever-useful steel swamp-hook, and it was yanked across the dray. Then the travoy took its careful way across the ice to where a dip in the shore gave access to a skidway.

Four logs had thus been safely hauled. The fifth was on its journey across the lake. Suddenly without warning, and with scarcely a sound, both horses sank through the ice, which bubbled up around them and over their backs in irregular rotted pieces. Little Fabian Laveque shouted, and jumped down from his log. Pat McGuire and young Henrys came running.

The horses had broken through an air-hole, about which the ice was strong. Fabian had already seized Molly by the bit, and was holding her head easily above water.

"Kitch Jenny by dat he't!" he cried to Pat.

Thus the two men, without exertion, sustained the noses of the team above the surface. The position demanded absolutely no haste, for it could have been maintained for a good half hour. Molly and Jenny, their soft eyes full of the intelligence of the situation, rested easily in full confidence. But Pat and Henrys, new to this sort of emergency, were badly frightened and excited. To them the affair had come to a deadlock.

"Oh, Lord!" cried Pat, clinging desperately to Jenny's headpiece. "What will we'z be doin'? We can't niver haul them two horses on the ice."

"Tak' de log-chain," said Fabian to Henrys, "an' tie him around de nec' of Jenny."

Henrys, after much difficulty and nervous fumbling, managed to loosen the swamp-hook; and after much more difficulty and nervous fumbling succeeded in making it fast about the gray mare's neck. Fabian intended with this to choke the animal to that peculiar state when she would float like a balloon on the water, and two men could with ease draw her over the edge of the ice. Then the unexpected happened.

The instant Henrys had passed the end of the chain through the knot, Pat, possessed by some Hibernian notion that now all was fast, let go of the bit. Jenny's head at once went under, and the end of the logging chain glided over the ice and fell plump in the hole.

Immediately all was confusion. Jenny kicked and struggled, churning the water, throwing it about, kicking out in every direction. Once a horse's head dips strongly, the game is over. No animal drowns more quickly. The two young boys scrambled away, and French oaths could not induce them to approach. Molly, still upheld by Fabian, looked at him piteously with her strange intelligent eyes, holding herself motionless and rigid with complete confidence in this master who had never failed her before. Fabian dug his heels into the ice, but could not hang on. The drowning horse was more than a dead weight. Presently it became a question of letting go or being dragged into the lake on top of the animals. With a sob the little Frenchman relinquished his hold. The water seemed slowly to rise and over-film the troubled look of pleading in Molly's eyes.

"Assassins!" hissed Laveque at the two unfortunate youths. That was all.

When the surface of the waters had again mirrored the clouds, they hauled the carcasses out on the ice and stripped the harness. Then they rolled the log from the dray, piled the tools on it, and took their way to camp. In the blue of the winter's sky was a single speck.

The speck grew. Soon it swooped. With a hoarse croak it lit on the snow at a wary distance, and began to strut back and forth. Presently, its suspicions at rest, the raven advanced, and with eager beak began its dreadful meal. By this time another, which had seen the first one's swoop, was in view through the ether; then another; then another. In an hour the brotherhood of ravens, thus telegraphically notified, was at feast.

### Chapter VIII

Fabian Laveque elaborated the details of the catastrophe with volubility.

"Hee's not fonny dat she bre'ks t'rough," he said. "I 'ave see dem bre'k t'rough two, t'ree tam in de day, but nevaire dat she get drown! W'en dose dam-fool can't t'ink wit' hees haid—sacre Dieu! eet is so easy, to chok' dat cheval—she make me cry wit' de eye!"

"I suppose it was a good deal my fault," commented Radway, doubtfully shaking his head, after Laveque had left the office. "I ought to have been surer about the ice."

"Eight inches is a little light, with so much snow atop," remarked the scaler carelessly.

By virtue of that same careless remark, however, Radway was so confirmed in his belief as to his own culpability that he quite overlooked Fabian's just contention—that the mere thinness of the ice was in reality no excuse for the losing of the horses. So Pat and Henrys were not discharged—were not instructed to "get their time." Fabian Laveque promptly demanded his.

"Sacre bleu!" said he to old Jackson. "I no work wid dat dam-fool dat no t'ink wit' hees haid."

This deprived the camp at once of a teamster and a team. When you reflect that one pair of horses takes care of the exertions of a crew of sawyers, several swampers, and three or four cant-hook men, you will readily see what a serious derangement their loss would cause. And besides, the animals themselves are difficult to replace. They are big strong beasts, selected for their power, staying qualities, and intelligence, worth anywhere from three to six hundred dollars a pair. They must be shipped in from a distance. And, finally, they require a very careful and patient training before they are of value in co-operating with the nicely adjusted efforts necessary to place the sawlog where it belongs. Ready-trained horses are never for sale during the season.

Radway did his best. He took three days to search out a big team of farm horses. Then it became necessary to find a driver. After some deliberation he decided to advance Bob Stratton to the post, that "decker" having had more or less experience the year before. Erickson, the Swede, while not a star cant-hook man, was nevertheless sure and reliable. Radway placed him in Stratton's place. But now he must find a swamper. He remembered Thorpe.

So the young man received his first promotion toward the ranks of skilled labor. He gained at last a field of application for the accuracy he had so intelligently acquired while road-making, for now a false stroke marred a saw-log; and besides, what was more to his taste, he found himself near the actual scene of operation, at the front, as it were. He had under his very eyes the process as far as it had been carried.

In his experience here he made use of the same searching analytical observation that had so quickly taught him the secret of the ax-swing. He knew that each of the things he saw, no matter how trivial, was either premeditated or the product of chance. If premeditated, he tried to find out its reason for being. If fortuitous, he wished to know the fact, and always attempted to figure out the possibility of its elimination.

So he learned why and when the sawyers threw a tree up or down hill; how much small standing timber they tried to fell it through; what consideration held for the cutting of different lengths of log; how the timber was skilfully decked on the skids in such a manner that the pile should not bulge and fall, and so that the scaler could easily determine the opposite ends of the same log;—in short, a thousand and one little details which ordinarily a man learns only as the exigencies arise to call in experience. Here, too, he first realized he was in the firing line.

Thorpe had assigned him as bunk mate the young fellow who assisted Tom Broadhead in the felling. Henry Paul was a fresh-complexioned, clear-eyed, quick-mannered young fellow with an air of steady responsibility about him. He came from the southern part of the State, where, during the summer, he worked on a little homestead farm of his own. After a few days he told Thorpe that he was married, and after a few days more he showed his bunk mate the photograph of a sweet-faced young woman who looked trustingly out of the picture.

"She's waitin' down there for me, and it ain't so very long till spring," said Paul wistfully. "She's the best little woman a man ever had, and there ain't nothin' too good for her, chummy!"

Thorpe, soul-sick after his recent experiences with the charity of the world, discovered a real pleasure in this fresh, clear passion. As he contemplated the abounding health, the upright carriage, the sparkling, bubbling spirits of the young woodsman, he could easily imagine the young girl and the young happiness, too big for a little backwoods farm.

Three days after the newcomer had started in at the swamping, Paul, during their early morning walk from camp to the scene of their operations, confided in him further.

"Got another letter, chummy," said he, "come in yesterday. She tells me," he hesitated with a blush, and then a happy laugh, "that they ain't going to be only two of us at the farm next year."

"You mean!" queried Thorpe.

"Yes," laughed Paul, "and if it's a girl she gets named after her mother, you bet."

The men separated. In a moment Thorpe found himself waist-deep in the pitchy aromatic top of an old bull-sap, clipping away at the projecting branches. After a time he heard Paul's gay halloo.

"TimBER!" came the cry, and then the swish-sh-sh,—CRASH of the tree's fall.

Thorpe knew that now either Hank or Tom must be climbing with the long measuring pole along the prostrate trunk, marking by means of shallow ax-clips where the saw was to divide the logs. Then Tom shouted something unintelligible. The other men seemed to understand, however, for they dropped their work and ran hastily in the direction of the voice. Thorpe, after a moment's indecision, did the same. He arrived to find a group about a prostrate man. The man was Paul.

Two of the older woodsmen, kneeling, were conducting coolly a hasty examination. At the front every man is more or less of a surgeon.

"Is he hurt badly?" asked Thorpe; "what is it?"

"He's dead," answered one of the other men soberly.

With the skill of ghastly practice some of them wove a litter on which the body was placed. The pathetic little procession moved in the solemn, inscrutable forest.

When the tree had fallen it had crashed through the top of another, leaving suspended in the branches of the latter a long heavy limb. A slight breeze dislodged it. Henry Paul was impaled as by a javelin.

This is the chief of the many perils of the woods. Like crouching pumas the instruments of a man's destruction poise on the spring, sometimes for days. Then swiftly, silently, the leap is made. It is a danger unavoidable, terrible, ever-present. Thorpe was destined in time to see men crushed and mangled in a hundred ingenious ways by the saw log, knocked into space and a violent death by the butts of trees, ground to powder in the mill of a jam, but never would he be more deeply impressed than by this ruthless silent taking of a life. The forces of nature are so tame, so simple, so obedient; and in the next instant so absolutely beyond human control or direction, so whirlingly contemptuous of puny human effort, that in time the wilderness shrouds itself to our eyes in the same impenetrable mystery as the sea.

That evening the camp was unusually quiet. Tellier let his fiddle hang. After supper Thorpe was approached by Purdy, the reptilian red-head with whom he had had the row some evenings before.

"You in, chummy?" he asked in a quiet voice. "It's a five apiece for Hank's woman."

"Yes," said Thorpe.

The men were earning from twenty to thirty dollars a month. They had, most of them, never seen Hank Paul before this autumn. He had not, mainly because of his modest disposition, enjoyed any extraordinary degree of popularity. Yet these strangers cheerfully, as a matter of course, gave up the proceeds of a week's hard work, and that without expecting the slightest personal credit. The money was sent "from the boys." Thorpe later read a heart-broken letter of thanks to the unknown benefactors. It touched him deeply, and he suspected the other men of the same emotions, but by that time they had regained the independent, self-contained poise of the frontiersman. They read it with unmoved faces, and tossed it aside with a more than ordinarily rough joke or oath. Thorpe understood their reticence. It was a part of his own nature. He felt more than ever akin to these men.

As swamper he had more or less to do with a cant-hook in helping the teamsters roll the end of the log on the little "dray." He soon caught the knack. Towards Christmas he had become a fairly efficient cant-hook man, and was helping roll the great sticks of timber up the slanting skids. Thus always intelligence counts, especially that rare intelligence which resolves into the analytical and the minutely observing.

On Sundays Thorpe fell into the habit of accompanying old Jackson Hines on his hunting expeditions. The ancient had been raised in the woods. He seemed to know by instinct the haunts and habits of all the wild animals, just as he seemed to know by instinct when one of his horses was likely to be troubled by the colic. His woodcraft was really remarkable.

So the two would stand for hours in the early morning and late evening waiting for deer on the edges of the swamps. They haunted the runways during the middle of the day. On soft moccasined feet they stole about in the evening with a bull's-eye lantern fastened on the head of one of them for a "jack." Several times they surprised the wolves, and shone the animals' eyes like the scattered embers of a camp fire.

Thorpe learned to shoot at a deer's shoulders rather than his heart, how to tell when the animal had sustained a mortal hurt from the way it leaped and the white of its tail. He even made progress in the difficult art of still hunting, where the man matches his senses against those of the creatures of the forest,—and sometimes wins. He soon knew better than to cut the animal's throat, and learned from Hines that a single stab at a certain point of the chest was much better for the purposes of bleeding. And, what is more, he learned not to over-shoot down hill.

Besides these things Jackson taught him many other, minor, details of woodcraft. Soon the young man could interpret the thousands of signs, so insignificant in appearance and so important in reality, which tell the history of the woods. He acquired the knack of winter fishing.

These Sundays were perhaps the most nearly perfect of any of the days of that winter. In them the young man drew more directly face to face with the wilderness. He called a truce with the enemy; and in return that great inscrutable power poured into his heart a portion of her grandeur. His ambition grew; and, as always with him, his determination became the greater and the more secret. In proportion as his ideas increased, he took greater pains to shut them in from expression. For failure in great things would bring keener disappointment than failure in little.

He was getting just the experience and the knowledge he needed; but that was about all. His wages were twenty-five dollars a month, which his van bill would reduce to the double eagle. At the end of the winter he would have but a little over a hundred dollars to show for his season's work, and this could mean at most only fifty dollars for Helen. But the future was his. He saw now more plainly what he had dimly perceived before, that for the man who buys timber, and logs it well, a sure future is waiting. And in this camp he was beginning to learn from failure the conditions of success.

### Chapter IX

They finished cutting on section seventeen during Thorpe's second week. It became necessary to begin on section fourteen, which lay two miles to the east. In that direction the character of the country changed somewhat.

The pine there grew thick on isolated "islands" of not more than an acre or so in extent,—little knolls rising from the level of a marsh. In ordinary conditions nothing would have been easier than to have ploughed roads across the frozen surface of this marsh. The peculiar state of the weather interposed tremendous difficulties.

The early part of autumn had been characterized by a heavy snow-fall immediately after a series of mild days. A warm blanket of some thickness thus overlaid the earth, effectually preventing the freezing which subsequent cold weather would have caused. All the season Radway had contended with this condition. Even in the woods, muddy swamp and spring-holes caused endless difficulty and necessitated a great deal of "corduroying," or the laying of poles side by side to form an artificial bottom. Here in the open some six inches of water and unlimited mud awaited the first horse that should break through the layer of snow and thin ice. Between each pair of islands a road had to be "tramped."

Thorpe and the rest were put at this disagreeable job. All day long they had to walk mechanically back and forth on diagonals between the marks set by Radway with his snowshoes. Early in the morning their feet were wet by icy water, for even the light weight of a man sometimes broke the frozen skin of the marsh. By night a road of trampled snow, of greater or less length, was marked out across the expanse. Thus the blanket was thrown back from the warm earth, and thus the cold was given a chance at the water beneath. In a day or so the road would bear a horse. A bridge of ice had been artificially constructed, on either side of which lay unsounded depths. This road was indicated by a row of firs stuck in the snow on either side.

It was very cold. All day long the restless wind swept across the shivering surface of the plains, and tore around the corners of the islands. The big woods are as good as an overcoat. The overcoat had been taken away.

When the lunch-sleigh arrived, the men huddled shivering in the lee of one of the knolls, and tried to eat with benumbed fingers before a fire that was but a mockery. Often it was nearly dark before their work had warmed them again. All of the skidways had to be placed on the edges of the islands themselves, and the logs had to be travoyed over the steep little knolls. A single misstep out on to the plain meant a mired horse. Three times heavy snows obliterated the roads, so that they had to be ploughed out before the men could go to work again. It was a struggle.

Radway was evidently worried. He often paused before a gang to inquire how they were "making it." He seemed afraid they might wish to quit, which was indeed the case, but he should never have taken before them any attitude but that of absolute confidence in their intentions. His anxiety was natural, however. He realized the absolute necessity of skidding and hauling this job before the heavy choking snows of the latter part of January should make it impossible to keep the roads open. So insistent was this necessity that he had seized the first respite in the phenomenal snow-fall of the early autumn to begin work. The cutting in the woods could wait.

Left to themselves probably the men would never have dreamed of objecting to whatever privations the task carried with it. Radway's anxiety for their comfort, however, caused them finally to imagine that perhaps they might have some just grounds for complaint after all. That is a great trait of the lumber-jack.

But Dyer, the scaler, finally caused the outbreak. Dyer was an efficient enough man in his way, but he loved his own ease. His habit was to stay in his bunk of mornings until well after daylight. To this there could be no objection—except on the part of the cook, who was supposed to attend to his business himself—for the scaler was active in his work, when once he began it, and could keep up with the skidding. But now he displayed a strong antipathy to the north wind on the plains. Of course he could not very well shirk the work entirely, but he did a good deal of talking on the very cold mornings.

"I don't pose for no tough son-of-a-gun," said he to Radway, "and I've got some respect for my ears and feet. She'll warm up a little by to-morrow, and perhaps the wind'll die. I can catch up on you fellows by hustling a little, so I guess I'll stay in and work on the books to-day."

"All right," Radway assented, a little doubtfully.

This happened perhaps two days out of the week. Finally Dyer hung out a thermometer, which he used to consult. The men saw it, and consulted it too. At once they felt much colder.

"She was stan' ten below," sputtered Baptiste Tellier, the Frenchman who played the fiddle. "He freeze t'rou to hees eenside. Dat is too cole for mak de work."

"Them plains is sure a holy fright," assented Purdy.

"Th' old man knows it himself," agreed big Nolan; "did you see him rammin' around yesterday askin' us if we found her too cold? He knows damn well he ought not to keep a man out that sort o' weather."

"You'd shiver like a dog in a briar path on a warm day in July," said Jackson Hines contemptuously.

"Shut up!" said they. "You're barn-boss. You don't have to be out in th' cold."

This was true. So Jackson's intervention went for a little worse than nothing.

"It ain't lak' he has nuttin' besides," went on Baptiste. "He can mak' de cut in de meedle of de fores'."

"That's right," agreed Bob Stratton, "they's the west half of eight ain't been cut yet."

So they sent a delegation to Radway. Big Nolan was the spokesman.

"Boss," said he bluntly, "she's too cold to work on them plains to-day. She's the coldest day we had."

Radway was too old a hand at the business to make any promises on the spot.

"I'll see, boys," said he.

When the breakfast was over the crew were set to making skidways and travoy roads on eight. This was a precedent. In time the work on the plains was grumblingly done in any weather. However, as to this Radway proved firm enough. He was a good fighter when he knew he was being imposed on. A man could never cheat or defy him openly without collecting a little war that left him surprised at the jobber's belligerency. The doubtful cases, those on the subtle line of indecision, found him weak. He could be so easily persuaded that he was in the wrong. At times it even seemed that he was anxious to be proved at fault, so eager was he to catch fairly the justice of the other man's attitude. He held his men inexorably and firmly to their work on the indisputably comfortable days; but gave in often when an able-bodied woodsman should have seen in the weather no inconvenience, even. As the days slipped by, however, he tightened the reins. Christmas was approaching. An easy mathematical computation reduced the question of completing his contract with Morrison & Daly to a certain weekly quota. In fact he was surprised at the size of it. He would have to work diligently and steadily during the rest of the winter.

Having thus a definite task to accomplish in a definite number of days, Radway grew to be more of a taskmaster. His anxiety as to the completion of the work overlaid his morbidly sympathetic human interest. Thus he regained to a small degree the respect of his men. Then he lost it again.

One morning he came in from a talk with the supply-teamster, and woke Dyer, who was not yet up.

"I'm going down home for two or three weeks," he announced to Dyer, "you know my address. You'll have to take charge, and I guess you'd better let the scaling go. We can get the tally at the banking grounds when we begin to haul. Now we ain't got all the time there is, so you want to keep the boys at it pretty well."

Dyer twisted the little points of his mustache. "All right, sir," said he with his smile so inscrutably insolent that Radway never saw the insolence at all. He thought this a poor year for a man in Radway's position to spend Christmas with his family, but it was none of his business.

"Do as much as you can in the marsh, Dyer," went on the jobber. "I don't believe it's really necessary to lay off any more there on account of the weather. We've simply got to get that job in before the big snows."

"All right, sir," repeated Dyer.

The scaler did what he considered his duty. All day long he tramped back and forth from one gang of men to the other, keeping a sharp eye on the details of the work. His practical experience was sufficient to solve readily such problems of broken tackle, extra expedients, or facility which the days brought forth. The fact that in him was vested the power to discharge kept the men at work.

Dyer was in the habit of starting for the marsh an hour or so after sunrise. The crew, of course, were at work by daylight. Dyer heard them often through his doze, just as he heard the chore-boy come in to build the fire and fill the water pail afresh. After a time the fire, built of kerosene and pitchy jack pine, would get so hot that in self-defense he would arise and dress. Then he would breakfast leisurely.

Thus he incurred the enmity of the cook and cookee. Those individuals have to prepare food three times a day for a half hundred heavy eaters; besides which, on sleigh-haul, they are supposed to serve a breakfast at three o'clock for the loaders and a variety of lunches up to midnight for the sprinkler men. As a consequence, they resent infractions of the little system they may have been able to introduce.

Now the business of a foreman is to be up as soon as anybody. He does none of the work himself, but he must see that somebody else does it, and does it well. For this he needs actual experience at the work itself, but above all zeal and constant presence. He must know how a thing ought to be done, and he must be on hand unexpectedly to see how its accomplishment is progressing. Dyer should have been out of bed at first horn-blow.

One morning he slept until nearly ten o'clock. It was inexplicable! He hurried from his bunk, made a hasty toilet, and started for the dining-room to get some sort of a lunch to do him until dinner time. As he stepped from the door of the office he caught sight of two men hurrying from the cook camp to the men's camp. He thought he heard the hum of conversation in the latter building. The cookee set hot coffee before him. For the rest, he took what he could find cold on the table.

On an inverted cracker box the cook sat reading an old copy of the Police Gazette. Various fifty-pound lard tins were bubbling and steaming on the range. The cookee divided his time between them and the task of sticking on the log walls pleasing patterns made of illustrations from cheap papers and the gaudy labels of canned goods. Dyer sat down, feeling, for the first time, a little guilty. This was not because of a sense of a dereliction in duty, but because he feared the strong man's contempt for inefficiency.

"I sort of pounded my ear a little long this morning," he remarked with an unwonted air of bonhomie.

The cook creased his paper with one hand and went on reading; the little action indicating at the same time that he had heard, but intended to vouchsafe no attention. The cookee continued his occupations.

"I suppose the men got out to the marsh on time," suggested Dyer, still easily.

The cook laid aside his paper and looked the scaler in the eye.

"You're the foreman; I'm the cook," said he. "You ought to know."

The cookee had paused, the paste brush in his hand.

Dyer was no weakling. The problem presenting, he rose to the emergency. Without another word he pushed back his coffee cup and crossed the narrow open passage to the men's camp

When he opened the door a silence fell. He could see dimly that the room was full of lounging and smoking lumbermen. As a matter of fact, not a man had stirred out that morning. This was more for the sake of giving Dyer a lesson than of actually shirking the work, for a lumber-jack is honest in giving his time when it is paid for.

"How's this, men!" cried Dyer sharply; "why aren't you out on the marsh?"

No one answered for a minute. Then Baptiste:

"He mak' too tam cole for de marsh. Meester Radway he spik dat we kip off dat marsh w'en he mak' cole."

Dyer knew that the precedent was indisputable.

"Why didn't you cut on eight then?" he asked, still in peremptory tones.

"Didn't have no one to show us where to begin," drawled a voice in the corner.

Dyer turned sharp on his heel and went out.

"Sore as a boil, ain't he!" commented old Jackson Hines with a chuckle.

In the cook camp Dyer was saying to the cook, "Well, anyway, we'll have dinner early and get a good start for this afternoon."

The cook again laid down his paper. "I'm tending to this job of cook," said he, "and I'm getting the meals on time. Dinner will be on time to-day not a minute early, and not a minute late."

Then he resumed his perusal of the adventures of ladies to whom the illustrations accorded magnificent calf-development.

The crew worked on the marsh that afternoon, and the subsequent days of the week. They labored conscientiously but not zealously. There is a deal of difference, and the lumber-jack's unaided conscience is likely to allow him a certain amount of conversation from the decks of skidways. The work moved slowly. At Christmas a number of the men "went out." Most of them were back again after four or five days, for, while men were not plenty, neither was work. The equilibrium was nearly exact.

But the convivial souls had lost to Dyer the days of their debauch, and until their thirst for recuperative "Pain Killer," "Hinckley" and Jamaica Ginger was appeased, they were not much good. Instead of keeping up to fifty thousand a day, as Radway had figured was necessary, the scale would not have exceeded thirty.

Dyer saw all this plainly enough, but was not able to remedy it. That was not entirely his fault. He did not dare give the delinquents their time, for he would not have known where to fill their places. This lay in Radway's experience. Dyer felt that responsibilities a little too great had been forced on him, which was partly true. In a few days the young man's facile conscience had covered all his shortcomings with the blanket excuse. He conceived that he had a grievance against Radway!

## Chapter X

Radway returned to camp by the 6th of January. He went on snowshoes over the entire job; and then sat silently in the office smoking "Peerless" in his battered old pipe. Dyer watched him amusedly, secure in his grievance in case blame should be attached to him. The jobber looked older. The lines of dry good-humor about his eyes had subtly changed to an expression of pathetic anxiety. He attached no blame to anybody, but rose the next morning at horn-blow, and the men found they had a new master over them.

And now the struggle with the wilderness came to grapples. Radway was as one possessed by a burning fever. He seemed everywhere at once, always helping with his own shoulder and arm, hurrying eagerly. For once luck seemed with him. The marsh was cut over; the "eighty" on section eight was skidded without a break. The weather held cold and clear.

Now it became necessary to put the roads in shape for hauling. All winter the blacksmith, between his tasks of shoeing and mending, had occupied his time in fitting the iron-work on eight log-sleighs which the carpenter had hewed from solid sticks of timber. They were tremendous affairs, these sleighs, with runners six feet apart, and bunks nine feet in width for the reception of logs. The bunks were so connected by two loosely-coupled rods that, when emptied, they could be swung parallel with the road, so reducing the width of the sleigh. The carpenter had also built two immense tanks on runners, holding each some seventy barrels of water, and with holes so arranged in the bottom and rear that on the withdrawal of plugs the water would flood the entire width of the road. These sprinklers were filled by horse power. A chain, running through blocks attached to a solid upper framework, like the open belfry of an Italian monastery, dragged a barrel up a wooden track from the water hole to the opening in the sprinkler. When in action this formidable machine weighed nearly two tons and resembled a moving house. Other men had felled two big hemlocks, from which they had hewed beams for a V plow.

The V plow was now put in action. Six horses drew it down the road, each pair superintended by a driver. The machine was weighted down by a number of logs laid across the arms. Men guided it by levers, and by throwing their weight against the fans of the plow. It was a gay, animated scene this, full of the spirit of winter—the plodding, straining horses, the brilliantly dressed, struggling men, the sullen-yielding snow thrown to either side, the shouts, warnings, and commands. To right and left grew white banks of snow. Behind stretched a broad white path in which a scant inch hid the bare earth.

For some distance the way led along comparatively high ground. Then, skirting the edge of a lake, it plunged into a deep creek bottom between hills. Here, earlier in the year, eleven bridges had been constructed, each a labor of accuracy; and perhaps as many swampy places had been "corduroyed" by carpeting them with long parallel poles. Now the first difficulty began.

Some of the bridges had sunk below the level, and the approaches had to be corduroyed to a practicable grade. Others again were humped up like tom-cats, and had to be pulled apart entirely. In spots the "corduroy" had spread, so that the horses thrust their hoofs far down into leg-breaking holes. The experienced animals were never caught, however. As soon as they felt the ground giving way beneath one foot, they threw their weight on the other.

Still, that sort of thing was to be expected. A gang of men who followed the plow carried axes and cant-hooks for the purpose of repairing extemporaneously just such defects, which never would have been discovered otherwise than by the practical experience. Radway himself accompanied the plow. Thorpe, who went along as one of the "road monkeys," saw now why such care had been required of him in smoothing the way of stubs, knots, and hummocks.

Down the creek an accident occurred on this account. The plow had encountered a drift. Three times the horses had plunged at it, and three times had been brought to a stand, not so much by the drag of the V plow as by the wallowing they themselves had to do in the drift.

"No use, break her through, boys," said Radway. So a dozen men hurled their bodies through, making an opening for the horses.

"Hi! YUP!" shouted the three teamsters, gathering up their reins.

The horses put their heads down and plunged. The whole apparatus moved with a rush, men clinging, animals digging their hoofs in, snow flying. Suddenly there came a check, then a CRACK, and then the plow shot forward so suddenly and easily that the horses all but fell on their noses. The flanging arms of the V, forced in a place too narrow, had caught between heavy stubs. One of the arms had broken square off.

There was nothing for it but to fell another hemlock and hew out another beam, which meant a day lost. Radway occupied his men with shovels in clearing the edge of the road, and started one of his sprinklers over the place already cleared. Water holes of suitable size had been blown in the creek bank by dynamite. There the machines were filled. It was a slow process. Stratton attached his horse to the chain and drove him back and forth, hauling the barrel up and down the slideway. At the bottom it was capsized and filled by means of a long pole shackled to its bottom and manipulated by old man Heath. At the top it turned over by its own weight. Thus seventy odd times.

Then Fred Green hitched his team on and the four horses drew the creaking, cumbrous vehicle spouting down the road. Water gushed in fans from the openings on either side and beneath; and in streams from two holes behind. Not for an instant as long as the flow continued dared the teamsters breathe their horses, for a pause would freeze the runners tight to the ground. A tongue at either end obviated the necessity of turning around.

While the other men hewed at the required beam for the broken V plow, Heath, Stratton, and Green went over the cleared road-length once. To do so required three sprinklerfuls. When the road should be quite free, and both sprinklers running, they would have to keep at it until after midnight.

And then silently the wilderness stretched forth her hand and pushed these struggling atoms back to their place.

That night it turned warmer. The change was heralded by a shift of wind. Then some blue jays appeared from nowhere and began to scream at their more silent brothers, the whisky jacks.

"She's goin' to rain," said old Jackson. "The air is kind o' holler."

"Hollow?" said Thorpe, laughing. "How is that?"

"I don' no," confessed Hines, "but she is. She jest feels that way."

In the morning the icicles dripped from the roof, and although the snow did not appreciably melt, it shrank into itself and became pock-marked on the surface.

Radway was down looking at the road.

"She's holdin' her own," said he, "but there ain't any use putting more water on her. She ain't freezing a mite. We'll plow her out."

So they finished the job, and plowed her out, leaving exposed the wet, marshy surface of the creek-bottom, on which at night a thin crust formed. Across the marsh the old tramped road held up the horses, and the plow swept clear a little wider swath.

"She'll freeze a little to-night," said Radway hopefully. "You sprinkler boys get at her and wet her down."

Until two o'clock in the morning the four teams and the six men creaked back and forth spilling hardly-gathered water—weird, unearthly, in the flickering light of their torches. Then they crept in and ate sleepily the food that a sleepy cookee set out for them.

By morning the mere surface of this sprinkled water had frozen, the remainder beneath had drained away, and so Radway found in his road considerable patches of shell ice, useless, crumbling. He looked in despair at the sky. Dimly through the gray he caught the tint of blue.

The sun came out. Nut-hatches and wood-peckers ran gayly up the warming trunks of the trees. Blue jays fluffed and perked and screamed in the hard-wood tops. A covey of grouse ventured from the swamp and strutted vainly, a pause of contemplation between each step. Radway, walking out on the tramped road of the marsh, cracked the artificial skin and thrust his foot through into icy water. That night the sprinklers stayed in.

The devil seemed in it. If the thaw would only cease before the ice bottom so laboriously constructed was destroyed! Radway vibrated between the office and the road. Men were lying idle; teams were doing the same. Nothing went on but the days of the year; and four of them had already ticked off the calendar. The deep snow of the unusually cold autumn had now disappeared from the tops of the stumps. Down in the swamp the covey of partridges were beginning to hope that in a few days more they might discover a bare spot in the burnings. It even stopped freezing during the night. At times Dyer's little thermometer marked as high as forty degrees.

"I often heard this was a sort 'v summer resort," observed Tom Broadhead, "but danged if I knew it was a summer resort all the year 'round."

The weather got to be the only topic of conversation. Each had his say, his prediction. It became maddening. Towards evening the chill of melting snow would deceive many into the belief that a cold snap was beginning.

"She'll freeze before morning, sure," was the hopeful comment.

And then in the morning the air would be more balmily insulting than ever.

"Old man is as blue as a whetstone," commented Jackson Hines, "an' I don't blame him. This weather'd make a man mad enough to eat the devil with his horns left on."

By and by it got to be a case of looking on the bright side of the affair from pure reaction.

"I don't know," said Radway, "it won't be so bad after all. A couple of days of zero weather, with all this water lying around, would fix things up in pretty good shape. If she only freezes tight, we'll have a good solid bottom to build on, and that'll be quite a good rig out there on the marsh."

The inscrutable goddess of the wilderness smiled, and calmly, relentlessly, moved her next pawn.

It was all so unutterably simple, and yet so effective. Something there was in it of the calm inevitability of fate. It snowed.

347

All night and all day the great flakes zig-zagged softly down through the air. Radway plowed away two feet of it. The surface was promptly covered by a second storm. Radway doggedly plowed it out again.

This time the goddess seemed to relent. The ground froze solid. The sprinklers became assiduous in their labor. Two days later the road was ready for the first sleigh, its surface of thick, glassy ice, beautiful to behold; the ruts cut deep and true; the grades sanded, or sprinkled with retarding hay on the descents. At the river the banking ground proved solid. Radway breathed again, then sighed. Spring was eight days nearer. He was eight days more behind.

### Chapter XI

As soon as loading began, the cook served breakfast at three o'clock. The men worked by the light of torches, which were often merely catsup jugs with wicking in the necks. Nothing could be more picturesque than a teamster conducting one of his great pyramidical loads over the little inequalities of the road, in the ticklish places standing atop with the bent knee of the Roman charioteer, spying and forestalling the chances of the way with a fixed eye and an intense concentration that relaxed not one inch in the miles of the haul. Thorpe had become a full-fledged cant-hook man.

He liked the work. There is about it a skill that fascinates. A man grips suddenly with the hook of his strong instrument, stopping one end that the other may slide; he thrusts the short, strong stock between the log and the skid, allowing it to be overrun; he stops the roll with a sudden sure grasp applied at just the right moment to be effective. Sometimes he allows himself to be carried up bodily, clinging to the cant-hook like an acrobat to a bar, until the log has rolled once; when, his weapon loosened, he drops lightly, easily to the ground. And it is exciting to pile the logs on the sleigh, first a layer of five, say; then one of six smaller; of but three; of two; until, at the very apex, the last is dragged slowly up the skids, poised, and, just as it is about to plunge down the other side, is gripped and held inexorably by the little men in blue flannel shirts.

Chains bind the loads. And if ever, during the loading, or afterwards when the sleigh is in motion, the weight of the logs causes the pyramid to break down and squash out;—then woe to the driver, or whoever happens to be near! A saw log does not make a great deal of fuss while falling, but it falls through anything that happens in its way, and a man who gets mixed up in a load of twenty-five or thirty of them obeying the laws of gravitation from a height of some fifteen to twenty feet, can be crushed into strange shapes and fragments. For this reason the loaders are picked and careful men.

At the banking grounds, which lie in and about the bed of the river, the logs are piled in a gigantic skidway to await the spring freshets, which will carry them down stream to the "boom." In that enclosure they remain until sawed in the mill.

Such is the drama of the saw log, a story of grit, resourcefulness, adaptability, fortitude and ingenuity hard to match. Conditions never repeat themselves in the woods as they do in the factory. The wilderness offers ever new complications to solve, difficulties to overcome. A man must think of everything, figure on everything, from the grand sweep of the country at large to the pressure on a king-bolt. And where another possesses the boundless resources of a great city, he has to rely on the material stored in one corner of a shed. It is easy to build a palace with men and tools; it is difficult to build a log cabin with nothing but an ax. His wits must help him where his experience fails; and his experience must push him mechanically along the track of habit when successive buffetings have beaten his wits out of his head. In a day he must construct elaborate engines, roads, and implements which old civilization considers the works of leisure. Without a thought of expense he must abandon as temporary, property which other industries cry out at being compelled to acquire as permanent. For this reason he becomes in time different from his fellows. The wilderness leaves something of her mystery in his eyes, that mystery of hidden, unknown but guessed, power. Men look after him on the street, as they would look after any other pioneer, in vague admiration of a scope more virile than their own.

Thorpe, in common with the other men, had thought Radway's vacation at Christmas time a mistake. He could not but admire the feverish animation that now characterized the jobber. Every mischance was as quickly repaired as aroused expedient could do the work.

The marsh received first attention. There the restless snow drifted uneasily before the wind. Nearly every day the road had to be plowed, and the sprinklers followed the teams almost constantly. Often it was bitter cold, but no one dared to suggest to the determined jobber that it might be better to remain indoors. The men knew as well as he that the heavy February snows would block traffic beyond hope of extrication.

As it was, several times an especially heavy fall clogged the way. The snow-plow, even with extra teams, could hardly force its path through. Men with shovels helped. Often but a few loads a day, and they small, could be forced to the banks by the utmost exertions of the entire crew. Esprit de corps awoke. The men sprang to their tasks with alacrity, gave more than an hour's exertion to each of the twenty-four, took a pride in repulsing the assaults of the great enemy, whom they personified under the generic "She." Mike McGovern raked up a saint somewhere whom he apostrophized in a personal and familiar manner.

He hit his head against an overhanging branch.

"You're a nice wan, now ain't ye?" he cried angrily at the unfortunate guardian of his soul. "Dom if Oi don't quit ye! Ye see!"

"Be the gate of Hivin!" he shouted, when he opened the door of mornings and discovered another six inches of snow, "Ye're a burrd! If Oi couldn't make out to be more of a saint than that, Oi'd quit the biznis! Move yor pull, an' get us some dacint weather! Ye awt t' be road monkeyin' on th' golden streets, thot's what ye awt to be doin'!"

348

Jackson Hines was righteously indignant, but with the shrewdness of the old man, put the blame partly where it belonged.

"I ain't sayin'," he observed judicially, "that this weather ain't hell. It's hell and repeat. But a man sort've got to expec' weather. He looks for it, and he oughta be ready for it. The trouble is we got behind Christmas. It's that Dyer. He's about as mean as they make 'em. The only reason he didn't die long ago is becuz th' Devil's thought him too mean to pay any 'tention to. If ever he should die an' go to Heaven he'd pry up th' golden streets an' use the infernal pit for a smelter."

With this magnificent bit of invective, Jackson seized a lantern and stumped out to see that the teamsters fed their horses properly.

"Didn't know you were a miner, Jackson," called Thorpe, laughing.

"Young feller," replied Jackson at the door, "it's a lot easier to tell what I AIN'T been."

So floundering, battling, making a little progress every day, the strife continued.

One morning in February, Thorpe was helping load a big butt log. He was engaged in "sending up"; that is, he was one of the two men who stand at either side of the skids to help the ascending log keep straight and true to its bed on the pile. His assistant's end caught on a sliver, ground for a second, and slipped back. Thus the log ran slanting across the skids instead of perpendicular to them. To rectify the fault, Thorpe dug his cant-hook into the timber and threw his weight on the stock. He hoped in this manner to check correspondingly the ascent of his end. In other words, he took the place, on his side, of the preventing sliver, so equalizing the pressure and forcing the timber to its proper position. Instead of rolling, the log slid. The stock of the cant-hook was jerked from his hands. He fell back, and the cant-hook, after clinging for a moment to the rough bark, snapped down and hit him a crushing blow on the top of the head.

Had a less experienced man than Jim Gladys been stationed at the other end, Thorpe's life would have ended there. A shout of surprise or horror would have stopped the horse pulling on the decking chain; the heavy stick would have slid back on the prostrate young man, who would have thereupon been ground to atoms as he lay. With the utmost coolness Gladys swarmed the slanting face of the load; interposed the length of his cant-hook stock between the log and it; held it exactly long enough to straighten the timber, but not so long as to crush his own head and arm; and ducked, just as the great piece of wood rumbled over the end of the skids and dropped with a thud into the place Norton, the "top" man, had prepared for it.

It was a fine deed, quickly thought, quickly dared. No one saw it. Jim Gladys was a hero, but a hero without an audience.

They took Thorpe up and carried him in, just as they had carried Hank Paul before. Men who had not spoken a dozen words to him in as many days gathered his few belongings and stuffed them awkwardly into his satchel. Jackson Hines prepared the bed of straw and warm blankets in the bottom of the sleigh that was to take him out.

"He would have made a good boss," said the old fellow. "He's a hard man to nick."

Thorpe was carried in from the front, and the battle went on without him.

## Chapter XII

Thorpe never knew how carefully he was carried to camp, nor how tenderly the tote teamster drove his hay-couched burden to Beeson Lake. He had no consciousness of the jolting train, in the baggage car of which Jimmy, the little brakeman, and Bud, and the baggage man spread blankets, and altogether put themselves to a great deal of trouble. When finally he came to himself, he was in a long, bright, clean room, and the sunset was throwing splashes of light on the ceiling over his head.

He watched them idly for a time; then turned on his pillow. At once he perceived a long, double row of clean white-painted iron beds, on which lay or sat figures of men. Other figures, of women, glided here and there noiselessly. They wore long, spreading dove-gray clothes, with a starched white kerchief drawn over the shoulders and across the breast. Their heads were quaintly white-garbed in stiff winglike coifs, fitting close about the oval of the face. Then Thorpe sighed comfortably, and closed his eyes and blessed the chance that he had bought a hospital ticket of the agent who had visited camp the month before. For these were Sisters, and the young man lay in the Hospital of St. Mary.

Time was when the lumber-jack who had the misfortune to fall sick or to meet with an accident was in a sorry plight indeed. If he possessed a "stake," he would receive some sort of unskilled attention in one of the numerous and fearful lumberman's boarding-houses,—just so long as his money lasted, not one instant more. Then he was bundled brutally into the street, no matter what his condition might be. Penniless, without friends, sick, he drifted naturally to the county poorhouse. There he was patched up quickly and sent out half-cured. The authorities were not so much to blame. With the slender appropriations at their disposal, they found difficulty in taking care of those who came legitimately under their jurisdiction. It was hardly to be expected that they would welcome with open arms a vast army of crippled and diseased men temporarily from the woods. The poor lumber-jack was often left broken in mind and body from causes which a little intelligent care would have rendered unimportant.

With the establishment of the first St. Mary's hospital, I think at Bay City, all this was changed. Now, in it and a half dozen others conducted on the same principles, the woodsman receives the best of medicines, nursing, and medical attendance. From one of the numerous agents who periodically visit the camps, he purchases for eight dollars a ticket which admits him at any time during the year to the hospital, where he is privileged to remain free of further charge until convalescent. So valuable are these institutions, and so excellently are they maintained by the Sisters, that a hospital agent is always welcome, even in those camps from which ordinary peddlers and insurance men are rigidly excluded. Like a great many other charities built on a common-sense self-supporting rational basis, the woods hospitals are under the Roman Catholic Church.

In one of these hospitals Thorpe lay for six weeks suffering from a severe concussion of the brain. At the end of the fourth, his fever had broken, but he was pronounced as yet too weak to be moved.

His nurse was a red-cheeked, blue-eyed, homely little Irish girl, brimming with motherly good-humor. When Thorpe found strength to talk, the two became friends. Through her influence he was moved to a bed about ten feet from the window. Thence his privileges were three roofs and a glimpse of the distant river.

The roofs were covered with snow. One day Thorpe saw it sink into itself and gradually run away. The tinkle tinkle tank tank of drops sounded from his own eaves. Down the far-off river, sluggish reaches of ice drifted. Then in a night the blue disappeared from the stream. It became a menacing gray, and even from his distance Thorpe could catch the swirl of its rising waters. A day or two later dark masses drifted or shot across the field of his vision, and twice he thought he distinguished men standing upright and bold on single logs as they rushed down the current.

"What is the date?" he asked of the Sister.

"The eleventh of March."

"Isn't it early for the thaw?"

"Listen to 'im!" exclaimed the Sister delightedly. "Early is it! Sure th' freshet co't thim all. Look, darlint, ye kin see th' drive from here."

"I see," said Thorpe wearily, "when can I get out?"

"Not for wan week," replied the Sister decidedly.

At the end of the week Thorpe said good-by to his attendant, who appeared as sorry to see him go as though the same partings did not come to her a dozen times a year; he took two days of tramping the little town to regain the use of his legs, and boarded the morning train for Beeson Lake. He did not pause in the village, but bent his steps to the river trail.

### Chapter XIII

Thorpe found the woods very different from when he had first traversed them. They were full of patches of wet earth and of sunshine; of dark pine, looking suddenly worn, and of fresh green shoots of needles, looking deliciously springlike. This was the contrast everywhere—stern, earnest, purposeful winter, and gay, laughing, careless spring. It was impossible not to draw in fresh spirits with every step.

He followed the trail by the river. Butterballs and scoters paddled up at his approach. Bits of rotten ice occasionally swirled down the diminishing stream. The sunshine was clear and bright, but silvery rather than golden, as though a little of the winter's snow,—a last ethereal incarnation,—had lingered in its substance. Around every bend Thorpe looked for some of Radway's crew "driving" the logs down the current. He knew from chance encounters with several of the men in Bay City that Radway was still in camp; which meant, of course, that the last of the season's operations were not yet finished. Five miles further Thorpe began to wonder whether this last conclusion might not be erroneous. The Cass Branch had shrunken almost to its original limits. Only here and there a little bayou or marsh attested recent freshets. The drive must have been finished, even this early, for the stream in its present condition would hardly float saw logs, certainly not in quantity.

Thorpe, puzzled, walked on. At the banking ground he found empty skids. Evidently the drive was over. And yet even to Thorpe's ignorance, it seemed incredible that the remaining million and a half of logs had been hauled, banked and driven during the short time he had lain in the Bay City hospital. More to solve the problem than in any hope of work, he set out up the logging road.

Another three miles brought him to camp. It looked strangely wet and sodden and deserted. In fact, Thorpe found a bare half dozen people in it,—Radway, the cook, and four men who were helping to pack up the movables, and who later would drive out the wagons containing them. The jobber showed strong traces of the strain he had undergone, but greeted Thorpe almost jovially. He seemed able to show more of his real nature now that the necessity of authority had been definitely removed.

"Hullo, young man," he shouted at Thorpe's mud-splashed figure, "come back to view, the remains? All well again, heigh? That's good!"

He strode down to grip the young fellow heartily by the hand. It was impossible not to be charmed by the sincere cordiality of his manner.

"I didn't know you were through," explained Thorpe, "I came to see if I could get a job."

"Well now I AM sorry!" cried Radway, "you can turn in and help though, if you want to."

Thorpe greeted the cook and old Jackson Hines, the only two whom he knew, and set to work to tie up bundles of blankets, and to collect axes, peavies, and tools of all descriptions. This was evidently the last wagon-trip, for little remained to be done.

"I ought by rights to take the lumber of the roofs and floors," observed Radway thoughtfully, "but I guess she don't matter."

Thorpe had never seen him in better spirits. He ascribed the older man's hilarity to relief over the completion of a difficult task. That evening the seven dined together at one end of the long table. The big room exhaled already the atmosphere of desertion.

"Not much like old times, is she?" laughed Radway. "Can't you just shut your eyes and hear Baptiste say, 'Mak' heem de soup one tam more for me'? She's pretty empty now."

Jackson Hines looked whimsically down the bare board. "More room than God made for geese in Ireland," was his comment.

After supper they even sat outside for a little time to smoke their pipes, chair-tilted against the logs of the cabins, but soon the chill of melting snow drove them indoors. The four teamsters played seven-up in the cook camp by the light of a barn lantern, while Thorpe and the cook wrote letters. Thorpe's was to his sister.

"I have been in the hospital for about a month," he wrote. "Nothing serious—a crack on the head, which is all right now. But I cannot get home this summer, nor, I am afraid, can we arrange about the school this year. I am about seventy dollars ahead of where I was last fall, so you see it is slow business. This summer I am going into a mill, but the wages for green labor are not very high there either," and so on.

When Miss Helen Thorpe, aged seventeen, received this document she stamped her foot almost angrily. "You'd think he was a day-laborer!" she cried. "Why doesn't he try for a clerkship or something in the city where he'd have a chance to use his brains!"

The thought of her big, strong, tanned brother chained to a desk rose to her, and she smiled a little sadly.

"I know," she went on to herself, "he'd rather be a common laborer in the woods than railroad manager in the office. He loves his out-of-doors."

"Helen!" called a voice from below, "if you're through up there, I wish you'd come down and help me carry this rug out."

The girl's eyes cleared with a snap.

"So do I!" she cried defiantly, "so do I love out-of-doors! I like the woods and the fields and the trees just as much as he does, only differently; but I don't get out!"

And thus she came to feeling rebelliously that her brother had been a little selfish in his choice of an occupation, that he sacrificed her inclinations to his own. She did not guess,—how could she?—his dreams for her. She did not see the future through his thoughts, but through his words. A negative hopelessness settled down on her, which soon her strong spirit, worthy counterpart of her brother's, changed to more positive rebellion. Thorpe had aroused antagonism where he craved only love. The knowledge of that fact would have surprised and hurt him, for he was entirely without suspicion of it. He lived subjectively to so great a degree that his thoughts and aims took on a certain tangible objectivity,—they became so real to him that he quite overlooked the necessity of communication to make them as real to others. He assumed unquestioningly that the other must know. So entirely had he thrown himself into his ambition of making a suitable position for Helen, so continually had he dwelt on it in his thoughts, so earnestly had he striven for it in every step of the great game he was beginning to play, that it never occurred to him he should also concede a definite outward manifestation of his feeling in order to assure its acceptance. Thorpe believed that he had sacrificed every thought and effort to his sister. Helen was becoming convinced that he had considered only himself.

After finishing the letter which gave occasion to this train of thought, Thorpe lit his pipe and strolled out into the darkness. Opposite the little office he stopped amazed.

Through the narrow window he could see Radway seated in front of the stove. Every attitude of the man denoted the most profound dejection. He had sunk down into his chair until he rested on almost the small of his back, his legs were struck straight out in front of him, his chin rested on his breast, and his two arms hung listless at his side, a pipe half falling from the fingers of one hand. All the facetious lines had turned to pathos. In his face sorrowed the anxious, questing, wistful look of the St. Bernard that does not understand.

"What's the matter with the boss, anyway?" asked Thorpe in a low voice of Jackson Hines, when the seven-up game was finished.

"H'aint ye heard?" inquired the old man in surprise.

"Why, no. What?"

"Busted," said the old man sententiously.

"How? What do you mean?"

"What I say. He's busted. That freshet caught him too quick. They's more'n a million and a half logs left in the woods that can't be got out this year, and as his contract calls for a finished job, he don't get nothin' for what he's done."

"That's a queer rig," commented Thorpe. "He's done a lot of valuable work here,—the timber's cut and skidded, anyway; and he's delivered a good deal of it to the main drive. The M. & D. outfit get all the advantage of that."

"They do, my son. When old Daly's hand gets near anything, it cramps. I don't know how the old man come to make such a contrac', but he did. Result is, he's out his expenses and time."

To understand exactly the catastrophe that had occurred, it is necessary to follow briefly an outline of the process after the logs have been piled on the banks. There they remain until the break-up attendant on spring shall flood the stream to a freshet. The rollways are then broken, and the saw logs floated down the river to the mill where they are to be cut into lumber.

If for any reason this transportation by water is delayed until the flood goes down, the logs are stranded or left in pools. Consequently every logger puts into the two or three weeks of freshet water a feverish activity which shall carry his product through before the ebb.

The exceptionally early break-up of this spring, combined with the fact that, owing to the series of incidents and accidents already sketched, the actual cutting and skidding had fallen so far behind, caught Radway unawares. He saw his rollways breaking out while his teams were still hauling in the woods. In order to deliver to the mouth of the Cass Branch the three million already banked, he was forced to drop everything else and attend strictly to the drive. This left still, as has been stated, a million and a half on skidways, which Radway knew he would be unable to get out that year.

In spite of the jobber's certainty that his claim was thus annulled, and that he might as well abandon the enterprise entirely for all he would ever get out of it, he finished the "drive" conscientiously and saved to the Company the logs already banked. Then he had interviewed Daly. The latter refused to pay him one cent. Nothing remained but to break camp and grin as best he might over the loss of his winter's work and expenses.

The next day Radway and Thorpe walked the ten miles of the river trail together, while the teamsters and the cook drove down the five teams. Under the influence of the solitude and a certain sympathy which Thorpe manifested, Radway talked—a very little.

"I got behind; that's all there is to it," he said. "I s'pose I ought to have driven the men a little; but still, I don't know. It gets pretty cold on the plains. I guess I bit off more than I could chew."

His eye followed listlessly a frenzied squirrel swinging from the tops of poplars.

"I wouldn't 'a done it for myself," he went on. "I don't like the confounded responsibility. They's too much worry connected with it all. I had a good snug little stake—mighty nigh six thousand. She's all gone now. That'd have been enough for me—I ain't a drinkin' man. But then there was the woman and the kid. This ain't no country for woman-folks, and I wanted t' take little Lida out o' here. I had lots of experience in the woods, and I've seen men make big money time and again, who didn't know as much about it as I do. But they got there, somehow. Says I, I'll make a stake this year—I'd a had twelve thousand in th' bank, if things'd have gone right—and then we'll jest move down around Detroit an' I'll put Lida in school."

Thorpe noticed a break in the man's voice, and glancing suddenly toward him was astounded to catch his eyes brimming with tears. Radway perceived the surprise.

"You know when I left Christmas?" he asked.

"Yes."

"I was gone two weeks, and them two weeks done me. We was going slow enough before, God knows, but even with the rank weather and all, I think we'd have won out, if we could have held the same gait."

Radway paused. Thorpe was silent.

"The boys thought it was a mighty poor rig, my leaving that way."

He paused again in evident expectation of a reply. Again Thorpe was silent.

"Didn't they?" Radway insisted.

"Yes, they did," answered Thorpe.

The older man sighed. "I thought so," he went on. "Well, I didn't go to spend Christmas. I went because Jimmy brought me a telegram that Lida was sick with diphtheria. I sat up nights with her for 'leven days."

"No bad after-effects, I hope?" inquired Thorpe.

"She died," said Radway simply.

The two men tramped stolidly on. This was too great an affair for Thorpe to approach except on the knees of his spirit. After a long interval, during which the waters had time to still, the young man changed the subject.

"Aren't you going to get anything out of M. & D.?" he asked.

"No. Didn't earn nothing. I left a lot of their saw logs hung up in the woods, where they'll deteriorate from rot and worms. This is their last season in this district."

"Got anything left?"

"Not a cent."

"What are you going to do?"

"Do!" cried the old woodsman, the fire springing to his eye. "Do! I'm going into the woods, by God! I'm going to work with my hands, and be happy! I'm going to do other men's work for them and take other men's pay. Let them do the figuring and worrying. I'll boss their gangs and make their roads and see to their logging for 'em, but it's got to be THEIRS. No! I'm going to be a free man by the G. jumping Moses!"

### Chapter XIV

Thorpe dedicated a musing instant to the incongruity of rejoicing over a freedom gained by ceasing to be master and becoming servant.

"Radway," said he suddenly, "I need money and I need it bad. I think you ought to get something out of this job of the M. & D.—not much, but something. Will you give me a share of what I can collect from them?"

"Sure!" agreed the jobber readily, with a laugh. "Sure! But you won't get anything. I'll give you ten per cent quick."

"Good enough!" cried Thorpe.

"But don't be too sure you'll earn day wages doing it," warned the other. "I saw Daly when I was down here last week."

"My time's not valuable," replied Thorpe. "Now when we get to town I want your power of attorney and a few figures, after which I will not bother you again."

The next day the young man called for the second time at the little red-painted office under the shadow of the mill, and for the second time stood before the bulky power of the junior member of the firm.

"Well, young man, what can I do for you?" asked the latter.

"I have been informed," said Thorpe without preliminary, "that you intend to pay John Radway nothing for the work done on the Cass Branch this winter. Is that true?"

Daly studied his antagonist meditatively. "If it is true, what is it to you?" he asked at length.

"I am acting in Mr. Radway's interest."

"You are one of Radway's men?"

"Yes."

"In what capacity have you been working for him?"

"Cant-hook man," replied Thorpe briefly.

"I see," said Daly slowly. Then suddenly, with an intensity of energy that startled Thorpe, he cried: "Now you get out of here! Right off! Quick!"

The younger man recognized the compelling and autocratic boss addressing a member of the crew.

"I shall do nothing of the kind!" he replied with a flash of fire.

The mill-owner leaped to his feet every inch a leader of men. Thorpe did not wish to bring about an actual scene of violence. He had attained his object, which was to fluster the other out of his judicial calm.

"I have Radway's power of attorney," he added.

Daly sat down, controlled himself with an effort, and growled out, "Why didn't you say so?"

"Now I would like to know your position," went on Thorpe. "I am not here to make trouble, but as an associate of Mr. Radway, I have a right to understand the case. Of course I have his side of the story," he suggested, as though convinced that a detailing of the other side might change his views.

Daly considered carefully, fixing his flint-blue eyes unswervingly on Thorpe's face. Evidently his scrutiny advised him that the young man was a force to be reckoned with.

"It's like this," said he abruptly, "we contracted last fall with this man Radway to put in five million feet of our timber, delivered to the main drive at the mouth of the Cass Branch. In this he was to act independently except as to the matter of provisions. Those he drew from our van, and was debited with the amount of the same. Is that clear?"

"Perfectly," replied Thorpe.

"In return we were to pay him, merchantable scale, four dollars a thousand. If, however, he failed to put in the whole job, the contract was void."

"That's how I understand it," commented Thorpe. "Well?"

"Well, he didn't get in the five million. There's a million and a half hung up in the woods."

"But you have in your hands three million and a half, which under the present arrangement you get free of any charge whatever."

"And we ought to get it," cried Daly. "Great guns! Here we intend to saw this summer and quit. We want to get in every stick of timber we own so as to be able to clear out of here for good and all at the close of the season; and now this condigned jobber ties us up for a million and a half."

"It is exceedingly annoying," conceded Thorpe, "and it is a good deal of Radway's fault, I am willing to admit, but it's your fault too."

"To be sure," replied Daly with the accent of sarcasm.

"You had no business entering into any such contract. It gave him no show."

"I suppose that was mainly his lookout, wasn't it? And as I already told you, we had to protect ourselves."

"You should have demanded security for the completion of the work. Under your present agreement, if Radway got in the timber, you were to pay him a fair price. If he didn't, you appropriated everything he had already done. In other words, you made him a bet."

"I don't care what you call it," answered Daly, who had recovered his good-humor in contemplation of the security of his position. "The fact stands all right."

"It does," replied Thorpe unexpectedly, "and I'm glad of it. Now let's examine a few figures. You owned five million feet of timber, which at the price of stumpage" (standing trees) "was worth ten thousand dollars."

"Well."

"You come out at the end of the season with three million and a half of saw logs, which with the four dollars' worth of logging added, are worth twenty-one thousand dollars."

"Hold on!" cried Daly, "we paid Radway four dollars; we could have done it ourselves for less."

"You could not have done it for one cent less than four-twenty in that country," replied Thorpe, "as any expert will testify."

"Why did we give it to Radway at four, then?"

"You saved the expense of a salaried overseer, and yourselves some bother," replied Thorpe. "Radway could do it for less, because, for some strange reason which you yourself do not understand, a jobber can always log for less than a company."

"We could have done it for four," insisted Daly stubbornly, "but get on. What are you driving at? My time's valuable."

"Well, put her at four, then," agreed Thorpe. "That makes your saw logs worth over twenty thousand dollars. Of this value Radway added thirteen thousand. You have appropriated that much of his without paying him one cent."

Daly seemed amused. "How about the million and a half feet of ours HE appropriated?" he asked quietly.

"I'm coming to that. Now for your losses. At the stumpage rate your million and a half which Radway 'appropriated' would be only three thousand. But for the sake of argument, we'll take the actual sum you'd have received for saw logs. Even then the million and a half would only have been worth between eight and nine thousand. Deducting this purely theoretical loss Radway has occasioned you, from the amount he has gained for you, you are still some four or five thousand ahead of the game. For that you paid him nothing."

"That's Radway's lookout."

"In justice you should pay him that amount. He is a poor man. He has sunk all he owned in this venture, some twelve thousand dollars, and he has nothing to live on. Even if you pay him five thousand, he has lost considerable, while you have gained."

"How have we gained by this bit of philanthropy?"

"Because you originally paid in cash for all that timber on the stump just ten thousand dollars and you get from Radway saw logs to the value of twenty," replied Thorpe sharply. "Besides you still own the million and a half which, if you do not care to put them in yourself, you can sell for something on the skids."

"Don't you know, young man, that white pine logs on skids will spoil utterly in a summer? Worms get into em."

"I do," replied Thorpe, "unless you bark them; which process will cost you about one dollar a thousand. You can find any amount of small purchasers at reduced price. You can sell them easily at three dollars. That nets you for your million and a half a little over four thousand dollars more. Under the circumstances, I do not think that my request for five thousand is at all exorbitant."

Daly laughed. "You are a shrewd figurer, and your remarks are interesting," said he.

"Will you give five thousand dollars?" asked Thorpe.

"I will not," replied Daly, then with a sudden change of humor, "and now I'll do a little talking. I've listened to you just as long as I'm going to. I have Radway's contract in that safe and I live up to it. I'll thank you to go plumb to hell!"

"That's your last word, is it?" asked Thorpe, rising.

"It is."

"Then," said he slowly and distinctly, "I'll tell you what I'll do. I intend to collect in full the four dollars a thousand for the three million and a half Mr. Radway has delivered to you. In return Mr. Radway will purchase of you at the stumpage rates of two dollars a thousand the million and a half he failed to put in. That makes a bill against you, if my figuring is correct, of just eleven thousand dollars. You will pay that bill, and I will tell you why: your contract will be classed in any court as a gambling contract for lack of consideration. You have no legal standing in the world. I call your bluff, Mr. Daly, and I'll fight you from the drop of the hat through every court in Christendom."

"Fight ahead," advised Daly sweetly, who knew perfectly well that Thorpe's law was faulty. As a matter of fact the young man could have collected on other grounds, but neither was aware of that.

"Furthermore," pursued Thorpe in addition, "I'll repeat my offer before witnesses; and if I win the first suit, I'll sue you for the money we could have made by purchasing the extra million and a half before it had a chance to spoil."

This statement had its effect, for it forced an immediate settlement before the pine on the skids should deteriorate. Daly lounged back with a little more deadly carelessness.

"And, lastly," concluded Thorpe, playing his trump card, "the suit from start to finish will be published in every important paper in this country. If you do not believe I have the influence to do this, you are at liberty to doubt the fact."

Daly was cogitating many things. He knew that publicity was the last thing to be desired. Thorpe's statement had been made in view of the fact that much of the business of a lumber firm is done on credit. He thought that perhaps a rumor of a big suit going against the firm might weaken confidence. As a matter of fact, this consideration had no weight whatever with the older man, although the threat of publicity actually gained for Thorpe what he demanded. The lumberman feared the noise of an investigation solely and simply because his firm, like so many others, was engaged at the time in stealing government timber in the upper peninsula. He did not call it stealing; but that was what it amounted to. Thorpe's shot in the air hit full.

"I think we can arrange a basis of settlement," he said finally. "Be here to-morrow morning at ten with Radway."

"Very well," said Thorpe.

"By the way," remarked Daly, "I don't believe I know your name?"

"Thorpe," was the reply.

"Well, Mr. Thorpe," said the lumberman with cold anger, "if at any time there is anything within my power or influence that you want—I'll see that you don't get it."

### Chapter XV

The whole affair was finally compromised for nine thousand dollars. Radway, grateful beyond expression, insisted on Thorpe's acceptance of an even thousand of it. With this money in hand, the latter felt justified in taking a vacation for the purpose of visiting his sister, so in two days after the signing of the check he walked up the straight garden path that led to Renwick's home.

It was a little painted frame house, back from the street, fronted by a precise bit of lawn, with a willow bush at one corner. A white picket fence effectually separated it from a broad, shaded, not unpleasing street. An osage hedge and a board fence respectively bounded the side and back.

Under the low porch Thorpe rang the bell at a door flanked by two long, narrow strips of imitation stained glass. He entered then a little dark hall from which the stairs rose almost directly at the door, containing with difficulty a hat-rack and a table on which rested a card tray with cards. In the course of greeting an elderly woman, he stepped into the parlor. This was a small square apartment carpeted in dark Brussels, and stuffily glorified in the bourgeois manner by a white marble mantel-piece, several pieces of mahogany furniture upholstered in haircloth, a table on which reposed a number of gift books in celluloid and other fancy bindings, an old-fashioned piano with a doily and a bit of china statuary, a cabinet or so containing such things as ore specimens, dried seaweed and coins, and a spindle-legged table or two upholding glass cases garnished with stuffed birds and wax flowers. The ceiling was so low that the heavy window hangings depended almost from the angle of it and the walls.

Thorpe, by some strange freak of psychology, suddenly recalled a wild, windy day in the forest. He had stood on the top of a height. He saw again the sharp puffs of snow, exactly like the smoke from bursting shells, where a fierce swoop of the storm struck the laden tops of pines; the dense swirl, again exactly like smoke but now of a great fire, that marked the lakes. The picture super-imposed itself silently over this stuffy bourgeois respectability, like the shadow of a dream. He heard plainly enough the commonplace drawl of the woman before him offering him the platitudes of her kind.

"You are lookin' real well, Mr. Thorpe," she was saying, "an' I just know Helen will be glad to see you. She had a hull afternoon out to-day and won't be back to tea. Dew set and tell me about what you've been a-doin' and how you're a-gettin' along."

"No, thank you, Mrs. Renwick," he replied, "I'll come back later. How is Helen?"

"She's purty well; and sech a nice girL I think she's getting right handsome."

"Can you tell me where she went?"

But Mrs. Renwick did not know. So Thorpe wandered about the maple-shaded streets of the little town.

For the purposes he had in view five hundred dollars would be none too much. The remaining five hundred he had resolved to invest in his sister's comfort and happiness. He had thought the matter over and come to his decision in that secretive, careful fashion so typical of him, working over every logical step of his induction so thoroughly that it ended by becoming part of his mental fiber. So when he reached the conclusion it had already become to him an axiom. In presenting it as such to his sister, he never realized that she had not followed with him the logical steps, and so could hardly be expected to accept the conclusion out-of-hand.

Thorpe wished to give his sister the best education possible in the circumstances. She was now nearly eighteen years old. He knew likewise that he would probably experience a great deal of difficulty in finding another family which would afford the young girl quite the same equality coupled with so few disadvantages. Admitted that its level of intellect and taste was not high, Mrs. Renwick was on the whole a good influence. Helen had not in the least the position of servant, but of a daughter. She helped around the house; and in return she was fed, lodged and clothed for nothing.

So though the money might have enabled Helen to live independently in a modest way for a year or so, Thorpe preferred that she remain where she was. His game was too much a game of chance. He might find himself at the end of the year without further means. Above all things he wished to assure Helen's material safety until such time as he should be quite certain of himself.

In pursuance of this idea he had gradually evolved what seemed to him an excellent plan. He had already perfected it by correspondence with Mrs. Renwick. It was, briefly, this: he, Thorpe, would at once hire a servant girl, who would make anything but supervision unnecessary in so small a household. The remainder of the money he had already paid for a year's tuition in the Seminary of the town. Thus Helen gained her leisure and an opportunity for study; and still retained her home in case of reverse.

Thorpe found his sister already a young lady. After the first delight of meeting had passed, they sat side by side on the haircloth sofa and took stock of each other.

Helen had developed from the school child to the woman. She was a handsome girl, possessed of a slender, well-rounded form, deep hazel eyes with the level gaze of her brother, a clean-cut patrician face, and a thorough-bred neatness of carriage that advertised her good blood. Altogether a figure rather aloof, a face rather impassive; but with the possibility of passion and emotion, and a will to back them.

"Oh, but you're tanned and—and BIG!" she cried, kissing her brother. "You've had such a strange winter, haven't you?"

"Yes," he replied absently.

Another man would have struck her young imagination with the wild, free thrill of the wilderness. Thus he would have gained her sympathy and understanding. Thorpe was too much in earnest.

"Things came a little better than I thought they were going to, toward the last," said he, "and I made a little money."

"Oh, I'm so glad!" she cried. "Was it much?"

"No, not much," he answered. The actual figures would have been so much better! "I've made arrangements with Mrs. Renwick to hire a servant girl, so you will have all your time free; and I have paid a year's tuition for you in the Seminary."

"Oh!" said the girl, and fell silent.

After a time, "Thank you very much, Harry dear." Then after another interval, "I think I'll go get ready for supper."

Instead of getting ready for supper, she paced excitedly up and down her room.

"Oh, why DIDN'T he say what he was about?" she cried to herself. "Why didn't he! Why didn't he!"

Next morning she opened the subject again.

"Harry, dear," said she, "I have a little scheme, and I want to see if it is not feasible. How much will the girl and the Seminary cost?"

"About four hundred dollars."

"Well now, see, dear. With four hundred dollars I can live for a year very nicely by boarding with some girls I know who live in a sort of a club; and I could learn much more by going to the High School and continuing with some other classes I am interested in now. Why see, Harry!" she cried, all interest. "We have Professor Carghill come twice a week to teach us English, and Professor Johns, who teaches us history, and we hope to get one or two more this winter. If I go to the Seminary, I'll have to miss all that. And Harry, really I don't want to go to the Seminary. I don't think I should like it. I KNOW I shouldn't."

"But why not live here, Helen?" he asked.

"Because I'm TIRED of it!" she cried; "sick to the soul of the stuffiness, and the glass cases, and the—the GOODNESS of it!"

Thorpe remembered his vision of the wild, wind-tossed pines, and sighed. He wanted very, very much to act in accordance with his sister's desires, although he winced under the sharp hurt pang of the sensitive man whose intended kindness is not appreciated. The impossibility of complying, however, reacted to shut his real ideas and emotions the more inscrutably within him.

"I'm afraid you would not find the girls' boarding-club scheme a good one, Helen," said he. "You'd find it would work better in theory than in practice."

"But it has worked with the other girls!" she cried.

"I think you would be better off here."

Helen bravely choked back her disappointment.

"I might live here, but let the Seminary drop, anyway. That would save a good deal," she begged. "I'd get quite as much good out of my work outside, and then we'd have all that money besides."

"I don't know; I'll see," replied Thorpe. "The mental discipline of class-room work might be a good thing."

He had already thought of this modification himself, but with his characteristic caution, threw cold water on the scheme until he could ascertain definitely whether or not it was practicable. He had already paid the tuition for the year, and was in doubt as to its repayment. As a matter of fact, the negotiation took about two weeks.

During that time Helen Thorpe went through her disappointment and emerged on the other side. Her nature was at once strong and adaptable. One by one she grappled with the different aspects of the case, and turned them the other way. By a tour de force she actually persuaded herself that her own plan was not really attractive to her. But what heart-breaks and tears this cost her, only those who in their youth have encountered such absolute negations of cherished ideas can guess.

Then Thorpe told her.

"I've fixed it, Helen," said he. "You can attend the High School and the classes, if you please. I have put the two hundred and fifty dollars out at interest for you."

"Oh, Harry!" she cried reproachfully. "Why didn't you tell me before!"

He did not understand; but the pleasure of it had all faded. She no longer felt enthusiasm, nor gratitude, nor anything except a dull feeling that she had been unnecessarily discouraged. And on his side, Thorpe was vaguely wounded.

The days, however, passed in the main pleasurably for them both. They were fond of one another. The barrier slowly rising between them was not yet cemented by lack of affection on either side, but rather by lack of belief in the other's affection. Helen imagined Thorpe's interest in her becoming daily more perfunctory. Thorpe fancied his sister cold, unreasoning, and ungrateful. As yet this was but the vague dust of a cloud. They could not forget that, but for each other, they were alone in the world. Thorpe delayed his departure from day to day, making all the preparations he possibly could at home.

Finally Helen came on him busily unpacking a box which a dray had left at the door. He unwound and laid one side a Winchester rifle, a variety of fishing tackle, and some other miscellanies of the woodsman. Helen was struck by the beauty of the sporting implements.

"Oh, Harry!" she cried, "aren't they fine! What are you going to do with them?"

"Going camping," replied Thorpe, his head in the excelsior.

"When?"

"This summer."

Helen's eyes lit up with a fire of delight. "How nice! May I go with you?" she cried.

Thorpe shook his head.

"I'm afraid not, little girl. It's going to be a hard trip a long ways from anywhere. You couldn't stand it."

"I'm sure I could. Try me."

"No," replied Thorpe. "I know you couldn't. We'll be sleeping on the ground and going on foot through much extremely difficult country."

"I wish you'd take me somewhere," pursued Helen. "I can't get away this summer unless you do. Why don't you camp somewhere nearer home, so I can go?"

Thorpe arose and kissed her tenderly. He was extremely sorry that he could not spend the summer with his sister, but he believed likewise that their future depended to a great extent on this very trip. But he did not say so.

"I can't, little girl; that's all. We've got our way to make."

She understood that he considered the trip too expensive for them both. At this moment a paper fluttered from the excelsior. She picked it up. A glance showed her a total of figures that made her gasp.

"Here is your bill," she said with a strange choke in her voice, and left the room.

"He can spend sixty dollars on his old guns; but he can't afford to let me leave this hateful house," she complained to the apple tree. "He can go 'way off camping somewhere to have a good time, but he leaves me sweltering in this miserable little town all summer. I don't care if he IS supporting me. He ought to. He's my brother. Oh, I wish I were a man; I wish I were dead!"

Three days later Thorpe left for the north. He was reluctant to go. When the time came, he attempted to kiss Helen good-by. She caught sight of the rifle in its new leather and canvas case, and on a sudden impulse which she could not explain to herself, she turned away her face and ran into the house. Thorpe, vaguely hurt, a little resentful, as the genuinely misunderstood are apt to be, hesitated a moment, then trudged down the street. Helen too paused at the door, choking back her grief.

"Harry! Harry!" she cried wildly; but it was too late.

Both felt themselves to be in the right. Each realized this fact in the other. Each recognized the impossibility of imposing his own point of view over the other's.

## PART II. THE LANDLOOKER

### Chapter XVI

In every direction the woods. Not an opening of any kind offered the mind a breathing place under the free sky. Sometimes the pine groves,—vast, solemn, grand, with the patrician aloofness of the truly great; sometimes the hardwood,—bright, mysterious, full of life; sometimes the swamps,—dark, dank, speaking with the voices of the shyer creatures; sometimes the spruce and balsam thickets,—aromatic, enticing. But never the clear, open sky.

And always the woods creatures, in startling abundance and tameness. The solitary man with the packstraps across his forehead and shoulders had never seen so many of them. They withdrew silently before him as he advanced. They accompanied him on either side, watching him with intelligent, bright eyes. They followed him stealthily for a little distance, as though escorting him out of their own particular territory. Dozens of times a day the traveller glimpsed the flaunting white flags of deer. Often the creatures would take but a few hasty jumps, and then would wheel, the beautiful embodiments of the picture deer, to snort and paw the leaves. Hundreds of birds, of which he did not know the name, stooped to his inspection, whirred away at his approach, or went about their business with hardy indifference under his very eyes. Blase porcupines trundled superbly from his path. Once a mother-partridge simulated a broken wing, fluttering painfully. Early one morning the traveller ran plump on a fat lolling bear, taking his ease from the new sun, and his meal from a panic stricken army of ants. As beseemed two innocent wayfarers they honored each other with a salute of surprise, and went their way. And all about and through, weaving, watching, moving like spirits, were the forest multitudes which the young man never saw, but which he divined, and of whose movements he sometimes caught for a single instant the faintest patter or rustle. It constituted the mystery of the forest, that great fascinating, lovable mystery which, once it steals into the heart of a man, has always a hearing and a longing when it makes its voice heard.

The young man's equipment was simple in the extreme. Attached to a heavy leather belt of cartridges hung a two-pound ax and a sheath knife. In his pocket reposed a compass, an air-tight tin of matches, and a map drawn on oiled paper of a district divided into sections. Some few of the sections were colored, which indicated that they belonged to private parties. All the rest was State or Government land. He carried in his hand a repeating rifle. The pack, if opened, would have been found to contain a woolen and a rubber blanket, fishing tackle, twenty pounds or so of flour, a package of tea, sugar, a slab of bacon carefully wrapped in oiled cloth, salt, a suit of underwear, and several extra pairs of thick stockings. To the outside of the pack had been strapped a frying pan, a tin pail, and a cup.

For more than a week Thorpe had journeyed through the forest without meeting a human being, or seeing any indications of man, excepting always the old blaze of the government survey. Many years before, officials had run careless lines through the country along the section-boundaries. At this time the blazes were so weather-beaten that Thorpe often found difficulty in deciphering the indications marked on them. These latter stated always the section, the township, and the range east or west by number. All Thorpe had to do was to find the same figures on his map. He knew just where he was. By means of his compass he could lay his course to any point that suited his convenience.

The map he had procured at the United States Land Office in Detroit. He had set out with the scanty equipment just described for the purpose of "looking" a suitable bunch of pine in the northern peninsula, which, at that time, was practically untouched. Access to its interior could be obtained only on foot or by river. The South Shore Railroad was already engaged in pushing a way through the virgin forest, but it had as yet penetrated only as far as Seney; and after all, had been projected more with the idea of establishing a direct route to Duluth and the copper districts than to aid the lumber industry. Marquette, Menominee, and a few smaller places along the coast were lumbering near at home; but they shipped entirely by water. Although the rest of the peninsula also was finely wooded, a general impression obtained among the craft that it would prove too inaccessible for successful operation.

Furthermore, at that period, a great deal of talk was believed as to the inexhaustibility of Michigan pine. Men in a position to know what they were talking about stated dogmatically that the forests of the southern peninsula would be adequate for a great many years to come. Furthermore, the magnificent timber of the Saginaw, Muskegon, and Grand River valleys in the southern peninsula occupied entire attention. No one cared to bother about property at so great a distance from home. As a consequence, few as yet knew even the extent of the resources so far north.

Thorpe, however, with the far-sightedness of the born pioneer, had perceived that the exploitation of the upper country was an affair of a few years only.

The forests of southern Michigan were vast, but not limitless, and they had all passed into private ownership. The north, on the other hand, would not prove as inaccessible as it now seemed, for the carrying trade would some day realize that the entire waterway of the Great Lakes offered an unrivalled outlet. With that elementary discovery would begin a rush to the new country. Tiring of a profitless employment further south he resolved to anticipate it, and by acquiring his holdings before general attention should be turned that way, to obtain of the best.

He was without money, and practically without friends; while Government and State lands cost respectively two dollars and a half and a dollar and a quarter an acre, cash down. But he relied on the good sense of capitalists to perceive, from the statistics which his explorations would furnish, the wonderful advantage of logging a new country with the chain of Great Lakes as shipping outlet at its very door. In return for his information, he would expect a half interest in the enterprise. This is the usual method of procedure adopted by landlookers everywhere.

We have said that the country was quite new to logging, but the statement is not strictly accurate. Thorpe was by no means the first to see the money in northern pine. Outside the big mill districts already named, cuttings of considerable size were already under way, the logs from which were usually sold to the mills of Marquette or Menominee. Here and there along the best streams, men had already begun operations.

But they worked on a small scale and with an eye to the immediate present only; bending their efforts to as large a cut as possible each season rather than to the acquisition of holdings for future operations. This they accomplished naively by purchasing one forty and cutting a dozen. Thorpe's map showed often near the forks of an important stream a section whose coloring indicated private possession. Legally the owners had the right only to the pine included in the marked sections; but if anyone had taken the trouble to visit the district, he would have found operations going on for miles up and down stream. The colored squares would prove to be nothing but so many excuses for being on the ground. The bulk of the pine of any season's cut he would discover had been stolen from unbought State or Government land.

This in the old days was a common enough trick. One man, at present a wealthy and respected citizen, cut for six years, and owned just one forty-acres! Another logged nearly fifty million feet from an eighty! In the State to-day live prominent business men, looked upon as models in every way, good fellows, good citizens, with sons and daughters proud of their social position, who, nevertheless, made the bulk of their fortunes by stealing Government pine.

"What you want to-day, old man?" inquired a wholesale lumber dealer of an individual whose name now stands for domestic and civic virtue.

"I'll have five or six million saw logs to sell you in the spring, and I want to know what you'll give for them."

"Go on!" expostulated the dealer with a laugh, "ain't you got that forty all cut yet?"

"She holds out pretty well," replied the other with a grin.

An official, called the Inspector, is supposed to report such stealings, after which another official is to prosecute. Aside from the fact that the danger of discovery is practically zero in so wild and distant a country, it is fairly well established that the old-time logger found these two individuals susceptible to the gentle art of "sugaring." The officials, as well as the lumberman, became rich. If worst came to worst, and investigation seemed imminent, the operator could still purchase the land at legal rates, and so escape trouble. But the intention to appropriate was there, and, to confess the truth, the whitewashing by purchase needed but rarely to be employed. I have time and again heard landlookers assert that the old Land Offices were rarely "on the square," but as to that I cannot, of course, venture an opinion.

Thorpe was perfectly conversant with this state of affairs. He knew, also, that in all probability many of the colored districts on his map represented firms engaged in steals of greater or less magnitude. He was further aware that most of the concerns stole the timber because it was cheaper to steal than to buy; but that they would buy readily enough if forced to do so in order to prevent its acquisition by another. This other might be himself. In his exploration, therefore, he decided to employ the utmost circumspection. As much as possible he purposed to avoid other men; but if meetings became inevitable, he hoped to mask his real intentions. He would pose as a hunter and fisherman.

During the course of his week in the woods, he discovered that he would be forced eventually to resort to this expedient. He encountered quantities of fine timber in the country through which he travelled, and some day it would be logged, but at present the difficulties were too great. The streams were shallow, or they did not empty into a good shipping port. Investors would naturally look first for holdings along the more practicable routes.

A cursory glance sufficed to show that on such waters the little red squares had already blocked a foothold for other owners. Thorpe surmised that he would undoubtedly discover fine unbought timber along their banks, but that the men already engaged in stealing it would hardly be likely to allow him peaceful acquisition.

For a week, then, he journeyed through magnificent timber without finding what he sought, working always more and more to the north, until finally he stood on the shores of Superior. Up to now the streams had not suited him. He resolved to follow the shore west to the mouth of a fairly large river called the Ossawinamakee.* It showed, in common with most streams of its size, land already taken, but Thorpe hoped to find good timber nearer the mouth. After several days' hard walking with this object in view, he found himself directly north of a bend in the river; so, without troubling to hunt for its outlet into Superior, he turned through the woods due south, with the intention of striking in on the stream. This he succeeded in accomplishing some twenty miles inland, where also he discovered a well-defined and recently used trail leading up the river. Thorpe camped one night at the bend, and then set out to follow the trail.

*Accent the last syllable.*

It led him for upwards of ten miles nearly due south, sometimes approaching, sometimes leaving the river, but keeping always in its direction. The country in general was rolling. Low parallel ridges of gentle declivity glided constantly across his way, their valleys sloping to the river. Thorpe had never seen a grander forest of pine than that which clothed them.

For almost three miles, after the young man had passed through a preliminary jungle of birch, cedar, spruce, and hemlock, it ran without a break, clear, clean, of cloud-sweeping altitude, without underbrush. Most of it was good bull-sap, which is known by the fineness of the bark, though often in the hollows it shaded gradually into the rough-skinned cork pine. In those days few people paid any attention to the Norway, and hemlock was not even thought of. With every foot of the way Thorpe became more and more impressed.

At first the grandeur, the remoteness, the solemnity of the virgin forest fell on his spirit with a kind of awe. The tall, straight trunks lifted directly upwards to the vaulted screen through which the sky seemed as remote as the ceiling of a Roman church. Ravens wheeled and croaked in the blue, but infinitely far away. Some lesser noises wove into the stillness without breaking the web of its splendor, for the pine silence laid soft, hushing fingers on the lips of those who might waken the sleeping sunlight.

Then the spirit of the pioneer stirred within his soul. The wilderness sent forth its old-time challenge to the hardy. In him awoke that instinct which, without itself perceiving the end on which it is bent, clears the way for the civilization that has been ripening in old-world hot-houses during a thousand years. Men must eat; and so the soil must be made productive. We regret, each after his manner, the passing of the Indian, the buffalo, the great pine forests, for they are of the picturesque; but we live gladly on the product of the farms that have taken their places. Southern Michigan was once a pine forest: now the twisted stump-fences about the most fertile farms of the north alone break the expanse of prairie and of trim "wood-lots."

Thorpe knew little of this, and cared less. These feathered trees, standing close-ranked and yet each isolate in the dignity and gravity of a sphinx of stone set to dancing his blood of the frontiersman. He spread out his map to make sure that so valuable a clump of timber remained still unclaimed. A few sections lying near the headwaters were all he found marked as sold. He resumed his tramp light-heartedly.

At the ten-mile point he came upon a dam. It was a crude dam,—built of logs,—whose face consisted of strong buttresses slanted up-stream, and whose sheer was made of unbarked timbers laid smoothly side by side at the required angle. At present its gate was open. Thorpe could see that it was an unusually large gate, with a powerful apparatus for the raising and the lowering of it.

The purpose of the dam in this new country did not puzzle him in the least, but its presence bewildered him. Such constructions are often thrown across logging streams at proper intervals in order that the operator may be independent of the spring freshets. When he wishes to "drive" his logs to the mouth of the stream, he first accumulates a head of water behind his dams, and then, by lifting the gates, creates an artificial freshet sufficient to float his timber to the pool formed by the next dam below. The device is common enough; but it is expensive. People do not build dams except in the certainty of some years of logging, and quite extensive logging at that. If the stream happens to be navigable, the promoter must first get an Improvement Charter from a board of control appointed by the State. So Thorpe knew that he had to deal, not with a hand-to-mouth-timber-thief, but with a great company preparing to log the country on a big scale.

He continued his journey. At noon he came to another and similar structure. The pine forest had yielded to knolls of hardwood separated by swamp-holes of blackthorn. Here he left his pack and pushed ahead in light marching order. About eight miles above the first dam, and eighteen from the bend of the river, he ran into a "slashing" of the year before. The decapitated stumps were already beginning to turn brown with weather, the tangle of tops and limbs was partially concealed by poplar growths and wild raspberry vines. Parenthetically, it may be remarked that the promptitude with which these growths succeed the cutting of the pine is an inexplicable marvel. Clear forty acres at random in the very center of a pine forest, without a tract of poplar within an hundred miles; the next season will bring up the fresh shoots. Some claim that blue jays bring the seeds in their crops. Others incline to the theory that the creative elements lie dormant in the soil, needing only the sun to start them to life. Final speculation is impossible, but the fact stands.

To Thorpe this particular clearing became at once of the greatest interest. He scrambled over and through the ugly debris which for a year or two after logging operations cumbers the ground. By a rather prolonged search he found what he sought,—the "section corners" of the tract, on which the government surveyor had long ago marked the "descriptions." A glance at the map confirmed his suspicions. The slashing lay some two miles north of the sections designated as belonging to private parties. It was Government land.

Thorpe sat down, lit a pipe, and did a little thinking.

As an axiom it may be premised that the shorter the distance logs have to be transported, the less it costs to get them in. Now Thorpe had that very morning passed through beautiful timber lying much nearer the mouth of the river than either this, or the sections further south. Why had these men deliberately ascended the stream? Why had they stolen timber eighteen miles from the bend, when they could equally well have stolen just as good fourteen miles nearer the terminus of their drive?

Thorpe ruminated for some time without hitting upon a solution. Then suddenly he remembered the two dams, and his idea that the men in charge of the river must be wealthy and must intend operating on a large scale. He thought he glimpsed it. After another pipe, he felt sure.

The Unknowns were indeed going in on a large scale. They intended eventually to log the whole of the Ossawinamakee basin. For this reason they had made their first purchase, planted their first foot-hold, near the headwaters. Furthermore, located as they were far from a present or an immediately future civilization, they had felt safe in leaving for the moment their holdings represented by the three sections already described. Some day they would buy all the standing Government pine in the basin; but in the meantime they would steal all they could at a sufficient distance from the lake to minimize the danger of discovery. They had not dared to appropriate the three mile tract Thorpe had passed through, because in that locality the theft would probably be remarked, so they intended eventually to buy it. Until that should become necessary, however, every stick cut meant so much less to purchase.

"They're going to cut, and keep on cutting, working down river as fast as they can," argued Thorpe. "If anything happens so they have to, they'll buy in the pine that is left; but if things go well with them, they'll take what they can for nothing. They're getting this stuff out up-river first, because they can steal safer while the country is still unsettled; and even when it does fill up, there will not be much likelihood of an investigation so far in-country,—at least until after they have folded their tents."

It seems to us who are accustomed to the accurate policing of our twentieth century, almost incredible that such wholesale robberies should have gone on with so little danger of detection. Certainly detection was a matter of sufficient simplicity. Someone happens along, like Thorpe, carrying a Government map in his pocket. He runs across a parcel of unclaimed land already cut over. It would seem easy to lodge a complaint, institute a prosecution against the men known to have put in the timber. BUT IT IS ALMOST NEVER DONE.

Thorpe knew that men occupied in so precarious a business would be keenly on the watch. At the first hint of rivalry, they would buy in the timber they had selected. But the situation had set his fighting blood to racing. The very fact that these men were thieves on so big a scale made him the more obstinately determined to thwart them. They undoubtedly wanted the tract down river. Well, so did he!

He purposed to look it over carefully, to ascertain its exact boundaries and what sections it would be necessary to buy in order to include it, and perhaps even to estimate it in a rough way. In the accomplishment of this he would have to spend the summer, and perhaps part of the fall, in that district. He could hardly expect to escape notice. By the indications on the river, he judged that a crew of men had shortly before taken out a drive of logs. After the timber had been rafted and towed to Marquette, they would return. He might be able to hide in the forest, but sooner or later, he was sure, one of the company's landlookers or hunters would stumble on his camp. Then his very concealment would tell them what he was after. The risk was too great. For above all things Thorpe needed time. He had, as has been said, to ascertain what he could offer. Then he had to offer it. He would be forced to interest capital, and that is a matter of persuasion and leisure.

Finally his shrewd, intuitive good-sense flashed the solution on him. He returned rapidly to his pack, assumed the straps, and arrived at the first dam about dark of the long summer day.

There he looked carefully about him. Some fifty feet from the water's edge a birch knoll supported, besides the birches, a single big hemlock. With his belt ax, Thorpe cleared away the little white trees. He stuck the sharpened end of one of them in the bark of the shaggy hemlock, fastened the other end in a crotch eight or ten feet distant, slanted the rest of the saplings along one side of this ridge pole, and turned in, after a hasty supper, leaving the completion of his permanent camp to the morrow.

## Chapter XVII

In the morning he thatched smooth the roof of the shelter, using for the purpose the thick branches of hemlocks; placed two green spruce logs side by side as cooking range; slung his pot on a rod across two forked sticks; cut and split a quantity of wood; spread his blankets; and called himself established. His beard was already well grown, and his clothes had become worn by the brush and faded by the sun and rain. In the course of the morning he lay in wait very patiently near a spot overflowed by the river, where, the day before, he had noticed lily-pads growing. After a time a doe and a spotted fawn came and stood ankle-deep in the water, and ate of the lily-pads. Thorpe lurked motionless behind his screen of leaves; and as he had taken the precaution so to station himself that his hiding-place lay downwind, the beautiful animals were unaware of his presence.

By and by a prong-buck joined them. He was a two-year-old, young, tender, with the velvet just off his antlers. Thorpe aimed at his shoulder, six inches above the belly-line, and pressed the trigger. As though by enchantment the three woods creatures disappeared. But the hunter had noticed that, whereas the doe and fawn flourished bravely the broad white flags of their tails, the buck had seemed but a streak of brown. By this he knew he had hit.

Sure enough, after two hundred yards of following the prints of sharp hoofs and occasional gobbets of blood on the leaves, he came upon his prey dead. It became necessary to transport the animal to camp. Thorpe stuck his hunting knife deep into the front of the deer's chest, where the neck joins, which allowed most of the blood to drain away. Then he fastened wild grape vines about the antlers, and, with a little exertion drew the body after him as though it had been a toboggan.

It slid more easily than one would imagine, along the grain; but not as easily as by some other methods with which Thorpe was unfamiliar.

At camp he skinned the deer, cut most of the meat into thin strips which he salted and placed in the sun to dry, and hung the remainder in a cool arbor of boughs. The hide he suspended over a pole.

All these things he did hastily, as though he might be in a hurry; as indeed he was.

At noon he cooked himself a venison steak and some tea. Then with his hatchet he cut several small pine poles, which he fashioned roughly in a number of shapes and put aside for the future. The brains of the deer, saved for the purpose, he boiled with water in his tin pail, wishing it were larger. With the liquor thus obtained he intended later to remove the hair and grain from the deer hide. Toward evening he caught a dozen trout in the pool below the dam. These he ate for supper.

Next day he spread the buck's hide out on the ground and drenched it liberally with the product of deer-brains. Later the hide was soaked in the river, after which, by means of a rough two-handled spatula, Thorpe was enabled after much labor to scrape away entirely the hair and grain. He cut from the edge of the hide a number of long strips of raw-hide, but anointed the body of the skin liberally with the brain liquor.

"Glad I don't have to do that every day!" he commented, wiping his brow with the back of his wrist.

As the skin dried he worked and kneaded it to softness. The result was a fair quality of white buckskin, the first Thorpe had ever made. If wetted, it would harden dry and stiff. Thorough smoking in the fumes of punk maple would obviate this, but that detail Thorpe left until later.

"I don't know whether it's all necessary," he said to himself doubtfully, "but if you're going to assume a disguise, let it be a good one."

In the meantime, he had bound together with his rawhide thongs several of the oddly shaped pine timbers to form a species of dead-fall trap. It was slow work, for Thorpe's knowledge of such things was theoretical. He had learned his theory well, however, and in the end arrived.

All this time he had made no effort to look over the pine, nor did he intend to begin until he could be sure of doing so in safety. His object now was to give his knoll the appearances of a trapper's camp.

Towards the end of the week he received his first visit. Evening was drawing on, and Thorpe was busily engaged in cooking a panful of trout, resting the frying pan across the two green spruce logs between which glowed the coals. Suddenly he became aware of a presence at his side. How it had reached the spot he could not imagine, for he had heard no approach. He looked up quickly.

"How do," greeted the newcomer gravely.

The man was an Indian, silent, solemn, with the straight, unwinking gaze of his race.

"How do," replied Thorpe.

The Indian without further ceremony threw his pack to the ground, and, squatting on his heels, watched the white man's preparations. When the meal was cooked, he coolly produced a knife, selected a clean bit of hemlock bark, and helped himself. Then he lit a pipe, and gazed keenly about him. The buckskin interested him.

"No good," said he, feeling of its texture.

Thorpe laughed. "Not very," he confessed.

"Good," continued the Indian, touching lightly his own moccasins.

"What you do?" he inquired after a long silence, punctuated by the puffs of tobacco.

"Hunt; trap; fish," replied Thorpe with equal sententiousness.

"Good," concluded the Indian, after a ruminative pause.

That night he slept on the ground. Next day he made a better shelter than Thorpe's in less than half the time; and was off hunting before the sun was an hour high. He was armed with an old-fashioned smooth-bore muzzle-loader; and Thorpe was astonished, after he had become better acquainted with his new companion's methods, to find that he hunted deer with fine bird shot. The Indian never expected to kill or even mortally wound his game; but he would follow for miles the blood drops caused by his little wounds, until the animals in sheer exhaustion allowed him to approach close enough for a dispatching blow. At two o'clock he returned with a small buck, tied scientifically together for toting, with the waste parts cut away, but every ounce of utility retained.

"I show," said the Indian:—and he did. Thorpe learned the Indian tan; of what use are the hollow shank bones; how the spinal cord is the toughest, softest, and most pliable sewing-thread known.

The Indian appeared to intend making the birch-knoll his permanent headquarters. Thorpe was at first a little suspicious of his new companion, but the man appeared scrupulously honest, was never intrusive, and even seemed genuinely desirous of teaching the white little tricks of the woods brought to their perfection by the Indian alone. He ended by liking him. The two rarely spoke. They merely sat near each other, and smoked. One evening the Indian suddenly remarked:

"You look 'um tree."

"What's that?" cried Thorpe, startled.

"You no hunter, no trapper. You look 'um tree, for make 'um lumber."

The white had not begun as yet his explorations. He did not dare until the return of the logging crew or the passing of someone in authority at the up-river camp, for he wished first to establish in their minds the innocence of his intentions.

"What makes you think that, Charley?" he asked.

"You good man in woods," replied Injin Charley sententiously, "I tell by way you look at him pine."

Thorpe ruminated.

"Charley," said he, "why are you staying here with me?"

"Big frien'," replied the Indian promptly.

"Why are you my friend? What have I ever done for you?"

"You gottum chief's eye," replied his companion with simplicity.

Thorpe looked at the Indian again. There seemed to be only one course.

"Yes, I'm a lumberman," he confessed, "and I'm looking for pine. But, Charley, the men up the river must not know what I'm after."

"They gettum pine," interjected the Indian like a flash.

"Exactly," replied Thorpe, surprised afresh at the other's perspicacity.

"Good!" ejaculated Injin Charley, and fell silent.

With this, the longest conversation the two had attempted in their peculiar acquaintance, Thorpe was forced to be content. He was, however, ill at ease over the incident. It added an element of uncertainty to an already precarious position.

Three days later he was intensely thankful the conversation had taken place.

After the noon meal he lay on his blanket under the hemlock shelter, smoking and lazily watching Injin Charley busy at the side of the trail. The Indian had terminated a long two days' search by toting from the forest a number of strips of the outer bark of white birch, in its green state pliable as cotton, thick as leather, and light as air. These he had cut into arbitrary patterns known only to himself, and was now sewing as a long shapeless sort of bag or sac to a slender beech-wood oval. Later it was to become a birch-bark canoe, and the beech-wood oval would be the gunwale.

So idly intent was Thorpe on this piece of construction that he did not notice the approach of two men from the down-stream side. They were short, alert men, plodding along with the knee-bent persistency of the woods-walker, dressed in broad hats, flannel shirts, coarse trousers tucked in high laced "cruisers "; and carrying each a bulging meal sack looped by a cord across the shoulders and chest. Both were armed with long slender scaler's rules. The first intimation Thorpe received of the presence of these two men was the sound of their voices addressing Injin Charley.

"Hullo Charley," said one of them, "what you doing here? Ain't seen you since th' Sturgeon district."

"Mak' 'um canoe," replied Charley rather obviously.

"So I see. But what you expect to get in this Godforsaken country?"

"Beaver, muskrat, mink, otter."

"Trapping, eh?" The man gazed keenly at Thorpe's recumbent figure.

"Who's the other fellow?"

Thorpe held his breath; then exhaled it in a long sigh of relief.

"Him white man," Injin Charley was replying, "him hunt too. He mak' 'um buckskin."

The landlooker arose lazily and sauntered toward the group. It was part of his plan to be well recognized so that in the future he might arouse no suspicions.

"Howdy," he drawled, "got any smokin'?"

"How are you," replied one of the scalers, eying him sharply, and tendering his pouch. Thorpe filled his pipe deliberately, and returned it with a heavy-lidded glance of thanks. To all appearances he was one of the lazy, shiftless white hunters of the backwoods. Seized with an inspiration, he said, "What sort of chances is they at your camp for a little flour? Me and Charley's about out. I'll bring you meat; or I'll make you boys moccasins. I got some good buckskin."

It was the usual proposition.

"Pretty good, I guess. Come up and see," advised the scaler. "The crew's right behind us."

"I'll send up Charley," drawled Thorpe, "I'm busy now makin' traps," he waved his pipe, calling attention to the pine and rawhide dead-falls.

They chatted a few moments, practically and with an eye to the strict utility of things about them, as became woodsmen. Then two wagons creaked lurching by, followed by fifteen or twenty men. The last of these, evidently the foreman, was joined by the two scalers.

"What's that outfit?" he inquired with the sharpness of suspicion.

"Old Injin Charley—you remember, the old boy that tanned that buck for you down on Cedar Creek."

"Yes, but the other fellow."

"Oh, a hunter," replied the scaler carelessly.

"Sure?"

The man laughed. "Couldn't be nothin' else," he asserted with confidence. "Regular old backwoods mossback."

At the same time Injin Charley was setting about the splitting of a cedar log.

"You see," he remarked, "I big frien'."

## Chapter XVIII

In the days that followed, Thorpe cruised about the great woods. It was slow business, but fascinating. He knew that when he should embark on his attempt to enlist considerable capital in an "unsight unseen" investment, he would have to be well supplied with statistics. True, he was not much of a timber estimator, nor did he know the methods usually employed, but his experience, observation, and reading had developed a latent sixth sense by which he could appreciate quality, difficulties of logging, and such kindred practical matters.

First of all he walked over the country at large, to find where the best timber lay. This was a matter of tramping; though often on an elevation he succeeded in climbing a tall tree whence he caught bird's-eye views of the country at large. He always carried his gun with him, and was prepared at a moment's notice to seem engaged in hunting,—either for game or for spots in which later to set his traps. The expedient was, however, unnecessary.

Next he ascertained the geographical location of the different clumps and forests, entering the sections, the quarter-sections, even the separate forties in his note-book; taking in only the "descriptions" containing the best pine.

Finally he wrote accurate notes concerning the topography of each and every pine district,—the lay of the land; the hills, ravines, swamps, and valleys; the distance from the river; the character of the soil. In short, he accumulated all the information he could by which the cost of logging might be estimated.

The work went much quicker than he had anticipated, mainly because he could give his entire attention to it. Injin Charley attended to the commissary, with a delight in the process that removed it from the category of work. When it rained, an infrequent occurrence, the two hung Thorpe's rubber blankets before the opening of the driest shelter, and waited philosophically for the weather to clear. Injin Charley had finished the first canoe, and was now leisurely at work on another. Thorpe had filled his note-book with the class of statistics just described. He decided now to attempt an estimate of the timber.

For this he had really too little experience. He knew it, but determined to do his best. The weak point of his whole scheme lay in that it was going to be impossible for him to allow the prospective purchaser a chance of examining the pine. That difficulty Thorpe hoped to overcome by inspiring personal confidence in himself. If he failed to do so, he might return with a landlooker whom the investor trusted, and the two could re-enact the comedy of this summer. Thorpe hoped, however, to avoid the necessity. It would be too dangerous. He set about a rough estimate of the timber.

Injin Charley intended evidently to work up a trade in buckskin during the coming winter. Although the skins were in poor condition at this time of the year, he tanned three more, and smoked them. In the day-time he looked the country over as carefully as did Thorpe. But he ignored the pines, and paid attention only to the hardwood and the beds of little creeks. Injin Charley was in reality a trapper, and he intended to get many fine skins in this promising district. He worked on his tanning and his canoe-making late in the afternoon.

One evening just at sunset Thorpe was helping the Indian shape his craft. The loose sac of birch-bark sewed to the long beech oval was slung between two tripods. Injin Charley had fashioned a number of thin, flexible cedar strips of certain arbitrary lengths and widths. Beginning with the smallest of these, Thorpe and his companion were catching one end under the beech oval, bending the strip bow-shape inside the sac, and catching again the other side of the oval. Thus the spring of the bent cedar, pressing against the inside of the birch-bark sac, distended it tightly. The cut of the sac and the length of the cedar strips gave to the canoe its graceful shape.

The two men bent there at their task, the dull glow of evening falling upon them. Behind them the knoll stood out in picturesque relief against the darker pine, the little shelters, the fire-places of green spruce, the blankets, the guns, a deer's carcass suspended by the feet from a cross pole, the drying buckskin on either side. The river rushed by with a never-ending roar and turmoil. Through its shouting one perceived, as through a mist, the still lofty peace of evening.

A young fellow, hardly more than a boy, exclaimed with keen delight of the picturesque as his canoe shot around the bend into sight of it.

The canoe was large and powerful, but well filled. An Indian knelt in the stern; amidships was well laden with duffle of all descriptions; then the young fellow sat in the bow. He was a bright-faced, eager-eyed, curly-haired young fellow, all enthusiasm and fire. His figure was trim and clean, but rather slender; and his movements were quick but nervous. When he stepped carefully out on the flat rock to which his guide brought the canoe with a swirl of the paddle, one initiated would have seen that his clothes, while strong and serviceable, had been bought from a sporting catalogue. There was a trimness, a neatness, about them.

"This is a good place," he said to the guide, "we'll camp here." Then he turned up the steep bank without looking back.

"Hullo!" he called in a cheerful, unembarrassed fashion to Thorpe and Charley. "How are you? Care if I camp here? What you making? By Jove! I never saw a canoe made before. I'm going to watch you. Keep right at it."

He sat on one of the outcropping boulders and took off his hat.

"Say! you've got a great place here! You here all summer? Hullo! you've got a deer hanging up. Are there many of 'em around here? I'd like to kill a deer first rate. I never have. It's sort of out of season now, isn't it?"

"We only kill the bucks," replied Thorpe.

"I like fishing, too," went on the boy; "are there any here? In the pool? John," he called to his guide, "bring me my fishing tackle."

In a few moments he was whipping the pool with long, graceful drops of the fly. He proved to be adept. Thorpe and Injin Charley stopped work to watch him. At first the Indian's stolid countenance seemed a trifle doubtful. After a time it cleared.

"Good! he grunted.

"You do that well," Thorpe remarked. "Is it difficult?"

"It takes practice," replied the boy. "See that riffle?" He whipped the fly lightly within six inches of a little suction hole; a fish at once rose and struck.

The others had been little fellows and easily handled. At the end of fifteen minutes the newcomer landed a fine two-pounder.

"That must be fun," commented Thorpe. "I never happened to get in with fly-fishing. I'd like to try it sometime."

"Try it now!" urged the boy, enchanted that he could teach a woodsman anything.

"No," Thorpe declined, "not to-night, to-morrow perhaps."

The other Indian had by now finished the erection of a tent, and had begun to cook supper over a little sheet-iron camp stove. Thorpe and Charley could smell ham.

"You've got quite a pantry," remarked Thorpe.

"Won't you eat with me?" proffered the boy hospitably.

But Thorpe declined. He could, however, see canned goods, hard tack, and condensed milk.

In the course of the evening the boy approached the older man's camp, and, with a charming diffidence, asked permission to sit awhile at their fire.

He was full of delight over everything that savored of the woods, or woodscraft. The most trivial and everyday affairs of the life interested him. His eager questions, so frankly proffered, aroused even the taciturn Charley to eloquence. The construction of the shelter, the cut of a deer's hide, the simple process of "jerking" venison,—all these awakened his enthusiasm.

"It must be good to live in the woods," he said with a sigh, "to do all things for yourself. It's so free!"

The men's moccasins interested him. He asked a dozen questions about them,—how they were cut, whether they did not hurt the feet, how long they would wear. He seemed surprised to learn that they are excellent in cold weather.

"I thought ANY leather would wet through in the snow!" he cried. "I wish I could get a pair somewhere!" he exclaimed. "You don't know where I could buy any, do you?" he asked of Thorpe.

"I don't know," answered he, "perhaps Charley here will make you a pair."

"WILL you, Charley?" cried the boy.

"I mak' him," replied the Indian stolidly.

The many-voiced night of the woods descended close about the little camp fire, and its soft breezes wafted stray sparks here and there like errant stars. The newcomer, with shining eyes, breathed deep in satisfaction. He was keenly alive to the romance, the grandeur, the mystery, the beauty of the littlest things, seeming to derive a deep and solid contentment from the mere contemplation of the woods and its ways and creatures.

"I just DO love this!" he cried again and again. "Oh, it's great, after all that fuss down there!" and he cried it so fervently that the other men present smiled; but so genuinely that the smile had in it nothing but kindliness.

"I came out for a month," said he suddenly, "and I guess I'll stay the rest of it right here. You'll let me go with you sometimes hunting, won't you?" he appealed to them with the sudden open-heartedness of a child. "I'd like first rate to kill a deer."

"Sure," said Thorpe, "glad to have you."

"My name is Wallace Carpenter," said the boy with a sudden unmistakable air of good-breeding.

"Well," laughed Thorpe, "two old woods loafers like us haven't got much use for names. Charley here is called Geezigut, and mine's nearly as bad; but I guess plain Charley and Harry will do."

"All right, Harry," replied Wallace.

After the young fellow had crawled into the sleeping bag which his guide had spread for him over a fragrant layer of hemlock and balsam, Thorpe and his companion smoked one more pipe. The whip-poor-wills called back and forth across the river. Down in the thicket, fine, clear, beautiful, like the silver thread of a dream, came the notes of the white-throat—the nightingale of the North. Injin Charley knocked the last ashes from his pipe.

"Him nice boy!" said he.

### Chapter XIX

The young fellow stayed three weeks, and was a constant joy to Thorpe. His enthusiasms were so whole-souled; his delight so perpetual; his interest so fresh! The most trivial expedients of woods lore seemed to him wonderful. A dozen times a day he exclaimed in admiration or surprise over some bit of woodcraft practiced by Thorpe or one of the Indians.

"Do you mean to say you have lived here six weeks and only brought in what you could carry on your backs!" he cried.

"Sure," Thorpe replied.

"Harry, you're wonderful! I've got a whole canoe load, and imagined I was travelling light and roughing it. You beat Robinson Crusoe! He had a whole ship to draw from."

"My man Friday helps me out," answered Thorpe, laughingly indicating Injin Charley.

Nearly a week passed before Wallace managed to kill a deer. The animals were plenty enough; but the young man's volatile and eager attention stole his patience. And what few running shots offered, he missed, mainly because of buck fever. Finally, by a lucky chance, he broke a four-year-old's neck, dropping him in his tracks. The hunter was delighted. He insisted on doing everything for himself—cruel hard work it was too—including the toting and skinning. Even the tanning he had a share in. At first he wanted the hide cured, "with the hair on." Injin Charley explained that the fur would drop out. It was the wrong season of the year for pelts.

"Then we'll have buckskin and I'll get a buckskin shirt out of it," suggested Wallace.

Injin Charley agreed. One day Wallace returned from fishing in the pool to find that the Indian had cut out the garment, and was already sewing it together.

"Oh!" he cried, a little disappointed, "I wanted to see it done!"

Injin Charley merely grunted. To make a buckskin shirt requires the hides of three deer. Charley had supplied the other two, and wished to keep the young man from finding it out.

Wallace assumed the woods life as a man would assume an unaccustomed garment. It sat him well, and he learned fast, but he was always conscious of it. He liked to wear moccasins, and a deer knife; he liked to cook his own supper, or pluck the fragrant hemlock browse for his pillow. Always he seemed to be trying to realize and to savor fully the charm, the picturesqueness, the romance of all that he was doing and seeing. To Thorpe these things were a part of everyday life; matters of expedient or necessity. He enjoyed them, but subconsciously, as one enjoys an environment. Wallace trailed the cloak of his glories in frank admiration of their splendor.

This double point of view brought the men very close together. Thorpe liked the boy because he was open-hearted, free from affectation, assumptive of no superiority,—in short, because he was direct and sincere, although in a manner totally different from Thorpe's own directness and sincerity. Wallace, on his part, adored in Thorpe the free, open-air life, the adventurous quality, the quiet hidden power, the resourcefulness and self-sufficiency of the pioneer. He was too young as yet to go behind the picturesque or romantic; so he never thought to inquire of himself what Thorpe did there in the wilderness, or indeed if he did anything at all. He accepted Thorpe for what he thought him to be, rather than for what he might think him to be. Thus he reposed unbounded confidence in him.

After a while, observing the absolute ingenuousness of the boy, Thorpe used to take him from time to time on some of his daily trips to the pines. Necessarily he explained partially his position and the need of secrecy. Wallace was immensely excited and important at learning a secret of such moment, and deeply flattered at being entrusted with it.

Some may think that here, considering the magnitude of the interests involved, Thorpe committed an indiscretion. It may be; but if so, it was practically an inevitable indiscretion. Strong, reticent characters like Thorpe's prove the need from time to time of violating their own natures, of running counter to their ordinary habits of mind and deed. It is a necessary relaxation of the strenuous, a debauch of the soul. Its analogy in the lower plane is to be found in the dissipations of men of genius; or still lower in the orgies of fighters out of training. Sooner or later Thorpe was sure to emerge for a brief space from that iron-bound silence of the spirit, of which he himself was the least aware. It was not so much a hunger for affection, as the desire of a strong man temporarily to get away from his strength. Wallace Carpenter became in his case the exception to prove the rule.

Little by little the eager questionings of the youth extracted a full statement of the situation. He learned of the timber-thieves up the river, of their present operations; and their probable plans; of the valuable pine lying still unclaimed; of Thorpe's stealthy raid into the enemy's country. It looked big to him, epic!—These were tremendous forces in motion, here was intrigue, here was direct practical application of the powers he had been playing with.

"Why, it's great! It's better than any book I ever read!"

He wanted to know what he could do to help.

"Nothing except keep quiet," replied Thorpe, already uneasy, not lest the boy should prove unreliable, but lest his very eagerness to seem unconcerned should arouse suspicion. "You mustn't try to act any different. If the men from up-river come by, be just as cordial to them as you can, and don't act mysterious and important."

"All right," agreed Wallace, bubbling with excitement. "And then what do you do—after you get the timber estimated?"

"I'll go South and try, quietly, to raise some money. That will be difficult, because, you see, people don't know me; and I am not in a position to let them look over the timber. Of course it will be merely a question of my judgment. They can go themselves to the Land Office and pay their money. There won't be any chance of my making way with that. The investors will become possessed of certain 'descriptions' lying in this country, all right enough. The rub is, will they have enough confidence in me and my judgment to believe the timber to be what I represent it?"

"I see," commented Wallace, suddenly grave.

That evening Injin Charley went on with his canoe building. He melted together in a pot, resin and pitch. The proportion he determined by experiment, for the mixture had to be neither hard enough to crack nor soft enough to melt in the sun. Then he daubed the mess over all the seams. Wallace superintended the operation for a time in silence.

"Harry," he said suddenly with a crisp decision new to his voice, "will you take a little walk with me down by the dam. I want to talk with you."

They strolled to the edge of the bank and stood for a moment looking at the swirling waters.

"I want you to tell me all about logging," began Wallace. "Start from the beginning. Suppose, for instance, you had bought this pine here we were talking about,—what would be your first move?"

They sat side by side on a log, and Thorpe explained. He told of the building of the camps, the making of the roads; the cutting, swamping, travoying, skidding; the banking and driving. Unconsciously a little of the battle clang crept into his narrative. It became a struggle, a gasping tug and heave for supremacy between the man and the wilderness. The excitement of war was in it. When he had finished, Wallace drew a deep breath.

"When I am home," said he simply, "I live in a big house on the Lake Shore Drive. It is heated by steam and lighted by electricity. I touch a button or turn a screw, and at once I am lighted and warmed. At certain hours meals are served me. I don't know how they are cooked, or where the materials come from. Since leaving college I have spent a little time down town every day; and then I've played golf or tennis or ridden a horse in the park. The only real thing left is the sailing. The wind blows just as hard and the waves mount just as high to-day as they did when Drake sailed. All the rest is tame. We do little imitations of the real thing with blue ribbons tied to them, and think we are camping or roughing it. This life of yours is glorious, is vital, it means something in the march of the world;—and I doubt whether ours does. You are subduing the wilderness, extending the frontier. After you will come the backwoods farmer to pull up the stumps, and after him the big farmer and the cities."

The young follow spoke with unexpected swiftness and earnestness. Thorpe looked at him in surprise.

"I know what you are thinking," said the boy, flushing. "You are surprised that I can be in earnest about anything. I'm out of school up here. Let me shout and play with the rest of the children."

Thorpe watched him with sympathetic eyes, but with lips that obstinately refused to say one word. A woman would have felt rebuffed. The boy's admiration, however, rested on the foundation of the more manly qualities he had already seen in his friend. Perhaps this very aloofness, this very silent, steady-eyed power appealed to him.

"I left college at nineteen because my father died," said he. "I am now just twenty-one. A large estate descended to me, and I have had to care for its investments all alone. I have one sister, that is all."

"So have I," cried Thorpe, and stopped.

"The estates have not suffered," went on the boy simply. "I have done well with them. But," he cried fiercely, "I HATE it! It is petty and mean and worrying and nagging! That's why I was so glad to get out in the woods."

He paused.

"Have some tobacco," said Thorpe.

Wallace accepted with a nod.

"Now, Harry, I have a proposal to make to you. It is this; you need thirty thousand dollars to buy your land. Let me supply it, and come in as half partner."

An expression of doubt crossed the landlooker's face.

"Oh PLEASE!" cried the boy, "I do want to get in something real! It will be the making of me!"

"Now see here," interposed Thorpe suddenly, "you don't even know my name."

"I know YOU," replied the boy.

"My name is Harry Thorpe," pursued the other. "My father was Henry Thorpe, an embezzler."

"Harry," replied Wallace soberly, "I am sorry I made you say that. I do not care for your name—except perhaps to put it in the articles of partnership,—and I have no concern with your ancestry. I tell you it is a favor to let me in on this deal. I don't know anything about lumbering, but I've got eyes. I can see that big timber standing up thick and tall, and I know people make profits in the business. It isn't a question of the raw material surely, and you have experience."

"Not so much as you think," interposed Thorpe.

"There remains," went on Wallace without attention to Thorpe's remark, "only the question of—"

"My honesty," interjected Thorpe grimly.

"No!" cried the boy hotly, "of your letting me in on a good thing!"

Thorpe considered a few moments in silence.

"Wallace," he said gravely at last, "I honestly do think that whoever goes into this deal with me will make money. Of course there's always chances against it. But I am going to do my best. I've seen other men fail at it, and the reason they've failed is because they did not demand success of others and of themselves. That's it; success! When a general commanding troops receives a report on something he's ordered done, he does not trouble himself with excuses;—he merely asks whether or not the thing was accomplished. Difficulties don't count. It is a soldier's duty to perform the impossible. Well, that's the way it ought to be with us. A man has no right to come to me and say, 'I failed because such and such things happened.' Either he should succeed in spite of it all; or he should step up and take his medicine without whining. Well, I'm going to succeed!"

The man's accustomed aloofness had gone. His eye flashed, his brow frowned, the muscles of his cheeks contracted under his beard. In the bronze light of evening he looked like a fire-breathing statue to that great ruthless god he had himself invoked,—Success.

Wallace gazed at him with fascinated admiration.

"Then you will?" he asked tremulously.

"Wallace," he replied again, "they'll say you have been the victim of an adventurer, but the result will prove them wrong. If I weren't perfectly sure of this, I wouldn't think of it, for I like you, and I know you want to go into this more out of friendship for me and because your imagination is touched, than from any business sense. But I'll accept, gladly. And I'll do my best!"

"Hooray!" cried the boy, throwing his cap up in the air. "We'll do 'em up in the first round!"

At last when Wallace Carpenter reluctantly quitted his friends on the Ossawinamakee, he insisted on leaving with them a variety of the things he had brought.

"I'm through with them," said he. "Next time I come up here we'll have a camp of our own, won't we, Harry? And I do feel that I am awfully in you fellows' debt. You've given me the best time I have ever had in my life, and you've refused payment for the moccasins and things you've made for me. I'd feel much better if you'd accept them,—just as keepsakes."

"All right, Wallace," replied Thorpe, "and much obliged."

"Don't forget to come straight to me when you get through estimating, now, will you? Come to the house and stay. Our compact holds now, honest Injin; doesn't it?" asked the boy anxiously.

"Honest Injin," laughed Thorpe. "Good-by."

The little canoe shot away down the current. The last Injin Charley and Thorpe saw of the boy was as he turned the curve. His hat was off and waving in his hand, his curls were blowing in the breeze, his eyes sparkled with bright good-will, and his lips parted in a cheery halloo of farewell.

"Him nice boy," repeated Injin Charley, turning to his canoe.

## Chapter XX

Thus Thorpe and the Indian unexpectedly found themselves in the possession of luxury. The outfit had not meant much to Wallace Carpenter, for he had bought it in the city, where such things are abundant and excite no remark; but to the woodsman each article possessed a separate and particular value. The tent, an iron kettle, a side of bacon, oatmeal, tea, matches, sugar, some canned goods, a box of hard-tack,—these, in the woods, represented wealth. Wallace's rifle chambered the .38 Winchester cartridge, which was unfortunate, for Thorpe's .44 had barely a magazineful left.

The two men settled again into their customary ways of life. Things went much as before, except that the flies and mosquitoes became thick. To men as hardened as Thorpe and the Indian, these pests were not as formidable as they would have been to anyone directly from the city, but they were sufficiently annoying. Thorpe's old tin pail was pressed into service as a smudge-kettle. Every evening about dusk, when the insects first began to emerge from the dark swamps, Charley would build a tiny smoky fire in the bottom of the pail, feeding it with peat, damp moss, punk maple, and other inflammable smoky fuel. This censer swung twice or thrice about the tent, effectually cleared it. Besides, both men early established on their cheeks an invulnerable glaze of a decoction of pine tar, oil, and a pungent herb. Towards the close of July, however, the insects began sensibly to diminish, both in numbers and persistency.

Up to the present Thorpe had enjoyed a clear field. Now two men came down from above and established a temporary camp in the woods half a mile below the dam. Thorpe soon satisfied himself that they were picking out a route for the logging road. Plenty which could be cut and travoyed directly to the banking ground lay exactly along the bank of the stream; but every logger possessed of a tract of timber tries each year to get in some that is easy to handle and some that is difficult. Thus the average of expense is maintained.

The two men, of course, did not bother themselves with the timber to be travoyed, but gave their entire attention to that lying further back. Thorpe was enabled thus to avoid them entirely. He simply transferred his estimating to the forest by the stream. Once he met one of the men; but was fortunately in a country that lent itself to his pose of hunter. The other he did not see at all.

But one day he heard him. The two up-river men were following carefully but noisily the bed of a little creek. Thorpe happened to be on the side-hill, so he seated himself quietly until they should have moved on down. One of the men shouted to the other, who, crashing through a thicket, did not hear. "Ho-o-o! DYER!" the first repeated. "Here's that infernal comer; over here!"

"Yop!" assented the other. "Coming!"

Thorpe recognized the voice instantly as that of Radway's scaler. His hand crisped in a gesture of disgust. The man had always been obnoxious to him.

Two days later he stumbled on their camp. He paused in wonder at what he saw.

The packs lay open, their contents scattered in every direction. The fire had been hastily extinguished with a bucket of water, and a frying pan lay where it had been overturned. If the thing had been possible, Thorpe would have guessed at a hasty and unpremeditated flight.

He was about to withdraw carefully lest he be discovered, when he was startled by a touch on his elbow. It was Injin Charley.

"Dey go up river," he said. "I come see what de row."

The Indian examined rapidly the condition of the little camp.

"Dey look for somethin'," said he, making his hand revolve as though rummaging, and indicating the packs.

"I t'ink dey see you in de woods," he concluded. "Dey go camp gettum boss. Boss he gone on river trail two t'ree hour."

"You're right, Charley," replied Thorpe, who had been drawing his own conclusions. "One of them knows me. They've been looking in their packs for their note-books with the descriptions of these sections in them. Then they piled out for the boss. If I know anything at all, the boss'll make tracks for Detroit."

367

"W'ot you do?" asked Injin Charley curiously.

"I got to get to Detroit before they do; that's all."

Instantly the Indian became all action.

"You come," he ordered, and set out at a rapid pace for camp.

There, with incredible deftness, he packed together about twelve pounds of the jerked venison and a pair of blankets, thrust Thorpe's waterproof match safe in his pocket, and turned eagerly to the young man.

"You come," he repeated.

Thorpe hastily unearthed his "descriptions" and wrapped them up. The Indian, in silence, rearranged the displaced articles in such a manner as to relieve the camp of its abandoned air.

It was nearly sundown. Without a word the two men struck off into the forest, the Indian in the lead. Their course was southeast, but Thorpe asked no questions. He followed blindly. Soon he found that if he did even that adequately, he would have little attention left for anything else. The Indian walked with long, swift strides, his knees always slightly bent, even at the finish of the step, his back hollowed, his shoulders and head thrust forward. His gait had a queer sag in it, up and down in a long curve from one rise to the other. After a time Thorpe became fascinated in watching before him this easy, untiring lope, hour after hour, without the variation of a second's fraction in speed nor an inch in length. It was as though the Indian were made of steel springs. He never appeared to hurry; but neither did he ever rest.

At first Thorpe followed him with comparative ease, but at the end of three hours he was compelled to put forth decided efforts to keep pace. His walking was no longer mechanical, but conscious. When it becomes so, a man soon tires. Thorpe resented the inequalities, the stones, the roots, the patches of soft ground which lay in his way. He felt dully that they were not fair. He could negotiate the distance; but anything else was a gratuitous insult.

Then suddenly he gained his second wind. He felt better and stronger and moved freer. For second wind is only to a very small degree a question of the breathing power. It is rather the response of the vital forces to a will that refuses to heed their first grumbling protests. Like dogs by the fire they do their utmost to convince their master that the limit of freshness is reached; but at last, under the whip, spring to their work.

At midnight Injin Charley called a halt. He spread his blanket; leaned on one elbow long enough to eat strip of dried meat, and fell asleep. Thorpe imitated his example. Three hours later the Indian roused his companion, and the two set out again.

Thorpe had walked a leisurely ten days through the woods far to the north. In that journey he had encountered many difficulties. Sometimes he had been tangled for hours at a time in a dense and almost impenetrable thicket. Again he had spent a half day in crossing a treacherous swamp. Or there had interposed in his trail abattises of down timber a quarter of a mile wide over which it had been necessary to pick a precarious way eight or ten feet from the ground.

This journey was in comparison easy. Most of the time the travellers walked along high beech ridges or through the hardwood forests. Occasionally they were forced to pass into the lowlands, but always little saving spits of highland reaching out towards each other abridged the necessary wallowing. Twice they swam rivers.

At first Thorpe thought this was because the country was more open; but as he gave better attention to their route, he learned to ascribe it entirely to the skill of his companion. The Indian seemed by a species of instinct to select the most practicable routes. He seemed to know how the land ought to lie, so that he was never deceived by appearances into entering a cul de sac. His beech ridges always led to other beech ridges; his hardwood never petered out into the terrible black swamps. Sometimes Thorpe became sensible that they had commenced a long detour; but it was never an abrupt detour, unforeseen and blind.

From three o'clock until eight they walked continually without a pause, without an instant's breathing spell. Then they rested a half hour, ate a little venison, and smoked a pipe.

An hour after noon they repeated the rest. Thorpe rose with a certain physical reluctance. The Indian seemed as fresh—or as tired—as when he started. At sunset they took an hour. Then forward again by the dim intermittent light of the moon and stars through the ghostly haunted forest, until Thorpe thought he would drop with weariness, and was mentally incapable of contemplating more than a hundred steps in advance.

"When I get to that square patch of light, I'll quit," he would say to himself, and struggle painfully the required twenty rods.

"No, I won't quit here," he would continue, "I'll make it that birch. Then I'll lie down and die."

And so on. To the actual physical exhaustion of Thorpe's muscles was added that immense mental weariness which uncertainty of the time and distance inflicts on a man. The journey might last a week, for all he knew. In the presence of an emergency these men of action had actually not exchanged a dozen words. The Indian led; Thorpe followed.

When the halt was called, Thorpe fell into his blanket too weary even to eat. Next morning sharp, shooting pains, like the stabs of swords, ran through his groin.

"You come," repeated the Indian, stolid as ever.

When the sun was an hour high the travellers suddenly ran into a trail, which as suddenly dived into a spruce thicket. On the other side of it Thorpe unexpectedly found himself in an extensive clearing, dotted with the blackened stumps of pines. Athwart the distance he could perceive the wide blue horizon of Lake Michigan. He had crossed the Upper Peninsula on foot!

"Boat come by to-day," said Injin Charley, indicating the tall stacks of a mill. "Him no stop. You mak' him stop take you with him. You get train Mackinaw City tonight. Dose men, dey on dat train."

Thorpe calculated rapidly. The enemy would require, even with their teams, a day to cover the thirty miles to the fishing village of Munising, whence the stage ran each morning to Seney, the present terminal of the South Shore

Railroad. He, Thorpe, on foot and three hours behind, could never have caught the stage. But from Seney only one train a day was despatched to connect at Mackinaw City with the Michigan Central, and on that one train, due to leave this very morning, the up-river man was just about pulling out. He would arrive at Mackinaw City at four o'clock of the afternoon, where he would be forced to wait until eight in the evening. By catching a boat at the mill to which Injin Charley had led him, Thorpe could still make the same train. Thus the start in the race for Detroit's Land Office would be fair.

"All right," he cried, all his energy returning to him. "Here goes! We'll beat him out yet!"

"You come back?" inquired the Indian, peering with a certain anxiety into his companion's eyes.

"Come back!" cried Thorpe. "You bet your hat!"

"I wait," replied the Indian, and was gone.

"Oh, Charley!" shouted Thorpe in surprise. "Come on and get a square meal, anyway."

But the Indian was already on his way back to the distant Ossawinamakee.

Thorpe hesitated in two minds whether to follow and attempt further persuasion, for he felt keenly the interest the other had displayed. Then he saw, over the headland to the east, a dense trail of black smoke. He set off on a stumbling run towards the mill.

### Chapter XXI

He arrived out of breath in a typical little mill town consisting of the usual unpainted houses, the saloons, mill, office, and general store. To the latter he addressed himself for information.

The proprietor, still sleepy, was mopping out the place.

"Does that boat stop here?" shouted Thorpe across the suds.

"Sometimes," replied the man somnolently.

"Not always?"

"Only when there's freight for her."

"Doesn't she stop for passengers?"

"Nope."

"How does she know when there's freight?"

"Oh, they signal her from the mill—" but Thorpe was gone.

At the mill Thorpe dove for the engine room. He knew that elsewhere the clang of machinery and the hurry of business would leave scant attention for him. And besides, from the engine room the signals would be given. He found, as is often the case in north-country sawmills, a Scotchman in charge.

"Does the boat stop here this morning?" he inquired.

"Weel," replied the engineer with fearful deliberation, "I canna say. But I hae received na orders to that effect."

"Can't you whistle her in for me?" asked Thorpe.

"I canna," answered the engineer, promptly enough this time.

"Why not?"

"Ye're na what a body might call freight."

"No other way out of it?"

"Na."

Thorpe was seized with an idea.

"Here!" he cried. "See that boulder over there? I want to ship that to Mackinaw City by freight on this boat."

The Scotchman's eyes twinkled appreciatively.

"I'm dootin' ye hae th' freight-bill from the office," he objected simply.

"See here," replied Thorpe, "I've just got to get that boat. It's worth twenty dollars to me, and I'll square it with the captain. There's your twenty."

The Scotchman deliberated, looking aslant at the ground and thoughtfully oiling a cylinder with a greasy rag.

"It'll na be a matter of life and death?" he asked hopefully. "She aye stops for life and death."

"No," replied Thorpe reluctantly. Then with an explosion, "Yes, by God, it is! If I don't make that boat, I'll kill YOU."

The Scotchman chuckled and pocketed the money. "I'm dootin' that's in order," he replied. "I'll no be party to any such proceedin's. I'm goin' noo for a fresh pail of watter," he remarked, pausing at the door, "but as a wee item of information: yander's th' wheestle rope; and a mon wheestles one short and one long for th' boat."

He disappeared. Thorpe seized the cord and gave the signal. Then he ran hastily to the end of the long lumber docks, and peered with great eagerness in the direction of the black smoke.

The steamer was as yet concealed behind a low spit of land which ran out from the west to form one side of the harbor. In a moment, however, her bows appeared, headed directly down towards the Straits of Mackinaw. When opposite the little bay Thorpe confidently looked to see her turn in, but to his consternation she held her course. He began to doubt whether his signal had been heard. Fresh black smoke poured from the funnel; the craft seemed to gather speed as she approached the eastern point. Thorpe saw his hopes sailing away. He wanted to stand up absurdly and wave his arms to attract attention at that impossible distance. He wanted to sink to the planks in apathy. Finally he sat down, and with dull eyes watched the distance widen between himself and his aims.

And then with a grand free sweep she turned and headed directly for him.

Other men might have wept or shouted. Thorpe merely became himself, imperturbable, commanding, apparently cold. He negotiated briefly with the captain, paid twenty dollars more for speed and the privilege of landing at Mackinaw City. Then he slept for eight hours on end and was awakened in time to drop into a small boat which deposited him on the broad sand beach of the lower peninsula.

## Chapter XXII

The train was just leisurely making up for departure. Thorpe, dressed as he was in old "pepper and salt" garments patched with buckskin, his hat a flopping travesty on headgear, his moccasins, worn and dirty, his face bearded and bronzed, tried as much as possible to avoid attention. He sent an instant telegram to Wallace Carpenter conceived as follows:

"Wire thirty thousand my order care Land Office, Detroit, before nine o'clock to-morrow morning. Do it if you have to rustle all night. Important."

Then he took a seat in the baggage car on a pile of boxes and philosophically waited for the train to start. He knew that sooner or later the man, provided he were on the train, would stroll through the car, and he wanted to be out of the way. The baggage man proved friendly, so Thorpe chatted with him until after bedtime. Then he entered the smoking car and waited patiently for morning.

So far the affair had gone very well. It had depended on personal exertions, and he had made it go. Now he was forced to rely on outward circumstances. He argued that the up-river man would have first to make his financial arrangements before he could buy in the land, and this would give the landlooker a chance to get in ahead at the office. There would probably be no difficulty about that. The man suspected nothing. But Thorpe had to confess himself fearfully uneasy about his own financial arrangements. That was the rub. Wallace Carpenter had been sincere enough in his informal striking of partnership, but had he retained his enthusiasm? Had second thought convicted him of folly? Had conservative business friends dissuaded him? Had the glow faded in the reality of his accustomed life? And even if his good-will remained unimpaired, would he be able, at such short notice, to raise so large a sum? Would he realize from Thorpe's telegram the absolute necessity of haste?

At the last thought, Thorpe decided to send a second message from the next station. He did so. It read: "Another buyer of timber on same train with me. Must have money at nine o'clock or lose land." He paid day rates on it to insure immediate delivery. Suppose the boy should be away from home!

Everything depended on Wallace Carpenter; and Thorpe could not but confess the chance slender. One other thought made the night seem long. Thorpe had but thirty dollars left.

Morning came at last, and the train drew in and stopped. Thorpe, being in the smoking car, dropped off first and stationed himself near the exit where he could look over the passengers without being seen. They filed past. Two only he could accord the role of master lumbermen—the rest were plainly drummers or hayseeds. And in these two Thorpe recognized Daly and Morrison themselves. They passed within ten feet of him, talking earnestly together. At the curb they hailed a cab and drove away. Thorpe with satisfaction heard them call the name of a hotel.

It was still two hours before the Land Office would be open. Thorpe ate breakfast at the depot and wandered slowly up Jefferson Avenue to Woodward, a strange piece of our country's medievalism in modern surroundings. He was so occupied with his own thoughts that for some time he remained unconscious of the attention he was attracting. Then, with a start, he felt that everyone was staring at him. The hour was early, so that few besides the working classes were abroad, but he passed one lady driving leisurely to an early train whose frank scrutiny brought him to himself. He became conscious that his broad hat was weather-soiled and limp, that his flannel shirt was faded, that his "pepper and salt" trousers were patched, that moccasins must seem as anachronistic as chain mail. It abashed him. He could not know that it was all wild and picturesque, that his straight and muscular figure moved with a grace quite its own and the woods', that the bronze of his skin contrasted splendidly with the clearness of his eye, that his whole bearing expressed the serene power that comes only from the confidence of battle. The woman in the carriage saw it, however.

"He is magnificent!" she cried. "I thought such men had died with Cooper!"

Thorpe whirled sharp on his heel and returned at once to a boarding-house off Fort Street, where he had "outfitted" three months before. There he reclaimed his valise, shaved, clothed himself in linen and cheviot once more, and sauntered slowly over to the Land Office to await its opening.

## Chapter XXIII

At nine o'clock neither of the partners had appeared. Thorpe entered the office and approached the desk.

"Is there a telegram here for Harry Thorpe?" he inquired.

The clerk to whom he addressed himself merely motioned with his head toward a young fellow behind the railing in a corner. The latter, without awaiting the question, shifted comfortably and replied:

"No."

At the same instant steps were heard in the corridor, the door opened, and Mr. Morrison appeared on the sill. Then Thorpe showed the stuff of which he was made.

"Is this the desk for buying Government lands?" he asked hurriedly.

"Yes," replied the clerk.

"I have some descriptions I wish to buy in."

"Very well," replied the clerk, "what township?"

Thorpe detailed the figures, which he knew by heart, the clerk took from a cabinet the three books containing them, and spread them out on the counter. At this moment the bland voice of Mr. Morrison made itself heard at Thorpe's elbow.

"Good morning, Mr. Smithers," it said with the deliberation of the consciously great man. "I have a few descriptions I would like to buy in the northern peninsula."

"Good morning, Mr. Morrison. Archie there will attend to you. Archie, see what Mr. Morrison wishes."

The lumberman and the other clerk consulted in a low voice, after which the official turned to fumble among the records. Not finding what he wanted, he approached Smithers. A whispered consultation ensued between these two. Then Smithers called:

"Take a seat, Mr. Morrison. This gentleman is looking over these townships, and will have finished in a few minutes."

Morrison's eye suddenly became uneasy.

"I am somewhat busy this morning," he objected with a shade of command in his voice.

"If this gentleman—?" suggested the clerk delicately.

"I am sorry," put in Thorpe with brevity, "my time, too, is valuable."

Morrison looked at him sharply.

"My deal is a big one," he snapped. "I can probably arrange with this gentleman to let him have his farm."

"I claim precedence," replied Thorpe calmly.

"Well," said Morrison swift as light, "I'll tell you, Smithers. I'll leave my list of descriptions and a check with you. Give me a receipt, and mark my lands off after you've finished with this gentleman."

Now Government and State lands are the property of the man who pays for them. Although the clerk's receipt might not give Morrison a valid claim; nevertheless it would afford basis for a lawsuit. Thorpe saw the trap, and interposed.

"Hold on," he interrupted, "I claim precedence. You can give no receipt for any land in these townships until after my business is transacted. I have reason to believe that this gentleman and myself are both after the same descriptions."

"What!" shouted Morrison, assuming surprise.

"You will have to await your turn, Mr. Morrison," said the clerk, virtuous before so many witnesses.

The business man was in a white rage of excitement.

"I insist on my application being filed at once!" he cried waving his check. "I have the money right here to pay for every acre of it; and if I know the law, the first man to pay takes the land."

He slapped the check down on the rail, and hit it a number of times with the flat of his hand. Thorpe turned and faced him with a steel look in his level eyes.

"Mr. Morrison," he said, "you are quite right. The first man who pays gets the land; but I have won the first chance to pay. You will kindly step one side until I finish my business with Mr. Smithers here."

"I suppose you have the amount actually with you," said the clerk, quite respectfully, "because if you have not, Mr. Morrison's claim will take precedence."

"I would hardly have any business in a land office, if I did not know that," replied Thorpe, and began his dictation of the description as calmly as though his inside pocket contained the required amount in bank bills.

Thorpe's hopes had sunk to zero. After all, looking at the matter dispassionately, why should he expect Carpenter to trust him, a stranger, with so large a sum? It had been madness. Only the blind confidence of the fighting man led him further into the struggle. Another would have given up, would have stepped aside from the path of this bona-fide purchaser with the money in his hand.

But Thorpe was of the kind that hangs on until the last possible second, not so much in the expectation of winning, as in sheer reluctance to yield. Such men shoot their last cartridge before surrendering, swim the last ounce of strength from their arms before throwing them up to sink, search coolly until the latest moment for a way from the burning building,— and sometimes come face to face with miracles.

Thorpe's descriptions were contained in the battered little note-book he had carried with him in the woods. For each piece of land first there came the township described by latitude and east-and-west range. After this generic description followed another figure representing the section of that particular district. So 49—17 W—8, meant section 8, of the township on range 49 north, 17 west. If Thorpe wished to purchase the whole section, that description would suffice. On the other hand, if he wished to buy only one forty, he described its position in the quarter-section. Thus SW—NW 49—17—8, meant the southwest forty of the northwest quarter of section 8 in the township already described.

The clerk marked across each square of his map as Thorpe read them, the date and the purchaser's name.

In his note-book Thorpe had, of course, entered the briefest description possible. Now, in dictating to the clerk, he conceived the idea of specifying each subdivision. This gained some time. Instead of saying simply, "Northwest quarter

371

of section 8," he made of it four separate descriptions, as follows:—Northwest quarter of northwest quarter; northeast of northwest quarter; southwest of northwest quarter; and southeast of northwest quarter.

He was not so foolish as to read the descriptions in succession, but so scattered them that the clerk, putting down the figures mechanically, had no idea of the amount of unnecessary work he was doing. The minute hands of the clock dragged around. Thorpe droned down the long column. The clerk scratched industriously, repeating in a half voice each description as it was transcribed.

At length the task was finished. It became necessary to type duplicate lists of the descriptions. While the somnolent youth finished this task, Thorpe listened for the messenger boy on the stairs.

A faint slam was heard outside the rickety old building. Hasty steps sounded along the corridor. The landlooker merely stopped the drumming of his fingers on the broad arm of the chair. The door flew open, and Wallace Carpenter walked quickly to him.

Thorpe's face lighted up as he rose to greet his partner. The boy had not forgotten their compact after all.

"Then it's all right?" queried the latter breathlessly.

"Sure," answered Thorpe heartily, "got 'em in good shape."

At the same time he was drawing the youth beyond the vigilant watchfulness of Mr. Morrison.

"You're just in time," he said in an undertone. "Never had so close a squeak. I suppose you have cash or a certified check: that's all they'll take here."

"What do you mean?" asked Carpenter blankly.

"Haven't you that money?" returned Thorpe quick as a hawk.

"For Heaven's sake, isn't it here?" cried Wallace in consternation. "I wired Duncan, my banker, here last night, and received a reply from him. He answered that he'd see to it. Haven't you seen him?"

"No," repeated Thorpe in his turn.

"What can we do?"

"Can you get your check certified here near at hand?"

"Yes."

"Well, go do it. And get a move on you. You have precisely until that boy there finishes clicking that machine. Not a second longer."

"Can't you get them to wait a few minutes?"

"Wallace," said Thorpe, "do you see that white whiskered old lynx in the corner? That's Morrison, the man who wants to get our land. If I fail to plank down the cash the very instant it is demanded, he gets his chance. And he'll take it. Now, go. Don't hurry until you get beyond the door: then FLY!"

Thorpe sat down again in his broad-armed chair and resumed his drumming. The nearest bank was six blocks away. He counted over in his mind the steps of Carpenter's progress; now to the door, now in the next block, now so far beyond. He had just escorted him to the door of the bank, when the clerk's voice broke in on him.

"Now," Smithers was saying, "I'll give you a receipt for the amount, and later will send to your address the title deeds of the descriptions."

Carpenter had yet to find the proper official, to identify himself, to certify the check, and to return. It was hopeless. Thorpe dropped his hands in surrender.

Then he saw the boy lay the two typed lists before his principal, and dimly he perceived that the youth, shamefacedly, was holding something bulky toward himself.

"Wh—what is it?" he stammered, drawing his hand back as though from a red-hot iron.

"You asked me for a telegram," said the boy stubbornly, as though trying to excuse himself, "and I didn't just catch the name, anyway. When I saw it on those lists I had to copy, I thought of this here."

"Where'd you get it?" asked Thorpe breathlessly.

"A fellow came here early and left it for you while I was sweeping out," explained the boy. "Said he had to catch a train. It's yours all right, ain't it?"

"Oh, yes," replied Thorpe.

He took the envelope and walked uncertainly to the tall window. He looked out at the chimneys. After a moment he tore open the envelope.

"I hope there's no bad news, sir?" said the clerk, startled at the paleness of the face Thorpe turned to the desk.

"No," replied the landlooker. "Give me a receipt. There's a certified check for your money!"

### Chapter XXIV

Now that the strain was over, Thorpe experienced a great weariness. The long journey through the forest, his sleepless night on the train, the mental alertness of playing the game with shrewd foes all these stretched his fibers out one by one and left them limp. He accepted stupidly the clerk's congratulations on his success, left the name of the little hotel off Fort Street as the address to which to send the deeds, and dragged himself off with infinite fatigue to his bed-room. There he fell at once into profound unconsciousness.

He was awakened late in the afternoon by the sensation of a strong pair of young arms around his shoulders, and the sound of Wallace Carpenter's fresh voice crying in his ears:

"Wake up, wake up! you Indian! You've been asleep all day, and I've been waiting here all that time. I want to hear about it. Wake up, I say!"

Thorpe rolled to a sitting posture on the edge of the bed, and smiled uncertainly. Then as the sleep drained from his brain, he reached out his hand.

"You bet we did 'em, Wallace," said he, "but it looked like a hard proposition for a while."

"How was it? Tell me about it!" insisted the boy eagerly. "You don't know how impatient I've been. The clerk at the Land Office merely told me it was all right. How did you fix it?"

While Thorpe washed and shaved and leisurely freshened himself, he detailed his experiences of the last week.

"And," he concluded gravely, "there's only one man I know or ever heard of to whom I would have considered it worth while even to think of sending that telegram, and you are he. Somehow I knew you'd come to the scratch."

"It's the most exciting thing I ever heard of," sighed Wallace drawing a full breath, "and I wasn't in it! It's the sort of thing I long for. If I'd only waited another two weeks before coming down!"

"In that case we couldn't have gotten hold of the money, remember," smiled Thorpe.

"That's so." Wallace brightened. "I did count, didn't I?"

"I thought so about ten o'clock this morning," Thorpe replied.

"Suppose you hadn't stumbled on their camp; suppose Injin Charley hadn't seen them go up-river; suppose you hadn't struck that little mill town JUST at the time you did!" marvelled Wallace.

"That's always the way," philosophized Thorpe in reply. "It's the old story of 'if the horse-shoe nail hadn't been lost,' you know. But we got there; and that's the important thing."

"We did!" cried the boy, his enthusiasm rekindling, "and to-night we'll celebrate with the best dinner we ran buy in town!"

Thorpe was tempted, but remembered the thirty dollars in his pocket, and looked doubtful.

Carpenter possessed, as part of his volatile enthusiastic temperament, keen intuitions.

"Don't refuse!" he begged. "I've set my heart on giving my senior partner a dinner. Surely you won't refuse to be my guest here, as I was yours in the woods!"

"Wallace," said Thorpe, "I'll go you. I'd like to dine with you; but moreover, I'll confess, I should like to eat a good dinner again. It's been more than a year since I've seen a salad, or heard of after-dinner coffee."

"Come on then," cried Wallace.

Together they sauntered through the lengthening shadows to a certain small restaurant near Woodward Avenue, then much in vogue among Detroit's epicures. It contained only a half dozen tables, but was spotlessly clean, and its cuisine was unrivalled. A large fireplace near the center of the room robbed it of half its restaurant air; and a thick carpet on the floor took the rest. The walls were decorated in dark colors after the German style. Several easy chairs grouped before the fireplace, and a light wicker table heaped with magazines and papers invited the guests to lounge while their orders were being prepared.

Thorpe was not in the least Sybaritic in his tastes, but he could not stifle a sigh of satisfaction at sinking so naturally into the unobtrusive little comforts which the ornamental life offers to its votaries. They rose up around him and pillowed him, and were grateful to the tired fibers of his being. His remoter past had enjoyed these things as a matter of course. They had framed the background to his daily habit. Now that the background had again slid into place on noiseless grooves, Thorpe for the first time became conscious that his strenuous life had indeed been in the open air, and that the winds of earnest endeavor, while bracing, had chilled. Wallace Carpenter, with the poet's insight and sympathy, saw and understood this feeling.

"I want you to order this dinner," said he, handing over to Thorpe the card which an impossibly correct waiter presented him. "And I want it a good one. I want you to begin at the beginning and skip nothing. Pretend you are ordering just the dinner you would like to offer your sister," he suggested on a sudden inspiration. "I assure you I'll try to be just as critical and exigent as she would be."

Thorpe took up the card dreamily.

"There are no oysters and clams now," said he, "so we'll pass right on to the soup. It seems to me a desecration to pretend to replace them. We'll have a bisque," he told the waiter, "rich and creamy. Then planked whitefish, and have them just a light crisp, brown. You can bring some celery, too, if you have it fresh and good. And for entree tell your cook to make some macaroni au gratin, but the inside must be soft and very creamy, and the outside very crisp. I know it's a queer dish for a formal dinner like ours," he addressed Wallace with a little laugh, "but it's very, very good. We'll have roast beef, rare and juicy;—if you bring it any way but a cooked red, I'll send it back;—and potatoes roasted with the meat and brown gravy. Then the breast of chicken with the salad, in the French fashion. And I'll make the dressing. We'll have an ice and some fruit for dessert. Black coffee."

"Yes, sir," replied the waiter, his pencil poised. "And the wines?"

Thorpe ruminated sleepily.

"A rich red Burgundy," he decided, "for all the dinner. If your cellar contains a very good smooth Beaune, we'll have that."

"Yes, sir," answered the waiter, and departed.

Thorpe sat and gazed moodily into the wood fire, Wallace respected his silence. It was yet too early for the fashionable world, so the two friends had the place to themselves. Gradually the twilight fell; strange shadows leaped and died on the wall. A boy dressed all in white turned on the lights. By and by the waiter announced that their repast awaited them.

Thorpe ate, his eyes half closed, in somnolent satisfaction. Occasionally he smiled contentedly across at Wallace, who smiled in response. After the coffee he had the waiter bring cigars. They went back between the tables to a little upholstered smoking room, where they sank into the depths of leather chairs, and blew the gray clouds of smoke towards the ceiling. About nine o'clock Thorpe spoke the first word.

"I'm stupid this evening, I'm afraid," said he, shaking himself. "Don't think on that account I am not enjoying your dinner. I believe," he asserted earnestly, "that I never had such an altogether comfortable, happy evening before in my life."

"I know," replied Wallace sympathetically.

"It seems just now," went on Thorpe, sinking more luxuriously into his armchair, "that this alone is living—to exist in an environment exquisitely toned; to eat, to drink, to smoke the best, not like a gormand, but delicately as an artist would. It is the flower of our civilization."

Wallace remembered the turmoil of the wilderness brook; the little birch knoll, yellow in the evening glow; the mellow voice of the summer night crooning through the pines. But he had the rare tact to say nothing.

"Did it ever occur to you that what you needed, when sort of tired out this way," he said abruptly after a moment, "is a woman to understand and sympathize? Wouldn't it have made this evening perfect to have seen opposite you a being whom you loved, who understood your moments of weariness, as well as your moments of strength?"

"No," replied Thorpe, stretching his arms over his head, "a woman would have talked. It takes a friend and a man, to know when to keep silent for three straight hours."

The waiter brought the bill on a tray, and Carpenter paid it.

"Wallace," said Thorpe suddenly after a long interval, "we'll borrow enough by mortgaging our land to supply the working expenses. I suppose capital will have to investigate, and that'll take time; but I can begin to pick up a crew and make arrangements for transportation and supplies. You can let me have a thousand dollars on the new Company's note for initial expenses. We'll draw up articles of partnership to-morrow."

### Chapter XXV

Next day the articles of partnership were drawn; and Carpenter gave his note for the necessary expenses. Then in answer to a pencilled card which Mr. Morrison had evidently left at Thorpe's hotel in person, both young men called at the lumberman's place of business. They were ushered immediately into the private office.

Mr. Morrison was a smart little man with an ingratiating manner and a fishy eye. He greeted Thorpe with marked geniality.

"My opponent of yesterday!" he cried jocularly. "Sit down, Mr. Thorpe! Although you did me out of some land I had made every preparation to purchase, I can't but admire your grit and resourcefulness. How did you get here ahead of us?"

"I walked across the upper peninsula, and caught a boat," replied Thorpe briefly.

"Indeed, INDEED!" replied Mr. Morrison, placing the tips of his fingers together. "Extraordinary! Well, Mr. Thorpe, you overreached us nicely; and I suppose we must pay for our carelessness. We must have that pine, even though we pay stumpage on it. Now what would you consider a fair price for it?"

"It is not for sale," answered Thorpe.

"We'll waive all that. Of course it is to your interest to make difficulties and run the price up as high as you can. But my time is somewhat occupied just at present, so I would be very glad to hear your top price—we will come to an agreement afterwards."

"You do not understand me, Mr. Morrison. I told you the pine is not for sale, and I mean it."

"But surely—What did you buy it for, then?" cried Mr. Morrison, with evidences of a growing excitement.

"We intend to manufacture it."

Mr. Morrison's fishy eyes nearly popped out of his head. He controlled himself with an effort.

"Mr. Thorpe," said he, "let us try to be reasonable. Our case stands this way. We have gone to a great deal of expense on the Ossawinamakee in expectation of undertaking very extensive operations there. To that end we have cleared the stream, built three dams, and have laid the foundations of a harbor and boom. This has been very expensive. Now your purchase includes most of what we had meant to log. You have, roughly speaking, about three hundred millions in your holding, in addition to which there are several millions scattering near it, which would pay nobody but yourself to get in. Our holdings are further up stream, and comprise only about the equal of yours."

"Three hundred millions are not to be sneezed at," replied Thorpe.

"Certainly not," agreed Morrison, suavely, gaining confidence from the sound of his own voice. "Not in this country. But you must remember that a man goes into the northern peninsula only because he can get something better there than here. When the firm of Morrison & Daly establishes itself now, it must be for the last time. We want enough timber to do us for the rest of the time we are in business."

"In that case, you will have to hunt up another locality," replied Thorpe calmly.

Morrison's eyes flashed. But he retained his appearance of geniality, and appealed to Wallace Carpenter.

"Then you will retain the advantage of our dams and improvements," said he. "Is that fair?"

"No, not on the face of it," admitted Thorpe. "But you did your work in a navigable stream for private purposes, without the consent of the Board of Control. Your presence on the river is illegal. You should have taken out a charter as an Improvement Company. Then as long as you 'tended to business and kept the concern in repair, we'd have paid you a toll per thousand feet. As soon as you let it slide, however, the works would revert to the State. I won't hinder your doing that yet; although I might. Take out your charter and fix your rate of toll."

"In other words, you force us to stay there and run a little two-by-four Improvement Company for your benefit, or else lose the value of our improvements?"

"Suit yourself," answered Thorpe carelessly. "You can always log your present holdings."

"Very well," cried Morrison, so suddenly in a passion that Wallace started back. "It's war! And let me tell you this, young man; you're a new concern and we're an old one. We'll crush you like THAT!" He crisped an envelope vindictively, and threw it in the waste-basket.

"Crush ahead," replied Thorpe with great good humor. "Good-day, Mr. Morrison," and the two went out.

Wallace was sputtering and trembling with nervous excitement. His was one of those temperaments which require action to relieve the stress of a stormy interview. He was brave enough, but he would always tremble in the presence of danger until the moment for striking arrived. He wanted to do something at once.

"Hadn't we better see a lawyer?" he asked. "Oughtn't we to look out that they don't take some of our pine? Oughtn't we—"

"You just leave all that to me," replied Thorpe. "The first thing we want to do is to rustle some money."

"And you can leave THAT to ME," echoed Wallace. "I know a little of such things, and I have business connections who know more. You just get the camp running."

"I'll start for Bay City to-night," submitted Thorpe. "There ought to be a good lot of lumber-jacks lying around idle at this time of year; and it's a good place to outfit from because we can probably get freight rates direct by boat. We'll be a little late in starting, but we'll get in SOME logs this winter, anyway."

## PART III. THE BLAZING OF THE TRAIL

### Chapter XXVI

A lumbering town after the drive is a fearful thing. Men just off the river draw a deep breath, and plunge into the wildest reactionary dissipation. In droves they invade the cities,—wild, picturesque, lawless. As long as the money lasts, they blow it in.

"Hot money!" is the cry. "She's burnt holes in all my pockets already!"

The saloons are full, the gambling houses overflow, all the places of amusement or crime run full blast. A chip rests lightly on everyone's shoulder. Fights are as common as raspberries in August. Often one of these formidable men, his muscles toughened and quickened by the active, strenuous river work, will set out to "take the town apart." For a time he leaves rack and ruin, black eyes and broken teeth behind him, until he meets a more redoubtable "knocker" and is pounded and kicked into unconsciousness. Organized gangs go from house to house forcing the peaceful inmates to drink from their bottles. Others take possession of certain sections of the street and resist "a l'outrance" the attempts of others to pass. Inoffensive citizens are stood on their heads, or shaken upside down until the contents of their pockets rattle on the street. Parenthetically, these contents are invariably returned to their owners. The riverman's object is fun, not robbery.

And if rip-roaring, swashbuckling, drunken glory is what he is after, he gets it. The only trouble is, that a whole winter's hard work goes in two or three weeks. The only redeeming feature is, that he is never, in or out of his cups, afraid of anything that walks the earth.

A man comes out of the woods or off the drive with two or three hundred dollars, which he is only too anxious to throw away by the double handful. It follows naturally that a crew of sharpers are on hand to find out who gets it. They are a hard lot. Bold, unprincipled men, they too are afraid of nothing; not even a drunken lumber-jack, which is one of the dangerous wild animals of the American fauna. Their business is to relieve the man of his money as soon as possible. They are experts at their business.

The towns of Bay City and Saginaw alone in 1878 supported over fourteen hundred tough characters. Block after block was devoted entirely to saloons. In a radius of three hundred feet from the famous old Catacombs could be numbered forty saloons, where drinks were sold by from three to ten "pretty waiter girls." When the boys struck town, the proprietors and waitresses stood in their doorways to welcome them.

"Why, Jack!" one would cry, "when did you drift in? Tickled to death to see you! Come in an' have a drink. That your chum? Come in, old man, and have a drink. Never mind the pay; that's all right."

And after the first drink, Jack, of course, had to treat, and then the chum.

Or if Jack resisted temptation and walked resolutely on, one of the girls would remark audibly to another.

"He ain't no lumber-jack! You can see that easy 'nuff! He's jest off th' hay-trail!"

Ten to one that brought him, for the woodsman is above all things proud and jealous of his craft.

In the center of this whirlpool of iniquity stood the Catacombs as the hub from which lesser spokes in the wheel radiated. Any old logger of the Saginaw Valley can tell you of the Catacombs, just as any old logger of any other valley will tell you of the "Pen," the "White Row," the "Water Streets" of Alpena, Port Huron, Ludington, Muskegon, and a dozen other lumber towns.

The Catacombs was a three-story building. In the basement were vile, ill-smelling, ill-lighted dens, small, isolated, dangerous. The shanty boy with a small stake, far gone in drunkenness, there tasted the last drop of wickedness, and thence was flung unconscious and penniless on the streets. A trap-door directly into the river accommodated those who were inconsiderate enough to succumb under rough treatment.

The second story was given over to drinking. Polly Dickson there reigned supreme, an anomaly. She was as pretty and fresh and pure-looking as a child; and at the same time was one of the most ruthless and unscrupulous of the gang. She could at will exercise a fascination the more terrible in that it appealed at once to her victim's nobler instincts of reverence, his capacity for what might be called aesthetic fascination, as well as his passions. When she finally held him, she crushed him as calmly as she would a fly.

Four bars supplied the drinkables. Dozens of "pretty waiter girls" served the customers. A force of professional fighters was maintained by the establishment to preserve that degree of peace which should look to the preservation of mirrors and glassware.

The third story contained a dance hall and a theater. The character of both would better be left to the imagination.

Night after night during the season, this den ran at top-steam.

By midnight, when the orgy was at its height, the windows brilliantly illuminated, the various bursts of music, laughing, cursing, singing, shouting, fighting, breaking in turn or all together from its open windows, it was, as Jackson Hines once expressed it to me, like hell let out for noon.

The respectable elements of the towns were powerless. They could not control the elections. Their police would only have risked total annihilation by attempting a raid. At the first sign of trouble they walked straightly in the paths of their own affairs, awaiting the time soon to come when, his stake "blown-in," the last bitter dregs of his pleasure gulped down, the shanty boy would again start for the woods.

### Chapter XXVII

Now in August, however, the first turmoil had died. The "jam" had boiled into town, "taken it apart," and left the inhabitants to piece it together again as they could; the "rear" had not yet arrived. As a consequence, Thorpe found the city comparatively quiet.

Here and there swaggered a strapping riverman, his small felt hat cocked aggressively over one eye, its brim curled up behind; a cigar stump protruding at an angle from beneath his sweeping moustache; his hands thrust into the pockets of his trousers, "stagged" off at the knee; the spikes of his river boots cutting little triangular pieces from the wooden sidewalk. His eye was aggressively humorous, and the smile of his face was a challenge.

For in the last month he had faced almost certain death a dozen times a day. He had ridden logs down the rapids where a loss of balance meant in one instant a ducking and in the next a blow on the back from some following battering-ram; he had tugged and strained and jerked with his peavey under a sheer wall of tangled timber twenty feet high,—behind which pressed the full power of the freshet,—only to jump with the agility of a cat from one bit of unstable footing to another when the first sharp CRACK warned him that he had done his work, and that the whole mass was about to break down on him like a wave on the shore; he had worked fourteen hours a day in ice-water, and had slept damp; he had pried at the key log in the rollways on the bank until the whole pile had begun to rattle down into the river like a cascade, and had jumped, or ridden, or even dived out of danger at the last second. In a hundred passes he had juggled with death as a child plays with a rubber balloon. No wonder that he has brought to the town and his vices a little of the lofty bearing of an heroic age. No wonder that he fears no man, since nature's most terrible forces of the flood have hurled a thousand weapons at him in vain. His muscles have been hardened, his eye is quiet and sure, his courage is undaunted, and his movements are as quick and accurate as a panther's. Probably nowhere in the world is a more dangerous man of his hands than the riverman. He would rather fight than eat, especially when he is drunk, as, like the cow-boy, he usually is when he gets into town. A history could be written of the feuds, the wars, the raids instituted by one camp or one town against another.

The men would go in force sometimes to another city with the avowed purpose of cleaning it out. One battle I know of lasted nearly all night. Deadly weapons were almost never resorted to, unless indeed a hundred and eighty pounds of muscle behind a fist hard as iron might be considered a deadly weapon. A man hard pressed by numbers often resorted to a billiard cue, or an ax, or anything else that happened to be handy, but that was an expedient called out by necessity. Knives or six-shooters implied a certain premeditation which was discountenanced.

On the other hand, the code of fair fighting obtained hardly at all. The long spikes of river-boots made an admirable weapon in the straight kick. I have seen men whose faces were punctured as thickly as though by small-pox, where the steel points had penetrated. In a free-for-all knock-down-and-drag-out, kicking, gouging, and biting are all legitimate. Anything to injure the other man, provided always you do not knife him. And when you take a half dozen of these enduring, active, muscular, and fiery men, not one entertaining in his innermost heart the faintest hesitation or fear, and set them at each other with the lightning tirelessness of so many wild-cats, you get as hard a fight as you could desire. And they seem to like it.

One old fellow, a good deal of a character in his way, used to be on the "drive" for a firm lumbering near Six Lakes. He was intensely loyal to his "Old Fellows," and every time he got a little "budge" in him, he instituted a raid on the town owned by a rival firm. So frequent and so severe did these battles become that finally the men were informed that another such expedition would mean instant discharge. The rule had its effect. The raids ceased.

But one day old Dan visited the saloon once too often. He became very warlike. The other men merely laughed, for they were strong enough themselves to recognize firmness in others, and it never occurred to them that they could disobey so absolute a command. So finally Dan started out quite alone.

He invaded the enemy's camp, attempted to clean out the saloon with a billiard cue single handed, was knocked down, and would have been kicked to death as he lay on the floor if he had not succeeded in rolling under the billiard table where the men's boots could not reach him. As it was, his clothes were literally torn to ribbons, one eye was blacked, his nose broken, one ear hung to its place by a mere shred of skin, and his face and flesh were ripped and torn everywhere by the "corks" on the boots. Any but a riverman would have qualified for the hospital. Dan rolled to the other side of the table, made a sudden break, and escaped.

But his fighting blood was not all spilled. He raided the butcher-shop, seized the big carving knife, and returned to the battle field.

The enemy decamped—rapidly—some of them through the window. Dan managed to get in but one blow. He ripped the coat down the man's back as neatly as though it had been done with shears, one clean straight cut from collar to bottom seam. A quarter of an inch nearer would have split the fellow's backbone. As it was, he escaped without even a scratch.

Dan commandeered two bottles of whisky, and, gory and wounded as he was, took up the six-mile tramp home, bearing the knife over his shoulder as a banner of triumph.

Next morning, weak from the combined effects of war and whisky, he reported to headquarters.

"What is it, Dan?" asked the Old Fellow without turning.

"I come to get my time," replied the riverman humbly.

"What for?" inquired the lumberman.

"I have been over to Howard City," confessed Dan.

The owner turned and looked him over.

"They sort of got ahead of me a little," explained Dan sheepishly.

The lumberman took stock of the old man's cuts and bruises, and turned away to hide a smile.

"I guess I'll let you off this trip," said he. "Go to work—when you can. I don't believe you'll go back there again."

"No, sir," replied Dan humbly.

And so the life of alternate work and pleasure, both full of personal danger, develops in time a class of men whose like is to be found only among the cowboys, scouts, trappers, and Indian fighters of our other frontiers. The moralists will always hold up the hands of horror at such types; the philosopher will admire them as the last incarnation of the heroic age, when the man is bigger than his work. Soon the factories, the machines, the mechanical structures and constructions, the various branches of co-operation will produce quasi-automatically institutions evidently more important than the genius or force of any one human being. The personal element will have become nearly eliminated. In the woods and on the frontier still are many whose powers are greater than their works; whose fame is greater than their deeds. They are men, powerful, virile, even brutal at times; but magnificent with the strength of courage and resource.

All this may seem a digression from the thread of our tale, but as a matter of fact it is necessary that you understand the conditions of the time and place in which Harry Thorpe had set himself the duty of success.

He had seen too much of incompetent labor to be satisfied with anything but the best. Although his ideas were not as yet formulated, he hoped to be able to pick up a crew of first-class men from those who had come down with the advance, or "jam," of the spring's drive. They should have finished their orgies by now, and, empty of pocket, should be found hanging about the boarding-houses and the quieter saloons. Thorpe intended to offer good wages for good men. He would not need more than twenty at first, for during the approaching winter he purposed to log on a very small scale indeed. The time for expansion would come later.

With this object in view he set out from his hotel about half-past seven on the day of his arrival, to cruise about in the lumber-jack district already described. The hotel clerk had obligingly given him the names of a number of the quieter saloons, where the boys "hung out" between bursts of prosperity. In the first of these Thorpe was helped materially in his vague and uncertain quest by encountering an old acquaintance.

From the sidewalk he heard the vigorous sounds of a one-sided altercation punctuated by frequent bursts of quickly silenced laughter. Evidently some one was very angry, and the rest amused. After a moment Thorpe imagined he recognized the excited voice. So he pushed open the swinging screen door and entered.

The place was typical. Across one side ran the hard-wood bar with foot-rest and little towels hung in metal clasps under its edge. Behind it was a long mirror, a symmetrical pile of glasses, a number of plain or ornamental bottles, and a miniature keg or so of porcelain containing the finer whiskys and brandies. The bar-keeper drew beer from two pumps immediately in front of him, and rinsed glasses in some sort of a sink under the edge of the bar. The center of the room was occupied by a tremendous stove capable of burning whole logs of cordwood. A stovepipe led from the stove here and there in wire suspension to a final exit near the other corner. On the wall were two sporting chromos, and a good variety of lithographed calendars and illuminated tin signs advertising beers and spirits. The floor was liberally sprinkled with damp sawdust, and was occupied, besides the stove, by a number of wooden chairs and a single round table.

The latter, a clumsy heavy affair beyond the strength of an ordinary man, was being deftly interposed between himself and the attacks of the possessor of the angry voice by a gigantic young riverman in the conventional stagged (i.e., chopped off) trousers, "cork" shoes, and broad belt typical of his craft. In the aggressor Thorpe recognized old Jackson Hines.

"Damn you!" cried the old man, qualifying the oath, "let me get at you, you great big sock-stealer, I'll make you hop high! I'll snatch you bald-headed so quick that you'll think you never had any hair!"

"I'll settle with you in the morning, Jackson," laughed the riverman.

"You want to eat a good breakfast, then, because you won't have no appetite for dinner."

The men roared, with encouraging calls. The riverman put on a ludicrous appearance of offended dignity.

"Oh, you needn't swell up like a poisoned pup!" cried old Jackson plaintively, ceasing his attacks from sheer weariness. "You know you're as safe as a cow tied to a brick wall behind that table."

Thorpe seized the opportunity to approach.

"Hello, Jackson," said he.

The old man peered at him out of the blur of his excitement.

"Don't you know me?" inquired Thorpe.

"Them lamps gives 'bout as much light as a piece of chalk," complained Jackson testily. "Knows you? You bet I do! How are you, Harry? Where you been keepin' yourself? You look 'bout as fat as a stall-fed knittin' needle."

"I've been landlooking in the upper peninsula," explained Thorpe, "on the Ossawinamakee, up in the Marquette country."

"Sho'" commented Jackson in wonder, "way up there where the moon changes!"

"It's a fine country," went on Thorpe so everyone could hear, "with a great cutting of white pine. It runs as high as twelve hundred thousand to the forty sometimes."

"Trees clean an' free of limbs?" asked Jackson.

"They're as good as the stuff over on seventeen; you remember that."

"Clean as a baby's leg," agreed Jackson.

"Have a glass of beer?" asked Thorpe.

"Dry as a tobacco box," confessed Hines.

"Have something, the rest of you?" invited Thorpe.

So they all drank.

On a sudden inspiration Thorpe resolved to ask the old man's advice as to crew and horses. It might not be good for much, but it would do no harm.

Jackson listened attentively to the other's brief recital.

"Why don't you see Tim Shearer? He ain't doin' nothin' since the jam came down," was his comment.

"Isn't he with the M. & D. people?" asked Thorpe.

"Nope. Quit."

"How's that?"

"'Count of Morrison. Morrison he comes up to run things some. He does. Tim he's getting the drive in shape, and he don't want to be bothered, but old Morrison he's as busy as hell beatin' tan-bark. Finally Tim, he calls him. '"Look here, Mr. Morrison,' says he, 'I'm runnin' this drive. If I don't get her there, all right; you can give me my time. 'Till then you ain't got nothin' to say.'

"Well, that makes the Old Fellow as sore as a scalded pup. He's used to bossin' clerks and such things, and don't have much of an idea of lumber-jacks. He has big ideas of respect, so he 'calls' Tim dignified like.

"Tim didn't hit him; but I guess he felt like th' man who met the bear without any weapon,—even a newspaper would 'a' come handy. He hands in his time t' once and quits. Sence then he's been as mad as a bar-keep with a lead quarter, which ain't usual for Tim. He's been filin' his teeth for M. & D. right along. Somethin's behind it all, I reckon."

"Where'll I find him?" asked Thorpe.

Jackson gave the name of a small boarding-house. Shortly after, Thorpe left him to amuse the others with his unique conversation, and hunted up Shearer's stopping-place.

### Chapter XXVIII

The boarding-house proved to be of the typical lumber-jack class, a narrow "stoop," a hall-way and stairs in the center, and an office and bar on either side. Shearer and a half dozen other men about his own age sat, their chairs on two legs and their "cork" boots on the rounds of the chairs, smoking placidly in the tepid evening air. The light came from inside the building, so that while Thorpe was in plain view, he could not make out which of the dark figures on the piazza was the man he wanted. He approached, and attempted an identifying scrutiny. The men, with the taciturnity of their class in the presence of a stranger, said nothing.

"Well, bub," finally drawled a voice from the corner, "blowed that stake you made out of Radway, yet?"

"That you, Shearer?" inquired Thorpe advancing. "You're the man I'm looking for."

"You've found me," replied the old man dryly.

Thorpe was requested elaborately to "shake hands" with the owners of six names. Then he had a chance to intimate quietly to Shearer that he wanted a word with him alone. The riverman rose silently and led the way up the straight, uncarpeted stairs, along a narrow, uncarpeted hall, to a square, uncarpeted bedroom. The walls and ceiling of this apartment were of unpainted planed pine. It contained a cheap bureau, one chair, and a bed and washstand to match the bureau. Shearer lit the lamp and sat on the bed.

"What is it?" he asked.

"I have a little pine up in the northern peninsula within walking distance of Marquette," said Thorpe, "and I want to get a crew of about twenty men. It occurred to me that you might be willing to help me."

The riverman frowned steadily at his interlocutor from under his bushy brows.

"How much pine you got?" he asked finally.

"About three hundred millions," replied Thorpe quietly.

The old man's blue eyes fixed themselves with unwavering steadiness on Thorpe's face.

"You're jobbing some of it, eh?" he submitted finally as the only probable conclusion. "Do you think you know enough about it? Who does it belong to?"

"It belongs to a man named Carpenter and myself."

The riverman pondered this slowly for an appreciable interval, and then shot out another question.

"How'd you get it?"

Thorpe told him simply, omitting nothing except the name of the firm up-river. When he had finished, Shearer evinced no astonishment nor approval.

"You done well," he commented finally. Then after another interval:

"Have you found out who was the men stealin' the pine?"

"Yes," replied Thorpe quietly, "it was Morrison & Daly."

The old man flickered not an eyelid. He slowly filled his pipe and lit it.

"I'll get you a crew of men," said he, "if you'll take me as foreman."

"But it's a little job at first," protested Thorpe. "I only want a camp of twenty. It wouldn't be worth your while."

"That's my look-out. I'll take th' job," replied the logger grimly. "You got three hundred million there, ain't you? And you're goin' to cut it? It ain't such a small job."

Thorpe could hardly believe his good-fortune in having gained so important a recruit. With a practical man as foreman, his mind would be relieved of a great deal of worry over unfamiliar detail. He saw at once that he would himself be able to perform all the duties of scaler, keep in touch with the needs of the camp, and supervise the campaign. Nevertheless he answered the older man's glance with one as keen, and said:

"Look here, Shearer, if you take this job, we may as well understand each other at the start. This is going to be my camp, and I'm going to be boss. I don't know much about logging, and I shall want you to take charge of all that, but I shall want to know just why you do each thing, and if my judgment advises otherwise, my judgment goes. If I want to discharge a man, he WALKS without any question. I know about what I shall expect of each man; and I intend to get it out of him. And in questions of policy mine is the say-so every trip. Now I know you're a good man, one of the best there is, and I presume I shall find your judgment the best, but I don't want any mistakes to start with. If you want to be my foreman on those terms, just say so, and I'll be tickled to death to have you."

For the first time the lumberman's face lost, during a single instant, its mask of immobility. His steel-blue eyes flashed, his mouth twitched with some strong emotion. For the first time, too, he spoke without his contemplative pause of preparation.

"That's th' way to talk!" he cried. "Go with you? Well I should rise to remark! You're the boss; and I always said it. I'll get you a gang of bully boys that will roll logs till there's skating in hell!"

Thorpe left, after making an appointment at his own hotel for the following day, more than pleased with his luck. Although he had by now fairly good and practical ideas in regard to the logging of a bunch of pine, he felt himself to be very deficient in the details. In fact, he anticipated his next step with shaky confidence. He would now be called upon to buy four or five teams of horses, and enough feed to last them the entire winter; he would have to arrange for provisions in abundance and variety for his men; he would have to figure on blankets, harness, cook-camp utensils, stoves, blacksmith tools, iron, axes, chains, cant-hooks, van-goods, pails, lamps, oil, matches, all sorts of hardware,—in short, all the thousand and one things, from needles to court-plaster, of which a self-sufficing community might come in need. And he would have to figure out his requirements for the entire winter. After navigation closed, he could import nothing more.

How could he know what to buy,—how many barrels of flour, how much coffee, raisins, baking powder, soda, pork, beans, dried apples, sugar, nutmeg, pepper, salt, crackers, molasses, ginger, lard, tea, corned beef, catsup, mustard,—to last twenty men five or six months? How could he be expected to think of each item of a list of two hundred, the lack of which meant measureless bother, and the desirability of which suggested itself only when the necessity arose? It is easy, when the mind is occupied with multitudinous detail, to forget simple things, like brooms or iron shovels. With Tim

Shearer to help his inexperience, he felt easy. He knew he could attend to advantageous buying, and to making arrangements with the steamship line to Marquette for the landing of his goods at the mouth of the Ossawinamakee.

Deep in these thoughts, he wandered on at random. He suddenly came to himself in the toughest quarter of Bay City.

Through the summer night shrilled the sound of cachinations painted to the colors of mirth. A cheap piano rattled and thumped through an open window. Men's and women's voices mingled in rising and falling gradations of harshness. Lights streamed irregularly across the dark.

Thorpe became aware of a figure crouched in the door-way almost at his feet. The sill lay in shadow so the bulk was lost, but the flickering rays of a distant street lamp threw into relief the high-lights of a violin, and a head. The face upturned to him was thin and white and wolfish under a broad white brow. Dark eyes gleamed at him with the expression of a fierce animal. Across the forehead ran a long but shallow cut from which blood dripped. The creature clasped both arms around a violin. He crouched there and stared up at Thorpe, who stared down at him.

"What's the matter?" asked the latter finally.

The creature made no reply, but drew his arms closer about his instrument, and blinked his wolf eyes.

Moved by some strange, half-tolerant whim of compassion, Thorpe made a sign to the unknown to rise.

"Come with me," said he, "and I'll have your forehead attended to."

The wolf eyes gleamed into his with a sudden savage concentration. Then their owner obediently arose.

Thorpe now saw that the body before him was of a cripple, short-legged, hunch-backed, long-armed, pigeon-breasted. The large head sat strangely top-heavy between even the broad shoulders. It confirmed the hopeless but sullen despair that brooded on the white countenance.

At the hotel Thorpe, examining the cut, found it more serious in appearance than in reality. With a few pieces of sticking plaster he drew its edges together.

Then he attempted to interrogate his find.

"What is your name?" he asked.

"Phil."

"Phil what?"

Silence.

"How did you get hurt?"

No reply.

"Were you playing your fiddle in one of those houses?"

The cripple nodded slowly.

"Are you hungry?" asked Thorpe, with a sudden thoughtfulness.

"Yes," replied the cripple, with a lightning gleam in his wolf eyes.

Thorpe rang the bell. To the boy who answered it he said:

"Bring me half a dozen beef sandwiches and a glass of milk, and be quick about it."

"Do you play the fiddle much?" continued Thorpe.

The cripple nodded again.

"Let's hear what you can do."

"They cut my strings!" cried Phil with a passionate wail.

The cry came from the heart, and Thorpe was touched by it. The price of strings was evidently a big sum.

"I'll get you more in the morning," said he. "Would you like to leave Bay City?"

"Yes" cried the boy with passion.

"You would have to work. You would have to be chore-boy in a lumber camp, and play fiddle for the men when they wanted you to."

"I'll do it," said the cripple.

"Are you sure you could? You will have to split all the wood for the men, the cook, and the office; you will have to draw the water, and fill the lamps, and keep the camps clean. You will be paid for it, but it is quite a job. And you would have to do it well. If you did not do it well, I would discharge you."

"I will do it!" repeated the cripple with a shade more earnestness.

"All right, then I'll take you," replied Thorpe.

The cripple said nothing, nor moved a muscle of his face, but the gleam of the wolf faded to give place to the soft, affectionate glow seen in the eyes of a setter dog. Thorpe was startled at the change.

A knock announced the sandwiches and milk. The cripple fell upon them with both hands in a sudden ecstacy of hunger. When he had finished, he looked again at Thorpe, and this time there were tears in his eyes.

A little later Thorpe interviewed the proprietor of the hotel.

"I wish you'd give this boy a good cheap room and charge his keep to me," said he. "He's going north with me."

Phil was led away by the irreverent porter, hugging tightly his unstrung violin to his bosom.

Thorpe lay awake for some time after retiring. Phil claimed a share of his thoughts.

Thorpe's winter in the woods had impressed upon him that a good cook and a fiddler will do more to keep men contented than high wages and easy work. So his protection of the cripple was not entirely disinterested. But his imagination persisted in occupying itself with the boy. What terrible life of want and vicious associates had he led in this terrible town? What treatment could have lit that wolf-gleam in his eyes? What hell had he inhabited that he was so eager to get away? In an hour or so he dozed. He dreamed that the cripple had grown to enormous proportions and was overshadowing his life. A slight noise outside his bed-room door brought him to his feet.

He opened the door and found that in the stillness of the night the poor deformed creature had taken the blankets from his bed and had spread them across the door-sill of the man who had befriended him.

## *Chapter XXIX*

Three weeks later the steam barge Pole Star sailed down the reach of Saginaw Bay.

Thorpe had received letters from Carpenter advising him of a credit to him at a Marquette bank, and inclosing a draft sufficient for current expenses. Tim Shearer had helped make out the list of necessaries. In time everything was loaded, the gang-plank hauled in, and the little band of Argonauts set their faces toward the point where the Big Dipper swings.

The weather was beautiful. Each morning the sun rose out of the frosty blue lake water, and set in a sea of deep purple. The moon, once again at the full, drew broad paths across the pathless waste. From the southeast blew daily the lake trades, to die at sunset, and then to return in the soft still nights from the west. A more propitious beginning for the adventure could not be imagined.

The ten horses in the hold munched their hay and oats as peaceably as though at home in their own stables. Jackson Hines had helped select them from the stock of firms changing locality or going out of business. His judgment in such matters was infallible, but he had resolutely refused to take the position of barn-boss which Thorpe offered him.

"No," said he, "she's too far north. I'm gettin' old, and the rheumatics ain't what you might call abandonin' of me. Up there it's colder than hell on a stoker's holiday."

So Shearer had picked out a barn-boss of his own. This man was important, for the horses are the mainstay of logging operations. He had selected also, a blacksmith, a cook, four teamsters, half a dozen cant-hook men, and as many handy with ax or saw.

"The blacksmith is also a good wood-butcher (carpenter)," explained Shearer. "Four teams is all we ought to keep going at a clip. If we need a few axmen, we can pick 'em up at Marquette. I think this gang'll stick. I picked 'em."

There was not a young man in the lot. They were most of them in the prime of middle life, between thirty and forty, rugged in appearance, "cocky" in manner, with the swagger and the oath of so many buccaneers, hard as nails. Altogether Thorpe thought them about as rough a set of customers as he had ever seen. Throughout the day they played cards on deck, and spat tobacco juice abroad, and swore incessantly. Toward himself and Shearer their manner was an odd mixture of independent equality and a slight deference. It was as much as to say, "You're the boss, but I'm as good a man as you any day." They would be a rough, turbulent, unruly mob to handle, but under a strong man they might accomplish wonders.

Constituting the elite of the profession, as it were,—whose swagger every lad new to the woods and river tried to emulate, to whom lesser lights looked up as heroes and models, and whose lofty, half-contemptuous scorn of everything and everybody outside their circle of "bully boys" was truly the aristocracy of class,—Thorpe might have wondered at their consenting to work for an obscure little camp belonging to a greenhorn. Loyalty to and pride in the firm for which he works is a strong characteristic of the lumber-jack. He will fight at the drop of a hat on behalf of his "Old Fellows"; brag loud and long of the season's cut, the big loads, the smart methods of his camps; and even after he has been discharged for some flagrant debauch, he cherishes no rancor, but speaks with a soft reminiscence to the end of his days concerning "that winter in '81 when the Old Fellows put in sixty million on Flat River."

For this reason he feels that he owes it to his reputation to ally himself only with firms of creditable size and efficiency. The small camps are for the youngsters. Occasionally you will see two or three of the veterans in such a camp, but it is generally a case of lacking something better.

The truth is, Shearer had managed to inspire in the minds of his cronies an idea that they were about to participate in a fight. He re-told Thorpe's story artistically, shading the yellows and the reds. He detailed the situation as it existed. The men agreed that the "young fellow had sand enough for a lake front." After that there needed but a little skillful maneuvering to inspire them with the idea that it would be a great thing to take a hand, to "make a camp" in spite of the big concern up-river.

Shearer knew that this attitude was tentative. Everything depended on how well Thorpe lived up to his reputation at the outset,—how good a first impression of force and virility he would manage to convey,—for the first impression possessed the power of transmuting the present rather ill-defined enthusiasm into loyalty or dissatisfaction. But Tim himself believed in Thorpe blindly. So he had no fears.

A little incident at the beginning of the voyage did much to reassure him. It was on the old question of whisky.

Thorpe had given orders that no whisky was to be brought aboard, as he intended to tolerate no high-sea orgies. Soon after leaving dock he saw one of the teamsters drinking from a pint flask. Without a word he stepped briskly forward, snatched the bottle from the man's lips, and threw it overboard. Then he turned sharp on his heel and walked away, without troubling himself as to how the fellow was going to take it.

The occurrence pleased the men, for it showed them they had made no mistake. But it meant little else. The chief danger really was lest they become too settled in the protective attitude. As they took it, they were about, good-naturedly, to help along a worthy greenhorn. This they considered exceedingly generous on their part, and in their own minds they were inclined to look on Thorpe much as a grown man would look on a child. There needed an occasion for him to prove himself bigger than they.

Fine weather followed them up the long blue reach of Lake Huron; into the noble breadth of the Detour Passage, past the opening through the Thousand Islands of the Georgian Bay; into the St. Mary's River. They were locked through after some delay on account of the grain barges from Duluth, and at last turned their prow westward in the Big Sea Water, beyond which lay Hiawatha's Po-ne-mah, the Land of the Hereafter.

Thorpe was about late that night, drinking in the mystic beauty of the scene. Northern lights, pale and dim, stretched their arc across beneath the Dipper. The air, soft as the dead leaves of spring, fanned his cheek. By and by the moon, like a red fire at sea, lifted itself from the waves. Thorpe made his way to the stern, beyond the square deck house, where he intended to lean on the rail in silent contemplation of the moon-path.

He found another before him. Phil, the little cripple, was peering into the wonderful east, its light in his eyes. He did not look at Thorpe when the latter approached, but seemed aware of his presence, for he moved swiftly to give room.

"It is very beautiful; isn't it, Phil?" said Thorpe after a moment.

"It is the Heart Song of the Sea," replied the cripple in a hushed voice.

Thorpe looked down surprised.

"Who told you that?" he asked.

But the cripple, repeating the words of a chance preacher, could explain himself no farther. In a dim way the ready-made phrase had expressed the smothered poetic craving of his heart,—the belief that the sea, the sky, the woods, the men and women, you, I, all have our Heart Songs, the Song which is most beautiful.

"The Heart Song of the Sea," he repeated gropingly. "I don't know ...I play it," and he made the motion of drawing a bow across strings, "very still and low." And this was all Thorpe's question could elicit.

Thorpe fell silent in the spell of the night, and pondered over the chances of life which had cast on the shores of the deep as driftwood the soul of a poet.

"Your Song," said the cripple timidly, "some day I will hear it. Not yet. That night in Bay City, when you took me in, I heard it very dim. But I cannot play it yet on my violin."

"Has your violin a song of its own?" queried the man.

"I cannot hear it. It tries to sing, but there is something in the way. I cannot. Some day I will hear it and play it, but—" and he drew nearer Thorpe and touched his arm—"that day will be very bad for me. I lose something." His eyes of the wistful dog were big and wondering.

"Queer little Phil!" cried Thorpe laughing whimsically. "Who tells you these things?"

"Nobody," said the cripple dreamily, "they come when it is like to-night. In Bay City they do not come."

At this moment a third voice broke in on them.

"Oh, it's you, Mr. Thorpe," said the captain of the vessel. "Thought it was some of them lumber-jacks, and I was going to fire 'em below. Fine night."

"It is that," answered Thorpe, again the cold, unresponsive man of reticence. "When do you expect to get in, Captain?"

"About to-morrow noon," replied the captain, moving away. Thorpe followed him a short distance, discussing the landing. The cripple stood all night, his bright, luminous eyes gazing clear and unwinking at the moonlight, listening to his Heart Song of the Sea.

## Chapter XXX

Next morning continued the traditions of its calm predecessors. Therefore by daybreak every man was at work. The hatches were opened, and soon between-decks was cumbered with boxes, packing cases, barrels, and crates. In their improvised stalls, the patient horses seemed to catch a hint of shore-going and whinnied. By ten o'clock there loomed against the strange coast line of the Pictured Rocks, a shallow bay and what looked to be a dock distorted by the northern mirage.

"That's her," said the captain.

Two hours later the steamboat swept a wide curve, slid between the yellow waters of two outlying reefs, and, with slackened speed, moved slowly toward the wharf of log cribs filled with stone.

The bay or the dock Thorpe had never seen. He took them on the captain's say-so. He knew very well that the structure had been erected by and belonged to Morrison & Daly, but the young man had had the foresight to purchase the land lying on the deep water side of the bay. He therefore anticipated no trouble in unloading; for while Morrison & Daly owned the pier itself, the land on which it abutted belonged to him.

From the arms of the bay he could make out a dozen figures standing near the end of the wharf. When, with propeller reversed, the Pole Star bore slowly down towards her moorings, Thorpe recognized Dyer at the head of eight or ten woodsmen. The sight of Radway's old scaler somehow filled him with a quiet but dangerous anger, especially since that official, on whom rested a portion at least of the responsibility of the jobber's failure, was now found in the employ of the very company which had attempted that failure. It looked suspicious.

"Catch this line!" sung out the mate, hurling the coil of a handline on the wharf.

No one moved, and the little rope, after a moment, slid overboard with a splash.

The captain, with a curse, signalled full speed astern.

"Captain Morse!" cried Dyer, stepping forward. "My orders are that you are to land here nothing but M. & D. merchandise."

"I have a right to land," answered Thorpe. "The shore belongs to me."

"This dock doesn't," retorted the other sharply, "and you can't set foot on her."

"You have no legal status. You had no business building in the first place—" began Thorpe, and then stopped with a choke of anger at the futility of arguing legality in such a case.

The men had gathered interestedly in the waist of the ship, cool, impartial, severely critical. The vessel, gathering speed astern, but not yet obeying her reversed helm, swung her bow in towards the dock. Thorpe ran swiftly forward, and during the instant of rubbing contact, leaped.

He alighted squarely upon his feet. Without an instant's hesitation, hot with angry energy at finding his enemy within reach of his hand, he rushed on Dyer, and with one full, clean in-blow stretched him stunned on the dock. For a moment there was a pause of astonishment. Then the woodsmen closed upon him.

During that instant Thorpe had become possessed of a weapon It came hurling through the air from above to fall at his feet. Shearer, with the cool calculation of the pioneer whom no excitement can distract from the main issue, had seen that it would be impossible to follow his chief, and so had done the next best thing,—thrown him a heavy iron belaying pin.

Thorpe was active, alert, and strong. The men could come at him only in front. As offset, he could not give ground, even for one step. Still, in the hands of a powerful man, the belaying pin is by no means a despicable weapon. Thorpe hit with all his strength and quickness. He was conscious once of being on the point of defeat. Then he had cleared a little space for himself. Then the men were on him again more savagely than ever. One fellow even succeeded in hitting him a glancing blow on the shoulder.

Then came a sudden crash. Thorpe was nearly thrown from his feet. The next instant a score of yelling men leaped behind and all around him. There ensued a moment's scuffle, the sound of dull blows; and the dock was clear of all but Dyer and three others who were, like himself, unconscious. The captain, yielding to the excitement, had run his prow plump against the wharf.

Some of the crew received the mooring lines. All was ready for disembarkation.

Bryan Moloney, a strapping Irish-American of the big-boned, red-cheeked type, threw some water over the four stunned combatants. Slowly they came to life. They were promptly yanked to their feet by the irate rivermen, who commenced at once to bestow sundry vigorous kicks and shakings by way of punishment. Thorpe interposed.

"Quit it!" he commanded. "Let them go!"

The men grumbled. One or two were inclined to be openly rebellious.

"If I hear another peep out of you," said Thorpe to these latter, "you can climb right aboard and take the return trip." He looked them in the eye until they muttered, and then went on: "Now, we've got to get unloaded and our goods ashore before those fellows report to camp. Get right moving, and hustle!"

If the men expected any comment, approval, or familiarity from their leader on account of their little fracas, they were disappointed. This was a good thing. The lumber-jack demands in his boss a certain fundamental unapproachability, whatever surface bonhomie he may evince.

So Dyer and his men picked themselves out of the trouble sullenly and departed. The ex-scaler had nothing to say as long as he was within reach, but when he had gained the shore, he turned.

"You won't think this is so funny when you get in the law-courts!" he shouted.

Thorpe made no reply. "I guess we'll keep even," he muttered.

"By the jumping Moses," snarled Scotty Parsons turning in threat.

"Scotty!" said Thorpe sharply.

Scotty turned back to his task, which was to help the blacksmith put together the wagon, the component parts of which the others had trundled out.

With thirty men at the job it does not take a great while to move a small cargo thirty or forty feet. By three o'clock the Pole Star was ready to continue her journey. Thorpe climbed aboard, leaving Shearer in charge.

"Keep the men at it, Tim," said he. "Put up the walls of the warehouse good and strong, and move the stuff in. If it rains, you can spread the tent over the roof, and camp in with the provisions. If you get through before I return, you might take a scout up the river and fix on a camp site. I'll bring back the lumber for roofs, floors, and trimmings with me, and will try to pick up a few axmen for swamping. Above all things, have a good man or so always in charge. Those fellows won't bother us any more for the present, I think; but it pays to be on deck. So long."

In Marquette, Thorpe arranged for the cashing of his time checks and orders; bought lumber at the mills; talked contract with old Harvey, the mill-owner and prospective buyer of the young man's cut; and engaged four axmen whom he found loafing about, waiting for the season to open.

When he returned to the bay he found the warehouse complete except for the roofs and gables. These, with their reinforcement of tar-paper, were nailed on in short order. Shearer and Andrews, the surveyor, were scouting up the river.

"No trouble from above, boys?" asked Thorpe.

"Nary trouble," they replied.

The warehouse was secured by padlocks, the wagon loaded with the tent and the necessaries of life and work. Early in the morning the little procession laughing, joking, skylarking with the high spirits of men in the woods took its way up the river-trail. Late that evening, tired, but still inclined to mischief, they came to the first dam, where Shearer and Andrews met them.

"How do you like it, Tim?" asked Thorpe that evening.

"She's all right," replied the riverman with emphasis; which, for him, was putting it strong.

At noon of the following day the party arrived at the second dam. Here Shearer had decided to build the permanent camp. Injin Charley was constructing one of his endless series of birch-bark canoes. Later he would paddle the whole string to Marquette, where he would sell them to a hardware dealer for two dollars and a half apiece.

To Thorpe, who had walked on ahead with his foreman, it seemed that he had never been away. There was the knoll; the rude camp with the deer hides; the venison hanging suspended from the pole; the endless broil and tumult of the clear north-country stream; the yellow glow over the hill opposite. Yet he had gone a nearly penniless adventurer; he returned at the head of an enterprise.

Injin Charley looked up and grunted as Thorpe approached.

"How are you, Charley?" greeted Thorpe reticently.

"You gettum pine? Good!" replied Charley in the same tone.

That was all; for strong men never talk freely of what is in their hearts. There is no need; they understand.

### Chapter XXXI

Two months passed away. Winter set in. The camp was built and inhabited. Routine had established itself, and all was going well.

The first move of the M. & D. Company had been one of conciliation. Thorpe was approached by the walking-boss of the camps up-river. The man made no reference to or excuse for what had occurred, nor did he pretend to any hypocritical friendship for the younger firm. His proposition was entirely one of mutual advantage. The Company had gone to considerable expense in constructing the pier of stone cribs. It would be impossible for the steamer to land at any other point. Thorpe had undisputed possession of the shore, but the Company could as indisputably remove the dock. Let it stay where it was. Both companies could then use it for their mutual convenience.

To this Thorpe agreed. Baker, the walking-boss, tried to get him to sign a contract to that effect. Thorpe refused.

"Leave your dock where it is and use it when you want to," said he. "I'll agree not to interfere as long as you people behave yourselves."

The actual logging was opening up well. Both Shearer and Thorpe agreed that it would not do to be too ambitious the first year. They set about clearing their banking ground about a half mile below the first dam; and during the six weeks before snow-fall cut three short roads of half a mile each. Approximately two million feet would be put in from these—roads which could be extended in years to come—while another million could be travoyed directly to the landing from its immediate vicinity.

"We won't skid them," said Tim. "We'll haul from the stump to the bank. And we'll tackle only a snowroad proposition:—we ain't got time to monkey with buildin' sprinklers and plows this year. We'll make a little stake ahead, and then next year we'll do it right and get in twenty million. That railroad'll get along a ways by then, and men'll be more plenty."

Through the lengthening evenings they sat crouched on wooden boxes either side of the stove, conversing rarely, gazing at one spot with a steady persistency which was only an outward indication of the persistency with which their minds held to the work in hand. Tim, the older at the business, showed this trait more strongly than Thorpe. The old man thought of nothing but logging. From the stump to the bank, from the bank to the camp, from the camp to the stump again, his restless intelligence travelled tirelessly, picking up, turning over, examining the littlest details with an ever-fresh curiosity and interest. Nothing was too small to escape this deliberate scrutiny. Nothing was in so perfect a state that it did not bear one more inspection. He played the logging as a chess player his game. One by one he adopted the various possibilities, remote and otherwise, as hypotheses, and thought out to the uttermost copper rivet what would be the best method of procedure in case that possibility should confront him.

Occasionally Thorpe would introduce some other topic of conversation. The old man would listen to his remark with the attention of courtesy; would allow a decent period of silence to intervene; and then, reverting to the old subject without comment on the new, would emit one of his terse practical suggestions, result of a long spell of figuring. That is how success is made.

In the men's camp the crew lounged, smoked, danced, or played cards. In those days no one thought of forbidding gambling. One evening Thorpe, who had been too busy to remember Phil's violin,—although he noticed, as he did every other detail of the camp, the cripple's industry, and the precision with which he performed his duties,—strolled over and looked through the window. A dance was in progress. The men were waltzing, whirling solemnly round and round, gripping firmly each other's loose sleeves just above the elbow. At every third step of the waltz they stamped one foot.

Perched on a cracker box sat Phil. His head was thrust forward almost aggressively over his instrument, and his eyes glared at the dancing men with the old wolf-like gleam. As he played, he drew the bow across with a swift jerk, thrust it back with another, threw his shoulders from one side to the other in abrupt time to the music. And the music! Thorpe unconsciously shuddered; then sighed in pity. It was atrocious. It was not even in tune. Two out of three of the notes were either sharp or flat, not so flagrantly as to produce absolute disharmony, but just enough to set the teeth on edge. And the rendition was as colorless as that of a poor hand-organ.

The performer seemed to grind out his fearful stuff with a fierce delight, in which appeared little of the esthetic pleasure of the artist. Thorpe was at a loss to define it.

"Poor Phil," he said to himself. "He has the musical soul without even the musical ear!"

Next day, while passing out of the cook camp he addressed one of the men:

"Well, Billy," he inquired, "how do you like your fiddler?"

"All RIGHT!" replied Billy with emphasis. "She's got some go to her."

In the woods the work proceeded finely. From the travoy sledges and the short roads a constant stream of logs emptied itself on the bank. There long parallel skidways had been laid the whole width of the river valley. Each log as it came was dragged across those monster andirons and rolled to the bank of the river. The cant-hook men dug their implements into the rough bark, leaned, lifted, or clung to the projecting stocks until slowly the log moved, rolling with gradually increasing momentum. Then they attacked it with fury lest the momentum be lost. Whenever it began to deviate from the straight rolling necessary to keep it on the center of the skids, one of the workers thrust the shoe of his cant-hook under one end of the log. That end promptly stopped; the other, still rolling, soon caught up; and the log moved on evenly, as was fitting.

At the end of the rollway the log collided with other logs and stopped with the impact of one bowling ball against another. The men knew that being caught between the two meant death or crippling for life. Nevertheless they escaped from the narrowing interval at the latest possible moment, for it is easier to keep a log rolling than to start it.

Then other men piled them by means of long steel chains and horses, just as they would have skidded them in the woods. Only now the logs mounted up and up until the skidways were thirty or forty feet high. Eventually the pile of logs would fill the banking ground utterly, burying the landing under a nearly continuous carpet of timber as thick as a two-story house is tall. The work is dangerous. A saw log containing six hundred board feet weighs about one ton. This is the weight of an ordinary iron safe. When one of them rolls or falls from even a moderate height, its force is irresistible. But when twenty or thirty cascade down the bold front of a skidway, carrying a man or so with them, the affair becomes a catastrophe.

Thorpe's men, however, were all old-timers, and nothing of the sort occurred. At first it made him catch his breath to see the apparent chances they took; but after a little he perceived that seeming luck was in reality a coolness of judgment and a long experience in the peculiar ways of that most erratic of inanimate cussedness—the pine log. The banks grew daily. Everybody was safe and sound.

The young lumberman had sense enough to know that, while a crew such as his is supremely effective, it requires careful handling to keep it good-humored and willing. He knew every man by his first name, and each day made it a point to talk with him for a moment or so. The subject was invariably some phase of the work. Thorpe never permitted himself the familiarity of introducing any other topic. By this course he preserved the nice balance between too great reserve, which chills the lumber-jack's rather independent enthusiasm, and the too great familiarity, which loses his respect. He never replied directly to an objection or a request, but listened to it non-committally; and later, without explanation or reasoning, acted as his judgment dictated. Even Shearer, with whom he was in most intimate contact, respected this trait in him. Gradually he came to feel that he was making a way with his men. It was a status, not assured as yet nor even very firm, but a status for all that.

Then one day one of the best men, a teamster, came in to make some objection to the cooking. As a matter of fact, the cooking was perfectly good. It generally is, in a well-conducted camp, but the lumber-jack is a great hand to growl, and he usually begins with his food.

Thorpe listened to his vague objections in silence.

"All right," he remarked simply.

Next day he touched the man on the shoulder just as he was starting to work.

"Step into the office and get your time," said he.

"What's the matter?" asked the man.

"I don't need you any longer."

The two entered the little office. Thorpe looked through the ledger and van book, and finally handed the man his slip.

"Where do I get this?" asked the teamster, looking at it uncertainly.

"At the bank in Marquette," replied Thorpe without glancing around.

"Have I got to go 'way up to Marquette?"

"Certainly," replied Thorpe briefly.

"Who's going to pay my fare south?"

"You are. You can get work at Marquette."

"That ain't a fair shake," cried the man excitedly.

"I'll have no growlers in this camp," said Thorpe with decision.

"By God!" cried the man, "you damned—"

"You get out of here!" cried Thorpe with a concentrated blaze of energetic passion that made the fellow step back.

"I ain't goin' to get on the wrong side of the law by foolin' with this office," cried the other at the door, "but if I had you outside for a minute—"

"Leave this office!" shouted Thorpe.

"S'pose you make me!" challenged the man insolently.

In a moment the defiance had come, endangering the careful structure Thorpe had reared with such pains. The young man was suddenly angry in exactly the same blind, unreasoning manner as when he had leaped single-handed to tackle Dyer's crew.

Without a word he sprang across the shack, seized a two-bladed ax from the pile behind the door, swung it around his head and cast it full at the now frightened teamster. The latter dodged, and the swirling steel buried itself in the snowbank beyond. Without an instant's hesitation Thorpe reached back for another. The man took to his heels.

"I don't want to see you around here again!" shouted Thorpe after him.

Then in a moment he returned to the office and sat down overcome with contrition.

"It might have been murder!" he told himself, awe-stricken.

But, as it happened, nothing could have turned out better.

Thorpe had instinctively seized the only method by which these strong men could be impressed. A rough-and-tumble attempt at ejectment would have been useless. Now the entire crew looked with vast admiration on their boss as a man who intended to have his own way no matter what difficulties or consequences might tend to deter him. And that is the kind of man they liked. This one deed was more effective in cementing their loyalty than any increase of wages would have been.

Thorpe knew that their restless spirits would soon tire of the monotony of work without ultimate interest. Ordinarily the hope of a big cut is sufficient to keep men of the right sort working for a record. But these men had no such hope—the camp was too small, and they were too few. Thorpe adopted the expedient, now quite common, of posting the results of each day's work in the men's shanty.

Three teams were engaged in travoying, and two in skidding the logs, either on the banking ground, or along the road. Thorpe divided his camp into four sections, which he distinguished by the names of the teamsters. Roughly speaking, each of the three hauling teams had its own gang of sawyers and skidders to supply it with logs and to take them from it, for of the skidding teams, one was split;—the horses were big enough so that one of them to a skidway sufficed. Thus three gangs of men were performing each day practically the same work. Thorpe scaled the results, and placed them conspicuously for comparison.

Red Jacket, the teamster of the sorrels, one day was credited with 11,000 feet; while Long Pine Jim and Rollway Charley had put in but 10,500 and 10,250 respectively. That evening all the sawyers, swampers, and skidders belonging to Red Jacket's outfit were considerably elated; while the others said little and prepared for business on the morrow.

Once Long Pine Jim lurked at the bottom for three days. Thorpe happened by the skidway just as Long Pine arrived with a log. The young fellow glanced solicitously at the splendid buckskins, the best horses in camp.

"I'm afraid I didn't give you a very good team, Jimmy," said he, and passed on.

That was all; but men of the rival gangs had heard. In camp Long Pine Jim and his crew received chaffing with balefully red glares. Next day they stood at the top by a good margin, and always after were competitors to be feared.

Injin Charley, silent and enigmatical as ever, had constructed a log shack near a little creek over in the hardwood. There he attended diligently to the business of trapping. Thorpe had brought him a deer knife from Detroit; a beautiful instrument made of the best tool steel, in one long piece extending through the buck-horn handle. One could even break bones with it. He had also lent the Indian the assistance of two of his Marquette men in erecting the shanty; and had given him a barrel of flour for the winter. From time to time Injin Charley brought in fresh meat, for which he was paid. This with his trapping, and his manufacture of moccasins, snowshoes and birch canoes, made him a very prosperous Indian indeed. Thorpe rarely found time to visit him, but he often glided into the office, smoked a pipeful of the white man's tobacco in friendly fashion by the stove, and glided out again without having spoken a dozen words.

Wallace made one visit before the big snows came, and was charmed. He ate with gusto of the "salt-horse," baked beans, stewed prunes, mince pie, and cakes. He tramped around gaily in his moccasins or on the fancy snowshoes he promptly purchased of Injin Charley. There was nothing new to report in regard to financial matters. The loan had been negotiated easily on the basis of a mortgage guaranteed by Carpenter's personal signature. Nothing had been heard from Morrison & Daly.

When he departed, he left behind him four little long-eared, short-legged beagle hounds. They were solemn animals, who took life seriously. Never a smile appeared in their questioning eyes. Wherever one went, the others followed, pattering gravely along in serried ranks. Soon they discovered that the swamp over the knoll contained big white hares. Their mission in life was evident. Thereafter from the earliest peep of daylight until the men quit work at night they chased rabbits. The quest was hopeless, but they kept obstinately at it, wallowing with contained excitement over a hundred paces of snow before they would get near enough to scare their quarry to another jump. It used to amuse the hares. All day long the mellow bell-tones echoed over the knoll. It came in time to be part of the color of the camp, just as were the pines and birches, or the cold northern sky. At the fall of night, exhausted, trailing their long ears almost to the ground, they returned to the cook, who fed them and made much of them. Next morning they were at it as hard as ever. To them it was the quest for the Grail,—hopeless, but glorious.

Little Phil, entrusted with the alarm clock, was the first up in the morning In the fearful biting cold of an extinct camp, he lighted his lantern and with numb hands raked the ashes from the stove. A few sticks of dried pine topped by split wood of birch or maple, all well dashed with kerosene, took the flame eagerly. Then he awakened the cook, and stole silently into the office, where Thorpe and Shearer and Andrews, the surveyor, lay asleep. There quietly he built another fire, and filled the water-pail afresh. By the time this task was finished, the cook sounded many times a conch, and the sleeping camp awoke.

Later Phil drew water for the other shanties, swept out all three, split wood and carried it in to the cook and to the living-camps, filled and trimmed the lamps, perhaps helped the cook. About half the remainder of the day he wielded an ax, saw and wedge in the hardwood, collecting painfully—for his strength was not great—material for the constant fires it was his duty to maintain. Often he would stand motionless in the vast frozen, creaking forest, listening with awe to the voices which spoke to him alone. There was something uncanny in the misshapen dwarf with the fixed marble white face and the expressive changing eyes,—something uncanny, and something indefinably beautiful.

He seemed to possess an instinct which warned him of the approach of wild animals. Long before a white man, or even an Indian, would have suspected the presence of game, little Phil would lift his head with a peculiar listening toss. Soon, stepping daintily through the snow near the swamp edge, would come a deer; or pat-apat-patting on his broad hairy paws, a lynx would steal by. Except Injin Charley, Phil was the only man in that country who ever saw a beaver in the open daylight.

At camp sometimes when all the men were away and his own work was done, he would crouch like a raccoon in the far corner of his deep square bunk with the board ends that made of it a sort of little cabin, and play to himself softly on his violin. No one ever heard him. After supper he was docilely ready to fiddle to the men's dancing. Always then he gradually worked himself to a certain pitch of excitement. His eyes glared with the wolf-gleam, and the music was vulgarly atrocious and out of tune.

As Christmas drew near, the weather increased in severity. Blinding snow-squalls swept whirling from the northeast, accompanied by a high wind. The air was full of it,—fine, dry, powdery, like the dust of glass. The men worked covered with it as a tree is covered after a sleet. Sometimes it was impossible to work at all for hours at a time, but Thorpe did not allow a bad morning to spoil a good afternoon. The instant a lull fell on the storm, he was out with his scaling rule, and he expected the men to give him something to scale. He grappled the fierce winter by the throat, and shook from it the price of success.

Then came a succession of bright cold days and clear cold nights. The aurora gleamed so brilliantly that the forest was as bright as by moonlight. In the strange weird shadow cast by its waverings the wolves stole silently, or broke into wild ululations as they struck the trail of game. Except for these weird invaders, the silence of death fell on the wilderness. Deer left the country. Partridges crouched trailing under the snow. All the weak and timid creatures of the woods shrank into concealment and silence before these fierce woods-marauders with the glaring famine-struck eyes.

Injin Charley found his traps robbed. In return he constructed deadfalls, and dried several scalps. When spring came, he would send them out for the bounty In the night, from time to time, the horses would awake trembling at an unknown terror. Then the long weird howl would shiver across the starlight near at hand, and the chattering man who rose hastily to quiet the horses' frantic kicking, would catch a glimpse of gaunt forms skirting the edge of the forest.

And the little beagles were disconsolate, for their quarry had fled. In place of the fan-shaped triangular trail for which they sought, they came upon dog-like prints. These they sniffed at curiously, and then departed growling, the hair on their backbones erect and stiff.

### Chapter XXXII

By the end of the winter some four million feet of logs were piled in the bed or upon the banks of the stream. To understand what that means, you must imagine a pile of solid timber a mile in length. This tremendous mass lay directly in the course of the stream. When the winter broke up, it had to be separated and floated piecemeal down the current. The process is an interesting and dangerous one, and one of great delicacy. It requires for its successful completion picked men of skill, and demands as toll its yearly quota of crippled and dead. While on the drive, men work fourteen hours a day, up to their waists in water filled with floating ice.

On the Ossawinamakee, as has been stated, three dams had been erected to simplify the process of driving. When the logs were in right distribution, the gates were raised, and the proper head of water floated them down.

Now the river being navigable, Thorpe was possessed of certain rights on it. Technically he was entitled to a normal head of water, whenever he needed it; or a special head, according to agreement with the parties owning the dam. Early in the drive, he found that Morrison & Daly intended to cause him trouble. It began in a narrows of the river between high, rocky banks. Thorpe's drive was floating through close-packed. The situation was ticklish. Men with spiked boots ran here and there from one bobbing log to another, pushing with their peaveys, hurrying one log, retarding another, working like beavers to keep the whole mass straight. The entire surface of the water was practically covered with the floating timbers. A moment's reflection will show the importance of preserving a full head of water. The moment the stream should drop an inch or so, its surface would contract, the logs would then be drawn close together in the narrow space; and, unless an immediate rise should lift them up and apart from each other, a jam would form, behind which the water, rapidly damming, would press to entangle it the more.

This is exactly what happened. In a moment, as though by magic, the loose wooden carpet ground together. A log in the advance up-ended; another thrust under it. The whole mass ground together, stopped, and began rapidly to pile up. The men escaped to the shore in a marvellous manner of their own.

Tim Shearer found that the gate at the dam above had been closed. The man in charge had simply obeyed orders. He supposed M. & D. wished to back up the water for their own logs.

Tim indulged in some picturesque language.

"You ain't got no right to close off more'n enough to leave us th' nat'ral flow unless by agreement," he concluded, and opened the gates.

Then it was a question of breaking the jam. This had to be done by pulling out or chopping through certain "key" logs which locked the whole mass. Men stood under the face of imminent ruin—over them a frowning sheer wall of bristling logs, behind which pressed the weight of the rising waters—and hacked and tugged calmly until the mass began to stir. Then they escaped. A moment later, with a roar, the jam vomited down on the spot where they had stood. It was dangerous work. Just one half day later it had to be done again, and for the same reason.

This time Thorpe went back with Shearer. No one was at the dam, but the gates were closed. The two opened them again.

That very evening a man rode up on horseback inquiring for Mr. Thorpe.

"I'm he," said the young fellow.

The man thereupon dismounted and served a paper. It proved to be an injunction issued by Judge Sherman enjoining Thorpe against interfering with the property of Morrison & Daly,—to wit, certain dams erected at designated points on the Ossawinamakee. There had not elapsed sufficient time since the commission of the offense for the other firm to secure the issuance of this interesting document, so it was at once evident that the whole affair had been pre-arranged by the up-river firm for the purpose of blocking off Thorpe's drive. After serving the injunction, the official rode away.

Thorpe called his foreman. The latter read the injunction attentively through a pair of steel-bowed spectacles.

"Well, what you going to do?" he asked.

"Of all the consummate gall!" exploded Thorpe. "Trying to enjoin me from touching a dam when they're refusing me the natural flow! They must have bribed that fool judge. Why, his injunction isn't worth the powder to blow it up!"

"Then you're all right, ain't ye?" inquired Tim.

"It'll be the middle of summer before we get a hearing in court," said he. "Oh, they're a cute layout! They expect to hang me up until it's too late to do anything with the season's cut!"

He arose and began to pace back and forth.

"Tim," said he, "is there a man in the crew who's afraid of nothing and will obey orders?"

"A dozen," replied Tim promptly.

"Who's the best?"

"Scotty Parsons."

"Ask him to step here."

In a moment the man entered the office.

"Scotty," said Thorpe, "I want you to understand that I stand responsible for whatever I order you to do."

"All right, sir," replied the man.

"In the morning," said Thorpe, "you take two men and build some sort of a shack right over the sluice-gate of that second dam,—nothing very fancy, but good enough to camp in. I want you to live there day and night. Never leave it, not even for a minute. The cookee will bring you grub. Take this Winchester. If any of the men from up-river try to go out on the dam, you warn them off. If they persist, you shoot near them. If they keep coming, you shoot at them. Understand?"

"You bet," answered Scotty with enthusiasm.

"All right," concluded Thorpe.

Next day Scotty established himself, as had been agreed. He did not need to shoot anybody. Daly himself came down to investigate the state of affairs, when his men reported to him the occupancy of the dam. He attempted to parley, but Scotty would have none of it.

"Get out!" was his first and last word.

Daly knew men. He was at the wrong end of the whip. Thorpe's game was desperate, but so was his need, and this was a backwoods country a long ways from the little technicalities of the law. It was one thing to serve an injunction; another to enforce it. Thorpe finished his drive with no more of the difficulties than ordinarily bother a riverman.

At the mouth of the river, booms of logs chained together at the ends had been prepared. Into the enclosure the drive was floated and stopped. Then a raft was formed by passing new manila ropes over the logs, to each one of which the line was fastened by a hardwood forked pin driven astride of it. A tug dragged the raft to Marquette.

Now Thorpe was summoned legally on two counts. First, Judge Sherman cited him for contempt of court. Second, Morrison & Daly sued him for alleged damages in obstructing their drive by holding open the dam-sluice beyond the legal head of water.

Such is a brief but true account of the coup-de-force actually carried out by Thorpe's lumbering firm in northern Michigan. It is better known to the craft than to the public at large, because eventually the affair was compromised. The manner of that compromise is to follow.

## Chapter XXXIII

Pending the call of trial, Thorpe took a three weeks' vacation to visit his sister. Time, filled with excitement and responsibility, had erased from his mind the bitterness of their parting. He had before been too busy, too grimly in earnest, to allow himself the luxury of anticipation. Now he found himself so impatient that he could hardly wait to get there. He pictured their meeting, the things they would say to each other.

As formerly, he learned on his arrival that she was not at home. It was the penalty of an attempted surprise. Mrs. Renwick proved not nearly so cordial as the year before; but Thorpe, absorbed in his eagerness, did not notice it. If he had, he might have guessed the truth: that the long propinquity of the fine and the commonplace, however safe at first from the insulation of breeding and natural kindliness, was at last beginning to generate sparks.

No, Mrs. Renwick did not know where Helen was: thought she had gone over to the Hughes's. The Hughes live two blocks down the street and three to the right, in a brown house back from the street. Very well, then; she would expect Mr. Thorpe to spend the night.

The latter wandered slowly down the charming driveways of the little western town. The broad dusty street was brown with sprinkling from numberless garden hose. A double row of big soft maples met over it, and shaded the sidewalk and part of the wide lawns. The grass was fresh and green. Houses with capacious verandas on which were glimpsed easy chairs and hammocks, sent forth a mild glow from a silk-shaded lamp or two. Across the evening air floated the sounds of light conversation and laughter from these verandas, the tinkle of a banjo, the thrum of a guitar. Automatic sprinklers whirled and hummed here and there. Their delicious artificial coolness struck refreshingly against the cheek.

Thorpe found the Hughes residence without difficulty, and turned up the straight walk to the veranda. On the steps of the latter a rug had been spread. A dozen youths and maidens lounged in well-bred ease on its soft surface. The gleam of white summer dresses, of variegated outing clothes, the rustle o frocks, the tinkle of low, well-bred laughter confused Thorpe, so that, as he approached the light from a tall lamp just inside the hall, he hesitated, vainly trying to make out the figures before him.

So it was that Helen Thorpe saw him first, and came fluttering to meet him.

"Oh, Harry! What a surprise!" she cried, and flung her arms about his neck to kiss him.

"How do you do, Helen," he replied sedately.

This was the meeting he had anticipated so long. The presence of others brought out in him, irresistibly, the repression of public display which was so strong an element of his character.

A little chilled, Helen turned to introduce him to her friends. In the cold light of her commonplace reception she noticed what in a warmer effusion of feelings she would never have seen,—that her brother's clothes were out of date and worn; and that, though his carriage was notably strong and graceful, the trifling constraint and dignity of his younger days had become almost an awkwardness after two years among uncultivated men. It occurred to Helen to be just a little ashamed of him.

He took a place on the steps and sat without saying a word all the evening. There was nothing for him to say. These young people talked thoughtlessly, as young people do, of the affairs belonging to their own little circle. Thorpe knew nothing of the cotillion, or the brake ride, or of the girl who visited Alice Southerland; all of which gave occasion for so much lively comment. Nor was the situation improved when some of them, in a noble effort at politeness, turned the conversation into more general channels. The topics of the day's light talk were absolutely unknown to him. The plays, the new books, the latest popular songs, jokes depending for their point on an intimate knowledge of the prevailing vaudeville mode, were as unfamiliar to him as Miss Alice Southerland's guest. He had thought pine and forest and the trail so long, that he found these square-elbowed subjects refusing to be jostled aside by any trivialities.

So he sat there silent in the semi-darkness. This man, whose lightest experience would have aroused the eager attention of the entire party, held his peace because he thought he had nothing to say.

He took Helen back to Mrs. Renwick's about ten o'clock. They walked slowly beneath the broad-leaved maples, whose shadows danced under the tall electric lights,—and talked.

Helen was an affectionate, warm-hearted girl. Ordinarily she would have been blind to everything except the delight of having her brother once more with her. But his apparently cold reception had first chilled, then thrown her violently into a critical mood. His subsequent social inadequacy had settled her into the common-sense level of everyday life.

"How have you done, Harry?" she inquired anxiously. "Your letters have been so vague."

"Pretty well," he replied. "If things go right, I hope some day to have a better place for you than this."

Her heart contracted suddenly. It was all she could do to keep from bursting into tears. One would have to realize perfectly her youth, the life to which she had been accustomed, the lack of encouragement she had labored under, the distastefulness of her surroundings, the pent-up dogged patience she had displayed during the last two years, the hopeless feeling of battering against a brick wall she always experienced when she received the replies to her attempts on Harry's confidence, to appreciate how the indefiniteness of his answer exasperated her and filled her with sullen despair. She said nothing for twenty steps. Then:

"Harry," she said quietly, "can't you take me away from Mrs. Renwick's this year?"

"I don't know, Helen. I can't tell yet. Not just now, at any rate."

"Harry," she cried, "you don't know what you're doing. I tell you I can't STAND Mrs. Renwick any longer." She calmed herself with an effort, and went on more quietly. "Really, Harry, she's awfully disagreeable. If you can't afford to keep me anywhere else—" she glanced timidly at his face and for the first time saw the strong lines about the jaw and the tiny furrows between the eyebrows. "I know you've worked hard, Harry dear," she said with a sudden sympathy, "and that you'd give me more, if you could. But so have I worked hard. Now we ought to change this in some way. I can get a position as teacher, or some other work somewhere. Won't you let me do that?"

Thorpe was thinking that it would be easy enough to obtain Wallace Carpenter's consent to his taking a thousand dollars from the profits of the year. But he knew also that the struggle in the courts might need every cent the new company could spare. It would look much better were he to wait until after the verdict. If favorable, there would be no difficulty about sparing the money. If adverse, there would be no money to spare. The latter contingency he did not seriously anticipate, but still it had to be considered. And so, until the thing was absolutely certain, he hesitated to explain the situation to Helen for fear of disappointing her!

"I think you'd better wait, Helen," said he. "There'll be time enough for all that later when it becomes necessary. You are very young yet, and it will not hurt you a bit to continue your education for a little while longer."

"And in the meantime stay with Mrs. Renwick?" flashed Helen.

"Yes. I hope it will not have to be for very long."

"How long do you think, Harry?" pleaded the girl.

"That depends on circumstances," replied Thorpe

"Oh!" she cried indignantly.

"Harry," she ventured after a time, "why not write to Uncle Amos?"

Thorpe stopped and looked at her searchingly.

"You can't mean that, Helen," he said, drawing a long breath.

"But why not?" she persisted.

"You ought to know."

"Who would have done any different? If you had a brother and discovered that he had—appropriated—most all the money of a concern of which you were president, wouldn't you think it your duty to have him arrested?"

"No!" cried Thorpe suddenly excited. "Never! If he was my brother, I'd help him, even if he'd committed murder!"

"We differ there," replied the girl coldly. "I consider that Uncle Amos was a strong man who did his duty as he saw it, in spite of his feelings. That he had father arrested is nothing against him in my eyes. And his wanting us to come to him since, seems to me very generous. I am going to write to him."

"You will do nothing of the kind," commanded Thorpe sternly. "Amos Thorpe is an unscrupulous man who became unscrupulously rich. He deliberately used our father as a tool, and then destroyed him. I consider that anyone of our family who would have anything to do with him is a traitor!"

The girl did not reply.

Next morning Thorpe felt uneasily repentant for his strong language. After all, the girl did lead a monotonous life, and he could not blame her for rebelling against it from time to time. Her remarks had been born of the rebellion; they had meant nothing in themselves. He could not doubt for a moment her loyalty to the family.

But he did not tell her so. That is not the way of men of his stamp. Rather he cast about to see what he could do.

Injin Charley had, during the winter just past, occupied odd moments in embroidering with beads and porcupine quills a wonderful outfit of soft buckskin gauntlets, a shirt of the same material, and moccasins of moose-hide. They were beautifully worked, and Thorpe, on receiving them, had at once conceived the idea of giving them to his sister. To this end he had consulted another Indian near Marquette, to whom he had confided the task of reducing the gloves and moccasins. The shirt would do as it was, for it was intended to be worn as a sort of belted blouse. As has been said, all were thickly beaded, and represented a vast quantity of work. Probably fifty dollars could not have bought them, even in the north country.

Thorpe tendered this as a peace offering. Not understanding women in the least, he was surprised to see his gift received by a burst of tears and a sudden exit from the room. Helen thought he had bought the things; and she was still sore from the pinch of the poverty she had touched the evening before. Nothing will exasperate a woman more than to be presented with something expensive for which she does not particularly care, after being denied, on the ground of economy, something she wants very much.

Thorpe stared after her in hurt astonishment. Mrs. Renwick sniffed.

That afternoon the latter estimable lady attempted to reprove Miss Helen, and was snubbed; she persisted, and an open quarrel ensued.

"I will not be dictated to by you, Mrs. Renwick," said Helen, "and I don't intend to have you interfere in any way with my family affairs."

"They won't stand MUCH investigation," replied Mrs. Renwick, goaded out of her placidity.

Thorpe entered to hear the last two speeches. He said nothing, but that night he wrote to Wallace Carpenter for a thousand dollars. Every stroke of the pen hurt him. But of course Helen could not stay here now.

"And to think, just to THINK that he let that woman insult me so, and didn't say a word!" cried Helen to herself.

Her method would have been to have acted irrevocably on the spot, and sought ways and means afterwards. Thorpe's, however, was to perfect all his plans before making the first step.

Wallace Carpenter was not in town. Before the letter had followed him to his new address, and the answer had returned, a week had passed. Of course the money was gladly put at Thorpe's disposal. The latter at once interviewed his sister.

"Helen," he said, "I have made arrangements for some money. What would you like to do this year?"

She raised her head and looked at him with clear bright gaze. If he could so easily raise the money, why had he not done so before? He knew how much she wanted it. Her happiness did not count. Only when his quixotic ideas of family honor were attacked did he bestir himself.

"I am going to Uncle Amos's," she replied distinctly.

"What?" asked Thorpe incredulously.

For answer she pointed to a letter lying open on the table. Thorpe took it and read:

"My dear Niece:

"Both Mrs. Thorpe and myself more than rejoice that time and reflection have removed that, I must confess, natural prejudice which the unfortunate family affair, to which I will not allude, raised in your mind against us. As we said long ago, our home is your's when you may wish to make it so. You state your present readiness to come immediately. Unless you wire to the contrary, we shall expect you next Tuesday evening on the four-forty train. I shall be at the Central Station myself to meet you. If your brother is now with you, I should be pleased to see him also, and will be most happy to give him a position with the firm.

"Aff. your uncle,

"Amos Thorpe.

"New York, June 6, 1883."

On finishing the last paragraph the reader crumpled the letter and threw it into the grate.

"I am sorry you did that, Helen," said he, "but I don't blame you, and it can't be helped. We won't need to take advantage of his 'kind offer' now."

"I intend to do so, however," replied the girl coldly.

"What do you mean?"

"I mean," she cried, "that I am sick of waiting on your good pleasure. I waited, and slaved, and stood unbearable things for two years. I did it cheerfully. And in return I don't get a civil word, not a decent explanation, not even a—caress," she fairly sobbed out the last word. "I can't stand it any longer. I have tried and tried and tried, and then when I've come to you for the littlest word of encouragement, you have pecked at me with those stingy little kisses, and have told me I was young and ought to finish my education. You put me in uncongenial surroundings, and go off into the woods camping yourself. You refuse me money enough to live in a three-dollar boarding-house, and you buy expensive rifles and fishing tackle for yourself. You can't afford to send me away somewhere for the summer, but you bring me back gee-gaws you have happened to fancy, worth a month's board in the country. You haven't a cent when it is a question of what I want; but you raise money quick enough when your old family is insulted. Isn't it my family too? And then you blame me because, after waiting in vain two years for you to do something, I start out to do the best I can for myself. I'm not of age but you're not my guardian!"

During this long speech Thorpe had stood motionless, growing paler and paler. Like most noble natures, when absolutely in the right, he was incapable of defending himself against misunderstandings. He was too wounded; he was hurt to the soul.

"You know that is not true, Helen," he replied, almost sternly.

"It IS true!" she asseverated, "and I'm THROUGH!"

"It's a little hard," said Thorpe passing his hand wearily before his eyes, "to work hard this way for years, and then—"
She laughed with a hard little note of scorn.

"Helen," said Thorpe with new energy, "I forbid you to have anything to do with Amos Thorpe. I think he is a scoundrel and a sneak."

"What grounds have you to think so?"

"None," he confessed, "that is, nothing definite. But I know men; and I know his type. Some day I shall be able to prove something. I do not wish you to have anything to do with him."

"I shall do as I please," she replied, crossing her hands behind her.

Thorpe's eyes darkened.

"We have talked this over a great many times," he warned, "and you've always agreed with me. Remember, you owe something to the family."

"Most of the family seem to owe something," she replied with a flippant laugh. "I'm sure I didn't choose the family. If I had, I'd have picked out a better one!"

The flippancy was only a weapon which she used unconsciously, blindly, in her struggle. The man could not know this. His face hardened, and his voice grew cold.

"You may take your choice, Helen," he said formally. "If you go into the household of Amos Thorpe, if you deliberately prefer your comfort to your honor, we will have nothing more in common."

They faced each other with the cool, deadly glance of the race, so similar in appearance but so unlike in nature.

"I, too, offer you a home, such as it is," repeated the man. "Choose!"

At the mention of the home for which means were so quickly forthcoming when Thorpe, not she, considered it needful, the girl's eyes flashed. She stooped and dragged violently from beneath the bed a flat steamer trunk, the lid of which she threw open. A dress lay on the bed. With a fine dramatic gesture she folded the garment and laid it in the bottom of the trunk. Then she knelt, and without vouchsafing another glance at her brother standing rigid by the door, she began feverishly to arrange the folds.

The choice was made. He turned and went out.

## Chapter XXXIV

With Thorpe there could be no half-way measure. He saw that the rupture with his sister was final, and the thrust attained him in one of his few unprotected points. It was not as though he felt either himself or his sister consciously in the wrong. He acquitted her of all fault, except as to the deadly one of misreading and misunderstanding. The fact argued not a perversion but a lack in her character. She was other than he had thought her.

As for himself, he had schemed, worked, lived only for her. He had come to her from the battle expecting rest and refreshment. To the world he had shown the hard, unyielding front of the unemotional; he had looked ever keenly outward; he had braced his muscles in the constant tension of endeavor. So much the more reason why, in the hearts of the few he loved, he, the man of action, should find repose; the man of sternness, should discover that absolute peace of the spirit in which not the slightest motion of the will is necessary, the man of repression should be permitted affectionate, care-free expansion of the natural affection, of the full sympathy which will understand and not mistake for weakness. Instead of this, he was forced into refusing where he would rather have given; into denying where he would rather have assented; and finally into commanding where he longed most ardently to lay aside the cloak of authority. His motives were misread; his intentions misjudged; his love doubted.

But worst of all, Thorpe's mind could see no possibility of an explanation. If she could not see of her own accord how much he loved her, surely it was a hopeless task to attempt an explanation through mere words. If, after all, she was capable of misconceiving the entire set of his motives during the past two years, expostulation would be futile. In his thoughts of her he fell into a great spiritual dumbness. Never, even in his moments of most theoretical imaginings, did he see himself setting before her fully and calmly the hopes and ambitions of which she had been the mainspring. And before a reconciliation, many such rehearsals must take place in the secret recesses of a man's being.

Thorpe did not cry out, nor confide in a friend, nor do anything even so mild as pacing the floor. The only outward and visible sign a close observer might have noted was a certain dumb pain lurking in the depths of his eyes like those of a wounded spaniel. He was hurt, but did not understand. He suffered in silence, but without anger. This is at once the noblest and the most pathetic of human suffering.

At first the spring of his life seemed broken. He did not care for money; and at present disappointment had numbed his interest in the game. It seemed hardly worth the candle.

Then in a few days, after his thoughts had ceased to dwell constantly on the one subject, he began to look about him mentally. Beneath his other interests he still felt constantly a dull ache, something unpleasant, uncomfortable. Strangely enough it was almost identical in quality with the uneasiness that always underlay his surface-thoughts when he was worried about some detail of his business. Unconsciously,—again as in his business,—the combative instinct aroused. In lack of other object on which to expend itself, Thorpe's fighting spirit turned with energy to the subject of the lawsuit.

Under the unwonted stress of the psychological condition just described, he thought at white heat. His ideas were clear, and followed each other quickly, almost feverishly.

After his sister left the Renwicks, Thorpe himself went to Detroit, where he interviewed at once Northrop, the brilliant young lawyer whom the firm had engaged to defend its case.

"I'm afraid we have no show," he replied to Thorpe's question. "You see, you fellows were on the wrong side of the fence in trying to enforce the law yourselves. Of course you may well say that justice was all on your side. That does not count. The only recourse recognized for injustice lies in the law courts. I'm afraid you are due to lose your case."

"Well," said Thorpe, "they can't prove much damage."

"I don't expect that they will be able to procure a very heavy judgment," replied Northrop. "The facts I shall be able to adduce will cut down damages. But the costs will be very heavy."

"Yes," agreed Thorpe.

"And," then pursued Northrop with a dry smile, "they practically own Sherman. You may be in for contempt of court at their instigation. As I understand it, they are trying rather to injure you than to get anything out of it themselves."

"That's it," nodded Thorpe.

"In other words, it's a case for compromise."

"Just what I wanted to get at," said Thorpe with satisfaction. "Now answer me a question. Suppose a man injures Government or State land by trespass. The land is afterwards bought by another party. Has the latter any claim for damage against the trespasser? Understand me, the purchaser bought AFTER the trespass was committed."

"Certainly," answered Northrop without hesitation.

"Provided suit is brought within six years of the time the trespass was committed."

"Good! Now see here. These M. & D. people stole about a section of Government pine up on that river, and I don't believe they've ever bought in the land it stood on. In fact I don't believe they suspect that anyone knows they've been stealing. How would it do, if I were to buy that section at the Land Office, and threaten to sue them for the value of the pine that originally stood on it?"

The lawyer's eyes glimmered behind the lenses of his pince-nez; but, with the caution of the professional man he made no other sign of satisfaction.

"It would do very well indeed," he replied, "but you'd have to prove they did the cutting, and you'll have to pay experts to estimate the probable amount of the timber. Have you the description of the section?"

"No," responded Thorpe, "but I can get it; and I can pick up witnesses from the woodsmen as to the cutting."

"The more the better. It is rather easy to discredit the testimony of one or two. How much, on a broad guess, would you estimate the timber to come to?"

"There ought to be about eight or ten million," guessed Thorpe after an instant's silence, "worth in the stump anywhere from sixteen to twenty thousand dollars. It would cost me only eight hundred to buy it."

"Do so, by all means. Get your documents and evidence all in shape, and let me have them. I'll see that the suit is discontinued then. Will you sue them?"

"No, I think not," replied Thorpe. "I'll just hold it back as a sort of club to keep them in line."

The next day, he took the train north. He had something definite and urgent to do, and, as always with practical affairs demanding attention and resource, he threw himself whole-souled into the accomplishment of it. By the time he had bought the sixteen forties constituting the section, searched out a dozen witnesses to the theft, and spent a week with the Marquette expert in looking over the ground, he had fallen into the swing of work again. His experience still ached; but dully.

Only now he possessed no interests outside of those in the new country; no affections save the half-protecting, good-natured comradeship with Wallace, the mutual self-reliant respect that subsisted between Tim Shearer and himself, and the dumb, unreasoning dog-liking he shared with Injin Charley. His eye became clearer and steadier; his methods more simple and direct. The taciturnity of his mood redoubled in thickness. He was less charitable to failure on the part of subordinates. And the new firm on the Ossawinamakee prospered.

## Chapter XXXV

Five years passed.

In that time Thorpe had succeeded in cutting a hundred million feet of pine. The money received for this had all been turned back into the Company's funds. From a single camp of twenty-five men with ten horses and a short haul of half a mile, the concern had increased to six large, well-equipped communities of eighty to a hundred men apiece, using nearly two hundred horses, and hauling as far as eight or nine miles.

Near the port stood a mammoth sawmill capable of taking care of twenty-two million feet a year, about which a lumber town had sprung up. Lake schooners lay in a long row during the summer months, while busy loaders passed the planks from one to the other into the deep holds. Besides its original holding, the company had acquired about a hundred and fifty million more, back near the headwaters of tributaries to the Ossawinamakee. In the spring and early summer months, the drive was a wonderful affair.

During the four years in which the Morrison & Daly Company shared the stream with Thorpe, the two firms lived in complete amity and understanding. Northrop had played his cards skillfully. The older capitalists had withdrawn suit. Afterwards they kept scrupulously within their rights, and saw to it that no more careless openings were left for Thorpe's shrewdness. They were keen enough business men, but had made the mistake, common enough to established power, of underrating the strength of an apparently insignificant opponent. Once they understood Thorpe's capacity, that young man had no more chance to catch them napping.

And as the younger man, on his side, never attempted to overstep his own rights, the interests of the rival firms rarely clashed. As to the few disputes that did arise, Thorpe found Mr. Daly singularly anxious to please. In the desire was no friendliness, however. Thorpe was watchful for treachery, and could hardly believe the affair finished when at the end of the fourth year the M. & D. sold out the remainder of its pine to a firm from Manistee, and transferred its operations to another stream a few miles east, where it had acquired more considerable holdings.

"They're altogether too confounded anxious to help us on that freight, Wallace," said Thorpe wrinkling his brow uneasily. "I don't like it. It isn't natural."

"No," laughed Wallace, "neither is it natural for a dog to draw a sledge. But he does it—when he has to. They're afraid of you, Harry: that's all."

Thorpe shook his head, but had to acknowledge that he could evidence no grounds for his mistrust.

The conversation took place at Camp One, which was celebrated in three states. Thorpe had set out to gather around him a band of good woodsmen. Except on a pinch he would employ no others.

"I don't care if I get in only two thousand feet this winter, and if a boy does that," he answered Shearer's expostulations, "it's got to be a good boy."

The result of his policy began to show even in the second year. Men were a little proud to say that they had put in a winter at "Thorpe's One." Those who had worked there during the first year were loyally enthusiastic over their boss's grit and resourcefulness, their camp's order, their cook's good "grub." As they were authorities, others perforce had to accept the dictum. There grew a desire among the better class to see what Thorpe's "One" might be like. In the autumn Harry had more applicants than he knew what to do with. Eighteen of the old men returned. He took them all, but when it came to distribution, three found themselves assigned to one or the other of the new camps. And quietly the rumor gained that these three had shown the least willing spirit during the previous winter. The other fifteen were sobered to the industry which their importance as veterans might have impaired.

Tim Shearer was foreman of Camp One; Scotty Parsons was drafted from the veterans to take charge of Two; Thorpe engaged two men known to Tim to boss Three and Four. But in selecting the "push" for Five he displayed most strikingly his keen appreciation of a man's relation to his environment. He sought out John Radway and induced him to accept the commission.

"You can do it, John," said he, "and I know it. I want you to try; and if you don't make her go, I'll call it nobody's fault but my own."

"I don't see how you dare risk it, after that Cass Branch deal, Mr. Thorpe," replied Radway, almost brokenly. "But I would like to tackle it, I'm dead sick of loafing. Sometimes it seems like I'd die, if I don't get out in the woods again."

"We'll call it a deal, then," answered Thorpe.

The result proved his sagacity. Radway was one of the best foremen in the outfit. He got more out of his men, he rose better to emergencies, and he accomplished more with the same resources than any of the others, excepting Tim Shearer. As long as the work was done for someone else, he was capable and efficient. Only when he was called upon to demand on his own account, did the paralyzing shyness affect him.

But the one feature that did more to attract the very best element among woodsmen, and so make possible the practice of Thorpe's theory of success, was Camp One. The men's accommodations at the other five were no different and but little better than those in a thousand other typical lumber camps of both peninsulas. They slept in box-like bunks filled with hay or straw over which blankets were spread; they sat on a narrow hard bench or on the floor; they read by the dim light of a lamp fastened against the big cross beam; they warmed themselves at a huge iron stove in the center of the room around which suspended wires and poles offered space for the drying of socks; they washed their clothes when the mood struck them. It was warm and comparatively clean. But it was dark, without ornament, cheerless.

The lumber-jack never expects anything different. In fact, if he were pampered to the extent of ordinary comforts, he would be apt at once to conclude himself indispensable; whereupon he would become worthless.

Thorpe, however, spent a little money—not much—and transformed Camp One. Every bunk was provided with a tick, which the men could fill with hay, balsam, or hemlock, as suited them. Cheap but attractive curtains on wires at once brightened the room and shut each man's "bedroom" from the main hall. The deacon seat remained but was supplemented by a half-dozen simple and comfortable chairs. In the center of the room stood a big round table over which glowed two hanging lamps. The table was littered with papers and magazines. Home life was still further suggested by a canary bird in a gilt cage, a sleepy cat, and two pots of red geraniums. Thorpe had further imported a washerwoman who dwelt in a separate little cabin under the hill. She washed the men's belongings at twenty-five cents a week, which amount Thorpe deducted from each man's wages, whether he had the washing done or not. This encouraged cleanliness. Phil scrubbed out every day, while the men were in the woods.

Such was Thorpe's famous Camp One in the days of its splendor. Old woodsmen will still tell you about it, with a longing reminiscent glimmer in the corners of their eyes as they recall its glories and the men who worked in it. To have "put in" a winter in Camp One was the mark of a master; and the ambition of every raw recruit to the forest. Probably Thorpe's name is remembered to-day more on account of the intrepid, skillful, loyal men his strange genius gathered about it, than for the herculean feat of having carved a great fortune from the wilderness in but five years' time.

But Camp One was a privilege. A man entered it only after having proved himself; he remained in it only as long as his efficiency deserved the honor. Its members were invariably recruited from one of the other four camps; never from applicants who had not been in Thorpe's employ. A raw man was sent to Scotty, or Jack Hyland, or Radway, or Kerlie. There he was given a job, if he happened to suit, and men were needed. By and by, perhaps, when a member of Camp One fell sick or was given his time, Tim Shearer would send word to one of the other five that he needed an axman or a sawyer, or a loader, or teamster, as the case might be. The best man in the other camps was sent up.

So Shearer was foreman of a picked crew. Probably no finer body of men was ever gathered at one camp. In them one could study at his best the American pioneer. It was said at that time that you had never seen logging done as it should be until you had visited Thorpe's Camp One on the Ossawinamakee.

Of these men Thorpe demanded one thing—success. He tried never to ask of them anything he did not believe to be thoroughly possible; but he expected always that in some manner, by hook or crook, they would carry the affair through. No matter how good the excuse, it was never accepted. Accidents would happen, there as elsewhere; a way to arrive in spite of them always exists, if only a man is willing to use his wits, unflagging energy, and time. Bad luck is a reality; but much of what is called bad luck is nothing but a want of careful foresight, and Thorpe could better afford to be harsh occasionally to the genuine for the sake of eliminating the false. If a man failed, he left Camp One.

The procedure was very simple. Thorpe never explained his reasons even to Shearer.

"Ask Tom to step in a moment," he requested of the latter.

"Tom," he said to that individual, "I think I can use you better at Four. Report to Kerlie there."

And strangely enough, few even of these proud and independent men ever asked for their time, or preferred to quit rather than to work up again to the glories of their prize camp.

For while new recruits were never accepted at Camp One, neither was a man ever discharged there. He was merely transferred to one of the other foremen.

It is necessary to be thus minute in order that the reader may understand exactly the class of men Thorpe had about his immediate person. Some of them had the reputation of being the hardest citizens in three States, others were mild as turtle doves. They were all pioneers. They had the independence, the unabashed eye, the insubordination even, of the man who has drawn his intellectual and moral nourishment at the breast of a wild nature. They were afraid of nothing alive. From no one, were he chore-boy or president, would they take a single word—with the exception always of Tim Shearer and Thorpe.

The former they respected because in their picturesque guild he was a master craftsman. The latter they adored and quoted and fought for in distant saloons, because he represented to them their own ideal, what they would be if freed from the heavy gyves of vice and executive incapacity that weighed them down.

And they were loyal. It was a point of honor with them to stay "until the last dog was hung." He who deserted in the hour of need was not only a renegade, but a fool. For he thus earned a magnificent licking if ever he ran up against a member of the "Fighting Forty." A band of soldiers they were, ready to attempt anything their commander ordered, devoted, enthusiastically admiring. And, it must be confessed, they were also somewhat on the order of a band of pirates. Marquette thought so each spring after the drive, when, hat-tilted, they surged swearing and shouting down to Denny Hogan's saloon. Denny had to buy new fixtures when they went away; but it was worth it.

Proud! it was no name for it. Boast! the fame of Camp One spread abroad over the land, and was believed in to about twenty per cent of the anecdotes detailed of it—which was near enough the actual truth. Anecdotes disbelieved, the class of men from it would have given it a reputation. The latter was varied enough, in truth. Some people thought Camp One must be a sort of hell-hole of roaring, fighting devils. Others sighed and made rapid calculations of the number of logs they could put in, if only they could get hold of help like that.

Thorpe himself, of course, made his headquarters at Camp One. Thence he visited at least once a week all the other camps, inspecting the minutest details, not only of the work, but of the everyday life. For this purpose he maintained a light box sleigh and pair of bays, though often, when the snow became deep, he was forced to snowshoes.

During the five years he had never crossed the Straits of Mackinaw. The rupture with his sister had made repugnant to him all the southern country. He preferred to remain in the woods. All winter long he was more than busy at his logging. Summers he spent at the mill. Occasionally he visited Marquette, but always on business. He became used to seeing only the rough faces of men. The vision of softer graces and beauties lost its distinctness before this strong, hardy northland, whose gentler moods were like velvet over iron, or like its own summer leaves veiling the eternal darkness of the pines.

He was happy because he was too busy to be anything else. The insistent need of success which he had created for himself, absorbed all other sentiments. He demanded it of others rigorously. He could do no less than demand it of himself. It had practically become one of his tenets of belief. The chief end of any man, as he saw it, was to do well and successfully what his life found ready. Anything to further this fore-ordained activity was good; anything else was bad. These thoughts, aided by a disposition naturally fervent and single in purpose, hereditarily ascetic and conscientious—for his mother was of old New England stock—gave to him in the course of six years' striving a sort of daily and familiar religion to which he conformed his life.

Success, success, success. Nothing could be of more importance. Its attainment argued a man's efficiency in the Scheme of Things, his worthy fulfillment of the end for which a divine Providence had placed him on earth. Anything that interfered with it—personal comfort, inclination, affection, desire, love of ease, individual liking,—was bad.

Luckily for Thorpe's peace of mind, his habit of looking on men as things helped him keep to this attitude of mind. His lumbermen were tools,—good, sharp, efficient tools, to be sure, but only because he had made them so. Their loyalty aroused in his breast no pride nor gratitude. He expected loyalty. He would have discharged at once a man who did not show it. The same with zeal, intelligence, effort—they were the things he took for granted. As for the admiration and affection which the Fighting Forty displayed for him personally, he gave not a thought to it. And the men knew it, and loved him the more from the fact.

Thorpe cared for just three people, and none of them happened to clash with his machine. They were Wallace Carpenter, little Phil, and Injin Charley.

Wallace, for reasons already explained at length, was always personally agreeable to Thorpe. Latterly, since the erection of the mill, he had developed unexpected acumen in the disposal of the season's cut to wholesale dealers in Chicago. Nothing could have been better for the firm. Thereafter he was often in the woods, both for pleasure and to get his partner's ideas on what the firm would have to offer. The entire responsibility at the city end of the business was in his hands.

Injin Charley continued to hunt and trap in the country round about. Between him and Thorpe had grown a friendship the more solid in that its increase had been mysteriously without outward cause. Once or twice a month the lumberman would snowshoe down to the little cabin at the forks. Entering, he would nod briefly and seat himself on a cracker-box.

"How do, Charley," said he.

"How do," replied Charley.

They filled pipes and smoked. At rare intervals one of them made a remark, tersely,

"Catch um three beaver las' week," remarked Charley.

"Good haul," commented Thorpe.

Or:

"I saw a mink track by the big boulder," offered Thorpe.

"H'm!" responded Charley in a long-drawn falsetto whine.

Yet somehow the men came to know each other better and better; and each felt that in an emergency he could depend on the other to the uttermost in spite of the difference in race.

As for Phil, he was like some strange, shy animal, retaining all its wild instincts, but led by affection to become domestic. He drew the water, cut the wood, none better. In the evening he played atrociously his violin—none worse—

bending his great white brow forward with the wolf-glare in his eyes, swaying his shoulders with a fierce delight in the subtle dissonances, the swaggering exactitude of time, the vulgar rendition of the horrible tunes he played. And often he went into the forest and gazed wondering through his liquid poet's eyes at occult things. Above all, he worshipped Thorpe. And in turn the lumberman accorded him a good-natured affection. He was as indispensable to Camp One as the beagles.

And the beagles were most indispensable. No one could have got along without them. In the course of events and natural selection they had increased to eleven. At night they slept in the men's camp underneath or very near the stove. By daylight in the morning they were clamoring at the door. Never had they caught a hare. Never for a moment did their hopes sink. The men used sometimes to amuse themselves by refusing the requested exit. The little dogs agonized. They leaped and yelped, falling over each other like a tangle of angleworms. Then finally, when the door at last flung wide, they precipitated themselves eagerly and silently through the opening. A few moments later a single yelp rose in the direction of the swamp; the band took up the cry. From then until dark the glade was musical with baying. At supper time they returned straggling, their expression pleased, six inches of red tongue hanging from the corners of their mouths, ravenously ready for supper.

Strangely enough the big white hares never left the swamp. Perhaps the same one was never chased two days in succession. Or it is possible that the quarry enjoyed the harmless game as much as did the little dogs.

Once only while the snow lasted was the hunt abandoned for a few days. Wallace Carpenter announced his intention of joining forces with the diminutive hounds.

"It's a shame, so it is, doggies!" he laughed at the tried pack. "We'll get one to-morrow."

So he took his shotgun to the swamp, and after a half hour's wait, succeeded in killing the hare. From that moment he was the hero of those ecstacized canines. They tangled about him everywhere. He hardly dared take a step for fear of crushing one of the open faces and expectant, pleading eyes looking up at him. It grew to be a nuisance. Wallace always claimed his trip was considerably shortened because he could not get away from his admirers.


### Chapter XXXVI

Financially the Company was rated high, and yet was heavily in debt. This condition of affairs by no means constitutes an anomaly in the lumbering business.

The profits of the first five years had been immediately reinvested in the business. Thorpe, with the foresight that had originally led him into this new country, saw farther than the instant's gain. He intended to establish in a few years more a big plant which would be returning benefices in proportion not only to the capital originally invested, but also in ratio to the energy, time, and genius he had himself expended. It was not the affair of a moment. It was not the affair of half-measures, of timidity.

Thorpe knew that he could play safely, cutting a few millions a year, expanding cautiously. By this method he would arrive, but only after a long period.

Or he could do as many other firms have done; start on borrowed money.

In the latter case he had only one thing to fear, and that was fire. Every cent, and many times over, of his obligations would be represented in the state of raw material. All he had to do was to cut it out by the very means which the yearly profits of his business would enable him to purchase. For the moment, he owed a great deal; without the shadow of a doubt mere industry would clear his debt, and leave him with substantial acquisitions created, practically, from nothing but his own abilities. The money obtained from his mortgages was a tool which he picked up an instant, used to fashion one of his own, and laid aside.

Every autumn the Company found itself suddenly in easy circumstances. At any moment that Thorpe had chosen to be content with the progress made, he could have, so to speak, declared dividends with his partner. Instead of undertaking more improvements, for part of which he borrowed some money, he could have divided the profits of the season's cut. But this he was not yet ready to do.

He had established five more camps, he had acquired over a hundred and fifty million more of timber lying contiguous to his own, he had built and equipped a modern high-efficiency mill, he had constructed a harbor break-water and the necessary booms, he had bought a tug, built a boarding-house. All this costs money. He wished now to construct a logging railroad. Then he promised himself and Wallace that they would be ready to commence paying operations.

The logging railroad was just then beginning to gain recognition. A few miles of track, a locomotive, and a number of cars consisting uniquely of wheels and "bunks," or cross beams on which to chain the logs, and a fairly well-graded right-of-way comprised the outfit. Its use obviated the necessity of driving the river—always an expensive operation. Often, too, the decking at the skidways could be dispensed with; and the sleigh hauls, if not entirely superseded for the remote districts, were entirely so in the country for a half mile on either side of the track, and in any case were greatly shortened. There obtained, too, the additional advantage of being able to cut summer and winter alike. Thus, the plant once established, logging by railroad was not only easier but cheaper. Of late years it has come into almost universal use in big jobs and wherever the nature of the country will permit. The old-fashioned, picturesque ice-road sleigh-haul will last as long as north-woods lumbering,—even in the railroad districts,—but the locomotive now does the heavy work.

With the capital to be obtained from the following winter's product, Thorpe hoped to be able to establish a branch which should run from a point some two miles behind Camp One, to a "dump" a short distance above the mill. For this he had made all the estimates, and even the preliminary survey. He was therefore the more grievously disappointed, when Wallace Carpenter made it impossible for him to do so.

He was sitting in the mill-office one day about the middle of July. Herrick, the engineer, had just been in. He could not keep the engine in order, although Thorpe knew that it could be done.

"I've sot up nights with her," said Herrick, "and she's no go. I think I can fix her when my head gets all right. I got headachy lately. And somehow that last lot of Babbit metal didn't seem to act just right."

Thorpe looked out of the window, tapping his desk slowly with the end of a lead pencil.

"Collins," said he to the bookkeeper, without raising his voice or altering his position, "make out Herrick's time."

The man stood there astonished.

"But I had hard luck, sir," he expostulated. "She'll go all right now, I think."

Thorpe turned and looked at him.

"Herrick," he said, not unkindly, "this is the second time this summer the mill has had to close early on account of that engine. We have supplied you with everything you asked for. If you can't do it, we shall have to get a man who can."

"But I had—" began the man once more.

"I ask every man to succeed in what I give him to do," interrupted Thorpe. "If he has a headache, he must brace up or quit. If his Babbit doesn't act just right he must doctor it up; or get some more, even if he has to steal it. If he has hard luck, he must sit up nights to better it. It's none of my concern how hard or how easy a time a man has in doing what I tell him to. I EXPECT HIM TO DO IT. If I have to do all a man's thinking for him, I may as well hire Swedes and be done with it. I have too many details to attend to already without bothering about excuses."

The man stood puzzling over this logic.

"I ain't got any other job," he ventured.

"You can go to piling on the docks," replied Thorpe, "if you want to."

Thorpe was thus explicit because he rather liked Herrick. It was hard for him to discharge the man peremptorily, and he proved the need of justifying himself in his own eyes.

Now he sat back idly in the clean painted little room with the big square desk and the three chairs. Through the door he could see Collins, perched on a high stool before the shelf-like desk. From the open window came the clear, musical note of the circular saw, the fresh aromatic smell of new lumber, the bracing air from Superior sparkling in the offing. He felt tired. In rare moments such as these, when the muscles of his striving relaxed, his mind turned to the past. Old sorrows rose before him and looked at him with their sad eyes; the sorrows that had helped to make him what he was. He wondered where his sister was. She would be twenty-two years old now. A tenderness, haunting, tearful, invaded his heart. He suffered. At such moments the hard shell of his rough woods life seemed to rend apart. He longed with a great longing for sympathy, for love, for the softer influences that cradle even warriors between the clangors of the battles.

The outer door, beyond the cage behind which Collins and his shelf desk were placed, flew open. Thorpe heard a brief greeting, and Wallace Carpenter stood before him.

"Why, Wallace, I didn't know you were coming!" began Thorpe, and stopped. The boy, usually so fresh and happily buoyant, looked ten years older. Wrinkles had gathered between his eyes. "Why, what's the matter?" cried Thorpe.

He rose swiftly and shut the door into the outer office. Wallace seated himself mechanically.

"Everything! everything!" he said in despair. "I've been a fool! I've been blind!"

So bitter was his tone that Thorpe was startled. The lumberman sat down on the other side of the desk.

"That'll do, Wallace," he said sharply. "Tell me briefly what is the matter."

"I've been speculating!" burst out the boy.

"Ah!" said his partner.

"At first I bought only dividend-paying stocks outright. Then I bought for a rise, but still outright. Then I got in with a fellow who claimed to know all about it. I bought on a margin. There came a slump. I met the margins because I am sure there will be a rally, but now all my fortune is in the thing. I'm going to be penniless. I'll lose it all."

"Ah!" said Thorpe.

"And the name of Carpenter is so old-established, so honorable!" cried the unhappy boy, "and my sister!"

"Easy!" warned Thorpe. "Being penniless isn't the worst thing that can happen to a man."

"No; but I am in debt," went on the boy more calmly. "I have given notes. When they come due, I'm a goner."

"How much?" asked Thorpe laconically.

"Thirty thousand dollars."

"Well, you have that amount in this firm."

"What do you mean?"

"If you want it, you can have it."

Wallace considered a moment.

"That would leave me without a cent," he replied.

"But it would save your commercial honor."

"Harry," cried Wallace suddenly, "couldn't this firm go on my note for thirty thousand more? Its credit is good, and that amount would save my margins."

"You are partner," replied Thorpe, "your signature is as good as mine in this firm."

"But you know I wouldn't do it without your consent," replied Wallace reproachfully. "Oh, Harry!" cried the boy, "when you needed the amount, I let you have it!"

Thorpe smiled.

"You know you can have it, if it's to be had, Wallace. I wasn't hesitating on that account. I was merely trying to figure out where we can raise such a sum as sixty thousand dollars. We haven't got it."

"But you'll never have to pay it," assured Wallace eagerly. "If I can save my margins, I'll be all right."

"A man has to figure on paying whatever he puts his signature to," asserted Thorpe. "I can give you our note payable at the end of a year. Then I'll hustle in enough timber to make up the amount. It means we don't get our railroad, that's all."

"I knew you'd help me out. Now it's all right," said Wallace, with a relieved air.

Thorpe shook his head. He was already trying to figure how to increase his cut to thirty million feet.

"I'll do it," he muttered to himself, after Wallace had gone out to visit the mill. "I've been demanding success of others for a good many years; now I'll demand it of myself."

## PART IV. THORPE'S DREAM GIRL

### Chapter XXXVII

The moment had struck for the woman. Thorpe did not know it, but it was true. A solitary, brooding life in the midst of grand surroundings, an active, strenuous life among great responsibilities, a starved, hungry life of the affections whence even the sister had withdrawn her love,—all these had worked unobtrusively towards the formation of a single psychological condition. Such a moment comes to every man. In it he realizes the beauties, the powers, the vastnesses which unconsciously his being has absorbed. They rise to the surface as a need, which, being satisfied, is projected into the visible world as an ideal to be worshipped. Then is happiness and misery beside which the mere struggle to dominate men becomes trivial, the petty striving with the forces of nature seems a little thing. And the woman he at that time meets takes on the qualities of the dream; she is more than woman, less than goddess; she is the best of that man made visible.

Thorpe found himself for the first time filled with the spirit of restlessness. His customary iron evenness of temper was gone, so that he wandered quickly from one detail of his work to another, without seeming to penetrate below the surface-need of any one task. Out of the present his mind was always escaping to a mystic fourth dimension which he did not understand. But a week before, he had felt himself absorbed in the component parts of his enterprise, the totality of which arched far over his head, shutting out the sky. Now he was outside of it. He had, without his volition, abandoned the creator's standpoint of the god at the heart of his work. It seemed as important, as great to him, but somehow it had taken on a strange solidarity, as though he had left it a plastic beginning and returned to find it hardened into the shapes of finality. He acknowledged it admirable,—and wondered how he had ever accomplished it! He confessed that it should be finished as it had begun,—and could not discover in himself the Titan who had watched over its inception.

Thorpe took this state of mind much to heart, and in combating it expended more energy than would have sufficed to accomplish the work. Inexorably he held himself to the task. He filled his mind full of lumbering. The millions along the bank on section nine must be cut and travoyed directly to the rollways. It was a shame that the necessity should arise. From section nine Thorpe had hoped to lighten the expenses when finally he should begin operations on the distant and inaccessible headwaters of French Creek. Now there was no help for it. The instant necessity was to get thirty millions of pine logs down the river before Wallace Carpenter's notes came due. Every other consideration had to yield before that. Fifteen millions more could be cut on seventeen, nineteen, and eleven,—regions hitherto practically untouched,—by the men in the four camps inland. Camp One and Camp Three could attend to section nine.

These were details to which Thorpe applied his mind. As he pushed through the sun-flecked forest, laying out his roads, placing his travoy trails, spying the difficulties that might supervene to mar the fair face of honest labor, he had always this thought before him,—that he must apply his mind. By an effort, a tremendous effort, he succeeded in doing so. The effort left him limp. He found himself often standing, or moving gently, his eyes staring sightless, his mind cradled on vague misty clouds of absolute inaction, his will chained so softly and yet so firmly that he felt no strength and hardly the desire to break from the dream that lulled him. Then he was conscious of the physical warmth of the sun, the faint sweet woods smells, the soothing caress of the breeze, the sleepy cicada-like note of the pine creeper. Through his half-closed lashes the tangled sun-beams made soft-tinted rainbows. He wanted nothing so much as to sit on the pine needles there in the golden flood of radiance, and dream—dream on—vaguely, comfortably, sweetly—dream of the summer—

Thorpe, with a mighty and impatient effort, snapped the silken cords asunder.

"Lord, Lord!" he cried impatiently. "What's coming to me? I must be a little off my feed!"

And he hurried rapidly to his duties. After an hour of the hardest concentration he had ever been required to bestow on a trivial subject, he again unconsciously sank by degrees into the old apathy.

"Glad it isn't the busy season!" he commented to himself. "Here, I must quit this! Guess it's the warm weather. I'll get down to the mill for a day or two."

There he found himself incapable of even the most petty routine work. He sat to his desk at eight o'clock and began the perusal of a sheaf of letters, comprising a certain correspondence, which Collins brought him. The first three he read carefully; the following two rather hurriedly; of the next one he seized only the salient and essential points; the seventh and eighth he skimmed; the remainder of the bundle he thrust aside in uncontrollable impatience. Next day he returned to the woods.

The incident of the letters had aroused to the full his old fighting spirit, before which no mere instincts could stand. He clamped the iron to his actions and forced them to the way appointed. Once more his mental processes became clear and incisive, his commands direct and to the point. To all outward appearance Thorpe was as before.

He opened Camp One, and the Fighting Forty came back from distant drinking joints. This was in early September, when the raspberries were entirely done and the blackberries fairly in the way of vanishing. That able-bodied and devoted band of men was on hand when needed. Shearer, in some subtle manner of his own, had let them feel that this year meant thirty million or "bust." They tightened their leather belts and stood ready for commands. Thorpe set them to work near the river, cutting roads along the lines he had blazed to the inland timber on seventeen and nineteen. After much discussion with Shearer the young man decided to take out the logs from eleven by driving them down French Creek.

To this end a gang was put to clearing the creekbed. It was a tremendous job. Centuries of forest life had choked the little stream nearly to the level of its banks. Old snags and stumps lay imbedded in the ooze; decayed trunks, moss-grown, blocked the current; leaning tamaracks, fallen timber, tangled vines, dense thickets gave to its course more the appearance of a tropical jungle than of a north country brook-bed. All these things had to be removed, one by one, and either piled to one side or burnt. In the end, however, it would pay. French Creek was not a large stream, but it could be driven during the time of the spring freshets.

Each night the men returned in the beautiful dreamlike twilight to the camp. There they sat, after eating, smoking their pipes in the open air. Much of the time they sang, while Phil, crouching wolf-like over his violin, rasped out an accompaniment of dissonances. From a distance it softened and fitted pleasantly into the framework of the wilderness. The men's voices lent themselves well to the weird minor strains of the chanteys. These times—when the men sang, and the night-wind rose and died in the hemlock tops—were Thorpe's worst moments. His soul, tired with the day's iron struggle, fell to brooding. Strange thoughts came to him, strange visions. He wanted something he knew not what; he longed, and thrilled, and aspired to a greater glory than that of brave deeds, a softer comfort than his old foster mother, the wilderness, could bestow.

The men were singing in a mighty chorus, swaying their heads in unison, and bringing out with a roar the emphatic words of the crude ditties written by some genius from their own ranks.

*"Come all ye sons of freedom throughout old Michigan,*
*Come all ye gallant lumbermen, list to a shanty man.*
*On the banks of the Muskegon, where the rapid waters flow,*
*OH!—we'll range the wild woods o'er while a-lumbering we go."*

Here was the bold unabashed front of the pioneer, here was absolute certainty in the superiority of his calling,—absolute scorn of all others. Thorpe passed his hand across his brow. The same spirit was once fully and freely his.

*"The music of our burnished ax shall make the woods resound,*
*And many a lofty ancient pine will tumble to the ground.*
*At night around our shanty fire we'll sing while rude winds blow,*
*OH!—we'll range the wild woods o'er while a-lumbering we go!"*

That was what he was here for. Things were going right. It would be pitiful to fail merely on account of this idiotic lassitude, this unmanly weakness, this boyish impatience and desire for play. He a woodsman! He a fellow with these big strong men!

A single voice, clear and high, struck into a quick measure:

*"I am a jolly shanty boy,*
*As you will soon discover;*
*To all the dodges I am fly,*
*A hustling pine-woods rover.*
*A peavey-hook it is my pride,*
*An ax I well can handle.*
*To fell a tree or punch a bull,*
*Get rattling Danny Randall."*

And then with a rattle and crash the whole Fighting Forty shrieked out the chorus:

*"Bung yer eye! bung yer eye!"*

Active, alert, prepared for any emergency that might arise; hearty, ready for everything, from punching bulls to felling trees—that was something like! Thorpe despised himself. The song went on.

*"I love a girl in Saginaw,*
*She lives with her mother.*

> I defy all Michigan
>   To find such another.
> She's tall and slim, her hair is red,
>   Her face is plump and pretty.
> She's my daisy Sunday best-day girl,
>   And her front name stands for Kitty."

And again as before the Fighting Forty howled truculently:

"Bung yer eye! bung yer eye!"

The words were vulgar, the air a mere minor chant. Yet Thorpe's mind was stilled. His aroused subconsciousness had been engaged in reconstructing these men entire as their songs voiced rudely the inner characteristics of their beings. Now his spirit halted, finger on lip. Their bravery, pride of caste, resource, bravado, boastfulness,—all these he had checked off approvingly. Here now was the idea of the Mate. Somewhere for each of them was a "Kitty," a "daisy Sunday best-day girl"; the eternal feminine; the softer side; the tenderness, beauty, glory of even so harsh a world as they were compelled to inhabit. At the present or in the past these woods roisterers, this Fighting Forty, had known love. Thorpe arose abruptly and turned at random into the forest. The song pursued him as he went, but he heard only the clear sweet tones, not the words. And yet even the words would have spelled to his awakened sensibilities another idea,— would have symbolized however rudely, companionship and the human delight of acting a part before a woman.

> "I took her to a dance one night,
>   A mossback gave the bidding—
> Silver Jack bossed the shebang,
>   and Big Dan played the fiddle.
> We danced and drank the livelong night
>   With fights between the dancing,
> Till Silver Jack cleaned out the ranch
>   And sent the mossbacks prancing."

And with the increasing war and turmoil of the quick water the last shout of the Fighting Forty mingled faintly and was lost.

> "Bung yer eye! bung yer eye!"

Thorpe found himself at the edge of the woods facing a little glade into which streamed the radiance of a full moon.

### Chapter XXXVIII

There he stood and looked silently, not understanding, not caring to inquire. Across the way a white-throat was singing, clear, beautiful, like the shadow of a dream. The girl stood listening.

Her small fair head was inclined ever so little sideways and her finger was on her lips as though she wished to still the very hush of night, to which impression the inclination of her supple body lent its grace. The moonlight shone full upon her countenance. A little white face it was, with wide clear eyes and a sensitive, proud mouth that now half parted like a child's. Here eyebrows arched from her straight nose in the peculiarly graceful curve that falls just short of pride on the one side and of power on the other, to fill the eyes with a pathos of trust and innocence. The man watching could catch the poise of her long white neck and the molten moon-fire from her tumbled hair,—the color of corn-silk, but finer.

And yet these words meant nothing. A painter might have caught her charm, but he must needs be a poet as well,—and a great poet, one capable of grandeurs and subtleties.

To the young man standing there rapt in the spell of vague desire, of awakened vision, she seemed most like a flower or a mist. He tried to find words to formulate her to himself, but did not succeed. Always it came back to the same idea—the flower and the mist. Like the petals of a flower most delicate was her questioning, upturned face; like the bend of a flower most rare the stalk of her graceful throat; like the poise of a flower most dainty the attitude of her beautiful, perfect body sheathed in a garment that outlined each movement, for the instant in suspense. Like a mist the glimmering of her skin, the shining of her hair, the elusive moonlike quality of her whole personality as she stood there in the ghost-like clearing listening, her fingers on her lips.

Behind her lurked the low, even shadow of the forest where the moon was not, a band of velvet against which the girl and the light-touched twigs and bushes and grass blades were etched like frost against a black window pane. There was something, too, of the frost-work's evanescent spiritual quality in the scene,—as though at any moment, with a puff of the balmy summer wind, the radiant glade, the hovering figure, the filagreed silver of the entire setting would melt into the accustomed stern and menacing forest of the northland, with its wolves, and its wild deer, and the voices of its sterner calling.

Thorpe held his breath and waited. Again the white-throat lifted his clear, spiritual note across the brightness, slow, trembling with. The girl never moved. She stood in the moonlight like a beautiful emblem of silence, half real, half fancy, part woman, wholly divine, listening to the little bird's message.

For the third time the song shivered across the night, then Thorpe with a soft sob, dropped his face in his hands and looked no more.

He did not feel the earth beneath his knees, nor the whip of the sumach across his face; he did not see the moon shadows creep slowly along the fallen birch; nor did he notice that the white-throat had hushed its song. His inmost spirit was shaken. Something had entered his soul and filled it to the brim, so that he dared no longer stand in the face of radiance until he had accounted with himself. Another drop would overflow the cup.

Ah, sweet God, the beauty of it, the beauty of it! That questing, childlike starry gaze, seeking so purely to the stars themselves! That flower face, those drooping, half parted lips! That inexpressible, unseizable something they had meant! Thorpe searched humbly—eagerly—then with agony through his troubled spirit, and in its furthermost depths saw the mystery as beautifully remote as ever. It approached and swept over him and left him gasping passion-racked. Ah, sweet God, the beauty of it! the beauty of it! the vision! the dream!

He trembled and sobbed with his desire to seize it, with his impotence to express it, with his failure even to appreciate it as his heart told him it should be appreciated.

He dared not look. At length he turned and stumbled back through the moonlit forest crying on his old gods in vain.

At the banks of the river he came to a halt. There in the velvet pines the moonlight slept calmly, and the shadows rested quietly under the breezeless sky. Near at hand the river shouted as ever its cry of joy over the vitality of life, like a spirited boy before the face of inscrutable nature. All else was silence. Then from the waste boomed a strange, hollow note, rising, dying, rising again, instinct with the spirit of the wilds. It fell, and far away sounded a heavy but distant crash. The cry lifted again. It was the first bull moose calling across the wilderness to his mate.

And then, faint but clear down the current of a chance breeze drifted the chorus of the Fighting Forty.

> *"The forests so brown at our stroke go down,*
>  *And cities spring up where they fell;*
> *While logs well run and work well done*
>  *Is the story the shanty boys tell."*

Thorpe turned from the river with a thrust forward of his head. He was not a religious man, and in his six years' woods experience had never been to church. Now he looked up over the tops of the pines to where the Pleiades glittered faintly among the brighter stars.

"Thanks, God," said he briefly.

### Chapter XXXIX

For several days this impression satisfied him completely. He discovered, strangely enough, that his restlessness had left him, that once more he was able to give to his work his former energy and interest. It was as though some power had raised its finger and a storm had stilled, leaving calm, unruffled skies.

He did not attempt to analyze this; he did not even make an effort to contemplate it. His critical faculty was stricken dumb and it asked no questions of him. At a touch his entire life had changed. Reality or vision, he had caught a glimpse of something so entirely different from anything his imagination or experience had ever suggested to him, that at first he could do no more than permit passively its influences to adjust themselves to his being.

Curiosity, speculation, longing,—all the more active emotions remained in abeyance while outwardly, for three days, Harry Thorpe occupied himself only with the needs of the Fighting Forty at Camp One.

In the early morning he went out with the gang. While they chopped or heaved, he stood by serene. Little questions of expediency he solved. Dilemmas he discussed leisurely with Tim Shearer. Occasionally he lent a shoulder when the peaveys lacked of prying a stubborn log from its bed. Not once did he glance at the nooning sun. His patience was quiet and sure. When evening came he smoked placidly outside the office, listening to the conversation and laughter of the men, caressing one of the beagles, while the rest slumbered about his feet, watching dreamily the night shadows and the bats. At about nine o'clock he went to bed, and slept soundly. He was vaguely conscious of a great peace within him, a great stillness of the spirit, against which the metallic events of his craft clicked sharply in vivid relief. It was the peace and stillness of a river before it leaps.

Little by little the condition changed. The man felt vague stirrings of curiosity. He speculated aimlessly as to whether or not the glade, the moonlight, the girl, had been real or merely the figments of imagination. Almost immediately the answer leaped at him from his heart. Since she was so certainly flesh and blood, whence did she come? what was she doing there in the wilderness? His mind pushed the query aside as unimportant, rushing eagerly to the essential point: When could he see her again? How find for the second time the vision before which his heart felt the instant need of prostrating itself. His placidity had gone. That morning he made some vague excuse to Shearer and set out blindly down the river.

He did not know where he was going, any more than did the bull moose plunging through the trackless wilderness to his mate. Instinct, the instinct of all wild natural creatures, led him. And so, without thought, without clear intention even,—most would say by accident,—he saw her again. It was near the "pole trail"; which was less like a trail than a rail-fence.

For when the snows are deep and snowshoes not the property of every man who cares to journey, the old-fashioned "pole trail" comes into use. It is merely a series of horses built of timber across which thick Norway logs are laid, about four feet from the ground, to form a continuous pathway. A man must be a tight-rope walker to stick to the pole trail when ice and snow have sheathed its logs. If he makes a misstep, he is precipitated ludicrously into feathery depths through which he must flounder to the nearest timber horse before he can remount. In summer, as has been said, it resembles nothing so much as a thick one-rail fence of considerable height, around which a fringe of light brush has grown.

Thorpe reached the fringe of bushes, and was about to dodge under the fence, when he saw her. So he stopped short, concealed by the leaves and the timber horse.

She stood on a knoll in the middle of a grove of monster pines. There was something of the cathedral in the spot. A hush dwelt in the dusk, the long columns lifted grandly to the Roman arches of the frond, faint murmurings stole here and there like whispering acolytes. The girl stood tall and straight among the tall, straight pines like a figure on an ancient tapestry. She was doing nothing—just standing there—but the awe of the forest was in her wide, clear eyes.

The great sweet feeling clutched the young man's throat again. But while the other,—the vision of the frost-work glade and the spirit-like figure of silence,—had been unreal and phantasmagoric, this was of the earth. He looked, and looked, and looked again. He saw the full pure curve of her cheek's contour, neither oval nor round, but like the outline of a certain kind of plum. He appreciated the half-pathetic downward droop of the corners of her mouth,—her red mouth in dazzling, bewitching contrast to the milk-whiteness of her skin. He caught the fineness of her nose, straight as a Grecian's, but with some faint suggestion about the nostrils that hinted at piquance. And the waving corn silk of her altogether charming and unruly hair, the superb column of her long neck on which her little head poised proudly like a flower, her supple body, whose curves had the long undulating grace of the current in a swift river, her slender white hand with the pointed fingers—all these he saw one after the other, and his soul shouted within him at the sight. He wrestled with the emotions that choked him. "Ah, God! Ah, God!" he cried softly to himself like one in pain. He, the man of iron frame, of iron nerve, hardened by a hundred emergencies, trembled in every muscle before a straight, slender girl, clad all in brown, standing alone in the middle of the ancient forest.

In a moment she stirred slightly, and turned. Drawing herself to her full height, she extended her hands over her head palm outward, and, with an indescribably graceful gesture, half mockingly bowed a ceremonious adieu to the solemn trees. Then with a little laugh she moved away in the direction of the river.

At once Thorpe proved a great need of seeing her again. In his present mood there was nothing of the awe-stricken peace he had experienced after the moonlight adventure. He wanted the sight of her as he had never wanted anything before. He must have it, and he looked about him fiercely as though to challenge any force in Heaven or Hell that would deprive him of it. His eyes desired to follow the soft white curve of her cheek, to dance with the light of her corn-silk hair, to delight in the poetic movements of her tall, slim body, to trace the full outline of her chin, to wonder at the carmine of her lips, red as a blood-spot on the snow. These things must be at once. The strong man desired it. And finding it impossible, he raged inwardly and tore the tranquillities of his heart, as on the shores of the distant Lake of Stars, the bull-moose trampled down the bushes in his passion.

So it happened that he ate hardly at all that day, and slept ill, and discovered the greatest difficulty in preserving the outward semblance of ease which the presence of Tim Shearer and the Fighting Forty demanded.

And next day he saw her again, and the next, because the need of his heart demanded it, and because, simply enough, she came every afternoon to the clump of pines by the old pole trail.

Now had Thorpe taken the trouble to inquire, he could have learned easily enough all there was to be known of the affair. But he did not take the trouble. His consciousness was receiving too many new impressions, so that in a manner it became bewildered. At first, as has been seen, the mere effect of the vision was enough; then the sight of the girl sufficed him. But now curiosity awoke and a desire for something more. He must speak to her, touch her hand, look into her eyes. He resolved to approach her, and the mere thought choked him and sent him weak.

When he saw her again from the shelter of the pole trail, he dared not, and so stood there prey to a novel sensation,— that of being baffled in an intention. It awoke within him a vast passion compounded part of rage at himself, part of longing for that which he could not take, but most of love for the girl. As he hesitated in one mind but in two decisions, he saw that she was walking slowly in his direction.

Perhaps a hundred paces separated the two. She took them deliberately, pausing now and again to listen, to pluck a leaf, to smell the fragrant balsam and fir tops as she passed them. Her progression was a series of poses, the one of which melted imperceptibly into the other without appreciable pause of transition. So subtly did her grace appeal to the sense of sight, that out of mere sympathy the other senses responded with fictions of their own. Almost could the young man behind the trail savor a faint fragrance, a faint music that surrounded and preceded her like the shadows of phantoms. He knew it as an illusion, born of his desire, and yet it was a noble illusion, for it had its origin in her.

In a moment she had reached the fringe of brush about the pole trail. They stood face to face.

She gave a little start of surprise, and her hand leaped to her breast, where it caught and stayed. Her childlike down-drooping mouth parted a little more, and the breath quickened through it. But her eyes, her wide, trusting, innocent eyes, sought his and rested.

He did not move. The eagerness, the desire, the long years of ceaseless struggle, the thirst for affection, the sob of awe at the moonlit glade, the love,—all these flamed in his eyes and fixed his gaze in an unconscious ardor that had nothing to do with convention or timidity. One on either side of the spike-marked old Norway log of the trail they stood, and for an appreciable interval the duel of their glances lasted,—he masterful, passionate, exigent; she proud, cool, defensive in the aloofness of her beauty. Then at last his prevailed. A faint color rose from her neck, deepened, and spread over her face and forehead. In a moment she dropped her eyes.

"Don't you think you stare a little rudely—Mr. Thorpe?" she asked.

## Chapter XL

The vision was over, but the beauty remained. The spoken words of protest made her a woman. Never again would she, nor any other creature of the earth, appear to Thorpe as she had in the silver glade or the cloistered pines. He had had his moment of insight. The deeps had twice opened to permit him to look within. Now they had closed again. But out of them had fluttered a great love and the priestess of it. Always, so long as life should be with him, Thorpe was destined to see in this tall graceful girl with the red lips and the white skin and the corn-silk hair, more beauty, more of the great mysterious spiritual beauty which is eternal, than her father or her mother or her dearest and best. For to them the vision had not been vouchsafed, while he had seen her as the highest symbol of God's splendor.

Now she stood before him, her head turned half away, a faint flush still tingeing the chalk-white of her skin, watching him with a dim, half-pleading smile in expectation of his reply.

"Ah, moon of my soul! light of my life!" he cried, but he cried it within him, though it almost escaped his vigilance to his lips. What he really said sounded almost harsh in consequence.

"How did you know my name?" he asked.

She planted both elbows on the Norway and framed her little face deliciously with her long pointed hands.

"If Mr. Harry Thorpe can ask that question," she replied, "he is not quite so impolite as I had thought him."

"If you don't stop pouting your lips, I shall kiss them!" cried Harry—to himself.

"How is that?" he inquired breathlessly.

"Don't you know who I am?" she asked in return.

"A goddess, a beautiful woman!" he answered ridiculously enough.

She looked straight at him. This time his gaze dropped.

"I am a friend of Elizabeth Carpenter, who is Wallace Carpenter's sister, who I believe is Mr. Harry Thorpe's partner."

She paused as though for comment. The young man opposite was occupied in many other more important directions. Some moments later the words trickled into his brain, and some moments after that he realized their meaning.

"We wrote Mr. Harry Thorpe that we were about to descend on his district with wagons and tents and Indians and things, and asked him to come and see us."

"Ah, heart o' mine, what clear, pure eyes she has! How they look at a man to drown his soul!"

Which, even had it been spoken, was hardly the comment one would have expected.

The girl looked at him for a moment steadily, then smiled. The change of countenance brought Thorpe to himself, and at the same moment the words she had spoken reached his comprehension.

"But I never received the letter. I'm so sorry," said he. "It must be at the mill. You see, I've been up in the woods for nearly a month."

"Then we'll have to forgive you."

"But I should think they would have done something for you at the mill—"

"Oh, we didn't come by way of your mill. We drove from Marquette."

"I see," cried Thorpe, enlightened. "But I'm sorry I didn't know. I'm sorry you didn't let me know. I suppose you thought I was still at the mill. How did you get along? Is Wallace with you?"

"No," she replied, dropping her hands and straightening her erect figure. "It's horrid. He was coming, and then some business came up and he couldn't get away. We are having the loveliest time though. I do adore the woods. Come," she cried impatiently, sweeping aside to leave a way clear, "you shall meet my friends."

Thorpe imagined she referred to the rest of the tenting party. He hesitated.

"I am hardly in fit condition," he objected.

She laughed, parting her red lips. "You are extremely picturesque just as you are," she said with rather embarrassing directness. "I wouldn't have you any different for the world. But my friends don't mind. They are used to it." She laughed again.

Thorpe crossed the pole trail, and for the first time found himself by her side. The warm summer odors were in the air, a dozen lively little birds sang in the brush along the rail, the sunlight danced and flickered through the openings.

Then suddenly they were among the pines, and the air was cool, the vista dim, and the bird songs inconceivably far away.

The girl walked directly to the foot of a pine three feet through, and soaring up an inconceivable distance through the still twilight.

"This is Jimmy," said she gravely. "He is a dear good old rough bear when you don't know him, but he likes me. If you put your ear close against him," she confided, suiting the action to the word, "you can hear him talking to himself. This little fellow is Tommy. I don't care so much for Tommy because he's sticky. Still, I like him pretty well, and here's Dick, and that's Bob, and the one just beyond is Jack."

"Where is Harry?" asked Thorpe.

"I thought one in a woods was quite sufficient," she replied with the least little air of impertinence.

"Why do you name them such common, everyday names?" he inquired.

"I'll tell you. It's because they are so big and grand themselves, that it did not seem to me they needed high-sounding names. What do you think?" she begged with an appearance of the utmost anxiety.

Thorpe expressed himself as in agreement. As the half-quizzical conversation progressed, he found their relations adjusting themselves with increasing rapidity. He had been successively the mystic devotee before his vision, the worshipper before his goddess; now he was unconsciously assuming the attitude of the lover before his mistress. It needs always this humanizing touch to render the greatest of all passions livable.

And as the human element developed, he proved at the same time greater and greater difficulty in repressing himself and greater and greater fear of the results in case he should not do so. He trembled with the desire to touch her long slender hand, and as soon as his imagination had permitted him that much he had already crushed her to him and had kissed passionately her starry face. Words hovered on his lips longing for flight. He withheld them by an effort that left him almost incoherent, for he feared with a deadly fear lest he lose forever what the vision had seemed to offer to his hand.

So he said little, and that lamely, for he dreaded to say too much. To her playful sallies he had no riposte. And in consequence he fell more silent with another boding—that he was losing his cause outright for lack of a ready word.

He need not have been alarmed. A woman in such a case hits as surely as a man misses. Her very daintiness and preciosity of speech indicated it. For where a man becomes stupid and silent, a woman covers her emotions with words and a clever speech. Not in vain is a proud-spirited girl stared down in such a contest of looks; brave deeds simply told by a friend are potent to win interest in advance; a straight, muscular figure, a brown skin, a clear, direct eye, a carriage of power and acknowledged authority, strike hard at a young imagination; a mighty passion sweeps aside the barriers of the heart. Such a victory, such a friend, such a passion had Thorpe.

And so the last spoken exchange between them meant nothing; but if each could have read the unsaid words that quivered on the other's heart, Thorpe would have returned to the Fighting Forty more tranquilly, while she would probably not have returned to the camping party at all for a number of hours.

"I do not think you had better come with me," she said. "Make your call and be forgiven on your own account. I don't want to drag you in at my chariot wheels."

"All right. I'll come this afternoon," Thorpe had replied.

"I love her, I must have her. I must go—at once," his soul had cried, "quick—now—before I kiss her!"

"How strong he is," she said to herself, "how brave-looking; how honest! He is different from the other men. He is magnificent."

### Chapter XLI

That afternoon Thorpe met the other members of the party, offered his apologies and explanations, and was graciously forgiven. He found the personnel to consist of, first of all, Mrs. Cary, the chaperone, a very young married woman of twenty-two or thereabouts; her husband, a youth of three years older, clean-shaven, light-haired, quiet-mannered; Miss Elizabeth Carpenter, who resembled her brother in the characteristics of good-looks, vivacious disposition and curly hair; an attendant satellite of the masculine persuasion called Morton; and last of all the girl whom Thorpe had already so variously encountered and whom he now met as Miss Hilda Farrand. Besides these were Ginger, a squab negro built to fit the galley of a yacht; and three Indian guides. They inhabited tents, which made quite a little encampment.

Thorpe was received with enthusiasm. Wallace Carpenter's stories of his woods partner, while never doing more than justice to the truth, had been of a warm color tone. One and all owned a lively curiosity to see what a real woodsman might be like. When he proved to be handsome and well mannered, as well as picturesque, his reception was no longer in doubt.

Nothing could exceed his solicitude as to their comfort and amusement. He inspected personally the arrangement of the tents, and suggested one or two changes conducive to the littler comforts. This was not much like ordinary woods-camping. The largest wall-tent contained three folding cots for the women, over which, in the daytime, were flung bright-colored Navajo blankets. Another was spread on the ground. Thorpe later, however, sent over two bear skins, which were acknowledgedly an improvement. To the tent pole a mirror of size was nailed, and below it stood a portable washstand. The second tent, devoted to the two men, was not quite so luxurious; but still boasted of little conveniences the true woodsman would never consider worth the bother of transporting. The third, equally large, was the dining tent. The other three, smaller, and on the A tent order, served respectively as sleeping rooms for Ginger and the Indians, and as a general store-house for provisions and impedimenta.

Thorpe sent an Indian to Camp One for the bearskins, put the rest to digging a trench around the sleeping tents in order that a rain storm might not cause a flood, and ordered Ginger to excavate a square hole some feet deep which he intended to utilize as a larder.

Then he gave Morton and Cary hints as to the deer they wished to capture, pointed out the best trout pools, and issued advice as to the compassing of certain blackberries, not far distant.

Simple things enough they were to do—it was as though a city man were to direct a newcomer to Central Park, or impart to him a test for the destinations of trolley lines—yet Thorpe's new friends were profoundly impressed with his knowledge of occult things. The forest was to them, as to most, more or less of a mystery, unfathomable except to the favored of genius. A man who could interpret it, even a little, into the speech of everyday comfort and expediency possessed a strong claim to their imaginations. When he had finished these practical affairs, they wanted him to sit down and tell them more things, to dine with them, to smoke about their camp fire in the evening. But here they encountered a decided check. Thorpe became silent, almost morose. He talked in monosyllables, and soon went away. They did not know what to make of him, and so were, of course, the more profoundly interested. The truth was, his habitual reticence would not have permitted a great degree of expansion in any case, but now the presence of Hilda made any but an attitude of hushed waiting for her words utterly impossible to him. He wished well to them all. If there was anything he could do for them, he would gladly undertake it. But he would not act the lion nor tell of his, to them, interesting adventures.

However, when he discovered that Hilda had ceased visiting the clump of pines near the pole trail, his desire forced him back among these people. He used to walk in swiftly at almost any time of day, casting quick glances here and there in search of his divinity.

"How do, Mrs. Cary," he would say. "Nice weather. Enjoying yourself?"

On receiving the reply he would answer heartily, "That's good!" and lapse into silence. When Hilda was about he followed every movement of hers with his eyes, so that his strange conduct lacked no explanation nor interpretation, in the minds of the women at least. Thrice he redeemed his reputation for being an interesting character by conducting the party on little expeditions here and there about the country. Then his woodcraft and resourcefulness spoke for him. They asked him about the lumbering operations, but he seemed indifferent.

"Nothing to interest you," he affirmed. "We're just cutting roads now. You ought to be here for the drive."

To him there was really nothing interesting in the cutting of roads nor the clearing of streams. It was all in a day's work.

Once he took them over to see Camp One. They were immensely pleased, and were correspondingly loud in exclamations. Thorpe's comments were brief and dry. After the noon dinner he had the unfortunate idea of commending the singing of one of the men.

"Oh, I'd like to hear him," cried Elizabeth Carpenter. "Can't you get him to sing for us, Mr. Thorpe?"

Thorpe went to the men's camp, where he singled out the unfortunate lumber-jack in question.

"Come on, Archie," he said. "The ladies want to hear you sing."

The man objected, refused, pleaded, and finally obeyed what amounted to a command. Thorpe reentered the office with triumph, his victim in tow.

"This is Archie Harris," he announced heartily. "He's our best singer just now. Take a chair, Archie."

The man perched on the edge of the chair and looked straight out before him.

"Do sing for us, won't you, Mr. Harris?" requested Mrs. Cary in her sweetest tones.

The man said nothing, nor moved a muscle, but turned a brick-red. An embarrassed silence of expectation ensued.

"Hit her up, Archie," encouraged Thorpe.

"I ain't much in practice no how," objected the man in a little voice, without moving.

"I'm sure you'll find us very appreciative," said Elizabeth Carpenter.

"Give us a song, Archie, let her go," urged Thorpe impatiently.

"All right," replied the man very meekly.

Another silence fell. It got to be a little awful. The poor woodsman, pilloried before the regards of this polite circle, out of his element, suffering cruelly, nevertheless made no sign nor movement one way or the other. At last when the situation had almost reached the breaking point of hysteria, he began.

His voice ordinarily was rather a good tenor. Now he pitched it too high; and went on straining at the high notes to the very end. Instead of offering one of the typical woods chanteys, he conceived that before so grand an audience he should give something fancy. He therefore struck into a sentimental song of the cheap music-hall type. There were nine verses, and he drawled through them all, hanging whiningly on the nasal notes in the fashion of the untrained singer. Instead of being a performance typical of the strange woods genius, it was merely an atrocious bit of cheap sentimentalism, badly rendered.

The audience listened politely. When the song was finished it murmured faint thanks.

"Oh, give us 'Jack Haggerty,' Archie," urged Thorpe.

But the woodsman rose, nodded his head awkwardly, and made his escape. He entered the men's camp, swearing, and for the remainder of the day made none but blasphemous remarks.

The beagles, however, were a complete success. They tumbled about, and lolled their tongues, and laughed up out of a tangle of themselves in a fascinating manner. Altogether the visit to Camp One was a success, the more so in that on the way back, for the first time, Thorpe found that chance—and Mrs. Cary—had allotted Hilda to his care.

A hundred yards down the trail they encountered Phil. The dwarf stopped short, looked attentively at the girl, and then softly approached. When quite near to her he again stopped, gazing at her with his soul in his liquid eyes.

"You are more beautiful than the sea at night," he said directly.

The others laughed. "There's sincerity for you, Miss Hilda," said young Mr. Morton.

"Who is he?" asked the girl after they had moved

"Our chore-boy," answered Thorpe with great brevity, for he was thinking of something much more important.

405

After the rest of the party had gone ahead, leaving them sauntering more slowly down the trail, he gave it voice.

"Why don't you come to the pine grove any more?" he asked bluntly.

"Why?" countered Hilda in the manner of women.

"I want to see you there. I want to talk with you. I can't talk with all that crowd around."

"I'll come to-morrow," she said—then with a little mischievous laugh, "if that'll make you talk."

"You must think I'm awfully stupid," agreed Thorpe bitterly.

"Ah, no! Ah, no!" she protested softly. "You must not say that."

She was looking at him very tenderly, if he had only known it, but he did not, for his face was set in discontented lines straight before him.

"It is true," he replied.

They walked on in silence, while gradually the dangerous fascination of the woods crept down on them. Just before sunset a hush falls on nature. The wind has died, the birds have not yet begun their evening songs, the light itself seems to have left off sparkling and to lie still across the landscape. Such a hush now lay on their spirits. Over the way a creeper was droning sleepily a little chant,—the only voice in the wilderness. In the heart of the man, too, a little voice raised itself alone.

"Sweetheart, sweetheart, sweetheart!" it breathed over and over again. After a while he said it gently in a half voice.

"No, no, hush!" said the girl, and she laid the soft, warm fingers of one hand across his lips, and looked at him from a height of superior soft-eyed tenderness as a woman might look at a child. "You must not. It is not right."

Then he kissed the fingers very gently before they were withdrawn, and she said nothing at all in rebuke, but looked straight before her with troubled eyes.

The voices of evening began to raise their jubilant notes. From a tree nearby the olive thrush sang like clockwork; over beyond carolled eagerly a black-throat, a myrtle warbler, a dozen song sparrows, and a hundred vireos and creepers. Down deep in the blackness of the ancient woods a hermit thrush uttered his solemn bell note, like the tolling of the spirit of peace. And in Thorpe's heart a thousand tumultuous voices that had suddenly roused to clamor, died into nothingness at the music of her softly protesting voice.

### Chapter XLII

Thorpe returned to Camp One shortly after dark. He found there Scotty Parsons, who had come up to take charge of the crew engaged in clearing French Creek. The man brought him a number of letters sent on by Collins, among which was one from Wallace Carpenter.

After commending the camping party to his companion's care, and giving minute directions as to how and where to meet it, the young fellow went on to say that affairs were going badly on the Board.

"Some interest that I haven't been able to make out yet has been hammering our stocks down day after day," he wrote. "I don't understand it, for the stocks are good—they rest on a solid foundation of value and intrinsically are worth more than is bid for them right now. Some powerful concern is beating them down for a purpose of its own. Sooner or later they will let up, and then we'll get things back in good shape. I am amply protected now, thanks to you, and am not at all afraid of losing my holdings. The only difficulty is that I am unable to predict exactly when the other fellows will decide that they have accomplished whatever they are about, and let up. It may not be before next year. In that case I couldn't help you out on those notes when they come due. So put in your best licks, old man. You may have to pony up for a little while, though of course sooner or later I can put it all back. Then, you bet your life, I keep out of it. Lumbering's good enough for yours truly.

"By the way, you might shine up to Hilda Farrand and join the rest of the fortune-hunters. She's got it to throw to the birds, and in her own right. Seriously, old fellow, don't put yourself into a false position through ignorance. Not that there is any danger to a hardened old woodsman like you."

Thorpe went to the group of pines by the pole trail the following afternoon because he had said he would, but with a new attitude of mind. He had come into contact with the artificiality of conventional relations, and it stiffened him. No wonder she had made him keep silence the afternoon before! She had done it gently and nicely, to be sure, but that was part of her good-breeding. Hilda found him formal, reserved, polite; and marvelled at it. In her was no coquetry. She was as straightforward and sincere as the look of her eyes.

They sat down on a log. Hilda turned to him with her graceful air of confidence.

"Now talk to me," said she.

"Certainly," replied Thorpe in a practical tone of voice, "what do you want me to talk about?"

She shot a swift, troubled glance at him, concluded herself mistaken, and said:

"Tell me about what you do up here—your life—all about it."

"Well—" replied Thorpe formally, "we haven't much to interest a girl like you. It is a question of saw logs with us"—and he went on in his driest, most technical manner to detail the process of manufacture. It might as well have been bricks.

The girl did not understand. She was hurt. As surely as the sun tangled in the distant pine frond, she had seen in his eyes a great passion. Now it was coldly withdrawn.

"What has happened to you?" she asked finally out of her great sincerity.

"Me? Nothing," replied Thorpe.

A forced silence fell upon him. Hilda seemed gradually to lose herself in reverie. After a time she said softly.

"Don't you love this woods?"

"It's an excellent bunch of pine," replied Thorpe bluntly. "It'll cut three million at least."

"Oh!" she cried drawing back, her hands pressed against the log either side of her, her eyes wide.

After a moment she caught her breath convulsively, and Thorpe became conscious that she was studying him furtively with a quickening doubt.

After that, by the mercy of God, there was no more talk between them. She was too hurt and shocked and disillusioned to make the necessary effort to go away. He was too proud to put an end to the position. They sat there apparently absorbed in thought, while all about them the accustomed life of the woods drew nearer and nearer to them, as the splash of their entrance into it died away.

A red squirrel poised thirty feet above them, leaped, and clung swaying to a sapling-top a dozen yards from the tree he had quitted. Two chickadees upside down uttering liquid undertones, searched busily for insects next their heads. Wilson's warblers, pine creepers, black-throats, myrtle and magnolia warblers, oven birds, peewits, blue jays, purple finches, passed silently or noisily, each according to his kind. Once a lone spruce hen dusted herself in a stray patch of sunlight until it shimmered on a tree trunk, raised upward, and disappeared, to give place to long level dusty shafts that shot here and there through the pines laying the spell of sunset on the noisy woods brawlers.

Unconsciously the first strain of opposition and of hurt surprise had relaxed. Each thought vaguely his thoughts. Then in the depths of the forest, perhaps near at hand, perhaps far away, a single hermit thrush began to sing. His song was of three solemn deep liquid notes; followed by a slight rhetorical pause as of contemplation; and then, deliberately, three notes more on a different key—and so on without haste and without pause. It is the most dignified, the most spiritual, the holiest of woods utterances. Combined with the evening shadows and the warm soft air, it offered to the heart an almost irresistible appeal. The man's artificial antagonism modified; the woman's disenchantment began to seem unreal.

Then subtly over and through the bird-song another sound became audible. At first it merely repeated the three notes faintly, like an echo, but with a rich, sad undertone that brought tears. Then, timidly and still softly, it elaborated the theme, weaving in and out through the original three the glitter and shimmer of a splendid web of sound, spreading before the awakened imagination a broad river of woods-imagery that reflected on its surface all the subtler moods of the forest. The pine shadows, the calls of the wild creatures, the flow of the brook, the splashes of sunlight through the trees, the sigh of the wind, the shout of the rapid,—all these were there, distinctly to be felt in their most ethereal and beautiful forms. And yet it was all slight and tenuous as though the crack of a twig would break it through—so that over it continually like a grand full organ-tone repeated the notes of the bird itself.

With the first sigh of the wonder-music the girl had started and caught her breath in the exquisite pleasure of it. As it went on they both forgot everything but the harmony and each other.

"Ah, beautiful!" she murmured.

"What is it?" he whispered marvelling.

"A violin,—played by a master."

The bird suddenly hushed, and at once the strain abandoned the woods-note and took another motif. At first it played softly in the higher notes, a tinkling, lightsome little melody that stirred a kindly surface-smile over a full heart. Then suddenly, without transition, it dropped to the lower register, and began to sob and wail in the full vibrating power of a great passion.

And the theme it treated was love. It spoke solemnly, fearfully of the greatness of it, the glory. These as abstractions it amplified in fine full-breathed chords that swept the spirit up and up as on the waves of a mighty organ. Then one by one the voices of other things were heard,—the tinkling of laughter, the roar of a city, the sob of a grief, a cry of pain suddenly shooting across the sound, the clank of a machine, the tumult of a river, the puff of a steamboat, the murmuring of a vast crowd,—and one by one, without seeming in the least to change their character, they merged imperceptibly into, and were part of the grand-breathed chords, so that at last all the fames and ambitions and passions of the world came, in their apotheosis, to be only parts of the master-passion of them all.

And while the echoes of the greater glory still swept beneath their uplifted souls like ebbing waves, so that they still sat rigid and staring with the majesty of it, the violin softly began to whisper. Beautiful it was as a spirit, beautiful beyond words, beautiful beyond thought. Its beauty struck sharp at the heart. And they two sat there hand in hand dreaming—dreaming—dreaming—

At last the poignant ecstacy seemed slowly, slowly to die. Fainter and fainter ebbed the music. Through it as through a mist the solemn aloof forest began to show to the consciousness of the two. They sought each other's eyes gently smiling. The music was very soft and dim and sad. They leaned to each other with a sob. Their lips met. The music ceased.

Alone in the forest side by side they looked out together for a moment into that eternal vision which lovers only are permitted to see. The shadows fell. About them brooded the inscrutable pines stretching a canopy over them enthroned. A single last shaft of the sun struck full upon them, a single light-spot in the gathering gloom. They were beautiful.

And over behind the trees, out of the light and the love and the beauty, little Phil huddled, his great shaggy head bowed in his arms. Beside him lay his violin, and beside that his bow, broken. He had snapped it across his knee. That day he had heard at last the Heart Song of the Violin, and uttering it, had bestowed love. But in accordance with his prophecy he had that day lost what he cared for most in all the world, his friend.

## Chapter XLIII

That was the moon of delight. The days passed through the hazy forest like stately figures from an old masque. In the pine grove on the knoll the man and the woman had erected a temple to love, and love showed them one to the other.

In Hilda Farrand was no guile, no coquetry, no deceit. So perfect was her naturalism that often by those who knew her least she was considered affected. Her trust in whomever she found herself with attained so directly its reward; her unconsciousness of pose was so rhythmically graceful; her ignorance and innocence so triumphantly effective, that the mind with difficulty rid itself of the belief that it was all carefully studied. This was not true. She honestly did not know that she was beautiful; was unaware of her grace; did not realize the potency of her wealth.

This absolute lack of self-consciousness was most potent in overcoming Thorpe's natural reticence. He expanded to her. She came to idolize him in a manner at once inspiring and touching in so beautiful a creature. In him she saw reflected all the lofty attractions of character which she herself possessed, but of which she was entirely unaware. Through his words she saw to an ideal. His most trivial actions were ascribed to motives of a dignity which would have been ridiculous, if it had not been a little pathetic. The woods-life, the striving of the pioneer kindled her imagination. She seized upon the great facts of them and fitted those facts with reasons of her own. Her insight perceived the adventurous spirit, the battle-courage, the indomitable steadfastness which always in reality lie back of these men of the frontier to urge them into the life; and of them constructed conscious motives of conduct. To her fancy the lumbermen, of whom Thorpe was one, were self-conscious agents of advance. They chose hardship, loneliness, the strenuous life because they wished to clear the way for a higher civilization. To her it seemed a great and noble sacrifice. She did not perceive that while all this is true, it is under the surface, the real spur is a desire to get on, and a hope of making money. For, strangely enough, she differentiated sharply the life and the reasons for it. An existence in subduing the forest was to her ideal; the making of a fortune through a lumbering firm she did not consider in the least important. That this distinction was most potent, the sequel will show.

In all of it she was absolutely sincere, and not at all stupid. She had always had all she could spend, without question. Money meant nothing to her, one way or the other. If need was, she might have experienced some difficulty in learning how to economize, but none at all in adjusting herself to the necessity of it. The material had become, in all sincerity, a basis for the spiritual. She recognized but two sorts of motives; of which the ideal, comprising the poetic, the daring, the beautiful, were good; and the material, meaning the sordid and selfish, were bad. With her the mere money-getting would have to be allied with some great and poetic excuse.

That is the only sort of aristocracy, in the popular sense of the word, which is real; the only scorn of money which can be respected.

There are some faces which symbolize to the beholder many subtleties of soul-beauty which by no other method could gain expression. Those subtleties may not, probably do not, exist in the possessor of the face. The power of such a countenance lies not so much in what it actually represents, as in the suggestion it holds out to another. So often it is with a beautiful character. Analyze it carefully, and you will reduce it generally to absolute simplicity and absolute purity—two elements common enough in adulteration; but place it face to face with a more complex personality, and mirror-like it will take on a hundred delicate shades of ethical beauty, while at the same time preserving its own lofty spirituality.

Thus Hilda Farrand reflected Thorpe. In the clear mirror of her heart his image rested transfigured. It was as though the glass were magic, so that the gross and material was absorbed and lost, while the more spiritual qualities reflected back. So the image was retained in its entirety, but etherealized, refined. It is necessary to attempt, even thus faintly and inadequately, a sketch of Hilda's love, for a partial understanding of it is necessary to the comprehension of what followed the moon of delight.

That moon saw a variety of changes.

The bed of French Creek was cleared. Three of the roads were finished, and the last begun. So much for the work of it.

Morton and Cary shot four deer between them, which was unpardonably against the law, caught fish in plenty, smoked two and a half pounds of tobacco, and read half of one novel. Mrs. Cary and Miss Carpenter walked a total of over a hundred miles, bought twelve pounds of Indian work of all sorts, embroidered the circle of two embroidery frames, learned to paddle a birch-bark canoe, picked fifteen quarts of berries, and gained six pounds in weight. All the party together accomplished five picnics, four explorations, and thirty excellent campfires in the evening. So much for the fun of it.

Little Phil disappeared utterly, taking with him his violin, but leaving his broken bow. Thorpe has it even to this day. The lumberman caused search and inquiry on all sides. The cripple was never heard of again. He had lived his brief hour, taken his subtle artist's vengeance of misplayed notes on the crude appreciation of men too coarse-fibered to recognize it, brought together by the might of sacrifice and consummate genius two hearts on the brink of misunderstanding;—now there was no further need for him, he had gone. So much for the tragedy of it.

"I saw you long ago," said Hilda to Thorpe. "Long, long ago, when I was quite a young girl. I had been visiting in Detroit, and was on my way all alone to catch an early train. You stood on the corner thinking, tall and straight and brown, with a weather-beaten old hat and a weather-beaten old coat and weather-beaten old moccasins, and such a proud, clear, undaunted look on your face. I have remembered you ever since."

**408**

And then he told her of the race to the Land Office, while her eyes grew brighter and brighter with the epic splendor of the story. She told him that she had loved him from that moment—and believed her telling; while he, the unsentimental leader of men, persuaded himself and her that he had always in some mysterious manner carried her image prophetically in his heart. So much for the love of it.

In the last days of the month of delight Thorpe received a second letter from his partner, which to some extent awakened him to the realities.

"My dear Harry," it ran. "I have made a startling discovery. The other fellow is Morrison. I have been a blind, stupid dolt, and am caught nicely. You can't call me any more names than I have already called myself. Morrison has been in it from the start. By an accident I learned he was behind the fellow who induced me to invest, and it is he who has been hammering the stock down ever since. They couldn't lick you at your game, so they tackled me at mine. I'm not the man you are, Harry, and I've made a mess of it. Of course their scheme is plain enough on the face of it. They're going to involve me so deeply that I will drag the firm down with me.

"If you can fix it to meet those notes, they can't do it. I have ample margin to cover any more declines they may be able to bring about. Don't fret about that. Just as sure as you can pay that sixty thousand, just so sure we'll be ahead of the game at this time next year. For God's sake get a move on you, old man. If you don't—good Lord! The firm'll bust because she can't pay; I'll bust because I'll have to let my stock go on margins—it'll be an awful smash. But you'll get there, so we needn't worry. I've been an awful fool, and I've no right to do the getting into trouble and leave you to the hard work of getting out again. But as partner I'm going to insist on your having a salary—etc."

The news aroused all Thorpe's martial spirit. Now at last the mystery surrounding Morrison & Daly's unnatural complaisance was riven. It had come to grapples again. He was glad of it. Meet those notes? Well I guess so! He'd show them what sort of a proposition they had tackled. Sneaking, underhanded scoundrels! taking advantage of a mere boy. Meet those notes? You bet he would; and then he'd go down there and boost those stocks until M. & D. looked like a last year's bird's nest. He thrust the letter in his pocket and walked buoyantly to the pines.

The two lovers sat there all the afternoon drinking in half sadly the joy of the forest and of being near each other, for the moon of delight was almost done. In a week the camping party would be breaking up, and Hilda must return to the city. It was uncertain when they would be able to see each other again, though there was talk of getting up a winter party to visit Camp One in January. The affair would be unique.

Suddenly the girl broke off and put her fingers to her lips. For some time, dimly, an intermittent and faint sound had been felt, rather than actually heard, like the irregular muffled beating of a heart. Gradually it had insisted on the attention. Now at last it broke through the film of consciousness.

"What is it?" she asked.

Thorpe listened. Then his face lit mightily with the joy of battle.

"My axmen," he cried. "They are cutting the road."

A faint call echoed. Then without warning, nearer at hand the sharp ring of an ax sounded through the forest.


## PART V. THE FOLLOWING OF THE TRAIL


### Chapter XLIV

For a moment they sat listening to the clear staccato knocking of the distant blows, and the more forceful thuds of the man nearer at hand. A bird or so darted from the direction of the sound and shot silently into the thicket behind them.

"What are they doing? Are they cutting lumber?" asked Hilda.

"No," answered Thorpe, "we do not cut saw logs at this time of year. They are clearing out a road."

"Where does it go to?"

"Well, nowhere in particular. That is, it is a logging road that starts at the river and wanders up through the woods where the pine is."

"How clear the axes sound. Can't we go down and watch them a little while?"

"The main gang is a long distance away; sound carries very clearly in this still air. As for that fellow you hear so plainly, he is only clearing out small stuff to get ready for the others. You wouldn't see anything different from your Indian chopping the cordwood for your camp fire. He won't chop out any big trees."

"Let's not go, then," said Hilda submissively.

"When you come up in the winter," he pursued, "you will see any amount of big timber felled."

"I would like to know more about it," she sighed, a quaint little air of childish petulance graving two lines between her eyebrows. "Do you know, Harry, you are a singularly uncommunicative sort of being. I have to guess that your life is interesting and picturesque,—that is," she amended, "I should have to do so if Wallace Carpenter had not told me a little something about it. Sometimes I think you are not nearly poet enough for the life you are living. Why, you are wonderful, you men of the north, and you let us ordinary mortals who have not the gift of divination imagine you entirely occupied with how many pounds of iron chain you are going to need during the winter." She said these things lightly as one who speaks things not for serious belief.

"It is something that way," he agreed with a laugh.

"Do you know, sir," she persisted, "that I really don't know anything at all about the life you lead here? From what I have seen, you might be perpetually occupied in eating things in a log cabin, and in disappearing to perform some mysterious rites in the forest." She looked at him with a smiling mouth but tender eyes, her head tilted back slightly.

"It's a good deal that way, too," he agreed again. "We use a barrel of flour in Camp One every two and a half days!"

She shook her head in a faint negation that only half understood what he was saying, her whole heart in her tender gaze.

"Sit there," she breathed very softly, pointing to the dried needles on which her feet rested, but without altering the position of her head or the steadfastness of her look.

He obeyed.

"Now tell me," she breathed, still in the fascinated monotone.

"What?" he inquired.

"Your life; what you do; all about it. You must tell me a story."

Thorpe settled himself more lazily, and laughed with quiet enjoyment. Never had he felt the expansion of a similar mood. The barrier between himself and self-expression had faded, leaving not the smallest debris of the old stubborn feeling.

"The story of the woods," he began, "the story of the saw log. It would take a bigger man than I to tell it. I doubt if any one man ever would be big enough. It is a drama, a struggle, a battle. Those men you hear there are only the skirmishers extending the firing line. We are fighting always with Time. I'll have to hurry now to get those roads done and a certain creek cleared before the snow. Then we'll have to keep on the keen move to finish our cutting before the deep snow; to haul our logs before the spring thaws; to float them down the river while the freshet water lasts. When we gain a day we have scored a victory; when the wilderness puts us back an hour, we have suffered a defeat. Our ammunition is Time; our small shot the minutes, our heavy ordnance the hours!"

The girl placed her hand on his shoulder. He covered it with his own.

"But we win!" he cried. "We win!"

"That is what I like," she said softly, "the strong spirit that wins!" She hesitated, then went on gently, "But the battlefields, Harry; to me they are dreadful. I went walking yesterday morning, before you came over, and after a while I found myself in the most awful place. The stumps of trees, the dead branches, the trunks lying all about, and the glaring hot sun over everything! Harry, there was not a single bird in all that waste, a single green thing. You don't know how it affected me so early in the morning. I saw just one lonesome pine tree that had been left for some reason or another, standing there like a sentinel. I could shut my eyes and see all the others standing, and almost hear the birds singing and the wind in the branches, just as it is here." She seized his fingers in her other hand. "Harry," she said earnestly, "I don't believe I can ever forget that experience, any more than I could have forgotten a battlefield, were I to see one. I can shut my eyes now, and can see this place our dear little wooded knoll wasted and blackened as that was."

The man twisted his shoulder uneasily and withdrew his hand.

"Harry," she said again, after a pause, "you must promise to leave this woods until the very last. I suppose it must all be cut down some day, but I do not want to be here to see after it is all over."

Thorpe remained silent.

"Men do not care much for keepsakes, do they, Harry?—they don't save letters and flowers as we girls do—but even a man can feel the value of a great beautiful keepsake such as this, can't he, dear? Our meeting-place—do you remember how I found you down there by the old pole trail, staring as though you had seen a ghost?—and that beautiful, beautiful music! It must always be our most sacred memory. Promise me you will save it until the very, very last."

Thorpe said nothing because he could not rally his faculties. The sentimental association connected with the grove had actually never occurred to him. His keepsakes were impressions which he carefully guarded in his memory. To the natural masculine indifference toward material bits of sentiment he had added the instinct of the strictly portable early developed in the rover. He had never even possessed a photograph of his sister. Now this sudden discovery that such things might be part of the woof of another person's spiritual garment came to him ready-grown to the proportions of a problem.

In selecting the districts for the season's cut, he had included in his estimates this very grove. Since then he had seen no reason for changing his decision. The operations would not commence until winter. By that time the lovers would no longer care to use it as at present. Now rapidly he passed in review a dozen expedients by which his plan might be modified to permit of the grove's exclusion. His practical mind discovered flaws in every one. Other bodies of timber promising a return of ten thousand dollars were not to be found near the river, and time now lacked for the cutting of roads to more distant forties.

"Hilda," he broke in abruptly at last, "the men you hear are clearing a road to this very timber."

"What do you mean?" she asked.

"This timber is marked for cutting this very winter."

She had not a suspicion of the true state of affairs. "Isn't it lucky I spoke of it!" she exclaimed. "How could you have forgotten to countermand the order! You must see to it to-day; now!"

She sprang up impulsively and stood waiting for him. He arose more slowly. Even before he spoke her eyes dilated with the shock from her quick intuitions.

"Hilda, I cannot," he said.

She stood very still for some seconds.

"Why not?" she asked quietly.

"Because I have not time to cut a road through to another bunch of pine. It is this or nothing."

"Why not nothing, then?"

"I want the money this will bring."

His choice of a verb was unfortunate. The employment of that one little word opened the girl's mind to a flood of old suspicions which the frank charm of the northland had thrust outside. Hilda Farrand was an heiress and a beautiful girl. She had been constantly reminded of the one fact by the attempts of men to use flattery of the other as a key to her heart and her fortune. From early girlhood she had been sought by the brilliant impecunious of two continents. The continued experience had varnished her self-esteem with a glaze of cynicism sufficiently consistent to protect it against any but the strongest attack. She believed in no man's protestations. She distrusted every man's motives as far as herself was concerned. This attitude of mind was not unbecoming in her for the simple reason that it destroyed none of her graciousness as regards other human relations besides that of love. That men should seek her in matrimony from a selfish motive was as much to be expected as that flies should seek the sugar bowl. She accepted the fact as one of nature's laws, annoying enough but inevitable; a thing to guard against, but not one of sufficient moment to grieve over.

With Thorpe, however, her suspicions had been lulled. There is something virile and genuine about the woods and the men who inhabit them that strongly predisposes the mind to accept as proved in their entirety all the other virtues. Hilda had fallen into this state of mind. She endowed each of the men whom she encountered with all the robust qualities she had no difficulty in recognizing as part of nature's charm in the wilderness. Now at a word her eyes were opened to what she had done. She saw that she had assumed unquestioningly that her lover possessed the qualities of his environment.

Not for a moment did she doubt the reality of her love. She had conceived one of those deep, uplifting passions possible only to a young girl. But her cynical experience warned her that the reality of that passion's object was not proven by any test besides the fallible one of her own poetizing imagination. The reality of the ideal she had constructed might be a vanishable quantity even though the love of it was not. So to the interview that ensued she brought, not the partiality of a loving heart, nor even the impartiality of one sitting in judgment, but rather the perverted prejudice of one who actually fears the truth.

"Will you tell me for what you want the money?" she asked.

The young man caught the note of distrust. At once, instinctively, his own confidence vanished. He drew within himself, again beyond the power of justifying himself with the needed word.

"The firm needs it in the business," said he.

Her next question countered instantaneously.

"Does the firm need the money more than you do me?"

They stared at each other in the silence of the situation that had so suddenly developed. It had come into being without their volition, as a dust cloud springs up on a plain.

"You do not mean that, Hilda," said Thorpe quietly. "It hardly comes to that."

"Indeed it does," she replied, every nerve of her fine organization strung to excitement. "I should be more to you than any firm."

"Sometimes it is necessary to look after the bread and butter," Thorpe reminded her gently, although he knew that was not the real reason at all.

"If your firm can't supply it, I can," she answered. "It seems strange that you won't grant my first request of you, merely because of a little money."

"It isn't a little money," he objected, catching manlike at the practical question. "You don't realize what an amount a clump of pine like this stands for. Just in saw logs, before it is made into lumber, it will be worth about thirty thousand dollars,—of course there's the expense of logging to pay out of that," he added, out of his accurate business conservatism, "but there's ten thousand dollars' profit in it."

The girl, exasperated by cold details at such a time, blazed out. "I never heard anything so ridiculous in my life!" she cried. "Either you are not at all the man I thought you, or you have some better reason than you have given. Tell me, Harry; tell me at once. You don't know what you are doing."

"The firm needs it, Hilda," said Thorpe, "in order to succeed. If we do not cut this pine, we may fail."

In that he stated his religion. The duty of success was to him one of the loftiest of abstractions, for it measured the degree of a man's efficiency in the station to which God had called him. The money, as such, was nothing to him.

Unfortunately the girl had learned a different language. She knew nothing of the hardships, the struggles, the delight of winning for the sake of victory rather than the sake of spoils. To her, success meant getting a lot of money. The name by which Thorpe labelled his most sacred principle, to her represented something base and sordid. She had more money herself than she knew. It hurt her to the soul that the condition of a small money-making machine, as she considered the lumber firm, should be weighed even for an instant against her love. It was a great deal Thorpe's fault that she so saw the firm. He might easily have shown her the great forces and principles for which it stood.

"If I were a man," she said, and her voice was tense, "if I were a man and loved a woman, I would be ready to give up everything for her. My riches, my pride, my life, my honor, my soul even,—they would be as nothing, as less than nothing to me,—if I loved. Harry, don't let me think I am mistaken. Let this miserable firm of yours fail, if fail it must for lack of my poor little temple of dreams," she held out her hands with a tender gesture of appeal. The affair had gone beyond the preservation of a few trees. It had become the question of an ideal. Gradually, in spite of herself, the conviction was forcing itself upon her that the man she had loved was no different from the rest; that the greed of the dollar had corrupted him too. By the mere yielding to her wishes, she wanted to prove the suspicion wrong.

Now the strange part of the whole situation was, that in two words Thorpe could have cleared it. If he had explained that he needed the ten thousand dollars to help pay a note given to save from ruin a foolish friend, he would have supplied to the affair just the higher motive the girl's clear spirituality demanded. Then she would have shared enthusiastically in the sacrifice, and been the more loving and repentant from her momentary doubt. All she needed was that the man should prove himself actuated by a noble, instead of a sordid, motive. The young man did not say the two words, because in all honesty he thought them unimportant. It seemed to him quite natural that he should go on Wallace Carpenter's note. That fact altered not a bit the main necessity of success. It was a man's duty to make the best of himself,—it was Thorpe's duty to prove himself supremely efficient in his chosen calling; the mere coincidence that his partner's troubles worked along the same lines meant nothing to the logic of the situation. In stating baldly that he needed the money to assure the firm's existence, he imagined he had adduced the strongest possible reason for his attitude. If the girl was not influenced by that, the case was hopeless.

It was the difference of training rather than the difference of ideas. Both clung to unselfishness as the highest reason for human action; but each expressed the thought in a manner incomprehensible to the other.

"I cannot, Hilda," he answered steadily.

"You sell me for ten thousand dollars! I cannot believe it! Harry! Harry! Must I put it to you as a choice? Don't you love me enough to spare me that?"

He did not reply. As long as it remained a dilemma, he would not reply. He was in the right.

"Do you need the money more than you do me? more than you do love?" she begged, her soul in her eyes; for she was begging also for herself. "Think, Harry; it is the last chance!"

Once more he was face to face with a vital decision. To his surprise he discovered in his mind no doubt as to what the answer should be. He experienced no conflict of mind; no hesitation; for the moment, no regret. During all his woods life he had been following diligently the trail he had blazed for his conduct. Now his feet carried him unconsciously to the same end. There was no other way out. In the winter of his trouble the clipped trees alone guided him, and at the end of them he found his decision. It is in crises of this sort, when a little reflection or consideration would do wonders to prevent a catastrophe, that all the forgotten deeds, decisions, principles, and thoughts of a man's past life combine solidly into the walls of fatality, so that in spite of himself he finds he must act in accordance with them. In answer to Hilda's question he merely inclined his head.

"I have seen a vision," said she simply, and lowered her head to conceal her eyes. Then she looked at him again. "There can be nothing better than love," she said.

"Yes, one thing," said Thorpe, "the duty of success."

The man had stated his creed; the woman hers. The one is born perfect enough for love; the other must work, must attain the completeness of a fulfilled function, must succeed, to deserve it.

She left him then, and did not see him again. Four days later the camping party left. Thorpe sent Tim Shearer over, as his most efficient man, to see that they got off without difficulty, but himself retired on some excuse to Camp Four. Three weeks gone in October he received a marked newspaper announcing the engagement of Miss Hilda Farrand to Mr. Hildreth Morton of Chicago.

He had burned his ships, and stood now on an unfriendly shore. The first sacrifice to his jealous god had been consummated, and now, live or die, he stood pledged to win his fight.


### Chapter XLV

Winter set in early and continued late; which in the end was a good thing for the year's cut. The season was capricious, hanging for days at a time at the brink of a thaw, only to stiffen again into severe weather. This was trying on the nerves. For at each of these false alarms the six camps fell into a feverish haste to get the job finished before the break-up. It was really quite extraordinary how much was accomplished under the nagging spur of weather conditions and the cruel rowelling of Thorpe.

The latter had now no thought beyond his work, and that was the thought of a madman. He had been stern and unyielding enough before, goodness knows, but now he was terrible. His restless energy permeated every molecule in the economic structure over which he presided, roused it to intense vibration. Not for an instant was there a resting spell. The veriest chore-boy talked, thought, dreamed of nothing but saw logs. Men whispered vaguely of a record cut. Teamsters looked upon their success or failure to keep near the top on the day's haul as a signal victory or a disgraceful defeat. The difficulties of snow, accident, topography which an ever-watchful nature threw down before the rolling car of this industry, were swept aside like straws. Little time was wasted and no opportunities. It did not matter how smoothly affairs happened to be running for the moment, every advantage, even the smallest, was eagerly seized to advance the work. A drop of five degrees during the frequent warm spells brought out the sprinklers, even in dead of night; an accident was white-hot in the forge almost before the crack of the iron had ceased to echo. At night the men fell into their bunks like sandbags, and their last conscious thought, if indeed they had any at all, was of eagerness for the morrow in order that they might push the grand total up another notch. It was madness; but it was the madness these men loved.

For now to his old religion Thorpe had added a fanaticism, and over the fanaticism was gradually creeping a film of doubt. To the conscientious energy which a sense of duty supplied, was added the tremendous kinetic force of a love turned into other channels. And in the wild nights while the other men slept, Thorpe's half-crazed brain was revolving over and over again the words of the sentence he had heard from Hilda's lips: "There can be nothing better than love."

His actions, his mind, his very soul vehemently denied the proposition. He clung as ever to his high Puritanic idea of man's purpose. But down deep in a very tiny, sacred corner of his heart a very small voice sometimes made itself heard when other, more militant voices were still: "It may be; it may be!"

The influence of this voice was practically nothing. It made itself heard occasionally. Perhaps even, for the time being, its weight counted on the other side of the scale; for Thorpe took pains to deny it fiercely, both directly and indirectly by increased exertions. But it persisted; and once in a moon or so, when the conditions were quite favorable, it attained for an instant a shred of belief.

Probably never since the Puritan days of New England has a community lived as sternly as did that winter of 1888 the six camps under Thorpe's management. There was something a little inspiring about it. The men fronted their daily work with the same grim-faced, clear-eyed steadiness of veterans going into battle;—with the same confidence, the same sure patience that disposes effectively of one thing before going on to the next. There was little merely excitable bustle; there was no rest. Nothing could stand against such a spirit. Nothing did. The skirmishers which the wilderness threw out, were brushed away. Even the inevitable delays seemed not so much stoppages as the instant's pause of a heavy vehicle in a snow drift, succeeded by the momentary acceleration as the plunge carried it through. In the main, and by large, the machine moved steadily and inexorably.

And yet one possessed of the finer spiritual intuitions could not have shaken off the belief in an impending struggle. The feel of it was in the air. Nature's forces were too mighty to be so slightly overcome; the splendid energy developed in these camps too vast to be wasted on facile success. Over against each other were two great powers, alike in their calm confidence, animated with the loftiest and most dignified spirit of enmity. Slowly they were moving toward each other. The air was surcharged with the electricity of their opposition. Just how the struggle would begin was uncertain; but its inevitability was as assured as its magnitude. Thorpe knew it, and shut his teeth, looking keenly about him. The Fighting Forty knew it, and longed for the grapple to come. The other camps knew it, and followed their leader with perfect trust. The affair was an epitome of the historic combats begun with David and Goliath. It was an affair of Titans. The little courageous men watched their enemy with cat's eyes.

The last month of hauling was also one of snow. In this condition were few severe storms, but each day a little fell. By and by the accumulation amounted to much. In the woods where the wind could not get at it, it lay deep and soft above the tops of bushes. The grouse ate browse from the slender hardwood tips like a lot of goldfinches, or precipitated themselves headlong down through five feet of snow to reach the ground. Often Thorpe would come across the irregular holes of their entrance. Then if he took the trouble to stamp about a little in the vicinity with his snowshoes, the bird would spring unexpectedly from the clear snow, scattering a cloud with its strong wings. The deer, herded together, tramped "yards" where the feed was good. Between the yards ran narrow trails. When the animals went from one yard to another in these trails, their ears and antlers alone were visible. On either side of the logging roads the snow piled so high as to form a kind of rampart. When all this water in suspense should begin to flow, and to seek its level in the water-courses of the district, the logs would have plenty to float them, at least.

So late did the cold weather last that, even with the added plowing to do, the six camps beat all records. On the banks at Camp One were nine million feet; the totals of all five amounted to thirty-three million. About ten million of this was on French Creek; the remainder on the main banks of the Ossawinamakee. Besides this the firm up-river, Sadler & Smith, had put up some twelve million more. The drive promised to be quite an affair.

About the fifteenth of April attention became strained. Every day the mounting sun made heavy attacks on the snow: every night the temperature dropped below the freezing point. The river began to show more air holes, occasional open places. About the center the ice looked worn and soggy. Someone saw a flock of geese high in the air. Then came rain.

One morning early, Long Pine Jim came into the men's camp bearing a huge chunk of tallow. This he held against the hot stove until its surface had softened, when he began to swab liberal quantities of grease on his spiked river shoes, which he fished out from under his bunk.

"She's comin', boys," said he.

He donned a pair of woolen trousers that had been chopped off at the knee, thick woolen stockings, and the river shoes. Then he tightened his broad leather belt about his heavy shirt, cocked his little hat over his ear, and walked over in the corner to select a peavey from the lot the blacksmith had just put in shape. A peavey is like a cant-hook except that it is pointed at the end. Thus it can be used either as a hook or a pike. At the same moment Shearer, similarly attired and equipped, appeared in the doorway. The opening of the portal admitted a roar of sound. The river was rising.

"Come on, boys, she's on!" said he sharply.

Outside, the cook and cookee were stowing articles in the already loaded wanigan. The scow contained tents, blankets, provisions, and a portable stove. It followed the drive, and made a camp wherever expediency demanded.

"Lively, boys, lively!" shouted Thorpe. "She'll be down on us before we know it!"

Above the soft creaking of dead branches in the wind sounded a steady roar, like the bellowing of a wild beast lashing itself to fury. The freshet was abroad, forceful with the strength of a whole winter's accumulated energy.

The men heard it and their eyes brightened with the lust of battle. They cheered.

413

At the banks of the river, Thorpe rapidly issued his directions. The affair had been all prearranged. During the week previous he and his foremen had reviewed the situation, examining the state of the ice, the heads of water in the three dams. Immediately above the first rollways was Dam Three with its two wide sluices through which a veritable flood could be loosened at will; then four miles farther lay the rollways of Sadler & Smith, the up-river firm; and above them tumbled over a forty-five foot ledge the beautiful Siscoe Falls; these first rollways of Thorpe's—spread in the broad marsh flat below the dam—contained about eight millions; the rest of the season's cut was scattered for thirty miles along the bed of the river.

Already the ice cementing the logs together had begun to weaken. The ice had wrenched and tugged savagely at the locked timbers until they had, with a mighty effort, snapped asunder the bonds of their hibernation. Now a narrow lane of black rushing water pierced the rollways, to boil and eddy in the consequent jam three miles below.

To the foremen Thorpe assigned their tasks, calling them to him one by one, as a general calls his aids.

"Moloney," said he to the big Irishman, "take your crew and break that jam. Then scatter your men down to within a mile of the pond at Dam Two, and see that the river runs clear. You can tent for a day or so at West Bend or some other point about half way down; and after that you had better camp at the dam. Just as soon as you get logs enough in the pond, start to sluicing them through the dam. You won't need more than four men there, if you keep a good head. You can keep your gates open five or six hours. And Moloney."

"Yes, sir."

"I want you to be careful not to sluice too long. There is a bar just below the dam, and if you try to sluice with the water too low, you'll center and jam there, as sure as shooting."

Bryan Moloney turned on his heel and began to pick his way down stream over the solidly banked logs. Without waiting the command, a dozen men followed him. The little group bobbed away irregularly into the distance, springing lightly from one timber to the other, holding their quaintly-fashioned peaveys in the manner of a rope dancer's balancing pole. At the lowermost limit of the rollways, each man pried a log into the water, and, standing gracefully erect on this unstable craft, floated out down the current to the scene of his dangerous labor.

"Kerlie," went on Thorpe, "your crew can break rollways with the rest until we get the river fairly filled, and then you can move on down stream as fast as you are needed. Scotty, you will have the rear. Tim and I will boss the river."

At once the signal was given to Ellis, the dam watcher. Ellis and his assistants thereupon began to pry with long iron bars at the ratchets of the heavy gates. The chore-boy bent attentively over the ratchet-pin, lifting it delicately to permit another inch of raise, dropping it accurately to enable the men at the bars to seize a fresh purchase. The river's roar deepened. Through the wide sluice-ways a torrent foamed and tumbled. Immediately it spread through the brush on either side to the limits of the freshet banks, and then gathered for its leap against the uneasy rollways. Along the edge of the dark channel the face of the logs seemed to crumble away. Farther in towards the banks where the weight of timber still outbalanced the weight of the flood, the tiers grumbled and stirred, restless with the stream's calling. Far down the river, where Bryan Moloney and his crew were picking at the jam, the water in eager streamlets sought the interstices between the logs, gurgling excitedly like a mountain brook.

The jam creaked and groaned in response to the pressure. From its face a hundred jets of water spurted into the lower stream. Logs up-ended here and there, rising from the bristling surface slowly, like so many arms from lower depths. Above, the water eddied back foaming; logs shot down from the rollways, paused at the slackwater, and finally hit with a hollow and resounding BOOM! against the tail of the jam. A moment later they too up-ended, so becoming an integral part of the "chevaux de frise."

The crew were working desperately. Down in the heap somewhere, two logs were crossed in such a manner as to lock the whole. They sought those logs.

Thirty feet above the bed of the river six men clamped their peaveys into the soft pine; jerking, pulling, lifting, sliding the great logs from their places. Thirty feet below, under the threatening face, six other men coolly picked out and set adrift, one by one, the timbers not inextricably imbedded. From time to time the mass creaked, settled, perhaps even moved a foot or two; but always the practiced rivermen, after a glance, bent more eagerly to their work.

Outlined against the sky, big Bryan Moloney stood directing the work. He had gone at the job on the bias of indirection, picking out a passage at either side that the center might the more easily "pull." He knew by the tenseness of the log he stood on that, behind the jam, power had gathered sufficient to push the whole tangle down-stream. Now he was offering it the chance.

Suddenly the six men below the jam scattered. Four of them, holding their peaveys across their bodies, jumped lightly from one floating log to another in the zigzag to shore. When they stepped on a small log they re-leaped immediately, leaving a swirl of foam where the little timber had sunk under them; when they encountered one larger, they hesitated for a barely perceptible instant. Thus their progression was of fascinating and graceful irregularity. The other two ran the length of their footing, and, overleaping an open of water, landed heavily and firmly on the very ends of two small floating logs. In this manner the force of the jump rushed the little timbers end-on through the water. The two men, maintaining marvellously their balance, were thus ferried to within leaping distance of the other shore.

In the meantime a barely perceptible motion was communicating itself from one particle to another through the center of the jam. A cool and observant spectator might have imagined that the broad timber carpet was changing a little its pattern, just as the earth near the windows of an arrested railroad train seems for a moment to retrogress. The crew redoubled its exertions, clamping its peaveys here and there, apparently at random, but in reality with the most definite of purposes. A sharp crack exploded immediately underneath. There could no longer exist any doubt as to the motion, although it was as yet sluggish, glacial. Then in silence a log shifted—in silence and slowly—but with irresistible force. Jimmy Powers quietly stepped over it, just as it menaced his leg. Other logs in all directions up-ended. The jam crew were forced continually to alter their positions, riding the changing timbers bent-kneed, as a circus rider treads his four galloping horses.

Then all at once down by the face something crashed. The entire stream became alive. It hissed and roared, it shrieked, groaned and grumbled. At first slowly, then more rapidly, the very forefront of the center melted inward and forward and downward until it caught the fierce rush of the freshet and shot out from under the jam. Far up-stream, bristling and formidable, the tons of logs, grinding savagely together, swept forward.

The six men and Bryan Moloney—who, it will be remembered, were on top—worked until the last moment. When the logs began to cave under them so rapidly that even the expert rivermen found difficulty in "staying on top," the foreman set the example of hunting safety.

"She 'pulls,' boys," he yelled.

Then in a manner wonderful to behold, through the smother of foam and spray, through the crash and yell of timbers protesting the flood's hurrying, through the leap of destruction, the drivers zigzagged calmly and surely to the shore.

All but Jimmy Powers. He poised tense and eager on the crumbling face of the jam. Almost immediately he saw what he wanted, and without pause sprang boldly and confidently ten feet straight downward, to alight with accuracy on a single log floating free in the current. And then in the very glory and chaos of the jam itself he was swept down-stream.

After a moment the constant acceleration in speed checked, then commenced perceptibly to slacken. At once the rest of the crew began to ride down-stream. Each struck the caulks of his river boots strongly into a log, and on such unstable vehicles floated miles with the current. From time to time, as Bryan Moloney indicated, one of them went ashore. There, usually at a bend of the stream where the likelihood of jamming was great, they took their stands. When necessary, they ran out over the face of the river to separate a congestion likely to cause trouble. The rest of the time they smoked their pipes.

At noon they ate from little canvas bags which had been filled that morning by the cookee. At sunset they rode other logs down the river to where their camp had been made for them. There they ate hugely, hung their ice-wet garments over a tall framework constructed around a monster fire, and turned in on hemlock branches.

All night long the logs slipped down the moonlit current, silently, swiftly, yet without haste. The porcupines invaded the sleeping camp. From the whole length of the river rang the hollow BOOM, BOOM, BOOM, of timbers striking one against the other.

The drive was on.

### Chapter XLVII

In the meantime the main body of the crew under Thorpe and his foremen were briskly tumbling the logs into the current. Sometimes under the urging of the peaveys, but a single stick would slide down; or again a double tier would cascade with the roar of a little Niagara. The men had continually to keep on the tension of an alert, for at any moment they were called upon to exercise their best judgment and quickness to keep from being carried downward with the rush of the logs. Not infrequently a frowning sheer wall of forty feet would hesitate on the brink of plunge. Then Shearer himself proved his right to the title of riverman.

Shearer wore caulks nearly an inch in length. He had been known to ride ten miles, without shifting his feet, on a log so small that he could carry it without difficulty. For cool nerve he was unexcelled.

"I don't need you boys here any longer," he said quietly.

When the men had all withdrawn, he walked confidently under the front of the rollway, glancing with practiced eye at the perpendicular wall of logs over him. Then, as a man pries jack-straws, he clamped his peavey and tugged sharply. At once the rollway flattened and toppled. A mighty splash, a hurl of flying foam and crushing timbers, and the spot on which the riverman had stood was buried beneath twenty feet of solid green wood. To Thorpe it seemed that Shearer must have been overwhelmed, but the riverman always mysteriously appeared at one side or the other, nonchalant, urging the men to work before the logs should have ceased to move. Tradition claimed that only once in a long woods life had Shearer been forced to "take water" before a breaking rollway: and then he saved his peavey. History stated that he had never lost a man on the river, simply and solely because he invariably took the dangerous tasks upon himself.

As soon as the logs had caught the current, a dozen men urged them on. With their short peaveys, the drivers were enabled to prevent the timbers from swirling in the eddies—one of the first causes of a jam. At last, near the foot of the flats, they abandoned them to the stream, confident that Moloney and his crew would see to their passage down the river.

In three days the rollways were broken. Now it became necessary to start the rear.

For this purpose Billy Camp, the cook, had loaded his cook-stove, a quantity of provisions, and a supply of bedding, aboard a scow. The scow was built of tremendous hewn timbers, four or five inches thick, to withstand the shock of the logs. At either end were long sweeps to direct its course. The craft was perhaps forty feet long, but rather narrow, in order that it might pass easily through the chute of a dam. It was called the "wanigan."

Billy Camp, his cookee, and his crew of two were now doomed to tribulation. The huge, unwieldy craft from that moment was to become possessed of the devil. Down the white water of rapids it would bump, smashing obstinately against boulders, impervious to the frantic urging of the long sweeps; against the roots and branches of the streamside it would scrape with the perverseness of a vicious horse; in the broad reaches it would sulk, refusing to proceed; and when expediency demanded its pause, it would drag Billy Camp and his entire crew at the rope's end, while they tried vainly to snub it against successively uprooted trees and stumps. When at last the wanigan was moored fast for the night,—usually a mile or so below the spot planned,—Billy Camp pushed back his battered old brown derby hat, the badge of his office, with a sigh of relief. To be sure he and his men had still to cut wood, construct cooking and camp fires, pitch tents, snip browse, and prepare supper for seventy men; but the hard work of the day was over. Billy Camp did not mind rain or cold—he would cheerfully cook away with the water dripping from his battered derby to his chubby and cold-purpled nose—but he did mind the wanigan. And the worst of it was, he got no sympathy nor aid from the crew. From either bank he and his anxious struggling assistants were greeted with ironic cheers and facetious remarks. The tribulations of the wanigan were as the salt of life to the spectators.

Billy Camp tried to keep back of the rear in clear water, but when the wanigan so disposed, he found himself jammed close in the logs. There he had a chance in his turn to become spectator, and so to repay in kind some of the irony and facetiousness.

Along either bank, among the bushes, on sandbars, and in trees, hundreds and hundreds of logs had been stranded when the main drive passed. These logs the rear crew were engaged in restoring to the current.

And as a man had to be able to ride any kind of a log in any water; to propel that log by jumping on it, by rolling it squirrel fashion with the feet, by punting it as one would a canoe; to be skillful in pushing, prying, and poling other logs from the quarter deck of the same cranky craft; as he must be prepared at any and all times to jump waist deep into the river, to work in ice-water hours at a stretch; as he was called upon to break the most dangerous jams on the river, representing, as they did, the accumulation which the jam crew had left behind them, it was naturally considered the height of glory to belong to the rear crew. Here were the best of the Fighting Forty,—men with a reputation as "white-water birlers"—men afraid of nothing.

Every morning the crews were divided into two sections under Kerlie and Jack Hyland. Each crew had charge of one side of the river, with the task of cleaning it thoroughly of all stranded and entangled logs. Scotty Parsons exercised a general supervisory eye over both crews. Shearer and Thorpe traveled back and forth the length of the drive, riding the logs down stream, but taking to a partly submerged pole trail when ascending the current. On the surface of the river in the clear water floated two long graceful boats called bateaux. These were in charge of expert boatmen,—men able to propel their craft swiftly forwards, backwards and sideways, through all kinds of water. They carried in racks a great supply of pike-poles, peaveys, axes, rope and dynamite, for use in various emergencies. Intense rivalry existed as to which crew "sacked" the farthest down stream in the course of the day. There was no need to urge the men. Some stood upon the logs, pushing mightily with the long pike-poles. Others, waist deep in the water, clamped the jaws of their peaveys into the stubborn timbers, and, shoulder bent, slid them slowly but surely into the swifter waters. Still others, lining up on either side of one of the great brown tree trunks, carried it bodily to its appointed place. From one end of the rear to the other, shouts, calls, warnings, and jokes flew back and forth. Once or twice a vast roar of Homeric laughter went up as some unfortunate slipped and soused into the water. When the current slacked, and the logs hesitated in their run, the entire crew hastened, bobbing from log to log, down river to see about it. Then they broke the jam, standing surely on the edge of the great darkness, while the ice water sucked in and out of their shoes.

Behind the rear Big Junko poled his bateau backwards and forwards exploding dynamite. Many of the bottom tiers of logs in the rollways had been frozen down, and Big Junko had to loosen them from the bed of the stream. He was a big man, this, as his nickname indicated, built of many awkwardnesses. His cheekbones were high, his nose flat, his lips thick and slobbery. He sported a wide, ferocious straggling mustache and long eye-brows, under which gleamed little fierce eyes. His forehead sloped back like a beast's, but was always hidden by a disreputable felt hat. Big Junko did not know much, and had the passions of a wild animal, but he was a reckless riverman and devoted to Thorpe. Just now he exploded dynamite.

The sticks of powder were piled amidships. Big Junko crouched over them, inserting the fuses and caps, closing the openings with soap, finally lighting them, and dropping them into the water alongside, where they immediately sank. Then a few strokes of a short paddle took him barely out of danger. He huddled down in his craft, waiting. One, two, three seconds passed. Then a hollow boom shook the stream. A cloud of water sprang up, strangely beautiful. After a moment the great brown logs rose suddenly to the surface from below, one after the other, like leviathans of the deep. And Junko watched, dimly fascinated, in his rudimentary animal's brain, by the sight of the power he had evoked to his aid.

When night came the men rode down stream to where the wanigan had made camp. There they slept, often in blankets wetted by the wanigan's eccentricities, to leap to their feet at the first cry in early morning. Some days it rained, in which case they were wet all the time. Almost invariably there was a jam to break, though strangely enough almost every one of the old-timers believed implicitly that "in the full of the moon logs will run free at night."

Thorpe and Tim Shearer nearly always slept in a dog tent at the rear; though occasionally they passed the night at Dam Two, where Bryan Moloney and his crew were already engaged in sluicing the logs through the chute.

The affair was simple enough. Long booms arranged in the form of an open V guided the drive to the sluice gate, through which a smooth apron of water rushed to turmoil in an eddying pool below. Two men tramped steadily backwards and forwards on the booms, urging the logs forward by means of long pike poles to where the suction could seize them. Below the dam, the push of the sluice water forced them several miles down stream, where the rest of Bryan Moloney's crew took them in charge.

Thus through the wide gate nearly three-quarters of a million feet an hour could be run—a quantity more than sufficient to keep pace with the exertions of the rear. The matter was, of course, more or less delayed by the necessity of breaking out such rollways as they encountered from time to time on the banks. At length, however, the last of the logs drifted into the wide dam pool. The rear had arrived at Dam Two, and Thorpe congratulated himself that one stage of his journey had been completed. Billy Camp began to worry about shooting the wanigan through the sluice-way.

## Chapter XLVIII

The rear had been tenting at the dam for two days, and was about ready to break camp, when Jimmy Powers swung across the trail to tell them of the big jam.

Ten miles along the river bed, the stream dropped over a little half-falls into a narrow, rocky gorge. It was always an anxious spot for the river drivers. In fact, the plunging of the logs head-on over the fall had so gouged out the soft rock below, that an eddy of great power had formed in the basin. Shearer and Thorpe had often discussed the advisability of constructing an artificial apron of logs to receive the impact. Here, in spite of all efforts, the jam had formed, first a little center of a few logs in the middle of the stream, dividing the current, and shunting the logs to right and left; then "wings" growing out from either bank, built up from logs shunted too violently; finally a complete stoppage of the channel, and the consequent rapid piling up as the pressure of the drive increased. Now the bed was completely filled, far above the level of the falls, by a tangle that defied the jam crew's best efforts.

The rear at once took the trail down the river. Thorpe and Shearer and Scotty Parsons looked over the ground.

"She may 'pull,' if she gets a good start," decided Tim.

Without delay the entire crew was set to work. Nearly a hundred men can pick a great many logs in the course of a day. Several times the jam started, but always "plugged" before the motion had become irresistible. This was mainly because the rocky walls narrowed at a slight bend to the west, so that the drive was throttled, as it were. It was hoped that perhaps the middle of the jam might burst through here, leaving the wings stranded. The hope was groundless.

"We'll have to shoot," Shearer reluctantly decided.

The men were withdrawn. Scotty Parsons cut a sapling twelve feet long, and trimmed it. Big Junko thawed his dynamite at a little fire, opening the ends of the packages in order that the steam generated might escape. Otherwise the pressure inside the oiled paper of the package was capable of exploding the whole affair. When the powder was warm, Scotty bound twenty of the cartridges around the end of the sapling, adjusted a fuse in one of them, and soaped the opening to exclude water. Then Big Junko thrust the long javelin down into the depths of the jam, leaving a thin stream of smoke behind him as he turned away. With sinister, evil eye he watched the smoke for an instant, then zigzagged awkwardly over the jam, the long, ridiculous tails of his brown cutaway coat flopping behind him as he leaped. A scant moment later the hoarse dynamite shouted.

Great chunks of timber shot to an inconceivable height; entire logs lifted bodily into the air with the motion of a fish jumping; a fountain of water gleamed against the sun and showered down in fine rain. The jam shrugged and settled. That was all; the "shot" had failed.

The men ran forward, examining curiously the great hole in the log formation.

"We'll have to flood her," said Thorpe.

So all the gates of the dam were raised, and the torrent tried its hand. It had no effect. Evidently the affair was not one of violence, but of patience. The crew went doggedly to work.

Day after day the CLANK, CLANK, CLINK of the peaveys sounded with the regularity of machinery. The only practicable method was to pick away the flank logs, leaving a long tongue pointing down-stream from the center to start when it would. This happened time and again, but always failed to take with it the main jam. It was cruel hard work; a man who has lifted his utmost strength into a peavey knows that. Any but the Fighting Forty would have grumbled.

Collins, the bookkeeper, came up to view the tangle. Later a photographer from Marquette took some views, which, being exhibited, attracted a great deal of attention, so that by the end of the week a number of curiosity seekers were driving over every day to see the Big Jam. A certain Chicago journalist in search of balsam health of lungs even sent to his paper a little item. This, unexpectedly, brought Wallace Carpenter to the spot. Although reassured as to the gravity of the situation, he remained to see.

The place was an amphitheater for such as chose to be spectators. They could stand or sit on the summit of the gorge cliffs, overlooking the river, the fall, and the jam. As the cliff was barely sixty feet high, the view lacked nothing in clearness.

At last Shearer became angry.

"We've been monkeying long enough," said he. "Next time we'll leave a center that WILL go out. We'll shut the dams down tight and dry-pick out two wings that'll start her."

The dams were first run at full speed, and then shut down. Hardly a drop of water flowed in the bed of the stream. The crews set laboriously to work to pull and roll the logs out in such flat fashion that a head of water should send them out.

This was even harder work than the other, for they had not the floating power of water to help them in the lifting. As usual, part of the men worked below, part above.

Jimmy Powers, curly-haired, laughing-faced, was irrepressible. He badgered the others until they threw bark at him and menaced him with their peaveys. Always he had at his tongue's end the proper quip for the occasion, so that in the long run the work was lightened by him. When the men stopped to think at all, they thought of Jimmy Powers with very kindly hearts, for it was known that he had had more trouble than most, and that the coin was not made too small for him to divide with a needy comrade. To those who had seen his mask of whole-souled good-nature fade into serious sympathy, Jimmy Powers's poor little jokes were very funny indeed.

"Did 'je see th' Swede at the circus las' summer?" he would howl to Red Jacket on the top tier.

"No," Red Jacket would answer, "was he there?"

"Yes," Jimmy Powers would reply; then, after a pause—"in a cage!"

It was a poor enough jest, yet if you had been there, you would have found that somehow the log had in the meantime leaped of its own accord from that difficult position.

Thorpe approved thoroughly of Jimmy Powers; he thought him a good influence. He told Wallace so, standing among the spectators on the cliff-top.

"He is all right," said Thorpe. "I wish I had more like him. The others are good boys, too."

Five men were at the moment tugging futilely at a reluctant timber. They were attempting to roll one end of it over the side of another projecting log, but were continually foiled, because the other end was jammed fast. Each bent his knees, inserting his shoulder under the projecting peavey stock, to straighten in a mighty effort.

"Hire a boy!" "Get some powder of Junko!" "Have Jimmy talk it out!" "Try that little one over by the corner," called the men on top of the jam.

Everybody laughed, of course. It was a fine spring day, clear-eyed and crisp, with a hint of new foliage in the thick buds of the trees. The air was so pellucid that one distinguished without difficulty the straight entrance to the gorge a mile away, and even the West Bend, fully five miles distant.

Jimmy Powers took off his cap and wiped his forehead.

"You boys," he remarked politely, "think you are boring with a mighty big auger."

"My God!" screamed one of the spectators on top of the cliff.

At the same instant Wallace Carpenter seized his friend's arm and pointed.

Down the bed of the stream from the upper bend rushed a solid wall of water several feet high. It flung itself forward with the headlong impetus of a cascade. Even in the short interval between the visitor's exclamation and Carpenter's rapid gesture, it had loomed into sight, twisted a dozen trees from the river bank, and foamed into the entrance of the gorge. An instant later it collided with the tail of the jam.

Even in the railroad rush of those few moments several things happened. Thorpe leaped for a rope. The crew working on top of the jam ducked instinctively to right and left and began to scramble towards safety. The men below, at first bewildered and not comprehending, finally understood, and ran towards the face of the jam with the intention of clambering up it. There could be no escape in the narrow canyon below, the walls of which rose sheer.

Then the flood hit square. It was the impact of resistible power. A great sheet of water rose like surf from the tail of the jam; a mighty cataract poured down over its surface, lifting the free logs; from either wing timbers crunched, split, rose suddenly into wracked prominence, twisted beyond the semblance of themselves. Here and there single logs were even projected bodily upwards, as an apple seed is shot from between the thumb and forefinger. Then the jam moved.

Scotty Parsons, Jack Hyland, Red Jacket, and the forty or fifty top men had reached the shore. By the wriggling activity which is a riverman's alone, they succeeded in pulling themselves beyond the snap of death's jaws. It was a narrow thing for most of them, and a miracle for some.

Jimmy Powers, Archie Harris, Long Pine Jim, Big Nolan, and Mike Moloney, the brother of Bryan, were in worse case. They were, as has been said, engaged in "flattening" part of the jam about eight or ten rods below the face of it. When they finally understood that the affair was one of escape, they ran towards the jam, hoping to climb out. Then the crash came. They heard the roar of the waters, the wrecking of the timbers, they saw the logs bulge outwards in anticipation of the break. Immediately they turned and fled, they knew not where.

All but Jimmy Powers. He stopped short in his tracks, and threw his battered old felt hat defiantly full into the face of the destruction hanging over him. Then, his bright hair blowing in the wind of death, he turned to the spectators standing helpless and paralyzed, forty feet above him.

It was an instant's impression,—the arrested motion seen in the flash of lightning—and yet to the onlookers it had somehow the quality of time. For perceptible duration it seemed to them they stared at the contrast between the raging hell above and the yet peaceable river bed below. They were destined to remember that picture the rest of their natural lives, in such detail that each one of them could almost have reproduced it photographically by simply closing his eyes. Yet afterwards, when they attempted to recall definitely the impression, they knew it could have lasted but a fraction of a second, for the reason that, clear and distinct in each man's mind, the images of the fleeing men retained definite attitudes. It was the instantaneous photography of events.

"So long, boys," they heard Jimmy Powers's voice. Then the rope Thorpe had thrown fell across a caldron of tortured waters and of tossing logs.

## Chapter XLIX

During perhaps ten seconds the survivors watched the end of Thorpe's rope trailing in the flood. Then the young man with a deep sigh began to pull it towards him.

At once a hundred surmises, questions, ejaculations broke out.

"What happened?" cried Wallace Carpenter.

"What was that man's name?" asked the Chicago journalist with the eager instinct of his profession.

"This is terrible, terrible, terrible!" a white-haired physician from Marquette kept repeating over and over.

A half dozen ran towards the point of the cliff to peer down stream, as though they could hope to distinguish anything in that waste of flood water.

"The dam's gone out," replied Thorpe. "I don't understand it. Everything was in good shape, as far as I could see. It didn't act like an ordinary break. The water came too fast. Why, it was as dry as a bone until just as that wave came along. An ordinary break would have eaten through little by little before it burst, and Davis should have been able to stop it. This came all at once, as if the dam had disappeared. I don't see."

His mind of the professional had already began to query causes.

"How about the men?" asked Wallace. "Isn't there something I can do?"

"You can head a hunt down the river," answered Thorpe. "I think it is useless until the water goes down. Poor Jimmy. He was one of the best men I had. I wouldn't have had this happen—"

The horror of the scene was at last beginning to filter through numbness into Wallace Carpenter's impressionable imagination.

"No, no!" he cried vehemently. "There is something criminal about it to me! I'd rather lose every log in the river!"

Thorpe looked at him curiously. "It is one of the chances of war," said he, unable to refrain from the utterance of his creed. "We all know it."

"I'd better divide the crew and take in both banks of the river," suggested Wallace in his constitutional necessity of doing something.

"See if you can't get volunteers from this crowd," suggested Thorpe. "I can let you have two men to show you trails. If you can make it that way, it will help me out. I need as many of the crew as possible to use this flood water."

"Oh, Harry," cried Carpenter, shocked. "You can't be going to work again to-day after that horrible sight, before we have made the slightest effort to recover the bodies!"

"If the bodies can be recovered, they shall be," replied Thorpe quietly. "But the drive will not wait. We have no dams to depend on now, you must remember, and we shall have to get out on freshet water."

"Your men won't work. I'd refuse just as they will!" cried Carpenter, his sensibilities still suffering.

Thorpe smiled proudly. "You do not know them. They are mine. I hold them in the hollow of my hand!"

"By Jove!" cried the journalist in sudden enthusiasm. "By Jove! that is magnificent!"

The men of the river crew had crouched on their narrow footholds while the jam went out. Each had clung to his peavey, as is the habit of rivermen. Down the current past their feet swept the debris of flood. Soon logs began to swirl by,—at first few, then many from the remaining rollways which the river had automatically broken. In a little time the eddy caught up some of these logs, and immediately the inception of another jam threatened. The rivermen, without hesitation, as calmly as though catastrophe had not thrown the weight of its moral terror against their stoicism, sprang, peavey in hand, to the insistent work.

"By Jove!" said the journalist again. "That is magnificent! They are working over the spot where their comrades died!"

Thorpe's face lit with gratification. He turned to the young man.

"You see," he said in proud simplicity.

With the added danger of freshet water, the work went on.

At this moment Tim Shearer approached from inland, his clothes dripping wet, but his face retaining its habitual expression of iron calmness. "Anybody caught?" was his first question as he drew near.

"Five men under the face," replied Thorpe briefly.

Shearer cast a glance at the river. He needed to be told no more.

"I was afraid of it," said he. "The rollways must be all broken out. It's saved us that much, but the freshet water won't last long. It's going to be a close squeak to get 'em out now. Don't exactly figure on what struck the dam. Thought first I'd go right up that way, but then I came down to see about the boys."

Carpenter could not understand this apparent callousness on the part of men in whom he had always thought to recognize a fund of rough but genuine feeling. To him the sacredness of death was incompatible with the insistence of work. To these others the two, grim necessity, went hand in hand.

"Where were you?" asked Thorpe of Shearer.

"On the pole trail. I got in a little, as you see."

In reality the foreman had had a close call for his life. A toughly-rooted basswood alone had saved him.

419

"We'd better go up and take a look," he suggested. "Th' boys has things going here all right."

The two men turned towards the brush.

"Hi, Tim," called a voice behind them.

Red Jacket appeared clambering up the cliff.

"Jack told me to give this to you," he panted, holding out a chunk of strangely twisted wood.

"Where'd he get this?" inquired Thorpe, quickly. "It's a piece of the dam," he explained to Wallace, who had drawn near.

"Picked it out of the current," replied the man.

The foreman and his boss bent eagerly over the morsel. Then they stared with solemnity into each other's eyes.

"Dynamite, by God!" exclaimed Shearer.

### *Chapter L*

For a moment the three men stared at each other without speaking.

"What does it mean?" almost whispered Carpenter.

"Mean? Foul play!" snarled Thorpe. "Come on, Tim."

The two struck into the brush, threading the paths with the ease of woodsmen. It was necessary to keep to the high inland ridges for the simple reason that the pole trail had by now become impassable. Wallace Carpenter, attempting to follow them, ran, stumbled, and fell through brush that continually whipped his face and garments, continually tripped his feet. All he could obtain was a vanishing glimpse of his companions' backs. Thorpe and his foreman talked briefly.

"It's Morrison and Daly," surmised Shearer. "I left them 'count of a trick like that. They wanted me to take charge of Perkinson's drive and hang her a purpose. I been suspecting something—they've been layin' too low."

Thorpe answered nothing. Through the site of the old dam they found a torrent pouring from the narrowed pond, at the end of which the dilapidated wings flapping in the current attested the former structure. Davis stood staring at the current.

Thorpe strode forward and shook him violently by the shoulder.

"How did this happen?" he demanded hoarsely. "Speak!"

The man turned to him in a daze. "I don't know," he answered.

"You ought to know. How was that 'shot' exploded? How did they get in here without you seeing them? Answer me!"

"I don't know," repeated the man. "I jest went over in th' bresh to kill a few pa'tridges, and when I come back I found her this way. I wasn't goin' to close down for three hours yet, and I thought they was no use a hangin' around here."

"Were you hired to watch this dam, or weren't you?" demanded the tense voice of Thorpe. "Answer me, you fool."

"Yes, I was," returned the man, a shade of aggression creeping into his voice.

"Well, you've done it well. You've cost me my dam, and you've killed five men. If the crew finds out about you, you'll go over the falls, sure. You get out of here! Pike! Don't you ever let me see your face again!"

The man blanched as he thus learned of his comrades' deaths. Thorpe thrust his face at him, lashed by circumstances beyond his habitual self-control.

"It's men like you who make the trouble," he stormed. "Damn fools who say they didn't mean to. It isn't enough not to mean to. They should MEAN NOT TO! I don't ask you to think. I just want you to do what I tell you, and you can't even do that."

He threw his shoulder into a heavy blow that reached the dam watcher's face, and followed it immediately by another. Then Shearer caught his arm, motioning the dazed and bloody victim of the attack to get out of sight. Thorpe shook his foreman off with one impatient motion, and strode away up the river, his head erect, his eyes flashing, his nostrils distended.

"I reckon you'd better mosey," Shearer dryly advised the dam watcher; and followed.

Late in the afternoon the two men reached Dam Three, or rather the spot on which Dam Three had stood. The same spectacle repeated itself here, except that Ellis, the dam watcher, was nowhere to be seen.

"The dirty whelps," cried Thorpe, "they did a good job!"

He thrashed about here and there, and so came across Ellis blindfolded and tied. When released, the dam watcher was unable to give any account of his assailants.

"They came up behind me while I was cooking," he said. "One of 'em grabbed me and the other one kivered my eyes. Then I hears the 'shot' and knows there's trouble."

Thorpe listened in silence. Shearer asked a few questions. After the low-voiced conversation Thorpe arose abruptly.

"Where you going?" asked Shearer.

But the young man did not reply. He swung, with the same long, nervous stride, into the down-river trail.

Until late that night the three men—for Ellis insisted on accompanying them—hurried through the forest. Thorpe walked tirelessly, upheld by his violent but repressed excitement. When his hat fell from his head, he either did not notice the fact, or did not care to trouble himself for its recovery, so he glanced through the trees bare-headed, his broad white brow gleaming in the moonlight. Shearer noted the fire in his eyes, and from the coolness of his greater age, counselled moderation.

"I wouldn't stir the boys up," he panted, for the pace was very swift. "They'll kill some one over there, it'll be murder on both sides."

He received no answer. About midnight they came to the camp.

Two great fires leaped among the trees, and the men, past the idea of sleep, grouped between them, talking. The lesson of twisted timbers was not lost to their experience, and the evening had brought its accumulation of slow anger against the perpetrators of the outrage. These men were not given to oratorical mouthings, but their low-voiced exchanges between the puffings of a pipe led to a steadier purpose than that of hysteria. Even as the woodsmen joined their group, they had reached the intensity of execution. Across their purpose Thorpe threw violently his personality.

"You must not go," he commanded.

Through their anger they looked at him askance.

"I forbid it," Thorpe cried.

They shrugged their indifference and arose. This was an affair of caste brotherhood; and the blood of their mates cried out to them.

"The work," Thorpe shouted hoarsely. "The work! We must get those logs out! We haven't time!"

But the Fighting Forty had not Thorpe's ideal. Success meant a day's work well done; while vengeance stood for a righting of the realities which had been unrighteously overturned. Thorpe's dry-eyed, burning, almost mad insistence on the importance of the day's task had not its ordinary force. They looked upon him from a standpoint apart, calmly, dispassionately, as one looks on a petulant child. The grim call of tragedy had lifted them above little mundane things.

Then swiftly between the white, strained face of the madman trying to convince his heart that his mind had been right, and the fanatically exalted rivermen, interposed the sanity of Radway. The old jobber faced the men calmly, almost humorously, and somehow the very bigness of the man commanded attention. When he spoke, his coarse, good-natured, everyday voice fell through the tense situation, clarifying it, restoring it to the normal.

"You fellows make me sick," said he. "You haven't got the sense God gave a rooster. Don't you see you're playing right in those fellows' hands? What do you suppose they dynamited them dams for? To kill our boys? Don't you believe it for a minute. They never dreamed we was dry pickin' that jam. They sent some low-lived whelp down there to hang our drive, and by smoke it looks like they was going to succeed, thanks to you mutton-heads.

"'Spose you go over and take 'em apart; what then? You have a scrap; probably you lick 'em." The men growled ominously, but did not stir. "You whale daylights out of a lot of men who probably don't know any more about this here shooting of our dams than a hog does about a ruffled shirt. Meanwhile your drive hangs. Well? Well? Do you suppose the men who were back of that shooting, do you suppose Morrison and Daly give a tinker's dam how many men of theirs you lick? What they want is to hang our drive. If they hang our drive, it's cheap at the price of a few black eyes."

The speaker paused and grinned good-humoredly at the men's attentive faces. Then suddenly his own became grave, and he swung into his argument all the impressiveness of his great bulk,

"Do you want to know how to get even?" he asked, shading each word. "Do you want to know how to make those fellows sing so small you can't hear them? Well, I'll tell you. TAKE OUT THIS DRIVE! Do it in spite of them! Show them they're no good when they buck up against Thorpe's One! Our boys died doing their duty—the way a riverman ought to. NOW HUMP YOURSELVES! Don't let 'em die in vain!"

The crew stirred uneasily, looking at each other for approval of the conversion each had experienced. Radway, seizing the psychological moment, turned easily toward the blaze.

"Better turn in, boys, and get some sleep," he said. "We've got a hard day to-morrow." He stooped to light his pipe at the fire. When he had again straightened his back after rather a prolonged interval, the group had already disintegrated. A few minutes later the cookee scattered the brands of the fire from before a sleeping camp.

Thorpe had listened non-committally to the colloquy. He had maintained the suspended attitude of a man who is willing to allow the trial of other methods, but who does not therefore relinquish his own. At the favorable termination of the discussion he turned away without comment. He expected to gain this result. Had he been in a more judicial state of mind he might have perceived at last the reason, in the complicated scheme of Providence, for his long connection with John Radway.

## Chapter LI

Before daylight Injin Charley drifted into the camp to find Thorpe already out. With a curt nod the Indian seated himself by the fire, and, producing a square plug of tobacco and a knife, began leisurely to fill his pipe. Thorpe watched him in silence. Finally Injin Charley spoke in the red man's clear-cut, imitative English, a pause between each sentence.

"I find trail three men," said he. "Both dam, three men. One man go down river. Those men have cork-boot. One man no have cork-boot. He boss." The Indian suddenly threw his chin out, his head back, half closed his eyes in a cynical squint. As by a flash Dyer, the scaler, leered insolently from behind the Indian's stolid mask.

"How do you know?" said Thorpe.

For answer the Indian threw his shoulders forward in Dyer's nervous fashion.

"He make trail big by the toe, light by the heel. He make trail big on inside."

Charley arose and walked, after Dyer's springy fashion, illustrating his point in the soft wood ashes of the immediate fireside.

Thorpe looked doubtful. "I believe you are right, Charley," said he. "But it is mighty little to go on. You can't be sure."

"I sure," replied Charley.

He puffed strongly at the heel of his smoke, then arose, and without farewell disappeared in the forest.

Thorpe ranged the camp impatiently, glancing often at the sky. At length he laid fresh logs on the fire and aroused the cook. It was bitter cold in the early morning. After a time the men turned out of their own accord, at first yawning with insufficient rest, and then becoming grimly tense as their returned wits reminded them of the situation.

From that moment began the wonderful struggle against circumstances which has become a by-word among rivermen everywhere. A forty-day drive had to go out in ten. A freshet had to float out thirty million feet of logs. It was tremendous; as even the men most deeply buried in the heavy hours of that time dimly realized. It was epic; as the journalist, by now thoroughly aroused, soon succeeded in convincing his editors and his public. Fourteen, sixteen, sometimes eighteen hours a day, the men of the driving crew worked like demons. Jams had no chance to form. The phenomenal activity of the rear crew reduced by half the inevitable sacking. Of course, under the pressure, the lower dam had gone out. Nothing was to be depended on but sheer dogged grit. Far up-river Sadler & Smith had hung their drive for the season. They had stretched heavy booms across the current, and so had resigned themselves to a definite but not extraordinary loss. Thorpe had at least a clear river.

Wallace Carpenter could not understand how human flesh and blood endured. The men themselves had long since reached the point of practical exhaustion, but were carried through by the fire of their leader. Work was dogged until he stormed into sight; then it became frenzied. He seemed to impart to those about him a nervous force and excitability as real as that induced by brandy. When he looked at a man from his cavernous, burning eyes, that man jumped.

It was all willing enough work. Several definite causes, each adequate alone to something extraordinary, focussed to the necessity. His men worshipped Thorpe; the idea of thwarting the purposes of their comrade's murderers retained its strength; the innate pride of caste and craft—the sturdiest virtue of the riverman—was in these picked men increased to the dignity of a passion. The great psychological forces of a successful career gathered and made head against the circumstances which such careers always arouse in polarity.

Impossibilities were puffed aside like thistles. The men went at them headlong. They gave way before the rush. Thorpe always led. Not for a single instant of the day nor for many at night was he at rest. He was like a man who has taken a deep breath to reach a definite goal, and who cannot exhale until the burst of speed be over. Instinctively he seemed to realize that a let-down would mean collapse.

After the camp had fallen asleep, he would often lie awake half of the few hours of their night, every muscle tense, staring at the sky. His mind saw definitely every detail of the situation as he had last viewed it. In advance his imagination stooped and sweated to the work which his body was to accomplish the next morning. Thus he did everything twice. Then at last the tension would relax. He would fall into uneasy sleep. But twice that did not follow. Through the dissolving iron mist of his striving, a sharp thought cleaved like an arrow. It was that after all he did not care. The religion of Success no longer held him as its devoutest worshiper. He was throwing the fibers of his life into the engine of toil, not because of moral duty, but because of moral pride. He meant to succeed in order to prove to himself that he had not been wrong.

The pain of the arrow-wound always aroused him from his doze with a start. He grimly laughed the thought out of court. To his waking moments his religion was sincere, was real. But deep down in his sub-consciousness, below his recognition, the other influence was growing like a weed. Perhaps the vision, not the waking, had been right. Perhaps that far-off beautiful dream of a girl which Thorpe's idealism had constructed from; the reactionary necessities of Thorpe's harsh life had been more real than his forest temples of his ruthless god! Perhaps there were greater things than to succeed, greater things than success. Perhaps, after all, the Power that put us here demands more that we cleave one to the other in loving-kindness than that we learn to blow the penny whistles it has tossed us. And then the keen, poignant memory of the dream girl stole into the young man's mind, and in agony was immediately thrust forth. He would not think of her. He had given her up. He had cast the die. For success he had bartered her, in the noblest, the loftiest spirit of devotion. He refused to believe that devotion fanatical; he refused to believe that he had been wrong. In the still darkness of the night he would rise and steal to the edge of the dully roaring stream. There, his eyes blinded and his throat choked with a longing more manly than tears, he would reach out and smooth the round rough coats of the great logs.

"We'll do it!" he whispered to them—and to himself. "We'll do it! We can't be wrong. God would not have let us!"

### *Chapter LII*

Wallace Carpenter's search expedition had proved a failure, as Thorpe had foreseen, but at the end of the week, when the water began to recede, the little beagles ran upon a mass of flesh and bones. The man was unrecognizable, either as an individual or as a human being. The remains were wrapped in canvas and sent for interment in the cemetery at Marquette. Three of the others were never found. The last did not come to light until after the drive had quite finished.

Down at the booms the jam crew received the drive as fast as it came down. From one crib to another across the broad extent of the river's mouth, heavy booms were chained end to end effectually to close the exit to Lake Superior. Against these the logs caromed softly in the slackened current, and stopped. The cribs were very heavy with slanting, instead of square, tops, in order that the pressure might be downwards instead of sidewise. This guaranteed their permanency. In a short time the surface of the lagoon was covered by a brown carpet of logs running in strange patterns like windrows of fallen grain. Finally, across the straight middle distance of the river, appeared little agitated specks leaping back and forth. Thus the rear came in sight and the drive was all but over.

Up till now the weather had been clear but oppressively hot for this time of year. The heat had come suddenly and maintained itself well. It had searched out with fierce directness all the patches of snow lying under the thick firs and balsams of the swamp edge, it had shaken loose the anchor ice of the marsh bottoms, and so had materially aided the success of the drive by increase of water. The men had worked for the most part in undershirts. They were as much in the water as out of it, for the icy bath had become almost grateful. Hamilton, the journalist, who had attached himself definitely to the drive, distributed bunches of papers, in which the men read that the unseasonable condition prevailed all over the country.

At length, however, it gave signs of breaking. The sky, which had been of a steel blue, harbored great piled thunder-heads. Occasionally athwart the heat shot a streak of cold air. Towards evening the thunder-heads shifted and finally dissipated, to be sure, but the portent was there.

Hamilton's papers began to tell of disturbances in the South and West. A washout in Arkansas derailed a train; a cloud-burst in Texas wiped out a camp; the cities along the Ohio River were enjoying their annual flood with the usual concomitants of floating houses and boats in the streets. The men wished they had some of that water here.

So finally the drive approached its end and all concerned began in anticipation to taste the weariness that awaited them. They had hurried their powers. The few remaining tasks still confronting them, all at once seemed more formidable than what they had accomplished. They could not contemplate further exertion. The work for the first time became dogged, distasteful. Even Thorpe was infected. He, too, wanted more than anything else to drop on the bed in Mrs. Hathaway's boarding house, there to sponge from his mind all colors but the dead gray of rest. There remained but a few things to do. A mile of sacking would carry the drive beyond the influence of freshet water. After that there would be no hurry.

He looked around at the hard, fatigue-worn faces of the men about him, and in the obsession of his wearied mood he suddenly felt a great rush of affection for these comrades who had so unreservedly spent themselves for his affair. Their features showed exhaustion, it is true, but their eyes gleamed still with the steady half-humorous purpose of the pioneer. When they caught his glance they grinned good-humoredly.

All at once Thorpe turned and started for the bank.

"That'll do, boys," he said quietly to the nearest group. "She's down!"

It was noon. The sackers looked up in surprise. Behind them, to their very feet, rushed the soft smooth slope of Hemlock Rapids. Below them flowed a broad, peaceful river. The drive had passed its last obstruction. To all intents and purposes it was over.

Calmly, with matter-of-fact directness, as though they had not achieved the impossible; as though they, a handful, had not cheated nature and powerful enemies, they shouldered their peaveys and struck into the broad wagon road. In the middle distance loomed the tall stacks of the mill with the little board town about it. Across the eye spun the thread of the railroad. Far away gleamed the broad expanses of Lake Superior.

The cook had, early that morning, moored the wanigan to the bank. One of the teamsters from town had loaded the men's "turkeys" on his heavy wagon. The wanigan's crew had thereupon trudged into town.

The men paired off naturally and fell into a dragging, dogged walk. Thorpe found himself unexpectedly with Big Junko. For a time they plodded on without conversation. Then the big man ventured a remark.

"I'm glad she's over," said he. "I got a good stake comin'."

"Yes," replied Thorpe indifferently.

"I got most six hundred dollars comin'," persisted Junko.

"Might as well be six hundred cents," commented Thorpe, "it'd make you just as drunk."

Big Junko laughed self-consciously but without the slightest resentment.

"That's all right," said he, "but you betcher life I don't blow this stake."

"I've heard that talk before," shrugged Thorpe.

"Yes, but this is different. I'm goin' to git married on this. How's THAT?"

Thorpe, his attention struck at last, stared at his companion. He noted the man's little twinkling animal eyes, his high cheek bones, his flat nose, his thick and slobbery lips, his straggling, fierce mustache and eyebrows, his grotesque long-tailed cutaway coat. So to him, too, this primitive man reaching dully from primordial chaos, the great moment had yielded its vision.

"Who is she?" he asked abruptly.

"She used to wash at Camp Four."

Thorpe dimly remembered the woman now—an overweighted creature with a certain attraction of elfishly blowing hair, with a certain pleasing full-cheeked, full-bosomed health.

The two walked on in re-established silence. Finally the giant, unable to contain himself longer, broke out again.

"I do like that woman," said he with a quaintly deliberate seriousness. "That's the finest woman in this district."

Thorpe felt the quick moisture rush to his eyes. There was something inexpressibly touching in those simple words as Big Junko uttered them.

"And when you are married," he asked, "what are you going to do? Are you going to stay on the river?"

"No, I'm goin' to clear a farm. The woman she says that's the thing to do. I like the river, too. But you bet when Carrie says a thing, that's plenty good enough for Big Junko."

"Suppose," suggested Thorpe, irresistibly impelled towards the attempt, "suppose I should offer you two hundred dollars a month to stay on the river. Would you stay?"

"Carrie don't like it," replied Junko.

"Two hundred dollars is big wages," persisted Thorpe. "It's twice what I give Radway."

"I'd like to ask Carrie."

"No, take it or leave it now."

"Well, Carrie says she don't like it," answered the riverman with a sigh.

Thorpe looked at his companion fixedly. Somehow the bestial countenance had taken on an attraction of its own. He remembered Big Junko as a wild beast when his passions were aroused, as a man whose honesty had been doubted.

"You've changed, Junko," said he.

"I know," said the big man. "I been a scalawag all right. I quit it. I don't know much, but Carrie she's smart, and I'm goin' to do what she says. When you get stuck on a good woman like Carrie, Mr. Thorpe, you don't give much of a damn for anything else. Sure! That's right! It's the biggest thing top o' earth!"

Here it was again, the opposing creed. And from such a source. Thorpe's iron will contracted again.

"A woman is no excuse for a man's neglecting his work," he snapped.

"Shorely not," agreed Junko serenely. "I aim to finish out my time all right, Mr. Thorpe. Don't you worry none about that. I done my best for you. And," went on the riverman in the expansion of this unwonted confidence with his employer, "I'd like to rise to remark that you're the best boss I ever had, and we boys wants to stay with her till there's skating in hell!"

"All right," murmured Thorpe indifferently.

His momentary interest had left him. Again the reactionary weariness dragged at his feet. Suddenly the remaining half mile to town seemed very long indeed.

### Chapter LIII

Wallace Carpenter and Hamilton, the journalist, seated against the sun-warmed bench of Mrs. Hathaway's boarding-house, commented on the band as it stumbled in to the wash-room.

"Those men don't know how big they are," remarked the journalist. "That's the way with most big men. And that man Thorpe belongs to another age. I'd like to get him to telling his experiences; he'd be a gold mine to me."

"And would require about as much trouble to 'work,'" laughed Wallace. "He won't talk."

"That's generally the trouble, confound 'em," sighed Hamilton. "The fellows who CAN talk haven't anything to say; and those who have something to tell are dumb as oysters. I've got him in though." He spread one of a roll of papers on his knees. "I got a set of duplicates for you. Thought you might like to keep them. The office tells me," he concluded modestly, "that they are attracting lots of attention, but are looked upon as being a rather clever sort of fiction."

Wallace picked up the sheet. His eye was at once met by the heading, "'So long, boys,'" in letters a half inch in height, and immediately underneath in smaller type, "said Jimmy Powers, and threw his hat in the face of death."

"It's all there," explained the journalist, "—the jam and the break, and all this magnificent struggle afterwards. It makes a great yarn. I feel tempted sometimes to help it out a little—artistically, you know—but of course that wouldn't do. She'd make a ripping yarn, though, if I could get up some motive outside mere trade rivalry for the blowing up of those dams. That would just round it off."

Wallace Carpenter was about to reply that such a motive actually existed, when the conversation was interrupted by the approach of Thorpe and Big Junko. The former looked twenty years older after his winter. His eye was dull, his shoulders drooped, his gait was inelastic. The whole bearing of the man was that of one weary to the bone.

"I've got something here to show you, Harry," cried Wallace Carpenter, waving one of the papers. "It was a great drive and here's something to remember it by."

"All right, Wallace, by and by," replied Thorpe dully. "I'm dead. I'm going to turn in for a while. I need sleep more than anything else. I can't think now."

He passed through the little passage into the "parlor bed-room," which Mrs. Hathaway always kept in readiness for members of the firm. There he fell heavily asleep almost before his body had met the bed.

In the long dining room the rivermen consumed a belated dinner. They had no comments to make. It was over.

The two on the veranda smoked. To the right, at the end of the sawdust street, the mill sang its varying and lulling keys. The odor of fresh-sawed pine perfumed the air. Not a hundred yards away the river slipped silently to the distant blue Superior, escaping between the slanting stone-filled cribs which held back the logs. Down the south and west the huge thunderheads gathered and flashed and grumbled, as they had done every afternoon for days previous.

"Queer thing," commented Hamilton finally, "these cold streaks in the air. They are just as distinct as though they had partitions around them."

"Queer climate anyway," agreed Carpenter.

Excepting always for the mill, the little settlement appeared asleep. The main booms were quite deserted. Not a single figure, armed with its picturesque pike-pole, loomed athwart the distance. After awhile Hamilton noticed something.

"Look here, Carpenter," said he, "what's happening out there? Have some of your confounded logs SUNK, or what? There don't seem to be near so many of them somehow."

"No, it isn't that," proffered Carpenter after a moment's scrutiny, "there are just as many logs, but they are getting separated a little so you can see the open water between them."

"Guess you're right. Say, look here, I believe that the river is rising!"

"Nonsense, we haven't had any rain."

"She's rising just the same. I'll tell you how I know; you see that spile over there near the left-hand crib? Well, I sat on the boom this morning watching the crew, and I whittled the spile with my knife—you can see the marks from here. I cut the thing about two feet above the water. Look at it now."

"She's pretty near the water line, that's right," admitted Carpenter.

"I should think that might make the boys hot," commented Hamilton. "If they'd known this was coming, they needn't have hustled so to get the drive down.

"That's so," Wallace agreed.

About an hour later the younger man in his turn made a discovery.

"She's been rising right along," he submitted. "Your marks are nearer the water, and, do you know, I believe the logs are beginning to feel it. See, they've closed up the little openings between them, and they are beginning to crowd down to the lower end of the pond."

"I don't know anything about this business," hazarded the journalist, "but by the mere look of the thing I should think there was a good deal of pressure on that same lower end. By Jove, look there! See those logs up-end? I believe you're going to have a jam right here in your own booms!"

"I don't know," hesitated Wallace, "I never heard of its happening."

"You'd better let someone know."

"I hate to bother Harry or any of the rivermen. I'll just step down to the mill. Mason—he's our mill foreman—he'll know."

Mason came to the edge of the high trestle and took one look.

"Jumping fish-hooks!" he cried. "Why, the river's up six inches and still a comin'! Here you, Tom!" he called to one of the yard hands, "you tell Solly to get steam on that tug double quick, and have Dave hustle together his driver crew."

"What you going to do?" asked Wallace.

"I got to strengthen the booms," explained the mill foreman. "We'll drive some piles across between the cribs."

"Is there any danger?"

"Oh, no, the river would have to rise a good deal higher than she is now to make current enough to hurt. They've had a hard rain up above. This will go down in a few hours."

After a time the tug puffed up to the booms, escorting the pile driver. The latter towed a little raft of long sharpened piles, which it at once began to drive in such positions as would most effectually strengthen the booms. In the meantime the thunder-heads had slyly climbed the heavens, so that a sudden deluge of rain surprised the workmen. For an hour it poured down in torrents; then settled to a steady gray beat. Immediately the aspect had changed. The distant rise of land was veiled; the brown expanse of logs became slippery and glistening; the river below the booms was picked into staccato points by the drops; distant Superior turned lead color and seemed to tumble strangely athwart the horizon.

Solly, the tug captain, looked at his mooring hawsers and then at the nearest crib.

"She's riz two inches in th' las' two hours," he announced, "and she's runnin' like a mill race." Solly was a typical north-country tug captain, short and broad, with a brown, clear face, and the steadiest and calmest of steel-blue eyes. "When she begins to feel th' pressure behind," he went on, "there's goin' to be trouble."

Towards dusk she began to feel that pressure. Through the rainy twilight the logs could be seen raising their ghostly arms of protest. Slowly, without tumult, the jam formed. In the van the logs crossed silently; in the rear they pressed in, were sucked under in the swift water, and came to rest at the bottom of the river. The current of the river began to protest, pressing its hydraulics through the narrowing crevices. The situation demanded attention.

A breeze began to pull off shore in the body of rain. Little by little it increased, sending the water by in gusts, ruffling the already hurrying river into greater haste, raising far from the shore dimly perceived white-caps. Between the roaring of the wind, the dash of rain, and the rush of the stream, men had to shout to make themselves heard.

"Guess you'd better rout out the boss," screamed Solly to Wallace Carpenter; "this damn water's comin' up an inch an hour right along. When she backs up once, she'll push this jam out sure."

Wallace ran to the boarding house and roused his partner from a heavy sleep. The latter understood the situation at a word. While dressing, he explained to the younger man wherein lay the danger.

"If the jam breaks once," said he, "nothing top of earth can prevent it from going out into the Lake, and there it'll scatter, Heaven knows where. Once scattered, it is practically a total loss. The salvage wouldn't pay the price of the lumber."

They felt blindly through the rain in the direction of the lights on the tug and pile-driver. Shearer, the water dripping from his flaxen mustache, joined them like a shadow.

"I heard you come in," he explained to Carpenter. At the river he announced his opinion. "We can hold her all right," he assured them. "It'll take a few more piles, but by morning the storm'll be over, and she'll begin to go down again."

The three picked their way over the creaking, swaying timber. But when they reached the pile-driver, they found trouble afoot. The crew had mutinied, and refused longer to drive piles under the face of the jam.

"If she breaks loose, she's going to bury us," said they.

"She won't break," snapped Shearer, "get to work."

"It's dangerous," they objected sullenly.

"By God, you get off this driver," shouted Solly. "Go over and lie down in a ten-acre lot, and see if you feel safe there!"

He drove them ashore with a storm of profanity and a multitude of kicks, his steel-blue eyes blazing.

"There's nothing for it but to get the boys out again," said Tim; "I kinder hate to do it."

But when the Fighting Forty, half asleep but dauntless, took charge of the driver, a catastrophe made itself known. One of the ejected men had tripped the lifting chain of the hammer after another had knocked away the heavy preventing block, and so the hammer had fallen into the river and was lost. None other was to be had. The pile driver was useless.

A dozen men were at once despatched for cables, chains, and wire ropes from the supply at the warehouse.

"I'd like to have those whelps here," cried Shearer, "I'd throw them under the jam."

"It's part of the same trick," said Thorpe grimly; "those fellows have their men everywhere among us. I don't know whom to trust."

"You think it's Morrison & Daly?" queried Carpenter astonished.

"Think? I know it. They know as well as you or I that if we save these logs, we'll win out in the stock exchange; and they're not such fools as to let us save them if it can be helped. I have a score to settle with those fellows; and when I get through with this thing I'll settle it all right."

"What are you going to do now?"

"The only thing there is to be done. We'll string heavy booms, chained together, between the cribs, and then trust to heaven they'll hold. I think we can hold the jam. The water will begin to flow over the bank before long, so there won't be much increase of pressure over what we have now; and as there won't be any shock to withstand, I think our heavy booms will do the business."

He turned to direct the boring of some long boom logs in preparation for the chains. Suddenly he whirled again to Wallace with so strange an expression in his face that the young man almost cried out. The uncertain light of the lanterns showed dimly the streaks of rain across his countenance, and, his eye flared with a look almost of panic.

"I never thought of it!" he said in a low voice. "Fool that I am! I don't see how I missed it. Wallace, don't you see what those devils will do next?"

"No, what do you mean?" gasped the younger man.

"There are twelve million feet of logs up river in Sadler & Smith's drive. Don't you see what they'll do?"

"No, I don't believe—"

"Just as soon as they find out that the river is booming, and that we are going to have a hard time to hold our jam, they'll let loose those twelve million on us. They'll break the jam, or dynamite it, or something. And let me tell you, that a very few logs hitting the tail of our jam will start the whole shooting match so that no power on earth can stop it."

"I don't imagine they'd think of doing that—" began Wallace by way of assurance.

"Think of it! You don't know them. They've thought of everything. You don't know that man Daly. Ask Tim, he'll tell you."

"Well, the—"

"I've got to send a man up there right away. Perhaps we can get there in time to head them off. They have to send their man over—By the way," he queried, struck with a new idea, "how long have you been driving piles?"

"Since about three o'clock."

"Six hours," computed Thorpe. "I wish you'd come for me sooner."

He cast his eye rapidly over the men.

"I don't know just who to send. There isn't a good enough woodsman in the lot to make Siscoe Falls through the woods a night like this. The river trail is too long; and a cut through the woods is blind. Andrews is the only man I know of who could do it, but I think Billy Mason said Andrews had gone up on the Gunther track to run lines. Come on; we'll see."

With infinite difficulty and caution, they reached the shore. Across the gleaming logs shone dimly the lanterns at the scene of work, ghostly through the rain. Beyond, on either side, lay impenetrable drenched darkness, racked by the wind.

"I wouldn't want to tackle it," panted Thorpe. "If it wasn't for that cursed tote road between Sadler's and Daly's, I wouldn't worry. It's just too EASY for them."

Behind them the jam cracked and shrieked and groaned. Occasionally was heard, beneath the sharper noises, a dull BOOM, as one of the heavy timbers forced by the pressure from its resting place, shot into the air, and fell back on the bristling surface.

Andrews had left that morning.

"Tim Shearer might do it," suggested Thorpe, "but I hate to spare him."

He picked his rifle from its rack and thrust the magazine full of cartridges.

"Come on, Wallace," said he, "we'll hunt him up."

They stepped again into the shriek and roar of the storm, bending their heads to its power, but indifferent in the already drenched condition of their clothing, to the rain. The saw-dust street was saturated like a sponge. They could feel the quick water rise about the pressure at their feet. From the invisible houses they heard a steady monotone of flowing from the roofs. Far ahead, dim in the mist, sprayed the light of lanterns.

Suddenly Thorpe felt a touch on his arm. Faintly he perceived at his elbow the high lights of a face from which the water streamed.

"Injin Charley!" he cried, "the very man!"

## Chapter LIV

Rapidly Thorpe explained what was to be done, and thrust his rifle into the Indian's hands. The latter listened in silence and stolidity, then turned, and without a word departed swiftly in the darkness. The two white men stood a minute attentive. Nothing was to be heard but the steady beat of rain and the roaring of the wind.

Near the bank of the river they encountered a man, visible only as an uncertain black outline against the glow of the lanterns beyond. Thorpe, stopping him, found Big Junko.

"This is no time to quit," said Thorpe, sharply.

"I ain't quittin'," replied Big Junko.

"Where are you going, then?"

Junko was partially and stammeringly unresponsive.

"Looks bad," commented Thorpe. "You'd better get back to your job."

"Yes," agreed Junko helplessly. In the momentary slack tide of work, the giant had conceived the idea of searching out the driver crew for purposes of pugilistic vengeance. Thorpe's suspicions stung him, but his simple mind could see no direct way to explanation.

All night long in the chill of a spring rain and windstorm the Fighting Forty and certain of the mill crew gave themselves to the labor of connecting the slanting stone cribs so strongly, by means of heavy timbers chained end to end, that the pressure of a break in the jam might not sweep aside the defenses. Wallace Carpenter, Shorty, the chore-boy, and Anderson, the barn-boss, picked a dangerous passage back and forth carrying pails of red-hot coffee which Mrs. Hathaway constantly prepared. The cold water numbed the men's hands. With difficulty could they manipulate the heavy chains through the auger holes; with pain they twisted knots, bored holes. They did not complain. Behind them the jam quivered, perilously near the bursting point. From it shrieked aloud the demons of pressure. Steadily the river rose, an inch an hour. The key might snap at any given moment, they could not tell,—and with the rush they knew very well that themselves, the tug, and the disabled piledriver would be swept from existence. The worst of it was that the blackness shrouded their experience into uselessness; they were utterly unable to tell by the ordinary visual symptoms how near the jam might be to collapse.

However, they persisted, as the old-time riverman always does, so that when dawn appeared the barrier was continuous and assured. Although the pressure of the river had already forced the logs against the defenses, the latter held the strain well.

The storm had settled into its gait. Overhead the sky was filled with gray, beneath which darker scuds flew across the zenith before a howling southwest wind. Out in the clear river one could hardly stand upright against the gusts. In the fan of many directions furious squalls swept over the open water below the booms, and an eager boiling current rushed to the lake.

Thorpe now gave orders that the tug and driver should take shelter. A few moments later he expressed himself as satisfied. The dripping crew, their harsh faces gray in the half-light, picked their way to the shore.

In the darkness of that long night's work no man knew his neighbor. Men from the river, men from the mill, men from the yard all worked side by side. Thus no one noticed especially a tall, slender, but well-knit individual dressed in a faded mackinaw and a limp slouch hat which he wore pulled over his eyes. This young fellow occupied himself with the chains. Against the racing current the crew held the ends of the heavy booms, while he fastened them together. He worked well, but seemed slow. Three times Shearer hustled him on after the others had finished, examining closely the work that had been done. On the third occasion he shrugged his shoulder somewhat impatiently.

The men straggled to shore, the young fellow just described bringing up the rear. He walked as though tired out, hanging his head and dragging his feet. When, however, the boarding-house door had closed on the last of those who preceded him, and the town lay deserted in the dawn, he suddenly became transformed. Casting a keen glance right and left to be sure of his opportunity, he turned and hurried recklessly back over the logs to the center booms. There he knelt and busied himself with the chains.

In his zigzag progression over the jam he so blended with the morning shadows as to seem one of them, and he would have escaped quite unnoticed had not a sudden shifting of the logs under his feet compelled him to rise for a moment to his full height. So Wallace Carpenter, passing from his bedroom, along the porch, to the dining room, became aware of the man on the logs.

His first thought was that something demanding instant attention had happened to the boom. He therefore ran at once to the man's assistance, ready to help him personally or to call other aid as the exigency demanded. Owing to the precarious nature of the passage, he could not see beyond his feet until very close to the workman. Then he looked up to find the man, squatted on the boom, contemplating him sardonically.

"Dyer!" he exclaimed

"Right, my son," said the other coolly.

"What are you doing?"

"If you want to know, I am filing this chain."

Wallace made one step forward and so became aware that at last firearms were taking a part in this desperate game.

"You stand still," commanded Dyer from behind the revolver. "It's unfortunate for you that you happened along, because now you'll have to come with me till this little row is over. You won't have to stay long; your logs'll go out in an hour. I'll just trouble you to go into the brush with me for a while."

The scaler picked his file from beside the weakened link.

"What have you against us, anyway, Dyer?" asked Wallace. His quick mind had conceived a plan. At the moment, he was standing near the outermost edge of the jam, but now as he spoke he stepped quietly to the boom log.

Dyer's black eyes gleamed at him suspiciously, but the movement appeared wholly natural in view of the return to shore.

"Nothing," he replied. "I didn't like your gang particularly, but that's nothing."

"Why do you take such nervy chances to injure us?" queried Carpenter.

"Because there's something in it," snapped the scaler. "Now about face; mosey!"

Like a flash Wallace wheeled and dropped into the river, swimming as fast as possible below water before his breath should give out. The swift current hurried him away. When at last he rose for air, the spit of Dyer's pistol caused him no uneasiness. A moment later he struck out boldly for shore.

What Dyer's ultimate plan might be, he could not guess. He had stated confidently that the jam would break "in an hour." He might intend to start it with dynamite. Wallace dragged himself from the water and commenced breathlessly to run toward the boarding-house.

Dyer had already reached the shore. Wallace raised what was left of his voice in a despairing shout. The scaler mockingly waved his hat, then turned and ran swiftly and easily toward the shelter of the woods. At their border he paused again to bow in derision. Carpenter's cry brought men to the boarding-house door. From the shadows of the forest two vivid flashes cut the dusk. Dyer staggered, turned completely about, seemed partially to recover, and disappeared. An instant later, across the open space where the scaler had stood, with rifle a-trail, the Indian leaped in pursuit.

### Chapter LV

"What is it?" "What's the matter?" "What's happened?" burst on Wallace in a volley.

"It's Dyer," gasped the young man. "I found him on the boom! He held me up with a gun while he filed the boom chains between the center piers. They're just ready to go. I got away by diving. Hurry and put in a new chain; you haven't much time!"

"He's a gone-er now," interjected Solly grimly.—"Charley is on his trail—and he is hit."

Thorpe's intelligence leaped promptly to the practical question.

"Injin Charley, where'd he come from? I sent him up Sadler & Smith's. It's twenty miles, even through the woods."

As though by way of colossal answer the whole surface of the jam moved inward and upward, thrusting the logs bristling against the horizon.

"She's going to break!" shouted Thorpe, starting on a run towards the river. "A chain, quick!"

The men followed, strung high with excitement. Hamilton, the journalist, paused long enough to glance up-stream. Then he, too, ran after them, screaming that the river above was full of logs. By that they all knew that Injin Charley's mission had failed, and that something under ten million feet of logs were racing down the river like so many battering rams.

At the boom the great jam was already a-tremble with eagerness to spring. Indeed a miracle alone seemed to hold the timbers in their place.

"It's death, certain death, to go out on that boom," muttered Billy Mason.

Tim Shearer stepped forward coolly, ready as always to assume the perilous duty. He was thrust back by Thorpe, who seized the chain, cold-shut and hammer which Scotty Parsons brought, and ran lightly out over the booms, shouting,

"Back! back! Don't follow me, on your lives! Keep 'em back, Tim!"

The swift water boiled from under the booms. BANG! SMASH! BANG! crashed the logs, a mile upstream, but plainly audible above the waters and the wind. Thorpe knelt, dropped the cold-shut through on either side of the weakened link, and prepared to close it with his hammer. He intended further to strengthen the connection with the other chain.

"Lem' me hold her for you. You can't close her alone," said an unexpected voice next his elbow.

Thorpe looked up in surprise and anger. Over him leaned Big Junko. The men had been unable to prevent his following. Animated by the blind devotion of the animal for its master, and further stung to action by that master's doubt of his fidelity, the giant had followed to assist as he might.

"You damned fool," cried Thorpe exasperated, then held the hammer to him, "strike while I keep the chain underneath," he commanded.

Big Junko leaned forward to obey, kicking strongly his caulks into the barked surface of the boom log. The spikes, worn blunt by the river work already accomplished, failed to grip. Big Junko slipped, caught himself by an effort, overbalanced in the other direction, and fell into the stream. The current at once swept him away, but fortunately in such a direction that he was enabled to catch the slanting end of a "dead head" log whose lower end was jammed in the crib. The dead head was slippery, the current strong; Big Junko had no crevice by which to assure his hold. In another moment he would be torn away.

"Let go and swim!" shouted Thorpe.

"I can't swim," replied Junko in so low a voice as to be scarcely audible.

For a moment Thorpe stared at him.

"Tell Carrie," said Big Junko.

Then there beneath the swirling gray sky, under the frowning jam, in the midst of flood waters, Thorpe had his second great Moment of Decision. He did not pause to weigh reasons or chances, to discuss with himself expediency, or the moralities of failure. His actions were foreordained, mechanical. All at once the great forces which the winter had been bringing to power, crystallized into something bigger than himself or his ideas. The trail lay before him; there was no choice.

Now clearly, with no shadow of doubt, he took the other view: There could be nothing better than Love. Men, their works, their deeds were little things. Success was a little thing; the opinion of men a little thing. Instantly he felt the truth of it.

And here was Love in danger. That it held its moment's habitation in clay of the coarser mould had nothing to do with the great elemental truth of it. For the first time in his life Thorpe felt the full crushing power of an abstraction. Without thought, instinctively, he threw before the necessity of the moment all that was lesser. It was the triumph of what was real in the man over that which environment, alienation, difficulties had raised up within him.

At Big Junko's words, Thorpe raised his hammer and with one mighty blow severed the chains which bound the ends of the booms across the opening. The free end of one of the poles immediately swung down with the current in the direction of Big Junko. Thorpe like a cat ran to the end of the boom, seized the giant by the collar, and dragged him through the water to safety.

"Run!" he shouted. "Run for your life!"

The two started desperately back, skirting the edge of the logs which now the very seconds alone seemed to hold back. They were drenched and blinded with spray, deafened with the crash of timbers settling to the leap. The men on shore could no longer see them for the smother. The great crush of logs had actually begun its first majestic sliding motion when at last they emerged to safety.

At first a few of the loose timbers found the opening, slipping quietly through with the current; then more; finally the front of the jam dove forward; and an instant later the smooth, swift motion had gained its impetus and was sweeping the entire drive down through the gap.

Rank after rank, like soldiers charging, they ran. The great fierce wind caught them up ahead of the current. In a moment the open river was full of logs jostling eagerly onward. Then suddenly, far out above the uneven tossing skyline of Superior, the strange northern "loom," or mirage, threw the specters of thousands of restless timbers rising and falling on the bosom of the lake.

## Chapter LVI

They stood and watched them go.

"Oh, the great man! Oh, the great man!" murmured the writer, fascinated.

The grandeur of the sacrifice had struck them dumb. They did not understand the motives beneath it all; but the fact was patent. Big Junko broke down and sobbed.

After a time the stream of logs through the gap slackened. In a moment more, save for the inevitably stranded few, the booms were empty. A deep sigh went up from the attentive multitude.

"She's GONE!" said one man, with the emphasis of a novel discovery; and groaned.

Then the awe broke from about their minds, and they spoke many opinions and speculations. Thorpe had disappeared. They respected his emotion and did not follow him.

"It was just plain damn foolishness;—but it was great!" said Shearer. "That no-account jackass of a Big Junko ain't worth as much per thousand feet as good white pine."

Then they noticed a group of men gathering about the office steps, and on it someone talking. Collins, the bookkeeper, was making a speech.

Collins was a little hatchet-faced man, with straight, lank hair, nearsighted eyes, a timid, order-loving disposition, and a great suitability for his profession. He was accurate, unemotional, and valuable. All his actions were as dry as the sawdust in the burner. No one had ever seen him excited. But he was human; and now his knowledge of the Company's affairs showed him the dramatic contrast. HE KNEW! He knew that the property of the firm had been mortgaged to the last dollar in order to assist expansion, so that not another cent could be borrowed to tide over present difficulty. He knew that the notes for sixty thousand dollars covering the loan to Wallace Carpenter came due in three months; he knew from the long table of statistics which he was eternally preparing and comparing that the season's cut should have netted a profit of two hundred thousand dollars—enough to pay the interest on the mortgages, to take up the notes, and to furnish a working capital for the ensuing year. These things he knew in the strange concrete arithmetical manner of the routine bookkeeper. Other men saw a desperate phase of firm rivalry; he saw a struggle to the uttermost. Other men cheered a rescue: he thrilled over the magnificent gesture of the Gambler scattering his stake in largesse to Death.

It was the simple turning of the hand from full breathed prosperity to lifeless failure.

His view was the inverse of his master's. To Thorpe it had suddenly become a very little thing in contrast to the great, sweet elemental truth that the dream girl had enunciated. To Collins the affair was miles vaster than the widest scope of his own narrow life.

The firm could not take up its notes when they came due; it could not pay the interest on the mortgages, which would now be foreclosed; it could not even pay in full the men who had worked for it—that would come under a court's adjudication.

He had therefore watched Thorpe's desperate sally to mend the weakened chain, in all the suspense of a man whose entire universe is in the keeping of the chance moment. It must be remembered that at bottom, below the outer consciousness, Thorpe's final decision had already grown to maturity. On the other hand, no other thought than that of accomplishment had even entered the little bookkeeper's head. The rescue and all that it had meant had hit him like a stroke of apoplexy, and his thin emotions had curdled to hysteria. Full of the idea he appeared before the men.

With rapid, almost incoherent speech he poured it out to them. Professional caution and secrecy were forgotten. Wallace Carpenter attempted to push through the ring for the purpose of stopping him. A gigantic riverman kindly but firmly held him back.

"I guess it's just as well we hears this," said the latter.

It all came out—the loan to Carpenter, with a hint at the motive: the machinations of the rival firm on the Board of Trade; the notes, the mortgages, the necessity of a big season's cut; the reasons the rival firm had for wishing to prevent that cut from arriving at the market; the desperate and varied means they had employed. The men listened silent. Hamilton, his eyes glowing like coals, drank in every word. Here was the master motive he had sought; here was the story great to his hand!

"That's what we ought to get," cried Collins, almost weeping, "and now we've gone and bust, just because that infernal river-hog had to fall off a boom. By God, it's a shame! Those scalawags have done us after all!"

Out from the shadows of the woods stole Injin Charley. The whole bearing and aspect of the man had changed. His eye gleamed with a distant farseeing fire of its own, which took no account of anything but some remote vision. He stole along almost furtively, but with a proud upright carriage of his neck, a backward tilt of his fine head, a distention of his nostrils that lent to his appearance a panther-like pride and stealthiness. No one saw him. Suddenly he broke through the group and mounted the steps beside Collins.

"The enemy of my brother is gone," said he simply in his native tongue, and with a sudden gesture held out before them—a scalp.

The medieval barbarity of the thing appalled them for a moment. The days of scalping were long since past, had been closed away between the pages of forgotten histories, and yet here again before them was the thing in all its living horror. Then a growl arose. The human animal had tasted blood.

All at once like wine their wrongs mounted to their heads. They remembered their dead comrades. They remembered the heart-breaking days and nights of toil they had endured on account of this man and his associates. They remembered the words of Collins, the little bookkeeper. They hated. They shook their fists across the skies. They turned and with one accord struck back for the railroad right-of-way which led to Shingleville, the town controlled by Morrison & Daly.

The railroad lay for a mile straight through a thick tamarack swamp, then over a nearly treeless cranberry plain. The tamarack was a screen between the two towns. When half-way through the swamp, Red Jacket stopped, removed his coat, ripped the lining from it, and began to fashion a rude mask.

"Just as well they don't recognize us," said he.

"Somebody in town will give us away," suggested Shorty, the chore-boy.

"No, they won't; they're all here," assured Kerlie.

It was true. Except for the women and children, who were not yet about, the entire village had assembled. Even old Vanderhoof, the fire-watcher of the yard, hobbled along breathlessly on his rheumatic legs. In a moment the masks were fitted. In a moment more the little band had emerged from the shelter of the swamp, and so came into full view of its objective point.

Shingleville consisted of a big mill; the yards, now nearly empty of lumber; the large frame boarding-house; the office; the stable; a store; two saloons; and a dozen dwellings. The party at once fixed its eyes on this collection of buildings, and trudged on down the right-of-way with unhastening grimness.

Their approach was not unobserved. Daly saw them; and Baker, his foreman, saw them. The two at once went forth to organize opposition. When the attacking party reached the mill-yard, it found the boss and the foreman standing alone on the saw-dust, revolvers drawn.

Daly traced a line with his toe.

"The first man that crosses that line gets it," said he.

They knew he meant what he said. An instant's pause ensued, while the big man and the little faced a mob. Daly's rivermen were still on drive. He knew the mill men too well to depend on them. Truth to tell, the possibility of such a raid as this had not occurred to him; for the simple reason that he did not anticipate the discovery of his complicity with the forces of nature. Skillfully carried out, the plan was a good one. No one need know of the weakened link, and it was the most natural thing in the world that Sadler & Smith's drive should go out with the increase of water.

The men grouped swiftly and silently on the other side of the sawdust line. The pause did not mean that Daly's defense was good. I have known of a crew of striking mill men being so bluffed down, but not such men as these.

"Do you know what's going to happen to you?" said a voice from the group. The speaker was Radway, but the contractor kept himself well in the background. "We're going to burn your mill; we're going to burn your yards; we're going to burn your whole shooting match, you low-lived whelp!"

"Yes, and we're going to string you to your own trestle!" growled another voice harshly.

"Dyer!" said Injin Charley, simply, shaking the wet scalp arm's length towards the lumbermen.

At this grim interruption a silence fell. The owner paled slightly; his foreman chewed a nonchalant straw. Down the still and deserted street crossed and recrossed the subtle occult influences of a half-hundred concealed watchers. Daly and his subordinate were very much alone, and very much in danger. Their last hour had come; and they knew it.

With the recognition of the fact, they immediately raised their weapons in the resolve to do as much damage as possible before being overpowered.

Then suddenly, full in the back, a heavy stream of water knocked them completely off their feet, rolled them over and over on the wet sawdust, and finally jammed them both against the trestle, where it held them, kicking and gasping for breath, in a choking cataract of water. The pistols flew harmlessly into the air. For an instant the Fighting Forty stared in paralyzed astonishment. Then a tremendous roar of laughter saluted this easy vanquishment of a formidable enemy.

Daly and Baker were pounced upon and captured. There was no resistance. They were too nearly strangled for that. Little Solly and old Vanderhoof turned off the water in the fire hydrant and disconnected the hose they had so effectively employed.

"There, damn you!" said Rollway Charley, jerking the millman to his feet. "How do YOU like too much water? hey?"

The unexpected comedy changed the party's mood.

It was no longer a question of killing. A number broke into the store, and shortly emerged, bearing pails of kerosene with which they deluged the slabs on the windward side of the mill. The flames caught the structure instantly. A thousand sparks, borne by the off-shore breeze, fastened like so many stinging insects on the lumber in the yard.

It burned as dried balsam thrown on a camp fire. The heat of it drove the onlookers far back in the village, where in silence they watched the destruction. From behind locked doors the inhabitants watched with them.

The billow of white smoke filled the northern sky. A whirl of gray wood ashes, light as air, floated on and ever on over Superior. The site of the mill, the squares where the piles of lumber had stood, glowed incandescence over which already a white film was forming.

Daly and his man were slapped and cuffed hither and thither at the men's will. Their faces bled, their bodies ached as one bruise.

"That squares us," said the men. "If we can't cut this year, neither kin you. It's up to you now!"

Then, like a destroying horde of locusts, they gutted the office and the store, smashing what they could not carry to the fire. The dwellings and saloons they did not disturb. Finally, about noon, they kicked their two prisoners into the river, and took their way stragglingly back along the right-of-way.

"I surmise we took that town apart SOME!" remarked Shorty with satisfaction.

"I should rise to remark," replied Kerlie. Big Junko said nothing, but his cavernous little animal eyes glowed with satisfaction. He had been the first to lay hands on Daly; he had helped to carry the petroleum; he had struck the first match; he had even administered the final kick.

At the boarding-house they found Wallace Carpenter and Hamilton seated on the veranda. It was now afternoon. The wind had abated somewhat, and the sun was struggling with the still flying scuds.

"Hello, boys," said Wallace, "been for a little walk in the woods?"

"Yes, sir," replied Jack Hyland, "we—"

"I'd rather not hear," interrupted Wallace. "There's quite a fire over east. I suppose you haven't noticed it."

Hyland looked gravely eastward.

"Sure 'nough!" said he.

"Better get some grub," suggested Wallace.

After the men had gone in, he turned to the journalist.

"Hamilton," he began, "write all you know about the drive, and the break, and the rescue, but as to the burning of the mill—"

The other held out his hand.

"Good," said Wallace offering his own.

And that was as far as the famous Shingleville raid ever got. Daly did his best to collect even circumstantial evidence against the participants, but in vain. He could not even get anyone to say that a single member of the village of Carpenter had absented himself from town that morning. This might have been from loyalty, or it might have been from fear of the vengeance the Fighting Forty would surely visit on a traitor. Probably it was a combination of both. The fact remains, however, that Daly never knew surely of but one man implicated in the destruction of his plant. That man was Injin Charley, but Injin Charley promptly disappeared.

After an interval, Tim Shearer, Radway and Kerlie came out again.

"Where's the boss?" asked Shearer.

"I don't know, Tim," replied Wallace seriously.

"I've looked everywhere. He's gone. He must have been all cut up. I think he went out in the woods to get over it. I am not worrying. Harry has lots of sense. He'll come in about dark."

"Sure!" said Tim.

"How about the boy's stakes?" queried Radway. "I hear this is a bad smash for the firm."

"We'll see that the men get their wages all right," replied Carpenter, a little disappointed that such a question should be asked at such a time.

"All right," rejoined the contractor. "We're all going to need our money this summer."

### Chapter LVII

Thorpe walked through the silent group of men without seeing them. He had no thought for what he had done, but for the triumphant discovery he had made in spite of himself. This he saw at once as something to glory in and as a duty to be fulfilled.

It was then about six o'clock in the morning. Thorpe passed the boarding-house, the store, and the office, to take himself as far as the little open shed that served the primitive town as a railway station. There he set the semaphore to flag the east-bound train from Duluth. At six thirty-two, the train happening on time, he climbed aboard. He dropped heavily into a seat and stared straight in front of him until the conductor had spoken to him twice.

"Where to, Mr. Thorpe?" he asked.

The latter gazed at him uncomprehendingly.

"Oh! Mackinaw City," he replied at last.

"How're things going up your way?" inquired the conductor by way of conversation while he made out the pay-slip.

"Good!" responded Thorpe mechanically.

The act of paying for his fare brought to his consciousness that he had but a little over ten dollars with him. He thrust the change back into his pocket, and took up his contemplation of nothing. The river water dripped slowly from his "cork" boots to form a pool on the car floor. The heavy wool of his short driving trousers steamed in the car's warmth. His shoulders dried in a little cloud of vapor. He noticed none of these things, but stared ahead, his gaze vacant, the bronze of his face set in the lines of a brown study, his strong capable hands hanging purposeless between his knees. The ride to Mackinaw City was six hours long, and the train in addition lost some ninety minutes; but in all this distance Thorpe never altered his pose nor his fixed attitude of attention to some inner voice.

The car-ferry finally landed them on the southern peninsula. Thorpe descended at Mackinaw City to find that the noon train had gone. He ate lunch at the hotel,—borrowed a hundred dollars from the agent of Louis Sands, a lumberman of his acquaintance; and seated himself rigidly in the little waiting room, there to remain until the nine-twenty that night. When the cars were backed down from the siding, he boarded the sleeper. In the doorway stood a disapproving colored porter.

"Yo'll fin' the smokin' cab up fo'wu'd, suh," said the latter, firmly barring the way.

"It's generally forward," answered Thorpe.

"This yeah's th' sleepah," protested the functionary. "You pays extry."

"I am aware of it," replied Thorpe curtly. "Give me a lower."

"Yessah!" acquiesced the darkey, giving way, but still in doubt. He followed Thorpe curiously, peering into the smoking room on him from time to time. A little after twelve his patience gave out. The stolid gloomy man of lower six seemed to intend sitting up all night.

"Yo' berth is ready, sah," he delicately suggested.

Thorpe arose obediently, walked to lower six, and, without undressing, threw himself on the bed. Afterwards the porter, in conscientious discharge of his duty, looked diligently beneath the seat for boots to polish. Happening to glance up, after fruitless search he discovered the boots still adorning the feet of their owner.

"Well, for th' LANDS sake!" ejaculated the scandalized negro, beating a hasty retreat.

He was still more scandalized when, the following noon, his strange fare brushed by him without bestowing the expected tip.

Thorpe descended at Twelfth Street in Chicago without any very clear notion of where he was going. For a moment he faced the long park-like expanse of the lake front, then turned sharp to his left and picked his way south up the interminable reaches of Michigan Avenue. He did this without any conscious motive—mainly because the reaches seemed interminable, and he proved the need of walking. Block after block he clicked along, the caulks of his boots striking fire from the pavement. Some people stared at him a little curiously. Others merely glanced in his direction, attracted more by the expression of his face than the peculiarity of his dress. At that time rivermen were not an uncommon sight along the water front.

After an interval he seemed to have left the smoke and dirt behind. The street became quieter. Boarding-houses and tailors' shops ceased. Here and there appeared a bit of lawn, shrubbery, flowers. The residences established an uptown crescendo of magnificence. Policemen seemed trimmer, better-gloved. Occasionally he might have noticed in front of one of the sandstone piles, a besilvered pair champing before a stylish vehicle. By and by he came to himself to find that he was staring at the deep-carved lettering in a stone horse-block before a large dwelling.

His mind took the letters in one after the other, perceiving them plainly before it accorded them recognition. Finally he had completed the word "Farrad." He whirled sharp on his heel, mounted the broad white stone steps, and rang the bell.

It was answered almost immediately by a cleanshaven, portly and dignified man with the most impassive countenance in the world. This man looked upon Thorpe with lofty disapproval.

"Is Miss Hilda Farrand at home?" he asked.

"I cannot say," replied the man. "If you will step to the back door, I will ascertain."

"The flowers will do. Now see that the south room is ready, Annie," floated a voice from within.

Without a word, but with a deadly earnestness, Thorpe reached forward, seized the astonished servant by the collar, yanked him bodily outside the door, stepped inside, and strode across the hall toward a closed portiere whence had come the voice. The riverman's long spikes cut little triangular pieces from the hardwood floor. Thorpe did not notice that. He thrust aside the portiere.

Before him he saw a young and beautiful girl. She was seated, and her lap was filled with flowers. At his sudden apparition, her hands flew to her heart, and her lips slightly parted. For a second the two stood looking at each other, just as nearly a year before their eyes had crossed over the old pole trail.

To Thorpe the girl seemed more beautiful than ever. She exceeded even his retrospective dreams of her, for the dream had persistently retained something of the quality of idealism which made the vision unreal, while the woman before him had become human flesh and blood, adorable, to be desired. The red of this violent unexpected encounter rushed to her face, her bosom rose and fell in a fluttering catch for breath; but her eyes were steady and inquiring.

Then the butler pounced on Thorpe from behind with the intent to do great bodily harm.

"Morris!" commanded Hilda sharply, "what are you doing?"

The man cut short his heroism in confusion.

"You may go," concluded Hilda.

Thorpe stood straight and unwinking by the straight portiere. After a moment he spoke.

"I have come to tell you that you were right and I was wrong," said he steadily. "You told me there could be nothing better than love. In the pride of my strength I told you this was not so. I was wrong."

He stood for another instant, looking directly at her, then turned sharply, and head erect walked from the room.

Before he had reached the outer door the girl was at his side.

"Why are you going?" she asked.

"I have nothing more to say."

"NOTHING?"

"Nothing at all."

She laughed happily to herself.

"But I have—much. Come back."

They returned to the little morning room, Thorpe's caulked boots gouging out the little triangular furrows in the hardwood floor. Neither noticed that. Morris, the butler, emerged from his hiding and held up the hands of horror.

"What are you going to do now?" she catechised, facing him in the middle of the room. A long tendril of her beautiful corn-silk hair fell across her eyes; her red lips parted in a faint wistful smile; beneath the draperies of her loose gown the pure slender lines of her figure leaned toward him.

"I am going back," he replied patiently.

"I knew you would come," said she. "I have been expecting you."

She raised one hand to brush back the tendril of hair, but it was a mechanical gesture, one that did not stir even the surface consciousness of the strange half-smiling, half-wistful, starry gaze with which she watched his face.

"Oh, Harry," she breathed, with a sudden flash of insight, "you are a man born to be much misunderstood."

He held himself rigid, but in his veins was creeping a molten fire, and the fire was beginning to glow dully in his eye. Her whole being called him. His heart leaped, his breath came fast, his eyes swam. With almost hypnotic fascination the idea obsessed him—to kiss her lips, to press the soft body of the young girl, to tumble her hair down about her flower face. He had not come for this. He tried to steady himself, and by an effort that left him weak he succeeded. Then a new flood of passion overcame him. In the later desire was nothing of the old humble adoration. It was elemental, real, almost a little savage. He wanted to seize her so fiercely as to hurt her. Something caught his throat, filled his lungs, weakened his knees. For a moment it seemed to him that he was going to faint.

And still she stood there before him, saying nothing, leaning slightly towards him, her red lips half parted, her eyes fixed almost wistfully on his face.

"Go away!" he whispered hoarsely at last. The voice was not his own. "Go away! Go away!"

Suddenly she swayed to him.

"Oh, Harry, Harry," she whispered, "must I TELL you? Don't you SEE?"

The flood broke through him. He seized her hungrily. He crushed her to him until she gasped; he pressed his lips against hers until she all but cried out with the pain of it, he ran his great brown hands blindly through her hair until it came down about them both in a cloud of spun light.

"Tell me!" he whispered. "Tell me!"

"Oh! Oh!" she cried. "Please! What is it?"

"I do not believe it," he murmured savagely.

She drew herself from him with gentle dignity.

"I am not worthy to say it," she said soberly, "but I love you with all my heart and soul!"

Then for the first and only time in his life Thorpe fell to weeping, while she, understanding, stood by and comforted him.

433

## Chapter LVIII

The few moments of Thorpe's tears eased the emotional strain under which, perhaps unconsciously, he had been laboring for nearly a year past. The tenseness of his nerves relaxed. He was able to look on the things about him from a broader standpoint than that of the specialist, to front life with saving humor. The deep breath after striving could at last be taken.

In this new attitude there was nothing strenuous, nothing demanding haste; only a deep glow of content and happiness. He savored deliberately the joy of a luxurious couch, rich hangings, polished floor, subdued light, warmed atmosphere. He watched with soul-deep gratitude the soft girlish curves of Hilda's body, the poise of her flower head, the piquant, half-wistful, half-childish set of her red lips, the clear starlike glimmer of her dusky eyes. It was all near to him; his.

"Kiss me, dear," he said.

She swayed to him again, deliciously graceful, deliciously unselfconscious, trusting, adorable. Already in the little nothingnesses of manner, the trifles of mental and bodily attitude, she had assumed that faint trace of the maternal which to the observant tells so plainly that a woman has given herself to a man.

She leaned her cheek against her hand, and her hand against his shoulder.

"I have been reading a story lately," said she, "that has interested me very much. It was about a man who renounced all he held most dear to shield a friend."

"Yes," said Thorpe.

"Then he renounced all his most valuable possessions because a poor common man needed the sacrifice."

"Sounds like a medieval story," said he with unconscious humor.

"It happened recently," rejoined Hilda. "I read it in the papers."

"Well, he blazed a good trail," was Thorpe's sighing comment. "Probably he had his chance. We don't all of us get that. Things go crooked and get tangled up, so we have to do the best we can. I don't believe I'd have done it."

"Oh, you are delicious!" she cried.

After a time she said very humbly: "I want to beg your pardon for misunderstanding you and causing you so much suffering. I was very stupid, and didn't see why you could not do as I wanted you to."

"That is nothing to forgive. I acted like a fool."

"I have known about you," she went on. "It has all come out in the Telegram. It has been very exciting. Poor boy, you look tired."

He straightened himself suddenly. "I have forgotten,—actually forgotten," he cried a little bitterly. "Why, I am a pauper, a bankrupt, I—"

"Harry," she interrupted gently, but very firmly, "you must not say what you were going to say. I cannot allow it. Money came between us before. It must not do so again. Am I not right, dear?"

She smiled at him with the lips of a child and the eyes of a woman.

"Yes," he agreed after a struggle, "you are right. But now I must begin all over again. It will be a long time before I shall be able to claim you. I have my way to make."

"Yes," said she diplomatically.

"But you!" he cried suddenly. "The papers remind me. How about that Morton?"

"What about him?" asked the girl, astonished. "He is very happily engaged."

Thorpe's face slowly filled with blood.

"You'll break the engagement at once," he commanded a little harshly.

"Why should I break the engagement?" demanded Hilda, eying him with some alarm.

"I should think it was obvious enough."

"But it isn't," she insisted. "Why?"

Thorpe was silent—as he always had been in emergencies, and as he was destined always to be. His was not a nature of expression, but of action. A crisis always brought him, like a bull-dog, silently to the grip.

Hilda watched him puzzled, with bright eyes, like a squirrel. Her quick brain glanced here and there among the possibilities, seeking the explanation. Already she knew better than to demand it of him.

"You actually don't think he's engaged to ME!" she burst out finally.

"Isn't he?" asked Thorpe.

"Why no, stupid! He's engaged to Elizabeth Carpenter, Wallace's sister. Now WHERE did you get that silly idea?"

"I saw it in the paper."

"And you believe all you see! Why didn't you ask Wallace—but of course you wouldn't! Harry, you are the most incoherent dumb old brute I ever saw! I could shake you! Why don't you say something occasionally when it's needed, instead of sitting dumb as a sphinx and getting into all sorts of trouble? But you never will. I know you. You dear old bear! You NEED a wife to interpret things for you. You speak a different language from most people." She said this between laughing and crying; between a sense of the ridiculous uselessness of withholding a single timely word, and a tender pathetic intuition of the suffering such a nature must endure. In the prospect of the future she saw her use. It gladdened her and filled her with a serene happiness possible only to those who feel themselves a necessary and integral part in the lives of the ones they love. Dimly she perceived this truth. Dimly beyond it she glimpsed that other great truth of nature, that the human being is rarely completely efficient alone, that in obedience to his greater use he must take to himself a mate before he can succeed.

Suddenly she jumped to her feet with an exclamation.

"Oh, Harry! I'd forgotten utterly!" she cried in laughing consternation. "I have a luncheon here at half-past one! It's almost that now. I must run and dress. Just look at me; just LOOK! YOU did that!"

"I'll wait here until the confounded thing is over," said Thorpe.

"Oh, no, you won't," replied Hilda decidedly. "You are going down town right now and get something to put on. Then you are coming back here to stay."

Thorpe glanced in surprise at his driver's clothes, and his spiked boots.

"Heavens and earth!" he exclaimed, "I should think so! How am I to get out without ruining the floor?"

Hilda laughed and drew aside the portiere.

"Don't you think you have done that pretty well already?" she asked. "There, don't look so solemn. We're not going to be sorry for a single thing we've done today, are we?" She stood close to him holding the lapels of his jacket in either hand, searching his face wistfully with her fathomless dusky eyes.

"No, sweetheart, we are not," replied Thorpe soberly.


### Chapter LIX

Surely it is useless to follow the sequel in detail, to tell how Hilda persuaded Thorpe to take her money. She aroused skillfully his fighting blood, induced him to use one fortune to rescue another. To a woman such as she this was not a very difficult task in the long run. A few scruples of pride; that was all.

"Do not consider its being mine," she answered to his objections. "Remember the lesson we learned so bitterly. Nothing can be greater than love, not even our poor ideals. You have my love; do not disappoint me by refusing so little a thing as my money."

"I hate to do it," he replied; "it doesn't look right."

"You must," she insisted. "I will not take the position of rich wife to a poor man; it is humiliating to both. I will not marry you until you have made your success."

"That is right," said Thorpe heartily.

"Well, then, are you going to be so selfish as to keep me waiting while you make an entirely new start, when a little help on my part will bring your plans to completion?"

She saw the shadow of assent in his eyes.

"How much do you need?" she asked swiftly.

"I must take up the notes," he explained. "I must pay the men. I may need something on the stock market. If I go in on this thing, I'm going in for keeps. I'll get after those fellows who have been swindling Wallace. Say a hundred thousand dollars."

"Why, it's nothing," she cried.

"I'm glad you think so," he replied grimly.

She ran to her dainty escritoire, where she scribbled eagerly for a few moments.

"There," she cried, her eyes shining, "there is my check book all signed in blank. I'll see that the money is there."

Thorpe took the book, staring at it with sightless eyes. Hilda, perched on the arm of his chair, watched his face closely, as later became her habit of interpretation.

"What is it?" she asked.

Thorpe looked up with a pitiful little smile that seemed to beg indulgence for what he was about to say.

"I was just thinking, dear. I used to imagine I was a strong man, yet see how little my best efforts amount to. I have put myself into seven years of the hardest labor, working like ten men in order to succeed. I have foreseen all that mortal could foresee. I have always thought, and think now, that a man is no man unless he works out the sort of success for which he is fitted. I have done fairly well until the crises came. Then I have been absolutely powerless, and if left to myself, I would have failed. At the times when a really strong man would have used effectively the strength he had been training, I have fallen back miserably on outer aid. Three times my affairs have become critical. In the crises I have been saved, first by a mere boy; then by an old illiterate man; now by a weak woman!"

She heard him through in silence.

"Harry," she said soberly when he had quite finished, "I agree with you that God meant the strong man to succeed; that without success the man hasn't fulfilled his reason for being. But, Harry, ARE YOU QUITE SURE GOD MEANT HIM TO SUCCEED ALONE?"

The dusk fell through the little room. Out in the hallway a tall clock ticked solemnly. A noiseless servant appeared in the doorway to light the lamps, but was silently motioned away.

"I had not thought of that," said Thorpe at last.

"You men are so selfish," went on Hilda. "You would take everything from us. Why can't you leave us the poor little privilege of the occasional deciding touch, the privilege of succor. It is all that weakness can do for strength."

"And why," she went on after a moment, "why is not that, too, a part of a man's success—the gathering about him of people who can and will supplement his efforts. Who was it inspired Wallace Carpenter with confidence in an unknown man? You. What did it? Those very qualities by which you were building your success. Why did John Radway join forces with you? How does it happen that your men are of so high a standard of efficiency? Why am I willing to give you everything, EVERYTHING, to my heart and soul? Because it is you who ask it. Because you, Harry Thorpe, have woven us into your fortune, so that we have no choice. Depend upon us in the crises of your work! Why, so are you dependent on your ten fingers, your eyes, the fiber of your brain! Do you think the less of your fulfillment for that?"

So it was that Hilda Farrand gave her lover confidence, brought him out from his fanaticism, launched him afresh into the current of events. He remained in Chicago all that summer, giving orders that all work at the village of Carpenter should cease. With his affairs that summer we have little to do. His common-sense treatment of the stock market, by which a policy of quiescence following an outright buying of the stock which he had previously held on margins, retrieved the losses already sustained, and finally put both partners on a firm financial footing. That is another story. So too is his reconciliation with and understanding of his sister. It came about through Hilda, of course. Perhaps in the inscrutable way of Providence the estrangement was of benefit,—even necessary, for it had thrown him entirely within himself during his militant years.

Let us rather look to the end of the summer. It now became a question of re-opening the camps. Thorpe wrote to Shearer and Radway, whom he had retained, that he would arrive on Saturday noon, and suggested that the two begin to look about for men. Friday, himself, Wallace Carpenter, Elizabeth Carpenter, Morton, Helen Thorpe, and Hilda Farrand boarded the north-bound train.

## *Chapter LX*

The train of the South Shore Railroad shot its way across the broad reaches of the northern peninsula. On either side of the right-of-way lay mystery in the shape of thickets so dense and overgrown that the eye could penetrate them but a few feet at most. Beyond them stood the forests. Thus Nature screened her intimacies from the impertinent eye of a new order of things.

Thorpe welcomed the smell of the northland. He became almost eager, explaining, indicating to the girl at his side.

"There is the Canada balsam," he cried. "Do you remember how I showed it to you first? And yonder the spruce. How stuck up your teeth were when you tried to chew the gum before it had been heated. Do you remember? Look! Look there! It's a white pine! Isn't it a grand tree? It's the finest tree in the forest, by my way of thinking, so tall, so straight, so feathery, and so dignified. See, Hilda, look quick! There's an old logging road all filled with raspberry vines. We'd find lots of partridges there, and perhaps a bear. Wouldn't you just like to walk down it about sunset?"

"Yes, Harry."

"I wonder what we're stopping for. Seems to me they are stopping at every squirrel's trail. Oh, this must be Seney. Yes, it is. Queer little place, isn't it? but sort of attractive. Good deal like our town. You have never seen Carpenter, have you? Location's fine, anyway; and to me it's sort of picturesque. You'll like Mrs. Hathaway. She's a buxom, motherly woman who runs the boarding-house for eighty men, and still finds time to mend my clothes for me. And you'll like Solly. Solly's the tug captain, a mighty good fellow, true as a gun barrel. We'll have him take us out, some still day. We'll be there in a few minutes now. See the cranberry marshes. Sometimes there's a good deal of pine on little islands scattered over it, but it's very hard to log, unless you get a good winter. We had just such a proposition when I worked for Radway. Oh, you'll like Radway, he's as good as gold. Helen!"

"Yes," replied his sister.

"I want you to know Radway. He's the man who gave me my start."

"All right, Harry," laughed Helen. "I'll meet anybody or anything from bears to Indians."

"I know an Indian too—Geezigut, an Ojibwa—we called him Injin Charley. He was my first friend in the north woods. He helped me get my timber. This spring he killed a man—a good job, too—and is hiding now. I wish I knew where he is. But we'll see him some day. He'll come back when the thing blows over. See! See!"

"What?" they all asked, breathless.

"It's gone. Over beyond the hills there I caught a glimpse of Superior."

"You are ridiculous, Harry," protested Helen Thorpe laughingly. "I never saw you so. You are a regular boy!"

"Do you like boys?" he asked gravely of Hilda.

"Adore them!" she cried.

"All right, I don't care," he answered his sister in triumph.

The air brakes began to make themselves felt, and shortly the train came to a grinding stop.

"What station is this?" Thorpe asked the colored porter.

"Shingleville, sah," the latter replied.

"I thought so. Wallace, when did their mill burn, anyway? I haven't heard about it."

"Last spring, about the time you went down."

"Is THAT so? How did it happen?"

"They claim incendiarism," parried Wallace cautiously.

436

Thorpe pondered a moment, then laughed. "I am in the mixed attitude of the small boy," he observed, "who isn't mean enough to wish anybody's property destroyed, but who wishes that if there is a fire, to be where he can see it. I am sorry those fellows had to lose their mill, but it was a good thing for us. The man who set that fire did us a good turn. If it hadn't been for the burning of their mill, they would have made a stronger fight against us in the stock market."

Wallace and Hilda exchanged glances. The girl was long since aware of the inside history of those days.

"You'll have to tell them that," she whispered over the back of her seat. "It will please them."

"Our station is next!" cried Thorpe, "and it's only a little ways. Come, get ready!"

They all crowded into the narrow passage-way near the door, for the train barely paused.

"All right, sah," said the porter, swinging down his little step.

Thorpe ran down to help the ladies. He was nearly taken from his feet by a wild-cat yell, and a moment later that result was actually accomplished by a rush of men that tossed him bodily onto its shoulders. At the same moment, the mill and tug whistles began to screech, miscellaneous fire-arms exploded. Even the locomotive engineer, in the spirit of the occasion, leaned down heartily on his whistle rope. The saw-dust street was filled with screaming, jostling men. The homes of the town were brilliantly draped with cheesecloth, flags and bunting.

For a moment Thorpe could not make out what had happened. This turmoil was so different from the dead quiet of desertion he had expected, that he was unable to gather his faculties. All about him were familiar faces upturned to his own. He distinguished the broad, square shoulders of Scotty Parsons, Jack Hyland, Kerlie, Bryan Moloney; Ellis grinned at him from the press; Billy Camp, the fat and shiny drive cook; Mason, the foreman of the mill; over beyond howled Solly, the tug captain, Rollway Charley, Shorty, the chore-boy; everywhere were features that he knew. As his dimming eyes travelled here and there, one by one the Fighting Forty, the best crew of men ever gathered in the northland, impressed themselves on his consciousness. Saginaw birlers, Flat River drivers, woodsmen from the forests of Lower Canada, bully boys out of the Muskegon waters, peavey men from Au Sable, white-water dare-devils from the rapids of the Menominee—all were there to do him honor, him in whom they had learned to see the supreme qualities of their calling. On the outskirts sauntered the tall form of Tim Shearer, a straw peeping from beneath his flax-white mustache, his eyes glimmering under his flax-white eyebrows. He did not evidence as much excitement as the others, but the very bearing of the man expressed the deepest satisfaction. Perhaps he remembered that zero morning so many years before when he had watched the thinly-clad, shivering chore-boy set his face for the first time towards the dark forest.

Big Junko and Anderson deposited their burden on the raised platform of the office steps. Thorpe turned and fronted the crowd.

At once pandemonium broke loose, as though the previous performance had been nothing but a low-voiced rehearsal.

The men looked upon their leader and gave voice to the enthusiasm that was in them. He stood alone there, straight and tall, the muscles of his brown face set to hide his emotion, his head thrust back proudly, the lines of his strong figure tense with power,—the glorification in finer matter of the hardy, reliant men who did him honor.

"Oh, aren't you PROUD of him?" gasped Hilda, squeezing Helen's arm with a little sob.

In a moment Wallace Carpenter, his countenance glowing with pride and pleasure, mounted the platform and stood beside his friend, while Morton and the two young ladies stopped half way up the steps.

At once the racket ceased. Everyone stood at attention.

"Mr. Thorpe," Wallace began, "at the request of your friends here, I have a most pleasant duty to fulfill. They have asked me to tell you how glad they are to see you; that is surely unnecessary. They have also asked me to congratulate you on having won the fight with our rivals."

"You done 'em good." "Can't down the Old Fellow," muttered joyous voices.

"But," said Wallace, "I think that I first have a story to tell on my own account.

"At the time the jam broke this spring, we owed the men here for a year's work. At that time I considered their demand for wages ill-timed and grasping. I wish to apologize. After the money was paid them, instead of scattering, they set to work under Jack Radway and Tim Shearer to salvage your logs. They have worked long hours all summer. They have invested every cent of their year's earnings in supplies and tools, and now they are prepared to show you in the Company's booms, three million feet of logs, rescued by their grit and hard labor from total loss."

At this point the speaker was interrupted. "Saw off," "Shut up," "Give us a rest," growled the audience. "Three million feet ain't worth talkin' about," "You make me tired," "Say your little say the way you oughter," "Found purty nigh two millions pocketed on Mare's Island, or we wouldn't a had that much," "Damn-fool undertaking, anyhow."

"Men," cried Thorpe, "I have been very fortunate. From failure success has come. But never have I been more fortunate than in my friends. The firm is now on its feet. It could afford to lose three times the logs it lost this year—"

He paused and scanned their faces.

"But," he continued suddenly, "it cannot now, nor ever can afford to lose what those three million feet represent,—the friends it has made. I can pay you back the money you have spent and the time you have put in—" Again he looked them over, and then for the first time since they have known him his face lighted up with a rare and tender smile of affection. "But, comrades, I shall not offer to do it: the gift is accepted in the spirit with which it was offered—"

He got no further. The air was rent with sound. Even the members of his own party cheered. From every direction the crowd surged inward. The women and Morton were forced up the platform to Thorpe. The latter motioned for silence.

"Now, boys, we have done it," said he, "and so will go back to work. From now on you are my comrades in the fight."

His eyes were dim; his breast heaved; his voice shook. Hilda was weeping from excitement. Through the tears she saw them all looking at their leader, and in the worn, hard faces glowed the affection and admiration of a dog for its master.

437

Something there was especially touching in this, for strong men rarely show it. She felt a great wave of excitement sweep over her. Instantly she was standing by Thorpe, her eyes streaming, her breast throbbing with emotion.

"Oh!" she cried, stretching her arms out to them passionately, "Oh! I love you; I love you all!"

# The Land of Footprints

## I. ON BOOKS OF ADVENTURE

Books of sporting, travel, and adventure in countries little known to the average reader naturally fall in two classes-neither, with a very few exceptions, of great value. One class is perhaps the logical result of the other.

Of the first type is the book that is written to make the most of far travels, to extract from adventure the last thrill, to impress the awestricken reader with a full sense of the danger and hardship the writer has undergone. Thus, if the latter takes out quite an ordinary routine permit to go into certain districts, he makes the most of travelling in "closed territory," implying that he has obtained an especial privilege, and has penetrated where few have gone before him. As a matter of fact, the permit is issued merely that the authorities may keep track of who is where. Anybody can get one. This class of writer tells of shooting beasts at customary ranges of four and five hundred yards. I remember one in especial who airily and as a matter of fact killed all his antelope at such ranges. Most men have shot occasional beasts at a quarter mile or so, but not airily nor as a matter of fact: rather with thanksgiving and a certain amount of surprise. The gentleman of whom I speak mentioned getting an eland at seven hundred and fifty yards. By chance I happened to mention this to a native Africander.

"Yes," said he, "I remember that; I was there."

This interested me-and I said so.

"He made a long shot," said I.

"A GOOD long shot," replied the Africander.

"Did you pace the distance?"

He laughed. "No," said he, "the old chap was immensely delighted. 'Eight hundred yards if it was an inch!' he cried."

"How far was it?"

"About three hundred and fifty. But it was a long shot, all right."

And it was! Three hundred and fifty yards is a very long shot. It is over four city blocks-New York size. But if you talk often enough and glibly enough of "four and five hundred yards," it does not sound like much, does it?

The same class of writer always gets all the thrills. He speaks of "blanched cheeks," of the "thrilling suspense," and so on down the gamut of the shilling shocker. His stuff makes good reading; there is no doubt of that. The spellbound public likes it, and to that extent it has fulfilled its mission. Also, the reader believes it to the letter-why should he not? Only there is this curious result: he carries away in his mind the impression of unreality, of a country impossible to be understood and gauged and savoured by the ordinary human mental equipment. It is interesting, just as are historical novels, or the copper-riveted heroes of modern fiction, but it has no real relation with human life. In the last analysis the inherent untruth of the thing forces itself on him. He believes, but he does not apprehend; he acknowledges the fact, but he cannot grasp its human quality. The affair is interesting, but it is more or less concocted of pasteboard for his amusement. Thus essential truth asserts its right.

All this, you must understand, is probably not a deliberate attempt to deceive. It is merely the recrudescence under the stimulus of a brand-new environment of the boyish desire to be a hero. When a man jumps back into the Pleistocene he digs up some of his ancestors' cave-qualities. Among these is the desire for personal adornment. His modern development of taste precludes skewers in the ears and polished wire around the neck; so he adorns himself in qualities instead. It is quite an engaging and diverting trait of character. The attitude of mind it both presupposes and helps to bring about is too complicated for my brief analysis. In itself it is no more blameworthy than the small boy's pretence at Indians in the back yard; and no more praiseworthy than infantile decoration with feathers.

In its results, however, we are more concerned. Probably each of us has his mental picture that passes as a symbol rather than an idea of the different continents. This is usually a single picture-a deep river, with forest, hanging snaky vines, anacondas and monkeys for the east coast of South America, for example. It is built up in youth by chance reading and chance pictures, and does as well as a pink place on the map to stand for a part of the world concerning which we know nothing at all. As time goes on we extend, expand, and modify this picture in the light of what knowledge we may acquire. So the reading of many books modifies and expands our first crude notions of Equatorial Africa. And the result is, if we read enough of the sort I describe above, we build the idea of an exciting, dangerous, extra-human continent, visited by half-real people of the texture of the historical-fiction hero, who have strange and interesting adventures which we could not possibly imagine happening to ourselves.

This type of book is directly responsible for the second sort. The author of this is deadly afraid of being thought to brag of his adventures. He feels constantly on him the amusedly critical eye of the old-timer. When he comes to describe the first time a rhino dashed in his direction, he remembers that old hunters, who have been so charged hundreds of times, may read the book. Suddenly, in that light, the adventure becomes pitifully unimportant. He sets down the fact that "we met a rhino that turned a bit nasty, but after a shot in the shoulder decided to leave us alone." Throughout he keeps before his mind's eye the imaginary audience of those who have done. He writes for them, to please them, to convince them that he is not "swelled head," nor "cocky," nor "fancies himself," nor thinks he has done, been, or seen anything wonderful. It is a good, healthy frame of mind to be in; but it, no more than the other type, can produce books that leave on the minds of the general public any impression of a country in relation to a real human being.

As a matter of fact, the same trouble is at the bottom of both failures. The adventure writer, half unconsciously perhaps, has been too much occupied play-acting himself into half-forgotten boyhood heroics. The more modest man, with even more self-consciousness, has been thinking of how he is going to appear in the eyes of the expert. Both have thought of themselves before their work. This aspect of the matter would probably vastly astonish the modest writer.

If, then, one is to formulate an ideal toward which to write, he might express it exactly in terms of man and environment. Those readers desiring sheer exploration can get it in any library: those in search of sheer romantic adventure can purchase plenty of it at any book-stall. But the majority want something different from either of these. They want, first of all, to know what the country is like-not in vague and grandiose "word paintings," nor in strange and foreign sounding words and phrases, but in comparison with something they know. What is it nearest like-Arizona? Surrey? Upper New York? Canada? Mexico? Or is it totally different from anything, as is the Grand Canyon? When you look out from your camp-any one camp-how far do you see, and what do you see?-mountains in the distance, or a screen of vines or bamboo near hand, or what? When you get up in the morning, what is the first thing to do? What does a rhino look like, where he lives, and what did you do the first time one came at you? I don't want you to tell me as though I were either an old hunter or an admiring audience, or as though you were afraid somebody might think you were making too much of the matter. I want to know how you REALLY felt. Were you scared or nervous? or did you become cool? Tell me frankly just how it was, so I can see the thing as happening to a common everyday human being. Then, even at second-hand and at ten thousand miles distance, I can enjoy it actually, humanly, even though vicariously, speculating a bit over my pipe as to how I would have liked it myself.

Obviously, to write such a book the author must at the same time sink his ego and exhibit frankly his personality. The paradox in this is only apparent. He must forget either to strut or to blush with diffidence. Neither audience should be forgotten, and neither should be exclusively addressed. Never should he lose sight of the wholesome fact that old hunters are to read and to weigh; never should he for a moment slip into the belief that he is justified in addressing the expert alone. His attitude should be that many men know more and have done more than he, but that for one reason or another these men are not ready to transmit their knowledge and experience.

To set down the formulation of an ideal is one thing: to fulfil it is another. In the following pages I cannot claim a fulfilment, but only an attempt. The foregoing dissertation must be considered not as a promise, but as an explanation. No one knows better than I how limited my African experience is, both in time and extent, bounded as it is by East Equatorial Africa and a year. Hundreds of men are better qualified than myself to write just this book; but unfortunately they will not do it.

## II. AFRICA

In looking back on the multitudinous pictures that the word Africa bids rise in my memory, four stand out more distinctly than the others. Strangely enough, these are by no means all pictures of average country-the sort of thing one would describe as typical. Perhaps, in a way, they symbolize more the spirit of the country to me, for certainly they represent but a small minority of its infinitely varied aspects. But since we must make a start somewhere, and since for some reason these four crowd most insistently in the recollection it might be well to begin with them.

Our camp was pitched under a single large mimosa tree near the edge of a deep and narrow ravine down which a stream flowed. A semicircle of low mountains hemmed us in at the distance of several miles. The other side of the semicircle was occupied by the upthrow of a low rise blocking off an horizon at its nearest point but a few hundred yards away. Trees marked the course of the stream; low scattered bushes alternated with open plain. The grass grew high. We had to cut it out to make camp.

Nothing indicated that we were otherwise situated than in a very pleasant, rather wide grass valley in the embrace of the mountains. Only a walk of a few hundred yards atop the upthrow of the low rise revealed the fact that it was in reality the lip of a bench, and that beyond it the country fell away in sheer cliffs whose ultimate drop was some fifteen hundred feet. One could sit atop and dangle his feet over unguessed abysses.

For a week we had been hunting for greater kudu. Each day Memba Sasa and I went in one direction, while Mavrouki and Kongoni took another line. We looked carefully for signs, but found none fresher than the month before. Plenty of other game made the country interesting; but we were after a shy and valuable prize, so dared not shoot lesser things. At last, at the end of the week, Mavrouki came in with a tale of eight lions seen in the low scrub across the stream. The kudu business was about finished, as far as this place went, so we decided to take a look for the lions.

We ate by lantern and at the first light were ready to start. But at that moment, across the slope of the rim a few hundred yards away, appeared a small group of sing-sing. These are a beautiful big beast, with widespread horns, proud and wonderful, like Landseer's stags, and I wanted one of them very much. So I took the Springfield, and dropped behind the line of some bushes. The stalk was of the ordinary sort. One has to remain behind cover, to keep down wind, to make no quick movements. Sometimes this takes considerable manoeuvring; especially, as now, in the case of a small band fairly well scattered out for feeding. Often after one has succeeded in placing them all safely behind the scattered cover, a straggler will step out into view. Then the hunter must stop short, must slowly, oh very, very slowly, sink down out of sight; so slowly, in fact, that he must not seem to move, but rather to melt imperceptibly away. Then he must take up his progress at a lower plane of elevation. Perhaps he needs merely to stoop; or he may crawl on hands and knees; or he may lie flat and hitch himself forward by his toes, pushing his gun ahead. If one of the beasts suddenly looks very intently in his direction, he must freeze into no matter what uncomfortable position, and so remain an indefinite time. Even a hotel-bred child to whom you have rashly made advances stares no longer nor more intently than a buck that cannot make you out.

I had no great difficulty with this lot, but slipped up quite successfully to within one hundred and fifty yards. There I raised my head behind a little bush to look. Three does grazed nearest me, their coats rough against the chill of early morning. Up the slope were two more does and two funny, fuzzy babies. An immature buck occupied the extreme left with three young ladies. But the big buck, the leader, the boss of the lot, I could not see anywhere. Of course he must be about, and I craned my neck cautiously here and there trying to make him out.

Suddenly, with one accord, all turned and began to trot rapidly away to the right, their heads high. In the strange manner of animals, they had received telepathic alarm, and had instantly obeyed. Then beyond and far to the right I at last saw the beast I had been looking for. The old villain had been watching me all the time!

The little herd in single file made their way rapidly along the face of the rise. They were headed in the direction of the stream. Now, I happened to know that at this point the stream-canyon was bordered by sheer cliffs. Therefore, the sing-sing must round the hill, and not cross the stream. By running to the top of the hill I might catch a glimpse of them somewhere below. So I started on a jog trot, trying to hit the golden mean of speed that would still leave me breath to shoot. This was an affair of some nicety in the tall grass. Just before I reached the actual slope, however, I revised my schedule. The reason was supplied by a rhino that came grunting to his feet about seventy yards away. He had not seen me, and he had not smelled me, but the general disturbance of all these events had broken into his early morning nap. He looked to me like a person who is cross before breakfast, so I ducked low and ran around him. The last I saw of him he was still standing there, quite disgruntled, and evidently intending to write to the directors about it.

Arriving at the top, I looked eagerly down. The cliff fell away at an impossible angle, but sheer below ran out a narrow bench fifty yards wide. Around the point of the hill to my right-where the herd had gone-a game trail dropped steeply to this bench. I arrived just in time to see the sing-sing, still trotting, file across the bench and over its edge, on some other invisible game trail, to continue their descent of the cliff. The big buck brought up the rear. At the very edge he came to a halt, and looked back, throwing his head up and his nose out so that the heavy fur on his neck stood forward like a ruff. It was a last glimpse of him, so I held my little best, and pulled trigger.

This happened to be one of those shots I spoke of-which the perpetrator accepts with a thankful and humble spirit. The sing-sing leaped high in the air and plunged over the edge of the bench. I signalled the camp-in plain sight-to come and get the head and meat, and sat down to wait. And while waiting, I looked out on a scene that has since been to me one of my four symbolizations of Africa.

The morning was dull, with gray clouds through which at wide intervals streamed broad bands of misty light. Below me the cliff fell away clear to a gorge in the depths of which flowed a river. Then the land began to rise, broken, sharp, tumbled, terrible, tier after tier, gorge after gorge, one twisted range after the other, across a breathlessly immeasurable distance. The prospect was full of shadows thrown by the tumult of lava. In those shadows one imagined stranger abysses. Far down to the right a long narrow lake inaugurated a flatter, alkali-whitened country of low cliffs in long straight lines. Across the distances proper to a dozen horizons the tumbled chaos heaved and fell. The eye sought rest at the bounds usual to its accustomed world-and went on. There was no roundness to the earth, no grateful curve to drop this great fierce country beyond a healing horizon out of sight. The immensity of primal space was in it, and the simplicity of primal things-rough, unfinished, full of mystery. There was no colour. The scene was done in slate gray, darkening to the opaque where a tiny distant rain squall started; lightening in the nearer shadows to reveal half-guessed peaks; brightening unexpectedly into broad short bands of misty gray light slanting from the gray heavens above to the sombre tortured immensity beneath. It was such a thing as Gustave Doré might have imaged to serve as an abiding place for the fierce chaotic spirit of the African wilderness.

I sat there for some time hugging my knees, waiting for the men to come. The tremendous landscape seemed to have been willed to immobility. The rain squalls forty miles or more away did not appear to shift their shadows; the rare slanting bands of light from the clouds were as constant as though they were falling through cathedral windows. But nearer at hand other things were forward. The birds, thousands of them, were doing their best to cheer things up. The roucoulements of doves rose from the bushes down the face of the cliffs; the bell bird uttered his clear ringing note; the chime bird gave his celebrated imitation of a really gentlemanly sixty-horse power touring car hinting you out of the way with the mellowness of a chimed horn; the bottle bird poured gallons of guggling essence of happiness from his silver jug. From the direction of camp, evidently jumped by the boys, a steinbuck loped gracefully, pausing every few minutes to look back, his dainty legs tense, his sensitive ears pointed toward the direction of disturbance.

And now, along the face of the cliff, I make out the flashing of much movement, half glimpsed through the bushes. Soon a fine old-man baboon, his tail arched after the dandified fashion of the baboon aristocracy stepped out, looked around, and bounded forward. Other old men followed him, and then the young men, and a miscellaneous lot of half-grown youngsters. The ladies brought up the rear, with the babies. These rode their mothers' backs, clinging desperately while they leaped along, for all the world like the pathetic monkey "jockeys" one sees strapped to the backs of big dogs in circuses. When they had approached to within fifty yards, remarked "hullo!" to them. Instantly they all stopped. Those in front stood up on their hind legs; those behind clambered to points of vantage on rocks and the tops of small bushes: They all took a good long look at me. Then they told me what they thought about me personally, the fact of my being there, and the rude way I had startled them. Their remarks were neither complimentary nor refined. The old men, in especial, got quite profane, and screamed excited billingsgate. Finally they all stopped at once, dropped on all fours, and loped away, their ridiculous long tails curved in a half arc. Then for the first time I noticed that, under cover of the insults, the women and children had silently retired. Once more I was left to the familiar gentle bird calls, and the vast silence of the wilderness beyond.

The second picture, also, was a view from a height, but of a totally different character. It was also, perhaps, more typical of a greater part of East Equatorial Africa. Four of us were hunting lions with natives-both wild and tame-and a scratch pack of dogs. More of that later. We had rummaged around all the morning without any results; and now at noon had climbed to the top of a butte to eat lunch and look abroad.

Our butte ran up a gentle but accelerating slope to a peak of big rounded rocks and slabs sticking out boldly from the soil of the hill. We made ourselves comfortable each after his fashion. The gunbearers leaned against rocks and rolled cigarettes. The savages squatted on their heels, planting their spears ceremonially in front of them. One of my friends lay on his back, resting a huge telescope over his crossed feet. With this he purposed seeing any lion that moved within ten miles. None of the rest of us could ever make out anything through the fearsome weapon. Therefore, relieved from responsibility by the presence of this Dreadnaught of a 'scope, we loafed and looked about us. This is what we saw:

Mountains at our backs, of course-at some distance; then plains in long low swells like the easy rise and fall of a tropical sea, wave after wave, and over the edge of the world beyond a distant horizon. Here and there on this plain, single hills lay becalmed, like ships at sea; some peaked, some cliffed like buttes, some long and low like the hulls of battleships. The brown plain flowed up to wash their bases, liquid as the sea itself, its tides rising in the coves of the hills, and ebbing in the valleys between. Near at hand, in the middle distance, far away, these fleets of the plain sailed, until at last hull-down over the horizon their topmasts disappeared. Above them sailed too the phantom fleet of the clouds, shot with light, shining like silver, airy as racing yachts, yet casting here and there exaggerated shadows below.

The sky in Africa is always very wide, greater than any other skies. Between horizon and horizon is more space than any other world contains. It is as though the cup of heaven had been pressed a little flatter; so that while the boundaries have widened, the zenith, with its flaming sun, has come nearer. And yet that is not a constant quantity either. I have seen one edge of the sky raised straight up a few million miles, as though some one had stuck poles under its corners, so that the western heaven did not curve cup-wise over to the horizon at all as it did everywhere else, but rather formed the proscenium of a gigantic stage. On this stage they had piled great heaps of saffron yellow clouds, and struck shafts of yellow light, and filled the spaces with the lurid portent of a storm-while the twenty thousand foot mountains below, crouched whipped and insignificant to the earth.

We sat atop our butte for an hour while H. looked through his 'scope. After the soft silent immensity of the earth, running away to infinity, with its low waves, and its scattered fleet of hills, it was with difficulty that we brought our gaze back to details and to things near at hand. Directly below us we could make out many different-hued specks. Looking closely, we could see that those specks were game animals. They fed here and there in bands of from ten to two hundred, with valleys and hills between. Within the radius of the eye they moved, nowhere crowded in big herds, but everywhere present. A band of zebras grazed the side of one of the earth waves, a group of gazelles walked on the skyline, a herd of kongoni rested in the hollow between. On the next rise was a similar grouping; across the valley a new variation. As far as the eye could strain its powers it could make out more and ever more beasts. I took up my field glasses, and brought them all to within a sixth of the distance. After amusing myself for some time in watching them, I swept the glasses farther on. Still the same animals grazing on the hills and in the hollows. I continued to look, and to look again, until even the powerful prismatic glasses failed to show things big enough to distinguish. At the limit of extreme vision I could still make out game, and yet more game. And as I took my glasses from my eyes, and realized how small a portion of this great land-sea I had been able to examine; as I looked away to the ship-hills hull-down over the horizon, and realized that over all that extent fed the Game; the ever-new wonder of Africa for the hundredth time filled my mind-the teeming fecundity of her bosom.

"Look here," said H. without removing his eye from the 'scope, "just beyond the edge of that shadow to the left of the bushes in the donga-I've been watching them ten minutes, and I can't make 'em out yet. They're either hyenas acting mighty queer, or else two lionesses."

We snatched our glasses and concentrated on that important detail.

To catch the third experience you must have journeyed with us across the "Thirst," as the natives picturesquely name the waterless tract of two days and a half. Our start had been delayed by a breakage of some Dutch-sounding essential to our ox wagon, caused by the confusion of a night attack by lions: almost every night we had lain awake as long as we could to enjoy the deep-breathed grumbling or the vibrating roars of these beasts. Now at last, having pushed through the dry country to the river in the great plain, we were able to take breath from our mad hurry, and to give our attention to affairs beyond the limits of mere expediency. One of these was getting Billy a shot at a lion.

Billy had never before wanted to shoot anything except a python. Why a python we could not quite fathom. Personally, I think she had some vague idea of getting even for that Garden of Eden affair. But lately, pythons proving scarcer than in that favoured locality, she had switched to a lion. She wanted, she said, to give the skin to her sister. In vain we pointed out that a zebra hide was very decorative, that lions go to absurd lengths in retaining possession of their own skins, and other equally convincing facts. It must be a lion or nothing; so naturally we had to make a try.

There are several ways of getting lions, only one of which is at all likely to afford a steady pot shot to a very small person trying to manipulate an over-size gun. That is to lay out a kill. The idea is to catch the lion at it in the early morning before he has departed for home. The best kill is a zebra: first, because lions like zebra; second, because zebra are fairly large; third, because zebra are very numerous.

Accordingly, after we had pitched camp just within a fringe of mimosa trees and of red-flowering aloes near the river; had eaten lunch, smoked a pipe and issued necessary orders to the men, C. and I set about the serious work of getting an appropriate bait in an appropriate place.

The plains stretched straight away from the river bank to some indefinite and unknown distance to the south. A low range of mountains lay blue to the left; and a mantle of scrub thornbush closed the view to the right. This did not imply that we could see far straight ahead, for the surface of the plain rose slowly to the top of a swell about two miles away. Beyond it reared a single butte peak at four or five times that distance.

We stepped from the fringe of red aloes and squinted through the dancing heat shimmer. Near the limit of vision showed a very faint glimmering whitish streak. A newcomer to Africa would not have looked at it twice: nevertheless, it could be nothing but zebra. These gaudily marked beasts take queer aspects even on an open plain. Most often they show pure white; sometimes a jet black; only when within a few hundred yards does one distinguish the stripes. Almost always they are very easily made out. Only when very distant and in heat shimmer, or in certain half lights of evening, does their so-called "protective colouration" seem to be in working order, and even then they are always quite visible to the least expert hunter's scrutiny.

It is not difficult to kill a zebra, though sometimes it has to be done at a fairly long range. If all you want is meat for the porters, the matter is simple enough. But when you require bait for a lion, that; is another affair entirely. In the first place, you must be able to stalk within a hundred yards of your kill without being seen; in the second place, you must provide two or three good lying-down places for your prospective trophy within fifteen yards of the carcass-and no more than two or three; in the third place, you must judge the direction of the probable morning wind, and must be able to approach from leeward. It is evidently pretty good luck to find an accommodating zebra in just such a spot. It is a matter of still greater nicety to drop him absolutely in his tracks. In a case of porters' meat it does not make any particular difference if he runs a hundred yards before he dies. With lion bait even fifty yards makes all the difference in the world.

C. and I talked it over and resolved to press Scallywattamus into service. Scallywattamus is a small white mule who is firmly convinced that each and every bush in Africa conceals a mule-eating rhinoceros, and who does not intend to be one of the number so eaten. But we had noticed that at times zebra would be so struck with the strange sight of Scallywattamus carrying a man, that they would let us get quite close. C. was to ride Scallywattamus while I trudged along under his lee ready to shoot.

We set out through the heat shimmer, gradually rising as the plain slanted. Imperceptibly the camp and the trees marking the river's course fell below us and into the heat haze. In the distance, close to the stream, we made out a blurred, brown-red solid mass which we knew for Masai cattle. Various little Thompson's gazelles skipped away to the left waggling their tails vigorously and continuously as Nature long since commanded "Tommies" to do. The heat haze steadied around the dim white line, so we could make out the individual animals. There were plenty of them, dozing in the sun. A single tiny treelet broke the plain just at the skyline of the rise. C. and I talked low-voiced as we went along. We agreed that the tree was an excellent landmark to come to, that the little rise afforded proper cover, and that in the morning the wind would in all likelihood blow toward the river. There were perhaps twenty zebra near enough to the chosen spot. Any of them would do.

But the zebra did not give a hoot for Scallywattamus. At five hundred yards three or four of them awoke with a start, stared at us a minute, and moved slowly away. They told all the zebra they happened upon that the three idiots approaching were at once uninteresting and dangerous. At four hundred and fifty yards a half dozen more made off at a trot. At three hundred and fifty yards the rest plunged away at a canter-all but one. He remained to stare, but his tail was up, and we knew he only stayed because he knew he could easily catch up in the next twenty seconds.

The chance was very slim of delivering a knockout at that distance, but we badly needed meat, anyway, after our march through the Thirst, so I tried him. We heard the well-known plunk of the bullet, but down went his head, up went his heels, and away went he. We watched him in vast disgust. He cavorted out into a bare open space without cover of any sort, and then flopped over. I thought I caught a fleeting grin of delight on Mavrouki's face; but he knew enough instantly to conceal his satisfaction over sure meat.

There were now no zebra anywhere near; but since nobody ever thinks of omitting any chances in Africa, I sneaked up to the tree and took a perfunctory look. There stood another, providentially absent-minded, zebra!

We got that one. Everybody was now happy. The boys raced over to the first kill, which soon took its dismembered way toward camp. C. and I carefully organized our plan of campaign. We fixed in our memories the exact location of each and every bush; we determined compass direction from camp, and any other bearings likely to prove useful in finding so small a spot in the dark. Then we left a boy to keep carrion birds off until sunset; and returned home.

We were out in the morning before even the first sign of dawn. Billy rode her little mule, C. and I went afoot, Memba Sasa accompanied us because he could see whole lions where even C.'s trained eye could not make out an ear, and the syce went along to take care of the mule. The heavens were ablaze with the thronging stars of the tropics, so we found we could make out the skyline of the distant butte over the rise of the plains. The earth itself was a pool of absolute blackness. We could not see where we were placing our feet, and we were continually bringing up suddenly to walk around an unexpected aloe or thornbush. The night was quite still, but every once in a while from the blackness came rustlings, scamperings, low calls, and once or twice the startled barking of zebra very near at hand. The latter sounded as ridiculous as ever. It is one of the many incongruities of African life that Nature should have given so large and so impressive a creature the petulant yapping of an exasperated Pomeranian lap dog. At the end of three quarters of an hour of more or less stumbling progress, we made out against the sky the twisted treelet that served as our landmark. Billy dismounted, turned the mule over to the syce, and we crept slowly forward until within a guessed two or three yards of our kill.

Nothing remained now but to wait for the daylight. It had already begun to show. Over behind the distant mountains some one was kindling the fires, and the stars were flickering out. The splendid ferocity of the African sunrise was at

443

hand. Long bands of slate dark clouds lay close along the horizon, and behind them glowed a heart of fire, as on a small scale the lamplight glows through a metal-worked shade. On either side the sky was pale green-blue, translucent and pure, deep as infinity itself. The earth was still black, and the top of the rise near at hand was clear edged. On that edge, and by a strange chance accurately in the centre of illumination, stood the uncouth massive form of a shaggy wildebeeste, his head raised, staring to the east. He did not move; nothing of that fire and black world moved; only instant by instant it changed, swelling in glory toward some climax until one expected at any moment a fanfare of trumpets, the burst of triumphant culmination.

Then very far down in the distance a lion roared. The wildebeeste, without moving, bellowed back an answer or a defiance. Down in the hollow an ostrich boomed. Zebra barked, and several birds chirped strongly. The tension was breaking not in the expected fanfare and burst of triumphal music, but in a manner instantly felt to be more fitting to what was indeed a wonder, but a daily wonder for all that. At one and the same instant the rim of the sun appeared and the wildebeeste, after the sudden habit of his kind, made up his mind to go. He dropped his head and came thundering down past us at full speed. Straight to the west he headed, and so disappeared. We could hear the beat of his hoofs dying into the distance. He had gone like a Warder of the Morning whose task was finished. On the knife-edged skyline appeared the silhouette of slim-legged little Tommies, flirting their rails, sniffing at the dewy grass, dainty, slender, confiding, the open-day antithesis of the tremendous and awesome lord of the darkness that had roared its way to its lair, and to the massive shaggy herald of morning that had thundered down to the west.

## III. THE CENTRAL PLATEAU

Now is required a special quality of the imagination, not in myself, but in my readers, for it becomes necessary for them to grasp the logic of a whole country in one mental effort. The difficulties to me are very real. If I am to tell you it all in detail, your mind becomes confused to the point of mingling the ingredients of the description. The resultant mental picture is a composite; it mixes localities wide apart; it comes out, like the snake-creeper-swamp-forest thing of grammar-school South America, an unreal and deceitful impression. If, on the other hand, I try to give you a bird's-eye view-saying, here is plain, and there follows upland, and yonder succeed mountains and hills-you lose the sense of breadth and space and the toil of many days. The feeling of onward outward extending distance is gone; and that impression so indispensable to finite understanding-"here am I, and what is beyond is to be measured by the length of my legs and the toil of my days." You will not stop long enough on my plains to realize their physical extent nor their influence on the human soul. If I mention them in a sentence, you dismiss them in a thought. And that is something the plains themselves refuse to permit you to do. Yet sometimes one must become a guide-book, and bespeak his reader's imagination.

The country, then, wherein we travelled begins at the sea. Along the coast stretches a low rolling country of steaming tropics, grown with cocoanuts, bananas, mangoes, and populated by a happy, half-naked race of the Swahilis. Leaving the coast, the country rises through hills. These hills are at first fertile and green and wooded. Later they turn into an almost unbroken plateau of thorn scrub, cruel, monotonous, almost impenetrable. Fix thorn scrub in your mind, with rhino trails, and occasional openings for game, and a few rivers flowing through palms and narrow jungle strips; fix it in your mind until your mind is filled with it, until you are convinced that nothing else can exist in the world but more and more of the monotonous, terrible, dry, onstretching desert of thorn.

Then pass through this to the top of the hills inland, and journey over these hills to the highland plains.

Now sense and appreciate these wide seas of and the hills and ranges of mountains rising from them, and their infinite diversity of country-their rivers marked by ribbons of jungle, their scattered-bush and their thick-bush areas, their grass expanses, and their great distances extending far over exceedingly wide horizons. Realize how many weary hours you must travel to gain the nearest butte, what days of toil the view from its top will disclose. Savour the fact that you can spend months in its veriest corner without exhausting its possibilities. Then, and not until then, raise your eyes to the low rising transverse range that bands it to the west as the thorn desert bands it to the east.

And on these ranges are the forests, the great bewildering forests. In what looks like a grove lying athwart a little hill you can lose yourself for days. Here dwell millions of savages in an apparently untouched wilderness. Here rises a snow mountain on the equator. Here are tangles and labyrinths, great bamboo forests lost in folds of the mightiest hills. Here are the elephants. Here are the swinging vines, the jungle itself.

Yet finally it breaks. We come out on the edge of things and look down on a great gash in the earth. It is like a sunken kingdom in itself, miles wide, with its own mountain ranges, its own rivers, its own landscape features. Only on either side of it rise the escarpments which are the true level of the plateau. One can spend two months in this valley, too, and in the countries south to which it leads. And on its farther side are the high plateau plains again, or the forests, or the desert, or the great lakes that lie at the source of the Nile.

So now, perhaps, we are a little prepared to go ahead. The guide-book work is finished for good and all. There is the steaming hot low coast belt, and the hot dry thorn desert belt, and the varied immense plains, and the high mountain belt of the forests, and again the variegated wide country of the Rift Valley and the high plateau. To attempt to tell you seriatim and in detail just what they are like is the task of an encyclopaedist. Perhaps more indirectly you may be able to fill in the picture of the country, the people, and the beasts.

# IV. THE FIRST CAMP

Our very first start into the new country was made when we piled out from the little train standing patiently awaiting the good pleasure of our descent. That feature strikes me with ever new wonder-the accommodating way trains of the Uganda Railway have of waiting for you. One day, at a little wayside station, C. and I were idly exchanging remarks with the only white man in sight, killing time until the engine should whistle to a resumption of the journey. The guard lingered about just out of earshot. At the end of five minutes C. happened to catch his eye, whereupon he ventured to approach.

"When you have finished your conversation," said he politely, "we are all ready to go on."

On the morning in question there were a lot of us to disembark-one hundred and twenty-two, to be exact-of which four were white. We were not yet acquainted with our men, nor yet with our stores, nor with the methods of our travel. The train went off and left us in the middle of a high plateau, with low ridges running across it, and mountains in the distance. Men were squabbling earnestly for the most convenient loads to carry, and as fast as they had gained undisputed possession, they marked the loads with some private sign of their own. M'ganga, the headman, tall, fierce, big-framed and bony, clad in fez, a long black overcoat, blue puttees and boots, stood stiff as a ramrod, extended a rigid right arm and rattled off orders in a high dynamic voice. In his left hand he clasped a bulgy umbrella, the badge of his dignity and the symbol of his authority. The four askaris, big men too, with masterful high-cheekboned countenances, rushed here and there seeing that the orders were carried out. Expostulations, laughter, the sound of quarrelling rose and fell. Never could the combined volume of it all override the firecracker stream of M'ganga's eloquence.

·We had nothing to do with it all, but stood a little dazed, staring at the novel scene. Our men were of many tribes, each with its own cast of features, its own notions of what befitted man's performance of his duties here below. They stuck together each in its clan. A fine free individualism of personal adornment characterized them. Every man dressed for his own satisfaction solely. They hung all sorts of things in the distended lobes of their ears. One had succeeded in inserting a fine big glittering tobacco tin. Others had invented elaborate topiary designs in their hair, shaving their heads so as to leave strange tufts, patches, crescents on the most unexpected places. Of the intricacy of these designs they seemed absurdly proud. Various sorts of treasure trove hung from them-a bunch of keys to which there were no locks, discarded hunting knives, tips of antelope horns, discharged brass cartridges, a hundred and one valueless trifles plucked proudly from the rubbish heap. They were all clothed. We had supplied each with a red blanket, a blue jersey, and a water bottle. The blankets they were twisting most ingeniously into turbans. Beside these they sported a great variety of garments. Shooting coats that had seen better days, a dozen shabby overcoats-worn proudly through the hottest noons-raggety breeches and trousers made by some London tailor, queer baggy homemades of the same persuasion, or quite simply the square of cotton cloth arranged somewhat like a short tight skirt, or nothing at all as the man's taste ran. They were many of them amusing enough; but somehow they did not look entirely farcical and ridiculous, like our negroes putting on airs. All these things were worn with a simplicity of quiet confidence in their entire fitness. And beneath the red blanket turbans the half-wild savage faces peered out.

Now Mahomet approached. Mahomet was my personal boy. He was a Somali from the Northwest coast, dusky brown, with the regular clear-cut features of a Greek marble god. His dress was of neat khaki, and he looked down on savages; but, also, as with all the dark-skinned races, up to his white master. Mahomet was with me during all my African stay, and tested out nobly. As yet, of course, I did not know him.

"Chakula taiari," said he.

That is Swahili. It means literally "food is ready." After one has hunted in Africa for a few months, it means also "paradise is opened," "grief is at an end," "joy and thanksgiving are now in order," and similar affairs. Those two words are never forgotten, and the veriest beginner in Swahili can recognize them without the slightest effort.

We followed Mahomet. Somehow, without orders, in all this confusion, the personal staff had been quietly and efficiently busy. Drawn a little to one side stood a table with four chairs. The table was covered with a white cloth, and was set with a beautiful white enamel service. We took our places. Behind each chair straight as a ramrod stood a neat khaki-clad boy. They brought us food, and presented it properly on the left side, waiting like well-trained butlers. We might have been in a London restaurant. As three of us were Americans, we felt a trifle dazed. The porters, having finished the distribution of their loads, squatted on their heels and watched us respectfully.

And then, not two hundred yards away, four ostriches paced slowly across the track, paying not the slightest attention to us-our first real wild ostriches, scornful of oranges, careless of tourists, and rightful guardians of their own snowy plumes. The passage of these four solemn birds seemed somehow to lend this strange open-air meal an exotic flavour. We were indeed in Africa; and the ostriches helped us to realize it.

We finished breakfast and arose from our chairs. Instantly a half dozen men sprang forward. Before our amazed eyes the table service, the chairs and the table itself disappeared into neat packages. M'ganga arose to his feet.

"Bandika!" he cried.

The askaris rushed here and there actively.

"Bandika! bandika! bandika!" they cried repeatedly.

The men sprang into activity. A struggle heaved the varicoloured multitude-and, lo! each man stood upright, his load balanced on his head. At the same moment the syces led up our horses, mounted and headed across the little plain whence had come the four ostriches. Our African journey had definitely begun.

Behind us, all abreast marched the four gunbearers; then the four syces; then the safari single file, an askari at the head bearing proudly his ancient musket and our banner, other askaris flanking, M'ganga bringing up the rear with his mighty umbrella and an unsuspected rhinoceros-hide whip. The tent boys and the cook scattered along the flank anywhere, as befitted the free and independent who had nothing to do with the serious business of marching. A measured sound of drumming followed the beating of loads with a hundred sticks; a wild, weird chanting burst from the ranks and died down again as one or another individual or group felt moved to song. One lot had a formal chant and response. Their leader, in a high falsetto, said something like,

"Kuna koma kuno,"

and all his tribesmen would follow with a single word in a deep gruff tone,

"Za-la-nee!"

All of which undoubtedly helped immensely.

The country was a bully country, but somehow it did not look like Africa. That is to say, it looked altogether too much like any amount of country at home. There was nothing strange and exotic about it. We crossed a little plain, and up over a small hill, down into a shallow canyon that seemed to be wooded with live oaks, across a grass valley or so, and around a grass hill. Then we went into camp at the edge of another grass valley, by a stream across which rose some ordinary low cliffs.

That is the disconcerting thing about a whole lot of this country-it is so much like home. Of course, there are many wide districts exotic enough in all conscience-the jungle beds of the rivers, the bamboo forests, the great tangled forests themselves, the banana groves down the aisles of which dance savages with shields-but so very much of it is familiar. One needs only church spires and a red-roofed village or so to imagine one's self in Surrey. There is any amount of country like Arizona, and more like the uplands of Wyoming, and a lot of it resembling the smaller landscapes of New England. The prospects of the whole world are there, so that somewhere every wanderer can find the countryside of his own home repeated. And, by the same token, that is exactly what makes a good deal of it so startling. When a man sees a file of spear-armed savages, or a pair of snorty old rhinos, step out into what has seemed practically his own back yard home, he is even more startled than if he had encountered them in quite strange surroundings.

We rode into the grass meadow and picked camp site. The men trailed in and dumped down their loads in a row.

At a signal they set to work. A dozen to each tent got them up in a jiffy. A long file brought firewood from the stream bed. Others carried water, stones for the cook, a dozen other matters. The tent boys rescued our boxes; they put together the cots and made the beds, even before the tents were raised from the ground. Within an incredibly short space of time the three green tents were up and arranged, each with its bed made, its mosquito bar hung, its personal box open, its folding washstand ready with towels and soap, the table and chairs unlimbered. At a discreet distance flickered the cook campfire, and at a still discreeter distance the little tents of the men gleamed pure white against the green of the high grass.

### V. MEMBA SASA

I wish I could plunge you at once into the excitements of big game in Africa, but I cannot truthfully do so. To be sure, we went hunting that afternoon, up over the low cliffs, and we saw several of a very lively little animal known as the Chandler's reedbuck. This was not supposed to be a game country, and that was all we did see. At these we shot several times-disgracefully. In fact, for several days we could not shoot at all, at any range, nor at anything. It was very sad, and very aggravating. Afterward we found that this is an invariable experience to the newcomer. The light is new, the air is different, the sizes of the game are deceiving. Nobody can at first hit anything. At the end of five days we suddenly began to shoot our normal gait. Why, I do not know.

But in this afternoon tramp around the low cliffs after the elusive reedbuck, I for the first time became acquainted with a man who developed into a real friend.

His name is Memba Sasa. Memba Sasa are two Swahili words meaning "now a crocodile." Subsequently, after I had learned to talk Swahili, I tried to find out what he was formerly, before he was a crocodile, but did not succeed.

He was of the tribe of the Monumwezi, of medium height, compactly and sturdily built, carried himself very erect, and moved with a concentrated and vigorous purposefulness. His countenance might be described as pleasing but not handsome, of a dark chocolate brown, with the broad nose of the negro, but with a firm mouth, high cheekbones, and a frowning intentness of brow that was very fine. When you talked to him he looked you straight in the eye. His own eyes were shaded by long, soft, curling lashes behind which they looked steadily and gravely-sometimes fiercely-on the world. He rarely smiled-never merely in understanding or for politeness' sake-and never laughed unless there was something really amusing. Then he chuckled from deep in his chest, the most contagious laughter you can imagine. Often we, at the other end of the camp, have laughed in sympathy, just at the sound of that deep and hearty ho! ho! ho! of Memba Sasa. Even at something genuinely amusing he never laughed much, nor without a very definite restraint. In fact, about him was no slackness, no sprawling abandon of the native in relaxation; but always a taut efficiency and a never-failing self-respect.

Naturally, behind such a fixed moral fibre must always be some moral idea. When a man lives up to a real, not a pompous, dignity some ideal must inform it. Memba Sasa's ideal was that of the Hunter.

He was a gunbearer; and he considered that a good gunbearer stood quite a few notches above any other human being, save always the white man, of course. And even among the latter Memba Sasa made great differences. These differences he kept to himself, and treated all with equal respect. Nevertheless, they existed, and Memba Sasa very well knew that fact. In the white world were two classes of masters: those who hunted well, and those who were considered by them as their friends and equals. Why they should be so considered Memba Sasa did not know, but he trusted the Hunter's judgment. These were the bwanas, or masters. All the rest were merely mazungos, or, "white men." To their faces he called them bwana, but in his heart he considered them not.

**446**

Observe, I say those who hunted well. Memba Sasa, in his profession as gunbearer, had to accompany those who hunted badly. In them he took no pride; from them he held aloof in spirit; but for them he did his conscientious best, upheld by the dignity of his profession.

For to Mamba Sasa that profession was the proudest to which a black man could aspire. He prided himself on mastering its every detail, in accomplishing its every duty minutely and exactly. The major virtues of a gunbearer are not to be despised by anybody; for they comprise great physical courage, endurance, and loyalty: the accomplishments of a gunbearer are worthy of a man's best faculties, for they include the ability to see and track game, to take and prepare properly any sort of a trophy, field taxidermy, butchering game meat, wood and plainscraft, the knowledge of how properly to care for firearms in all sorts of circumstances, and a half hundred other like minutiae. Memba Sasa knew these things, and he performed them with the artist's love for details; and his keen eyes were always spying for new ways.

At a certain time I shot an egret, and prepared to take the skin. Memba Sasa asked if he might watch me do it. Two months later, having killed a really gaudy peacocklike member of the guinea fowl tribe, I handed it over to him with instructions to take off the breast feathers before giving it to the cook. In a half hour he brought me the complete skin, I examined it carefully, and found it to be well done in every respect. Now in skinning a bird there are a number of delicate and unusual operations, such as stripping the primary quills from the bone, cutting the ear cover, and the like. I had explained none of them; and yet Memba Sasa, unassisted, had grasped their method from a single demonstration and had remembered them all two months later! C. had a trick in making the second skin incision of a trophy head that had the effect of giving a better purchase to the knife. Its exact description would be out of place here, but it actually consisted merely in inserting the point of the knife two inches away from the place it is ordinarily inserted. One day we noticed that Memba Sasa was making his incisions in that manner. I went to Africa fully determined to care for my own rifle. The modern high-velocity gun needs rather especial treatment; mere wiping out will not do. I found that Memba Sasa already knew all about boiling water, and the necessity for having it really boiling, about subsequent metal sweating, and all the rest. After watching him at work I concluded, rightly, that he would do a lot better job than I.

To the new employer Memba Sasa maintained an attitude of strict professional loyalty. His personal respect was upheld by the necessity of every man to do his job in the world. Memba Sasa did his. He cleaned the rifles; he saw that everything was in order for the day's march; he was at my elbow all ways with more cartridges and the spare rifle; he trailed and looked conscientiously. In his attitude was the stolidity of the wooden Indian. No action of mine, no joke on the part of his companions, no circumstance in the varying fortunes of the field gained from him the faintest flicker of either approval, disapproval, or interest. When we returned to camp he deposited my water bottle and camera, seized the cleaning implements, and departed to his own campfire. In the field he pointed out game that I did not see, and waited imperturbably the result of my shot.

As I before stated, the result of that shot for the first five days was very apt to be nil. This, at the time, puzzled and grieved me a lot. Occasionally I looked at Memba Sasa to catch some sign of sympathy, disgust, contempt, or-rarely-triumph at a lucky shot. Nothing. He gently but firmly took away my rifle, reloaded it, and handed it back; then waited respectfully for my next move. He knew no English, and I no Swahili.

But as time went on this attitude changed. I was armed with the new Springfield rifle, a weapon with 2,700 feet velocity, and with a marvellously flat trajectory. This commanding advantage, combined with a very long familiarity with firearms, enabled me to do some fairish shooting, after the strangeness of these new conditions had been mastered. Memba Sasa began to take a dawning interest in me as a possible source of pride. We began to develop between us a means of communication. I set myself deliberately to learn his language, and after he had cautiously determined that I really meant it, he took the greatest pains-always gravely-to teach me. A more human feeling sprang up between us.

But we had still the final test to undergo-that of danger and the tight corner.

In close quarters the gunbearer has the hardest job in the world. I have the most profound respect for his absolute courage. Even to a man armed and privileged to shoot and defend himself, a charging lion is an awesome thing, requiring a certain amount of coolness and resolution to face effectively. Think of the gunbearer at his elbow, depending not on himself but on the courage and coolness of another. He cannot do one solitary thing to defend himself. To bolt for the safety of a tree is to beg the question completely, to brand himself as a shenzi forever; to fire a gun in any circumstances is to beg the question also, for the white man must be able to depend absolutely on his second gun in an emergency. Those things are outside consideration, even, of any respectable gunbearer. In addition, he must keep cool. He must see clearly in the thickest excitement; must be ready unobtrusively to pass up the second gun in the position most convenient for immediate use, to seize the other and to perform the finicky task of reloading correctly while some rampageous beast is raising particular thunder a few yards away. All this in absolute dependence on the ability of his bwana to deal with the situation. I can confess very truly that once or twice that little unobtrusive touch of Memba Sasa crouched close to my elbow steadied me with the thought of how little right I-with a rifle in my hand-had to be scared. And the best compliment I ever received I overheard by chance. I had wounded a lion when out by myself, and had returned to camp for a heavier rifle and for Memba Sasa to do the trailing. From my tent I overheard the following conversation between Memba Sasa and the cook:

"The grass is high," said the cook. "Are you not afraid to go after a wounded lion with only one white man?"

"My one white man is enough," replied Memba Sasa.

It is a quality of courage that I must confess would be quite beyond me-to depend entirely on the other fellow, and not at all on myself. This courage is always remarkable to me, even in the case of the gunbearer who knows all about the man whose heels he follows. But consider that of the gunbearer's first experience with a stranger. The former has no idea of how the white man will act; whether he will get nervous, get actually panicky, lose his shooting ability, and generally mess things up. Nevertheless, he follows his master in, and he stands by. If the hunter fails, the gunbearer will probably die. To me it is rather fine: for he does it, not from the personal affection and loyalty which will carry men far, but from a sheer sense of duty and pride of caste. The quiet pride of the really good men, like Memba Sasa, is easy to understand.

And the records are full of stories of the white man who has not made good: of the coward who bolts, leaving his black man to take the brunt of it, or who sticks but loses his head. Each new employer must be very closely and interestedly scrutinized. In the light of subsequent experience, I can no longer wonder at Memba Sasa's first detached and impersonal attitude.

As time went on, however, and we grew to know each other better, this attitude entirely changed. At first the change consisted merely in dropping the disinterested pose as respects game. For it was a pose. Memba Sasa was most keenly interested in game whenever it was an object of pursuit. It did not matter how common the particular species might be: if we wanted it, Memba Sasa would look upon it with eager ferocity; and if we did not want it, he paid no attention to it at all. When we started in the morning, or in the relaxation of our return at night, I would mention casually a few of the things that might prove acceptable.

"To-morrow we want kongoni for boys' meat, or zebra; and some meat for masters-Tommy, impala, oribi," and Memba Sasa knew as well as I did what we needed to fill out our trophy collection. When he caught sight of one of these animals his whole countenance changed. The lines of his face set, his lips drew back from his teeth, his eyes fairly darted fire in the fixity of their gaze. He was like a fine pointer dog on birds, or like the splendid savage he was at heart.

"M'palla!" he hissed; and then after a second, in a restrained fierce voice, "Na-ona? Do you see?"

If I did not see he pointed cautiously. His own eyes never left the beast. Rarely he stayed put while I made the stalk. More often he glided like a snake at my heels. If the bullet hit, Memba Sasa always exhaled a grunt of satisfaction-"hah!"-in which triumph and satisfaction mingled with a faint derision at the unfortunate beast. In case of a trophy he squatted anxiously at the animal's head while I took my measurements, assisting very intelligently with the tape line. When I had finished, he always looked up at me with wrinkled brow.

"Footie n'gapi?" he inquired. This means literally, "How many feet?", footie being his euphemistic invention of a word for the tape. I would tell him how many "footie" and how many "inchie" the measurement proved to be. From the depths of his wonderful memory he would dig up the measurements of another beast of the same sort I had killed months back, but which he had remembered accurately from a single hearing.

The shooting of a beast he always detailed to his few cronies in camp: the other gunbearers, and one or two from his own tribe. He always used the first person plural, "we" did so and so; and took an inordinate pride in making out his bwana as being an altogether superior person to any of the other gunbearer's bwanas. Over a miss he always looked sad; but with a dignified sadness as though we had met with undeserved misfortune sent by malignant gods. If there were any possible alleviating explanation, Memba Sasa made the most of it, provided our fiasco was witnessed. If we were alone in our disgrace, he buried the incident fathoms deep. He took an inordinate pride in our using the minimum number of cartridges, and would explain to me in a loud tone of voice that we had cartridges enough in the belt. When we had not cartridges enough, he would sneak around after dark to get some more. At times he would even surreptitiously "lift" a few from B.'s gunbearer!

When in camp, with his "cazi" finished, Memba Sasa did fancy work! The picture of this powerful half-savage, his fierce brows bent over a tiny piece of linen, his strong fingers fussing with little stitches, will always appeal to my sense of the incongruous. Through a piece of linen he punched holes with a porcupine quill. Then he "buttonhole" stitched the holes, and embroidered patterns between them with fine white thread. The result was an openwork pattern heavily encrusted with beautiful fine embroidery. It was most astounding stuff, such as you would expect from a French convent, perhaps, but never from an African savage. He did a circular piece and a long narrow piece. They took him three months to finish, and then he sewed them together to form a skull cap. Billy, entranced with the lacelike delicacy of the work, promptly captured it; whereupon Memba Sasa philosophically started another.

By this time he had identified himself with my fortunes. We had become a firm whose business it was to carry out the affairs of a single personality-me. Memba Sasa, among other things, undertook the dignity. When I walked through a crowd, Memba Sasa zealously kicked everybody out of my royal path. When I started to issue a command, Memba Sasa finished it and amplified it and put a snapper on it. When I came into camp, Memba Sasa saw to it personally that my tent went up promptly and properly, although that was really not part of his "cazi" at all. And when somewhere beyond my ken some miserable boy had committed a crime, I never remained long in ignorance of that fact.

Perhaps I happened to be sitting in my folding chair idly smoking a pipe and reading a book. Across the open places of the camp would stride Memba Sasa, very erect, very rigid, moving in short indignant jerks, his eye flashing fire. Behind him would sneak a very hang-dog boy. Memba Sasa marched straight up to me, faced right, and drew one side, his silence sparkling with honest indignation.

"Just look at THAT!" his attitude seemed to say, "Could you believe such human depravity possible? And against OUR authority?"

He always stood, quite rigid, waiting for me to speak.

"Well, Memba Sasa?" I would inquire, after I had enjoyed the show a little.

In a few restrained words he put the case before me, always briefly, always with a scornful dignity. This shenzi has done so-and-so.

We will suppose the case fairly serious. I listened to the man's story, if necessary called a few witnesses, delivered judgment. All the while Memba Sasa stood at rigid attention, fairly bristling virtue, like the good dog standing by at the punishment of the bad dogs. And in his attitude was a subtle triumph, as one would say: "You see! Fool with my bwana, will you! Just let anybody try to get funny with US!" Judgment pronounced-we have supposed the case serious, you remember-Memba Sasa himself applied the lash. I think he really enjoyed that; but it was a restrained joy. The whip descended deliberately, without excitement.

The man's devotion in unusual circumstances was beyond praise. Danger or excitement incite a sort of loyalty in any good man; but humdrum, disagreeable difficulty is a different matter.

One day we marched over a country of thorn-scrub desert. Since two days we had been cut loose from water, and had been depending on a small amount carried in zinc drums. Now our only reasons for faring were a conical hill, over the horizon, and the knowledge of a river somewhere beyond. How far beyond, or in what direction, we did not know. We had thirty men with us, a more or less ragtag lot, picked up anyhow in the bazaars. They were soft, ill-disciplined and uncertain. For five or six hours they marched well enough. Then the sun began to get very hot, and some of them began to straggle. They had, of course, no intention of deserting, for their only hope of surviving lay in staying with us; but their loads had become heavy, and they took too many rests. We put a good man behind, but without much avail. In open country a safari can be permitted to straggle over miles, for always it can keep in touch by sight; but in this thorn-scrub desert, that looks all alike, a man fifty yards out of sight is fifty yards lost. We would march fifteen or twenty minutes, then sit down to wait until the rearmost men had straggled in, perhaps a half hour later. And we did not dare move on until the tale of our thirty was complete. At this rate progress was very slow, and as the fierce equatorial sun increased in strength, became always slower still. The situation became alarming. We were quite out of water, and we had no idea where water was to be found. To complicate matters, the thornbrush thickened to a jungle.

My single companion and I consulted. It was agreed that I was to push on as rapidly as possible to locate the water, while he was to try to hold the caravan together. Accordingly, Memba Sasa and I marched ahead. We tried to leave a trail to follow; and we hoped fervently that our guess as to the stream's course would prove to be a good one. At the end of two hours and a half we found the water-a beautiful jungle-shaded stream-and filled ourselves up therewith. Our duty was accomplished, for we had left a trail to be followed. Nevertheless, I felt I should like to take back our full canteens to relieve the worst cases. Memba Sasa would not hear of it, and even while I was talking to him seized the canteens and disappeared.

At the end of two hours more camp was made, after a fashion; but still four men had failed to come in. We built a smudge in the hope of guiding them; and gave them up. If they had followed our trail, they should have been in long ago; if they had missed that trail, heaven knows where they were, or where we should go to find them. Dusk was falling, and, to tell the truth, we were both very much done up by a long day at 115 degrees in the shade under an equatorial sun. The missing men would climb trees away from the beasts, and we would organize a search next day. As we debated these things, to us came Memba Sasa.

"I want to take 'Winchi,'" said he. "Winchi" is his name for my Winchester 405.

"Why?" we asked.

"If I can take Winchi, I will find the men," said he.

This was entirely voluntary on his part. He, as well as we, had had a hard day, and he had made a double journey for part of it. We gave him Winchi and he departed. Sometime after midnight he returned with the missing men.

Perhaps a dozen times all told he volunteered for these special services; once in particular, after a fourteen-hour day, he set off at nine o'clock at night in a soaking rainstorm, wandered until two o'clock, and returned unsuccessful, to rouse me and report gravely that he could not find them. For these services he neither received nor expected special reward. And catch him doing anything outside his strict "cazi" except for US.

We were always very ceremonious and dignified in our relations on such occasions. Memba Sasa would suddenly appear, deposit the rifle in its place, and stand at attention.

"Well, Memba Sasa?" I would inquire.

"I have found the men; they are in camp."

Then I would give him his reward. It was either the word "assanti," or the two words "assanti sana," according to the difficulty and importance of the task accomplished. They mean simply "thank you" and "thank you very much."

Once or twice, after a particularly long and difficult month or so, when Memba Sasa has been almost literally my alter ego, I have called him up for special praise. "I am very pleased with you, Memba Sasa," said I. "You have done your cazi well. You are a good man."

He accepted this with dignity, without deprecation, and without the idiocy of spoken gratitude. He agreed perfectly with everything I said! "Yes" was his only comment. I liked it.

On our ultimate success in a difficult enterprise Memba Sasa set great store; and his delight in ultimate success was apparently quite apart from personal considerations. We had been hunting greater kudu for five weeks before we finally landed one. The greater kudu is, with the bongo, easily the prize beast in East Africa, and very few are shot. By a piece of bad luck, for him, I had sent Memba Sasa out in a different direction to look for signs the afternoon we finally got one. The kill was made just at dusk. C. and I, with Mavrouki, built a fire and stayed, while Kongoni went to camp after men. There he broke the news to Memba Sasa that the great prize had been captured, and he absent. Memba Sasa was hugely delighted, nor did he in any way show what must have been a great disappointment to him. After repeating the news triumphantly to every one in camp, he came out to where we were waiting, arrived quite out of breath, and grabbed me by the hand in heartiest congratulation.

Memba Sasa went in not at all for personal ornamentation, any more than he allowed his dignity to be broken by anything resembling emotionalism. No tattoo marks, no ear ornaments, no rings nor bracelets. He never even picked up an ostrich feather for his head. On the latter he sometimes wore an old felt hat; sometimes, more picturesquely, an orange-coloured fillet. Khaki shirt, khaki "shorts," blue puttees, besides his knife and my own accoutrements: that was all. In town he was all white clad, a long fine linen robe reaching to his feet; and one of the lacelike skull caps he was so very skilful at making.

That will do for a preliminary sketch. If you follow these pages, you will hear more of him; he is worth it.

## VI. THE FIRST GAME CAMP

In the review of "first" impressions with which we are concerned, we must now skip a week or ten days to stop at what is known in our diaries as the First Ford of the Guaso Nyero River.

These ten days were not uneventful. We had crossed the wide and undulating plains, had paused at some tall beautiful falls plunging several hundred feet into the mysteriousness of a dense forest on which we looked down. There we had enjoyed some duck, goose and snipe shooting; had made the acquaintance of a few of the Masai, and had looked with awe on our first hippo tracks in the mud beside a tiny ditchlike stream. Here and there were small game herds. In the light of later experience we now realize that these were nothing at all; but at the time the sight of full-grown wild animals out in plain sight was quite wonderful. At the close of the day's march we always wandered out with our rifles to see what we could find. Everything was new to us, and we had our men to feed. Our shooting gradually improved until we had overcome the difficulties peculiar to this new country and were doing as well as we could do anywhere.

Now, at the end of a hard day through scrub, over rolling bold hills, and down a scrub brush slope, we had reached the banks of the Guaso Nyero.

At this point, above the junction of its principal tributary rivers, it was a stream about sixty or seventy feet wide, flowing swift between high banks. A few trees marked its course, but nothing like a jungle. The ford was in swift water just above a deep still pool suspected of crocodiles. We found the water about waist deep, stretched a rope across, and forcibly persuaded our eager boys that one at a time was about what the situation required. On the other side we made camp on an open flat. Having marched so far continuously, we resolved to settle down for a while. The men had been without sufficient meat; and we desired very much to look over the country closely, and to collect a few heads as trophies.

Perhaps a word might not come amiss as to the killing of game. The case is here quite different from the condition of affairs at home. Here animal life is most extraordinarily abundant; it furnishes the main food supply to the traveller; and at present is probably increasing slightly, certainly holding its own. Whatever toll the sportsman or traveller take is as nothing compared to what he might take if he were an unscrupulous game hog. If his cartridges and his shoulder held out, he could easily kill a hundred animals a day instead of the few he requires. In that sense, then, no man slaughters indiscriminately. During the course of a year he probably shoots from two hundred to two hundred and fifty beasts, provided he is travelling with an ordinary sized caravan. This, the experts say, is about the annual toll of one lion. If the traveller gets his lion, he plays even with the fauna of the country; if he gets two or more lions, he has something to his credit. This probably explains why the game is still so remarkably abundant near the road and on the very outskirts of the town.

We were now much in need of a fair quantity of meat, both for immediate consumption of our safari, and to make biltong or jerky. Later, in like circumstances, we should have sallied forth in a businesslike fashion, dropped the requisite number of zebra and hartebeeste as near camp as possible, and called it a job. Now, however, being new to the game, we much desired good trophies in variety. Therefore, we scoured the country far and wide for desirable heads; and the meat waited upon the acquisition of the trophy.

This, then, might be called our first Shooting Camp. Heretofore we had travelled every day. Now the boys settled down to what the native porter considers the height of bliss: a permanent camp with plenty to eat. Each morning we were off before daylight, riding our horses, and followed by the gunbearers, the syces, and fifteen or twenty porters. The country rose from the river in a long gentle slope grown with low brush and scattered candlestick euphorbias. This slope ended in a scattered range of low rocky buttes. Through any one of the various openings between them, we rode to find ourselves on the borders of an undulating grass country of low rounded hills with wide valleys winding between them. In these valleys and on these hills was the game.

Daylight of the day I would tell about found us just at the edge of the little buttes. Down one of the slopes the growing half light revealed two oryx feeding, magnificent big creatures, with straight rapier horns three feet in length. These were most exciting and desirable, so off my horse I got and began to sneak up on them through the low tufts of grass. They fed quite calmly. I congratulated myself, and slipped nearer. Without even looking in my direction, they trotted away. Somewhat chagrined, I returned to my companions, and we rode on.

Then across a mile-wide valley we saw two dark objects in the tall grass; and almost immediately identified these as rhinoceroses, the first we had seen. They stood there side by side, gazing off into space, doing nothing in a busy morning world. After staring at them through our glasses for some time, we organized a raid. At the bottom of the valley we left the horses and porters; lined up, each with his gunbearer at his elbow; and advanced on the enemy. B. was to have the shot According to all the books we should have been able, provided we were downwind and made no noise, to have approached within fifty or sixty yards undiscovered. However, at a little over a hundred yards they both turned tail and departed at a swift trot, their heads held well up and their tails sticking up straight and stiff in the most ridiculous fashion. No good shooting at them in such circumstances, so we watched them go, still keeping up their slashing trot, growing smaller and smaller in the distance until finally they disappeared over the top of a swell.

We set ourselves methodically to following them. It took us over an hour of steady plodding before we again came in sight of them. They were this time nearer the top of a hill, and we saw instantly that the curve of the slope was such that we could approach within fifty yards before coming in sight at all. Therefore, once more we dismounted, lined up in battle array, and advanced.

Sensations? Distinctly nervous, decidedly alert, and somewhat self-congratulatory that I was not more scared. No man can predicate how efficient he is going to be in the presence of really dangerous game. Only the actual trial will show. This is not a question of courage at all, but of purely involuntary reaction of the nerves. Very few men are physical cowards. They will and do face anything. But a great many men are rendered inefficient by the way their nervous systems act under stress. It is not a matter for control by will power in the slightest degree. So the big game hunter must determine by actual trial whether it so happens that the great excitement of danger renders his hand shaky or steady. The excitement in either case is the same. No man is ever "cool" in the sense that personal danger is of the same kind of indifference to him as clambering aboard a street car. He must always be lifted above himself, must enter an extra normal condition to meet extra normal circumstances. He can always control his conduct; but he can by no means always determine the way the inevitable excitement will affect his coordinations. And unfortunately, in the final result it does not matter how brave a man is, but how closely he can hold. If he finds that his nervous excitement renders him unsteady, he has no business ever to tackle dangerous game alone. If, on the other hand, he discovers that IDENTICALLY THE SAME nervous excitement happens to steady his front sight to rocklike rigidity-a rigidity he could not possibly attain in normal conditions-then he will probably keep out of trouble.

To amplify this further by a specific instance: I hunted for a short time in Africa with a man who was always eager for exciting encounters, whose pluck was admirable in every way, but whose nervous reaction so manifested itself that he was utterly unable to do even decent shooting at any range. Furthermore, his very judgment and power of observation were so obscured that he could not remember afterward with any accuracy what had happened-which way the beast was pointing, how many there were of them, in which direction they went, how many shots were fired, in short all the smaller details of the affair. He thought he remembered. After the show was over it was quite amusing to get his version of the incident. It was almost always so wide of the fact as to be little recognizable. And, mind you, he was perfectly sincere in his belief, and absolutely courageous. Only he was quite unfitted by physical make-up for a big game hunter; and I was relieved when, after a short time, his route and mine separated.

Well, we clambered up that slope with a fine compound of tension, expectation, and latent uneasiness as to just what was going to happen, anyway. Finally, we raised the backs of the beasts, stooped, sneaked a little nearer, and finally at a signal stood upright perhaps forty yards from the brutes.

For the first time I experienced a sensation I was destined many times to repeat-that of the sheer size of the animals. Menagerie rhinoceroses had been of the smaller Indian variety; and in any case most menagerie beasts are more or less stunted. These two, facing us, their little eyes blinking, looked like full-grown ironclads on dry land. The moment we stood erect B. fired at the larger of the two. Instantly they turned and were off at a tearing run. I opened fire, and B. let loose his second barrel. At about two hundred and fifty yards the big rhinoceros suddenly fell on his side, while the other continued his flight. It was all over-very exciting because we got excited, but not in the least dangerous.

The boys were delighted, for here was meat in plenty for everybody. We measured the beast, photographed him, marvelled at his immense size, and turned him over to the gunbearers for treatment. In half an hour or so a long string of porters headed across the hills in the direction of camp, many miles distant, each carrying his load either of meat, or the trophies. Rhinoceros hide, properly treated, becomes as transparent as amber, and so from it can be made many very beautiful souvenirs, such as bowls, trays, paper knives, table tops, whips, canes, and the like. And, of course, the feet of one's first rhino are always saved for cigar boxes or inkstands.

Already we had an admiring and impatient audience. From all directions came the carrion birds. They circled far up in the heavens; they shot downward like plummets from a great height with an inspiring roar of wings; they stood thick in a solemn circle all around the scene of the kill; they rose with a heavy flapping when we moved in their direction. Skulking forms flashed in the grass, and occasionally the pointed ears of a jackal would rise inquiringly.

It was by now nearly noon. The sun shone clear and hot; the heat shimmer rose in clouds from the brown surface of the hills. In all directions we could make out small gameherds resting motionless in the heat of the day, the mirage throwing them into fantastic shapes. While the final disposition was being made of the defunct rhinoceros I wandered over the edge of the hill to see what I could see, and fairly blundered on a herd of oryx at about a hundred and fifty yards range. They looked at me a startled instant, then leaped away to the left at a tremendous speed. By a lucky shot, I bowled one over. He was a beautiful beast, with his black and white face and his straight rapierlike horns nearly three feet long, and I was most pleased to get him. Memba Sasa came running at the sound of the shot. We set about preparing the head.

Then through a gap in the hills far to the left we saw a little black speck moving rapidly in our direction. At the end of a minute we could make it out as the second rhinoceros. He had run heaven knows how many miles away, and now he was returning; whether with some idea of rejoining his companion or from sheer chance, I do not know. At any rate, here he was, still ploughing along at his swinging trot. His course led him along a side hill about four hundred yards from where the oryx lay. When he was directly opposite I took the Springfield and fired, not at him, but at a spot five or six feet in front of his nose. The bullet threw up a column of dust. Rhino brought up short with astonishment, wheeled to the left, and made off at a gallop. I dropped another bullet in front of him. Again he stopped, changed direction, and made off. For the third time I hit the ground in front of him. Then he got angry, put his head down and charged the spot.

Five more shots I expended on the amusement of that rhinoceros; and at the last had run furiously charging back and forth in a twenty-yard space, very angry at the little puffing, screeching bullets, but quite unable to catch one. Then he made up his mind and departed the way he had come, finally disappearing as a little rapidly moving black speck through the gap in the hills where we had first caught sight of him.

We finished caring for the oryx, and returned to camp. To our surprise we found we were at least seven or eight miles out.

In this fashion days passed very quickly. The early dewy start in the cool of the morning, the gradual grateful warming up of sunrise, and immediately after, the rest during the midday heats under a shady tree, the long trek back to camp at sunset, the hot bath after the toilsome day-all these were very pleasant. Then the swift falling night, and the gleam of many tiny fires springing up out of the darkness; with each its sticks full of meat roasting, and its little circle of men, their skins gleaming in the light. As we sat smoking, we would become aware that M'ganga, the headman, was standing silent awaiting orders. Some one would happen to see the white of his eyes, or perhaps he might smile so that his teeth would become visible. Otherwise he might stand there an hour, and no one the wiser, for he was respectfully silent, and exactly the colour of the night.

We would indicate to him our plans for the morrow, and he would disappear. Then at a distance of twenty or thirty feet from the front of our tents a tiny tongue of flame would lick up. Dark figures could be seen manipulating wood. A blazing fire sprang up, against which we could see the motionless and picturesque figure of Saa-sita (Six o'Clock), the askari of the first night watch, leaning on his musket. He was a most picturesque figure, for his fancy ran to original headdresses, and at the moment he affected a wonderful upstanding structure made of marabout wings.

At this sign that the night had begun, we turned in. A few hyenas moaned, a few jackals barked: otherwise the first part of the night was silent, for the hunters were at their silent business, and the hunted were "layin' low and sayin' nuffin'."

Day after day we rode out, exploring the country in different directions. The great uncertainty as to what of interest we would find filled the hours with charm. Sometimes we clambered about the cliffs of the buttes trying to find klipspringers; again we ran miles pursuing the gigantic eland. I in turn got my first rhinoceros, with no more danger than had attended the killing of B.'s. On this occasion, however, I had my first experience of the lightning skill of the first-class gunbearer. Having fired both barrels, and staggered the beast, I threw open the breech and withdrew the empty cartridges, intending, of course, as my next move to fish two more out of my belt. The empty shells were hardly away from the chambers, however, when a long brown arm shot over my right shoulder and popped two fresh cartridges in the breech. So astonished was I at this unexpected apparition, that for a second or so I actually forgot to close the gun.

### VII. ON THE MARCH

After leaving the First Game Camp, we travelled many hours and miles over rolling hills piling ever higher and higher until they broke through a pass to illimitable plains. These plains were mantled with the dense scrub, looking from a distance and from above like the nap of soft green velvet. Here and there this scrub broke in round or oval patches of grass plain. Great mountain ranges peered over the edge of a horizon. Lesser mountain peaks of fantastic shapes-sheer Yosemite cliffs, single buttes, castles-had ventured singly from behind that same horizon barricade. The course of a river was marked by a meandering line of green jungle.

It took us two days to get to that river. Our intermediate camp was halfway down the pass. We ousted a hundred indignant straw-coloured monkeys and twice as many baboons from the tiny flat above the water hole. They bobbed away cursing over their shoulders at us. Next day we debouched on the plains. They were rolling, densely grown, covered with volcanic stones, swarming with game of various sorts. The men marched well. They were happy, for they had had a week of meat; and each carried a light lunch of sun-dried biltong or jerky. Some mistaken individuals had attempted to bring along some "fresh" meat. We found it advisable to pass to windward of these; but they themselves did not seem to mind.

It became very hot; for we were now descending to the lower elevations. The marching through long grass and over volcanic stones was not easy. Shortly we came out on stumbly hills, mostly rock, very dry, grown with cactus and discouraged desiccated thorn scrub. Here the sun reflected powerfully and the bearers began to flag.

Then suddenly, without warning, we pitched over a little rise to the river.

No more marvellous contrast could have been devised. From the blasted barren scrub country we plunged into the lush jungle. It was not a very wide jungle, but it was sufficient. The trees were large and variegated, reaching to a high and spacious upper story above the ground tangle. From the massive limbs hung vines, festooned and looped like great serpents. Through this upper corridor flitted birds of bright hue or striking variegation. We did not know many of them by name, nor did we desire to; but were content with the impression of vivid flashing movement and colour. Various monkeys swung, leaped and galloped slowly away before our advance; pausing to look back at us curiously, the ruffs of fur standing out all around their little black faces. The lower half of the forest jungle, however, had no spaciousness at all, but a certain breathless intimacy. Great leaved plants as tall as little trees, and trees as small as big plants, bound together by vines, made up the "deep impenetrable jungle" of our childhood imagining. Here were rustlings, sudden scurryings, half-caught glimpses, once or twice a crash as some greater animal made off. Here and there through the thicket wandered well beaten trails, wide, but low, so that to follow them one would have to bend double. These were the paths of rhinoceroses. The air smelt warm and moist and earthy, like the odour of a greenhouse.

We skirted this jungle until it gave way to let the plain down to the river. Then, in an open grove of acacias, and fairly on the river's bank, we pitched our tents.

These acacia trees were very noble big chaps, with many branches and a thick shade. In their season they are wonderfully blossomed with white, with yellow, sometimes even with vivid red flowers. Beneath them was only a small matter of ferns to clear away.

Before us the sodded bank rounded off ten feet the river itself. At this point far up in its youth it was a friendly river. Its noble width ran over shallows of yellow sand or of small pebbles. Save for unexpected deep holes one could wade across it anywhere. Yet it was very wide, with still reaches of water, with islands of gigantic papyrus, with sand bars dividing the current, and with always the vista for a greater or lesser distance down through the jungle along its banks. From our canvas chairs we could look through on one side to the arid country, and on the other to this tropical wonderland.

Yes, at this point in its youth it was indeed a friendly river in every sense of the word. There are three reasons, ordinarily, why one cannot bathe in the African rivers. In the first place, they are nearly all disagreeably muddy; in the second place, cold water in a tropical climate causes horrible congestions; in the third place they swarm with crocodiles and hippos. But this river was as yet unpolluted by the alluvial soil of the lower countries; the sun on its shallows had warmed its waters almost to blood heat; and the beasts found no congenial haunts in these clear shoals. Almost before our tents were up the men were splashing. And always my mental image of that river's beautiful expanse must include round black heads floating like gourds where the water ran smoothest.

Our tents stood all in a row facing the stream, the great trees at their backs. Down in the grove the men had pitched their little white shelters. Happily they settled down to ease. Settling down to ease, in the case of the African porter, consists in discarding as many clothes as possible. While on the march he wears everything he owns; whether from pride or a desire to simplify transportation I am unable to say. He is supplied by his employer with a blanket and jersey. As supplementals he can generally produce a half dozen white man's ill-assorted garments: an old shooting coat, a ragged pair of khaki breeches, a kitchen tablecloth for a skirt, or something of the sort. If he can raise an overcoat he is happy, especially if it happen to be a long, thick WINTER overcoat. The possessor of such a garment will wear it conscientiously throughout the longest journey and during the hottest noons. But when he relaxes in camp, he puts away all these prideful possessions and turns out in the savage simplicity of his red blanket. Draped negligently, sometimes very negligently, in what may be termed semi-toga fashion, he stalks about or squats before his little fire in all the glory of a regained savagery. The contrast of the red with his red bronze or black skin, the freedom and grace of his movements, the upright carriage of his fine figure, and the flickering savagery playing in his eyes are very effective.

Our men occupied their leisure variously and happily. A great deal of time they spent before their tiny fires roasting meat and talking. This talk was almost invariably of specific personal experiences. They bathed frequently and with pleasure. They slept. Between times they fashioned ingenious affairs of ornament or use: bows and arrows, throwing clubs, snuff-boxes of the tips of antelope horns, bound prettily with bright wire, wooden swords beautifully carved in exact imitation of the white man's service weapon, and a hundred other such affairs. At this particular time also they were much occupied in making sandals against the thorns. These were flat soles of rawhide, the edges pounded to make them curl up a trifle over the foot, fastened by thongs; very ingenious, and very useful. To their task they brought song. The labour of Africa is done to song; weird minor chanting starting high in the falsetto to trickle unevenly down to the lower registers, or where the matter is one of serious effort, an antiphony of solo and chorus. From all parts of the camp come these softly modulated chantings, low and sweet, occasionally breaking into full voice as the inner occasion swells, then almost immediately falling again to the murmuring undertone of more concentrated attention.

The red blanket was generally worn knotted from one shoulder or bound around the waist Malay fashion. When it turned into a cowl, with a miserable and humpbacked expression, it became the Official Badge of Illness. No matter what was the matter that was the proper thing to do-to throw the blanket over the head and to assume as miserable a demeanour as possible. A sore toe demanded just as much concentrated woe as a case of pneumonia. Sick call was cried after the day's work was finished. Then M'ganga or one of the askaris lifted up his voice.

"N'gonjwa! n'gonjwa!" he shouted; and at the shout the red cowls gathered in front of the tent. Three things were likely to be the matter: too much meat, fever, or pus infection from slight wounds. To these in the rainy season would be added the various sorts of colds. That meant either Epsom salts, quinine, or a little excursion with the lancet and permanganate. The African traveller gets to be heap big medicine man within these narrow limits.

All the red cowls squatted miserably, oh, very miserably, in a row. The headman stood over them rather fiercely. We surveyed the lot contemplatively, hoping to heaven that nothing complicated was going to turn up. One of the tent boys hovered in the background as dispensing chemist.

"Well," said F. at last, "what's the matter with you?"

The man indicated pointed to his head and the back of his neck and groaned. If he had a slight headache he groaned just as much as though his head were splitting. F. asked a few questions, and took his temperature. The clinical thermometer is in itself considered big medicine, and often does much good.

"Too much meat, my friend," remarked F. in English, and to his boy in Swahili, "bring the cup."

He put in this cup a triple dose of Epsom salts. The African requires three times a white man's dose. This, pathologically, was all that was required: but psychologically the job was just begun. Your African can do wonderful things with his imagination. If he thinks he is going to die, die he will, and very promptly, even though he is ailing of the most trivial complaint. If he thinks he is going to get well, he is very apt to do so in face of extraordinary odds. Therefore the white man desires not only to start his patient's internal economy with Epsom salts, but also to stir his faith. To this end F. added to that triple dose of medicine a spoonful of Chutney, one of Worcestershire sauce, a few grains of quinine, Sparklets water and a crystal or so of permanganate to turn the mixture a beautiful pink. This assortment the patient drank with gratitude-and the tears running down his cheeks.

"He will carry a load to-morrow," F. told the attentive M'ganga.

The next patient had fever. This one got twenty grains of quinine in water.

"This man carries no load to-morrow," was the direction, "but he must not drop behind."

453

Two or three surgical cases followed. Then a big Kavirondo rose to his feet.

"Nini?" demanded F.

"Homa-fever," whined the man.

F. clapped his hand on the back of the other's neck.

"I think," he remarked contemplatively in English, "that you're a liar, and want to get out of carrying your load."

The clinical thermometer showed no evidence of temperature.

"I'm pretty near sure you're a liar," observed F. in the pleasantest conversational tone and still in English, "but you may be merely a poor diagnostician. Perhaps your poor insides couldn't get away with that rotten meat I saw you lugging around. We'll see."

So he mixed a pint of medicine.

"There's Epsom salts for the real part of trouble," observed F., still talking to himself, "and here's a few things for the fake."

He then proceeded to concoct a mixture whose recoil was the exact measure of his imagination. The imagination was only limited by the necessity of keeping the mixture harmless. Every hot, biting, nauseous horror in camp went into that pint measure.

"There," concluded F., "if you drink that and come back again to-morrow for treatment, I'll believe you ARE sick."

Without undue pride I would like to record that I was the first to think of putting in a peculiarly nauseous gun oil, and thereby acquired a reputation of making tremendous medicine.

So implicit is this faith in white man's medicine that at one of the Government posts we were approached by one of the secondary chiefs of the district. He was a very nifty savage, dressed for calling, with his hair done in ropes like a French poodle's, his skin carefully oiled and reddened, his armlets and necklets polished, and with the ceremonial ball of black feathers on the end of his long spear. His gait was the peculiar mincing teeter of savage conventional society. According to custom, he approached unsmiling, spat carefully in his palm, and shook hands. Then he squatted and waited.

"What is it?" we asked after it became evident he really wanted something besides the pleasure of our company.

"N'dowa-medicine," said he.

"Why do you not go the Government dispensary?" we demanded.

"The doctor there is an Indian; I want REAL medicine, white man's medicine," he explained.

Immensely flattered, of course, we wanted further to know what ailed him.

"Nothing," said he blandly, "nothing at all; but it seemed an excellent chance to get good medicine."

After the clinic was all attended to, we retired to our tents and the screeching-hot bath so grateful in the tropics. When we emerged, in our mosquito boots and pajamas, the daylight was gone. Scores of little blazes licked and leaped in the velvet blackness round about, casting the undergrowth and the lower branches of the trees into flat planes like the cardboard of a stage setting. Cheerful, squatted figures sat in silhouette or in the relief of chance high light. Long switches of meat roasted before the fires. A hum of talk, bursts of laughter, the crooning of minor chants mingled with the crackling of thorns. Before our tents stood the table set for supper. Beyond it lay the pile of firewood, later to be burned on the altar of our safety against beasts. The moonlight was casting milky shadows over the river and under the trees opposite. In those shadows gleamed many fireflies. Overhead were millions of stars, and a little breeze that wandered through upper branches.

But in Equatorial Africa the simple bands of velvet black, against the spangled brightnesses that make up the visual night world, must give way in interest to the other world of sound. The air hums with an undertone of insects; the plain and hill and jungle are populous with voices furtive or bold. In daytime one sees animals enough, in all conscience, but only at night does he sense the almost oppressive feeling of the teeming life about him. The darkness is peopled. Zebra bark, bucks blow or snort or make the weird noises of their respective species; hyenas howl; out of an immense simian silence a group of monkeys suddenly break into chatterings; ostriches utter their deep hollow boom; small things scurry and squeak; a certain weird bird of the curlew or plover sort wails like a lonesome soul. Especially by the river, as here, are the boomings of the weirdest of weird bullfrogs, and the splashings and swishings of crocodile and hippopotamus. One is impressed with the busyness of the world surrounding him; every bird or beast, the hunter and the hunted, is the centre of many important affairs. The world swarms.

And then, some miles away a lion roars, the earth and air vibrating to the sheer power of the sound. The world falls to a blank dead silence. For a full minute every living creature of the jungle or of the veldt holds its breath. Their lord has spoken.

After dinner we sat in our canvas chairs, smoking. The guard fire in front of our tent had been lit. On the other side of it stood one of our askaris leaning on his musket. He and his three companions, turn about, keep the flames bright against the fiercer creatures.

After a time we grew sleepy. I called Saa-sita and entrusted to him my watch. On the crystal of this I had pasted a small piece of surgeon's plaster. When the hour hand reached the surgeon's plaster, he must wake us up. Saa-sita was a very conscientious and careful man. One day I took some time hitching my pedometer properly to his belt: I could not wear it effectively myself because I was on horseback. At the end of the ten-hour march it registered a mile and a fraction. Saa-sita explained that he wished to take especial care of it, so he had wrapped it in a cloth and carried it all day in his hand!

We turned in. As I reached over to extinguish the lantern I issued my last command for the day.

"Watcha kalele, Saa-sita," I told the askari; at once he lifted up his voice to repeat my words. "Watcha kalele!" Immediately from the Responsible all over camp the word came back-from gunbearers, from M'ganga, from tent boys-"kalele! kalele! kalele!"

Thus commanded, the boisterous fun, the croon of intimate talk, the gently rising and falling tide of melody fell to complete silence. Only remained the crackling of the fire and the innumerable voices of the tropical night.

## VIII. THE RIVER JUNGLE

We camped along this river for several weeks, poking indefinitely and happily around the country in all directions to see what we could see. Generally we went together, for neither B. nor myself had been tried out as yet on dangerous game-those easy rhinos hardly counted-and I think we both preferred to feel that we had backing until we knew what our nerves were going to do with us. Nevertheless, occasionally, I would take Memba Sasa and go out for a little purposeless stroll a few miles up or down river. Sometimes we skirted the jungle, sometimes we held as near as possible to the river's bank, sometimes we cut loose and rambled through the dry, crackling scrub over the low volcanic hills of the arid country outside.

Nothing can equal the intense interest of the most ordinary walk in Africa. It is the only country I know of where a man is thoroughly and continuously alive. Often when riding horseback with the dogs in my California home I have watched them in envy of the keen, alert interest they took in every stone, stick, and bush, in every sight, sound, and smell. With equal frequency I have expressed that envy, but as something unattainable to a human being's more phlegmatic make-up. In Africa one actually rises to continuous alertness. There are dozy moments-except you curl up in a safe place for the PURPOSE of dozing; again just like the dog! Every bush, every hollow, every high tuft of grass, every deep shadow must be scrutinized for danger. It will not do to pass carelessly any possible lurking place. At the same time the sense of hearing must be on guard; so that no break of twig or crash of bough can go unremarked. Rhinoceroses conceal themselves most cannily, and have a deceitful habit of leaping from a nap into their swiftest stride. Cobras and puff adders are scarce, to be sure, but very deadly. Lions will generally give way, if not shot at or too closely pressed; nevertheless there is always the chance of cubs or too close a surprise. Buffalo lurk daytimes in the deep thickets, but occasionally a rogue bull lives where your trail will lead. These things do not happen often, but in the long run they surely do happen, and once is quite enough provided the beast gets in.

At first this continual alertness and tension is rather exhausting; but after a very short time it becomes second nature. A sudden rustle the other side a bush no longer brings you up all standing with your heart in your throat; but you are aware of it, and you are facing the possible danger almost before your slower brain has issued any orders to that effect.

In rereading the above, I am afraid that I am conveying the idea that one here walks under the shadow of continual uneasiness. This is not in the least so. One enjoys the sun, and the birds and the little things. He cultivates the great leisure of mind that shall fill the breadth of his outlook abroad over a newly wonderful world. But underneath it all is the alertness, the responsiveness to quick reflexes of judgment and action, the intimate correlations to immediate environment which must characterize the instincts of the higher animals. And it is good to live these things.

Along the edge of that river jungle were many strange and beautiful affairs. I could slip along among the high clumps of the thicker bushes in such a manner as to be continually coming around unexpected bends. Of such maneouvres are surprises made. The graceful red impalla were here very abundant. I would come on them, their heads up, their great ears flung forward, their noses twitching in inquiry of something they suspected but could not fully sense. When slightly alarmed or suspicious the does always stood compactly in a herd, while the bucks remained discreetly in the background, their beautiful, branching, widespread horns showing over the backs of their harems. The impalla is, in my opinion, one of the most beautiful and graceful of the African bucks, a perpetual delight to watch either standing or running. These beasts are extraordinarily agile, and have a habit of breaking their ordinary fast run by unexpectedly leaping high in the air. At a distance they give somewhat the effect of dolphins at sea, only their leaps are higher and more nearly perpendicular. Once or twice I have even seen one jump over the back of another. On another occasion we saw a herd of twenty-five or thirty cross a road of which, evidently, they were a little suspicious. We could not find a single hoof mark in the dust! Generally these beasts frequent thin brush country; but I have three or four times seen them quite out in the open flat plains, feeding with the hartebeeste and zebra. They are about the size of our ordinary deer, are delicately fashioned, and can utter the most incongruously grotesque of noises by way of calls or ordinary conversation.

The lack of curiosity, or the lack of gallantry, of the impalla bucks was, in my experience, quite characteristic. They were almost always the farthest in the background and the first away when danger threatened. The ladies could look out for themselves. They had no horns to save; and what do the fool women mean by showing so little sense, anyway! They deserve what they get! It used to amuse me a lot to observe the utter abandonment of all responsibility by these handsome gentlemen. When it came time to depart, they departed. Hang the girls! They trailed along after as fast as they could.

The waterbuck-a fine large beast about the size of our caribou, a well-conditioned buck resembling in form and attitude the finest of Landseer's stags-on the other hand, had a little more sense of responsibility, when he had anything to do with the sex at all. He was hardly what you might call a strictly domestic character. I have hunted through a country for several days at a time without seeing a single mature buck of this species, although there were plenty of does, in herds of ten to fifty, with a few infants among them just sprouting horns. Then finally, in some small grassy valley, I would come on the Men's Club. There they were, ten, twenty, three dozen of them, having the finest kind of an untramelled masculine time all by themselves. Generally, however, I will say for them, they took care of their own peoples. There would quite likely be one big old fellow, his harem of varying numbers, and the younger subordinate

455

bucks all together in a happy family. When some one of the lot announced that something was about, and they had all lined up to stare in the suspected direction, the big buck was there in the foreground of inquiry. When finally they made me out, it was generally the big buck who gave the signal. He went first, to be sure, but his going first was evidently an act of leadership, and not merely a disgraceful desire to get away before the rest did.

But the waterbuck had to yield in turn to the plains gazelles; especially to the Thompson's gazelle, familiarly-and affectionately-known as the "Tommy." He is a quaint little chap, standing only a foot and a half tall at the shoulder, fawn colour on top, white beneath, with a black, horizontal stripe on his side, like a chipmunk, most lightly and gracefully built. When he was first made, somebody told him that unless he did something characteristic, like waggling his little tail, he was likely to be mistaken by the undiscriminating for his bigger cousin, the Grant's gazelle. He has waggled his tail ever since, and so is almost never mistaken for a Grant's gazelle, even by the undiscriminating. Evidently his religion is Mohammedan, for he always has a great many wives. He takes good care of them, however. When danger appears, even when danger threatens, he is the last to leave the field. Here and there he dashes frantically, seeing that the women and children get off. And when the herd tops the hill, Tommy's little horns bring up the rear of the procession. I like Tommy. He is a cheerful, gallant, quaint little person, with the air of being quite satisfied with his own solution of this complicated world.

Among the low brush at the edge of the river jungle dwelt also the dik-dik, the tiniest miniature of a deer you could possibly imagine. His legs are lead pencil size, he stands only about nine inches tall, he weighs from five to ten pounds; and yet he is a perfect little antelope, horns and all. I used to see him singly or in pairs standing quite motionless and all but invisible in the shade of bushes; or leaping suddenly to his feet and scurrying away like mad through the dry grass. His personal opinion of me was generally expressed in a loud clear whistle. But then nobody in this strange country talks the language you would naturally expect him to talk! Zebra bark, hyenas laugh, impallas grunt, ostriches boom like drums, leopards utter a plaintive sigh, hornbills cry like a stage child, bushbucks sound like a cross between a dog and a squawky toy-and so on. There is only one safe rule of the novice in Africa: NEVER BELIEVE A WORD THE JUNGLE AND VELDT PEOPLE TELL YOU.

These two-the impalla and the waterbuck-were the principal buck we would see close to the river. Occasionally, however, we came on a few oryx, down for a drink, beautiful big antelope, with white and black faces, roached manes, and straight, nearly parallel, rapier horns upward of three feet long. A herd of these creatures, the light gleaming on their weapons, held all at the same slant, was like a regiment of bayonets in the sun. And there were also the rhinoceroses to be carefully espied and avoided. They lay obliterated beneath the shade of bushes, and arose with a mighty blow-off of steam. Whereupon we withdrew silently, for we wanted to shoot no more rhinos, unless we had to.

Beneath all these obvious and startling things, a thousand other interesting matters were afoot. In the mass and texture of the jungle grew many strange trees and shrubs. One most scrubby, fat and leafless tree, looking as though it were just about to give up a discouraged existence, surprised us by putting forth, apparently directly from its bloated wood, the most wonderful red blossoms. Another otherwise self-respecting tree hung itself all over with plump bologna sausages about two feet long and five inches thick. A curious vine hung like a rope, with Turk's-head knots about a foot apart on its whole length, like the hand-over-hand ropes of gymnasiums. Other ropes were studded all over with thick blunt bosses, resembling much the outbreak on one sort of Arts-and-Crafts door: the sort intended to repel Mail-clad Hosts.

The monkeys undoubtedly used such obvious highways through the trees. These little people were very common. As we walked along, they withdrew before us. We could make out their figures galloping hastily across the open places, mounting bushes and stubs to take a satisfying backward look, clambering to treetops, and launching themselves across the abysses between limbs. If we went slowly, they retired in silence. If we hurried at all, they protested in direct ratio to the speed of our advance. And when later the whole safari, loads on heads, marched inconsiderately through their jungle! We happened to be hunting on a parallel course a half mile away, and we could trace accurately the progress of our men by the outraged shrieks, chatterings, appeals to high heaven for at least elemental justice to the monkey people.

Often, too, we would come on concourses of the big baboons. They certainly carried on weighty affairs of their own according to a fixed polity. I never got well enough acquainted with them to master the details of their government, but it was indubitably built on patriarchal lines. When we succeeded in approaching without being discovered, we would frequently find the old men baboons squatting on their heels in a perfect circle, evidently discussing matters of weight and portent. Seen from a distance, their group so much resembled the council circles of native warriors that sometimes, in a native country, we made that mistake. Outside this solemn council, the women, young men and children went about their daily business, whatever that was. Up convenient low trees or bushes roosted sentinels.

We never remained long undiscovered. One of the sentinels barked sharply. At once the whole lot loped away, speedily but with a curious effect of deliberation. The men folks held their tails in a proud high sideways arch; the curious youngsters clambered up bushes to take a hasty look; the babies clung desperately with all four feet to the thick fur on their mothers' backs; the mothers galloped along imperturbably unheeding of infantile troubles aloft. The side hill was bewildering with the big bobbing black forms.

In this lower country the weather was hot, and the sun very strong. The heated air was full of the sounds of insects; some of them comfortable, like the buzzing of bees, some of them strange and unusual to us. One cicada had a sustained note, in quality about like that of our own August-day's friend, but in quantity and duration as the roar of a train to the gentle hum of a good motor car. Like all cicada noises it did not usurp the sound world, but constituted itself an underlying basis, so to speak. And when it stopped the silence seemed to rush in as into a vacuum!

We had likewise the aeroplane beetle. He was so big that he would have made good wing-shooting. His manner of flight was the straight-ahead, heap-of-buzz, plenty-busy, don't-stop-a-minute-or-you'll-come-down method of the aeroplane; and he made the same sort of a hum. His first-cousin, mechanically, was what we called the wind-up-the-watch insect. This specimen possessed a watch-an old-fashioned Waterbury, evidently-that he was continually winding. It must have been hard work for the poor chap, for it sounded like a very big watch.

All these things were amusing. So were the birds. The African bird is quite inclined to be didactic. He believes you need advice, and he means to give it. To this end he repeats the same thing over and over until he thinks you surely cannot misunderstand. One chap especially whom we called the lawyer bird, and who lived in the treetops, had four phrases to impart. He said them very deliberately, with due pause between each; then he repeated them rapidly; finally he said them all over again with an exasperated bearing-down emphasis. The joke of it is I cannot now remember just how they went! Another feathered pedagogue was continually warning us to go slow; very good advice near an African jungle. "Poley-poley! Poley-poley!" he warned again and again; which is good Swahili for "slowly! slowly!" We always minded him. There were many others, equally impressed with their own wisdom, but the one I remember with most amusement was a dilatory person who apparently never got around to his job until near sunset. Evidently he had contracted to deliver just so many warnings per diem; and invariably he got so busy chasing insects, enjoying the sun, gossiping with a friend and generally footling about that the late afternoon caught him unawares with never a chirp accomplished. So he sat in a bush and said his say over and over just as fast as he could without pause for breath or recreation. It was really quite a feat. Just at dusk, after two hours of gabbling, he would reach the end of his contracted number. With final relieved chirp he ended.

It has been said that African birds are "songless." This is a careless statement that can easily be read to mean that African birds are silent. The writer evidently must have had in mind as a criterion some of our own or the English great feathered soloists. Certainly the African jungle seems to produce no individual performers as sustained as our own bob-o-link, our hermit thrush, or even our common robin. But the African birds are vocal enough, for all that. Some of them have a richness and depth of timbre perhaps unequalled elsewhere. Of such is the chime-bird with his deep double note; or the bell-bird tolling like a cathedral in the blackness of the forest; or the bottle bird that apparently pours gurgling liquid gold from a silver jug. As the jungle is exceedingly populous of these feathered specialists, it follows that the early morning chorus is wonderful. Africa may not possess the soloists, but its full orchestral effects are superb.

Naturally under the equator one expects and demands the "gorgeous tropical plumage" of the books. He is not disappointed. The sun-birds of fifty odd species, the brilliant blue starlings, the various parrots, the variegated hornbills, the widower-birds, and dozens of others whose names would mean nothing flash here and there in the shadow and in the open. With them are hundreds of quiet little bodies just as interesting to one who likes birds. From the trees and bushes hang pear-shaped nests plaited beautifully of long grasses, hard and smooth as hand-made baskets, the work of the various sorts of weaver-birds. In the tops of the trees roosted tall marabout storks like dissipated, hairless old club-men in well-groomed, correct evening dress.

And around camp gathered the swift brown kites. They were robbers and villains, but we could not hate them. All day long they sailed back and forth spying sharply. When they thought they saw their chance, they stooped with incredible swiftness to seize a piece of meat. Sometimes they would snatch their prize almost from the hands of its rightful owner, and would swoop triumphantly upward again pursued by polyglot maledictions and a throwing stick. They were very skilful on their wings. I have many times seen them, while flying, tear up and devour large chunks of meat. It seems to my inexperience as an aviator rather a nice feat to keep your balance while tearing with your beak at meat held in your talons. Regardless of other landmarks, we always knew when we were nearing camp, after one of our strolls, by the gracefully wheeling figures of our kites.

### IX. THE FIRST LION

One day we all set out to make our discoveries: F., B., and I with our gunbearers, Memba Sasa, Mavrouki, and Simba, and ten porters to bring in the trophies, which we wanted very much, and the meat, which the men wanted still more. We rode our horses, and the syces followed. This made quite a field force-nineteen men all told. Nineteen white men would be exceedingly unlikely to get within a liberal half mile of anything; but the native has sneaky ways.

At first we followed between the river and the low hills, but when the latter drew back to leave open a broad flat, we followed their line. At this point they rose to a clifflike headland a hundred and fifty feet high, flat on top. We decided to investigate that mesa, both for the possibilities of game, and for the chance of a view abroad.

The footing was exceedingly noisy and treacherous, for it was composed of flat, tinkling little stones. Dried-up, skimpy bushes just higher than our heads made a thin but regular cover. There seemed not to be a spear of anything edible, yet we caught the flash of red as a herd of impalla melted away at our rather noisy approach. Near the foot of the hill we dismounted, with orders to all the men but the gunbearers to sit down and make themselves comfortable. Should we need them we could easily either signal or send word. Then we set ourselves toilsomely to clamber up that volcanic hill.

It was not particularly easy going, especially as we were trying to walk quietly. You see, we were about to surmount a skyline. Surmounting a skyline is always most exciting anywhere, for what lies beyond is at once revealed as a whole and contains the very essence of the unknown; but most decidedly is this true in Africa. That mesa looked flat, and almost anything might be grazing or browsing there. So we proceeded gingerly, with due regard to the rolling of the loose rocks or the tinkling of the little pebbles.

But long before we had reached that alluring skyline we were halted by the gentle snapping of Mavrouki's fingers. That, strangely enough, is a sound to which wild animals seem to pay no attention, and is therefore most useful as a signal. We looked back. The three gunbearers were staring to the right of our course. About a hundred yards away, on the steep side hill, and partly concealed by the brush, stood two rhinoceroses.

457

They were side by side, apparently dozing. We squatted on our heels for a consultation.

The obvious thing, as the wind was from them, was to sneak quietly by, saying nuffin' to nobody. But although we wanted no more rhino, we very much wanted rhino pictures. A discussion developed no really good reason why we should not kodak these especial rhinos-except that there were two of them. So we began to worm our way quietly through the bushes in their direction.

F. and B. deployed on the flanks, their double-barrelled rifles ready for instant action. I occupied the middle with that dangerous weapon the 3A kodak. Memba Sasa followed at my elbow, holding my big gun.

Now the trouble with modern photography is that it is altogether too lavish in its depiction of distances. If you do not believe it, take a picture of a horse at as short a range as twenty-five yards. That equine will, in the development, have receded to a respectable middle distance. Therefore it had been agreed that the advance of the battle line was to cease only when those rhinoceroses loomed up reasonably large in the finder. I kept looking into the finder, you may be sure. Nearer and nearer we crept. The great beasts were evidently basking in the sun. Their little pig eyes alone gave any sign of life. Otherwise they exhibited the complete immobility of something done in granite. Probably no other beast impresses one with quite this quality. I suppose it is because even the little motions peculiar to other animals are with the rhinoceros entirely lacking. He is not in the least of a nervous disposition, so he does not stamp his feet nor change his position. It is useless for him to wag his tail; for, in the first place, the tail is absurdly inadequate; and, in the second place, flies are not among his troubles. Flies wouldn't bother you either, if you had a skin two inches thick. So there they stood, inert and solid as two huge brown rocks, save for the deep, wicked twinkle of their little eyes.

Yes, we were close enough to "see the whites of their eyes," if they had had any: and also to be within the range of their limited vision. Of course we were now stalking, and taking advantage of all the cover.

Those rhinoceroses looked to me like two Dreadnaughts. The African two-horned rhinoceros is a bigger animal anyway than our circus friend, who generally comes from India. One of these brutes I measured went five feet nine inches at the shoulder, and was thirteen feet six inches from bow to stern. Compare these dimensions with your own height and with the length of your motor car. It is one thing to take on such beasts in the hurry of surprise, the excitement of a charge, or to stalk up to within a respectable range of them with a gun at ready. But this deliberate sneaking up with the hope of being able to sneak away again was a little too slow and cold-blooded. It made me nervous. I liked it, but I knew at the time I was going to like it a whole lot better when it was triumphantly over.

We were now within twenty yards (they were standing starboard side on), and I prepared to get my picture. To do so I would either have to step quietly out into sight, trusting to the shadow and the slowness of my movements to escape observation, or hold the camera above the bush, directing it by guess work. It was a little difficult to decide. I knew what I OUGHT to do—

Without the slightest premonitory warning those two brutes snorted and whirled in their tracks to stand facing in our direction. After the dead stillness they made a tremendous row, what with the jerky suddenness of their movements, their loud snorts, and the avalanche of echoing stones and boulders they started down the hill.

This was the magnificent opportunity. At this point I should boldly have stepped out from behind my bush, levelled my trusty 3A, and coolly snapped the beasts, "charging at fifteen yards." Then, if B.'s and F.'s shots went absolutely true, or if the brutes didn't happen to smash the camera as well as me, I, or my executors as the case might be, would have had a fine picture.

But I didn't. I dropped that expensive 3A Special on some hard rocks, and grabbed my rifle from Memba Sasa. If you want really to know why, go confront your motor car at fifteen or twenty paces, multiply him by two, and endow him with an eagerly malicious disposition.

They advanced several yards, halted, faced us for perhaps five or six seconds, uttered snort, whirled with the agility of polo ponies, departed at a swinging trot and with surprising agility along the steep side hill.

I recovered the camera, undamaged, and we continued our climb.

The top of the mesa was disappointing as far as game was concerned. It was covered all over with red stones, round, and as large as a man's head. Thornbushes found some sort of sustenance in the interstices.

But we had gained to a magnificent view. Below us lay the narrow flat, then the winding jungle of our river, then long rolling desert country, gray with thorn scrub, sweeping upward to the base of castellated buttes and one tremendous riven cliff mountain, dropping over the horizon to a very distant blue range. Behind us eight or ten miles away was the low ridge through which our journey had come. The mesa on which we stood broke back at right angles to admit another stream flowing into our own. Beyond this stream were rolling hills, and scrub country, the hint of blue peaks and illimitable distances falling away to the unknown Tara Desert and the sea.

There seemed to be nothing much to be gained here, so we made up our minds to cut across the mesa, and from the other edge of it to overlook the valley of the tributary river. This we would descend until we came to our horses.

Accordingly we stumbled across a mile or so of those round and rolling stones. Then we found ourselves overlooking a wide flat or pocket where the stream valley widened. It extended even as far as the upward fling of the barrier ranges. Thick scrub covered it, but erratically, so that here and there were little openings or thin places. We sat down, manned our trusty prism glasses, and gave ourselves to the pleasing occupation of looking the country over inch by inch.

This is great fun. It is a game a good deal like puzzle pictures. Re-examination generally develops new and unexpected beasts. We repeated to each other aloud the results of our scrutiny, always without removing the glasses from our eyes.

"Oryx, one," said F.; "oryx, two."

"Giraffe," reported B., "and a herd of impala."

I saw another giraffe, and another oryx, then two rhinoceroses.

The three bearers squatted on their heels behind us, their fierce eyes staring straight ahead, seeing with the naked eye what we were finding with six-power glasses.

We turned to descend the hill. In the very centre of the deep shade of a clump of trees, I saw the gleam of a waterbuck's horns. While I was telling of this, the beast stepped from his concealment, trotted a short distance upstream and turned to climb a little ridge parallel to that by which we were descending. About halfway up he stopped, staring in our direction, his head erect, the slight ruff under his neck standing forward. He was a good four hundred yards away. B., who wanted him, decided the shot too chancy. He and F. slipped backward until they had gained the cover of the little ridge, then hastened down the bed of the ravine. Their purpose was to follow the course already taken by the waterbuck until they should have sneaked within better range. In the meantime I and the gunbearers sat down in full view of the buck. This was to keep his attention distracted.

We sat there a long time. The buck never moved but continued to stare at what evidently puzzled him. Time passes very slowly in such circumstances, and it seemed incredible that the beast should continue much longer to hold his fixed attitude. Nevertheless B. and F. were working hard. We caught glimpses of them occasionally slipping from bush to bush. Finally B. knelt and levelled his rifle. At once I turned my glasses on the buck. Before the sound of the rifle had reached me, I saw him start convulsively, then make off at the tearing run that indicates a heart hit. A moment later the crack of the rifle and the dull plunk of the hitting bullet struck my ear.

We tracked him fifty yards to where he lay dead. He was a fine trophy, and we at once set the boys to preparing it and taking the meat. In the meantime we sauntered down to look at the stream. It was a small rapid affair, but in heavy papyrus, with sparse trees, and occasional thickets, and dry hard banks. The papyrus should make a good lurking place for almost anything; but the few points of access to the water failed to show many interesting tracks. Nevertheless we decided to explore a short distance.

For an hour we walked among high thornbushes, over baking hot earth. We saw two or three dik-dik and one of the giraffes. At that time it had become very hot, and the sun was bearing down on us as with the weight of a heavy hand. The air had the scorching, blasting quality of an opened furnace door. Our mouths were getting dry and sticky in that peculiar stage of thirst on which no luke-warm canteen water in necessarily limited quantity has any effect. So we turned back, picked up the men with the waterbuck, and plodded on down the little stream, or, rather, on the red-hot dry valley bottom outside the stream's course, to where the syces were waiting with our horses. We mounted with great thankfulness. It was now eleven o'clock, and we considered our day as finished.

The best way for a distance seemed to follow the course of the tributary stream to its point of junction with our river. We rode along, rather relaxed in the suffocating heat. F. was nearest the stream. At one point it freed itself of trees and brush and ran clear, save for low papyrus, ten feet down below a steep eroded bank. F. looked over and uttered a startled exclamation. I spurred my horse forward to see.

Below us, about fifteen yards away, was the carcass of a waterbuck half hidden in the foot-high grass. A lion and two lionesses stood upon it, staring up at us with great yellow eyes. That picture is a very vivid one in my memory, for those were the first wild lions I had ever seen. My most lively impression was of their unexpected size. They seemed to bulk fully a third larger than my expectation.

The magnificent beasts stood only long enough to see clearly what had disturbed them, then turned, and in two bounds had gained the shelter of the thicket.

Now the habit in Africa is to let your gunbearers carry all your guns. You yourself stride along hand free. It is an English idea, and is pretty generally adopted out there by every one, of whatever nationality. They will explain it to you by saying that in such a climate a man should do only necessary physical work, and that a good gunbearer will get a weapon into your hand so quickly and in so convenient a position that you will lose no time. I acknowledge the gunbearers are sometimes very skilful at this, but I do deny that there is no loss of time. The instant of distracted attention while receiving a weapon, the necessity of recollecting the nervous correlations after the transfer, very often mark just the difference between a sure instinctive snapshot and a lost opportunity. It reasons that the man with the rifle in his hand reacts instinctively, in one motion, to get his weapon into play. If the gunbearer has the gun, HE must first react to pass it up, the master must receive it properly, and THEN, and not until then, may go on from where the other man began. As for physical labour in the tropics: if a grown man cannot without discomfort or evil effects carry an eight-pound rifle, he is too feeble to go out at all. In a long Western experience I have learned never to be separated from my weapon; and I believe the continuance of this habit in Africa saved me a good number of chances.

At any rate, we all flung ourselves off our horses. I, having my rifle in my hand, managed to throw a shot after the biggest lion as he vanished. It was a snap at nothing, and missed. Then in an opening on the edge a hundred yards away appeared one of the lionesses. She was trotting slowly, and on her I had time to draw a hasty aim. At the shot she bounded high in the air, fell, rolled over, and was up and into the thicket before I had much more than time to pump up another shell from the magazine. Memba Sasa in his eagerness got in the way-the first and last time he ever made a mistake in the field.

By this time the others had got hold of their weapons. We fronted the blank face of the thicket.

The wounded animal would stand a little waiting. We made a wide circle to the other side of the stream. There we quickly picked up the trail of the two uninjured beasts. They had headed directly over the hill, where we speedily lost all trace of them on the flint-like surface of the ground. We saw a big pack of baboons in the only likely direction for a lion to go. Being thus thrown back on a choice of a hundred other unlikely directions, we gave up that slim chance and returned to the thicket.

This proved to be a very dense piece of cover. Above the height of the waist the interlocking branches would absolutely prevent any progress, but by stooping low we could see dimly among the simpler main stems to a distance of perhaps fifteen or twenty feet. This combination at once afforded the wounded lioness plenty of cover in which to hide, plenty of room in which to charge home, and placed us under the disadvantage of a crouched or crawling attitude with limited vision. We talked the matter over very thoroughly. There was only one way to get that lioness out; and that was to go after her. The job of going after her needed some planning. The lion is cunning and exceeding fierce. A flank attack, once we were in the thicket, was as much to be expected as a frontal charge.

We advanced to the thicket's edge with many precautions. To our relief we found she had left us a definite trail. B. and I kneeling took up positions on either side, our rifles ready. F. and Simba crawled by inches eight or ten feet inside the thicket. Then, having executed this manoeuvre safely, B. moved up to protect our rear while I, with Memba Sasa, slid down to join F.

From this point we moved forward alternately. I would crouch, all alert, my rifle ready, while F. slipped by me and a few feet ahead. Then he get organized for battle while I passed him. Memba Sasa and Simba, game as badgers, their fine eyes gleaming with excitement, their faces shining, crept along at the rear. B. knelt outside the thicket, straining his eyes for the slightest movement either side of the line of our advance. Often these wily animals will sneak back in a half circle to attack their pursuers from behind. Two or three of the bolder porters crouched alongside B., peering eagerly. The rest had quite properly retired to the safe distance where the horses stood.

We progressed very, very slowly. Every splash of light or mottled shadow, every clump of bush stems, every fallen log had to be examined, and then examined again. And how we did strain our eyes in a vain attempt to penetrate the half lights, the duskinesses of the closed-in thicket not over fifteen feet away! And then the movement forward of two feet would bring into our field of vision an entirely new set of tiny vistas and possible lurking places.

Speaking for myself, I was keyed up to a tremendous tension. I stared until my eyes ached; every muscle and nerve was taut. Everything depended on seeing the beast promptly, and firing quickly. With the manifest advantage of being able to see us, she would spring to battle fully prepared. A yellow flash and a quick shot seemed about to size up that situation. Every few moments, I remember, I surreptitiously held out my hand to see if the constantly growing excitement and the long-continued strain had affected its steadiness.

The combination of heat and nervous strain was very exhausting. The sweat poured from me; and as F. passed me I saw the great drops standing out on his face. My tongue got dry, my breath came laboriously. Finally I began to wonder whether physically I should be able to hold out. We had been crawling, it seemed, for hours. I dared not look back, but we must have come a good quarter mile. Finally F. stopped.

"I'm all in for water," he gasped in a whisper.

Somehow that confession made me feel a lot better. I had thought that I was the only one. Cautiously we settled back on our heels. Memba Sasa and Simba wiped the sweat from their faces. It seemed that they too had found the work severe. That cheered me up still more.

Simba grinned at us, and, worming his way backward with the sinuousity of a snake, he disappeared in the direction from which we had come. F. cursed after him in a whisper both for departing and for taking the risk. But in a moment he had returned carrying two canteens of blessed water. We took a drink most gratefully.

I glanced at my watch. It was just under two hours since I had fired my shot. I looked back. My supposed quarter mile had shrunk to not over fifty feet!

After resting a few moments longer, we again took up our systematic advance. We made perhaps another fifty feet. We were ascending a very gentle slope. F. was for the moment ahead. Right before us the lion growled; a deep rumbling like the end of a great thunder roll, fathoms and fathoms deep, with the inner subterranean vibrations of a heavy train of cars passing a man inside a sealed building. At the same moment over F.'s shoulder I saw a huge yellow head rise up, the round eyes flashing anger, the small black-tipped ears laid back, the great fangs snarling. The beast was not over twelve feet distant. F. immediately fired. His shot, hitting an intervening twig, went wild. With the utmost coolness he immediately pulled the other trigger of his double barrel. The cartridge snapped.

"If you will kindly stoop down-" said I, in what I now remember to be rather an exaggeratedly polite tone. As F.'s head disappeared, I placed the little gold bead of my 405 Winchester where I thought it would do the most good, and pulled trigger. She rolled over dead.

The whole affair had begun and finished with unbelievable swiftness. From the growl to the fatal shot I don't suppose four seconds elapsed, for our various actions had followed one another with the speed of the instinctive. The lioness had growled at our approach, had raised her head to charge, and had received her deathblow before she had released her muscles in the spring. There had been no time to get frightened.

We sat back for a second. A brown hand reached over my shoulder.

"Mizouri-mizouri sana!" cried Memba Sasa joyously. I shook the hand.

"Good business!" said F. "Congratulate you on your first lion."

We then remembered B., and shouted to him that all was over. He and the other men wriggled in to where we were lying. He made this distance in about fifteen seconds. It had taken us nearly an hour.

We had the lioness dragged out into the open. She was not an especially large beast, as compared to most of the others I killed later, but at that time she looked to me about as big as they made them. As a matter of fact she was quite big enough, for she stood three feet two inches at the shoulder-measure that against the wall-and was seven feet and six inches in length. My first bullet had hit her leg, and the last had reached her heart.

Every one shook me by the hand. The gunbearers squatted about the carcass, skilfully removing the skin to an undertone of curious crooning that every few moments broke out into one or two bars of a chant. As the body was uncovered, the men crouched about to cut off little pieces of fat. These they rubbed on their foreheads and over their chests, to make them brave, they said, and cunning, like the lion.

We remounted and took up our interrupted journey to camp. It was a little after two, and the heat was at its worst. We rode rather sleepily, for the reaction from the high tension of excitement had set in. Behind us marched the three gunbearers, all abreast, very military and proud. Then came the porters in single file, the one carrying the folded lion skin leading the way; those bearing the waterbuck trophy and meat bringing up the rear. They kept up an undertone of humming in a minor key; occasionally breaking into a short musical phrase in full voice.

We rode an hour. The camp looked very cool and inviting under its wide high trees, with the river slipping by around the islands of papyrus. A number of black heads bobbed about in the shallows. The small fires sent up little wisps of smoke. Around them our boys sprawled, playing simple games, mending, talking, roasting meat. Their tiny white tents gleamed pleasantly among the cool shadows.

I had thought of riding nonchalantly up to our own tents, of dismounting with a careless word of greeting—

"Oh, yes," I would say, "we did have a good enough day. Pretty hot. Roy got a fine waterbuck. Yes, I got a lion." (Tableau on part of Billy.)

But Memba Sasa used up all the nonchalance there was. As we entered camp he remarked casually to the nearest man.

"Bwana na piga simba-the master has killed a lion."

The man leaped to his feet.

"Simba! simba! simba!" he yelled. "Na piga simba!"

Every one in camp also leaped to his feet, taking up the cry. From the water it was echoed as the bathers scrambled ashore. The camp broke into pandemonium. We were surrounded by a dense struggling mass of men. They reached up scores of black hands to grasp my own; they seized from me everything portable and bore it in triumph before me-my water bottle, my rifle, my camera, my whip, my field glasses, even my hat, everything that was detachable. Those on the outside danced and lifted up their voices in song, improvised for the most part, and in honor of the day's work. In a vast swirling, laughing, shouting, triumphant mob we swept through the camp to where Billy-by now not very much surprised-was waiting to get the official news. By the measure of this extravagant joy could we gauge what the killing of a lion means to these people who have always lived under the dread of his rule.

## X. LIONS

A very large lion I killed stood three feet and nine inches at the withers, and of course carried his head higher than that. The top of the table at which I sit is only two feet three inches from the floor. Coming through the door at my back that lion's head would stand over a foot higher than halfway up. Look at your own writing desk; your own door. Furthermore, he was nine feet and eleven inches in a straight line from nose to end of tail, or over eleven feet along the contour of the back. If he were to rise on his hind feet to strike a man down, he would stand somewhere between seven and eight feet tall, depending on how nearly he straightened up. He weighed just under six hundred pounds, or as much as four well-grown specimens of our own "mountain lion." I tell you this that you may realize, as I did not, the size to which a wild lion grows. Either menagerie specimens are stunted in growth, or their position and surroundings tend to belittle them, for certainly until a man sees old Leo in the wilderness he has not understood what a fine old chap he is.

This tremendous weight is sheer strength. A lion's carcass when the skin is removed is a really beautiful sight. The great muscles lie in ropes and bands; the forearm thicker than a man's leg, the lithe barrel banded with brawn; the flanks overlaid by the long thick muscles. And this power is instinct with the nervous force of a highly organized being. The lion is quick and intelligent and purposeful; so that he brings to his intenser activities the concentration of vivid passion, whether of anger, of hunger or of desire.

So far the opinions of varied experience will jog along together. At this point they diverge.

Just as the lion is one of the most interesting and fascinating of beasts, so concerning him one may hear the most diverse opinions. This man will tell you that any lion is always dangerous. Another will hold the king of beasts in the most utter contempt as a coward and a skulker.

In the first place, generalization about any species of animal is an exceedingly dangerous thing. I believe that, in the case of the higher animals at least, the differences in individual temperament are quite likely to be more numerous than the specific likenesses. Just as individual men are bright or dull, nervous or phlegmatic, cowardly or brave, so individual animals vary in like respect. Our own hunters will recall from their personal experiences how the big bear may have sat down and bawled harmlessly for mercy, while the little unconsidered fellow did his best until finished off: how one buck dropped instantly to a wound that another would carry five miles: how of two equally matched warriors of the herd one will give way in the fight, while still uninjured, before his perhaps badly wounded antagonist. The casual observer might-and often does-say that all bears are cowardly, all bucks are easily killed, or the reverse, according as the god of chance has treated him to one spectacle or the other. As well try to generalize on the human race-as is a certain ecclesiastical habit-that all men are vile or noble, dishonest or upright, wise or foolish.

The higher we go in the scale the truer this individualism holds. We are forced to reason not from the bulk of observations, but from their averages. If we find ten bucks who will go a mile wounded to two who succumb in their tracks from similar hurts, we are justified in saying tentatively that the species is tenacious of life. But as experience broadens we may modify that statement; for strange indeed are runs of luck.

For this reason a good deal of the wise conclusion we read in sportsmen's narratives is worth very little. Few men have experience enough with lions to rise to averages through the possibilities of luck. ESPECIALLY is this true of lions. No beast that roams seems to go more by luck than felis leo. Good hunters may search for years without seeing hide nor hair of one of the beasts. Selous, one of the greatest, went to East Africa for the express purpose of getting some of the fine beasts there, hunted six weeks and saw none. Holmes of the Escarpment has lived in the country six years, has hunted a great deal and has yet to kill his first. One of the railroad officials has for years gone up and down the Uganda Railway on his handcar, his rifle ready in hopes of the lion that never appeared; though many are there seen by those with better fortune. Bronson hunted desperately for this great prize, but failed. Rainsford shot no lions his first trip, and ran into them only three years later. Read Abel Chapman's description of his continued bad luck at even seeing the beasts. MacMillan, after five years' unbroken good fortune, has in the last two years failed to kill a lion, although he has made many trips for the purpose. F. told me he followed every rumour of a lion for two years before he got one. Again, one may hear the most marvellous of yarns the other way about-of the German who shot one from the train on the way up from Mombasa; of the young English tenderfoot who, the first day out, came on three asleep, across a river, and potted the lot; and so on. The point is, that in the case of lions the element of sheer chance seems to begin earlier and last longer than is the case with any other beast. And, you must remember, experience must thrust through the luck element to the solid ground of averages before it can have much value in the way of generalization. Before he has reached that solid ground, a man's opinions depend entirely on what kind of lions he chances to meet, in what circumstances, and on how matters happen to shape in the crowded moments.

But though lack of sufficiently extended experience has much to do with these decided differences of opinion, I believe that misapprehension has also its part. The sportsman sees lions on the plains. Likewise the lions see him, and promptly depart to thick cover or rocky butte. He comes on them in the scrub; they bound hastily out of sight. He may even meet them face to face, but instead of attacking him, they turn to right and left and make off in the long grass. When he follows them, they sneak cunningly away. If, added to this, he has the good luck to kill one or two stone dead at a single shot each, he begins to think there is not much in lion shooting after all, and goes home proclaiming the king of beasts a skulking coward.

After all, on what grounds does he base this conclusion? In what way have circumstances been a test of courage at all? The lion did not stand and fight, to be sure; but why should he? What was there in it for lions? Behind any action must a motive exist. Where is the possible motive for any lion to attack on sight? He does not-except in unusual cases-eat men; nothing has occurred to make him angry. The obvious thing is to avoid trouble, unless there is a good reason to seek it. In that one evidences the lion's good sense, but not his lack of courage. That quality has not been called upon at all.

But if the sportsman had done one of two or three things, I am quite sure he would have had a taste of our friend's mettle. If he had shot at and even grazed the beast; if he had happened upon him where an exit was not obvious; or IF HE HAD EVEN FOLLOWED THE LION UNTIL THE LATTER HAD BECOME TIRED OF THE ANNOYANCE, he would very soon have discovered that Leo is not all good nature, and that once on his courage will take him in against any odds. Furthermore, he may be astonished and dismayed to discover that of a group of several lions, two or three besides the wounded animal are quite likely to take up the quarrel and charge too. In other words, in my opinion, the lion avoids trouble when he can, not from cowardice but from essential indolence or good nature; but does not need to be cornered* to fight to the death when in his mind his dignity is sufficiently assailed.

> * This is an important distinction in estimating the inherent
> courage of man or beast. Even a mouse will fight when
> cornered.

For of all dangerous beasts the lion, when once aroused, will alone face odds to the end. The rhinoceros, the elephant, and even the buffalo can often be turned aside by a shot. A lion almost always charges home.* Slower and slower he comes, as the bullets strike; but he comes, until at last he may be just hitching himself along, his face to the enemy, his fierce spirit undaunted. When finally he rolls over, he bites the earth in great mouthfuls; and so passes fighting to the last. The death of a lion is a fine sight.

> * I seem to be generalizing here, but all these conclusions
> must be understood to take into consideration the liability
> of individual variation.

No, I must confess, to me the lion is an object of great respect; and so, I gather, he is to all who have had really extensive experience. Those like Leslie Tarleton, Lord Delamere, W. N. MacMillan, Baron von Bronsart, the Hills, Sir Alfred Pease, who are great lion men, all concede to the lion a courage and tenacity unequalled by any other living beast. My own experience is of course nothing as compared to that of these men. Yet I saw in my nine months afield seventy-one lions. None of these offered to attack when unwounded or not annoyed. On the other hand, only one turned tail once the battle was on, and she proved to be a three quarters grown lioness, sick and out of condition.

It is of course indubitable that where lions have been much shot they become warier in the matter of keeping out of trouble. They retire to cover earlier in the morning, and they keep more than a perfunctory outlook for the casual human being. When hunters first began to go into the Sotik the lions there would stand imperturbable, staring at the intruder with curiosity or indifference. Now they have learned that such performances are not healthy-and they have probably satisfied their curiosity. But neither in the Sotik, nor even in the plains around Nairobi itself, does the lion refuse the challenge once it has been put up to him squarely. Nor does he need to be cornered. He charges in quite blithely from the open plain, once convinced that you are really an annoyance.

462

As to habits! The only sure thing about a lion is his originality. He has more exceptions to his rules than the German language. Men who have been mighty lion hunters for many years, and who have brought to their hunting close observation, can only tell you what a lion MAY do in certain circumstances. Following very broad principles, they may even predict what he is APT to do, but never what he certainly WILL do. That is one thing that makes lion hunting interesting.

In general, then, the lion frequents that part of the country where feed the great game herds. From them he takes his toll by night, retiring during the day into the shallow ravines, the brush patches, or the rocky little buttes. I have, however, seen lions miles from game, slumbering peacefully atop an ant hill. Indeed, occasionally, a pack of lions likes to live high in the tall-grass ridges where every hunt will mean for them a four- or five-mile jaunt out and back again. He needs water, after feeding, and so rarely gets farther than eight or ten miles from that necessity.

He hunts at night. This is as nearly invariable a rule as can be formulated in regard to lions. Yet once, and perhaps twice, I saw lionesses stalking through tall grass as early as three o'clock in the afternoon. This eagerness may, or may not, have had to do with the possession of hungry cubs. The lion's customary harmlessness in the daytime is best evidenced, however, by the comparative indifference of the game to his presence then. From a hill we watched three of these beasts wandering leisurely across the plains below. A herd of kongonis feeding directly in their path, merely moved aside right and left, quite deliberately, to leave a passage fifty yards or so wide, but otherwise paid not the slightest attention. I have several times seen this incident, or a modification of it. And yet, conversely, on a number of occasions we have received our first intimation of the presence of lions by the wild stampeding of the game away from a certain spot.

However, the most of his hunting is done by dark. Between the hours of sundown and nine o'clock he and his comrades may be heard uttering the deep coughing grunt typical of this time of night. These curious, short, far-sounding calls may be mere evidences of intention, or they may be a sort of signal by means of which the various hunters keep in touch. After a little they cease. Then one is quite likely to hear the petulant, alarmed barking of zebra, or to feel the vibrations of many hoofs. There is a sense of hurried, flurried uneasiness abroad on the veldt.

The lion generally springs on his prey from behind or a little off the quarter. By the impetus his own weight he hurls his victim forward, doubling its head under, and very neatly breaking its neck. I have never seen this done, but the process has been well observed and attested; and certainly, of the many hundreds of lion kills I have taken the pains to inspect, the majority had had their necks broken. Sometimes, but apparently more rarely, the lion kills its prey by a bite in the back of the neck. I have seen zebra killed in this fashion, but never any of the buck. It may be possible that the lack of horns makes it more difficult to break a zebra's neck because of the corresponding lack of leverage when its head hits the ground sidewise; the instances I have noted may have been those in which the lion's spring landed too far back to throw the victim properly; or perhaps they were merely examples of the great variability in the habits of felis leo.

Once the kill is made, the lion disembowels the beast very neatly indeed, and drags the entrails a few feet out of the way. He then eats what he wants, and, curiously enough, seems often to be very fond of the skin. In fact, lacking other evidence, it is occasionally possible to identify a kill as being that of a lion by noticing whether any considerable portion of the hide has been devoured. After eating he drinks. Then he is likely to do one of two things: either he returns to cover near the carcass and lies down, or he wanders slowly and with satisfaction toward his happy home. In the latter case the hyenas, jackals, and carrion birds seize their chance. The astute hunter can often diagnose the case by the general actions and demeanour of these camp followers. A half dozen sour and disgusted looking hyenas seated on their haunches at scattered intervals, and treefuls of mournfully humpbacked vultures sunk in sadness, indicate that the lion has decided to save the rest of his zebra until to-morrow and is not far away. On the other hand, a grand flapping, snarling Kilkenny-fair of an aggregation swirling about one spot in the grass means that the principal actor has gone home.

It is ordinarily useless to expect to see the lion actually on his prey. The feeding is done before dawn, after which the lion enjoys stretching out in the open until the sun is well up, and then retiring to the nearest available cover. Still, at the risk of seeming to be perpetually qualifying, I must instance finding three lions actually on the stale carcass of a waterbuck at eleven o'clock in the morning of a piping hot day! In an undisturbed country, or one not much hunted, the early morning hours up to say nine o'clock are quite likely to show you lions sauntering leisurely across the open plains toward their lairs. They go a little, stop a little, yawn, sit down a while, and gradually work their way home. At those times you come upon them unexpectedly face to face, or, seeing them from afar, ride them down in a glorious gallop. Where the country has been much hunted, however, the lion learns to abandon his kill and seek shelter before daylight, and is almost never seen abroad. Then one must depend on happening upon him in his cover.

In the actual hunting of his game the lion is apparently very clever. He understands the value of cooperation. Two or more will manoeuvre very skilfully to give a third the chance to make an effective spring; whereupon the three will share the kill. In a rough country, or one otherwise favourable to the method, a pack of lions will often deliberately drive game into narrow ravines or cul de sacs where the killers are waiting.

At such times the man favoured by the chance of an encampment within five miles or so can hear a lion's roar.

Otherwise I doubt if he is apt often to get the full-voiced, genuine article. The peculiar questioning cough of early evening is resonant and deep in vibration, but it is a call rather than a roar. No lion is fool enough to make a noise when he is stalking. Then afterward, when full fed, individuals may open up a few times, but only a few times, in sheer satisfaction, apparently, at being well fed. The menagerie row at feeding time, formidable as it sounds within the echoing walls, is only a mild and gentle hint. But when seven or eight lions roar merely to see how much noise they can make, as when driving game, or trying to stampede your oxen on a wagon trip, the effect is something tremendous. The very substance of the ground vibrates; the air shakes. I can only compare it to the effect of a very large deep organ in a very small church. There is something genuinely awe-inspiring about it; and when the repeated volleys rumble into silence, one can imagine the veldt crouched in a rigid terror that shall endure.

## XI. LIONS AGAIN

As to the dangers of lion hunting it is also difficult to write. There is no question that a cool man, using good judgment as to just what he can or cannot do, should be able to cope with lion situations. The modern rifle is capable of stopping the beast, provided the bullet goes to the right spot. The right spot is large enough to be easy to hit, if the shooter keeps cool. Our definition of a cool man must comprise the elements of steady nerves under super-excitement, the ability to think quickly and clearly, and the mildly strategic quality of being able to make the best use of awkward circumstances. Such a man, barring sheer accidents, should be able to hunt lions with absolute certainty for just as long as he does not get careless, slipshod or over-confident. Accidents-real accidents, not merely unexpected happenings-are hardly to be counted. They can occur in your own house.

But to the man not temperamentally qualified, lion shooting is dangerous enough. The lion, when he takes the offensive, intends to get his antagonist. Having made up his mind to that, he charges home, generally at great speed. The realization that it is the man's life or the beast's is disconcerting. Also the charging lion is a spectacle much more awe-inspiring in reality than the most vivid imagination can predict. He looks very large, very determined, and has uttered certain rumbling, blood-curdling threats as to what he is going to do about it. It suddenly seems most undesirable to allow that lion to come any closer, not even an inch! A hasty, nervous shot misses—

An unwounded lion charging from a distance is said to start rather slowly, and to increase his pace only as he closes. Personally I have never been charged by an unwounded beast, but I can testify that the wounded animal comes very fast. Cuninghame puts the rate at about seven seconds to the hundred yards. Certainly I should say that a man charged from fifty yards or so would have little chance for a second shot, provided he missed the first. A hit seemed, in my experience, to the animal, by sheer force of impact, long enough to permit me to throw in another cartridge. A lioness thus took four frontal bullets starting at about sixty yards. An initial miss would probably have permitted her to close.

Here, as can be seen, is a great source of danger to a flurried or nervous beginner. He does not want that lion to get an inch nearer; he fires at too long a range, misses, and is killed or mauled before he can reload. This happened precisely so to two young friends of MacMillan. They were armed with double-rifles, let them off hastily as the beast started at them from two hundred yards, and never got another chance. If they had possessed the experience to have waited until the lion had come within fifty yards they would have had the almost certainty of four barrels at close range. Though I have seen a lion missed clean well inside those limits.

From such performances are so-called lion accidents built. During my stay in Africa I heard of six white men being killed by lions, and a number of others mauled. As far as possible I tried to determine the facts of each case. In every instance the trouble followed either foolishness or loss of nerve. I believe I should be quite safe in saying that from identically the same circumstances any of the good lion men-Tarleton, Lord Delamere, the Hills, and others-would have extricated themselves unharmed.

This does not mean that accidents may not happen. Rifles jam, but generally because of flurried manipulation! One may unexpectedly meet the lion at too close quarters; a foot may slip, or a cartridge prove defective. So may one fall downstairs or bump one's head in the dark. Sufficient forethought and alertness and readiness would go far in either case to prevent bad results.

The wounded beast, of course, offers the most interesting problem to the lion hunter. If it sees the hunter, it is likely to charge him at once. If hit while making off, however, it is more apt to take cover. Then one must summon all his good sense and nerve to get it out. No rules can be given for this; nor am I trying to write a text book for lion hunters. Any good lion hunter knows a lot more about it than I do. But always a man must keep in mind three things: that a lion can hide in cover so short that it seems to the novice as though a jack-rabbit would find scant concealment there; that he charges like lightning, and that he can spring about fifteen feet. This spring, coming unexpectedly from an unseen beast, is about impossible to avoid. Sheer luck may land a fatal shot; but even then the lion will probably do his damage before he dies. The rush from a short distance a good quick shot ought to be able to cope with.

Therefore the wise hunter assures himself of at least twenty feet-preferably more-of neutral zone all about him. No matter how long it takes, he determines absolutely that the lion is not within that distance. The rest is alertness and quickness.

As I have said, the amount of cover necessary to conceal a lion is astonishingly small. He can flatten himself out surprisingly; and his tawny colour blends so well with the brown grasses that he is practically invisible. A practised man does not, of course, look for lions at all. He is after unusual small patches, especially the black ear tips or the black of the mane. Once guessed at, it is interesting to see how quickly the hitherto unsuspected animal sketches itself out in the cover.

I should, before passing on to another aspect of the matter, mention the dangerous poisons carried by the lion's claws. Often men have died from the most trivial surface wounds. The grooves of the claws carry putrefying meat from the kills. Every sensible man in a lion country carries a small syringe, and either permanganate or carbolic. And those mild little remedies he uses full strength!

The great and overwhelming advantage is of course with the hunter. He possesses as deadly a weapon: and that weapon will kill at a distance. This is proper, I think. There are more lions than hunters; and, from our point of view, the man is more important than the beast. The game is not too hazardous. By that I mean that, barring sheer accident, a man is sure to come out all right provided he does accurately the right thing. In other words, it is a dangerous game of skill, but it does not possess the blind danger of a forest in a hurricane, say. Furthermore, it is a game that no man need play unless he wants to. In the lion country he may go about his business-daytime business-as though he were home at the farm.

Such being the case, may I be pardoned for intruding one of my own small ethical ideas at this point, with the full realization that it depends upon an entirely personal point of view. As far as my own case goes, I consider it poor sportsmanship ever to refuse a lion-chance merely because the advantages are not all in my favour. After all, lion hunting is on a different plane from ordinary shooting: it is a challenge to war, a deliberate seeking for mortal combat. Is it not just a little shameful to pot old felis leo at long range, in the open, near his kill, and wherever we have him at an advantage-nine times, and then to back out because that advantage is for once not so marked? I have so often heard the phrase, "I let him (or them) alone. It was not good enough," meaning that the game looked a little risky.

Do not misunderstand. I am not advising that you bull ahead into the long grass, or that alone you open fire on a half dozen lions in easy range. Kind providence endowed you with strategy, and certainly you should never go in where there is no show for you to use your weapon effectively. But occasionally the odds will be against you and you will be called upon to take more or less of a chance. I do not think it is quite square to quit playing merely because for once your opponent has been dealt the better cards. If here are too many of them see if you cannot manoeuvre them; if the grass is long, try every means in your power to get them out. Stay with them. If finally you fail, you will at least have the satisfaction of knowing that circumstances alone have defeated you. If you do not like that sort of a game, stay out of it entirely.

## XII. MORE LIONS

Nor do the last remarks of the preceding chapter mean that you shall not have your trophy in peace. Perhaps excitement and a slight doubt as to whether or not you are going to survive do not appeal to you; but nevertheless you would like a lion skin or so. By all means shoot one lion, or two, or three in the safest fashion you can. But after that you ought to play the game.

The surest way to get a lion is to kill a zebra, cut holes in him, fill the holes with strychnine, and come back next morning. This method is absolutely safe.

The next safest way is to follow the quarry with a pack of especially trained dogs. The lion is so busy and nervous over those dogs that you can walk up and shoot him in the ear. This method has the excitement of riding and following, the joy of a grand and noisy row, and the fun of seeing a good dog-fight. The same effect can be got chasing wart-hogs, hyenas, jackals-or jack-rabbits. The objection is that it wastes a noble beast in an inferior game. My personal opinion is that no man is justified in following with dogs any large animal that can be captured with reasonable certainty without them. The sport of coursing is another matter; but that is quite the same in essence whatever the size of the quarry. If you want to kill a lion or so quite safely, and at the same time enjoy a glorious and exciting gallop with lots of accompanying row, by all means follow the sport with hounds. But having killed one or two by that method, quit. Do not go on and clean up the country. You can do it. Poison and hounds are the SURE methods of finding any lion there may be about; and AFTER THE FIRST FEW, one is about as justifiable as the other. If you want the undoubtedly great joy of cross country pursuit, send your hounds in after less noble game.

The third safe method of killing a lion is nocturnal. You lay out a kill beneath a tree, and climb the tree. Or better, you hitch out a pig or donkey as live bait. When the lion comes to this free lunch, you try to see him; and, if you succeed in that, you try to shoot him. It is not easy to shoot at night; nor is it easy to see in the dark. Furthermore, lions only occasionally bother to come to bait. You may roost up that tree many nights before you get a chance. Once up, you have to stay up; for it is most decidedly not safe to go home after dark. The tropical night in the highlands is quite chilly. Branches seem to be quite as cramping and abrasive under the equator as in the temperate zones. Still, it is one method.

Another is to lay out a kill and visit it in the early morning. There is more to this, for you are afoot, must generally search out your beast in nearby cover, and can easily find any amount of excitement in the process.

The fourth way is to ride the lion. The hunter sees his quarry returning home across the plains, perhaps; or jumps it from some small bushy ravine. At once he spurs his horse in pursuit. The lion will run but a short distance before coming to a stop, for he is not particularly long either of wind or of patience. From this stand he almost invariably charges. The astute hunter, still mounted, turns and flees. When the lion gets tired of chasing, which he does in a very short time, the hunter faces about. At last the lion sits down in the grass, waiting for the game to develop. This is the time for the hunter to dismount and to take his shot. Quite likely he must now stand a charge afoot, and drop his beast before it gets to him.

This is real fun. It has many elements of safety, and many of danger.

To begin with, the hunter at this game generally has companions to back him: often he employs mounted Somalis to round the lion up and get it to stand. The charging lion is quite apt to make for the conspicuous mounted men-who can easily escape-ignoring the hunter afoot. As the game is largely played in the open, the movements of the beast are easily followed.

On the other hand, there is room for mistake. The hunter, for example, should never follow directly in the rear of his lion, but rather at a parallel course off the beast's flank. Then, if the lion stops suddenly, the man does not overrun before he can check his mount. He should never dismount nearer than a hundred and fifty yards from the embayed animal; and should never try to get off while the lion is moving in his direction. Then, too, a hard gallop is not conducive to the best of shooting. It is difficult to hold the front bead steady; and it is still more difficult to remember to wait, once the lion charges, until he has come near enough for a sure shot. A neglect in the inevitable excitement of the moment to remember these and a dozen other small matters may quite possibly cause trouble.

465

Two or three men together can make this one of the most exciting mounted games on earth; with enough of the give and take of real danger and battle to make it worth while. The hunter, however, who employs a dozen Somalis to ride the beast to a standstill, after which he goes to the front, has eliminated much of the thrill. Nor need that man's stay-at-home family feel any excessive uneasiness over Father Killing Lions in Africa.

The method that interested me more than any other is one exceedingly difficult to follow except under favourable circumstances. I refer to tracking them down afoot. This requires that your gunbearer should be an expert trailer, for, outside the fact that following a soft-padded animal over all sorts of ground is a very difficult thing to do, the hunter should be free to spy ahead. It is necessary also to possess much patience and to endure under many disappointments. But on the other hand there is in this sport a continuous keen thrill to be enjoyed in no other; and he who single handed tracks down and kills his lion thus, has well earned the title of shikari-the Hunter.

And the last method of all is to trust to the God of Chance. The secret of success is to be always ready to take instant advantage of what the moment offers.

An occasional hunting story is good in itself: and the following will also serve to illustrate what I have just been saying.

We were after that prize, the greater kudu, and in his pursuit had penetrated into some very rough country. Our hunting for the time being was over broad bench, perhaps four or five miles wide, below a range of mountains. The bench itself broke down in sheer cliffs some fifteen hundred feet, but one did not appreciate that fact unless he stood fairly on the edge of the precipice. To all intents and purposes we were on a rolling grassy plain, with low hills and cliffs, and a most beautiful little stream running down it beneath fine trees.

Up to now our hunting had gained us little beside information: that kudu had occasionally visited the region, that they had not been there for a month, and that the direction of their departure had been obscure. So we worked our way down the stream, trying out the possibilities. Of other game there seemed to be a fair supply: impalla, hartebeeste, zebra, eland, buffalo, wart-hog, sing-sing, and giraffe we had seen. I had secured a wonderful eland and a very fine impalla, and we had had a gorgeous close-quarters fight with a cheetah.* Now C. had gone out, a three weeks' journey, carrying to medical attendance a porter injured in the cheetah fracas. Billy and I were continuing the hunt alone.

*This animal quite disproved the assertion that cheetahs*
*never assume the aggressive. He charged repeatedly.*

We had marched two hours, and were pitching camp under a single tree near the edge of the bench. After seeing everything well under way, I took the Springfield and crossed the stream, which here ran in a deep canyon. My object was to see if I could get a sing-sing that had bounded away at our approach. I did not bother to take a gunbearer, because I did not expect to be gone five minutes.

The canyon proved unexpectedly deep and rough, and the stream up to my waist. When I had gained the top, I found grass growing patchily from six inches to two feet high; and small, scrubby trees from four to ten feet tall, spaced regularly, but very scattered. These little trees hardly formed cover, but their aggregation at sufficient distance limited the view.

The sing-sing had evidently found his way over the edge of the bench. I turned to go back to camp. A duiker-a small grass antelope-broke from a little patch of the taller grass, rushed, head down headlong after their fashion, suddenly changed his mind, and dashed back again. I stepped forward to see why he had changed his mind-and ran into two lions!

They were about thirty yards away, and sat there on their haunches, side by side, staring at me with expressionless yellow eyes. I stared back. The Springfield is a good little gun, and three times before I had been forced to shoot lions with it, but my real "lion gun" with which I had done best work was the 405 Winchester. The Springfield is too light for such game. Also there were two lions, very close. Also I was quite alone.

As the game stood, it hardly looked like my move; so I held still and waited. Presently one yawned, they looked at each other, turned quite leisurely, and began to move away at a walk.

This was a different matter. If I had fired while the two were facing me, I should probably have had them both to deal with. But now that their tails were turned toward me, I should very likely have to do with only the one: at the crack of the rifle the other would run the way he was headed. So I took a careful bead at the lioness and let drive.

My aim was to cripple the pelvic bone, but, unfortunately, just as I fired, the beast wriggled lithely sidewise to pass around a tuft of grass, so that the bullet inflicted merely a slight flesh wound on the rump. She whirled like a flash, and as she raised her head high to locate me, I had time to wish that the Springfield hit a trifle harder blow. Also I had time to throw another cartridge in the barrel.

The moment she saw me she dropped her head and charged. She was thoroughly angry and came very fast. I had just enough time to steady the gold bead on her chest and to pull trigger.

At the shot, to my great relief, she turned bottom up, and I saw her tail for an instant above the grass-an almost sure indication of a bad hit. She thrashed around, and made a tremendous hullabaloo of snarls and growls. I backed out slowly, my rifle ready. It was no place for me, for the grass was over knee high.

Once at a safe distance I blazed a tree with my hunting knife and departed for camp, well pleased to be out of it. At camp I ate lunch and had a smoke; then with Memba Sasa and Mavrouki returned to the scene of trouble. I had now the 405 Winchester, a light and handy weapon delivering a tremendous blow.

We found the place readily enough. My lioness had recovered from the first shock and had gone. I was very glad I had gone first.

The trail was not very plain, but it could be followed a foot or so at a time, with many faults and casts back. I walked a yard to one side while the men followed the spoor. Owing to the abundance of cover it was very nervous work, for the beast might be almost anywhere, and would certainly charge. We tried to keep a neutral zone around ourselves by tossing stones ahead of and on both sides of our line of advance. My own position was not bad, for I had the rifle ready in my hand, but the men were in danger. Of course I was protecting them as well as I could, but there was always a chance that the lioness might spring on them in such a manner that I would be unable to use my weapon. Once I suggested that as the work was dangerous, they could quit if they wanted to.

"Hapana!" they both refused indignantly.

We had proceeded thus for half a mile when to our relief, right ahead of us, sounded the commanding, rumbling half-roar, half-growl of the lion at bay.

Instantly Memba Sasa and Mavrouki dropped back to me. We all peered ahead. One of the boys made her out first, crouched under a bush thirty-two yards away. Even as I raised the rifle she saw us and charged. I caught her in the chest before she had come ten feet. The heavy bullet stopped her dead. Then she recovered and started forward slowly, very weak, but game to the last. Another shot finished her.

The remarkable point of this incident was the action of the little Springfield bullet. Evidently the very high velocity of this bullet from its shock to the nervous system had delivered a paralyzing blow sufficient to knock out the lioness for the time being. Its damage to tissue, however, was slight. Inasmuch as the initial shock did not cause immediate death, the lioness recovered sufficiently to be able, two hours later, to take the offensive. This point is of the greatest interest to the student of ballistics; but it is curious to even the ordinary reader.

That is a very typical example of finding lions by sheer chance. Generally a man is out looking for the smallest kind of game when he runs up against them. Now happened to follow an equally typical example of tracking.

The next day after the killing of the lioness Memba Sasa, Kongoni and I dropped off the bench, and hunted greater kudu on a series of terraces fifteen hundred feet below. All we found were two rhino, some sing-sing, a heard of impalla, and a tremendous thirst. In the meantime, Mavrouki had, under orders, scouted the foothills of the mountain range at the back. He reported none but old tracks of kudu, but said he had seen eight lions not far from our encounter of the day before.

Therefore, as soon next morning as we could see plainly, we again crossed the canyon and the waist-deep stream. I had with me all three of the gun men, and in addition two of the most courageous porters to help with the tracking and the looking.

About eight o'clock we found the first fresh pad mark plainly outlined in an isolated piece of soft earth. Immediately we began that most fascinating of games-trailing over difficult ground. In this we could all take part, for the tracks were some hours old, and the cover scanty. Very rarely could we make out more than three successive marks. Then we had to spy carefully for the slightest indication of direction. Kongoni in especial was wonderful at this, and time and again picked up a broken grass blade or the minutest inch-fraction of disturbed earth. We moved slowly, in long hesitations and castings about, and in swift little dashes forward of a few feet; and often we went astray on false scents, only to return finally to the last certain spot. In this manner we crossed the little plain with the scattered shrub trees and arrived at the edge of the low bluff above the stream bottom.

This bottom was well wooded along the immediate bank of the stream itself, fringed with low thick brush, and in the open spaces grown to the edges with high, green, coarse grass.

As soon as we had managed to follow without fault to this grass, our difficulties of trailing were at an end. The lions' heavy bodies had made distinct paths through the tangle. These paths went forward sinuously, sometimes separating one from the other, sometimes intertwining, sometimes combining into one for a short distance. We could not determine accurately the number of beasts that had made them.

"They have gone to drink water," said Memba Sasa.

We slipped along the twisting paths, alert for indications; came to the edge of the thicket, stooped through the fringe, and descended to the stream under the tall trees. The soft earth at the water's edge was covered with tracks, thickly overlaid one over the other. The boys felt of the earth, examined, even smelled, and came to the conclusion that the beasts must have watered about five o'clock. If so, they might be ten miles away, or as many rods.

We had difficulty in determining just where the party left this place, until finally Kongoni caught sight of suspicious indications over the way. The lions had crossed the stream. We did likewise, followed the trail out of the thicket, into the grass, below the little cliffs parallel to the stream, back into the thicket, across the river once more, up the other side, in the thicket for a quarter mile, then out into the grass on that side, and so on. They were evidently wandering, rather idly, up the general course of the stream. Certainly, unlike most cats, they did not mind getting their feet wet, for they crossed the stream four times.

At last the twining paths in the shoulder-high grass fanned out separately. We counted.

"You were right, Mavrouki," said I, "there were eight."

At the end of each path was a beaten-down little space where evidently the beasts had been lying down. With an exclamation the three gunbearers darted forward to investigate. The lairs were still warm! Their occupants had evidently made off only at our approach!

Not five minutes later we were halted by a low warning growl right ahead. We stopped. The boys squatted on their heels close to me, and we consulted in whispers.

Of course it would be sheer madness to attack eight lions in grass so high we could not see five feet in front of us. That went without saying. On the other hand, Mavrouki swore that he had yesterday seen no small cubs with the band, and our examination of the tracks made in soft earth seemed to bear him out. The chances were therefore that, unless themselves attacked or too close pressed, the lions would not attack us. By keeping just in their rear we might be able to urge them gently along until they should enter more open cover. Then we could see.

Therefore we gave the owner of that growl about five minutes to forget it, and then advanced very cautiously. We soon found where the objector had halted, and plainly read by the indications where he had stood for a moment or so, and then moved on. We slipped along after.

For five hours we hung at the heels of that band of lions, moving very slowly, perfectly willing to halt whenever they told us to, and going forward again only when we became convinced that they too had gone on. Except for the first half hour, we were never more than twenty or thirty yards from the nearest lion, and often much closer. Three or four times I saw slowly gliding yellow bodies just ahead of me, but in the circumstances it would have been sheer stark lunacy to have fired. Probably six or eight times-I did not count-we were commanded to stop, and we did stop.

It was very exciting work, but the men never faltered. Of course I went first, in case one of the beasts had the toothache or otherwise did not play up to our calculations on good nature. One or the other of the gunbearers was always just behind me. Only once was any comment made. Kongoni looked very closely into my face.

"There are very many lions," he remarked doubtfully.

"Very many lions," I agreed, as though assenting to a mere statement of fact.

Although I am convinced there was no real danger, as long as we stuck to our plan of campaign, nevertheless it was quite interesting to be for so long a period so near these great brutes. They led us for a mile or so along the course of the stream, sometimes on one side, sometimes on the other. Several times they emerged into better cover, and even into the open, but always ducked back into the thick again before we ourselves had followed their trail to the clear.

At noon we were halted by the usual growl just as we had reached the edge of the river. So we sat down on the banks and had lunch.

Finally our chance came. The trail led us, for the dozenth time, from the high grass into the thicket along the river. We ducked our heads to enter. Memba Sasa, next my shoulder, snapped his fingers violently. Following the direction of the brown arm that shot over my shoulder, I strained my eyes into the dimness of the thicket. At first I could see nothing at all, but at length a slight motion drew my eye. Then I made out the silhouette of a lion's head, facing us steadily. One of the rear guard had again turned to halt us, but this time where he and his surroundings could be seen.

Luckily I always use a Sheard gold bead sight, and even in the dimness of the tree-shaded thicket it showed up well. The beast was only forty yards away, so I fired at his head. He rolled over without a sound.

We took the usual great precautions in determining the genuineness of his demise, then carried him into the open. Strangely enough the bullet had gone so cleanly into his left eye that it had not even broken the edge of the eyelid; so that when skinned he did not show a mark. He was a very decent maned lion, three feet four inches at the shoulder, and nine feet long as he lay. We found that he had indeed been the rear guard, and that the rest, on the other side of the thicket, had made off at the shot. So in spite of the APPARENT danger of the situation, our calculations had worked out perfectly. Also we had enjoyed a half day's sport of an intensity quite impossible to be extracted from any other method of following the lion.

In trying to guess how any particular lions may act, however, you will find yourself often at fault. The lion is a very intelligent and crafty beast, and addicted to tricks. If you follow a lion to a small hill, it is well to go around that hill on the side opposite to that taken by your quarry. You are quite likely to meet him for he is clever enough thus to try to get in your rear. He will lie until you have actually passed him before breaking off. He will circle ahead, then back to confuse his trail. And when you catch sight of him in the distance, you would never suspect that he knew of your presence at all. He saunters slowly, apparently aimlessly, along pausing often, evidently too bored to take any interest in life. You wait quite breathlessly for him to pass behind cover. Then you are going to make a very rapid advance, and catch his leisurely retreat. But the moment old Leo does pass behind the cover, his appearance of idle stroller vanishes. In a dozen bounds he is gone.

That is what makes lion hunting delightful. There are some regions, very near settlements, where it is perhaps justifiable to poison these beasts. If you are a true sportsman you will confine your hound-hunting to those districts. Elsewhere, as far as playing fair with a noble beast is concerned, you may as well toss a coin to see which you shall take-your pack or a strychnine bottle.

### XIII. ON THE MANAGING OF A SAFARI

We made our way slowly down the river. As the elevation dropped, the temperature rose. It was very hot indeed during the day, and in the evening the air was tepid and caressing, and musical with the hum of insects. We sat about quite comfortably in our pajamas, and took our fifteen grains of quinine per week against the fever.

The character of the jungle along the river changed imperceptibly, the dhum palms crowding out the other trees; until, at our last camp, were nothing but palms. The wind in them sounded variously like the patter or the gathering onrush of rain. On either side the country remained unchanged, however. The volcanic hills rolled away to the distant ranges. Everywhere grew sparsely the low thornbrush, opening sometimes into clear plains, closing sometimes into dense thickets. One morning we awoke to find that many supposedly sober-minded trees had burst into blossom fairly over night. They were red, and yellow and white that before were green, a truly gorgeous sight.

Then we turned sharp to the right and began to ascend a little tributary brook coming down the wide flats from a cleft in the hills. This was prettily named the Isiola, and, after the first mile or so, was not big enough to afford the luxury of a jungle of its own. Its banks were generally grassy and steep, its thickets few, and its little trees isolated in parklike spaces. To either side of it, and almost at its level, stretched plains, but plains grown with scattered brush and shrubs so that at a mile or two one's vista was closed. But for all its scant ten feet of width the Isiola stood upon its dignity as a stream. We discovered that when we tried to cross. The men floundered waist-deep on uncertain bottom; the syces received much unsympathetic comment for their handling of the animals, and we had to get Billy over by a melodramatic "bridge of life" with B., F., myself, and Memba Sasa in the title roles.

Then we pitched camp in the open on the other side, sent the horses back from the stream until after dark, in fear of the deadly tsetse fly, and prepared to enjoy a good exploration of the neighbourhood. Whereupon M'ganga rose up to his gaunt and terrific height of authority, stretched forth his bony arm at right angles, and uttered between eight and nine thousand commands in a high dynamic monotone without a single pause for breath. These, supplemented by about as many more, resulted in (a) a bridge across the stream, and (b) a banda.

A banda is a delightful African institution. It springs from nothing in about two hours, but it takes twenty boys with a vitriolic M'ganga back of them to bring it about. Some of them carry huge backloads of grass, or papyrus, or cat-tail rushes, as the case may be; others lug in poles of various lengths from where their comrades are cutting them by means of their panga. A panga, parenthetically, is the safari man's substitute for axe, shovel, pick, knife, sickle, lawn-mower, hammer, gatling gun, world's library of classics, higher mathematics, grand opera, and toothpicks. It looks rather like a machete with a very broad end and a slight curved back. A good man can do extraordinary things with it. Indeed, at this moment, two boys are with this apparently clumsy implement delicately peeling some of the small thorn trees, from the bared trunks of which they are stripping long bands of tough inner bark.

With these three raw materials-poles, withes, and grass-M'ganga and his men set to work. They planted their corner and end poles, they laid their rafters, they completed their framework, binding all with the tough withes; then deftly they thatched it with the grass. Almost before we had settled our own affairs, M'ganga was standing before us smiling. Gone now was his mien of high indignation and swirling energy.

"Banda naquisha," he informed us.

And we moved in our table and our canvas chairs; hung up our water bottles; Billy got out her fancy work. Nothing could be pleasanter nor more appropriate to the climate than this wide low arbour, open at either end to the breezes, thatched so thickly that the fierce sun could nowhere strike through.

The men had now settled down to a knowledge of what we were like; and things were going smoothly. At first the African porter will try it on to see just how easy you are likely to prove. If he makes up his mind that you really are easy, then you are in for infinite petty annoyance, and possibly open mutiny. Therefore, for a little while, it is necessary to be extremely vigilant, to insist on minute performance in all circumstances where later you might condone an omission. For the same reason punishment must be more frequent and more severe at the outset. It is all a matter of watching the temper of the men. If they are cheerful and willing, you are not nearly as particular as you would be were their spirit becoming sullen. Then the infraction is not so important in itself as an excuse for the punishment. For when your men get sulky, you watch vigilantly for the first and faintest EXCUSE to inflict punishment.

This game always seemed to me very fascinating, when played right. It is often played wrong. People do not look far enough. Because they see that punishment has a most salutary effect on morale, and is sometimes efficacious in getting things done that otherwise would lag, they jump to the conclusion that the only effective way to handle a safari is by penalties. By this I do not at all mean that they act savagely, or punish to brutal excess. Merely they hold rigidly to the letter of the work and the day's discipline. Because it is sometimes necessary to punish severely slight infractions when the men's tempers need sweetening, they ALWAYS punish slight infractions severely.

And in ordinary circumstances this method undoubtedly results in a very efficient safari. Things are done smartly, on time, with a snap. The day's march begins without delay; there is a minimum of straggling; on arrival the tents are immediately got up and the wood and water fetched. But in a tight place, men so handled by invariable rule are very apt to sit down apathetically, and put the whole thing up to the white man. When it comes time to help out they are not there. The contrast with a well-disposed safari cannot be appreciated by one who has not seen both.

The safari-man loves a master. He does not for a moment understand any well-meant but misplaced efforts on your part to lighten his work below the requirements of custom. Always he will beg you to ease up on him, to accord him favour; and always he will despise you if you yield. The relations of man to man, of man to work, are all long since established by immemorial distauri-custom-and it is not for you or him to change them lightly. If you know what he should or can do, and hold him rigidly to it, he will respect and follow you.

But in order to keep him up to the mark, it is not always advisable to light into him with a whip, necessary as the whip often is. If he is sullen, or inclined to make mischief, then that is the crying requirement. But if he is merely careless, or a little slow, or tired, you can handle him in other ways. Ridicule before his comrades is very effective: a sort of good-natured guying, I mean. "Ah! very tired!" uttered in the right tone of voice has brought many a loiterer to his feet as effectively as the kick some men feel must always be bestowed, and quite without anger, mind you! For days at a time we have kept our men travelling at good speed by commenting, as though by the way, after we had arrived in camp, on which tribe happened to come in at the head.

"Ah! Kavirondos came in first to-night," we would remark. "Last night the Monumwezis were ahead."

And once, actually, by this method we succeeded in working up such a feeling of rivalry that the Kikuyus, the unambitious, weak and despised Kikuyus, led the van!

But the first hint of insubordination, of intended insolence, of willful shirking must be met by instant authority. Occasionally, when the situation is of the quick and sharp variety, the white man may have to mix in the row himself. He must never hesitate an instant; for the only reason he alone can control so many is that he has always controlled them. F.

had a very effective blow, or shove, which I found well worth adopting. It is delivered with the heel of the palm to the man's chin, and is more of a lifting, heaving shove than an actual blow. Its effect is immediately upsetting. Impertinence is best dealt with in this manner on the spot. Evidently intended slowness in coming when called is also best treated by a flick of the whip-and forgetfulness. And so with a half dozen others. But any more serious matter should be decided from the throne of the canvas chair, witness should be heard, judgment formally pronounced, and execution intrusted to the askaris or gunbearers.

It is, as I have said, a most interesting game. It demands three sorts of knowledge: first what a safari man is capable of doing; second, what he customarily should or should not do; third, an ability to read the actual intention or motive back of his actions. When you are able to punish or hold your hand on these principles, and not merely because things have or have not gone smoothly or right, then you are a good safari manager. There are mighty few of them.

As for punishment, that is quite simply the whip. The average writer on the country speaks of this with hushed voice and averted face as a necessity but as something to be deprecated and passed over as quickly as possible. He does this because he thinks he ought to. As a matter of fact, such an attitude is all poppycock. In the flogging of a white man, or a black who suffers from such a punishment in his soul as well as his body, this is all very well. But the safari man expects it, it doesn't hurt his feelings in the least, it is ancient custom. As well sentimentalize over necessary schoolboy punishment, or over father paddy-whacking little Willie when little Willie has been a bad boy. The chances are your porter will leap to his feet, crack his heels together and depart with a whoop of joy, grinning from ear to ear. Or he may draw himself up and salute you, military fashion, again with a grin. In any case his "soul" is not "scared" a little bit, and there is no sense in yourself feeling about it as though it were.

At another slant the justice you will dispense to your men differs from our own. Again this is because of the teaching long tradition has made part of their mental make-up. Our own belief is that it is better to let two guilty men go than to punish one innocent. With natives it is the other way about. If a crime is committed the guilty MUST be punished. Preferably he alone is to be dealt with; but in case it is impossible to identify him, then all the members of the first inclusive unit must be brought to account. This is the native way of doing things; is the only way the native understands; and is the only way that in his mind true justice is answered. Thus if a sheep is stolen, the thief must be caught and punished. Suppose, however it is known to what family the thief belongs, but the family refuses to disclose which of its members committed the theft: then each member must be punished for sheep stealing; or, if not the family, then the tribe must make restitution. But punishment MUST be inflicted.

There is an essential justice to recommend this, outside the fact that it has with the native all the solidity of accepted ethics, and it certainly helps to run the real criminal to earth. The innocent sometimes suffers innocently, but not very often; and our own records show that in that respect with us it is the same. This is not the place to argue the right or wrong of the matter from our own standpoint but to recognize the fact that it is right from theirs, and to act accordingly. Thus in cast of theft of meat, or something that cannot be traced, it is well to call up the witnesses, to prove the alibis, and then to place the issue squarely up to those that remain. There may be but two, or there may be a dozen.

"I know you did not all steal the meat," you must say, "but I know that one of you did. Unless I know which one that is by to-morrow morning, I will kiboko all of you. Bass!"

Perhaps occasionally you may have to kiboko the lot, in the full knowledge that most are innocent. That seems hard; and your heart will misgive you. Harden it. The "innocent" probably know perfectly well who the guilty man is. And the incident builds for the future.

I had intended nowhere to comment on the politics or policies of the country. Nothing is more silly than the casual visitor's snap judgments on how a country is run. Nevertheless, I may perhaps be pardoned for suggesting that the Government would strengthen its hand, and aid its few straggling settlers by adopting this native view of retributions. For instance, at present it is absolutely impossible to identify individual sheep and cattle stealers. They operate stealthily and at night. If the Government cannot identify the actual thief, it gives the matter up. As a consequence a great hardship is inflicted on the settler and an evil increases. If, however, the Government would hold the village, the district, or the tribe responsible, and exact just compensation from such units in every case, the evil would very suddenly come to an end. And the native's respect for the white man would climb in the scale.

Once the safari man gets confidence in his master, that confidence is complete. The white man's duties are in his mind clearly defined. His job is to see that the black man is fed, is watered, is taken care of in every way. The ordinary porter considers himself quite devoid of responsibility. He is also an improvident creature, for he drinks all his water when he gets thirsty, no matter how long and hot the journey before him; he eats his rations all up when he happens to get hungry, two days before next distribution time; he straggles outrageously at times and has to be rounded up; he works three months and, on a whim, deserts two days before the end of his journey, thus forfeiting all his wages. Once two porters came to us for money.

"What for?" asked C.

"To buy a sheep," said they.

For two months we had been shooting them all the game meat they could eat, but on this occasion two days had intervened since the last kill. If they had been on trading safari they would have had no meat at all. A sheep cost six rupees in that country, and they were getting but ten rupees a month as wages. In view of the circumstances, and for their own good, we refused. Another man once insisted on purchasing a cake of violet-scented soap for a rupee. Their chief idea of a wild time in Nairobi, after return from a long safari, is to SIT IN A CHAIR and drink tea. For this they pay exorbitantly at the Somali so-called "hotels." It is a strange sight. But then, I have seen cowboys off the range or lumberjacks from the river do equally extravagant and foolish things.

On the other hand they carry their loads well, they march tremendously, they know their camp duties and they do them. Under adverse circumstances they are good-natured. I remember C. and I, being belated and lost in a driving rain. We wandered until nearly midnight. The four or five men with us were loaded heavily with the meat and trophy of a roan. Certainly they must have been very tired; for only occasionally could we permit them to lay down their loads. Most of the time we were actually groping, over boulders, volcanic rocks, fallen trees and all sorts of tribulation. The men took it as a huge joke, and at every pause laughed consumedly.

In making up a safari one tries to mix in four or five tribes. This prevents concerted action in case of trouble, for no one tribe will help another. They vary both in tribal and individual characteristics, of course. For example, the Kikuyus are docile but mediocre porters; the Kavirondos strong carriers but turbulent and difficult to handle. You are very lucky if you happen on a camp jester, one of the sort that sings, shouts, or jokes while on the march. He is probably not much as a porter, but he is worth his wages nevertheless. He may or may not aspire to his giddy eminence. We had one droll-faced little Kavirondo whose very expression made one laugh, and whose rueful remarks on the harshness of his lot finally ended by being funny. His name got to be a catchword in camp.

"Mualo! Mualo!" the men would cry, as they heaved their burdens to their heads; and all day long their war cry would ring out, "Mualo!" followed by shrieks of laughter.

Of the other type was Sulimani, a big, one-eyed Monumwezi, who had a really keen wit coupled with an earnest, solemn manner. This man was no buffoon, however; and he was a good porter, always at or near the head of the procession. In the great jungle south of Kenia we came upon Cuninghame. When the head of our safari reached the spot Sulimani left the ranks and, his load still aloft danced solemnly in front of Cuninghame, chanting something in a loud tone of voice. Then with a final deep "Jambo!" to his old master he rejoined the safari. When the day had stretched to weariness and the men had fallen to a sullen plodding, Sulimani's vigorous song could always set the safari sticks tapping the sides of the chop boxes.

He carried part of the tent, and the next best men were entrusted with the cook outfit and our personal effects. It was a point of honour with these men to be the first in camp. The rear, the very extreme and straggling rear, was brought up by worthless porters with loads of cornmeal-and the weary askaris whose duty it was to keep astern and herd the lot in.

## XIV. A DAY ON THE ISIOLA

Early one morning-we were still on the Isiola-we set forth on our horses to ride across the rolling, brush-grown plain. Our intention was to proceed at right angles to our own little stream until we had reached the forest growth of another, which we could dimly make out eight or ten miles distant. Billy went with us, so there were four a-horseback. Behind us trudged the gunbearers, and the syces, and after them straggled a dozen or fifteen porters.

The sun was just up, and the air was only tepid as yet. From patches of high grass whirred and rocketed grouse of two sorts. They were so much like our own ruffed grouse and prairie chicken that I could with no effort imagine myself once more a boy in the coverts of the Middle West. Only before us we could see the stripes of trotting zebra disappearing; and catch the glint of light on the bayonets of the oryx. Two giraffes galumphed away to the right. Little grass antelope darted from clump to clump of grass. Once we saw gerenuk-oh, far away in an impossible distance. Of course we tried to stalk them; and as usual we failed. The gerenuk we had come to look upon as our Lesser Hoodoo.

The beast is a gazelle about as big as a black-tailed deer. His peculiarity is his excessively long neck, a good deal on the giraffe order. With it he crops browse above high tide mark of other animals, especially when as often happens he balances cleverly on his hind legs. By means of it also he can, with his body completely concealed, look over the top of ordinary cover and see you long before you have made out his inconspicuous little head. Then he departs. He seems to have a lamentable lack of healthy curiosity about you. In that respect he should take lessons from the kongoni. After that you can follow him as far as you please; you will get only glimpses at three or four hundred yards.

We remounted sadly and rode on. The surface of the ground was rather soft, scattered with round rocks the size of a man's head, and full of pig holes.

"Cheerful country to ride over at speed," remarked Billy. Later in the day we had occasion to remember that statement.

The plains led us ever on. First would be a band of scattered brush growing singly and in small clumps: then a little open prairie; then a narrow, long grass swale; then perhaps a low, long hill with small single trees and rough, volcanic footing. Ten thousand things kept us interested. Game was everywhere, feeding singly, in groups, in herds, game of all sizes and descriptions. The rounded ears of jackals pointed at us from the grass. Hundreds of birds balanced or fluttered about us, birds of all sizes from the big ground hornbill to the littlest hummers and sun birds. Overhead, across the wonderful variegated sky of Africa the broad-winged carrion hunters and birds of prey wheeled. In all our stay on the Isiola we had not seen a single rhino track, so we rode quite care free and happy.

Finally, across a glade, not over a hundred and fifty yards away, we saw a solitary bull oryx standing under a bush. B. wanted an oryx. We discussed this one idly. He looked to be a decent oryx, but nothing especial. However, he offered a very good shot; so B., after some hesitation, decided to take it. It proved to be by far the best specimen we shot, the horns measuring thirty-six and three fourths inches! Almost immediately after, two of the rather rare striped hyenas leaped from the grass and departed rapidly over the top of a hill. We opened fire, and F. dropped one of them. By the time these trophies were prepared, the sun had mounted high in the heavens, and it was getting hot.

Accordingly we abandoned that still distant river and swung away in a wide circle to return to camp.

Several minor adventures brought us to high noon and the heat of the day. B. had succeeded in drawing a prize, one of the Grevy's or mountain zebra. He and the gunbearers engaged themselves with that, while we sat under the rather scanty shade of a small thorn tree and had lunch. Here we had a favourable chance to observe that very common, but always wonderful phenomenon, the gathering of the carrion birds. Within five minutes after the stoop of the first vulture above the carcass, the sky immediately over that one spot was fairly darkened with them. They were as thick as midges-or as ducks used to be in California. All sizes were there from the little carrion crows to the great dignified vultures and marabouts and eagles. The small fry flopped and scolded, and rose and fell in a dense mass; the marabouts walked with dignified pace to and fro through the grass all about. As far as the eye could penetrate the blue, it could make out more and yet more of the great soarers stooping with half bent wings. Below we could see uncertainly through the shimmer of the mirage the bent forms of the men.

We ate and waited; and after a little we dozed. I was awakened suddenly by a tremendous rushing roar, like the sound of a not too distant waterfall. The group of men were plodding toward us carrying burdens. And like plummets the birds were dropping straight down from the heavens, spreading wide their wings at the last moment to check their speed. This made the roaring sound that had awakened me.

A wide spot in the shimmer showed black and struggling against the ground. I arose and walked over, meeting halfway B. and the men carrying the meat. It took me probably about two minutes to reach the place where the zebra had been killed. Hundreds, perhaps thousands, of the great birds were standing idly about; a dozen or so were flapping and scrambling in the centre. I stepped into view. With a mighty commotion they all took wing clumsily, awkwardly, reluctantly. A trampled, bloody space and the larger bones, picked absolutely clean, was all that remained! In less than two minutes the job had been done!

"You're certainly good workmen!" I exclaimed, "but I wonder how you all make a living!"

We started the men on to camp with the meat, and ourselves rested under the shade. The day had been a full and interesting one; but we considered it as finished. Remained only the hot journey back to camp.

After a half hour we mounted again and rode on slowly. The sun was very strong and a heavy shimmer clothed the plain. Through this shimmer we caught sight of something large and black and flapping. It looked like a crow-or, better, a scare-crow-crippled, half flying, half running, with waving wings or arms, now dwindling, now gigantic as the mirage caught it up or let it drop. As we watched, it developed, and we made it out to be a porter, clad in a long, ragged black overcoat, running zigzag through the bushes in our direction.

The moment we identified it we spurred our horses forward. As my horse leaped, Memba Sasa snatched the Springfield from my left hand and forced the 405 Winchester upon me. Clever Memba Sasa! He no more than we knew what was up, but shrewdly concluded that whatever it was it needed a heavy gun.

As we galloped to meet him, the porter stopped. We saw him to be a very long-legged, raggedy youth whom we had nicknamed the Marabout because of his exceedingly long, lean legs, the fact that his breeches were white, short and baggy, and because he kept his entire head shaved close. He called himself Fundi, which means The Expert, a sufficient indication of his confidence in himself.

He awaited us leaning on his safari stick, panting heavily, the sweat running off his face in splashes. "Simba!"* said he, and immediately set off on a long, easy lope ahead of us. We pulled down to a trot and followed him.

* *Lion*

At the end of a half mile we made out a man up a tree. Fundi, out of breath, stopped short and pointed to this man. The latter, as soon as he had seen us, commenced to scramble down. We spurred forward to find out where the lions had been last seen.

Then Billy covered herself with glory by seeing them first. She apprised us of that fact with some excitement. We saw the long, yellow bodies of two of them disappearing in the edge of the brush about three hundred yards away. With a wild whoop we tore after them at a dead run.

Then began a wild ride. Do you remember Billy's remark about the nature of the footing? Before long we closed in near enough to catch occasional glimpses of the beasts, bounding easily along. At that moment B.'s horse went down in a heap. None of us thought for a moment of pulling up. I looked back to see B. getting up again, and thought I caught fragments of encouraging-sounding language. Then my horse went down. I managed to hold my rifle clear, and to cling to the reins. Did you ever try to get on a somewhat demoralized horse in a frantic hurry, when all your friends were getting farther away every minute, and so lessening your chances of being in the fun? I began to understand perfectly B.'s remarks of a moment before. However, on I scrambled, and soon overtook the hunt.

We dodged in and out of bushes, and around and over holes. Every few moments we would catch a glimpse of one of those silently bounding lions, and then we would let out a yell. Also every few moments one or the other of us would go down in a heap, and would scramble up and curse, and remount hastily. Billy had better luck. She had no gun, and belonged a little in the rear anyway, but was coming along game as a badger for all that.

My own horse had the legs of the others quite easily, and for that reason I was ahead far enough to see the magnificent sight of five lions sideways on, all in a row, standing in the grass gazing at me with a sort of calm and impersonal dignity. I wheeled my horse immediately so as to be ready in case of a charge, and yelled to the others to hurry up. While I sat there, they moved slowly off one after the other, so that by the time the men had come, the lions had gone. We now had no difficulty in running into them again. Once more my better animal brought me to the lead, so that for the second time I drew up facing the lions, and at about one hundred yards range. One by one they began to leave as before, very leisurely and haughtily, until a single old maned fellow remained. He, however, sat there, his great round head peering over the top of the grass.

"Well," he seemed to say, "here I am, what do you intend to do about it?"

The others arrived, and we all dismounted. B. had not yet killed his lion, so the shot was his. Billy very coolly came up behind and held his horse. I should like here to remark that Billy is very terrified of spiders. F. and I stood at the ready, and B. sat down.

Riding fast an exciting mile or so, getting chucked on your head two or three times, and facing your first lion are none of them conducive to steady shooting. The first shot therefore went high, but the second hit the lion square in the chest, and he rolled over dead.

We all danced a little war dance, and congratulated B. and turned to get the meaning of a queer little gurgling gasp behind us. There was Fundi! That long-legged scarecrow, not content with running to get us and then back again, had trailed us the whole distance of our mad chase over broken ground at terrific speed in order to be in at the death. And he was just about all in at the death. He could barely gasp his breath, his eyes stuck out; he looked close to apoplexy.

"Bwana! bwana!" was all he could say. "Master! master!"

We shook hands with Fundi.

"My son," said I, "you're a true sport, and you'll surely get yours later."

He did not understand me, but he grinned. The gunbearers began to drift in, also completely pumped. They set up a feeble shout when they saw the dead lion. It was a good maned beast, three feet six inches at the shoulder, and nine feet long.

We left Fundi with the lion, instructing him to stay there until some of the other men came up. We remounted and pushed on slowly in hopes of coming on one of the others.

Here and there we rode, our courses interweaving, looking eagerly. And lo! through a tiny opening in the brush we espied one of those elusive gerenuk standing not over one hundred yards away. Whereupon I dismounted and did some of the worst shooting I perpetrated in Africa, for I let loose three times at him before I landed. But land I did, and there was one Lesser Hoodoo broken. Truly this was our day.

We measured him and started to prepare the trophy, when to us came Mavrouki and a porter, quite out of breath, but able to tell us that they had been scouting around and had seen two of the lions. Then, instead of leaving one up a tree to watch, both had come pell-mell to tell us all about it. We pointed this out to them, and called their attention to the fact that the brush was wide, that lions are not stationary objects, and that, unlike the leopard, they can change their spots quite readily. However, we remounted and went to take a look.

Of course there was nothing. So we rode on, rather aimlessly, weaving in and out of the bushes and open spaces. I think we were all a little tired from the long day and the excitement, and hence a bit listless. Suddenly we were fairly shaken out of our saddles by an angry roar just ahead. Usually a lion growls, low and thunderous, when he wants, to warn you that you have gone about far enough; but this one was angry all through at being followed about so much, and he just plain yelled at us.

He crouched near a bush forty yards away, and was switching his tail. I had heard that this was a sure premonition of an instant charge, but I had not before realized exactly what "switching the tail" meant. I had thought of it as a slow sweeping from side to side, after the manner of the domestic cat. This lion's tail was whirling perpendicularly from right to left, and from left to right with the speed and energy of a flail actuated by a particularly instantaneous kind of machinery. I could see only the outline of the head and this vigorous tail; but I took instant aim and let drive. The whole affair sank out of sight.

We made a detour around the dead lion without stopping to examine him, shouting to one of the men to stay and watch the carcass. Billy alone seemed uninfected with the now prevalent idea that we were likely to find lions almost anywhere. Her skepticism was justified. We found no more lions; but another miracle took place for all that. We ran across the second imbecile gerenuk, and B. collected it! These two were the only ones we ever got within decent shot of, and they sandwiched themselves neatly with lions. Truly, it WAS our day.

After a time we gave it up, and went back to measure and photograph our latest prize. It proved to be a male, maneless, two inches shorter than that killed by B., and three feet five and one half inches tall at the shoulder. My bullet had reached the brain just over the left eye.

Now, toward sunset, we headed definitely toward camp. The long shadows and beautiful lights of evening were falling across the hills far the other side the Isiola. A little breeze with a touch of coolness breathed down from distant unseen Kenia. We plodded on through the grass quite happily, noting the different animals coming out to the cool of the evening. The line of brush that marked the course of the Isiola came imperceptibly nearer until we could make out the white gleam of the porters' tents and wisps of smoke curling upward.

Then a small black mass disengaged itself from the camp and came slowly across the prairie in our direction. As it approached we made it out to be our Monumwezis, twenty strong. The news of the lions had reached them, and they were coming to meet us. They were huddled in a close knot, their heads inclined toward the centre. Each man carried upright a peeled white wand. They moved in absolute unison and rhythm, on a slanting zigzag in our direction: first three steps to the right, then three to the left, with a strong stamp of the foot between. Their bodies swayed together. Sulimani led them, dancing backward, his wand upheld.

"Sheeka!" he enunciated in a piercing half whistle.

And the swaying men responded in chorus, half hushed, rumbling, with strong aspiration.

"Goom zoop! goom zoop!"

When fifty yards from us, however, the formation broke and they rushed us with a yell. Our horses plunged in astonishment, and we had hard work to prevent their bolting, small blame to 'em! The men surrounded us, shaking our hands frantically. At once they appropriated everything we or our gunbearers carried. One who got left otherwise insisted on having Billy's parasol. Then we all broke for camp at full speed, yelling like fiends, firing our revolvers in the air. It was a grand entry, and a grand reception. The rest of the camp poured out with wild shouts. The dark forms thronged about us, teeth flashing, arms waving. And in the background, under the shadows of the trees were the Monumwezis, their formation regained, close gathered, heads bent, two steps swaying to the right-stamp! two steps swaying to the left-stamp!-the white wands gleaming, and the rumble of their lion song rolling in an undertone:

"Goom zoop! goom zoop!"

## XV. THE LION DANCE

We took our hot baths and sat down to supper most gratefully, for we were tired. The long string of men, bearing each a log of wood, filed in from the darkness to add to our pile of fuel. Saa-sita and Shamba knelt and built the night fire. In a moment the little flame licked up through the carefully arranged structure. We finished the meal, and the boys whisked away the table.

Then out in the blackness beyond our little globe of light we became aware of a dull confusion, a rustling to and fro. Through the shadows the eye could guess at movement. The confusion steadied to a kind of rhythm, and into the circle of the fire came the group of Monumwezis. Again they were gathered together in a compact little mass; but now they were bent nearly double, and were stripped to the red blankets about their waists. Before them writhed Sulimani, close to earth, darting irregularly now to right, now to left, wriggling, spreading his arms abroad. He was repeating over and over two phrases; or rather the same phrase in two such different intonations that they seemed to convey quite separate meanings.

"Ka soompeele?" he cried with a strongly appealing interrogation.

"Ka soompeele!" he repeated with the downward inflection of decided affirmation.

And the bent men, their dark bodies gleaming in the firelight, stamping in rhythm every third step, chorused in a deep rumbling bass:

"Goom zoop! goom zoop!"

Thus they advanced; circled between us and the fire, and withdrew to the half darkness, where tirelessly they continued the same reiterations.

Hardly had they withdrawn when another group danced forward in their places. These were the Kikuyus. They had discarded completely their safari clothes, and now came forth dressed out in skins, in strips of white cloth, with feathers, shells and various ornaments. They carried white wands to represent spears, and they sang their tribal lion song. A soloist delivered the main argument in a high wavering minor and was followed by a deep rumbling emphatic chorus of repetition, strongly accented so that the sheer rhythm of it was most pronounced:

"An-gee a Ka ga An-gee a Ka ga An-gee a Ka ga Ki ya Ka ga Ka ga an gee ya!"

Solemnly and loftily, their eyes fixed straight before them they made the circle of the fire, passed before our chairs, and withdrew to the half light. There, a few paces from the stamping, crouching Monumwezis, they continued their performance.

The next to appear were the Wakambas. These were more histrionic. They too were unrecognizable as our porters, for they too had for the lion discarded their work-a-day garments in favour of savage. They produced a pantomime of the day's doings, very realistic indeed, ending with a half dozen of dark swaying bodies swinging and shuddering in the long grass as lions, while the "horses" wove in and out among the crouching forms, all done to the beat of rhythm. Past us swept the hunt, and in its turn melted into the half light.

The Kavirondos next appeared, the most fantastically caparisoned of the lot, fine big black men, their eyes rolling with excitement. They had captured our flag from its place before the big tent, and were rallied close about this, dancing fantastically. Before us they leaped and stamped and shook their spears and shouted out their full-voiced song, while the other three tribes danced each its specialty dimly in the background.

The dance thus begun lasted for fully two hours. Each tribe took a turn before us, only to give way to the next. We had leisure to notice minutiae, such as the ingenious tail one of the "lions" had constructed from a sweater. As time went on, the men worked themselves to a frenzy. From the serried ranks every once in a while one would break forth with a shriek to rush headlong into the fire, to beat the earth about him with his club, to rush over to shake one of us violently by the hand, or even to seize one of our feet between his two palms. Then with equal abruptness back he darted to regain his place among the dancers. Wilder and wilder became the movements, higher rose the voices. The mock lion hunt grew more realistic, and the slaughter on both sides something tremendous. Lower and lower crouched the Monumwezi, drawing apart with their deep "goom"; drawing suddenly to a common centre with the sharp "zoop!" Only the Kikuyus held their lofty bearing as they rolled forth their chant, but the mounting excitement showed in their tense muscles and the rolling of their eyes. The sweat glistened on naked black and bronze bodies. Among the Monumwezi to my astonishment I saw Memba Sasa, stripped like the rest, and dancing with all abandon. The firelight leaped high among the logs that eager hands cast on it; and the shadows it threw from the swirling, leaping figures wavered out into a great, calm darkness.

The night guard understood a little of the native languages, so he stood behind our chairs and told us in Swahili the meaning of some of the repeated phrases.

"This has been a glorious day; few safaris have had so glorious a day."

"The masters looked upon the fierce lions and did not run away."

"Brave men without other weapons will nevertheless kill with a knife."

"The masters' mothers must be brave women, the masters are so brave."

"The white woman went hunting, and so were many lions killed."

The last one pleased Billy. She felt that at last she was appreciated.

We sat there spellbound by the weird savagery of the spectacle-the great licking fire, the dancing, barbaric figures, the rise and fall of the rhythm, the dust and shuffle, the ebb and flow of the dance, the dim, half-guessed groups swaying in the darkness-and overhead the calm tropic night.

At last, fairly exhausted, they stopped. Some one gave a signal. The men all gathered in one group, uttered a final yell, very like a cheer, and dispersed.

We called up the heroes of the day-Fundi and his companion-and made a little speech, and bestowed appropriate reward. Then we turned in.

## XVI. FUNDI

Fundi, as I have suggested, was built very much on the lines of the marabout stork. He was about twenty years old, carried himself very erect, and looked one straight in the eye. His total assets when he came to us were a pair of raggedy white breeches, very baggy, and an old mesh undershirt, ditto ditto. To this we added a jersey, a red blanket, and a water bottle. At the first opportunity he constructed himself a pair of rawhide sandals.

Throughout the first part of the trip he had applied himself to business and carried his load. He never made trouble. Then he and his companion saw five lions; and the chance Fundi had evidently long been awaiting came to his hand. He ran himself almost into coma, exhibited himself game, and so fell under our especial and distinguished notice. After participating whole-heartedly in the lion dance he and his companion were singled out for Our Distinguished Favour, to the extent of five rupees per. Thus far Fundi's history reads just like the history of any ordinary Captain of Industry.

Next morning, after the interesting ceremony of rewarding the worthy, we moved on to a new camp. When the line-up was called for, lo! there stood Fundi, without a load, but holding firmly my double-barrelled rifle. Evidently he had seized the chance of favour-and the rifle-and intended to be no longer a porter but a second gunbearer.

This looked interesting, so we said nothing. Fundi marched the day through very proudly. At evening he deposited the rifle in the proper place, and set to work with a will at raising the big tent.

The day following he tried it again. It worked. The third day he marched deliberately up past the syce to take his place near me. And the fourth day, as we were going hunting, Fundi calmly fell in with the rest. Nothing had been said, but Fundi had definitely grasped his chance to rise from the ranks. In this he differed from his companion in glory. That worthy citizen pocketed his five rupees and was never heard from again; I do not even remember his name nor how he looked.

I killed a buck of some sort, and Memba Sasa, as usual, stepped forward to attend to the trophy. But I stopped him.

"Fundi," said I, "if you are a gunbearer, prepare this beast."

He stepped up confidently and set to work. I watched him closely. He did it very well, without awkwardness, though he made one or two minor mistakes in method.

"Have you done this before?" I inquired.

"No, bwana."

"How did you learn to do it?"

"I have watched the gunbearers when I was a porter bringing in meat."*

> * Except in the greatest emergencies a gunbearer would never
> think of carrying any sort of a burden.

This was pleasing, but it would never do, at this stage of the game, to let him think so, neither on his own account nor that of the real gunbearers.

"You will bring in meat today also," said I, for I was indeed a little shorthanded, "and you will learn how to make the top incision straighter."

When we had reached camp I handed him the Springfield.

"Clean this," I told him.

He departed with it, returning it after a time for my inspection. It looked all right. I catechized him on the method he had employed-for high velocities require very especial treatment-and found him letter perfect.

"You learned this also by watching?"

"Yes, bwana, I watched the gunbearers by the fire, evenings."

Evidently Fundi had been preparing for his chance.

Next day, as he walked alongside, I noticed that he had not removed the leather cap, or sight protector, that covers the end of the rifle and is fastened on by a leather thong. Immediately I called a halt.

"Fundi," said I, "do you know that the cover should be in your pocket? Suppose a rhinoceros jumps up very near at hand: how can you get time to unlace the thong and hand me the rifle?"

He thrust the rifle at me suddenly. In some magical fashion the sight cover had disappeared!

"I have thought of this," said he, "and I have tied the thong, so, in order that it come away with one pull; and I snatch it off, so, with my left hand while I am giving you the gun with my right hand. It seemed good to keep the cover on, for there are many branches, and the sight is very easy to injure."

Of course this was good sense, and most ingenious; Fundi bade fair to be quite a boy, but the native African is very easily spoiled. Therefore, although my inclination was strongly to praise him, I did nothing of the sort.

"A gunbearer carries the gun away from the branches," was my only comment.

Shortly after occurred an incident by way of deeper test. We were all riding rather idly along the easy slope below the foothills. The grass was short, so we thought we could see easily everything there was to be seen; but, as we passed some thirty yards from a small tree, an unexpected and unnecessary rhinoceros rose from an equally unexpected and unnecessary green hollow beneath the tree, and charged us. He made straight for Billy. Her mule, panic-stricken, froze with terror in spite of Billy's attack with a parasol. I spurred my own animal between her and the charging brute, with some vague idea of slipping off the other side as the rhino struck. F. and B. leaped from their own animals, and F., with a little.28 calibre rifle, took a hasty shot at the big brute. Now, of course a.28 calibre rifle would hardly injure a rhino, but the bullet happened to catch his right shoulder just as he was about to come down on his right foot. The shock tripped him up as neatly as though he had been upset by a rope. At the same instant Billy's mule came to its senses and bolted, whereupon I too jumped off. The whole thing took about two finger snaps of time. At the instant I hit the ground, Fundi passed the double rifle across the horse's back to me.

Note two things to the credit of Fundi: in the first place, he had not bolted; in the second place, instead of running up to the left side of my mount and perhaps colliding with and certainly confusing me, he had come up on the right side and passed the rifle to me ACROSS the horse. I do not know whether or not he had figured this out beforehand, but it was cleverly done.

The rhinoceros rolled over and over, like a shot rabbit, kicked for a moment, and came to his feet. We were now all ready for him, in battle array, but he had evidently had enough. He turned at right angles and trotted off, apparently-and probably-none the worse for the little bullet in his shoulder.

Fundi now began acquiring things that he supposed befitting to his dignity. The first of these matters was a faded fez, in which he stuck a long feather. From that he progressed in worldly wealth. How he got it all, on what credit, or with what hypnotic power, I do not know. Probably he hypothecated his wages, certainly he had his five rupees.

At any rate he started out with a ragged undershirt and a pair of white, baggy breeches. He entered Nairobi at the end of the trip with a cap, a neat khaki shirt, two water bottles, a cartridge belt, a sash with a tassel, a pair of spiral puttees, an old pair of shoes, and a personal private small boy, picked up en route from some of the savage tribes, to carry his cooking pot, make his fires, draw his water, and generally perform his lordly behests. This was indeed "more-than-oriental-splendour!"

From now on Fundi considered himself my second gunbearer. I had no use for him, but Fundi's development interested me, and I wanted to give him a chance. His main fault at first was eagerness. He had to be rapped pretty sharply and a good number of times before he discovered that he really must walk in the rear. His habit of calling my attention to perfectly obvious things I cured by liberal sarcasm. His intense desire to take his own line as perhaps opposed to mine when we were casting about on trail, I abated kindly but firmly with the toe of my boot. His evident but mistaken tendency to consider himself on an equality with Memba Sasa we both squelched by giving him the hard and dirty work to do. But his faults were never those of voluntary omission, and he came on surprisingly; in fact so surprisingly that he began to get quite cocky over it. Not that he was ever in the least aggressive or disrespectful or neglectful-it would have been easy to deal with that sort of thing-but he carried his head pretty high, and evidently began to have mental reservations. Fundi needed a little wholesome discipline. He was forgetting his porter days, and was rapidly coming to consider himself a full-fledged gunbearer.

The occasion soon arose. We were returning from a buffalo hunt and ran across two rhinoceroses, one of which carried a splendid horn. B. wanted a well developed specimen very much, so we took this chance. The approach was easy enough, and at seventy yards or so B. knocked her flat with a bullet from his.465 Holland. The beast was immediately afoot, but was as promptly smothered by shots from us all. So far the affair was very simple, but now came complication. The second rhinoceros refused to leave. We did not want to kill it, so we spent a lot of time and pains shooing it away. We showered rocks and clods of earth in his direction; we yelled sharply and whistled shrilly. The brute faced here and there, his pig eyes blinking, his snout upraised, trying to locate us, and declining to budge. At length he gave us up as hopeless, and trotted away slowly. We let him go, and when we thought he had quite departed, we approached to examine B.'s trophy.

Whereupon the other craftily returned; and charged us, snorting like an engine blowing off steam. This was a genuine premeditated charge, as opposed to a blind rush, and it is offered as a good example of the sort.

The rhinoceros had come fairly close before we got into action. He headed straight for F. and myself, with B. a little to one side. Things happened very quickly. F. and I each planted a heavy bullet in his head; while B. sent a lighter Winchester bullet into the ribs. The rhino went down in a heap eleven yards away, and one of us promptly shot him in the spine to finish him.

Personally I was entirely concentrated in the matter at hand-as is always the way in crises requiring action-and got very few impressions from anything outside. Nevertheless I imagined, subconsciously that I had heard four shots. F. and B. disclaimed more than one apiece, so I concluded myself mistaken, exchanged my heavy rifle with Fundi for the lighter Winchester, and we started for camp, leaving all the boys to attend to the dead rhinos. At camp I threw down the lever of my Winchester-and drew out an exploded shell!

Here was a double crime on Fundi's part. In the first place, he had fired the gun, a thing no bearer is supposed ever to do in any circumstances short of the disarmament and actual mauling of his master. Naturally this is so, for the white man must be able in an emergency to depend ABSOLUTELY on his second gun being loaded and ready for his need. In the second place, Fundi had given me an empty rifle to carry home. Such a weapon is worse than none in case of trouble; at least I could have gone up a tree in the latter case. I would have looked sweet snapping that old cartridge at anything dangerous!

Therefore after supper we stationed ourselves in a row before the fire, seated in our canvas chairs, and with due formality sent word that we wanted all the gunbearers. They came and stood before us. Memba Sasa erect, military, compact, looking us straight in the eye; Mavrouki slightly bent forward, his face alive with the little crafty, calculating smile peculiar to him; Simba, tall and suave, standing with much social ease; and Fundi, a trifle frightened, but uncertain as to whether or not he had been found out.

We stated the matter in a few words.

"Gunbearers, this man Fundi, when the rhinoceros charged, fired Winchi. Was this the work of a gunbearer?"

The three seasoned men looked at each other with shocked astonishment that such depravity could exist.

"And being frightened, he gave back Winchi with the exploded cartridge in her. Was that the work of a gunbearer?"

"No, bwana," said Fundi humbly.

"You, the gunbearers, have been called because we wish to know what should be done with this man Fundi."

It should be here explained that it is not customary to kiboko, or flog, men of the gunbearer class. They respect themselves and their calling, and would never stand that sort of punishment. When one blunders, a sarcastic scolding is generally sufficient; a more serious fault may be punished on the spot by the white man's fist; or a really bad dereliction may cause the man's instant degradation from the post. With this in mind we had called the council of gunbearers. Memba Sasa spoke.

"Bwana," said he, "this man is not a true gunbearer. He is no longer a true porter. He carries a gun in the field, like a gunbearer; and he knows much of the duty of gunbearer. Also he does not run away nor climb trees. But he carries in the meat; and he is not a real gunbearer. He is half porter and half gunbearer."

"What punishment shall he have?"

"Kiboko," said they.

"Thank you. Bass!"

They went, leaving Fundi. We surveyed him, quietly.

"You a gunbearer!" said we at last. "Memba Sasa says you are half gunbearer. He was wrong. You are all porter; and you know no more than they do. It is in our mind to put you back to carrying a load. If you do not wish to taste the kiboko, you can take a load to-morrow."

"The kiboko, bwana," pleaded Fundi, very abashed and humble.

"Furthermore," we added crushingly, "you did not even hit the rhinoceros!"

So with all ceremony he got the kiboko. The incident did him a lot of good, and toned down his exuberance somewhat. Nevertheless he still required a good deal of training, just as does a promising bird dog in its first season. Generally his faults were of over-eagerness. Indeed, once he got me thoroughly angry in face of another rhinoceros by dancing just out of reach with the heavy rifle, instead of sticking close to me where I could get at him. I temporarily forgot the rhino, and advanced on Fundi with the full intention of knocking his fool head off. Whereupon this six feet something of most superb and insolent pride wilted down to a small boy with his elbow before his face.

"Don't hit, bwana! Don't hit!" he begged.

The whole thing was so comical, especially with Memba Sasa standing by virtuous and scornful, that I had hard work to keep from laughing. Fortunately the rhinoceros behaved himself.

The proud moment of Fundi's life was when safari entered Nairobi at the end of the first expedition. He had gone forth with a load on his head, rags on his back, and his only glory was the self-assumed one of the name he had taken-Fundi, the Expert. He returned carrying a rifle, rigged from top to toe in new garments and fancy accoutrements, followed by a toro, or small boy, he had bought from some of the savage tribes to carry his blanket and cooking pot for him. To the friends who darted out to the line of march, he was gracious, but he held his head high, and had no time for mere persiflage.

I did not take Fundi on my second expedition, for I had no real use for a second gunbearer. Several times subsequently I saw him on the streets of Nairobi. Always he came up to greet me, and ask solicitously if I would not give him a job. This I was unable to do. When we paid off, I had made an addition to his porter's wages, and had written him a chit. This said that the boy had the makings of a gunbearer with further training. It would have been unfair to possible white employers to have said more. Fundi was, when I left the country, precisely in the position of any young man who tries to rise in the world. He would not again take a load as porter, and he was not yet skilled enough or known enough to pick up more than stray jobs as gunbearer. Before him was struggle and hard times, with a certainty of a highly considered profession if he won through. Behind him was steady work without outlets for ambition. It was distinctly up to him to prove whether he had done well to reach for ambition, or whether he would have done better in contentment with his old lot. And that is in essence a good deal like our own world isn't it?

## XVII. NATIVES

Up to this time, save for a few Masai at the very beginning of our trip, we had seen no natives at all. Only lately, the night of the lion dance, one of the Wanderobo-the forest hunters-had drifted in to tell us of buffalo and to get some meat. He was a simple soul, small and capable, of a beautiful red-brown, with his hair done up in a tight, short queue. He wore three skewers about six inches long thrust through each of his ears, three strings of blue beads on his neck, a bracelet tight around his upper arm, a bangle around his ankle, a pair of rawhide sandals, and about a half yard of cotton cloth which he hung from one shoulder. As weapons he carried a round-headed, heavy club, or runga, and a long-bladed spear. He led us to buffalo, accepted a thirty-three cent blanket, and made fire with two sticks in about thirty seconds. The only other evidences of human life we had come across were a few beehives suspended in the trees. These were logs, bored hollow and stopped at either end. Some of them were very quaintly carved. They hung in the trees like strange fruits.

Now, however, after leaving the Isiola, we were to quit the game country and for days travel among the swarming millions of the jungle.

A few preliminary and entirely random observations may be permitted me by way of clearing the ground for a conception of these people. These observations do not pretend to be ethnological, nor even common logical.

The first thing for an American to realize is that our own negro population came mainly from the West Coast, and differed utterly from these peoples of the highlands in the East. Therefore one must first of all get rid of the mental image of our own negro "dressed up" in savage garb. Many of these tribes are not negro at all-the Somalis, the Nandi, and the Masai, for example-while others belong to the negroid and Nilotic races. Their colour is general cast more on the red-bronze than the black, though the Kavirondos and some others are black enough. The texture of their skin is very satiny and wonderful. This perfection is probably due to the constant anointing of the body with oils of various sorts. As a usual thing they are a fine lot physically. The southern Masai will average between six and seven feet in height, and are almost invariably well built. Of most tribes the physical development is remarkably strong and graceful; and a great many of the women will display a rounded, firm, high-breasted physique in marked contrast to the blacks of the lowlands. Of the different tribes possibly the Kikuyus are apt to count the most weakly and spindly examples: though some of these people, perhaps a majority, are well made.

Furthermore, the native differentiates himself still further in impression from our negro in his carriage and the mental attitude that lies behind it. Our people are trying to pattern themselves on white men, and succeed in giving a more or less shambling imitation thereof. The native has standards, ideas, and ideals that perfectly satisfy him, and that antedated the white man's coming by thousands of years. The consciousness of this reflects itself in his outward bearing. He does not shuffle; he is not either obsequious or impudent. Even when he acknowledges the white man's divinity and pays it appropriate respect, he does not lose the poise of his own well-worked-out attitude toward life and toward himself.

We are fond of calling these people primitive. In the world's standard of measurement they are primitive, very primitive indeed. But ordinarily by that term, we mean also undeveloped, embryonic. In that sense we are wrong. Instead of being at the very dawn of human development, these people are at the end-as far as they themselves are concerned. The original racial impulse that started them down the years toward development has fulfilled its duty and spent its force. They have worked out all their problems, established all their customs, arranged the world and its phenomena in a philosophy to their complete satisfaction. They have lived, ethnologists tell us, for thousands, perhaps hundreds of thousands of years, just as we find them to-day. From our standpoint that is in a hopeless intellectual darkness, for they know absolutely nothing of the most elementary subjects of knowledge. From their standpoint, however, they have reached the highest DESIRABLE pinnacle of human development. Nothing remains to be changed. Their customs, religions, and duties have been worked out and immutably established long ago; and nobody dreams of questioning either their wisdom or their imperative necessity. They are the conservatives of the world.

Nor must we conclude-looking at them with the eyes of our own civilization-that the savage is, from his standpoint, lazy and idle. His life is laid out more rigidly than ours will be for a great many thousands of years. From childhood to old age he performs his every act in accord with prohibitions and requirements. He must remember them all; for ignorance does not divert consequences. He must observe them all; in pain of terrible punishments. For example, never may he cultivate on the site of a grave; and the plants that spring up from it must never be cut.* He must make certain complicated offerings before venturing to harvest a crop. On crossing the first stream of a journey he must touch his lips with the end of his wetted bow, wade across, drop a stone on the far side, and then drink. If he cuts his nails, he must throw the parings into a thicket. If he drink from a stream, and also cross it, he must eject a mouthful of water back into the stream. He must be particularly careful not to look his mother-in-law in the face. Hundreds of omens by the manner of their happening may modify actions, as, on what side of the road a woodpecker calls, or in which direction a hyena or jackal crosses the path, how the ground hornbill flies or alights, and the like. He must notice these things, and change his plans according to their occurrence. If he does not notice them, they exercise their influence just the same. This does not encourage a distrait mental attitude. Also it goes far to explain otherwise unexplainable visitations. Truly, as Hobley says in his unexcelled work on the A-Kamba, "the life of a savage native is a complex matter, and he is hedged round by all sorts of rules and prohibitions, the infringement of which will probably cause his death, if only by the intense belief he has in the rules which guide his life."

*Customs are not universal among the different tribes. I am
merely illustrating.*

For these rules and customs he never attempts to give a reason. They are; and that is all there is to it. A mere statement: "This is the custom" settles the matter finally. There is no necessity, nor passing thought even, of finding any logical cause. The matter was worked out in the mental evolution of remote ancestors. At that time, perhaps, insurgent and Standpatter, Conservative and Radical fought out the questions of the day, and the Muckrakers swung by their tails and chattered about it. Those days are all long since over. The questions of the world are settled forever. The people have passed through the struggles of their formative period to the ultimate highest perfection of adjustment to material and spiritual environment of which they were capable under the influence of their original racial force.

Parenthetically, it is now a question whether or not an added impulse can be communicated from without. Such an impulse must (a) unsettle all the old beliefs, (b) inspire an era of skepticism, (c) reintroduce the old struggle of ideas between the Insurgent and the Standpatter, and Radical and the Conservative, (d) in the meantime furnish, from the older

478

civilization, materials, both in the thought-world and in the object-world, for building slowly a new set of customs more closely approximating those we are building for ourselves. This is a longer and slower and more complicated affair than teaching the native to wear clothes and sing hymns; or to build houses and drink gin; but it is what must be accomplished step by step before the African peoples are really civilized. I, personally, do not think it can be done.

Now having, a hundred thousand years or so ago, worked out the highest good of the human race, according to them, what must they say to themselves and what must their attitude be when the white man has come and has unrolled his carpet of wonderful tricks? The dilemma is evident. Either we, as black men, must admit that our hundred-thousand-year-old ideas as to what constitutes the highest type of human relation to environment is all wrong, or else we must evolve a new attitude toward this new phenomena. It is human nature to do the latter. Therefore the native has not abandoned his old gods; nor has he adopted a new. He still believes firmly that his way is the best way of doing things, but he acknowledges the Superman.

To the Superman, with all races, anything is possible. Only our Superman is an idea, and ideal. The native has his Superman before him in the actual flesh.

We will suppose that our own Superman has appeared among us, accomplishing things that apparently contravene all our established tenets of skill, of intellect, of possibility. It will be readily acknowledged that such an individual would at first create some astonishment. He wanders into a crowded hotel lobby, let us say, evidently with the desire of going to the bar. Instead of pushing laboriously through the crowd, he floats just above their heads, gets his drink, and floats out again! That is levitation, and is probably just as simple to him as striking a match is to you and me. After we get thoroughly accustomed to him and his life, we are no longer vastly astonished, though always interested, at the various manifestations of his extraordinary powers. We go right along using the marvellous wireless, aeroplanes, motor cars, constructive machinery, and the like that make us confident-justly, of course-in that we are about the smartest lot of people on earth. And if we see red, white, and blue streamers of light crossing the zenith at noon, we do not manifest any very profound amazement. "There's that confounded Superman again," we mutter, if we happen to be busy. "I wonder what stunt he's going to do now!"

A consideration of the above beautiful fable may go a little way toward explaining the supposed native stolidity in the face of the white man's wonders. A few years ago some misguided person brought a balloon to Nairobi. The balloon interested the white people a lot, but everybody was chiefly occupied wondering what the natives would do when they saw THAT! The natives did not do anything. They gathered in large numbers, and most interestedly watched it go up, and then went home again. But they were not stricken with wonder to any great extent. So also with locomotives, motor cars, telephones, phonographs-any of our modern ingenuities. The native is pleased and entertained, but not astonished. "Stupid creature, no imagination," say we, because our pride in showing off is a wee bit hurt.

Why should he be astonished? His mental revolution took place when he saw the first match struck. It is manifestly impossible for any one to make fire instantaneously by rubbing one small stick. When for the first time he saw it done, he was indeed vastly astounded. The immutable had been changed. The law had been transcended. The impossible had been accomplished. And then, as logical sequence, his mind completed the syllogism. If the white man can do this impossibility, why not all the rest? To defy the laws of nature by flying in the air or forcing great masses of iron to transport one, is no more wonderful than to defy them by striking a light. Since the white man can provedly do one, what earthly reason exists why he should not do anything else that hits his fancy? There is nothing to get astonished at.

This does not necessarily mean that the native looks on the white man as a god. On the contrary, your African is very shrewd in the reading of character. But indubitably white men possess great magic, uncertain in its extent.

That is as far as I should care to go, without much deeper acquaintance, into the attitude of the native mind toward the whites. A superficial study of it, beyond the general principals I have enunciated, discloses many strange contradictions. The native respects the white man's warlike skill, he respects his physical prowess, he certainly acknowledges tacitly his moral superiority in the right to command. In case of dispute he likes the white man's adjudication; in case of illness the man's medicine; in case of trouble the white man's sustaining hand. Yet he almost never attempts to copy the white man's appearance or ways of doing things. His own savage customs and habits he fulfils with as much pride as ever in their eternal fitness. Once I was badgering Memba Sasa, asking him whether he thought the white skin or the black skin the more ornamental. "You are not white," he retorted at last. "That," pointing to a leaf of my notebook, "is white. You are red. I do not like the looks of red people."

They call our speech the "snake language," because of its hissing sound. Once this is brought to your attention, indeed, you cannot help noticing the superabundance of the sibilants.

A queer melange the pigeonholes of an African's brain must contain-fear and respect, strongly mingled with clear estimate of intrinsic character of individuals and a satisfaction with his own standards.

Nor, I think, do we realize sufficiently the actual fundamental differences between the African and our peoples. Physically they must be in many ways as different from our selves as though they actually belonged to a different species. The Masai are a fine big race, enduring, well developed and efficient. They live exclusively on cow's milk mixed with blood; no meat, no fruit, no vegetables, no grain; just that and nothing more. Obviously they must differ from us most radically, or else all our dietetic theories are wrong. It is a well-known fact that any native requires a triple dose of white man's medicine. Furthermore a native's sensitiveness to pain is very much less than the white man's. This is indubitable. For example, the Wakamba file-or, rather, chip, by means of a small chisel-all their front teeth down to needle points, When these happen to fall out, the warrior substitutes an artificial tooth which he drives down into the socket. If the savage got the same effects from such a performance that a white man's dental system would arouse, even "savage stoicism" would hardly do him much good. There is nothing to be gained by multiplying examples. Every African traveller can recall a thousand.

Incidentally, and by the way, I want to add to the milk-and-blood joke on dietetics another on the physical culturists. We are all familiar with the wails over the loss of our toe nails. You know what I mean; they run somewhat like this: shoes are the curse of civilization; if we wear them much longer we shall not only lose the intended use of our feet, but we shall lose our toe nails as well; the savage man, etc., etc., etc. Now I saw a great many of said savage men in Africa, and I got much interested in their toe nails, because I soon found that our own civilized "imprisoned" toe nails were very much better developed. In fact, a large number of the free and untramelled savages have hardly any toe nails at all! Whether this upsets a theory, nullifies a sentimental protest, or merely stands as an exception, I should not dare guess. But the fact is indubitable.

## XVIII. IN THE JUNGLE

### (a) THE MARCH TO MERU

Now, one day we left the Isiola River and cut across on a long upward slant to the left. In a very short time we had left the plains, and were adrift in an ocean of brown grass that concealed all but the bobbing loads atop the safari, and over which we could only see when mounted. It was glorious feed, apparently, but it contained very few animals for all that. An animal could without doubt wax fat and sleek therein: but only to furnish light and salutary meals to beasts of prey. Long grass makes easy stalking. We saw a few ostriches, some giraffe, and three or four singly adventurous oryx. The ripening grasses were softer than a rippling field grain; and even more beautiful in their umber and browns. Although apparently we travelled a level, nevertheless in the extreme distance the plains of our hunting were dropping below, and the far off mountains were slowly rising above the horizon. On the other side were two very green hills, looking nearly straight up and down, and through a cleft the splintered snow-clad summit of Mt. Kenia.

At length this gentle foothill slope broke over into rougher country. Then, in the pass, we came upon many parallel beaten paths, wider and straighter than the game trails-native tracks. That night we camped in a small, round valley under some glorious trees, with green grass around us; a refreshing contrast after the desert brown. In the distance ahead stood a big hill, and at its base we could make out amid the tree-green, the straight slim smoke of many fires and the threads of many roads.

We began our next morning's march early, and we dropped over the hill into a wide, cultivated valley. Fields of grain, mostly rape, were planted irregularly among big scattered trees. The morning air, warming under the sun, was as yet still, and carried sound well. The cooing, chattering and calling of thousands of birds mingled with shouts and the clapping together of pieces of wood. As we came closer we saw that every so often scaffolds had been erected overlooking the grain, and on these scaffolds naked boys danced and yelled and worked clappers to scare the birds from the crops. They seemed to put a great deal of rigour into the job; whether from natural enthusiasm or efficient direful supervision I could not say. Certainly they must have worked in watches, however; no human being could keep up that row continuously for a single day, let alone the whole season of ripening grain. As we passed they fell silent and stared their fill.

On the banks of a boggy little stream that we had to flounder across we came on a gentleman and lady travelling. They were a tall, well formed pair, mahogany in colour, with the open, pleasant expression of most of these jungle peoples. The man wore a string around his waist into which was thrust a small leafy branch; the woman had on a beautiful skirt made by halving a banana leaf, using the stem as belt, and letting the leaf part hang down as a skirt. Shortly after meeting these people we turned sharp to the right on a well beaten road.

For nearly two weeks we were to follow this road, so it may be as well to get an idea of it. Its course was a segment of about a sixth of the circle of Kenia's foothills. With Kenia itself as a centre, this road swung among the lower elevations about the base of that great mountain. Its course was mainly down and up hundreds of the canyons radiating from the main peak, and over the ridges between them. No sooner were we down, than we had to climb up; and no sooner were we up, than once more down we had to plunge. At times, however, we crossed considerable plateaus. Most of this country was dense jungle, so dense that we could not see on either side more than fifteen or twenty feet. Occasionally, atop the ridges, however, we would come upon small open parks. In these jungles live millions of human beings.

At once, as soon as we had turned into the main road, we began to meet people. In the grain fields of the valley we saw only the elevated boys, and a few men engaged in weaving a little house perched on stilts. We came across some of these little houses all completed, with conical roofs. They were evidently used for granaries. As we mounted the slope on the other side, however, the trees closed in, and we found ourselves marching down the narrow aisle of the jungle itself.

It was a dense and beautiful jungle, with very tall trees and the deepest shade; and the impenetrable tangle to the edge of the track. Among the trees were the broad leaves of bananas and palms, the fling of leafy vines. Over the track these leaned, so that we rode through splashing and mottling shade. Nothing could have seemed wilder than this apparently impenetrable and yet we had ridden but a short distance before we realized that we were in fact passing through cultivated land. It was, again, only a difference in terms. Native cultivation in this district rarely consists of clearing land and planting crops in due order, but in leaving the forest proper as it is, and in planting foodstuffs haphazard wherever a tiny space can be made for even three hills of corn or a single banana. Thus they add to rather than subtract from the typical density of the jungle. At first, we found, it took some practice to tell a farm when we saw it.

From the track narrow little paths wound immediately out of sight. Sometimes we saw a wisp of smoke rising above the undergrowth and eddying in the tops of the trees. Long vine ropes swung from point to point, hung at intervals with such matters as feathers, bones, miniature shields, carved sticks, shells and clappers: either as magic or to keep off the birds. From either side the track we were conscious always of bright black eyes watching us. Sometimes we caught a glimpse of their owners crouched in the bush, concealed behind banana leaves, motionless and straight against a tree trunk. When they saw themselves observed they vanished without a sound.

The upper air was musical with birds, and bright with the flutter of their wings. Rarely did we see them long enough to catch a fair idea of their size and shape. They flashed from shade to shade, leaving only an impression of brilliant colour. There were some exceptions: as the widower-bird, dressed all in black, with long trailing wing-plumes of which he seemed very proud; and the various sorts of green pigeons and parrots. There were many flowering shrubs and trees, and the air was laden with perfume. Strange, too, it seemed to see tall trees with leaves three or four feet long and half as many wide.

We were riding a mile or so ahead of the safari. At first we were accompanied only by our gunbearers and syces. Before long, however, we began to accumulate a following.

This consisted at first of a very wonderful young man, probably a chief's son. He carried a long bright spear, wore a short sword thrust through a girdle, had his hair done in three wrapped queues, one over each temple and one behind, and was generally brought to a high state of polish by means of red earth and oil. About his knee he wore a little bell that jingled pleasingly at every step. From one shoulder hung a goat-skin cloak embroidered with steel beads. A small package neatly done up in leaves probably contained his lunch. He teetered along with a mincing up and down step, every movement, and the expression of his face displaying a fatuous self-satisfaction. When we looked back again this youth had magically become two. Then appeared two women and a white goat. All except the goat were dressed for visiting, with long chains of beads, bracelets and anklets, and heavy ornaments in the distended ear lobes. The manner people sprang apparently out of the ground was very disconcerting. It was a good deal like those fairy-story moving pictures where a wave of the wand produces beautiful ladies. By half an hour we had acquired a long retinue-young warriors, old men, women and innumerable children. After we had passed, the new recruits stepped quietly from the shadow of the jungle and fell in. Every one with nothing much to do evidently made up his mind he might as well go to Meru now as any other time.

Also we met a great number of people going in the other direction. Women were bearing loads of yams. Chiefs' sons minced along, their spears poised in their left hands at just the proper angle, their bangles jingling, their right hands carried raised in a most affected manner. Their social ease was remarkable, especially in contrast with the awkwardness of the lower poverty-stricken or menial castes. The latter drew one side to let us pass, and stared. Our chiefs' sons, on the other hand, stepped springingly and beamingly forward; spat carefully in their hands (we did the same); shook hands all down the line: exchanged a long-drawn "moo-o-ga!" with each of us; and departed at the same springing rapid gait. The ordinary warriors greeted us, but did not offer to shake hands, thank goodness! There were a great many of them. Across the valleys and through the open spaces the sun, as it struck down the trail, was always flashing back from distant spears. Twice we met flocks of sheep being moved from one point to another. Three or four herdsmen and innumerable small boys seemed to be in charge. Occasionally we met a real chief or headman of a village, distinguished by the fact that he or a servant carried a small wooden stool. With these dignitaries we always stopped to exchange friendly words.

These comprised the travelling public. The resident public also showed itself quite in evidence. Once our retainers had become sufficiently numerous to inspire confidence, the jungle people no longer hid. On the contrary, they came out to the very edge of the track to exchange greetings. They were very good-natured, exceedingly well-formed, and quite jocular with our boys. Especially did our suave and elegant Simba sparkle. This resident public, called from its daily labours and duties, did not always show as gaudy a make-up as did the dressed-up travelling public. Banana leaves were popular wear, and seemed to us at once pretty and fresh. To be sure some had rather withered away; but even wool will shrink. We saw some grass skirts, like the Sunday-school pictures.

At noon we stopped under a tree by a little stream for lunch. Before long a dozen women were lined up in front of us staring at Billy with all their might. She nodded and smiled at them. Thereupon they sent one of their number away. The messenger returned after a few moments carrying a bunch of the small eating bananas which she laid at our feet. Billy fished some beads out of her saddle bags, and presented them. Friendly relations having been thus fully established, two or three of the women scurried hastily away, to return a few moments later each with her small child. To these infants they carefully and earnestly pointed out Billy and her wonders, talking in a tongue unknown to us. The admonition undoubtedly ran something like this:

"Now, my child, look well at this: for when you get to be a very old person you will be able to look back at the day when with your own eyes you beheld a white woman. See all the strange things she wears-and HASN'T she a funny face?"

We offered these bung-eyed and totally naked youngsters various bribes in the way of beads, the tinfoil from chocolate, and even a small piece of the chocolate itself. Most of them howled and hid their faces against their mothers. The mothers looked scandalized, and hypocritically astounded, and mortified.

They made remarks, still in an unknown language, but which much past experience enabled me to translate very readily:

"I don't know what has got into little Willie," was the drift of it. "I have never known him to act this way before. Why, only yesterday I was saying to his father that it really seemed as though that child NEVER cried-"

It made me feel quite friendly and at home.

Now at last came two marvellous and magnificent personages before whom the women and children drew back to a respectful distance. These potentates squatted down and smiled at us engagingly. Evidently this was a really important couple, so we called up Simba, who knew the language, and had a talk.

481

They were old men, straight, and very tall, with the hawk-faced, high-headed dignity of the true aristocrat. Their robes were voluminous, of some short-haired skins, beautifully embroidered. Around their arms were armlets of polished buffalo horn. They wore most elaborate ear ornaments, and long cased marquise rings extending well beyond the first joints of the fingers. Very fine old gentlemen. They were quite unarmed.

After appropriate greetings, we learned that these were the chief and his prime minister of a nearby village hidden in the jungle. We exchanged polite phrases; then offered tobacco. This was accepted. From the jungle came a youth carrying more bananas. We indicated our pleasure. The old men arose with great dignity and departed, sweeping the women and children before them.

We rode on. Our acquired retinue, which had waited at a respectful distance, went on too. I suppose they must have desired the prestige of being attached to Our Persons. In the depths of the forest Billy succumbed to the temptation to bargain, and made her first trade. Her prize was a long water gourd strapped with leather and decorated with cowry shells. Our boys were completely scandalized at the price she paid for it, so I fear the wily savage got ahead of her.

About the middle of the afternoon we sat down to wait for the safari to catch up. It would never do to cheat our boys out of their anticipated grand entrance to the Government post at Meru. We finally debouched from the forest to the great clearing at the head of a most impressive procession, flags flying, oryx horns blowing, boys chanting and beating the sides of their loads with the safari sticks. As there happened to be gathered, at this time, several thousand of warriors for the purpose of a council, or shauri, with the District Commissioner we had just the audience to delight our barbaric hearts.

(b) MERU

The Government post at Meru is situated in a clearing won from the forest on the first gentle slopes of Kenia's ranges. The clearing is a very large one, and on it the grass grows green and short, like a lawn. It resembles, as much as anything else, the rolling, beautiful downs of a first-class country club, and the illusion is enhanced by the Commissioner's house among some trees atop a hill. Well-kept roadways railed with rustic fences lead from the house to the native quarters lying in the hollow and to the Government offices atop another hill. Then also there are the quarters of the Nubian troops; round low houses with conical grass roofs.

These, and the presence everywhere of savages, rather take away from the first country-club effect. A corral seemed full of a seething mob of natives; we found later that this was the market, a place of exchange. Groups wandered idly here and there across the greensward; and other groups sat in circles under the shade of trees, each man's spear stuck in the ground behind him. At stated points were the Nubians, fine, tall, black, soldierly men, with red fez, khaki shirt, and short breeches, bare knees and feet, spiral puttees, and a broad red sash of webbing. One of these soldiers assigned us a place to camp. We directed our safari there, and then immediately rode over to pay our respects to the Commissioner.

The latter, Horne by name, greeted us with the utmost cordiality, and offered us cool drinks. Then we accompanied him to a grand shauri or council of chiefs.

Horne was a little chap, dressed in flannels and a big slouch hat, carrying only a light rawhide whip, with very little of the dignity and "side" usually considered necessary in dealing with wild natives. The post at Meru had been established only two years, among a people that had always been very difficult, and had only recently ceased open hostilities. Nevertheless in that length of time Horne's personal influence had won them over to positive friendliness. He had, moreover, done the entire construction work of the post itself; and this we now saw to be even more elaborate than we had at first realized. Irrigating ditches ran in all directions brimming with clear mountain water; the roads and paths were rounded, graded and gravelled; the houses were substantial, well built and well kept; fences, except of course the rustic, were whitewashed; the native quarters and "barracks" were well ranged and in perfect order. The place looked ten years old instead of only two.

We followed Horne to an enclosure, outside the gate of which were stacked a great number of spears. Inside we found the owners of those spears squatted before the open side of a small, three-walled building containing a table and a chair. Horne placed himself in the chair, lounged back, and hit the table smartly with his rawhide whip. From the centre of the throng an old man got up and made quite a long speech. When he had finished another did likewise. All was carried out with the greatest decorum. After four or five had thus spoken, Horne, without altering his lounging attitude, spoke twenty or thirty words, rapped again on the table with his rawhide whip, and immediately came over to us.

"Now," said he cheerfully, "we'll have a game of golf."

That was amusing, but not astonishing. Most of us have at one time or another laid out a scratch hole or so somewhere in the vacant lot. We returned to the house, Horne produced a sufficiency of clubs, and we sallied forth. Then came the surprise of our life! We played eighteen holes-eighteen, mind you-over an excellently laid-out and kept-up course! The fair greens were cropped short and smooth by a well-managed small herd of sheep; the putting greens were rolled, and in perfect order; bunkers had been located at the correct distances; there were water hazards in the proper spots. In short, it was a genuine, scientific, well-kept golf course. Over it played Horne, solitary except on the rare occasions when he and his assistant happened to be at the post at the same time. The nearest white man was six days' journey; the nearest small civilization 196 miles.* The whole affair was most astounding.

*Which was, in turn, over three hundred miles from the
next.

Our caddies were grinning youngsters a good deal like the Gold Dust Twins. They wore nothing but our golf bags. Afield were other supernumerary caddies: one in case we sliced, one in case we pulled, and one in case we drove straight ahead. Horne explained that unlimited caddies were easier to get than unlimited golf balls. I can well believe it.

482

F. joined forces with Horne against B. and me for a grand international match. I regret to state that America was defeated by two holes.

We returned to find our camp crowded with savages. In a short time we had established trade relations and were doing a brisk business. Two years before we should have had to barter exclusively; but now, thanks to Horne's attempt to collect an annual hut tax, money was some good. We had, however, very good luck with bright blankets and cotton cloth. Our beads did not happen here to be in fashion. Probably three months earlier or later we might have done better with them. The feminine mind here differs in no basic essential from that of civilization. Fashions change as rapidly, as often and as completely in the jungle as in Paris. The trader who brings blue beads when blue beads have "gone out" might just as well have stayed at home. We bought a number of the pretty "marquise" rings for four cents apiece (our money), some war clubs or rungas for the same, several spears, armlets, stools and the like. Billy thought one of the short, soft skin cloaks embroidered with steel beads might be nice to hang on the wall. We offered a youth two rupees for one. This must have been a high price, for every man in hearing of the words snatched off his cloak and rushed forward holding it out. As that reduced his costume to a few knick-knacks, Billy retired from the busy mart until we could arrange matters.

We dined with Horne. His official residence was most interesting. The main room was very high to beams and a grass-thatched roof, with a well-brushed earth floor covered with mats. It contained comfortable furniture, a small library, a good phonograph, tables, lamps and the like. When the mountain chill descended, Horne lit a fire in a coal-oil can with a perforated bottom. What little smoke was produced by the clean burning wood lost itself far aloft. Leopard skins and other trophies hung on the wall. We dined in another room at a well-appointed table. After dinner we sat up until the unheard of hour of ten o'clock discussing at length many matters that interested us. Horne told us of his personal bodyguard consisting of one son from each chief of his wide district. These youths were encouraged to make as good an appearance as possible, and as a consequence turned out in the extreme of savage gorgeousness. Horne spoke of them carelessly as a "matter of policy in keeping the different tribes well disposed," but I thought he was at heart a little proud of them. Certainly, later and from other sources, we heard great tales of their endurance, devotion and efficiency. Also we heard that Horne had cut in half his six months' leave (earned by three years' continuous service in the jungle) to hurry back from England because he could not bear the thought of being absent from the first collection of the hut tax! He is a good man.

We said good-night to him and stepped from the lighted house into the vast tropical night. The little rays of our lantern showed us the inequalities of the ground, and where to step across the bubbling, little irrigation streams. But thousands of stars insisted on a simplification. The broad, rolling meadows of the clearing lay half guessed in the dim light; and about its edge was the velvet band of the forest, dark and mysterious, stretching away for leagues into the jungle. From it near at hand, far away, came the rhythmic beating of solemn great drums, and the rising and falling chants of the savage peoples.

(C) THE CHIEFS

We left Meru well observed by a very large audience, much to the delight of our safari boys, who love to show off. We had acquired fourteen more small boys, or totos, ranging in age from eight to twelve years. These had been fitted out by their masters to alleviate their original shenzi appearance of savagery. Some had ragged blankets, which they had already learned to twist turban wise around their heads; others had ragged old jerseys reaching to their knees, or the wrecks of full-grown undershirts; one or two even sported baggy breeches a dozen sizes too large. Each carried his little load, proudly, atop his head like a real porter, sufurias or cooking pots, the small bags of potio, and the like. Inside a mile they had gravitated together and with the small boy's relish for imitation and for playing a game, had completed a miniature safari organization of their own. Thenceforth they marched in a compact little company, under orders of their "headman." They marched very well, too, straight and proud and tireless. Of course we inspected their loads to see that they were not required to carry too much for their strength; but, I am bound to say, we never discovered an attempt at overloading. In fact, the toto brigade was treated very well indeed. M'ganga especially took great interest in their education and welfare. One of my most vivid camp recollections is that of M'ganga, very benign and didactic, seated on a chop box and holding forth to a semicircle of totos squatted on the ground before him. On reaching camp totos had several clearly defined duties: they must pick out good places for their masters' individual camps, they must procure cooking stones, they must collect kindling wood and start fires, they must fill the sufurias with water and set them over to boil. In the meantime, their masters were attending to the pitching of the bwana's camp. The rest of the time the toto played about quite happily, and did light odd jobs, or watched most attentively while his master showed him small details of a safari-boy's duty, or taught him simple handicraft. Our boys seemed to take great pains with their totos and to try hard to teach them.

Also at Meru we had acquired two cocks and four hens of the ridiculously small native breed. These rode atop the loads: their feet were tied to the cords and there they swayed and teetered and balanced all day long, apparently quite happy and interested. At each new camp site they were released and went scratching and clucking around among the tents. They lent our temporary quarters quite a settled air of domesticity. We named the cocks Gaston and Alphonse and somehow it was rather fine, in the blackness before dawn, to hear these little birds crowing stout-heartedly against the great African wilderness. Neither Gaston, Alphonse nor any of their harem were killed and eaten by their owners; but seemed rather to fulfil the function of household pets.

Along the jungle track we met swarms of people coming in to the post. One large native safari composed exclusively of women were transporting loads of trade goods for the Indian trader. They carried their burdens on their backs by means of a strap passing over the top of the head; our own "tump line" method. The labour seemed in no way to have dashed their spirits, for they grinned at us, and joked merrily with our boys. Along the way, every once in a while, we came upon people squatted down behind small stocks of sugarcane, yams, bananas, and the like. With these our boys did a brisk trade. Little paths led mysteriously into the jungle. Down them came more savages to greet us. Everybody was most friendly and cheerful, thanks to Horne's personal influence. Two years before this same lot had been hostile. From every hidden village came the headmen or chiefs. They all wanted to shake hands-the ordinary citizen never dreamed of aspiring to that honour-and they all spat carefully into their palms before they did so. This all had to be done in passing; for ordinary village headmen it was beneath Our Dignity to draw rein. Once only we broke over this rule. That was in the case of an old fellow with white hair who managed to get so tangled up in the shrubbery that he could not get to us. He was so frantic with disappointment that we made an exception and waited.

About three miles out, we lost one of our newly acquired totos. Reason: an exasperated parent who had followed from Meru for the purpose of reclaiming his runaway offspring. The latter was dragged off howling. Evidently he, like some of his civilized cousins, had "run away to join the circus." As nearly as we could get at it, the rest of the totos, as well as the nine additional we picked up before we quitted the jungle, had all come with their parents' consent. In fact, we soon discovered that we could buy any amount of good sound totos, not house broke however, for an average of half a rupee (16-1/2 cents) apiece.

The road was very much up and down hill over the numerous ridges that star-fish out from Mt. Kenia. We would climb down steep trails from 200 to 800 feet (measured by aneroid), cross an excellent mountain stream of crystalline dashing water, and climb out again. The trails of course had no notion of easy grades. It was very hard work, especially for men with loads; and it would have been impossible on account of the heat were it not for the numerous streams. On the slopes and in the bottoms were patches of magnificent forest; on the crests was the jungle, and occasionally an outlook over extended views. The birds and the strange tropical big-leaved trees were a constant delight-exotic and strange. Billy was in a heaven of joy, for her specialty in Africa was plants, seeds and bulbs, for her California garden. She had syces, gunbearers and tent boys all climbing, shaking branches, and generally pawing about.

This idiosyncracy of Billy's puzzled our boys hugely. At first they tried telling her that everything was poisonous; but when that did not work, they resigned themselves to their fate. In fact, some of the most enterprising like Memba Sasa, Kitaru, and, later, Kongoni used of their own accord to hunt up and bring in seeds and blossoms. They did not in the least understand what it was for; and it used to puzzle them hugely until out of sheer pity for their uneasiness, I implied that the Memsahib collected "medicine." That was rational, so the wrinkled brow of care was smoothed. From this botanical trait, Billy got her native name of "Beebee Kooletta"-"The Lady Who Says: Go Get That." For in Africa every white man has a name by which he is known among the native people. If you would get news of your friends, you must know their local cognomens-their own white man names will not do at all. For example, I was called either Bwana Machumwani or Bwana N'goma. The former means merely Master Four-eyes, referring to my glasses. The precise meaning of the latter is a matter much disputed between myself and Billy. An N'goma is a native dance, consisting of drum poundings, chantings, and hoppings around. Therefore I translate myself (most appropriately) as the Master who Makes Merry. On the other hand, Billy, with true feminine indirectness, insists that it means "The Master who Shouts and Howls." I leave it to any fairminded reader.

About the middle of the morning we met a Government runner, a proud youth, young, lithe, with many ornaments and bangles; his red skin glistening; the long blade of his spear, bound around with a red strip to signify his office, slanting across his shoulder; his buffalo hide shield slung from it over his back; the letter he was bearing stuck in a cleft stick and carried proudly before him as a priest carries a cross to the heathen-in the pictures. He was swinging along at a brisk pace, but on seeing us drew up and gave us a smart military salute.

At one point where the path went level and straight for some distance, we were riding in an absolute solitude. Suddenly from the jungle on either side and about fifty yards ahead of us leaped a dozen women. They were dressed in grass skirts, and carried long narrow wooden shields painted white and brown. These they clashed together, shrieked shrilly, and charged down on us at full speed. When within a few yards of our horses noses they came to a sudden halt, once more clashed their shields, shrieked, turned and scuttled away as fast as their legs could carry them. At a hundred yards they repeated the performance; and charged back at us again. Thus advancing and retreating, shrieking high, hitting the wooden shields with resounding crash, they preceded our slow advance for a half mile or so. Then at some signal unperceived by us they vanished abruptly into the jungle. Once more we rode forward in silence and in solitude. Why they did it I could not say.

Of this tissue were our days made. At noon our boys plucked us each two or three banana leaves which they spread down for us to lie on. Then we dozed through the hot hours in great comfort, occasionally waking to blue sky through green trees, or to peer idly into the tangled jungle. At two o'clock or a little later we would arouse ourselves reluctantly and move on. The safari we had dimly heard passing us an hour before. In this country of the direct track we did not attempt to accompany our men.

The end of the day's march found us in a little clearing where we could pitch camp. Generally this was atop a ridge, so that the boys had some distance to carry water; but that disadvantage was outweighed by the cleared space. Sometimes we found ourselves hemmed in by a wall of jungle. Again we enjoyed a broad outlook. One such in especial took in the magnificent, splintered, snow-capped peak of Kenia on the right, a tremendous gorge and rolling forested mountains straight ahead, and a great drop to a plain with other and distant mountains to the left. It was as fine a panoramic view as one could imagine.

Our tents pitched, and ourselves washed and refreshed, we gave audience to the resident chief, who had probably been waiting. With this potentate we conversed affably, after the usual expectoratorial ceremonies. Billy, being a mere

484

woman, did not always come in for this; but nevertheless she maintained what she called her "quarantine gloves," and kept them very handy. We had standing orders with our boys for basins of hot water to be waiting always behind our tents. After the usual polite exchanges we informed the chief of our needs-firewood, perhaps, milk, a sheep or the like. These he furnished. When we left we made him a present of a few beads, a knife, a blanket or such according to the value of his contribution.

To me these encounters were some of the most interesting of our many experiences, for each man differed radically from every other in his conceptions of ceremony, in his ideas, and in his methods. Our coming was a good deal of an event, always, and each chief, according to his temperament and training, tried to do things up properly. And in that attempt certain basic traits of human nature showed in the very strongest relief. Thus there are three points of view to take in running any spectacle: that of the star performer, the stage manager, or the truly artistic. We encountered well-marked specimens of each. I will tell you about them.

The star performer knew his stagecraft thoroughly; and in the exposition of his knowledge he showed incidentally how truly basic are the principles of stagecraft anywhere.

We were seated under a tree near the banks of a stream eating our lunch. Before us appeared two tall and slender youths, wreathed in smiles, engaging, and most attentive to the small niceties of courtesy. We returned their greeting from our recumbent positions, whereupon they made preparation to squat down beside us.

"Are you sultans?" we demanded sternly, "that you attempt to sit in Our Presence," and we lazily kicked the nearest.

Not at all abashed, but favourably impressed with our transcendent importance-as we intended-they leaned gracefully on their spears and entered into conversation. After a few trifles of airy persiflage they got down to business.

"This," said they, indicating the tiny flat, "is the most beautiful place to camp in all the mountains."

We doubted it.

"Here is excellent water."

We agreed to that.

"And there is no more water for a journey."

"You are liars," we observed politely.

"And near is the village of our chief, who is a great warrior, and will bring you many presents; the greatest man in these parts."

"Now you're getting to it," we observed in English; "you want trade." Then in Swahili, "We shall march two hours longer."

After a few polite phrases they went away. We finished lunch, remounted, and rode up the trail. At the edge of the canyon we came to a wide clearing, at the farther side of which was evidently the village in question. But the merry villagers, down to the last toro, were drawn up at the edge of the track in a double line through which we rode. They were very wealthy savages, and wore it all. Bright neck, arm, and leg ornaments, yards and yards of cowry shells in strings, blue beads of all sizes (blue beads were evidently "in"), odd scraps and shapes of embroidered skins, clean shaves and a beautiful polish characterized this holiday gathering. We made our royal progress between the serried ranks. About eight or ten seconds after we had passed the last villager-just the proper dramatic pause, you observe-the bushes parted and a splendid, straight, springy young man came into view and stepped smilingly across the space that separated us. And about eight or ten seconds after his emergence-again just the right dramatic pause-the bushes parted again to give entrance to four of the quaintest little dolls of wives. These advanced all abreast, parted, and took up positions two either side the smiling chief. This youth was evidently in the height of fashion, his hair braided in a tight queue bound with skin, his ears dangling with ornaments, heavy necklaces around his neck, and armlets etc., ad lib. His robe was of fine monkey skin embroidered with rosettes of beads, and his spear was very long, bright and keen. He was tall and finely built carried himself with a free, lithe swing. As the quintette came to halt, the villagers fell silent and our shauri began.

We drew up and dismounted. We all expectorated as gentlemen.

"These," said he proudly, "are my beebees."

We replied that they seemed like excellent beebees and politely inquired the price of wives thereabout, and also the market for totos. He gave us to understand that such superior wives as these brought three cows and twenty sheep apiece, but that you could get a pretty good toto for half a rupee.

"When we look upon our women," he concluded grandly, "we find them good; but when we look upon the white women they are as nothing!" He completely obliterated the poor little beebees with a magnificent gesture. They looked very humble and abashed. I was, however, a bit uncertain as to whether this was intended as a genuine tribute to Billy, or was meant to console us for having only one to his four.

Now observe the stagecraft of all this: entrance of diplomats, preliminary conversation introducing the idea of the greatness of N'Zahgi (for that was his name), chorus of villagers, and, as climax, dramatic entrance of the hero and heroines. It was pretty well done.

Again we stopped about the middle of the afternoon in an opening on the rounded top of a hill. While waiting for the safari to come up, Billy wandered away fifty or sixty yards to sit under a big tree. She did not stay long. Immediately she was settled, a dozen women and young girls surrounded her. They were almost uproariously good-natured, but Billy was probably the first white woman they had ever seen, and they intended to make the most of her. Every item of her clothes and equipment they examined minutely, handled and discussed. When she told them with great dignity to go away, they laughed consumedly, fairly tumbling into each other's arms with excess of joy. Billy tried to gather her effects for a masterly retreat, but found the press of numbers too great. At last she had to signal for help. One of us wandered over with a kiboko with which lightly he flicked the legs of such damsels as he could reach. They scattered like quail, laughing hilariously. Billy was escorted back to safety.

Shortly after the Chief and his Prime Minister came in. He was a little old gray-haired gentleman, as spry as a cricket, quite nervous, and very chatty. We indicated our wants to him, and he retired after enunciating many words. The safari came in, made camp. We had tea and a bath. The darkness fell; and still no Chief, no milk, no firewood, no promises fulfilled. There were plenty of natives around camp, but when we suggested that they get out and rustle on our behalf, they merely laughed good-naturedly. We seriously contemplated turning the whole lot out of camp.

Finally we gave it up, and sat down to our dinner. It was now quite dark. The askaris had built a little campfire out in front.

Then, far in the distance of the jungle's depths, we heard a faint measured chanting as of many people coming nearer. From another direction this was repeated. The two processions approached each other; their paths converged; the double chanting became a chorus that grew moment by moment. We heard beneath the wild weird minors the rhythmic stamping of feet, and the tapping of sticks. The procession debouched from the jungle's edge into the circle of the firelight. Our old chief led, accompanied by a bodyguard in all the panoply of war: ostrich feather circlets enclosing the head and face, shields of bright heraldry, long glittering spears. These were followed by a dozen of the quaintest solemn dolls of beebees dressed in all the white cowry shells, beads and brass the royal treasury afforded, very earnest, very much on inspection, every little head uplifted, singing away just as hard as ever they could. Each carried a gourd of milk, a bunch of bananas, some sugarcane, yams or the like. Straight to the fire marched the pageant. Then the warriors dividing right and left, drew up facing each other in two lines, struck their spears upright in the ground, and stood at attention. The quaint brown little women lined up to close the end of this hollow square, of which our group was, roughly speaking, the fourth side. Then all came to attention. The song now rose to a wild and ecstatic minor chanting. The beebees, still singing, one by one cast their burdens between the files and at our feet in the middle of the hollow square. Then they continued their chant, singing away at the tops of their little lungs, their eyes and teeth showing, their pretty bodies held rigidly upright. The warriors, very erect and military, stared straight ahead.

And the chief? Was he the centre of the show, the important leading man, to the contemplation of whom all these glories led? Not at all! This particular chief did not have the soul of a leading man, but rather the soul of a stage manager. Quite forgetful of himself and his part in the spectacle, his brow furrowed with anxiety, he was flittering from one to another of the performers. He listened carefully to each singer in turn, holding his hand behind his ear to catch the individual note, striking one on the shoulder in admonition, nodding approval at another. He darted unexpectedly across to scrutinize a warrior, in the chance of catching a flicker of the eyelid even. Nary a flicker! They did their stage manager credit, and stood like magnificent bronzes. He even ran across to peer into our own faces to see how we liked it.

With a sudden crescendo the music stopped. Involuntarily we broke into handclapping. The old boy looked a bit startled at this, but we explained to him, and he seemed very pleased. We then accepted formally the heap of presents, by touching them-and in turn passed over a blanket, a box of matches, and two needles, together with beads for the beebees. Then F., on an inspiration, produced his flashlight. This made a tremendous sensation. The women tittered and giggled and blinked as its beams were thrown directly into their eyes; the chief's sons grinned and guffawed; the chief himself laughed like a pleased schoolboy, and seemed never to weary of the sudden shutting on and off of the switch. But the trusty Spartan warriors, standing still in their formation behind their planted spears, were not to be shaken. They glared straight in front of them, even when we held the light within a few inches of their eyes, and not a muscle quivered!

"It is wonderful! wonderful!" the old man repeated. "Many Government men have come here, but none have had anything like that! The bwanas must be very great sultans!"

After the departure of our friends, we went rather grandly to bed. We always did after any one had called us sultans.

But our prize chief was an individual named M'booley.* Our camp here also was on a fine cleared hilltop between two streams. After we had traded for a while with very friendly and prosperous people M'booley came in. He was young, tall, straight, with a beautiful smooth lithe form, and his face was hawklike and cleverly intelligent. He carried himself with the greatest dignity and simplicity, meeting us on an easy plane of familiarity. I do not know how I can better describe his manner toward us than to compare it to the manner the member of an exclusive golf club would use to one who is a stranger, but evidently a guest. He took our quality for granted; and supposed we must do the same by him, neither acting as though he considered us "great white men," nor yet standing aloof and too respectful. And as the distinguishing feature of all, he was absolutely without personal ornament.

* *Pronounce each o separately.*

Pause for a moment to consider what a real advance in esthetic taste that one little fact stands for. All M'booley's attendants were the giddiest and gaudiest savages we had yet seen, with more colobus fur, sleighbells, polished metal, ostrich plumes, and red paint than would have fitted out any two other royal courts of the jungle. The women too were wealthy and opulent without limit. It takes considerable perception among our civilized people to realize that severe simplicity amid ultra magnificence makes the most effective distinguishing of an individual. If you do not believe it, drop in at the next ball to which you are invited. M'booley had fathomed this, and what was more he had the strength of mind to act on it. Any savage loves finery for its own sake. His hair was cut short, and shaved away at the edges to leave what looked like an ordinary close-fitting skull cap. He wore one pair of plain armlets on his left upper arm and small simple ear-rings. His robe was black. He had no trace of either oil or paint, nor did he even carry a spear.

He greeted us with good-humoured ease, and inquired conversationally if we wanted anything. We suggested wood and milk, whereupon still smiling, he uttered a few casual words in his own language to no one in particular. There was no earthly doubt that he was chief. Three of the most gorgeous and haughty warriors ran out of camp. Shortly long files of women came in bringing loads of firewood; and others carrying bananas, yams, sugarcane and a sheep. Truly M'booley did things on a princely scale. We thanked him. He accepted the thanks with a casual smile, waved his hand and went on to talk of something else. In due order our M'ganga brought up one of our best trade blankets, to which we added a half dozen boxes of matches and a razor.

Now into camp filed a small procession: four women, four children, and two young men. These advanced to where M'booley was standing smoking with great satisfaction one of B's tailor-made cigarettes. M'booley advanced ten feet to meet them, and brought them up to introduce them one by one in the most formal fashion. These were of course his family, and we had to confess that they "saw" N'Zahgi's outfit of ornaments and "raised" him beyond the ceiling. We gave them each in turn the handshake of ceremony, first with the palms as we do it, and then each grasping the other's upright thumb. The "little chiefs" were proud, aristocratic little fellows, holding themselves very straight and solemn. I think one would have known them for royalty anywhere.

It was quite a social occasion. None of our guests was in the least ill at ease; in fact, the young ladies were quite coy and flirtatious. We had a great many jokes. Each of the little ladies received a handful of prevailing beads. M'booley smiled benignly at these delightful femininities. After a time he led us to the edge of the hill and showed us his houses across the cation, perched on a flat about halfway up the wall. They were of the usual grass-thatched construction, but rather larger and neater than most. Examining them through the glasses we saw that a little stream had been diverted to flow through the front yard. M'booley waved his hand abroad and gave us to understand that he considered the outlook worth looking at. It was; but an appreciation of that fact is foreign to the average native. Next morning, when we rode by very early, we found the little flat most attractively cleared and arranged. M'booley was out to shake us by the hand in farewell, shivering in the cold of dawn. The flirtatious and spoiled little beauties were not in evidence.

One day after two very deep canyons we emerged from the forest jungle into an up and down country of high jungle bush-brush. From the top of a ridge it looked a good deal like a northern cut-over pine country grown up very heavily to blackberry vines; although, of course, when we came nearer, the "blackberry vines" proved to be ten or twenty feet high. This was a district of which Horne had warned us. The natives herein were reported restless and semi-hostile; and in fact had never been friendly. They probably needed the demonstration most native tribes seem to require before they are content to settle down and be happy. At any rate safaris were not permitted in their district; and we ourselves were allowed to go through merely because we were a large party, did not intend to linger, and had a good reputation with natives.

It is very curious how abruptly, in Central Africa, one passes from one condition to another, from one tribe or race to the next. Sometimes, as in the present case, it is the traversing of a deep cation; at others the simple crossing of a tiny brook is enough. Moreover the line of demarcation is clearly defined, as boundaries elsewhere are never defined save in wartime.

Thus we smiled our good-bye to a friendly numerous people, descended a hill, and ascended another into a deserted track. After a half mile we came unexpectedly on to two men carrying each a load of reeds. These they abandoned and fled up the hillside through the jungle, in spite of our shouted assurances. A moment later they reappeared at some distance above us, each with a spear he had snatched from somewhere; they were unarmed when we first caught sight of them. Examined through the glasses they proved to be sullen looking men, copper coloured, but broad across the cheekbones, broad in the forehead, more decidedly of the negro type than our late hosts.

Aside from these two men we travelled through an apparently deserted jungle. I suspect, however, that we were probably well watched; for when we stopped for noon we heard the gunbearers beyond the screen of leaves talking to some one. On learning from our boys that these were some of the shenzis, we told them to bring the savages in for a shauri; but in this our men failed, nor could they themselves get nearer than fifty yards or so to the wild people. So until evening our impression remained that of two distant men, and the indistinct sound of voices behind a leafy screen.

We made camp comparatively early in a wide open space surrounded by low forest. Almost immediately then the savages commenced to drift in, very haughty and arrogant. They were fully armed. Besides the spear and decorated shield, some of them carried the curious small grass spears. These are used to stab upward from below, the wielder lying flat in the grass. Some of these men were fantastically painted with a groundwork ochre, on which had been drawn intricate wavy designs on the legs, like stockings, and varied stripes across the face. One particularly ingenious individual, stark naked, had outlined a roughly entire skeleton! He was a gruesome object! They stalked here and there through the camp, looking at our men and their activities with a lofty and silent contempt.

You may be sure we had our arrangements, though they did not appear on the surface. The askaris, or native soldiers, were posted here and there with their muskets; the gunbearers also kept our spare weapons by them. The askaris could not hit a barn, but they could make a noise. The gunbearers were fair shots.

Of course the chief and his prime minister came in. They were evil-looking savages. To them we paid not the slightest attention, but went about our usual business as though they did not exist. At the end of an hour they of their own initiative greeted us. We did not hear them. Half an hour later they disappeared, to return after an interval, followed by a string of young men bearing firewood. Evidently our bearing had impressed them, as we had intended. We then unbent far enough to recognize them, carried on a formal conversation for a few moments, gave them adequate presents and dismissed them. Then we ordered the askaris to clear camp and to keep it clear. No women had appeared. Even the gifts of firewood had been carried by men, a most unusual proceeding.

As soon as dark fell the drums began roaring in the forest all about our clearing, and the chanting to rise. We instructed our men to shoot first and inquire afterward, if a shenzi so much as showed himself in the clearing. This was not as bad as it sounded; the shenzi stood in no immediate danger. Then we turned in to a sleep rather light and broken by uncertainty. I do not think we were in any immediate danger of a considered attack, for these people were not openly hostile; but there was always a chance that the savages might by their drum pounding and dancing work themselves into a frenzy. Then we might have to do a little rapid shooting. Not for one instant the whole night long did those misguided savages cease their howling and dancing. At any rate we cost them a night's sleep.

Next morning we took up our march through the deserted tracks once more. Not a sign of human life did we encounter. About ten o'clock we climbed down a tremendous gash of a box canyon with precipitous cliffs. From below we looked back to see, perched high against the skyline, the motionless figures of many savages watching us from the crags. So we had had company after all, and we had not known it. This canyon proved to be the boundary line. With the same abruptness we passed again into friendly country.

(d) OUT THE OTHER SIDE

We left the jungle finally when we turned on a long angle away from Kenia. At first the open country of the foothills was closely cultivated with fields of rape and maize. We saw some of the people breaking new soil by means of long pointed sticks. The plowmen quite simply inserted the pointed end in the ground and pried. It was very slow hard work. In other fields the grain stood high and good. From among the stalks, as from a miniature jungle, the little naked totos stared out, and the good-natured women smiled at us. The magnificent peak of Kenia had now shaken itself free of the forests. On its snow the sunrises and sunsets kindled their fires. The flames of grass fires, too, could plainly be made out, incredible distances away, and at daytime, through the reek, were fascinating suggestions of distant rivers, plains, jungles, and hills. You see, we were still practically on the wide slope of Kenia's base, though the peak was many days away, and so could look out over wide country.

The last half day of this we wandered literally in a rape field. The stalks were quite above our heads, and we could see but a few yards in any direction. In addition the track had become a footpath not over two feet wide. We could occasionally look back to catch glimpses of a pack or so bobbing along on a porter's head. From our own path hundreds of other paths branched; we were continually taking the wrong fork and moving back to set the safari right before it could do likewise. This we did by drawing a deep double line in the earth across the wrong trail. Then we hustled on ahead to pioneer the way a little farther; our difficulties were further complicated by the fact that we had sent our horses back to Nairobi for fear of the tsetse fly, so we could not see out above the corn. All we knew was that we ought to go down hill.

At the ends of some of our false trails we came upon fascinating little settlements: groups of houses inside brush enclosures, with low wooden gateways beneath which we had to stoop to enter. Within were groups of beehive houses with small naked children and perhaps an old woman or old man seated cross-legged under a sort of veranda. From them we obtained new-and confusing-directions.

After three o'clock we came finally out on the edge of a cliff fifty or sixty feet high, below which lay uncultivated bottom lands like a great meadow and a little meandering stream. We descended the cliff, and camped by the meandering stream.

By this time we were fairly tired from long walking in the heat, and so were content to sit down under our tent-fly before our little table, and let Mahomet bring us sparklets and lime juice. Before us was the flat of a meadow below the cliffs and the cliffs themselves. Just below the rise lay a single patch of standing rape not over two acres in extent, the only sign of human life. It was as though this little bit had overflowed from the countless millions on the plateau above. Beyond it arose a thin signal of smoke.

We sipped our lime juice and rested. Soon our attention was attracted by the peculiar actions of a big flock of very white birds. They rose suddenly from one side of the tiny rape field, wheeled and swirled like leaves in the wind, and dropped down suddenly on the other side the patch. After a few moments they repeated the performance. The sun caught the dazzling white of their plumage. At first we speculated on what they might be, then on what they were doing, to behave in so peculiar a manner. The lime juice and the armchair began to get in their recuperative work. Somehow the distance across that flat did not seem quite as tremendous as at first. Finally I picked up the shotgun and sauntered across to investigate. The cause of action I soon determined. The owner of that rape field turned out to be an emaciated, gray-haired but spry old savage. He was armed with a spear; and at the moment his chief business in life seemed to be chasing a large flock of white birds off his grain. Since he had no assistance, and since the birds held his spear in justifiable contempt as a fowling piece, he was getting much exercise and few results. The birds gave way before his direct charge, flopped over to the other side, and continued their meal. They had already occasioned considerable damage; the rape heads were bent and destroyed for a space of perhaps ten feet from the outer edge of the field. As this grain probably constituted the old man's food supply for a season, I did not wonder at the vehemence with which he shook his spear at his enemies, nor the apparent flavour of his language, though I did marvel at his physical endurance. As for the birds, they had become cynical and impudent; they barely fluttered out of the way.

I halted the old gentleman and hastened to explain that I was neither a pirate, a robber, nor an oppressor of the poor. This as counter-check to his tendency to flee, leaving me in sole charge. He understood a little Swahili, and talked a few words of something he intended for that language. By means of our mutual accomplishment in that tongue, and through a more efficient sign language, I got him to understand the plan of campaign. It was very simple. I squatted down inside the rape, while he went around the other side to scare them up.

The white birds uttered their peculiarly derisive cackle at the old man and flapped over to my side. Then they were certainly an astonished lot of birds. I gave them both barrels and dropped a pair; got two more shots as they swung over me and dropped another pair, and brought down a straggling single as a grand finale. The flock, with shrill, derogatory remarks, flew in an airline straight away. They never deviated, as far as I could follow them with the eye. Even after they had apparently disappeared, I could catch an occasional flash of white in the sun.

Now the old gentleman came whooping around with long, undignified bounds to fall on his face and seize my foot in an excess of gratitude. He rose and capered about, he rushed out and gathered in the slain one by one and laid them in a pile at my feet. Then he danced a jig-step around them and reviled them, and fell on his face once more, repeating the word "Bwana! bwana! bwana!" over and over-"Master! master! master!" We returned to camp together, the old gentleman carrying the birds, and capering about like a small boy, pouring forth a flood of his sort of Swahili, of which I could understand only a word here and there. Memba Sasa, very dignified and scornful of such performances, met us halfway and took my gun. He seemed to be able to understand the old fellow's brand of Swahili, and said it over again in a brand I could understand. From it I gathered that I was called a marvellously great sultan, a protector of the poor, and other Arabian Nights titles.

The birds proved to be white egrets. Now at home I am strongly against the killing of these creatures, and have so expressed myself on many occasions. But, looking from the beautiful white plumage of these villainous mauraders, to the wrinkled countenance of the grateful weary old savage, I could not fan a spark of regret. And from the straight line of their retreating flight I like to think that the rest of the flock never came back, but took their toll from the wider fields of the plateau above.

Next day we reentered the game-haunted wilderness, nor did we see any more native villages until many weeks later we came into the country of the Wakamba.

## XIX. THE TANA RIVER

Our first sight of the Tana River was from the top of a bluff. It flowed below us a hundred feet, bending at a sharp elbow against the cliff on which we stood. Out of the jungle it crept sluggishly and into the jungle it crept again, brown, slow, viscid, suggestive of the fevers and the lurking beasts by which, indeed, it was haunted. From our elevation we could follow its course by the jungle that grew along its banks. At first this was intermittent, leaving thin or even open spaces at intervals, but lower down it extended away unbroken and very tall. The trees were many of them beginning to come into flower.

Either side of the jungle were rolling hills. Those to the left made up to the tremendous slopes of Kenia. Those to the right ended finally in a low broken range many miles away called the Ithanga Hills. The country gave one the impression of being clothed with small trees; although here and there this growth gave space to wide grassy plains. Later we discovered that the forest was more apparent than real. The small trees, even where continuous, were sparse enough to permit free walking in all directions, and open enough to allow clear sight for a hundred yards or so. Furthermore, the shallow wide valleys between the hills were almost invariably treeless and grown to very high thick grass.

Thus the course of the Tana possessed advantages to such as we. By following in general the course of the stream we were always certain of wood and water. The river itself was full of fish-not to speak of hundreds of crocodiles and hippopotamuses. The thick river jungle gave cover to such animals as the bushbuck, leopard, the beautiful colobus, some of the tiny antelope, waterbuck, buffalo and rhinoceros. Among the thorn and acacia trees of the hillsides one was certain of impalla, eland, diks-diks, and giraffes. In the grass bottoms were lions, rhinoceroses, a half dozen varieties of buck, and thousands and thousands of game birds such as guinea fowl and grouse. On the plains fed zebra, hartebeeste, wart-hog, ostriches, and several species of the smaller antelope. As a sportsman's paradise this region would be hard to beat.

We were now afoot. The dreaded tsetse fly abounded here, and we had sent our horses in via Fort Hall. F. had accompanied them, and hoped to rejoin us in a few days or weeks with tougher and less valuable mules. Pending his return we moved on leisurely, camping long at one spot, marching short days, searching the country far and near for the special trophies of which we stood in need.

It was great fun. Generally we hunted each in his own direction and according to his own ideas. The jungle along the river, while not the most prolific in trophies, was by all odds the most interesting. It was very dense, very hot, and very shady. Often a thorn thicket would fling itself from the hills right across to the water's edge, absolutely and hopelessly impenetrable save by way of the rhinoceros tracks. Along these then we would slip, bent double, very quietly and gingerly, keeping a sharp lookout for the rightful owners of the trail. Again we would wander among lofty trees through the tops of which the sun flickered on festooned serpent-like vines. Every once in a while we managed a glimpse of the sullen oily river through the dense leaf screen on its banks. The water looked thick as syrup, of a deadly menacing green. Sometimes we saw a loathsome crocodile lying with his nose just out of water, or heard the snorting blow of a hippopotamus coming up for air. Then the thicket forced us inland again. We stepped very slowly, very alertly, our ears cocked for the faintest sound, our eyes roving. Generally, of course, the creatures of the jungle saw us first. We became aware of them by a crash or a rustling or a scamper. Then we stood stock listening with all our ears for some sound distinguishing to the species. Thus I came to recognize the queer barking note of the bushbuck, for example, and to realize how profane and vulgar that and the beautiful creature, the impalla, can be when he forgets himself. As for the rhinoceros, he does not care how much noise he makes, nor how badly he scares you.

Personally, I liked very well to circle out in the more open country until about three o'clock, then to enter the river jungle and work my way slowly back toward camp. At that time of day the shadows were lengthening, the birds and animals were beginning to stir about. In the cooling nether world of shadow we slipped silently from thicket to thicket, from tree to tree; and the jungle people fled from us, or withdrew, or gazed curiously, or cursed us as their dispositions varied.

While thus returning one evening I saw my first colobus. He was swinging rapidly from one tree to another, his long black and white fur shining against the sun. I wanted him very much, and promptly let drive at him with the 405 Winchester. I always carried this heavier weapon in the dense jungle. Of course I missed him, but the roar of the shot so surprised him that he came to a stand. Memba Sasa passed me the Springfield, and I managed to get him in the head. At the shot another flashed into view, high up in the top of a tree. Again I aimed and fired. The beast let go and fell like a plummet. "Good shot," said I to myself. Fifty feet down the colobus seized a limb and went skipping away through the branches as lively as ever. In a moment he stopped to look back, and by good luck I landed him through the body. When we retrieved him we found that the first shot had not hit him at all!

At the time I thought he must have been frightened into falling; but many subsequent experiences showed me that this sheer let-go-all-holds drop is characteristic of the colobus and his mode of progression. He rarely, as far as my observation goes, leaps out and across as do the ordinary monkeys, but prefers to progress by a series of slanting ascents followed by breath-taking straight drops to lower levels. When closely pressed from beneath, he will go as high as he can, and will then conceal himself in the thick leaves.

B. and I procured our desired number of colobus by taking advantage of this habit-as soon as we had learned it. Shooting the beasts with our rifles we soon found to be not only very difficult, but also destructive of the skins. On the other hand, a man could not, save by sheer good fortune, rely on stalking near enough to use a shotgun. Therefore we evolved a method productive of the maximum noise, row, barked shins, thorn wounds, tumbles, bruises-and colobus! It was very simple. We took about twenty boys into the jungle with us, and as soon as we caught sight of a colobus we chased him madly. That was all there was to it.

And yet this method, simple apparently to the point of imbecility, had considerable logic back of it after all; for after a time somebody managed to get underneath that colobus when he was at the top of a tree. Then the beast would hide.

Consider then a tumbling riotous mob careering through the jungle as fast as the jungle would let it, slipping, stumbling, falling flat, getting tangled hopelessly, disentangling with profane remarks, falling behind and catching up again, everybody yelling and shrieking. Ahead of us we caught glimpses of the sleek bounding black and white creature, running up the long slanting limbs, and dropping like a plummet into the lower branches of the next tree. We white men never could keep up with the best of our men at this sort of work, although in the open country I could hold them well enough. We could see them dashing through the thick cover at a great rate of speed far ahead of us. After an interval came a great shout in chorus. By this we knew that the quarry had been definitely brought to a stand. Arriving at the spot we craned our heads backward, and proceeded to get a crick in the neck trying to make out invisible colobus in the very tops of the trees above us. For gaudily marked beasts the colobus were extraordinarily difficult to see. This was in no sense owing to any far-fetched application of protective colouration; but to the remarkable skill the animals possessed in concealing themselves behind apparently the scantiest and most inadequate cover. Fortunately for us our boys' ability to see them was equally remarkable. Indeed, the most difficult part of their task was to point the game out to us. We squinted, and changed position, and tried hard to follow directions eagerly proffered by a dozen of the men. Finally one of us would, by the aid of six power-glasses, make out, or guess at a small tuft of white or black hair showing beyond the concealment of a bunch of leaves. We would unlimber the shotgun and send a charge of BB into that bunch. Then down would plump the game, to the huge and vociferous delight of all the boys. Or, as occasionally happened, the shot was followed merely by a shower of leaves and a chorus of expostulations indicating that we had mistaken the place, and had fired into empty air.

In this manner we gathered the twelve we required between us. At noon we sat under the bank, with the tangled roots of trees above us, and the smooth oily river slipping by. You may be sure we always selected a spot protected by very shoal water, for the crocodiles were numerous. I always shot these loathsome creatures whenever I got a chance, whenever the sound of a shot would not alarm more valuable game. Generally they were to be seen in midstream, just the tip of their snouts above water, and extraordinarily like anything but crocodiles. Often it took several close scrutinies through the glass to determine the brutes. This required rather nice shooting. More rarely we managed to see them on the banks, or only half submerged. In this position, too, they were all but undistinguishable as living creatures. I think this is perhaps because of their complete immobility. The creatures of the woods, standing quite still, are difficult enough to see; but I have a notion that the eye, unknown to itself, catches the sum total of little flexings of the muscles, movements of the skin, winkings, even the play of wind and light in the hair of the coat, all of which, while impossible of analysis, together relieve the appearance of dead inertia. The vitality of a creature like the crocodile, however, seems to have withdrawn into the inner recesses of its being. It lies like a log of wood, and for a log of wood it is mistaken.

Nevertheless the crocodile has stored in it somewhere a fearful vitality. The swiftness of its movements when seizing prey is most astonishing; a swirl of water, the sweep of a powerful tail, and the unfortunate victim has disappeared. For this reason it is especially dangerous to approach the actual edge of any of the great rivers, unless the water is so shallow that the crocodile could not possibly approach under cover, as is its cheerful habit. We had considerable difficulty in impressing this elementary truth on our hill-bred totos until one day, hearing wild shrieks from the direction of the river, I rushed down to find the lot huddled together in the very middle of a sand spit that-reached well out into the stream. Inquiry developed that while paddling in the shallows they had been surprised by the sudden appearance of an ugly snout and well drenched by the sweep of an eager tail. The stroke fortunately missed. We stilled the tumult, sat down quietly to wait, and at the end of ten minutes had the satisfaction of abating that croc.

Generally we killed the brutes where we found them and allowed them to drift away with the current. Occasionally however we wanted a piece of hide, and then tried to retrieve them. One such occasion showed very vividly the tenacity of life and the primitive nervous systems of these great saurians.

I discovered the beast, head out of water, in a reasonable sized pool below which were shallow rapids. My Springfield bullet hit him fair, whereupon he stood square on his head and waved his tail in the air, rolled over three or four times, thrashed the water, and disappeared. After waiting a while we moved on downstream. Returning four hours later I sneaked up quietly. There the crocodile lay sunning himself on the sand bank. I supposed he must be dead; but when I accidentally broke a twig, he immediately commenced to slide off into the water. Thereupon I stopped him with a bullet in the spine. The first shot had smashed a hole in his head, just behind the eye, about the size of an ordinary coffee cup. In spite of this wound, which would have been instantly fatal to any warm-blooded animal, the creature was so little affected that it actually reacted to a slight noise made at some distance from where it lay. Of course the wound would probably have been fatal in the long run.

The best spot to shoot at, indeed, is not the head but the spine immediately back of the head.

These brutes are exceedingly powerful. They are capable of taking down horses and cattle, with no particular effort. This I know from my own observation. Mr. Fleischman, however, was privileged to see the wonderful sight of the capture and destruction of a full-grown rhinoceros by a crocodile. The photographs he took of this most extraordinary affair leave no room for doubt. Crossing a stream was always a matter of concern to us. The boys beat the surface of the water vigorously with their safari sticks. On occasion we have even let loose a few heavy bullets to stir up the pool before venturing in.

A steep climb through thorn and brush would always extricate us from the river jungle when we became tired of it. Then we found ourselves in a continuous but scattered growth of small trees. Between the trunks of these we could see for a hundred yards or so before their numbers closed in the view. Here was the favourite haunt of numerous beautiful impalla. We caught glimpses of them, flashing through the trees; or occasionally standing, gazing in our direction, their slender necks stretched high, their ears pointed for us. These curious ones were generally the does. The bucks were either more cautious or less inquisitive. A herd or so of eland also liked this covered country; and there were always a few waterbuck and rhinoceroses about. Often too we here encountered stragglers from the open plains-zebra or hartebeeste, very alert and suspicious in unaccustomed surroundings.

A great deal of the plains country had been burned over; and a considerable area was still afire. The low bright flames licked their way slowly through the grass in a narrow irregular band extending sometimes for miles. Behind it was blackened soil, and above it rolled dense clouds of smoke. Always accompanied it thousands of birds wheeling and dashing frantically in and out of the murk, often fairly at the flames themselves. The published writings of a certain worthy and sentimental person waste much sympathy over these poor birds dashing frenziedly about above their destroyed nests. As a matter of fact they are taking greedy advantage of a most excellent opportunity to get insects cheap. Thousands of the common red-billed European storks patrolled the grass just in front of the advancing flames, or wheeled barely above the fire. Grasshoppers were their main object, although apparently they never objected to any small mammals or reptiles that came their way. Far overhead wheeled a few thousand more assorted soarers who either had no appetite or had satisfied it.

The utter indifference of the animals to the advance of a big conflagration always impressed me. One naturally pictures the beasts as fleeing wildly, nostrils distended, before the devouring element. On the contrary I have seen kongoni grazing quite peacefully with flames on three sides of them. The fire seems to travel rather slowly in the tough grass; although at times and for a short distance it will leap to a wild and roaring life. Beasts will then lope rapidly away to right or left, but without excitement.

On these open plains we were more or less pestered with ticks of various sizes. These clung to the grass blades; but with no invincible preference for that habitat; trousers did them just as well. Then they ascended looking for openings. They ranged in size from little red ones as small as the period of a printed page to big patterned fellows the size of a pea. The little ones were much the most abundant. At times I have had the front of my breeches so covered with them that their numbers actually imparted a reddish tinge to the surface of the cloth. This sounds like exaggeration, but it is a measured statement. The process of de-ticking (new and valuable word) can then be done only by scraping with the back of a hunting knife.

Some people, of tender skin, are driven nearly frantic by these pests. Others, of whom I am thankful to say I am one, get off comparatively easy. In a particularly bad tick country, one generally appoints one of the youngsters as "tick toto." It is then his job in life to de-tick any person or domestic animal requiring his services. His is a busy existence. But though at first the nuisance is excessive, one becomes accustomed to it in a remarkably short space of time. The adaptability of the human being is nowhere better exemplified. After a time one gets so that at night he can remove a marauding tick and cast it forth into the darkness without even waking up. Fortunately ticks are local in distribution. Often one may travel weeks or months without this infliction.

I was always interested and impressed to observe how indifferent the wild animals seem to be to these insects. Zebra, rhinoceros and giraffe seem to be especially good hosts. The loathsome creatures fasten themselves in clusters wherever they can grip their fangs. Thus in a tick country a zebra's ears, the lids and corners of his eyes, his nostrils and lips, the soft skin between his legs and body, and between his hind legs, and under his tail are always crusted with ticks as thick as they can cling. One would think the drain on vitality would be enormous, but the animals are always plump and in condition. The same state of affairs obtains with the other two beasts named. The hartebeeste also carries ticks but not nearly in the same abundance; while such creatures as the waterbuck, impalla, gazelles and the smaller bucks seem either to be absolutely free from the pests, or to have a very few. Whether this is because such animals take the trouble to rid themselves, or because they are more immune from attack it would be difficult to say. I have found ticks clinging to the hair of lions, but never fastened to the flesh. It is probable that they had been brushed off from the grass in passing.

Perhaps ticks do not like lions, waterbuck, Tommies, et al., or perhaps only big coarse-grained common brutes like zebra and rhinos will stand them at all.

## XX. DIVERS ADVENTURES ALONG THE TANA

Late one afternoon I shot a wart-hog in the tall grass. The beast was an unusually fine specimen, so I instructed Fundi and the porters to take the head, and myself started for camp with Memba Sasa. I had gone not over a hundred yards when I was recalled by wild and agonized appeals of "Bwana! bwana!" The long-legged Fundi was repeatedly leaping straight up in the air to an astonishing height above the long grass, curling his legs up under him at each jump, and yelling like a steam-engine. Returning promptly, I found that the wart-hog had come to life at the first prick of the knife. He was engaged in charging back and forth in an earnest effort to tusk Fundi, and the latter was jumping high in an equally earnest effort to keep out of the way. Fortunately he proved agile enough to do so until I planted another bullet in the aggressor.

These wart-hogs are most comical brutes from whatever angle one views them. They have a patriarchal, self-satisfied, suburban manner of complete importance. The old gentleman bosses his harem outrageously, and each and every member of the tribe walks about with short steps and a stuffy parvenu small-town self-sufficiency. One is quite certain that it is only by accident that they have long tusks and live in Africa, instead of rubber-plants and self-made business and a pug-dog within commuters' distance of New York. But at the slightest alarm this swollen and puffy importance breaks down completely. Away they scurry, their tails held stiffly and straightly perpendicular, their short legs scrabbling the small stones in a frantic effort to go faster than nature had intended them to go. Nor do they cease their flight at a reasonable distance, but keep on going over hill and dale, until they fairly vanish in the blue. I used to like starting them off this way, just for the sake of contrast, and also for the sake of the delicious but impossible vision of seeing their human prototypes do likewise.

When a wart-hog is at home, he lives down a hole. Of course it has to be a particularly large hole. He turns around and backs down it. No more peculiar sight can be imagined than the sardonically toothsome countenance of a wart-hog fading slowly in the dimness of a deep burrow, a good deal like Alice's Cheshire Cat. Firing a revolver, preferably with smoky black powder, just in front of the hole annoys the wart-hog exceedingly. Out he comes full tilt, bent on damaging some one, and it takes quick shooting to prevent his doing so.

Once, many hundreds of miles south of the Tana, and many months later, we were riding quite peaceably through the country, when we were startled by the sound of a deep and continuous roaring in a small brush patch to our left. We advanced cautiously to a prospective lion, only to discover that the roaring proceeded from the depths of a wart-hog burrow. The reverberation of our footsteps on the hollow ground had alarmed him. He was a very nervous wart-hog.

On another occasion, when returning to camp from a solitary walk, I saw two wart-hogs before they saw me. I made no attempt to conceal myself, but stood absolutely motionless. They fed slowly nearer and nearer until at last they were not over twenty yards away. When finally they made me out, their indignation and amazement and utter incredulity were very funny. In fact, they did not believe in me at all for some few snorty moments. Finally they departed, their absurd tails stiff upright.

One afternoon F. and I, hunting along one of the wide grass bottom lands, caught sight of a herd of an especially fine impalla. The animals were feeding about fifty yards the other side of a small solitary bush, and the bush grew on the sloping bank of the slight depression that represented the dry stream bottom. We could duck down into the depression, sneak along it, come up back of the little bush, and shoot from very close range. Leaving the gunbearers, we proceeded to do this.

So quietly did we move that when we rose up back of the little bush a lioness lying under it with her cub was as surprised as we were!

Indeed, I do not think she knew what we were, for instead of attacking, she leaped out the other side the bush, uttering a startled snarl. At once she whirled to come at us, but the brief respite had allowed us to recover our own scattered wits. As she turned I caught her broadside through the heart. Although this shot knocked her down, F. immediately followed it with another for safety's sake. We found that actually we had just missed stepping on her tail!

The cub we caught a glimpse of. He was about the size of a setter dog. We tried hard to find him, but failed. The lioness was an unusually large one, probably about as big as the female ever grows, measuring nine feet six inches in length, and three feet eight inches tall at the shoulder.

Billy had her funny times housekeeping. The kitchen department never quite ceased marvelling at her. Whenever she went to the cook-camp to deliver her orders she was surrounded by an attentive and respectful audience. One day, after holding forth for some time in Swahili, she found that she had been standing hobnailed on one of the boy's feet.

"Why, Mahomet!" she cried. "That must hurt you! Why didn't you tell me?"

"Memsahib," he smiled politely, "I think perhaps you move some time!"

On another occasion she was trying to tell the cook, through Mahomet as interpreter, that she wanted a tough old buffalo steak pounded, boarding-house style. This evidently puzzled all hands. They turned to in an earnest discussion of what it was all about, anyway. Billy understood Swahili well enough at that time to gather that they could not understand the Memsahib's wanting the meat "kiboked"-FLOGGED. Was it a religious rite, or a piece of revenge? They gave it up.

"All right," said Mahomet patiently at last. "He say he do it. WHICH ONE IS IT?"

Part of our supplies comprised tins of dehydrated fruit. One evening Billy decided to have a grand celebration, so she passed out a tin marked "rhubarb" and some cornstarch, together with suitable instructions for a fruit pudding. In a little while the cook returned.

*"Nataka m'tund-I want fruit,"* said he.

Billy pointed out, severely, that he already had fruit. He went away shaking his head. Evening and the pudding came. It looked good, and we congratulated Billy on her culinary enterprise. Being hungry, we took big mouthfuls. There followed splutterings and investigations. The rhubarb can proved to be an old one containing heavy gun grease!

When finally we parted with our faithful cook we bought him a really wonderful many bladed knife as a present. On seeing it he slumped to the ground-six feet of lofty dignity-and began to weep violently, rocking back and forth in an excess of grief.

"Why, what is it?" we inquired, alarmed.

"Oh, Memsahib!" he wailed, the tears coursing down his cheeks, "I wanted a watch!"

One morning about nine o'clock we were riding along at the edge of a grass-grown savannah, with a low hill to our right and another about four hundred yards ahead. Suddenly two rhinoceroses came to their feet some fifty yards to our left out in the high grass, and stood looking uncertainly in our direction.

"Look out! Rhinos!" I warned instantly.

"Why-why!" gasped Billy in an astonished tone of voice, "they have manes!"

In some concern for her sanity I glanced in her direction. She was staring, not to her left, but straight ahead. I followed the direction of her gaze, to see three lions moving across the face of the hill.

Instantly we dropped off our horses. We wanted a shot at those lions very much indeed, but were hampered in our efforts by the two rhinoceroses, now stamping, snorting, and moving slowly in our direction. The language we muttered was racy, but we dropped to a kneeling position and opened fire on the disappearing lions. It was most distinctly a case of divided attention, one eye on those menacing rhinos, and one trying to attend to the always delicate operation of aligning sights and signalling from a rather distracted brain just when to pull the trigger. Our faithful gunbearers crouched by us, the heavy guns ready.

One rhino seemed either peaceable or stupid. He showed no inclination either to attack or to depart, but was willing to back whatever play his friend might decide on. The friend charged toward us until we began to think he meant battle, stopped, thought a moment, and then, followed by his companion, trotted slowly across our bows about eighty yards away, while we continued our long range practice at the lions over their backs.

In this we were not winning many cigars. F. had a 280-calibre rifle shooting the Ross cartridge through the much advertised grooveless oval bore. It was little accurate beyond a hundred yards. Memba Sasa had thrust the 405 into my hand, knowing it for the "lion gun," and kept just out of reach with the long-range Springfield. I had no time to argue the matter with him. The 405 has a trajectory like a rainbow at that distance, and I was guessing at it, and not making very good guesses either. B. had his Springfield and made closer practice, finally hitting a leg of one of the beasts. We saw him lift his paw and shake it, but he did not move lamely afterward, so the damage was probably confined to a simple scrape. It was a good shot anyway. Then they disappeared over the top of the hill.

We walked forward, regretting rhinos. Thirty yards ahead of me came a thunderous and roaring growl, and a magnificent old lion reared his head from a low bush. He evidently intended mischief, for I could see his tail switching. However, B. had killed only one lion and I wanted very much to give him the shot. Therefore, I held the front sight on the middle of his chest, and uttered a fervent wish to myself that B. would hurry up. In about ten seconds the muzzle of his rifle poked over my shoulder, so I resigned the job.

At B.'s shot the lion fell over, but was immediately up and trying to get at us. Then we saw that his hind quarters were paralyzed. He was a most magnificent sight as he reared his fine old head, roaring at us full mouthed so that the very air trembled. Billy had a good look at a lion in action. B. took up a commanding position on an ant hill to one side with his rifle levelled. F. and I advanced slowly side by side. At twelve feet from the wounded beast stopped, F. unlimbered the kodak, while I held the bead of the 405 between the lion's eyes, ready to press trigger at the first forward movement, however slight. Thus we took several exposures in the two cameras. Unfortunately one of the cameras fell in the river the next day. The other contained but one exposure. While not so spectacular as some of those spoiled, it shows very well the erect mane, the wicked narrowing of the eyes, the flattening of the ears of an angry lion. You must imagine, furthermore, the deep rumbling diapason of his growling.

We backed away, and B. put in the finishing shot. The first bullet, we then found, had penetrated the kidneys, thus inflicting a temporary paralysis.

When we came to skin him we found an old-fashioned lead bullet between the bones of his right forepaw. The entrance wound had so entirely healed over that hardly the trace of a scar remained. From what I know of the character of these beasts, I have no doubt that this ancient injury furnished the reason for his staying to attack us instead of departing with the other three lions over the hill.

Following the course of the river, we one afternoon came around a bend on a huge herd of mixed game that had been down to water. The river, a quite impassable barrier lay to our right, and an equally impassable precipitous ravine barred their flight ahead. They were forced to cross our front, quite close, within the hundred yards. We stopped to watch them go, a seemingly endless file of them, some very much frightened, bounding spasmodically as though stung; others more philosophical, loping easily and unconcernedly; still others to a few-even stopping for a moment to get a good view of us. The very young creatures, as always, bounced along absolutely stiff-legged, exactly like wooden animals suspended by an elastic, touching the ground and rebounding high, without a bend of the knee nor an apparent effort of the muscles. Young animals seem to have to learn how to bend their legs for the most efficient travel. The same is true of human babies as well. In this herd were, we estimated, some four or five hundred beasts.

While hunting near the foothills I came across the body of a large eagle suspended by one leg from the crotch of a limb. The bird's talon had missed its grip, probably on alighting, the tarsus had slipped through the crotch beyond the joint, the eagle had fallen forward, and had never been able to flop itself back to an upright position!

## XXI. THE RHINOCEROS

The rhinoceros is, with the giraffe, the hippopotamus, the gerenuk, and the camel, one of Africa's unbelievable animals. Nobody has bettered Kipling's description of him in the Just-so Stories: "A horn on his nose, piggy eyes, and few manners." He lives a self-centred life, wrapped up in the porcine contentment that broods within nor looks abroad over the land. When anything external to himself and his food and drink penetrates to his intelligence he makes a flurried fool of himself, rushing madly and frantically here and there in a hysterical effort either to destroy or get away from the cause of disturbance. He is the incarnation of a living and perpetual Grouch.

Generally he lives by himself, sometimes with his spouse, more rarely still with a third that is probably a grown-up son or daughter. I personally have never seen more than three in company. Some observers have reported larger bands, or rather collections, but, lacking other evidence, I should be inclined to suspect that some circumstances of food or water rather than a sense of gregariousness had attracted a number of individuals to one locality.

The rhinoceros has three objects in life: to fill his stomach with food and water, to stand absolutely motionless under a bush, and to imitate ant hills when he lies down in the tall grass. When disturbed at any of these occupations he snorts. The snort sounds exactly as though the safety valve of a locomotive had suddenly opened and as suddenly shut again after two seconds of escaping steam. Then he puts his head down and rushes madly in some direction, generally upwind. As he weighs about two tons, and can, in spite of his appearance, get over the ground nearly as fast as an ordinary horse, he is a truly imposing sight, especially since the innocent bystander generally happens to be upwind, and hence in the general path of progress. This is because the rhino's scent is his keenest sense, and through it he becomes aware, in the majority of times, of man's presence. His sight is very poor indeed; he cannot see clearly even a moving object much beyond fifty yards. He can, however, hear pretty well.

The novice, then, is subjected to what he calls a "vicious charge" on the part of the rhinoceros, merely because his scent was borne to the beast from upwind, and the rhino naturally runs away upwind. He opens fire, and has another thrilling adventure to relate. As a matter of fact, if he had approached from the other side, and then aroused the animal with a clod of earth, the beast would probably have "charged" away in identically the same direction. I am convinced from a fairly varied experience that this is the basis for most of the thrilling experiences with rhinoceroses.

But whatever the beast's first mental attitude, the danger is quite real. In the beginning he rushes, upwind in instinctive reaction against the strange scent. If he catches sight of the man at all, it must be after he has approached to pretty close range, for only at close range are the rhino's eyes effective. Then he is quite likely to finish what was at first a blind dash by a genuine charge. Whether this is from malice or from the panicky feeling that he is now too close to attempt to get away, I never was able determine. It is probably in the majority of cases the latter. This seems indicated by the fact that the rhino, if avoided in his first rush, will generally charge right through and keep on going. Occasionally, however, he will whirl and come back to the attack. There can then be no doubt that he actually intends mischief.

Nor must it be forgotten that with these animals, AS WITH ALL OTHERS, not enough account is taken of individual variation. They, as well as man, and as well as other animals, have their cowards, their fighters, their slothful and their enterprising. And, too, there seem to be truculent and peaceful districts. North of Mt. Kenia, between that peak and the Northern Guaso Nyero River, we saw many rhinos, none of which showed the slightest disposition to turn ugly. In fact, they were so peaceful that they scrabbled off as fast as they could go every time they either scented, heard, or SAW us; and in their flight they held their noses up, not down. In the wide angle between the Tana and Thika rivers, and comprising the Yatta Plains, and in the thickets of the Tsavo, the rhinoceroses generally ran nose down in a position of attack and were much inclined to let their angry passions master them at the sight of man. Thus we never had our safari scattered by rhinoceroses in the former district, while in the latter the boys were up trees six times in the course of one morning! Carl Akeley, with a moving picture machine, could not tease a charge out of a rhino in a dozen tries, while Dugmore, in a different part of the country, was so chivied about that he finally left the district to avoid killing any more of the brutes in self-defence!

The fact of the matter is that the rhinoceros is neither animated by the implacable man-destroying passion ascribed to him by the amateur hunter, nor is he so purposeless and haphazard in his rushes as some would have us believe. On being disturbed his instinct is to get away. He generally tries to get away in the direction of the disturbance, or upwind, as the case may be. If he catches sight of the cause of disturbance he is apt to try to trample and gore it, whatever it is. As his sight is short, he will sometimes so inflict punishment on unoffending bushes. In doing this he is probably not animated by a consuming destructive blind rage, but by a naturally pugnacious desire to eliminate sources of annoyance. Missing a definite object, he thunders right through and disappears without trying again to discover what has aroused him.

This first rush is not a charge in the sense that it is an attack on a definite object. It may not, and probably will not, amount to a charge at all, for the beast will blunder through without ever defining more clearly the object of his blind dash. That dash is likely, however, at any moment, to turn into a definite charge should the rhinoceros happen to catch sight of his disturber. Whether the impelling motive would then be a mistaken notion that on the part of the beast he was so close he had to fight, or just plain malice, would not matter. At such times the intended victim is not interested in the rhino's mental processes.

Owing to his size, his powerful armament, and his incredible quickness the rhinoceros is a dangerous animal at all times, to be treated with respect and due caution. This is proved by the number of white men, out of a sparse population, that are annually tossed and killed by the brutes, and by the promptness with which the natives take to trees-thorn trees at that!-when the cry of faru! is raised. As he comes rushing in your direction, head down and long weapon pointed, tail rigidly erect, ears up, the earth trembling with his tread and the air with his snorts, you suddenly feel very small and ineffective.

If you keep cool, however, it is probable that the encounter will result only in a lot of mental perturbation for the rhino and a bit of excitement for yourself. If there is any cover you should duck down behind it and move rapidly but quietly to one side or another of the line of advance. If there is no cover, you should crouch low and hold still. The chances are he will pass to one side or the other of you, and go snorting away into the distance. Keep your eye on him very closely. If he swerves definitely in your direction, AND DROPS HIS HEAD A LITTLE LOWER, it would be just as well to open fire. Provided the beast was still far enough away to give me "sea-room," I used to put a small bullet in the flesh of the outer part of the shoulder. The wound thus inflicted was not at all serious, but the shock of the bullet usually turned the beast. This was generally in the direction of the wounded shoulder, which would indicate that the brute turned toward the apparent source of the attack, probably for the purpose of getting even. At any rate, the shot turned the rush to one side, and the rhinoceros, as usual, went right on through. If, however, he seemed to mean business, or was too close for comfort, the point to aim for was the neck just above the lowered horn.

In my own experience I came to establish a "dead line" about twenty yards from myself. That seemed to be as near as I cared to let the brutes come. Up to that point I let them alone on the chance that they might swerve or change their minds, as they often did. But inside of twenty yards, whether the rhinoceros meant to charge me, or was merely running blindly by, did not particularly matter. Even in the latter case he might happen to catch sight of me and change his mind. Thus, looking over my notebook records, I find that I was "charged" forty odd times-that is to say, the rhinoceros rushed in my general direction. Of this lot I can be sure of but three, and possibly four, that certainly meant mischief. Six more came so directly at us, and continued so to come, that in spite of ourselves we were compelled to kill them. The rest were successfully dodged.

As I have heard old hunters of many times my experience, affirm that only in a few instances have they themselves been charged indubitably and with malice aforethought, it might be well to detail my reasons for believing myself definitely and not blindly attacked.

The first instance was that when B. killed his second trophy rhinoceros. The beast's companion refused to leave the dead body for a long time, but finally withdrew. On our approaching, however, and after we had been some moments occupied with the trophy, it returned and charged viciously. It was finally killed at fifteen yards.

The second instance was of a rhinoceros that got up from the grass sixty yards away, and came headlong in my direction. At the moment I was standing on the edge of a narrow eroded ravine, ten feet deep, with perpendicular sides. The rhinoceros came on bravely to the edge of this ravine-and stopped. Then he gave an exhibition of unmitigated bad temper most amusing to contemplate-from my safe position. He snorted, and stamped, and pawed the earth, and tramped up and down at a great rate. I sat on the opposite bank and laughed at him. This did not please him a bit, but after many short rushes to the edge of the ravine, he gave it up and departed slowly, his tail very erect and rigid. From the persistency with which he tried to get at me, I cannot but think he intended something of the sort from the first.

The third instance was much more aggravating. In company with Memba Sasa and Fundi I left camp early one morning to get a waterbuck. Four or five hundred yards out, however, we came on fresh buffalo signs, not an hour old. To one who knew anything of buffaloes' habits this seemed like an excellent chance, for at this time of the morning they should be feeding not far away preparatory to seeking cover for the day. Therefore we immediately took up the trail.

It led us over hills, through valleys, high grass, burned country, brush, thin scrub, and small woodland alternately. Unfortunately we had happened on these buffalo just as they were about changing district, and they were therefore travelling steadily. At times the trail was easy to follow and at other times we had to cast about very diligently to find traces of the direction even such huge animals had taken. It was interesting work, however, and we drew on steadily, keeping a sharp lookout ahead in case the buffalo had come to a halt in some shady thicket out of the sun. As the latter ascended the heavens and the scorching heat increased, our confidence in nearing our quarry ascended likewise, for we knew that buffaloes do not like great heat. Nevertheless this band continued straight on its way. I think now they must have got scent of our camp, and had therefore decided to move to one of the alternate and widely separated feeding grounds every herd keeps in its habitat. Only at noon, and after six hours of steady trailing, covering perhaps a dozen miles, did we catch them up.

From the start we had been bothered with rhinoceroses. Five times did we encounter them, standing almost squarely on the line of the spoor we were following. Then we had to make a wide quiet circle to leeward in order to avoid disturbing them, and were forced to a very minute search in order to pick up the buffalo tracks again on the other side. This was at once an anxiety and a delay, and we did not love those rhino.

Finally, at the very edge of the Yatta Plains we overtook the herd, resting for noon in a scattered thicket. Leaving Fundi, I, with Memba Sasa, stalked down to them. We crawled and crept by inches flat to the ground, which was so hot that it fairly burned the hand. The sun beat down on us fiercely, and the air was close and heavy even among the scanty grass tufts in which we were trying to get cover. It was very hard work indeed, but after a half hour of it we gained a thin bush not over thirty yards from a half dozen dark and indeterminate bodies dozing in the very centre of a brush patch. Cautiously I wiped the sweat from my eyes and raised my glasses. It was slow work and patient work, picking out and examining each individual beast from the mass. Finally the job was done. I let fall my glasses.

495

"Monumookee y'otey-all cows," I whispered to Memba Sasa.

We backed out of there inch by inch, with intention of circling a short distance to the leeward, and then trying the herd again lower down. But some awkward slight movement, probably on my part, caught the eye of one of those blessed cows. She threw up her head; instantly the whole thicket seemed alive with beasts. We could hear them crashing and stamping, breaking the brush, rushing headlong and stopping again; we could even catch momentary glimpses of dark bodies. After a few minutes we saw the mass of the herd emerge from the thicket five hundred yards away and flow up over the hill. There were probably a hundred and fifty of them, and, looking through my glasses, I saw among them two fine old bulls. They were of course not much alarmed, as only the one cow knew what it was all about anyway, and I suspected they would stop at the next thicket.

We had only one small canteen of water with us, but we divided that. It probably did us good, but the quantity was not sufficient to touch our thirst. For the remainder of the day we suffered rather severely, as the sun was fierce.

After a short interval we followed on after the buffaloes. Within a half mile beyond the crest of the hill over which they had disappeared was another thicket. At the very edge of the thicket, asleep under an outlying bush, stood one of the big bulls!

Luck seemed with us at last. The wind was right, and between us and the bull lay only four hundred yards of knee-high grass. All we had to do was to get down on our hands and knees, and, without further precautions, crawl up within range and pot him. That meant only a bit of hard, hot work.

When we were about halfway a rhinoceros suddenly arose from the grass between us and the buffalo, and about one hundred yards away.

What had aroused him, at that distance and upwind, I do not know. It hardly seemed possible that he could have heard us, for we were moving very quietly, and, as I say, we were downwind. However, there he was on his feet, sniffing now this way, now that, in search for what had alarmed him. We sank out of sight and lay low, fully expecting that the brute would make off.

For just twenty-five minutes by the watch that rhinoceros looked and looked deliberately in all directions while we lay hidden waiting for him to get over it. Sometimes he would start off quite confidently for fifty or sixty yards, so that we thought at last we were rid of him, but always he returned to the exact spot where we had first seen him, there to stamp, and blow. The buffalo paid no attention to these manifestations. I suppose everybody in jungleland is accustomed to rhinoceros bad temper over nothing. Twice he came in our direction, but both times gave it up after advancing twenty-five yards or so. We lay flat on our faces, the vertical sun slowly roasting us, and cursed that rhino.

Now the significance of this incident is twofold: first, the fact that, instead of rushing off at the first intimation of our presence, as would the average rhino, he went methodically to work to find us; second, that he displayed such remarkable perseverance as to keep at it nearly a half hour. This was a spirit quite at variance with that finding its expression in the blind rush or in the sudden passionate attack. From that point of view it seems to me that the interest and significance of the incident can hardly be overstated.

Four or five times we thought ourselves freed of the nuisance, but always, just as we were about to move on, back he came, as eager as ever to nose us out. Finally he gave it up, and, at a slow trot, started to go away from there. And out of the three hundred and sixty degrees of the circle where he might have gone he selected just our direction. Note that this was downwind for him, and that rhinoceroses usually escape upwind.

We laid very low, hoping that, as before, he would change his mind as to direction. But now he was no longer looking, but travelling. Nearer and nearer he came. We could see plainly his little eyes, and hear the regular swish, swish, swish of his thick legs brushing through the grass. The regularity of his trot never varied, but to me lying there directly in his path, he seemed to be coming on altogether too fast for comfort. From our low level he looked as big as a barn. Memba Sasa touched me lightly on the leg. I hated to shoot, but finally when he loomed fairly over us I saw it must be now or never. If I allowed him to come closer, he must indubitably catch the first movement of my gun and so charge right on us before I would have time to deliver even an ineffective shot. Therefore, most reluctantly, I placed the ivory bead of the great Holland gun just to the point of his shoulder and pulled the trigger. So close was he that as he toppled forward I instinctively, though unnecessarily of course, shrank back as though he might fall on me. Fortunately I had picked my spot properly, and no second shot was necessary. He fell just twenty-seven feet-nine yards—from where we lay!

The buffalo vanished into the blue. We were left with a dead rhino, which we did not want, twelve miles from camp, and no water. It was a hard hike back, but we made it finally, though nearly perished from thirst.

This beast, be it noted, did not charge us at all, but I consider him as one of the three undoubtedly animated by hostile intentions. Of the others I can, at this moment, remember five that might or might not have been actually and maliciously charging when they were killed or dodged. I am no mind reader for rhinoceros. Also I am willing to believe in their entirely altruistic intentions. Only, if they want to get the practical results of their said altruistic intentions they must really refrain from coming straight at me nearer than twenty yards. It has been stated that if one stands perfectly still until the rhinoceros is just six feet away, and then jumps sideways, the beast will pass him. I never happened to meet anybody who had acted on this theory. I suppose that such exist: though I doubt if any persistent exponent of the art is likely to exist long. Personally I like my own method, and stoutly maintain that within twenty yards it is up to the rhinoceros to begin to do the dodging.

At first the traveller is pleased and curious over rhinoceros. After he has seen and encountered eight or ten, he begins to look upon them as an unmitigated nuisance. By the time he has done a week in thick rhino-infested scrub he gets fairly to hating them.

They are bad enough in the open plains, where they can be seen and avoided, but in the tall grass or the scrub they are a continuous anxiety. No cover seems small enough to reveal them. Often they will stand or lie absolutely immobile until you are within a very short distance, and then will outrageously break out. They are, in spite of their clumsy build, as quick and active as polo ponies, and are the only beasts I know of capable of leaping into full speed ahead from a recumbent position. In thorn scrub they are the worst, for there, no matter how alert the traveller may hold himself, he is likely to come around a bush smack on one. And a dozen times a day the throat-stopping, abrupt crash and smash to right or left brings him up all standing, his heart racing, the blood pounding through his veins. It is jumpy work, and is very hard on the temper. In the natural reaction from being startled into fits one snaps back to profanity. The cumulative effects of the epithets hurled after a departing and inconsiderately hasty rhinoceros may have done something toward ruining the temper of the species. It does not matter whether or not the individual beast proves dangerous; he is inevitably most startling. I have come in at night with my eyes fairly aching from spying for rhinos during a day's journey through high grass.

And, as a friend remarked, rhinos are such a mussy death. One poor chap, killed while we were away on our first trip, could not be moved from the spot where he had been trampled. A few shovelfuls of earth over the remains was all the rhinoceros had left possible.

Fortunately, in the thick stuff especially, it is often possible to avoid the chance rhinoceros through the warning given by the rhinoceros birds. These are birds about the size of a robin that accompany the beast everywhere. They sit in a row along his back occupying themselves with ticks and a good place to roost. Always they are peaceful and quiet until a human being approaches. Then they flutter a few feet into the air uttering a peculiar rapid chattering. Writers with more sentiment than sense of proportion assure us that this warns the rhinoceros of approaching danger! On the contrary, I always looked at it the other way. The rhinoceros birds thereby warned ME of danger, and I was duly thankful.

The safari boys stand quite justly in a holy awe of the rhino. The safari is strung out over a mile or two of country, as a usual thing, and a downwind rhino is sure to pierce some part of the line in his rush. Then down go the loads with a smash, and up the nearest trees swarm the boys. Usually their refuges are thorn trees, armed, even on the main trunk, with long sharp spikes. There is no difficulty in going up, but the gingerly coming down, after all the excitement has died, is a matter of deliberation and of voices uplifted in woe. Cuninghame tells of an inadequate slender and springy, but solitary, sapling into which swarmed half his safari on the advent of a rambunctious rhino. The tree swayed and bent and cracked alarmingly, threatening to dump the whole lot on the ground. At each crack the boys yelled. This attracted the rhinoceros, which immediately charged the tree full tilt. He hit square, the tree shivered and creaked, the boys wound their arms and legs around the slender support and howled frantically. Again and again rhinoceros drew back to repeat his butting of that tree. By the time Cuninghame reached the spot, the tree, with its despairing burden of black birds, was clinging to the soil by its last remaining roots.

In the Nairobi Club I met a gentleman with one arm gone at the shoulder. He told his story in a slightly bored and drawling voice, picking his words very carefully, and evidently most occupied with neither understating nor overstating the case. It seems he had been out, and had killed some sort of a buck. While his men were occupied with this, he strolled on alone to see what he could find. He found a rhinoceros, that charged viciously, and into which he emptied his gun.

"When I came to," he said, "it was just coming on dusk, and the lions were beginning to grunt. My arm was completely crushed, and I was badly bruised and knocked about. As near as I could remember I was fully ten miles from camp. A circle of carrion birds stood all about me not more than ten feet away, and a great many others were flapping over me and fighting in the air. These last were so close that I could feel the wind from their wings. It was rawther gruesome." He paused and thought a a moment, as though weighing his words. "In fact," he added with an air of final conviction, "it was QUITE gruesome!"

The most calm and imperturbable rhinoceros I ever saw was one that made us a call on the Thika River. It was just noon, and our boys were making camp after a morning's march. The usual racket was on, and the usual varied movement of rather confused industry. Suddenly silence fell. We came out of the tent to see the safari gazing spellbound in one direction. There was a rhinoceros wandering peaceably over the little knoll back of camp, and headed exactly in our direction. While we watched, he strolled through the edge of camp, descended the steep bank to the river's edge, drank, climbed the bank, strolled through camp again and departed over the hill. To us he paid not the slightest attention. It seems impossible to believe that he neither scented nor saw any evidences of human life in all that populated flat, especially when one considers how often these beasts will SEEM to become aware of man's presence by telepathy.* Perhaps he was the one exception to the whole race, and was a good-natured rhino.

* Opposing theories are those of "instinct," and of slight
causes, such a grasshoppers leaping before the hunter's
feet, not noticed by the man approaching.

The babies are astonishing and amusing creatures, with blunt noses on which the horns are just beginning to form, and with even fewer manners than their parents. The mere fact of an 800-pound baby does not cease to be curious. They are truculent little creatures, and sometimes rather hard to avoid when they get on the warpath. Generally, as far as my observation goes, the mother gives birth to but one at a time. There may be occasional twin births, but I happen never to have met so interesting a family.

Rhinoceroses are still very numerous-too numerous. I have seen as many as fourteen in two hours, and probably could have found as many more if I had been searching for them. There is no doubt, however, that this species must be the first to disappear of the larger African animals. His great size combined with his 'orrid 'abits mark him for early destruction. No such dangerous lunatic can be allowed at large in a settled country, nor in a country where men are travelling constantly. The species will probably be preserved in appropriate restricted areas. It would be a great pity to have so perfect an example of the Prehistoric Pinhead wiped out completely. Elsewhere he will diminish, and finally disappear.

For one thing, and for one thing only, is the traveller indebted to the rhinoceros. The beast is lazy, large, and has an excellent eye for easy ways through. For this reason, as regards the question of good roads, he combines the excellent qualities of Public Sentiment, the Steam Roller, and the Expert Engineer. Through thorn thickets impenetrable to anything less armoured than a Dreadnaught like himself he clears excellent paths. Down and out of eroded ravines with perpendicular sides he makes excellent wide trails, tramped hard, on easy grades, often with zigzags to ease the slant. In some of the high country where the torrential rains wash hundreds of such gullies across the line of march it is hardly an exaggeration to say that travel would be practically impossible without the rhino trails wherewith to cross. Sometimes the perpendicular banks will extend for miles without offering any natural break down to the stream-bed. Since this is so I respectfully submit to Government the following proposal:

(a) That a limited number of these beasts shall be licensed as Trail Rhinos; and that all the rest shall be killed from the settled and regularly travelled districts.

(b) That these Trail Rhinos shall be suitably hobbled by short steel chains.

(c) That each Trail Rhino shall carry painted conspicuously on his side his serial number.

(d) That as a further precaution for public safety each Trail Rhino shall carry firmly attached to his tail a suitable red warning flag. Thus the well-known habit of the rhinoceros of elevating his tail rigidly when about to charge, or when in the act of charging, will fly the flag as a warning to travellers.

(e) That an official shall be appointed to be known as the Inspector of Rhinos whose duty it shall be to examine the hobbles, numbers and flags of all Trail Rhinos, and to keep the same in due working order and repair.

And I do submit to all and sundry that the above resolutions have as much sense to them as have most of the petitions submitted to Government by settlers in a new country.

## XXIII. THE HIPPO POOL

For a number of days we camped in a grove just above a dense jungle and not fifty paces from the bank of a deep and wide river. We could at various points push through light low undergrowth, or stoop beneath clear limbs, or emerge on tiny open banks and promontories to look out over the width of the stream. The river here was some three or four hundred feet wide. It cascaded down through various large boulders and sluiceways to fall bubbling and boiling into deep water; it then flowed still and sluggish for nearly a half mile and finally divided into channels around a number of wooded islands of different sizes. In the long still stretch dwelt about sixty hippopotamuses of all sizes.

During our stay these hippos led a life of alarmed and angry care. When we first arrived they were distributed picturesquely on banks or sandbars, or were lying in midstream. At once they disappeared under water. By the end of four or five minutes they began to come to the surface. Each beast took one disgusted look, snorted, and sank again. So hasty was his action that he did not even take time to get a full breath; consequently up he had to come in not more than two minutes, this time. The third submersion lasted less than a minute; and at the end of half hour of yelling we had the hippos alternating between the bottom of the river and the surface of the water about as fast as they could make a round trip, blowing like porpoises. It was a comical sight. And as some of the boys were always out watching the show, those hippos had no respite during the daylight hours. From a short distance inland the explosive blowing as they came to the surface sounded like the irregular exhaust of a steam-engine.

We camped at this spot four days; and never, in that length of time, during the daytime, did those hippopotamuses take any recreation and rest. To be sure after a little they calmed down sufficiently to remain on the surface for a half minute or so, instead of gasping a mouthful of air and plunging below at once; but below was where they considered they belonged most of the time. We got to recognize certain individuals. They would stare at us fixedly for a while; and then would glump down out of sight like submarines.

When I saw them thus floating with only the very top of the head and snout out of water, I for the first time appreciated why the Greeks had named them hippopotamuses-the river horses. With the heavy jowl hidden; and the prominent nostrils, the long reverse-curved nose, the wide eyes, and the little pointed ears alone visible, they resembled more than a little that sort of conventionalized and noble charger seen on the frieze of the Parthenon, or in the prancy paintings of the Renaissance.

There were hippopotamuses of all sizes and of all colours. The little ones, not bigger than a grand piano, were of flesh pink. Those half-grown were mottled with pink and black in blotches. The adults were almost invariably all dark, though a few of them retained still a small pink spot or so-a sort of persistence in mature years of the eternal boy-, I suppose. All were very sleek and shiny with the wet; and they had a fashion of suddenly and violently wiggling one or the other or both of their little ears in ridiculous contrast to the fixed stare of their bung eyes. Generally they had nothing to say as to the situation, though occasionally some exasperated old codger would utter a grumbling bellow.

The ground vegetation for a good quarter mile from the river bank was entirely destroyed, and the earth beaten and packed hard by these animals. Landing trails had been made leading out from the water by easy and regular grades.

These trails were about two feet wide and worn a foot or so deep. They differed from the rhino trails, from which they could be easily distinguished, in that they showed distinctly two parallel tracks separated from each other by a slight ridge. In other words, the hippo waddles. These trails we found as far as four and five miles inland. They were used, of course, only at night; and led invariably to lush and heavy feed. While we were encamped there, the country on our side the river was not used by our particular herd of hippos. One night, however, we were awakened by a tremendous rending crash of breaking bushes, followed by an instant's silence and then the outbreak of a babel of voices. Then we heard a prolonged sw-i-sh-sh-sh, exactly like the launching of a big boat. A hippo had blundered out the wrong side the river, and fairly into our camp.

In rivers such as the Tana these great beasts are most extraordinarily abundant. Directly in front of our camp, for example, were three separate herds which contained respectively about sixty, forty, and twenty-five head. Within two miles below camp were three other big pools each with its population; while a walk of a mile above showed about as many more. This sort of thing obtained for practically the whole length of the river-hundreds of miles. Furthermore, every little tributary stream, no matter how small, provided it can muster a pool or so deep enough to submerge so large an animal, has its faithful band. I have known of a hippo quite happily occupying a ditch pool ten feet wide and fifteen feet long. There was literally not room enough for the beast to turn around; he had to go in at one end and out at the other! Each lake, too, is alive with them; and both lakes and rivers are many.

Nobody disturbs hippos, save for trophies and an occasional supply of meat for the men or of cooking fat for the kitchen. Therefore they wax fat and sassy, and will long continue to flourish in the land.

It takes time to kill a hippo, provided one is wanted. The mark is small, and generally it is impossible to tell whether or not the bullet has reached the brain. Harmed or whole the beast sinks anyway. Some hours later the distention of the stomach will float the body. Therefore the only decent way to do is to take the shot, and then wait a half day to see whether or not you have missed. There are always plenty of volunteers in camp to watch the pool, for the boys are extravagantly fond of hippo meat. Then it is necessary to manoeuvre a rope on the carcass, often a matter of great difficulty, for the other hippos bellow and snort and try to live up to the circus posters of the Blood-sweating Behemoth of Holy Writ, and the crocodiles like dark meat very much. Usually one offers especial reward to volunteers, and shoots into the water to frighten the beasts. The volunteer dashes rapidly across the shallows, makes a swift plunge, and clambers out on the floating body as onto a raft.

Then he makes fast the rope, and everybody tails on and tows the whole outfit ashore. On one occasion the volunteer produced a fish line and actually caught a small fish from the floating carcass! This sounds like a good one; but I saw it with my own two eyes.

It was at the hippo pool camp that we first became acquainted with Funny Face.

Funny Face was the smallest, furriest little monkey you ever saw. I never cared for monkeys before; but this one was altogether engaging. He had thick soft fur almost like that on a Persian cat, and a tiny human black face, and hands that emerged from a ruff; and he was about as big as old-fashioned dolls used to be before they began to try to imitate real babies with them. That is to say, he was that big when we said farewell to him. When we first knew him, had he stood in a half pint measure he could just have seen over the rim. We caught him in a little thorn ravine all by himself, a fact that perhaps indicates that his mother had been killed, or perhaps that he, like a good little Funny Face, was merely staying where he was told while she was away. At any rate he fought savagely, according to his small powers. We took him ignominiously by the scruff of the neck, haled him to camp, and dumped him down on Billy. Billy constructed him a beautiful belt by sacrificing part of a kodak strap (mine), and tied him to a chop box filled with dry grass. Thenceforth this became Funny Face's castle, at home and on the march.

Within a few hours his confidence in life was restored. He accepted small articles of food from our hands, eyeing us intently, retired and examined them. As they all proved desirable, he rapidly came to the conclusion that these new large strange monkeys, while not so beautiful and agile as his own people, were nevertheless a good sort after all. Therefore he took us into his confidence. By next day he was quite tame, would submit to being picked up without struggling, and had ceased trying to take an end off our various fingers. In fact when the finger was presented, he would seize it in both small black hands; convey it to his mouth; give it several mild and gentle love-chews; and then, clasping it with all four hands, would draw himself up like a little athlete and seat himself upright on the outspread palm. Thence he would survey the world, wrinkling up his tiny brow.

This chastened and scholarly attitude of mind lasted for four or five days. Then Funny Face concluded that he understood all about it, had settled satisfactorily to himself all the problems of the world and his relations to it, and had arrived at a good working basis for life. Therefore these questions ceased to occupy him. He dismissed them from his mind completely, and gave himself over to light-hearted frivolity.

His disposition was flighty but full of elusive charm. You deprecated his lack of serious purpose in life, disapproved heartily of his irresponsibility, but you fell to his engaging qualities. He was a typical example of the lovable good-for-naught. Nothing retained his attention for two consecutive minutes. If he seized a nut and started for his chop box with it, the chances were he would drop it and forget all about it in the interest excited by a crawling ant or the colour of a flower. His elfish face was always alight with the play of emotions and of flashing changing interests. He was greatly given to starting off on very important errands, which he forgot before he arrived.

In this he contrasted strangely with his friend Darwin. Darwin was another monkey of the same species, caught about a week later. Darwin's face was sober and pondering, and his methods direct and effective. No side excursions into the brilliant though evanescent fields of fancy diverted him from his ends. These were, generally, to get the most and best food and the warmest corner for sleep. When he had acquired a nut, a kernel of corn, or a piece of fruit, he sat him down and examined it thoroughly and conscientiously and then, conscientiously and thoroughly, he devoured it. No extraneous interest could distract his attention; not for a moment. That he had sounded the seriousness of life is proved by the fact that he had observed and understood the flighty character of Funny Face. When Funny Face acquired a titbit, Darwin took up a hump-backed position near at hand, his bright little eyes fixed on his friend's activities. Funny Face would nibble relishingly at his prune for a moment or so; then an altogether astonishing butterfly would flitter by just overhead. Funny Face, lost in ecstasy would gaze skyward after the departing marvel. This was Darwin's opportunity. In two hops he was at Funny Face's side. With great deliberation, but most businesslike directness, Darwin disengaged Funny Face's unresisting fingers from the prune, seized it, and retired. Funny Face never knew it; his soul was far away after the blazoned wonder, and when it returned, it was not to prunes at all. They were forgotten, and his wandering eye focussed back to a bright button in the grass. Thus by strict attention to business did Darwin prosper.

Darwin's attitude was always serious, and his expression grave. When he condescended to romp with Funny Face one could see that it was not for the mere joy of sport, but for the purposes of relaxation. If offered a gift he always examined it seriously before finally accepting it, turning it over and over in his hands, and considering it with wrinkled brow. If you offered anything to Funny Face, no matter what, he dashed up, seized it on the fly, departed at speed uttering grateful low chatterings; probably dropped and forgot it in the excitement of something new before he had even looked to see what it was.

"These people," said Darwin to himself, "on the whole, and as an average, seem to give me appropriate and pleasing gifts. To be sure, it is always well to see that they don't try to bunco me with olive stones or such worthless trash, but still I believe they are worth cultivating and standing in with."

"It strikes me," observed Funny Face to himself, "that my adorable Memsahib and my beloved bwana have been very kind to me to-day, though I don't remember precisely how. But I certainly do love them!"

We cut good sized holes on each of the four sides of their chop box to afford them ventilation on the march. The box was always carried on one of the safari boy's heads: and Funny Face and Darwin gazed forth with great interest. It was very amusing to see the big negro striding jauntily along under his light burden; the large brown winking eyes glued to two of the apertures. When we arrived in camp and threw the box cover open, they hopped forth, shook themselves, examined their immediate surroundings and proceeded to take a little exercise. When anything alarmed them, such as the shadow of a passing hawk, they skittered madly up the nearest thing in sight-tent pole, tree, or human form— and scolded indignantly or chittered in a low tone according to the degree of their terror. When Funny Face was very young, indeed, the grass near camp caught fire. After the excitement was over we found him completely buried in the straw of his box, crouched, and whimpering like a child. As he could hardly, at his tender age, have had any previous experience with fire, this instinctive fear was to me very interesting.

The monkeys had only one genuine enemy. That was an innocent plush lion named Little Simba. It had been given us in joke before we left California, we had tucked it into an odd corner of our trunk, had discovered it there, carried it on safari out of sheer idleness, and lo! it had become an important member of the expedition. Every morning Mahomet or Yusuf packed it-or rather him-carefully away in the tin box. Promptly at the end of the day's march Little Simba was haled forth and set in a place of honour in the centre of the table, and reigned there-or sometimes in a little grass jungle constructed by his faithful servitors-until the march was again resumed. His job in life was to look after our hunting luck. When he failed to get us what we wanted, he was punished; when he procured us what we desired he was rewarded by having his tail sewed on afresh, or by being presented with new black thread whiskers, or even a tiny blanket of Mericani against the cold. This last was an especial favour for finally getting us the greater kudu. Naturally as we did all this in the spirit of an idle joke our rewards and punishments were rather desultory. To our surprise, however, we soon found that our boys took Little Simba quite seriously. He was a fetish, a little god, a power of good or bad luck. We did not appreciate this point until one evening, after a rather disappointing day, Mahomet came to us bearing Little Simba in his hand.

"Bwana," said he respectfully, "is it enough that I shut Simba in the tin box, or do you wish to flog him?"

On one very disgraceful occasion, when everything went wrong, we plucked Little Simba from his high throne and with him made a beautiful drop-kick out into the tall grass. There, in a loud tone of voice, we sternly bade him lie until the morrow. The camp was bung-eyed. It is not given to every people to treat its gods in such fashion: indeed, in very deed, great is the white man! To be fair, having published Little Simba's disgrace, we should publish also Little Simba's triumph: to tell how, at the end of a certain very lucky three months' safari he was perched atop a pole and carried into town triumphantly at the head of a howling, singing procession of a hundred men. He returned to America, and now, having retired from active professional life, is leading an honoured old age among the trophies he helped to procure.

Funny Face first met Little Simba when on an early investigating tour. With considerable difficulty he had shinnied up the table leg, and had hoisted himself over the awkwardly projecting table edge. When almost within reach of the fascinating affairs displayed atop, he looked straight up into the face of Little Simba! Funny Face shrieked aloud, let go all holds and fell off flat on his back. Recovering immediately, he climbed just as high as he could, and proceeded, during the next hour, to relieve his feelings by the most insulting chatterings and grimaces. He never recovered from this initial experience. All that was necessary to evoke all sorts of monkey talk was to produce Little Simba. Against his benign plush front then broke a storm of remonstrance. He became the object of slow advances and sudden scurrying, shrieking retreats, that lasted just as long as he stayed there, and never got any farther than a certain quite conservative point. Little Simba did not mind. He was too busy being a god.

The Cape Buffalo is one of the four dangerous kinds of African big game; of which the other three are the lion, the rhinoceros, and the elephant. These latter are familiar to us in zoological gardens, although the African and larger form of the rhinoceros and elephant are seldom or never seen in captivity. But buffaloes are as yet unrepresented in our living collections. They are huge beasts, tremendous from any point of view, whether considered in height, in mass, or in power. At the shoulder they stand from just under five feet to just under six feet in height; they are short legged, heavy bodied bull necked, thick in every dimension. In colour they are black as to hair, and slate gray as to skin; so that the individual impression depends on the thickness of the coat. They wear their horns parted in the middle, sweeping smoothly away in the curves of two great bosses either side the head. A good trophy will measure in spread from forty inches to four feet. Four men will be required to carry in the head alone. As buffaloes when disturbed or suspicious have a habit of thrusting their noses up and forward, that position will cling to one's memory as the most typical of the species.

A great many hunters rank the buffalo first among the dangerous beasts. This is not my own opinion, but he is certainly dangerous enough. He possesses the size, power, and truculence of the rhinoceros, together with all that animal's keenness of scent and hearing but with a sharpness of vision the rhinoceros has not. While not as clever as either the lion or the elephant, he is tricky enough when angered to circle back for the purpose of attacking his pursuers in the rear or flank, and to arrange rather ingenious ambushes for the same purpose. He is rather more tenacious of life than the rhinoceros, and will carry away an extraordinary quantity of big bullets. Add to these considerations the facts that buffaloes go in herds; and that, barring luck, chances are about even they will have to be followed into the thickest cover, it can readily be seen that their pursuit is exciting.

The problem would be simplified were one able or willing to slip into the thicket or up to the grazing herd and kill the nearest beast that offers. As a matter of fact an ordinary herd will contain only two or three bulls worth shooting; and it is the hunter's delicate task to glide and crawl here and there, with due regard for sight, scent and sound, until he has picked one of these from the scores of undesirables. Many times will he worm his way by inches toward the great black bodies half defined in the screen of thick undergrowth only to find that he has stalked cows or small bulls. Then inch by inch he must back out again, unable to see twenty yards to either side, guiding himself by the probabilities of the faint chance breezes in the thicket. To right and left he hears the quiet continued crop, crop, crop, sound of animals grazing. The sweat runs down his face in streams, and blinds his eyes, but only occasionally and with the utmost caution can he raise his hand-or, better, lower his head-to clear his vision. When at last he has withdrawn from the danger zone, he wipes his face, takes a drink from the canteen, and tries again. Sooner or later his presence comes to the notice of some old cow. Behind the leafy screen where unsuspected she has been standing comes the most unexpected and heart-jumping crash! Instantly the jungle all about roars into life. The great bodies of the alarmed beasts hurl themselves through the thicket, smash! bang! crash! smash! as though a tornado were uprooting the forest. Then abruptly a complete silence! This lasts but ten seconds or so; then off rushes the wild stampede in another direction; only again to come to a listening halt of breathless stillness. So the hunter, unable to see anything, and feeling very small, huddles with his gunbearers in a compact group, listening to the wild surging short rushes, now this way, now that, hoping that the stampede may not run over him. If by chance it does, he has his two shots and the possibility of hugging a tree while the rush divides around him. The latter is the most likely; a single buffalo is hard enough to stop with two shots, let alone a herd. And yet, sometimes, the mere flash and noise will suffice to turn them, provided they are not actually trying to attack, but only rushing indefinitely about. Probably a man can experience few more thrilling moments than he will enjoy standing in one of the small leafy rooms of an African jungle while several hundred tons of buffalo crash back and forth all around him.

In the best of circumstances it is only rarely that having identified his big bull, the hunter can deliver a knockdown blow. The beast is extraordinarily vital, and in addition it is exceedingly difficult to get a fair, open shot. Then from the danger of being trampled down by the blind and senseless stampede of the herd he passes to the more defined peril from an angered and cunning single animal. The majority of fatalities in hunting buffaloes happen while following wounded beasts. A flank charge at close range may catch the most experienced man; and even when clearly seen, it is difficult to stop. The buffalo's wide bosses are a helmet to his brain, and the body shot is always chancy. The beast tosses his victim, or tramples him, or pushes him against a tree to crush him like a fly.

He who would get his trophy, however, is not always-perhaps is not generally-forced into the thicket to get it. When not much disturbed, buffaloes are in the habit of grazing out into the open just before dark; and of returning to their thicket cover only well after sunrise. If the hunter can arrange to meet his herd at such a time, he stands a very good chance of getting a clear shot. The job then requires merely ordinary caution and manoeuvring; and the only danger, outside the ever-present one from the wounded beast, is that the herd may charge over him deliberately. Therefore it is well to keep out of sight.

The difficulty generally is to locate your beasts. They wander all night, and must be blundered upon in the early morning before they have drifted back into the thickets. Sometimes, by sending skilled trackers in several directions, they can be traced to where they have entered cover. A messenger then brings the white man to the place, and every one tries to guess at what spot the buffaloes are likely to emerge for their evening stroll. It is remarkably easy to make a wrong guess, and the remaining daylight is rarely sufficient to repair a mistake. And also, in the case of a herd ranging a wide country with much tall grass and several drinking holes, it is rather difficult, without very good luck, to locate them on any given night or morning. A few herds, a very few, may have fixed habits, and so prove easy hunting.

These difficulties, while in no way formidable, are real enough in their small way; but they are immensely increased when the herds have been often disturbed. Disturbance need not necessarily mean shooting. In countries unvisited by white men often the pastoral natives will so annoy the buffalo by shoutings and other means, whenever they appear near the tame cattle, that the huge beasts will come practically nocturnal. In that case only the rankest luck will avail to get a man a chance in the open. The herds cling to cover until after sundown and just at dusk; and they return again very soon after the first streaks of dawn. If the hunter just happens to be at the exact spot, he may get a twilight shot when the glimmering ivory of his front sight is barely visible. Otherwise he must go into the thicket.

As an illustration of the first condition might be instanced an afternoon on the Tana. The weather was very hot. We had sent three lots of men out in different directions, each under the leadership of one of the gunbearers, to scout, while we took it easy in the shade of our banda, or grass shelter, on the bank of the river. About one o'clock a messenger came into camp reporting that the men under Mavrouki had traced a herd to its lying-down place. We took our heavy guns and started.

The way led through thin scrub up the long slope of a hill that broke on the other side into undulating grass ridges that ended in a range of hills. These were about four or five miles distant, and thinly wooded on sides and lower slopes with what resembled a small live-oak growth. Among these trees, our guide told us, the buffalo had first been sighted.

The sun was very hot, and all the animals were still. We saw impalla in the scrub, and many giraffes and bucks on the plains. After an hour and a half's walk we entered the parklike groves at the foot of the hills, and our guide began to proceed more cautiously. He moved forward a few feet, peered about, retraced his steps. Suddenly his face broke into a broad grin. Following his indication we looked up, and there in a tree almost above us roosted one of our boys sound asleep! We whistled at him. Thereupon he awoke, tried to look very alert, and pointed in the direction we should go. After an interval we picked up another sentinel, and another, and another until, passed on thus from one to the next, we traced the movements of the herd. Finally we came upon Mavrouki and Simba under a bush. From them, in whispers, we learned that the buffalo were karibu sana-very near; that they had fed this far, and were now lying in the long grass just ahead. Leaving the men, we now continued our forward movement on hands and knees, in single file. It was very hot work, for the sun beat square down on us, and the tall grass kept off every breath of air. Every few moments we rested, lying on our faces. Occasionally, when the grass shortened, or the slant of ground tended to expose us, we lay quite flat and hitched forward an inch at a time by the strength of our toes. This was very severe work indeed, and we were drenched in perspiration. In fact, as I had been feeling quite ill all day, it became rather doubtful whether I could stand the pace.

However after a while we managed to drop down into an eroded deep little ravine. Here the air was like that of a furnace, but at least we could walk upright for a few rods. This we did, with the most extraordinary precautions against even the breaking of a twig or the rolling of a pebble. Then we clambered to the top of the bank, wormed our way forward another fifty feet to the shelter of a tiny bush, and stretched out to recuperate. We lay there some time, sheltered from the sun. Then ahead of us suddenly rumbled a deep bellow. We were fairly upon the herd!

Cautiously F., who was nearest the centre of the bush, raised himself alongside the stem to look. He could see where the beasts were lying, not fifty yards away, but he could make out nothing but the fact of great black bodies taking their ease in the grass under the shade of trees. So much he reported to us; then rose again to keep watch.

Thus we waited the rest of the afternoon. The sun dipped at last toward the west, a faint irregular breeze wandered down from the hills, certain birds awoke and uttered their clear calls, an unsuspected kongoni stepped from the shade of a tree over the way and began to crop the grass, the shadows were lengthening through the trees. Then ahead of us an uneasiness ran through the herd. We in the grass could hear the mutterings and grumblings of many great animals. Suddenly F. snapped his fingers, stooped low and darted forward. We scrambled to our feet and followed.

Across a short open space we ran, bent double to the shelter of a big ant hill. Peering over the top of this we found ourselves within sixty yards of a long compact column of the great black beasts, moving forward orderly to the left, the points of the cow's horns, curved up and in, tossing slowly as the animals walked. On the flank of the herd was a big gray bull.

It had been agreed that B. was to have the shot. Therefore he opened fire with his 405 Winchester, a weapon altogether too light for this sort of work. At the shot the herd dashed forward to an open grass meadow a few rods away, wheeled and faced back in a compact mass, their noses thrust up and out in their typical fashion, trying with all their senses to locate the cause of the disturbance.

Taking advantage both of the scattered cover, and the half light of the shadows we slipped forward as rapidly and as unobtrusively as we could to the edge of the grass meadow. Here we came to a stand eighty yards from the buffaloes. They stood compactly like a herd of cattle, staring, tossing their heads, moving slightly, their wild eyes searching for us. I saw several good bulls, but always they moved where it was impossible to shoot without danger of getting the wrong beast. Finally my chance came; I planted a pair of Holland bullets in the shoulder of one of them.

The herd broke away to the right, sweeping past us at close range. My bull ran thirty yards with them, then went down stone dead. When we examined him we found the hole made by B.'s Winchester bullet; so that quite unintentionally and by accident I had fired at the same beast. This was lucky. The trophy, by hunter's law, of course, belonged to B.

Therefore F. and I alone followed on after the herd. It was now coming on dusk. Within a hundred yards we began to see scattered beasts. The formation of the herd had broken. Some had gone on in flight, while others in small scattered groups would stop to stare back, and would then move slowly on for a few paces before stopping again. Among these I made out a bull facing us about a hundred and twenty-five yards away, and managed to stagger him, but could not bring him down.

Now occurred an incident which I should hesitate to relate were it not that both F. and myself saw it. We have since talked it over, compared our recollections, and found them to coincide in every particular.

502

As we moved cautiously in pursuit of the slowly retreating herd three cows broke back and came running down past us. We ducked aside and hid, of course, but noticed that of the three two were very young, while one was so old that she had become fairly emaciated, a very unusual thing with buffaloes. We then followed the herd for twenty minutes, or until twilight, when we turned back. About halfway down the slope we again met the three cows, returning. They passed us within twenty yards, but paid us no attention whatever. The old cow was coming along very reluctantly, hanging back at every step, and every once in a while swinging her head viciously at one or the other of her two companions. These escorted her on either side, and a little to the rear. They were plainly urging her forward, and did not hesitate to dig her in the ribs with their horns whenever she turned especially obstinate. In fact they acted exactly like a pair of cowboys HERDING a recalcitrant animal back to its band and I have no doubt at all that when they first by us the old lady was making a break for liberty in the wrong direction, AND THAT THE TWO YOUNGER COWS WERE TRYING TO ROUND HER BACK! Whether they were her daughters or not is problematical; but it certainly seemed that they were taking care of her and trying to prevent her running back where it was dangerous to go. I never heard of a similar case, though Herbert Ward* mentions, without particulars that elephants AND BUFFALOES will assist each other WHEN WOUNDED.

* *A Voice from the Congo.*

After passing these we returned to where B. and the men, who had now come up, had prepared the dead bull for transportation. We started at once, travelling by the stars, shouting and singing to discourage the lions, but did not reach camp until well into the night.

### XXV. THE BUFFALO-continued

Some months later, and many hundreds of miles farther south, Billy and I found ourselves alone with twenty men, and two weeks to pass until C.-our companion at the time-should return from a long journey out with a wounded man. By slow stages, and relaying back and forth, we landed in a valley so beautiful in every way that we resolved to stay as long as possible. This could be but five days at most. At the end of that time we must start for our prearranged rendezvous with C.

The valley was in the shape of an ellipse, the sides of which were formed by great clifflike mountains, and the other two by hills lower, but still of considerable boldness and size. The longest radius was perhaps six or eight miles, and the shortest three or four. At one end a canyon dropped away to a lower level, and at the other a pass in the hills gave over to the country of the Narassara River. The name of the valley was Lengeetoto.

From the great mountains flowed many brooks of clear sparkling water, that ran beneath the most beautiful of open jungles, to unite finally in one main stream that disappeared down the canyon. Between these brooks were low broad rolling hills, sometimes grass covered, sometimes grown thinly with bushes. Where they headed in the mountains, long stringers of forest trees ran up to blocklike groves, apparently pasted like wafers against the base of the cliffs, but in reality occupying spacious slopes below them.

We decided to camp at the foot of a long grass slant within a hundred yards of the trees along one of the small streams. Before us we had the sweep of brown grass rising to a clear cut skyline; and all about us the distant great hills behind which the day dawned and fell. One afternoon a herd of giraffes stood silhouetted on this skyline quite a half hour gazing curiously down on our camp. Hartebeeste and zebra swarmed in the grassy openings; and impalla in the brush. We saw sing-sing and steinbuck, and other animals, and heard lions nearly every night. But principally we elected to stay because a herd of buffaloes ranged the foothills and dwelt in the groves of forest trees under the cliffs. We wanted a buffalo; and as Lengeetoto is practically unknown to white men, we thought this a good chance to get one. In that I reckoned without the fact that at certain seasons the Masai bring their cattle in, and at such times annoy the buffalo all they can.

We started out well enough. I sent Memba Sasa with two men to locate the herd. About three o'clock a messenger came to camp after me. We plunged through our own jungle, crossed a low swell, traversed another jungle, and got in touch with the other two men. They reported the buffalo had entered the thicket a few hundred yards below us. Cautiously reconnoitering the ground it soon became evident that we would be forced more definitely to locate the herd. To be sure, they had entered the stream jungle at a known point, but there could be no telling how far they might continue in the thicket, nor on what side of it they would emerge at sundown. Therefore we commenced cautiously and slowly follow the trail.

The going was very thick, naturally, and we could not see very far ahead. Our object was not now to try for a bull, but merely to find where the herd was feeding, in order that we might wait for it to come out. However, we were brought to a stand, in the middle of a jungle of green leaves, by the cropping sound of a beast grazing just the other side of a bush. We could not see it, and we stood stock still in the hope of escaping discovery ourselves. But an instant later a sudden crash of wood told us we had been seen. It was near work. The gunbearers crouched close to me. I held the heavy double gun ready. If the beast had elected to charge I would have had less than ten yards within which to stop it. Fortunately it did not do so. But instantly the herd was afoot and off at full speed. A locomotive amuck in a kindling pile could have made no more appalling a succession of rending crashes than did those heavy animals rushing here and there through the thick woody growth. We could see nothing. Twice the rush started in our direction, but stopped as suddenly as it had begun, to be succeeded by absolute stillness when everything, ourselves included, held its breath to listen. Finally, the first panic over, the herd started definitely away downstream. We ran as fast as we could out of the jungle to a commanding position on the hill. Thence we could determine the course of the herd. It continued on downstream as far as we could follow the sounds in the convolutions of the hills. Realizing that it would improbably recover enough from its alarmed condition to resume its regular habits that day, we returned to camp.

Next morning Memba Sasa and I were afield before daylight. We took no other men. In hunting I am a strong disbeliever in the common habit of trailing along a small army. It is simple enough, in case the kill is made, to send back for help. No matter how skilful your men are at stalking, the chances of alarming the game are greatly increased by numbers; while the possibilities of misunderstanding the plan of campaign, and so getting into the wrong place at the wrong time, are infinite. Alone, or with one gunbearer, a man can slip in and out a herd of formidable animals with the least chances of danger. Merely going out after camp meat is of course a different matter.

We did not follow in the direction taken by the herd the night before, but struck off toward the opposite side of the valley. For two hours we searched the wooded country at the base of the cliff mountains, working slowly around the circle, examining every inlet, ravine and gully. Plenty of other sorts of game we saw, including elephant tracks not a half hour old; but no buffalo. About eight o'clock, however, while looking through my glasses, I caught sight of some tiny chunky black dots crawling along below the mountains diagonally across the valley, and somewhat over three miles away. We started in that direction as fast as we could walk. At the end of an hour we surmounted the last swell, and stood at the edge of a steep drop. Immediately below us flowed a good-sized stream through a high jungle over the tops of which we looked to a triangular gentle slope overgrown with scattered bushes and high grass. Beyond this again ran another jungle, angling up hill from the first, to end in a forest of trees about thirty or forty acres in extent. This jungle and these trees were backed up against the slope of the mountain. The buffaloes we had first seen above the grove: they must now have sought cover among either the trees or the lower jungle, and it seemed reasonable that the beasts would emerge on the grass and bush area late in the afternoon. Therefore Memba Sasa and I selected good comfortable sheltered spots, leaned our backs against rocks, and resigned ourselves to long patience. It was now about nine o'clock in the morning, and we could not expect our game to come out before half past three at earliest. We could not, however, go away to come back later because of the chance that the buffaloes might take it into their heads to go travelling. I had been fooled that way before. For this reason, also, it was necessary, every five minutes or so, to examine carefully all our boundaries; lest the beasts might be slipping away through the cover.

The hours passed very slowly. We made lunch last as long as possible. I had in my pocket a small edition of Hawthorne's "The House of the Seven Gables," which I read, pausing every few minutes to raise my glasses for the periodical examination of the country. The mental focussing back from the pale gray half light of Hawthorne's New England to the actuality of wild Africa was a most extraordinary experience.

Through the heat of the day the world lay absolutely silent. At about half-past three, however, we heard rumblings and low bellows from the trees a half mile away. I repocketed Hawthorne, and aroused myself to continuous alertness.

The ensuing two hours passed more slowly than all the rest of the day, for we were constantly on the lookout. The buffaloes delayed most singularly, seemingly reluctant to leave their deep cover. The sun dropped behind the mountains, and their shadow commenced to climb the opposite range. I glanced at my watch. We had not more than a half hour of daylight left.

Fifteen minutes of this passed. It began to look as though our long and monotonous wait had been quite in vain; when, right below us, and perhaps five hundred yards away, four great black bodies fed leisurely from the bushes. Three of them we could see plainly. Two were bulls of fair size. The fourth, half concealed in the brush, was by far the biggest of the lot.

In order to reach them we would have to slip down the face of the hill on which we sat, cross the stream jungle at the bottom, climb out the other side, and make our stalk to within range. With a half hour more of daylight this would have been comparatively easy, but in such circumstances it is difficult to move at the same time rapidly and unseen. However, we decided to make the attempt. To that end we disencumbered ourselves of all our extras-lunch box, book, kodak, glasses, etc.-and wormed our way as rapidly as possible toward the bottom of the hill. We utilized the cover as much as we were able, but nevertheless breathed a sigh of relief when we had dropped below the line of the jungle. We wasted very little time crossing the latter, save for precautions against noise. Even in my haste, however, I had opportunity to notice its high and austere character, with the arching overhead vines, and the clear freedom from undergrowth in its heart. Across this cleared space we ran at full speed, crouching below the grasp of the vines, splashed across the brook and dashed up the other bank. Only a faint glimmer of light lingered in the jungle. At the upper edge we paused, collected ourselves, and pushed cautiously through the thick border-screen of bush.

The twilight was just fading into dusk. Of course we had taken our bearings from the other hill; so now, after reassuring ourselves of them, we began to wriggle our way at a great pace through the high grass. Our calculations were quite accurate. We stalked successfully, and at last, drenched in sweat, found ourselves lying flat within ten yards of a small bush behind which we could make out dimly the black mass of the largest beast we had seen from across the way.

Although it was now practically dark, we had the game in our own hands. From our low position the animal, once it fed forward from behind the single small bush, would be plainly outlined against the sky, and at ten yards I should be able to place my heavy bullets properly, even in the dark. Therefore, quite easy in our minds, we lay flat and rested. At the end of twenty seconds the animal began to step forward. I levelled my double gun, ready to press trigger the moment the shoulder appeared in the clear. Then against the saffron sky emerged the ugly outline and two upstanding horns of a rhinoceros!

"Faru!" I whispered disgustedly to Memba Sasa. With infinite pains we backed out, then retreated to a safe distance. It was of course now too late to hunt up the three genuine buffaloes of this ill-assorted group.

In fact our main necessity was to get through the river jungle before the afterglow had faded from the sky, leaving us in pitch darkness. I sent Memba Sasa across to pick up the effects we had left on the opposite ridge, while I myself struck directly across the flat toward camp.

I had plunged ahead thus, for two or three hundred yards, when I was brought up short by the violent snort of a rhinoceros just off the starboard bow. He was very close, but I was unable to locate him in the dusk. A cautious retreat and change of course cleared me from him, and I was about to start on again full speed when once more I was halted by another rhinoceros, this time dead ahead. Attempting to back away from him, I aroused another in my rear; and as though this were not enough a fourth opened up to the left.

It was absolutely impossible to see anything ten yards away unless it happened to be silhouetted against the sky. I backed cautiously toward a little bush, with a vague idea of having something to dodge around. As the old hunter said when, unarmed, he met the bear, "Anything, even a newspaper, would have come handy." To my great joy I backed against a conical ant hill four or five feet high. This I ascended and began anti-rhino demonstrations. I had no time to fool with rhinos, anyway. I wanted to get through that jungle before the leopards left their family circles. I hurled clods of earth and opprobrious shouts and epithets in the four directions of my four obstreperous friends, and I thought I counted four reluctant departures. Then, with considerable doubt, I descended from my ant hill and hurried down the slope, stumbling over grass hummocks, colliding with bushes, tangling with vines, but progressing in a gratifyingly rhinoless condition. Five minutes cautious but rapid feeling my way brought me through the jungle. Shortly after I raised the campfires; and so got home.

The next two days were repetitions, with slight variation, of this experience, minus the rhinos! Starting from camp before daylight we were only in time to see the herd-always aggravatingly on the other side of the cover, no matter which side we selected for our approach, slowly grazing into the dense jungle. And always they emerged so late and so far away that our very best efforts failed to get us near them before dark. The margin always so narrow, however, that our hopes were alive.

On the fourth day, which must be our last in Longeetoto, we found that the herd had shifted to fresh cover three miles along the base of the mountains. We had no faith in those buffaloes, but about half-past three we sallied forth dutifully and took position on a hill overlooking the new hiding place. This consisted of a wide grove of forest trees varied by occasional open glades and many dense thickets. So eager were we to win what had by now developed into a contest that I refused to shoot a lioness with a three-quarters-grown cub that appeared within easy shot from some reeds below us.

Time passed as usual until nearly sunset. Then through an opening into one of the small glades we caught sight of the herd travelling slowly but steadily from right to left. The glimpse was only momentary, but it was sufficient to indicate the direction from which we might expect them to emerge. Therefore we ran at top speed down from our own hill, tore through the jungle at its foot, and hastily, but with more caution, mounted the opposite slope through the scattered groves and high grass. We could hear occasionally indications of the buffaloes' slow advance, and we wanted to gain a good ambuscade above them before they emerged. We found it in the shape of a small conical hillock perched on the side hill itself, and covered with long grass. It commanded open vistas through the scattered trees in all directions. And the thicket itself ended not fifty yards away. No buffalo could possibly come out without our seeing him; and we had a good half hour of clear daylight before us. It really seemed that luck had changed at last.

We settled ourselves, unlimbered for action, and got our breath. The buffaloes came nearer and nearer. At length, through a tiny opening a hundred yards away, we could catch momentary glimpses of their great black bodies. I thrust forward the safety catch and waited. Finally a half dozen of the huge beasts were feeding not six feet inside the circle of brush, and only thirty-odd yards from where we lay.

And they came no farther! I never passed a more heart-breaking half hour of suspense than that in which little by little the daylight and our hopes faded, while those confounded buffaloes moved slowly out to the very edge of the thicket, turned, and moved as slowly back again. At times they came actually into view. We could see their sleek black bodies rolling lazily into sight and back again, like seals on the surface of water, but never could we make out more than that. I could have had a dozen good shots, but I could not even guess what I would be shooting at. And the daylight drained away and the minutes ticked by!

Finally, as I could see no end to this performance save that to which we had been so sickeningly accustomed in the last four days, I motioned to Memba Sasa, and together we glided like shadows into the thicket.

There it was already dusk. We sneaked breathlessly through the small openings, desperately in a hurry, almost painfully on the alert. In the dark shadow sixty yards ahead stood a half dozen monstrous bodies all facing our way. They suspected the presence of something unusual, but in the darkness and the stillness they could neither identify it nor locate it exactly. I dropped on one knee and snatched my prism glasses to my eyes. The magnification enabled me to see partially into the shadows. Every one of the group carried the sharply inturned points to the horns: they were all cows!

An instant after I had made out this fact, they stampeded across our face. The whole band thundered and crashed away.

Desperately we sprang after them, our guns atrail, our bodies stooped low to keep down in the shadow of the earth. And suddenly, without the slightest warning we plumped around a bush square on top of the entire herd. It had stopped and was staring back in our direction. I could see nothing but the wild toss of a hundred pair of horns silhouetted against such of the irregular saffron afterglow as had not been blocked off by the twigs and branches of the thicket. All below was indistinguishable blackness.

They stood in a long compact semicircular line thirty yards away, quite still, evidently staring intently into the dusk to find out what had alarmed them. At any moment they were likely to make another rush; and if they did so in the direction they were facing, they would most certainly run over us and trample us down.

Remembering the dusk I thought it likely that the unexpected vivid flash of the gun might turn them off before they got started. Therefore I raised the big double Holland, aimed below the line of heads, and was just about to pull trigger when my eye caught the silhouette of a pair of horns whose tips spread out instead of turning in. This was a bull, and I immediately shifted the gun in his direction. At the heavy double report, the herd broke wildly to right and left and thundered away. I confess I was quite relieved.

A low moaning bellow told us that our bull was down. The last few days' experience at being out late had taught us wisdom so Memba Sasa had brought a lantern. By the light of this, we discovered our bull down, and all but dead. To make sure, I put a Winchester bullet into his backbone.

We felt ourselves legitimately open to congratulations, for we had killed this bull from a practically nocturnal herd, in the face of considerable danger and more than considerable difficulty. Therefore we shook hands and made appropriate remarks to each other, lacking anybody to make them for us.

By now it was pitch dark in the thicket, and just about so outside. We had to do a little planning. I took the Holland gun, gave Memba Sasa the Winchester, and started him for camp after help. As he carried off the lantern, it was now up to me to make a fire and to make it quickly.

For the past hour a fine drizzle had been falling; and the whole country was wet from previous rains. I hastily dragged in all the dead wood I could find near, collected what ought to be good kindling, and started in to light a fire. Now, although I am no Boy Scout, I have lit several fires in my time. But never when I was at the same time in such a desperate need and hurry; and in possession of such poor materials. The harder I worked, the worse things sputtered and smouldered. Probably the relief from the long tension of the buffalo hunt had something to do with my general piffling inefficiency. If I had taken time to do a proper job once instead of a halfway job a dozen times, as I should have done and usually would have done, I would have had a fire in no time. I imagine I was somewhat scared. The lioness and her hulking cub had smelled the buffalo and were prowling around. I could hear them purring and uttering their hollow grunts. However, at last the flame held. I fed it sparingly, lit a pipe, placed the Holland gun next my hand, and resigned myself to waiting. For two hours this was not so bad. I smoked, and rested up, and dried out before my little fire. Then my fuel began to run low. I arose and tore down all the remaining dead limbs within the circle of my firelight. These were not many, so I stepped out into the darkness for more. Immediately I was warned back by a deep growl!

The next hour was not one of such solid comfort. I began to get parsimonious about my supply of firewood, trying to use it in such a manner as to keep up an adequate blaze, and at the same time to make it last until Memba Sasa should return with the men. I did it, though I got down to charred ends before I was through. The old lioness hung around within a hundred yards or so below, and the buffalo herd, returning, filed by above, pausing to stamp and snort at the fire. Finally, about nine o'clock, I made out two lanterns bobbing up to me through the trees.

The last incident to be selected from many experiences with buffaloes took place in quite an unvisited district over the mountains from the Loieta Plains. For nearly two months we had ranged far in this lovely upland country of groves and valleys and wide grass bottoms between hills, hunting for greater kudu. One day we all set out from camp to sweep the base of a range of low mountains in search of a good specimen of Newman's hartebeeste, or anything else especially desirable that might happen along. The gentle slope from the mountains was of grass cut by numerous small ravines grown with low brush. This brush was so scanty as to afford but indifferent cover for anything larger than one of the small grass antelopes. All the ravines led down a mile or so to a deeper main watercourse paralleling the mountains. Some water stood in the pools here; and the cover was a little more dense, but consisted at best of but a "stringer" no wider than a city street. Flanking the stringer were scattered high bushes for a few yards; and then the open country. Altogether as unlikely a place for the shade-loving buffalo as could be imagined.

We collected our Newmanii after rather a long hunt; and just at noon, when the heat of the day began to come on, we wandered down to the water for lunch. Here we found a good clear pool and drank. The boys began to make themselves comfortable by the water's edge; C. went to superintend the disposal of Billy's mule. Billy had sat down beneath the shade of the most hospitable of the bushes a hundred feet or so away, and was taking off her veil and gloves. I was carrying to her the lunch box. When I was about halfway from where the boys were drinking at the stream's edge to where she sat, a buffalo bull thrust his head from the bushes just the other side of her. His head was thrust up and forward, as he reached after some of the higher tender leaves on the bushes. So close was he that I could see plainly the drops glistening on his moist black nose. As for Billy, peacefully unwinding her long veil, she seemed fairly under the beast.

I had no weapon, and any moment might bring some word or some noise that would catch the animal's attention. Fortunately, for the moment, every one, relaxed in the first reaction after the long morning, was keeping silence. If the buffalo should look down, he could not fail to see Billy; and if he saw her, he would indubitably kill her.

As has been explained, snapping the fingers does not seem to reach the attention of wild animals. Therefore I snapped mine as vigorously as I knew how. Billy heard, looked toward me, turned in the direction of my gaze, and slowly sank prone against the ground. Some of the boys heard me also, and I could see the heads of all of them popping up in interest from the banks of the stream. My cautious but very frantic signals to lie low were understood: the heads dropped back. Mavrouki, a rifle in each hand, came worming his way toward me through the grass with incredible quickness and agility. A moment later he thrust the 405 Winchester into my hand.

This weapon, powerful and accurate as it is, the best of the lot for lions, was altogether too small for the tremendous brute before me. However, the Holland was in camp; and I was very glad in the circumstances to get this. The buffalo had browsed slowly forward into the clear, and was now taking the top off a small bush, and facing half away from us. It seemed to me quite the largest buffalo I had ever seen, though I should have been willing to have acknowledged at that moment that the circumstances had something to do with the estimate. However, later we found that the impression was correct. He was verily a giant of his kind. His height at the shoulder was five feet ten inches; and his build was even chunkier than the usual solid robust pattern of buffaloes. For example, his neck, just back of the horns, was two feet eight inches thick! He weighed not far from three thousand pounds.

Once the rifle was in my hands I lost the feeling of utter helplessness, and began to plan the best way out of the situation. As yet the beast was totally unconscious of our presence; but that could not continue long. There were too many men about. A chance current of air from any one of a half dozen directions could not fail to give him the scent. Then there would be lively doings. It was exceedingly desirable to deliver the first careful blow of the engagement while he was unaware. On the other hand, his present attitude-half away from me-was not favourable; nor, in my exposed position dared I move to a better place. There seemed nothing better than to wait; so wait we did. Mavrouki crouched close at my elbow, showing not the faintest indication of a desire to be anywhere but there.

The buffalo browsed for a minute or so; then swung slowly broadside on. So massive and low were the bosses of his horns that the brain shot was impossible. Therefore I aimed low in the shoulder. The shock of the bullet actually knocked that great beast off his feet! My respect for the hitting power of the 405 went up several notches. The only trouble was that he rebounded like a rubber ball. Without an instant's hesitation I gave him another in the same place. This brought him to his knees for an instant; but he was immediately afoot again. Billy had, with great good sense and courage, continued to lie absolutely flat within a few yards of the beast, Mavrouki and I had kept low, and C. and the men were out of sight. The buffalo therefore had seen none of his antagonists. He charged at a guess, and guessed wrong. As he went by I fired at his head, and, as we found out afterward, broke his jaw. A moment later C.'s great elephant gun roared from somewhere behind me as he fired by a glimpse through the brush at the charging animal. It was an excellent snapshot, and landed back of the ribs.

When the buffalo broke through the screen of brush I dashed after him, for I thought our only chance of avoiding danger lay in keeping close track of where that buffalo went. On the other side the bushes I found a little grassy opening, and then a small but dense thicket into which the animal had plunged. To my left, C. was running up, followed closely by Billy, who, with her usual good sense, had figured out the safest place to be immediately back of the guns. We came together at the thicket's edge.

The animal's movements could be plainly followed by the sound of his crashing. We heard him dash away some distance, pause, circle a bit to the right, and then come rushing back in our direction. Stooping low we peered into the darkness of the thicket. Suddenly we saw him, not a dozen yards away. He was still afoot, but very slow. I dropped the magazine of five shots into him as fast as I could work the lever. We later found all the bullet-holes in a spot as big as the palm of your hand. These successive heavy blows delivered all in the same place were too much for even his tremendous vitality; and slowly he sank on his side.

## XXVI. JUJA

Most people have heard of Juja, the modern dwelling in the heart of an African wilderness, belonging to our own countryman, Mr. W. N. McMillan. If most people are as I was before I saw the place, they have considerable curiosity and no knowledge of what it is and how it looks.

We came to Juja at the end of a wide circle that had lasted three months, and was now bringing us back again toward our starting point. For five days we had been camped on top a high bluff at the junction of two rivers. When we moved we dropped down the bluff, crossed one river, and, after some searching, found our way up the other bluff. There we were on a vast plain bounded by mountains thirty miles away. A large white and unexpected sign told us we were on Juja Farm, and warned us that we should be careful of our fires in the long grass.

For an hour we plodded slowly along. Herds of zebra and hartebeeste drew aside before us, dark heavy wildebeeste-the gnu-stood in groups at a safe distance their heads low, looking exactly like our vanished bison; ghostlike bands of Thompson's gazelles glided away with their smooth regular motion. On the vast and treeless plains single small objects standing above the general uniformity took an exaggerated value; so that, before it emerged from the swirling heat mirage, a solitary tree might easily be mistaken for a group of buildings or a grove. Finally, however, we raised above the horizon a dark straight clump of trees. It danced in the mirage, and blurred and changed form, but it persisted. A strange patch of white kept appearing and disappearing again. This resolved itself into the side of a building. A spider-legged water tower appeared above the trees.

Gradually we drew up on these. A bit later we swung to the right around a close wire fence ten feet high, passed through a gate, and rode down a long slanting avenue of young trees. Between the trees were century plants and flowers, and a clipped border ran before them. The avenue ended before a low white bungalow, with shady verandas all about it, and vines. A formal flower garden lay immediately about it, and a very tall flag pole had been planted in front. A hundred feet away the garden dropped off steep to one of the deep river canyons.

Two white-robed Somalis appeared on the veranda to inform us that McMillan was off on safari. Our own boys approaching at this moment, we thereupon led them past the house, down another long avenue of trees and flowers, out into an open space with many buildings at its edges, past extensive stables, and through another gate to the open plains once more. Here we made camp. After lunch we went back to explore.

Juja is situated on the top of a high bluff overlooking a river. In all directions are tremendous grass plains. Donya Sabuk-the Mountain of Buffaloes-is the only landmark nearer than the dim mountains beyond the edge of the world, and that is a day's journey away. A rectangle of possibly forty acres has been enclosed on three sides by animal-proof wire fence. The fourth side is the edge of the bluff. Within this enclosure have been planted many trees, now of good size; a pretty garden with abundance of flowers, ornamental shrubs, a sundial, and lawns. In the river bottom land below the bluff is a very extensive vegetable and fruit garden, with cornfields, and experimental plantings of rubber, and the like. For the use of the people of Juja here are raised a great variety and abundance of vegetables, fruits, and grains.

Juja House, as has been said, stands back a hundred feet from a bend in the bluffs that permits a view straight up the river valley. It is surrounded by gardens and trees, and occupies all one end of the enclosed rectangle. Farther down and perched on the edge of a bluff, are several pretty little bungalows for the accommodation of the superintendent and his family, for the bachelors' mess, for the farm offices and dispensary, and for the dairy room, the ice-plant and the post-office and telegraph station. Back of and inland from this row on the edge of the cliff, and scattered widely in open space, are a large store stocked with everything on earth, the Somali quarters of low whitewashed buildings, the cattle corrals, the stables, wild animal cages, granaries, blacksmith and carpenter shops, wagon sheds and the like. Outside the enclosure, and a half mile away, are the conical grass huts that make up the native village. Below the cliff is a concrete dam, an electric light plant, a pumping plant and a few details of the sort.

Such is a relief map of Juja proper. Four miles away, and on another river, is Long Juja, a strictly utilitarian affair where grow ostriches, cattle, sheep, and various irrigated things in the bottom land. All the rest of the farm, or estate, or whatever one would call it, is open plain, with here and there a river bottom, or a trifle of brush cover. But never enough to constitute more than an isolated and lonesome patch.

Before leaving London we had received from McMillan earnest assurances that he kept open house, and that we must take advantage of his hospitality should we happen his way. Therefore when one of his white-robed Somalis approached us to inquire respectfully as to what we wanted for dinner, we yielded weakly to the temptation and told him. Then we marched us boldly to the house and took possession.

All around the house ran a veranda, shaded bamboo curtains and vines, furnished with the luxurious teakwood chairs of the tropics of which you can so extend the arms as to form two comfortable and elevated rests for your feet. Horns of various animals ornamented the walls. A megaphone and a huge terrestrial telescope on a tripod stood in one corner. Through the latter one could examine at favourable times the herds of game on the plains.

And inside-mind you, we were fresh from three months in the wilderness-we found rugs, pictures, wall paper, a pianola, many books, baths, beautiful white bedrooms with snowy mosquito curtains, electric lights, running water, and above all an atmosphere of homelike comfort. We fell into easy chairs, and seized books and magazines. The Somalis brought us trays with iced and fizzy drinks in thin glasses. When the time came we crossed the veranda in the rear to enter a spacious separate dining-room. The table was white with napery, glittering with silver and glass, bright with flowers. We ate leisurely of a well-served course dinner, ending with black coffee, shelled nuts, and candied fruit. Replete and satisfied we strolled back across the veranda to the main house. F. raised his hand.

"Hark!" he admonished us.

We held still. From the velvet darkness came the hurried petulant barking of zebra; three hyenas howled.

## XXVII. A VISIT AT JUJA

Next day we left all this; and continued our march. About a month later, however, we encountered McMillan himself in Nairobi. I was just out from a very hard trip to the coast-Billy not with me-and wanted nothing so much as a few days' rest. McMillan's cordiality was not to be denied, however, so the very next day found us tucking ourselves into a buckboard behind four white Abyssinian mules. McMillan, some Somalis and Captain Duirs came along in another similar rig. Our driver was a Hottentot half-caste from South Africa. He had a flat face, a yellow skin, a quiet manner, and a competent hand. His name was Michael. At his feet crouched a small Kikuyu savage, in blanket ear ornaments and all the fixings, armed with a long lashed whip and raucous voice. At any given moment he was likely to hop out over the moving wheel, run forward, bat the off leading mule, and hop back again, all with the most extraordinary agility. He likewise hurled what sounded like very opprobrious epithets at such natives as did not get out the way quickly enough to suit him. The expression of his face, which was that of a person steeped in woe, never changed.

We rattled out of Nairobi at a great pace, and swung into the Fort Hall Road. This famous thoroughfare, one of the three or four made roads in all East Africa, is about sixty miles long. It is a strategic necessity but is used by thousands of natives on their way to see the sights of the great metropolis. As during the season there is no water for much of the distance, a great many pay for their curiosity with their lives. The road skirts the base of the hills, winding in and out of shallow canyons and about the edges of rounded hills. To the right one can see far out across the Athi Plains.

We met an almost unbroken succession of people. There were long pack trains of women, quite cheerful, bent over under the weight of firewood or vegetables, many with babies tucked away in the folds of their garments; mincing dandified warriors with poodle-dog hair, skewers in their ears, their jewelery brought to a high polish a fatuous expression of self-satisfaction on their faces, carrying each a section of sugarcane which they now used as a staff but would later devour for lunch; bearers, under convoy of straight soldierly red-sashed Sudanese, transporting Government goods; wild-eyed staring shenzis from the forest, with matted hair and goatskin garments, looking ready to bolt aside at the slightest alarm; coveys of marvellous and giggling damsels, their fine-grained skin anointed and shining with red oil, strung with beads and shells, very coquettish and sure of their feminine charm; naked small boys marching solemnly like their elders; camel trains from far-off Abyssinia or Somaliland under convoy of white-clad turbaned grave men of beautiful features; donkey safaris in charge of dirty degenerate looking East Indians carrying trade goods to some distant post-all these and many more, going one way or the other, drew one side, at the sight of our white faces, to let us pass.

About two o'clock we suddenly turned off from the road, apparently quite at random, down the long grassy interminable incline that dipped slowly down and slowly up again over great distance to form the Athi Plains. Along the road, with its endless swarm of humanity, we had seen no game, but after a half mile it began to appear. We encountered herds of zebra, kongoni, wildebeeste, and "Tommies" standing about or grazing, sometimes almost within range from the moving buckboard. After a time we made out the trees and water tower of Juja ahead; and by four o'clock had turned into the avenue of trees. Our approach had been seen. Tea was ready, and a great and hospitable table of bottles, ice, and siphons.

The next morning we inspected the stables, built of stone in a hollow square, like a fort, with box stalls opening directly into the courtyard and screened carefully against the deadly flies. The horses, beautiful creatures, were led forth each by his proud and anxious syce. We tried them all, and selected our mounts for the time of our stay. The syces were small black men, lean and well formed, accustomed to running afoot wherever their charges went, at walk, lope or gallop. Thus in a day they covered incredible distances over all sorts of country; but were always at hand to seize the bridle reins when the master wished to dismount. Like the rickshaw runners in Nairobi, they wore their hair clipped close around their bullet heads and seemed to have developed into a small compact hard type of their own. They ate and slept with their horses.

Just outside the courtyard of the stables a little barred window had been cut through. Near this were congregated a number of Kikuyu savages wrapped in their blankets, receiving each in turn a portion of cracked corn from a dusty white man behind the bars. They were a solemn, unsmiling, strange type of savage, and they performed all the manual work within the enclosure, squatting on their heels and pulling methodically but slowly at the weeds, digging with their pangas, carrying loads: to and fro, or solemnly pushing a lawn mower, blankets wrapped shamelessly about their necks. They were harried about by a red-faced beefy English gardener with a marvellous vocabulary of several native languages and a short hippo-hide whip. He talked himself absolutely purple in the face without, as far as my observation went, penetrating an inch below the surface. The Kikuyus went right on doing what they were already doing in exactly the same manner. Probably the purple Englishman was satisfied with that, but I am sure apoplexy of either the heat or thundering variety has him by now.

Before the store building squatted another group of savages. Perhaps in time one of the lot expected to buy something; or possibly they just sat. Nobody but a storekeeper would ever have time to find out. Such is the native way. The storekeeper in this case was named John. Besides being storekeeper, he had charge of the issuing of all the house supplies, and those for the white men's mess; he must do all the worrying about the upper class natives; he must occasionally kill a buck for the meat supply; and he must be prepared to take out any stray tenderfeet that happen along during McMillan's absence, and persuade them that they are mighty hunters. His domain was a fascinating place, for it contained everything from pianola parts to patent washstands. The next best equipped place of the kind I know of is the property room of a moving picture company.

We went to mail a letter, and found the postmaster to be a gentle-voiced, polite little Hindu, who greeted us smilingly, and attempted to conceal a work of art. We insisted; whereupon he deprecatingly drew forth a copy of a newspaper cartoon having to do with Colonel Roosevelt's visit. It was copied with mathematical exactness, and highly coloured in a manner to throw into profound melancholy the chauffeur of a coloured supplement press. We admired and praised; whereupon, still shyly, he produced more, and yet again more copies of the same cartoon. When we left, he was reseating himself to the painstaking valueless labour with which he filled his days. Three times a week such mail as Juja gets comes in via native runner. We saw the latter, a splendid figure, almost naked, loping easily, his little bundle held before him.

Down past the office and dispensary we strolled, by the comfortable, airy, white man's clubhouse. The headman of the native population passed us with a dignified salute; a fine upstanding deep-chested man, with a lofty air of fierce pride. He and his handful of soldiers alone of the natives, except the Somalis and syces, dwelt within the compound in a group of huts near the gate. There when off duty they might be seen polishing their arms, or chatting with their women. The latter were ladies of leisure, with wonderful chignons, much jewelery, and patterned Mericani wrapped gracefully about their pretty figures.

By the time we had seen all these things it was noon. We ate lunch. The various members of the party decided to do various things. I elected to go out with McMillan while he killed a wildebeeste, and I am very glad I did. It was a most astonishing performance.

You must imagine us driving out the gate in a buckboard behind four small but lively white Abyssinian mules. In the front seat were Michael, the Hottentot driver, and McMillan's Somali gunbearer. In the rear seat were McMillan and myself, while a small black syce perched precariously behind. Our rifles rested in a sling before us. So we jogged out on the road to Long Juju, examining with a critical eye the herds of game to right and left of us. The latter examined us, apparently, with an eye as critical. Finally, in a herd of zebra, we espied a lone wildebeeste.

The wildebeeste is the Jekyll and Hyde of the animal kingdom. His usual and familiar habit is that of a heavy, sluggish animal, like our vanished bison. He stands solid and inert, his head down; he plods slowly forward in single file, his horns swinging, each foot planted deliberately. In short, he is the personification of dignity, solid respectability, gravity of demeanour. But then all of a sudden, at any small interruption, he becomes the giddiest of created beings. Up goes his head and tail, he buck jumps, cavorts, gambols, kicks up his heels, bounds stiff-legged, and generally performs like an irresponsible infant. To see a whole herd at once of these grave and reverend seigneurs suddenly blow up into such light-headed capers goes far to destroy one's faith in the stability of institutions.

Also the wildebeeste is not misnamed. He is a conservative, and he sees no particular reason for allowing his curiosity to interfere with his preconceived beliefs. The latter are distrustful. Therefore he and his females and his young-I should say small-depart when one is yet far away. I say small, because I do not believe that any wildebeeste is ever young. They do not resemble calves, but are exact replicas of the big ones, just as Niobe's daughters are in nothing childlike, but merely smaller women.

When we caught sight of this lone wildebeeste among the zebra, I naturally expected that we would pull up the buckboard, descend, and approach to within some sort of long range. Then we would open fire. Barring luck, the wildebeeste would thereupon depart "wilder and beestier than ever," as John McCutcheon has it. Not at all! Michael, the Hottentot, turned the buckboard off the road, headed toward the distant quarry, and charged at full speed! Over stones we went that sent us feet into the air, down and out of shallow gullies that seemed as though they would jerk the pole from the vehicle with a grand rattlety-bang, every one hanging on for his life. I was entirely occupied with the state of my spinal column and the retention of my teeth, but McMillan must have been keeping his eye on the game. One peculiarity of the wildebeeste is that he cannot see behind him, and another is that he is curious. It would not require a very large bump of curiosity, however, to cause any animal to wonder what all the row was about. There could be no doubt that this animal would sooner or later stop for an instant to look for the purpose of seeing what was up in jungleland; and just before doing so he would, for a few steps, slow down from a gallop to a trot. McMillan was watching for this symptom.

"Now!" he yelled, when he saw it.

Instantly Michael threw his weight into the right rein and against the brake. We swerved so violently to the right and stopped so suddenly that I nearly landed on the broad prairies. The manoeuvre fetched us up broadside. The small black syce-and heaven knows how HE had managed to hang on-darted to the heads of the leading mules. At the same moment the wildebeeste turned, and stopped; but even before he had swung his head, McMillan had fired. It was extraordinarily good, quick work, the way he picked up the long range from the spurts of dust where the bullets hit. At the third or fourth shots he landed one. Immediately the beast was off again at a tearing run pursued by a rapid fusillade from the remaining shots. Then with a violent jerk and a wild yell we were off again.

This time, since the animal was wounded, he made for rougher country. And everywhere that wildebeeste went we too were sure to go. We hit or shaved boulders that ought to have smashed a wheel, we tore through thick brush regardless. Twice we charged unhesitatingly over apparent precipices. I do not know the name of the manufacturer of the buckboard. If I did, I should certainly recommend it here. Twice more we swerved to our broadside and cut loose the port batteries. Once more McMillan hit. Then, on the fourth "run," we gained perceptibly. The beast was weakening. When he came to a stumbling halt we were not over a hundred yards from him, and McMillan easily brought him down. We had chased him four or five miles, and McMillan had fired nineteen shots, of which two had hit. The rifle practice throughout had been remarkably good, and a treat to watch. Personally, besides the fun of attending the show, I got a mighty good afternoon's exercise.

We loaded the game aboard and jogged slowly back to the house, for the mules were pretty tired. We found a neighbour, Mr. Heatley of Kamiti Ranch who had "dropped down" twelve miles to see us. On account of a theft McMillan now had all the Somalis assembled for interrogation on the side verandas. The interrogation did not amount to much, but while it was going on the Sudanese headman and his askaris were quietly searching the boys' quarters. After a time they appeared. The suspected men had concealed nothing, but the searchers brought with them three of McMillan's shirts which they had found among the effects of another, and entirely unsuspected, boy named Abadie.

"How is this, Abadie?" demanded McMillan sternly.

Abadie hesitated. Then he evidently reflected that there is slight use in having a deity unless one makes use of him.

"Bwana," said he with an engaging air of belief and candour, "God must have put them there!"

That evening we planned a "general day" for the morrow. We took boys and buckboards and saddle-horses, beaters, shotguns, rifles, and revolvers, and we sallied forth for a grand and joyous time. The day from a sporting standpoint was entirely successful, the bag consisting of two waterbuck, a zebra, a big wart-hog, six hares, and six grouse. Personally I was a little hazy and uncertain. By evening the fever had me, and though I stayed at Juja for six days longer, it was as a patient to McMillan's unfailing kindness rather than as a participant in the life of the farm.

## XXVIII. A RESIDENCE AT JUJA

A short time later, at about middle of the rainy season, McMillan left for a little fishing off Catalina Island. The latter is some fourteen thousand miles of travel from Juja. Before leaving on this flying trip, McMillan made us a gorgeous offer.

"If," said he, "you want to go it alone, you can go out and use Juja as long as you please."

This offer, or, rather, a portion of it, you may be sure, we accepted promptly. McMillan wanted in addition to leave us his servants; but to this we would not agree. Memba Sasa and Mahomet were, of course, members of our permanent staff. In addition to them we picked up another house boy, named Leyeye. He was a Masai. These proud and aristocratic savages rarely condescend to take service of any sort except as herders; but when they do they prove to be unusually efficient and intelligent. We had also a Somali cook, and six ordinary bearers to do general labour. This small safari we started off afoot for Juja. The whole lot cost us about what we would pay one Chinaman on the Pacific Coast.

Next day we ourselves drove out in the mule buckboard. The rains were on, and the road was very muddy. After the vital tropical fashion the grass was springing tall in the natural meadows and on the plains and the brief-lived white lilies and an abundance of ground flowers washed the slopes with colour. Beneath the grass covering, the entire surface of the ground was an inch or so deep in water. This was always most surprising, for, apparently, the whole country should have been high and dry. Certainly its level was that of a plateau rather than a bottom land; so that one seemed always to be travelling at an elevation. Nevertheless walking or riding we were continually splashing, and the only dry going outside the occasional rare "islands" of the slight undulations we found near the very edge of the bluffs above the rivers. There the drainage seemed sufficient to carry off the excess. Elsewhere the hardpan or bedrock must have been exceptionally level and near the top of the ground.

Nothing nor nobody seemed to mind this much. The game splashed around merrily, cropping at the tall grass; the natives slopped indifferently, and we ourselves soon became so accustomed to two or three inches of water and wet feet that after the first two days we never gave those phenomena a thought.

The world above at this season of the year was magnificent. The African heavens are always widely spacious, but now they seemed to have blown even vaster than usual. In the sweep of the vision four or five heavy black rainstorms would be trailing their skirts across an infinitely remote prospect; between them white piled scud clouds and cumuli sailed like ships; and from them reflected so brilliant a sunlight and behind all showed so dazzling a blue sky that the general impression was of a fine day. The rainstorms' gray veils slanted; tremendous patches of shadow lay becalmed on the plains; bright sunshine poured abundantly its warmth and yellow light.

So brilliant with both direct and reflected light and the values of contrast were the heavens, that when one happened to stand within one of the great shadows it became extraordinarily difficult to make out game on the plains. The pupils contracted to the brilliancy overhead. Often too, near sunset, the atmosphere would become suffused with a lurid saffron light that made everything unreal and ghastly. At such times the game seemed puzzled by the unusual aspect of things. The zebra especially would bark and stamp and stand their ground, and even come nearer out of sheer curiosity. I have thus been within fifty yards of them, right out in the open. At such times it was as though the sky, instead of rounding over in the usual shape, had been thrust up at the western horizon to the same incredible height as the zenith. In the space thus created were piled great clouds through which slanted broad bands of yellow light on a diminished world.

It rained with great suddenness on our devoted heads, and with a curious effect of metamorphosing the entire universe. One moment all was clear and smiling, with the trifling exception of distant rain squalls that amounted to nothing in the general scheme. Then the horizon turned black, and with incredible swiftness the dark clouds materialized out of nothing, rolled high to the zenith like a wave, blotted out every last vestige of brightness. A heavy oppressive still darkness breathed over the earth. Then through the silence came a faraway soft drumming sound, barely to be heard. As we bent our ears to catch this it grew louder and louder, approaching at breakneck speed like a troop of horses. It became a roar fairly terrifying in its mercilessly continued crescendo. At last the deluge of rain burst actually as a relief.

And what a deluge! Facing it we found difficulty in breathing. In six seconds every stitch we wore was soaked through, and only the notebook, tobacco, and matches bestowed craftily in the crown of the cork helmet escaped. The visible world was dark and contracted. It seemed that nothing but rain could anywhere exist; as though this storm must fill all space to the horizon and beyond. Then it swept on and we found ourselves steaming in bright sunlight. The dry flat prairie (if this was the first shower for some time) had suddenly become a lake from the surface of which projected bushes and clumps of grass. Every game trail had become the water course of a swiftly running brook.

But most pleasant were the evenings at Juja, when, safe indoors, we sat and listened to the charge of the storm's wild horsemen, and the thunder of its drumming on the tin roof. The onslaughts were as fierce and abrupt as those of Cossacks, and swept by as suddenly. The roar died away in the distance, and we could then hear the steady musical dripping of waters.

Pleasant it was also to walk out from Juja in almost any direction. The compound, and the buildings and trees within it, soon dwindled in the distances of the great flat plain. Herds of game were always in sight, grazing, lying down, staring in our direction. The animals were incredibly numerous. Some days they were fairly tame, and others exceedingly wild, without any rhyme or reason. This shyness or the reverse seemed not to be individual to one herd; but to be practically universal. On a "wild day" everything was wild from the Lone Tree to Long Juju. It would be manifestly absurd to guess at the reason. Possibly the cause might be atmospheric or electrical; possibly days of nervousness might follow nights of unusual activity by the lions; one could invent a dozen possibilities. Perhaps the kongonis decided it.

At Juja we got to know the kongonis even better than we had before. They are comical, quizzical beasts, with long-nosed humorous faces, a singularly awkward construction, a shambling gait; but with altruistic dispositions and an ability to get over the ground at an extraordinary speed. Every move is a joke; their expression is always one of grieved but humorous astonishment. They quirk their heads sidewise or down and stare at an intruder with the most comical air of skeptical wonder. "Well, look who's here!" says the expression.

"Pooh!" says the kongoni himself, after a good look, "pooh! pooh!" with the most insulting inflection.

He is very numerous and very alert. One or more of a grazing herd are always perched as sentinels atop ant hills or similar small elevations. On the slightest intimation of danger they give the alarm, whereupon the herd makes off at once, gathering in all other miscellaneous game that may be in the vicinity. They will go out of their way to do this, as every African hunter knows. It immensely complicates matters; for the sportsman must not only stalk his quarry, but he must stalk each and every kongoni as well. Once, in another part of the country, C. and I saw a kongoni leave a band of its own species far down to our right, gallop toward us and across our front, pick up a herd of zebra we were trying to approach and make off with them to safety. We cursed that kongoni, but we admired him, for he deliberately ran out of safety into danger for the purpose of warning those zebra. So seriously do they take their job as policemen of the plains that it is very common for a lazy single animal of another species to graze in a herd of kongonis simply for the sake of protection. Wildebeeste are much given to this.

The kongoni progresses by a series of long high bounds. While in midair he half tucks up his feet, which gives him the appearance of an automatic toy. This gait looks deliberate, but is really quite fast, as the mounted sportsman discovers when he enters upon a vain pursuit. If the horse is an especially good one, so that the kongoni feels himself a trifle closely pressed, the latter stops bouncing and runs. Then he simply fades away into the distance.

**511**

These beasts are also given to chasing each other all over the landscape. When a gentleman kongoni conceives a dislike for another gentleman kongoni, he makes no concealment of his emotions, but marches up and prods him in the ribs. The ensuing battle is usually fought out very stubbornly with much feinting, parrying, clashing of the lyre-shaped horns; and a good deal of crafty circling for a favourable opening. As far as I was ever able to see not much real damage is inflicted; though I could well imagine that only skilful fence prevented unpleasant punctures in soft spots. After a time one or the other feels himself weakening. He dashes strongly in, wheels while his antagonist is braced, and makes off. The enemy pursues. Then, apparently, the chase is on for the rest of the day. The victor is not content merely to drive his rival out of the country; he wants to catch him. On that object he is very intent; about as intent as the other fellow is of getting away. I have seen two such beasts almost run over a dozen men who were making no effort to keep out of sight. Long after honour is satisfied, indeed, as it seems to me, long after the dictates of common decency would call a halt that persistent and single-minded pursuer bounds solemnly and conscientiously along in the wake of his disgusted rival.

These and the zebra and wildebeeste were at Juja the most conspicuous game animals. If they could not for the moment be seen from the veranda of the house itself, a short walk to the gate was sufficient to reveal many hundreds. Among them fed herds of the smaller Thompson's gazelle, or "Tommies." So small were they that only their heads could be seen above the tall grass as they ran.

To me there was never-ending fascination in walking out over those sloppy plains in search of adventure, and in the pleasure of watching the beasts. Scarcely less fascination haunted a stroll down the river canyons or along the tops of the bluffs above them. Here the country was broken into rocky escarpments in which were caves; was clothed with low and scattered brush; or was wooded in the bottom lands. Naturally an entirely different set of animals dwelt here; and in addition one was often treated to the romance of surprise. Herds of impalla haunted these edges; graceful creatures, trim and pretty with wide horns and beautiful glowing red coats. Sometimes they would venture out on the open plains, in a very compact band, ready to break back for cover at the slightest alarm; but generally fed inside the fringe of bushes. Once from the bluff above I saw a beautiful herd of over a hundred pacing decorously along the river bottom below me, single file, the oldest buck at the head, and the miscellaneous small buck bringing up the rear after the does. I shouted at them. Immediately the solemn procession broke. They began to leap, springing straight up into the air as though from a released spring, or diving forward and upward in long graceful bounds like dolphins at sea. These leaps were incredible. Several even jumped quite over the backs of others; and all without a semblance of effort.

Along the fringe of the river, too, dwelt the lordly waterbuck, magnificent and proud as the stags of Landseer; and the tiny steinbuck and duiker, no bigger than jack-rabbits, but perfect little deer for all that. The incredibly plebeian wart-hog rooted about; and down in the bottom lands were leopards. I knocked one off a rock one day. In the river itself dwelt hippopotamuses and crocodiles. One of the latter dragged under a yearling calf just below the house itself, and while we were there. Besides these were of course such affairs as hyenas and jackals, and great numbers of small game: hares, ducks, three kinds of grouse, guinea fowl, pigeons, quail, and jack snipe, not to speak of a variety of plover.

In the drier extents of dry grass atop the bluffs the dance birds were especially numerous; each with his dance ring nicely trodden out, each leaping and falling rhythmically for hours at a time. Toward sunset great flights of sand grouse swarmed across the yellowing sky from some distant feeding ground.

Near Juja I had one of the three experiences that especially impressed on my mind the abundance of African big game. I had stalked and wounded a wildebeeste across the N'derogo River, and had followed him a mile or so afoot, hoping to be able to put in a finishing shot. As sometimes happens the animal rather gained strength as time went on; so I signalled for my horse, mounted, and started out to run him down. After a quarter mile we began to pick up the game herds. Those directly in our course ran straight away; other herds on either side, seeing them running, came across in a slant to join them. Inside of a half mile I was driving before me literally thousands of head of game of several varieties. The dust rose in a choking cloud that fairly obscured the landscape, and the drumming of the hooves was like the stampeding of cattle. It was a wonderful sight.

On the plains of Juja, also, I had my one real African Adventure, when, as in the Sunday Supplements, I Stared Death in the Face-also everlasting disgrace and much derision. We were just returning to the farm after an afternoon's walk, and as we approached I began to look around for much needed meat. A herd of zebra stood in sight; so leaving Memba Sasa I began to stalk them. My usual weapon for this sort of thing was the Springfield, for which I carried extra cartridges in my belt. On this occasion, however, I traded with Memba Sasa for the 405, simply for the purpose of trying it out. At a few paces over three hundred yards I landed on the zebra, but did not knock him down. Then I set out to follow. It was a long job and took me far, for again and again he joined other zebra, when, of course, I could not tell one from t'other. My only expedient was to frighten the lot. There upon the uninjured ones would distance the one that was hurt. The latter kept his eye on me. Whenever I managed to get within reasonable distance, I put up the rear sight of the 405, and let drive. I heard every shot hit, and after each hit was more than a little astonished to see the zebra still on his feet, and still able to wobble on.* The fifth shot emptied the rifle. As I had no more cartridges for this arm, I approached to within sixty yards, and stopped to wait either for him to fall, or for a very distant Memba Sasa to come up with more cartridges. Then the zebra waked up. He put his ears back and came straight in my direction. This rush I took for a blind death flurry, and so dodged off to one side, thinking that he would of course go by me. Not at all! He swung around on the circle too, and made after me. I could see that his ears were back, eyes blazing, and his teeth snapping with rage. It was a malicious charge, and, as such, with due deliberation, I offer it to sportsman's annals. As I had no more cartridges I ran away as fast as I could go. Although I made rather better time than ever I had attained to before, it was evident that the zebra would catch me; and as the brute could paw, bite, and kick, I did not much care for the situation. Just as he had nearly reached me, and as I was trying to figure on what kind of a fight I could put up with a clubbed rifle barrel, he fell dead. To be killed by a lion is at least a dignified death; but to be mauled by a zebra!

I am sorry I did not try out this heavy-calibred rifle oftener at long range. It was a marvellously effective weapon at close quarters; but I have an idea-but only a tentative idea-that above three hundred yards its velocity is so reduced by air resistance against the big blunt bullet as greatly to impair its hitting powers.

We generally got back from our walks or rides just before dark to find the house gleaming with lights, a hot bath ready, and a tray of good wet drinks next the easy chairs. There, after changing our clothes, we sipped and read the papers-two months off the press, but fresh arrived for all that-until a white-robed, dignified figure appeared in the doorway to inform us that dinner was ready. Our ways were civilized and soft, then, until the morrow when once again, perhaps, we went forth into the African wilderness.

Juja is a place of startling contrasts-of naked savages clipping formal hedges, of windows opening from a perfectly appointed brilliantly lighted dining-room to a night whence float the lost wails of hyenas or the deep grumbling of lions, of cushioned luxurious chairs in reach of many books, but looking out on hills where the game herds feed, of comfortable beds with fine linen and soft blankets where one lies listening to the voices of an African night, or the weirder minor house noises whose origin and nature no man could guess, of tennis courts and summer houses, of lawns and hammocks, of sundials and clipped hedges separated only by a few strands of woven wire from fields identical with those in which roamed the cave men of the Pleistocene. But to Billy was reserved the most ridiculous contrast of all. Her bedroom opened to a veranda a few feet above a formal garden. This was a very formal garden, with a sundial, gravelled walks, bordered flower beds, and clipped border hedges. One night she heard a noise outside. Slipping on a warm wrap and seizing her trusty revolver she stole out on the veranda to investigate. She looked over the veranda rail. There just below her, trampling the flower beds, tracking the gravel walks, endangering the sundial, stood a hippopotamus!

We had neighbours six or seven miles away. At times they came down to spend the night and luxuriate in the comforts of civilization. They were a Lady A., and her nephew, and a young Scotch acquaintance the nephew had taken into partnership. They had built themselves circular houses of papyrus reeds with conical thatched roofs and earth floors, had purchased ox teams and gathered a dozen or so Kikuyus, and were engaged in breaking a farm in the wilderness. The life was rough and hard, and Lady A. and her nephew gently bred, but they seemed to be having quite cheerfully the time of their lives. The game furnished them meat, as it did all of us, and they hoped in time that their labours would make the land valuable and productive. Fascinating as was the life, it was also one of many deprivations. At Juja were a number of old copies of Life, the pretty girls in which so fascinated the young men that we broke the laws of propriety by presenting them, though they did not belong to us. C., the nephew, was of the finest type of young Englishman, clean cut, enthusiastic, good looking, with an air of engaging vitality and optimism. His partner, of his own age, was an insufferable youth. Brought up in some small Scottish valley, his outlook had never widened. Because he wanted to buy four oxen at a cheaper price, he tried desperately to abrogate quarantine regulations. If he had succeeded, he would have made a few rupees, but would have introduced disease in his neighbours' herds. This consideration did not affect him. He was much given to sneering at what he could not understand; and therefore, a great deal met with his disapproval. His reading had evidently brought him down only to about the middle sixties; and affairs at that date were to him still burning questions. Thus he would declaim vehemently over the Alabama claims.

"I blush with shame," he would cry, "when I think of England's attitude in that matter."

We pointed out that the dispute had been amicably settled by the best minds of the time, had passed between the covers of history, and had given way in immediate importance to several later topics.

"This vacillating policy," he swept on, "annoys me. For my part, I should like to see so firm a stand taken on all questions that in any part of the world, whenever a man, and wherever a man, said 'I am an Englishman? everybody else would draw back!'"

He was an incredible person. However, I was glad to see him; he and a few others of his kind have consoled me for a number of Americans I have met abroad. Lady A., with the tolerant philosophy of her class, seemed merely amused. I have often since wondered how this ill-assorted partnership turned out.

Two other neighbours of ours dropped in once or twice-twenty-six miles on bicycles, on which they could ride only a portion of the distance. They had some sort of a ranch up in the Ithanga Hills; and were two of the nicest fellows one would want to meet, brimful of energy, game for anything, and had so good a time always that the grumpiest fever could not prevent every one else having a good time too. Once they rode on their bicycles forty miles to Nairobi, danced half the night at a Government House ball, rode back in the early morning, and did an afternoon's plowing! They explained this feat by pointing out most convincingly that the ground was just right for plowing, but they did not want to miss the ball!

Occasionally a trim and dapper police official would drift in on horseback looking for native criminals; and once a safari came by. Twelve miles away was the famous Kamiti Farm of Heatly, where Roosevelt killed his buffalo; and once or twice Heatly himself, a fine chap, came to see us. Also just before I left with Duirs for a lion hunt on Kapiti, Lady Girouard, wife of the Governor, and her nephew and niece rode out for a hunt. In the African fashion, all these people brought their own personal servants. It makes entertaining easy. Nobody knows where all these boys sleep; but they manage to tuck away somewhere, and always show up after a mysterious system of their own whenever there is anything to be done.

We stayed at Juja a little over three weeks. Then most reluctantly said farewell and returned to Nairobi in preparation for a long trip to the south.

513

## XXIX. CHAPTER THE LAST

With our return from Juja to Nairobi for a breathing space, this volume comes to a logical conclusion. In it I have tried to give a fairly comprehensive impression-it could hardly be a picture of so large a subject-of a portion of East Equatorial Africa, its animals, and its people. Those who are sufficiently interested will have an opportunity in a succeeding volume of wandering with us even farther afield. The low jungly coast region; the fierce desert of the Serengetti; the swift sullen rhinoceros-haunted stretches of the Tsavo; Nairobi, the strangest mixture of the twentieth centuries A.D. and B.C.; Mombasa with its wild, barbaric passionate ebb and flow of life, of colour, of throbbing sound, the great lions of the Kapiti Plains, the Thirst of the Loieta, the Masai spearmen, the long chase for the greater kudu; the wonderful, high unknown country beyond the Narossara and other affairs will there be detailed. If the reader of this volume happens to want more, there he will find it.

## APPENDIX I

Most people are very much interested in how hot it gets in such tropics as we traversed. Unfortunately it is very difficult to tell them. Temperature tables have very little to do with the matter, for humidity varies greatly. On the Serengetti at lower reaches of the Guaso Nyero I have seen it above 110 degrees. It was hot, to be sure, but not exhaustingly so. On the other hand, at 90 or 95 degrees the low coast belt I have had the sweat run from me literally in streams; so that a muddy spot formed wherever I stood still. In the highlands, moreover, the nights were often extremely cold. I have recorded night temperatures as low as 40 at 7000 feet of elevation; and noon temperatures as low 65.

Of more importance than the actual or sensible temperature of the air is the power of the sun's rays. At all times of year this is practically constant; for the orb merely swings a few degrees north and south of the equator, and the extreme difference in time between its risings or settings is not more than twenty minutes. This power is also practically constant whatever the temperature of the air and is dangerous even on a cloudy day, when the heat waves are effectually screened off, but when the actinic rays are as active as ever. For this reason the protection of helmet and spine pad should never be omitted, no matter what the condition of the weather, between nine o'clock and four. A very brief exposure is likely to prove fatal. It should be added that some people stand these actinic rays better than others.

Such being the case, mere temperature tables could have little interest to the general reader. I append a few statistics, selected from many, and illustrative of the different conditions.

| Locality. | Elevation | 6am | noon | 8pm | Apparent conditions |
|---|---|---|---|---|---|
| Coast | — | 80 | 90 | 76 | Very hot and sticky |
| Isiola River | 2900 | 65 | 94 | 84 | Hot but not exhausting |
| Tans River | 3350 | 68 | 98 | 79 | Hot but not exhausting |
| Near Meru | 5450 | 62 | 80 | 70 | Very pleasant |
| Serengetti Plains | 2200 | 78 | 106 | 86 | Hot and humid |
| Narossara River | 5450 | 54 | 89 | 69 | Very pleasant |
| Narossara Mts. | 7400 | 42 | 80 | 50 | Chilly |
| Narossara Mts. | 6450 | 40 | 62 | 52 | Cold |

## APPENDIX II
### GAME ANIMALS COLLECTED

| | | |
|---|---|---|
| Lion | Bush pig | Grant's gazelle |
| Serval cat | Baboon | Thompson's gazelle |
| Cheetah | Colobus | Gerenuk gazelle |
| Black-backed jackal | Hippopotamus | Coke's hartebeests |
| Silver jackal | Rhinoceros | Jackson's hartebeests |
| Striped hyena | Crocodile | Neuman's hartebeests |
| Spotted hyena | Python | Chandler's reedbuck |
| Fennec fox | Ward's zebra | Bohur reedbuck |
| Honey badger | Grevy's zebra | Beisa ox |
| Aardewolf | Notata gazelle | Fringe-eared oryx |
| Wart-hog | Roberts' gazelle | Duiker |
| Waterbuck | Klipspringer | Harvey's duiker |
| Sing-sing | Dik-dik | Greater kudu |
| Oribi (3 varieties) | Wildebeeste | Lesser kudu |
| Eland | Roosevelt's wildebeests | Sable antelope |

| Roan antelope | Buffalo |
|---|---|
| Bushbuck | Topi |

*Total, fifty-four kinds*

GAME BIRDS COLLECTED

| Marabout | Gadwall | Lesser bustard |
|---|---|---|
| Egret | European stork | Guinea fowl |
| Glossy ibis | Quail | Giant guinea fowl |
| Egyptian goose | Sand grouse | Green pigeon |
| White goose | Francolin | Blue pigeon |
| English snipe | Spur fowl | Dove (2 species) |
| Mallard duck | Greater bustard | |

*Total, twenty-two kinds*

## APPENDIX III

For the benefit of the sportsman and gun crank who want plain facts and no flapdoodle, the following statistics are offered. To the lay reader this inclusion will be incomprehensible; but I know my gun crank as I am one myself!

Army Springfield, model 1903 to take the 1906 cartridge, shooting the Spitzer sharp point bullet. Stocked to suit me by Ludwig Wundhammer, and fitted with Sheard gold bead front sight and Lyman aperture receiver sight. With this I did most my shooting, as the trajectory was remarkably good, and the killing power remarkable. Tried out both the old-fashioned soft point bullets and the sharp Spitzer bullets, but find the latter far the more effective. In fact the paralyzing shock given by the Spitzer is almost beyond belief. African animals are notably tenacious of life; but the Springfield dropped nearly half the animals dead with one shot; a most unusual record, as every sportsman will recognize. The bullets seemed on impact always to flatten slightly at the base, the point remaining intact-to spin widely on the axis, and to plunge off at an angle. This action of course depended on the high velocity. The requisite velocity, however seemed to keep up within all shooting ranges. A kongoni I killed at 638 paces (measured), and another at 566 paces both exhibited this action of the bullet. I mention these ranges because I have seen the statement in print that the remaining velocity beyond 350 yards would not be sufficient in this arm to prevent the bullet passing through cleanly. I should also hasten to add that I do not habitually shoot at game at the above ranges; but did so in these two instances for the precise purpose of testing the arm. Metal fouling did not bother me at all, though I had been led to expect trouble from it. The weapon was always cleaned with water so boiling hot that the heat of the barrel dried it. When occasionally flakes of metal fouling became visible a Marble brush always sufficed to remove enough of it. It was my habit to smear the bullets with mobilubricant before placing them in the magazine. This was not as much of a nuisance as it sounds. A small tin box about the size of a pill box lasted me the whole trip; and only once did I completely empty the magazine at one time. On my return I tested the rifle very thoroughly for accuracy. In spite of careful cleaning the barrel was in several places slightly corroded. For this the climate was responsible. The few small pittings, however, did not seem in any way to have affected the accuracy, as the rifle shot the following groups: 3-1/2 inches at 200 yards; 7-1/4 inches at 300 yards; and 11-1/2 inches at 500 yards.*

> \* It shot one five-shot 1-2/3 inch group at 200 yds., and
> several others at all distances less than the figures given,
> but I am convinced these must have been largely accidental.

These groups were not made from a machine rest, however; as none was available. The complete record with this arm for my whole stay in Africa was 307 hits out of 395 cartridges fired, representing 185 head of game killed. Most of this shooting was for meat and represented also all sorts of "varmints" as well.

The 405 Winchester. This weapon was sighted like the Springfield, and was constantly in the field as my second gun. For lions it could not be beaten; as it was very accurate, delivered a hard blow, and held five cartridges. Beyond 125 to 150 yards one had to begin to guess at distance, so for ordinary shooting I preferred the Springfield. In thick brush country, however, where one was likely to come suddenly on rhinoceroes, but where one wanted to be ready always for desirable smaller game, the Winchester was just the thing. It was short, handy, and reliable. One experience with a zebra 300-350 yards has made me question whether at long (hunting) ranges the remaining velocity of the big blunt nosed bullet is not seriously reduced; but as to that I have not enough data for a final conclusion. I have no doubt, however, that at such ranges, and beyond, the little Springfield has more shocking power. Of course at closer ranges the Winchester is by far the more powerful. I killed one rhinoceros with the 405, one buffalo and one hippo; but should consider it too light for an emergency gun against the larger dangerous animals, such as buffalo and rhinoceros. If one has time for extreme accuracy, and can pick the shot, it is plenty big; but I refer now to close quarters in a hurry. I had no trouble whatever with the mechanism of this arm; nor have I ever had trouble with any of the lever actions, although I have used them for many years. As regards speed of fire the controversy between the lever and bolt action advocates seems to me foolish in the extreme. Either action can be fired faster than it should be fired in the presence of game. It is my belief that any man,

**515**

no matter how practised or how cool, can stampede himself beyond his best accuracy by pumping out his shots too rapidly. This is especially true in the face of charging dangerous game. So firmly do I believe this that I generally take the rifle from my shoulder between each shot. Even aimed rapid fire is of no great value as compared with better aimed slower fire. The first bullet delivers to an animal's nervous system about all the shock it can absorb. If the beast is not thereby knocked down and held down, subsequent shots can accomplish that desirable result only by reaching a vital spot or by tearing tissue. As an example of this I might instance a waterbuck into which I saw my companion empty five heavy 465 and double 500 bullets from cordite rifles before it fell! Thus if the game gets to its feet after the first shock, it is true that the hunter will often empty into it six or seven more bullets without apparent result, unless he aims carefully for a centrally vital point. It follows that therefore a second shot aimed with enough care to land it in that point is worth a lot more than a half dozen delivered in three or four seconds with only the accuracy necessary to group decently at very short range, even if all of them hit the beast. I am perfectly aware that this view will probably be disputed; but it is the result of considerable experience, close observation and real interest in the game. The whole record of the Winchester was 56 hits out of 70 cartridges fired; representing 27 head of game.

The 465 Holland & Holland double cordite rifle. This beautiful weapon, built and balanced like a fine hammerless shotgun, was fitted with open sights. It was of course essentially a close range emergency gun, but was capable of accurate work at a distance. I killed one buffalo dead with it, across a wide canyon, with the 300-yard leaf up on the back sight. Its game list however was limited to rhinoceroses, hippopotamuses, buffaloes and crocodiles. The recoil in spite of its weight of twelve and one half pounds, was tremendous; but unnoticeable when I was shooting at any of these brutes. Its total record was 31 cartridges fired with 29 hits representing 13 head of game.

The conditions militating against marksmanship are often severe. Hard work in the tropics is not the most steadying regime in the world, and outside a man's nerves, he is often bothered by queer lights, and the effects of the mirage that swirls from the sun-heated plain. The ranges, too, are rather long. I took the trouble to pace out about every kill, and find that antelope in the plains averaged 245 yards; with a maximum of 638 yards, while antelope in covered country averaged 148 yards, with a maximum of 311.

### APPENDIX IV. THE AMERICAN IN AFRICA
### IN WHICH HE APPEARS AS DIFFERENT FROM THE ENGLISHMAN

It is always interesting to play the other fellow's game his way, and then, in light of experience, to see wherein our way and his way modify each other.

The above proposition here refers to camping. We do considerable of it in our country, especially in our North and West. After we have been at it for some time, we evolve a method of our own. The basis of that method is to do without; to GO LIGHT. At first even the best of us will carry too much plunder, but ten years of philosophy and rainstorms, trails and trials, will bring us to an irreducible minimum. A party of three will get along with two pack horses, say; or, on a harder trip, each will carry the necessities on his own back. To take just as little as is consistent with comfort is to play the game skilfully. Any article must pay in use for its transportation.

With this ideal deeply ingrained by the test of experience, the American camper is appalled by the caravan his British cousins consider necessary for a trip into the African back country. His said cousin has, perhaps, very kindly offered to have his outfit ready for him when he arrives. He does arrive to find from one hundred to one hundred and fifty men gathered as his personal attendants.

"Great Scot!" he cries, "I want to go camping; I don't want to invade anybody's territory. Why the army?"

He discovers that these are porters, to carry his effects.

"What effects?" he demands, bewildered. As far as he knows, he has two guns, some ammunition, and a black tin box, bought in London, and half-filled with extra clothes, a few medicines, a thermometer, and some little personal knick-knacks. He has been wondering what else he is going to put in to keep things from rattling about. Of course he expected besides these to take along a little plain grub, and some blankets, and a frying pan and kettle or so.

The English friend has known several Americans, so he explains patiently.

"I know this seems foolish to you," he says, "but you must remember you are under the equator and you must do things differently here. As long as you keep fit you are safe; but if you get run down a bit you'll go. You've got to do yourself well, down here, rather better than you have to in any other climate. You need all the comfort you can get; and you want to save yourself all you can."

This has a reasonable sound and the American does not yet know the game. Recovering from his first shock, he begins to look things over. There is a double tent, folding camp chair, folding easy chair, folding table, wash basin, bath tub, cot, mosquito curtains, clothes hangers; there are oil lanterns, oil carriers, two loads of mysterious cooking utensils and cook camp stuff; there is an open fly, which his friend explains is his dining tent; and there are from a dozen to twenty boxes standing in a row, each with its padlock. "I didn't go in for luxury," apologizes the English friend. "Of course we can easily add anything you want but I remember you wrote me that you wanted to travel light."

"What are those?" our American inquires, pointing to the locked boxes.

He learns that they are chop boxes, containing food and supplies. At this he rises on his hind legs and paws the air.

"Food!" he shrieks. "Why, man alive, I'm alone, and I am only going to be out three months! I can carry all I'll ever eat in three months in one of those boxes."

516

But the Englishman patiently explains. You cannot live on "bacon and beans" in this country, so to speak. You must do yourself rather well, you know, to keep in condition. And you cannot pack food in bags, it must be tinned. And then, of course, such things as your sparklet siphons and lime juice require careful packing-and your champagne.

"Champagne," breathes the American in awestricken tones.

"Exactly, dear boy, an absolute necessity. After a touch of sun there's nothing picks you up better than a mouthful of fizz. It's used as a medicine, not a drink, you understand."

The American reflects again that this is the other fellow's game, and that the other fellow has been playing it for some time, and that he ought to know. But he cannot yet see why the one hundred and fifty men. Again the Englishman explains. There is the Headman to run the show. Correct: we need him. Then there are four askaris. What are they? Native soldiers. No, you won't be fighting anything; but they keep the men going, and act as sort of sub-foremen in bossing the complicated work. Next is your cook, and your own valet and that of your horse. Also your two gunbearers.

"Hold on!" cries our friend. "I have only two guns, and I'm going to carry one myself."

But this, he learns, is quite impossible. It is never done. It is absolutely necessary, in this climate, to avoid all work.

That makes how many? Ten already, and there seem to be three tent loads, one bed load, one chair and table load, one lantern load, two miscellaneous loads, two cook loads, one personal box, and fifteen chop boxes-total twenty-six, plus the staff, as above, thirty-six. Why all the rest of the army?

Very simple: these thirty-six men have, according to regulation, seven tents, and certain personal effects, and they must have "potio" or a ration of one and a half pounds per diem. These things must be carried by more men.

"I see," murmurs the American, crushed, "and these more men have more tents and more potio, which must also be carried. It's like the House that Jack Built."

So our American concludes still once again that the other fellow knows his own game, and starts out. He learns he has what is called a "modest safari"; and spares a fleeting wonder as to what a really elaborate safari must be. The procession takes the field. He soon sees the value of the four askaris-the necessity of whom he has secretly doubted. Without their vigorous seconding the headman would have a hard time indeed. Also, when he observes the labour of tent-making, packing, washing, and general service performed by his tent boy, he abandons the notion that that individual could just as well take care of the horse as well, especially as the horse has to have all his grass cut and brought to him. At evening our friend has a hot bath, a long cool fizzly drink of lime juice and soda; he puts on the clean clothes laid out for him, assumes soft mosquito boots, and sits down to dinner. This is served to him in courses, and on enamel ware. Each course has its proper-sized plate and cutlery. He starts with soup, goes down through tinned whitebait or other fish, an entree, a roast, perhaps a curry, a sweet, and small coffee. He is certainly being "done well," and he enjoys the comfort of it.

There comes a time when he begins to wonder a little. It is all very pleasant, of course, and perhaps very necessary; they all tell him it is. But, after all, it is a little galling to the average man to think that of him. Your Englishman doesn't mind that; he enjoys being taken care of: but the sportsman of American training likes to stand on his own feet as far as he is able and conditions permit. Besides, it is expensive. Besides that, it is a confounded nuisance, especially when potio gives out and more must be sought, near or far. Then, if he is wise, he begins to do a little figuring on his own account.

My experience was very much as above. Three of us went out for eleven weeks with what was considered a very "modest" safari indeed. It comprised one hundred and eighteen men. My fifth and last trip, also with two companions, was for three months. Our personnel consisted, all told, forty men.

In essentials the Englishman is absolutely right. One cannot camp in Africa as one would at home. The experimenter would be dead in a month. In his application of that principle, however, he seems to the American point of view to overshoot. Let us examine his proposition in terms of the essentials-food, clothing, shelter. There is no doubt but that a man must keep in top condition as far as possible; and that, to do so, he must have plenty of good food. He can never do as we do on very hard trips at home: take a little tea, sugar, coffee, flour, salt, oatmeal. But on the other hand, he certainly does not need a five-course dinner every night, nor a complete battery of cutlery, napery and table ware to eat it from. Flour, sugar, oatmeal, tea and coffee, rice, beans, onions, curry, dried fruits, a little bacon, and some dehydrated vegetables will do him very well indeed-with what he can shoot. These will pack in waterproof bags very comfortably. In addition to feeding himself well, he finds he must not sleep next to the ground, he must have a hot bath every day, but never a cold one, and he must shelter himself with a double tent against the sun.

Those are the absolute necessities of the climate. In other words, if he carries a double tent, a cot, a folding bath; and gives a little attention to a properly balanced food supply, he has met the situation.

If, in addition, he takes canned goods, soda siphons, lime juice, easy chairs and all the rest of the paraphernalia, he is merely using a basic principle as an excuse to include sheer luxuries. In further extenuation of this he is apt to argue that porters are cheap, and that it costs but little more to carry these extra comforts. Against this argument, of course, I have nothing to say. It is the inalienable right of every man to carry all the luxuries he wants. My point is that the average American sportsman does not want them, and only takes them because he is overpersuaded that these things are not luxuries, but necessities. For, mark you, he could take the same things into the Sierras or the North-by paying; but he doesn't.

I repeat, it is the inalienable right of any man to travel as luxuriously as he pleases. But by the same token it is not his right to pretend that luxuries are necessities. That is to put himself into the same category with the man who always finds some other excuse for taking a drink than the simple one that he wants it.

The Englishman's point of view is that he objects to "pigging it," as he says. "Pigging it" means changing your home habits in any way. If you have been accustomed to eating your sardines after a meal, and somebody offers them to you first, that is "pigging it." In other words, as nearly as I can make out, "pigging it" does not so much mean doing things in an inadequate fashion as DOING THEM DIFFERENTLY. Therefore, the Englishman in the field likes to approximate as closely as may be his life in town, even if it takes one hundred and fifty men to do it. Which reduces the "pigging it" argument to an attempt at condemnation by calling names.

The American temperament, on the contrary, being more experimental and independent, prefers to build anew upon its essentials. Where the Englishman covers the situation blanket-wise with his old institutions, the American prefers to construct new institutions on the necessities of the case. He objects strongly to being taken care of too completely. He objects strongly to losing the keen enjoyment of overcoming difficulties and enduring hardships. The Englishman by habit and training has no such objections. He likes to be taken care of, financially, personally, and everlastingly. That is his ideal of life. If he can be taken care of better by employing three hundred porters and packing eight tin trunks of personal effects-as I have seen it done-he will so employ and take. That is all right: he likes it.

But the American does not like it. A good deal of the fun for him is in going light, in matching himself against his environment. It is no fun to him to carry his complete little civilization along with him, laboriously. If he must have cotton wool, let it be as little cotton wool as possible. He likes to be comfortable; but he likes to be comfortable with the minimum of means. Striking just the proper balance somehow adds to his interest in the game. And how he DOES object to that ever-recurring thought-that he is such a helpless mollusc that it requires a small regiment to get him safely around the country!

Both means are perfectly legitimate, of course; and neither view is open to criticism. All either man is justified in saying is that he, personally, wouldn't get much fun out of doing it the other way. As a matter of fact, human nature generally goes beyond its justifications and is prone to criticise. The Englishman waxes a trifle caustic on the subject of "pigging it"; and the American indulges in more than a bit of sarcasm on the subject of "being led about Africa like a dog on a string."

By some such roundabout mental process as the above the American comes to the conclusion that he need not necessarily adopt the other fellow's method of playing this game. His own method needs modification, but it will do. He ventures to leave out the tables and easy chair, takes a camp stool and eats off a chop box. To the best of his belief his health does not suffer from this. He gets on with a camper's allowance of plate, cup and cutlery, and so cuts out a load and a half of assorted kitchen utensils and table ware. He even does without a tablecloth and napkins! He discards the lime juice and siphons, and purchases a canvas evaporation bag to cool the water. He fires one gunbearer, and undertakes the formidable physical feat of carrying one of his rifles himself. And, above all, he modifies that grub list. The purchase of waterproof bags gets rid of a lot of tin: the staple groceries do quite as well as London fancy stuff. Golden syrup takes the place of all the miscellaneous jams, marmalades and other sweets. The canned goods go by the board. He lays in a stock of dried fruit. At the end, he is possessed of a grub list but little different from that of his Rocky Mountain trips. Some few items he has cut down; and some he has substituted; but bulk and weight are the same. For his three months' trip he has four or five chop boxes all told.

And then suddenly he finds that thus he has made a reduction all along the line. Tent load, two men; grub and kitchen, five men; personal, one man; bed, one man; miscellaneous, one or two. There is now no need for headmen and askaris to handle this little lot. Twenty more to carry food for the men-he is off with a quarter of the number of his first "modest safari."

You who are sportsmen and are not going to Africa, as is the case with most, will perhaps read this, because we are always interested in how the other fellow does it. To the few who are intending an exploration of the dark continent this concentration of a year's experience may be valuable. Remember to sleep off the ground, not to starve yourself, to protect yourself from the sun, to let negroes do all hard work but marching and hunting. Do these things your own way, using your common-sense on how to get at it. You'll be all right.

That, I conceive, covers the case. The remainder of your equipment has to do with camp affairs, and merely needs listing. The question here is not of the sort to get, but of what to take. The tents, cooking affairs, etc., are well adapted to the country. In selecting your tent, however, you will do very well to pick out one whose veranda fly reaches fairly to the ground, instead of stopping halfway.

*1 tent and ground sheet*
*1 folding cot and cork mattress,*
*1 pillow, 3 single blankets*
*1 combined folding bath and ashstand ("X" brand)*
*1 camp stool*
*3 folding candle lanterns*
*1 gallon turpentine*
*3 lbs. alum*
*1 river rope*
*Sail needles and twine*
*3 pangas (native tools for chopping and digging)*
*Cook outfit (select these yourself, and cut out the extras)*
*2 axes (small)*
*Plenty laundry soap*
*Evaporation bag*
*2 pails*
*10 yards cotton cloth ("Mericani")*

These things, your food, your porters' outfits and what trade goods you may need are quite sufficient. You will have all you want, and not too much. If you take care of yourself, you ought to keep in good health. Your small outfit permits greater mobility than does that of the English cousin, infinitely less nuisance and expense. Furthermore, you feel that once more you are "next to things," instead of "being led about Africa like a dog on a string."

## APPENDIX V. THE AMERICAN IN AFRICA
### WHAT HE SHOULD TAKE

Before going to Africa I read as many books as I could get hold of on the subject, some of them by Americans. In every case the authors have given a chapter detailing the necessary outfit. Invariably they have followed the Englishman's ideas almost absolutely. Nobody has ventured to modify those ideas in any essential manner. Some have deprecatingly ventured to remark that it is as well to leave out the tinned carfare-if you do not like carfare; but that is as far as they care to go. The lists are those of the firms who make a business of equipping caravans. The heads of such firms are generally old African travellers. They furnish the equipment their customers demand; and as English sportsmen generally all demand the same thing, the firms end by issuing a printed list of essentials for shooting parties in Africa, including carfare. Travellers follow the lists blindly, and later copy them verbatim into their books. Not one has thought to empty out the whole bag of tricks, to examine them in the light of reason, and to pick out what a man of American habits, as contrasted to one of English habits, would like to have. This cannot be done a priori; it requires the test of experience to determine how to meet, in our own way, the unusual demands of climate and conditions.

And please note, when the heads of these equipment firms, these old African travellers, take the field for themselves, they pay no attention whatever to their own printed lists of "essentials."

Now, premising that the English sportsman has, by many years' experience, worked out just what he likes to take into the field; and assuring you solemnly that his ideas are not in the least the ideas of American sportsman, let us see if we cannot do something for ourselves.

At present the American has either to take over in toto the English idea, which is not adapted to him, and is-TO HIM-a nuisance, or to go it blind, without experience except that acquired in a temperate climate, which is dangerous. I am not going to copy out the English list again, even for comparison. I have not the space; and if curious enough, you can find it in any book on modern African travel. Of course I realize well that few Americans go to Africa; but I also realize well that the sportsman is a crank, a wild and eager enthusiast over items of equipment anywhere. He-and I am thinking emphatically of him-would avidly devour the details of the proper outfit for the gentle art of hunting the totally extinct whiffenpoof.

Let us begin, first of all, with:

Personal Equipment Clothes. On the top of your head you must have a sun helmet. Get it of cork, not of pith. The latter has a habit of melting unobtrusively about your ears when it rains. A helmet in brush is the next noisiest thing to a circus band, so it is always well to have, also, a double terai. This is not something to eat. It is a wide felt hat, and then another wide felt hat on top of that. The vertical-rays-of-the-tropical-sun (pronounced as one word to save time after you have heard and said it a thousand times) are supposed to get tangled and lost somewhere between the two hats. It is not, however, a good contraption to go in all day when the sun is strong.

As underwear you want the lightest Jaeger wool. Doesn't sound well for tropics, but it is an essential. You will sweat enough anyway, even if you get down to a brass wire costume like the natives. It is when you stop in the shade, or the breeze, or the dusk of evening, that the trouble comes. A chill means trouble, SURE. Two extra suits are all you want. There is no earthly sense in bringing more. Your tent boy washes them out whenever he can lay hands on them-it is one of his harmless manias.

Your shirt should be of the thinnest brown flannel. Leather the shoulders, and part way down the upper arm, with chamois. This is to protect your precious garment against the thorns when you dive through them. On the back you have buttons sewed wherewith to attach a spine pad. Before I went to Africa I searched eagerly for information or illustration of a spine pad. I guessed what it must be for, and to an extent what it must be like, but all writers maintained a conservative reticence as to the thing itself. Here is the first authorized description. A spine pad is a quilted affair in consistency like the things you are supposed to lift hot flat-irons with. On the outside it is brown flannel, like the shirt; on the inside it is a gaudy orange colour. The latter is not for aesthetic effect, but to intercept actinic rays. It is eight or ten inches wide, is shaped to button close up under your collar, and extends halfway down your back. In addition it is well to wear a silk handkerchief around the neck; as the spine and back of the head seem to be the most vulnerable to the sun.

For breeches, suit yourself as to material. It will have to be very tough, and of fast colour. The best cut is the "semi-riding," loose at the knees, which should be well faced with soft leather, both for crawling, and to save the cloth in grass and low brush. One pair ought to last four months, roughly speaking. You will find a thin pair of ordinary khaki trousers very comfortable as a change for wear about camp. In passing I would call your attention to "shorts." Shorts are loose, bobbed off khaki breeches, like knee drawers. With them are worn puttees or leather leggings, and low boots. The knees are bare. They are much affected by young Englishmen. I observed them carefully at every opportunity, and my private opinion is that man has rarely managed to invent as idiotically unfitted a contraption for the purpose in hand. In a country teeming with poisonous insects, ticks, fever-bearing mosquitoes; in a country where vegetation is unusually well armed with thorns, spines and hooks, mostly poisonous; in a country where, oftener than in any other a man is called upon to get down on his hands and knees and crawl a few assorted abrading miles, it would seem an obvious necessity to protect one's bare skin as much as possible. The only reason given for these astonishing garments is that they are cooler and freer to walk in. That I can believe. But they allow ticks and other insects to crawl up, mosquitoes to bite, thorns to tear, and assorted troubles to enter. And I can vouch by experience that ordinary breeches are not uncomfortably hot or tight. Indeed, one does not get especially hot in the legs anyway. I noticed that none of the old-time hunters like Cuninghame or Judd wore shorts. The real reason is not that they are cool, but that they are picturesque. Common belief to the contrary, your average practical, matter-of-fact Englishman loves to dress up. I knew one engaged in farming-picturesque farming-in our own West, who used to appear at afternoon tea in a clean suit of blue overalls! It is a harmless amusement. Our own youths do it, also, substituting chaps for shorts, perhaps. I am not criticising the spirit in them; but merely trying to keep mistaken shorts off you.

For leg gear I found that nothing could beat our American combination of high-laced boots and heavy knit socks. Leather leggings are noisy, and the rolled puttees hot and binding. Have your boots ten or twelve inches high, with a flap to buckle over the tie of the laces, with soles of the mercury-impregnated leather called "elk hide," and with small Hungarian hobs. Your tent boy will grease these every day with "dubbin," of which you want a good supply. It is not my intention to offer free advertisements generally, but I wore one pair of boots all the time I was in Africa, through wet, heat, and long, long walking. They were in good condition when I gave them away finally, and had not started a stitch. They were made by that excellent craftsman, A. A. Cutter, of Eau Claire, Wis., and he deserves and is entirely welcome to this puff. Needless to remark, I have received no especial favours from Mr. Cutter.

Six pairs of woollen socks, knit by hand, if possible-will be enough. For evening, when you come in, I know nothing better than a pair of very high moosehide moccasins. They should, however, be provided with thin soles against the stray thorn, and should reach well above the ankle by way of defence against the fever mosquito. That festive insect carries on a surreptitious guerrilla warfare low down. The English "mosquito boot" is simply an affair like a riding boot, made of suede leather, with thin soles. It is most comfortable. My objection is that it is unsubstantial and goes to pieces in a very brief time even under ordinary evening wear about camp.

You will also want a coat. In American camping I have always maintained the coat is a useless garment. There one does his own work to a large extent. When at work or travel the coat is in the way. When in camp the sweater or buckskin shirt is handier, and more easily carried. In Africa, however, where the other fellow does most of the work, a coat is often very handy. Do not make the mistake of getting an unlined light-weight garment. When you want it at all, you want it warm and substantial. Stick on all the pockets possible, and have them button securely.

For wet weather there is nothing to equal a long and voluminous cape. Straps crossing the chest and around the waist permit one to throw it off the shoulders to shoot. It covers the hands, the rifle-most of the little horses or mules one gets out there. One can sleep in or on it, and it is a most effective garment against heavy winds. One suit of pajamas is enough, considering your tent boy's commendable mania for laundry work. Add handkerchiefs and you are fixed.

You will wear most of the above, and put what remains in your "officer's box." This is a thin steel, air-tight affair with a wooden bottom, and is the ticket for African work.

Sporting. Pick out your guns to suit yourself. You want a light one and a heavy one.

When I came to send out my ammunition, I was forced again to take the other fellow's experience. I was told by everybody that I should bring plenty, that it was better to have too much than too little, etc. I rather thought so myself, and accordingly shipped a trifle over 1,500 rounds of small bore cartridges. Unfortunately, I never got into the field with any of my numerous advisers on this point, so cannot state their methods from first-hand information. Inductive reasoning leads me to believe that they consider it unsportsmanlike to shoot at a standing animal at all, or at one running nearer than 250 yards. Furthermore, it is etiquette to continue firing until the last cloud of dust has died down on the distant horizon. Only thus can I conceive of getting rid of that amount of ammunition. In eight months of steady shooting, for example-shooting for trophies, as well as to feed a safari of fluctuating numbers, counting jackals, marabout and such small trash-I got away with 395 rounds of small bore ammunition and about 100 of large. This accounted for 225 kills. That should give one an idea. Figure out how many animals you are likely to want for ANY purpose, multiply by three, and bring that many cartridges.

To carry these cartridges I should adopt the English system of a stout leather belt on which you slip various sized pockets and loops to suit the occasion. Each unit has loops for ten cartridges. You rarely want more than that; and if you do, your gunbearer is supplied. In addition to the loops, you have leather pockets to carry your watch; your money, your matches and tobacco, your compass-anything you please. They are handy and safe. The tropical climate is too "sticky" to get much comfort, or anything else, out of ordinary pockets.

In addition, you supply your gunbearer with a cartridge belt, a leather or canvas carrying bag, water bottle for him and for yourself, a sheath knife and a whetstone. In the bag are your camera, tape line, the whetstone, field cleaners and lunch. You personally carry your field glasses, sun glasses, a knife, compass, matches, police whistle and notebook. The field glasses should not be more than six power; and if possible you should get the sort with detachable prisms. The prisms are apt to cloud in a tropical climate, and the non-detachable sort are almost impossible for a layman to clean. Hang these glasses around your neck by a strap only just long enough to permit you to raise them to your eyes. The best notebook is the "loose-leaf" sort. By means of this you can keep always a fresh leaf on top; and at night can transfer your day's notes to safe keeping in your tin box. The sun glasses should not be smoked or dark-you can do nothing with them-but of the new amberol, the sort that excludes the ultra-violet rays, but otherwise makes the world brighter and gayer. Spectacle frames of non-corrosive white metal, not steel, are the proper sort.

To clean your guns you must supply plenty of oil, and then some more. The East African gunbearer has a quite proper and gratifying, but most astonishing horror for a suspicion of rust; and to use oil any faster he would have to drink it.

Other Equipment. All this has taken much time to tell about, it has not done much toward filling up that tin box. Dump in your toilet effects and a bath towel, two or three scalpels for taxidermy, a ball of string, some safety-pins, a small tool kit, sewing materials, a flask of brandy, kodak films packed in tin, a boxed thermometer, an aneroid (if you are curious as to elevations), journal, tags for labelling trophies, a few yards of gun cloth, and the medicine kit.

The latter divides into two classes: for your men and for yourself. The men will suffer from certain well defined troubles: "tumbo," or overeating; diarrhaea, bronchial colds, fever and various small injuries. For "tumbo" you want a liberal supply of Epsom's salts; for diarrhaea you need chlorodyne; any good expectorant for the colds; quinine for the fever; permanganate and plenty of bandages for the injuries. With this lot you can do wonders. For yourself you need, or may need, in addition, a more elaborate lot: Laxative, quinine, phenacetin, bismuth and soda, bromide of ammonium, morphia, camphor-ice, and aspirin. A clinical thermometer for whites and one for blacks should be included. A tin of malted milk is not a bad thing to take as an emergency ration after fever.

By this time your tin box is fairly well provided. You may turn to general supplies.

521

# The Riverman

## *I*

The time was the year 1872, and the place a bend in the river above a long pond terminating in a dam. Beyond this dam, and on a flat lower than it, stood a two-story mill structure. Save for a small, stump-dotted clearing, and the road that led from it, all else was forest. Here in the bottom-lands, following the course of the stream, the hardwoods grew dense, their uppermost branches just beginning to spray out in the first green of spring. Farther back, where the higher lands arose from the swamp, could be discerned the graceful frond of white pines and hemlock, and the sturdy tops of Norways and spruce.

A strong wind blew up the length of the pond. It ruffled the surface of the water, swooping down in fan-shaped, scurrying cat's-paws, turning the dark-blue surface as one turns the nap of velvet. At the upper end of the pond it even succeeded in raising quite respectable wavelets, which LAP LAP LAPPED eagerly against a barrier of floating logs that filled completely the mouth of the inlet river. And behind this barrier were other logs, and yet others, as far as the eye could see, so that the entire surface of the stream was carpeted by the brown timbers. A man could have walked down the middle of that river as down a highway.

On the bank, and in a small woods-opening, burned two fires, their smoke ducking and twisting under the buffeting of the wind. The first of these fires occupied a shallow trench dug for its accommodation, and was overarched by a rustic framework from which hung several pails, kettles, and pots. An injured-looking, chubby man in a battered brown derby hat moved here and there. He divided his time between the utensils and an indifferent youth—his "cookee." The other, and larger, fire centred a rectangle composed of tall racks, built of saplings and intended for the drying of clothes. Two large tents gleamed white among the trees.

About the drying-fire were gathered thirty-odd men. Some were half-reclining before the blaze; others sat in rows on logs drawn close for the purpose; still others squatted like Indians on their heels, their hands thrown forward to keep the balance. Nearly all were smoking pipes.

Every age was represented in this group, but young men predominated. All wore woollen trousers stuffed into leather boots reaching just to the knee. These boots were armed on the soles with rows of formidable sharp spikes or caulks, a half and sometimes even three quarters of an inch in length. The tight driver's shoe and "stagged" trousers had not then come into use. From the waist down these men wore all alike, as though in a uniform, the outward symbol of their calling. From the waist up was more latitude of personal taste. One young fellow sported a bright-coloured Mackinaw blanket jacket; another wore a red knit sash, with tasselled ends; a third's fancy ran to a bright bandana about his neck. Head-gear, too, covered wide variations of broader or narrower brim, of higher or lower crown; and the faces beneath those hats differed as everywhere the human countenance differs. Only when the inspection, passing the gradations of broad or narrow, thick or thin, bony or rounded, rested finally on the eyes, would the observer have caught again the caste-mark which stamped these men as belonging to a distinct order, and separated them essentially from other men in other occupations. Blue and brown and black and gray these eyes were, but all steady and clear with the steadiness and clarity that comes to those whose daily work compels them under penalty to pay close and undeviating attention to their surroundings. This is true of sailors, hunters, plainsmen, cowboys, and tugboat captains. It was especially true of the old-fashioned river-driver, for a misstep, a miscalculation, a moment's forgetfulness of the sullen forces shifting and changing about him could mean for him maiming or destruction. So, finally, to one of an imaginative bent, these eyes, like the "cork boots," grew to seem part of the uniform, one of the marks of their caste, the outward symbol of their calling.

"Blow, you son of a gun!" cried disgustedly one young fellow with a red bandana, apostrophising the wind. "I wonder if there's ANY side of this fire that ain't smoky!"

"Keep your hair on, bub," advised a calm and grizzled old-timer. "There's never no smoke on the OTHER side of the fire—whichever that happens to be. And as for wind—she just makes holiday for the river-hogs."

"Holiday, hell!" snorted the younger man. "We ought to be down to Bull's Dam before now—"

"And Bull's Dam is half-way to Redding," mocked a reptilian and red-headed giant on the log, "and Redding is the happy childhood home of—"

The young man leaped to his feet and seized from a pile of tools a peavy—a dangerous weapon, like a heavy cant-hook, but armed at the end with a sharp steel shoe.

"That's about enough!" he warned, raising his weapon, his face suffused and angry. The red-headed man, quite unafraid, rose slowly from the log and advanced, bare-handed, his small eyes narrowed and watchful.

But immediately a dozen men interfered.

"Dry up!" advised the grizzled old-timer—Tom North by name. "You, Purdy, set down; and you, young squirt, subside! If you're going to have ructions, why, have 'em, but not on drive. If you don't look out, I'll set you both to rustling wood for the doctor."

At this threat the belligerents dropped muttering to their places. The wind continued to blow, the fire continued to flare up and down, the men continued to smoke, exchanging from time to time desultory and aimless remarks. Only Tom North carried on a consecutive, low-voiced conversation with another of about his own age.

"Just the same, Jim," he was saying, "it is a little tough on the boys—this new sluice-gate business. They've been sort of expectin' a chance for a day or two at Redding, and now, if this son of a gun of a wind hangs out, I don't know when we'll make her. The shallows at Bull's was always bad enough, but this is worse."

"Yes, I expected to pick you up 'way below," admitted Jim, whose "turkey," or clothes-bag, at his side proclaimed him a newcomer. "Had quite a tramp to find you."

"This stretch of slack water was always a terror," went on North, "and we had fairly to pike-pole every stick through when the wind blew; but now that dam's backed the water up until there reely ain't no current at all. And this breeze has just stopped the drive dead as a smelt."

"Don't opening the sluice-gates give her a draw?" inquired the newcomer.

"Not against this wind—and not much of a draw, anyway, I should guess."

"How long you been hung?"

"Just to-day. I expect Jack will be down from the rear shortly. Ought to see something's wrong when he runs against the tail of this jam of ours."

At this moment the lugubrious, round-faced man in the derby hat stepped aside from the row of steaming utensils he had been arranging.

"Grub pile," he remarked in a conversational tone of voice.

The group arose as one man and moved upon the heap of cutlery and of tin plates and cups. From the open fifty-pound lard pails and kettles they helped themselves liberally; then retired to squat in little groups here and there near the sources of supply. Mere conversation yielded to an industrious silence. Sadly the cook surveyed the scene, his arms folded across the dirty white apron, an immense mental reservation accenting the melancholy of his countenance. After some moments of contemplation he mixed a fizzling concoction of vinegar and soda, which he drank. His rotundity to the contrary notwithstanding, he was ravaged by a gnawing dyspepsia, and the sight of six eggs eaten as a side dish to substantials carried consternation to his interior.

So busily engaged was each after his own fashion that nobody observed the approach of a solitary figure down the highway of the river. The man appeared tiny around the upper bend, momently growing larger as he approached. His progress was jerky and on an uneven zigzag, according as the logs lay, by leaps, short runs, brief pauses, as a riverman goes. Finally he stepped ashore just below the camp, stamped his feet vigorously free of water, and approached the group around the cooking-fire.

No one saw him save the cook, who vouchsafed him a stately and lugubrious inclination of the head.

The newcomer was a man somewhere about thirty years of age, squarely built, big of bone, compact in bulk. His face was burly, jolly, and reddened rather than tanned by long exposure. A pair of twinkling blue eyes and a humorously quirked mouth redeemed his countenance from commonplaceness.

He spread his feet apart and surveyed the scene.

"Well, boys," he remarked at last in a rollicking big voice, "I'm glad to see the situation hasn't spoiled your appetites."

At this they looked up with a spontaneous answering grin. Tom North laid aside his plate and started to arise.

"Sit still, Tom," interposed the newcomer. "Eat hearty. I'm going to feed yet myself. Then we'll see what's to be done. I think first thing you'd better see to having this wind turned off."

After the meal was finished, North and his principal sauntered to the water's edge, where they stood for a minute looking at the logs and the ruffled expanse of water below.

"Might as well have sails on them and be done with it," remarked Jack Orde reflectively. "Couldn't hold 'em any tighter. It's a pity that old mossback had to put in a mill. The water was slack enough before, but now there seems to be no current at all."

"Case of wait for the wind," agreed Tom North. "Old Daly will be red-headed. He must be about out of logs at the mill. The flood-water's going down every minute, and it'll make the riffles above Redding a holy fright. And I expect Johnson's drive will be down on our rear most any time."

"It's there already. Let's go take a look," suggested Orde.

They picked their way around the edge of the pond to the site of the new mill.

"Sluice open all right," commented Orde. "Thought she might be closed."

"I saw to that," rejoined North in an injured tone.

"'Course," agreed Orde, "but he might have dropped her shut on you between times, when you weren't looking."

He walked out on the structure and looked down on the smooth water rushing through.

"Ought to make a draw," he reflected. Then he laughed. "Tom, look here," he called. "Climb down and take a squint at this."

North clambered to a position below.

"The son of a gun!" he exclaimed.

The sluice, instead of bedding at the natural channel of the river, had been built a good six feet above that level; so that, even with the gates wide open, a "head" of six feet was retained in the slack water of the pond.

"No wonder we couldn't get a draw," said Orde. "Let's hunt up old What's-his-name and have a pow-wow."

"His name is plain Reed," explained North. "There he comes now."

"Sainted cats!" cried Orde, with one of his big, rollicking chuckles. "Where did you catch it?"

The owner of the dam flapped into view as a lank and lengthy individual dressed in loose, long clothes and wearing a-top a battered old "plug" hat, the nap of which seemed all to have been rubbed off the wrong way.

As he bore down on the intruders with tremendous, nervous strides, they perceived him to be an old man, white of hair, cadaverous of countenance, with thin, straight lips, and burning, fanatic eyes beneath stiff and bushy brows.

"Good-morning, Mr. Reed," shouted Orde above the noise of the water.

"Good-morning, gentlemen," replied the apparition.

"Nice dam you got here," went on Orde.

Reed nodded, his fiery eyes fixed unblinking on the riverman.

"But you haven't been quite square to us," said Orde. "You aren't giving us much show to get our logs out."

"How so?" snapped the owner, his thin lips tightening.

"Oh, I guess you know, all right," laughed Orde, clambering leisurely back to the top of the dam. "That sluice is a good six foot too high."

"Is that so!" cried the old man, plunging suddenly into a craze of excitement. "Well, let me tell you this, Mr. Man, I'm giving you all the law gives you, and that's the natural flow of the river, and not a thing more will you get! You that comes to waste and destroy, to arrogate unto yourselves the kingdoms of the yearth and all the fruits thereof, let me tell you you can't override Simeon Reed! I'm engaged here in a peaceful and fittin' operation, which is to feed the hungry by means of this grist-mill, not to rampage and bring destruction to the noble forests God has planted! I've give you what the law gives you, and nothin' more!"

Somewhat astonished at this outbreak, the two rivermen stood for a moment staring at the old man. Then a steely glint crept into Orde's frank blue eye and the corners of his mouth tightened.

"We want no trouble with you, Mr. Reed," said he, "and I'm no lawyer to know what the law requires you to do and what it requires you not to do. But I do know that this is the only dam on the river with sluices built up that way, and I do know that we'll never get those logs out if we don't get more draw on the water. Good-day."

Followed by the reluctant North he walked away, leaving the gaunt figure of the dam owner gazing after them, his black garments flapping about him, his hands clasped behind his back, his ruffled plug hat thrust from his forehead.

"Well!" burst out North, when they were out of hearing.

"Well!" mimicked Orde with a laugh.

"Are you going to let that old high-banker walk all over you?"

"What are you going to do about it, Tom? It's his dam."

"I don't know. But you ain't going to let him bang us up here all summer—"

"Sure not. But the wind's shifting. Let's see what the weather's like to-morrow. To-day's pretty late."

## II

The next morning dawned clear and breathless. Before daylight the pessimistic cook was out, his fire winking bravely against the darkness. His only satisfaction of the long day came when he aroused the men from the heavy sleep into which daily toil plunged them. With the first light the entire crew were at the banks of the river.

As soon as the wind died the logs had begun to drift slowly out into the open water. The surface of the pond was covered with the scattered timbers floating idly. After a few moments the clank of the bars and ratchet was heard as two of the men raised the heavy sluice-gate on the dam. A roar of water, momently increasing, marked the slow rise of the barrier. A very imaginative man might then have made out a tendency forward on the part of those timbers floating nearest the centre of the pond. It was a very sluggish tendency, however, and the men watching critically shook their heads.

Four more had by this time joined the two men who had raised the gate, and all together, armed with long pike poles, walked out on the funnel-shaped booms that should concentrate the logs into the chute. Here they prodded forward the few timbers within reach, and waited for more.

These were a long time coming. Members of the driving crew leaped shouting from one log to another. Sometimes, when the space across was too wide to jump, they propelled a log over either by rolling it, paddling it, or projecting it by the shock of a leap on one end. In accomplishing these feats of tight-rope balance, they stood upright and graceful, quite unconscious of themselves, their bodies accustomed by long habit to nice and instant obedience to the almost unconscious impulses of the brain. Only their eyes, intent, preoccupied, blazed out by sheer will-power the unstable path their owners should follow. Once at the forefront of the drive, the men began vigorously to urge the logs forward. This they accomplished almost entirely by main strength, for the sluggish current gave them little aid. Under the pressure of their feet as they pushed against their implements, the logs dipped, rolled, and plunged. Nevertheless, they worked as surely from the decks of these unstable craft as from the solid earth itself.

In this manner the logs in the centre of the pond were urged forward until, above the chute, they caught the slightly accelerated current which should bring them down to the pike-pole men at the dam. Immediately, when this stronger influence was felt, the drivers zigzagged back up stream to start a fresh batch. In the meantime a great many logs drifted away to right and left into stagnant water, where they lay absolutely motionless. The moving of them was deferred for the "sacking crew," which would bring up the rear.

Jack Orde wandered back and forth over the work, his hands clasped behind his back, a short pipe clenched between his teeth. To the edge of the drive he rode the logs, then took to the bank and strolled down to the dam. There he stood for a moment gazing aimlessly at the water making over the apron, after which he returned to the work. No cloud obscured the serene good-nature of his face. Meeting Tom North's troubled glance, he grinned broadly.

"Told you we'd have Johnson on our necks," he remarked, jerking his thumb up river toward a rapidly approaching figure.

This soon defined itself as a tall, sun-reddened, very blond individual with a choleric blue eye.

"What in hell's the matter here?" he yelled, as soon as he came within hearing distance.

Orde made no reply, but stood contemplating the newcomer with a flicker of amusement.

"What in hell's the matter?" repeated the latter violently.

"Better go there and inquire," rejoined Orde drolly. "What ails you, Johnson?"

"We're right at your rear," cried the other, "and you ain't even made a start gettin' through this dam! We'll lose the water next! Why in hell ain't you through and gone?"

"Keep your shirt on," advised Orde. "We're getting through as fast as we can. If you want these logs pushed any faster, come down and do it yourself."

Johnson vouchsafed no reply, but splashed away over the logs, examining in detail the progress of the work. After a little he returned within hailing distance.

"If you can't get out logs, why do you take the job?" he roared, with a string of oaths. "If you hang my drive, damn you, you'll catch it for damages! It's gettin' to a purty pass when any old highbanker from anywheres can get out and play jackstraws holdin' up every drive in the river! I tell you our mills need logs, and what's more they're agoin' to GIT them!"

He departed in a rumble of vituperation.

Orde laughed humorously at his foreman.

"Johnson gets so mad sometimes, his skin cracks," he remarked. "However," he went on more seriously, "there's a heap in what he means, if there ain't so much in what he says. I'll go labour with our old friend below."

He regained the bank, stopped to light his pipe, and sauntered, with every appearance of leisure, down the bank, past the dam, to the mill structure below.

Here he found the owner occupying a chair tilted back against the wall of the building. His ruffled plug hat was thrust, as usual, well away from his high and narrow forehead; the long broadcloth coat fell back to reveal an unbuttoned waistcoat the flapping black trousers were hitched up far enough to display woollen socks wrinkled about bony shanks. He was whittling a pine stick, which he held pointing down between his spread knees, and conversing animatedly with a young fellow occupying another chair at his side.

"And there comes one of 'em now," declaimed the old man dramatically.

Orde nodded briefly to the stranger, and came at once to business.

"I want to talk this matter over with you," he began. "We aren't making much progress. We can't afford to hang up the drive, and the water is going down every day. We've got to have more water. I'll tell you what we'll do: If you'll let us cut down the new sill, we'll replace it in good shape when we get all our logs through."

"No, sir!" promptly vetoed the old man.

"Well, we'll give you something for the privilege. What do you think is fair?"

"I tell ye I'll give you your legal rights, and not a cent more," replied the old man, still quietly, but with quivering nostrils.

"What is your name?" asked Orde.

"My name is Reed, sir."

"Well, Mr. Reed, stop and think what this means. It's a more serious matter than you think. In a little while the water will be so low in the river that it will be impossible to take out the logs this year. That means a large loss, of course, as you know."

"I don't know nothin' about the pesky business, and I don't wan to," snorted Reed.

"Well, there's borers, for one thing, to spoil a good many of the logs. And think what it will mean to the mills. No logs means no lumber. That is bankruptcy for a good many who have contracts to fulfil. And no logs means the mills must close. Thousands of men will be thrown out of their jobs, and a good many of them will go hungry. And with the stream full of the old cutting, that means less to do next winter in the woods—more men thrown out. Getting out a season's cut with the flood-water is a pretty serious matter to a great many people, and if you insist on holding us up here in this slack water the situation will soon become alarming."

"Ye finished?" demanded Reed grimly.

"Yes," replied Orde.

The old man cast from him his half-whittled piece of pine. He closed his jack-knife with a snap and thrust it in his pocket. He brought to earth the front legs of his chair with a thump, and jammed his ruffled plug hat to its proper place.

"And if the whole kit and kaboodle of ye starved out-right," said he, "it would but be the fulfillin' of the word of the prophet who says, 'So will I send upon you famine and evil beasts, and they shall bereave thee, and pestilence and blood shall pass through thee; and I will bring the sword upon thee. I the Lord have spoken it!'"

"That's your last word?" inquired Orde.

"That's my last word, and my first. Ye that make of God's smilin' land waste places and a wilderness, by your own folly shall ye perish."

"Good-day," said Orde, whirling on his heel without further argument.

The young man, who had during this colloquy sat an interested and silent spectator, arose and joined him. Orde looked at his new companion a little curiously. He was a very slender young man, taut-muscled, taut-nerved, but impassive in demeanour. He possessed a shrewd, thin face, steel-gray, inscrutable eyes behind glasses. His costume was quite simply an old gray suit of business clothes and a gray felt hat. At the moment he held in his mouth an unlighted and badly chewed cigar.

"Nice, amiable old party," volunteered Orde with a chuckle.

"Seems to be," agreed the young man drily.

"Well, I reckon we'll just have to worry along without him," remarked Orde, striking his steel caulks into the first log and preparing to cross out into the river where the work was going on.

"Wait a minute," said the young fellow. "Have you any objections to my hanging around a little to watch the work? My name is Newmark—Joseph Newmark. I'm out in this country a good deal for my health. This thing interests me."

"Sure," replied Orde, puzzled. "Look all you want to. The scenery's free."

"Yes. But can you put me up? Can I get a chance to stay with you a little while?"

"Oh, as far as I'm concerned," agreed Orde heartily. "But," he supplemented with one of his contagious chuckles, "I'm only river-boss. You'll have to fix it up with the doctor—the cook, I mean," he explained, as Newmark look puzzled. "You'll find him at camp up behind that brush. He's a slim, handsome fellow, with a jolly expression of countenance."

He leaped lightly out over the bobbing timbers, leaving Newmark to find his way.

In the centre of the stream the work had been gradually slowing down to a standstill with the subsidence of the first rush of water after the sluice-gate was opened. Tom North, leaning gracefully against the shaft of a peavy, looked up eagerly as his principal approached.

"Well, Jack," he inquired, "is it to be peace or war?"

"War," replied Orde briefly.

### III

At this moment the cook stepped into view, and, making a trumpet of his two hands, sent across the water a long, weird, and not unmusical cry. The men at once began slowly to drift in the direction of the camp. There, when the tin plates had all been filled, and each had found a place to his liking, Orde addressed them. His manner was casual and conversational.

"Boys," said he, "the old mossback who owns that dam has come up here loaded to scatter. He's built up the sill of that gate until we can't get a draw on the water, and he refuses to give, lend, or sell us the right to cut her out. I've made him every reasonable proposition, but all I get back is quotations from the prophets. Now, we've got to get those logs out— that's what we're here for. A fine bunch of whitewater birlers we'd look if we got hung up by an old mossback in a plug hat. Johnny Sims, what's the answer?"

"Cut her out," grinned Johnny Sims briefly.

"Correct!" replied Orde with a chuckle. "Cut her out. But, my son, it's against the law to interfere with another man's property."

This was so obviously humourous in intent that its only reception consisted of more grins from everybody.

"But," went on Orde more seriously, "it's quite a job. We can't work more than six or eight men at it at a time. We got to work as fast as we can before the old man can interfere."

"The nearest sheriff's at Spruce Rapids," commented some one philosophically.

"We have sixty men, all told," said Orde. "We ought to be able to carry it through."

He filled his plate and walked across to a vacant place. Here he found himself next to Newmark.

"Hello!" he greeted that young man, "fixed it with the doctor all right?"

"Yes," replied Newmark, in his brief, dry manner, "thanks! I think I ought to tell you that the sheriff is not at Spruce Rapids, but at the village—expecting trouble."

Orde whistled, then broke into a roar of delight.

"Boys," he called, "old Plug Hat's got the sheriff right handy. I guess he sort of expected we'd be thinking of cutting through that dam. How'd you like to go to jail?"

"I'd like to see any sheriff take us to jail, unless he had an army with him," growled one of the river-jacks.

"Has he a posse?" inquired Orde of Newmark.

"I didn't see any; but I understood in the village that the governor had been advised to hold State troops in readiness for trouble."

Orde fell into a brown study, eating mechanically. The men began an eager and somewhat truculent discussion full of lawless and bloodthirsty suggestion. Some suggested the kidnapping and sequestration of Reed until the affair should be finished.

"How'd he get hold of his old sheriff, then?" they inquired with some pertinence.

Orde, however, paid no attention to all this talk, but continued to frown into space. At last his face cleared, and he slapped down his tin plate so violently that the knife and fork jumped off into the dirt.

"I have it!" he cried aloud.

But he would not tell what he had. After the noon hour he instructed a half-dozen men to provide themselves with saws, axes, picks, and shovels, and all marched in the direction of the mill.

When within a hundred yards or so of that structure the advancing riverman saw the lank, black figure of the mill owner flap into sight, astride a bony old horse, and clatter away, coat-tails flying, up the road and into the waiting forest.

"Now, boys!" cried Orde crisply. "He'll be back in an hour with the sheriff. Lively!" He rapidly designated ten men of his crew. "You boys get to work and make things hum. Get as much done as you can before the sheriff comes."

"He'll have to bring all of Spruce County to get me," commented one of those chosen, spitting on his hands.

"Me, too!" said others.

"Now, listen," said Orde, holding them with an impressive gesture. "When that sheriff comes, with or without a posse, I want you to go peaceably. Understand?"

"Cave in? Not much!" cried Purdy.

"See here," and Orde drew them aside to an earnest, low-voiced conversation that lasted several minutes. When he had finished he clapped each of them on the back, and all moved off, laughing, to the dam.

"Now, boys," he commanded the others, "no row without orders. Understand? If there's going to be a fight, I'll give you the word when."

The chopping crew descended to the bottom of the sluice, the gate of which had been shut, and began immediately to chop away at the apron. As the water in the pond above had been drawn low by the morning's work, none overflowed the gate, so the men were enabled to work dry. Below the apron, of course, had been filled in with earth and stones. As soon as the axe-men had effected an entry to this deposit, other men with shovels and picks began to remove the filling.

The work had continued nearly an hour when Orde commanded the fifty or more idlers back to camp.

"Get out, boys," he ordered. "The sheriff will be here pretty quick now, and I don't want any row. Get out of sight."

"And leave them to fight her out alone? Guess not!" grumbled a tall, burly individual with a red face.

Orde immediately walked directly to this man.

"Am I bossing this drive, or am I not?" he demanded.

The riverman growled something.

SMACK! SMACK! sounded Orde's fists. The man, taken by surprise, went down in a heap, but immediately rebounded to his feet as though made of rubber. But Orde had seized a peavy, and stood over against his antagonist, the murderous weapon upraised.

"Lie down, you hound, or I'll brain you!" he roared at the top strength of his great voice. "Want fight, do you? Well, you won't have to wait till the sheriff gets here! You make a move!"

For a full half minute the man crouched breathless, and Orde, his ruddy face congested, held his threatening attitude. Then he dropped his peavy and stepped aside.

"March!" he commanded. "Get your turkey and hit the hay trail. You'll get your time at Redding."

The man sullenly arose and slouched away, grumbling under his breath. Orde watched him from sight, then turned to the silent group, a new crispness in his manner.

"Well?" he demanded.

Hesitating, they turned to the river trail, leaving the ten still working at the sluice. When well within the fringe of the brush, Orde called a halt. His customary good-humour seemed quite restored.

"Now, boys," he commanded, "squat down and lay low. You give me an ache! Don't you suppose I got this thing all figured out? If fight would do any good, you know mighty well I'd fight. And the boys won't be in jail any longer than it takes to get a wire to Daly to bail them out. Smoke up, and don't bother."

They filled their pipes and settled down to an enjoyment of the situation. Ordinarily from very early in the morning until very late at night the riverman is busy every instant at his dangerous and absorbing work. Those affairs which do not immediately concern his task—as the swiftness of rapids, the state of flood, the curves of streams, the height of water, the obstructions of channels, the quantities of logs—pass by the outer fringe of his consciousness, if indeed they reach him at all. Thus, often he works all day up to his waist in a current bearing the rotten ice of the first break-up, or endures the drenching of an early spring rain, or battles the rigours of a belated snow with apparent indifference. You or I would be exceedingly uncomfortable; would require an effort of fortitude to make the plunge. Yet these men, absorbed in the mighty problems of their task, have little attention to spare to such things. The cold, the wet, the discomfort, the hunger, the weariness, all pass as shadows on the background. In like manner the softer moods of the spring rarely penetrate through the concentration of faculties on the work. The warm sun shines; the birds by thousands flutter and twitter and sing their way north; the delicate green of spring, showered from the hand of the passing Sower, sprinkles the tops of the trees, and gradually sifts down through the branches; the great, beautiful silver clouds sail down the horizon like ships of a statelier age, as totally without actual existence to these men. The logs, the river—those are enough to strain all the faculties a man possesses, and more.

So when, as now, a chance combination of circumstances brings them leisure to look about them, the forest and the world of out-of-doors comes to them with a freshness impossible for the city dweller to realise. The surroundings are accustomed, but they bring new messages. To most of them, these impressions never reach the point of coherency. They brood, and muse, and expand in the actual and figurative warmth, and proffer the general opinion that it is a damn fine day!

Another full half hour elapsed before the situation developed further. Then Tom North's friend Jim, who had gathered his long figure on the top of a stump, unclasped his knees and remarked that old Plug Hat was back.

The men arose to their feet and peered cautiously through the brush. They saw Reed, accompanied by a thick-set man whom some recognised as the sheriff of the county, approach the edge of the dam. A moment later the working crew mounted to the top, stacked their tools neatly, resumed their coats and jackets, and departed up the road in convoy of the sheriff.

A gasp of astonishment broke from the concealed rivermen.

"Well, I'll be damned!" ejaculated one. "What are we comin' to? That's the first time I ever see one lonesome sheriff gather in ten river-hogs without the aid of a gatlin' or an ambulance! What's the matter with that chicken-livered bunch, anyway?"

Orde watched them, his eyes expressionless, until they had disappeared in the fringe of the forest Then he turned to the astonished group.

"Jim," said he, "and you, Ellis, and you, and you, and you, and you, get to work on that dam. And remember this, if you are arrested, go peaceably. Any resistance will spoil the whole game."

The men broke into mingled cheers and laughter as the full significance of Orde's plan reached them. They streamed back to the dam, where they perched proffering advice and encouragement to those about to descend.

Immediately, however, Reed was out, his eyes blazing either side his hawk nose.

"Here!" he cried, "quit that! I'll have ye arrested!"

"Arrest ahead," replied Orde coldly.

Reed stormed back and forth for a moment, then departed at full speed up the road.

"Now, boys, get as much done as possible," urged Orde. "We better get back in the brush, or he may try to take in the whole b'iling of us on some sort of a blanket warrant."

"How about the other boys?" inquired North.

"I gave one of them a telegram to send to Daly," replied Orde. "Daly will be up to bail them out."

Once more they hid in the woods; and again, after a longer interval, the mill owner and the sheriff reappeared. Reed appeared to be expostulating violently, and a number of times pointed up river; but the sheriff went ahead stolidly to the dam, summoned those working below, and departed up the road as before. Reed stood uncertain until he saw the rivermen beginning to re-emerge from the brush, then followed the officer at top speed.

Without the necessity of command, a half-dozen men leaped down on the apron. The previous crews had made considerable progress in weakening the heavy supports. As soon as these should be cut out and the backing removed, the mere sawing through of the massive sill should carry away the whole obstruction.

"Next time will decide it," remarked Orde. "If the sheriff brings a posse and sits down to lay for us, of course we won't be able to get near to finish the job."

"I didn't think that of George Morris," commented Sims in an aggrieved way. "He was a riverman himself once before he was sheriff."

"He's got to obey orders, and serve a warrant when it's issued, of course," replied Orde to this. "What did you expect?"

At the end of another hour, which brought the time to four o'clock, the sheriff made his third appearance—this time in a side-bar buggy.

"I wish I dared join that confab," said Orde, "and hear what's going on, but I'm afraid he'd jug me sure."

"He wouldn't jug me," spoke up Newmark. "I'll go down."

"Bully for you!" agreed Orde.

The young man departed in his precise, methodical manner, picking his way rather mincingly among the inequalities of the trail. In spite of the worn and wrinkled condition of his garments, they retained something of a city hang and smartness that sharply differentiated their wearer from even the well-dressed citizens of a smaller town. They seemed to match the refined, shrewd, but cold intelligence of his lean and nervous face.

About sunset he returned from a scene which the distant spectators had watched with breathless interest. It was in essence only a repetition of the two that had preceded it, but Reed had evidently gone almost to the point of violence in his insistence, and the sheriff had shaken him off rudely. Finally, Morris and his six prisoners had trailed away. The sheriff and North's friend occupied the seat of the buggy, while the other five trudged peaceably alongside. Once again Reed clattered away on his bony steed, but this time ahead of the official party.

With a whoop the river crew, now reduced to a scant dozen, rushed down to meet the too deliberate Newmark.

"Well?" they demanded, crowding about him.

"Reed wanted the sheriff to stay and protect the dam," reported Newmark in his brief, dry manner. "Sheriff refused. Said his duty was simply to arrest on warrant, and as often as Reed got out warrants, he'd serve them. Reed said, then, he should get a posse and hunt up Orde and the rest of them. Sheriff replied that as far as he could see, the terms of his warrant were covered by the men he found working on the dam, Reed demanded protection, Sheriff said for him to get an injunction, and it would be enforced."

"Well, that's all right," interjected Orde with satisfaction. "We'll have her cut through before he gets that injunction, and I guess I've got men enough here and down river to get through before we're ALL arrested."

"Yes," said Newmark, "that's all very well. But now he's gone to telegraph the governor to send the troops."

Orde whistled a jig tune.

"Kind of expected that, boys," said he. "Let's see. The next train out from Redding—They'll be here by five in the morning at soonest. Hope it'll be later."

"What will you do?" asked Newmark.

"Take chances," replied Orde. "All you boys get to work. Zeke," he commanded one of the cookees, "go up road, and report if Morris comes back. I reckon this time we'll have to scatter if he comes after us. I hope we won't have to, though. Like to keep everything square on account of this State troop business."

The sun had dropped below the fringe of trees, which immediately etched their delicate outlines against a pale, translucent green sky. Two straight, thin columns of smoke rose from the neglected camp-fires. Orde, glancing around him, noticed these.

"Doctor," he commanded sharply, "get at your grub! Make some coffee right off, and bring it down. Get the lanterns from the wanigan, and bring them to the dam. Come on, boys!"

Over a score of men attacked the sluice-way, for by now part of the rear crew had come down river. The pond above had recovered its volume. Water was beginning to trickle over the top of the gate. In a short time progress became difficult, almost impossible, The men worked up to their knees in swift water. They could not see, and the strokes of axe or pick lost much of their force against the liquid. Dusk fell. The fringe of the forest became mysterious in its velvet dark. Silver streaks, of a supernal calm, suggested the reaches of the pond. Above, the sky's day surface unfolded and receded and dissolved and melted away until, through the pale afterglow, one saw beyond into the infinities. Down by the sluice a dozen lanterns flickered and blinked yellow against the blue-blackness of the night.

After some time Orde called his crew off and opened the sluice-gates. The water had become too deep for effective work, and a half hour's flow would reduce the pressure. The time was occupied in eating and in drying off about the huge fire the second cookee had built close at hand.

"Water cold, boys?" asked Orde.

"Some," was his reply.

"Want to quit?" he inquired, with mock solicitude.

"Nary quit."

Orde's shout of laughter broke the night silence of the whispering breeze and the rushing water.

"We'll stick to 'em like death to a dead nigger," was his comment.

Newmark, having extracted a kind of cardigan jacket from the bag he had brought with him as far as the mill, looked at the smooth, iron-black water and shivered.

When the meal was finished, the men lit their pipes and went back to work philosophically. With entire absorption in the task, they dug, chopped, and picked. The dull sound of blows, the gurgle and trickle of the water, the occasional grunt or brief comment of a riverman alone broke the calm of evening. Now that the sluice-gate was down and the water had ceased temporarily to flow over it, the work went faster. Orde, watching with the eye of an expert, vouchsafed to the taciturn Newmark that he thought they'd make it.

Near midnight, however, a swaying lantern was seen approaching. Orde, leaping to his feet with a curse at the boy on watch, heard the sound of wheels. A moment later, Daly's bulky form stepped into the illumination of the fire.

Orde wandered over to where his principal stood peering about him.

"Hullo!" said he.

"Oh, there you are!" cried Daly angrily. "What in hell you up to here?"

"Running logs," replied Orde coolly.

"Running logs!" shouted Daly, tugging at his overcoat pocket, and finally producing a much-folded newspaper. "How about this?"

Orde unfolded the paper and lowered it to the campfire. It was an extra, screaming with wood type. He read it deliberately over.

WAR!

the headline ran.

RIOTING AND BLOODSHED IN THE WOODS RIVERMEN AND DAM OWNERS CLASH!

There followed a vague and highly coloured statement to the effect that an initial skirmish had left the field in possession of the rivermen, in spite of the sheriff and a large posse, but that troops were being rushed to the spot, and that this "high-handed defiance of authority" would undoubtedly soon be suppressed. It concluded truthfully with the statement that the loss of life was as yet unknown.

Orde folded up the paper and handed it back.

"Don't you know any better than to get into that kind of a row down here?" Daly had been saying. "Do you want to bring us up for good here? Don't you realise that this isn't the northern peninsula? What are you trying to do, any way?"

"Sure I do," replied Orde placidly. "Come along here till I show you the situation."

Ten minutes later, Daly, relieved in his mind, was standing by the fire drinking hot coffee and laughing at Orde's description of Reed's plug hat.

To Orde's satisfaction, the sheriff did not reappear. Reed evidently now pinned his faith to the State troops.

All night the work went on, the men spelling each other at intervals of every few hours. By three o'clock the main abutments had been removed. The gate was then blocked to prevent its fall when its nether support should be withdrawn, and two men, leaning over cautiously, began at arm's-length to deliver their axe-strokes against the middle of the sill-timbers of the sluice itself, notching each heavy beam deeply that the force of the current might finally break it in two. The night was very dark, and very still. Even the night creatures had fallen into the quietude that precedes the first morning hours. The muffled, spaced blows of the axes, the low-voiced comments or directions of the workers, the crackle of the fire ashore were thrown by contrast into an undue importance. Men in blankets, awaiting their turn, slept close to the blaze.

Suddenly the vast silence of before dawn was broken by a loud and exultant yell from one of the axemen. At once the two scrambled to the top of the dam. The blanketed figures about the fire sprang to life. A brief instant later the snapping of wood fibres began like the rapid explosions of infantry fire; a crash and bang of timbers smote the air; and then the river, exultant, roaring with joy, rushed from its pent quietude into the new passage opened for it. At the same moment, as though at the signal, a single bird, premonitor of the yet distant day, lifted up his voice, clearly audible above the tumult.

Orde stormed into the camp up stream, his eyes bright, his big voice booming exultantly.

"Roll out, you river-hogs!" he shouted to those who had worked out their shifts earlier in the night. "Roll out, you web-footed sons of guns, and hear the little birds sing praise!"

Newmark, who had sat up the night through, and now shivered sleepily by the fire, began to hunt around for the bed-roll he had, earlier in the evening, dumped down somewhere in camp.

"I suppose that's all," said he. "Just a case of run logs now. I'll turn in for a little."

But Orde, a thick slice of bread half-way to his lips, had frozen in an attitude of attentive listening.

"Hark!" said he.

Faint, still in the depths of the forest, the wandering morning breeze bore to their ears a sound whose difference from the louder noises nearer at hand alone rendered it audible.

"The troops!" exclaimed Orde.

He seized a lantern and returned down the trail, followed eagerly by Newmark and every man in camp.

"Troops coming!" said Orde to Daly.

The men drew a little to one side, watching the dim line of the forest, dark against the paling sky. Shadows seemed to stir in its blackness. They heard quite distinctly the clink of metal against metal. A man rode out of the shadow and reined up by the fire. "Halt!" commanded a harsh voice. The rivermen could make out the troops—three or four score of them—standing rigid at attention. Reed, afoot now in favour of the commanding officer, pushed forward.

"Who is in charge here?" inquired the officer crisply.

"I am," replied Orde, stepping forward.

"I wish to inquire, sir, if you have gone mad to counsel your men to resist civil authority?"

"I have not resisted civil authority," replied Orde respectfully.

"It has been otherwise reported."

"The reports have been false. The sheriff of this county has arrested about twenty of my men single-handed and without the slightest trouble."

"Mr. Morris," cried the officer sharply.

"Yes?" replied the sheriff.

"Is what this man says true?"

"It sure is. Never had so little fuss arrestin' rivermen before in my life."

The officer's face turned a slow brick-red. For a moment he said nothing, then exploded with the utmost violence.

"Then why the devil am I dragged up here with my men in the night?" he cried. "Who's responsible for this insanity, anyway? Don't you know," he roared at Reed, who that moment swung within his range of vision, "that I have no standing in the presence of civil law? What do you mean getting me up here to your miserable little backwoods squabbles?"

Reed started to say something, but was immediately cut short by the irate captain.

"I've nothing to do with that; settle it in court. And what's more, you'll have something yourself to settle with the State! About, face! Forward, march!"

The men faded into the gray light as though dissolved by it.

A deep and respectful silence fell upon the men, which was broken by Orde's solemn and dramatic declamation.

> *"The King of France and twice ten thousand men*
> *Marched up the hill, and then marched down again,"*

he recited; then burst into his deep roar of laughter.

"Now you see, boys," he said, digging his fists into his eyes, "if you'd put up a row, what we'd have got into. No blue-coats in mine, thank you. Well, push the grub pile, and then get at those logs. It's a case of flood-water now."

But Reed, having recovered from his astonishment, had still his say.

"I tell ye, I'm not done with ye yet," he threatened, shaking his bony forefinger in Orde's face. "I'll sue ye for damages, and I'll GIT 'em, too."

"See here, you old mossback," said Orde, thrusting his bulky form to the fore, "you sue just as soon as you want to. You can't get at it any too quick to suit us. But just now you get out of this camp, and you stay out. You're an old man, and we don't want to be rough with you, but you're biting off more than you can chew. Skedaddle!"

Reed hesitated, waving his long arms about, flail-like, as though to begin a new oration.

"Now, do hop along," urged Orde. "We'll pay you any legitimate damages, of course, but you can't expect to hang up a riverful of logs just on a notion. And we're sick of you. Oh, hell, then! See here, you two; just see that this man leaves camp."

Orde turned square on his heel. Reed, after a glance at the two huge rivermen approaching, beat a retreat to his mill, muttering and wrathful still.

"Well, good-bye, boys," said Daly, pulling on his overcoat; "I'll just get along and bail the boys out of that village calaboose. I reckon they've had a good night's rest. Be good!"

The fringe of trees to eastward showed clearly against the whitening sky. Hundreds of birds of all kinds sang in an ecstasy. Another day had begun. Already men with pike-poles were guiding the sullen timbers toward the sluice-way.

When Newmark awoke once more to interest in affairs, the morning was well spent. On the river the work was going forward with the precision of clockwork. The six-foot lowering of the sluice-way had produced a fine current, which sucked the logs down from above. Men were busily engaged in "sacking" them from the sides of the pond toward its centre, lest the lowering water should leave them stranded. Below the dam the jam crew was finding plenty to do in keeping them moving in the white-water and the shallows. A fine sun, tempered with a prophetic warmth of later spring, animated the scene. Reed had withdrawn to the interior of his mill, and appeared to have given up the contest.

Some of the logs shot away down the current, running freely. To these the crews were not required to pay any attention. With luck, a few of the individual timbers would float ten, even twenty, miles before some chance eddy or fortuitous obstruction would bring them to rest. Such eddies and obstructions, however, drew a constant toll from the ranks of the free-moving logs, so that always the volume of timbers floating with the current diminished, and always the number of logs caught and stranded along the sides of the river increased. To restore these to the faster water was the especial province of the last and most expert crew—the rear.

Orde discovered about noon that the jam crew was having its troubles. Immediately below Reed's dam ran a long chute strewn with boulders, which was alternately a shallow or a stretch of white-water according as the stream rose or fell. Ordinarily the logs were flushed over this declivity by opening the gate, behind which a head of water had been accumulated. Now, however, the efficiency of the gate had been destroyed. Orde early discovered that he was likely to have trouble in preventing the logs rushing through the chute from grounding into a bad jam on the rapids below.

For a time the jam crew succeeded in keeping the "wings" clear. In the centre of the stream, however, a small jam formed, like a pier. Along the banks logs grounded, and were rolled over by their own momentum into places so shallow as to discourage any hope of refloating them unless by main strength. As the sluicing of the nine or ten million feet that constituted this particular drive went forward, the situation rapidly became worse.

"Tom, we've got to get flood-water unless we want to run into an awful job there," said Orde to the foreman. "I wonder if we can't drop that gate 'way down to get something for a head."

The two men examined the chute and the sluice-gate attentively for some time.

"If we could clear out the splinters and rubbish, we might spike a couple of saplings on each side for the gate to slide down into," speculated North. "Might try her on."

The logs were held up in the pond, and a crew of men set to work to cut away, as well as they might in the rush of water, the splintered ends of the old sill and apron. It was hard work. Newmark, watching, thought it impracticable. The current rendered footing impossible, so all the work had to be done from above. Wet wood gripped the long saws vice-like, so that a man's utmost strength could scarcely budge them. The water deadened the force of axe-blows. Nevertheless, with the sure persistence of the riverman, they held to it. Orde, watching them a few moments, satisfied himself that they would succeed, and so departed up river to take charge of the rear.

This crew he found working busily among some overflowed woods. They were herding the laggards of the flock. The subsidence of the water consequent upon the opening of the sluice-gate had left stranded and in shallows many hundreds of the logs. These the men sometimes, waist deep in the icy water, owing to the extreme inequality of the bottom, were rolling over and over with their peavies until once more they floated. Some few the rivermen were forced to carry bodily, ten men to a side, the peavies clamped in as handles. When once they were afloat, the task became easier. From the advantage of deadwood, stumps, or other logs the "sackers" pushed the unwieldy timbers forward, leaping, splashing, heaving, shoving, until at last the steady current of the main river seized the logs and bore them away. With marvellous skill they topped the dripping, bobby, rolling timbers, treading them over and over, back and forth, in unconscious preservation of equilibrium.

There was a good deal of noise and fun at the rear. The crew had been divided, and a half worked on either side the river. A rivalry developed as to which side should advance fastest in the sacking. It became a race. Momentary success in getting ahead of the other fellow was occasion for exultant crowing, while a mishap called forth ironic cheers and catcalls from the rival camp. Just as Orde came tramping up the trail, one of the rivermen's caulks failed to "bite" on an unusually smooth, barked surface. His foot slipped; the log rolled; he tried in vain to regain his balance, and finally fell in with a heavy splash.

The entire river suspended work to send up a howl of delight. As the unfortunate crawled out, dripping from head to foot, he was greeted by a flood of sarcasm and profane inquiry that left no room for even his acknowledged talents of repartee. Cursing and ashamed, he made his way ashore over the logs, spirting water at every step. There he wrung out his woollen clothes as dry as he could, and resumed work.

Hardly had Orde the opportunity to look about at the progress making, however, before he heard his name shouted from the bank. Looking up, to his surprise he saw the solemn cook waving a frantic dish-towel at him. Nothing could induce the cook to attempt the logs.

"What is it, Charlie?" asked Orde, leaping ashore and stamping the loose water from his boots.

"It's all off," confided the cook pessimistically. "It's no good. He's stopped us now."

"What's off? Who's stopped what?"

"Reed. He's druv the men from the dam with a shotgun. We might as well quit."

"Shotgun, hey!" exclaimed Orde. "Well, the old son of a gun!" He thought a moment, his lips puckered as though to whistle; then, as usual, he laughed amusedly. "Let's go take a look at the army," said he.

He swung away at a round pace, followed rather breathlessly by the cook. The trail led through the brush across a little flat point, up over a high bluff where the river swung in, down to another point, and across a pole trail above a marsh to camp.

A pole trail consists of saplings laid end to end, and supported three or four feet above wet places by means of sawbuck-like structures at their extremities. To a river-man or a tight-rope dancer they are easy walks. All others must proceed cautiously in contrite memory of their sins.

Orde marched across the first two lengths confidently enough. Then he heard a splash and lamentations. Turning, he perceived Charlie, covered with mud, in the act of clambering up one of the small trestles.

"Ain't got no caulks!" ran the lamentations. "The —— of a —— of a pole-trail, anyways!"

He walked ahead gingerly, threw his hands aloft, bent forward, then suddenly protruded his stomach, held out one foot in front of him, spasmodically half turned, and then, realising the case hopeless, wilted like a wet rag, to clasp the pole trail both by arm and leg. This saved him from falling off altogether, but swung him underneath, where he hung like the sloths in the picture-books. A series of violent wriggles brought him, red-faced and panting, astride the pole, whence, his feelings beyond mere speech, he sadly eyed his precious derby, which lay, crown up, in the mud below.

Orde contemplated the spectacle seriously.

"Sorry I haven't got time to enjoy you just now, Charlie," he remarked. "I'd take it slower, if I were you."

He departed, catching fragments of vows anent never going on any more errands for nobody, and getting his time if ever again he went away from his wanigan.

Orde stopped short outside the fringe of brush to utter another irrepressible chuckle of amusement.

The centre of the dam was occupied by Reed. The old man was still in full regalia, his plug hat fuzzier than ever, and thrust even farther back on his head, his coat-tails and loose trousers flapping at his every movement as he paced back and forth with military precision. Over his shoulder he carried a long percussion-lock shotgun. Not thirty feet away, perched along the bank, for all the world like a row of cormorants, sat the rivermen, watching him solemnly and in silence.

"What's the matter?" inquired Orde, approaching.

The old man surveyed him with a snort of disgust.

"If the law of the land don't protect me, I'll protect myself, sir," he proclaimed. "I give ye fair warning! I ain't a-going to have my property interfered with no more."

"But surely," said Orde, "we have a right to run our logs through. It's an open river."

"And hev ye been running your logs through?" cried the old man excitedly. "Hev ye? First off ye begin to tear down my dam; and then, when the river begins a-roarin' and a-ragin' through, then you tamper with my improvements furthermore, a-lowerin' the gate and otherwise a-modifyin' my structure."

Orde stepped forward to say something further. Immediately Reed wheeled, his thumb on the hammer.

"All right, old Spirit of '76," replied Orde. "Don't shoot; I'll come down."

He walked back to the waiting row, smiling quizzically.

"Well, you calamity howlers, what do you think of it?"

Nobody answered, but everybody looked expectant.

"Think he'd shoot?" inquired Orde of Tom North.

"I know he would," replied North earnestly. "That crazy-headed kind are just the fellers to rip loose."

"I think myself he probably would," agreed Orde.

"Surely," spoke up Newmark, "whatever the status of the damage suits, you have the legal right to run your logs."

Orde rolled a quizzical eye in his direction.

"Per-fect-ly correct, son," he drawled, "but we're engaged in the happy occupation of getting out logs. By the time the law was all adjusted and a head of steam up, the water'd be down. In this game, you get out logs first, and think about law afterward."

"How about legal damages?" insisted Newmark.

"Legal damages!" scoffed Orde. "Legal damages! Why, we count legal damages as part of our regular expenses—like potatoes. It's lucky it's so," he added. "If anybody paid any attention to legal technicalities, there'd never be a log delivered. A man always has enemies.

"Well, what are you going to do?" persisted Newmark.

Orde thrust back his felt hat and ran his fingers through his short, crisp hair.

"There you've got me," he confessed, "but, if necessary, we'll pile the old warrior."

He walked to the edge of the dam and stood looking down current. For perhaps a full minute he remained there motionless, his hat clinging to one side, his hand in his hair. Then he returned to the grimly silent rivermen.

"Boys," he commanded briefly, "get your peavies and come along."

He led the way past the mill to the shallows below.

"There's a trifle of wading to do," he announced. "Bring down two logs—fairly big—and hold them by that old snag," he ordered. "Whoa-up! Easy! Hold them end on—no, pointing up stream—fix 'em about ten foot apart—that's it! George, drive a couple of stakes each side of them to hold 'em. Correct! Now, run down a couple dozen more and pile them across those two—side on to the stream, of course. Roll 'em up—that's the ticket!"

Orde had been splashing about in the shallow water, showing where each timber was to be placed. He drew back, eyeing the result with satisfaction. It looked rather like a small and bristly pier.

Next he cast his eye about and discovered a partially submerged boulder on a line with the newly completed structure. Against this he braced the ends of two more logs, on which he once more caused to be loaded at right angles many timbers. An old stub near shore furnished him the basis of a third pier. He staked a thirty-inch butt for a fourth; and so on, until the piers, in conjunction with the small centre jam already mentioned, extended quite across the river.

All this was accomplished in a very short time, and immediately below the mill, but beyond sight from the sluice-gate of the dam.

"Now, boys," commanded Orde, "shove off some shore logs, and let them come down."

"We'll have a jam sure," objected Purdy stupidly.

"No, my son, would we?" mocked Orde. "I surely hope not!"

The stray logs floating down with the current the rivermen caught and arranged to the best possible advantage about the improvised piers. A good riverman understands the correlation of forces represented by saw-logs and water-pressure. He knows how to look for the key-log in breaking jams; and by the inverse reasoning, when need arises he can form a jam as expertly as Koosy-oonek himself—that bad little god who brings about the disagreeable and undesired—"who hides our pipes, steals our last match, and brings rain on the just when they want to go fishing."

So in ten seconds after the shore logs began drifting down from above, the jam was taking shape. Slowly it formed, low and broad. Then, as the water gathered pressure, the logs began to slip over one another. The weight of the topmost sunk those beneath to the bed of the stream. This to a certain extent dammed back the water. Immediately the pressure increased. More logs were piled on top. The piers locked the structure. Below the improvised dam the water fell almost to nothing, and above it, swirling in eddies, grumbling fiercely, bubbling, gurgling, searching busily for an opening, the river, turned back on itself, gathered its swollen and angry forces.

"That will do, boys," said Orde with satisfaction.

He led the way to the bank and sat down. The men followed his example. Every moment the water rose, and each instant, as more logs came down the current, the jam became more formidable.

"Nothing can stand that pressure," breathed Newmark, fascinated.

"The bigger the pressure the tighter she locks," replied Orde, lighting his pipe.

The high bank where the men sat lay well above the reach of the water. Not so the flat on which stood Reed's mill. In order to take full advantage of the water-power developed by the dam, the old man had caused his structure to be built nearly at a level with the stream. Now the river, backing up, rapidly overflowed this flat. As the jam tightened by its own weight and the accumulation of logs, the water fairly jumped from the lowest floor of the mill to the one above.

Orde had not long to wait for Reed's appearance. In less than five minutes the old man descended on the group, somewhat of his martial air abated, and something of a vague anxiety manifest in his eye.

"What's the matter here?" he demanded.

"Matter?" inquired Orde easily. "Oh, nothing much, just a little jam."

"But it's flooding my mill!"

"So I perceive," replied Orde, striking a match.

"Well, why don't you break it?"

"Not interested."

The old warrior ran up the bank to where he could get a good view of his property. The water was pouring into the first-floor windows.

"Here!" he cried, running back. "I've a lot of grain up-stairs. It'll be ruined!"

"Not interested," repeated Orde.

Reed was rapidly losing control of himself.

"But I've got a lot of money invested here!" he shouted. "You miserable blackguard, you're ruining me!"

Orde replaced his pipe.

Reed ran back and forth frantically, disappeared, returned bearing an antiquated pike-pole, and single-handed and alone attacked the jam!

Astonishment and delight held the rivermen breathless for a moment. Then a roar of laughter drowned even the noise of the waters. Men pounded each other on the back, rolled over and over, clutching handfuls of earth, struggled weak and red-faced for breath as they saw against the sky-line of the bristling jam the lank, flapping figure with the old plug hat pushing frantically against the immovable statics of a mighty power. The exasperation of delay, the anxiety lest success be lost through the mulish and narrow-minded obstinacy of one man, the resentment against another obstacle not to be foreseen and not to be expected in a task redundantly supplied with obstacles of its own—these found relief at last.

"By Jove!" breathed Newmark softly to himself. "Don Quixote and the windmills!" Then he added vindictively, "The old fool!" although, of course, the drive was not his personal concern.

Only Orde seemed to see the other side. And on Orde the responsibility, uncertainty, and vexation had borne most heavily, for the success of the undertaking was in his hands. With a few quick leaps he had gained the old man's side.

"Look here, Reed," he said kindly, "you can't break this jam. Come ashore now, and let up. You'll kill yourself."

Reed turned to him, a wild light in his eye.

"Break it!" he pleaded. "You're ruining me. I've got all my money in that mill."

"Well," said Orde, "we've got a lot of money in our logs too. You haven't treated us quite right."

Reed glanced frantically toward the flood up stream.

"Come," said Orde, taking him gently by the arm. "There's no reason you and I shouldn't get along together all right. Maybe we're both a little hard-headed. Let's talk it over."

533

He led the old man ashore, and out of earshot of the rivermen.

At the end of ten minutes he returned.

"War's over, boys!" he shouted cheerfully. "Get in and break that jam."

At once the crew swarmed across the log barrier to a point above the centre pier. This they attacked with their peavies, rolling the top logs off into the current below. In less than no time they had torn out quite a hole in the top layer. The river rushed through the opening. Immediately the logs in the wings were tumbled in from either side. At first the men had to do all of the work, but soon the river itself turned to their assistance. Timbers creaked and settled, or rose slightly buoyant as the water loosened the tangle. Men trod on the edge of expectation. Constantly the logs shifted, and as constantly the men shifted also, avoiding the upheavals and grindings together, wary eyes estimating the correlation of the forces into whose crushing reach a single misstep would bring them. The movement accelerated each instant, as the music of the play hastens to the climax. Wood fibres smashed. The whole mass seemed to sink down and forward into a boiling of waters. Then, with a creak and a groan, the jam moved, hesitated, moved again; finally, urged by the frantic river, went out in a majestic crashing and battering of logs.

At the first movement Newmark expected the rivermen to make their escape. Instead, they stood at attention, their peavies poised, watching cat-eyed the symptoms of the break. Twice or thrice several of the men, observing something not evident to Newmark's unpractised eye, ran forward, used their peavies vigorously for a moment or so, and stood back to watch the result. Only at the very last, when it would seem that some of them must surely he caught, did the river-jacks, using their peavy-shafts as balancing poles, zigzag calmly to shore across the plunging logs. Newmark seemed impressed.

"That was a close shave," said he to the last man ashore.

"What?" inquired the riverman. "Didn't see it. Somebody fall down?"

"Why, no," explained Newmark; "getting in off those logs without getting caught."

"Oh!" said the man indifferently, turning away.

The going out of the jam drained the water from the lower floors of the mill; the upper stories and the grain were still safe.

By evening the sluice-gate had been roughly provided with pole guides down which to slide to the bed of the river. The following morning saw the work going on as methodically as ever. During the night a very good head of water had gathered behind the lowered gate. The rear crew brought down the afterguard of logs to the pond. The sluicers with their long pike-poles thrust the logs into the chute. The jam crew, scattered for many miles along the lower stretches, kept the drive going; running out over the surface of the river like water-bugs to thrust apart logs threatening to lock; leaning for hours on the shafts of their peavies watching contemplatively the orderly ranks as they drifted by, sleepy, on the bosom of the river; occasionally gathering, as the filling of the river gave warning, to break a jam. By the end of the second day the pond was clear, and as Charlie's wanigan was drifting toward the chute, the first of Johnson's drive floated into the head of the pond.

## V

Charlie's wanigan, in case you do not happen to know what such a thing may be, was a scow about twenty feet long by ten wide. It was very solidly constructed of hewn timbers, square at both ends, was inconceivably clumsy, and weighed an unbelievable number of pounds. When loaded, it carried all the bed-rolls, tents, provisions, cooking utensils, tools, and a chest of tobacco, clothes, and other minor supplies. It was managed by Charlie and his two cookees by means of pike-poles and a long sweep at either end. The pike-poles assured progress when the current slacked; the sweeps kept her head-on when drifting with the stream.

Charlie's temperament was pessimistic at best. When the wanigan was to be moved, he rose fairly to the heights of what might be called destructive prophecy.

The packing began before the men had finished breakfast. Shortly after daylight the wanigan, pushed strongly from shore by the pike-poles, was drifting toward the chute. When the heavy scow threatened to turn side-on, the sweeps at either end churned the water frantically in an endeavour to straighten her out. Sometimes, by a misunderstanding, they worked against each other. Then Charlie, raging from one to the other of his satellites, frothed and roared commands and vituperations. His voice rose to a shriek. The cookees, bewildered by so much violence, lost their heads completely. Then Charlie abruptly fell to an exaggerated calm. He sat down amidships on a pile of bags, and gazed with ostentatious indifference out over the pond. Finally, in a voice fallen almost to a whisper, and with an elaborate politeness, Charlie proffered a request that his assistants acquire the sense God gave a rooster. Newmark, who had elected to accompany the wanigan on its voyage, evidently found it vastly amusing, for his eyes twinkled behind his glasses. As the wanigan neared the sluice through which it must shoot the flood-water, the excitement mounted to fever pitch. The water boiled under the strokes of the long steering oars. The air swirled with the multitude and vigour of Charlie's commands. As many of the driving crew as were within distance gathered to watch. It was a supreme moment. As Newmark looked at the smooth rim of the water sucking into the chute, he began to wonder why he had come.

However, the noble ship was pointed right at last, and caught the faster water head-on. Even Charlie managed to look cheerful for an instant, and to grin at his passenger as he wiped his forehead with a very old, red handkerchief.

"All right now," he shouted.

Zeke and his mate took in the oars. The wanigan shot forward below the gate—

WHACK! BUMP! BANG! and the scow stopped so suddenly that its four men plunged forward in a miscellaneous heap, while Zeke narrowly escaped going overboard. Almost immediately the water, backed up behind the stern, began to overflow into the boat. Newmark, clearing his vision as well as he could for lack of his glasses, saw that the scow had evidently run her bow on an obstruction, and had been brought to a standstill square beneath the sluice-gate. Men seemed to be running toward them. The water was beginning to flow the entire length of the boat. Various lighter articles shot past him and disappeared over the side. Charlie had gone crazy and was grabbing at these, quite uselessly, for as fast as he had caught one thing he let it go in favour of another. The cookees, retaining some small degree of coolness, were pushing uselessly with pike-poles.

Newmark had an inspiration. The more important matters, such as the men's clothes-bags, the rolls of bedding, and the heavier supplies of provisions, had not yet cut loose from their moorings, although the rapid backing of the water threatened soon to convert the wanigan into a chute for nearly the full volume of the current. He seized one of the long oars, thrust the blade under the edge of a thwart astern laid the shaft of the oar across the cargo, and by resting his weight on the handle attempted to bring it down to bind the contents of the wanigan to their places. The cookees saw what he was about, and came to his assistance. Together they succeeded in bending the long hickory sweep far enough to catch its handle-end under another, forward, thwart. The second oar was quickly locked alongside the first, and not a moment too soon. A rush of water forced them all to cling for their lives. The poor old wanigan was almost buried by the river.

But now help was at hand. Two or three rivermen appeared at the edge of the chute. A moment later old man Reed ran up, carrying a rope. This, after some difficulty, was made fast to the bow of the wanigan. A dozen men ran with the end of it to a position of vantage from which they might be able to pull the bow away from the sunken obstruction, but Orde, appearing above, called a halt. After consultation with Reed, another rope was brought and the end of it tossed down to the shipwrecked crew. Orde pointed to the stern of the boat, revolving his hands in pantomime to show that the wanigan would be apt to upset if allowed to get side-on when freed. A short rope led to the top of the dam allowed the bow to be lifted free of the obstruction; a cable astern prevented the current from throwing her broadside to the rush of waters; another cable from the bow led her in the way she should go. Ten minutes later she was pulled ashore out of the eddy below, very much water-logged, and manned by a drenched and disgruntled crew.

But Orde allowed them little chance for lamentation.

"Hard luck!" he said briefly. "Hope you haven't lost much. Now get a move on you and bail out. You've got to get over the shallows while this head is on."

"That's all the thanks you get," grumbled Charlie to himself and the other three as Orde moved away. "Work, slave, get up in the night, drownd yourself—"

He happily discovered that the pails under the forward thwart had not been carried away, and all started in to bail. It was a back-breaking job, and consumed the greater part of two hours. Even at the end of that time the wanigan, though dry of loose water, floated but sluggishly.

"'Bout two ton of water in them bed-rolls and turkeys," grumbled Charlie. "Well, get at it!"

Newmark soon discovered that the progress of the wanigan was looked upon in the light of a side-show by the rivermen. Its appearance was signal for shouts of delighted and ironic encouragement; its tribulations—which at first, in the white-water, were many—the occasion for unsympathetic and unholy joy. Charlie looked on all spectators as enemies. Part of the time he merely glowered. Part of the time he tried to reply in kind. To his intense disgust, he was taken seriously in neither case.

In a couple of hours' run the wanigan had overtaken and left far behind the rear of the drive. All about floated the logs, caroming gently one against the other, shifting and changing the pattern of their brown against the blue of the water. The current flowed strongly and smoothly, but without obstruction. Everything went well. The banks slipped by silently and mysteriously, like the unrolling of a panorama—little strips of marshland, stretches of woodland where the great trees leaned out over the river, thickets of overflowed swampland with the water rising and draining among roots in a strange regularity of its own. The sun shone warm. There was no wind. Newmark wrung out his outer garments, and basked below the gunwale. Zeke and his companion pulled spasmodically on the sweeps. Charlie, having regained his equanimity together with his old brown derby, which he came upon floating sodden in an eddy, marched up and down the broad gunwale with his pike-pole, thrusting away such logs as threatened interference.

"Well," said he at last, "we better make camp. We'll be down in the jam pretty soon."

The cookees abandoned the sweeps in favour of more pike-poles. By pushing and pulling on the logs floating about them, they managed to work the wanigan in close to the bank.

Charlie, a coil of rope in his hand, surveyed the prospects.

"We'll stop right down there by that little knoll," he announced.

He leaped ashore, made a turn around a tree, and braced himself to snub the boat, but unfortunately he had not taken into consideration the "two ton" of water soaked up by the cargo. The weight of the craft relentlessly dragged him forward. In vain he braced and struggled. The end of the rope came to the tree; he clung for a moment, then let go, and ran around the tree to catch it before it should slip into the water.

By this time the wanigan had caught the stronger current at the bend and was gathering momentum. Charlie tried to snub at a sapling, and broke the sapling; on a stub, and uprooted the stub. Down the banks and through the brush he tore at the end of his rope, clinging desperately, trying at every solid tree to stop the career of his runaway, but in every instance being forced by the danger of jamming his hands to let go. Again he lost his derby. The landscape was a blur.

Dimly he made out the howls of laughter as the outfit passed a group of rivermen. Then abruptly a ravine yawned before him, and he let go just in time to save himself a fall. The wanigan, trailing her rope, drifted away.

Nor did she stop until she had overtaken the jam. There, her momentum reduced by the closer crowding of the logs, she slowed down enough so that Newmark and the cookees managed to work her to the bank and make her fast.

That evening, after the wanigan's crew had accomplished a hard afternoon's work pitching camp and drying blankets, the first of the rear drifted in very late after a vain search for camp farther up stream.

"For God's sake, Charlie," growled one, "it's a wonder you wouldn't run through to Redding and be done with it."

Whereupon Charlie, who had been preternaturally calm all the afternoon, uttered a shriek of rage, and with a carving-knife chased that man out into the brush. Nor would he be appeased to the point of getting supper until Orde himself had intervened.

"Well," said Orde to Newmark later, around the campfire, "how does river-driving strike you?"

"It is extremely interesting," replied Newmark.

"Like to join the wanigan crew permanently?"

"No, thanks," returned Newmark drily.

"Well, stay with us as long as you're having a good time," invited Orde heartily, but turning away from his rather uncommunicative visitor.

"Thank you," Newmark acknowledged this, "I believe I will."

"Well, Tommy," called Orde across the fire to North, "I reckon we've got to rustle some more supplies. That shipwreck of ours to-day mighty near cleaned us out of some things. Lucky Charlie held his head and locked in the bedding with those sweeps, or we'd have been strapped."

"I didn't do it," grumbled Charlie. "It was him."

"Oh!" Orde congratulated Newmark. "Good work! I'm tickled to death you belonged to that crew."

"That old mossback Reed was right on deck with his rope," remarked Johnny Simms. "That was pretty decent of him."

"Old skunk!" growled North. "He lost us two days with his damn nonsense. You let him off too easy, Jack."

"Oh, he's a poor old devil," replied Orde easily. "He means well enough. That's the way the Lord made him. He can't help how he's made."

## VI

During the thirty-three days of the drive, Newmark, to the surprise of everybody, stayed with the work. Some of these days were very disagreeable. April rains are cold and persistent—the proverbs as to showers were made for another latitude. Drenched garments are bad enough when a man is moving about and has daylight; but when night falls, and the work is over, he likes a dry place and a change with which to comfort himself. Dry places there were none. Even the interior of the tents became sodden by continual exits and entrances of dripping men, while dry garments speedily dampened in the shiftings of camp which, in the broader reaches of the lower river, took place nearly every day. Men worked in soaked garments, slept in damp blankets. Charlie cooked only by virtue of persistence. The rivermen ate standing up, as close to the sputtering, roaring fires as they could get. Always the work went forward.

But there were other times when a golden sun rose each morning a little earlier on a green and joyous world. The river ran blue. Migratory birds fled busily northward—robins, flute-voiced blue-birds, warblers of many species, sparrows of different kinds, shore birds and ducks, the sweet-songed thrushes. Little tepid breezes wandered up and down, warm in contrast to the faint snow-chill that even yet lingered in the shadows. Sounds carried clearly, so that the shouts and banter of the rivermen were plainly audible up the reaches of the river. Ashore moist and aggressive green things were pushing up through the watery earth from which, in shade, the last frost had not yet departed. At camp the fires roared invitingly. Charlie's grub was hot and grateful. The fir beds gave dreamless sleep.

Newmark followed the work of the log-drive with great interest. All day long he tramped back and forth—on jam one day, on rear the next. He never said much, but watched keenly, and listened to the men's banter both on the work and about the evening's fire as though he enjoyed it. Gradually the men got used to him, and ceased to treat him as an outsider. His thin, eager face, his steel-blue, inquiring eyes behind the glasses, his gray felt hat, his lank, tense figure in its gray, became a familiar feature. They threw remarks to him, to which he replied briefly and drily. When anything interesting was going on, somebody told him about it. Then he hurried to the spot, no matter how distant it might be. He used always the river trail; he never attempted to ride the logs.

He seemed to depend most on observation, for he rarely asked any questions. What few queries he had to proffer, he made to Orde himself, waiting sometimes until evening to interview that busy and good-natured individual. Then his questions were direct and to the point. They related generally to the advisability of something he had seen done; only rarely did they ask for explanation of the work itself. That Newmark seemed capable of puzzling out for himself.

The drive, as has been said, went down as far as Redding in thirty-three days. It had its share of tribulation. The men worked fourteen and sixteen hours at times. Several bad jams relieved the monotony. Three dams had to be sluiced through. Problems of mechanics arose to be solved on the spot; problems that an older civilisation would have attacked deliberately and with due respect for the seriousness of the situation and the dignity of engineering. Orde solved them by a rough-and-ready but very effective rule of thumb. He built and abandoned structures which would have furnished opportunity for a winter's discussion to some committees; just as, earlier in the work, the loggers had built through a rough country some hundreds of miles of road better than railroad grade, solid in foundation, and smooth as a turnpike, the quarter of which would have occupied the average county board of supervisors for five years. And while he was at it, Orde kept his men busy and satisfied. Your white-water birler is not an easy citizen to handle. Yet never once did the boss appear hurried or flustered. Always he wandered about, his hands in his pockets, chewing a twig, his round, wind-reddened face puckered humorously, his blue eyes twinkling, his square, burly form lazily relaxed. He seemed to meet his men almost solely on the plane of good-natured chaffing. Yet the work was done, and done efficiently, and Orde was the man responsible.

The drive of which Orde had charge was to be delivered at the booms of Morrison and Daly, a mile or so above the city of Redding. Redding was a thriving place of about thirty thousand inhabitants, situated on a long rapids some forty miles from Lake Michigan. The water-power developed from the rapids explained Redding's existence. Most of the logs floated down the river were carried through to the village at the lake coast, where, strung up the river for eight or ten miles, stood a dozen or so big saw-mills, with concomitant booms, yards, and wharves. Morrison and Daly, however, had built a saw and planing mill at Redding, where they supplied most of the local trade and that of the surrounding country-side.

The drive, then, was due to break up as soon as the logs should be safely impounded.

The last camp was made some six or eight miles above the mill. From that point a good proportion of the rivermen, eager for a taste of the town, tramped away down the road, to return early in the morning, more or less drunk, but faithful to their job. One or two did not return.

Among the revellers was the cook, Charlie, commonly called The Doctor. The rivermen early worked off the effects of their rather wild spree, and turned up at noon chipper as larks. Not so the cook. He moped about disconsolately all day; and in the evening, after his work had been finished, he looked so much like a chicken with the pip that Orde's attention was attracted.

"Got that dark-brown taste, Charlie?" he inquired with mock solicitude.

The cook mournfully shook his head.

"Large head? Let's feel your pulse. Stick out your tongue, sonny."

"I ain't been drinking, I tell you!" growled Charlie.

"Drinking!" expostulated Orde, horrified. "Of course not! I hope none of MY boys ever take a drink! But that lemon-pop didn't agree with your stomach—now did it, Charlie?"

"I tell you I only had two glasses of beer!" cried Charlie, goaded, "and I can prove it by Johnny Challan."

Orde turned to survey the pink-cheeked, embarrassed young boy thus designated.

"How many glasses did Johnny Challan have?" he inquired.

"He didn't drink none to speak of," spoke up the boy.

"Then why this joyless demeanour?" begged Orde.

Charlie grumbled, fiercely inarticulate; but Johnny Challan interposed with a chuckle of enjoyment.

"He got 'bunked.'"

"Tell us!" cried Orde delightedly.

"It was down at McNeill's place," explained Johnny Challan; encouraged by the interest of his audience. "They was a couple of sports there who throwed out three cards on the table and bet you couldn't pick the jack. They showed you where the jack was before they throwed, and it surely looked like a picnic, but it wasn't."

"Three-card monte," said Newmark.

"How much?" asked Simms.

"About fifty dollars," replied the boy.

Orde turned on the disgruntled cook.

"And you had fifty in your turkey, camping with this outfit of hard citizens!" he cried. "You ought to lose it."

Johnny Challan was explaining to his companions exactly how the game was played.

"It's a case of keep your eye on the card, I should think," said big Tim Nolan. "If you got a quick enough eye to see him flip the card around, you ought to be able to pick her."

"That's what this sport said," agreed Challan. "'Your eye agin my hand,' says he."

"Well, I'd like to take a try at her," mused Tim.

But at this point Newmark broke into the discussion. "Have you a pack of cards?" he asked in his dry, incisive manner.

Somebody rummaged in a turkey and produced the remains of an old deck.

"I don't believe this is a full deck," said he, "and I think they's part of two decks in it."

"I only want three," assured Newmark, reaching his hand for the pack.

The men crowded around close, those in front squatting, those behind looking over their shoulders.

Newmark cleared a cracker-box of drying socks and drew it to him.

"These three are the cards," he said, speaking rapidly. "There is the jack of hearts. I pass my hands—so. Pick the jack, one of you," he challenged, leaning back from the cracker-box on which lay the three cards, back up. "Any of you," he urged. "You, North."

Thus directly singled out, the foreman leaned forward and rather hesitatingly laid a blunt forefinger on one of the bits of pasteboard.

Without a word, Newmark turned it over. It was the ten of spades.

"Let me try," interposed Tim Nolan, pressing his big shoulders forward. "I bet I know which it was that time; and I bet I can pick her next time."

"Oh, yes, you BET!" shrugged Newmark. "And that's where the card-sharps get you fellows every time. Well, pick it," said he, again deftly flipping the cards.

Nolan, who had watched keenly, indicated one without hesitation. Again it proved to be the ten of spades.

"Anybody else ambitious?" inquired Newmark. Everybody was ambitious; and the young man, with inexhaustible patience, threw out the cards, the corners of his mouth twitching sardonically at each wrong guess.

At length he called a halt.

"By this time I'd have had all your money," he pointed out. "Now, I'll pick the jack."

For the last time he made his swift passes and distributed the cards. Then quite calmly, without disturbing the three on the cracker-box, he held before their eyes the jack of hearts.

An exclamation broke from the interested group. Tim Nolan, who was the nearest, leaned forward and turned over the three on the board. They were the eight of diamonds and two tens of spades.

"That's how the thing is worked nine times out of ten," announced Newmark. "Once in a while you'll run against a straight game, but not often."

"But you showed us the jack every time before you throwed them!" puzzled Johnny Simms.

"Sleight of hand," explained Newmark. "The simplest kind of palming."

"Well, Charlie," said big Tim, "looks to me as if you had just about as much chance as a snowball in hell."

"Where'd you get onto doing all that, Newmark?" inquired North. "You ain't a tin horn yourself?"

Newmark laughed briefly. "Not I," said he. "I learned a lot of those tricks from a travelling magician in college."

During this demonstration Orde had sat well in the background, his chin propped on his hand, watching intently all that was going on. After the comment and exclamations following the exposure of the method had subsided, he spoke.

"Boys," said he, "how game are you to get Charlie's money back—and then some?"

"Try us," returned big Tim.

"This game's at McNeill's, and McNeill's is a tough hole," warned Orde. "Maybe everything will go peaceful, and maybe not. And you boys that go with me have got to keep sober. There isn't going to be any row unless I say so, and I'm not taking any contract to handle a lot of drunken river-hogs as well as go against a game."

"All right," agreed Nolan, "I'm with you."

The thirty or so men of the rear crew then in camp signified their intention to stay by the procession.

"You can't make those sharps disgorge," counselled Newmark. "At the first look of trouble they will light out. They have it all fixed. Force won't do you much good—and may get some of you shot."

"I'm not going to use force," denied Orde. "I'm just going to play their game. But I bet I can make it go. Only I sort of want the moral support of the boys."

"I tell you, you CAN'T win!" cried Newmark disgustedly. "It's a brace game pure and simple."

"I don't know about it's being pure," replied Orde drolly, "but it's simple enough, if you know how to make the wheels go 'round. How is it, boys—will you back my play?"

And such was their confidence that, in face of Newmark's demonstration, they said they would.

## VII

After the men had been paid off, perhaps a dozen of them hung around the yards awaiting evening and the rendezvous named by Orde. The rest drifted away full of good intentions, but did not show up again. Orde himself was busy up to the last moment, but finally stamped out of the office just as the boarding-house bell rang for supper. He surveyed what remained of his old crew and grinned.

"Well, boys, ready for trouble?" he greeted them. "Come on."

They set out up the long reach of Water Street, their steel caulks biting deep into the pitted board-walks.

For nearly a mile the street was flanked solely by lumber-yards, small mills, and factories. Then came a strip of unimproved land, followed immediately by the wooden, ramshackle structures of Hell's Half-Mile.

In the old days every town of any size had its Hell's Half-Mile, or the equivalent. Saginaw boasted of its Catacombs; Muskegon, Alpena, Port Huron, Ludington, had their "Pens," "White Rows," "River Streets," "Kilyubbin," and so forth. They supported row upon row of saloons, alike stuffy and squalid; gambling hells of all sorts; refreshment "parlours," where drinks were served by dozens of "pretty waiter-girls," and huge dance-halls.

The proprietors of these places were a bold and unscrupulous lot. In their everyday business they had to deal with the most dangerous rough-and-tumble fighters this country has ever known; with men bubbling over with the joy of life, ready for quarrel if quarrel also spelled fun, drinking deep, and heavy-handed and fearless in their cups. But each of these rivermen had two or three hundred dollars to "blow" as soon as possible. The pickings were good. Men got rich very quickly at this business. And there existed this great advantage in favour of the dive-keeper: nobody cared what happened to a riverman. You could pound him over the head with a lead pipe, or drug his drink, or choke him to insensibility, or rob him and throw him out into the street, or even drop him tidily through a trap-door into the river flowing conveniently beneath. Nobody bothered—unless, of course, the affair was so bungled as to become public. The police knew enough to stay away when the drive hit town. They would have been annihilated if they had not. The only fly in the divekeeper's ointment was that the riverman would fight back.

And fight back he did, until from one end of his street to the other he had left the battered evidences of his skill as a warrior. His constant heavy lifting made him as hard as nails and as strong as a horse; the continual demand on his agility in riding the logs kept him active and prevented him from becoming muscle-bound; in his wild heart was not the least trace of fear of anything that walked, crawled, or flew. And he was as tireless as machinery, and apparently as indifferent to punishment as a man cast in iron.

Add to this a happy and complete disregard of consequences—to himself or others—of anything he did, and, in his own words, he was a "hard man to nick."

As yet the season was too early for much joy along Hell's Half-Mile. Orde's little crew, and the forty or fifty men of the drive that had preceded him, constituted the rank and file at that moment in town. A little later, when all the drives on the river should be in, and those of its tributaries, and the men still lingering at the woods camps, at least five hundred woods-weary men would be turned loose. Then Hell's Half-Mile would awaken in earnest from its hibernation. The lights would blaze from day to day. From its opened windows would blare the music, the cries of men and women, the shuffle of feet, the noise of fighting, the shrieks of wild laughter, curses deep and frank and unashamed, songs broken and interrupted. Crews of men, arms locked, would surge up and down the narrow sidewalks, their little felt hats cocked one side, their heads back, their fearless eyes challenging the devil and all his works—and getting the challenge accepted. Girls would flit across the lit windows like shadows before flames, or stand in the doorways hailing the men jovially by name. And every few moments, above the roar of this wild inferno, would sound the sudden crash and the dull blows of combat. Only, never was heard the bark of the pistol. The fighting was fierce, and it included kicking with the sharp steel boot-caulks, biting and gouging; but it barred knives and firearms. And when Hell's Half-Mile was thus in full eruption, the citizens of Redding stayed away from Water Street after dark. "Drive's in," said they, and had business elsewhere. And the next group of rivermen, hurrying toward the fun, broke into an eager dog-trot. "Taking the old town apart to-night," they told each other. "Let's get in the game."

To-night, however, the street was comparatively quiet. The saloons were of modified illumination. In many of them men stood drinking, but in a sociable rather than a hilarious mood. Old friends of the two drives were getting together for a friendly glass. The barkeepers were listlessly wiping the bars. The "pretty waiter-girls" gossiped with each other and yawned behind their hands. From several doorways Orde's little compact group was accosted by the burly saloonkeepers.

"Hullo, boys!" said they invariably, "glad to see you back. Come in and have a drink on me."

Well these men knew that one free drink would mean a dozen paid for. But the rivermen merely shook their heads.

"Huh!" sneered one of the girls. "Them's no river-jacks! Them's just off the hay trail, I bet!"

But even this time-honoured and generally effective taunt was ignored.

In the middle of the third block Orde wheeled sharp to the left down a dark and dangerous-looking alley. Another turn to the right brought him into a very narrow street. Facing this street stood a three-story wooden structure, into which led a high-arched entrance up a broad half-flight of wooden steps. This was McNeill's.

As Orde and his men turned into the narrow street, a figure detached itself from the shadow and approached. Orde uttered an exclamation.

"You here, Newmark?" he cried.

"Yes," replied that young man. "I want to see this through."

"With those clothes?" marvelled Orde. "It's a wonder some of these thugs haven't held you up long ago! I'll get Johnny here to go back with you to the main street."

"No," argued Newmark, "I want to go in with you."

"It's dangerous," explained Orde. "You're likely to get slugged."

"I can stand it if you can," returned Newmark.

"I doubt it," said Orde grimly. "However, it's your funeral. Come on, if you want to."

McNeill's lower story was given over entirely to drinking. A bar ran down all one side of the room. Dozens of little tables occupied the floor. "Pretty waiter-girls" were prepared to serve drinks at these latter—and to share in them, at a commission. The second floor was a theatre, and the third a dance-hall. Beneath the building were still viler depths. From this basement the riverman and the shanty boy generally graduated penniless, and perhaps unconscious, to the street. Now, your lumber-jack did not customarily arrive at this stage without more or less lively doings en route; therefore McNeill's maintained a force of fighters. They were burly, sodden men, in striking contrast to the clean-cut, clear-eyed rivermen, but strong in their experience and their discipline. To be sure, they might not last quite as long as their antagonists could—a whisky training is not conducive to long wind—but they always lasted plenty long enough. Sand-bags and brass knuckles helped some, ruthless singleness of purpose counted, and team work finished the job. At times the storm rose high, but up to now McNeill had always ridden it.

Orde and his men entered the lower hall, as though sauntering in without definite aim. Perhaps a score of men were in the room. Two tables of cards were under way—with a great deal of noisy card-slapping that proclaimed the game merely friendly. Eight or ten other men wandered about idly, chaffing loudly with the girls, pausing to overlook the card games, glancing with purposeless curiosity at the professional gamblers sitting quietly behind their various lay-outs. It was a dull evening.

Orde wandered about with the rest, a wide, good-natured smile on his face.

"Start your little ball to rolling for that," he instructed the roulette man, tossing down a bill. "Dropped again!" he lamented humorously. "Can't seem to have any luck."

He drifted on to the crap game.

"Throw us the little bones, pardner," he said. "I'll go you a five on it."

He lost here, and so found himself at the table presided over by the three-card monte men. The rest of his party, who had according to instructions scattered about the place, now began quietly to gravitate in his direction.

"What kind of a lay-out is this?" inquired Orde.

The dealer held up the three cards face out.

"What kind of an eye have you got, bub?" he asked.

"Oh, I don't know. A pretty fair eye. Why?"

"Do you think you could pick out the jack when I throw them out like this?" asked the dealer.

"Sure! She's that one."

"Well," exclaimed the gambler with a pretence of disgust, "damn if you didn't! I bet you five dollars you can't do it again."

"Take you!" replied Orde. "Put up your five."

Again Orde was permitted to pick the jack.

"You've got the best eye that's been in this place since I got here," claimed the dealer admiringly. "Here, Dennis," said he to his partner, "try if you can fool this fellow."

Dennis obligingly took the cards, threw them, and lost. By this time the men, augmented by the idlers not busy with the card games, had drawn close.

"Sail into 'em, bub," encouraged one.

Whether it was that the gamblers, expert in the reading of a man's mood and intentions, sensed the fact that Orde might be led to plunge, or whether, more simply, they were using him as a capper to draw the crowd into their game, it would be difficult to say, but twice more they bungled the throw and permitted him to win.

Newmark plucked him at the sleeve.

"You're twenty dollars ahead," he muttered. "Quit it! I never saw anybody beat this game that much before."

Orde merely shrugged him off with an appearance of growing excitement, while an HABITUE of the place, probably one of the hired fighters, growled into Newmark's ear.

"Shut up, you damn dude!" warned this man. "Keep out of what ain't none of your business."

"What limit do you put on this game, anyway?" Orde leaned forward, his eyes alight.

The two gamblers spoke swiftly apart.

"How much do you want to bet?" asked one.

"Would you stand for five hundred dollars?" asked Orde.

A dead silence fell on the group. Plainly could be heard the men's quickened breathing. The shouts and noise from the card parties blundered through the stillness. Some one tiptoed across and whispered in the ear of the nearest player. A moment later the chairs at the two tables scraped back. One of them fell violently to the floor. Their occupants joined the tense group about the monte game. All the girls drew near. Only behind the bar the white-aproned bartenders wiped their glasses with apparent imperturbability, their eyes, however, on their brass knuckles hanging just beneath the counter, their ears pricked up for the riot call.

The gambler pretended to deliberate, his cool, shifty eyes running over the group before him. A small door immediately behind him swung slowly ajar an inch or so.

"Got the money?" he asked.

"Have you?" countered Orde.

Apparently satisfied, the man nodded.

"I'll go you, bub, if I lose," said he. "Lay out your money."

Orde counted out nine fifty-dollar bills and five tens. Probably no one in the group of men standing about had realised quite how much money five hundred dollars meant until they saw it thus tallied out before them.

"All right," said the gambler, taking up the cards.

"Hold on!" cried Orde. "Where's yours?"

"Oh, that's all right," the gambler reassured him. "I'm with the house. I guess McNeill's credit is good," he laughed.

"That may all be," insisted Orde, "but I'm putting up my good money, and I expect to see good money put up in return."

They wrangled over this point for some time, but Orde was obstinate. Finally the gamblers yielded. A canvass of the drawer, helped out by the bar and the other games, made up the sum. It bulked large on the table beside Orde's higher denominations.

The interested audience now consisted of the dozen men comprised by Orde's friends; nearly twice as many strangers, evidently rivermen; eight hangers-on of the joint, probably fighters and "bouncers"; half a dozen professional gamblers, and several waitresses. The four barkeepers still held their positions. Of these, the rivermen were scattered loosely back of Orde, although Orde's own friends had by now gathered compactly enough at his shoulder. The mercenaries and gamblers had divided, and flanked the table at either side. Newmark, a growing wonder and disgust creeping into his usually unexpressive face, recognised the strategic advantage of this arrangement. In case of difficulty, a determined push would separate the rivermen from the gamblers long enough for the latter to disappear quietly through the small door at the back.

"Satisfied?" inquired the gambler briefly.

"Let her flicker," replied Orde with equal brevity.

A gasp of anticipation went up. Quite coolly the gambler made his passes. With equal coolness and not the slightest hesitation, Orde planted his great red fist on one of the cards.

"That is the jack," he announced, looking the gambler in the eye.

"Oh, is it?" sneered the dealer. "Well, turn it over and let's see."

"No!" roared Orde. "YOU TURN OVER THE OTHER TWO!"

A low oath broke from the gambler, and his face contorted in a spasm. The barkeepers slid out from behind the bar. For a moment the situation was tense and threatening. The dealer with a sweeping glance again searched the faces of those before him. In that moment, probably, he made up his mind that an open scandal must be avoided. Force and broken bones, even murder, might be all right enough under colour of right. If Orde had turned up for a jack the card on which he now held his fist, and then had attempted to prove cheating, a cry of robbery and a lively fight would have given opportunity for making way with the stakes. But McNeill's could not afford to be shown up before thirty interested rivermen as running an open-and-shut brace-game. However, the gambler made a desperate try at what he must have known was a very forlorn hope.

"That isn't the way this game is played," said he. "Show up your jack."

"It's the way I play it," replied Orde sternly. "These gentlemen heard the bet." He reached over and dexterously flipped over the other two cards. "You see, neither of these is the jack; this must be."

"You win," assented the gambler, after a pause.

Orde, his fist still on the third card, began pocketing the stakes with the other hand. The gambler reached, palm up, across the table.

"Give me the other card," said he.

Orde picked it up, laughing. For a moment he seemed to hesitate, holding the bit of pasteboard tantalisingly outstretched, as though he were going to turn also this one face up. Then, quite deliberately he looked to right and to left where the fighters awaited their signal, laughed again, and handed the card to the gambler.

At once pandemonium broke loose. The rivermen of Orde's party fairly shouted with joy over the unexpected trick; the employees of the resort whispered apart; the gambler explained, low-voiced and angry, his reasons for not putting up a fight for so rich a stake.

"All to the bar!" yelled Orde.

They made a rush, and lined up and ordered their drinks. Orde poured his on the floor and took the glass belonging to the man next him.

"Get them to give you another, Tim," said he. "No knock-out drops, if I can help it."

The men drank, and some one ordered another round.

"Tim," said Orde, low-voiced, "get the crowd together and we'll pull out. I've a thousand dollars on me, and they'll sand-bag me sure if I go alone. And let's get out right off."

Ten minutes later they all stood safely on the lighted thoroughfare of Water Street.

"Good-night, boys," said Orde. "Go easy, and show up at the booms Monday."

He turned up the street toward the main part of the town. Newmark joined him.

"I'll walk a little ways with you," he explained. "And I say, Orde, I want to apologise to you. 'Most of the evening I've been thinking you the worst fool I ever saw, but you can take care of yourself at every stage of the game. The trick was good, but your taking the other fellow's drink beat it."

## VIII

Orde heard no more of Newmark—and hardly thought of him—until over two weeks later.

In the meantime the riverman, assuming the more conventional garments of civilisation, lived with his parents in the old Orde homestead at the edge of town. This was a rather pretentious two-story brick structure, in the old solid, square architecture, surrounded by a small orchard, some hickories, and a garden. Orde's father had built it when he arrived in the pioneer country from New England forty years before. At that time it was considered well out in the country. Since then the town had crept to it, so that the row of grand old maples in front shaded a stone-guttered street. A little patch of corn opposite, and many still vacant lots above, placed it, however, as about the present limit of growth.

Jack Orde was the youngest and most energetic of a large family that had long since scattered to diverse cities and industries. He and Grandpa and Grandma Orde dwelt now in the big, echoing, old-fashioned house alone, save for the one girl who called herself the "help" rather than the servant. Grandpa Orde, now above sixty, was tall, straight, slender. His hair was quite white, and worn a little long. His features were finely chiselled and aquiline. From them looked a pair of piercing, young, black eyes. In his time, Grandpa Orde had been a mighty breaker of the wilderness; but his time had passed, and with the advent of a more intensive civilisation he had fallen upon somewhat straitened ways. Grandma Orde, on the other hand, was a very small, spry old lady, with a small face, a small figure, small hands and feet. She dressed in the then usual cap and black silk of old ladies. Half her time she spent at her housekeeping, which she loved, jingling about from cellar to attic store-room, seeing that Amanda, the "help," had everything in order. The other half she sat in a wooden "Dutch" rocking-chair by a window overlooking the garden. Her silk-shod feet rested neatly side by side on a carpet-covered hassock, her back against a gay tapestried cushion. Near her purred big Jim, a maltese rumoured to weigh fifteen pounds. Above her twittered a canary.

And the interior of the house itself was in keeping. The low ceilings, the slight irregularities of structure peculiar to the rather rule-of-thumb methods of the earlier builders, the deep window embrasures due to the thickness of the walls, the unexpected passages leading to unsuspected rooms, and the fact that many of these apartments were approached by a step or so up or a step or so down—these lent to it a quaint, old-fashioned atmosphere enhanced further by the steel engravings, the antique furnishings, the many-paned windows, and all the belongings of old people who have passed from a previous generation untouched by modern ideas.

To this house and these people Orde came direct from the greatness of the wilderness and the ferocity of Hell's Half-Mile. Such contrasts were possible even ten or fifteen years ago. The untamed country lay at the doors of the most modern civilisation.

Newmark, reappearing one Sunday afternoon at the end of the two weeks, was apparently bothered. He examined the Orde place for some moments; walked on beyond it; finding nothing there, he returned, and after some hesitation turned in up the tar sidewalk and pulled at the old-fashioned wire bell-pull. Grandma Orde herself answered the door.

At sight of her fine features, her dainty lace cap and mitts, and the stiffness of her rustling black silks, Newmark took off his gray felt hat.

"Good-afternoon," said he. "Will you kindly tell me where Mr. Orde lives?"

"This is Mr. Orde's," replied the little old lady.

"Pardon me," persisted Newmark, "I am looking for Mr. Jack Orde, and I was directed here. I am sorry to have troubled you."

"Mr. Jack Orde lives here," returned Grandma Orde. "He is my son. Would you like to see him?"

"If you please," assented Newmark gravely, his thin, shrewd face masking itself with its usual expression of quizzical cynicism.

"Step this way, please, and I'll call him," requested his interlocutor, standing aside from the doorway.

Newmark entered the cool, dusky interior, and was shown to the left into a dim, long room. He perched on a mahogany chair, and had time to notice the bookcases with the white owl atop, the old piano with the yellowing keys, the haircloth sofa and chairs, the steel engravings, and the two oil portraits, when Orde's large figure darkened the door.

For an instant the young man, who must just have come in from the outside sunshine, blinked into the dimness. Newmark, too, blinked back, although he could by this time see perfectly well.

Newmark had known Orde only as a riverman. Like most Easterners, then and now, he was unable to imagine a man in rough clothes as being anything but essentially a rough man. The figure he saw before him was decently and correctly dressed in what was then the proper Sunday costume. His big figure set off the cloth to advantage, and even his wind-reddened face seemed toned down and refined by the change in costume and surroundings.

"Oh, it's you, Mr. Newmark!" cried Orde in his hearty way, and holding out his hand. "I'm glad to see you. Where you been? Come on out of there. This is the 'company place.'" Without awaiting a reply, he led the way into the narrow hall, whence the two entered another, brighter room, in which Grandma Orde sat, the canary singing above her head.

"Mother," said Orde, "this is Mr. Newmark, who was with us on the drive this spring."

Grandma Orde laid her gold-bowed glasses and her black leather Bible on the stand beside her.

"Mr. Newmark and I spoke at the door," said she, extending her frail hand with dignity. "If you were on the drive, Mr. Newmark, you must have been one of the High Privates in this dreadful war we all read about."

Newmark laughed and made some appropriate reply. A few moments later, at Orde's suggestion, the two passed out a side door and back into the remains of the old orchard.

"It's pretty nice here under the trees," said Orde. "Sit down and light up. Where you been for the last couple of weeks?"

"I caught Johnson's drive and went on down river with him to the lake," replied Newmark, thrusting the offered cigar in one corner of his mouth and shaking his head at Orde's proffer of a light.

"You must like camp life."

"I do not like it at all," negatived Newmark emphatically, "but the drive interested me. It interested me so much that I've come back to talk to you about it."

"Fire ahead," acquiesced Orde.

"I'm going to ask you a few questions about yourself, and you can answer them or not, just as you please."

"Oh, I'm not bashful about my career," laughed Orde.

"How old are you?" inquired Newmark abruptly.

"Thirty."

"How long have you been doing that sort of thing—driving, I mean?"

"Off and on, about six years."

"Why did you go into that particular sort of thing?"

Orde selected a twig and carefully threw it at a lump in the turf.

"Because there's nothing ahead of shovelling but dirt," he replied with a quaint grin.

"I see," said Newmark, after a pause. "Then you think there's more future to that sort of thing than the sort of thing the rest of your friends go in for—law, and wholesale groceries, and banking and the rest of it?"

"There is for me," replied Orde simply.

"Yet you're merely river-driving on a salary at thirty."

Orde flushed slowly, and shifted his position.

"Exactly so—Mr. District Attorney," he said drily.

Newmark started from his absorption in his questioning and shifted his unlighted cigar.

"Does sound like it," he admitted; "but I'm not asking all this out of idle curiosity. I've got a scheme in my head that I think may work out big for us both."

"Well," assented Orde reservedly, "in that case—I'm foreman on this drive because my outfit went kerplunk two years ago, and I'm making a fresh go at it."

"Failed?" inquired Newmark.

"Partner skedaddled," replied Orde. "Now, if you're satisfied with my family history, suppose you tell me what the devil you're driving at."

He was plainly restive under the cross-examination to which he had been subjected.

"Look here," said Newmark, abruptly changing the subject, "you know that rapids up river flanked by shallows, where the logs are always going aground?"

"I do," replied Orde, still grim.

"Well, why wouldn't it help to put a string of piers down both sides, with booms between them to hold the logs in the deeper water?"

"It would," said Orde.

"Why isn't it done, then?"

"Who would do it?" countered Orde, leaning back more easily in the interest of this new discussion. "If Daly did it, for instance, then all the rest of the drivers would get the advantage of it for nothing."

"Get them to pay their share."

Orde grinned. "I'd like to see you get any three men to agree to anything on this river."

"And a sort of dam would help at that Spruce Rapids?"

"Sure! If you improved the river for driving, she'd be easier to drive. That goes without saying."

"How many firms drive logs on this stream?"

"Ten," replied Orde, without hesitation.

"How many men do they employ?"

"Driving?" asked Orde.

"Driving."

"About five hundred; a few more or less."

"Now suppose," Newmark leaned forward impressively, "suppose a firm should be organised to drive ALL the logs on the river. Suppose it improved the river with necessary piers, dams, and all the rest of it, so that the driving would be easier. Couldn't it drive with less than five hundred men, and couldn't it save money on the cost of driving?"

"It might," agreed Orde.

"You know the conditions here. If such a firm should be organised and should offer to drive the logs for these ten firms at so much a thousand, do you suppose it would get the business?"

"It would depend on the driving firm," said Orde. "You see, mill men have got to have their logs. They can't afford to take chances. It wouldn't pay."

"Then that's all right," agreed Newmark, with a gleam of satisfaction across his thin face. "Would you form a partnership with me having such an object in view?"

Orde threw back his head and laughed with genuine amusement.

"I guess you don't realise the situation," said he. "We'd have to have a few little things like distributing booms, and tugs, and a lot of tools and supplies and works of various kinds."

"Well, we'd get them."

It was now Orde's turn to ask questions.

"How much are you worth?" he inquired bluntly.

"About twenty thousand dollars," replied Newmark.

"Well, if I raise very much more than twenty thousand cents, I'm lucky just now."

"How much capital would we have to have?" asked Newmark.

Orde thought for several minutes, twisting the petal of an old apple-blossom between his strong, blunt fingers.

"Somewhere near seventy-five thousand dollars," he estimated at last.

"That's easy," cried Newmark. "We'll make a stock company—say a hundred thousand shares. We'll keep just enough between us to control the company—say fifty-one thousand. I'll put in my pile, and you can pay for yours out of the earnings of the company."

"That doesn't sound fair," objected Orde.

"You pay interest," explained Newmark. "Then we'll sell the rest of the stock to raise the rest of the money."

"If we can," interjected Orde.

"I think we can," asserted Newmark.

Orde fell into a brown study, occasionally throwing a twig or a particle of earth at the offending lump in the turf. Overhead the migratory warblers balanced right-side up or up-side down, searching busily among the new leaves, uttering their simple calls. The air was warm and soft and still, the sky bright. Fat hens clucked among the grasses. A feel of Sunday was in the air.

"I must have something to live on," said he thoughtfully at last.

"So must I," said Newmark. "We'll have to pay ourselves salaries, of course, but the smaller the better at first. You'll have to take charge of the men and the work and all the rest of it—I don't know anything about that. I'll attend to the incorporating and the routine, and I'll try to place the stock. You'll have to see, first of all, whether you can get contracts from the logging firms to drive the logs."

"How can I tell what to charge them?"

"We'll have to figure that very closely. You know where these different drives would start from, and how long each of them would take?"

"Oh, yes; I know the river pretty well."

"Well, then we'll figure how many days' driving there is for each, and how many men there are, and what it costs for wages, grub, tools—we'll just have to figure as near as we can to the actual cost, and then add a margin for profit and for interest on our investment."

"It might work out all right," admitted Orde.

"I'm confident it would," asserted Newmark. "And there'd be no harm figuring it all out, would there?"

"No," agreed Orde, "that would be fun all right."

543

At this moment Amanda appeared at the back door and waved an apron.

"Mr. Jack!" she called. "Come in to dinner."

Newmark looked puzzled, and, as he arose, glanced surreptitiously at his watch. Orde seemed to take the summons as one to be expected, however. In fact, the strange hour was the usual Sunday custom in the Redding of that day, and had to do with the late-church freedom of Amanda and her like.

"Come in and eat with us," invited Orde. "We'd be glad to have you."

But Newmark declined.

"Come up to-morrow night, then, at half-past six, for supper," Orde urged him. "We can figure on these things a little. I'm in Daly's all day, and hardly have time except evenings."

To this Newmark assented. Orde walked with him down the deep-shaded driveway with the clipped privet hedge on one side, to the iron gate that swung open when one drove over a projecting lever. There he said good-bye.

A moment later he entered the long dining-room, where Grandpa and Grandma Orde were already seated. An old-fashioned service of smooth silver and ivory-handled steel knives gave distinction to the plain white linen. A tea-pot smothered in a "cosey" stood at Grandma Orde's right. A sirloin roast on a noble platter awaited Grandpa Orde's knife.

Orde dropped into his place with satisfaction.

"Shut up, Cheep!" he remarked to a frantic canary hanging in the sunshine.

"Your friend seems a nice-appearing young man," said Grandma Orde. "Wouldn't he stay to dinner?"

"I asked him," replied Orde, "but he couldn't. He and I have a scheme for making our everlasting fortunes."

"Who is he?" asked grandma.

Orde dropped his napkin into his lap with a comical chuckle of dismay.

"Blest if I have the slightest idea, mother," he said. "Newmark joined us on the drive. Said he was a lawyer, and was out in the woods for his health. He's been with us, studying and watching the work, ever since."

## IX

"I think I'll go see Jane Hubbard this evening," Orde remarked to his mother, as he arose from the table. This was his method of announcing that he would not be home for supper.

Jane Hubbard lived in a low one-story house of blue granite, situated amid a grove of oaks at the top of the hill. She was a kindly girl, whose parents gave her free swing, and whose house, in consequence, was popular with the younger people. Every Sunday she offered to all who came a "Sunday-night lunch," which consisted of cold meats, cold salad, bread, butter, cottage cheese, jam, preserves, and the like, warmed by a cup of excellent tea. These refreshments were served by the guests themselves. It did not much matter how few or how many came.

On the Sunday evening in question Orde found about the usual crowd gathered. Jane herself, tall, deliberate in movement and in speech, kindly and thoughtful, talked in a corner with Ernest Colburn, who was just out of college, and who worked in a bank. Mignonne Smith, a plump, rather pretty little body with a tremendous aureole of hair like spun golden fire, was trying to balance a croquet-ball on the end of a ruler. The ball regularly fell off. Three young men, standing in attentive attitudes, thereupon dove forward in an attempt to catch it before it should hit the floor—which it generally did with a loud thump. A collapsed chair of slender lines stacked against the wall attested previous acrobatics. This much Orde, standing in the doorway, looked upon quite as the usual thing. Only he missed the Incubus. Searching the room with his eyes, he at length discovered that incoherent, desiccated, but persistent youth VIS-A-VIS with a stranger. Orde made out the white of her gown in the shadows, the willowy outline of her small and slender figure, and the gracious forward bend of her head.

The company present caught sight of Orde standing in the doorway, and suspended occupations to shout at him joyfully. He was evidently a favourite. The strange girl in the corner turned to him a white, long face, of which he could see only the outline and the redness of the lips where the lamplight reached them. She leaned slightly forward and the lips parted. Orde's muscular figure, standing square and uncompromising in the doorway, the out-of-door freshness of his complexion, the steadiness of his eyes laughing back a greeting, had evidently attracted her. Or perhaps anything was a relief from the Incubus.

"So you're back at last, are you, Jack?" drawled Jane in her lazy, good-natured way. "Come and meet Miss Bishop. Carroll, I want to present Mr. Orde."

Orde bowed ceremoniously into the penumbra cast by the lamp's broad shade. The girl inclined gracefully her small head with the glossy hair. The Incubus, his thin hands clasped on his knee, his sallow face twisted in one of its customary wry smiles, held to the edge of his chair with characteristic pertinacity.

"Well, Walter," Orde addressed him genially, "are you having a good time?"

"Yes-indeed!" replied the Incubus as though it were one word.

His chair was planted squarely to exclude all others. Orde surveyed the situation with good-humour.

"Going to keep the other fellow from getting a chance, I see."

"Yes-indeed!" replied the Incubus.

Orde bent over, and with great ease lifted Incubus, chair, and all, and set him facing Mignonne Smith and the croquet-ball.

"Here, Mignonne," said he, "I've brought you another assistant."

He returned to the lamp, to find the girl, her dark eyes alight with amusement, watching him intently. She held the tip of a closed fan against her lips, which brought her head slightly forward in an attitude as though she listened. Somehow there was about her an air of poise, of absolute balanced repose quite different from Jane's rather awkward statics, and in direct contrast to Mignonne's dynamics.

"Walter is a very bright man in his own line," said Orde, swinging forward a chair, "but he mustn't be allowed any monopolies."

"How do you know I want him so summarily removed?" the girl asked him, without changing either her graceful attitude of suspended motion or the intentness of her gaze.

"Well," argued Orde, "I got him to say all he ever says to any girl—'Yes-indeed!'—so you couldn't have any more conversation from him. If you want to look at him, why, there he is in plain sight. Besides, I want to talk to you myself."

"Do you always get what you want?" inquired the girl.

Orde laughed.

"Any one can get anything he wants, if only he wants it bad enough," he asserted.

The girl pondered this for a moment, and finally lowered and opened her fan, and threw back her head in a more relaxed attitude.

"Some people," she amended. "However, I forgive you. I will even flatter you by saying I am glad you came. You look to have reached the age of discretion. I venture to say that these boys' idea of a lively evening is to throw bread about the table."

Orde flushed a little. The last time he had supped at Jane Hubbard's, that was exactly what they did do.

"They are young, of course," he said, "and you and I are very old and wise. But having a noisy, good time isn't such a great crime—or is it where you came from?"

The girl leaned forward, a sparkle of interest in her eyes.

"Are you and I going to fight?" she demanded.

"That depends on you," returned Orde squarely, but with perfect good-humour.

They eyed each other a moment. Then the girl closed her fan, and leaned forward to touch him on the arm with it.

"You are quite right not to allow me to say mean things about your friends, and I am a nasty little snip."

Orde bowed with sudden gravity.

"And they do throw bread," said he.

They both laughed. She leaned back with a movement of satisfaction, seeming to sink into the shadows.

"Now, tell me; what do you do?"

"What do I do?" asked Orde, puzzled.

"Yes. Everybody does something out West here. It's a disgrace not to do something, isn't it?"

"Oh, my business! I'm a river-driver just now."

"A river-driver?" she repeated, once more leaning forward. "Why, I've just been hearing a great deal about you."

"That so?" he inquired.

"Yes, from Mrs. Baggs."

"Oh!" said Orde. "Then you know what a drunken, swearing, worthless lot of bums and toughs we are, don't you?"

For the first time, in some subtle way she broke the poise of her attitude.

"There is Hell's Half-Mile," she reminded him.

"Oh, yes," said Orde bitterly, "there's Hell's Half-Mile! Whose fault is that? My rivermen's? My boys? Look here! I suppose you couldn't understand it, if you tried a month; but suppose you were working out in the woods nine months of the year, up early in the morning and in late at night. Suppose you slept in rough blankets, on the ground or in bunks, ate rough food, never saw a woman or a book, undertook work to scare your city men up a tree and into a hole too easy, risked your life a dozen times a week in a tangle of logs, with the big river roaring behind just waiting to swallow you; saw nothing but woods and river, were cold and hungry and wet, and so tired you couldn't wiggle, until you got to feeling like the thing was never going to end, and until you got sick of it way through in spite of the excitement and danger. And then suppose you hit town, where there were all the things you hadn't had—and the first thing you struck was Hell's Half-Mile. Say! you've seen water behind a jam, haven't you? Water-power's a good thing in a mill course, where it has wheels to turn; but behind a jam it just RIPS things—oh, what's the use talking! A girl doesn't know what it means. She couldn't understand."

He broke off with an impatient gesture. She was looking at him intently, her lips again half-parted.

"I think I begin to understand a little," said she softly. She smiled to herself. "But they are a hard and heartless class in spite of all their energy and courage, aren't they?" she drew him out.

"Hard and heartless!" exploded Orde. "There's no kinder lot of men on earth, let me tell you. Why, there isn't a man on that river who doesn't chip in five or ten dollars when a man is hurt or killed; and that means three or four days' hard work for him. And he may not know or like the injured man at all! Why—"

"What's all the excitement?" drawled Jane Hubbard behind them. "Can't you make it a to-be-continued-in-our-next? We're 'most starved."

"Yes-indeed!" chimed in the Incubus.

The company trooped out to the dining-room where the table, spread with all the good things, awaited them.

"Ernest, you light the candles," drawled Jane, drifting slowly along the table with her eye on the arrangements, "and some of you boys go get the butter and the milk-pitcher from the ice-box."

To Orde's relief, no one threw any bread, although the whole-hearted fun grew boisterous enough before the close of the meal. Miss Bishop sat directly across from him. He had small chance of conversation with her in the hubbub that raged, but he gained full leisure to examine her more closely in the fuller illumination. Throughout, her note was of fineness. Her hands, as he had already noticed, were long, the fingers tapering; her wrists were finely moulded, but slender, and running without abrupt swelling of muscles into the long lines of her forearm; her figure was rounded, but built on the curves of slenderness; her piled, glossy hair was so fine that though it was full of wonderful soft shadows denied coarser tresses, its mass hardly did justice to its abundance. Her face, again, was long and oval, with a peculiar transparence to the skin and a peculiar faint, healthy circulation of the blood well below the surface, which relieved her complexion of pallor, but did not give her a colour. The lips, on the contrary, were satin red, and Orde was mildly surprised, after his recent talk, to find them sensitively moulded, and with a quaint, child-like quirk at the corners. Her eyes were rather contemplative, and so black as to resemble spots.

In spite of her half-scornful references to "bread-throwing," she joined with evident pleasure in the badinage and more practical fun which struck the note of the supper. Only Orde thought to discern even in her more boisterous movements a graceful, courteous restraint, to catch in the bend of her head a dainty concession to the joy of the moment, to hear in the tones of her laughter a reservation of herself, which nevertheless was not at all a reservation, against the others.

After the meal was finished, each had his candle to blow out, and then all returned to the parlour, leaving the debris for the later attention of the "hired help."

Orde with determination made his way to Miss Bishop's side. She smiled at him.

"You see, I am a hypocrite as well as a mean little snip," said she. "I threw a little bread myself."

"Threw bread?" repeated Orde. "I didn't see you."

"The moon is made of green cheese," she mocked him, "and there are countries where men's heads do grow beneath their shoulders." She moved gracefully away toward Jane Hubbard. "Do you Western 'business men' never deal in figures of speech as well as figures of the other sort?" she wafted back to him over her shoulder.

"I was very stupid," acknowledged Orde, following her.

She stopped and faced him in the middle of the room, smiling quizzically.

"Well?" she challenged.

"Well, what?" asked Orde, puzzled.

"I thought perhaps you wanted to ask me something."

"Why?"

"Your following me," she explained, the corners of her mouth smiling. "I had turned away—"

"I just wanted to talk to you," said Orde.

"And you always get what you want," she repeated. "Well?" she conceded, with a shrug of mock resignation. But the four other men here cut in with a demand.

"Music!" they clamoured. "We want music!"

With a nod, Miss Bishop turned to the piano, sweeping aside her white draperies as she sat. She struck a few soft chords, and then, her long hands wandering idly and softly up and down the keys, she smiled at them over her shoulder.

"What shall it be?" she inquired.

Some one thrust an open song-book on the rack in front of her. The others gathered close about, leaning forward to see.

Song followed song, at first quickly, then at longer intervals. At last the members of the chorus dropped away one by one to occupations of their own. The girl still sat at the piano, her head thrown back idly, her hands wandering softly in and out of melodies and modulations. Watching her, Orde finally saw only the shimmer of her white figure, and the white outline of her head and throat. All the rest of the room was gray from the concentration of his gaze. At last her hands fell in her lap. She sat looking straight ahead of her.

Orde at once arose and came to her.

"That was a wonderfully quaint and beautiful thing," said he. "What was it?"

She turned to him, and he saw that the mocking had gone from her eyes and mouth, leaving them quite simple, like a child's.

"Did you like it?" she asked.

"Yes," said Orde. He hesitated and stammered awkwardly. "It was so still and soothing, it made me think of the river sometimes about dusk. What was it?"

"It wasn't anything. I was improvising."

"You made it up yourself?"

"It was myself, I suppose. I love to build myself a garden, and wander on until I lose myself in it. I'm glad there was a river in the garden—a nice, still, twilight river."

She flashed up at him, her head sidewise.

"There isn't always." She struck a crashing discord on the piano.

Every one looked up at the sudden noise of it.

"Oh, don't stop!" they cried in chorus, as though each had been listening intently.

The girl laughed up at Orde in amusement. Somehow this flash of an especial understanding between them to the exclusion of the others sent a warm glow to his heart.

"I do wish you had your harp here," said Jane Hubbard, coming indolently forward. "You just ought to hear her play the harp," she told the rest. "It's just the best thing you ever DID hear!"

At this moment the outside door opened to admit Mr and Mrs. Hubbard, who had, according to their usual Sunday custom, been spending the evening with a neighbour. This was the signal for departure. The company began to break up.

Orde pushed his broad shoulders in to screen Carroll Bishop from the others.

"Are you staying here?" he asked.

She opened her eyes wide at his brusqueness.

"I'm visiting Jane," she replied at length, with an affectation of demureness.

"Are you going to be here long?" was Orde's next question.

"About a month."

"I am coming to see you," announced Orde. "Good-night."

He took her hand, dropped it, and followed the others into the hall, leaving her standing by the lamp. She watched him until the outer door had closed behind him. Not once did he look back. Jane Hubbard, returning after a moment from the hall, found her at the piano again, her head slightly one side, playing with painful and accurate exactness a simple one-finger melody.

Orde walked home down the hill in company with the Incubus. Neither had anything to say; Orde because he was absorbed in thought, the Incubus because nothing occurred to draw from him his one remark. Their feet clipped sharply against the tar walks, or rang more hollow on the boards. Overhead the stars twinkled through the still-bare branches of the trees. With few exceptions the houses were dark. People "retired" early in Redding. An occasional hall light burned dimly, awaiting some one's return. At the gate of the Orde place, Orde roused himself to say good-night. He let himself into the dim-lighted hall, hung up his hat, and turned out the gas. For some time he stood in the dark, quite motionless; then, with the accuracy of long habitude, he walked confidently to the narrow stairs and ascended them. Subconsciously he avoided the creaking step, but outside his mother's door he stopped, arrested by a greeting from within.

"That you, Jack?" queried Grandma Orde.

For answer Orde pushed open the door, which stood an inch or so ajar, and entered. A dim light from a distant street-lamp, filtered through the branches of a tree, flickered against the ceiling. By its aid he made out the great square bed, and divined the tiny figure of his mother. He seated himself sidewise on the edge of the bed.

"Go to Jane's?" queried grandma in a low voice, to avoid awakening grandpa, who slept in the adjoining room.

"Yes," replied Orde, in the same tone.

"Who was there?"

"Oh, about the usual crowd."

He fell into an abstracted silence, which endured for several minutes.

"Mother," said he abruptly, at last, "I've met the girl I want for my wife."

Grandma Orde sat up in bed.

"Who is she?" she demanded.

"Her name is Carroll Bishop," said Orde, "and she's visiting Jane Hubbard."

"Yes, but WHO is she?" insisted Grandma Orde. "Where is she from?"

Orde stared at her in the dim light.

"Why, mother," he repeated for the second time that day, "blest if I know that!"

## X

Orde was up and out at six o'clock the following morning. By eight he had reported for work at Daly's mill, where, with the assistance of a portion of the river crew, he was occupied in sorting the logs in the booms. Not until six o'clock in the evening did the whistle blow for the shut-down. Then he hastened home, to find that Newmark had preceded him by some few moments and was engaged in conversation with Grandma Orde. The young man was talking easily, though rather precisely and with brevity. He nodded to Orde and finished his remark.

After supper Orde led the way up two flights of narrow stairs to his own room. This was among the gables, a chamber of strangely diversified ceiling, which slanted here and there according to the demands of the roof outside.

"Well," said he, "I've made up my mind to-day to go in with you. It may not work out, but it's a good chance, and I want to get in something that looks like money. I don't know who you are, nor how much of a business man you are or what your experience is, but I'll risk it."

"I'm putting in twenty thousand dollars," pointed out Newmark.

"And I'm putting in my everlasting reputation," said Orde. "If we tell these fellows that we'll get out their logs for them, and then don't do it, I'll be DEAD around here."

"So that's about a stand-off," said Newmark. "I'm betting twenty thousand on what I've seen and heard of you, and you're risking your reputation that I don't want to drop my money."

Orde laughed.

"And I reckon we're both right," he responded.

"Still," Newmark pursued the subject, "I've no objection to telling you about myself. New York born and bred; experience with Cooper and Dunne, brokers, eight years. Money from a legacy. Parents dead. No relatives to speak to."

Orde nodded gravely twice in acknowledgment.

"Now," said Newmark, "have you had time to do any figuring?"

"Well," replied Orde, "I got at it a little yesterday afternoon, and a little this noon. I have a rough idea." He produced a bundle of scribbled papers from his coat-pocket. "Here you are. I take Daly as a sample, because I've been with his outfit. It costs him to run and deliver his logs one hundred miles about two dollars a thousand feet. He's the only big manufacturer up here; the rest are all at Monrovia, where they can get shipping by water. I suppose it costs the other nine firms doing business on the river from two to two and a half a thousand."

Newmark produced a note-book and began to jot down figures.

"Do these men all conduct separate drives?" he inquired.

"All but Proctor and old Heinzman. They pool in together."

"Now," went on Newmark, "if we were to drive the whole river, how could we improve on that?"

"Well, I haven't got it down very fine, of course," Orde told him, "but in the first place we wouldn't need so many men. I could run the river on three hundred easy enough. That saves wages and grub on two hundred right there. And, of course, a few improvements on the river would save time, which in our case would mean money. We would not need so many separate cook outfits and all that. Of course, that part of it we'd have to get right down and figure on, and it will take time. Then, too, if we agreed to sort and deliver, we'd have to build sorting booms down at Monrovia."

"Suppose we had all that. What, for example, do you reckon you could bring Daly's logs down for?"

Orde fell into deep thought, from which he emerged occasionally to scribble on the back of his memoranda.

"I suppose somewhere about a dollar," he announced at last. He looked up a trifle startled. "Why," he cried, "that looks like big money! A hundred per cent!"

Newmark watched him for a moment, a quizzical smile wrinkling the corners of his eyes.

"Hold your horses," said he at last. "I don't know anything about this business, but I can see a few things. In the first place, close figuring will probably add a few cents to that dollar. And then, of course, all our improvements will be absolutely valueless to anybody after we've got through using them. You said yesterday they'd probably stand us in seventy-five thousand dollars. Even at a dollar profit, we'd have to drive seventy-five million before we got a cent back. And, of course, we've got to agree to drive for a little less than they could themselves."

"That's so," agreed Orde, his crest falling.

"However," said Newmark briskly, as he arose, "there's good money in it, as you say. Now, how soon can you leave Daly?"

"By the middle of the week we ought to be through with this job."

"That's good. Then we'll go into this matter of expense thoroughly, and establish our schedule of rates to submit to the different firms."

Newmark said a punctilious farewell to Mr. and Mrs. Orde.

"By the way," said Orde to him at the gate, "where are you staying?"

"At the Grand."

"I know most of the people here—all the young folks. I'd be glad to take you around and get you acquainted."

"Thank you," replied Newmark, "you are very kind. But I don't go in much for that sort of thing, and I expect to be very busy now on this new matter; so I won't trouble you."

XI

The new partners, as soon as Orde had released himself from Daly, gave all their time to working out a schedule of tolls. Orde drew on his intimate knowledge of the river and its tributaries, and the locations of the different rollways, to estimate as closely as possible the time it would take to drive them. He also hunted up Tom North and others of the older men domiciled in the cheap boarding-houses of Hell's Half-Mile, talked with them, and verified his own impressions. Together, he and Newmark visited the supply houses, got prices, obtained lists. All the evenings they figured busily, until at last Newmark expressed himself as satisfied.

"Now, Orde," said he, "here is where you come in. It's now your job to go out and interview these men and get their contracts for driving their next winter's cut."

But Orde drew back.

"Look here, Joe," he objected, "that's more in your line. You can talk business to them better than I can."

"Not a bit," negatived Newmark. "They don't know me from Adam, and they do know you, and all about you. We've got to carry this thing through at first on our face, and they'd be more apt to entrust the matter to you personally."

"All right," agreed Orde. "I'll start in on Daly."

He did so the following morning. Daly swung his bulk around in his revolving office-chair and listened attentively.

"Well, Jack," said he, "I think you're a good riverman, and I believe you can do it. I'd be only too glad to get rid of the nuisance of it, let alone get it done cheaper. If you'll draw up your contract and bring it in here, I'll sign it. I suppose you'll break out the rollways?"

"No," said Orde; "we hadn't thought of doing more than the driving and distributing. You'll have to deliver the logs in the river. Maybe another year, after we get better organised, we'll be able to break rollways—at a price per thousand—but until we get a-going we'll have to rush her through."

Orde repeated this to his associate.

"That was smooth enough sailing," he exulted.

"Yes," pondered Newmark, removing his glasses and tapping his thumb with their edge. "Yes," he repeated, "that was smooth sailing. What was that about rollways?"

"Oh, I told him we'd expect him to break out his own," said Orde.

"Yes, but what does that mean exactly?"

"Why," explained Orde, with a slight stare of surprise, "when the logs are cut and hauled during the winter, they are banked on the river-banks, and even in the river-channel itself. Then, when the thaws come in the spring, these piles are broken down and set afloat in the river."

"I see," said Newmark. "Well, but why shouldn't we undertake that part of it? I should think that would be more the job of the river-drivers."

"It would hold back our drive too much to have to stop and break rollways," explained Orde.

548

The next morning they took the early train for Monrovia, where were situated the big mills and the offices of the nine other lumber companies. Within an hour they had descended at the small frame terminal station, and were walking together up the village street.

Monrovia was at that time a very spread-out little place of perhaps two thousand population. It was situated a half mile from Lake Michigan, behind the sparsely wooded sand hills of its shore. From the river, which had here grown to a great depth and width, its main street ran directly at right angles. Four brick blocks of three stories lent impressiveness to the vista. The stores in general, however, were low frame structures. All faced broad plank sidewalks raised above the street to the level of a waggon body. From this main street ran off, to right and left, other streets, rendered lovely by maple trees that fairly met across the way. In summer, over sidewalk and roadway alike rested a dense, refreshing dark shadow that seemed to throw from itself an odour of coolness. This was rendered further attractive by the warm spicy odour of damp pine that arose from the resilient surface of sawdust and shingles broken beneath the wheels of traffic. Back from these trees, in wide, well-cultivated lawns, stood the better residences. They were almost invariably built of many corners, with steep roofs meeting each other at all angles, with wide and ornamented red chimneys, numerous windows, and much scroll work adorning each apex and cornice. The ridge poles bristled in fancy foot-high palisades of wood. Chimneys were provided with lightning-rods. Occasionally an older structure, on square lines, recorded the era of a more dignified architecture. Everywhere ran broad sidewalks and picket fences. Beyond the better residence districts were the board shanties of the mill workers.

Orde and Newmark tramped up the plank walk to the farthest brick building. When they came to a cross street, they had to descend to it by a short flight of steps on one side, and ascend from it by a corresponding flight on the other. At the hotel, Newmark seated himself in a rocking-chair next the big window.

"Good luck!" said he.

Orde mounted a wide, dark flight of stairs that led from the street to a darker hall. The smell of stale cigars and cocoa matting was in the air. Down the dim length of this hall he made his way to a door, which without ceremony he pushed open.

He found himself in a railed-off space, separated from the main part of the room by a high walnut grill.

"Mr. Heinzman in?" he asked of a clerk.

"I think so," replied the clerk, to whom evidently Orde was known.

Orde spent the rest of the morning with Heinzman, a very rotund, cautious person of German extraction and accent. Heinzman occupied the time in asking questions of all sorts about the new enterprise. At twelve he had not in any way committed himself nor expressed an opinion. He, however, instructed Orde to return the afternoon of the following day.

"I vill see Proctor," said he.

Orde, rather exhausted, returned to find Newmark still sitting in the rocking-chair with his unlighted cigar. The two had lunch together, after which Orde, somewhat refreshed, started out. He succeeded in getting two more promises of contracts and two more deferred interviews.

"That's going a little faster," he told Newmark cheerfully.

The following morning, also, he was much encouraged by the reception his plan gained from the other lumbermen. At lunch he recapitulated to Newmark.

"That's four contracts already," said he, "and three more practically a sure thing. Proctor and Heinzman are slower than molasses about everything, and mean as pusley, and Johnson's up in the air, the way he always is, for fear some one's going to do him."

"It isn't a bad outlook," admitted Newmark.

But Heinzman offered a new problem for Orde's consideration.

"I haf talked with Proctor," said he, "and ve like your scheme. If you can deliffer our logs here for two dollars and a quarter, why, that is better as ve can do it; but how do ve know you vill do it?"

"I'll guarantee to get them here all right," laughed Orde.

"But what is your guarantee good for?" persisted Heinzman blandly, locking his fingers over his rotund little stomach. "Suppose the logs are not deliffered—what then? How responsible are you financially?"

"Well, we're investing seventy-five thousand dollars or so."

Heinzman rubbed his thumb and forefinger together and wafted the imaginary pulverisation away.

"Worth that for a judgment," said he.

He allowed a pause to ensue.

"If you vill give a bond for the performance of your contract," pursued Heinzman, "that vould be satisfactory."

Orde's mind was struck chaotic by the reasonableness of this request, and the utter impossibility of acceding to it.

"How much of a bond?" he asked.

"Twenty-fife thousand vould satisfy us," said Heinzman. "Bring us a suitable bond for that amount and ve vill sign your contract."

Orde ran down the stairs to find Newmark. "Heinzman won't sign unless we give him a bond for performance," he said in a low tone, as he dropped into the chair next to Newmark.

Newmark removed his unlighted cigar, looked at the chewed end, and returned it to the corner of his mouth.

"Heinzman has sense," said he drily. "I was wondering if ordinary business caution was unknown out here."

"Can we get such a bond? Nobody would go on my bond for that amount."

"Mine either," said Newmark. "We'll just have to let them go and drive ahead without them. I only hope they won't spread the idea. Better get those other contracts signed up as soon as we can."

With this object in view, Orde started out early the next morning, carrying with him the duplicate contracts on which Newmark had been busy.

"Rope 'em in," advised Newmark. "It's Saturday, and we don't want to let things simmer over Sunday, if we can help it."

About eleven o'clock a clerk of the Welton Lumber Co. entered Mr. Welton's private office to deliver to Orde a note.

"This just came by special messenger," he explained.

Orde, with an apology, tore it open. It was from Heinzman, and requested an immediate interview. Orde delayed only long enough to get Mr. Welton's signature, then hastened as fast as his horse could take him across the drawbridge to the village.

Heinzman he found awaiting him. The little German, with his round, rosy cheeks, his dot of a nose, his big spectacles, and his rotund body, looked even more than usual like a spider or a Santa Clause—Orde could not decide which.

"I haf been thinking of that bond," he began, waving a pudgy hand toward a seat, "and I haf been talking with Proctor."

"Yes," said Orde hopefully.

"I suppose you would not be prepared to gif a bond?"

"I hardly think so."

"Vell, suppose ve fix him this way," went on Heinzman, clasping his hands over his stomach and beaming through his spectacles. "Proctor and I haf talked it ofer, and ve are agreet that the probosition is a good one. Also ve think it is vell to help the young fellers along." He laughed silently in such a manner as to shake himself all over. "Ve do not vish to be too severe, and yet ve must be assured that ve get our logs on time. Now, I unterstood you to say that this new concern is a stock company."

Orde did not remember having said so, but he nodded.

"Vell, if you gif us a bond secured with stock in the new company, that would be satisfactory to us."

Orde's face cleared.

"Do you mean that, Mr. Heinzman?"

"Sure. Ve must haf some security, but ve do not vish to be too hard on you boys."

"Now, I call that a mighty good way out!" cried Orde.

"Make your contract out according to these terms, then," said Heinzman, handing him a paper, "and bring it in Monday."

Orde glanced over the slip. It recited two and a quarter as the agreed price; specified the date of delivery at Heinzman and Proctor's booms; named twenty-five thousand dollars as the amount of the bond, to be secured by fifty thousand dollars' worth of stock in the new company. This looked satisfactory. Orde arose.

"I'm much obliged to you, Mr. Heinzman," said he. "I'll bring it around Monday."

He had reached the gate to the grill before Heinzman called him back.

"By the vay," the little German beamed up at him, swinging his fat legs as the office-chair tipped back on its springs, "if it is to be a stock company, you vill be selling some of the stock to raise money, is it not so?"

"Yes," agreed Orde, "I expect so."

"How much vill you capitalise for?"

"We expect a hundred thousand ought to do the trick," replied Orde.

"Vell," said Heinzman, "ven you put it on the market, come and see me." He nodded paternally at Orde, beaming through his thick spectacles.

That evening, well after six, Orde returned to the hotel. After freshening up in the marbled and boarded washroom, he hunted up Newmark.

"Well, Joe," said he, "I'm as hungry as a bear. Come on, eat, and I'll tell you all about it."

They deposited their hats on the racks and pushed open the swinging screen doors that led into the dining-room. There they were taken in charge by a marvellously haughty and redundant head-waitress, who signalled them to follow down through ranks of small tables watched by more stately damsels. Newmark, reserved and precise, irreproachably correct in his neat gray, seemed enveloped in an aloofness as impenetrable as that of the head-waitress herself. Orde, however, was as breezy as ever. He hastened his stride to overtake the head-waitress.

"Annie, be good!" he said in his jolly way. "We've got business to talk. Put us somewhere alone."

Newmark nodded approval, and thrust his hand in his pocket. But Annie looked up into Orde's frank, laughing face, and her lips curved ever so faintly in the condescension of a smile.

"Sure, sorr," said she, in a most unexpected brogue.

"Well, I've got 'em all," said Orde, as soon as the waitress had gone with the order. "But the best stroke of business you'd never guess. I roped in Heinzman."

"Good!" approved Newmark briefly.

"It was really pretty decent of the little Dutchman. He agreed to let us put up our stock as security. Of course, that security is good only if we win out; and if we win out, why, then he'll get his logs, so he won't have any use for security. So it's just one way of beating the devil around the bush. He evidently wanted to give us the business, but he hated like the devil to pass up his rules—you know how those old shellbacks are."

"H'm, yes," said Newmark.

The waitress sailed in through a violently kicked swinging door, bearing aloft a tin tray heaped perilously. She slanted around a corner in graceful opposition to the centrifugal, brought the tray to port on a sort of landing stage by a pillar, and began energetically to distribute small "iron-ware" dishes, each containing a dab of something. When the clash of arrival had died, Orde went on:

"I got into your department a little, too."

"How's that?" asked Newmark, spearing a baked potato. "Heinzman said he'd buy some of our stock. He seems to think we have a pretty good show."

Newmark paused, his potato half-way to his plate.

"Kind of him," said he after a moment. "Did he sign a contract?"

"It wasn't made out," Orde reminded him. "I've the memoranda here. We'll make it out to-night. I am to bring it in Monday."

"I see we're hung up here over Sunday," observed Newmark. "No Sunday trains to Redding."

Orde became grave.

"I know it. I tried to hurry matters to catch the six o'clock, but couldn't make it." His round, jolly face fell sombre, as though a light within had been extinguished. After a moment the light returned. "Can't be helped," said he philosophically.

They ate hungrily, then drifted out into the office again, where Orde lit a cigar.

"Now, let's see your memoranda," said Newmark.

He frowned over the three simple items for some time.

"It's got me," he confessed at last.

"What?" inquired Orde.

"What Heinzman is up to."

"What do you mean?" asked Orde, turning in his chair with an air of slow surprise.

"It all looks queer to me. He's got something up his sleeve. Why should he take a bond with that security from us? If we can't deliver the logs, our company fails; that makes the stock worthless; that makes the bond worthless—just when it is needed. Of course, it's as plain as the nose on your face that he thinks the proposition a good one and is trying to get control."

"Oh, no!" cried Orde, astounded.

"Orde, you're all right on the river," said Newmark, with a dry little laugh, "but you're a babe in the woods at this game."

"But Heinzman is honest," cried Orde. "Why, he is a church member, and has a class in Sunday-school."

Newmark selected a cigar from his case, examined it from end to end, finally put it between his lips. The corners of his mouth were twitching quietly with amusement.

"Besides, he is going to buy some stock," added Orde, after a moment.

"Heinzman has not the slightest intention of buying a dollar's worth of stock," asserted Newmark.

"But why—"

"—Did he make that bluff?" finished Newmark. "Because he wanted to find out how much stock would be issued. You told him it would be a hundred thousand dollars, didn't you?"

"Why—yes, I believe I did," said Orde, pondering. Newmark threw back his head and laughed noiselessly.

"So now he knows that if we forfeit the bond he'll have controlling interest," he pointed out.

Orde smoked rapidly, his brow troubled.

"But what I can't make out," reflected Newmark, "is why he's so sure we'll have to forfeit."

"I think he's just taking a long shot at it," suggested Orde, who seemed finally to have decided against Newmark's opinion. "I believe you're shying at mare's nests."

"Not he. He has some good reason for thinking we won't deliver the logs. Why does he insist on putting in a date for delivery? None of the others does."

"I don't know," replied Orde. "Just to put some sort of a time limit on the thing, I suppose."

"You say you surely can get the drive through by then?"

Orde laughed.

"Sure? Why, it gives me two weeks' leeway over the worst possible luck I could have. You're too almighty suspicious, Joe."

Newmark shook his head.

"You let me figure this out," said he.

But bedtime found him without a solution. He retired to his room under fire of Orde's good-natured raillery. Orde himself shut his door, the smile still on his lips. As he began removing his coat, however, the smile died. The week had been a busy one. Hardly had he exchanged a dozen words with his parents, for he had even been forced to eat his dinner and supper away from home. This Sunday he had promised himself to make his deferred but much-desired call on Jane Hubbard—and her guest. He turned out the gas with a shrug of resignation. For the first time his brain cleared of its turmoil of calculations, of guesses, of estimates, and of men. He saw clearly the limited illumination cast downward by the lamp beneath its wide shade, the graceful, white figure against the shadow of the easy chair, the oval face cut in half by the lamplight to show plainly the red lips with the quaint upward quirks at the corners, and dimly the inscrutable eyes and the hair with the soft shadows. With a sigh he fell asleep.

Some time in the night he was awakened by a persistent tapping on the door. In the woodsman's manner, he was instantly broad awake. He lit the gas and opened the door to admit Newmark, partially dressed over his night gown.

"Orde," said he briefly and without preliminary, "didn't you tell me the other day that rollways were piled both on the banks and IN the river?"

"Yes, sometimes," said Orde. "Why?"

"Then they might obstruct the river?"

"Certainly."

"I thought so!" cried Newmark, with as near an approach to exultation as he ever permitted himself. "Now, just one other thing: aren't Heinzman's rollways below most of the others?"

"Yes, I believe they are," said Orde.

"And, of course, it was agreed, as usual, that Heinzman was to break out his own rollways?"

"I see," said Orde slowly. "You think he intends to delay things enough so we can't deliver on the date agreed on."

"I know it," stated Newmark positively.

"But if he refuses to deliver the logs, no court of law will—"

"Law!" cried Newmark. "Refuse to deliver! You don't know that kind. He won't refuse to deliver. There'll just be a lot of inevitable delays, and his foreman will misunderstand, and all that. You ought to know more about that than I do."

Orde nodded, his eye abstracted.

"It's a child-like scheme," commented Newmark. "If I'd had more knowledge of the business, I'd have seen it sooner."

"I'd never have seen it at all," said Orde humbly. "You seem to be the valuable member of this firm, Joe."

"In my way," said Newmark, "you in yours. We ought to make a good team."

## XII

Sunday afternoon, Orde, leaving Newmark to devices of his own, walked slowly up the main street, turned to the right down one of the shaded side residence streets that ended finally in a beautiful glistening sand-hill. Up this he toiled slowly, starting at every step avalanches and streams down the slope. Shortly he found himself on the summit, and paused for a breath of air from the lake.

He was just above the tops of the maples, which seen from this angle stretched away like a forest through which occasionally thrust roofs and spires. Some distance beyond a number of taller buildings and the red of bricks were visible. Beyond them still were other sand-hills, planted raggedly with wind-twisted and stunted trees. But between the brick buildings and these sand-hills flowed the river—wide, deep, and still—bordered by the steamboat landings on the town side and by fishermen's huts and net-racks and small boats on the other. Orde seated himself on the smooth, clean sand and removed his hat. He saw these things, and in imagination the far upper stretches of the river, with the mills and yards and booms extending for miles; and still above them the marshes and the flats where the river widened below the Big Bend. That would be the location for the booms of the new company—a cheap property on which the partners had already secured a valuation. And below he dropped in imagination with the slackening current until between two greater sand-hills than the rest the river ran out through the channel made by two long piers to the lake—blue, restless, immeasurable. To right and left stretched the long Michigan coast, with its low yellow hills topped with the green of twisted pines, firs, and beeches, with always its beach of sand, deep and dry to the very edge of its tideless sea, strewn with sawlogs, bark, and the ancient remains of ships.

After he had cooled he arose and made his way back to a pleasant hardwood forest of maple and beech. Here the leaves were just bursting from their buds. Underfoot the early spring flowers—the hepaticas, the anemones, the trilium, the dog-tooth violets, the quaint, early, bright-green undergrowths—were just reaching their perfection. Migration was in full tide. Birds, little and big, flashed into view and out again, busy in the mystery of their northward pilgrimage, giving the appearance of secret and silent furtiveness, yet each uttering his characteristic call from time to time, as though for a signal to others of the host. The woods were swarming as city streets, yet to Orde these little creatures were as though invisible. He stood in the middle of a great multitude, he felt himself under the observation of many bright eyes, he heard the murmuring and twittering that proclaimed a throng, he sensed an onward movement that flowed slowly but steadily toward the pole; nevertheless, a flash of wings, a fluttering little body, the dip of a hasty short flight, represented the visible tokens. Across the pale silver sun of April their shadows flickered, and with them flickered the tracery of new leaves and the delicacy of the lace-like upper branches.

Orde walked slowly farther and farther into the forest, lost in an enjoyment which he could not have defined accurately, but which was so integral a portion of his nature that it had drawn him from the banks and wholesale groceries to the woods. After a while he sat down on a log and lit his pipe. Ahead the ground sloped upward. Dimly through the half-fronds of the early season he could make out the yellow of sands and the deep complementary blue of the sky above them. He knew the Lake to lie just beyond. With the thought he arose. A few moments later he stood on top the hill, gazing out over the blue waters.

Very blue they were, with a contrasting snowy white fringe of waves breaking gently as far up the coast as the eye could reach. The beach, on these tideless waters, was hard and smooth only in the narrow strip over which ran the wash of the low surf. All the rest of the expanse of sand back to the cliff-like hills lay dry and tumbled into hummocks and drifts, from which projected here a sawlog cast inland from a raft by some long-past storm, there a slab, again a ship's rib sticking gaunt and defiant from the shifting, restless medium that would smother it. And just beyond the edge of the hard sand, following the long curves of the wash, lay a dark, narrow line of bark fragments.

The air was very clear and crystalline. The light-houses on the ends of the twin piers, though some miles distant, seemed close at hand. White herring gulls, cruising against the blue, flashed white as the sails of a distant ship. A fresh breeze darkened the blue velvet surface of the water, tumbled the white foam hissing up the beach, blew forward over the dunes a fine hurrying mist of sand, and bore to Orde at last the refreshment of the wide spaces. A woman, walking slowly, bent her head against the force of this wind.

Orde watched her idly. She held to the better footing of the smooth sand, which made it necessary that she retreat often before the inrushing wash, sometimes rather hastily. Orde caught himself admiring the grace of her deft and sudden movements, and the sway of her willowy figure. Every few moments she turned and faced the lake, her head thrown back, the wind whipping her garments about her.

As she drew nearer, Orde tried in vain to catch sight of her face. She looked down, watching the waters advance and recede; she wore a brimmed hat bent around her head by means of some sort of veil tied over the top and beneath her chin. When she had arrived nearly opposite Orde she turned abruptly inland, and a moment later began laboriously to climb the steep sand.

The process seemed to amuse her. She turned her head sidewise to watch with interest the hurrying, tumbling little cascades that slid from her every step. From time to time she would raise her skirts daintily with the tips of her fingers, and lean far over in order to observe with interest how her feet sank to the ankles, and how the sand rushed from either side to fill in the depressions. The wind carried up to Orde low, joyous chuckles of delight, like those of a happy child.

As though directed by some unseen guide, her course veered more and more until it led directly to the spot where Orde stood. When she was within ten feet of him she at last raised her head so the young man could see something besides the top of her hat. Orde looked plump into her eyes.

"Hullo!" she said cheerfully and unsurprised, and sank down cross-legged at his feet.

Orde stood quite motionless, overcome by astonishment. Her face, its long oval framed in the bands of the gray veil and the down-turned brim of the hat, looked up smiling into his. The fresh air had deepened the colour beneath her skin and had blown loose stray locks of the fine shadow-filled hair. Her red lips, with the quaintly up-turned corners, smiled at him with a new frankness, and the black eyes—the eyes so black as to resemble spots—had lost their half-indolent reserve and brimmed over quite frankly with the joy of life. She scooped up a handful of the dry, clean sand from either side of her, raised it aloft, and let it trickle slowly between her fingers. The wind snatched at the sand and sprayed it away in a beautiful plume.

"Isn't this REAL fun?" she asked him.

"Why, Miss Bishop!" cried Orde, finding his voice. "What are you doing here?"

A faint shade of annoyance crossed her brow.

"Oh, I could ask the same of you; and then we'd talk about how surprised we are, world without end," said she. "The important thing is that here is sand to play in, and there is the Lake, and here are we, and the day is charmed, and it's good to be alive. Sit down and dig a hole! We've all the common days to explain things in."

Orde laughed and seated himself to face her. Without further talk, and quite gravely, they commenced to scoop out an excavation between them, piling the sand over themselves and on either side as was most convenient. As the hole grew deeper they had to lean over more and more. Their heads sometimes brushed ever so lightly, their hands perforce touched. Always the dry sand flowed from the edges partially to fill in the result their efforts. Faster and faster they scooped it out again. The excavation thus took on the shape of a funnel. Her cheeks glowed pink, her eyes shone like stars. Entirely was she absorbed in the task. At last a tiny commotion manifested itself in the bottom of the funnel. Impulsively she laid her hand on Orde's, to stop them. Fascinated, they watched. After incredible though lilliputian upheavals, at length appeared a tiny black insect, struggling against the rolling, overwhelming sands. With great care the girl scooped this newcomer out and set him on the level ground. She looked up happily at Orde, thrusting the loose hair from in front of her eyes.

"I was convinced we ought to dig a hole," said she gravely. "Now, let's go somewhere else."

She arose to her feet, shaking the sand free from her skirts.

"I think, through these woods," she decided. "Can we get back to town this way?"

Receiving Orde's assurance, she turned at once down the slope through the fringe of scrub spruces and junipers into the tall woods. Here the air fell still. She remarked on how warm it seemed, and began to untie from over her ears the narrow band of veil that held close her hat.

"Yes," replied Orde. "The lumber-jacks say that the woods are the poor man's overcoat."

She paused to savour this, her head on one side, her arms upraised to the knot.

"Oh, I like that!" said she, continuing her task. In a moment or so the veil hung free. She removed it and the hat, and swung them both from one finger, and threw back her head.

"Hear all the birds!" she said.

Softly she began to utter a cheeping noise between her lips and teeth, low and plaintive. At once the volume of bird-sounds about increased; the half-seen flashes became more frequent. A second later the twigs were alive with tiny warblers and creepers, flirting from branch to branch, with larger, more circumspect chewinks, catbirds, and finches hopping down from above, very silent, very grave. In the depths of the thickets the shyer hermit and olive thrushes and the oven birds revealed themselves ghost-like, or as sea-growths lift into a half visibility through translucent shadows the colour of themselves. All were very intent, very earnest, very interested, each after his own manner, in the comradeship of the featherhood he imagined to be uttering distressful cries. A few, like the chickadees, quivered their wings, opened their little mouths, fluttered down tiny but aggressive against the disaster. Others hopped here and there restlessly, uttering plaintive, low-toned cheeps. The shyest contented themselves by a discreet, silent, and distant sympathy. Three or four freebooting Jays, attracted not so much by the supposed calls for help as by curiosity, fluttered among the tops of the trees, uttering their harsh notes.

553

Finally, the girl ended her performance in a musical laugh.

"Run away, Brighteyes," she called. "It's all right; nobody's damaged."

She waved her hand. As though at a signal, the host she had evoked melted back into the shadows of the forest. Only the chickadee, impudent as ever, retreated scolding rather ostentatiously, and the jays, splendid in their ornate blue, screamed opinions at each other from the tops of trees.

"How would you like to be a bird?" she inquired.

"Hadn't thought," replied Orde.

"Don't you ever indulge in vain and idle speculations?" she inquired. "Never mind, don't answer. It's too much to expect of a man."

She set herself in idle motion down the slope, swinging the hat at the end of its veil, pausing to look or listen, humming a little melody between her closed lips, throwing her head back to breathe deep the warm air, revelling in the woods sounds and woods odours and woods life with entire self-abandonment. Orde followed her in silence. She seemed to be quite without responsibility in regard to him; and yet an occasional random remark thrown in his direction proved that he was not forgotten. Finally they emerged from the beach woods.

They faced an open rolling country. As far as the eye could reach were the old stumps of pine trees. Sometimes they stood in place, burned and scarred, but attesting mutely the abiding place of a spirit long since passed away. Sometimes they had been uprooted and dragged to mark the boundaries of fields, where they raised an abatis of twisted roots to the sky.

The girl stopped short as she came face to face with this open country. The inner uplift, that had lent to her aspect the wide-eyed, careless joy of a child, faded. In its place came a new and serious gravity. She turned on him troubled eyes.

"You do this," she accused him quite simply.

For answer he motioned to the left where below them lay a wide and cultivated countryside—farmhouses surrounded by elms; compact wood lots of hardwood; crops and orchards, all fair and pleasant across the bosom of a fertile nature.

"And this," said he. "That valley was once nothing but a pine forest—and so was all the southern part of the State, the peach belt and the farms. And for that matter Indiana, too, and all the other forest States right out to the prairies. Where would we be now, if we HADN'T done that?" he pointed across at the stump-covered hills.

Mischief had driven out the gravity from the girl's eyes. She had lowered her head slightly sidewise as though to conceal their expression from him.

"I was beginning to be afraid you'd say 'yes-indeed,'" said she.

Orde looked bewildered, then remembered the Incubus, and laughed.

"I haven't been very conversational," he acknowledged.

"Certainly NOT!" she said severely. "That would have been very disappointing. There has been nothing to say." She turned and waved her hat at the beech woods falling sombre against the lowering sun.

"Good-bye," she said gravely, "and pleasant dreams to you. I hope those very saucy little birds won't keep you awake." She looked up at Orde. "He was rather nice to us this afternoon," she explained, "and it's always well to be polite to them anyway." She gazed steadily at Orde for signs of amusement. He resolutely held his face sympathetic.

"Now I think we'll go home," said she.

They made their way between the stumps to the edge of the sand-hill overlooking the village. With one accord they stopped. The low-slanting sun cast across the vista a sleepy light of evening.

"How would you like to live in a place like that all your life?" asked Orde.

"I don't know." She weighed her words carefully. "It would depend. The place isn't of so much importance, it seems to me. It's the life one is called to. It's whether one finds her soul's realm or not that a place is liveable or not. I can imagine entering my kingdom at a railway water-tank," she said quaintly, "or missing it entirely in a big city."

Orde looked out over the raw little village with a new interest.

"Of course I can see how a man's work can lie in a small place," said he; "but a woman is different."

"Why is a woman different?" she challenged. "What is her 'work,' as you call it; and why shouldn't it, as well as a man's, lie in a small place? What is work—outside of drudgery—unless it is correspondence of one's abilities to one's task?"

"But the compensations—" began Orde vaguely.

"Compensations?" she cried. "What do you mean? Here are the woods and fields, the river, the lake, the birds, and the breezes. We'll check them off against the theatre and balls. Books can be had here as well as anywhere. As to people: in a large city you meet a great many, and they're all busy, and unless you make an especial and particular effort—which you're not likely to—you'll see them only casually and once in a great while. In a small place you know fewer people; but you know them intimately." She broke off with a half-laugh. "I'm from New York," she stated humorously, "and you've magicked me into an eloquent defense of Podunk!" She laughed up at Orde quite frankly. "Giant Strides!" she challenged suddenly. She turned off the edge of the sand-hill, and began to plunge down its slope, leaning far back, her arms extended, increasing as much as possible the length of each step. Orde followed at full speed. When the bottom was reached, he steadied her to a halt. She shook herself, straightened her hat, and wound the veil around it. Her whole aspect seemed to have changed with the descent into the conventionality of the village street. The old, gentle though capable and self-contained reserve had returned. She moved beside Orde with dignity.

"I came down with Jane and Mrs. Hubbard to see Mr. Hubbard off on the boat for Milwaukee last night," she told him. "Of course we had to wait over Sunday. Mrs. Hubbard and Jane had to see some relative or other; but I preferred to take a walk."

"Where are you staying?" asked Orde.

"At the Bennetts'. Do you know where it is?"

"Yes," replied Orde.

They said little more until the Bennetts' gate was reached. Orde declined to come in.

"Good-night," she said. "I want to thank you. You did not once act as though you thought I was silly or crazy. And you didn't try, as all the rest of them would, to act silly too. You couldn't have done it; and you didn't try. Oh, you may have felt it—I know!" She smiled one of her quaint and quizzical smiles. "But men aren't built for foolishness. They have to leave that to us. You've been very nice this afternoon; and it's helped a lot. I'm good for quite a long stretch now. Good-night."

She nodded to him and left him tongue-tied by the gate.

Orde, however, walked back to the hotel in a black rage with himself over what he termed his imbecility. As he remembered it, he had made just one consecutive speech that afternoon.

"Joe," said he to Newmark, at the hotel office, "what's the plural form of Incubus? I dimly remember it isn't 'busses.'"

"Incubi," answered Newmark.

"Thanks," said Orde gloomily.

## XIII

"I have Heinzman's contract all drawn," said Newmark the next morning, "and I think I'll go around with you to the office."

At the appointed time they found the little German awaiting them, a rotund smile of false good-nature illuminating his rosy face. Orde introduced his partner. Newmark immediately took charge of the interview.

"I have executed here the contract, and the bonds secured by Mr. Orde's and my shares of stock in the new company," he explained. "It is only necessary that you affix your signature and summon the required witnesses."

Heinzman reached his hands for the papers, beaming over his glasses at the two young men.

As he read, however, his smile vanished, and he looked up sharply.

"Vat is this?" he inquired, a new crispness in his voice. "You tolt me," he accused Orde, "dot you were not brepared to break out the rollways. You tolt me you would egspect me to do that for myself."

"Certainly," agreed Orde.

"Vell, why do you put in this?" demanded Heinzman, reading from the paper in his hand. "'In case said rollways belonging to said parties of the second part are not broken out by the time the drive has reached them, and in case on demand said parties of the second part do refuse or do not exercise due diligence in breaking out said rollways, the said parties of the first part shall themselves break out said rollways, and the said parties of the second part do hereby agree to reimburse said parties of the first part at the rate of a dollar per thousand board feet.'"

"That is merely to protect ourselves," struck in Newmark.

"But," exploded Heinzman, his face purpling, "a dollar a tousand is absurd!"

"Of course it is," agreed Newmark. "We expect it to be. But also we expect you to break out your own rollways in time. It is intended as a penalty in case you don't."

"I vill not stand for such foolishness," pounded Heinzman on the arm of his chair.

"Very well," said Newmark crisply, reaching for the contract.

But Heinzman clung to it.

"It is absurd," he repeated in a milder tone. "See, I vill strike it out." He did so with a few dashes of the pen.

"We have no intention," stated Newmark with decision, "of giving you the chance to hang up our drive."

Heinzman caught his breath like a child about to cry out.

"So that is what you think!" he shouted at them. "That's the sort of men you think we are! I'll show you you cannot come into honest men's offices to insoolt them by such insinuations!" He tore the contract in pieces and threw it in the waste basket. "Get oudt of here!" he cried.

Newmark arose as dry and precise as ever. Orde was going red and white by turns, and his hands twitched.

"Then I understand you to refuse our offer?" asked Newmark coolly.

"Refuse! Yes! You and your whole kapoodle!" yelled Heinzman.

He hopped down and followed them to the grill door, repeating over and over that he had been insulted. The clerks stared in amazement.

Once at the foot of the dark stairs and in the open street, Orde looked up at the sky with a deep breath of relief.

"Whew!" said he, "that was a terror! We've gone off the wrong foot that time."

Newmark looked at him with some amusement.

"You don't mean to say that fooled you!" he marvelled.

"What?" asked Orde.

"All that talk about insults, and the rest of the rubbish. He saw we had spotted his little scheme; and he had to retreat somehow. It was as plain as the nose on your face."

"You think so?" doubted Orde.

"I know so. If he was mad at all, it was only at being found out."

"Maybe," said Orde.

"We've got an enemy on our hands in any case," concluded Newmark, "and one we'll have to look out for, I don't know how he'll do it; but he'll try to make trouble on the river. Perhaps he'll try to block the stream by not breaking his rollways."

"One of the first things we'll do will be to boom through a channel where Mr. Man's rollways will be," said Orde.

A faint gleam of approval lit Newmark's eyes.

"I guess you'll be equal to the occasion," said he drily.

Before the afternoon train, there remained four hours. The partners at once hunted out the little one-story frame building near the river in which Johnson conducted his business.

Johnson received them with an evident reserve of suspicion.

"I see no use in it," said he, passing his hand over his hair "slicked" down in the lumber-jack fashion. "I can run me own widout help from any man."

"Which seems to settle that!" said Newmark to Orde after they had left.

"Oh, well, his drive is small; and he's behind us," Orde pointed out.

"True," said Newmark thoughtfully.

"Now," said Newmark, as they trudged back to their hotel to get lunch and their hand-bags. "I'll get to work at my part of it. This proposition of Heinzman's has given me an idea. I'm not going to try to sell this stock outside, but to the men who own timber along the river. Then they won't be objecting to the tolls; for if the company makes any profits, part will go to them."

"Good idea!" cried Orde.

"I'll take these contracts, to show we can do the business."

"All correct."

"And I'll see about incorporation. Also I'll look about and get a proper office and equipments, and get hold of a book-keeper. Of course we'll have to make this our headquarters."

"I suppose so," said Orde a little blankly. After an instant he laughed. "Do you know, I hadn't thought of that? We'll have to live here, won't we?"

"Also," went on Newmark calmly, "I'll buy the supplies to the best advantage I can, and see that they get here in good shape. I have our preliminary lists, and as fast as you think you need anything, send a requisition in to me, and I'll see to it."

"And I?" inquired Orde.

"You'll get right at the construction. Get the booms built and improve the river where it needs it. Begin to get your crew—I'm not going to tell you how; you know better than I do. Only get everything in shape for next spring's drive. You can start right off. We have my money to begin on."

Orde laughed and stretched his arms over his head.

"My! She's a nice big job, isn't she?" he cried joyously.

*XIV*

Orde, in spite of his activities, managed to see Carroll Bishop twice during the ensuing week.

On his return home late Monday afternoon, Grandma Orde informed him with a shrewd twinkle that she wanted him surely at home the following evening.

"I've asked in three or four of the young people for a candy pull," said she.

"Who, mother?" asked Orde.

"Your crowd. The Smiths, Collinses, Jane Hubbard, and Her," said Grandma Orde, which probably went to show that she had in the meantime been making inquiries, and was satisfied with them.

"Do you suppose they'll care for candy pulling?" hazarded Orde a little doubtfully.

"You mean, will she?" countered Grandma. "Well, I hope for both your sakes she is not beyond a little old-fashioned fun."

So it proved. The young people straggled in at an early hour after supper—every one had supper in those days. Carroll Bishop and Jane arrived nearly the last. Orde stepped into the hall to help them with their wraps. He was surprised as he approached Miss Bishop to lift her cloak from her shoulders, to find that the top of her daintily poised head, with its soft, fine hair, came well below the level of his eyes. Somehow her poise, her slender grace of movement and of attitude, had lent her the impression of a stature she did not possess. To-night her eyes, while fathomless as ever, shone quietly in anticipation.

"Do you know," she told Orde delightedly, "I have never been to a real candy pull in my life. It was so good of your mother to ask me. What a dear she looks to-night. And is that your father? I'm going to speak to him."

She turned through the narrow door into the lighted, low-ceilinged parlour where the company were chatting busily. Orde mechanically followed her. He was arrested by the sound of Jane Hubbard's slow good-humoured voice behind him.

"Now, Jack," she drawled, "I agree with you perfectly; but that is NO reason why I should be neglected entirely. Come and hang up my coat."

Full of remorse, Orde turned. Jane Hubbard stood accusingly in the middle of the hall, her plain, shrewd, good-humoured face smiling faintly. Orde met her frank wide eyes with some embarrassment.

"Here it is," said Jane, holding out the coat. "I don't much care whether you hang it up or not. I just wanted to call you back to wish you luck." Her slow smile widened, and her gray eyes met his still more knowingly.

556

Orde seized the coat and her hand at the same time.

"Jane, you're a trump," said he. "No wonder you're the most popular girl in town."

"Of course I am, Jack," she agreed indolently. She entered the parlour.

The candy pulling was a success. Of course everybody got burned a little and spattered a good deal; but that was to be expected. After the product had been broken and been piled on dishes, all trooped to the informal "back sitting-room," where an open fire invited to stories and games of the quieter sort. Some of the girls sat in chairs, though most joined the men on the hearth.

Carroll Bishop, however, seemed possessed of a spirit of restlessness. The place seemed to interest her. She wandered here and there in the room, looking now at the walnut-framed photograph of Uncle Jim Orde, now at the great pink conch shells either side the door, now at the marble-topped table with its square paper-weight of polished agate and its glass "bell," beneath which stood a very life-like robin. This "back sitting-room" contained little in the way of ornament. It was filled, on the contrary, with old comfortable chairs, and worn calf-backed books. The girl peered at the titles of these; but the gas-jets had been turned low in favour of the firelight, and she had to give over the effort to identify the volumes. Once she wandered close to Grandma Orde's cushioned wooden rocker, and passed her hand lightly over the old lady's shoulder.

"Do you mind if I look at things?" she asked. "It's so dear and sweet and old and different from our New York homes."

"Look all you want to, dearie," said Grandma Orde.

After a moment she passed into the dining-room. Here Orde found her, her hands linked in front of her.

"Oh, it is so quaint and delightful," she exhaled slowly. "This dear, dear old house with its low ceilings and its queer haphazard lines, and its deep windows, and its old pictures, and queer unexpected things that take your breath away."

"It is one of the oldest houses in town," said Orde, "and I suppose it is picturesque. But, you see, I was brought up here, so I'm used to it."

"Wait until you leave it," said she prophetically, "and live away from it. Then all these things will come back to you to make your heart ache for them."

They rambled about together, Orde's enthusiasm gradually kindling at the flame of her own. He showed her the marvellous and painstaking pencil sketch of Napoleon looking out over a maltese-cross sunset done by Aunt Martha at the age of ten. It hung framed in the upper hall.

"It has always been there, ever since I can remember," said Orde, "and it has seemed to belong there. I've never thought of it as good or bad, just as belonging."

"I know," she nodded.

In this spirit also they viewed the plaster statue of Washington in the lower hall, and the Roger's group in the parlour. The glass cabinet of "curiosities" interested her greatly—the carved ivory chessmen, the dried sea-weeds, the stone from Sugar Loaf Rock, the bit from the wreck of the NORTH STAR, the gold and silver shells, the glittering geodes and pyrites, the sandal-wood fan, and all the hundred and one knick-knacks it was then the custom to collect under glass. They even ventured part way up the creaky attic stairs, but it was too dark to enter that mysterious region.

"I hear the drip of water," she whispered, her finger on her lips.

"It's the tank," said Orde.

"And has it a Dark Place behind it?" she begged.

"That's just what it has," said he.

"And—tell me—are there real hair trunks with brass knobs on 'em?"

"Yes, mother has two or three."

"O-o-h!" she breathed softly. "Don't tell me what's in them. I want to believe in brocades and sashes. Do you know," she looked at him soberly, "I never had any dark places behind the tank, nor mysterious trunks, when I was a child."

"You might begin now," suggested Orde.

"Do you mean to insinuate I haven't grown up?" she mocked. "Thank you! Look OUT!" she cried suddenly, "the Boojum will catch us," and picking up her skirts she fairly flew down the narrow stairs. Orde could hear the light swish of her draperies down the hall, and then the pat of her feet on the stair carpet of the lower flight.

He followed rather dreamily. A glance into the sitting-room showed the group gathered close around the fire listening to Lem Collin's attempt at a ghost story. She was not there. He found her, then, in the parlour. She was kneeling on the floor before the glass cabinet of curiosities, and she had quite flattened her little nose against the pane. At his exclamation she looked up with a laugh.

"This is the proper altitude from which to view a cabinet of curiosities," said she, "and something tells me you ought to flatten your nose, too." She held out both hands to be helped up. "Oh, WHAT a house for a child!" she cried.

After the company had gone, Orde stood long by the front gate looking up into the infinite spaces. Somehow, and vaguely, he felt the night to be akin to her elusive spirit. Farther and farther his soul penetrated into its depths; and yet other depths lay beyond, other mysteries, other unguessed realms. And yet its beauty was the simplicity of space and dark and the stars.

The next time he saw her was at her own house—or rather the house of the friend she visited. Orde went to call on Friday evening and was lucky enough to find the girls home and alone. After a decent interval Jane made an excuse and went out. They talked on a great variety of subjects, and with a considerable approach toward intimacy. Not until nearly time to go did Orde stumble upon the vital point of the evening. He had said something about a plan for the week following.

"But you forget that by that time I shall be gone," said she.

"Gone!" he echoed blankly. "Where?"

"Home," said she. "Don't you remember I am to go Sunday morning?"

"I thought you were going to stay a month."

"I was, but I—certain things came up that made it necessary for me to leave sooner."

"I—I'm sorry you're going," stammered Orde.

"So am I," said she. "I've had a very nice time here."

"Then I won't see you again," said Orde, still groping for realisation. "I must go to Monrovia to-morrow. But I'll be down to see you off."

"Do come," said she.

"It's not to be for good?" he expostulated. "You'll be coming back."

She threw her hands palm out, with a pretty gesture of ignorance.

"That is in the lap of the gods," said she.

"Will you write me occasionally?" he begged.

"As to that—" she began—"I'm a very poor correspondent."

"But won't you write?" he insisted.

"I do not make it a custom to write to young men."

"Oh!" he cried, believing himself enlightened. "Will you answer if I write you?"

"That depends."

"On what?"

"On whether there is a reply to make."

"But may I write you?"

"I suppose I couldn't very well prevent you, if you were sure to put on a three-cent stamp."

"Do you want me to?" persisted Orde.

She began gently to laugh, quite to herself, as though enjoying a joke entirely within her own personal privilege.

"You are so direct and persistent and boy-like," said she presently. "Now if you'll be very good, and not whisper to the other little pupils, I'll tell you how they do such things usually." She sat up straight from the depths of her chair, her white, delicately tapering forearms resting lightly on her knees. "Young men desiring to communicate with young ladies do not ask them bluntly. They make some excuse, like sending a book, a magazine, a marked newspaper, or even a bit of desired information. At the same time, they send notes informing the girl of the fact. The girl is naturally expected to acknowledge the politeness. If she wishes the correspondence to continue, she asks a question, or in some other way leaves an opening. Do you see?"

"Yes, I see," said Orde, slightly crestfallen. "But that's a long time to wait. I like to feel settled about a thing. I wanted to know."

She dropped back against the cushioned slant of her easy chair, and laughed again.

"And so you just up and asked!" she teased.

"I beg your pardon if I was rude," he said humbly.

The laughter died slowly from her eyes.

"Don't," she said. "It would be asking pardon for being yourself. You wanted to know: so you asked. And I'm going to answer. I shall be very glad to correspond with you and tell you about my sort of things, if you happen to be interested in them. I warn you: they are not very exciting."

"They are yours," said he.

She half rose to bow in mock graciousness, caught herself, and sank back.

"No, I won't," she said, more than half to herself. She sat brooding for a moment; then suddenly her mood changed. She sprang up, shook her skirts free, and seated herself at the piano. To Orde, who had also arisen, she made a quaint grimace over her shoulder.

"Admire your handiwork!" she told him. "You are rapidly bringing me to 'tell the truth and shame the devil.' Oh, he must be dying of mortification this evening!" She struck a great crashing chord, holding the keys while the strings reverberated and echoed down slowly into silence again. "It isn't fair," she went on, "for you big simple men to disarm us. I don't care! I have my private opinion of such brute strength. JE ME MOQUE!"

She wrinkled her nose and narrowed her eyes. Then ruthlessly she drowned his reply in a torrent of music. Like mad she played, rocking her slender body back and forth along the key-board; holding rigid her fingers, her hands, and the muscles of her arms. The bass notes roared like the rumbling of thunder; the treble flashed like the dart of lightnings. Abruptly she muted the instrument. Silence fell as something that had been pent and suddenly released. She arose from the piano stool quite naturally, both hands at her hair.

"Aren't Mr. and Mrs. Hubbard dear old people?" said she.

"What is your address in New York?" demanded Orde. She sank into a chair nearby with a pretty uplifted gesture of despair.

"I surrender!" she cried, and then she laughed until the tears started from her eyes and she had to brush them away with what seemed to Orde an absurd affair to call a handkerchief. "Oh, you are delicious!" she said at last. "Well, listen. I live at 12 West Ninth Street. Can you remember that?" Orde nodded. "And now any other questions the prisoner can reply to without incriminating herself, she is willing to answer." She folded her hands demurely in her lap.

Two days later Orde saw the train carry her away. He watched the rear car disappear between the downward slopes of two hills, and then finally the last smoke from the locomotive dissipate in the clear blue.

Declining Jane's kindly meant offer of a lift, he walked back to town.

## XV

The new firm plunged busily into its more pressing activities. Orde especially had an infinitude of details on his hands. The fat note-book in his side pocket filled rapidly with rough sketches, lists, and estimates. Constantly he interviewed men of all kinds—rivermen, mill men, contractors, boat builders, hardware dealers, pile-driver captains, builders, wholesale grocery men, cooks, axe-men, chore boys—all a little world in itself.

The signs of progress soon manifested themselves. Below Big Bend the pile-drivers were at work, the square masses of their hammers rising rapidly to the tops of the derricks, there to pause a moment before dropping swiftly to a dull THUMP! They were placing a long, compact row, which should be the outer bulwarks separating the sorting-booms from the channel of the river. Ashore the carpenters were knocking together a long, low structure for the cook-house and a larger building, destined to serve as bunk-house for the regular boom-crew. There would also be a blacksmith's forge, a storehouse, a tool and supply-house, a barn, and small separate shanties for the married men. Below more labourers with picks, shovels, axes, and scrapers were cutting out and levelling a road which would, when finished, meet the county road to town. The numerous bayous of great marsh were crossed by "float-bridges," lying flat on the surface of the water, which spurted up in rhythmical little jets under the impact of hoofs. Down stream eight miles, below the mills, and just beyond where the drawbridge crossed over to Monrovia, Duncan McLeod's shipyards clipped and sawed, and steamed and bent and bolted away at two tugboats, the machinery for which was already being stowed in the hold of a vessel lying at wharf in Chicago. In the storerooms of hardware firms porters carried and clerks checked off chains, strap iron, bolts, spikes, staples, band iron, bar iron, peavies, cant-hooks, pike-poles, sledge-hammers, blocks, ropes, and cables.

These things took time and attention to details; also a careful supervision. The spring increased, burst into leaf and bloom, and settled into summer. Orde was constantly on the move. As soon as low water came with midsummer, however, he arranged matters to run themselves as far as possible, left with Newmark minute instructions as to personal supervision, and himself departed to Redding. Here he joined a crew which Tom North had already collected, and betook himself to the head of the river.

He knew exactly what he intended to do. Far back on the head-waters he built a dam. The construction of it was crude, consisting merely of log cribs filled with stone and debris placed at intervals across the bed of the stream, against which slanted logs made a face. The gate operated simply, and could be raised to let loose an entire flood. And indeed this was the whole purpose of the dam. It created a reservoir from which could be freed new supplies of water to eke out the dropping spring freshets.

Having accomplished this formidable labour—for the trees had to be cut and hauled, the stone carted, and the earth shovelled—the crew next moved down a good ten miles to where the river dropped over a rapids rough and full of boulders. Here were built and placed a row of stone-filled log cribs in a double row down stream to define the channel and to hold the drive in it and away from the shallows near either bank. The profile of these cribs was that of a right-angled triangle, the slanting side up stream. Booms chained between them helped deflect the drive from the shoals. Their more important office, however, was to give footing to the drivers.

For twenty-five miles then nothing of importance was undertaken. Two or three particularly bad boulders were split out by the explosion of powder charges; a number of snags and old trees were cut away and disposed of; the channel was carefully examined for obstructions of any kind whatever. Then the party came to the falls.

Here Orde purposed his most elaborate bit of rough engineering. The falls were only about fifteen feet high, but they fell straight down to a bed of sheer rock. This had been eaten by the eddies into pot-holes and crannies until a jagged irregular scoop-hollow had formed immediately underneath the fall. Naturally this implied a ledge below.

In flood time the water boiled and roared through this obstruction in a torrent. The saw logs, caught in the rush, plunged end on into the scoop-hollow, hit with a crash, and were spewed out below more or less battered, barked, and stripped. Sometimes, however, when the chance of the drive brought down a hundred logs together, they failed to shoot over the barrier of the ledge. Then followed a jam, a bad jam, difficult and dangerous to break. The falls had taken her usurious share of the lives the river annually demands as her toll.

This condition of affairs Orde had determined, if possible, to obviate. From the thirty-five or forty miles of river that lay above, and from its tributaries would come the bulk of the white and Norway pine for years to follow. At least two thirds of each drive Orde figured would come from above the fall.

"If," said he to North, "we could carry an apron on a slant from just under the crest and over the pot-holes, it would shoot both the water and the logs off a better angle."

"Sure," agreed North, "but you'll have fun placing your apron with all that water running through. Why, it would drown us!"

"I've got a notion on that," said Orde. "First thing is to get the material together."

A hardwood forest topped the slope. Into this went the axe-men. The straightest trees they felled, trimmed, and dragged, down travoy trails they constructed, on sleds they built for the purpose, to the banks of the river. Here they bored the two holes through either end to receive the bolts when later they should be locked together side by side in their places. As fast as they were prepared, men with cant-hooks rolled them down the slope to a flat below the falls. They did these things swiftly and well, because they were part of the practised day's work, but they shook their heads at the falls.

After the trees had been cut in sufficient number—there were seventy-five of them, each twenty-six feet long—Orde led the way back up stream a half mile to a shallows, where he commanded the construction of a number of exaggerated sawhorses with very widespread slanting legs. In the meantime the cook-wagon and the bed-wagon had evidently been

**559**

making many trips to Sand Creek, fifteen miles away, as was attested by a large pile of heavy planks. When the sawhorses were completed, Orde directed the picks and shovels to be brought up.

At this point the river, as has been hinted, widened over shoals. The banks at either hand, too, were flat and comparatively low. As is often the case in bends of rivers subject to annual floods, the banks sloped back for some distance into a lower black-ash swamp territory.

Orde set his men to digging a channel through this bank. It was no slight job, from one point of view, as the slope down into the swamp began only at a point forty or fifty feet inland; but on the other hand the earth was soft and free from rocks. When completed the channel gave passage to a rather feeble streamlet from the outer fringe of the river. The men were puzzled, but Orde, by the strange freak of his otherwise frank and open nature, as usual told nothing of his plans, even to Tom North.

"He can't expect to turn that river," said Tim Nolan, who was once more with the crew. "He'd have to dig a long ways below that level to catch the main current—and then some."

"Let him alone," advised North, puffing at his short pipe. "He's wiser than a tree full of owls."

Next Orde assigned two men to each of the queer-shaped sawhorses, and instructed them to place the horses in a row across the shallowest part of the river, and broadside to the stream. This was done. The men, half-way to their knees in the swift water, bore down heavily to keep their charges in place. Other men immediately began to lay the heavy planks side by side, perpendicular to and on the up-stream side of the horses. The weight of the water clamped them in place; big rocks and gravel shovelled on in quantity prevented the lower ends from rising; the wide slant of the legs directed the pressure so far downward that the horses were prevented from floating away. And slowly the bulk of the water, thus raised a good three feet above its former level, turned aside into the new channel and poured out to inundate the black-ash swamp beyond.

A good volume still poured over the top of the temporary dam and down to the fall; but it was by this expedient so far reduced that work became possible.

"Now, boys!" cried Orde. "Lively, while we've got the chance!"

By means of blocks and tackles and the team horses the twenty-six-foot logs were placed side by side, slanting from a point two feet below the rim of the fall to the ledge below. They were bolted together top and bottom through the four holes bored for that purpose. This was a confusing and wet business. Sufficient water still flowed in the natural channel of the river to dash in spray over the entire work. Men toiled, wet to the skin, their garments clinging to them, their eyes full of water, barely able to breathe, yet groping doggedly at it, and arriving at last. The weather was warm with the midsummer. They made a joke of the difficulty, and found inexhaustible humour in the fact that one of their number was an Immersion Baptist. When the task was finished, they pried the flash-boards from the improvised dam; piled them neatly beyond reach of high water; rescued the sawhorses and piled them also for a possible future use; blocked the temporary channel with a tree or so—and earth. The river, restored to its immemorial channel by these men who had so nonchalantly turned it aside, roared on, singing again the song it had until now sung uninterruptedly for centuries. Orde and his crew tramped back to the falls, and gazed on their handiwork with satisfaction. Instead of plunging over an edge into a turmoil of foam and eddies, now the water flowed smoothly, almost without a break, over an incline of thirty degrees.

"Logs'll slip over that slick as a gun barrel," said Tom North. "How long do you think she'll last?"

"Haven't an idea," replied Orde. "We may have to do it again next summer, but I don't think it. There's nothing but the smooth of the water to wear those logs until they begin to rot."

Quite cheerfully they took up their long, painstaking journey back down the river.

Travel down the river was at times very pleasant, and at times very disagreeable. The ground had now hardened so that a wanigan boat was unnecessary. Instead, the camp outfit was transported in waggons, which often had to journey far inland, to make extraordinary detours, but which always arrived somehow at the various camping places. Orde and his men, of course, took the river trail.

The river trail ran almost unbroken for over a hundred miles of meandering way. It climbed up the high banks at the points, it crossed the bluffs along their sheer edges, it descended to the thickets in the flats, it crossed the swamps on pole-trails, it skirted the great, solemn woods. Sometimes, in the lower reaches, its continuity was broken by a town, but always after it recovered from its confusion it led on with purpose unvarying. Never did it desert for long the river. The cool, green still reaches, or the tumbling of the white-water, were always within its sight, sometimes beneath its very tread. When occasionally it cut in across a very long bend, it always sent from itself a little tributary trail which traced all the curves, and returned at last to its parent, undoubtedly with a full report of its task. And the trail was beaten hard by the feet of countless men, who, like Orde and his crew, had taken grave, interested charge of the river from her birth to her final rest in the great expanses of the Lake. It is there to-day, although the life that brought it into being has been gone from it these many years.

In midsummer Orde found the river trail most unfamiliar in appearance. Hardly did he recognise it in some places. It possessed a wide, leisurely expansiveness, an indolent luxury, a lazy invitation born of broad green leaves, deep and mysterious shadows, the growth of ferns, docks, and the like cool in the shade of the forest, the shimmer of aspens and poplars through the heat, the green of tangling vines, the drone of insects, the low-voiced call of birds, the opulent splashing of sun-gold through the woods, quite lacking to the hard, tight season in which his river work was usually performed. What, in the early year, had been merely a whip of brush, now had become a screen through whose waving, shifting interstices he caught glimpses of the river flowing green and cool. What had been bare timber amongst whose twigs and branches the full daylight had shone unobstructed, now had clothed itself in foliage and leaned over to make black and mysterious the water that flowed beneath. Countless insects hovered over the polished surface of that water. Dragon-flies cruised about. Little birds swooped silently down and fluttered back, intent on their tiny prey. Water-bugs skated hither and thither in apparently purposeless diagonals. Once in a great while the black depths were stirred. A bass rolled lazily over, carrying with him his captured insect, leaving on the surface of the water concentric rings which widened and died away.

The trail led the crew through many minor labours, all of which consumed time. At Reed's Mill Orde entered into diplomatic negotiations with Old Man Reed, whom he found singularly amenable. The skirmish in the spring seemed to have taken all the fight out of him; or perhaps, more simply, Orde's attitude toward him at that time had won him over to the young man's side. At any rate, as soon as he understood that Orde was now in business for himself, he readily came to an agreement. Thereupon Orde's crew built a new sluiceway and gate far enough down to assure a good head in the pond above. Other dam owners farther down the stream also signed agreements having to do with supplying water over and above what the law required of them. Above one particularly shallow rapid Orde built a dam of his own.

All this took time, and the summer months slipped away. Orde had fallen into the wild life as into a habit. He lived on the river or the trail. His face took on a ruddier hue than ever; his clothes faded to a nondescript neutral colour of their own; his hair below his narrow felt hat bleached three shades. He did his work, and figured on his schemes, and smoked his pipe, and occasionally took little trips to the nearest town, where he spent the day at the hotel desks reading and answering his letters. The weather was generally very warm. Thunder-storms were not infrequent. Until the latter part of August, mosquitoes and black flies were bad.

About the middle of September the crew had worked down as far as Redding, leaving behind them a river tamed, groomed, and harnessed for their uses. Remained still the forty miles between Redding and the Lake to be improved. As, however, navigation for light draught vessels extended as far as that city, Orde here paid off his men. A few days' work with a pile driver would fence the principal shoals from the channel.

He stayed over night with his parents, and at once took the train for Monrovia. There he made his way immediately to the little office the new firm had rented. Newmark had just come down.

"Hullo, Joe," greeted Orde, his teeth flashing in contrast to the tan of his face. "I'm done. Anything new since you wrote last?"

Newmark had acquired his articles of incorporation and sold his stock. How many excursions, demonstrations, representations, and arguments that implied, only one who has undertaken the floating of a new and untried scheme can imagine. Perhaps his task had in it as much of difficulty as Orde's taming of the river. Certainly he carried it to as successful a conclusion. The bulk of the stock he sold to the log-owners themselves; the rest he scattered here and there and everywhere in small lots, as he was able. Some five hundred and thousand dollar blocks even went to Chicago. His own little fortune of twenty thousand he paid in for the shares that represented his half of the majority retained by himself and Orde. The latter gave a note at ten per cent for his proportion of the stock. Newmark then borrowed fifteen thousand more, giving as security a mortgage on the company's newly acquired property—the tugs, booms, buildings, and real estate. Thus was the financing determined. It left the company with obligations of fifteen hundred dollars a year in interest, expenses which would run heavily into the thousands, and an obligation to make good outside stock worth at par exactly forty-nine thousand dollars. In addition, Orde had charged against his account a burden of two thousand dollars a year interest on his personal debt. To offset these liabilities—outside the river improvements and equipments, which would hold little or no value in case of failure—the firm held contracts to deliver about one hundred million feet of logs. After some discussion the partners decided to allow themselves twenty-five hundred dollars apiece by way of salary.

"If we don't make any dividends at first," Orde pointed out, "I've got to keep even on my interest."

"You can't live on five hundred," objected Newmark.

"I'll be on the river and at the booms six months of the year," replied Orde, "and I can't spend much there."

"I'm satisfied," said Newmark thoughtfully, "I'm getting a little better than good interest on my own investment from the start. And in a few years after we've paid up, there'll be mighty big money in it."

He removed his glasses and tapped his palm with their edge.

"The only point that is at all risky to me," said he, "is that we have only one-season contracts. If for any reason we hang up the drive, or fail to deliver promptly, we're going to get left the year following. And then it's B-U-S-T, bust."

"Well, we'll just try not to hang her," replied Orde.

## XVI

Orde's bank account, in spite of his laughing assertion to Newmark, contained some eleven hundred dollars. After a brief but comprehensive tour of inspection over all the works then forward, he drew a hundred of this and announced to Newmark that business would take him away for about two weeks.

"I have some private affairs to attend to before settling down to business for keeps," he told Newmark vaguely.

At Redding, whither he went to pack his little sole-leather trunk, he told Grandma Orde the same thing. She said nothing at the time, but later, when Grandpa Orde's slender figure had departed, very courteous, very erect, very dignified, with its old linen duster flapping around it, she came and stood by the man leaning over the trunk.

"Speak to her, Jack," said she quietly. "She cares for you."

Orde looked up in astonishment, but he did not pretend to deny the implied accusation as to his destination.

"Why, mother!" he cried. "She's only seen me three or four times! It's absurd—yet."

"I know," nodded Grandma Orde, wisely. "I know. But you mark my words; she cares for you."

She said nothing more, but stood looking while Orde folded and laid away, his head bent low in thought. Then she placed her hand for an instant on his shoulder and went away. The Ordes were not a demonstrative people.

The journey to New York was at that time very long and disagreeable, but Orde bore it with his accustomed stoicism. He had visited the metropolis before, so it was not unfamiliar to him. He was very glad, however, to get away from the dust and monotony of the railroad train. The September twilight was just falling. Through its dusk the street lamps were popping into illumination as the lamp-lighter made his rapid way. Orde boarded a horse-car and jingled away down Fourth Avenue. He was pleased at having arrived, and stretched his legs and filled his lungs twice with so evident an enjoyment that several people smiled.

His comfort was soon disturbed, however, by an influx of people boarding the car at Twenty-third Street. The seats were immediately filled, and late comers found themselves obliged to stand in the aisle. Among these were several women. The men nearest buried themselves in the papers after the almost universal metropolitan custom. Two or three arose to offer their seats, among them Orde. When, however, the latter had turned to indicate to one of the women the vacated seat, he discovered it occupied by a chubby and flashily dressed youth of the sort common enough in the vicinity of Fourteenth Street; impudent of eye, cynical of demeanour, and slightly contemptuous of everything unaccustomed. He had slipped in back of Orde when that young man arose, whether under the impression that Orde was about to get off the car or from sheer impudence, it would be impossible to say.

Orde stared at him, a little astonished.

"I intended that seat for this lady," said Orde, touching him on the shoulder.

The youth looked up coolly.

"You don't come that!" said he.

Orde wasted no time in discussion, which no doubt saved the necessity of a more serious disturbance. He reached over suddenly, seized the youth by the collar, braced his knee against the seat, and heaved the interloper so rapidly to his feet that he all but plunged forward among the passengers sitting opposite.

"Your seat, madam," said Orde.

The woman, frightened, unwilling to become the participant of a scene of any sort, stood looking here and there. Orde, comprehending her embarrassment, twisted his antagonist about, and, before he could recover his equilibrium sufficiently to offer resistance, propelled him rapidly to the open door, the passengers hastily making way for them.

"Now, my friend," said Orde, releasing his hold on the other's collar, "don't do such things any more. They aren't nice."

Trivial as the incident was, it served to draw Orde to the particular notice of an elderly man leaning against the rear rail. He was a very well-groomed man, dressed in garments whose fit was evidently the product of the highest art, well buttoned up, well brushed, well cared for in every way. In his buttonhole he wore a pink carnation, and in his gloved hand he carried a straight, gold-headed cane. A silk hat covered his head, from beneath which showed a slightly empurpled countenance, with bushy white eyebrows, a white moustache, and a pair of rather bloodshot, but kindly, blue eyes. In spite of his somewhat pudgy rotundity, he carried himself quite erect, in a manner that bespoke the retired military man.

"You have courage, sir," said this gentleman, inclining his head gravely to Orde.

The young man laughed in his good-humoured fashion.

"Not much courage required to root out that kind of a skunk," said he cheerfully.

"I refer to the courage of your convictions. The young men of this generation seem to prefer to avoid public disturbances. That breed is quite capable of making a row, calling the police, raising the deuce, and all that."

"What of it?" said Orde.

The elderly gentleman puffed out his cheeks.

"You are from the West, are you not?" he stated, rather than asked.

"We call it the East out there," said Orde. "It's Michigan."

"I should call that pretty far west," said the old gentleman.

Nothing more was said. After a block or two Orde descended on his way to a small hotel just off Broadway. The old gentleman saluted. Orde nodded good-humouredly. In his private soul he was a little amused at the old boy. To his view a man and clothes carried to their last refinement were contradictory terms.

Orde ate, dressed, and set out afoot in search of Miss Bishop's address. He arrived in front of the house a little past eight o'clock, and, after a moment's hesitation, mounted the steps and rang the bell.

The door swung silently back to frame an impassive man-servant dressed in livery. To Orde's inquiry he stated that Miss Bishop had gone out to the theatre. The young man left his name and a message of regret. At this the footman, with an irony so subtle as to be quite lost on Orde, demanded a card. Orde scribbled a line in his note-book, tore it out, folded it, and left it. In it he stated his regret, his short residence in the city, and desired an early opportunity to call. Then he departed down the brownstone steps, totally unconscious of the contempt he had inspired in the heart of the liveried man behind him.

He retired early and arose early, as had become his habit. When he descended to the office the night clerk, who had not yet been relieved, handed him a note delivered the night before. Orde ripped it open eagerly.

"MY DEAR MR. ORDE:

"I was so sorry to miss you that evening because of a stupid play. Come around as early as you can to-morrow morning. I shall expect you.

"Sincerely yours,

"CARROLL BISHOP."

Orde glanced at the clock, which pointed to seven. He breakfasted, read the morning paper, finally started leisurely in the direction of West Ninth Street. He walked slowly, so as to consume more time, then at University Place was seized with a panic, and hurried rapidly to his destination. The door was answered by the same man who had opened the night before, but now, in some indefinable way, his calm, while flawless externally, seemed to have lifted to a mere surface, as though he might hastily have assumed his coat. To Orde's inquiry he stated with great brevity that Miss Bishop was not yet visible, and prepared to close the door.

"You are mistaken," said Orde, with equal brevity, and stepped inside. "I have an engagement with Miss Bishop. Tell her Mr. Orde is here."

The man departed in some doubt, leaving Orde standing in the gloomy hall. That young man, however, quite cheerfully parted the heavy curtains leading into a parlour, and sat down in a spindle-legged chair. At his entrance, a maid disappeared out another door, carrying with her the implements of dusting and brushing.

Orde looked around the room with some curiosity. It was long, narrow, and very high. Tall windows admitted light at one end. The illumination was, however, modified greatly by hangings of lace covering all the windows, supplemented by heavy draperies drawn back to either side. The embrasure was occupied by a small table, over which seemed to flutter a beautiful marble Psyche. A rubber plant, then as now the mark of the city and suburban dweller, sent aloft its spare, shiny leaves alongside a closed square piano. The lack of ornaments atop the latter bespoke the musician. Through the filtered gloom of the demi-light Orde surveyed with interest the excellent reproductions of the Old World masterpieces framed on the walls—"Madonnas" by Raphael, Murillo, and Perugino, the "Mona Lisa," and Botticelli's "Spring"—the three oil portraits occupying the large spaces; the spindle-legged chairs and tables, the tea service in the corner, the tall bronze lamp by the piano, the neat little grate-hearth, with its mantel of marble; the ormolu clock, all the decorous and decorated gentility which marked the irreproachable correctness of whoever had furnished the apartment. Dark and heavy hangings depended in front of a double door leading into another room beyond. Equally dark and heavy hangings had closed behind Orde as he entered. An absolute and shrouded stillness seemed to settle down upon him. The ormolu clock ticked steadily. Muffled sounds came at long intervals from behind the portieres. Orde began to feel oppressed and subdued.

For quite three quarters of an hour he waited without hearing any other indications of life than the muffled sounds just remarked upon. Occasionally he shifted his position, but cautiously, as though he feared to awaken some one. The three oil portraits stared at him with all the reserved aloofness of their painted eyes. He began to doubt whether the man had announced him at all.

Then, breaking the stillness with almost startling abruptness, he heard a clear, high voice saying something at the top of the stairs outside. A rhythmical SWISH of skirts, punctuated by the light PAT-PAT of a girl tripping downstairs, brought him to his feet. A moment later the curtains parted and she entered, holding out her hand.

"Oh, I did keep you waiting such a long time!" she cried.

He stood holding her hand, suddenly unable to say a word, looking at her hungrily. A flood of emotion, of which he had had no prevision, swelled up within him to fill his throat. An almost irresistible impulse all but controlled him to crush her to him, to kiss her lips and her throat, to lose his fingers in the soft, shadowy fineness of her hair. The crest of the wave passed almost immediately, but it left him shaken. A faint colour deepened under the transparence of her skin; her fathomless black eyes widened ever so little; she released her hand.

"It was good of you to come so promptly," said she. "I'm so anxious to hear all about the dear people at Redding."

She settled gracefully in one of the little chairs. Orde sat down, once more master of himself, but still inclined to devour her with his gaze. She was dressed in a morning gown, all laces and ribbons and long, flowing lines. Her hair was done low on the back of her head and on the nape of her neck. The blood ebbed and flowed beneath her clear skin. A faint fragrance of cleanliness diffused itself about her—the cool, sweet fragrance of daintiness. They entered busily into conversation. Her attitudes were no longer relaxed and languidly graceful as in the easy chairs under the lamplight. She sat forward, her hands crossed on her lap, a fire smouldering deep beneath the cool surface lights of her eyes.

The sounds in the next room increased in volume, as though several people must have entered that apartment. In a moment or so the curtains to the hall parted to frame the servant.

"Mrs. Bishop wishes to know, miss," said that functionary, "if you're not coming to breakfast."

Orde sprang to his feet.

"Haven't you had your breakfast yet?" he cried, conscience stricken.

"Didn't you gather the fact that I'm just up?" she mocked him. "I assure you it doesn't matter. The family has just come down."

"But," cried Orde, "I wasn't here until nine o'clock. I thought, of course, you'd be around. I'm mighty sorry—"

"Oh, la la!" she cried, cutting him short. "What a bother about nothing. Don't you see—I'm ahead a whole hour of good talk."

"You see, you told me in your note to come early," said Orde.

"I forgot you were one of those dreadful outdoor men. You didn't see any worms, did you? Next time I'll tell you to come the day after."

Orde was for taking his leave, but this she would not have.

"You must meet my family," she negatived. "For if you're here for so short a time we want to see something of you. Come right out now."

Orde thereupon followed her down a narrow, dark hall, squeezed between the stairs and the wall, to a door that opened slantwise into a dining-room the exact counterpart in shape to the parlour at the other side of the house. Only in this case

563

the morning sun and more diaphanous curtains lent an air of brightness, further enhanced by a wire stand of flowers in the bow-windows.

The centre of the room was occupied by a round table, about which were grouped several people of different ages. With her back to the bow-window sat a woman well beyond middle age, but with evidently some pretensions to youth. She was tall, desiccated, quick in movement. Dark rings below her eyes attested either a nervous disease, an hysterical temperament, or both. Immediately at her left sat a boy of about fourteen years of age, his face a curious contradiction between a naturally frank and open expression and a growing sullenness. Next him stood a vacant chair, evidently for Miss Bishop. Opposite lolled a young man, holding a newspaper in one hand and a coffee cup in the other. He was very handsome, with a drooping black moustache, dark eyes, under lashes almost too luxuriant, and a long, oval face, dark in complexion, and a trifle sardonic in expression. In the VIS-A-VIS to Mrs. Bishop, Orde was surprised to find his ex-military friend of the street car. Miss Bishop performed the necessary introductions, which each acknowledged after his fashion, but with an apparent indifference that dashed Orde, accustomed to a more Western cordiality. Mrs. Bishop held out a languidly graceful hand, the boy mumbled a greeting, the young man nodded lazily over his newspaper. Only General Bishop, recognising him, arose and grasped his hand, with a real, though rather fussy, warmth.

"My dear sir," he cried, "I am honoured to see you again. This, my dear," he addressed his wife, "is the young man I was telling you about—in the street car," he explained.

"How very interesting," said Mrs. Bishop, with evidently no comprehension and less interest.

Gerald Bishop cast an ironically amused glance across at Orde. The boy looked up at him quickly, the sullenness for a moment gone from his face.

Carroll Bishop appeared quite unconscious of an atmosphere which seemed to Orde strained, but sank into her place at the table and unfolded her napkin. The silent butler drew forward a chair for Orde, and stood looking impassively in Mrs. Bishop's direction.

"You will have some breakfast with us?" she inquired. "No? A cup of coffee, at least?"

She began to manipulate the coffee pot, without paying the slightest attention to Orde's disclaimer. The general puffed out his cheeks, and coughed a bit in embarrassment.

"A good cup of coffee is never amiss to an old campaigner," he said to Orde. "It's as good as a full meal in a pinch. I remember when I was a major in the Eleventh, down near the City of Mexico, in '48, the time Hardy's command was so nearly wiped out by that viaduct—" He half turned toward Orde, his face lighting up, his fingers reaching for the fork with which, after the custom of old soldiers, to trace the chart of his reminiscences.

Mrs. Bishop rattled her cup and saucer with an uncontrollably nervous jerk of her slender body. For some moments she had awaited a chance to get the general's attention. "Spare us, father," she said brusquely. "Will you have another cup of coffee?"

The old gentleman, arrested in mid-career, swallowed, looked a trifle bewildered, but subsided meekly.

"No, thank you, my dear," said he, and went furiously at his breakfast.

Orde, overwhelmed by embarrassment, discovered that none of the others had paid the incident the slightest attention. Only on the lips of Gerald Bishop he surprised a fine, detached smile.

At this moment the butler entered bearing the mail. Mrs. Bishop tore hers open rapidly, dropping the mangled envelopes at her side. The contents of one seemed to vex her.

"Oh!" she cried aloud. "That miserable Marie! She promised me to have it done to-day, and now she puts it off until Monday. It's too provoking!" She turned to Orde for sympathy. "Do you know ANYTHING more aggravating than to work and slave to the limit of endurance, and then have everything upset by the stupidity of some one else?"

Orde murmured an appropriate reply, to which Mrs. Bishop paid no attention whatever. She started suddenly up from the table.

"I must see about it!" she cried. "I plainly see I shall have to do it myself. I WILL do it myself. I promised it for Sunday."

"You mustn't do another stitch, mother," put in Carroll Bishop decidedly. "You know what the doctor told you. You'll have yourself down sick."

"Well, see for yourself!" cried Mrs. Bishop. "That's what comes of leaving things to others! If I'd done it myself, it would have saved me all this bother and fuss, and it would have been done. And now I've got to do it anyway."

"My dear," put in the general, "perhaps Carroll can see Marie about it. In any case, there's nothing to work yourself up into such an excitement about."

"It's very easy for you to talk, isn't it?" cried Mrs. Bishop, turning on him. "I like the way you all sit around like lumps and do nothing, and then tell me how I ought to have done it. John, have the carriage around at once." She turned tensely to Orde. "I hope you'll excuse me," she said very briefly; "I have something very important to attend to."

Carroll had also risen. Orde held out his hand.

"I must be going," said he.

"Well," she conceded, "I suppose I'd better see if I can't help mother out. But you'll come in again. Come and dine with us this evening. Mother will be delighted."

As Mrs. Bishop had departed from the room, Orde had to take for granted the expression of this delight. He bowed to the other occupants of the table. The general was eating nervously. Gerald's eyes were fixed amusedly on Orde.

To Orde's surprise, he was almost immediately joined on the street by young Mr. Bishop, most correctly appointed.

"Going anywhere in particular?" he inquired. "Let's go up the avenue, then. Everybody will be out."

They turned up the great promenade, a tour of which was then, even more than now, considered obligatory on the gracefully idle. Neither said anything—Orde because he was too absorbed in the emotions this sudden revelation of Carroll's environment had aroused in him; Gerald, apparently, because he was too indifferent. Nevertheless it was the young exquisite who finally broke the silence.

"It was an altar cloth," said he suddenly.

"What?" asked Orde, rather bewildered.

"Mother is probably the most devout woman in New York," went on Gerald's even voice. "She is one of the hardest workers in the church. She keeps all the fast days, and attends all the services. Although she has no strength to speak of, she has just completed an elaborate embroidered altar cloth. The work she accomplished while on her knees. Often she spent five or six hours a day in that position. It was very devout, but against the doctor's orders, and she is at present much pulled down. Finally she gave way to persuasion to the extent of sending the embroidery out to be bound and corded. As a result, the altar cloth will not be done for next Sunday."

He delivered this statement in a voice absolutely colourless, without the faintest trace discernible of either approval or disapproval, without the slightest irony, yet Orde felt vaguely uncomfortable.

"It must have been annoying to her," he said gravely, "and I hope she will get it done in time. Perhaps Miss Bishop will be able to do it."

"That," said Gerald, "is Madison Square—or perhaps you know New York? My sister would, of course, be only too glad to finish the work, but I fear that my mother's peculiarly ardent temperament will now insist on her own accomplishment of the task. But perhaps you do not understand temperaments?"

"Very little, I'm afraid," confessed Orde.

They walked on for some distance farther.

"Your father was in the Mexican War?" said Orde, to change the trend of his own thoughts.

"He was a most distinguished officer. I believe he received the Medal of Honour for a part in the affair of the Molina del Rey."

"What command had he in the Civil War?" asked Orde. "I fooled around the outskirts of that a little myself."

"My father resigned from the army in '54," replied Gerald, with his cool, impersonal courtesy.

"That was too bad; just before the chance for more service," said Orde.

"Army life was incompatible with my mother's temperament," stated Gerald.

Orde said nothing more. It was Gerald's turn to end the pause.

"You are from Redding, of course," said he. "My sister is very enthusiastic about the place. You are in business there?"

Orde replied briefly, but, forced by the direct, cold, and polite cross-questioning of his companion, he gave the latter a succinct idea of the sort of operations in which he was interested.

"And you," he said at last; "I suppose you're either a broker or lawyer; most men are down here."

"I am neither one nor the other," stated Gerald. "I am possessed of a sufficient income from a legacy to make business unnecessary."

"I don't believe I'd care to—be idle," said Orde vaguely.

"There is plenty to occupy one's time," replied Gerald. "I have my clubs, my gymnasium, my horse, and my friends."

"Isn't there anything that particularly attracts you?" asked Orde.

The young man's languid eyes grew thoughtful, and he puffed more strongly on his cigarette.

"I should like," said he slowly, at last, "to enter the navy."

"Why don't you?" asked Orde bluntly.

"Certain family reasons make it inexpedient at present," said Gerald. "My mother is in a very nervous state; she depends on us, and any hint of our leaving her is sufficient to render her condition serious."

By this time the two young men were well uptown. On Gerald's initiative, they turned down a side street, and shortly came to a stop.

"That is my gymnasium," said Gerald, pointing to a building across the way. "Won't you come in with me? I am due now for my practice."

## XVII

Orde's evening was a disappointment to him. Mrs. Bishop had, by Carroll's report, worked feverishly at the altar cloth all the afternoon. As a consequence, she had gone to bed with a bad headache. This state of affairs seemed to throw the entire family into a state of indecision. It was divided in mind as to what to do, the absolute inutility of any effort balancing strongly against a sense of what the invalid expected.

"I wonder if mother wouldn't like just a taste of this beef," speculated the general, moving fussily in his chair. "I believe somebody ought to take some up. She MIGHT want it."

The man departed with the plate, but returned a few moments later, impassive—but still with the plate.

"Has she got her hot-water bag?" asked the boy unexpectedly.

"Yes, Master Kendrick," replied the butler.

After a preoccupied silence the general again broke out:

"Seems to me somebody ought to be up there with her."

"You know, father, that she can't stand any one in the room," said Carroll equably.

Toward the close of the meal, however, a distant bell tinkled faintly. Every one jumped as though guilty. Carroll said a hasty excuse and ran out. After ringing the bell, the invalid had evidently anticipated its answer by emerging from her room to the head of the stairs, for Orde caught the sharp tones of complaint, and overheard something about "take all night to eat a simple meal, when I'm lying here suffering."

At the end of an interval a maid appeared in the doorway to say that Miss Carroll sent word she would not be down again for a time, and did not care for any more dinner. This seemed to relieve the general's mind of responsibility. He assumed his little fussy air of cheerfulness, told several stories of the war, and finally, after Kendrick had left, brought out some whisky and water. He winked slyly at Orde.

"Can't do this before the youngsters, you know," he chirruped craftily.

Throughout the meal Gerald had sat back silent, a faint amusement in his eye. After dinner he arose, yawned, consulted his watch, and departed, pleading an engagement. Orde lingered some time, listening to the general, in the hope that Carroll would reappear. She did not, so finally he took his leave.

He trudged back to his hotel gloomily. The day had passed in a most unsatisfactory manner, according to his way of looking at it. Yet he had come more clearly to an understanding of the girl; her cheerfulness, her unselfishness, and, above all, the sweet, beautiful philosophy of life that must lie back, to render her so uncomplainingly the slave of the self-willed woman, yet without the indifferent cynicism of Gerald, the sullen, yet real, partisanship of Kendrick, or the general's week-kneed acquiescence.

The next morning he succeeded in making an arrangement by letter for an excursion to the newly projected Central Park. Promptly at two o'clock he was at the Bishops' house. To his inquiry the butler said that Mrs. Bishop had recovered from her indisposition, and that Miss Bishop would be down immediately. Orde had not long to wait for her. The SWISH, PAT-PAT of her joyous descent of the stairs brought him to his feet. She swept aside the portieres, and stood between their folds, bidding him welcome.

"I'm so sorry about last night," said she, "but poor mother does depend on me so at such times. Isn't it a gorgeous day to walk? It won't be much like OUR woods, will it? But it will be something. OH, I'm so glad to get out!"

She was in one of her elfish moods, the languid grace of her sleepy-eyed moments forgotten. With a little cry of rapture she ran to the piano, and dashed into a gay, tinkling air with brilliancy and abandon. Her head, surmounted by a perky, high-peaked, narrow-brimmed hat, with a flaming red bird in front, glorified by the braid and "waterfall" of that day, bent forward and turned to flash an appeal for sympathy toward Orde.

"There, I feel more able to stay on earth!" she cried, springing to her feet. "Now I'll get on my gloves and we'll start."

She turned slowly before the mirror, examining quite frankly the hang of her skirt, the fit of her close-cut waist, the turn of the adorable round, low-cut collars that were then the mode.

"It pays to be particular; we are in New York," she answered, or parried, Orde's glance of admiration.

The gloves finally drawn on and buttoned, Orde held aside the portieres, and she passed fairly under his uplifted hand. He wanted to drop his arm about her, this slender girl with her quaint dignity, her bird-like ways, her gentle, graceful, mysterious, feminine soul. The flame-red bird lent its colour to her cheeks; her eyes, black and fathomless, the pupils wide in this dim light, shone with two stars of delight.

But, as they moved toward the massive front doors, Mrs. Bishop came down the stairs behind them. She, too, was dressed for the street. She received Orde's greeting and congratulation over her improved health in rather an absent manner. Indeed, as soon as she could hurry this preliminary over, she plunged into what evidently she considered a more important matter.

"You aren't thinking of going out, are you?" she asked Carroll.

"I told you, mother; don't you remember? Mr. Orde and I are going to get a little air in the park."

"I'm sorry," said Mrs. Bishop, with great brevity and decision, "but I'm going to the rectory to help Mr. Merritt, and I shall want you to go too, to see about the silver."

"But, mother," expostulated Carroll, "wouldn't Marie do just as well?"

"You know very well she can't be trusted without direction."

"I DO so want to go to the park," said Carroll wistfully. Mrs. Bishop's thin, nervous figure jerked spasmodically. "There is very little asked of you from morning until night," she said, with some asperity, "and I should think you'd have some slight consideration for the fact that I'm just up from a sick bed to spare me all you could. Besides which, you do very little for the church. I won't insist. Do exactly as you think best."

Carroll threw a pathetic glance at Orde.

"How soon are you going?" she asked her mother.

"In about ten minutes," replied Mrs. Bishop; "as soon as I've seen Honorine about the dinner." She seemed abruptly to realise that the amenities demanded something of her. "I'm sorry we must go so soon," she said briefly to Orde, "but of course church business—We shall hope to see you often."

Once more Orde held aside the curtains. The flame-bird drooped from the twilight of the hall into the dimness of the parlour. All the brightness seemed to have drained from the day, and all the joy of life seemed to have faded from the girl's soul. She sank into a chair, and tried pathetically to smile across at Orde.

"I'm such a baby about disappointments," said she.

"I know," he replied, very gently.

"And it's such a blue and gold day."

"I know," he repeated.

She twisted her glove in her lap, a bright spot of colour burning in each cheek.

"Mother is not well, and she has a great deal to try her. Poor mother!" she said softly, her head cast down.

"I know," said Orde in his gentle tones.

566

After a moment he arose to go. She remained seated, her head down.

"I'm sorry about this afternoon," said he cheerfully, "but it couldn't be helped, could it? Jane used to tell me about your harp playing. I'm going to come in to hear you this evening. May I?"

"Yes," she said, in a stifled voice, and held out her hand. She sat quite still until she heard the front door close after him; then she ran to the curtains and looked after his sturdy, square figure, as it swung up the street.

"Well done; oh, well done, gentle heart!" she breathed after him. Then she went back to the piano.

But Orde's mouth, could she have seen it, was set in grim lines, and his feet, could she have heard them, rang on the pavement with quite superfluous vigour. He turned to the left, and, without pause, walked some ten or twelve miles.

The evening turned out very well, fortunately; Orde could not have stood much more. They had the parlour quite to themselves. Carroll took the cover from the tall harp, and, leaning her cheek against it, she played dreamily for a half hour. Her arms were bare, and as her fingers reached out lingeringly and caressingly to draw the pure, golden chords from the golden instrument, her soft bosom pressed against the broad sounding board. There is about the tones of a harp well played something luminous, like rich, warm sunlight. When the girl muted the strings at last, it seemed to Orde as though all at once the room had perceptibly darkened. He took his leave finally, his spirit soothed and restored.

Tranquillity was not for long, however. Orde's visits were, naturally, as frequent as possible. To them almost instantly Mrs. Bishop opposed the strong and intuitive jealousy of egotism. She had as yet no fears as to the young man's intentions, but instinctively she felt an influence that opposed her own supreme dominance. In consequence, Orde had much time to himself. Carroll and the rest of the family, with the possible exception of Gerald, shared the belief that the slightest real opposition to Mrs. Bishop would suffice to throw her into one of her "spells," a condition of alarming and possibly genuine collapse. "To drive mother into a spell" was an expression of the worst possible domestic crime. It accused the perpetrator—through Mrs. Bishop—of forgetting the state of affairs, of ingratitude for care and affection, of common inhumanity, and of impiety in rendering impossible of performance the multifarious church duties Mrs. Bishop had invented and assumed as so many particularly shining virtues. Orde soon discovered that Carroll went out in society very little for the simple reason that she could never give an unqualified acceptance to an invitation. At the last moment, when she had donned her street wraps and the carriage was at the door, she was liable to be called back, either to assist at some religious function, which, by its sacred character, was supposed to have precedence over everything, or to attend a nervous crisis, brought on by some member of the household, or by mere untoward circumstances. The girl always acquiesced most sweetly in these recurrent disappointments. And the very fact that she accepted few invitations gave Orde many more chances to see her, in spite of Mrs. Bishop's increasing exactions. He did not realise this fact, however, but ground his teeth and clung blind-eyed to his temper whenever the mother cut short his visits or annulled his engagements on some petty excuse of her own. He could almost believe these interruptions malicious, were it not that he soon discovered Mrs. Bishop well disposed toward him personally whenever he showed himself ready to meet her even quarter way on the topics that interested her—the church and her health.

In this manner the week passed. Orde saw as much as he could of Miss Bishop. The remainder of the time he spent walking the streets and reading in the club rooms to which Gerald's courtesy had given him access. Gerald himself seemed to be much occupied. Precisely at eleven every morning, however, he appeared at the gymnasium for his practice; and in this Orde dropped into the habit of joining him. When the young men first stripped in each other's presence, they eyed each other with a secret surprise. Gerald's slender and elegant body turned out to be smoothly and gracefully muscled on the long lines of the Flying Mercury. His bones were small, but his flesh was hard, and his skin healthy with the flow of blood beneath. Orde, on the other hand, had earned from the river the torso of an ancient athlete. The round, full arch of his chest was topped by a mass of clean-cut muscle; across his back, beneath the smooth skin, the muscles rippled and ridged and dimpled with every movement; the beautiful curve of the deltoids, from the point of the shoulder to the arm, met the other beautiful curve of the unflexed biceps and that fulness of the back arm so often lacking in a one-sided development; the surface of the abdomen showed the peculiar corrugation of the very strong man; the round, columnar neck arose massive.

"By Jove!" said Gerald, roused at last from his habitual apathy.

"What's the matter?" asked Orde, looking up from tying the rubber-soled shoes that Gerald had lent him.

"Murphy," called Gerald, "come here."

A very hairy, thick-set, bullet-headed man, the type of semi-professional "handlers," emerged from somewhere across the gymnasium.

"Do you think you could down this fellow?" asked Gerald.

Murphy looked Orde over critically.

"Who ye ringin' in on me?" he inquired.

"This is a friend of mine," said Gerald severely.

"Beg your pardon. The gentleman is well put up. How much experience has he had?"

"Ever box much?" Gerald asked Orde.

"Box?" Orde laughed. "Never had time for that sort of thing. Had the gloves on a few times."

"Where did you get your training, sir?" asked the handler.

"My training?" repeated Orde, puzzled. "Oh, I see! I was always pretty heavy, and I suppose the work on the river keeps a man in pretty good shape."

Gerald's languor had vanished, and a glint had appeared in his eye that would have reminded Orde of Miss Bishop's most mischievous mood could he have seen it.

"Put on the gloves with Murphy," he suggested, "will you? I'd like to see you two at it."

"Surely," agreed Orde good-naturedly. "I'm not much good at it, but I'd just as soon try." He was evidently not in the least afraid to meet the handler, though as evidently without much confidence in his own skill.

"All right; I'll be with you in a second," said Gerald, disappearing. In the anteroom he rung a bell, and to the boy who leisurely answered its summons he said rapidly:

"Run over to the club and find Mr. Winslow, Mr. Clark, and whoever else is in the smoking room, and tell them from me to come over to the gymnasium. Tell them there's some fun on."

Then he returned to the gymnasium floor, where Murphy was answering Orde's questions as to the apparatus. While the two men were pulling on the gloves, Gerald managed a word apart with the trainer.

"Can you do him, Murph?" he whispered.

"Sure!" said the handler. "Them kind's always as slow as dray-horses. They gets muscle-bound."

"Give it to him," said Gerald, "but don't kill him. He's a friend of mine."

Then he stepped back, the same joy in his soul that inspires a riverman when he encounters a high-banker; a hunter when he takes out a greenhorn, or a cowboy as he watches the tenderfoot about to climb the bronco.

"Time!" said he.

The first round was sharp. When Gerald called the end, Orde grinned at him cheerfully.

"Don't look like I was much at this game, does it?" said he. "I wouldn't pull down many persimmons out of that tree. Your confounded man's too lively; I couldn't hit him with a shotgun."

Orde had stood like a rock, his feet planted to the floor, while Murphy had circled around him hitting at will. Orde hit back, but without landing. Nevertheless Murphy, when questioned apart, did not seem satisfied.

"The man's pig-iron," said he. "I punched him plenty hard enough, and it didn't seem to jar him."

The gallery at one end the running track had by now half filled with interested spectators.

"Time!" called Gerald for round two.

This time Murphy went in more viciously, aiming and measuring his blows accurately. Orde stood as before, a humourous smile of self-depreciation on his face, hitting back at the elusive Murphy, but without much effect, his feet never stirring in their tracks. The handler used his best tactics and landed almost at will, but without apparent damage. He grew ugly—finally lost his head.

"Well, if ye will have it!" he muttered, and aimed what was intended as a knockout blow.

Gerald uttered a half cry of warning as his practised eye caught Murphy's intention. The blow landed. Orde's head snapped back, but to the surprise of every one the punch had no other effect, and a quick exchange of infighting sent Murphy staggering back from the encounter. The smile had disappeared from Orde's face, and his eye had calmed.

"Look here," he called to Gerald, "I don't understand this game very well. At school we used 'taps.' Is a man supposed to hit hard?"

Gerald hesitated, then looked beyond Orde to the gallery. To a man it made frantic and silent demonstration.

"Of course you hit," he replied. "You can't hurt any one with those big gloves."

Orde turned back to his antagonist. The latter advanced once more, his bullet head sunk between his shoulders, his little eyes twinkling. Evidently Mr. Bishop's friend would now take the aggressive, and forward movement would deliver an extra force to the professional's blows.

Orde did not wait for Murphy, however. Like a tiger he sprang forward, hitting out fiercely, first with one hand then with the other. Murphy gave ground, blocked, ducked, exerted all a ring general's skill either to stop or avoid the rush. Orde followed him insistent. Several times he landed, but always when Murphy was on the retreat, so the blows had not much weight. Several times Murphy ducked in and planted a number of short-arm jabs at close range. The round ended almost immediately to a storm of applause from the galleries.

"What do you think of his being muscle-bound?" Gerald asked Murphy, as the latter flung himself panting on the wrestling mat for his rest.

"He's quick as chained lightning," acknowledged the other grudgingly. "But I'll get him. He can't keep that up; he'll be winded in half a minute."

Orde sat down on a roll of mat. His smile had quite vanished, and he seemed to be awaiting eagerly the beginning of the next round.

"Time!" called Gerald for the third.

Orde immediately sprang at his adversary, repeating the headlong rush with which the previous round had ended. Murphy blocked, ducked, and kept away, occasionally delivering a jolt as opportunity offered, awaiting the time when Orde's weariness would leave him at the other's mercy. That moment did not come. The young man hammered away tirelessly, insistently, delivering a hurricane of his two-handed blows, pressing relentlessly in as Murphy shifted and gave ground, his head up, his eyes steady, oblivious to the return hammering the now desperate handler opposed to him. Two minutes passed without perceptible slackening in this terrific pace. The gallery was in an uproar, and some of the members were piling down the stairs to the floor. Perspiration stood out all over Murphy's body. His blows failed of their effect, and some of Orde's were landing. At length, bewildered more by the continuance than the violence of the attack, he dropped his ring tactics and closed in to straight slugging, blow against blow, stand up, give and take.

As he saw his opponent stand, Orde uttered a sound of satisfaction. He dropped slightly his right shoulder behind his next blow. The glove crashed straight as a pile-driver through Murphy's upraised hands to his face, which it met with a smack. The trainer, lifted bodily from the ground, was hurled through the air, to land doubled up against the supports of a parallel bars. There he lay quite still, his palms up, his head sunk forward.

Orde stared at him a moment in astonishment, as though expecting him to arise. When, however, he perceived that Murphy was in reality unconscious, he tore off the gloves and ran forward to kneel by the professional's side.

"I didn't suppose one punch like that would hurt him," he muttered to the men crowding around. "Especially with the gloves. Do you suppose he's killed?"

But already Murphy's arms were making aimless motions, and a deep breath raised his chest.

"He's just knocked out," reassured one of the men, examining the prostrate handler with a professional attention. "He'll be as good as ever in five minutes. Here," he commanded one of the gymnasium rubbers who had appeared, "lend a hand here with some water."

The clubmen crowded about, all talking at once.

"You're a wonder, my friend," said one.

"By Jove, he's hardly breathing fast after all that rushing," said a second.

"So you didn't think one punch like that would hurt him," quoted another with good-natured sarcasm.

"No," said Orde, simply. "I've hit men that hard before with my bare fist."

"Did they survive?"

"Surely."

"What kind of armour-plates were they, in heaven's name?"

Orde had recovered his balance and humour.

"Just plain ordinary rivermen," said he with a laugh.

"Gentlemen," struck in Gerald, "I want to introduce you to my friend." He performed the introductions. It was necessary for him to explain apart that Orde was in reality his friend, an amateur, a chance visitor in the city. All in all, the affair made quite a little stir, and went far to give Orde a standing with these sport-loving youths.

Finally Gerald and Orde were permitted to finish their gymnasium practice. Murphy had recovered, and came forward.

"You have a strong punch, sir, and you're a born natural fighter, sir," said he. "If you had a few lessons in boxing, sir, I'd put you against the best."

But later, when the young men were resting, each under his sheet after a rub-down, the true significance of the affair for Orde came out. Since the fight, Gerald's customary lassitude of manner seemed quite to have left him. His eye was bright, a colour mounted beneath the pale olive of his skin, the almost effeminate beauty of his countenance had animated. He looked across at Orde several times, hesitated, and at last decided to speak.

"Look here, Orde," said he, "I want to confess something to you. When you first came here three days ago, I had lots of fun with myself about you. You know your clothes aren't quite the thing, and I thought your manner was queer, and all that. I was a cad. I want to apologise. You're a man, and I like you better than any fellow I've met for a long time. And if there's any trouble—in the future—that is—oh, hang it, I'm on your side—you know what I mean!"

Orde smiled slowly.

"Bishop," was his unexpected reply, "you're not near so much of a dandy as you think you are."

## XVIII

Affairs went thus for a week. Orde was much at the Bishop residence, where he was cordially received by the general, where he gained an occasional half-hour with Carroll, and where he was almost ignored by Mrs. Bishop in her complete self-absorption. Indeed, it is to be doubted whether he attained any real individuality to that lady, who looked on all the world outside her family as useful or useless to the church.

In the course of the happy moments he had alone with Carroll, he arrived at a more intimate plane of conversation with her. He came to an understanding of her unquestioning acceptance of Mrs. Bishop's attitude. Carroll truly believed that none but herself could perform for her mother the various petty offices that lady demanded from her next of kin, and that her practical slavery was due by every consideration of filial affection. To Orde's occasional tentative suggestion that the service was of a sort better suited to a paid companion or even a housemaid, she answered quite seriously that it made mother nervous to have others about her, and that it was better to do these things than to throw her into a "spell." Orde chafed at first over seeing his precious opportunities thus filched from him; later he fretted because he perceived that Carroll was forced, however willingly, to labours beyond her strength, to irksome confinement, and to that intimate and wearing close association with the abnormal which in the long run is bound to deaden the spirit. He lost sight of his own grievance in the matter. With perhaps somewhat of exaggeration he came mightily to desire for her more of the open air, both of body and spirit. Often when tramping back to his hotel he communed savagely with himself, turning the problem over and over in his mind until, like a snowball, it had gathered to itself colossal proportions.

And in his hotel room he brooded over the state of affairs until his thoughts took a very gloomy tinge indeed. To begin with, in spite of his mother's assurance, he had no faith in his own cause. His acquaintance with Carroll was but an affair of months, and their actual meetings comprised incredibly few days. Orde was naturally humble-minded. It did not seem conceivable to him that he could win her without a long courtship. And superadded was the almost intolerable weight of Carroll's ideas as to her domestic duties. Although Orde held Mrs. Bishop's exactions in very slight esteem, and was most sceptical in regard to the disasters that would follow their thwarting, nevertheless he had to confess to himself that all Carroll's training, life, the very purity and sweetness of her disposition lent the situation an iron reality for her. He became much discouraged.

Nevertheless, at the very moment when he had made up his mind that it would be utterly useless even to indulge in hope for some years to come, he spoke. It came about suddenly, and entirely without premeditation.

The two had escaped for a breath of air late in the evening. Following the conventions, they merely strolled to the end of the block and back, always within sight of the house. Fifth Avenue was gay with illumination and the prancing of horses returning uptown or down to the Washington Square district. In contrast the side street, with its austere rows of brownstone houses, each with its area and flight of steps, its spaced gas lamps, its deserted roadway, seemed very still and quiet. Carroll was in a tired and pensive mood. She held her head back, breathing deeply.

"It's only a little strip, but it's the stars," said she, looking up to the sky between the houses. "They're so quiet and calm and big."

She seemed to Orde for the first time like a little girl. The maturer complexities which we put on with years, with experience, and with the knowledge of life had for the moment fallen from her, leaving merely the simple soul of childhood gazing in its eternal wonder at the stars. A wave of tenderness lifted Orde from his feet. He leaned over, his breath coming quickly.

"Carroll!" he said.

She looked up at him, and shrank back.

"No, no! You mustn't," she cried. She did not pretend to misunderstand. The preliminaries seemed in some mysterious fashion to have been said long ago.

"It's life or death with me," he said.

"I must not," she cried, fluttering like a bird. "I promised myself long ago that I must always, ALWAYS take care of mother."

"Please, please, dear," pleaded Orde. He had nothing more to say than this, just the simple incoherent symbols of pleading; but in such crises it is rather the soul than the tongue that speaks. His hand met hers and closed about it. It did not respond to his grasp, nor did it draw away, but lay limp and warm and helpless in his own.

She shook her head slowly.

"Don't you care for me, dear?" asked Orde very gently.

"I have no right to tell you that," answered she. "I have tried, oh, so hard, to keep you from saying this, for I knew I had no right to hear you."

Orde's heart leaped with a wild exultation.

"You do care for me!" he cried.

They had mounted the steps and stood just within the vestibule. Orde drew her toward him, but she repulsed him gently.

"No," she shook her head. "Please be very good to me. I'm very weak."

"Carroll!" cried Orde. "Tell me that you love me! Tell me that you'll marry me!"

"It would kill mother if I should leave her," she said sadly.

"But you must marry me," pleaded Orde. "We are made for each other. God meant us for each other."

"It would have to be after a great many years," she said doubtfully.

She pulled the bell, which jangled faintly in the depths of the house.

"Good-night," she said. "Come to me to-morrow. No, you must not come in." She cut short Orde's insistence and the eloquence that had just found its life by slipping inside the half-open door and closing it after her.

Orde stood for a moment uncertain; then turned away and walked up the street, his eyes so blinded by the greater glory that he all but ran down an inoffensive passer-by.

At the hotel he wrote a long letter to his mother. The first part was full of the exultation of his discovery. He told of his good fortune quite as something just born, utterly forgetting his mother's predictions before he came East. Then as the first effervescence died, a more gloomy view of the situation came uppermost. To his heated imagination the deadlock seemed complete. Carroll's devotion to what she considered her duty appeared unbreakable. In the reaction Orde doubted whether he would have it otherwise. And then his fighting blood surged back to his heart. All the eloquence, the arguments, the pleadings he should have commanded earlier in the evening hurried belated to their posts. After the manner of the young and imaginative when in the white fire of emotion, he began dramatising scenes between Carroll and himself. He saw them plainly. He heard the sound of his own voice as he rehearsed the arguments which should break her resolution. A woman's duty to her own soul; her obligation toward the man she could make or mar by her love; her self-respect; the necessity of a break some time; the advantage of having the crisis over with now rather than later; a belief in the ultimate good even to Mrs. Bishop of throwing that lady more on her own resources; and so forth and so on down a list of arguments obvious enough or trivial enough, but all inspired by the soul of fervour, all ennobled by the spirit of truth that lies back of the major premise that a woman should cleave to a man, forsaking all others. Orde sat back in his chair, his eyes vacant, his pen all but falling from his hand. He did not finish the letter to his mother. After a while he went upstairs to his own room.

The fever of the argument coursed through his veins all that long night. Over and over again he rehearsed it in wearisome repetition until it had assumed a certain and almost invariable form. And when he had reached the end of his pleading he began it over again, until the daylight found him weary and fevered. He arose and dressed himself. He could eat no breakfast. By a tremendous effort of the will he restrained himself from going over to Ninth Street until the middle of the morning.

He entered the drawing-room to find her seated at the piano. His heart bounded, and for an instant he stood still, summoning his forces to the struggle for which he had so painfully gathered his ammunition. She did not look up as he approached until he stood almost at her shoulder. Then she turned to him and held out both her hands.

"It is no use, Jack," she said. "I care for you too much. I will marry you whenever you say."

Orde left that evening early. This was at Carroll's request. She preferred herself to inform her family of the news.

"I don't know yet how mother is going to get along," said she. "Come back to-morrow afternoon and see them all."

The next morning Orde, having at last finished and despatched the letter to his mother, drifted up the avenue and into the club. As he passed the smoking room he caught sight of Gerald seated in an armchair by the window. He entered the room and took a seat opposite the young fellow.

Gerald held out his hand silently, which the other took.

"I'm glad to hear it," said Gerald at last. "Very glad. I told you I was on your side." He hesitated, then went on gravely: "Poor Carroll is having a hard time, though. I think it's worse than she expected. It's no worse than I expected. You are to be one of the family, so I am going to give you a piece of advice. It's something, naturally, I wouldn't speak of otherwise. But Carroll is my only sister, and I want her to be happy. I think you are the man to make her so, but I want you to avoid one mistake. Fight it out right now, and never give back the ground you win."

"I feel that," replied Orde quietly.

"Mother made father resign from the army; and while he's a dear old boy, he's never done anything since. She holds me—although I see through her—possibly because I'm weak or indifferent, possibly because I have a silly idea I can make a bad situation better by hanging around. She is rapidly turning Kendrick into a sullen little prig, because he believes implicitly all the grievances against the world and the individual she pours out to him. You see, I have no illusions concerning my family. Only Carroll has held to her freedom of soul, because that's the joyous, free, sweet nature of her, bless her! For the first time she's pitted her will against mother's, and it's a bad clash."

"Your mother objected?" asked Orde.

Gerald laughed a little bitterly. "It was very bad," said he. "You've grown horns, hoofs, and a tail overnight. There's nothing too criminal to have escaped your notice. I have been forbidden to consort with you. So has the general. The battle of last night had to do with your coming to the house at all. As it is not Carroll's house, naturally she has no right to insist."

"I shall not be permitted to see her?" cried Orde.

"I did not say that. Carroll announced then quite openly that she would see you outside. I fancy that was the crux of the matter. Don't you see? The whole affair shifted ground. Carroll has offered direct disobedience. Oh, she's a bully little fighter!" he finished in admiring accents. "You can't quite realise what she's doing for your sake; she's not only fighting mother, but her own heart."

Orde found a note at the hotel, asking him to be in Washington Square at half-past two.

Carroll met him with a bright smile.

"Things aren't quite right at home," she said. "It is a great shock to poor mother at first, and she feels very strongly. Oh, it isn't you, dear; it's the notion that I can care for anybody but her. You see, she's been used to the other idea so long that I suppose it seemed a part of the universe to her. She'll get used to it after a little, but it takes time."

Orde examined her face anxiously. Two bright red spots burned on her cheeks; her eyes flashed with a nervous animation, and a faint shade had sketched itself beneath them.

"You had a hard time," he murmured, "you poor dear!"

She smiled up at him.

"We have to pay for the good things in life, don't we, dear? And they are worth it. Things will come right after a little. We must not be too impatient. Now, let's enjoy the day. The park isn't so bad, is it?"

At five o'clock Orde took her back to her doorstep, where he left her.

This went on for several days.

At the end of that time Orde could not conceal from himself that the strain was beginning to tell. Carroll's worried expression grew from day to day, while the animation that characterised her manner when freed from the restraint became more and more forced. She was as though dominated by some inner tensity, which she dared not relax even for a moment. To Orde's questionings she replied as evasively as she could, assuring him always that matters were going as well as she had expected; that mother was very difficult; that Orde must have patience, for things would surely come all right. She begged him to remain quiescent until she gave him the word; and she implored it so earnestly that Orde, though he chafed, was forced to await the turn of events. Every afternoon she met him, from two to five. The situation gave little opportunity for lovers' demonstrations. She seemed entirely absorbed by the inner stress of the struggle she was going through, so that hardly did she seem able to follow coherently even plans for the future. She appeared, however, to gain a mysterious refreshment from Orde's mere proximity; so gradually he, with that streak of almost feminine intuition which is the especial gift to lovers, came to the point of sitting quite silent with her, clasping her hand out of sight of the chance passer-by. When the time came to return, they arose and walked back to Ninth Street, still in silence. At the door they said good-bye. He kissed her quite soberly.

"I wish I could help, sweetheart," said he.

She shook her head at him.

"You do help," she replied.

From Gerald at the club, Orde sought more intimate news of what was going on. For several days, however, the young man absented himself from his usual haunts. It was only at the end of the week that Orde succeeded in finding him.

"No," Gerald answered his greeting, "I haven't been around much. I've been sticking pretty close home."

Little by little, Orde's eager questions drew out the truth of the situation. Mrs. Bishop had shut herself up in a blind and incredible obstinacy, whence she sallied with floods of complaints, tears, accusations, despairs, reproaches, vows, hysterics—all the battery of the woman misunderstood, but in which she refused to listen to a consecutive conversation. If Carroll undertook to say anything, the third word would start her mother off into one of her long and hysterical tirades. It was very wearing, and there seemed to be nothing gained from day to day. Her child had disobeyed her. And as a climax, she had assumed the impregnable position of a complete prostration, wherein she demanded the minute care of an invalid in the crisis of a disorder. She could bear no faintest ray of illumination, no lightest footfall. In a hushed twilight she lay, her eyes swathed, moaning feebly that her early dissolution at the hands of ingratitude was imminent. Thus she established a deadlock which was likely to continue indefinitely. The mere mention of the subject nearest Carroll's heart brought the feeble complaint:

"Do you want to kill me?"

The only scrap of victory to be snatched from this stricken field was the fact that Carroll insisted on going to meet her lover every afternoon. The invalid demanded every moment of her time, either for personal attendance or in fulfilment of numerous and exacting church duties. An attempt, however, to encroach thus on the afternoon hours met a stone wall of resolution on Carroll's part.

This was the situation Orde gathered from his talk with Gerald. Though he fretted under the tyranny exacted, he could see nothing which could relieve the situation save his own withdrawal. He had already long over-stayed his visit; important affairs connected with his work demanded his attention, he had the comfort of Carroll's love assured; and the lapse of time alone could be depended on to change Mrs. Bishop's attitude, a consummation on which Carroll seemed set. Although Orde felt all the lively dissatisfaction natural to a newly accepted lover who had gained slight opportunity for favours, for confidences, even for the making of plans, nevertheless he could see for the present nothing else to do.

The morning after he had reached this conclusion he again met Gerald at the gymnasium. That young man, while as imperturbable and languid in movement as ever, concealed an excitement. He explained nothing until the two, after a shower and rub-down, were clothing themselves leisurely in the empty couch-room.

"Orde," said Gerald suddenly, "I'm worried about Carroll."

Orde straightened his back and looked steadily at Gerald, but said nothing.

"Mother has commenced bothering her again. It wasn't so bad as long as she stuck to daytime, but now she's taken to prowling in a dozen times a night. I hear their voices for an hour or so at a time. I'm afraid it's beginning to wear on Carroll more than you realise."

"Thank you," said Orde briefly.

That afternoon with Carroll he took the affair firmly in hand.

"This thing has come to the point where it must stop," said he, "and I'm going to stop it. I have some rights in the matter of the health and comfort of the girl I love."

"What do you intend to do?" asked Carroll, frightened.

"I shall have it out with your mother," replied Orde.

"You mustn't do that," implored Carroll. "It would do absolutely no good, and would just result in a quarrel that could never be patched up."

"I don't know as I care particularly," said Orde.

"But I do. Think—she is my mother."

Orde stirred uneasily with a mental reservation as to selfishness, but said nothing.

"And think what it means to a girl to be married and go away from home finally without her parent's consent. It's the most beautiful and sacred thing in her life, and she wants it to be perfect. It's worth waiting and fighting a little for. After all, we are both young, and we have known each other such a very short time."

So she pleaded with him, bringing forward all the unanswerable arguments built by the long average experience of the world—arguments which Orde could not refute, but whose falsity to the situation he felt most keenly. He could not specify without betraying Gerald's confidence. Raging inwardly, he consented to a further armistice.

At his hotel he found a telegram. He did not open it until he had reached his own room. It was from home, urging his immediate return for the acceptance of some contracted work.

"To hell with the contracted work!" he muttered savagely, and calling a bell-boy, sent an answer very much to that effect. Then he plunged his hands into his pockets, stretched out his legs, and fell into a deep and gloomy meditation.

He was interrupted by a knock on the door.

"Come in!" he called, without turning his head.

He heard the door open and shut. After a moment he looked around. Kendrick Bishop stood watching him.

Orde lit the gas.

"Hello, Kendrick!" said he. "Sit down." The boy made no reply. Orde looked at him curiously, and saw that he was suffering from an intense excitement. His frame trembled convulsively, his lips were white, his face went red and pale by turns. Evidently he had something to say, but could not yet trust his voice. Orde sat down and waited.

"You've got to let my mother alone," he managed to say finally.

"I have done nothing to your mother, Kendrick," said Orde kindly.

"You've brought her to the point of death," asserted Keudrick violently. "You're hounding her to her grave. You're turning those she loves best against her."

Orde thought to catch the echo of quotation in these words.

"Did your mother send you to me?" he asked.

"If we had any one else worth the name of man in the family, I wouldn't have to come," said Kendrick, almost in the manner of one repeating a lesson.

"What do you want me to do?" asked Orde after a moment of thought.

"Go away," cried Kendrick. "Stop this unmanly contest against a defenceless woman."

"I cannot do that," replied Orde quietly.

Kendrick's face assumed a livid pallor, and his eyes seemed to turn black with excitement. Trembling in every limb, but without hesitation, he advanced on Orde, drew a short riding-whip from beneath his coat, and slashed the young man across the face. Orde made an involuntary movement to arise, but sank back, and looked steadily at the boy. Once again Kendrick hit; raised his arm for the third time; hesitated. His lips writhed, and then, with a sob, he cast the little whip from him and burst from the room.

Orde sat without moving, while two red lines slowly defined themselves across his face. The theatrical quality of the scene and the turgid rhetorical bathos of the boy's speeches attested his youth and the unformed violence of his emotions. Did they also indicate a rehearsal, or had the boy merely been goaded to vague action by implicit belief in a woman's vagaries? Orde did not know, but the incident brought home to him, as nothing else could, the turmoil of that household.

"Poor youngster!" he concluded his reverie, and went to wash his face in hot water.

He had left Carroll that afternoon in a comparatively philosophical and hopeful frame of mind. The next day she came to him with hurried, nervous steps, her usually pale cheeks mounting danger signals of flaming red, her eyes swimming. When she greeted him she choked, and two of the tears overflowed. Quite unmindful of the nursemaids across the square, Orde put his arm comfortingly about her shoulder. She hid her face against his sleeve and began softly to cry.

Orde did not attempt as yet to draw from her the cause of this unusual agitation. A park bench stood between two dense bushes, screened from all directions save one. To this he led her. He comforted her as one comforts a child, stroking clumsily her hair, murmuring trivialities without meaning, letting her emotion relieve itself. After awhile she recovered somewhat her control of herself and sat up away from him, dabbing at her eyes with a handkerchief dampened into a tiny wad. But even after she had shaken her head vigorously at last, and smiled up at him rather tremulously in token that the storm was over, she would not tell him that anything definite had happened to bring on the outburst.

"I just needed you," she said, "that's all. It's just nothing but being a woman, I think. You'll get used to little things like that."

"This thing has got to quit!" said he grimly.

She said nothing, but reached up shyly and touched his face where Kendrick's whip had stung, and her eyes became very tender. A carriage rolled around Washington Arch, and, coming to a stand, discharged its single passenger on the pavement.

"Why, it's Gerald!" cried Carroll, surprised.

The young man, catching sight of them, picked his way daintily and leisurely toward them. He was, as usual, dressed with meticulous nicety, the carnation in his button-hole, the gloss on his hat and shoes, the freshness on his gloves, the correct angle on his stick. His dark, long face with its romantic moustache, and its almost effeminate soft eyes, was as unemotional and wearied as ever. As he approached, he raised his stick slightly by way of salutation.

"I have brought," said he, "a carriage, and I wish you would both do me the favour to accompany me on a short excursion."

Taking their consent for granted, he signalled the vehicle, which rapidly approached.

The three—Carroll and Orde somewhat bewildered—took their seats. During a brief drive, Gerald made conversation on different topics, apparently quite indifferent as to whether or not his companions replied. After an interval the carriage drew up opposite a brown-stone dwelling on a side street. Gerald rang the bell, and a moment later the three were ushered by a discreet and elderly maid into a little square reception-room immediately off the hall. The maid withdrew.

Gerald carefully deposited his top hat on the floor, placed in it his gloves, and leaned his stick against its brim.

"I have brought you here, among other purposes, to hear from me a little brief wisdom drawn from experience and the observation of life," he began, addressing his expectant and curious guests. "That wisdom is briefly this: there comes a time in the affairs of every household when a man must assert himself as the ruler. In all the details he may depend on the woman's judgment, experience, and knowledge, but when it comes to the big crises, where life is deflected into one channel or the other, then, unless the man does the deciding, he is lost for ever, and his happiness, and the happiness of those who depend on him. This is abstruse, but I come to the particular application shortly.

"But moments of decision are always clouded by many considerations. The decision is sure to cut across much that is expedient, much that seems to be necessary, much that is dear. Carroll remembers the case of our own father. The general would have made a name for himself in the army; his wife demanded his retirement; he retired, and his career ended. That was the moment of his decision. It is very easy to say, in view of that simple statement, that the general was weak in yielding to his wife, but a consideration of the circumstances—"

"Why do you say all this?" interrupted Orde.

Gerald raised his hand.

"Believe me, it is necessary, as you will agree when you have heard me through. Mrs. Bishop was in poor health; the general in poor financial circumstances. The doctors said the Riviera. Mrs. Bishop's parents, who were wealthy, furnished the money for her sojourn in that climate. She could not bear to be separated from her husband. A refusal to resign then, a refusal to accept the financial aid offered, would have been cast against him as a reproach—he did not love his wife enough to sacrifice his pride, his ambition, his what-you-will. Nevertheless, that was his moment of decision.

"I could multiply instances, yet it would only accumulate needless proof. My point is that in these great moments a man can afford to take into consideration only the affair itself. Never must he think of anything but the simple elements of the problem—he must ignore whose toes are trodden upon, whose feelings are hurt, whose happiness is apparently marred. For note this: if a man does fearlessly the right thing, I am convinced that in the readjustment all these conflicting interests find themselves bettered instead of injured. You want a concrete instance? I believe firmly that if the general had kept to his army life, and made his wife conform to it, after the storm had passed she would have settled down to a happy existence. I cannot prove it—I believe it."

"This may be all very true, Gerald," said Orde, "but I fail to see why you have brought us to this strange house to tell it."

"In a moment," replied Gerald. "Have patience. Believing that thoroughly, I have come in the last twenty-four hours to a decision. That this happens not to affect my own immediate fortunes does not seem to me to invalidate my philosophy."

He carefully unbuttoned his frock coat, crossed his legs, produced a paper and a package from his inside pocket, and eyed the two before him.

"I have here," he went on suddenly, "marriage papers duly made out; in this package is a plain gold ring; in the next room is waiting, by prearrangement, a very good friend of mine in the clergy. Personally I am at your disposal."

He looked at them expectantly.

"The very thing!" "Oh, no!" cried Orde and Carroll in unison.

Nevertheless, in spite of this divergence of opinion, ten minutes later the three passed through the door into the back apartment—Carroll still hesitant, Orde in triumph, Gerald as correct and unemotional as ever.

In this back room they found waiting a young clergyman conversing easily with two young girls. At the sight of Carroll, these latter rushed forward and overwhelmed her with endearments. Carroll broke into a quickly suppressed sob and clasped them close to her.

"Oh, you dears!" she cried, "I'm so glad you're here!" She flashed a grateful look in Gerald's direction, and a moment later took occasion to press his arm and whisper:

"You've thought of everything! You're the dearest brother in the world!"

Gerald received this calmly, and set about organising the ceremony. In fifteen minutes the little party separated at the front door, amid a chatter of congratulations and good wishes. Mr. and Mrs. Orde entered the cab and drove away.

## XX

"Oh, it IS the best way, dear, after all!" cried Carroll, pressing close to her husband. "A few minutes ago I was all doubts and fears, but now I feel so safe and settled," she laughed happily. "It is as though I had belonged to you always, you old Rock of Gibraltar! and anything that happens now will come from the outside, and not from the inside, won't it, dear?"

"Yes, sweetheart," said Orde.

"Poor mother! I wonder how she'll take it."

"We'll soon know, anyway," replied Orde, a little grimly.

In the hallway of the Bishop house Orde kissed her.

"Be brave, sweetheart," said he, "but remember that now you're my wife."

She nodded at him gravely and disappeared.

Orde sat in the dim parlour for what seemed to be an interminable period. Occasionally the sounds of distant voices rose to his ear and died away again. The front door opened to admit some one, but Orde could not see who it was. Twice a scurrying of feet overhead seemed to indicate the bustle of excitement. The afternoon waned. A faint whiff of cooking, escaping through some carelessly open door, was borne to his nostrils. It grew dark, but the lamps remained unlighted. Finally he heard the rustle of the portieres, and turned to see the dim form of the general standing there.

"Bad business! bad business!" muttered the old man. "It's very hard on me. Perhaps you did the right thing—you must be good to her—but I cannot countenance this affair. It was most high-handed, sir!"

The portieres fell again, and he disappeared.

Finally, after another interval, Carroll returned. She went immediately to the gas-fixture, which she lit. Orde then saw that she was sobbing violently. She came to him, and for a moment hid her face against his breast. He patted her hair, waiting for her to speak. After a little she controlled herself.

"How was it?" asked Orde, then.

She shivered.

"I never knew people could be so cruel," she complained in almost a bewildered manner. "Jack, we must go to-night. She—she has ordered me out of the house, and says she never wants to see my face again." She broke down for a second. "Oh, Jack! she can't mean that. I've always been a good daughter to her. And she's very bitter against Gerald. Oh! I told her it wasn't his fault, but she won't listen. She sent for that odious Mr. Merritt—her rector, you know—and he supported her. I believe he's angry because we did not go to him. Could you believe such a thing! And she's shut herself up in her air of high virtue, and underneath it she's, oh, so angry!"

"Well, it's natural she should be upset," comforted Orde. "Don't think too much of what she does now. Later she'll get over it."

Carroll shivered again.

"You don't know, dear, and I'm not going to tell you. Why," she cried, "she told me that you and I were in a conspiracy to drive her to her grave so we could get her money!"

"She must be a little crazy," said Orde, still pacifically.

"Come, help me," said Carroll. "I must get my things."

574

"Can't you just pack a bag and leave the rest until tomorrow? It's about hungry time."

"She says I must take every stitch belonging to me tonight."

They packed trunks until late that night, quite alone. Gerald had departed promptly after breaking the news, probably without realising to what a pass affairs would come. A frightened servant, evidently in disobedience of orders and in fear of destruction, brought them a tray of food, which she put down on a small table and hastily fled. In a room down the hall they could hear the murmur of voices where Mrs. Bishop received spiritual consolation from her adviser. When the trunks were packed, Orde sent for a baggage waggon. Carroll went silently from place to place, saying farewell to such of her treasures as she had made up her mind to leave. Orde scribbled a note to Gerald, requesting him to pack up the miscellanies and send them to Michigan by freight. The baggage man and Orde carried the trunks downstairs. No one appeared. Carroll and Orde walked together to the hotel. Next morning an interview with Gerald confirmed them in their resolution of immediate departure.

"She is set in her opposition now, and at present she believes firmly that her influence will separate you. Such a state of mind cannot be changed in an hour."

"And you?" asked Carroll.

"Oh, I," he shrugged, "will go on as usual. I have my interests."

"I wish you would come out in our part of the country," ventured Orde.

Gerald smiled his fine smile.

"Good-bye," said he. "Going to a train is useless, and a bore to everybody."

Carroll threw herself on his neck in an access of passionate weeping.

"You WILL write and tell me of everything, won't you?" she begged.

"Of course. There now, good-bye."

Orde followed him into the hall.

"It would be quite useless to attempt another interview?" he inquired.

Gerald made a little mouth.

"I am in the same predicament as yourselves," said he, "and have since nine this morning taken up my quarters at the club. Please do not tell Carroll; it would only pain her."

At the station, just before they passed in to the train, the general appeared.

"There, there!" he fussed. "If your mother should hear of my being here, it would be a very bad business, very bad. This is very sad; but—well, good-bye, dear; and you, sir, be good to her. And write your daddy, Carroll. He'll be lonesome for you." He blew his nose very loudly and wiped his glasses. "Now, run along, run along," he hurried them. "Let us not have any scenes. Here, my dear, open this envelope when you are well started. It may help cheer the journey. Not a word!"

He hurried them through the gate, paying no heed to what they were trying to say. Then he steamed away and bustled into a cab without once looking back.

When the train had passed the Harlem River and was swaying its uneven way across the open country, Carroll opened the envelope. It contained a check for a thousand dollars.

"Dear old daddy!" she murmured. "Our only wedding present!"

"You are the capitalist of the family," said Orde. "You don't know how poor a man you've married. I haven't much more than the proverbial silver watch and bad nickel."

She reached out to press his hand in reassurance. He compared it humorously with his own.

"What a homely, knotted, tanned old thing it is by yours," said he.

"It's a strong hand," she replied soberly, "it's a dear hand." Suddenly she snatched it up and pressed it for a fleeting instant against her cheek, looking at him half ashamed.

## XXI

The winter months were spent at Monrovia, where Orde and his wife lived for a time at the hotel. This was somewhat expensive, but Orde was not quite ready to decide on a home, and he developed unexpected opposition to living at Redding in the Orde homestead.

"No, I've been thinking about it," he told Grandma Orde. "A young couple should start out on their own responsibility. I know you'd be glad to have us, but I think it's better the other way. Besides, I must be at Monrovia a good deal of the time, and I want Carroll with me. She can make you a good long visit in the spring, when I have to go up river."

To this Grandma Orde, being a wise old lady, had to nod her assent, although she would much have liked her son near her.

At Monrovia, then, they took up their quarters. Carroll soon became acquainted with the life of the place. Monrovia, like most towns of its sort and size, consisted of an upper stratum of mill owners and lumber operators, possessed of considerable wealth, some cultivation, and definite social ideas; a gawky, countrified, middle estate of storekeepers, catering both to the farm and local trade and the lumber mill operatives, generally of Holland extraction, who dwelt in simple unpainted board shanties. The class first mentioned comprised a small coterie, among whom Carroll soon found two or three congenials—Edith Fuller, wife of the young cashier in the bank; Valerie Cathcart, whose husband had been killed in the Civil War; Clara Taylor, wife of the leading young lawyer of the village; and, strangely enough, Mina Heinzman, the sixteen-year-old daughter of old Heinzman, the lumberman. Nothing was more indicative of the absolute divorce of business and social life than the unbroken evenness of Carroll's friendship for the younger girl. Though later the old German and Orde locked in serious struggle on the river, they continued to meet socially quite as usual; and the daughter of one and the wife of the other never suspected anything out of the ordinary. This impersonality of struggle has always been characteristic of the pioneer business man's good-nature.

Newmark received the news of his partner's sudden marriage without evincing any surprise, but with a sardonic gleam in one corner of his eye. He called promptly, conversed politely for a half hour, and then took his leave.

"How do you like him?" asked Orde, when he had gone.

"He looks like a very shrewd man," replied Carroll, picking her words for fear of saying the wrong thing.

Orde laughed.

"You don't like him," he stated.

"I don't dislike him," said Carroll. "I've not a thing against him. But we could never be in the slightest degree sympathetic. He and I don't—don't—"

"Don't jibe," Orde finished for her. "I didn't much think you would. Joe never was much of a society bug." It was on the tip of Carroll's tongue to reply that "society bugs" were not the only sort she could appreciate, but she refrained. She had begun to realise the extent of her influence over her husband's opinion.

Newmark did not live at the hotel. Early in the fall he had rented a small one-story house situated just off Main Street, set well back from the sidewalk among clumps of oleanders. Into this he retired as a snail into its shell. At first he took his meals at the hotel, but later he imported an impassive, secretive man-servant, who took charge of him completely. Neither master nor man made any friends, and in fact rebuffed all advances. One Sunday, Carroll and Orde, out for a walk, passed this quaint little place, with its picket fence.

"Let's go in and return Joe's call," suggested Orde.

Their knock at the door brought the calm valet.

"Mr. Newmark is h'out, sir," said he. "Yes, sir, I'll tell him that you called."

They turned away. As they sauntered down the little brick-laid walk, Carroll suddenly pressed close to her husband's arm.

"Jack," she begged, "I want a little house like that, for our very own."

"We can't afford it, sweetheart."

"Not to own," she explained, "just to rent. It will be next best to having a home of our own."

"We'd have to have a girl, dear," said Orde, "and we can't even afford that, yet."

"A girl!" cried Carroll indignantly. "For us two!"

"You couldn't do the housework and the cooking," said Orde. "You've never done such a thing in your life, and I won't have my little girl slaving."

"It won't be slaving, it will be fun—just like play-housekeeping," protested Carroll. "And I've got to learn some time. I was brought up most absurdly, and I realise it now."

"We'll see," said Orde vaguely.

The subject was dropped for the time being. Later Carroll brought it up again. She was armed with several sheets of hotel stationery, covered with figures showing how much cheaper it would be to keep house than to board.

"You certainly make out a strong case—on paper," laughed Orde. "If you buy a rooster and a hen, and she raises two broods, at the end of a year you'll have twenty-six; and if they all breed—even allowing half roosters—you'll have over three hundred; and if they all breed, you'll have about thirty-five hundred; and if—"

"Stop! stop!" cried Carroll, covering her ears.

"All right," agreed Orde equably, "but that's the way it figures. Funny the earth isn't overrun with chickens, isn't it?"

She thrust her tables of figures into her desk drawer. "You're just making fun of me always," she said reproachfully.

Two days later Orde took her one block up the street to look at a tiny little house tucked on a fifty-foot lot beneath the shadow of the church.

"It's mighty little," said he. "I'll have to go out in the hall to change my collar, and we couldn't have more than two people at a time to call on us."

"It's a dear!" said she, "and I'm not so e-nor-mous myself, whatever YOU may be."

They ended by renting the little house, and Carroll took charge of it delightedly. What difficulties she overcame, and what laughable and cryable mistakes she made only those who have encountered a like situation could realise. She learned fast, however, and took a real pride in her tiny box of a home. A piano was, of course, out of the question, but the great golden harp occupied one corner, or rather one side, of the parlour. Standing thus enshrouded in its covering, it rather resembled an august and tremendous veiled deity. To Carroll's great delight, Orde used solemnly to go down on all fours and knock his forehead thrice on the floor before it when he entered the house at evening. When the very cold weather came and they had to light the base-burner stove, which Orde stoutly maintained occupied all the other half of the parlour, the harp's delicate constitution necessitated its standing in the hall. Nevertheless, Carroll had great comfort from it. While Orde was away at the office, she whispered through its mellow strings her great happiness, the dreams for her young motherhood which would come in the summer, the vague and lingering pain over the hapless but beloved ones she had left behind her in her other life. Then she arose refreshed, and went about the simple duties of her tiny domain.

The winter was severe. All the world was white. The piles of snow along the sidewalks grew until Carroll could hardly look over them. Great fierce winds swept in from the lake. Sometimes Orde and his wife drove two miles to the top of the sand hills, where first they had met in this their present home, and looked out beyond the tumbled shore ice to the steel-gray, angry waters. The wind pricked their faces, and, going home, the sleigh-bells jingled, the snowballs from the horses' hoofs hit against the dash, the cold air seared the inside of their nostrils. When Orde helped Carroll from beneath the warm buffalo robes, she held up to him a face glowing with colour, framed in the soft fluffy fur of a hood.

"You darling!" he cried, and stooped to kiss her smooth, cold cheek.

When he had returned from the stable around the corner, he found the lit lamp throwing its modified light and shade over the little round table. He shook down the base-burner vigorously, thrust several billets of wood in its door, and turned to meet her eyes across the table.

"Kind of fun being married, isn't it?" said he.

"Kind of," she admitted, nodding gravely.

The business of the firm was by now about in shape. All the boom arrangements had been made; the two tugs were in the water and their machinery installed; supplies and equipments were stored away; the foremen of the crews engaged, and the crews themselves pretty well picked out. Only there needed to build the wanigan, and to cart in the supplies for the upper river works before the spring break-up and the almost complete disappearance of the roads. Therefore, Orde had the good fortune of unusual leisure to enjoy these first months with his bride. They entered together the Unexplored Country, and found it more wonderful than they had dreamed. Almost before they knew it, January and February had flown.

"We must pack up, sweetheart," said Orde.

"It's only yesterday that we came," she cried regretfully.

They took the train for Redding, were installed in the gable room, explored together for three days the delights of the old-fashioned house, the spicy joys of Grandma Orde's and Amanda's cookery, the almost adoring adulation of the old folks. Then Orde packed his "turkey," assumed his woods clothes, and marched off down the street carrying his bag on his back.

"He looks like an old tramp in that rig," said Grandma Orde, closing the storm door.

"He looks like a conqueror of wildernesses!" cried Carroll, straining her eyes after his vanishing figure. Suddenly she darted after him, calling in her high, bird-like tones. He turned and came back to her. She clasped him by the shoulders, reluctant to let him go.

"Good-bye," she said at last. "You'll take better care of my sweetheart than you ever did of Jack Orde, won't you, dear?"

## XXII

Orde had reconnoitred the river as a general reconnoitres his antagonist, and had made his dispositions as the general disposes of his army, his commissary, his reserves. At this point five men could keep the river clear; at that rapid it would require twenty; there a dozen would suffice for ordinary contingencies, and yet an emergency might call for thirty—those thirty must not be beyond reach. In his mind's eye he apportioned the sections of the upper river. Among the remoter wildernesses every section must have its driving camp. The crews of each, whether few or many, would be expected to keep clear and running their own "beats" on the river. As far as the rear crew should overtake these divisions, either it would absorb them or the members of them would be thrown forward beyond the lowermost beat, to take charge of a new division down stream. When the settled farm country or the little towns were reached, many of the driving camps would become unnecessary; the men could be boarded out at farms lying in their beats. A continual advance would progress toward the Lake, the drive crews passing and repassing each other like pigeons in the sown fields. Each of these sections would be in charge of a foreman, whose responsibility ceased with the delivery of the logs to the men next below. A walking boss would trudge continually the river trail, or ride the logs down stream, holding the correlation of these many units. Orde himself would drive up and down the river, overseeing the whole plan of campaign, throwing the camps forward, concentrating his forces here, spreading them elsewhere, keeping accurately in mind the entire situation so that he could say with full confidence: "Open Dam Number One for three hours at nine o'clock; Dam Number Two for two hours and a half at ten thirty," and so on down the line; sure that the flood waters thus released would arrive at the right moment, would supplement each other, and would so space themselves as to accomplish the most work with the least waste. In that one point more than in any other showed the expert. The water was his ammunition, a definite and limited quantity of it. To "get the logs out with the water" was the last word of praise to be said for the river driver. The more logs, the greater the glory.

Thus it can readily be seen, this matter was rather a campaign than a mere labour, requiring the men, the munitions, the organisation, the tactical ability, the strategy, the resourcefulness, the boldness, and the executive genius of a military commander.

To all these things, and to the distribution of supplies and implements among the various camps, Orde had attended. The wanigan for the rear crew was built. The foremen and walking boss had been picked out. Everything was in readiness. Orde was satisfied with the situation except that he found himself rather short-handed. He had counted on three hundred men for his crews, but scrape and scratch as he would, he was unable to gather over two hundred and fifty. This matter was not so serious, however, as later, when the woods camps should break up, he would be able to pick up more workmen.

"They won't be rivermen like my old crew, though," said Orde regretfully to Tom North, the walking boss. "I'd like to steal a few from some of those Muskegon outfits."

Until the logs should be well adrift, Orde had resolved to boss the rear crew himself.

As the rear was naturally the farthest up stream, Orde had taken also the contract to break the rollways belonging to Carlin, which in the season's work would be piled up on the bank. Thus he could get to work immediately at the break-up, and without waiting for some one else. The seven or eight million feet of lumber comprised in Carlin's drive would keep the men below busy until the other owners, farther down and up the tributaries, should also have put their season's cut afloat.

The ice went out early, to Orde's satisfaction. As soon as the river ran clear in its lower reaches he took his rear crew in to Carlin's rollways.

This crew was forty in number, and had been picked from the best—a hard-bitten, tough band of veterans, weather beaten, scarred in numerous fights or by the backwoods scourge of small-pox, compact, muscular, fearless, loyal, cynically aloof from those not of their cult, out-spoken and free to criticise—in short, men to do great things under the strong leader, and to mutiny at the end of three days under the weak. They piled off the train at Sawyer's, stamped their feet on the board platform of the station, shouldered their "turkeys," and straggled off down the tote-road. It was an eighteen-mile walk in. The ground had loosened its frost. The footing was ankle-deep in mud and snow-water.

Next morning, bright and early, the breaking of the rollways began. During the winter the logs had been hauled down ice roads to the river, where they were "banked" in piles twenty, and even thirty, feet in height. The bed of the stream itself was filled with them for a mile, save in a narrow channel left down through the middle to allow for some flow of water; the banks were piled with them, side on, ready to roll down at the urging of the men.

First of all, the entire crew set itself, by means of its peavies, to rolling the lower logs into the current, where they were rapidly borne away. As the waters were now at flood, this was a quick and easy labour. Occasionally some tiers would be stuck together by ice, in which case considerable prying and heaving was necessary in order to crack them apart. But forty men, all busily at work, soon had the river full. Orde detailed some six or eight to drop below in order that the river might run clear to the next section, where the next crew would take up the task. These men, quite simply, walked to the edges of the rollway, rolled a log apiece into the water, stepped aboard, leaned against their peavies, and were swept away by the swift current. The logs on which they stood whirled in the eddies, caromed against other timbers, slackened speed, shot away; never did the riders alter their poses of easy equilibrium. From time to time one propelled his craft ashore by hooking to and pushing against other logs. There he stood on some prominent point, leaning his chin contemplatively against the thick shaft of his peavy, watching the endless procession of the logs drifting by. Apparently he was idle, but in reality his eyes missed no shift of the ordered ranks. When a slight hitch or pause, a subtle change in the pattern of the brown carpet caught his attention, he sprang into life. Balancing his peavy across his body, he made his way by short dashes to the point of threatened congestion. There, working vigorously, swept down stream with the mass, he pulled, hauled, and heaved, forcing the heavy, reluctant timbers from the cohesion that threatened trouble later. Oblivious to his surroundings, he wrenched and pried desperately. The banks of the river drifted by. Point succeeded point, as though withdrawn up stream by some invisible manipulator. The river appeared stationary, the banks in motion. Finally he heard at his elbow the voice of the man stationed below him, who had run out from his own point.

"Hullo, Bill," he replied to this man, "you old slough hog! Tie into this this!"

"All the time!" agreed Bill cheerfully.

In a few moments the danger was averted, the logs ran free. The rivermen thereupon made their uncertain way back to shore, where they took the river trail up stream again to their respective posts.

At noon they ate lunches they had brought with them in little canvas bags, snatched before they left the rollways from a supply handy by the cook. In the meantime the main crew were squatting in the lea of the brush, devouring a hot meal which had been carried to them in wooden boxes strapped to the backs of the chore boys. Down the river and up its tributaries other crews, both in the employ of Newmark and Orde and of others, were also pausing from their cold and dangerous toil. The river, refreshed after its long winter, bent its mighty back to the great annual burden laid upon it.

By the end of the second day the logs actually in the bed of the stream had been shaken loose, and a large proportion of them had floated entirely from sight. It now became necessary to break down the rollways piled along the tops of the banks.

The evening of this day, however, Orde received a visit from Jim Denning, the foreman of the next section below, bringing with him Charlie, the cook of Daly's last year's drive. Leaving him by the larger fire, Jim Denning drew his principal one side.

"This fellow drifted in to-night two days late after a drunk, and he tells an almighty queer story," said he. "He says a crew of bad men from the Saginaw, sixty strong, have been sent in by Heinzman. He says Heinzman hired them to come over not to work, but just to fight and annoy us."

"That so?" said Orde. "Well, where are they?"

"Don't know. But he sticks by his story, and tells it pretty straight."

"Bring him over, and let's hear it," said Orde.

"Hullo, Charlie!" he greeted the cook when the latter stood before him. "What's this yarn Jim's telling me?"

"It's straight, Mr. Orde," said the cook. "There's a big crew brought in from the Saginaw Waters to do you up. They're supposed to be over here to run his drive, but really they're goin' to fight and raise hell. For why would he want sixty men to break out them little rollways of his'n up at the headwaters?"

"Is that where they've gone?" asked Orde like a flash.

"Yes, sir. And he only owns a 'forty' up there, and it ain't more'n half cut, anyway."

"I didn't know he owned any."

"Yes, sir. He bought that little Johnson piece last winter. I been workin' up there with a little two-horse crew since January. We didn't put up more'n a couple hundred thousand."

"Is he breaking out his rollways below?" Orde asked Denning.

"No, sir," struck in Charlie, "he ain't."

"How do you happen to be so wise?" inquired Orde, "Seems to me you know about as much as old man Solomon."

"Well," explained Charlie, "you see it's like this. When I got back from the woods last week, I just sort of happened into McNeill's place. I wasn't drinkin' a drop!" he cried virtuously, in answer to Orde's smile.

"Of course not," said Orde. "I was just thinking of the last time we were in there together."

"That's just it!" cried Charlie. "They was always sore at you about that. Well, I was lyin' on one of those there benches back of the 'Merican flags in the dance hall 'cause I was very sleepy, when in blew old man Heinzman and McNeill himself. I just lay low for black ducks and heard their talk. They took a look around, but didn't see no one, so they opened her up wide."

"What did you hear?" asked Orde.

"Well, McNeill he agreed to get a gang of bad ones from the Saginaw to run in on the river, and I heard Heinzman tell him to send 'em in to headwaters. And McNeill said, 'That's all right about the cash, Mr. Heinzman, but I been figgerin' on gettin' even with Orde for some myself.'"

"Is that all?" inquired Orde.

"That's about all," confessed Charlie.

"How do you know he didn't hire them to carry down his drive for him? He'd need sixty men for his lower rollways, and maybe they weren't all to go to headwaters?" asked Orde by way of testing Charlie's beliefs.

"He's payin' them four dollars a day," replied Charlie simply. "Now, who'd pay that fer just river work?"

Orde nodded at Jim Denning.

"Hold on, Charlie," said he. "Why are you giving all this away if you were working for Heinzman?"

"I'm working for you now," replied Charlie with dignity. "And, besides, you helped me out once yourself."

"I guess it's a straight tip all right," said Orde to Denning, when the cook had resumed his place by the fire.

"That's what I thought. That's why I brought him up."

"If that crew's been sent in there, it means only one thing at that end of the line," said Orde.

"Sure. They're sent up to waste out the water in the reservoir and hang this end of the drive," replied Denning.

"Correct," said Orde. "The old skunk knows his own rollways are so far down stream that he's safe, flood water or no flood water."

A pause ensued, during which the two smoked vigorously.

"What are you going to do about it?" asked Denning at last.

"What would you do?" countered Orde.

"Well," said Denning slowly, and with a certain grim joy, "I don't bet those Saginaw river-pigs are any more two-fisted than the boys on this river. I'd go up and clean 'em out."

"Won't do," negatived Orde briefly. "In the first place, as you know very well, we're short-handed now, and we can't spare the men from the work. In the second place, we'd hang up sure, then; to go up in that wilderness, fifty miles from civilisation, would mean a first-class row of too big a size to handle. Won't do!"

"Suppose you get a lawyer," suggested Denning sarcastically.

Orde laughed with great good-humour

"Where'd our water be by the time he got an injunction for us?"

He fell into a brown study, during which his pipe went out.

"Jim," he said finally, "it isn't a fair game. I don't know what to do. Delay will hang us; taking men off the work will hang us. I've just got to go up there myself and see what can be done by talking to them."

"Talking to them!" Denning snorted. "You might as well whistle down the draught-pipe of hell! If they're just up there for a row, there'll be whisky in camp; and you can bet McNeill's got some of 'em instructed on YOUR account. They'll kill you, sure!"

"I agree with you it's risky," replied Orde. "I'm scared; I'm willing to admit it. But I don't see what else to do. Of course he's got no rights, but what the hell good does that do us after our water is gone? And Jim, my son, if we hang this drive, I'll be buried so deep I never will dig out. No; I've got to go. You can stay up here in charge of the rear until I get back. Send word by Charlie who's to boss your division while you're gone."

## XXIII

Orde tramped back to Sawyer's early next morning, hitched into the light buckboard the excellent team with which later, when the drive should spread out, he would make his longest jumps, and drove to head-waters. He arrived in sight of the dam about three o'clock. At the edge of the clearing he pulled up to survey the scene.

A group of three small log-cabins marked the Johnson, and later the Heinzman, camp. From the chimneys a smoke arose. Twenty or thirty rivermen lounged about the sunny side of the largest structure. They had evidently just arrived, for some of their "turkeys" were still piled outside the door. Orde clucked to his horses, and the spidery wheels of the buckboard swung lightly over the wet hummocks of the clearing, to come to a stop opposite the men. Orde leaned forward against his knees.

"Hullo, boys!" said he cheerfully.

No one replied, though two or three nodded surlily. Orde looked them over with some interest.

They were a dirty, unkempt, unshaven, hard-looking lot, with bloodshot eyes, a flicker of the dare-devil in expression, beyond the first youth, hardened into an enduring toughness of fibre—bad men from the Saginaw, in truth, and, unless Orde was mistaken, men just off a drunk, and therefore especially dangerous; men eager to fight at the drop of the hat, or sooner, to be accommodating, and ready to employ in their assaults all the formidable and terrifying weapons of the rough-and-tumble; reckless, hard, irreverrent, blasphemous, to be gained over by no words, fair or foul; absolutely scornful of any and all institutions imposed on them by any other but the few men whom they acknowledged as their leaders. And to master these men's respect there needed either superlative strength, superlative recklessness, or superlative skill.

"Who's your boss?" asked Orde.

"The Rough Red," growled one of the men without moving.

Orde had heard of this man, of his personality and his deeds. Like Silver Jack of the Muskegon, his exploits had been celebrated in song. A big, broad-faced man, with a red beard, they had told him, with little, flickering eyes, a huge voice that bellowed through the woods in a torrent of commands and imprecations, strong as a bull, and savage as a wild beast. A hint of his quality will suffice from the many stories circulated about him. It was said that while jobbing for Morrison and Daly, in some of that firm's Saginaw Valley holdings, the Rough Red had discovered that a horse had gone lame. He called the driver of that team before him, seized an iron starting bar, and with it broke the man's leg. "Try th' lameness yourself, Barney Mallan," said he. To appeal to the charity of such a man would be utterly useless. Orde saw this point. He picked up his reins and spoke to his team.

But before the horses had taken three steps, a huge riverman had planted himself squarely in the way. The others rising, slowly surrounded the rig.

"I don't know what you're up here for," growled the man at the horses' heads, "but you wanted to see the boss, and I guess you'd better see him."

"I intend to see him," said Orde sharply. "Get out of the way and let me hitch my team."

He drove deliberately ahead, forcing the man to step aside, and stopped his horses by a stub. He tied them there and descended, to lean his back also against the log walls of the little house.

After a few moments a huge form appeared above the river bank at some forty rods' distance.

"Yonder he comes now," vouchsafed the man nearest Orde.

Orde made out the great square figure of the boss, his soft hat, his flaming red beard, his dingy mackinaw coat, his dingy black-and-white checked flannel shirt, his dingy blue trousers tucked into high socks, and, instead of driving boots, his ordinary lumberman's rubbers. As a spot of colour, he wore a flaming red knit sash, with tassels. Before he had approached near enough to be plainly distinguishable, he began to bellow at the men, commanding them, with a mighty array of oaths, to wake up and get the sluice-gate open. In a moment or so he had disappeared behind some bushes that intervened in his approach to the house. His course through them could be traced by the top of his cap, which just showed above them. In a moment he thrust through the brush and stood before Orde.

For a moment he stared at the young man, and then, with a wild Irish yell, leaped upon him. Orde, caught unawares and in an awkward position, was hardly able even to struggle against the gigantic riverman. Indeed, before he had recovered his faculties to the point of offering determined resistance, he was pinned back against the wall by his shoulders, and the Rough Red's face was within two feet of his own.

"And how are ye, ye ould darlint?" shouted the latter, with a roll of oaths.

"Why, Jimmy Bourke!" cried Orde, and burst into a laugh.

The Rough Red jerked him to his feet, delivered a bear hug that nearly crushed his ribs, and pounded him mightily on the back.

"You ould snoozer!" he bellowed. "Where the blankety blank in blank did you come from? Byes," he shouted to the men, "it's me ould boss on th' Au Sable six year back—that time, ye mind, whin we had th' ice jam! Glory be! but I'm glad to see ye!"

Orde was still laughing.

"I didn't know you'd turned into the Rough Red, Jimmy," said he. "I don't believe we were either of us old enough for whiskers then, were we?"

The Rough Red grinned.

"Thrue for ye!" said he. "And what have ye been doing all these years?"

"That's just it, Jimmy," said Orde, drawing the giant one side, out of ear-shot. "All my eggs are in one basket, and it's a mean trick of you to hire out for filthy lucre to kick that basket."

"What do ye mane?" asked the Rough Red, fixing his twinkling little eyes on Orde.

"You don't mean to tell me," countered Orde, glancing down at the other's rubber-shod feet, "that this crew has been sent up here just to break out those measly little rollways?"

"Thim?" said the Rough Red. "Thim? Hell, NO! Thim's my bodyguard. They can lick their weight in wild cats, and I'd loike well to see the gang of highbankers that infists this river thry to pry thim out. We weren't sint here to wurrk; we were sint here to foight."

"Fight? Why?" asked Orde.

"Oh, I dunno," replied the Rough Red easily. "Me boss and the blank of a blank blanked blank that's attimptin' to droive this river has some sort of a row."

"Jimmy," said Orde, "didn't you know that I am the gentleman last mentioned?"

"What!"

"I'm driving this river, and that's my dam-keeper you've got hid away somewhere here, and that's my water you're planning to waste!"

"What?" repeated the Rough Red, but in a different tone of voice.

"That's right," said Orde.

In a tone of vast astonishment, the Rough Red mentioned his probable deserts in the future life.

"Luk here, Jack," said he after a moment, "here's a crew of white-water birlers that ye can't beat nowheres. What do you want us to do? We're now gettin' four dollars a day AN' board from that murderin' ould villain, Heinzman, SO WE CAN AFFORD TO WURRK FOR YOU CHEAP."

Orde hesitated.

"Oh, please do now, darlint!" wheedled the Rough Red, his little eyes agleam with mischief. "Sind us some oakum and pitch and we'll caulk yure wanigan for ye. Or maybe some more peavies, and we'll hilp ye on yure rollways. And till us, afore ye go, how ye want this dam, and that's the way she'll be. Come, now, dear! and ain't ye short-handed now?"

Orde slapped his knee and laughed.

"This is sure one hell of a joke!" he cried.

"And ain't it now?" said the Rough Red, smiling with as much ingratiation as he was able.

"I'll take you boys on," said Orde at last, "at the usual wages—dollar and a half for the jam, three for the rear. I doubt if you'll see much of Heinzman's money when this leaks out."

## XXIV

Thus Orde, by the sheer good luck that sometimes favours men engaged in large enterprises, not only frustrated a plan likely to bring failure to his interests, but filled up his crews. It may be remarked here, as well as later, that the "terrors of the Saginaw" stayed with the drive to its finish, and proved reliable and tractable in every particular. Orde scattered them judiciously, so there was no friction with the local men. The Rough Red he retained on the rear.

Here the breaking of the rollways had reached a stage more exciting both to onlooker and participant than the mere opening of the river channel. Huge stacks of logs piled sidewise to the bank lined the stream for miles. When the lowermost log on the river side was teased and pried out, the upper tiers were apt to cascade down with a roar, a crash, and a splash. The man who had done the prying had to be very quick-eyed, very cool, and very agile to avoid being buried under the tons of timber that rushed down on him. Only the most reliable men were permitted at this initial breaking down. Afterwards the crew rolled in what logs remained.

The Rough Red's enormous strength, dare-devil spirit, and nimbleness of body made him invaluable at this dangerous work. Orde, too, often took a hand in some of the more ticklish situations. In old days, before he had attained the position of responsibility that raised the value of his time beyond manual work, he had been one of the best men on the river at breaking bank rollways. A slim, graceful, handsome boy of twenty, known as "Rollway Charlie," also distinguished himself by the quickness and certainty of his work. Often the men standing near lost sight of him entirely in the spray, the confusion, the blur of the breaking rollways, until it seemed certain he must have perished. Nevertheless, always he appeared at right or left, sometimes even on a log astream, nonchalant, smiling, escaped easily from the destructive power he had loosed. Once in the stream the logs ran their appointed course, watched by the men who herded them on their way. And below, from the tributaries, from the other rollways a never-ending procession of recruits joined this great brown army on its way to the lake, until for miles and miles the river was almost a solid mass of logs.

The crews on the various beats now had their hands full to keep the logs running. The slightest check at any one point meant a jam, for there was no way of stopping the unending procession. The logs behind floated gently against the obstruction and came to rest. The brown mass thickened. As far as the eye could reach the surface of the water was concealed. And then, as the slow pressure developed from the three or four miles of logs forced against each other by the pushing of the current, the breast of the jam began to rise. Timbers up-ended, crossed, interlocked, slid one over the other, mounted higher and higher in the formidable game of jack-straws the loss of which spelled death to the players.

Immediately, and with feverish activity, the men nearest at hand attacked the work. Logs on top they tumbled and rolled into the current below. Men beneath the breast tugged and pried in search of the key logs causing all the trouble. Others "flattened out the wings," hoping to get a "draw" around the ends. As the stoppage of the drive indicated to the men up and down stream that a jam had formed, they gathered at the scene—those from above over the logs, those from below up the river trail.

Rarely, unless in case of unusual complications, did it take more than a few hours at most to break the jam. The breast of it went out with a rush. More slowly the wings sucked in. Reluctantly the mass floating on the surface for miles up stream stirred, silently moved forward. For a few minutes it was necessary to watch carefully until the flow onward steadied itself, until the congestion had spaced and ordered as before. Then the men moved back to their posts; the drive was resumed. At night the river was necessarily left to its own devices. Rivermen, with the touch of superstition inseparably connected with such affairs, believe implicitly that "logs run free at night." Certainly, though it might be expected that each morning would reveal a big jam to break, such was rarely the case. The logs had usually stopped, to be sure, but generally in so peaceful a situation as easily to be started on by a few minutes' work. Probably this was because they tended to come to rest in the slow, still reaches of the river, through which, in daytime, they would be urged by the rivermen.

Jams on the river, contrary to general belief, are of very common occurrence. Throughout the length of the drive there were probably three or four hang-ups a day. Each of these had to be broken, and in the breaking was danger. The smallest misstep, the least slowness in reading the signs of the break, the slightest lack of promptness in acting on the hint or of agility in leaping from one to the other of the plunging timbers, the faintest flicker from rigid attention to the antagonist crouching on the spring, would mean instant death to the delinquent. Thus it was literally true that each one of these men was called upon almost daily to wager his personal skill against his destruction.

**581**

In the meantime the rear was "sacking" its way as fast as possible, moving camp with the wanigan whenever necessary, working very hard and very cold and very long. In its work, however, beyond the breaking of the rollways, was little of the spectacular.

Orde, after the rear was well started, patrolled the length of the drive in his light buckboard. He had a first-class team of young horses—high-spirited, somewhat fractious, but capable on a pinch of their hundred miles in a day. He handled them well over the rough corduroys and swamp roads. From jam to rear and back again he travelled, pausing on the river banks to converse earnestly with one of the foremen, surveying the situation with the bird's-eye view of the general. At times he remained at one camp for several days watching the trend of the work. The improvements made during the preceding summer gave him the greatest satisfaction, especially the apron at the falls.

"We'd have had a dozen bad jams here before now with all these logs in the river," said he to Tim Nolan, who was in charge of that beat.

"And as it is," said Tim, "we've had but the one little wing jam."

The piers to define the channel along certain shallows also saved the rear crew much labour in the matter of stranded logs. Everything was very satisfactory. Even old man Reed held to his chastened attitude, and made no trouble. In fact, he seemed glad to turn an honest penny by boarding the small crew in charge of sluicing the logs.

No trouble was experienced until Heinzman's rollways were reached. Here Orde had, as he had promised his partner, boomed a free channel to prevent Heinzman from filling up the entire river-bed with his rollways. When the jam of the drive had descended the river as far as this, Orde found that Heinzman had not yet begun to break out. Hardly had Orde's first crew passed, however, when Heinzman's men began to break down the logs into the drive. Long before the rear had caught up, all Heinzman's drive was in the water, inextricably mingled with the sixty or eighty million feet Orde had in charge.

The situation was plain. All Heinzman now had to do was to retain a small crew, which should follow after the rear in order to sack what logs the latter should leave stranded. This amounted practically to nothing. As it was impossible in so great a mass of timbers, and in the haste of a pressing labour, to distinguish or discriminate against any single brand, Heinzman was in a fair way to get his logs sent down stream with practically no expense.

"Vell, my boy," remarked the German quite frankly to Orde as they met on the road one day, "looks like I got you dis time, eh?"

Orde laughed, also with entire good-humour.

"If you mean your logs are going down with ours, why I guess you have. But you paste this in your hat: you're going to keep awful busy, and it's going to cost you something yet to get 'em down."

To Newmark, on one of his occasional visits to the camps, Orde detailed the situation.

"It doesn't amount to much," said he, "except that it complicates matters. We'll make him scratch gravel, if we have to sit up nights and work overtime to do it. We can't injure him or leave his logs, but we can annoy him a lot."

The state of affairs was perfectly well known to the men, and the entire river entered into the spirit of the contest. The drivers kept a sharp lookout for "H" logs, and whenever possible thrust them aside into eddies and backwaters. This, of course, merely made work for the sackers Heinzman had left above the rear. Soon they were in charge of a very fair little drive of their own. Their lot was not enviable. Indeed, only the pressure of work prevented some of the more aggressive of Orde's rear—among whom could be numbered the Rough Red—from going back and "cleaning out" this impertinent band of hangers-on. One day two of the latter, conducting the jam of the miniature drive astern, came within reach of the Rough Red. The latter had lingered in hopes of rescuing his peavy, which had gone overboard. To lose one's peavy is, among rivermen, the most mortifying disgrace. Consequently, the Rough Red was in a fit mood for trouble. He attacked the two single-handed. A desperate battle ensued, which lasted upward of an hour. The two rivermen punched, kicked, and battered the Rough Red in a manner to tear his clothes, deprive him to some extent of red whiskers, bloody his face, cut his shoulder, and knock loose two teeth. The Rough Red, more than the equal of either man singly, had reciprocated in kind. Orde, driving in toward the rear from a detour to avoid a swamp, heard, and descended from his buckboard. Tying his horses to trees, he made his way through the brush to the scene of conflict. So winded and wearied were the belligerents by now that he had no difficulty in separating them. He surveyed their wrecks with a sardonic half smile.

"I call this a draw," said he finally. His attitude became threatening as the two up-river men, recovering somewhat, showed ugly symptoms. "Git!" he commanded. "Scat! I guess you don't know me. I'm Jack Orde. Jimmy and I together could do a dozen of you." He menaced them until, muttering, they had turned away.

"Well, Jimmy," said he humorously, "you look as if you'd been run through a thrashing machine."

"Those fellers make me sick!" growled the Rough Red.

Orde looked him over again.

"You look sick," said he.

When the buckboard drew into camp, Orde sent Bourke away to repair damages while he called the cookee to help unpack several heavy boxes of hardware. They proved to contain about thirty small hatchets, well sharpened, and each with a leather guard. When the rear crew had come in that night, Orde distributed the hatchets.

"Boys," said he, "while you're on the work, I want you all to keep a watch-out for these "H" logs, and whenever you strike one I want you to blaze it plainly, so there won't be any mistake about it."

"What for?" asked one of the Saginaw men as he received his hatchet.

But the riverman who squatted next nudged him with his elbow.

"The less questions you ask Jack, the more answers you'll get. Just do what you're told to on this river and you'll see fun sure."

Three days later the rear crew ran into the head of the pond above Reed's dam. To every one's surprise, Orde called a halt on the work and announced a holiday.

Now, holidays are unknown on drive. Barely is time allowed for eating and sleeping. Nevertheless, all that day the men lay about in complete idleness, smoking, talking, sleeping in the warm sun. The river, silenced by the closed sluice-gates, slept also. The pond filled with logs. From above, the current, aided by a fair wind, was driving down still other logs—the forerunners of the little drive astern. At sight of these, some of the men grumbled. "We're losin' what we made," said they. "We left them logs, and sorted 'em out once already."

Orde sent a couple of axe-men to blaze the newcomers. A little before sundown he ordered the sluice-gates of the dam opened.

"Night work," said the men to one another. They knew, of course, that in sluicing logs, the gate must be open a couple of hours before the sluicing begins in order to fill the river-bed below. Logs run ahead faster than the water spreads.

Sure enough, after supper Orde suddenly appeared among them, the well-known devil of mischief dancing in his eyes and broadening his good-natured face.

"Get organised, boys," said he briskly. "We've got to get this pond all sluiced before morning, and there's enough of us here to hustle it right along."

The men took their places. Orde moved here and there, giving his directions.

"Sluice through everything but the "H" logs," he commanded. "Work them off to the left and leave them."

Twilight, then dark, fell. After a few moments the moon, then just past its full, rose behind the new-budding trees. The sluicing, under the impetus of a big crew, went rapidly.

"I bet there's mighty near a million an hour going through there," speculated Orde, watching the smooth, swift, but burdened waters of the chute.

And in this work the men distinguished easily the new white blaze-marks on Heinzman's logs; so they were able without hesitation to shunt them one side into the smoother water, as Orde had commanded.

About two o'clock the last log shot through.

"Now, boys," said Orde, "tear out the booms."

The chute to the dam was approached, as has been earlier explained, by two rows of booms arranged in a V, or funnel, the apex of which emptied into the sluice-way, and the wide, projecting arms of which embraced the width of the stream. The logs, floating down the pond, were thus concentrated toward the sluice. Also, the rivermen, walking back and forth the length of the booms, were able easily to keep the drive moving.

Now, however, Orde unchained these boom logs. The men pushed them ashore. There as many as could find room on either side the boom-poles clamped in their peavies, and, using these implements as handles, carried the booms some distance back into the woods. Then everybody tramped back and forth, round and about, to confuse the trail. Orde was like a mischievous boy at a school prank. When the last timber had been concealed, he lifted up his deep voice in a roar of joy, in which the crew joined.

"Now let's turn in for a little sleep," said be.

This situation, perhaps a little cloudy in the reader's mind, would have cleared could he have looked out over the dam pond the following morning. The blazed logs belonging to Heinzman, drifting slowly, had sucked down into the corner toward the power canal where, caught against the grating, they had jammed. These logs would have to be floated singly, and pushed one by one against the current across the pond and into the influence of the sluice-gate. Some of them would be hard to come at.

"I guess that will keep them busy for a day or two," commented Orde, as he followed the rear down to where it was sacking below the dam.

This, as Orde had said, would be sufficiently annoying to Heinzman, but would have little real effect on the main issue, which was that the German was getting down his logs with a crew of less than a dozen men. Nevertheless, Orde, in a vast spirit of fun, took delight in inventing and executing practical jokes of the general sort just described. For instance, at one spot where he had boomed the deeper channel from the rocks on either side, he shunted as many of Heinzman's logs as came by handily through an opening he had made in the booms. There they grounded on the shallows—more work for the men following. Many of the logs in charge of the latter, however, catching the free current, overtook the rear, so that the number of the "H" logs in the drive was not materially diminished.

At first, as has been hinted, these various tactics had little effect. One day, however, the chore boy, who had been over to Spruce Rapids after mail, reported that an additional crew of twenty had been sent in to Heinzman's drive. This was gratifying.

"We're making him scratch gravel, boys, anyway," said Orde.

The men entered into the spirit of the thing. In fact, their enthusiasm was almost too exuberant. Orde had constantly to negative new and ingenious schemes.

"No, boys," said he, "I want to keep on the right side of the law. We may need it later."

Meanwhile the entire length of the river was busy and excited. Heinzman's logs were all blazed inside a week. The men passed the hatchets along the line, and slim chance did a marked log have of rescue once the poor thing fell into difficulties. With the strange and interesting tendency rivermen and woodsmen have of personifying the elements of their daily work, the men addressed the helpless timbers in tones of contempt.

"Thought you'd ride that rock, you —— —— ——," said they, "and got left, did you? Well, lie there and be —— to you!"

And if chance offered, and time was not pressing, the riverman would give his helpless victim a jerk or so into a more difficult position. Times of rising water—when the sluice-gates above had been opened—were the most prolific of opportunities. Logs rarely jam on rising water, for the simple reason that constantly the surface area of the river is increasing, thus tending to separate the logs. On the other hand, falling water, tending to crowd the drive closer together, is especially prolific of trouble. Therefore, on flood water the watchers scattered along the stretches of the river had little to do—save strand Heinzman's logs for him. And when flood water had passed, some of those logs were certainly high and dry.

Up to a certain point this was all very well. Orde took pains not to countenance it officially, and caused word to be passed about, that while he did not expect his men to help drive Heinzman's logs, they must not go out of their way to strand them.

"If things get too bad, he'll have spies down here to collect evidence on us," said Orde, "and he'll jug some of us for interference with his property. We don't own the river."

"How about them booms?" asked the Rough Red.

"I did own them," explained Orde, "and I had a right to take them up when I had finished with them."

This hint was enough. The men did not cease from a labour that tickled them mightily, but they adopted a code of signals. Strangers were not uncommon. Spectators came out often from the little towns and from the farms round-about. When one of these appeared the riverman nearest raised a long falsetto cry. This was taken up by his next neighbour and passed on. In a few minutes all that section of the drive knew that it would be wise to "lie low." And inside of two weeks Orde had the great satisfaction of learning that Heinzman was working—and working hard—a crew of fifty men.

"A pretty fair crew, even if he was taking out his whole drive," commented Orde.

The gods of luck seemed to be with the new enterprise. Although Orde had, of course, taken the utmost pains to foresee every contingency possible to guard against, nevertheless, as always when dealing with Nature's larger forces, he anticipated some of those gigantic obstacles which continually render uncertain wilderness work. Nothing of the kind happened. There formed none of the tremendous white-water jams that pile up several million feet of logs, tax every resource of men, horses, and explosives, and require a week or so to break. No men were killed, and only two injured. No unexpected floods swept away works on which the drive depended. The water held out to carry the last stick of timber over the shallowest rapids. Weather conditions were phenomenal—and perfect. All up and down the river the work went with that vim and dash that is in itself an assurance of success. The Heinzman affair, which under auspices of evil augury might have become a serious menace to the success of the young undertaking, now served merely to add a spice of humour to the situation. Among the men gained currency a half-affectionate belief in "Orde's luck."

After this happy fashion the drive went, until at last it entered the broad, deep, and navigable stretches of the river from Redding to the lake. Here, barring the accident of an extraordinary flood, the troubles were over. On the broad, placid bosom of the stream the logs would float. A crew, following, would do the easy work of sacking what logs would strand or eddy in the lazy current; would roll into the faster waters the component parts of what were by courtesy called jams, but which were in reality pile-ups of a few hundred logs on sand bars mid-stream; and in the growing tepid warmth of summer would tramp pleasantly along the river trail. Of course, a dry year would make necessary a larger crew and more labour; of course, a big flood might sweep the logs past all defences into the lake for an irretrievable loss. But such floods come once in a century, and even the dryest of dry years could not now hang the drive. As Orde sat in his buckboard, ready to go into town for a first glimpse of Carroll in more than two months, he gazed with an immense satisfaction over the broad river moving brown and glacier-like as though the logs that covered it were viscid and composed all its substance. The enterprise was practically assured of success.

For a while now Orde was to have a breathing spell. A large number of men were here laid off. The remainder, under the direction of Jim Denning, would require little or no actual supervision. Until the jam should have reached the distributing booms above Monrovia, the affair was very simple. Before he left, however, he called Denning to him.

"Jim," said he, "I'll be down to see you through the sluiceways at Redding, of course. But now that you have a good, still stretch of river, I want you to have the boys let up on sacking out those "H" logs. And I want you to include in our drive all the Heinzman logs from above you possibly can. If you can fix it, let their drive drift down into ours."

"Then we'll have to drive their logs for them," objected Denning.

"Sure," rejoined Orde, "but it's easy driving; and if that crew of his hasn't much to do, perhaps he'll lay most of them off here at Redding."

Denning looked at his principal for a moment, then a slow grin overspread his face. Without comment he turned back to camp, and Orde took up his reins.

## XXV

"Oh, I'm so GLAD to get you back!" cried Carroll over and over again, as she clung to him. "I don't live while you're away. And every drop of rain that patters on the roof chills my heart, because I think of it as chilling you; and every creak of this old house at night brings me up broad awake, because I hear in it the crash of those cruel great timbers. Oh, oh, OH! I'm so glad to get you! You're the light of my life; you're my whole life itself!"—she smiled at him from her perch on his knee—"I'm silly, am I not?" she said. "Dear heart, don't leave me again."

"I've got to support an extravagant wife, you know," Orde reminded her gravely.

"I know, of course," she breathed, bending lightly to him. "You have your work in the world to do, and I would not have it otherwise. It is great work—wonderful work—I've been asking questions."

Orde laughed.

"It's work, just like any other. And it's hard work," said he.

She shook her head at him slowly, a mysterious smile on her lips. Without explaining her thought, she slipped from his knee and glided across to the tall golden harp, which had been brought from Monrovia. The light and diaphanous silk of her loose peignoir floated about her, defining the maturing grace of her figure. Abruptly she struck a great crashing chord.

Then, with an abandon of ecstasy she plunged into one of those wild and sea-blown saga-like rhapsodies of the Hungarians, full of the wind in rigging, the storm in the pines, of shrieking, vast forces hurtling unchained through a resounding and infinite space, as though deep down in primeval nature the powers of the world had been loosed. Back and forth, here and there, erratic and swift and sudden as lightning the theme played breathless. It fell.

"What is that?" gasped Orde, surprised to find himself tense, his blood rioting, his soul stirred.

She ran to him to hide her face in his neck.

"Oh, it's you, you, you!" she cried.

He held her to him closely until her excitement had died.

"Do you think it is good to get quite so nervous, sweetheart?" he asked gently, then. "Remember—"

"Oh, I do, I do!" she broke in earnestly. "Every moment of my waking and sleeping hours I remember him. Always I keep his little soul before me as a light on a shrine. But to-night—oh! to-night I could laugh and shout aloud like the people in the Bible, with clapping of hands." She snuggled herself close to Orde with a little murmur of happiness. "I think of all the beautiful things," she whispered, "and of the noble things, and of the great things. He is going to be sturdy, like his father; a wonderful boy, a boy all of fire—"

"Like his mother," said Orde.

She smiled up at him. "I want him just like you, dear," she pleaded.

## XXVI

Three days later the jam of the drive reached the dam at Redding. Orde took Carroll downtown in the buckboard. There a seat by the dam-watcher's little house was given her, back of the brick factory buildings next the power canal, whence for hours she watched the slow onward movement of the sullen brown timbers, the smooth, polished-steel rush of the waters through the chute, the graceful certain movements of the rivermen. Some of the latter were brought up by Orde and introduced. They were very awkward, and somewhat embarrassed, but they all looked her straight in the eye, and Carroll felt somehow that back of their diffidence they were quite dispassionately appraising her. After a few gracious speeches on her part and monosyllabic responses on theirs, they blundered away. In spite of the scant communication, these interviews left something of a friendly feeling on both sides.

"I like your Jim Denning," she told Orde; "he's a nice, clean-cut fellow. And Mr. Bourke," she laughed. "Isn't he funny with his fierce red beard and his little eyes? But he simply adores you."

Orde laughed at the idea of the Rough Red's adoring anybody.

"It's so," she insisted, "and I like him for it—only I wish he were a little cleaner."

She thought the feats of "log-riding" little less than wonderful, and you may be sure the knowledge of her presence did not discourage spectacular display. Finally, Johnny Challan, uttering a loud whoop, leaped aboard a log and went through the chute standing bolt upright. By a marvel of agility, he kept his balance through the white-water below, and emerged finally into the lower waters still proudly upright, and dry above the knees.

Carroll had arisen, the better to see.

"Why," she cried aloud, "it's marvellous! Circus riding is nothing to it!"

"No, ma'am," replied a gigantic riverman who was working near at hand, "that ain't nothin'. Ordinary, however, we travel that way on the river. At night we have the cookee pass us out each a goose-ha'r piller, and lay down for the night."

Carroll looked at him in reproof. He grinned slowly.

"Don't git worried about me, ma'am," said he, "I'm hopeless. For twenty year now I been wearin' crape on my hat in memory of my departed virtues."

After the rear had dropped down river from Redding, Carroll and Orde returned to their deserted little box of a house at Monrovia.

Orde breathed deep of a new satisfaction in walking again the streets of this little sandy, sawdust-paved, shantyfied town, with its yellow hills and its wide blue river and its glimpse of the lake far in the offing. It had never meant anything to him before. Now he enjoyed every brick and board of it; he trod the broken, aromatic shingles of the roadway with pleasure; he tramped up the broad stairs and down the dark hall of the block with anticipation; he breathed the compounded office odour of ledgers, cocoa matting, and old cigar smoke in a long, reminiscent whiff; he took his seat at his roll-top desk, enchanted to be again in these homely though familiar surroundings.

"Hanged if I know what's struck me," he mused. "Never experienced any remarkable joy before in getting back to this sort of truck."

Then, with a warm glow at the heart, the realisation was brought to him. This was home, and over yonder, under the shadow of the heaven-pointing spire, a slip of a girl was waiting for him.

He tried to tell her this when next he saw her.

"I felt that I ought to make you a little shrine, and burn candles to you, the way the Catholics do—"

"To the Mater Dolorosa?" she mocked.

He looked at her dark eyes so full of the sweetness of content, at her sensitive lips with the quaintly upturned corners, and he thought of what her home life had been and of the real sorrow that even yet must smoulder somewhere down in the deeps of her being.

"No," said he slowly, "not that. I think my shrine will be dedicated to Our Lady of the Joyous Soul."

The rest of the week Orde was absent up the river, superintending in a general way the latter progress of the drive, looking into the needs of the crews, arranging for supplies. The mills were all working now, busily cutting into the residue of last season's logs. Soon they would need more.

At the booms everything was in readiness to receive the jam. The long swing arm slanting across the river channel was attached to its winch which would operate it. When shut it would close the main channel and shunt into the booms the logs floating in the river. There, penned at last by the piles driven in a row and held together at the top by bolted timbers, they would lie quiet. Men armed with pike-poles would then take up the work of distribution according to the brands stamped on the ends. Each brand had its own separate "sorting pens," the lower end leading again into the open river. From these each owner's property was rafted and towed to his private booms at his mill below.

Orde spent the day before the jam appeared in constructing what he called a "boomerang."

"Invention of my own," he explained to Newmark. "Secret invention just yet. I'm going to hold up the drive in the main river until we have things bunched, then I'm going to throw a big crew down here by the swing. Heinzman anticipates, of course, that I'll run the entire drive into the booms and do all my sorting there. Naturally, if I turn his logs loose into the river as fast as I run across them, he will be able to pick them up one at a time, for he'll only get them occasionally. If I keep them until everything else is sorted, only Heinzman's logs will remain; and as we have no right to hold logs, we'll have to turn them loose through the lower sorting booms, where he can be ready to raft them. In that way he gets them all right without paying us a cent. See?"

"Yes, I see," said Newmark.

"Well," said Orde, with a laugh, "here is where I fool him. I'm going to rush the drive into the booms all at once, but I'm going to sort out Heinzman's logs at these openings near the entrance and turn them into the main channel."

"What good will that do?" asked Newmark sceptically. "He gets them sorted just the same, doesn't he?"

"The current's fairly strong," Orde pointed out, "and the river's almighty wide. When you spring seven or eight million feet on a man, all at once and unexpected, and he with no crew to handle them, he's going to keep almighty busy. And if he don't stop them this side his mill, he'll have to raft and tow them back; and if he don't stop 'em this side the lake, he may as well kiss them all good bye—except those that drift into the bayous and inlets and marshes, and other ungodly places."

"I see," said Newmark drily.

"But don't say a word anywhere," warned Orde. "Secrecy is the watchword of success with this merry little joke."

The boomerang worked like a charm. The men had been grumbling at an apparently peaceful yielding of the point at issue, and would have sacked out many of the blazed logs if Orde had not held them rigidly to it. Now their spirits flamed into joy again. The sorting went like clockwork. Orde, in personal charge, watched that through the different openings in his "boomerang" the "H" logs were shunted into the river. Shortly the channel was full of logs floating merrily away down the little blue wavelets. After a while Orde handed over his job to Tom North.

"Can't stand it any longer, boys," said he. "I've got to go down and see how the Dutchman is making it."

"Come back and tell us!" yelled one of the crew.

"You bet I will!" Orde shouted back.

He drove the team and buckboard down the marsh road to Heinzman's mill. There he found evidences of the wildest excitement. The mill had been closed down, and all the men turned in to rescue logs. Boats plied in all directions. A tug darted back and forth. Constantly the number of floating logs augmented, however. Many had already gone by.

"If you think you're busy now," said Orde to himself with a chuckle, "just wait until you begin to get LOGS."

He watched for a few moments in silence.

"What's he doing with that tug?" thought he. "O-ho! He's stringing booms across the river to hold the whole outfit."

He laughed aloud, turned his team about, and drove frantically back to the booms. Every few moments he chuckled. His eyes danced. Hardly could he wait to get there. Once at the camp, he leaped from the buckboard, with a shout to the stableman, and ran rapidly out over the booms to where the sorting of "H" logs was going merrily forward.

"He's shut down his mill," shouted Orde, "and he's got all that gang of highbankers out, and every old rum-blossom in Monrovia, and I bet if you say 'logs' to him, he'd chase his tail in circles."

"Want this job?" North asked him.

"No," said Orde, suddenly fallen solemn, "haven't time. I'm going to take Marsh and the SPRITE and go to town. Old Heinzman," he added as an afterthought, "is stringing booms across the river—obstructing navigation."

He ran down the length of the whole boom to where lay the two tugs.

"Marsh," he called when still some distance away, "got up steam?"

There appeared a short, square, blue-clad man, with hard brown cheeks, a heavy bleached flaxen moustache, and eyes steady, unwavering, and as blue as the sky.

"Up in two minutes," he answered, and descended from the pilot house to shout down a low door leading from the deck into the engine room.

"Harvey," he commanded, "fire her up!"

A tall, good-natured negro reached the upper half of his body from the low door to seize an armful of the slabs piled along the narrow deck. Ten minutes later the SPRITE, a cloud of white smoke pouring from her funnel, was careening down the stretch of the river.

Captain Marsh guided his energetic charge among the logs floating in the stream with the marvellous second instinct of the expert tugboat man. A whirl of the wheel to the right, a turn to the left—the craft heeled strongly under the forcing of her powerful rudder to avoid by an arm's-length some timbers fairly flung aside by the wash. The displacement of the rapid running seemed almost to press the water above the level of the deck on either side and about ten feet from the gunwale. As the low marshes and cat-tails flew past, Orde noted with satisfaction that many of the logs, urged one side by the breeze, had found lodgment among the reeds and in the bayous and inlets. One at a time, and painfully, these would have to be salvaged.

In a short time the mills' tall smokestacks loomed in sight. The logs thickened until it was with difficulty that Captain Marsh could thread his way among them at all. Shortly Orde, standing by the wheel in the pilot-house, could see down the stretches of the river a crowd of men working antlike.

"They've got 'em stopped," commented Orde. "Look at that gang working from boats! They haven't a dozen 'cork boots' among 'em."

"What do you want me to do?" asked Captain Marsh.

"This is a navigable river, isn't it?" replied Orde. "Run through!"

Marsh rang for half-speed and began to nose his way gently through the loosely floating logs. Soon the tug had reached the scene of activity, and headed straight for the slender line of booms hitched end to end and stretching quite across the river.

"I'm afraid we'll just ride over them if we hit them too slow," suggested Marsh.

Orde looked at his watch.

"We'll be late for the mail unless we hurry," said he. Marsh whirled the spokes of his wheel over and rang the engine-room bell. The water churned white behind, the tug careened.

"Vat you do! Stop!" cried Heinzman from one of the boats.

Orde stuck his head from the pilot-house door.

"You're obstructing navigation!" he yelled. "I've got to go to town to buy a postage-stamp."

The prow of the tug, accurately aimed by Marsh, hit square in the junction of two of the booms. Immediately the water was agitated on both sides and for a hundred feet or so by the pressure of the long poles sidewise. There ensued a moment of strain; then the links snapped, and the SPRITE plunged joyously through the opening. The booms, swept aside by the current, floated to either shore. The river was open.

Orde, his head still out the door, looked back. "Slow down, Marsh," said he. "Let's see the show." Already the logs caught by the booms had taken their motion and had swept past the opening. Although the lonesome tug Heinzman had on the work immediately picked up one end of the broken boom, and with it started out into the river, she found difficulty in making headway against the sweep of the logs. After a long struggle she reached the middle of the river, where she was able to hold her own.

"Wonder what next?" speculated Orde. "How are they going to get the other end of the booms out from the other bank?"

Captain Marsh had reversed the SPRITE. The tug lay nearly motionless amidstream, her propeller slowly revolving.

Up river all the small boats gathered in a line, connected one to the other by a rope. The tug passed over to them the cable attached to the boom. Evidently the combined efforts of the rowboats were counted on to hold the half-boom across the current while the tug brought out the other half. When the tug dropped the cable, Orde laughed.

"Nobody but a Dutchman would have thought of that!" he cried. "Now for the fun!"

Immediately the weight fell on the small boats, they were dragged irresistibly backward. Even from a distance the three men on the SPRITE could make out the white-water as the oars splashed and churned and frantically caught crabs in a vain effort to hold their own. Marsh lowered his telescope, the tears streaming down his face.

"It's better than a goat fight," said he.

Futilely protesting, the rowboats were dragged backward, turned as a whip is snapped, and strung out along the bank below.

"They'll have to have two tugs before they can close the break that way," commented Orde.

"Sure thing," replied Captain Marsh.

But at that moment a black smoke rolled up over the marshes, and shortly around the bend from above came the LUCY BELLE.

The LUCY BELLE was the main excuse for calling the river navigable. She made trips as often as she could between Redding and Monrovia. In luck, she could cover the forty miles in a day. It was no unusual thing, however, for the LUCY BELLE to hang up indefinitely on some one of the numerous shifting sand bars. For that reason she carried more imperishable freight than passengers. In appearance she was two-storied, with twin smokestacks, an iron Indian on her top, and a "splutter-behind" paddle-wheel.

"There comes his help," said Orde. "Old Simpson would stop to pick up a bogus three-cent piece."

Sure enough, on hail from one of the rowboats, the LUCY BELLE slowed down and stopped. After a short conference, she steamed clumsily over to get hold of one end of the booms. The tug took the other. In time, and by dint of much splashing, some collisions, and several attempts, the ends of the booms were united.

By this time, however, nearly all the logs had escaped. The tug, towing a string of rowboats, set out in pursuit.

The SPRITE continued on her way until beyond sight. Then she slowed down again. The LUCY BELLE churned around the bend, and turned in toward the tug.

"She's going to speak us," marvelled Orde. "I wonder what the dickens she wants."

"Tug ahoy!" bellowed a red-faced individual from the upper deck. He was dressed in blue and brass buttons, carried a telescope in one hand, and was liberally festooned with gold braid and embroidered anchors.

"Answer him," Orde commanded Marsh.

"Hullo there, commodore! what is it?" replied the tug captain.

The red-faced figure glared down for a moment.

"They want a tug up there at Heinzman's. Can you go?"

"Sure!" cried Marsh, choking.

The LUCY BELLE sheered off magnificently.

"What do you think of that?" Marsh asked Orde.

"The commodore always acts as if that old raft was a sixty-gun frigate," was Orde's non-committal answer. "Head up stream again."

Heinzman saw the SPRITE coming, and rowed out frantically, splashing at every stroke and yelling with every breath.

"Don't you go through there! Vait a minute! Stop, I tell you!"

"Hold up!" said Orde to Marsh.

Heinzman rowed alongside, dropped his oars and mopped his brow.

"Vat you do?" he demanded heatedly.

"I forgot the money to buy my stamp with," said Orde sweetly. "I'm going back to get it."

"Not through my pooms!" cried Heinzman.

"Mr. Heinzman," said Orde severely, "you are obstructing a navigable stream. I am doing business, and I cannot be interfered with."

"But my logs!" cried the unhappy mill man.

"I have nothing to do with your logs. You are driving your own logs," Orde reminded him.

Heinzman vituperated and pounded the gunwale.

"Go ahead, Marsh!" said Orde.

The tug gathered way. Soon Heinzman was forced to let go. For a second time the chains were snapped. Orde and Marsh looked back over the churning wake left by the SPRITE. The severed ends of the booms were swinging back toward either shore. Between them floated a rowboat. In the rowboat gesticulated a pudgy man. The river was well sprinkled with logs. Evidently the sorting was going on well.

"May as well go back to the works," said Orde. "He won't string them together again to-day—not if he waits for that tug he sent Simpson for."

Accordingly, they returned to the booms, where work was suspended while Orde detailed to an appreciative audience the happenings below. This tickled the men immensely.

"Why, we hain't sorted out more'n a million feet of his logs," cried Rollway Charlie. "He hain't SEEN no logs yet!"

They turned with new enthusiasm to the work of shunting "H" logs into the channel.

In ten minutes, however, the stableman picked his way out over the booms with a message for Orde.

"Mr. Heinzman's ashore, and wants to see you," said he.

Orde and Jim Denning exchanged glances.

"'Coon's come down," said the latter.

Orde found the mill man pacing restlessly up and down before a steaming pair of horses. Newmark, perched on a stump, was surveying him sardonically and chewing the end of an unlighted cigar.

"Here you poth are!" burst out Heinzman, when Orde stepped ashore. "Now, this must stop. I must not lose my logs! Vat is your proposition?"

Newmark broke in quickly before Orde could speak.

"I've told Mr. Heinzman," said he, "that we would sort and deliver the rest of his logs for two dollars a thousand."

"That will be about it," agreed Orde.

"But," exploded Heinzman, "that is as much as you agreet to drive and deliffer my whole cut!"

"Precisely," said Newmark.

"Put I haf all the eggspence of driving the logs myself. Why shoult I pay you for doing what I haf alretty paid to haf done?"

Orde chuckled.

"Heinzman," said he, "I told you I'd make you scratch gravel. Now it's time to talk business. You thought you were boring with a mighty auger, but it's time to revise. We aren't forced to bother with your logs, and you're lucky to get out so easy. If I turn your whole drive into the river, you'll lose more than half of it outright, and it'll cost you a heap to salvage the rest. And what's more, I'll turn 'em in before you can get hold of a pile-driver. I'll sort night and day," he bluffed, "and by to-morrow morning you won't have a stick of timber above my booms." He laughed again. "You want to get down to business almighty sudden."

When finally Heinzman had driven sadly away, and the whole drive, "H" logs included, was pouring into the main boom, Orde stretched his arms over his head in a luxury of satisfaction.

"That just about settles that campaign," he said to Newmark.

"Oh, no, it doesn't," replied the latter decidedly.

"Why?" asked Orde, surprised. "You don't imagine he'll do anything more?"

"No, but I will," said Newmark.

## XXVII

Early in the fall the baby was born. It proved to be a boy. Orde, nervous as a cat after the ordeal of doing nothing, tiptoed into the darkened room. He found his wife weak and pale, her dark hair framing her face, a new look of rapt inner contemplation rendering even more mysterious her always fathomless eyes. To Orde she seemed fragile, aloof, enshrined among her laces and dainty ribbons. Hardly dared he touch her when she held her hand out to him weakly, but fell on his knees beside the bed and buried his face in the clothes. She placed a gentle hand caressingly on his head.

So they remained for some time. Finally he raised his eyes. She held her lips to him. He kissed them.

"It seems sort of make-believe even yet, sweetheart," she smiled at him whimsically, "that we have a real, live baby all of our own."

"Like other people," said Orde.

"Not like other people at all!" she disclaimed, with a show of indignation.

Grandma Orde brought the newcomer in for Orde's inspection. He looked gravely down on the puckered, discoloured bit of humanity with some feeling of disappointment, and perhaps a faint uneasiness. After a moment he voiced the latter.

"Is—do you think—that is—" he hesitated, "does the doctor say he's going to be all right?"

"All right!" cried Grandma Orde indignantly. "I'd like to know if he isn't all right now! What in the world do you expect of a new-born baby?"

But Carroll was laughing softly to herself on the bed. She held out her arms for the baby, and cuddled it close to her breast.

"He's a little darling," she crooned, "and he's going to grow up big and strong, just like his daddy." She put her cheek against the sleeping babe's and looked up sidewise at the two standing above her. "But I know how you feel," she said to her husband. "When they first showed him to me, I thought he looked like a peanut a thousand years old."

Grandma Orde fairly snorted with indignation.

"Come to your old grandmother, who appreciates you!" she cried, possessing herself of the infant. "He's a beautiful baby; one of the best-looking new-born babies I ever saw!"

Orde escaped to the open air. He had to go to the office to attend to some details of the business. With every step his elation increased. At the office he threw open his desk with a slam. Newmark jumped nervously and frowned. Orde's big, open, and brusque manners bothered him as they would have bothered a cat.

"Got a son and heir over at my place," called Orde in his big voice.

"This old firm's got to rustle now, I tell you."

"Congratulate you, I'm sure," said Newmark rather shortly. "Mrs. Orde is doing well, I hope?"

"Fine, fine!" cried Orde.

Newmark dropped the subject and plunged into a business matter. Orde's attention, however, was flighty. After a little while he closed his desk with another bang.

"No use!" said he. "Got to make it a vacation. I'm going to run over to see how the family is."

Strangely enough, the young couple had not discussed before the question of a name. One evening at twilight, when Orde was perched at the foot of the bed, Carroll brought up the subject.

"He ought to be named for you," she began timidly. "I know that, Jack, and I'd love to have another Jack Orde in the family; but, dear, I've been thinking about father. He's a poor, forlorn old man, who doesn't get much out of life. And it would please him so—oh, more than you can imagine such a thing could please anybody!"

She looked up at him doubtfully. Orde said nothing, but walked around the bed to where the baby lay in his little cradle. He leaned over and took the infant up in his gingerly awkward fashion.

"How are you to-day, Bobby Orde?" he inquired of the blinking mite.

## XXVIII

The first season of the Boom Company was most successful. Its prospects for the future were bright. The drive had been delivered to its various owners at a price below what it had cost them severally, and without the necessary attendant bother. Therefore, the loggers were only too willing to renew their contracts for another year. This did not satisfy Newmark, however.

"What we want," he told Orde, "is a charter giving us exclusive rights on the river, and authorising us to ask toll. I'm going to try and get one out of the legislature."

He departed for Lansing as soon as the Assembly opened, and almost immediately became lost in one of those fierce struggles of politics not less bitter because concealed. Heinzman was already on the ground.

Newmark had the shadow of right on his side, for he applied for the charter on the basis of the river improvements already put in by his firm. Heinzman, however, possessed much political influence, a deep knowledge of the subterranean workings of plot and counterplot, and a "barrel." Although armed with an apparently incontestable legal right, Newmark soon found himself fighting on the defensive. Heinzman wanted the improvements already existing condemned and sold as a public utility to the highest bidder. He offered further guarantees as to future improvements. In addition were other and more potent arguments proffered behind closed doors. Many cases resolved themselves into a bald question of cash. Others demanded diplomacy. Jobs, fat contracts, business favours, influence were all flung out freely—bribes as absolute as though stamped with the dollar mark. Newspapers all over the State were pressed into service. These, bought up by Heinzman and his prospective partners in a lucrative business, spoke virtuously of private piracy of what are now called public utilities, the exploiting of the people's natural wealths, and all the rest of a specious reasoning the more convincing in that it was in many other cases only too true. The independent journals, uninformed of the rights of the case, either remained silent on the matter, or groped in a puzzled and undecided manner on both sides.

Against this secret but effective organisation Newmark most unexpectedly found himself pitted. He had anticipated being absent but a week; he became involved in an affair of months.

With decision he applied himself to the problem. He took rooms at the hotel, sent for Orde, and began at once to set in motion the machinery of opposition. The refreshed resources of the company were strained to the breaking point in order to raise money for this new campaign opening before it. Orde, returning to Lansing after a trip devoted to the carrying out of Newmark's directions as to finances, was dismayed at the tangle of strategy and cross-strategy, innuendo, vague and formless cobweb forces by which he was surrounded. He could make nothing of them. They brushed his face, he felt their influence, yet he could place his finger on no tangible and comprehensible solidity. Among these delicate and complicated cross-currents Newmark moved silent, cold, secret. He seemed to understand them, to play with them, to manipulate them as elements of the game. Above them was the hollow shock of the ostensible battle—the speeches, the loud talk in lobbies, the newspaper virtue, indignation, accusations; but the real struggle was here in the furtive ways, in whispered words delivered hastily aside, in hotel halls on the way to and from the stairs, behind closed doors of rooms without open transoms.

Orde in comic despair acknowledged that it was all "too deep for him." Nevertheless, it was soon borne in on him that the new company was struggling for its very right to existence. It had been doing that from the first; but now, to Orde the fight, the existence, had a new importance. The company up to this point had been a scheme merely, an experiment that might win or lose. Now, with the history of a drive behind it, it had become a living entity. Orde would have fought against its dissolution as he would have fought against a murder. Yet he had practically to stand one side, watching Newmark's slender, gray-clad, tense figure gliding here and there, more silent, more reserved, more watchful every day.

The fight endured through most of the first half of the session. When finally it became evident to Heinzman that Newmark would win, he made the issue of toll rates the ditch of his last resistance, trying to force legal charges so low as to eat up the profits. At the last, however, the bill passed the board. The company had its charter.

At what price only Newmark could have told. He had fought with the tense earnestness of the nervous temperament that fights to win without count of the cost. The firm was established, but it was as heavily in debt as its credit would stand. Newmark himself, though as calm and reserved and precise as ever, seemed to have turned gray, and one of his eyelids had acquired a slight nervous twitch which persisted for some months. He took his seat at the desk, however, as calmly as ever. In three days the scandalised howls of bribery and corruption had given place in the newspapers to some other sensation.

"Joe," said Orde to his partner, "how about all this talk? Is there really anything in it? You haven't gone in for that business, have you?"

Newmark stretched his arms wearily.

"Press bought up," he replied. "I know for a fact that old Stanford got five hundred dollars from some of the Heinzman interests. I could have swung him back for an extra hundred, but it wasn't worth while. They howl bribery at us to distract attention from their own performances."

With this evasive reply Orde contented himself. Whether it satisfied him or whether he was loath to pursue the subject further it would be impossible to say.

"It's cost us plenty, anyway," he said, after a moment. "The proposition's got a load on it. It will take us a long time to get out of debt. The river driving won't pay quite so big as we thought it would," he concluded, with a rueful little laugh.

"It will pay plenty well enough," replied Newmark decidedly, "and it gives us a vantage point to work from. You don't suppose we are going to quit at river driving, do you? We want to look around for some timber of our own; there's where the big money is. And perhaps we can buy a schooner or two and go into the carrying trade—the country's alive with opportunity. Newmark and Orde means something to these fellows now. We can have anything we want, if we just reach out for it."

His thin figure, ordinarily slightly askew, had straightened; his steel-gray, impersonal eyes had lit up behind the bowed glasses and were seeing things beyond the wall at which they gazed. Orde looked up at him with a sudden admiration.

"You're the brains of this concern," said he.

"We'll get on," replied Newmark, the fire dying from his eyes.

## XXIX

In the course of the next eight years Newmark and Orde floated high on that flood of apparent prosperity that attends a business well conceived and passably well managed. The Boom and Driving Company made money, of course, for with the margin of fifty per cent or thereabouts necessitated by the temporary value of the improvements, good years could hardly fail to bring good returns. This, it will be remembered, was a stock company. With the profits from that business the two men embarked on a separate copartnership. They made money at this, too, but the burden of debt necessitated by new ventures, constantly weighted by the heavy interest demanded at that time, kept affairs on the ragged edge.

In addition, both Orde and Newmark were more inclined to extension of interests than to "playing safe." The assets gained in one venture were promptly pledged to another. The ramifications of debt, property, mortgages, and expectations overlapped each other in a cobweb of interests.

Orde lived at ease in a new house of some size surrounded by grounds. He kept two servants: a blooded team of horses drew the successor to the original buckboard. Newmark owned a sail yacht of five or six tons, in which, quite solitary, he took his only pleasure. Both were considered men of substance and property, as indeed they were. Only, they risked dollars to gain thousands. A succession of bad years, a panic-contraction of money markets, any one of a dozen possible, though not probable, contingencies would render it difficult to meet the obligations which constantly came due, and which Newmark kept busy devising ways and means of meeting. If things went well—and it may be remarked that legitimately they should—Newmark and Orde would some day be rated among the millionaire firms. If things went ill, bankruptcy could not be avoided. There was no middle ground. Nor were Orde and his partner unique in this; practically every firm then developing or exploiting the natural resources of the country found itself in the same case.

Immediately after the granting of the charter to drive the river the partners had offered them an opportunity of acquiring about thirty million feet of timber remaining from Morrison and Daly's original holdings. That firm was very anxious to begin development on a large scale of its Beeson Lake properties in the Saginaw waters. Daly proposed to Orde that he take over the remnant, and having confidence in the young man's abilities, agreed to let him have it on long-time notes. After several consultations with Newmark, Orde finally completed the purchase. Below the booms they erected a mill, the machinery for which they had also bought of Daly, at Redding. The following winter Orde spent in the woods. By spring he had banked, ready to drive, about six million feet.

For some years these two sorts of activity gave the partners about all they could attend to. As soon as the drive had passed Redding, Orde left it in charge of one of his foremen while he divided his time between the booms and the mill. Late in the year his woods trips began, the tours of inspection, of surveying for new roads, the inevitable preparation for the long winter campaigns in the forest. As soon as the spring thaws began, once more the drive demanded his attention. And in marketing the lumber, manipulating the firm's financial affairs, collecting its dues, paying its bills, making its purchases, and keeping oiled the intricate bearing points of its office machinery, Newmark was busy—and invaluable.

At the end of the fifth year the opportunity came, through a combination of a bad debt and a man's death, to get possession of two lake schooners. Orde at once suggested the contract for a steam barge. Towing was then in its infancy. The bulk of lake traffic was by means of individual sailing ships—a method uncertain as to time. Orde thought that a steam barge could be built powerful enough not only to carry its own hold and deck loads, but to tow after it the two schooners. In this manner the crews could be reduced, and an approximate date of delivery could be guaranteed. Newmark agreed with him. Thus the firm, in accordance with his prophecy, went into the carrying trade, for the vessels more than sufficed for its own needs. The freighting of lumber added much to the income, and the carrying of machinery and other heavy freight on the return trip grew every year.

But by far the most important acquisition was that of the northern peninsula timber. Most operators called the white pine along and back from the river inexhaustible. Orde did not believe this. He saw the time, not far distant, when the world would be compelled to look elsewhere for its lumber supply, and he turned his eyes to the almost unknown North. After a long investigation through agents, and a month's land-looking on his own account, he located and purchased three hundred million feet. This was to be paid for, as usual, mostly by the firm's notes secured by its other property. It would become available only in the future, but Orde believed, as indeed the event justified, this future would prove to be not so distant as most people supposed.

As these interests widened, Orde became more and more immersed in them. He was forced to be away all of every day, and more than the bulk of every year. Nevertheless, his home life did not suffer for it.

To Carroll he was always the same big, hearty, whole-souled boy she had first learned to love. She had all his confidence. If this did not extend into business affairs, it was because Orde had always tried to get away from them when at home. At first Carroll had attempted to keep in the current of her husband's activities, but as the latter broadened in scope and became more complex, she perceived that their explanation wearied him. She grew out of the habit of asking him about them. Soon their rapid advance had carried them quite beyond her horizon. To her, also, as to most women, the word "business" connoted nothing but a turmoil and a mystery.

In all other things they were to each other what they had been from the first. No more children had come to them. Bobby, however, had turned out a sturdy, honest little fellow, with more than a streak of his mother's charm and intuition. His future was the subject of all Orde's plans.

"I want to give him all the chance there is," he explained to Carroll. "A boy ought to start where his father left off, and not have to do the same thing all over again. But being a rich man's son isn't much of a job."

"Why don't you let him continue your business?" smiled Carroll, secretly amused at the idea of the small person before them ever doing anything.

"By the time Bobby's grown up this business will all be closed out," replied Orde seriously.

He continued to look at his minute son with puckered brow, until Carroll smoothed out the wrinkles with the tips of her fingers.

"Of course, having only a few minutes to decide," she mocked, "perhaps we'd better make up our minds right now to have him a street-car driver."

"Yes!" agreed Bobby unexpectedly, and with emphasis.

Three years after this conversation, which would have made Bobby just eight, Orde came back before six of a summer evening, his face alight with satisfaction.

"Hullo, bub!" he cried to Bobby, tossing him to his shoulder. "How's the kid?"

They went out together, while awaiting dinner, to see the new setter puppy in the woodshed.

"Named him yet?" asked Orde.

"Duke," said Bobby.

Orde surveyed the animal gravely.

"Seems like a good name," said he.

After dinner the two adjourned to the library, where they sat together in the "big chair," and Bobby, squirmed a little sidewise in order the better to see, watched the smoke from his father's cigar as it eddied and curled in the air.

"Tell a story," he commanded finally.

"Well," acquiesced Orde, "there was once a man who had a cow—"

"Once upon a time," corrected Bobby.

He listened for a moment or so.

"I don't like that story," he then announced. "Tell the story about the bears."

"But this is a new story," protested Orde, "and you've heard about the bears so many times."

"Bears," insisted Bobby.

"Well, once upon a time there were three bears—a big bear and a middle-sized bear and a little bear—" began Orde obediently.

Bobby, with a sigh of rapture and content, curled up in a snug, warm little ball. The twilight darkened.

"Blind-man's holiday!" warned Carroll behind them so suddenly that they both jumped. "And the sand man's been at somebody, I know!"

She bore him away to bed. Orde sat smoking in the darkness, staring straight ahead of him into the future. He believed he had found the opportunity—twenty years distant—for which he had been looking so long.

## XXX

After a time Carroll descended the stairs, chuckling. "Jack," she called into the sitting-room, "come out on the porch. What do you suppose the young man did to-night?"

"Give it up," replied Orde promptly. "No good guessing when it's a question of that youngster's performances. What was it?"

"He said his 'Now I lay me,' and asked blessings on you and me, and the grandpas and grandmas, and Auntie Kate, as usual. Then he stopped. 'What else?' I reminded him. 'And,' he finished with a rush, 'make-Bobby-a-good-boy-and-give-him-plenty-of-bread-'n-butter-'n apple-sauce!'"

They laughed delightedly over this, clinging together like two children. Then they stepped out on the little porch and looked into the fathomless night. The sky was full of stars, aloof and calm, but waiting breathless on the edge of action, attending the word of command or the celestial vision, or whatever it is for which stars seem to wait. Along the street the dense velvet shade of the maples threw the sidewalks into impenetrable blackness. Sounds carried clearly. From the Welton's, down the street, came the tinkle of a mandolin and an occasional low laugh from the group of young people that nightly frequented the front steps. Tree toads chirped in unison or fell abruptly silent as though by signal. All up and down the rows of houses whirred the low monotone of the lawn sprinklers, and the aroma of their wetness was borne cool and refreshing through the tepid air.

Orde and his wife sat together on the top step. He slipped his arm about her. They said nothing, but breathed deep of the quiet happiness that filled their lives.

The gate latch clicked and two shadowy figures defined themselves approaching up the concrete walk.

"Hullo!" called Orde cheerfully into the darkness.

"Hullo!" a man's voice instantly responded.

"Taylor and Clara," said Orde to Carroll with satisfaction. "Just the man I wanted to see."

The lawyer and his wife mounted the steps. He was a quick, energetic, spare man, with lean cheeks, a bristling, clipped moustache, and a slight stoop to his shoulders. She was small, piquant, almost child-like, with a dainty up-turned nose, a large and lustrous eye, a constant, bird-like animation of manner—the Folly of artists, the adorable, lovable, harmless Folly standing tiptoe on a complaisant world.

"Just the man I wanted to see," repeated Orde, as the two approached.

Clara Taylor stopped short and considered him for a moment.

"Let us away," she said seriously to Carroll. "My prophetic soul tells me they are going to talk business, and if any more business is talked in my presence, I shall EXPIRE!"

Both men laughed, but Orde explained apologetically:

"Well, you know, Mrs. Taylor, these are my especially busy days for the firm, and I have to work my private affairs in when I can."

"I thought Frank was very solicitous about my getting out in the air," cried Clara. "Come, Carroll, let's wander down the street and see Mina Heinzman."

The two interlocked arms and sauntered along the walk. Both men lit cigars and sat on the top step of the porch.

"Look here, Taylor," broke in Orde abruptly, "you told me the other day you had fifteen or twenty thousand you wanted to place somewhere."

"Yes," replied Taylor.

"Well, I believe I have just the proposition."

"What is it?"

"California pine," replied Orde.

"California pine?" repeated Taylor, after a slight pause. "Why California? That's a long way off. And there's no market, is there? Why way out there?"

"It's cheap," replied Orde succinctly. "I don't say it will be good for immediate returns, nor even for returns in the near future, but in twenty or thirty years it ought to pay big on a small investment made now."

Taylor shook his head doubtfully.

"I don't see how you figure it," he objected. "We have more timber than we can use in the East. Why should we go several thousand miles west for the same thing?"

"When our timber gives out, then we'll HAVE to go west," said Orde.

Taylor laughed.

"Laugh all you please," rejoined Orde, "but I tell you Michigan and Wisconsin pine is doomed. Twenty or thirty years from now there won't be any white pine for sale."

"Nonsense!" objected Taylor. "You're talking wild. We haven't even begun on the upper peninsula. After that there's Minnesota. And I haven't observed that we're quite out of timber on the river, or the Muskegon, or the Saginaw, or the Grand, or the Cheboygan—why, Great Scott! man, our children's children's children may be thinking of investing in California timber, but that's about soon enough."

"All tight," said Orde quietly. "Well, what do you think of Indiana as a good field for timber investment?"

"Indiana!" cried Taylor, amazed. "Why, there's no timber there; it's a prairie."

"There used to be. And all the southern Michigan farm belt was timbered, and around here. We have our stumps to show for it, but there are no evidences at all farther south. You'd have hard work, for instance, to persuade a stranger that Van Buren County was once forest."

"Was it?" asked Taylor doubtfully.

"It was. You take your map and see how much area has been cut already, and how much remains. That'll open your eyes. And remember all that has been done by crude methods for a relatively small demand. The demand increases as the country grows and methods improve. It would not surprise me if some day thirty or forty millions would constitute an average cut. * 'Michigan pine exhaustless!'—those fellows make me sick!"

> * At the present day some firms cut as high as 150,000,000 feet.

"Sounds a little more reasonable," said Taylor slowly.

"It'll sound a lot more reasonable in five or ten years," insisted Orde, "and then you'll see the big men rushing out into that Oregon and California country. But now a man can get practically the pick of the coast. There are only a few big concerns out there."

"Why is it that no one—"

"Because," Orde cut him short, "the big things are for the fellow who can see far enough ahead."

"What kind of a proposition have you?" asked Taylor after a pause.

"I can get ten thousand acres at an average price of eight dollars an acre," replied Orde.

"Acres? What does that mean in timber?"

"On this particular tract it means about four hundred million feet."

"That's about twenty cents a thousand."

Orde nodded.

"And of course you couldn't operate for a long time?"

"Not for twenty, maybe thirty, years," replied Orde calmly.

"There's your interest on your money, and taxes, and the risk of fire and—"

"Of course, of course," agreed Orde impatiently, "but you're getting your stumpage for twenty cents or a little more, and in thirty years it will be worth as high as a dollar and a half." *

> * At the present time (1908) sugar pine such as Orde described would cost $3.50 to $4.

"What!" cried Taylor.

"That is my opinion," said Orde.

Taylor relapsed into thought.

"Look here, Orde," he broke out finally, "how old are you?"

"Thirty-eight. Why?"

"How much timber have you in Michigan?"

"About ten million that we've picked up on the river since the Daly purchase and three hundred million in the northern peninsula."

"Which will take you twenty years to cut, and make you a million dollars or so?"

"Hope so."

"Then why this investment thirty years ahead?"

"It's for Bobby," explained Orde simply. "A man likes to have his son continue on in his business. I can't do it here, but there I can. It would take fifty years to cut that pine, and that will give Bobby a steady income and a steady business."

"Bobby will be well enough off, anyway. He won't have to go into business."

Orde's brow puckered.

"I know a man—Bobby is going to work. A man is not a success in life unless he does something, and Bobby is going to be a success. Why, Taylor," he chuckled, "the little rascal fills the wood-box for a cent a time, and that's all the pocket-money he gets. He's saving now to buy a thousand-dollar boat. I've agreed to pool in half. At his present rate of income, I'm safe for about sixty years yet."

"How soon are you going to close this deal?" asked Taylor, rising as he caught sight of two figures coming up the walk.

"I have an option until November 1," replied Orde. "If you can't make it, I guess I can swing it myself. By the way, keep this dark."

Taylor nodded, and the two turned to defend themselves as best they could against Clara's laughing attack.

## XXXI

Orde had said nothing to Newmark concerning this purposed new investment, nor did he intend doing so.

"It is for Bobby," he told himself, "and I want Bobby, and no one else, to run it. Joe would want to take charge, naturally. Taylor won't. He knows nothing of the business."

He walked downtown next morning busily formulating his scheme. At the office he found Newmark already seated at his desk, a pile of letters in front of him. Upon Orde's boisterous greeting his nerves crisped slightly, but of this there was no outward sign beyond a tightening of his hands on the letter he was reading. Behind his eye-glasses his blue, cynical eyes twinkled like frost crystals. As always, he was immaculately dressed in neat gray clothes, and carried in one corner of his mouth an unlighted cigar.

"Joe," said Orde, spinning a chair to Newmark's roll-top desk and speaking in a low tone, "just how do we stand on that upper peninsula stumpage?"

"What do you mean? How much of it is there? You know that as well as I do—about three hundred million."

"No; I mean financially."

"We've made two payments of seventy-five thousand each, and have still two to make of the same amount."

"What could we borrow on it?"

"We don't want to borrow anything on it," returned Newmark in a flash.

"Perhaps not; but if we should?"

"We might raise fifty or seventy-five thousand, I suppose."

"Joe," said Orde, "I want to raise about seventy-five thousand dollars on my share in this concern, if it can be done."

"What's up?" inquired Newmark keenly.

"It's a private matter."

Newmark said nothing, but for some time thought busily, his light blue eyes narrowed to a slit.

"I'll have to figure on it a while," said he at last, and turned back to his mail. All day he worked hard, with only a fifteen-minute intermission for a lunch which was brought up from the hotel below. At six o'clock he slammed shut the desk. He descended the stairs with Orde, from whom he parted at their foot, and walked precisely away, his tall, thin figure held rigid and slightly askew, his pale eyes slitted behind his eye-glasses, the unlighted cigar in one corner of his straight lips. To the occasional passerby he bowed coldly and with formality. At the corner below he bore to the left, and after a short walk entered the small one-story house set well back from the sidewalk among the clumps of oleanders. Here he turned into a study, quietly and richly furnished ten years in advance of the taste then prevalent in Monrovia, where he sank into a deep-cushioned chair and lit the much-chewed cigar. For some moments he lay back with his eyes shut. Then he opened them to look with approval on the dark walnut book-cases, the framed prints and etchings, the bronzed student's lamp on the square table desk, the rugs on the polished floor. He picked up a magazine, into which he dipped for ten minutes.

The door opened noiselessly behind him.

"Mr. Newmark, sir," came a respectful voice, "it is just short of seven."

"Very well," replied Newmark, without looking around.

The man withdrew as softly as he had come. After a moment, Newmark replaced the magazine on the table, yawned, threw aside the cigar, of which he had smoked but an inch, and passed from his study into his bedroom across the hall. This contained an exquisite Colonial four-poster, with a lowboy and dresser to match, and was papered and carpeted in accordance with these, its chief ornaments. Newmark bathed in the adjoining bathroom, shaved carefully between the two wax lights which were his whim, and dressed in what were then known as "swallow-tail" clothes. Probably he was the only man in Monrovia at that moment so apparelled. Then calmly, and with all the deliberation of one under fire of a hundred eyes, he proceeded to the dining-room, where waited the man who had a short time before reminded him of the hour. He was a solemn, dignified man, whose like was not to be found elsewhere this side the city. He, too, wore the "swallow-tail," but its buttons were of gilt.

Newmark seated himself in a leather-upholstered mahogany chair before a small, round, mahogany table. The room was illuminated only by four wax candles with red shades. They threw into relief the polish of mahogany, the glitter of glass, the shine of silver, but into darkness the detail of massive sideboard, dull panelling, and the two or three dark-toned sporting prints on the wall.

"You may serve dinner, Mallock," said Newmark.

He ate deliberately and with enjoyment the meal, exquisitely prepared and exquisitely presented to him. With it he drank a single glass of Burgundy—a deed that would, in the eyes of Monrovia, have condemned him as certainly as driving a horse on Sunday or playing cards for a stake. Afterward he returned to the study, whither Mallock brought coffee. He lit another cigar, opened a drawer in his desk, extracted therefrom some bank-books and small personal account books. From these he figured all the evening. His cigar went out, but he did not notice that, and chewed away quite contentedly on the dead butt. When he had finished, his cold eye exhibited a gleam of satisfaction. He had resolved on a course of action. At ten o'clock he went to bed.

Next morning Mallock closed the door behind him promptly upon the stroke of eight. It was strange that not one living soul but Mallock had ever entered Newmark's abode. Curiosity had at first brought a few callers; but these were always met by the imperturbable servant with so plausible a reason for his master's absence that the visitors had departed without a suspicion that they had been deliberately excluded. And as Newmark made no friends and excited little interest, the attempts to cultivate him gradually ceased.

"Orde," said Newmark, as the former entered the office, "I think I can arrange this matter."

Orde drew up a chair.

"I talked last evening with a man from Detroit named Thayer, who thinks he may advance seventy-five thousand dollars on a mortgage on our northern peninsula stumpage. For that, of course, we will give the firm's note with interest at ten per cent. I will turn this over to you."

"That's—" began Orde.

"Hold on," interrupted Newmark. "As collateral security you will deposit for me your stock in the Boom Company, indorsed in blank. If you do not pay the full amount of the firm's note to Thayer, then the stock will be turned in to me."

"I see," said Orde.

"Now, don't misunderstand me," said Newmark drily. "This is your own affair, and I do not urge it on you. If we raise as much as seventy-five thousand dollars on that upper peninsula stumpage, it will be all it can stand, for next year we must make a third payment on it. If you take that money, it is of course proper that you pay the interest on it."

"Certainly," said Orde.

"And if there's any possibility of the foreclosure of the mortgage, it is only right that you run all the risk of loss—not myself."

"Certainly," repeated Orde.

"From another point of view," went on Newmark, "you are practically mortgaging your interest in the Boom Company for seventy-five thousand dollars. That would make, on the usual basis of a mortgage, your share worth above two hundred thousand—and four hundred thousand is a high valuation of our property."

"That looks more than decent on your part," said Orde.

"Of course, it's none of my business what you intend to do with this," went on Newmark, "but unless you're SURE you can meet these notes, I should strongly advise against it."

"The same remark applies to any mortgage," rejoined Orde.

"Exactly."

"For how long a time could I get this?" asked Orde at length.

"I couldn't promise it for longer than five years," replied Newmark.

"That would make about fifteen thousand a year?"

"And interest."

"Certainly—and interest. Well, I don't see why I can't carry that easily on our present showing and prospects."

"If nothing untoward happens," insisted Newmark determined to put forward all objections possible.

"It's not much risk," said Orde hopefully. "There's nothing surer than lumber. We'll pay the notes easily enough as we cut, and the Boom Company's on velvet now. What do our earnings figure, anyway?"

"We're driving one hundred and fifty million at a profit of about sixty cents a thousand," said Newmark.

"That's ninety thousand dollars—in five years, four hundred and fifty thousand," said Orde, sucking his pencil.

"We ought to clean up five dollars a thousand on our mill."

"That's about a hundred thousand on what we've got left."

"And that little barge business nets us about twelve or fifteen thousand a year."

"For the five years about sixty thousand more. Let's see—that's a total of say six hundred thousand dollars in five years."

"We will have to take up in that time," said Newmark, who seemed to have the statistics at his finger-tips, "the two payments on our timber, the note on the First National, the Commercial note, the remaining liabilities on the Boom Company—about three hundred thousand all told, counting the interest."

Orde crumpled the paper and threw it into the waste basket.

"Correct," said he. "Good enough. I ought to get along on a margin like that."

He went over to his own desk, where he again set to figuring on his pad. The results he eyed a little doubtfully. Each year he must pay in interest the sum of seven thousand five hundred dollars. Each year he would have to count on a proportionate saving of fifteen thousand dollars toward payment of the notes. In addition, he must live.

"The Orde family is going to be mighty hard up," said he, whistling humorously.

But Orde was by nature and training sanguine and fond of big risks.

"Never mind; it's for Bobby," said he to himself. "And maybe the rate of interest will go down. And I'll be able to borrow on the California tract if anything does go wrong."

He put on his hat, thrust a bundle of papers into his pocket, and stepped across the hall into Taylor's office.

The lawyer he found tipped back in his revolving chair, reading a printed brief.

"Frank," began Orde immediately, "I came to see you about that California timber matter."

Taylor laid down the brief and removed his eye-glasses, with which he began immediately to tap the fingers of his left hand.

"Sit down, Jack," said he. "I'm glad you came in. I was going to try to see you some time to-day. I've been thinking the matter over very carefully since the other day, and I've come to the conclusion that it is too steep for me. I don't doubt the investment a bit, but the returns are too far off. Fifteen thousand means a lot more to me than it does to you, and I've got to think of the immediate future. I hope you weren't counting on me—"

"Oh, that's all right," broke in Orde. "As I told you, I can swing the thing myself, and only mentioned it to you on the off chance you might want to invest. Now, what I want is this—" he proceeded to outline carefully the agreement between himself and Newmark while the lawyer took notes and occasionally interjected a question.

"All right," said the latter, when the details had been mastered. "I'll draw the necessary notes and papers."

"Now," went on Orde, producing the bundle of papers from his pocket, "here's the abstract of title. I wish you'd look it over. It's a long one, but not complicated, as near as I can make out. Trace seems to have acquired this tract mostly from the original homesteaders and the like, who, of course, take title direct from the government. But naturally there are a heap of them, and I want you to look it over to be sure everything's shipshape."

"All right," agreed Taylor, reaching for the papers.

"One other thing," concluded Orde, uncrossing his legs. "I want this investment to get no further than the office door. You see, this is for Bobby, and I've given a lot of thought to that sort of thing; and nothing spoils a man sooner than to imagine the thing's all cut and dried for him, and nothing keeps him going like the thought that he's got to rustle his own opportunities. You and I know that. Bobby's going to have the best education possible; he's going to learn to be a lumberman by practical experience, and that practical experience he'll get with other people. No working for his dad in Bobby's, I can tell you. When he gets through college, I'll get him a little job clerking with some good firm, and he'll have a chance to show what is in him and to learn the business from the ground up, the way a man ought to. Of course, I'll make arrangements that he has a real chance. Then, when he's worked into the harness a little, the old man will take him out and show him the fine big sugar pine and say to him, 'There, my boy, there's your opportunity, and you've earned it. How does ORDE AND SON sound to you?' What do you think of it, Frank?"

Taylor nodded several times.

"I believe you're on the right track, and I'll help you all I can," said he briefly.

"So, of course, I want to keep the thing dead secret," continued Orde. "You're the only man who knows anything about it. I'm not even going to buy directly under my own name. I'm going to incorporate myself," he said, with a grin. "You know how those things will get out, and how they always get back to the wrong people."

"Count on me," Taylor assured him.

As Orde walked home that evening, after a hot day, his mind was full of speculation as to the immediate future. He had a local reputation for wealth, and no one knew better than himself how important it is for a man in debt to keep up appearances. Nevertheless, decided retrenchment would be necessary. After Bobby had gone to bed, he explained this to his wife.

"What's the matter?" she asked quickly. "Is the firm losing money?"

"No," replied Orde, "it's a matter of reinvestment." He hesitated. "It's a dead secret, which I don't want to get out, but I'm thinking of buying some western timber for Bobby when he grows up."

Carroll laughed softly.

"You so relieve my mind," she smiled at him. "I was afraid you'd decided on the street-car-driver idea. Why, sweetheart, you know perfectly well we could go back to the little house next the church and be as happy as larks."

## XXXII

In the meantime Newmark had closed his desk, picked his hat from the nail, and marched precisely down the street to Heinzman's office. He found the little German in. Newmark demanded a private interview, and without preliminary plunged into the business that had brought him. He had long since taken Heinzman's measure, as, indeed, he had taken the measure of every other man with whom he did or was likely to do business.

"Heinzman," said he abruptly, "my partner wants to raise seventy-five thousand dollars for his personal use. I have agreed to get him that money from the firm."

Heinzman sat immovable, his round eyes blinking behind his big spectacles.

"Proceed," said he shrewdly.

"As security in case he cannot pay the notes the firm will have to give, he has signed an agreement to turn over to me his undivided one-half interest in our enterprises."

"Vell? You vant to borrow dot money of me?" asked Heinzman. "I could not raise it."

"I know that perfectly well," replied Newmark coolly. "You are going to have difficulty meeting your July notes, as it is."

Heinzman hardly seemed to breathe, but a flicker of red blazed in his eye.

"Proceed," he repeated non-committally, after a moment. "I intend," went on Newmark, "to furnish this money myself. It must, however, seem to be loaned by another. I want you to lend this money on mortgage."

"What for?" asked Heinzman.

"For a one tenth of Orde's share in case he does not meet those notes."

"But he vill meet the notes," objected Heinzman. "You are a prosperous concern. I know somethings of YOUR business, also."

"He thinks he will," rejoined Newmark grimly. "I will merely point out to you that his entire income is from the firm, and that from this income he must save twenty-odd thousand a year.

"If the firm has hard luck—" said Heinzman.

"Exactly," finished Newmark.

"Vy you come to me?" demanded Heinzman at length.

"Well, I'm offering you a chance to get even with Orde. I don't imagine you love him?"

"Vat's de matter mit my gettin' efen with you, too?" cried Heinzman. "Ain't you beat me out at Lansing?"

Newmark smiled coldly under his clipped moustache.

"I'm offering you the chance of making anywhere from thirty to fifty thousand dollars."

"Perhaps. And suppose this liddle scheme don't work out?"

"And," pursued Newmark calmly, "I'll carry you over in your present obligations." He suddenly hit the arm of his chair with his clenched fist. "Heinzman, if you don't make those July payments, what's to become of you? Where's your timber and your mills and your new house—and that pretty daughter of yours?"

Heinzman winced visibly.

"I vill get an extension of time," said he feebly.

"Will you?" countered Newmark.

The two men looked each other in the eye for a moment.

"Vell, maybe," laughed Heinzman uneasily. "It looks to me like a winner."

"All right, then," said Newmark briskly. "I'll make out a mortgage at ten per cent for you, and you'll lend the money on it. At the proper time, if things happen that way, you will foreclose. That's all you have to do with it. Then, when the timber land comes to you under the foreclose, you will reconvey an undivided nine-tenths' interest—for proper consideration, of course, and without recording the deed."

Heinzman laughed with assumed lightness.

"Suppose I fool you," said he. "I guess I joost keep it for mineself."

Newmark looked at him coldly.

"I wouldn't," he advised. "You may remember the member from Lapeer County in that charter fight? And the five hundred dollars for his vote? Try it on, and see how much evidence I can bring up. It's called bribery in this State, and means penitentiary usually."

"You don't take a joke," complained Heinzman.

Newmark arose.

"It's understood, then?" he asked.

"How so I know you play fair?" asked the German.

"You don't. It's a case where we have to depend more or less on each other. But I don't see what you stand to lose—and anyway you'll get carried over those July payments," Newmark reminded him.

Heinzman was plainly uneasy and slightly afraid of these new waters in which he swam.

"If you reduce the firm's profits, he iss going to suspect," he admonished.

"Who said anything about reducing the firm's profits?" said Newmark impatiently. "If it does work out that way, we'll win a big thing; if it does not, we'll lose nothing."

He nodded to Heinzman and left the office. His demeanour was as dry and precise as ever. No expression illuminated his impassive countenance. If he felt the slightest uneasiness over having practically delivered his intentions to the keeping of another, he did not show it. For one thing, an accomplice was absolutely essential. And, too, he held the German by his strongest passions—his avarice, his dread of bankruptcy, his pride, and his fear of the penitentiary. As he entered the office of his own firm, his eye fell on Orde's bulky form seated at the desk. He paused involuntarily, and a slight shiver shook his frame from head to foot—the dainty, instinctive repulsion of a cat for a large robustious dog. Instantly controlling himself, he stepped forward.

"I've made the loan," he announced.

Orde looked up with interest.

"The banks wouldn't touch northern peninsula," said Newmark steadily, "so I had to go to private individuals."

"So you said. Don't care who deals it out," laughed Orde.

"Thayer backed out, so finally I got the whole amount from Heinzman," Newmark announced.

"Didn't know the old Dutchman was that well off," said Orde, after a slight pause.

"Can't tell about those secretive old fellows," said Newmark.

Orde hesitated.

"I didn't know he was friendly enough to lend us money."

"Business is business," replied Newmark.

There exists the legend of an eastern despot who, wishing to rid himself of a courtier, armed the man and shut him in a dark room. The victim knew he was to fight something, but whence it was to come, when, or of what nature he was unable to guess. In the event, while groping tense for an enemy, he fell under the fatal fumes of noxious gases.

From the moment Orde completed the secret purchase of the California timber lands from Trace, he became an unwitting participant in one of the strangest duels known to business history. Newmark opposed to him all the subtleties, all the ruses and expedients to which his position lent itself. Orde, sublimely unconscious, deployed the magnificent resources of strength, energy, organisation, and combative spirit that animated his pioneer's soul. The occult manoeuverings of Newmark called out fresh exertions on the part of Orde.

Newmark worked under this disadvantage: he had carefully to avoid the slightest appearance of an attitude inimical to the firm's very best prosperity. A breath of suspicion would destroy his plans. If the smallest untoward incident should ever bring it clearly before Orde that Newmark might have an interest in reducing profits, he could not fail to tread out the logic of the latter's devious ways. For this reason Newmark could not as yet fight even in the twilight. He did not dare make bad sales, awkward transactions. In spite of his best efforts, he could not succeed, without the aid of chance, in striking a blow from which Orde could not recover. The profits of the first year were not quite up to the usual standard, but they sufficed. Newmark's finesse cut in two the firm's income of the second year. Orde roused himself. With his old-time energy of resource, he hurried the woods work until an especially big cut gave promise of recouping the losses of the year before. Newmark found himself struggling against a force greater than he had imagined it to be. Blinded and bound, it nevertheless made head against his policy. Newmark was forced to a temporary quiescence. He held himself watchful, intent, awaiting the opportunity which chance should bring.

Chance seemed by no means in haste. The end of the fourth year found Newmark puzzled. Orde had paid regularly the interest on his notes. How much he had been able to save toward the redemption of the notes themselves his partner was unable to decide. It depended entirely on how much the Ordes had disbursed in living expenses, whether or not Orde had any private debts, and whether or not he had private resources. In the meantime Newmark contented himself with tying up the firm's assets in such a manner as to render it impossible to raise money on its property when the time should come.

What Orde regarded as a series of petty annoyances had made the problem of paying for the California timber a matter of greater difficulty than he had supposed it would be. A pressure whose points of support he could not place was closing slowly on him. Against this pressure he exerted himself. It made him a trifle uneasy, but it did not worry him. The margin of safety was not as broad as he had reckoned, but it existed. And in any case, if worse came to worst, he could always mortgage the California timber for enough to make up the difference—and more. Against this expedient, however, he opposed a sentimental obstinacy. It was Bobby's, and he objected to encumbering it. In fact, Orde was capable of a prolonged and bitter struggle to avoid doing so. Nevertheless, it was there—an asset. A loan on its security would, with what he had set aside, more than pay the notes on the northern peninsula stumpage. Orde felt perfectly easy in his mind. He was in the position of many of our rich men's sons who, quite sincerely and earnestly, go penniless to the city to make their way. They live on their nine dollars a week, and go hungry when they lose their jobs. They stand on their own feet, and yet—in case of severe illness or actual starvation—the old man is there! It gives them a courage to be contented on nothing. So Orde would have gone to almost any lengths to keep free "Bobby's tract," but it stood always between himself and disaster. And a loan on western timber could be paid off just as easily as a loan on eastern timber; when you came right down to that. Even could he have known his partner's intentions, they would, on this account, have caused him no uneasiness, however angry they would have made him, or however determined to break the partnership. Even though Newmark destroyed utterly the firm's profits for the remaining year and a half the notes had to run, he could not thereby ruin Orde's chances. A loan on the California timber would solve all problems now. In this reasoning Orde would have committed the mistake of all large and generous temperaments when called upon to measure natures more subtle than their own. He would have underestimated both Newmark's resources and his own grasp of situations. *

*The author has considered it useless to burden the course of the narrative with a detailed account of Newmark's financial manoeuvres. Realising, however, that a large class of his readers might be interested in the exact particulars, he herewith gives a sketch of the transactions.*

*It will be remembered that at the time—1878—Orde first came in need of money for the purpose of buying the California timber, the firm, Newmark and Orde, owned in the northern peninsula 300,000,000 feet of pine. On this they had paid $150,000, and owed still a like amount. They borrowed $75,000 on it, giving a note secured by mortgage due in 1883. Orde took this, giving in return his note secured by the Boom Company's stock. In 1879 and 1880 they made the two final payments on the timber; so that by the latter date they owned the land free of encumbrance save for the mortgage of $75,000. Since Newmark's plan had always* *contemplated the eventual foreclosure of this mortgage, it now became necessary further to encumber the property. Otherwise, since a property worth considerably above $300,000 carried only a $75,000 mortgage, it would be possible, when the latter came due, to borrow a further sum on a second mortgage with which to meet the obligations of the first. Therefore Newmark, in 1881, approached Orde with the request that the firm raise $70,000 by means of a second mortgage on the timber. This $70,000 he proposed to borrow personally, giving his note due in 1885 and putting up the same collateral as Orde had—that is to say, his stock in the Boom Company. To this Orde could hardly in reason oppose an objection, as it nearly duplicated his own transaction of 1878. Newmark therefore, through Heinzman, lent this sum to himself.*

*It may now be permitted to forecast events in the line of Newmark's reasoning.*

*If his plans should work out, this is what would happen: in 1883 the firm's note for $75,000 would come due. Orde would be unable to pay it. Therefore at once his stock in the Boom Company would become the property of Newmark and Orde. Newmark would profess himself unable to raise enough from the firm to pay the mortgage. The second mortgage from which he had drawn his personal loan would render it impossible for the firm to raise more money on the land. A foreclosure would follow. Through Heinzman, Newmark would buy in. As he had himself loaned the money to himself—again through Heinzman—on the second mortgage, the latter would occasion him no loss.*

*The net results of the whole transaction would be: first, that Newmark would have acquired personally the 300,000,000 feet of northern peninsula timber; and, second, that Orde's personal share in the stock company would flow be held in partnership by the two. Thus, in order to gain so large a stake, it would pay Newmark to suffer considerable loss jointly with Orde in the induced misfortunes of the firm.*

*Incidentally it might be remarked that Newmark, of course, purposed paying his own note to the firm when it should fall due in 1885, thus saving for himself the Boom Company stock which he had put up as collateral.*

Affairs stood thus in the autumn before the year the notes would come due. The weather had been beautiful. A perpetual summer seemed to have embalmed the world in its forgetfulness of times and seasons. Navigation remained open through October and into November. No severe storms had as yet swept the lakes. The barge and her two tows had made one more trip than had been thought possible. It had been the intention to lay them up for the winter, but the weather continued so mild that Orde suggested they be laden with a consignment for Jones and Mabley, of Chicago.

"Did intend to ship by rail," said he. "They're all 'uppers,' so it would pay all right. But we can save all kinds of money by water, and they ought to skip over there in twelve to fifteen hours."

Accordingly, the three vessels were laid alongside the wharves at the mill, and as fast as possible the selected lumber was passed into their holds. Orde departed for the woods to start the cutting as soon as the first belated snow should fall.

This condition seemed, however, to delay. During each night it grew cold. The leaves, after their blaze and riot of colour, turned crisp and crackly and brown. Some of the little, still puddles were filmed with what was almost, but not quite ice. A sheen of frost whitened the house roofs and silvered each separate blade of grass on the lawns. But by noon the sun, rising red in the veil of smoke that hung low in the snappy air, had mellowed the atmosphere until it lay on the cheek like a caress. No breath of wind stirred. Sounds came clearly from a distance. Long V-shaped flights of geese swept athwart the sky, very high up, but their honking came faintly to the ear. And yet, when the sun, swollen to the great dimensions of the rising moon, dipped blood-red through the haze; the first premonitory tingle of cold warned one that the grateful warmth of the day had been but an illusion of a season that had gone. This was not summer, but, in the quaint old phrase, Indian summer, and its end would be as though the necromancer had waved his wand.

To Newmark, sitting at his desk, reported Captain Floyd of the steam barge NORTH STAR.

"All loaded by noon, sir," he said.

Newmark looked up in surprise.

"Well, why do you tell me?" he inquired.

"I want your orders."

"My orders? Why?"

"This is a bad time of year," explained Captain Floyd, "and the storm signal's up. All the signs are right for a blow."

Newmark whirled in his chair.

"A blow!" he cried. "What of it? You don't come in every time it blows, do you?"

"You don't know the lakes, sir, at this time of year," insisted Captain Floyd.

"Are you afraid?" sneered Newmark.

Captain Floyd's countenance burned a dark red.

"I only want your orders," was all he said. "I thought we might wait to see."

"Then go," snapped Newmark. "That lumber must get to the market. You heard Mr. Orde's orders to sail as soon as you were loaded."

Captain Floyd nodded curtly and went out without further comment.

Newmark arose and looked out of the window. The sun shone as balmily soft as ever. English sparrows twittered and fought outside. The warm smell of pine shingles rose from the street. Only close down to the horizon lurked cold, flat, greasy-looking clouds; and in the direction of the Government flag-pole he caught the flash of red from the lazily floating signal. He was little weatherwise, and he shook his head sceptically. Nevertheless it was a chance, and he took it, as he had taken a great many others.

## XXXIV

To Carroll's delight, Orde returned unexpectedly from the woods late that night. He was so busy these days that she welcomed any chance to see him. Much to his disappointment, Bobby had been taken duck-hunting by his old friend, Mr. Kincaid. Next morning, however, Orde told Carroll his stay would be short and that his day would be occupied.

"I'd take old Prince and get some air," he advised. "You're too much indoors. Get some friend and drive around. It's fine and blowy out, and you'll get some colour in your cheeks."

After breakfast Carroll accompanied her husband to the front door. When they opened it a blast of air rushed in, whirling some dead leaves with it.

"I guess the fine weather's over," said Orde, looking up at the sky.

A dull lead colour had succeeded the soft gray of the preceding balmy days. The heavens seemed to have settled down closer to the earth. A rising wind whistled through the branches of the big maple trees, snatching the remaining leaves in handfuls and tossing them into the air. The tops swayed like whips. Whirlwinds scurried among the piles of dead leaves on the lawns, scattering them, chasing them madly around and around in circles.

"B-r-r-r!" shivered Carroll. "Winter's coming."

She kept herself busy about the house all the morning; ate her lunch in solitude. Outside, the fierce wind, rising in a crescendo shriek, howled around the eaves. The day darkened, but no rain fell. At last Carroll resolved to take her husband's advice. She stopped for Mina Heinzman, and the two walked around to the stable, where the men harnessed old Prince into the phaeton.

They drove, the wind at their backs, across the drawbridge, past the ship-yards, and out beyond the mills to the Marsh Road. There, on either side the causeway, miles and miles of cat-tails and reeds bent and recovered under the snatches of the wind. Here and there showed glimpses of ponds or little inlets, the surface of the water ruffled and dark blue. Occasionally one of these bayous swung in across the road. Then the two girls could see plainly the fan-like cat's-paws skittering here and there as though panic-stricken by the swooping, invisible monster that pursued them.

Carroll and Mina Heinzman had a good time. They liked each other very much, and always saw a great deal to laugh at in the things about them and in the subjects about which they talked. When, however, they turned toward home, they were forced silent by the mighty power of the wind against them. The tears ran from their eyes as though they were crying; they had to lower their heads. Hardly could Carroll command vision clear enough to see the road along which she was driving. This was really unnecessary, for Prince was buffeted to a walk. Thus they crawled along until they reached the turn-bridge, where the right-angled change in direction gave them relief. The river was full of choppy waves, considerable in size. As they crossed, the SPRITE darted beneath them, lowering her smokestack as she went under the bridge.

They entered Main Street, where was a great banging and clanging of swinging signs and a few loose shutters. All the sidewalk displays of vegetables and other goods had been taken in, and the doors, customarily wide open, were now shut fast. This alone lent to the street quite a deserted air, which was emphasised by the fact that actually not a rig of any sort stood at the curbs. Up the empty roadway whirled one after the other clouds of dust hurried by the wind.

"I wonder where all the farmers' wagons are?" marvelled the practical Mina. "Surely they would not stay home Saturday afternoon just for this wind!"

Opposite Randall's hardware store her curiosity quite mastered her.

"Do stop!" she urged Carroll. "I want to run in and see what's the matter."

She was gone but a moment, and returned, her eyes shining with excitement.

"Oh, Carroll!" she cried, "there are three vessels gone ashore off the piers. Everybody's gone to see."

"Jump in!" said Carroll. "We'll drive out. Perhaps they'll get out the life-saving crew."

They drove up the plank road over the sand-hill, through the beech woods, to the bluff above the shore. In the woods they were somewhat sheltered from the wind, although even there the crash of falling branches and the whirl of twigs and dead leaves advertised that the powers of the air were abroad; but when they topped the last rise, the unobstructed blast from the open Lake hit them square between the eyes.

Probably a hundred vehicles of all descriptions were hitched to trees just within the fringe of woods. Carroll, however, drove straight ahead until Prince stood at the top of the plank road that led down to the bath houses. Here she pulled up.

Carroll saw the lake, slate blue and angry, with white-capped billows to the limit of vision. Along the shore were rows and rows of breakers, leaping, breaking, and gathering again, until they were lost in a tumble of white foam that rushed and receded on the sands. These did not look to be very large until she noticed the twin piers reaching out from the river's mouth. Each billow, as it came in, rose sullenly above them, broke tempestuously to overwhelm the entire structure of their ends, and ripped inshore along their lengths, the crest submerging as it ran every foot of the massive structures. The piers and the light-houses at their ends looked like little toys, and the compact black crowd of people on the shore below were as small as Bobby's tin soldiers.

"Look there—out farther!" pointed Mina.

Carroll looked, and rose to her feet in excitement.

Three little toy ships—or so they seemed compared to the mountains of water—lay broadside-to, just inside the farthest line of breakers. Two were sailing schooners. These had been thrown on their beam ends, their masts pointing at an angle toward the beach. Each wave, as it reached, stirred them a trifle, then broke in a deluge of water that for a moment covered their hulls completely from sight. With a mighty suction the billow drained away, carrying with it wreckage. The third vessel was a steam barge. She, too, was broadside to the seas, but had caught in some hole in the bar so that she lay far down by the head. The shoreward side of her upper works had, for some freakish reason, given away first, so now the interior of her staterooms and saloons was exposed to view as in the cross-section of a model ship. Over her, too, the great waves hurled themselves, each carrying away its spoil. To Carroll it seemed fantastically as though the barge were made of sugar, and that each sea melted her precisely as Bobby loved to melt the lump in his chocolate by raising and lowering it in a spoon.

And the queer part of it all was that these waves, so mighty in their effects, appeared to the woman no different from those she had often watched in the light summer blows that for a few hours raise the "white caps" on the lake. They came in from the open in the same swift yet deliberate ranks; they gathered with the same leisurely pauses; they broke with the same rush and roar. They seemed no larger, but everything else had been struck small—the tiny ships, the toy piers, the ant-like swarm of people on the shore. She looked on it as a spectacle. It had as yet no human significance.

"Poor fellows!" cried Mina.

"What?" asked Carroll.

"Don't you see them?" queried the other.

Carroll looked, and in the rigging of the schooner she made out a number of black objects.

"Are those men?—up the masts?" she cried.

She set Prince in motion toward the beach.

At the foot of the bluff the plank road ran out into the deep sand. Through this the phaeton made its way heavily. The fine particles were blown in the air like a spray, mingling with the spume from the lake, stinging Carroll's face like so many needles. Already the beach was strewn with pieces of wreckage, some of it cast high above the wash, others still thrown up and sucked back by each wave, others again rising and falling in the billows. This wreckage constituted a miscellaneous jumble, although most of it was lumber from the deck-loads of the vessels. Intermingled with the split and broken yellow boards were bits of carving and of painted wood. Carroll saw one piece half buried in the sand which bore in gilt two huge letters, A R. A little farther, bent and twisted, projected the ornamental spear which had pointed the way before the steamer's bow. Portions of the usual miscellaneous freight cargo carried on every voyage were scattered along the shore—boxes, barrels, and crates. Five or six men had rolled a whisky barrel beyond the reach of the water, had broached it, and now were drinking in turn from a broken and dingy fragment of a beer-schooner. They were very dirty; their hair had fallen over their eyes, which were bloodshot; the expression of their faces was imbecile. As the phaeton passed, they hailed its occupants in thick voices, shouting against the wind maudlin invitations to drink.

The crowd gathered at the pier comprised fully half the population of Monrovia. It centred about the life saving crew, whose mortar was being loaded. A stove-in lifeboat mutely attested the failure of other efforts. The men worked busily, ramming home the powder sack, placing the projectile with the light line attached, attending that the reel ran freely. Their chief watched the seas and winds through his glasses. When the preparations were finished, he adjusted the mortar, and pulled the string. Carroll had seen this done in practice. Now, with the recollection of that experience in mind, she was astonished at the feeble report of the piece, and its freedom from the dense white clouds of smoke that should have enveloped it. The wind snatched both noise and vapour away almost as soon as they were born. The dart with its trailer of line rose on a long graceful curve. The reel sang. Every member of the crowd unconsciously leaned forward in attention. But the resistance of the wind and the line early made itself felt. Slower and slower hummed the reel. There came a time when the missile seemed to hesitate, then fairly to stand in equilibrium. Finally, in an increasingly abrupt curve, it descended into the sea. By a good three hundred yards the shot had failed to carry the line over the vessels.

"There's Mr. Bradford," said Carroll, waving her hand. "I wish he'd come and tell us something about it."

The banjo-playing village Brummell saw the signal and came, his face grave.

"Couldn't they get the lifeboats out to them?" asked Carroll as he approached.

"You see that one," said Bradford, pointing. "Well, the other's in kindling wood farther up the beach."

601

"Anybody drowned?" asked Mina quickly.

"No, we got 'em out. Mr. Cam's shoulder is broken." He glanced down at himself comically, and the girls for the first time noticed that beneath the heavy overcoat his garments were dripping.

"But surely they'll never get a line over with the mortar!" said Carroll. "That last shot fell so far short!"

"They know it. They've shot a dozen times. Might as well do something."

"I should think," said Mina, "that they'd shoot from the end of the pier. They'd be ever so much nearer."

"Tried it," replied Bradford succinctly. "Nearly lost the whole business."

Nobody said anything for some time, but all looked helplessly to where the vessels—from this elevation insignificant among the tumbling waters—were pounding to pieces.

At this moment from the river a trail of black smoke became visible over the point of sand-hill that ran down to the pier. A smokestack darted into view, slowed down, and came to rest well inside the river-channel. There it rose and fell regularly under the influence of the swell that swung in from the lake. The crowd uttered a cheer, and streamed in the direction of the smokestack.

"Come and see what's up," suggested Bradford.

He hitched Prince to a log sticking up at an angle from the sand, and led the way to the pier.

There they had difficulty in getting close enough to see; but Bradford, preceding the two women, succeeded by patience and diplomacy in forcing a way. The SPRITE was lying close under the pier, the top of her pilot-house just about level with the feet of the people watching her. She rose and fell with the restless waters. Fat rope-yarn bumpers interposed between her sides and the piling. The pilot-house was empty, but Harvey, the negro engineer, leaned, elbows crossed against the sill of his little square door, smoking his pipe.

"I wouldn't go out there for a million dollars!" cried a man excitedly to Carroll and Bradford. "Nothing on earth could live in that sea! Nothing! I've run a tug myself in my time, and I know what I'm talking about!"

"What are they going to do?" asked Carroll.

"Haven't you heard!" cried the other, turning to her. "Where you been? This is one of Orde's tugs, and she's going to try to get a line to them vessels. But I wouldn't—"

Bradford did not wait for him to finish. He turned abruptly, and with an air of authority brushed toward the tug, followed closely by Carroll and Mina. At the edge of the pier was the tug's captain, Marsh, listening to earnest expostulation by a half-dozen of the leading men of the town, among whom were both Newmark and Orde.

As the three came within earshot Captain Marsh spit forth the stump of cigar he had been chewing.

"Gentlemen," said he crisply, "that isn't the question. I think I can do it; and I'm entirely willing to take all personal risks. The thing is hazardous and it's Mr. Orde's tug. It's for him to say whether he wants to risk her."

"Good Lord, man, what's the tug in a case like this!" cried Orde, who was standing near. Carroll looked at him proudly, but she did not attempt to make her presence known.

"I thought so," replied Captain Marsh. "So it's settled. I'll take her out, if I can get a crew. Harvey, step up here!"

The engineer slowly hoisted his long figure through the breast-high doorway, dragged his legs under him, then with extraordinary agility swung to the pier, his teeth shining like ivory in his black face.

"Yas, suh!" said he.

"Harvey," said Captain Marsh briskly, "we're going to try to get a line aboard those vessels out there. It's dangerous. You don't have to go if you don't want to. Will you go?"

Harvey removed his cap and scratched his wool. The grin faded from his good-natured countenance.

"You-all goin', suh?" he asked.

"Of course."

"I reckon I'll done haif to go, too," said Harvey simply. Without further word he swung lightly back to the uneasy craft below him, and began to toss the slabs from the deck into the hold.

"I want a man with me at the wheel, two to handle the lines, and one to fire for Harvey," said Captain Marsh to the crowd in general.

"That's our job," announced the life-saving captain.

"Well, come on then. No use in delay," said Captain Marsh.

The four men from the life-saving service dropped aboard. The five then went over the tug from stem to stern, tossing aside all movables, and lashing tight all essentials. From the pilot-house Captain Marsh distributed life preservers. Harvey declined his.

"Whaf-for I want dat?" he inquired. "Lots of good he gwine do me down here!"

Then all hatches were battened down. Captain Marsh reached up to shake the hand which Orde, stooping, offered him.

"I'll try to bring her back all right, sir," said he.

"To hell with the tug!" cried Orde, impatient at this insistence on the mere property aspect. "Bring yourself back."

Captain Marsh deliberately lit another cigar and entered the pilot-house with the other men.

"Cast off!" he cried; and the silent crowd heard clearly the single sharp bell ringing for attention, and then the "jangler" that called for full speed ahead. Awed, they watched the tiny sturdy craft move out into the stream and point to the fury of the open lake.

"Brave chaps! Brave chaps!" said Dr. McMullen to Carroll as they turned away. The physician drew his tall slender figure to its height. "Brave chaps, every one of them. But, do you know, to my mind, the bravest of them all are that nigger—and his fireman—nailed down in the hold where they can't see nor know what's going on, and if—if—" the good doctor blew his nose vigorously five or six times—"well, it's just like a rat in a hole." He shook his head vigorously and looked out to sea. "I read last evening, sir," said he to Bradford, "in a blasted fool medical journal I take, that the race is degenerating. Good God!"

The tug had rounded the end of the pier. The first of her thousand enemies, sweeping in from the open, had struck her fair. A great sheet of white water, slanting back and up, shot with terrific impact against the house and beyond. For an instant the little craft seemed buried; but almost immediately the gleam of her black hull showed her plunging forward dauntlessly.

"That's nothin'!" said the tug captain who had first spoken. "Wait 'til she gets outside!" The watchers streamed down from the pier for a better view. Carroll and Miss Heinzman followed. They saw the staunch little craft drive into three big seas, each of which appeared to bury her completely, save for her upper works. She managed, however, to keep her headway.

"She can stand that, all right," said one of the life-saving crew who had been watching her critically. "The trouble will come when she drops down to the vessels."

In spite of the heavy smashing of head-on seas the SPRITE held her course straight out.

"Where's she going, anyway?" marvelled little Mr. Smith, the stationer. "She's away beyond the wrecks already."

"Probably Marsh has found the seas heavier than he thought and is afraid to turn her broadside," guessed his companion.

"Afraid, hell!" snorted a riverman who overheard.

Nevertheless the SPRITE was now so distant that the loom of the great seas on the horizon swallowed her from view, save when she rose on the crest of some mighty billow.

"Well, what is he doing 'way out there then?" challenged Mr. Smith's friend with some asperity.

"Do'no," replied the riverman, "but whatever it is, it's all right as long as Buck Marsh is at the wheel."

"There, she's turned now," Mr. Smith interposed.

Beneath the trail of black smoke she had shifted direction. And then with startling swiftness the SPRITE darted out of the horizon into full view. For the first time the spectators realised the size and weight of the seas. Not even the sullen pounding to pieces of the vessels on the bar had so impressed them as the sight of the tug coasting with railroad speed down the rush of a comber like a child's toy-boat in the surf. One moment the whole of her deck was visible as she was borne with the wave; the next her bow alone showed high as the back suction caught her and dragged her from the crest into the hollow. A sea rose behind. Nothing of the tug was to be seen. It seemed that no power or skill could prevent her feeling overwhelmed. Yet somehow always she staggered out of the gulf until she caught the force of the billow and was again cast forward like a chip.

"Maybe they ain't catchin' p'ticular hell at that wheel to hold her from yawing!" muttered the tug captain to his neighbour, who happened to be Mr. Duncan, the minister.

Almost before Carroll had time to see that the little craft was coming in, she had arrived at the outer line of breakers. Here the combers, dragged by the bar underneath, crested, curled over, and fell with a roar, just as in milder weather the surf breaks on the beach. When the SPRITE rushed at this outer line of white-water, a woman in the crowd screamed.

But at the edge of destruction the SPRITE came to a shuddering stop. Her powerful propellers had been set to the reverse. They could not hold her against the forward fling of the water, but what she lost thus she regained on the seaward slopes of the waves and in their hollows. Thus she hovered on the edge of the breakers, awaiting her chance.

As long as the seas rolled in steadily, and nothing broke, she was safe. But if one of the waves should happen to crest and break, as many of them did, the weight of water catching the tug on her flat, broad stern deck would indubitably bury her. The situation was awful in its extreme simplicity. Would Captain Marsh see his opportunity before the law of chances would bring along the wave that would overwhelm him?

A realisation of the crisis came to the crowd on the beach. At once the terrible strain of suspense tugged at their souls. Each conducted himself according to his nature. The hardy men of the river and the woods set their teeth until the cheek muscles turned white, and blasphemed softly and steadily. Two or three of the townsmen walked up and down the space of a dozen feet. One, the woman who had screamed, prayed aloud in short hysterical sentences.

"O God! Save them, O Lord! O Lord!"

Orde stood on top of a half-buried log, his hat in his hand, his entire being concentrated on the manoeuvre being executed. Only Newmark apparently remained as calm as ever, leaning against an upright timber, his arms folded, and an unlighted cigar as usual between his lips.

Methodically every few moments he removed his eyeglasses and wiped the lenses free of spray.

Suddenly, without warning, occurred one of those inexplicable lulls that interpose often amid the wildest uproars. For the briefest instant other sounds than the roar of the wind and surf were permitted the multitude on the beach. They heard the grinding of timbers from the stricken ships, and the draining away of waters. And distinctly they heard the faint, far tinkle of the jangler calling again for "full speed ahead."

Between two waves the SPRITE darted forward directly for the nearest of the wrecks. Straight as an arrow's flight she held until from the crowd went up a groan.

"She'll collide!" some one put it into words.

But at the latest moment the tug swerved, raced past, and turned on a long diagonal across the end of the bar toward the piers.

Captain Marsh had chosen his moment with exactitude. To the utmost he had taken advantage of the brief lull of jumbled seas after the "three largest waves" had swept by. Yet in shallow water and with the strong inshore set, even that lull was all too short. The SPRITE was staggered by the buffets of the smaller breakers; her speed was checked, her stern was dragged around. For an instant it seemed that the back suction would hold her in its grip. She tore herself from the grasp of the current. Enveloped in a blinding hail of spray she struggled desperately to extricate herself from the maelstrom in which she was involved before the resumption of the larger seas should roll her over and over to destruction.

Already these larger seas were racing in from the open. To Carroll, watching breathless and wide-eyed in that strange passive and receptive state peculiar to imaginative natures, they seemed alive. And the SPRITE, too, appeared to be, not a fabric and a mechanism controlled by men, but a sentient creature struggling gallantly on her own volition.

Far out in the lake against the tumbling horizon she saw heave up for a second the shoulder of a mighty wave. And instinctively she perceived this wave as a deadly enemy of the little tug, and saw it bending all its great energies to hurrying in on time to catch the victim before it could escape. To this wave she gave all her attention, watching for it after it had sunk momentarily below its fellows, recognising it instantly as it rose again. The spasms of dismay and relief among the crowd about her she did not share at all. The crises they indicated did not exist for her. Until the wave came in, Carroll knew, the SPRITE, no matter how battered and tossed, would be safe. Her whole being was concentrated in a continually shifting calculation of the respective distances between the tug and the piers, the tug and the relentlessly advancing wave.

"Oh, go!" she exhorted the SPRITE under her breath.

Then the crowd, too, caught with its slower perceptions the import of the wave. Carroll felt the electric thrill of apprehension shiver through it. Huge and towering, green and flecked with foam the wave came on now calmly and deliberately as though sure. The SPRITE was off the end of the pier when the wave lifted her, just in the position her enemy would have selected to crush her life out against the cribs. Slowly the tug rose against its shoulder, was lifted onward, poised; and then with a swift forward thrust the wave broke, smothering the pier and lighthouse beneath tons of water.

A low, agonised wail broke from the crowd. And then—and then—over beyond the pier down which the wave, broken and spent but formidable still, was ripping its way, they saw gliding a battered black stack from which still poured defiantly clouds of gray smoke.

For ten seconds the spectators could not believe their eyes. They had distinctly seen the SPRITE caught between a resistless wall of water and the pier; where she should have been crushed like the proverbial egg-shell. Yet there she was—or her ghost.

Then a great cheer rose up against the wind. The crowd went crazy. Mere acquaintances hugged each other and danced around and around through the heavy sands. Several women had hysterics. The riverman next to Mr. Duncan opened his mouth and swore so picturesquely that, as he afterward told his chum, "I must've been plumb inspired for the occasion." Yet it never entered Mr. Duncan's ministerial head to reprove the blasphemy. Orde jumped down from his half-buried log and clapped his hat on his head. Newmark did not alter his attitude nor his expression.

The SPRITE was safe. For the few moments before she glided the length of the long pier to stiller water this fact sufficed.

"I wonder if she got the line aboard," speculated the tug-boat captain at last.

The crowd surged over to the piers again. Below them rose and fell the SPRITE. All the fancy scroll-work of her upper works, the cornice of her deck house, the light rigging of her cabin had disappeared, leaving raw and splintered wood to mark their attachments. The tall smokestack was bent awry, but its supports had held, which was fortunate since otherwise the fires would have been drowned out. At the moment, Captain Marsh was bending over examining a bad break in the overhang—the only material damage the tug had sustained.

At sight of him the crowd set up a yell. He paid no attention. One of the life-saving men tossed a mooring line ashore. It was seized by a dozen men. Then for the first time somebody noticed that although the tug had come to a standstill, her screw was still turning slowly over and over, holding her against the erratic strong jerking of a slender rope that ran through her stern chocks and into the water.

"He got it aboard!" yelled the man, pointing.

Another cheer broke out. The life-saving crew leaped to the deck. They were immediately followed by a crowd of enthusiasts eager to congratulate and question. But Captain Marsh would have none of them.

"Get off my tug!" he shouted. "Do you want to swamp her? What do you suppose we put that line aboard for? Fun? Get busy and use it! Rescue that crew now!"

Abashed, the enthusiasts scrambled back. The life-saving crew took charge. It was necessary to pass the line around the end of the pier and back to the beach. This was a dangerous job, and one requiring considerable power and ingenuity, for the strain on the line imposed by the waters was terrific; and the breaking seas rendered work on the piers extremely hazardous. However, the life-saving captain took charge confidently enough. His crew began to struggle out the pier, while volunteers, under his personal direction, manipulated the reel.

A number of the curious lingered about the SPRITE. Marsh and Orde were in consultation over the smashed stern, and did not look as though they cared to be disturbed. Harvey leaned out his little square door.

"Don' know nuffin 'bout it," said he, "'ceptin' she done rolled 'way over 'bout foh times. Yass she did, suh! I know. I felt her doin' it."

"No," he answered a query. "I wasn't what you-all would call scairt, that is, not really SCAIRT—jess a little ne'vous. All I had to do was to feed her slabs and listen foh my bell. You see, Cap'n Ma'sh, he was in cha'ge."

"No, sir," Captain Marsh was saying emphatically to his employer. "I can't figure it out except on one thing. You see it's stove from UNDERNEATH. A sea would have smashed it from above."

"Perhaps you grounded in between seas out there," suggested Orde.

Marsh smiled grimly.

"I reckon I'd have known it," said he. "No, sir! It sounds wild, but it's the only possible guess. That last sea must've lifted us bodily right over the corner of the pier."

"Well—maybe," assented Orde doubtfully.

"Sure thing," repeated Marsh with conviction.

"Well, you'd better not tell 'em so unless you want to rank in with Old Man Ananias," ended Orde. "It was a good job. Pretty dusty out there, wasn't it?"

"Pretty dusty," grinned Marsh.

They turned away together and were at once pounced on by Leopold Lincoln Bunn, the local reporter, a callow youth aflame with the chance for a big story of more than local interest.

"Oh, Captain Marsh!" he cried. "How did you get around the pier? It looked as though the wave had you caught."

Orde glanced at his companion in curiosity.

"On roller skates," replied Marsh.

Leopold tittered nervously.

"Could you tell me how you felt when you were out there in the worst of it?" he inquired.

"Oh, hell!" said Marsh grumpily, stalking away.

"Don't interview for a cent, does he?" grinned Orde.

"Oh, Mr. Orde! Perhaps you—"

"Don't you think we'd better lend a hand below?" suggested Orde, pointing to the beach.

The wild and picturesque work of rescue was under way. The line had been successfully brought to the left of the lighthouse. To it had been attached the rope, and to that the heavy cable. These the crew of the schooner had dragged out and made fast to a mast. The shore end passed over a tall scissors. When the cable was tightened the breeches buoy was put into commission, and before long the first member of the crew was hauled ashore, plunging in and out of the waves as the rope tightened or slackened. He was a flaxen-haired Norwegian, who stamped his feet, shook his body and grinned comically at those about him. He accepted with equanimity a dozen drinks of whisky thrust at him from all sides, swigged a mug of the coffee a few practical women were making over an open fire, and opposed to Leopold Lincoln Bunn's frantic efforts a stolid and baffling density. Of none of these attentions did he seem to stand in especial need.

The crew and its volunteers worked quickly. When the last man had come ashore, the captain of the life-saving service entered the breeches buoy and caused himself to be hauled through the smother to the wreck. After an interval, a signal jerked back. The buoy was pulled in empty and the surf car substituted. In it were piled various utensils of equipment. One man went with it, and several more on its next trip, until nearly the whole crew were aboard the wreck.

Carroll and Mina stayed until dusk and after, watching the long heavy labour of rescue. Lines had to be rocketed from the schooner to the other vessels. Then by their means cable communication had to be established with the shore. After this it was really a matter of routine to run the crew to the beach, though cruel, hard work, and dangerous. The wrecks were continually swept by the great seas; and at any moment the tortured fabrics might give way, might dissolve completely in the elements that so battered them. The women making the hot coffee found their services becoming valuable. Big fires of driftwood were ignited. They were useful for light as well as warmth.

By their illumination finally Orde discovered the two girls standing, and paused long enough in his own heavy labour of assistance to draw Carroll one side.

"You'd better go home now, sweetheart," said he. "Bobby'll be waiting for you, and the girls may be here in the crowd somewhere. There'll be nobody to take care of him."

"I suppose so," she assented. "But hasn't it been exciting? Whose vessels were they; do you know?"

Orde glanced at her strangely.

"They were ours," said he.

She looked up at him, catching quickly the wrinkles of his brow and the harassed anxiety in his eyes. Impulsively she pulled him down to her and kissed him.

"Never mind, dear," said she. "I care only if you do."

She patted his great shoulders lightly and smiled up at him.

"Run, help!" she cried. "And come home as soon as you can. I'll have something nice and hot all ready for you."

She turned away, the smile still on her lips; but as soon as she was out of sight, her face fell grave.

"Come, Mina!" she said to the younger girl. "Time to go."

They toiled through the heavy sand to where, hours ago, they had left Prince. That faithful animal dozed in his tracks and awoke reluctantly.

Carroll looked back. The fires leaped red and yellow. Against them were the silhouettes of people, and in the farther circle of their illumination were more people cast in bronze that flickered red. In contrast to their glow the night was very dark. Only from the lake there disengaged a faint gray light where the waters broke. The strength of the failing wind still lifted the finer particles of sand. The organ of the pounding surf filled the night with the grandeur of its music.

605

Orde mounted the office stairs next day with a very heavy step. The loss of the NORTH STAR and of the two schooners meant a great deal to him at that time.

"It kicks us into somewhat of a hole," he grumbled to Newmark.

"A loss is never pleasant," replied the latter, "and it puts us out of the carrying business for awhile. But we're insured."

"I can't understand why Floyd started," said Orde. "He ought to know better than to face sure prospects of a fall blow. I'll tan his soul for that, all right!"

"I'm afraid I'm partly responsible for his going," put in Newmark.

"You!" cried Orde.

"Yes. You see that Smith and Mabley shipment was important enough to strain a point for—and it's only twenty-four hours or so—and it certainly didn't look to see me as if it were going to blow very soon. Poor Floyd feels bad enough. He's about sick."

Orde for the first time began to appreciate the pressure of his circumstances. The loss on the cargo of "uppers" reached about 8,000,000 feet; which represented $20,000 in money. As for the NORTH STAR and her consorts, save for the insurance, they were simply eliminated. They had represented property. Now they were gone. The loss of $60,000 or so on them, however, did not mean a diminution of the company's present cash resources to that amount; and so did not immediately affect Orde's calculations as to the payment of the notes which were now soon to come due.

At this time the woods work increasingly demanded his attention. He disappeared for a week, his organising abilities claimed for the distribution of the road crews. When he returned to the office, Newmark, with an air of small triumph, showed him contracts for the construction of three new vessels.

"I get them for $55,000," said he, "with $30,000 of it on long time."

"Without consulting me!" cried Orde.

Newmark explained carefully that the action, seemingly so abrupt, had really been taking advantage of a lucky opportunity.

"Otherwise," he finished, "we shouldn't have been able to get the job done for another year, at least. If that big Cronin contract goes through—well, you know what that would mean in the shipyards—nobody would get even a look-in. And McLeod is willing, in the meantime, to give us a price to keep his men busy. So you see I had to close at once. You can see what a short chance it was."

"It's a good chance, all right," admitted Orde; "but—why—that is, I thought perhaps we'd job our own freighting for awhile—it never occurred to me we'd build any more vessels until we'd recovered a little."

"Recovered," Newmark repeated coldly. "I don't see what 'recovered' has to do with it. If the mill burned down, we'd rebuild, wouldn't we? Even if we were embarrassed—which we're not—we'd hardly care to acknowledge publicly that we couldn't keep up our equipment. And as we're making twelve or fifteen thousand a year out of our freighting, it seems to me too good a business to let slip into other hands."

"I suppose so," agreed Orde, a trifle helplessly.

"Therefore I had to act without you," Newmark finished. "I knew you'd agree. That's right: isn't it?" he insisted.

"Yes, that's right," agreed Orde drearily.

"You'll find copies of the contract on your desk," Newmark closed the matter. "And there's the tax lists. I wish you'd run them over."

"Joe," replied Orde, "I—I don't think I'll stay down town this morning. I—"

Newmark glanced up keenly.

"You don't look a bit well," said he; "kind of pale around the gills. Bilious. Don't believe that camp grub quite agrees with you for a steady diet."

"Yes, that must be it," assented Orde.

He closed his desk and went out. Newmark turned back to his papers. His face was expressionless. From an inner pocket he produced a cigar which he thrust between his teeth. The corners of his mouth slowly curved in a grim smile.

Orde did not go home. Instead, he walked down Main Street to the docks where he jumped into a rowboat lying in a slip, and with a few rapid strokes shot out on the stream. In his younger days he had belonged to a boat club, and had rowed in the "four." He still loved the oar, and though his racing days were past, he maintained a clean-lined, rather unstable little craft which it was his delight to propel rapidly with long spoon-oars whenever he needed exercise. To-day, however, he was content to drift.

The morning was still and golden. The crispness of late fall had infused a wine into the air. The sky was a soft, blue-gray; the sand-hills were a dazzling yellow. Orde did not try to think; he merely faced the situation, staring it in the face until it should shrink to its true significance.

One thing he felt distinctly; yet could not without a struggle bring himself to see. The California lands must be mortgaged. If he could raise a reasonable sum of money on them, he would still be perfectly able to meet his notes. He hated fiercely to raise that money.

It was entirely a matter of sentiment. Orde realised the fact clearly, and browbeat his other self with a savage contempt. Nevertheless his dream had been to keep the western timber free and unencumbered—for Bobby. Dreams are harder to give up than realities.

He fell into the deepest reflections which were broken only when the pounding of surf warned him he had drifted almost to the open lake. After all, there was no essential difference between owing money to a man in Michigan and to a man in California. That was the net result of his struggle.

"When the time comes, we'll just borrow that money on a long-time mortgage, like sensible people," he said aloud, "and quit this everlasting scrabbling."

Back to town he pulled with long vigorous strokes, skittering his feathered spoon-oars lightly over the tops of the wavelets. At the slip he made fast the boat, and a few minutes later re-entered the office, his step springy, his face glowing. Newmark glanced up.

"Hullo!" said he. "Back again? You look better."

"Exercise," said Orde, in his hearty manner. "Exercise, old boy! You ought to try it. Greatest thing in the world. Just took a row to the end of the piers and back, and I'm as fit as a fiddle!"

## XXXVI

Orde immediately set into motion the machinery of banking to borrow on the California timber. Taylor took charge of this, as the only man in Monrovia who had Orde's confidence. At the end of a necessary delay Orde received notice that the West had been heard from. He stepped across the hall to the lawyer's office.

"Well, Frank," said he, "glad we managed to push it through with so little trouble."

Taylor arose, shut carefully the door into his outer office, walked to the window, looked contemplatively out upon the hotel backyard, and returned to his desk.

"But there is trouble," said he curtly.

"What's the matter?" asked Orde.

"The banks refuse the loan."

Orde stared at him in blank astonishment.

"Refuse!" he echoed.

"Absolutely."

"What grounds can they possibly have for that?"

"I can't make out exactly from these advices. It's something about the title."

"But I thought you went over the title."

"I did," stated Taylor emphatically; "and I'll stake my reputation as a lawyer that everything is straight and clear from the Land Office itself. I've wired for an explanation; and we ought surely to know something definite by tomorrow."

With this uncertainty Orde was forced to be content. For the first time in his business career a real anxiety gnawed at his vitals. He had been in many tight places; but somehow heretofore success or failure had seemed to him about immaterial, like points gained or conceded in the game; a fresh start was always so easy, and what had been already won as yet unreal. Now the game itself was at issue. Property, reputation, and the family's future were at stake. When the three had lived in the tiny house by the church, it had seemed that no adversity could touch them. But now that long use had accustomed them to larger quarters, servants, luxuries, Orde could not conceive the possibility of Carroll's ever returning to that simplest existence. Carroll could have told him otherwise; but of course he did not as yet bring the possibility before her. She had economised closely, these last few years. Orde was proud of her. He was also fiercely resentful that his own foolishness, or untoward circumstances, or a combination of both should jeopardise her future. Therefore he awaited further news with the greatest impatience.

The message came the following day, as Taylor had predicted. Taylor handed it to him without comment.

"Land Office under investigation," Orde read. "Fraudulent entries suspected. All titles clouded until decision is reached."

"What do you suppose that means?" asked Orde, although he knew well enough.

Taylor glanced up at his dull eyes with commiseration.

"They simply won't lend good money on an uncertainty," said he.

"Frank," said Orde, rousing himself with an effort, "I've got to be here. I couldn't get away this winter if my life depended on it. And I won't even have time to pay much attention to it from here. I want you to go to California and look after those interests for me. Never mind your practice, man," as Taylor tried to interrupt him. "Make what arrangements you please; but go. It'll be like a sort of vacation to you. You need one. And I'll make it worth your while. Take Clara with you. She'll like California. Now don't say no. It's important. Straighten it out as quick as you can: and the minute it IS straight borrow that money on it, and send it on p.d.q."

Taylor thoughtfully tapped his palm with the edge of his eye-glasses.

"All right," he said at last.

"Good!" cried Orde, rising and holding out his hand.

He descended the dark stairs to the street, where he turned down toward the river. There he sat on a pile for nearly an hour, quite oblivious to the keen wind of latter November which swept up over the scum ice from the Lake. At length he hopped down and made his way to the office of the Welton Lumber Co.

"Look here, Welton," he demanded abruptly when he had reached that operator's private office, "how much of a cut are you going to make this year?"

"About twenty million," replied Welton. "Why?"

"Just figuring on the drive," said Orde, nodding a farewell.

He had the team harnessed, and, assuming his buffalo-fur coat, drove to the offices of all the men owning timber up and down the river. When he had collected his statistics, he returned to his desk, where he filled the backs of several envelopes with his characteristically minute figures. At the close of his calculations he nodded his head vigorously several times.

"Joe," he called across to his partner, "I'm going to cut that whole forty million we have left."

Newmark did not turn. After a moment his dry expressionless voice came back.

"I thought that we figured that as a two-years' job."

"We did, but I'm going to clean up the whole thing this year."

"Do you think you can do it?"

"Sure thing," replied Orde. Then under his breath, and quite to himself, he added: "I've got to!"

## XXXVII

The duel had now come to grapples. Orde was fighting for his very life. The notes given by Newmark and Orde would come due by the beginning of the following summer. Before that time Orde must be able to meet them personally, or, as by the agreement with Newmark, his stock in the Boom Company would be turned in to the firm. This would, of course, spell nearly a total loss of it, as far as Orde was concerned.

The chief anxiety under which the riverman laboured, however, was the imminent prospect of losing under the mortgage all the Northern Peninsula timber. He had thought that the firm would be able to step in for its redemption, even if he personally found himself unable to meet the obligation. Three hundred million feet would seem to be too important a matter to let go under so small a mortgage. Now as the time approached, he realised that if he could not pay the notes, the firm would certainly be unable to do so. What with the second mortgage, due two years later, and to be met by Newmark; with the outstanding obligations; with the new enterprise of the vessels ordered from Duncan McLeod, Newmark and Orde would be unable to raise anything like the necessary amount. To his personal anxieties Orde added a deep and bitter self-reproach at having involved his partner in what amounted to a total loss.

Spurred doubly by these considerations, then, he fell upon the woods work with unparalleled ferocity. A cut and sale of the forty million feet remaining of the firm's up-river holdings, together with the tolls to be collected for driving the river that spring would, if everything went right and no change in the situation took place, bring Orde through the venture almost literally by "the skin of his teeth." To cut forty million feet, even in these latter days of improvements then unknown, would be a task to strain to the utmost every resource of energy, pluck, equipment and organisation. In 1880-81 the operators on the river laughed good-humouredly over an evident madness.

Nevertheless Orde accomplished the task. To be sure he was largely helped by a favourable winter. The cold weather came early and continued late. Freezing preceded the snow, which was deep enough for good travoying and to assure abundant freshet water in the spring, but not too deep to interfere with the work. Orde increased his woods force; and, contrary to his custom, he drove them mercilessly. He was that winter his own walking-boss, and lived constantly in the woods. The Rough Red had charge of the banking, where his aggressive, brutal personality kept the rollways free from congestion. For congestion there means delay in unloading the sleighs; and that in turn means a drag in the woods work near the skidways at the other end of the line. Tom North and Tim Nolan and Johnny Sims and Jim Denning were foremen back in the forest. Every one had an idea, more or less vague, that the Old Fellow had his back to the wall. Late into the night the rude torches, made quite simply from brown stone jugs full of oil and with wicks in their necks, cast their flickering glare over the ice of the haul-roads. And though generally in that part of Michigan the thaws begin by the first or second week in March, this year zero weather continued even to the eighth of April. When the drive started, far up toward headwaters, the cut was banked for miles along the stream, forty million feet of it to the last timber.

The strain over, Orde slept the clock around and awoke to the further but familiar task of driving the river. He was very tired; but his spirit was at peace. As always after the event, he looked back on his anxieties with a faint amusement over their futility.

From Taylor he had several communications. The lawyer confessed himself baffled as to the purpose and basis of the Land Office investigation. The whole affair appeared to be tangled in a maze of technicalities and a snarl of red-tape which it would take some time to unravel. In the meantime Taylor was enjoying himself; and was almost extravagant in his delight over the climate and attractions of Southern California.

Orde did not much care for this delay. He saw his way clear to meeting his obligations without the necessity of hypothecating the California timber; and was the better pleased for it. With the break-up of spring he started confidently with the largest drive in the history of the river, a matter of over two hundred million feet.

This tremendous mass of timber moved practically in three sections. The first, and smallest, comprised probably thirty millions. It started from the lowermost rollways on the river, drove rapidly through the more unobstructed reaches, and was early pocketed above Monrovia in the Company's distributing booms. The second and largest section of a hundred million came from the main river and its largest tributaries. It too made a safe drive; and was brought to rest in the main booms and in a series of temporary or emergency booms built along the right bank and upstream from the main works. The third section containing a remainder of about seventy million had by the twenty-sixth of June reached the slack water above the city of Redding.

## XXXVIII

The morning of June twenty-sixth dawned clear. Orde was early on the road before the heat of the day. He drove his buckboard rapidly over the twelve miles that separated his home from the distributing booms, for he wanted at once to avoid the heat of the first sun and to arrive at the commencement of the day's work. After a glance at the river, he entered the tiny office and set about the examination of the tally sheets left by the foreman. While he was engaged in this checking, the foreman, Tom North, entered.

"The river's rising a little"? he remarked conversationally as he reached for the second set of tally boards.

"You're crazy," muttered Orde, without looking up. "It's clear as a bell; and there have been no rains reported from anywhere."

"It's rising a little, just the same," insisted North, going out.

An hour later Orde, having finished his clerical work, walked out over the booms. The water certainly had risen; and considerably at that. A decided current sucked through the interstices in the piling. The penned logs moved uneasily.

"I should think it was rising!" said Orde to himself, as he watched the slowly moving water. "I wonder what's up. It can't be merely those rains three days ago."

He called one of the younger boys to him, Jimmy Powers by name.

"Here, Jimmy," said he, "mark one of these piles and keep track of how fast the water rises."

For some time the river remained stationary, then resumed its slow increase. Orde shook his head.

"I don't like June floods," he told Tom North. "A fellow can understand an ordinary spring freshet, and knows about how far it will go; but these summer floods are so confounded mysterious. I can't figure out what's struck the old stream, unless they're having almighty heavy rains up near headwaters."

By three o'clock in the afternoon Jimmy Powers reported a rise since morning of six inches. The current had proportionately increased in power.

"Tom," said Orde to the old riverman, "I'm going to send Marsh down for the pile-drivers and some cable. The barge company has some fifteen inch manilla."

North laughed.

"What in blazes do you expect to do with that?" he inquired.

"We may need them," Orde stated with conviction. "Everything's safe enough now; and probably will continue so; but I can't afford to take chances. If those logs ever break through they'll go on out to Lake Michigan and there they wouldn't be worth the salvage."

Tom North stared at his principal in surprise.

"That's a mighty long chance," he commented. "Never knew you to come so near croaking before, Jack."

"If this drive goes out, it surely busts me," replied Orde, "and I'm not taking even long chances."

Captain Marsh, returning with the SPRITE, brought an evening paper and news from the telegraph offices. A cloudburst in the China Creek district followed by continued heavy rains was responsible for the increased water. The papers mentioned this only incidentally, and in explanation. Their columns were filled with an account of the big log jam that had formed above the iron railroad bridge. The planing mill's booms had given way under pressure and the contents had piled down stream against the buttresses. Before steps could be taken to clear the way, the head of the drive, hurried by the excess water, had piled in on top. Immediately a jam formed, increasing in weight each moment, until practically the entire third section had piled up back of the bridge.

The papers occupied themselves with the picturesque side of the affair. None expressed any anxiety as to the bridge. It was a new structure, each of whose bents weighed over a hundred tons. A fall of a few inches only would suffice to lock the jam solidly, thus relieving whatever pressure the mass exerted against the iron bridge. That the water would shortly go down was of course inevitable at this time of year. It would be a big jam for the rivermen to break, however.

"Do you think you'll go up there?" asked North.

Orde shook his head.

"They're in a nice pickle," he acknowledged; "but Nolan's in charge and will do his best. I think we may have troubles of our own right here at home."

He slept that night at the booms. The water, contrary to all expectation, rose steadily. By morning it had crept so far up the piles that there began to be danger that it would overflow their tops. In that case, of course, the logs in the booms would also run out.

"Guess it's time we did a little work," remarked Orde.

He set a crew of men to raising the height of the piling by tying logs firmly to the bolted timbers atop. This would take care of an extra two feet of water; a two feet beyond all previous records. Another crew stretched the fifteen inch manilla cables across the field of logs in order to segregate them into several units of mass, and so prevent them from piling up at the down-stream end of the enclosure. The pile-driver began to drop its hammer at spots of weakness. In spite of the accelerated current and the increased volume of the river, everything was soon shipshape and safe.

"We're all right now," said Orde. "The only thing I'm a little uneasy about is those confounded temporary booms upstream. Still they're all right unless they get to piling up. Then we'll have to see what we can do to hold them. I think as soon as the driver is through down at the sorting end, she'd better drive a few clumps of piles to strengthen the swing when it is shut. Then if the logs pile down on us from above, we can hold them there."

About two hours later the pile-driver moved up. The swing was opened; and the men began to drive clumps of piles in such a position as to strengthen the swing when the latter should be shut. It was a slow job. Each pile had to be taken from the raft at the stern of the scow, erected in the "carrier," and pounded into place by the heavy hammer raised and let drop in the derrick at the bow.

Long before the task was finished, the logs in the temporary booms had begun to slide atop one another, to cross and tangle, until at last the river bed inside the booms was filled with a jam of formidable dimensions. From beneath it the water boiled in eddies. Orde, looking at it, roused himself to sudden activity.

"Get a move on," he advised Captain Aspinwall of the driver. "If that jam breaks on us, we want to be ready; and if it don't break before you get this swing strengthened, maybe we can hold her where she is. There's no earthly doubt that those boom piles will never stand up when they get the full pressure of the freshet."

He departed up river on a tour of inspection from which he returned almost immediately.

"Hurry up! Hurry up!" he cried. "She can't last much longer!"

Indeed even to the men on the pile-driver, evidences of the pressure sustained by the slender boom piles were not wanting. Above the steady gurgle of the water and the intermittent puffing and other noises of the work, they could hear a creaking and groaning of timbers full of portent to those who could read the signs.

The driver's crew laboured desperately, hoisting the piles into the carriage, tripping the heavy hammer, sending it aloft again, binding feverishly the clumps of piles together by means of cables. Each man worked with an eye over his shoulder, fearful of the power that menaced him.

Two of the clumps had been placed and bound; a third was nearly finished, when suddenly, with a crack and a roar the upper booms gave way, projecting their logs upon the opening and the driver.

The half dozen members of the crew, caught utterly unaware in spite of the half warning they had been receiving for an hour past, were scattered by the winds of a panic. Two or three flung themselves on their faces; several ran from one end of the scow to the other; one leaped into the river! Imminent destruction seemed upon them.

Tom North, at the winch that operated the arm of the swing, however, retained his presence of mind. At the first sag outward of the boom piles he set in operation the machinery that closed the gate. Clumsy and slow as was his mechanism, he nevertheless succeeded in getting the long arm started. The logs, rushing in back of it, hurried it shut. Immediately they jammed again, and heaped up in a formidable tangle behind the barrier. Tom North, his little black pipe between his teeth, stood calm, the lever of his winch in his hand. A short three feet from the spot on which he stood, the first saw log of the many that might have overwhelmed him thrust forward its ugly head. The wash of the water lifted the huge pile-driver bodily and deposited it with a crash half on the bank and half in the water.

Instantly after the first break Orde had commenced running out over the booms from the shore.

"Good boy, Tom!" he shot at North as he passed.

Across the breast of the jam he hurried, and to the other bank where the pile-driver lay. The crew had recovered from their panic, and were ashore gazing curiously underneath the scow. Captain Aspinwall examined the supports of the derrick on deck.

"That was lucky," said Orde briefly to Aspinwall. "How's the damage? Stove you in?"

"I—I don't think so," replied the captain, turning a rather perturbed face to Orde.

"That's good. I'll send over the tug to help get her afloat. We've got our work cut out for us now. As soon as you're afloat, blow your whistle and I'll come over to tell you what to do."

"You don't expect me to work my driver under the face of that jam!" cried the captain.

"Certainly," snapped Orde, wheeling.

"Not me!" said Aspinwall positively. "I know when I've got enough!"

"What's the matter?" asked Orde.

"It isn't safe," replied the captain; "and I don't intend to risk my men or my driver."

Orde stood for a moment stock-still; then with a snort of anger he leaped to the deck, seized the man by the neck and thrust him bodily over the side to the bank.

"Safe, you white-livered skunk!" he roared. "Safe! Go over in the middle of that ten-acre lot and lie down on your face and see if you feel safe there! Get out; the whole pack of you! I'm in charge here now."

Captain Aspinwall picked himself up, his face red with anger.

"Get off my driver," he snarled. "Put that man off."

Orde seized a short heavy bar.

"This driver is requisitioned," said he. "Get out! I haven't time to fool with you. I've got to save my logs."

They hesitated; and while they did so Tom North and some others of the crew came running across the jam.

"Get a cable to the winch," Orde shouted at these as soon as they were within hearing. "And get Marsh up here with the SPRITE. We've got to get afloat."

He paid no more attention to the ejected crew. The latter, overawed by the rivermen, who now gathered in full force, took the part of spectators.

A few minutes' hard work put the driver afloat. Fortunately its raft of piles had not become detached in the upheaval.

"Tom," said Orde briskly to North, "you know the pile-driver business. Pick out your crew, and take charge."

In ten seconds of time the situation had changed from one of comparative safety to one of extreme gravity. The logs, broken loose from the upper temporary booms, now jammed against the swing and against the other logs already filling the main booms. Already the pressure was beginning to tell, as the water banked up behind the mass. The fifteen-inch cables tightened slowly but mightily; some of the piles began to groan and rub one against the other; here and there a log deliberately up-ended above the level.

Orde took charge of the situation in its entirety, as a general might. He set North immediately to driving clumps each of sixteen piles, bound to solidity by chains, and so arranged in angles and slants as to direct the enormous pressure toward either bank, thus splitting the enemy's power. The small driver owned by the Boom Company drove similar clumps here, there and everywhere that need arose or weakness developed. Seventy-five men opposed, to the weight of twenty million tons of logs and a river of water, the expedients invented by determination and desperation.

As in a virulent disease, the symptoms developed rapidly when once the course of the malady was assured. After the first rush, when the upper booms broke, nothing spectacular occurred. Steadily and relentlessly the logs, packed close together down to the very bed of the stream, pressed outward against the frail defences. Orde soon found himself forced from the consideration of definite plans of campaign. He gave over formal defences, and threw his energies to saving the weak places which rapidly developed. By the most tremendous exertions he seemed but just able to keep even. So closely balanced was the equilibrium between the improvisation of defence and the increase of pressure behind the jam that it seemed as if even a moment's breathing spell would bring the deluge. Piles quivered, bent slowly outward—immediately, before the logs behind them could stir, the pile-driver must do its work. Back and forth darted the SPRITE and her sister-tug the SPRAY towing the pile-drivers or the strings of piles. Under the frowning destruction that a breath might loosen, the crews had to do their work. And if ever that breath should come, there would be no chance for escape. Crushed and buried, the men and their craft alike would be borne with the breaking jam to an unknown grave in the Lake. Every man knew it.

Darkness came. No one stopped for food. By the light of lanterns the struggle went on, doubly terrifying in the mystery of night. By day the men, practised in such matters, could at least judge of the probabilities of a break. At night they had to work blindly, uncertain at what moment the forces they could not see would cut loose to overwhelm them.

Morning found no change in the situation. The water rose steadily; the logs grew more and more restive; the defences weaker and more inadequate. Orde brought out steaming pails of coffee which the men gulped down between moments. No one thought of quitting. They were afire with the flame of combat, and were set obstinately on winning even in the face of odds. About ten o'clock they were reinforced by men from the mills downstream. The Owners of those mills had no mind to lose their logs. Another pile-driver was also sent up from the Government work. Without this assistance the jam must surely have gone out. Spectators marvelled how it held as it did. The mass seemed constantly to quiver on the edge of motion. Here and there over the surface of the jam single logs could be seen popping suddenly into the air, propelled as an apple seed is projected from between a boy's thumb and forefinger. Some of the fifteen-inch cables stretched to the shore parted. One, which passed once around an oak tree before reaching its shore anchorage, actually buried itself out of sight in the hard wood. Bunches of piles bent, twisted, or were cut off as though they had been but shocks of Indian corn. The current had become so swift that the tugs could not hold the drivers against it; and as a consequence, before commencing operations, special mooring piles had to be driven. Each minute threatened to bring an end to the jam, yet it held; and without rest the dogged little insects under its face toiled to gain an inch on the waters.

## XXXIX

All that day and the next night the fight was hand to hand, without the opportunity of a breathing space. Then Orde, bareheaded and dishevelled, strung to a high excitement, but cool as a veteran under fire, began to be harassed by annoyances. The piles provided for the drivers gave out. Newmark left, ostensibly to purchase more. He did not return. Tom North and Jim Denning, their eyes burning deep in their heads for lack of sleep, came to Orde holding to him symbolically their empty hands.

"No more piles," they said briefly.

"Get 'em," said Orde with equal brevity. "Newmark will have enough here shortly. In the meantime, get them."

North and his friend disappeared, taking with them the crews of the drivers and the two tugs. After an interval they returned towing small rafts of the long timbers. Orde did not make any inquiries; nor until days later did he see a copy of the newspaper telling how a lawless gang of rivermen had driven away the railroad men and stolen the railroad's property. These piles lasted five or six hours. Tom North placed and drove them accurately and deliberately, quite unmindful of the constant danger. A cold fire seemed to consume the man, inflaming his courage and his dogged obstinacy. Once a wing of the jam broke suddenly just as his crew had placed a pile in the carrier. The scow was picked up, whirled around, carried bodily a hundred feet, and deposited finally with a crash. The instant the craft steadied and even before any one could tell whether or no the danger was past, Tom cut loose the hammer and drove that pile!

"I put you in that carrier to be DROVE!" he shouted viciously, "and drove you'll be, if we ARE goin' to hell!"

When the SPRAY shouldered the scow back to position that one pile was left standing upright in the channel, a monument to the blind determination of the man.

Fortunately the wing break carried with it but a few logs; but it sufficed to show, if demonstration were needed, what would happen if any more serious break should occur.

Orde was everywhere. Long since he had lost his hat; and over his forehead and into his eyes the strands of his hair whipped tousled and unkempt. Miles and miles he travelled; running along the tops of the booms, over the surface of the jam, spying the weakening places, and hurrying to them a rescue. He seemed tireless, omnipresent, alive to every need. It was as though his personality alone held in correlation these struggling forces; as though were he to relax for an instant his effort they would burst forth with the explosion of long-pent energies.

Toward noon the piles gave out again.

"Where in HELL is Newmark!" exploded Orde, and immediately was himself again, controlled and resourceful. He sent North and a crew of men to cut piles from standing timber in farm wood lots near the river.

"Haul them out with your winch," said he. "If the owners object, stand them off with your peavies. Get them anyway."

About three of the afternoon the LUCY BELLE splattered up stream from the village, carrying an excursion to see the jam. Captain Simpson brought her as close in as possible. The waves raised by her awkward paddle-wheel and her clumsy lines surged among the logs and piles. Orde looked on this with distrust.

"Go tell him to pull out of that," he instructed Jimmy Powers "The confounded old fool ought to know better than that. Tell him it's dangerous. If the jam goes out, it'll carry him to Kingdom Come."

Jimmy Powers returned red-faced from his interview.

"He told me to go to hell," he said shortly.

"Oh, he did," snapped Orde. "I should think we had enough without that old idiot!"

With the short nervous leaps of a suppressed anger he ran down to where the SPRITE had just towed the Number One driver into a new position.

"Lay me alongside the LUCY BELLE," he told Marsh.

But Simpson, in a position of importance at last, was disinclined to listen. He had worn his blue clothes and brass buttons for a good many years in charge only of boxes and barrels. Now at a stroke he found himself commander over tenscore people. Likewise, at fifty cents a head, he foresaw a good thing as long as high water should last. He had risen nobly to the occasion; for he had even hoisted his bunting and brought with him the local brass band. Orde, brusque in his desire to hurry through an affair of minor importance, rubbed the man the wrong way.

"I reckon I've some rights on this river," Captain Simpson concluded the argument, "and I ain't agoin' to be bulldozed out of them."

The excursionists, typical "trippers" from Redding, Holland, Monrovia and Muskegon, cheered this sentiment and jeered at Orde.

Orde nodded briefly.

"Marsh," said he to his captain in a low voice, "get a crew and take them in charge. Run 'em off."

As soon as the tug touched the piling, he was off and away, paying no further attention to a matter already settled. Captain Marsh called a dozen rivermen to him; laid the SPRITE alongside the LUCY BELLE, and in spite of Simpson's scandalised protests and an incipient panic among the passengers, thrust aside the regular crew of the steamship and took charge. Quite calmly he surveyed the scene. From the height of the steamer's bridge he could see abroad over the country. A warm June sun flooded the landscape which was filled with the peace of early summer. The river seemed to flow smoothly and quietly enough, in spite of the swiftness of its current and the swollen volume of its waters. Only up stream where the big jam shrugged and groaned did any element jar on the peace of the scene; and even that, in contrast to the rest of the landscape, afforded small hint to the inexperienced eye of the imminence of a mighty destruction.

Captain Marsh paid little attention to all this. His eye swept rapidly up and down where the banks used to be until he saw a cross current deeper than the rest sweeping in athwart the inundated fields. He swung over the wheel and rang to the engine-room for half speed ahead. Slowly the LUCY BELLE answered. Quite calmly Captain Marsh rammed her through the opening and out over the cornfields. The LUCY BELLE was a typical river steamboat, built light in the draught in order to slide over the numerous shifting bars to be encountered in her customary business. When Captain Marsh saw that he had hit the opening, he rang for full speed, and rammed the poor old LUCY BELLE hard aground in about a foot of water through which a few mournful dried cornstalks were showing their heads. Then, his hands in his pockets, he sauntered out of the pilot-house to the deck.

"Now if you want to picnic," he told the astonished and frightened excursionists, "go to it!"

With entire indifference to the water, he vaulted over the low rail and splashed away. The rivermen and the engineer who had accompanied him lingered only long enough to start up the band.

"Now you're safe as a cow tied to a brick wall," said the Rough Red, whose appearance alone had gone far toward overawing the passengers. "Be joyful. Start up the music. Start her up, I tell you!"

The band hastily began to squawk, very much out of time, and somewhat out of tune.

"That's right," grinned the Rough Red savagely, "keep her up. If you quit before I get back to work, I'll come back and take you apart."

They waded through the shallow water in the cornfield. After them wafted the rather disorganised strains of WHOA, EMMA. Captain Simpson was indulging in what resembled heat apoplexy. After a time the LUCY BELLE'S crew recovered their scattered wits sufficiently to transport the passengers in small boats to a point near the county road, whence all trudged to town. The LUCY BELLE grew in the cornfield until several weeks later, when time was found to pull her off on rollers.

Arrived at the booms Captain Marsh shook the loose water from his legs.

"All right, sir," he reported to Orde. "I ran 'em ashore yonder."

Orde looked up, brushing the hair from his eyes. He glanced in the direction of the cornfield, and a quick grin flickered across the absorbed expression of his face.

"I should think you did," said he briefly. "I guess that'll end the excursion business. Now take Number Two up below the swing; and then run down and see if you can discover Tom. He went somewhere after piles about an hour ago."

Down river the various mill owners were busy with what men they had left in stringing defences across the river in case Orde's works should go out. When Orde heard this he swore vigourously.

"Crazy fools," he spat out. "They'd be a lot better off helping here. If this goes out, their little booms won't amount to a whiff of wind."

He sent word to that effect; but, lacking the enforcement of his personal presence his messages did not carry conviction, and the panic-stricken owners continued to labour, each according to his ideas, on what Orde's clearer vision saw to be a series of almost comical futilities. However, Welton answered the summons. Orde hailed his coming with a shout.

"I want a dredge," he yelled, as soon as the lumberman was within distance. "I believe we can relieve the pressure somewhat by a channel into Steam's bayou. Get that Government dredge up and through the bayou as soon as you can."

"All right," said Welton briefly. "Can you hold her?"

"I've got to hold her," replied Orde between his clenched teeth. "Have you seen Newmark? Where in HELL is Newmark? I need him for fifty things, and he's disappeared off the face of the earth! Purdy! that second cable! She's snapped a strand! Get a reinforcing line on her!" He ran in the direction of the new danger without another thought of Welton.

By the late afternoon casual spectators from the countryside had gathered in some number. The bolder or more curious of these added a further touch of anxiety to the situation by clambering out over the jam for a better view. Orde issued instructions that these should keep off the logs; but in spite of that, with the impertinent perseverance of the sight-seer, many persisted from time to time, when the rivermen were too busily engaged to attend to them, in venturing out where they were not only in danger but also in the way. Tom North would have none of this on his pile-driver. If a man was not actually working, he had no business on Number One.

"But," protested a spectator mildly, "I OWN this driver. I haven't any objections to your grabbing her in this emergency, even if you did manhandle my captain; but surely you are not going to keep me off my own property?"

"I don't give a tinker's damn who you are," replied North sturdily. "If you're not working, you get off."

And get off he did.

The broad deck of the pile-driver scow was a tempting point from which to survey the work, and the ugly jam, and the water boiling angrily, and the hollow-eyed, dishevelled maniacs who worked doggedly with set teeth as though they had not already gone without two nights' sleep. North had often to order ashore intruders, until his temper shortened to the vanishing point. One big hulking countryman attempted to argue the point. North promptly knocked him overboard into the shallow water between the driver and the bank. He did not rise; so North fished for him in the most matter-of-fact way with a boat hook, threw him on the bank unconscious, and went on driving piles! The incident raised a laugh among the men.

But flesh and blood has its limit of endurance; and that limit was almost reached. Orde heard the first premonitions of reaction in the mild grumblings that arose. He knew these men well from his long experience with them. Although the need for struggle against the tireless dynamics of the river was as insistent as ever; although it seemed certain that a moment's cessation of effort would permit the enemy an irretrievable gain, he called a halt on the whole work.

"Boys," said he, irrelevantly, "let's have a smoke?"

He set the example by throwing himself full length against a slanting pile and most leisurely filling his pipe. The men stared a moment; then followed his example. A great peace of evening filled the sky. The horizon lay low and black against the afterglow. Beneath it the river shone like silver. Only the groaning, the heave and shrugging of the jam, and the low threatening gurgle of hurrying waters reminded the toil-weary men of the enemy's continued activity. Over beyond the rise of land that lay between the river and Stearn's Bayou could be seen the cloud of mingled smoke and steam that marked the activities of the dredge. For ten minutes they rested in the solace of tobacco. Orde was apparently more at ease than any of the rest, but each instant he expected to hear the premonitory CRACK that would sound the end of everything. Finally he yawned, knocked the ashes from his pipe, and got to his feet.

"Now," said he, a new ring in his voice, "come on and let's get something DONE!"

They responded to a man.

## XL

By midnight the water seemed to have gone down slightly. Half the crew snatched a little sleep. For several hours more the issue hung aggravatingly in equilibrium. Then, with the opening of the channel into Stearn's Bayou the heaviest pressure was relieved. For the moment the acute danger point was passed.

Orde spent the next two days in strengthening the defences. The men were able to take their quota of meals and of sleep. Merely the working hours were longer than usual. Orde himself slept little, and was still possessed by a feverish activity. The flood continued at about the same volume. Until the water should subside, the danger could not be considered completely over with.

In these few days of comparative leisure Orde had time to look about him and to receive news. The jam had been successfully held at the iron railroad bridge above Redding; but only by the most strenuous efforts. Braces of oak beams had been slanted where they would do the most good; chains strengthened the weaker spots; and on top of all ton after ton of railroad iron held the whole immovably. Nolan had enjoyed the advantage of a "floating" jam; of convenient facilities incident to a large city; and of an aroused public sentiment that proffered him all the help he could use. Monrovia, little village that it was, had not grasped the situation. Redding saw it clearly. The loss of the timber alone—representing some millions of dollars' worth of the sawed product—would mean failure of mill companies, of banks holding their paper, and so of firms in other lines of business; and besides would throw thousands of men out of employment. Furthermore, what was quite as serious, should the iron bridge give way, the wooden bridges below could hardly fail to go out. Railroad communication between eastern and western Michigan would be entirely cut off. For a season industry of every description would be practically paralysed. Therefore Nolan had all the help he required. Every device known was employed to strengthen the jam. For only a few hours was the result in doubt. Then as the CLARION jubilantly expressed it, "It's a hundred dollars to an old hat she holds!"

Orde received all this with satisfaction, but with a slight scepticism.

"It's a floating jam; and it gets a push from underneath," he pointed out. "It's probably safe; but another flood might send it out."

"The floods are going down," said North.

"Good Lord; I hope so!" said Orde.

Newmark sent word that a sudden fit of sickness had confined him to the house.

"Didn't think of a little thing like piles," said Orde to himself. "Well, that's hardly fair. Joe couldn't have realised when he left here just how bad things were."

For two days, as has been said, nothing happened. Then Orde decided to break out a channel through the jam itself. This was a necessary preliminary to getting the logs in shape for distribution. An opening was made in the piles, and the rivermen, with pike-pole and peavy, began cautiously to dig their way through the tangled timbers. The Government pile-driver, which had finally been sent up from below, began placing five extra booms at intervals down stream to capture the drift as fast as it was turned loose. From the mills and private booms crews came to assist in the labour. The troubles appeared to be quite over, when word came from Redding that the waters were again rising. Ten minutes later Leopold Lincoln Bunn, the local reporter, came flapping in on Randall's old white horse, like a second Paul Revere, crying that the iron bridge had gone, and the logs were racing down river toward the booms.

"It just went out!" he answered the eager exclamations of the men who crowded around him. "That's all I know. It went out! And the other bridges! Sure! All but the Lake Shore! Don't know why that didn't go out. No; the logs didn't jam there; just slid right under!"

"That settles it," said Welton, turning away.

"You aren't going to quit!" cried Orde.

"Certainly. You're crazy!" said Welton with some asperity. "If they can't stop a little jam with iron, what are your wooden defences going to amount to against the whole accumulation? When those logs hit the tail of this jam, she'll go out before you can wink."

He refused to listen to argument.

"It's sure death," said he, "and I'm not going to sacrifice my men for nothing, even if they'd stay."

Other owners among the bystanders said the same thing. An air of profound discouragement had fallen on them all. The strain of the fight was now telling. The utmost that human flesh and blood was capable of had been accomplished; a hard-won victory had been gained by the narrowest of narrow margins. In this new struggle the old odds were still against them, and in addition the strength that had pushed aside Redding's best effort, augmented by the momentum of a powerful current. It was small wonder they gave up.

Already the news was spreading among the workers on the jams. As man shouted to man, each shouldered his peavy and came running ashore, eager question on his lips. Orde saw the Government driver below casting loose from her moorings. A moment later her tug towed her away to some side bayou of safety out of the expected rush to the Lake.

"But we can hold her!" cried Orde in desperation. "Have a little nerve with you. You aren't going to quit like that!"

He swept them with his eye; then turned away from them with a gesture of despair. They watched him gravely and silently.

"It's no use, boy," said old Carlin; "it's sure death."

"Sure death!" Orde laughed bitterly. "All right; sure death, then. Isn't there a man in this crowd that will tackle this sort of sure death with me?"

"I'm with you."

"And me," said North and the Rough Red in a breath.

"Good!" cried Orde. "You, too, Johnny Sims? and Purdy? and Jimmy Powers? Bully boys!"

"I reckon you'll need the tug," said Marsh.

A dozen more of Orde's personal following volunteered. At once his good humour returned; and his easy leisurely confidence in himself.

"We've got to close that opening, first thing," said he. "Marsh, tow the pile-driver up there."

He caused a heavy line to be run from a tree, situated around the bend down stream, to the stern of the driver.

"Now if you have to," he told North, who had charge, "let go all holds, and the line will probably swing you around out of danger. We on the tug will get out as best we can."

The opening was to be closed by piles driven in groups of sixteen bound together by chains. The clumps were connected one to the other by a system of boom logs and ropes to interpose a continuous barrier. The pile-driver placed the clumps; while the tug attended to the connecting defences.

"Now, boys," said Orde as his last word, "if she starts to go, save yourselves the best way you can. Never mind the driver. STAY ON TOP!"

Slowly the tug and her consort nosed up through the boiling water.

"She's rising already," said Orde to Marsh, watching the water around the piles.

"Yes, and that jam's going out before many minutes," supplemented the tugboat captain grimly.

Both these statements were only too true. Although not fifteen minutes before, the jam had lain locked in perfect safety, now the slight rise of the waters had lifted and loosened the mass until it rose fairly on the quiver.

"Work fast!" Orde called to the men on the pile-driver. "If we can close the opening before those Redding logs hit us, we may be able to turn them into our new channel."

He did not add that if the opening were not closed before the jam broke, as break it would in a very few moments, the probabilities were that both pile-driver and tug would be destroyed. Every man knew that already.

Tom North ordered a pile placed in the carriage; the hammer descended. At once, like battering rams logs began to shoot up from the depths of the river end foremost all about them. These timbers were projected with tremendous force, leaping sometimes half their length above the surface of the water. If any of them had hit either the tug or the pile-driver squarely, it would have stove and sunk the craft. Fortunately this did not happen; but Marsh hastily towed the scow back to a better position. The pile had evidently been driven into the foot of the jam itself, thus loosening timbers lying at the bottom of the river.

The work went forward as rapidly as possible. Four times the jam shrugged and settled; but four times it paused on the brink of discharge. Three of the clumps had been placed and bound; and fifteen piles of the last clump had been driven.

"One more pile!" breathed Orde, his breath quickening a trifle as he glanced up stream.

The hammer in the high derrick ran smoothly to the top, paused, and fell. A half dozen times more it ripped. Then without delay the heavy chains were thrown around the winch, and the steam power began to draw the clumps together.

"Done!" cried Tom North, straightening his back.

"And a job in time, too," said Johnny Sims, indicating the creaking and tottering jam.

North unmoored, and the driver dropped back with the current and around the bend where she was snubbed by the safety line already mentioned.

Immediately the tug churned forward to accomplish the last duty, that of binding the defences together by means of chains and cables. Two men leaped to the floating booms and moved her fore and aft. Orde and the Rough Red set about the task. Methodically they worked from either end toward the middle. When they met finally, Orde directed his assistant to get aboard the tug.

"I'll tie this one, Jimmy," said he.

Aboard the tug all was tense preparation. Marsh grasped alertly the spokes of the wheel. In the engine-room Harvey, his hand on the throttle, stood ready to throw her wide open at the signal. Armed with sharp axes two men prepared to cut the mooring lines on a sign from the Rough Red. They watched his upraised hand. When it should descend, their axes must fall.

"Look out," the Rough Red warned Orde, who was methodically tying the last cumbersome knot, "she's getting ready!"

Orde folded the knot over without reply. Up stream the jam creaked, groaned, settled deliberately forward, cutting a clump of piles like straw.

"She's coming!" cried the Rough Red.

"Give me every second you can," said Orde, without looking up. He was just making the last turns.

The mass toppled slowly, fell into the swift current, and leaped with a roar. The Rough Red watched with cat-like attention.

"Jump!" he cried at last, and his right arm descended.

With the shout and the motion several things happened simultaneously. Orde leaped blindly for the rail, where he was seized and dragged aboard by the Rough Red; the axes fell, Marsh whirled over the wheel, Harvey threw open his throttle. The tug sprang from its leash like a hound. And behind the barrier the logs, tossing and tumbling, the white spray flying before their onslaught, beat in vain against the barrier, like raging wild beasts whose prey has escaped.

"Close call," said Orde briefly.

"Bet you," replied Marsh.

Neither referred to the tug's escape; but to the fortunate closing of the opening.

## XLI

Orde now took steps to deflect into the channel recently dredged to Stearn's Bayou the mass of the logs racing down stream from Redding. He estimated that he had still two hours or so in which to do the work. In this time he succeeded by the severest efforts in establishing a rough shunt into the new channel. The logs would come down running free. Only the shock of their impact against the tail of the jam already formed was to be feared. Orde hoped to be able to turn the bulk of them aside.

This at first he succeeded in doing; and very successfully as affecting the pressure on the jam below. The first logs came scattering. Then in a little while the surface of the river was covered with them; they shouldered each other aside in their eagerness to outstrip the rushing water; finally they crowded down more slowly, hardly able to make their way against the choking of the river banks, but putting forth in the very effort to proceed a tremendous power. To the crew working in the channel dredged through to Steam's Bayou the affair was that of driving a rather narrow and swift stream, only exaggerated. By quick and skilful work they succeeded in keeping the logs in motion. A large proportion of the timbers found their way into the bayou. Those that continued on down the river could hardly have much effect on the jam.

The work was breathless in its speed. From one to another sweat-bathed, panting man the logs were handed on. As yet only the advance of the big jam had arrived at the dredged channel.

Orde looked about him and realised this.

"We can't keep this up when the main body hits us," he panted to his neighbour, Jim Denning. "We'll have to do some more pile-driver work."

He made a rapid excursion to the boom camp, whence he returned with thirty or forty of the men who had given up work on the jam below.

"Here, boys," said he, "you can at least keep these logs moving in this channel for a couple of hours. This isn't dangerous."

He spoke quite without sarcastic intent; but the rivermen, already over their first panic, looked at each other a trifle shamefacedly.

"I'll tie into her wherever you say," said one big fellow. "If you fellows are going back to the jam, I'm with you."

Two or three more volunteered. The remainder said nothing, but in silence took charge of the dredged channel.

Orde and his men now returned to the jam where, on the pile-driver, the tugs, and the booms, they set methodically to strengthening the defences as well as they were able.

"She's holding strong and dandy," said Orde to Tom North, examining critically the clumps of piles. "That channel helps a lot in more ways than one. It takes an awful lot of water out of the river. As long as those fellows keep the logs moving, I really believe we're all right."

But shortly the water began to rise again, this time fairly by leaps. In immediate response the jam increased its pressure. For the hundredth time the frail wooden defences opposed to millions of pounds were tested to the very extreme of their endurance. The clumps of piles sagged outward; the network of chains and cables tightened and tightened again, drawing ever nearer the snapping point. Suddenly, almost without warning, the situation had become desperate.

And for the first time Orde completely lost his poise and became fluently profane. He shook his fist against the menacing logs; he apostrophised the river, the high water, the jam, the deserters, Newmark and his illness, ending finally in a general anathema against any and all streams, logs, and floods. Then he stormed away to see if anything had gone wrong at the dredged channel.

"Well," said Tom North, "they've got the old man real good and mad this time."

The crew went on driving piles, stringing cables, binding chains, although, now that the inspiration of Orde's combative spirit was withdrawn the labours seemed useless, futile, a mere filling in of the time before the supreme moment when they would be called upon to pay the sacrifice their persistence and loyalty had proffered for the altar of self-respect and the invincibility of the human Soul.

At the dredged channel Orde saw the rivermen standing idle, and, half-blind with anger he burst upon them demanding by this, that and the other what they meant. Then he stopped short and stared.

Square across the dredged channel and completely blocking it lay a single span of an iron bridge. Although twisted and misshapen, it was still intact, the framework of its overhead truss-work retaining its cage-like shape. Behind it the logs had of course piled up in a jam, which, sinking rapidly to the bed of the channel, had dammed back the water.

"Where in hell did that drop from?" cried Orde.

"Come down on top the jam," explained a riverman. "Must have come way from Redding. We just couldn't SCARE her out of here."

Orde, suddenly fallen into a cold rage, stared at the obstruction, both fists clenched at his side.

"Too bad, boy," said Welton at his elbow. "But don't take it too hard. You've done more than any of the rest of us could. And we're all losers together."

Orde looked at him strangely.

"That about settles it," repeated Welton.

"Settle!" cried Orde. "I should think not."

Welton smiled quaintly.

"Don't you know when you're licked?"

"Licked, hell!" said Orde. "We've just begun to fight."

"What can you do?"

"Get that bridge span out of there, of course."

"How?"

"Can't we blow her up with powder?"

"Ever try to blow up iron?"

"There must be some way."

"Oh, there is," replied Welton. "Of course—take her apart bolt by bolt and nut by nut."

"Send for the wrenches, then," snapped Orde.

"But it would take two or three days, even working night and day."

"What of it?"

"But it would be too late—it would do no good—"

"Perhaps not," interrupted Orde; "but it will be doing something, anyway. Look here, Welton, are you game? If you'll get that bridge out in two days I'll hold the jam."

"You can't hold that jam two hours, let alone two days," said Welton decidedly.

"That's my business. You're wasting time. Will you send for lanterns and wrenches and keep this crew working?"

"I will," said Welton.

"Then do it."

During the next two days the old scenes were all relived, with back of them the weight of the struggle that had gone before. The little crew worked as though mad. Excepting them, no one ventured on the river, for to be caught in the imminent break meant to die. Old spars, refuse timbers of all sorts—anything and everything was requisitioned that might help form an obstruction above or below water. Piles were taken where they could be found. Farmer's trees were cut down. Pines belonging to divers and protesting owners were felled and sharpened. Some were brought in by rail. Even the inviolate Government supply was commandeered. The Railroad Company had a fine lot which, with remarkable shortsightedness and lack of public spirit, they refused to sell at any price. The crew took them by force. Once Captain Marsh was found up to his waist in water, himself felling the trees of a wood, and dragging them to the river by a cable attached to the winch of his tug. Night followed day; and day night again. None of the crews realised the fact. The men were caught in the toils of a labour ceaseless and eternal. Never would it end, just as never had it begun. Always were they to handle piles, steam hammers and the implements of their trade, menaced by a jam on the point of breaking, wet by a swollen and angry flood, over-arched by a clear calm sky or by the twinkling peaceful stars. Long since had they ceased to reckon with the results of what they did, the consequences either to themselves or to the jam. Mechanically they performed their labour. Perhaps the logs would kill them. Perhaps these long, black, dripping piles they drove were having some effect on the situation. Neither possibility mattered.

Then all at once, as though a faucet had been turned off, the floods slackened.

"They've opened the channel," said Orde dully. His voice sounded to himself very far away. Suddenly the external world, too, seemed removed to a distance, far from his centre of consciousness. He felt himself moving in strange and distorted surroundings; he heard himself repeating to each of a number of wavering, gigantic figures the talismanic words that had accomplished the dissolution of the earth for himself: "They've opened the channel." At last he felt hard planks beneath his feet, and, shaking his head with an effort, he made out the pilot-house of the SPRITE and a hollow-eyed man leaning against it. "They've opened the channel, Marsh," he repeated. "I guess that'll be all." Then quite slowly he sank to the deck, sound asleep.

Welton, returning from his labours with the iron bridge and the jam, found them thus. Men slept on the deck of the tug, aboard the pile-driver. Two or three had even curled up in the crevices of the jam, resting in the arms of the monster they had subdued.

## XLII

When Newmark left, in the early stages of the jam, he gave scant thought to the errand on which he had ostensibly departed. Whether or nor Orde got a supply of piles was to him a matter of indifference. His hope, or rather preference was that the jam should go out; but he saw clearly what Orde, blinded by the swift action of the struggle, was as yet unable to perceive. Even should the riverman succeed in stopping the jam, the extraordinary expenses incidental to the defence and to the subsequent salvaging, untangling and sorting would more than eat up the profits of the drive. Orde would then be forced to ask for an extension of time on his notes.

On arriving in Monrovia, he drove to his own house. To Mallock he issued orders.

"Go to the office and tell them I am ill," said he, "and then hunt up Mr. Heinzman, wherever he is, and tell him I want to see him immediately."

He did not trouble to send word directly to Orde, up river; but left him to be informed by the slow process of filtration through the bookkeepers. The interim of several hours before Heinzman appeared he spent very comfortably in his easy chair, dipping into a small volume of Montaigne.

At length the German was announced. He entered rather red and breathless, obviously surprised to find Newmark at home.

"Dot was a terrible jam," said he, mopping his brow and sinking into a chair. "I got lots of logs in it."

Newmark dismissed the subject with an abrupt flip of his unlighted cigar.

"Heinzman," said he, "in three weeks at the latest Orde will come to you asking for a renewal of the notes you hold against our firm. You must refuse to make such a renewal."

"All righdt," agreed Heinzman.

"He'll probably offer you higher interest. You must refuse that. Then when the notes are overdue you must begin suit in foreclosure."

"All righdt," repeated Heinzman a little restlessly. "Do you think he vill hold that jam?"

Newmark shrugged his shoulders swiftly.

"I got lots of logs in that jam. If that jam goes out I vill lose a heap of money."

"Well, you'll make quite a heap on this deal," said Newmark carelessly.

"Suppose he holds it," said Heinzman, pausing. "I hate like the mischief to joomp on him."

"Rot!" said Newmark decisively. "That's what he's there for." He looked at the German sharply. "I suppose you know just how deep you're in this?"

"Oh, I ain't backing oudt," negatived Heinzman. "Not a bit."

"Well, then, you know what to do," said Newmark, terminating the interview.

## XLIII

Little by little the water went down. The pressure, already considerably relieved by the channel into Stearn's Bayou, slackened every hour. Orde, still half dazed with his long-delayed sleep, drove back along the marsh road to town.

His faculties were still in the torpor that follows rest after exhaustion. The warm July sun, the breeze from the Lake, the flash of light from the roadside water, these were all he had room for among his perceptions. He was content to enjoy them, and to anticipate drowsily the keen pleasure of seeing Carroll again. In the rush of the jam he had heard nothing from her. For all he knew she and Bobby might have been among the spectators on the bank; he had hardly once left the river. It did not seem to him strange that Carroll should not have been there to welcome him after the struggle was over. Rarely did she get to the booms in ordinary circumstances. This episode of the big jam was, after all, nothing but part of the day's work to Orde; a crisis, exaggerated it is true, but like many other crises a man must meet and cope with on the river. There was no reason why Carroll should drive the twelve miles between Monrovia and the booms, unless curiosity should take her.

As the team left the marsh road for the county turnpike past the mills and lumberyards, Orde shook himself fully awake. He began to review the situation. As Newmark had accurately foreseen, he came almost immediately to a realisation that the firm would not be able to meet the notes given to Heinzman. Orde had depended on the profits from the season's drive to enable him to make up the necessary amount. Those profits would be greatly diminished, if not wiped out entirely, by the expenses, both regular and irregular, incurred in holding the jam; by the damage suits surely to be brought by the owners of the piles, trees, pile-drivers and other supplies and materials requisitioned in the heat of the campaign; and by the extra labour necessary to break out the jam and to sort the logs according to their various destinations.

"I'll have to get an extension of time," said Orde to himself. "Of course Joe will let me have more time on my own personal note to the firm. And Heinzman surely ought to—I saved a lot of his logs in that jam. And if he doesn't want to, I guess an offer of a little higher interest will fetch him."

Ordinarily the state of affairs would have worried him, for it was exactly the situation he had fought against so hard. But now he was too wearied in soul and body. He dismissed the subject from his mind. The horses, left almost to themselves, lapsed into a sleepy jog. After a little they passed the bridge and entered the town. Warm spicy odours of pine disengaged themselves from the broken shingles and sawdust of the roadway, and floated upward through the hot sunshine. The beautiful maples with their dense shadows threw the sidewalks into coolness. Up one street and down another the horses took their accustomed way. Finally they pulled up opposite the Orde house. Orde hitched the horses, and, his step quickening in anticipation, sprang up the walk and into the front door.

"Hullo, sweetheart!" he called cheerily.

The echoes alone answered him. He cried again, and yet again, with a growing feeling of disappointment that Carroll should happen to be from home. Finally a door opened and shut in the back part of the house. A moment later Mary, the Irish servant girl, came through the dining-room, caught sight of Orde, threw her apron over her head, and burst into one of those extravagant demonstrations of grief peculiar to the warm-hearted of her class.

Orde stopped short, a sinking at his heart.

"What is it, Mary?" he asked very quietly.

But the girl only wept the louder, rocking back and forth in a fresh paroxysm of grief. Beside himself with anxiety Orde sprang forward to shake her by the arm, to shower her with questions. These elicited nothing but broken and incoherent fragments concerning "the missus," "oh, the sad day!" "and me lift all alone with Bobby, me heart that heavy," and the like, which served merely to increase Orde's bewilderment and anxiety. At this moment Bobby himself appeared from the direction of the kitchen. Orde, frantic with alarm, fell upon his son. Bobby, much bewildered by all this pother, could only mumble something about "smallpox," and "took mamma away with doctor."

"Where? where, Bobby?" cried Orde, fairly shaking the small boy by the shoulder. He felt like a man in a bad dream, trying to reach a goal that constantly eluded him.

At this moment a calm, dry voice broke through the turmoil of questions and exclamations. Orde looked up to see the tall, angular form of Doctor McMullen standing in the doorway.

"It's all right," said the doctor in answer to Orde's agonised expression. "Your wife was exposed to smallpox and is at my house to avoid the danger of spreading contagion. She is not ill."

Having thus in one swift decisive sentence covered the ground of Orde's anxiety, he turned to the sniffling servant.

"Mary," said he sternly, "I'm ashamed of you! What kind of an exhibition is this? Go out to the kitchen and cook us some lunch!" He watched her depart with a humourous quirk to his thin lips. "Fool Irish!" he said with a Scotchman's contempt. "I meant to head you off before you got home, but I missed you. Come in and sit down, and I'll tell you about it."

"You're quite sure Mrs. Orde is well?" insisted Orde.

"Absolutely. Never better. As well as you are."

"Where was she exposed?"

"Down at Heinzman's. You know—or perhaps you don't—that old Heinzman is the worst sort of anti-vaccination crank. Well, he's reaped the reward."

"Has he smallpox?" asked Orde. "Why, I thought I remembered seeing him up river only the other day."

"No; his daughter."

"Mina?"

"Yes. Lord knows where she got it. But get it she did. Mrs. Orde happened to be with her when she was taken with the fever and distressing symptoms that begin the disease. As a neighbourly deed she remained with the girl. Of course no one could tell it was smallpox at that time. Next day, however, the characteristic rash appeared on the thighs and armpits, and I diagnosed the case." Dr. McMullen laughed a little bitterly. "Lord, you ought to have seen them run! Servants, neighbours, friends—they all skedaddled, and you couldn't have driven them back with a steam-roller! I telegraphed to Redding for a nurse. Until she came Mrs. Orde stayed by, like a brick. Don't know what I should have done without her. There was nobody to do anything at all. As soon as the nurse came Mrs. Orde gave up her post. I tell you," cried Doctor McMullen with as near an approach to enthusiasm as he ever permitted himself, "there's a sensible woman! None of your story-book twaddle about nursing through the illness, and all that. When her usefulness was ended, she knew enough to step aside gracefully. There was not much danger as far as she was concerned. I had vaccinated her myself, you know, last year. But she MIGHT take the contagion and she wanted to spare the youngster. Quite right. So I offered her quarters with us for a couple of weeks."

"How long ago was this?" asked Orde, who had listened with a warm glow of pride to the doctor's succinct statement.

"Seven days."

"How is Mina getting on?"

"She'll get well. It was a mild case. Fever never serious after the eruption appeared. I suppose I'll have old Heinzman on my hands, though."

"Why; has he taken it?"

"No; but he will. Emotional old German fool. Rushed right in when he heard his daughter was sick. Couldn't keep him out. And he's been with her or near her ever since."

"Then you think he's in for it?"

"Sure to be," replied Dr. McMullen. "Unless a man has been vaccinated, continuous exposure means infection in the great majority of cases."

"Hard luck," said Orde thoughtfully. "I'm going to step up to your house and see Mrs. Orde."

"You can telephone her," said the doctor. "And you can see her if you want to. Only in that case I should advise your remaining away from Bobby until we see how things turn out."

"I see," said Orde. "Well," he concluded with a sigh, after a moment's thought, "I suppose I'd better stay by the ship."

He called up Dr. McMullen's house on the telephone.

"Oh, it's good to hear your voice again," cried Carroll, "even if I can't see you! You must promise me right after lunch to walk up past the house so I can see you. I'll wave at you from the window."

"You're a dear, brave girl, and I'm proud of you," said Orde.

"Nonsense! There was no danger at all. I'd been vaccinated recently. And somebody had to take care of poor Mina until we could get help. How's Bobby?"

## XLIV

After lunch Orde went downtown to his office where for some time he sat idly looking over the mail. About three o'clock Newmark came in.

"Hullo, Joe," said Orde with a slight constraint, "sorry to hear you've been under the weather. You don't look very sick now."

"I'm better," replied Newmark, briefly; "this is my first appearance."

"Too bad you got sick just at that time," said Orde; "we needed you."

"So I hear. You may rest assured I'd have been there if possible."

"Sure thing," said Orde, heartily, his slight resentment dissipating, as always, in the presence of another's personality. "Well, we had a lively time, you bet, all right; and got through about by the skin of our teeth." He arose and walked over to Newmark's desk, on the edge of which he perched. "It's cost us considerable; and it's going to cost us a lot more, I'll have to get an extension on those notes."

"What's that?" asked Newmark, quickly.

Orde picked up a paper knife and turned it slowly between his fingers.

"I don't believe I'll be able to meet those notes. So many things have happened—"

"But," broke in Newmark, "the firm certainly cannot do so. I've been relying on your assurance that you would take them up personally. Our resources are all tied up."

"Can't we raise anything more on the Northern Peninsula timber?" asked Orde.

"You ought to know we can't," cried Newmark, with an appearance of growing excitement. "The last seventy-five thousand we borrowed for me finishes that."

"Can't you take up part of your note?"

"My note comes due in 1885," rejoined Newmark with cold disgust. "I expect to take it up then. But I can't until then. I hadn't expected anything like this."

"Well, don't get hot," said Orde vaguely. "I only thought that Northern Peninsula stuff might be worth saving any way we could figure it."

"Worth saving!" snorted Newmark, whirling in his chair.

"Well, keep your hair on," said Orde, on whom Newmark's manner was beginning to have its effect, as Newmark intended it should. "You have my Boom Company stock as security."

"Pretty security for the loss of a tract like the Upper Peninsula timber!"

"Well, it's the security you asked for, and suggested," said Orde.

"I thought you'd surely be able to pay it," retorted Newmark, now secure in the position he desired to take, that of putting Orde entirely in the wrong.

"Well, I expected to pay it; and I'll pay it yet," rejoined Orde. "I don't think Heinzman will stand in his own light rather than renew the notes."

He seized his hat and departed. Once in the street, however, his irritation passed. As was the habit of the man, he began more clearly to see Newmark's side, and so more emphatically to blame himself. After all, when he got right down to the essentials, he could not but acknowledge that Newmark's anger was justified. For his own private ends he had jeopardised the firm's property. More of a business man might have reflected that Newmark, as financial head, should have protected the firm against all contingencies; should have seen to it that it met Heinzman's notes, instead of tying up its resources in unnecessary ways. Orde's own delinquency bulked too large in his eyes to admit his perception of this. By the time he had reached Heinzman's office, the last of his irritation had vanished. Only he realised clearly now that it would hardly do to ask Newmark for a renewal of the personal note on which depended his retention of his Boom Company stock unless he could renew the Heinzman note also. This is probably what Newmark intended.

"Mr. Heinzman?" he asked briefly of the first clerk.

"Mr. Heinzman is at home ill," replied the bookkeeper.

"Already?" said Orde. He drummed on the black walnut rail thoughtfully. The notes came due in ten days. "How bad is he?"

The clerk looked up curiously. "Can't say. Probably won't be back for a long time. It's smallpox, you know."

"True," said Orde. "Well, who's in charge?"

"Mr. Lambert. You'll find him in the private office."

Orde passed through the grill into the inner room.

"Hullo, Lambert," he addressed the individual seated at Heinzman's desk. "So you're the boss, eh?"

Lambert turned, showing a perfectly round face, ornamented by a dot of a nose, two dots of eyes set rather close together, and a pursed up mouth. His skin was very brown and shiny, and was so filled by the flesh beneath as to take the appearance of having been inflated.

"Yes, I'm the boss," said he non-committally.

Orde dropped into a chair.

"Heinzman holds some notes due against our people in ten days," said he. "I came in to see about their renewal. Can you attend to it?"

"Yes, I can attend to it," replied Lambert. He struck a bell; and to the bookkeeper who answered he said: "John, bring me those Newmark and Orde papers."

Orde heard the clang of the safe door. In a moment the clerk returned and handed to Lambert a long manilla envelope. Lambert opened this quite deliberately, spread its contents on his knee, and assumed a pair of round spectacles.

"Note for seventy-five thousand dollars with interest at ten per cent. Interest paid to January tenth. Mortgage deed on certain lands described herein."

"That's it," said Orde.

Lambert looked up over his spectacles.

"I want to renew the note for another year," Orde explained.

"Can't do it," replied Lambert, removing and folding the glasses.

"Why not?"

"Mr. Heinzman gave me especial instructions in regard to this matter just before his daughter was taken sick. He told me if you came when he was not here—he intended to go to Chicago yesterday—to tell you he would not renew."

"Why not?" asked Orde blankly.

"I don't know that."

"But I'll give him twelve per cent for another year."

"He said not to renew, even if you offered higher interest."

"Do you happen to know whether he intends anything in regard to this mortgage?"

"He instructed me to begin suit in foreclosure immediately."

"I don't understand this," said Orde.

Lambert shook his head blandly. Orde thought for a moment.

"Where's your telephone?" he demanded abruptly.

He tried in vain to get Heinzman at his house. Finally the telephone girl informed him that although messages had come from the stricken household, she had been unable to get an answer to any of her numerous calls, and suspected the bell had been removed. Finally Orde left the office at a loss how to proceed next. Lambert, secretly overjoyed at this opportunity of exercising an unaccustomed and autocratic power, refused to see beyond his instructions. Heinzman's attitude puzzled Orde. A foreclosure could gain Heinzman no advantage of immediate cash. Orde was forced to the conclusion that the German saw here a good opportunity to acquire cheap a valuable property. In that case a personal appeal would avail little.

Orde tramped out to the end of the pier and back, mulling over the tangled problem. He was pressed on all sides—by the fatigue after his tremendous exertions of the past two weeks; by his natural uneasiness in regard to Carroll; and finally by this new complication which threatened the very basis of his prosperity. Nevertheless the natural optimism of the man finally won its ascendency.

"There's the year of redemption on that mortgage," he reminded himself. "We may be able to do something in that time. I don't know just what," he added whimsically, with a laugh at himself. He became grave. "Poor Joe," he said, "this is pretty tough on him. I'll have to make it up to him somehow. I can let him in on that California deal, when the titles are straightened out."

Orde did not return to the office; he felt unwilling to face Newmark until he had a little more thoroughly digested the situation. He spent the rest of the afternoon about the place, picking up the tool house, playing with Bobby, training Duke, the black and white setter dog. Three or four times he called up Carroll by telephone; and three or four times he passed Dr. McMullen's house to shout his half of a long-distance and fragmentary conversation with her. He ate solemnly with Bobby at six o'clock, the two quite subdued over the vacant chair at the other end of the table. After dinner they sat on the porch until Bobby's bed-time. Orde put his small son to bed, and sat talking with the youngster as long as his conscience would permit. Then he retired to the library, where, for a long time, he sat in twilight and loneliness. Finally, when he could no longer distinguish objects across the room, he arose with a sigh, lit the lamp, and settled himself to read.

The last of the twilight drained from the world, and the window panes turned a burnished black. Through the half-open sashes sucked a warm little breeze, swaying the long lace curtains back and forth. The hum of lawn-sprinklers and the chirping of crickets and tree-frogs came with it.

One by one the lawn-sprinklers fell silent. Gradually there descended upon the world the deep slumbrous stillness of late night; a stillness compounded of a thousand and one mysterious little noises repeated monotonously over and over until their identity was lost in accustomedness. Occasionally the creak of timbers or the sharp scurrying of a mouse in the wall served more to accentuate than to break this night silence.

Orde sat lost in reverie, his book in his lap. At stated intervals the student lamp at his elbow flared slightly, then burned clear again after a swallow of satisfaction in its reservoir. These regular replenishments of the oil supply alone marked the flight of time.

Suddenly Orde leaned forward, his senses at the keenest attention. After a moment he arose and quietly walked toward the open window. Just as he reached the casement and looked out, a man looked in. The two stared at each other not two feet apart.

"Good Lord! Heinzman!" cried Orde in a guarded voice. He stepped decisively through the window, seized the German by the arm, and drew him one side.

"What are you doing here?" he demanded.

Heinzman was trembling violently as though from a chill.

"Dake me somewheres," he whispered hoarsely. "Somewheres quick. I haf broke quarantine, and dey vill be after me."

"The place for you is at your own house," said Orde, his anger rising. "What do you mean by coming here and exposing my house to infection?"

Heinzman began to blubber; choked, shivered all over, and cried aloud with an expression of the greatest agony:

"You must dake me somewheres. I must talk with you and your goot wife. I haf somedings to say to you." He in his turn grasped Orde by the arm. "I haf broke quarantine to gome and tell you. Dey are dere mit shotguns to kill me if I broke quarantine. And I haf left my daughter, my daughter Mina, all alone mit dose people to come and tell you. And now you don't listen."

He wrung his hands dramatically, his soft pudgy body shaking.

"Come with me," said Orde briefly.

He led the way around the house to the tool shed. Here he lit a lantern, thrust forward one nail keg, and sat down on another.

Heinzman sat down on the nail keg, almost immediately arose, walked up and down two or three times, and resumed his seat.

Orde looked at him curiously. He was half dressed, without a collar, his thin hair unkempt. The usual bright colour of his cheeks had become livid, and the flesh, ordinarily firm and elastic, had fallen in folds and wrinkles. His eyes burned bright as though from some internal fire. A great restlessness possessed him. Impulsively Orde leaned forward to touch his hand. It was dry and hot.

"What is it, Heinzman?" he asked quietly, fully prepared for the vagaries of a half delirium.

"Ach, Orde!" cried the German, "I am tortured mit HOLLENQUALLE—what you call?—hell's fire. You, whose wife comes in and saves my Mina when the others runs away. You, my best friends! It is SCHRECKLICH! She vas the noblest, the best, the most kindest—"

"If you mean Mrs. Orde's staying with Mina," broke in Orde, "it was only what any one should have done, in humanity; and I, for one, am only too glad she had the chance. You mustn't exaggerate. And now you'd better get home where you can be taken care of. You're sick."

"No, no, my friend," said Heinzman, vigourously shaking his head. "She might take the disease. She might die. It vas noble." He shuddered. "My Mina left to die all alone!"

Orde rose to his feet with decision.

"That is all right," said he. "Carroll was glad of the chance. Now let me get you home."

But Heinzman's excitement had suddenly died.

"No," said he, extending his trembling hand; "sit down. I want to talk business."

"You are in no condition to talk business," said Orde.

"No!" cried Heinzman with unexpected vigour. "Sit down! Listen to me! Dot's better. I haf your note for sefenty-five t'ousand dollars. No?"

Orde nodded.

"Dot money I never lent you. NO! I'm not crazy. Sit still! I know my name is on dot note. But the money came from somewheres else. It came from your partner, Joseph Newmark."

Orde half rose from his keg.

"Why? What?" he asked in bewilderment.

"Den ven you could not pay the note, I vas to foreclose and hand over dot Northern Peninsula land to Joseph Newmark, your partner."

"Impossible!" cried Orde.

"I vas to get a share. It vas a trick."

"Go on," said Orde grimly.

"Dere is no go on. Dot is all."

"Why do you come to tell me now?"

"Because for more than one year now I say to mineself, 'Carl Heinzman, you vas one dirty scoundrel. You vas dishonest; a sneak; a thief'; I don't like to call myself names like dose. It iss all righdt to be smart; but to be a thief!"

"Why didn't you pull out?" asked Orde.

"I couldn't!" cried Heinzman piteously. "How could I? He haf me cold. I paid Stanford five hundred dollars for his vote on the charter; and Joseph Newmark, he know dot; he can PROVE it. He tell me if I don't do what he say, he put me in jail. Think of dot! All my friends go back on me; all my money gone; maybe my daughter Mina go back on me, too. How could I?"

"Well, he can still put you in prison," said Orde.

"Vot I care?" cried Heinzman, throwing up both his arms. "You and your wife are my friends. She save my Mina. DU LIEBER GOTT! If my daughter had died, vot good iss friends and money? Vot good iss anything? I don't vant to live! And ven I sit dere by her always something ask me: 'Vy you do dot to the peoples dot safe your Mina?' And ven she look at me, her eyes say it; and in the night everything cry out at me; and I get sick, and I can't stand it no longer, and I don't care if he send me to prison or to hell, no more."

His excitement died. He sat listless, his eyes vacant, his hands between his knees.

"Vell, I go," he said at last.

"Have you that note?" asked Orde.

"Joseph Newmark, he keeps it most times," replied Heinzman, "but now it is at my office for the foreclosure. I vill not foreclose; he can send me to the penitentiary."

"Telephone Lambert in the morning to give it to me. No; here. Write an order in this notebook."

Heinzman wrote the required order.

"I go," said he, suddenly weary.

Orde accompanied him down the street. The German was again light-headed with the fever, mumbling about his daughter, the notes, Carroll, the voices that had driven him to righteousness. By some manoeuvring Orde succeeded in slipping him through the improvised quarantine without discovery. Then the riverman with slow and thoughtful steps returned to where the lamp in the study still marked off with the spaced replenishments from its oil reservoir the early morning hours.

## XLVI

Morning found Orde still seated in the library chair. His head was sunk forward on his chest; his hands were extended listless, palms up, along the arms of the chair; his eyes were vacant and troubled. Hardly once in the long hours had he shifted by a hair's breadth his position. His body was suspended in an absolute inaction while his spirit battered at the walls of an impasse. For, strangely enough, Orde did not once, even for a single instant, give a thought to the business aspects of the situation—what it meant to him and his prospects or what he could do about it. Hurt to the soul he stared at the wreck of a friendship. Nothing will more deeply sicken the heart of a naturally loyal man than to discover baseless his faith in some one he has thoroughly trusted.

Orde had liked Newmark. He had admired heartily his clearness of vision, his financial skill, his knowledge of business intricacies, his imperturbable coolness, all the abilities that had brought him to success. With a man of Orde's temperament, to admire is to like; and to like is to invest with all good qualities. He had constructed his ideal of a friend, with Newmark as a basis; and now that this, which had seemed to him as solid a reality as a brick block, had dissolved into nothing, he found himself in the necessity of refashioning his whole world. He was not angry at Newmark. But he was grieved down to the depths of his being.

When the full sun shone into the library, he aroused himself to change his clothes. Then, carrying those he had just discarded, he slipped out of the house and down the street. Duke, the black and white setter dog, begged to follow him. Orde welcomed the animal's company. He paused only long enough to telephone from the office telling Carroll he would be out of town all day. Then he set out at a long swinging gait over the hills. By the time the sun grew hot, he was some miles from the village and in the high beech woods. There he sat down, his back to a monster tree. All day long he gazed steadily on the shifting shadows and splotches of sunlight; on the patches of blue sky, the dazzling white clouds that sailed across them; on the waving, whispering frond that over-arched him, and the deep cool shadows beneath. The woods creatures soon became accustomed to his presence. Squirrels of the several varieties that abounded in the Michigan forests scampered madly after each other in spirals around the tree trunks, or bounded across the ground in long undulating leaps. Birds flashed and called and disappeared mysteriously. A chewink, brave in his black and white and tan uniform, scratched mightily with great two-footed swoops that threw the vegetable mould over Orde's very feet.

Blazoned butterflies—the yellow and black turnus, the dark troilus, the shade-loving nymphalis—flickered in and out of the patches of sunlight. Orde paid them no attention. The noon heat poured down through the forest isles like an incense. Overhead swung the sun, and down the slope until the long shafts of its light lifted wand-like across the tree trunks.

At this hint of evening Orde shook himself and arose. He was little nearer the readjustment he sought than he had been the previous night.

He reached home a little before six o'clock. To his surprise he found Taylor awaiting him. The lawyer had written nothing as to his return.

"I had things pretty well in shape," he said, after the first greetings had been exchanged, "and it would do no good to stay away any longer."

"Then the trouble is over?" asked Orde.

"I wouldn't say that," replied Taylor; "but you can rest easy as to the title to your lands. The investigation had no real basis to it. There may have been some small individual cases of false entry; but nothing on which to ground a real attack."

"When can I borrow on it?"

"Not for a year or two, I should say. There's an awful lot of red-tape to unwind, as there always is in such cases."

"Oh," said Orde in some disappointment.

Taylor hesitated, removed his eye-glasses, wiped them carefully, and replaced them. He glanced at Orde sidelong through his keen, shrewd eyes.

"I have something more to tell you; something that will be painful," said he.

Orde looked up quickly.

"Well; what is it?" he asked.

"The general cussedness of all this investigation business had me puzzled, until at last I made up my mind to do a little investigating on my own account. It all looked foolish to me. Somebody or something must be back of all this performance. I was at it all the time I was West, between times on regular business, of course. I didn't make much out of my direct efforts—they cover things up well in those matters—but at last I got on a clue by sheer accident. There was one man behind all this. He was—"

"Joe Newmark," said Orde quietly.

"How did you know that?" cried Taylor in astonishment.

"I didn't know, Frank; I just guessed."

"Well, you made a good guess. It was Newmark. He'd tied up the land in this trumped-up investigation so you could not borrow on it."

"How did he find out I owned any land?" asked Orde.

"That I couldn't tell you. Must have been a leak somewhere."

"Quite likely," said Orde calmly.

Taylor looked at his principal in some wonder.

"Well, I must say you take it coolly enough," said he at last.

Orde smiled.

"Do I?" said he.

"Of course," went on Taylor after a moment, "we have a strong presumption of conspiracy to get hold of your Boom Company stock, which I believe you put up as security. But I don't see how we have any incontestable proof of it."

"Proof? What more do we want?"

"We'd have no witness to any of these transactions; nor have we documentary proofs. It's merely moral certainty; and moral certainty isn't much in a court of law. I'll see him, if you say so, though, and scare him into some sort of an arrangement."

Orde shook his head.

"No," said he decidedly. "Rather not. I'll run this. Please say nothing."

"Of course not!" interjected Taylor, a trifle indignantly.

"And I'll figure out what I want to do."

Orde pressed Taylor to stay to supper; but the latter declined. After a few moments' conversation on general topics the lawyer took his departure, secretly marvelling over the phlegmatic way in which Orde had taken what had been to Taylor, when he first stumbled against it, a shocking piece of news.

## XLVII

Orde did not wish to return to the office until he had worked his problem out; so, to lend his absence the colour of naturalness, he drove back next morning to the booms. There he found enough to keep him occupied all that day and the next. As in those times the long distance telephone had not yet been attempted, he was cut off from casual communication with the village. Late in the afternoon he returned home.

A telephone to Carroll apprised him that all was well with her. A few moments later the call sounded, and Orde took a message that caused him to look grave and to whistle gently with surprise. He ate supper with Bobby. About star-time he took his hat and walked slowly down the street beneath the velvet darkness of the maples. At Newmark's he turned in between the oleanders.

Mallock answered his ring.

"No, sir, Mr. Newmark is out, sir," said Mallock. "I'll tell him you called, sir," and started respectfully but firmly to close the door.

But Orde thrust his foot and knee in the opening.

"I'll come in and wait," said he quietly.

"Yes, sir, this way, sir," said Mallock, trying to indicate the dining-room, where he wished Orde to sit until he could come at his master's wishes in the matter.

Orde caught the aroma of tobacco and the glimmer of light to the left. Without reply he turned the knob of the door and entered the library.

There he found Newmark in evening dress, seated in a low easy chair beneath a lamp, smoking, and reading a magazine. At Orde's appearance in the doorway, he looked up calmly, his paper knife poised, keeping the place.

"Oh, it's you, Orde," said he.

"Your man told me you were not in," said Orde.

"He was mistaken. Won't you sit down?"

Orde entered the room and mechanically obeyed Newmark's suggestion, his manner preoccupied. For some time he stared with wrinkled brow at a point above the illumination of the lamp. Newmark, over the end of his cigar, poised a foot from his lips, watched the riverman with a cool calculation.

"Newmark," Orde began abruptly at last, "I know all about this deal."

"What deal?" asked Newmark, after a barely perceptible pause.

"This arrangement you made with Heinzman."

"I borrowed some money from Heinzman for the firm."

"Yes; and you supplied that money yourself."

Newmark's eyes narrowed, but he said nothing. Orde glanced toward him, then away again, as though ashamed.

"Well," said Newmark at last, "what of it?"

"If you had the money to lend why didn't you lend it direct?"

"Because it looks better to mortgage to an outside holder."

An expression of profound disgust flitted across Orde's countenance. Newmark smiled covertly, and puffed once or twice strongly on his nearly extinct cigar.

"That was not the reason," went on Orde. "You agreed with Heinzman to divide when you succeeded in foreclosing me out of the timber lands given as security. Furthermore you instructed Floyd to go out on the eve of that blow in spite of his warnings; and you contracted with McLeod for the new vessels; and you've tied us up right and left for the sole purpose of pinching us down where we couldn't meet those notes. That's the only reason you borrowed the seventy-five thousand on your own account; so we couldn't borrow it to save ourselves."

"It strikes me you are interesting but inconclusive," said Newmark, as Orde paused again.

"That sort of thing is somewhat of a facer," went on Orde without the slightest attention to the interjection. "It took me some days to work it out in all its details; but I believe I understand it all now. I don't quite understand how you discovered about my California timber. That 'investigation' was a very pretty move."

"How the devil did you get onto that?" cried Newmark, startled for a moment out of his cool attitude of cynical aloofness.

"Then you acknowledge it?" shot in Orde quick as a flash.

Newmark laughed in amusement.

"Why shouldn't I? Of course Heinzman blabbed. You couldn't have got it all anywhere else."

Orde arose to his feet, and half sat again on the arm of his chair.

"Now I'll tell you what we will do in this matter," said he crisply.

But Newmark unexpectedly took the aggressive.

"We'll follow," said he, "the original programme, as laid down by myself. I'm tired of dealing with blundering fools. Heinzman's mortgage will be foreclosed; and you will hand over as per the agreement your Boom Company stock."

Orde stared at him in amazement.

"I must say you have good nerve," he said; "you don't seem to realise that you are pretty well tangled up. I don't know what they call it: criminal conspiracy, or something of that sort, I suppose. So far from handing over to you the bulk of my property, I can send you to the penitentiary."

"Nonsense," rejoined Newmark, leaning forward in his turn. "I know you too well, Jack Orde. You're a fool of more kinds than I care to count, and this is one of the kinds. Do you seriously mean to say that you dare try to prosecute me? Just as sure as you do, I'll put Heinzman in the pen too. I've got it on him, COLD. He's a bribe giver—and somewhat of a criminal conspirator himself."

"Well," said Orde.

Newmark leaned back with an amused little chuckle. "If the man hadn't come to you and given the whole show away, you'd have lost every cent you owned. He did you the biggest favour in his power. And for your benefit I'll tell you what you can easily substantiate; I forced him into this deal with me. I had this bribery case on him; and in addition his own affairs were all tied up."

"I knew that," replied Orde.

"What had the man to gain by telling you?" pursued Newmark. "Nothing at all. What had he to lose? Everything: his property, his social position, his daughter's esteem, which the old fool holds higher than any of them. You could put me in the pen, perhaps—with Heinzman's testimony. But the minute Heinzman appears on the stand, I'll land him high and dry and gasping, without a chance to flop."

He paused a moment to puff at his cigar. Finding it had gone out, he laid the butt carefully on the ash tray at his elbow.

"I'm not much used to giving advice," he went on, "least of all when it is at all likely to be taken. But I'll offer you some. Throw Heinzman over. Let him go to the pen. He's been crooked, and a fool."

"That's what you'd do, I suppose," said Orde.

"Exactly that. You owe nothing to Heinzman; but something to what you would probably call repentance, but which is in reality a mawkish sentimentality of weakness. However, I know you, Jack Orde, from top to bottom; and I know you're fool enough not to do it. I'm so sure of it that I dare put it to you straight; you could never bring yourself to the point of destroying a man who had sacrificed himself for you."

"You seem to have this game all figured out," said Orde with contempt.

Newmark leaned back in his chair. Two bright red spots burned in his ordinarily sallow cheeks. He half closed his eyes.

"You're right," said he with an ill-concealed satisfaction. "If you play a game, play it through. Each man is different; for each a different treatment is required. The game is infinite, wonderful, fascinating to the skilful." He opened his eyes and looked over at Orde with a mild curiosity. "I suppose men are about all of one kind to you."

"Two," said Orde grimly; "the honest men and the scoundrels."

"Well," said the other, "let's settle this thing. The fact remains that the firm owes a note to Heinzman, which it cannot pay. You owe a note to the firm which you cannot pay. All this may be slightly irregular; but for private reasons you do not care to make public the irregularity. Am I right so far?"

Orde, who had been watching him with a slightly sardonic smile, nodded.

"Well, what I want out of this—"

"You might hear the other side," interrupted Orde. "In the first place," said he, producing a bundle of papers, "I have the note and the mortgage in my possession."

"Whence Heinzman will shortly rescue them, as soon as I get to see him," countered Newmark. "You acknowledge that I can force Heinzman; and you can hardly refuse him."

"If you force Heinzman, he'll land you," Orde pointed out.

"There is Canada for me, with no extradition. He travels with heavier baggage. I have the better trumps."

"You'd lose everything."

"Not quite," smiled Newmark. "And, as usual, you are forgetting the personal equation. Heinzman is—Heinzman. And I am I."

"Then I suppose this affidavit from Heinzman as to the details of all this is useless for the same reason?"

Newmark's thin lips parted in another smile.

"Correct," said he.

"But you're ready to compromise below the face of the note?"

"I am."

"Why?"

Newmark hesitated.

"I'll tell you," said he; "because I know you well enough to realise that there is a point where your loyalty to Heinzman would step aside in favour of your loyalty to your family."

"And you think you know where that point is?"

"It's the basis of my compromise."

Orde began softly to laugh. "Newmark, you're as clever as the devil," said he. "But aren't you afraid to lay out your cards this way?"

"Not with you," replied Newmark, boldly; "with anybody else on earth, yes. With you, no."

Orde continued to laugh, still in the low undertone.

"The worst of it is, I believe you're right," said he at last. "You have the thing sized up; and there isn't a flaw in your reasoning. I always said that you were the brains of this concern. If it were not for one thing, I'd compromise sure; and that one thing was beyond your power to foresee."

He paused. Newmark's eyes half-closed again, in a quick darting effort of his brain to run back over all the elements of the game he was playing. Orde waited in patience for him to speak.

"What is it?" asked Newmark at last. "Heinzman died of smallpox at four o'clock this afternoon," said Orde.

### XLVIII

Newmark did not alter his attitude nor his expression, but his face slowly went gray. For a full minute he sat absolutely motionless, his breath coming and going noisily through his contracted nostrils. Then he arose gropingly to his feet, and started toward one of the two doors leading from the room.

"Where are you going?" asked Orde quietly.

Newmark steadied himself with an effort.

"I'm going to get myself a drink in my bedroom," he snapped. "Any objections?"

"No," replied Orde. "None. After you get your drink, come back. I want to talk to you."

Newmark snarled at him: "You needn't be afraid I'll run away. How'd I get out of town?"

"I know it wouldn't pay you to run away," said Orde.

Newmark passed out through the door. Orde looked thoughtfully at Heinzman's affidavit, which, duly disinfected, had been handed him by Dr. McMullen as important; and thrust it and the other papers into his inside pocket. Then he arose to his feet and glided softly across the room to take a position close to the door through which Newmark had departed in quest of his drink. For a half minute he waited. Finally the door swung briskly inward. Like a panther, as quickly and as noiselessly, Orde sprang forward. A short but decisive struggle ensued. In less than ten seconds Orde had pinioned Newmark's arms to his side where he held them immovable with one of his own. The other hand he ran down Newmark's right arm to the pocket. There followed an instant of silent resistance. Then with a sharp cry of mingled anger and pain Newmark snatched his hand out and gazed a trifle amazedly at the half crushed fingers. Orde drew forth the revolver Newmark had grasped concealed in the coat pocket.

Without hesitation he closed and locked the bedroom door; turned the key in the lock of the other; tried and fastened the window. The revolver he opened; spilled out the cartridges into his hand; and then tossed the empty weapon to Newmark, who had sunk into the chair by the lamp.

"There's your plaything," said he. "So you wanted that affidavit, did you? Now we have the place to ourselves; and we'll thresh this matter out."

He paused, collecting his thoughts.

"I don't need to tell you that I've got you about where you live," said he finally. "Nor what I think of you. The case is open and shut; and I can send you over the road for the best part of your natural days. Also I've got these notes and the mortgage."

"Quit it," growled Newmark, "you've got me. Send me up; and be damned."

"That's the question," went on Orde slowly. "I've been at it three days, without much time off for sleep. You hurt me pretty bad, Joe. I trusted you; and I thought of you as a friend."

Newmark stirred slightly with impatience.

"I had a hard time getting over that part of it; and about three-quarters of what was left in the world looked mighty like ashes for awhile. Then I began to see this thing a little clearer. We've been together a good many years now; and as near as I can make out you've been straight as a string with me for eight of them. Then I suppose the chance came and before you knew it you were in over your neck."

He looked, half-pleading toward Newmark. Newmark made no sign.

"I know that's the way it might be. A man thinks he's mighty brave; and so he is, as long as he can see what's coming, and get ready for it. But some day an emergency just comes up and touches him on the shoulder, and he turns around and sees it all of a sudden. Then he finds he's a coward. It's pretty hard for me to understand dishonesty, or how a man can be dishonest. I've tried, but I can't do it. Crookedness isn't my particular kind of fault. But I do know this: that we every one of us have something to be forgiven for by some one. I guess I've got a temper that makes me pretty sorry sometimes. Probably you don't see how it's possible for a man to get crazy mad about little things. That isn't your particular kind of fault."

"Oh, for God's sake, drop that preaching. It makes me sick!" broke out Newmark.

Orde smiled whimsically.

"I'm not preaching," he said; "and even if I were, I've paid a good many thousands of dollars, it seems, to buy the right to say what I damn please. And if you think I'm working up to a Christian forgiveness racket, you're very much mistaken. I'm not. I don't forgive you; and I surely despise your sort. But I'm explaining to you—no, to myself—just what I've been at for three days."

"Well, turn me over to your sheriff, and let's get through with this," said Newmark sullenly. "I suppose you've got that part of it all fixed."

Orde rose.

"Look here, Newmark, that's just what I've been coming to, just what I've had such a hard time to get hold of. I felt it, but I couldn't put my finger on it. Now I know. I'm not going to hand you over to any sheriff; I'm going to let you off. No," he continued, in response to Newmark's look of incredulous amazement, "it isn't from any fool notion of forgiveness. I told you I didn't forgive you. But I'm not going to burden my future life with you. That's just plain, ordinary selfishness. I suppose I really ought to jug you; but if I do, I'll always carry with me the thought that I've taken it on myself to judge a man. And I don't believe any man is competent to judge another. I told you why—or tried to—a minute or so ago. I've lived clean, and I've enjoyed the world as a clean open-air sort of proposition—like a windy day— and I always hope to. I'd rather drop this whole matter. In a short time I'd forget you; you'd pass out of my life entirely. But if we carry this thing through to a finish, I'd always have the thought with me that I'd put you in the pen; that you are there now. I don't like the notion. I'd rather finish this up right here and now and get it over and done with and take a fresh start." He paused and wiped his brow, wet with the unusual exertion of this self-analysis. "I think a fellow ought to act always as if he was making the world. He ought to try not to put things in it that are going to make it an unpleasant or an evil world. We don't always do it; but we ought to try. Now if I were making a world, I wouldn't put a man in a penitentiary in it. Of course there's dangerous criminals." He glanced at Newmark a little anxiously. "I don't believe you're that. You're sharp and dishonest, and need punishment; but you don't need extinction. Anyway, I'm not going to bother my future with you."

Newmark, who had listened to this long and rambling exposition with increasing curiosity and interest, broke into a short laugh.

"You've convicted me," he said. "I'm a most awful failure. I thought I knew you; but this passes all belief."

Orde brushed this speech aside as irrelevant.

"Our association, of course, comes to an end. There remain the terms of settlement. I could fire you out of this without a cent, and you'd have to git. But that wouldn't be fair. I don't give a damn for you; but it wouldn't be fair to me. Now as for the Northern Peninsula timber, you have had seventy-five thousand out of that and have lent me the same amount. Call that quits. I will take up your note when it comes due; and destroy the one given to Heinzman. For all your holdings in our common business I will give you my note without interest and without time for one hundred thousand dollars. That is not its face value, nor anything like it, but you have caused me directly and indirectly considerable loss. I don't know how soon I can pay this note; but it will be paid."

"All right," agreed Newmark.

"Does that satisfy you?"

"I suppose it's got to."

"Very well. I have the papers here all made out. They need simply to be signed and witnessed. Timbull is the nearest notary."

He unlocked the outside door.

"Come," said he.

In silence the two walked the block and a half to the notary's house. Here they were forced to wait some time while Timbull dressed himself and called the necessary witnesses. Finally the papers were executed. In the street Newmark paused significantly. But Orde did not take the hint.

"Are you coming with me?" asked Newmark.

"I am," replied Orde. "There is one thing more."

In silence once more they returned to the shadowy low library filled with its evidences of good taste. Newmark threw himself into the armchair. He was quite recovered, once again the imperturbable, coldly calculating, cynical observer. Orde relocked the door, and turned to face him.

"You have five days to leave town," he said crisply. "Don't ever show up here again. Let me have your address for the payment of this note."

He took two steps forward.

"I've let you off from the pen because I didn't want my life bothered with the thought of you. But you've treated me like a hound. I've been loyal to the firm's interests from the start; and I've done my best by it. You knifed me in the back. You're a dirty, low-lived skunk. If you think you're going to get off scot-free, you're mightily mistaken."

He advanced two steps more. Newmark half arose.

"What do you mean?" he asked in some alarm.

"I mean that I'm going to give you about the worst licking you ever heard TELL of," replied Orde, buttoning his coat.

## XLIX

Five minutes later Orde emerged from Newmark's house, softly rubbing the palm of one hand over the knuckles of the other. At the front gate he paused to look up at the stars. Then he shut it decisively behind him.

Up through the maple shaded streets he walked at a brisk pace, breathing deep, unconsciously squaring back his shoulders. The incident was behind him. In his characteristic decisive manner he had wiped the whole disagreeable affair off the slate. The copartnership with its gains and losses, its struggles and easy sailing was a thing of the past. Only there remained, as after a flood the sediment, a final result of it all, the balance between successes and failures, a ground beneath the feet of new aspirations. Orde had the Northern Peninsula timber; the Boom Company; and the carrying trade. They were all burdened with debt, it is true, but the riverman felt surging within him the reawakened and powerful energy for which optimism is another name. He saw stretching before him a long life of endeavour, the sort of endeavour he enjoyed, exulted in; and in it he would be untrammelled and alone. The idea appealed to him. Suddenly he was impatient for the morrow that he might begin.

He turned out of the side street. His own house lay before him, dark save for the gas jet in the hallway and the single lamp in the library. A harmony of softly touched chords breathed out through the open window. He stopped; then stole forward softly until he stood looking in through the doorway.

Carroll sat leaning against the golden harp, her shining head with the soft shadows bent until it almost touched the strings. Her hands were straying idly over accustomed chords and rich modulations, the plaintive half-music of reverie. A soft light fell on her slender figure; half revealed the oval of her cheek and the sweep of her lashes.

Orde crept to her unheard. Gently he clasped her from behind. Unsurprised she relinquished the harp strings and sank back against his breast with a happy little sigh.

"Kind of fun being married, isn't it, sweetheart?" he repeated their quaint formula.

"Kind of," she replied; and raised her face to his.

Made in United States
Orlando, FL
23 January 2025

57671454R00343